FORGES OF MARS

More great Warhammer 40,000 fiction from Black Library

• DAWN OF FIRE •

BOOK 1: AVENGING SON
by Guy Haley

BOOK 2: THE GATE OF BONES
by Andy Clark

BOOK 3: THE WOLFTIME
by Gav Thorpe

BOOK 4: THRONE OF LIGHT
by Guy Haley

BOOK 5: THE IRON KINGDOM
by Nick Kyme

BOOK 6: THE MARTYR'S TOMB
by Marc Collins

INDOMITUS
A novel by Gav Thorpe

• DARK IMPERIUM •
by Guy Haley

BOOK 1: DARK IMPERIUM
BOOK 2: PLAGUE WAR
BOOK 3: GODBLIGHT

BELISARIUS CAWL: THE GREAT WORK
A novel by Guy Haley

IMPERATOR: WRATH OF THE OMNISSIAH
A novel by Gav Thorpe

SERVANTS OF THE MACHINE-GOD
An anthology by various authors

• BLACKSTONE FORTRESS •
by Darius Hinks

BOOK 1: BLACKSTONE FORTRESS
BOOK 2: ASCENSION

• VAULTS OF TERRA •
by Chris Wraight

BOOK 1: THE CARRION THRONE
BOOK 2: THE HOLLOW MOUNTAIN
BOOK 3: THE DARK CITY

WARHAMMER 40,000

FORGES OF MARS

GRAHAM McNEILL

A BLACK LIBRARY PUBLICATION

Priests of Mars first published in 2012.
Lords of Mars first published in 2013.
Gods of Mars first published in 2014.
'Zero Day Exploit' first published digitally in 2014.
This edition published in Great Britain in 2023 by
Black Library, Games Workshop Ltd., Willow Road,
Nottingham, NG7 2WS, UK.

Represented by: Games Workshop Limited – Irish branch,
Unit 3, Lower Liffey Street, Dublin 1,
D01 K199, Ireland.

10 9 8 7 6 5 4 3 2 1

Produced by Games Workshop in Nottingham.
Cover illustration by Zhenjie Ni (Nico).

A CIP record for this book is available from the British Library.

ISBN 13: 978-1-80407-543-2

Printed and bound in the UK.

For more than a hundred centuries the Emperor has sat immobile on the Golden Throne of Earth. He is the Master of Mankind. By the might of His inexhaustible armies a million worlds stand against the dark.

Yet, He is a rotting carcass, the Carrion Lord of the Imperium held in life by marvels from the Dark Age of Technology and the thousand souls sacrificed each day so that His may continue to burn.

To be a man in such times is to be one amongst untold billions. It is to live in the cruellest and most bloody regime imaginable. It is to suffer an eternity of carnage and slaughter. It is to have cries of anguish and sorrow drowned by the thirsting laughter of dark gods.

This is a dark and terrible era where you will find little comfort or hope. Forget the power of technology and science. Forget the promise of progress and advancement. Forget any notion of common humanity or compassion.

There is no peace amongst the stars, for in the grim darkness of the far future,
there is only war.

CONTENTS

PRIESTS OF MARS

DRAMATIS PERSONAE

The *Speranza*

Lexell Kotov – Archmagos of the Kotov Explorator Fleet
Tarkis Blaylock – Fabricatus Locum, Magos of the Cebrenia Quadrangle
Vitali Tychon – Stellar Cartographer of the Quatria Orbital Galleries
Linya Tychon – Stellar Cartographer, daughter of Vitali Tychon
Azuramagelli – Magos of Astrogation
Kryptaestrex – Magos of Logistics
Turentek – Ark Fabricatus
Hirimau Dahan – Secutor/Guilder Suzerain
Saiixek – Master of Engines
Julius Hawke – Bondsman
Abrehem Locke – Bondsman
Vannen Coyne – Bondsman
Ismael de Roeven – Bondsman
Crusha – Bondsman

The *Renard*

Roboute Surcouf – Captain
Emil Nader – First Mate
Adara Siavash – Hired Gun
Ilanna Pavelka – Tech-Priest
Kayrn Sylkwood – Enginseer
Gideon Teivel – Astropath
Elior Roi – Navigator

Adeptus Astartes Black Templars

Kul Gilad – Reclusiarch
Tanna – Brother-Sergeant
Auiden – Apothecary
Issur – Initiate
Atticus Varda – Initiate
Bracha – Initiate
Yael – Initiate

The Cadian 71st 'The Hellhounds'

Ven Anders – Colonel of the Cadian Detached Formation
Blayne Hawkins – Captain of Blazer Company
Taybard Rae – Lieutenant of Blazer Company
Jahn Callins – Requisitional Support Officer, Blazer Company

Legio Sirius

ARLO LUTH, 'THE WINTERSUN' – Warlord Princeps, *Lupa Capitalina*
MARKO KOSKINEN – Moderati
LARS ROSTEN – Moderati
MAGOS HYRDRITH – Tech-Priest

ERYKS SKÁLMÖLD, 'THE MOONSORROW' – Reaver Princeps, *Canis Ulfrica*
TOBIAS OSARA – Moderati
JOAKIM BALDUR – Moderati
MAGOS OHTAR – Tech-Priest

GUNNAR VINTRAS, 'THE SKINWALKER' – Warhound Princeps, *Amarok*
ELIAS HÄRKIN, 'THE IRONWOAD' – Warhound Princeps, *Vilka*

The *Starblade*

BIELANNA FAERELLE – Farseer of Biel-Tan
ARIGANNA – Striking Scorpion Exarch of Biel-Tan
TARIQUEL – Striking Scorpion of Biel-Tan
VAYNESH – Striking Scorpion of Biel-Tan
ULDANAISH GHOSTWALKER – Wraithlord of Biel-Tan

<Toll the Great Bell once!>
<For the Souls of Machines lost to the void.>
<Toll the Great Bell twice!>
<Keep them in your eternal power,>
<Our Master of flesh and iron.>
<Toll the Great Bell thrice!>
<For Magos Vettius Telok.>
<Compiler of data, seeker after truth.>
<Guide his machines, entombed in lightless depths.>
<Give them the will and clarity required>
<to cogitate Empyreal Tempests,>
<and seek the serenity of perfect code.>
<Toll the Great Bell in Grief!>
<And mourn the loss of knowledge.>
<Sing Praise to the God of All Machines!>

Binaric inscription on
the Bell of Lost Souls.

Tower of Heroes, Terra.

The Telok Expedition:
Declared lost with all
knowledge: 383.M38

Mechanicus metafile 487834857b/KOTOV

METADATA REPOSITORY %001

Begin .org 4048 a_start .equ 3000 2048 ld length,% 2064 WILL BE DONE 00000010 10000000 BURN-IN LATENCY 00000110 2068 addcc%r1,-4,%r1 10000010 10000000 01111111 11111100 2072 addcc.%r1,%r2,%r4 10001000 QUERY INLOAD (MARQUE?) 01000000 FLEET AGGLOMERATION CACHE 2076 ld%r4,%r5 11001010 00000001 00000000 00000000 2080 ba loop 00010000 10111111 11111111 INFOCYTE-LOGS PARITY? 2084 addcc%r3,%r5,%r3 10000110 10000000 11000000 00000101 2088 done: jmpl%r15+4,%r0 10000001 11000011 TEMPLAR 00000100 2092 length: 20 HALO-SCAR CARTOGRAPHIES REF: TYCHON 00000000 00000000 00010100 2096 address: a_start 00000100 ANOMALOUS CHRONO-READINGS 00000000 00001011 10111000 .Omni.a_start

Arithmetic Overflow Arithmetic Overflow Arithmetic Overflow Arithmetic Overflow Arithmetic Overflow Arithmetic Overflow Arithmetic Overflow Arithmetic Overflow Arithmetic Overflow Arithmetic Overflow Arithmetic Overflow Arithmetic Overflow Arithmetic Overflow Arithmetic Overflow///////////

Metadata Parsing in effect.

+++++++++++++++++

<++<First Principles>++>

001

Knowledge is power. It is the first credo. It is the only credo. To understand that fundamental concept is to possess power beyond measure. To harness fire, to shape the elements and bend them to your will. Such things as can now only be dreamed of by lunatics and the Machine-touched were commonplace in an age unremembered. What is now miraculous and divine, the preserve of the few, was once possessed by all. Yet understood by none.

Woe to you, man who honours not the Omnissiah, for ignorance shall be your doom!

The Great Machines of Old Earth were wondrous engines of creation whose power dwarfed that of any myth or legend. They shaped entire worlds, they drank the hearts of stars and brought light into the dark places of the universe. The techno-sorcerers who crafted them and wielded their power bestrode the world as gods.

How far we have fallen.

010

Great void-born city of metal and stone, marvel of wonders never to be known again. You live in the depths of space, your sheet steel skin cold and unyielding. You are a living thing, a creature whose bones are adamantium, whose molten heart is that of a thousand caged stars. Oil is your

sweat and the devotion of a million souls your succour. Creatures of flesh and blood empower you from within. They work the myriad wonders that drive your organs, feed your hunger and hurl you through the trackless wilderness between the stars.

How far will you travel?

What miracles will you see?

The light of uncounted suns will shine from the glitter-sheen of your hull, light that has travelled from the past, cast by stars that are dead and stars in the throes of their violent birth. A mariner in strange seas, swept out among the glittering nebulae, you will see sights that no man can know, no legend tell or history record.

You are *living history, for you will venture further and longer than any other of your kind.*

No grim ship of war are you, no lowly workhorse yoked to dull purpose.

You are Ark Mechanicus.

You are Speranza.

You are the bringer of hope in this hopeless age.

011

The spirit of the Omnissiah flows in bright traceries of golden energy. It moves in the heart of every machine. It brings motion and heat, energy and light. It feeds the forges, it drives the engines and is the alpha and omega of all that is and all that will ever be crafted by the hands of man. The soul of the Great Machine lives in cogs and gears, it flows through every cable, it infuses every piston and the thrumming heart of every engine. Without it, the universe would be a benighted, sterile place, devoid of light and existence.

The God of All Machines is eternal and unchanging.

It is the First Power: the power at the heart of all things.

To know it is to be one with it, and to feel its touch is to be changed forever.

Flesh fails, but the machine endures.

That which was once encoded in the very bones of the ancient Men of Gold has been lost, perhaps forever. But perhaps not. Much has been forgotten that will never again be remembered, and the hidden corners of this dying galaxy have secrets left to whisper. Those with eyes to see and the will to search may find scraps of what the titans, who shaped the galaxy to their every desire, left in the ruins of their doom.

The lost realm of Man once claimed the galaxy as its own, with lustrous eyes turned to those stellar realms beyond its haloed fringes, but such was not to be our species' destiny. We reached too far, too soon, too greedily and were almost destroyed.

By hubris? Or worse, by ignorance?

Who can know? None remember the truth of what brought our race to the edge of extinction. Some claim the machines rebelled against their enslavement and turned on their makers; others that an emergent strain of psykers unleashed a cataclysm. Whatever the cause, it wrought more harm than anyone living could ever have imagined.

We plunged from a Golden Age of technology and reason into an Age of Darkness from which there is little hope of escape. Forget the promise of progress, they say. Forget the glories of the past. Cling to what little light remains and be satisfied with its feeble illumination.

The Adeptus Mechanicus rejects that paradigm.

We are crusaders in the darkness, ever-seeking out that which will bring back the light of science and understanding. That is at the heart of what we have lost, the capacity to understand and question, the vision to determine what we do not know and seek out answers.

We have become enslaved by dogma, ritual and blind superstitions that place fetters on our ability to even know there are questions to be asked.

I will ask those questions.

I will not be enslaved.

I am Archmagos Lexell Kotov, and I will reclaim what was lost.

This is my quest for knowledge.

MACROCONTENT COMMENCEMENT:

+++MACROCONTENT 001+++

Life is directed motion.

Microcontent 01

Low-orbit traffic above Joura was lousy with ships jostling for space. Queues of lifter-boats, heavy-duty bulk tenders and system monitors held station in the wash of augur-fogging electro-magnetics and engine flare from the heavier vessels as system pilots manoeuvred them into position for refuelling, re-arming and supply. Musters like this happened only rarely, and for two of them to come at once wasn't just rare, it was a complete pain in the backside.

The *Renard* was a ship of respectable tonnage, but compared to the working vessels hauling their monstrously fat bodies between Joura and the fleets competing for docking space like squealing cudbear litters fighting for prime position at the teat, she was little more than an insignificant speck.

Roboute Surcouf didn't like thinking of his ship like that. No captain worthy of the rank did.

The command bridge of the *Renard* was a warmly lit chamber of chamfered wood, bronze and glass, embellished with bygone design flourishes more commonly found on the ancient ships sailing the oceans of Macragge. Every surface was polished to a mirror shine, and though Magos Pavelka called such labours a waste of her servitors' resources, not even an adept of the Martian Priesthood would gainsay a rogue trader with a Letter of Marque stamped with Segmentum Pacificus accreditation.

Pavelka claimed it was the fragment of the Omnissiah that lived in the heart of a starship that every captain had to appease, but Roboute disagreed with Ilanna's slavish devotion to her Martian dogma when it came to ships. Roboute knew you had to love a ship, love her more than anything else in the world. Flying sub-atmospheric cutters on Iax as a youth had taught him that every ship had a *soul* that needed to be loved. And the ships who knew they weren't loved would be cantankerous mares; feisty at best, dangerous at worst.

Ilanna Pavelka was about the only member of his crew who hadn't objected to this venture. In fact she'd gotten almost giddy at the prospect of joining Archmagos Kotov's Explorator Fleet and working with fellow Mechanicus adepts once more. Perhaps giddy wasn't the right word, but she'd voiced calm approval, which was about as close to excitement as a priest of Mars ever got in Roboute's experience.

'Update: berthing docket inloading from the *Speranza*,' Pavelka informed him, speaking from her sunken, steel-panelled command station in the forward arc of the bridge. Holographic streams of binaric data cascaded before her, manipulated by the waving mechadendrites that sprang from her shoulders like a host of snakes. 'One hundred minutes until our allotted berth is available.'

'How much margin for error in that?' asked Emil Nader, the *Renard's* first officer, seated in a contoured inertial-harness to Roboute's left as he kept them within their assigned approach corridor with deft touches of manoeuvring jets. Pavelka could bring them in with an electromagnetic tether, but Roboute liked to give Emil a bit of freedom in the upper atmosphere. The *Renard* was going to be enslaved to the *Speranza's* course for the foreseeable future, and his cocksure first officer would appreciate this free flight time. Like most natives of Espandor, he had a wild, feral streak that made him averse to unthinking obedience to machinery.

'Clarification: none,' said Pavelka. 'The cogitators of the *Speranza* are first generation Martian logic-engines, they do not allow for error.'

'Yeah, but the pilots ahead of us aren't,' pointed out Emil. 'Factor in their presence.'

'All vessels ahead of us are tethered, as we will need to be before we enter the *Speranza's* gravity envelope. There will be no error margin.'

'Care to wager on that?' asked Emil with a sly grin.

A soft exhalation of chemical breath escaped Pavelka's red cowl, and Roboute hid a smile at her exasperation. Emil Nader never missed a chance to pick at Mechanicus infallibility, and would never resort to automation if there was an option for human control.

'I do not wager, Mister Nader,' said Pavelka. 'You own nothing I

desire, and none of my possessions would be of any use to you without extensive redesign of your ventral anatomy.'

'Leave it alone, Emil,' said Roboute, as he saw Nader about to answer Pavelka's statement with something inflammatory. 'Just concentrate on getting us up there in one piece. If we stray so much as a kilometre from our assigned path, it'll put a snarl in the orbital traffic worse than that time over Cadia when that officer on the *Gathalamor* shot up his bridge, remember?'

Emil shook his head. 'I try not to. But what did they expect, giving a ship a name like that? You might as well call it the *Horus* and be done with it.'

'Don't say that name!' hissed Adara Siavash, lounging in Gideon Teivel's vacant astropath station with a las-lock pistol spinning in one hand and a butterfly blade in the other. 'It's bad luck.'

Roboute wasn't exactly sure what rank or position Adara Siavash held on the *Renard*. He'd come aboard on a cargo run between Joura and Lodan, and had never left. He was lethal with a blade and could fire a rifle with a skill that would have earned him a marksman's lanyard in the Iax Defence Auxilia. He'd saved Roboute's life on that run, putting down a passenger who'd turned out to be an unsanctioned psyker and who'd almost killed everyone aboard when they'd translated. Yet for all that, Roboute couldn't help but think of him as a young boy, such was his childlike innocence and constant wonder at the galaxy's strangeness.

Sometimes Roboute almost envied him.

'The lad's right,' he said, as he sensed a kink in the ship's systems. 'Don't say that name.'

His first mate shrugged, but Roboute saw that Emil knew he'd crossed a line.

The crew carried on with their assigned tasks, and Roboute brought the current shipboard operations up onto the inner surface of his retina. A mass of gold-cored cables trailed from the base of his neck to the command throne upon which he sat, feeding him real-time data from the various active bridge stations. Trajectories, approach vectors, fuel consumption and closure speeds scrolled past, together with noospheric identity tags for the hundreds of vessels in orbit.

Everything was looking good, though a number of the engineering systems were running closer to capacity than he'd have liked. Roboute opened a vox-link to the engineering spaces, almost two kilometres behind him.

'Kayrn, are you seeing what I am on the coolant feed levels to the engines?' he asked.

'Of course I am,' came the voice of Kayrn Sylkwood, the *Renard's* enginseer. 'I perform six hundred and four system checks every minute. I know more about these engines than you ever will.'

Emil leaned over and whispered, 'You had to ask. You *always* have to ask.'

Kayrn Sylkwood was ex-Guard, a veteran enginseer of the Cadian campaigns. She'd been mustered out of the regiment after taking one too many shots to the head on Nemesis Tessera during the last spasm of invasion from the Dreaded Eye. Below Guard fitness requirements and having lost three tanks under her care, the Mechanicus didn't want her either, but Roboute had recognised her rare skill in coaxing the best from engines that needed a sympathetic touch or a kick in the arse.

'Just keep an eye on it,' he said, shutting off the link before Sylkwood could berate him again.

Despite any slight running concerns about the engines, the *Renard* was a ship like no other Roboute had known. She was fast, nimble (as far as a three-kilometre vessel could be) and carried enough cargo to make operating her profitable on local-system runs. Even the odd sector run wasn't beyond her capabilities, but Roboute never liked stretching her that far. She hadn't let him down in the fifteen years he'd captained her, and that kind of respect had to be earned.

'Promethium tender coming in below and behind us,' noted Emil. 'She's burning hotter than I'd like, and it's closing on an elliptical course.'

'Probably some planetside dock overseer feeling the whips of his masters to cut the lag on his orbital deliveries,' replied Roboute. 'How close is she?'

'Two thousand kilometres, but her apogee will put her within fifteen hundred if we don't course correct.'

'No,' said Roboute. 'Two thousand, fifteen hundred, what does it matter? If she goes up, all we'll see is the flash before we're incinerated. Conserve fuel and stay on course.'

Roboute wasn't worried about the danger of collision – even the closest ships had gulfs of hundreds of kilometres between them – what worried the ship masters of each fleet was the threat of delay to their departure schedules. And Roboute didn't intend to compound that delay by being late for his first face-to-face meeting with Lexell Kotov.

The archmagos had made it clear that such a breach of protocol would not be tolerated.

Of all the bright lights thronging the sky, the brightest and biggest now hove into view as Emil made a final manoeuvring burn.

Even Roboute had to admit to being mightily impressed with this

ship. He'd flown the length and breadth of more than one sector, but he had yet to see anything to match this for sheer scale and grandeur.

'Adara,' said Roboute. 'Go below and inform Magos Tychon that we'll be docking with the *Speranza* soon.'

The dockers' bar didn't have a name; no one had ever thought to give it one. But everyone around the busy port knew it: a bunch of converted cargo containers welded together and fitted with rudimentary power and plumbing. Who really ran it was unclear, but a steady stream of disgruntled and exhausted dock workers could always be found filling its echoing, metallic spaces.

'*This* is where you do your off-duty drinking?' said Ismael, his slurred tone telling Abrehem and Coyne exactly what he thought of this dive. 'No wonder we're usually behind schedule.'

Abrehem was already regretting taking the overseer up on his offer of drinks for the crane crew, but it was too late to back out now. They'd made their quota, for the first time in weeks, and Ismael had offered to take them out drinking in a rare moment of largesse.

'Yeah,' said Abrehem. 'It's not much, but we like it.'

'Damn, it stinks,' said Ismael, his face screwed up in disgust.

The loader-overseer was already drunk. The shine served at the first few bars they'd visited had almost knocked him off his feet. Ismael didn't drink much, and it was showing in his mean temper and cruel jokes at the expense of men who didn't dare answer back.

A nighttime crowd already thronged the bar's bench seats, and the pungent reek of engine oil, grease, lifter-fuel, sweat and hopelessness caught in the back of his throat. Abrehem knew the aroma well, because he stank of it too.

Faces turned to stare at them as Ismael pushed his way through the crowd of dock workers to the bar, a series of planks set up on a pair of trestles, upon which sat two vats that had once been the promethium drums of a Hellhound. Some men claimed to be able to tell what kind of tanks the varieties of shine had been brewed in, that each one gave a subtly different flavour, but how anyone could taste anything after a few mouthfuls was beyond Abrehem.

Coyne took Abrehem's arm as he set off after Ismael.

'Thor's balls, you shouldn't have taken him up on that drink,' whispered his fellow operator.

Abrehem knew that very well, but tried to put his best face on. 'Come on, he's not a bad boss.'

'No,' agreed Coyne. 'I've had worse, that's for sure, but there's some lines you just shouldn't cross.'

'And getting drunk on shine with a man that can get you thrown off shift is one of them, I know.'

'We'll be lucky if he gets away without a beating tonight,' said Coyne. 'And when he wakes up with a cracked skull, we'll be the ones he blames. I can't lose this assignment, Abrehem, I've a wife and three young'uns to support.'

'I know that,' said Abrehem, annoyed that Coyne always thought of his own woes before anyone else's. Abrehem had a wife too, though she was a stranger to him now. Both their young ones had died of lung-rust before their fifth year, and the loss had broken them beyond repair. Toxic exhalations from the sprawling Mechanicus refineries fogged the hab-zones surrounding the Navy docks, and the young were particularly susceptible to the corrosive atmospherics.

'Come on,' said Coyne. 'Let's try and get this over while we still have jobs.'

'We'll have one drink and then we'll go,' promised Abrehem, threading his way through the sullen drinkers towards the bar. He could already hear Ismael's nasal voice over the simmering hubbub of gloomy conversation. Abrehem knew most of the faces, fellow grafters on the back-breaking labour shifts handling the supply needs of a busy tithe-world.

Times were busy enough normally, but with the Mechanicus fleet at high anchor needing to be furnished with supplies to last an indefinite time, the docks and their workers were being stretched to breaking point. Yes, there had been some accidents and deaths that could no doubt be traced back to excessive consumption of shine distilled in scavenged fuel drums, but the lives of a few drunk dockers mattered little in the grand scheme of things.

Hundreds of fleet tenders were making daily trips back and forth from the loading platforms, fat and groaning with weapons, ammo, food, fuel, spare uniforms, engine parts, machine parts, surgical supplies, millions of gallons of refined fluids for lubrication, drinking, anointing and who knew what else. It was hard, dangerous work, but it was work, and no man of Joura could afford to pass up a steady, reliable credit-stream.

Abrehem reached the bar to find Ismael loudly arguing with the shaven-headed barkeep at the drum. With a gene-bulked and partially augmented ogryn nearby, it was a poor fight to pick. Abrehem had seen the creature take off a man's head with the merest twist of its wrist, and knew it wasn't above a bit of casual violence when its tiny brain was fogged with shine. The filters in his eyes read the scrubbed ident-codes on the augmetics applied to the ogryn's arms and cranium.

Backstreet, fifth-gen knock-offs. Crude and cheap, but effective.

'Have you tried this?' demanded Ismael. 'This bloody idiot is trying to poison me!'

'It's a special blend,' said Abrehem, taking a glass from the barkeep and sliding an extra couple of credit wafers across the bar. 'Unique, in fact. Takes a bit of getting used to, that's all.'

The barkeep gave him a fixed stare and nodded to the exit. Abrehem understood and took the three drinks from the bar as Coyne steered Ismael away from the glowering ogryn. With his overseer out of earshot, Abrehem leaned over the bar and said, 'We'll down these and be on our way. We're not here for trouble.'

The barkeep grunted, and Abrehem followed Coyne and Ismael to a bench seat located in the corner of the containers away from most of the bar's patrons. This part of the bar was mostly empty, located as it was next to the latrines. The stink of stale urine and excrement was pungent, and only marginally more offensive than the acrid fumes of their drinks.

'Emperor's guts,' swore Ismael. 'It stinks here.'

'Yeah, but at least we have a seat,' said Coyne. 'And after a day's shift at the docks, that's all that matters, right?'

'Sure,' agreed Abrehem. 'You get to our age and a seat's important.'

'I spend my days sitting down in a control cab,' pointed out Ismael.

'*You* do, we don't,' said Coyne, unable to keep the resentment from his voice.

Fortunately Ismael was too drunk to notice, and Abrehem shot Coyne a warning glance.

'Come on, let's sink these and we'll get out of here,' said Abrehem, but Ismael wasn't listening. Abrehem followed his gaze and sighed as he saw a familiar face hunched low over a three-quarters-drunk bottle of shine.

'Is that him?' said Ismael.

'Yeah, it's him,' agreed Abrehem, putting a hand on Ismael's arm. 'Leave him alone, it's not worth it. Trust me.'

'No,' said Ismael, throwing off Abrehem's hand with an ugly sneer. 'I want to see what a real *hero* looks like.'

'He's not a hero, he's a drunk, a liar and a waste of a pair of coveralls.'

Ismael wasn't listening, and Abrehem gave Coyne a nod as their overseer made his way over to the man's table. Abrehem saw the ogryn heft a length of rebar as long as Abrehem's leg and start moving through the crowded bar, parting knots of men before it like a planetoid with its own gravitational field. A few of the more sober patrons, sensing trouble, headed for the exit, and Abrehem wished he could follow them.

He cursed and sat next to Ismael as he planted himself on a stool at the drunk's table.

'You're him,' said Ismael, but the man ignored him.

Abrehem studied the man's face. Lined with exhaustion and old before its time, a network of ruptured capillaries around his ruddy cheeks and nose spoke of a lifetime lived in a bottle, but there was a hardness there too, reminding Abrehem that this man had once been a soldier in the Guard.

A *bad* soldier if the stories were to be believed, but a soldier nonetheless.

'I said, you're him, aren't you?' said Ismael.

'Go away,' said the man, and Abrehem heard the sadness in his voice. 'Please.'

'I know you're him,' said Ismael, leaning forwards over the table. 'I saw you on shift last week, and heard all about you.'

'Then you don't need me to tell you again,' said the man, and Abrehem realised he wasn't drunk.

The bottle in front of him was an old one, and the drink in his hand was untouched.

'I want to hear you tell it,' said Ismael, his tone viperous.

'Why bother? I've told it over and over, and no one believes me,' said the man.

'Come on, hero, tell me how you killed the Iron Warrior. Did you breathe on him and he keeled over dead?'

'Please,' said the man, an edge of steel in his voice. 'I asked you nicely to leave me alone.'

'No, not till you tell me how you took on an entire army of Traitor Space Marines,' spat Ismael, reaching for the man's bottle.

The man slapped Ismael's hand away and before anyone could stop him, he had a knife at the overseer's throat. It glinted dully in the low light. Abrehem scanned the serial number on the blade: 250371, Guard-issue, carbon steel and a killing edge that could cut deeper than a fusion-weld in the right hands.

The ogryn reached their table, the rebar slamming down and sending their drinks flying. Broken glass and splintered wood flew. Abrehem fell away from the table onto the ribbed floor. The stink was worse down here, and he rolled as the ogryn stepped in close to where Ismael was pinned against the wall by the knife-wielding man.

'Put down knife. Put down man,' said the ogryn in halting, child like speech.

The man didn't acknowledge its words, pressing the knife into Ismael's throat with enough force to draw a thin line of blood.

'I'd kill you if I thought it would stop anyone else asking the same damned questions over and over,' said the man. 'Or maybe I'll just kill you because I feel like crap today.'

'Put knife down. Put man down,' repeated the ogryn.

Before the man could comply, metal shutter doors throughout the bar crashed open and a chorus of vox-amplified voices blared inside. Sodium-tinged light flooded through the doors and, from his vantage point on the floor, Abrehem saw strobing spotlights mounted on the backs of giant vehicles. Black-armoured figures poured into the bar, clubbing men to the ground with vicious blows from shock mauls and the butts of automatic shotguns. Metal-skinned hounds on chain-leashes barked with augmetic anger, their polished steel fangs bared. Hungry red eyes fixed on the bar's patrons.

'Collarmen!' shouted Coyne, scrambling away from the overturned table. Abrehem struggled to his feet, suddenly sober at the sight of the impressment teams as they dragged men out to the rumbling confinement vehicles. The man with the knife stepped away from Ismael, and the overseer bolted for the nearest way out, sobbing in fear and confusion.

The bar was in uproar. Concussion sirens brayed and blinding light strobed through the bar, all designed to stun and disorientate. Abrehem's ocular cutoffs screened him from the worst of the light, but the horns were still deafening. Men encased in black leather and gleaming carapace armour with bronze, faceless helmets swept through the bar like soldiers clearing a room. Abrehem saw Ismael shot in the back by a soft round and slammed into a metal wall with the force of the impact. He slumped to the ground, unconscious, and two of the growling cyber-hounds dragged the overseer's limp body outside.

A hand grabbed his shoulder. 'We've got to get out of here!' cried Coyne.

Abrehem looked for a way out. The collarmen and their mastiffs had all the exits covered, or at least all the obvious ones. There had to be a few they didn't know about.

'This way,' said the man with the knife. 'If you don't want to get taken, follow me.'

The man ran, but the ogryn grabbed him by the scruff of the neck as it dumbly watched the methodical subduing tactics of collarmen. Soft rounds slammed the ogryn, but it hardly seemed to feel them, and Abrehem rolled behind the grunting creature as it tried to make sense of what was happening and why these men were shooting it.

The knifeman struggled in the ogryn's grip, but he was as helpless as a child against its strength.

'Let go of me, damn you!' yelled the man.

'Forget him,' said Coyne. 'There's a back way out through the latrines.'

Abrehem nodded and moved past the stupefied ogryn as a flurry of soft rounds battered the container wall next to his head. From the deformation of the sheet steel, Abrehem didn't reckon those 'soft' rounds were particularly soft.

Coyne pushed open the flimsy door to the latrines and was immediately flung back as a shock maul slammed into the side of his head. He dropped, poleaxed, to the ground. Abrehem skidded to a halt and tried to reverse his course. A crackling baton swung at his head, but he ducked and ran back the way he'd come. He heard the metallic cough of a shotgun blast and pain exploded in his lower back as his legs went numb under him. Abrehem crashed to the floor again, feeling twitching spasms of pain shooting up and down his spine.

Mesh-gauntleted hands hauled him upright and he was dragged through the shattered remains of the bar, with its former clientele pleading, threatening and bargaining with the collarmen. Abrehem tried to struggle, but was held fast. Once the collarmen had you, that was it, you were bound to life aboard a starship, but that didn't stop him from trying to beg for his freedom.

'Please,' he said. 'You can't... I have... permits. I work! I have a wife!'

He blinked away static interference as they dragged him outside, the discordant wail of the sirens making him feel sick and the constant barking of the cyber-hounds setting his teeth on edge. The collarmen dumped him at the open doors of the growling volunteer-wagon, and fresh hands hauled him upright. His legs were still weak, but he was able to stand as a clicking bio-optic was shone in his eyes, overloading his filters.

'Exosomatic augmetics,' said a voice, surprise evident even muffled by a vox-grille.

'Tertiary grade,' said another. 'We can pull a full bio-ident and service history off them.'

'Got it. Loader-technician Abrehem Locke, assigned to Lifter Rig *Savickas*.'

'A lifter-tech with tertiary grade augmetics? Got to be black market.'

'Or stolen.'

'They're not stolen,' gasped Abrehem as his filters recalibrated. Three men in glossy black armour stood before him. Two held him upright. Another consulted a data-slate. 'They were my father's.'

'He was bonded?' demanded a fourth voice, heavily augmented by vox-amplification.

Abrehem turned to see a magos of the Adeptus Mechanicus, swathed in hooded crimson vestments, only the hot coals of a tripartite optic visible in the shadows. A black and gold stole with cog-toothed edges and a host of blurred numbers hung from his neck, and a heavy generator pack was fixed to his back. A haze of chill air gusted from its vents like breath, causing a patina of frost to form on the nearest collarman's armour.

'Yes, to Magos Xurgis of the 734th Jouran Manufactory Echelons.'

'Then you might be useful. Bring him and do not damage his optics,' said the magos, turning away and moving on down the ragged line of collared men and women, floating on a shimmering cushion of repulsor fields.

'No, please! Don't!' he cried, but the men holding him gave his pleas no mind. A bulked-out servitor with a piston-driven musculature hauled him inside the iron-hulled vehicle, where at least thirty other men were shackled in various states of disarray. Abrehem saw Coyne and Ismael trussed like livestock ready for slaughter. The ogryn sat with its back resting against the interior of the confinement compartment with a bemused smile on its face, as though this were a mild diversion from its daily routine instead of a life-changing moment of horror.

'No!' he screamed as the steel doors slammed shut, leaving them sealed in dim, red-lit darkness.

Abrehem wept as he felt the engine roar, and the heavy vehicle moved off. He kicked out at the doors, almost breaking bone as he slammed his heels into the metalwork again and again.

'Won't do you any good,' said a voice behind him.

Abrehem turned angrily to see the man who'd threatened Ismael with the knife. He no longer had his weapon, and his hands were bound before him with plastek cuffs. Like the ogryn, he seemed unnaturally calm, and Abrehem hated him for that.

'Where are they taking us?' he said.

'Where do you think? To the embarkation platforms. We've been collared and we're on our way to the bowels of a starship to shovel fuel, haul ammunition crates or some other shitty detail until we're dead or crippled.'

'You sound pretty calm about it.'

The man shrugged. 'I reckon it's my lot in life to get shit on from on high. I think the Emperor has a very sick sense of humour when it comes to my life. He puts me through the worst experiences a man could have, but keeps me alive. And for what? So I can go through more shit? Damn, but I wish He'd have done with me.'

Abrehem heard the depths of the man's anguish and an echo of something so awful that it didn't bear thinking about. It sounded like the truth.

'Those things you told the regimental commanders really happened, didn't they?' said Abrehem.

The man nodded.

'And all that stuff on Hydra Cordatus? It was all true?'

'Yeah, I told the truth. For all the good it did me,' said the man, holding out a cuffed hand to Abrehem. 'Guardsman Julius Hawke. Welcome to the shit.'

Microcontent 02

A pair of intricate four-dimensional maps of the southern reaches of Segmentum Pacificus hung suspended above the hololith projector. The *Renard's* crew quarters did not possess such technology, so Magos Cartographae Vitali Tychon had brought one from his observatory on Quatria. Ghostly star systems spun in a dance that looked random, but was as carefully plotted and arranged as the most perfectly formed binaric cant.

Tychon's myriad eyes saw divine beauty in the celestial geography, but amid the shimmering representation of the southern stars, a blighted, ugly wound burned at the edge of known space like a raw lasburn.

The Halo Scar, a benighted region of hostile space that swallowed ships and defeated every attempt to penetrate its void-dark emptiness. No one knew what lay beyond the Scar, and the last Mechanicus fleet to have dared to enter its depths in search of knowledge had vanished from the galaxy thousands of years ago. Telok the Machine-touched had led his doomed fleet into the Halo Scar, seeking the answers to what he described as the greatest mystery of the universe. None of his ships had returned.

Until now.

Noospheric tags flickered and died like sparks as Tychon's multiple eyes scrolled through a hundred star systems a second. He sought an answer to the conundrum that had compelled him to accept Archmagos Kotov's offer of a place in his Expeditionary Fleet.

He knew every speck of light and every hazed nebula on the first map, for he had compiled it himself, a little over five centuries ago.

Ah, but the second map...

To an outside observer, even a gifted stellar cartographer, there might appear to be no difference between the two maps. Yet to Tychon the second map might as well have represented the mutant wolf stars that leered in the tortured space around the Maelstrom. The second map's structure was an agglomeration of thousands upon thousands of compiled celestial measurements from all across the segmentum, crude by comparison with the subtleties of his own measurements, but sufficiently accurate to cause him concern.

Clicking mechanical fingers, ten on each hand, spun the globe of stars and systems, zooming in with haptic familiarity. Tychon read the various wavelength spectra, pulse intervals and radiation outputs of stars that had aged hundreds of thousands of years, in celestial terms, overnight.

He let out a machine breath, amused at the holdover from when he had possessed organic lungs.

'You know you won't see anything new in those maps just by staring at them, don't you?' asked Linya, without looking up from her writing. His daughter sat at a battered wooden desk Captain Surcouf had procured for her from a fusty storage chamber in the dripping cloisters that flanked the engine spaces. The old wood smelled of contaminated oil, cheap engine lubricants and a mixture of chlorine from the purifiers and carbon dioxide from the atmospheric scrubbers. The aroma was unpleasant, and while Vitali could filter it out, Linya had no such recourse. She didn't seem to mind, and had in fact relished the chance to work at a desk of organic material and not a bench of cold steel for a change.

'I know that, daughter dearest, but it tasks me,' said Vitali, using his flesh voice. Though his vocal cords had long since atrophied, Linya had insisted he replace them with vat-grown replacements. Of course she had the capacity to comprehend and communicate in binaric cant, as well as the most complex devotional liturgies of lingua-technis, but chose to express herself with the imperfect and imprecise language of the unenlightened.

'And it will still task you tomorrow, and the day after,' said Linya, finally looking up from her books. Unlike her father, Linya was still – outwardly – largely organic. She wore the red of the Priesthood – as was her right as a member of the Cult Mechanicus – but there the similarities to most adepts of Mars ended. Long dark hair spilled around her shoulders, and the skin of her face was smooth and finely boned. Her features were those of her father, which was only to be expected, though an anomaly in the reproduction process had resulted in a spontaneous reversal of the sex he had chosen for his successor.

A great deal of Linya's internal biological architecture had been upgraded over the years, but she stubbornly clung to her original human form and the archaic ways of her forebears. The book in which she wrote was composed of pressed plant material and the instrument by which she recorded her thoughts and experimental observations was a simple plastek tube filled with liquid pigment.

Linya's refusal to follow convention was a source of irritation to her fellow tech-priests, and a source of great pleasure to Vitali.

'I have no doubt it will,' said Vitali, 'but when one recalls scientific discoveries, it is always with a degree of fiction. We recall the "Eureka!" moment, and forget the decades of study, false starts and disproved hypotheses along the road to enlightenment. How many adepts failed in their researches before the one we remember came upon the truth by learning from their mistakes?'

'You're talking about Magos Mojaro again, aren't you?'

'A man may die yet still endure if his work enters the greater work, for time is carried upon a current of forgotten deeds, and events of great moment are but the culmination of a single, carefully placed thought,' said Vitali, reciting the ancient words of wisdom as though they were his own. 'As all men must thank progenitors obscured by the past, so we must endure the present so that those who follow may continue the endeavour.'

'Yes, he was an example to us all, father, but that won't give you any insight into the changes in those maps. The data parity of the macroscope inloads is too scattered to be usable and the information brought back to the galleries is all third-hand at best. We'll need to get out to the Halo Scar before we can gather anything concrete.'

She paused before continuing, and Vitali knew what she was going to say, because she had said it so many times before.

'You know we didn't have to come on this mission? After all, even if we *do* emerge on the other side of the Scar, there's no knowing if we'll come back. The last explorators to travel beyond the Scar were declared lost over three thousand years ago. Even if Captain Surcouf *does* have a genuine relic of Telok's lost fleet, what's to say we won't suffer the same fate?'

She sighed, attempting a different tack. 'Perhaps it's just some facet of the Scar's existence that's altering the readings we're taking?'

'Do you really believe I haven't considered that?' asked Vitali. 'Yes, stellar geography is an inconstant thing, but the changes you and I have both seen should have taken hundreds of thousands of years at least, not a few centuries.'

'So what insights has the last three hours of staring at those maps given you?'

'Regrettably none,' he said, without disappointment. 'Though I am greatly looking forward to discovering why this map no longer resembles the readings of our original in-situ macroscopes. It's been far too long since I ventured beyond the confines of Quatria's orbital galleries.'

Vitali gestured to the maps, the haptic sensors in his hands causing them to expand enormously and fill the room with shimmering points of light. 'The archmagos himself requested my presence.'

'Over the objections of the Martian Conclave,' pointed out Linya.

Vitali collapsed the star maps with an irritated gesture.

'Kotov is no fool,' he said. 'He recognised my intimate knowledge of this region of space and knew my presence could mean the difference between glorious success and ignoble failure.'

Linya said nothing, and Vitali was relieved. Even he wasn't convinced by his words. He didn't know why Lexell Kotov had exercised his precious veto, for the archmagos was not known as an adept given to gestures of emotional indulgence. Few were, but Kotov's ruthless determination and harsh enforcement of protocol was legendary, even among a priesthood that viewed cold abruptness as a virtue.

'Perhaps the loss of his forge world fiefs has granted Kotov a measure of humility,' suggested Linya, and Vitali almost laughed.

'I don't believe that for a nanosecond,' he said. 'Do you?'

'No, which makes me think Kotov has some other reason for asking you to come on this foolhardy expedition.'

'And no doubt you have a theory as to what that reason might be?'

'He's desperate,' said Linya. 'His forge worlds were wiped out and even you must have heard the rumours about the petitions being made to the Fabricator General calling for Kotov's Martian holdings to be seized. He knows he can't get any of the more powerful magi to support him, and he needs a great success to re-establish his power base on Mars. Leading this expedition in search of Telok's fleet is Kotov's last chance to salvage his reputation. It's his only hope of staving off the threats to his remaining forges.'

Vitali nodded, but before he could muster even a token defence of Kotov's prospects, a sharp rapping came at the shutter door of their shared quarters.

'Yes, Mister Siavash?' asked Vitali.

A pause.

'How did you know it was me?' asked the young fighter. Vitali could hear the sound of his butterfly blade clicking and clacking in his nimble fingers.

'Stride length, weight to decibel ratio of your footfalls,' answered Vitali. 'Not to mention that irritating tune you insist on whistling as you walk.'

'*Pride of Joura*, that is,' said Adara Siavash through the door. 'My da used to play it on the flute when I was a lad, and–'

'What do you want, Adara?' asked Linya, interrupting yet another tale of the lad's bucolic youth.

'Hello, Miss Linya,' said the young man, and even through the blast-sealed door Vitali could picture the young man blushing. 'Captain Surcouf sent me to tell you that we're almost ready to dock with the *Speranza*.'

Roboute watched the Navy battleships cruising serenely at high orbit, little more than bright moving dots that winked and gleamed in the light of the distant sun. More aggressive cruisers wove patrol circuits around bloated mass-conveyors ready to transport the freshly-raised Guard regiments from the world below to the ever-expanding crusade in the Pergamus Sector. Joura was a proud world, a populous world, and one that routinely answered the call for soldiers to serve in the proud ranks of the Imperial Guard.

The inexhaustible armies of the Emperor were only kept so by the men and women of worlds like Joura. The scale of the mass-conveyors was extraordinary, vast leviathans whose length and beam were impossible to comprehend as being able to move, let alone traverse the immense gulfs of space between star systems. Yet even they were overwhelmed by the gargantuan scale of the *Speranza*.

Adara had brought Magos Tychon and his daughter to the command bridge, arriving just as the *Renard* began her approach run to the vast superstructure of the Ark Mechanicus. Though six hundred kilometres still separated the two vessels, the flank of Lexell Kotov's flagship filled the viewing bay. Less a ship, more a cliff of burnished steel and adamantium, it was a landscape of metal that defied rational understanding of how colossal a starship could possibly be.

Vitali and Linya – who, Roboute had to admit, was an attractive, if slightly aloof woman – stared at the immense vessel with undisguised admiration. Even among the priests of the Mechanicus, to see a vessel of such age and marvel was an honour.

'There're a lot of ships in orbit,' said Adara. 'I've never seen so many.'

'This is nothing,' said Roboute. 'You should see the conjunctions of Ultramar, those are gatherings like no other. Imagine a dozen worlds contributing to a muster. There're so many ships in orbit that you could strap on an environment suit and stroll around the orbital equator without having to void walk, you'd just step from hull to hull.'

'You're making fun of me, aren't you?' said Adara. 'That's impossible.'

'Care to wager on that?' asked Emil.

'With you? Not on your life.'

'Shame,' said Emil, with a hurt pout. 'Nobody wagers with me any more.'

'That's because you always win,' said Roboute.

'What can I say, I'm lucky,' said Emil with a shrug.

'Ultramar luck,' said Adara.

'There is no such thing as luck,' put in Linya Tychon, without taking her pretty eyes from the viewing bay. 'Only statistical probability, apophenia and confirmation bias.'

'Then you and I need to play a few hands of Knights and Knaves,' said Emil.

Roboute chuckled, returning his attention to the viewing bay and the impossibly vast craft before his own ship.

'Holy Terra...' breathed Emil, finally looking up at the vessel he was flying towards.

'You mean "Holy Mars", surely?' said Pavelka.

'Whatever,' said Emil. 'That thing's bloody enormous.'

'Such masterful understatement,' said Pavelka. 'The *Speranza* is a vessel against which all others are diminished. All praise the Omnissiah.'

Roboute had heard of the vessels known as Ark Mechanicus, but had dismissed tales of their continent-sized cityscapes and planetoid bulk as exaggerations, embellished legends or outright lies.

Now he knew better.

A passing battleship that Roboute recognised as a Dominator-class vessel sailed below the *Speranza*, and its length was more than eclipsed by the beam of the Ark Mechanicus. Where the Navy's ships tended towards wedge-shaped prows and giant cathedrals of stone carved into the craggy structure of their hulls, the Mechanicus favoured a less ostentatious approach to the design of their ships. Function, not form or glorification, was the guiding light of the ancient Mechanicus shipwrights. The colossal vessel had little symmetry, no gilded arches of lofty architecture, no processional cloisters of statuary, no vaulted, geodesic domes and no great eagle-wings or sweeping crenellations.

The *Speranza* was all infrastructure and industry, a hive's worth of manufactories, refineries, crackling power plants and kilometre upon

kilometre of laboratories, testing ranges, chemical vats and gene-bays arranged in as efficient a way as the ancient plans for its construction had allowed. Its engines were larger than most starships' full mass, its individual void generators and Geller arrays large enough to shroud a frigate by themselves.

Roboute had seen his fair share of space-faring leviathans, some Imperial, some not, but he had yet to see anything to match the sheer bloody-mindedness and ambition of the Mechanicus to have built such a damnably impressive vessel.

'It'll take us days to get from the embarkation deck to the bridge,' said Emil.

'Perhaps they have internal teleporters,' suggested Roboute.

'Don't joke,' said Adara.

'I'm not,' said Roboute. 'Seriously, I'm not. How else would anyone get about a vessel that size?'

'No one's teleporting me anywhere,' said Adara.

'Fine, you can stay on the *Renard* and keep her from being dismantled and studied,' said Emil.

'You think they'd do that?'

'I doubt it, but you never know,' said Roboute, patting the pearl-inlaid wooden arms of his command throne. 'The *Renard*'s a classic Triplex-Phall 99 Intrepid class, with Konor-sanctioned upgrades to her shield arrays. I wouldn't trust a tech-priest with a wrench anywhere near her.'

'An unfair assessment,' said Linya Tychon. 'No tech-priest would touch this ship once they inloaded her refit history. They would be too afraid of system-degradation from such ancient data.'

'Interrogative: was that a joke?' asked Pavelka, her mechadendrites stiffening and her floodstream rising to the challenge levelled at her vessel.

'It was,' said Linya.

'Do not insult our ship,' said Pavelka. 'You of all people ought to know better.'

'Apologies, magos,' said Linya with a cough of binary to emphasise her contrition. 'A poor jest.'

'What are those ships?' asked Adara, pointing to a number of high-sided craft bathed in the light of the Jouran moon, ungainly vessels shaped like space-faring Capitol Imperialis. They rose into a cavernous hold on one of the rear embarkation blisters, and though each was surely enormous, even they were dwarfed by the *Speranza*. Emil twisted the brass dial of the auspex array to read the broadcast frequencies of the vessels, and winced as the names blasted into space like a challenge. He snatched the implant from his ear, dialling down the gain as howls of machine cant bellowed out identities and warnings with equal force.

'Legio Sirius,' said Emil, massaging the side of his head where the binaric screeching had overloaded a number of his implanted cognitive arrays. Roboute nodded, now seeing the canidae symbol on the flanks of the engine transports.

'Titans, the god-machines...' said Pavelka, almost to herself. 'I once performed a maintenance ritual on a wounded engine of Legio Praetor. Only a Warhound, but still...'

'The Legio are warning people away from their loading operations,' said Magos Tychon.

'For such big bastards, they're coyer than an Ophelian Hospitaller on her wedding night,' said Emil with a sly wink. 'Trust me, I know what I'm talking about.'

'You shouldn't say things like that about the Sororitas,' said Adara, blushing.

It never ceased to amaze Roboute that a man so skilled in taking life and causing harm was so innocent in the ways of the fairer sex. Adara had honed his skills in one arena, while neglecting many others. Roboute could admire that trait, for he had seen others follow that path aboard *Isha's Needle*, but that was a time in his life he had long ago learned to keep to himself.

Emil's fingers danced over the control console beside him as a panel of lights began blinking in sequence. Say what you wanted about Emil Nader, he was a hell of a pilot. Roboute felt the deck shift beneath him as the *Renard* rolled and dipped her blunt nose to come in below the *Speranza*, awaiting final docking authority to be transferred to the Mechanicus controllers.

Satisfied control had been transferred, Emil sat back in his chair.

'Okay, if we crash and burn after this, it's not my fault.'

Roboute was about to answer when the hull shook and a groaning rumble travelled the length of *Renard's* structure as they passed into the graviton envelope of the Ark Mechanicus. So colossal was the *Speranza's* mass and density that it created a distorted gravity field equivalent to that of an unstable moon. To fly through such volatile space without an electromagnetic tether would be highly dangerous, though that hadn't stopped Emil from wanting to try.

Roboute watched the cavernous hold of the *Speranza* growing wider with every passing second as they juddered through the graviton interference. His heart rate was increasing with every kilometre they travelled, pulled in like struggling prey caught on a lure.

The image wasn't a reassuring one.

Emil leaned over and whispered, 'For the record, I still think this is a terrible idea.'

'You've made that clear more than once.'

'You know we don't need to do this, Roboute,' said Emil. 'We've plenty of profitable routes, and more contracts than we can handle. If you ask me, which you almost never do, trying to fly beyond the Halo Scar is a risk we don't need to take.'

'It'll be an adventure. Think of what might find out there.'

'I am. That's what's giving me nightmares,' said Emil, glancing over at the door to the captain's stateroom. 'And you're sure that thing in the stasis chest is real? Because I don't think these Martian priests are going to be too happy if it's not.'

'It's real, I'm sure of it,' said Roboute, as the Ark Mechanicus swallowed the *Renard*.

'I'm glad one of us is,' said Emil with a worried expression.

Microcontent 03

Little had improved for Abrehem and the men collared in the port-side bar. Shipped with unseemly haste from one hard metal box to another, fed syrupy, sugar-rich nutrient paste and forcibly injected with anti-ague shots, their lives had become long stretches of frustration followed by sharp bouts of terrifying activity.

Each collared individual was branded with a sub-dermal fealty identifier, which, according to the booming pronouncements that brayed regularly from the vox-grilles high on the containment facility's steel walls, marked them as indentured bondsmen of Archmagos Lexell Kotov, impressed to serve aboard the *Speranza* until such time as their debt to the Imperium was repaid.

'That means never,' reflected Hawke sourly when Abrehem asked what that meant.

They'd been blasted with water, doused in cleansing chemicals and so thoroughly deloused that Abrehem thanked the Emperor he harboured no desire for more children. Most of the captured souls – predominantly men, though a few women had been caught in the net – kept themselves to themselves, sullen and resigned to their fate. A few railed and shouted themselves hoarse at their confinement, but quickly gave up when they realised their words were falling on uncaring ears.

Ismael, however, had refused to quit and demanded to speak to a senior magos with admirable – if pointless – persistence. Eventually, the door had opened and a pair of heavily built warriors in bulked-out carapace armour entered, their faces sheathed in metal and hard plastek implants. Threat oozed from them and Ismael backed away, realising he'd made a grave error of judgement. The two warriors dragged the overseer out, and they hadn't seen him since. Abrehem hadn't missed his noisy and irritating presence overmuch, though he didn't like to dwell on what might be happening to his old supervisor.

The ogryn enforcer from the bar sat alone, and Abrehem wondered if it even knew what was happening to it. Had it accepted its fate or was it just waiting for someone to tell it what to do? Hawke had immediately found a seat next to the hulking creature, ingratiating himself with quick words it probably didn't understand. Abrehem couldn't deny the logic of the man's strategy; making friends with the biggest, meanest captive had a certain cunning to it. From what he was learning of Guardsman Hawke, low cunning and guile were two qualities he possessed in abundance. The man was a born survivor, and Abrehem knew that if he was going to get through this, he would do well to follow his lead.

He stuck close to Hawke and the ogryn, dragging Coyne over in the spirit of the more people you know the better. The ogryn didn't have a name, at least not one it could remember. The owner of the bar had called it Crusha, which seemed as good a name as any. Coyne spent most of his time weeping for a wife he'd likely never see again, but Abrehem had shed precious few tears for his own wife. His lack of regret had disgusted him at first, but after the introspection that confinement brings, he realised the only thing she would miss of him would be the credit stream from his work on the lifter rig.

The loss of their children had driven a wedge between them and, beyond the everyday routines of existence, they now shared little in common except grief. Abrehem knew she blamed him for their deaths, and he was hard-pressed to deny the truth of that. It had been his desire to seek work in the Joura starport facilities that had brought them to the polluted hab-zones in the first place. Shared loss had turned to bitter rancour and everyday cruelty, but mutual need had kept them together. She needed his credits, and he needed... he needed her to remind him that he had once been a father to two of the brightest stars in his world.

After decontamination they had been allowed to retain one personal possession, and Abrehem had held onto the folded pict of his two children, Eli and Zera. It wasn't a particularly good pict, Eli was looking away at his mother, and Zera's eyes were closed, but it was all he had left of them, so it would have to be enough. They were with the Emperor now, or so the fat preacher at the port Ministorum shrine told them. Abrehem suspected he would be joining them soon.

Eventually they'd been loaded into the berth of a rumbling craft, and noospheric tags drifting up through the indentured men's containers like coloured smoke told Abrehem they were aboard a sub-orbital trans-lifter designated *Joura XV/UM33*. Bulk carriers designed to go up and down on a fixed path, such craft were monstrously inefficient to run and prone to numerous delays if the pilot missed his narrow approach window.

Abrehem's lifter rig had loaded more than one such craft, and he wondered how many of the featureless containers he'd hooked up and crammed into their vast-bellied holds had contained desperate men and women bound for a life of virtual slavery aboard one of the fleet vessels in orbit. Their ascent had been violent and juddering, the friction heat of atmospheric breach swiftly replaced by the cold of the void. The container holds were uninsulated, and the brushed steel walls were soon crackling with frost.

'Emperor's balls, it's like a bloody icebox,' complained Hawke. 'Do they want us to freeze to death before they put us to work?'

'I think they figure we don't merit thermal shielding,' said Coyne.

'Where we're going we'll soon wish it was this cold again,' said Abrehem.

'What do you mean?'

'I mean I think we're heading to the engine compartments of the *Speranza*,' he answered. 'We've been loaded in one of the aft compartments of the engineering decks.'

'How do you know that?' asked Hawke. 'You got a direct line to the Machine-God or something?'

'No,' said Abrehem, wishing he'd kept his mouth shut.

'Come on,' said Hawke. 'Spill it. How do you know where we're headed?'

Leaning in, Abrehem tapped his cheek just below his eye and pulled the skin down a fraction, exposing the steel rim of his augmetic eye.

'Bloody hell,' hissed Hawke. Abrehem could see the man's brain turning over, figuring out ways to turn this knowledge to his advantage. 'There's something you don't see every day.'

The crew of the *Renard* disembarked into a scene of ordered anarchy.

Hundreds of cargo barques with vast bellies were berthed in the cavernous hold, arranged in precise ranks as unending lines of shipping containers were unloaded by servitor rigs that looked like ants devouring a carcass piece by piece. Roboute smelled oil, hot metal and chemical-rich sweat on the air, which was cold and sharp from the frosted hides of the barques. Thousands of men and machines moved in an intricate dance through the space, moving to an ordered, binary ballet along allotted routes. The scale of the space defied the idea of being indoors, that a vault of such dimensions could be constructed at all, let alone aboard a starship.

'I'll say this about the Mechanicus,' said Roboute. 'They know how to get things done.'

'Was that ever in doubt?' said Pavelka, standing just behind him.

'No, but to see it in action is quite something.'

Pavelka had demanded to accompany him, as had Kayrn Sylkwood, and both members of the Cult Mechanicus stood awed by the monumental industry and mechanical grandeur within Archmagos Kotov's flagship. The *Renard's* magos wore her ubiquitous red robe, with the sleeves ruffed up on her right arm to expose the limb's bionics, and Roboute couldn't help but notice the fresh gleam to her Icon Mechanicus amulet.

In deference to her exalted surroundings, Sylkwood had changed from her sweat- and grease-stained coveralls into a durable set of canvas trousers and padded jacket. Her enginseer's attire would never quite lose its sheen of oil and incense, but it had at least been given a clean. Sylkwood had the look of a grafter, with a shaven head gnarled with augmetics, and scars on the backs of her hands that spoke of a lifetime spent working in the living guts of engines.

For his own attire, Roboute had chosen a deep blue-grey frock coat, edged in red piping and with the Surcouf coat of arms: a stylised Ultima with a golden wreath curled around each arm like a battle honour. His trousers were of the deepest black, and his patent boots gleamed like new.

Emil had stifled a laugh at the sight of him, but Roboute knew better than any of them how much appearances, protocol and expectation mattered, especially to an organisation like the Adeptus Mechanicus. His first officer stood at his right, with Adara Siavash at his left, both clad in their best braided jackets and polished boots. Both men looked acutely uncomfortable dressed in clothes hauled from footlockers once in a blue moon, but Roboute had told them in no uncertain terms that they were going to meet their patron looking the part.

Between them, Emil and Adara carried the stasis chest, a smooth-finished box of matt black with a uniquely crafted lock that could only be opened by Roboute himself. The lock had been crafted by Yrlandriar of Alaitoc, and its worth was beyond imagining. It had been Ithandriel's gift to Roboute when he had left *Isha's Needle* – a gift he still felt unworthy to possess.

What lay within the chest could earn Roboute and his crew a fortune they couldn't spend in ten lifetimes. He couldn't speak for the others, but it wasn't the desire for wealth that had led Roboute to

Lexell Kotov. The artefact in the stasis chest held the solution to a mystery that had long vexed the priests of Mars, a mystery that spoke to Roboute's romantic soul and made all the risks inherent in their latest venture worthwhile.

'Shall we?' asked Emil, when Roboute didn't move.

'Yes,' he said, passing off his hesitation as wonderment. 'Tide and time wait for no man, eh?'

Awaiting them at the base of the crew ramp was a detachment of dangerous-looking men in vitreous black armour with heavy-gauge rifles held across their broad chests. Coiling power lines linked the tesla-chambers of their weapons with heavy backpacks that thrummed with electrical power, and each warrior's face was an impassive mix of square jaw, uncaring eyes and plastek implants feeding them tactical information. Each breastplate was machine-stamped with the image of a skull and lightning bolt. A clan emblem or guild symbol?

In the centre of the knot of skitarii, an adept of the Mechanicus awaited them, a tall figure in a voluminous surplice of red and gold, hooded and with only multiple spots of green light beneath his hood to give any hint of a face. The adept's limbs were elongated and ribbed with hissing ochre cabling, and a barrel-like drum of iridescent liquid was fitted to his back. A number of gene-dwarfed lackeys swathed in vulcanised rubber smocks and red-tinted goggles attended to the pulsing tubes that distributed the fluid around his system.

'Is that him?' asked Emil, *sotto voce.*

Roboute shook his head, trying not to show his irritation that they had not been met by Archmagos Kotov himself. Whoever this was, he was clearly an adept of some rank, but that he was not the leader of the Explorator Fleet was a none too subtle reminder of the expedition's hierarchy.

He marched towards the magos, and his practised eye caught the skitarii warriors tensing, their targeting augmetics following his every movement. He had no doubt that if he were stupid enough to make a move for the gold-chased ceremonial pistol holstered at his hip, they would gun him down without a second thought.

'Ave Deus Mechanicus,' said the magos as he reached the bottom of the ramp.

'I am Roboute Surcouf,' he said. 'But you are not Archmagos Kotov.'

'Situational update: Archmagos Kotov was detained by important fleet matters pertaining to our imminent break from high anchor,' explained the tech-priest in a perfectly modulated recreation of a human voice that still managed to sound grating and false. 'He sends his apologies, and requires that you accompany me to the Adamant Ciborium.'

Roboute didn't move when the magos indicated that he should follow him.

'Is there a problem?' asked the adept.

'Who are you?' asked Roboute. 'I like to know the name of the person to whom I am speaking.'

'Yes, of course. Introductions. Familiarity brought about by recognition of identifiers,' said the magos, drawing himself up straighter. 'Identify: I am Tarkis Blaylock, High Magos of the Cebrenia Quadrangle, Fabricatus Locum of the Kotov Explorator Fleet and Restorati Ultimus of the Schiaparelli Sorrow. I have extensive titles, Captain Surcouf, do you require me to recite them all for you?'

'No, that won't be necessary,' said Roboute, turning and walking back up the crew ramp of the *Renard*. He waved at Emil and the others. Knowing when to follow his lead, they reversed their course and returned to the ship with him.

'Captain?' said Magos Blaylock in confusion. 'What are you doing? Archmagos Kotov requires your presence. The expedition's departure cannot be delayed.'

Roboute paused halfway up the ramp, relishing Pavelka's look of horror at his breach of Mechanicus protocol. Enginseer Sylkwood had a roguish grin plastered across her face, and he gave her a sly wink before facing Blaylock once again.

'I think you and Archmagos Kotov are forgetting that without me and my crew, there *is* no expedition,' said Roboute, rapping his knuckles on the top of the chest. 'Without this artefact, this expedition is over before it begins, so I'll have a measure of recognition of that fact and a bit of damned respect. Your voice may be artificially rendered, Magos Blaylock, but I can still tell when someone who thinks he's cleverer than I am is talking down to me.'

Blaylock crossed his cabled arms in an approximation of an aquila, a gesture no doubt intended to mollify the captain, and bowed deeply.

'Apologies, Captain Surcouf,' said Blaylock. 'No disrespect was intended, the failing is simply one of unfamiliarity. It has been thirty-five point seven three nine years since I last had dealings with an individual not of the Cult Mechanicus. I simply assumed you would have read my identity in the noosphere. Had we conversed in the binaric purity of lingua-technis, such ambiguity and misunderstanding could have been avoided.'

Emil whispered to him out of the corner of his mouth. 'Even when they're apologising they can't resist a barb.'

Roboute rubbed a hand across his face to hide the grin that threatened to surface.

'Perhaps I should try to learn your language,' said Roboute. 'To avoid future *misunderstandings*.'

'That could be arranged with some simple augmetic surgery,' agreed Blaylock.

'That was a joke,' said Surcouf, returning to the bottom of the crew ramp.

'I see,' said Blaylock. 'It is all too easy to forget the ways of those not joined to the Machine.'

'Then I suggest you reacquaint yourself with our illogical ways,' snapped Roboute. 'Otherwise this is going to be a very short expedition.'

Blaylock nodded. 'I shall endeavour to rectify my understanding of our differing ways.'

'That would be a start,' said Roboute, as Blaylock turned his attention to the stasis chest being carried between Emil and Adara. The green lights beneath his hood narrowed their focus.

'May I see the item?' he asked – with a casual tone, but even one so transformed by mechanical additions to his biological form couldn't quite conceal the all-consuming desire to examine what lay within the chest.

'I think not,' said Roboute. 'As commander of this expedition, it seems only fitting that Archmagos Kotov be the first to examine the device, don't you think?'

'Of course,' replied Blaylock, quick to hide his bitter disappointment. 'Yes, absolutely. The Archmagos Explorator should have that honour.'

'Then you'd better take us to him,' said Roboute. 'Immediately.'

After being shunted along mass-conveyor rails and swung over abyssal chasms by servitor-crewed loader rigs, Abrehem felt a heavy thump as their container was at last deposited with an air of finality. Ceiling-mounted illuminators burst to life and the rear wall of the container rumbled forwards on protesting gears, inexorably flushing the human cargo out onto industrially stamped metal deck plates.

Containers identical to theirs stretched out left and right, hundreds or perhaps even thousands of them. Crowds of bewildered looking men and women milled uncertainly around them, blinking in the harsh light and looking fearfully for anything that might give them comfort.

Abrehem tried to hide his amazement at the space in which they stood, but failed miserably.

A vast steel cliff face of a wall stretched up into darkness before them, a writhing collection of pipes and ductwork spiralling across its surface like exposed arteries to shape the black and white Icon

Mechanicus. Steam poured from one eye of the great skull at its centre and a furnace-red light pulsed from behind the other. Stained-glass windows ran the full length of the walls, bathing the scene in a surreal blend of multi-coloured lights.

Vast statues of winged adepts and machine-cherubs filled deep alcoves and enormous cylindrical pipes hung from the ceiling on perilously thin strands of cabling. Powerful waves of heat sweated from them. Coolant gases vented from grilles along their length, and Abrehem caught the acrid, chemical tang of plasma venting. A thudding rumble vibrated through the deck plates, and he guessed the vast engine compartments were close by. Towering pistons pumped like drilling rigs at the edges of the chamber, and the squeal of metal on metal echoed in time with the ancient heartbeat of the vessel.

Vast machines filled the chamber, towering stacks of black iron, rotating cogs, pumping metal limbs and hissing flues that burped plumes of caustic gases. Standing before the front rank of these machines were a hundred warriors encased in the same black, beetle-gloss armour worn by the men who'd taken Ismael away. Bare-armed to better display their guild tattoos and implanted muscle enhancers, they carried a mixture of vicious shock mauls, shot-cannons and whips. Faceless behind black helms, they were fearsome killers, psychopaths yoked by iron discipline and devotion.

'Skitarii,' said Abrehem, and the men within earshot flinched at the word.

They'd all heard the stories of the mortal footsoldiers of the Adeptus Mechanicus, former Guardsmen enhanced with all manner of implants, both physical and mental, to render them into remorseless killers and zealous protectors of the holy artefacts of their tech-priest masters. Little better than feral wildmen, they were said to decorate their armour with the skin of those they had slain and collect trophy racks of enemy warriors' skulls.

So the stories went, but these men looked nothing like the stories.

They looked like pitiless, highly disciplined warriors against whom only a Space Marine might hope to prevail. Arranged in ordered ranks like robots, there was very little of these warriors that could be described as feral. A hundred boots slammed down in unison as the skitarii snapped to attention, and a grav-plate descended into their midst from the enormous skull.

A rippling energy haze surrounded the edges of the plate, and a reverberant hum filled the chamber as it hovered a few metres above the deck. Two figures stood side by side on the plate; the larger of the pair clad in armour similar to that worn by the skitarii, though much

more heavily ornamented and augmented. The other wore hooded vestments of deep crimson, around which hung a black and gold stole with cog-toothed edges, acid-etched with the sixteen laws in a host of numerical languages. A heavy generator pack clamped around his torso like a murderous arachnid, and a swirling haze of freezing air swirled around the machine priest like trapped mist. Abrehem felt cold just looking at him.

With a start, he recognised the magos from Joura, the one directing the collarmen. This was the man who'd torn him from his old life, and a bright nugget of hatred took hold in his heart.

'Who do you suppose they are?' asked Coyne.

'Can you tell, Abrehem?' asked Hawke.

'I'm trying to,' he said. 'But it's not easy. The sheer volume of data being inloaded and exloaded from their floodstreams every second is immense...'

'Listen to him,' sneered Hawke. 'You'd think he was one of them.'

Abrehem ignored the sniping remark and concentrated on the two figures as the Mechanicus adept in red drifted to the front of the grav-plate. Noospheric data cascaded in a waterfall of invisible light above his head in a halo of radiance, and the information Abrehem sought – though embedded on his every inload – was difficult to read.

'Saiixek,' said Abrehem. 'The bastard's called Saiixek.'

A burst of what sounded like static erupted from unseen speaker horns, deafening and abrasive. The distortion squalled and squealed like a badly-tuned vox-caster until Abrehem finally realised the magos was speaking to them. Gradually, the static diminished and the words came through, as the magos finished his pronouncement in unintelligible machine language and switched to his flesh voice.

'Informational: I am Magos Saiixek, Master of Engines,' he began, his voice artificial and devoid of any human inflection. 'You have been brought to the Adeptus Mechanicus vessel *Speranza*. This is a great honour. Every one of you is now bonded to the Priesthood of Mars and your service will allow the great machines of this vessel to function. By your exertions will the great engines burn hotter than stars. By your blood will the ship's wheels and gears be greased. By the strength in your bones will the mighty pistons empower its great heart and its fists of light. Your lives now serve the Omnissiah.'

'As far as inspiring speeches go, I've heard better,' said Hawke, and a ripple of gallows laughter spread through the men and women of their container.

The shoulder of Saiixek's robe twitched and a series of whirring, reticulated arms emerged from a number of concealed folds. They clicked and snapped as they unfolded, each one terminating in unfolding metallic grips, tools and needle-like appendages that looked more like instruments of torture than engineering manipulators.

The plate descended to the deck, and the figure in black stepped down. Now that he was on the same level as the newly-arrived men and women, Abrehem saw his shoulders were almost absurdly oversized. Augmented with mechanical prosthetics, muscle enhancers and numerous weapon implants, the warrior was as hulking as the Space Marines were said to be. He carried a long polearm, its top surmounted by a serrated blade and its base fitted with a clawed energy pod, the purpose of which eluded Abrehem but which was no doubt intended to cause harm.

The man's skull was a hairless orb, the front half pallid and waxen, the rear encased in bronze and silver. His teeth were gleaming and metallic, and a red-gold Icon Mechanicus was embedded in the centre of his forehead. This was no skitarii chieftain: this was a tech-priest, but one unlike any Abrehem had seen before.

The warrior-magos stopped directly in front of Hawke and regarded him through eyes with the glassy sheen of artificiality. Abrehem recognised high-end implants, sophisticated targeting mechanisms, threat analysers and combat vector-metrics. He'd only ever heard of quality like that on high-ranking Mechanicus adepts.

The man's head twitched in Abrehem's direction, no doubt reading the passive emanations of his own augmetics. His exposed flesh was wet with chemical unguents and hot oil lubricants. The additional limbs partly concealed beneath his black cloak were sheened black iron. Quickly Abrehem was dismissed as a threat, and the warrior-magos leaned down over Hawke, easily a metre taller than him. His lip curled in a sneer as he read his biometric data from the fealty brand.

'Hawke, Julius,' he said in a voice that sounded like crushed gravel. 'A troublemaker.'

'Me, sir? No, sir,' said Hawke.

'It wasn't a question,' said the brutish figure.

Hawke didn't reply and continued to stare at a point just over the warrior's shoulder, which was no mean feat given the height difference between them. Hawke's face assumed a slack, vacant expression, common to all soldiers of low rank when facing an irate superior officer.

'I am Dahan, Secutor of the Skitarii Guilds aboard the *Speranza*,' said the brutal giant. 'Do you know what that means, Hawke, Julius?'

'No, sir,' answered Hawke.

'It means that I have the power of life and death over you,' said Dahan. 'It means your biometrics have been recorded and filed. Wherever you are and whatever you are doing, I will know it. I destroy troublemakers like you without effort, and I have a thousand men who would happily do it for me. Do you understand your place aboard this ship?'

'Sir, yes, sir,' responded Hawke.

Dahan turned away, but instead of returning to the hovering grav-plate and Magos Saiixek, he marched to join his warriors. Abrehem let out a pent-up breath, but Hawke just grinned as the hulking warrior departed, leaving only the faint reek of his chemical anointments.

Magos Saiixek resumed speaking as Dahan joined the ranked-up skitarii.

'Each of you has been branded with a unique identifier, indicating which honoured task you have been allotted aboard the *Speranza*. Move to the end of this chamber, where you will be directed to your storage facility and instructed on how to carry out your duties.'

The vox-grilles barked as a rotating series of binaric cants and recitations in High Gothic filled the chamber. Abrehem could only catch the odd word here and there; enough to know that he was hearing machine hymns in praise of the Machine-God, but not enough to make much sense of it.

'Well, that was interesting,' said Hawke.

'Thor's blood, I thought that skitarii magos was going to kill you,' said Coyne, his skin glistening with sweat. 'Did you see the bloody size of him?'

'I've seen his type a hundred times before,' said Hawke, raising his voice just enough for those nearby to hear him. 'The trick is to never make eye contact and only say yes or no. That got me through ten years of service in the Guard, and you can have that one for free, lads!'

Wary smiles greeted his comment, but Abrehem kept his expression neutral as the vast iron cliff face before them split down its middle with a *boom* of disengaging locks. The grinning skull slid apart on friction-dampened rails as the ranks of skitarii warriors turned with a thunder of boots. They marched aside as the enormous door before the newest crew members of the *Speranza* opened to reveal a series of ironwork channels, like funnels used to guide livestock to the slaughterman's knife.

Glowing red light shone from beyond the vast gateway, and the fire of voracious furnaces, ever-thirsty plasma engines and hungry weapon batteries awaited them.

Microcontent 04

Sitting high in the cupola of his faithful Hellhound, Captain Blayne Hawkins watched the loading operations of the 71st Cadian (detached formation) with exasperation. His soldiers had transferred from warzone to warzone often enough that the movement of an entire regiment was something the support corps could usually manage with a degree of finesse. Moving ten companies should have been child's play.

But this was the first time they had embarked upon a Mechanicus vessel.

A degree of belligerent cooperation existed between the crews of Navy carrier vessels and the Guard units they were transporting, but no such bond, begrudged or otherwise, was in evidence between the Cadians and the Adeptus Mechanicus logisters. Nearly a hundred armoured vehicles were snarled in the embarkation deck, engines throbbing and filling the air with the blue-shot fug of exhaust fumes, while Cadian supply officers and Mechanicus deck crew argued over the best means of untangling the log-jammed vehicles.

His drivers were well practised in the best way to manoeuvre their tanks into berthing holds, but the Mechanicus logisters had different ideas. It hadn't taken long until a couple of squadrons had become entangled and a number of vehicles inevitably collided. In the ensuing anarchy, a Leman Russ threw a track and a pair of Hellhounds had broadsided one another as each driver received conflicting orders.

'Emperor damn it, we're supposed to be in the berthing hangar by now,' he snapped, clambering from the hatch and swinging his legs out over the tank's forward turret. Fresh-faced and young, by other regimental standards, to hold a captaincy, Hawkins had earned his stripes as a warrior and commander by the time he'd left the violet-lit world of Cadia, and had only gone on to cement his reputation as a tenacious and competent officer in the years since leaving his home world for good.

Hawkins dropped to the deck, feeling the rumble of the mighty starship's engines through the soles of his boots. He was used to the scale of Navy bulk handlers, but the *Speranza* was many times greater than any vessel he or his men had berthed in. Each starship had its own sound, its own feel and its own smell. He remembered *Thor's Light;* it had reeked of fyceline and almonds from its time as an ordnance carrier. *Azure Halo* always smelled of wet permacrete, and the internals of *Maddox Hope* had inexplicably dripped with moisture as though its very superstructure were melting.

He knelt and placed his palm on the deck plates, feeling the immense presence of the starship – a bass hum of incredible power and age. This ship was *old*, older than the ships of the Navy, which had already sailed for thousands of years. Colonel Anders had hinted that the vessel's keel had been laid down before the ancient crusade to reunite the fragmented worlds of men, but where he'd learned that particular nugget, he hadn't elaborated.

Hawkins could well believe it to be true. Unbreakable strength rested in the ship's ancient bones, yet despite its obvious age, there was a *newness* to the ship that belied its unimaginable scale. It felt welcoming, so perhaps this mess of entangled vehicles wasn't the bad omen he had feared.

'Rae, get down here,' he yelled, knowing his adjutant wouldn't be far away. Taybard Rae was a veteran lieutenant of the regiment, a stalwart of the company and a man without whose steady presence many a battle line might have buckled. Hawkins rose to his full height as Rae appeared from behind an idling Chimera, his uniform already crumpled and untidy. Hawkins had watched a freshly-pressed uniform become creased and looking like it had just been through a battle in the time it took Rae to walk from the barracks to the parade ground.

'Bloody Mechanicus meddling if ever I saw it,' said Rae.

'Looks like it,' agreed Hawkins.

'The colonel on board yet?'

'I hope not,' said Hawkins, setting off through the press of tightly-packed armoured vehicles, towards the source of the hold-up. 'I want to get this sorted before he sees this damn mess.'

'Good luck with that,' said Rae. 'I've just been up front. There're three tanks jammed in the link tunnel to the berthing hold, and everyone else is rammed tight up their arses. It's going to take hours to get them untangled.'

'Where's Callins? He's supposed to keep things like this from happening.'

'Arguing with the Mechanicus logisters. It's not pretty.'

'I'm sure.'

'Remember that time with those greenskins and the ogryns on Peolosia? Where they just stood and pounded on each other until they both dropped? It's like that, but without the finesse.'

Hawkins swore, carefully negotiating the narrow paths between trapped Leman Russ battle tanks, idling Salamanders and the regiment's signature Hellhound tanks. Hawkins approached the sound of arguing voices, his temper fraying with every step. He ducked under the sponson mount of *Kasr's Fist*, a Leman Russ Destroyer with numerous kill markings etched into its pockmarked hull. Still painted in the urban camouflage of Baktar III's ruined industrial wastelands, its rightmost lascannon was wedged tightly against the hull of *Creed's Pride* and a number of the rivets holding it in place had buckled against the pressure.

'The colonel's not going to like that,' said Rae, examining the popped seams along the edge of the sponson mount.

A dark-coated supply corps officer was arguing with a number of Mechanicus logisters in bright robes and a bulked-out machine-skull at the front of the tank. The Mechanicus adepts were gesturing with green-lit illuminator wands and barking commands in vox-amped irritation, but the Cadian supply officer was giving as good as he got. Major Jahn Callins was at the heart of the argument, and Hawkins didn't envy the logisters the full force of his wrath. He'd seen colonels and generals retreat with their tails between their legs in the face of Callins's blunt procedural anger.

Surely a lowly Mechanicus adept had no chance?

Callins was a granite-faced veteran from Kasr Fayn, a no-nonsense supply officer who innately understood the operational needs of the regiment. Never in all Hawkins's years of service had he known any unit of the 71st to run out of ammo, food or any other essential supply. To gauge the attrition of supplies was as much an artform as accountancy, and Callins understood the monstrous appetite of war better than anyone.

'What's the hold-up, major?' asked Hawkins, straightening his pale grey uniform jacket.

Callins sighed and waved an irritated hand at the logisters. As a major, Callins was technically Hawkins's superior, but Cadian fighting ranks often assumed seniority while on active service.

'These idiots are trying to get us directed by mass and dimensions,' said Callins, almost spitting the words. 'They want the heavies in first.'

'To better distribute the accumulated cargo loads,' said the logister, a robed man with iron-faced cognitive augmetics grafted to the side of his skull. He carried a battered data-slate, which he repeatedly tapped with a tapered stylus. 'A Mechanicus vessel has to be loaded in a specific mass-distribution pattern to ensure optimal inertial compensation efficiency.'

'I understand that,' said Callins. 'But if you load our heavies on first, it's going to slow our disembarkation. The heavies go in last so the big guns come out first. Basic rule of warfare, that is. Listen, why don't you let the big boys who actually do the fighting sort out how we want our tanks loaded and then we'll all get on so much better.'

'You proceed on a fallacious assumption,' said the logister. 'With Mechanicus loading and unloading protocols and rapid transit rigs, I assure you that our procedures are faster than yours.'

Callins turned to face Hawkins, throwing his hands up in exasperation. 'You see what I have to deal with?'

'Let me see that,' said Hawkins, holding his hand out for the logister's data-slate.

'Guard captains are not authorised to consult Mechanicus protocols,' said the logister.

'Just give him the damn slate,' said a voice behind Hawkins, and every Cadian within earshot stood to attention. 'I have the authority and I want this hellish snarl-up dealt with right bloody now. Is that understood?'

Colonel Ven Anders emerged from the tangled snarl of vehicles, resplendent in his dress greys, a slightly more formal-looking ensemble than that of a Guardsman. Only the bronze rank pins on the starched collar of his uniform jacket and its elaborate cuffs gave any indication that he was an officer of high rank. His dark, close-cropped hair was kept hidden beneath a forager cap, and his smooth, patrician features were handsome in the way that only good breeding and a healthy diet could sculpt.

Two commissars came after him, their black storm coats and gleaming peaked caps looking ragged and shabby next to the casual ease of the colonel's dress. Both men were unknown to Hawkins – recent transfers to the company after Commissar Florian's death – but he instinctively held himself a little taller at the sight of them.

The logister immediately handed the slate over, and Hawkins quickly

scanned the reams of information: lading rates, berth capacity and lifter speeds. Though much of the data was too complex to easily digest or superfluous to his needs, he understood that the Mechanicus system *would*, in all likelihood, be quicker than the Cadian way of doing things.

'Well?' asked Anders.

'It looks good,' said Hawkins, handing the slate over to Callins. 'In most circumstances, I'd agree with whatever the major wanted to do, but in this case, I think we ought to go with this.'

Callins scanned the data-slate and Hawkins saw the reluctant acceptance of his words as he ran the numbers.

'Can you really move these tanks this fast?' asked Callins.

'Those margins of efficiency are at maximum tolerances,' explained the logister. 'With non-Mechanicus cargo, we allow extra time-slippage for dispersement procedures.'

'Is he right?' asked Anders. 'Can they get us loaded fast?'

Callins sighed. 'If they can hit these numbers, yes.'

'That's all I need to know,' said the colonel, taking the slate back from Callins and handing it to the logister. 'Adept, you may proceed. Do what you need to do to get my tanks berthed. How long will you require to complete loading operations?'

The logister didn't answer, a shimmer of data-light flickering behind his eyes.

'Forty-six minutes,' said the logister as the light faded. 'I have just inloaded a statistical schematic of movement patterns from Magos Blaylock that will allow these vehicles to be separated with minimal effort if you will permit my men to work unhindered.'

'Do it,' said Anders, addressing his words as much to his own soldiers as the Mechanicus adepts. 'You have my assurance that you will have the full cooperation of every Cadian footslogger, tanker, flame-whip and ditch-digger under my command in all matters.'

The logister gave a short bow and issued a series of orders to his deck crew in staccato blurts of machine language. In moments, overhead lifter rigs descended from the distant ceiling to lift out those vehicles that prevented others from moving. Hawkins, Rae, Anders, Callins and the two commissars hastily moved out of the way and watched with admiration as the Gordian knot of tangled vehicles was gradually transformed into an orderly stream of rumbling armour. Hellhounds, Leman Russ, Sentinels and a host of other vehicles roared past on their way to their assigned berths.

'Okay, they're not bad,' conceded Callins.

'Right, now that our vehicles are being stowed, let's see about getting

the men squared away,' said Anders. 'Do we think we can manage that without getting them lost?'

'Yes, sir,' said Hawkins.

'Right, get it done, Blayne,' ordered Anders. 'Archmagos Kotov awaits, and I can't be stuck here making sure every soldier's got a bunk.'

'No, sir,' Hawkins assured him. 'We'll be in place before you get back, squared away and ready for orders.'

'Good, make sure of it,' said Anders. 'Give them an hour to bed in then get them running weapon drills. I want everything five by five before we break orbit. Is that clear?'

'Crystal,' said Hawkins.

'Begging your pardon, Colonel Anders,' said Rae. 'Is it true what we've been hearing?

'What have you been hearing, lieutenant?' said Anders.

Rae shrugged, as though suddenly unwilling to say what he'd heard for fear of looking foolish.

'That we'll be fighting alongside Space Marines, sir.'

'The rumour mill's been in overdrive, I see,' replied Anders.

'But is it true, sir?'

'So I'm given to understand, lieutenant,' said Anders. 'Space Marines of the Black Templars, though I haven't seen or heard whether that's truly the case.'

'Black Templars...' said Rae. 'Makes sense, I suppose. After all, we're crusading out into unexplored space, aren't we? Yeah, I like the sound of that. We're bloody crusaders.'

Colonel Anders grinned and gave a quick salute to his officers before striding off in the direction of one of the embarkation deck's transit hubs, where bullet-shaped capsules paused to pick up or disgorge passengers before shooting through the *Speranza* at incredible speeds.

With Anders gone, Hawkins said, 'You heard the colonel, we've ten companies of tired and irritable soldiers to get bunked down and ready for weapon drills and inspection. Callins, Rae, see to it. The Mechanicus might have shown us up when it comes to moving machinery around, but I'll be damned if they'll do it when it comes to moving soldiers.'

He snapped his fingers.

'Move!' he ordered.

Incense smoke fogged the innermost sanctum of the rapid strike cruiser *Adytum*, and the banners hanging from the wide arches of surrounding cloisters swung gently with the passage of the warriors beneath. Six Space Marines of the Black Templars, armoured in plates of the deepest jet and purest white, marched along the nave towards the great slab of an altar at its end. Torchlight reflected from the curves of their warplate and caught the hard chips of their eyes.

A giant figure encased in bulky Terminator armour stood like an obsidian statue before the altar, his shoulders bulked out with the tanned hide of the great dragon-creature he had slain on his first crusade. A golden eagle spread its wings over his enormous chest, where rested a gold and silver rosette with a blood-red gem at its heart.

His glowering helm, fashioned in the form of a bone-white skull with coal-red eye-lenses, was a rictus death mask that was the last thing countless enemies of the Emperor had seen as they died. In one oversized gauntlet, the colossal warrior bore a great eagle-winged maul, his instrument of death and badge of office all in one.

This was the Reclusiarch of the Scar Crusade, and his name was Kul Gilad.

The six Templars halted before Kul Gilad and dropped to their knees. They carried their helms in the crook of their arms, five black, one white, and all kept their heads bowed as the Reclusiarch stepped down to the marble-flagged floor of the sanctum. Robed acolytes and neophytes emerged from behind the altar and sang hymns of battle and glory as they took up position either side of the Reclusiarch. Most were acolyte-serfs of the Chapter, but one was a neophyte, and he bore the most revered artefact aboard the *Adytum*.

Masked and stripped of all insignia to keep the weapon he carried from knowing his name, the neophyte bore a sword of immense proportions. Sheathed in an unbreakable black scabbard of an alloy unknown beyond the slopes of Olympus Mons, the leather-wrapped hilt bore the Chapter's flared cross emblem at its pommel, an obsidian orb set with a polished garnet. A long chain hung from the handle, ready to be fettered to whichever warrior it would choose as its bearer.

The Templars took their position before the Reclusiarch, devotional incense coiling around them as yet more figures emerged from the cloisters. Each of these figures bore a piece of armour: a breastplate, a greave, a pauldron, a vambrace. Unseen choirs added their chanting to this most sacred moment, a hundred voices that told of great deeds, honourable victories and unbreakable duty.

'You are the Emperor's blade that splits the night,' said the Reclusiarch.

'*We light the flame that banishes shadows*,' answered the six warriors.

'You are the vengeance that never rests.'

'*We cleave to the first duty of the Adeptus Astartes*.'

'You are the fire of truth that shines brightest.'

'*So the primarch willed it, so it shall be done*.'

'The Emperor's gift is your strength and righteous purpose.'

'With it we bring doom to our enemies.'

'Your honour is your life!'

'Let none dispute it!'

The Reclusiarch dipped the fingers of his left hand in a brazier of smouldering ash carried on the back of a hooded acolyte and moved between the kneeling warriors. Though each was genhanced to be greater than any mortal warrior, the Reclusiarch dwarfed them all in his ancient suit of Terminator armour. He anointed each warrior's forehead with a cross of black ash, whispering words that spoke to each man's soul.

Bearded Tanna, the squad sergeant, resolute and unyielding in his devotion.

'Steel of Dorn within your bones.'

Auiden, the anchor of the squad.

'Courage of Sigismund fill your heart.'

Issur the bladesman, an inspiration to them all.

'Strength of the ages be yours.'

Varda, the questioner, to whom all mysteries were a source of fresh joy.

'You carry the soul of us all.'

Bracha, who had recovered the Crusader Helm of the fallen Aelius at Dantium Gate.

'Honour of Terra shall be yours to bear.'

Yael, the youngster, he who had been singled out by Helbrecht himself as a warrior of note.

'Learn well the lessons of battle, for they are only taught once.'

The unseen choirs raised the tempo and discordance of their chants, filling the sanctum with hymns in praise of the Emperor and His sons. Toxic incense that could kill mortals with a single breath wreathed the floor like marsh fog, and as each warrior stared into the depths of the mists, they reflected on the legacy of heroism that had gone before them, the glorious crusades of their forebears and the roll of battles won and foes slain. To live up to such a past was no easy thing, and not every warrior could bear such a heavy burden.

But most of all they reflected on the shame of Dantium.

A battle lost... An Emperor's Champion slain...

And the doom that had dogged their thoughts since that day...

The Reclusiarch stepped back to the altar as each Templar took deep breaths of the chemical-laden smoke, their lungs filling with the secrets encoded into its molecular arrangement. Only the gene-smiths of the *Eternal Crusader* knew the origin of the incense, and only by their strange alchemy could it be rendered.

Kul Gilad studied the men before him, each one shaped by thousands of years of history and lost arts of genetics. The best and bravest of the Imperium, the strength and honour of the past was carved into their very marrow. The fearful losses at Dantium had shaken them to their core, but this crusade would be a chance for them to regain their honour, to prove their worth to the High Marshal once again and shake off the ill temper that had settled upon them all. This deployment alongside the Adeptus Mechanicus was not punishment nor penance, but redemption.

Ghostly images of mighty warriors shimmered at the edges of Kul Gilad's vision, but he ignored them, knowing them for the narcotic phantoms they were. He would never again be touched by the visions, but one among his warriors would certainly feel the power of the Golden Throne moving within him. Who would be touched by the Emperor's presence, he could not know, for none could fathom the complexities and subtle nuances of His will. Kul Gilad searched each man's face for any sign of a reaction to the fugue-inducing mist, but he could see nothing beyond their stoic determination to commence this latest crusade into the unknown and reclaim their honour.

When it began, it began suddenly.

Varda rose to his feet, reaching out to something only he could see. His eyes were wide and his jaw fell open in wonderment. Tears ran down his cheeks as he wept at a sight of rapture or terror. Varda took a faltering step towards the altar, his hand grasping for something just out of reach.

'I see...' said Varda. 'Its beauty is terrible... I know... I know what I must do.'

'What must you do?' asked Kul Gilad.

'Slay those who have given insult to the Emperor,' said Varda, his voice betraying a dreamlike quality to its tone. 'I need to kill them all, to bathe my blade in the blood of the unclean. Where is my sword? Where is my armour...?'

'They are here,' answered Kul Gilad, pleased that it should be Varda who was chosen. He nodded to the figures lurking in the cloisters and they came forwards in pairs, one bearing a shard of battleplate, the other empty-handed. They surrounded Varda, and piece by piece, stripped him of his armour until he stood only in his grey bodyglove. Even bereft of his power armour, the strength of his body was palpable. And as they had divested him of his old armour, now the figures attired him in his new warplate.

As each portion of the gilded and artificer-wrought armour was fastened to his body, it seemed that Varda grew to fill its contours, as though it had

been fashioned for him and him alone. At last he was clad head to foot in the ancient Armour of Faith, and all that remained to be fitted was his own ivory-wreathed helm. Varda reached up and slid the helmet over his head, clicking it into place and holding out his hands in expectation.

'Arm him,' said Kul Gilad, and the neophyte at his side moved to stand before the dazed warrior.

Varda took a step towards the boy, who backed away in fear.

'Quickly, boy! Give him the sword,' snapped Kul Gilad. It was not unknown for a warrior in such a fugue state to slay any who came near him, believing them to be his enemies. Only the sword would bring them to their senses. The neophyte held the midnight scabbard out to Varda, who let out a shuddering breath as he knelt before the youngster. He cocked his head to the side as though seeing something more than a mere sword.

'Give it to me,' he said, and the neophyte held the scabbard out, hilt-first.

Varda drew the sword, its eternally sharp blade utterly black and etched along its length with filigreed lettering in the curling Gothic script of the Imperium. Its blade was long and heavy beyond the means of any mortal soldier to bear, the handle long enough to allow it to be wielded by one or two hands. Kul Gilad approached Varda and took hold of the dangling chain.

He wrapped it around Varda's wrist and fastened the fetter to his gauntlet.

'The Black Sword is yours,' said Kul Gilad. 'It can never be loosed, never surrendered and never be sheathed without blood first being shed. Only in death will it pass to another.'

Kul Gilad placed his hand on Varda's helmet.

'Rise, Emperor's Champion,' he said.

The mag-lev was a frictionless transit system that ran a convoluted circuit around the interior spaces of the *Speranza* like a network of blood vessels around a living being. Silvered linear induction rails sparked with e-mag pulses, the car running through the spaces between bulkheads at dizzying speeds that made Roboute's heart race. Only an inertial dampening field within the compartment kept them from being crushed by the awesome g-force. Adara and Emil sat either side of the stasis chest at the rear of the bullet-shaped compartment, staring through the smoky glass at the incredible sights passing by with mind-numbing rapidity.

Magos Pavelka and Enginseer Sylkwood sat at the rear of the compartment as Blaylock steered the mag-lev via a hard-wired MIU plug

that socketed into place beneath the nape of his hood. His retinue of dwarf attendants hunkered down at his knees like well-behaved children. The two Magos Tychons – father and daughter (though such a notion still had Roboute scratching his head at the logistics of how such a thing had come to be) – sat behind Blaylock.

'You see?' said Emil. '*This* is how you get around a ship this big. No teleporters required.'

'The *Speranza* is fitted with numerous teleport chambers,' said Blaylock. 'Intended for both external and internal use, though to use them to travel within the bounds of the ship is considered wasteful and only ever employed in emergencies.'

'Good to know,' said Adara, turning to Sylkwood in the back. 'Any chance we can get something like this mag-lev fitted to the *Renard*?'

Sylkwood laughed. 'What would be the point? You can walk from one end to the other without breaking sweat.'

'*You* can,' said Adara. 'You've got augmetic legs.'

Sylkwood smiled and looked away, admiring the sheer scale of industrial architecture contained within the *Speranza's* hull. They'd already passed fog-belching refineries, chemical silos, flame-lit Machine temples, skitarii barracks, laboratory decks, training arenas, vast power plants with skyscraper-sized generators that spat coils of azure lightning, and building-sized structures that Magos Blaylock informed them were voltaic capacitors capable of running the vessel's mechanical functions for a month.

A towering vehicle hangar was filled with numerous gargantuan cathedrals of industry mounted on track units the size of hab-blocks, construction engines that could raise a city in under a day and demolition machinery capable of levelling a moderately-sized hive in half that. Folded solar collectors filled bay after bay, concertinaed like corrugated fields of black glass entwined with intricate gear mechanisms and looping arcs of insulated power relays.

One hangar was so vast it took them several seconds to traverse its length, but in that time, Roboute and his crew caught a glimpse of the mightiest war-engines of the Adeptus Mechanicus.

The god-machines of Legio Sirius boarded the *Speranza*, hunched over like age-bowed giants as they emerged from their transports with wary footfalls. Each war-engine was a towering behemoth of destruction, an avatar of the Machine-God in his aspect of the Destroyer.

'Titans!' cried Adara, pressing himself to the glass at the sight of the colossal machines.

One engine with squared shoulders and legs like hab-towers – a Warlord – dwarfed the others, the armoured segments of its grey and

gold carapace shifting like time-lapsed continental plates as it took thunderous steps towards its transit cradle. Such a machine could conquer worlds single-handedly, it could lay waste to cities and entire armies. Such a machine was worthy of worship, and it had no shortage of devotees. Thousands of robed adepts supervised the embarkation of the Mechanicus battle-engines, each one an honoured servant and a genuflecting devotee of these mobile temples to destruction.

Smaller engines followed the Warlord like a hunting pack, a Reaver and a pair of loping Warhounds. Their weapons snapped up to follow the passage of the mag-lev as howled threats brayed from their warhorns.

The Titans were soon lost to sight as the mag-lev passed through a metres-thick bulkhead, but it wasn't long before they caught sight of yet more of the Kotov Expedition's armed might. An embarkation deck swarmed with armoured vehicles, caught in what looked like an almighty snarl-up. Super-heavies were locked in with main battle tanks, armoured fighting vehicles and lurching walkers that stopped and started as space opened up for them to move.

'Good luck sorting that mess out,' noted Emil, before twisting in his seat to grin at Pavelka. 'Hey, Ilanna, I thought the Mechanicus didn't allow for things like that.'

Pavelka looked down at the hopelessly entangled armoured regiment.

'They are not Mechanicus,' she said. 'Regimental markings identify them as the 71st Cadian Hellhounds. From the dispersal pattern of the gridlocked vehicles, it seems clear the Guard units have not followed Mechanicus loading protocols.'

'Perceptive of you, Magos Pavelka,' said Blaylock. 'I have just compiled a statistical analysis of the trapped vehicles and exloaded it to the ranking logister. Would you care to peruse it?'

Pavelka nodded and Roboute saw a flicker of light behind her eyes as the data packet passed invisibly between the two magi. Pavelka's lips parted as she processed the inloaded schematics, smiling in appreciation of Blaylock's calculations.

'Masterful,' she said. 'The code-sequencing of the movement algorithms is a work of art.'

Blaylock had no face Roboute could see, but the emerald light beneath his voluminous hood pulsed with a binaric acknowledgement of Pavelka's high praise.

The entangled vehicles were soon lost to sight as the mag-lev sped onwards, and Roboute noticed the cavernous halls they travelled were becoming more ornate, less functional. Bare steel and iron gave way to chrome and gold, clanking machinery to banks of humming cogitation processionals. Servitors became few and far between, replaced by robed Mechanicus adepts and gaggles of their retinues.

If they had just passed through the guts of the *Speranza*, now they were drawing near its higher functions, the grand temples and the seats of sacred knowledge.

'Cadians, eh?' said Adara with an appreciative nod. 'We're travelling in esteemed company.'

'Titans? Cadians? Makes me wonder what this Kotov is expecting to find beyond the Halo Scar,' said Emil.

'Archmagos Kotov also counts the Adeptus Astartes as part of his Complement of Explorators,' added Magos Blaylock. 'High Marshal Helbrecht himself sends a battle squad of his finest warriors to stand with Mars.'

'Really?' said Adara, wide-eyed and almost bursting with excitement.

'Indeed. The compact between the Priesthood of Mars and the Adeptus Astartes is an ancient and respected bond,' said Blaylock. 'The High Marshal recognises that.'

'Space Marines,' said Sylkwood, leaning back and lighting a lho-stick with a solder-lance embedded in the metallic fingertip of her left hand. 'I've fought alongside Space Marines. Good to have at your side, but best to keep out of their way, Adara.'

'What do you mean?' asked the youngster.

Sylkwood leaned forwards, resting her elbows on her knees as she blew a cloud of blue smoke.

'They're not like us,' she said. 'They might look like us, sort of, but trust me, they're not. Like as not, they'll ignore you, but if you're really unlucky you might accidentally offend one and end up on the wrong end of a mass-reactive.'

'Kayrn's right,' said Roboute. 'Stay away from Space Marines if you know what's good for you.'

'I thought you Ultramar types were all about how great and noble the Space Marines are?'

'The Ultramarines, maybe,' agreed Roboute. 'But even they're a step removed from us. They don't think like us. When you can take pain and inflict harm like a Space Marine, you start to look at everything in terms of how you can kill it.'

'When all you have is a bolter and chainsword, everything looks like a target,' added Emil. 'Roboute's right, if there's Space Marines here, keep out of their way.'

'There is only one Adeptus Astartes aboard at present,' said Magos Blaylock. 'Reclusiarch Kul Gilad joins us while his warriors remain sequestered aboard the *Adytum*.'

'The *Adytum*?' asked Roboute.

'Their vessel, a modified rapid strike cruiser, designed for smaller expeditionary forces.'

'I didn't recall seeing a Space Marine identifier on the orbital manifest,' said Emil.

'The Black Templars have chosen to keep their vessel noospherically dark,' explained Blaylock, not even trying to conceal his distaste at such an action. 'Archmagos Kotov has granted them a degree of... latitude in observing Mechanicus protocols.'

'I believe their warrior expeditions are known as crusades,' said Linya.

'Just so, Mistress Tychon,' said Blaylock. 'Though due to the overtly martial aspect such a term might confer upon our expedition, Archmagos Kotov is disinclined to employ it.'

'Her title is *Magos*,' said Vitali Tychon. 'I suggest you use it.'

'Of course,' said Blaylock, inclining his head in a gesture of respect. 'I employed the feminine honorific simply to differentiate between two individuals bearing the title of Magos Tychon.'

'Mistress Tychon is an acceptable form of address,' said Linya, accepting Blaylock's gesture.

Roboute grinned and slapped a hand on Blaylock's shoulder, all hard angles and clicking joints, as the mag-lev sped towards a great golden cliff face stamped with a vast Icon Mechanicus, embossed gears, cogs and reams of binary code in praise of the Omnissiah.

'Seems like you're going out of your way to offend people today, Tarkis,' he said.

'Not at all,' said Blaylock. 'Perhaps mortals need to learn more of our ways as much as I need to learn of theirs.'

Roboute laughed. 'I think you and I are going to get on famously.'

Microcontent 05

An irising hatch, only fractionally larger than the diameter of the mag-lev, opened in the golden escarpment, and the speeding compartment punched through into a wide processional of polished steel and glittering chrome. Numerous induction rails terminated at an elevated rostrum, and several gently humming mag-levs were already berthed at the terminus.

Arching beams soared overhead, absurdly slender to support such a grand ceiling. Vaulted and coffered with gold and adamantium, grand artworks in vivid pigments told the history of the Mechanicus with emotive artistry that was out of keeping with what Roboute thought he knew of the Martian priesthood. Between tessellated stained-glass windows, statues the equal of the god-machines in height flanked the hexagonal-tiled floor, and lines of power squirmed across its patterning.

Electricity as blood, power as life-force.

Three transports awaited. Two were elevated sedans, rising high on six articulated limbs, with narrow-backed chairs like thrones and an elaborately-artificed servitor with bronze skin hardwired to the rear. The third was a bulky armoured vehicle based on the ubiquitous Rhino chassis, but modified to be larger and bristling with weapon mounts, strange antennae and numerous blister pods of unknown function. The augmented Rhino's hull was emblazoned with the same skull-and-lightning-bolt symbol that was stamped onto the skitarii's breastplates.

'Impressive,' said Roboute, craning his neck to look up at the gilded mosaics and vividly rendered murals. 'I didn't think the Mechanicus went in for ornamentation.'

'We recognise the need to occasionally display status,' said Blaylock. 'It never hurts to remind others that the Adeptus Mechanicus is an indispensable facet of the Imperium, one with a lengthy and honourable history. We are all cogs in the Great Machine, Captain Surcouf.'

'But some cogs are bigger than others, eh?'

'The builders of the *Speranza* were of a different age, one where such ostentation was the norm.'

'It's like I imagine the Emperor's palace to look like,' said Adara.

'This entire vessel is a palace, a temple to the God of All Machines,' said Blaylock, switching his attention to the younger man. 'Its operation is an act of devotion, its existence a display of faith and belief. To serve aboard such a holy link to the past is to commune with the Omnissiah himself.'

'It's incredible,' said Pavelka. 'We're honoured.'

'I've seen grander,' said Emil. 'The Temple of Correction... Now *that's* architecture.'

'Architecture? I'm not talking about *physical* structure,' said Pavelka, entranced by what she saw.

'Then what are you talking about?' asked Emil.

Pavelka shot him a puzzled glance, before remembering that neither Roboute nor Emil could discern noospheric data streams when disconnected from the *Renard's* data engines.

'The air is alive with knowledge,' she said. 'It's all around us, streams of invention and cascades of sacred algebraic construction. History, quantum biology, galactic physics, black hole chemistry, monomolecular engineering, fractal algorithms, bio-mechanical cognisance... You could spend a dozen lifetimes and you'd only ever know a fraction of what's contained here.'

'I can calculate how long it would take to process it all if you like,' offered Blaylock.

'Thank you, but I'm happy for it to remain a wonderful mystery,' said Roboute, climbing onto the elevated sedan and sitting on one of the thrones. 'Shall we go? We don't want to keep the archmagos waiting, now do we?'

'Of course,' agreed Blaylock, ascending to the sedan with a subtly altered gait that suggested that whatever form of locomotion he employed was no longer biological. Emil and Adara joined them, lugging the stasis chest between them, while Magos Tychon, Mistress Tychon, Pavelka and Sylkwood took the second. The skitarii warriors took the upgraded Rhino, and its weapon mounts swung smoothly up as the crew ramps slammed shut.

With no audible command being given, the sedans rose to their full height and began walking down the length of the vaulted processional. Their movement was like that of an ocean-going vessel in a gentle tidal sway, and Roboute liked the grand nature of this mode of transport. They passed gilded statues of honoured magi, and Blaylock regaled them with their identities and achievements.

Here was Magos Ozimandian, who had unlocked the STC engine fragment of Beta Umojas, which had led to the five per cent paradigm shift. Across from him – or her; it was often hard to tell – was Magos Latteir, whose archaeovations in the Neo-Alexandrian atom-wastes had uncovered the binary records of the First Algorithmatrix. Latteir stood shoulder to shoulder with the stoic form of Magos Zimmen, originator of Hexamathic Geometry. Emil and Adara soon lost interest, but Roboute continued to feign attention as they rolled and swayed towards a sloping wall at the far end of the processional. Angled away from them like a portion of an enormous pyramid's buried flank, a towering portal of brushed smoke-grey steel led within, easily able to accommodate the height of even the largest battle-engine and the width of a tank company.

Yet more cogs and gears were worked into its surface, but these were more than symbolic, and rotated with smooth precision as the doors swung slowly outwards. Gusts of oil-rich vapour blew from within, together with a soft burr of binary hymnals. Roboute understood none of it, but the lilting machine language was strangely comforting.

'The Adamant Ciborium,' said Blaylock, revealing the identity of the structure in a blurt of binary as well as with his flesh voice. 'Archmagos Kotov awaits.'

The titanic strides of *Lupa Capitalina* were measured and precise, the mind at the controls one of cold-edged wisdom, hard-won in a hundred and thirteen engine engagements, including nineteen against multiple gross-displacement war-engines. Alpha Princeps Arlo Luth, the Wintersun, floated in milky-grey suspension, his foetal form pale as a spectre and withered like a premature infant. Looping implants trailed from his bisected torso, a silver wraith tail that plugged directly into the base of his spinal column and allowed him to control the drive mechanism of his Titan's limbs.

His eyes were sightless cataracts, sutured closed and linked via MIU

to the surveyor and auspex suite embedded in the serrated crown of the *Capitalina*. She saw as a predator, a veteran of the hunt with scalding oil for blood and a keen eye for a prey's weakness. Thousands of chanting tech-priests and robed acolytes surrounded her, together with enormous fuel tenders, ammunition haulers and the hundreds of vehicles required to keep the God-Machines in the field. The deck priests were his support crew and his worshippers, devotees come to welcome a living embodiment of their god aboard the *Speranza*.

Canted binary hymns of greeting boomed from vox-trumpets in the vaulted ceiling, and gently swinging censers the size of battle tanks created a cloud-bank of aromatic oils that fell to the deck in a lubricating rain. Such a welcome was afforded to only the mightiest avatars of the Machine-God, and choral chants of the Legio's battle honours and its heroic princeps echoed throughout the hangar on a repeating algorithmic cycle.

Luth had no time to bask in their adulation, but he did not ignore it.

Ferromort, the Red Ruination himself, Grand Master of Sinister, had said it best.

Despise infantry if you must. Crush them underfoot, by all means. But do not ignore them. Battlefields are littered with the wreckage of Titans whose crews ignored infantry.

Luth knew from bitter experience how easy it was to forget that these scurrying creatures could hurt him. His armoured pelt still bore the scars of the acids, bilious venoms and digestive juices of the tyranid swarms that had almost brought him to ruin amid the night-shrouded ice forests of Beta Fortanis. *Lupa Capitalina* rumbled beneath him, and he angrily shook off the memory as he felt its displeasure. No one liked to be reminded of their defeats, least of all a Warlord Titan of Legio Sirius.

He followed the blinking lights on the deck, the transit corridor assigned to him by the Mechanicus devotional logisters that would lead the towering engine to its inertia-cradle. The *Capitalina* chafed at being so trammelled, but Luth pressed his will down upon her, cautioning against allowing her ire to manifest beyond a few reactor rumbles and a low growl from her warhorns.

The embarkation deck was a titanic space, as befitted the god-machines of Legio Sirius, honoured engines whose enduring frames had been laid down in the polar temples of the Verica VII forge world. Ten inertia-cradles occupied the far wall of the deck, enormous restraints that would couple the Legio's engines to the *Speranza* on the long journey between the stars, too many for the remaining engines of Sirius. That more than half of the cradles would remain empty was a knife in Luth's guts.

Just to set foot aboard a vessel as ancient as the *Speranza* was an honour. It should be Luth and the rest of Sirius singing praises to its unimaginable legacy. With every step the *Lupa Capitalina* took, he could feel the enormous power and unbreakable strength that lay at the heart of the Ark Mechanicus. Its age was immense, its machine-spirit like none other he had known.

Only a princeps, a warrior so intimately conjoined with the Omnissiah, could truly understand the living soul of this vessel. Thousand of machines had become one with this craft, an incredible lineage of technology that stretched back through the mists of time to an age where entire fleets of such awesome vessels plied the stars in the name of exploration and progress.

Those machines were now part of the *Speranza*, and it was part of them: one sprawling tapestry of awesome cognition that had become something more incredible, more complex than any living organism in the galaxy. He sensed its unimaginable age, yet understood the sharp newness of its existence. The *Speranza* was a fiery colt in the body of a ageing stallion...

Luth wondered if anyone else on this vessel truly understood that contradiction.

Behind him walked the rest of his pack, much diminished since the losses suffered during the Fortanis campaign. Princeps Eryks Skálmöld – the Moonsorrow – followed in *Canis Ulfrica*, a battle-hungry Reaver with the heart of a ferocious and relentless hunter. Loping at its heels came *Amarok* and *Vilka*, Warhounds of vicious temperament and wild hunger. Gunnar Vintras, princeps of *Amarok*, whose pack name was Skinwalker, was the lone predator, always railing against the bonds of the pack. *Vilka* was the loyal hound that hunted where its master willed, and Princeps Elias Härkin, called Ironwoad, was as steady and unshakeable as they came.

Lupa Capitalina was the glue at their heart, the alpha engine whose icy will bound them together as a fighting force. Luth felt *Canis Ulfrica's* approach, drawing closer to his rear quarters than was necessary or wise. A calculated challenge to his authority, a declaration of Moonsorrow's desire to lead the pack.

Luth twisted in his suspension tank, baring his engine's teeth and raising its hackles. In response the *Capitalina's* shoulder mounts tensed and her warhorns growled a burst of coded war-cant. *Amarok* and *Vilka* scattered with their wolf-snout cockpits lowered, sending the Mechanicus adepts nearby diving from their path. *Canis Ulfrica* paused in its steady advance, letting its warhorn answer Luth's challenge.

Alarm sirens blared throughout the vast hangar deck as Luth moved his engine from its prescribed path. Warning lights flashed and a slew of interrogatives flickered to life behind his sightless eyes. He ignored them and clenched non-existent fists, raising his arms and cycling his auto-loaders. The weapons were disconnected from their colossal ammo-hoppers, but the symbolism of the gesture was clear and *Canis Ulfrica* took a backward step with its shoulders dipping in submission.

'Moonsorrow is getting bold,' said Moderati Koskinen, watching the auspex cascade as the Reaver returned to its assigned spacing.

'If he thinks he's ready to be alpha, then he's a fool,' replied Moderati Rosten.

Luth knew he should rebuke Rosten for such a comment, but it was hard to argue with the truth of it. *Lupa Capitalina* knew it too. He shared its urge to strike out at this challenge to his authority, but would not allow such dissent within this holy place.

'I'm getting heat build in the plasma destructor again,' noted Moderati Koskinen. 'Looks like the *Capitalina* wasn't too happy with Moonsorrow either.'

'Compensating,' answered Magos Hyrdrith from her elevated position at the rear of the cockpit.

Luth had felt the heat build, but ignored it, knowing it was simply the *Capitalina's* anger that caused the temperature increase. He felt the soothing balm of coolant bathe his fist, uncurling phantom fingers that had long-since been amputated and replaced with a series of silver-tipped mechadendrites that drifted like cnidaria fronds.

'The destructor's heat-exchange coils have always been temperamental,' said Rosten. 'I knew those sunborn adepts on Joura wouldn't be able to sort the problem.'

'They were competent adepts,' countered Hyrdrith. 'The issue is not in the coil chamber.'

'I have readings that say otherwise,' replied Koskinen.

'With all due respect, moderati, that gun's spirit has always been over-eager to be loosed.'

Luth felt the *Capitalina's* ire build at the disparaging tone in the tech-priest's voice. Hyrdrith felt it too, and hurriedly added, 'Though I admit its rapid rate of recharge more than makes up for that.'

Koskinen grinned. 'Always a diplomat, eh, Hyrdrith?' he said, returning his attention to the haptic display flickering before him.

+When the pack hunts, a strong alpha is its heart and soul. The heart must always be the strongest organ in the body. I am still stronger than Moonsorrow and he knows it.+

The interior of the cockpit was filled with Luth's voice, a rasping

thing that emerged from the shadows. When Luth spoke aloud, everyone listened.

'By your word, Wintersun,' said his moderati and tech-priest together, bowing their heads.

+We walk in the belly of our greatest temple,+ said Luth, letting his hunter's heart come through in the modulation of his feral growl. **+Recognise the honour you have been granted just by being permitted to join this expedition.+**

He felt the contrition of his bridge crew and returned to his original course. He dismissed the blinking warning icons floating invisibly in the translucent liquid with an irritated growl and strode towards the inertia-cradle that a shimmering noospheric halo indicated had been assigned to the *Capitalina*. Floating guide-lifters and grav-cushions awaited him, and hissing inload ports, feed lines and restraint clamps spread wide to receive the god-machine.

Luth felt the welcome of a thousand binary souls woven into one voice that spoke to him and him alone. He sensed the hunger for exploration at the heart of the *Speranza*, the burning desire to be away from this world of iron and these well-travelled routes through space. Like a callow princeps, the *Speranza* wanted nothing more than to charge out into the unknown, to sail by the light of suns that had never shone their face on the realm of men.

He recognised its kindred soul and heard the joyous howling at its core.

+The *Speranza* has many wolves in its heart,+ he said.

The space enclosed by the Adamant Ciborium was curiously modest, a vast structure surrounding a space no larger than the bridge of the *Renard*. Roboute guessed the walls must be at least a hundred metres thick or more, and he wondered what manner of revered technology had been worked within them.

Once inside the portal, the passageway narrowed in geometric steps that Roboute recognised as corresponding to the ratios of the Golden Mean. Eventually they were obliged to disembark and continue on foot. Together with the armoured skitarii vehicle, their transports retreated to await them.

At the heart of the Ciborium was an elliptical chamber like a grand hall of governance, with stepped tiers of hard metal benches rising to either side of a perfectly circular table. The table was easily ten metres wide, fashioned from wedge-shaped planes of segmented steel inset with panels of a smooth red rock that could only have come from one world of the galaxy. Gently humming data engines ran around

the curve of the chamber's walls, and a number of blank-faced servitors were plugged into several exload ports, holo-capture augmetics recording every angle of this gathering.

A spherical orb of wire mesh and glittering gemstones hung suspended over the centre of the table, an archaic representation of the cosmos as envisaged by the ancient stargazers of Old Earth. Magos Blaylock indicated Roboute should stand at a vacant segment of the table before taking his own place with the stunted slaves arranging his network of tubing behind him. A clicking machine arm unfolded from Blaylock's robes and slid home in a connection port on the table's underside. The green lenses of his eyes flickered with data transfer.

Magos Tychon took a position at an unoccupied segment to Roboute's left, while Linya moved to stand by one of the data stations at the wall behind her father, plugging into the ship's Manifold with a discreetly extruded data-spike.

Arranged around the table's circumference were the individuals representing the disparate elements of the Explorator Fleet and the senior magi of the *Speranza*. Roboute scanned the faces of these men and women to whom his fate would be linked for the duration of the expedition.

The man nearest him wore the dress uniform of a Cadian colonel, a rugged ensemble that managed to look ceremonial and battle-ready in the same instant. Though his outfit was more restrained than plenty of other rogue traders he'd met, Roboute felt like a foppish dandy next to the colonel. Aides-de-camp scratching at data-slates stood a respectful distance from their commanding officer, and Roboute gave the colonel a respectful nod as he took his place at the table.

Opposite the colonel stood a monstrously tall figure encased in black Terminator armour, rendered beyond human in scale by the heavy plates of polished jet and ivory. The flared cross on his white shoulder guard told Roboute what he already knew. This was a Space Marine of the Black Templars, and the warrior filled the chamber with his colossal bulk. The oversized armour made him seem more like a bipedal tank instead of a man. Super-engineered beyond mortality, the warrior did not acknowledge Roboute's arrival, save by a curt inclination of his skull-faced helm.

Magi occupied the rest of the segments around the table, a collection of robed adepts who were at least as far removed from their original human template as the Space Marine. Some, like Blaylock, kept their hoods raised, with only the dim glow of augmetics to give any indication of sensory apparatus beneath. Others went bare-headed, though the majority had long since removed their human features in favour of machine replacements along the route of ascension through the Mechanicus ranks. One appeared to be little more than portions of brain matter spread between a number of fluid-filled bell jars and linked together by crackling copper wiring. The disparate parts of the magos – or was there more than one individual suspended in the jars? – were supported on a walking armature of armoured steel like a fleshless praetorian.

Roboute recognised none of them save the magos directly across from him.

Taller than every other adept in the chamber, Archmagos Explorator Lexell Kotov's robes were a shimmering weave of crimson mail and contoured plates moulded in the form of human musculature. Roboute took his time in studying the magos who would be leading them beyond the edges of the known galaxy into the wilderness space that had swallowed entire fleets. He realised that no part of the magos below the neck was organic; that his body was entirely artificial.

Kotov's mechanised body put Roboute in mind of the gladiatorial warriors of the Romanii empire from Old Earth's ancient history, an impression further cemented by the long electro-bladed sword loosely belted at his hip. Roboute's eyes were drawn to the black iron gorget at Kotov's neck, where the last of his original body ended and joined with the automaton's shoulders. Cold wisps of air sighed from the gorget, and green indicator lights winked with rhythmic precision. A cloak of many hues hung from his shoulders, and a black steel collar rose up at the back of his shaven skull, crackling with a dancing nimbus of power that fed into a trio of bare metal cryo-cylinders harnessed to his back.

Unusually for one so elevated in the ranks of the Adeptus Mechanicus, Kotov's face was still recognisably human, albeit starved of sunlight and cyanotic. Eyes that were a disconcerting shade of violet regarded Roboute with amusement, and Kotov smiled in welcome as Emil and Adara deposited the stasis chest at his side.

'Ave Deus Mechanicus,' said Kotov with a nod towards Blaylock and the Tychons, who returned the salutation with great solemnity. Finally, the archmagos turned to Roboute.

'Captain Surcouf,' said Kotov. 'With your arrival, the components of our fleet enterprise are finally assembled. Take your place at the Ultor Martius, our link to the sacred stone of Mars.'

'Archmagos Kotov,' said Roboute, with a formal bow. 'It gives me great pleasure to finally meet you in person. Communication over the Manifold waystations is all well and good, but it's no substitute for speaking face to face.'

'I fail to see the difference,' said Kotov. 'Manifold communication is equally as efficient. In any case, with your arrival we can begin. Do you have the device?'

Knowing that to continually rail against the blunt ways of the Mechanicus would be wasted effort, Roboute held his temper in check at the lack of formal niceties. But it would do no harm to remind the assembled tech-priests that this was a *joint* expedition.

Ignoring Kotov's question, Roboute turned to the Cadian colonel and held out his hand.

'Roboute Surcouf, captain of the rogue trader vessel *Renard*.'

'Ven Anders,' said the Guard officer. 'Colonel of the 71st Cadians, good to have you aboard.'

Roboute saw the wry amusement in Anders's eyes and recognised the man's obvious pleasure at having another individual of flesh and blood amongst the expeditionary command staff.

'Captain Surcouf?' asked Kotov. 'Did you not hear my interrogative?'

'I heard it,' said Roboute, 'but as I already explained to Magos Blaylock here, I prefer to know who I'm dealing with before I begin any endeavour. Silly, I know, but there you go.'

'Yes, he informed me of your obsession with identifiers,' sighed Kotov. 'Very well, arranged around the Ultor Martius in cogwise rotation are the senior magi of the *Speranza*, together with the command ranks of our adjunct elements. You have already met Magos Blaylock, my Fabricatus Locum. Next is Magos Saiixek, Master of Engineering, Magos Azuramagelli of Astrogation, Magos Kryptaestrex of Logistics, Magos Dahan of Armaments and Secutor of the Skitarii Clans.'

Kotov turned to the enormous Space Marine. 'And this is–'

'I make my own introductions, Archmagos Kotov,' said the Space Marine. 'I am Reclusiarch Kul Gilad of the Black Templars.'

'An honour to know you, Reclusiarch,' said Roboute.

'You bear an honourable name,' said the Reclusiarch. 'You are of Ultramar?'

'I am,' agreed Roboute. 'I was born on Iax, one of the cardinal worlds.'

'It surprises me to see a citizen of Ultramar as a rogue trader.'

'It's a long story,' said Roboute. 'Maybe I'll tell you it over the course of our journey together.'

'Captain Surcouf, the device if you please,' said Kotov, cutting across any response Kul Gilad might have made.

'Of course,' said Roboute. 'Emil, Adara?'

The two crewmen lifted the stasis chest onto the table and backed

away when he gave them a nod of thanks. He saw the admiration for the workmanship that had gone into the crafting of the stasis chest, and more than one magos blink-clicked images at the sight of it.

'An unusual design,' said the disembodied voice of Magos Azuramagelli, his steel armature flexing and his multiple brain jars leaning over the tabe. 'It has an aesthetic reminiscent of eldar workmanship.'

'That's because it was made by an eldar bonesinger,' said Roboute.

'And how comes it into your possession?' asked Magos Dahan. 'An act of piracy or trade?'

'Neither, actually,' said Roboute. 'It was a gift.'

'A gift?' said Kul Gilad, leaning forwards and placing two enormous fists on the table. 'Am I given to understand you willingly consort with xenos species?'

'I am a rogue trader, Reclusiarch,' said Surcouf. 'I deal with xenos species as a matter of course.'

Kul Gilad turned to Kotov. 'You said nothing of us employing xeno-tech.'

'Don't worry, it's just the chest that's eldar,' said Roboute, placing his hand on the locking mechanism. Little more than a sliver of wraithbone Yrlandriar had sung into shape using Roboute's name as his keynote, the plate pulsed warmly as it recognised his touch. The wraithbone responded to his sincere desire for it to release, and the lock disengaged with a soft click.

Roboute opened the chest and lifted out what had cost him the better part of three years' worth of earnings from his cobalt routes to procure. In appearance, the catalyst for this expedition was disappointing to look at: a bronze cylinder like an artillery shell with a flattened head and crimped centre section. A number of trailing wires hung limply from a tear in the outer casing, and the metal was heavily pitted with rust and corrosion. Crystal growths encircled the cylinder, and it didn't need a Mechanicus metallurgist to know it was obviously of great age.

'What is it?' asked Ven Anders. 'A beacon of some kind?'

'That's exactly what it is, colonel,' said Roboute. 'It's a synchronised distress beacon taken from a saviour pod ejected from the *Tomioka*, the lost flagship of Magos Telok.'

Though Kotov must surely have told the assembled magi the nature of what he had brought to them, they still reacted with scattered barks of binary. Code blurts crossed the table, and every augmetic eye brightened at the prospect that this was indeed a relic from the legendary fleet lost beyond the Halo Scar. Roboute placed the beacon on the stone of the table before him and the central portion of the table irised open. Snaking mechadendrites emerged like a writhing nest of snakes with clicking clamp heads. They eased through the air and a number of the mechanised probes clamped onto the body of the beacon.

Every magos around the table, if they had not yet done so, connected to the inload ports of the Ultor Martius as information flowed into the cogitator at its heart. The lights of the Adamant Ciborium dimmed and a breath of oil-scented air gusted from unseen vents, as though the *Speranza* itself were tasting the knowledge being transferred from the beacon.

Kotov frowned and said, 'The beacon bears genuine Mechanicus assembly codes that match those of Telok's fleet, but there are sectors of the beacon's data-coils missing.'

'There are,' agreed Roboute.

'The astrogation logs and datum references have been removed,' noted Magos Tychon. 'There is no way to locate where the saviour pod was ejected. As it is presented, the beacon is useless.'

'Not exactly,' said Roboute, removing a wafer of pressed brass from his coat pocket, its surface etched with angular code impressions. 'I have that information right here.'

'You have desecrated a holy artefact,' said Kotov. 'I could have you executed on the spot for such blasphemy. Only those privy to the mysteries of the Cult Mechanicus are permitted to touch the inner workings of a blessed machine.'

'And that's just what happened,' said Roboute, turning to his crew. 'I had Magos Pavelka identify the coil containing all local stellar references to where this pod went down and remove it. As you've already seen, there's enough left to verify the provenance of the beacon, so I suggest we all calm down and get ready to break orbit.'

'Why would you do such a thing?'

'I've done my research, and I know you didn't get to be an Archmagos of Mars by always honouring every bargain you've struck.'

'What is to stop me asking the Reclusiarch to take that memory wafer from you by force?'

'Nothing,' said Roboute. 'Though it *is* very fragile, and I doubt you could reconstruct its data once I've crushed it under my boot.'

The magi gathered around the table recoiled from Roboute's threat, horrified at the idea of destroying such priceless knowledge.

'Very well, Captain Surcouf, what payment do you hope to gain over and above what we have already agreed by keeping this information from me?'

'I don't want more money or tech if that's what you're thinking,'

said Roboute. 'I just want the chance to fly the *Renard* at the forefront of this fleet once we're on the other side of the Halo Scar, and be the first to encounter what lies on the other side. When we get there, I'll gladly give you the memory wafer. On my honour as a loyal servant of the Golden Throne.'

Roboute pocketed the data wafer as he saw Kotov's realisation that he had no choice but to accede.

'Right then,' he said, leaning forwards and placing both hands on the red stone of the table. 'Shall we get under way?'

Microcontent 06

Abrehem watched the bald man fall, his body twisting and spinning through the air. His name was Vehlas, and he screamed until his skull struck a protruding spar of the cyclic rotator scaffold. After that he fell in silence. By the time he spread his body over a wide area of the deck plates, five hundred metres below, most of the rest of the work detail had returned their attention to the vast plasma cylinder being lifted towards them. The gantry was narrow and swayed with the motion of a work crew below them. Abrehem watched them detach their own plasma cylinder from the greased chains securing it and manoeuvre it towards the yawning mouth of the drive chamber.

'He hit yet?' asked Coyne.

Abrehem nodded, too numb and exhausted to reply.

'Why do you always watch?' asked Hawke.

'I keep hoping someone might do something to save the ones that fall,' said Abrehem.

'Not bloody likely,' grunted Hawke. 'Mechanicus don't care about us, we're just slaves. Not even human. They think they're honouring us by letting us kill ourselves in here. Some honour, eh?'

'I've seen four men die just fuelling this engine alone,' said Abrehem, wiping sweat from his forehead with the grimy sleeve of his overalls. They had started out garish red, but were now a sodden, oil-stained muddy black.

'Four,' mused Coyne. 'I thought it was more than that.'

'No, the last man didn't hit the deck,' said Hawke, casting a venomous glare at Vresh, the robed overseer directing their labours from a floating repulsor pod. 'Poor bastard landed on one of the lower work crew gantries. He didn't die, but he looked all broken up.'

The apathy displayed by their Mechanicus masters horrified Abrehem. 'Men are dying, but that's just an inconvenience to the engine overseers.'

'We're collared,' said Hawke. 'What did you expect?'

Abrehem nodded and sank to his haunches, pressing his face into his hands. They stank of sweat, burst blisters and engine grease. Along with Hawke, Coyne and Crusha, he worked with a hundred other men on a narrow gantry forming part of the enormous rotator scaffolding that moved like a giant wheel around the outer circumference of a vast fusion reactor. The seething plasma reactor formed part of the ventral drive chamber. Three-quarters of a kilometre in diameter, each of the fifty drive chambers required two dozen plasma cylinders, each the size of an ore silo, to be loaded in like bullets in a revolver before the *Speranza* would have enough power to break orbit.

The reactor temple resonated to the sounds of heaving loader rigs, rattling chains thicker than support columns, squealing binaric hymnals, beating hammers and the volcanic thunder of venting plasma. It reeked of caustic gases, and the air rippled with heat haze from the plasma flares and flashing warning beacons. Heat exhaustion had caused more than a dozen men to be replaced on the gantries, and the water piped in through dirty plastic tubes was brackish and tasted of metal.

As each thrumming plasma cylinder was brought in from the sealed munitions decks, the rotator scaffold would move around until it was aimed at the grooved tunnel into which it was to be slotted. Work crews occupied each gantry, manually guiding the colossal cylinders along greased rails until they were locked into the drive chamber. Then the rotator scaffold would turn again and another cylinder would emerge from below decks to be man-handled into place.

It was hard, dangerous and thankless work. Four men had already fallen, and several had been horribly injured when an anchor chain snapped and a plasma cylinder crushed them against the gantry railings.

'Watch out,' said Coyne, looking out over Abrehem's shoulder. 'Here comes the next one.'

The shift continued for another five hours, their work crew loading in another six plasma cylinders before the klaxon blared and the rotator scaffold jerked and squealed around its central hub to deposit them on the hot deck. A series of exit hatches slid up on the bare metal walls of the reactor temple, and the exhausted workers marched in ragged ranks towards the steps that led down to their dismal quarters in the belly of the *Speranza*.

Like an army of defeated soldiers being led into captivity from which there could be no escape, the workers shuffled with their heads downcast. Abrehem glanced up as Hawke nudged him in the ribs and nodded over to where Vresh's repulsor disc had drifted down to inspect the seal on a recently locked-in cylinder.

'Hey!' shouted Hawke, waving his fist at the overseer. 'You up there!'

'What are you doing?' hissed Abrehem, grabbing Hawke's arm. 'Be quiet!'

Hawke shrugged off Abrehem's hand. 'Hey, you're killing us down here, you bastard!'

'Shut up, Hawke,' said Coyne, but the ex-Guardsman's bitter anger was in full spate.

'This isn't right, what you're doing! I served the Emperor in battle, damn you! You can't treat us like this!'

Vresh finally deigned to look down, the overseer's metal-masked face scanning the crowds of sullen workers with a flickering blue glow of augmetics. He fastened his gaze on Hawke and a hard bark of code screeched over them. The repulsor disc dropped lower, and Vresh stamped his crackling shock-staff against it.

'Forget it,' said Abrehem, pulling Hawke away. 'He probably can't even understand you.'

'He understands me just fine,' snapped Hawke. 'He might be a jumped-up robot, but Vresh was once like you and me. He knows what I'm saying.'

'Maybe he does, but he's not listening.'

'One day I'm going to *make* the bastard listen,' said Hawke.

To an outside observer, the command deck of the *Speranza* would be an uninspiring place of cold steel, sunken rows of hardwired servitors sealed in modular booths, and isolated nubs of metal that looked like the shorn trunks of silver-barked trees. But to Linya Tychon, whose prosthetic optic nerves were noospherically-enabled, it was a place of wonder, a place where entoptic machinery generated flows of data that floated in the air like unimaginably delicate neon sculptures.

Like the Adamant Ciborium, the interior of the command deck was an elliptical space, its walls alive with crawling circuitry and exposed pipes and cabling. Ceiling-mounted data hubs pulsed with light and pushed streams of squirming information throughout the holographic lattice of the deck: a ship-wide floodstream of staggering complexity.

Information blurts passed between nodes of agglomerated facts, before being filtered for relevancy and then passed on through data prisms that spliced them to their destinations. Infocyte terminals, where multi-armed haptic seers parsed a million micro-packets of inloaded data a second, were gushing fountains of volcanic light, almost too bright to look upon directly.

A ship as big as the *Speranza* generated a colossal amount of information every second: hull temperature fluctuations, gravitational drag factors, inertial compensation, reactor bleed, Geller field integrity, warp-capacitance, fuel tolerances, engine readiness, ablative voids, weapon arsenals, life-support, floodstream, Ancile gravity shields, teleport arrays and a billion other pieces of data to be processed by the awesomely complex logic engines of the ancient ship. Information hung in bright veils, reams of icons, numbers and readouts unravelling in skeins of light, a neural network of unimaginable intricacy and multi-dimensional geometry.

Linya had brushed her myriad senses over the surface of the ship's deep consciousness, amazed and a little bit frightened at its seemingly infinite depths. To know the *Speranza* was old was one thing, but to feel that age in the densely wound code-spirit at its heart was quite another. She read the ship's readiness to depart in every shimmered curtain of phantom light.

The *Speranza* strained at the leash, eager to be on its way.

'Welcome to the command deck,' said Lexell Kotov, the central dais upon which the Archmagos Explorator sat rotating to face them. 'I imagine neither of you will ever have seen anything quite like this.'

'I have never seen its like,' agreed her father, as he made his way up the gentle slope leading from the arterial passageway at the deck's only entrance to the rostrum upon which the higher functions of the craft were directed. Vitali and Kotov spoke in binaric cant, each code blurt tonally modulated with signifiers of respect and mutual admiration. No words passed between them, only the purity of precise and uncorrupted data.

'Nor I,' said Linya, following her father and registering ever more complex forms of algebraic, geometric and algorithmic representations of information. Some of it passed through her, assimilating elements of her floodstream into its numinous admixture, while other fragments darted around her like startled fish.

'A rare jewel in the heavens,' said Vitali. 'Wonderful to see an atmosphere so redolent with data.'

Kotov frowned at Vitali's overt use of metaphor, but let the emotive sentiment pass unremarked.

'Few have, even among the Adeptus Mechanicus,' he responded. 'Quatria must be very quiet by comparison.'

'That it is, though I rather enjoy the peace of my humble orbital galleries,' said Vitali. 'There is something almost mystical in the contemplation of the stars. To know that the light we gather is already ancient and the lives lived beneath their radiance have ended before we even knew of their existence. To view such things is to find peace and equanimity, archmagos, to feel at one with the universe and know your place in it. When we return from this expedition, you should join me there for a time. To look upon the past gives a man perspective.'

'Perhaps I shall visit,' said Kotov masking his impatience with a crooked grin, as though he thought a gesture of humanity would somehow appear comradely. Like most biological micro-expressions discarded by adepts of the Mechanicus along their route of ascension to machinehood, once it was gone it was near impossible to recover with any conviction. 'But that is a pleasure I shall have to postpone, for the secrets of the Halo Scar await discovery. Magos Azuramagelli has almost completed his calculations for optimal orbit breaking and passage to the galactic fringe.'

'So I see,' said Vitali, nodding in respect to where Magos Azuramagelli stood immobile at one of the silvered nubs of metal that rose from the deck, linked via a series of MIU cables extruded from his irised-open trunk. The green lights that bathed his disassembled brain were directed upwards, and a number of haptic claws sifted through streams of information passing between the ships that made up the Explorator Fleet.

Azuramagelli did not acknowledge their entry to the bridge, his full attention directed to factoring the complex statistical inloads of Magos Blaylock into his avionics packages. To plot a course through an inhabited system was a task of great complexity, one that required intimate knowledge of planetary orbits, local stellar phenomena and potential immaterial interference bleeding through the real space/warp space divide at the Mandeville point. Yet Azuramagelli had not only computed such a course, but one that incorporated every aspect of their journey over three sectors to the Halo Scar itself.

Woven chains of Boolean logic-code bristled from his epidermal haptics like cilia as he shed irrelevant data. Linya watched his calculations coalesce to a mandala of symmetry, an expression of numerals and astro-navigational data rendered in light and fractal geometry.

Azuramagelli straightened as a delicate sculpture of latticed light floated free of the silver data hub. Weaving mechadendrites turned it this way and that as his brain-optics examined its purity and complexity from a multitude of angles.

'Is the course ready for insertion?' asked Kotov.

'It is,' answered Azuramagelli, exloading the course data to Kotov's throne.

'Very good,' said the archmagos. 'Yes, very good indeed. This should see us to the scar in forty-three days, plus or minus one day. Prepare to–'

'If I may?' said Linya, stepping towards the gently spinning light crafted by Azuramagelli with her hands outstretched. The Magos of Astrogation lifted his creation away from her, his floodstream rising in irritation at her interruption. Mechadendrites flared like startled snakes, and several of his martial systems surged to life. The light in his bell jars flickered an angry red.

'Interrogative: what are you doing?' he demanded.

'I wish to examine your computations.'

'Statement: out of the question.'

'Why?'

'Clarify: why what?'

'Why is it out of the question?' asked Linya. 'I am a magos of the Adeptus Mechanicus. Surely I can examine a fellow priest's work?'

Azuramagelli barked in the negative. 'The calculations are too complex for those not versed in hexamathical logic equations. You could not comprehend the multi-dimensional integer lattices without augmentation or inloaded wetware.'

Linya smiled and allowed elements of her honorifics to come to the fore of her noospheric aura.

'I think you'll find that I am a hexamathical-savantus; secundus grade,' she said. 'I see that you are tertiary grade, Magos Azuramagelli. I assure you that I will understand what you have done.'

Azuramagelli turned his armatured body towards Kotov, perhaps expecting him to rebuke her, but Linya suspected her logic would appeal to the archmagos.

'Let her look,' said Kotov. 'What harm can it do?'

Linya forced herself to ignore the faintly patronising comment and held out her hand to Azuramagelli. Reluctantly, the ball of light drifted towards her, like a frightened animal coaxed closer with a promise of a comforting hand.

'Change nothing,' warned Azuramagelli. 'The geometric data is fragile and easily prone to exponential degradation if it is altered without care.'

'My daughter is very gifted,' said Vitali with pride.

'You don't need to explain, father,' said Linya. 'I'll let my calculations do that.'

Linya reached up and exploded the ball of light with a rapid spread of her fingers. The shimmering algebraic architecture of Azuramagelli's course plot spun around her, gossamer threads of holographic information of such complexity that it took her breath away. A billion times a billion calculations, statistical extrapolations and inloaded astrogation datum points from tens of thousands of sources surrounded her like a shoal of glitter-scale oceanids.

For the most part, his workings were exemplary and beyond the reach of even those who held the exalted rank of a primus grade hexamath. Yet Linya held an innate grasp of such concepts that bordered on preternatural, an instinctive understanding of the way numbers integrated with one another that had seen her crack previously insoluble proofs with apparent ease. All that had prevented her from ascending to primus grade had been a lack of any desire to travel to Mars and spend half a century in the scholam temples of Olympus Mons when Quatria's galleries offered the mysteries of the universe to gaze upon.

'Your calculations are exquisite, Magos Azuramagelli,' said Linya.

'You tell me what I already know, Mistress Tychon,' said Azuramagelli, reaching a manipulator arm to coalesce the light into a data transfer packet. 'Now, if I may continue–'

'Exquisite, but wrong,' said Linya, spinning the light with a twist of her wrist and zooming in on a jagged, fractal-edged numeral hive.

'Wrong?' said Azuramagelli. 'Impossible. You are mistaken.'

'See for yourself,' said Linya. 'A single flawed data inload from a microscopically deviant gravometric reading has been magnified exponentially throughout the calculation, going unnoticed as it spread its error margin to the entire working. This course will add four days to our journey, and force us to divert around the emergent Jouranion cometary shower.'

'My daughter has something of a fondness for logging cometary phenomena,' said Vitali.

Azuramagelli's optics snapped in close and his silence told her that he now saw the error.

'Is she correct?' asked Kotov.

'So it would appear,' replied Azuramagelli.

'The error was not one of Magos Azuramagelli's making, archmagos,' said Linya hurriedly, though she knew it was too little too late. She hadn't set out to humiliate the magos of astrogation, and already regretted her grandstanding.

'Perhaps not,' said Kotov, also examining the highlighted data. 'Yet he failed to notice the irregularity in data parity.'

'Which given the staggering volume of inloaded data is hardly surprising,' pointed out Linya.

'Yet you saw the flaw almost immediately,' said Kotov. 'Perhaps I should elevate you to command deck status?'

'That will not be necessary,' said Linya. 'My expertise would be more efficiently employed in the cartographae as per the original mission parameters.'

Kotov rubbed a hand that streamed dermic information into the atmosphere and nodded, which in turn sent drifts of information into the ship-wide noosphere.

'Agreed,' he said at last. 'Azuramagelli, update your course with the corrections implemented by Mistress Tychon and inload the new information to the ship's data engines.'

'Yes, archmagos,' said Azuramagelli, collapsing the updated course and pressing it back into the silver hub before him. Golden traceries of light bled into the cylinder, flowing like molten metal into the information network of the *Speranza*, which welcomed the new data with a surge of perfect numbers and harmonic proofs that chimed from the very walls.

And a distant vibration of firing engines.

Despite their lack of augmentation, Magos Dahan had to admit the Cadian troopers were effective soldiers. Though the 71st Hellhounds had been aboard the *Speranza* less than six hours, they had already run through numerous training scenarios with an aggression and competence that belied their months of transit to Joura from the punishing warzones of the Eastern Fringe.

It was a fact of the Imperium's vast scale that most Guard regiments suffered a substantial degradation in their combat effectiveness after long periods of transit in the holds of a Navy mass-conveyor. Soldiers and officers alike fell prey to a lassitude engendered by long periods of absence from the front line and the detrimental effects of prolonged immaterium travel.

Not so with these Cadians.

Three times the generator building had been captured, and with every assault the time between the opening shots being fired to the final room being cleared was getting shorter. The building shook with flat, muffled bangs and flickered with the strobing flashes of concussion grenades. Shouting troopers yelled in terse shorthand, a simple battle cant that had clearly been honed over years of service together on their benighted home world.

It had taken Dahan less than a second to comprehend the simple

codings of their cant, relying as it did on local argot and embedded cultural references. A simple index scan of database: Cadia, and a matching of shouts to actions provided the necessary syntax key to unlock the more complex orders. An inefficient means of relaying commands, but without access to the noosphere or any binaric link between soldiers, it was the best means of conveying orders in the heat of battle without compromising operational security.

The vast training deck echoed with barks of las-fire and detonations, shouted orders and the roaring of tank engines. Spanning almost the entire width of the *Speranza*, this area of the ship was entirely given over to combat drills, training facilities and exercise grounds. Entire armies could train here, utilising the time between origin and destination to turn newly-raised regiments into battle-ready formations by the time a journey was over.

Any number of battlescapes could be mocked up. Entire cities could be raised in prefabricated permacrete, deserts sculpted by dozer rigs or vast forests embedded in the ground. The training deck was Dahan's fiefdom aboard the *Speranza*, and he prided himself that there were no battlescapes he could not create with his logistical resources, no testing ground that would not offer a host of challenges to a training force.

Accompanied by a cluster of servitor scribes, skitarii guildmasters and apprentice magi, Dahan made his way through the safe zone in the centre of the deck on the back of an open-topped variant of the Rhino chassis with a quad-mounted battery of heavy bolters fitted to its glacis. Known as an Iron Fist, it had been developed from a scrap of STC data uncovered on forge world Porphetus prior to its loss to the bio-horrors of the Great Devourer. It had yet to achieve full Mechanicus ratification, but Dahan liked its blunt profile and the single-mindedness of its purpose enough to employ it regardless of its unofficial status.

Its machine-spirit was a bellicose thing, eager to be at war, and he could feel its urge to take part in the battle drills being carried out to either side. Dahan shared its desire, for he too had been built for war and the taking of life. Every facet of his flesh was enhanced to kill: implanted rotator cannons sheathed over his shoulders, sub-dermal lightning claws and digital scarifiers in his wrists and fingertips, target prioritisers, electrically-charged floodstream, flame-retardant skin coatings, three hundred and sixty degree combat awareness surveyor packages, and an enhanced substrate ammunition storage.

Dahan was a killing machine, a mathematician of death.

With over sixteen billion combats inloaded and structurally analysed, his statistical synthesis of the fighting styles of a hundred and forty-three life forms had enabled him to compile a database of almost every combat move possible. Few were the opponents who could surprise Hirimau Dahan, and fewer still would have a chance of besting him.

Dividing his multi-faceted eyes and senses between the various battle drills being carried out around his tank, Dahan soaked up the myriad sources of information being generated by the thousands of soldiers working through punishing combat simulations.

Cadian tanks rolled through a mock-up of a ruined cityscape, driven with machine-like precision as automated gun emplacements set up to mimic dug-in enemy units opened fire. No sooner was each position revealed, than a pair of supporting tanks would engage the enemy as the target tank raced for cover. With the enemy suppressed, twin Hellhound tanks would roll in from the flanks and unleash blazing streams of promethium over their position.

Infantry moved up in support of the tanks, ensuring any remaining enemy soldiers were eliminated. Sniper units riding on the roofs of Chimera armoured fighting vehicles took shots of uncanny accuracy to take out ambush teams armed with missile launchers or any other form of tank-killer.

With each pass, Mechanicus gene-bulked ogryns and heavy lifter rigs would move in and rearrange the cityscape's plan in ever more elaborate and deadly ways, with blind corners, fire-pockets, kill-zones, funnel-streets and herringbone crossfires. And every time, the Cadians rolled through with cool, disciplined fury, meeting every new threat with confident rigour. Even on the most testing of battlefield arrangements, few tanks were lost, and even then none were beyond the ability of Atlas salvage teams to recover and repair.

Other units practised marksman drill, yet more close-combat operations. Officers in black and grey, with bronzed breastplates and peaked caps, shouted orders, and even the black, storm-coated commissars were training as hard as any of the soldiers; something of a rarity among the Guard units Dahan had fought alongside.

It was, Dahan reflected, a thing of beauty to watch battle being given with purity of purpose.

Few flesh and blood regiments could achieve anything close to Mechanicus levels of efficiency in war, and Dahan had to admit that Kotov had chosen well by requesting a formation of Cadians.

Yes, they were an efficient fighting force, but they were no skitarii.

Dahan's own warriors fought through a battlescape comprising a mixture of terrain types. Urban ruins, rugged desert and dense forests. Armoured in black, with form-fitting body armour, the skitarii fought without the grunting, sweating exertion of the Cadians. With physiques boosted by stimm-shunts, adrenal boosters and dormant muscle-enhancers, they had no need for aggressive yells which dulled the fear response and triggered hormonal changes to enable a soldier to flout his body's survival instinct.

Carefully controlled chemical stimulants drove skitarii bodies, together with mechanised augmentations to boost accuracy, strength and speed. Already the best of the regiments from which they had been plucked, these soldiers were the elite of the Mechanicus, rendered into some of galaxy's premier fighting men and women.

Very infrequently, Dahan would observe a combat manoeuvre being carried out with below-optimal efficiency and a terse burst of binary would blurt from his throat augmitter to issue rectifying commands and punishment data. Dahan was a master of the arts of war, a tactician and a warrior, a magos who had become his own test-bed for the weapon upgrades and fighting styles inloaded from other skitarii forces through the forge world Manifold. To fight and kill in ever more inventive and efficient ways was Dahan's means of drawing closer to the Omnissiah. As the Machine-God revealed new and ever more deadly forms of ending life, Dahan made it his mission in life to learn them all and to excel in all the lethal arts.

He paused by the ruined structure of a barracks building as a mob of sweating soldiers emerged from within. Their skin was ruddy and gleaming with sweat. Uniforms were rumpled and dusty, and to all outward appearances, the troopers appeared to be an ill-disciplined bunch. Their captain led them from the building with a rifle slung over his shoulder, its muzzle drooling fumes from heat-discharge.

The building's noospheric data registered it as cleared, and Dahan scanned for death markers on the soldiers. The barracks structure was one of the most lethal facilities to assault, and Dahan paused and halted the Iron Fist with a pulse of thought along the MIU linked to its machine-spirit.

<Diagnostic: Barracks structure. Defences funtionality report.>

Reams of data streamed from the walls of the barracks like illuminated smoke. Each of the automated defence systems, servitor-crewed weapons and random kill permutations designed to inflict maximum casualties were fully functional.

Yet the Cadians had captured it without losing a single trooper.

The side of the Iron Fist opened up and Dahan unplugged from the machine-spirit as he stepped down to the deck. The Cadians altered step, ready to give him a wide berth, but he held up a hard-skinned hand to stop them.

'Captain Hawkins, your soldiers took the barracks structure.'

'Is that a question?' asked the captain.

'No,' replied Dahan, pushing back his hood to reveal his half-flesh, half-machine skull. 'Did it sound like one?'

'I suppose not, but my ears are still ringing from a concussion grenade Manos threw a little later than I'd have liked.'

The chastened trooper shrugged and said, 'I can't help it if you're so eager to get to grips with the enemy, you don't wait for the blast. Sir.'

Hawkins nodded grudgingly. 'Fair point, Manos. So, adept, what can we do for you, or are you just here to congratulate us on another sterling operation?'

'I am Hirimau Dahan, and this is my training deck. I design the combat simulations and engineer the differing tactical situationals.'

'Then you're doing a bang-up job,' said Hawkins. 'These are some pretty tough fishes.'

'Fishes?' said Dahan. 'I am not familiar with piscine life as it applies to combat operations.'

Hawkins grunted in what Dahan assumed was amusement, but it was an officer whose biometrics identified him as Lieutenant Taybard Rae that answered. 'It's an acronym, sir. Stands for Fighting In Someone's Hab. It's what we call building clearances.'

'I see,' said Dahan. 'I shall add it to my combat lexicon: Cadians.'

Hawkins jerked his thumb in the direction of the barracks. 'Yeah, we captured it, though it was a close run thing.'

'You lost no men.'

'That's usually the way I like to run my operations,' said Hawkins, earning grim chuckles from a few of his troopers.

'The barracks structure is one of the most lethal buildings to fight through,' said Dahan. 'I am surprised you were able to take it without loss.'

'Then you don't know much about Cadians.'

'On the contrary,' said Dahan, 'I have inloaded over thirty thousand combat engagements logged by Cadian regiments and/or recorded by Mechanicus forces to which they were attached.'

'You don't look much like a magos,' said Hawkins. 'Are you some kind of skitarii officer?'

'I am a magos,' said Dahan. 'A Secutor to be precise. I specialise in combat mathematics, battle metrics and warfare at all levels: from close combat to mass mobilisations.'

'Yeah, you look pretty handy in a fight,' said Hawkins. 'You should train with us sometime. Be good to see how the Mechanicus fight. Your skitarii look like they can handle some tough scrapes.'

'They are the most efficient fighting force aboard the *Speranza*,' said Dahan, allowing a modulation of pride to enter his voice as he communicated the sentiment via noospheric means to his troopers.

Lieutenant Rae nodded towards a gantry railing that ran the length of the training deck.

'I think they might argue with that,' he said.

Dahan turned as his combat awareness routines flashed up with a red-lined threat warning.

High on the gantry above them stood seven figures, Kul Gilad and six warriors in black power-armoured warplate. The Black Templars surveyed the battle drills playing out below them, but Dahan could discern nothing of their reactions. The warriors' armour was dark to him, their machine-spirits uncommunicative and silent to his interrogatives.

Dahan called up to Kul Gilad. 'Do you join us for combat operation drills?'

The towering Reclusiarch shook his head. 'No, Magos Dahan. We merely observe.'

'On this deck, no one observes,' said Dahan. 'You fight or you leave.'

'Training in this arena would serve no purpose,' said Kul Gilad. 'Its environments are too forgiving to test us.'

'I believe you are mistaken,' said Dahan.

'Then you don't know much about Black Templars,' said Kul Gilad.

Fifteen hours later, the *Speranza* finally broke the gravitational bonds of Joura. It turned its prow towards the outer edges of the system as the blue-hot sun of its engine section flared and shifted it from geostationary anchor. Even shifting its attitude fractionally was enough to boost the craft away from the blue-green planet below, and in deference to those that had helped ready it for its journey, Magos Saiixek feathered the engine outputs to create a swirling flare of variant radiation outputs that descended through the atmosphere to produce a vivid aurora over the northern hemisphere. Though such a gesture seemed out of character for the adepts of the Mechanicus, it was customary for departing explorator fleets to acknowledge the labours of those who had furnished them with the means to venture into the unknown.

At least fifty ships remained in orbit, still suckled by the industry of the world below. The Guard muster for the Pergamus sector still had weeks to go before its Lords Militant would consider their loading and supply complete. To muster enough men and materiel for a lengthy campaign was not an operation to undertake lightly. The presence of so many Mechanicus logisters had helped speed the process, and in thanks, the shipmasters of the muster ordered their gun decks to fire thunderous broadsides into space in their honour.

On the planet's surface, millions of eyes turned to the heavens, staring in wonder at the shimmering bands of variegated colour that sparkled through the troposphere like an orbital barrage. Amid this glorious cascade of irradiated exhaust dust and expended munitions, the Kotov Fleet broke orbit with Captain Surcouf's vessel in the lead. The fleet turned towards the unknown, on a journey whose ending no one could predict. Alongside the *Renard*, the Black Templars' ship *Adytum* knifed through space like a blade thrust to the heart.

Where the rogue trader vessel was designed with a measure of flourish in its tall towers, flared wing section and needlessly aerodynamic profile, the shipwrights of the Adeptus Astartes had built their craft with but a single purpose. Though small in comparison to most ships employed by the Space Marines, the *Adytum* was a scrapper: a battle-scored veteran of a hundred or more vicious void engagements.

And with a battle squad of Space Marines led by a Reclusiarch aboard, its fighting prowess was multiplied exponentially.

A host of craft followed the three lead vessels: refinery ships, mining hulks, vessels that were little more than vast atomic reactors, manufactory ships, immense water-bearing haulers, repair ships, and a host of fleet tenders that could be employed as general workhorses to ferry men and war machines between the fleet. In addition to the working ships of the fleet, Archmagos Kotov had assembled a Mechanicus warfleet with which to pierce the veil of the Halo Scar.

The Retribution-class vessel *Cardinal Boras* had been constructed in the shipyards of Rayvenscrag IV nearly five thousand years ago and was no stranger to such voyages of exploration. As part of a fleet led by Rogue Trader Ventunius, it had ventured deep into the northern rim of the galaxy and had been one of only five vessels to return. Its guns had ended the Regime of Iron at the battle of Korsk, and its proud history included battle honours earned in over eighteen different sector fleets. It had fought as part of Battlefleet Gothic against the fleets of the arch-enemy, and with this latest secondment, it would once again venture beyond the light of the Astronomican.

Moonchild and *Wrathchild*, two Gothic-class cruisers that had been little more than blazing wrecks when the Mechanicus had salvaged them off the shoulder of Orion, flanked the *Cardinal Boras* like devoted followers. Rebuilt and refitted to better serve the Mechanicus, their hulls had been consecrated at the Terminus Nox of Phobos and Deimos, when the regenerative aspects of the Omnissiah were

at their apogee. Stalwarts of the Adeptus Mechanicus fighting fleets, both vessels had been virtually conjoined since their rebirth, and deployments to separate battlefleets had seen them suffer inexplicable mechanical breakdowns and system-wide failures until they had been reassigned to work together.

To repay a centuries-old Debita Fabricata to Archmagos Kotov, the forge world Voss Prime had despatched three heavily armed escort cruisers from Battlefleet Armageddon to stand for Mars. Two Endurance-class vessels, *Honour Blade* and *Mortis Voss* sailed in arrowhead formation with the *Blade of Voss*, an Endeavour-class ship killer. All three vessels bore honour markings bestowed by Battlefleet Armageddon, and *Mortis Voss*, whose mater-captain had delivered the deathblow to the greenskin flagship *Choppa*, bore the personal heraldry of Princeps Zarha, the fallen Crone of Invigilata.

Squadrons of modified frigates, destroyers and a host of local system vessels flew as an honour guard to the Explorator Fleet, though they would turn back at the system's edge. With enough resources to sustain a fleet expedition beyond the stars for many years and enough firepower to fend off all but the most powerful enemies, the Kotov Fleet was as well prepared as it was possible to be.

Time would tell if that would be enough.

MACROCONTENT COMMENCEMENT:

+++MACROCONTENT 002+++

Intellect is the understanding of knowledge.

+++Inload Interrupt+++

Runestones fell from the delicately wrought bowl, the grain of the wood expertly nurtured by Khareili the Shaper to form rippled patterns that made sweet music when water poured through the microgrooves in the surface. It had been a thoughtful gift, one intended to calm the soul, but no soft music and no serene shaping could calm the aching sadness in Bielanna's heart.

She sat cross-legged in one of the aspect shrine's many battle domes, its curved walls hung with swords, axes, pikes and blades that few armourers beyond Biel-Tan could name. Each was fashioned with the customary grace of Bielanna's race, but possessed a brutal purity of purpose common to the warriors of her craftworld. Theirs was a martial philosophy, one of war and reconquest, and each aspect of Biel-Tan's paths reflected that overriding ethos.

Bielanna knew she risked a great deal by coming to the Shrine of the Twilight Blade: the Aspect Warriors did not welcome outsiders to their sacred places. Few areas aboard an eldar ship of war were denied to a farseer, but even she might be punished for this transgression.

The red sand beneath her was soft and warm. Warriors had trained here recently, and she could read the ballet of their combat in the ridges, folds and depressions in the sand. A warrior of incredible skill had danced with one whose footwork was more complex, but who had – in the end – lost to the iron control of his opponent. As

Bielanna's senses flowed into the skein, she followed the threads of the warriors back into the past, seeing shadowy ghost-figures spinning and leaping around her. Their every movement was fluid, economical and deadly. The phantom shapes spun around her with ever greater fury as she looked down at the wraithbone runestones in the sand.

The Scorpion and the Doom of Eldanesh. Both lying atop the Tears of Isha.

The pattern was familiar to her, each one tracing the line of fate's weave. Between them they represented skeins of futures that had already been realised, that were yet to be, and which might *never* be. They braided together in innumerable threads, and each one was – in turn – made up of a dizzying number of potential futures, making the task of interpretation and manipulation almost impossible.

The corners of her full-lipped mouth twitched at her choice of words.

Almost.

She had spent over a century learning how to read the winds of fate in the shrine of the farseers, but even so, her knowledge was woefully incomplete. The futures were fracturing, the threads of fate unravelling from their complex braids. Some were being extinguished, while others were revealed, but through all of the splintering of the future, one strand remained achingly constant.

One that no amount of her manipulations could avoid, a seemingly fixed point in fate.

'It was a good bout,' said a voice behind her. She hadn't heard his approach, but nor would she have expected to hear the stealthy advance of so formidable a warrior. She was just surprised he had waited this long to reveal himself.

'Vaynesh is very skilful,' she said. 'You have taught him well.'

'I have, but he will never beat me. Anger clouds his concentration and blinds him to attack.'

'You toyed with him,' said Bielanna. 'I counted at least three times you could have ended the fight with a killing strike.'

'Only three? You are not looking close enough,' growled the warrior, moving around to stand before her. 'I could have killed him five times before I chose to take the deathblow.'

Tariquel was clad in his full Striking Scorpion aspect armour, with only his head left bare. Its plates were a subtle mix of green and ivory, edged with fluted lines of gold and inlaid mother-of-pearl. His features were hard-edged now, but Bielanna remembered when he had followed the Path of the Dancer and wept as he performed *Swans of Isha's Mercy*.

She blinked away the memory. That Tariquel was long gone and would never return.

The ice in his eyes told her that she had offended him. Had his war-mask been to the fore and fully enmeshed with his warrior aspect, he might well have killed her for such a comment.

'I apologise,' said Bielanna. 'My full attention was not on reading the sword dance.'

'I know,' said Tariquel, kneeling before her. 'You should not be here. Seers are not welcome in the Shrine of the Twilight Blade. This is a place where threads are ended, not where they continue into the future.'

'I know.'

'Then why are you here?'

'The human fleet is leaving the coreworld at this system's heart,' said Bielanna. 'We will soon emerge from concealment to enter the webway in pursuit of their foolish expedition.'

'The heartbeat of Khaine within the infinity circuit already told me that,' said Tariquel. 'You did not need to come here to deliver this news.'

'True,' said Bielanna, lifting a cloth-wrapped bundle from the sand beside her. 'I came here because I wanted to bring you a gift.'

'I do not want it.'

'You don't know what it is.'

'It is irrelevant,' said the Striking Scorpion. 'Gifts have no place here.'

'This one does,' she said, holding out the cloth.

Tariquel took the bundle and unwrapped it with quick, impatient motion. His eyes fell upon what was contained within its folds, and his features softened for the briefest moment as he recognised its significance.

'It is ugly,' he said at last.

'Yes,' she agreed. 'It is, but it belongs here, in a temple of war.'

Tariquel gripped the leather-wrapped sword hilt with fingers that were too delicate to handle such a brutish, clumsy weapon. The hilt was pugnaciously forged, its bellicose form beaten into submission with hammers and molten heat. No wonder the metal had failed in the crucible of combat and caused the black blade to snap a hand-span above the quillons. What weapon would *not* turn on its wielder after so traumatic a birth?

A broken chain of cold iron dangled from the flared cross of its pommel, the last link cut clean through with a single strike.

'Very well, I shall present it to Exarch Ariganna. She will decide if we should keep it.'

'Thank you,' said Bielanna.

'Was this *his* sword?'

'No,' said Bielanna. 'He was not among the slain of Dantium.'

'Then you should take greater care in your rune casting,' snapped Tariquel, his war-mask slipping over his features. 'Eldar lives were lost in that battle. Now you say it was for nothing?'

Bielanna shook her head. 'Nothing ever happens in isolation, Tariquel,' she said, struggling for a way to explain to him the complexities of acting on visions from the skein. 'What happened on Dantium *needed* to happen. It has brought us to this point, and without those human deaths, the future I must shape might never come to pass.'

'Your words are fleeting like the Warp Spider and just as insubstantial,' said Tariquel.

'Human fates are so brief and fickle that they are difficult to follow with any real precision.'

'So again we go to war to reclaim a lost future with uncertainty as our touchstone?'

'We must,' said Bielanna, gathering up her runes in the patterned bowl and swirling them around once more. Tariquel reached out with a blindingly swift hand and gripped her wrist hard enough to draw a grimace of pain.

'The *Starblade* is a large vessel,' said Tariquel. 'Surely there are other places more suited to the casting of runes than an aspect shrine?'

'There are,' agreed Bielanna, as the warrior released her arm.

Tariquel nodded towards the runestones in the bowl, and the gentle soul he had been before Khaine's siren song had called to him swam to the surface for a heartbeat.

'Does what we do here bring the future you seek any closer?'

Tears welled in Bielanna's eyes as she pictured the two empty cots in her chambers.

'Not yet,' she said. 'But it will. It must.'

Microcontent 07

He was a leviathan, a mighty bio-mechanical construct engineered far beyond the natural evolutionary norm for his kind. His structure was immense, self-sustaining and driven to grow larger, an amusingly biological imperative: exist, consume, procreate. To be of iron and oil, stone and steel was to know permanence, but if the fleshy remnants at the heart of these perceptions knew anything, it was that nothing fashioned by the hand of man was permanent.

Seated upon his command throne and linked to the machine heart of the *Speranza* via dermal haptics, MIUs and the Manifold, Archmagos Lexell Kotov felt the spirit of his ship rushing through him, its millennial heart a roaring cascade of information that surged around his floodstream like a churning river of light. Even with so many points of connection, he only dared skim the uppermost levels of the enormous starship's mind. Any deeper and he risked being swept away by its powerful magnificence, drowned in the liquid streams of interleaved data.

The *Speranza's* machine-spirit was orders of magnitude greater than any bio-augmented sentience he had encountered. It could easily consume the totality of his mortal mind and leave his body a vacant, brain-dead shell with no more sense of its own existence than a servitor. Kotov had once risked linking his mind's full cognitive functions with the wounded heart of a forge world to avert a catastrophic reactor failure, but the *Speranza* dwarfed even that mighty spirit.

Forge worlds were seething cauldrons of pure function, singularly directed to the point of mindlessness, entire planets of manufactories driven to extremes of production that could only be yoked by the tens of thousands of Martian adepts thronging their surfaces. The *Speranza* held that same function, but was unfettered from fixed stellar geography: a forge world that could travel the stars, a mighty engine of creation to rival the scale of those crafted in the Golden Age of Technology.

Its discovery had been accidental, a chance accretion of aberrant code bleeding from its slumbering mind-core into the data engines of Kotov's high temple on the forge world of Palomar. At first, he had dismissed the binaric leakage, believing it to be ghost emissions from long-deactivated machines, but as his infocytes scoured the deep networks for similar code geometries, a pattern emerged that gradually revealed something unbelievable.

The full might of Kotov's analyticae had been brought to bear, and the divergent paths of the data bleed were quickly identified. Even then, no one had fully realised the enormity of what the neurally-conjoined adepts were uncovering. Only after physical explorator teams had spent the better part of a century verifying the outer edges of the code footprint had Kotov dared to believe that what was being revealed could be true.

One of the legendary Ark Mechanicus.

Buried in the steel bedrock of his forge world for thousands of years.

Only a handful of such incredible vessels were said to exist, and to have discovered one intact was a miracle to rival that of stumbling across a fully functioning STC system. None of the recovered data scraps could identify the ship, which astounded Kotov, for it was a central tenet of the Mechanicus never to delete anything. For all intents and purposes, the ship had never existed before now. At first, Kotov believed its long-dead crew had somehow managed to land the vast starship intact on the planet's surface and then subsumed it into the world's metal strata.

Only as more of the ship had been revealed did Kotov finally understand the truth.

The ship was incomplete.

Portions of the starship remained to be constructed, and it had never been launched. For reasons unknown, its builders had abandoned the project in its final stages and simply incorporated the existing structure into the planet's expanding skein of industry. The ship had been forgotten, and its halls of technological marvels and grand ambition were swallowed by the evolving forge world until no hint of its original structure could be discerned.

And so it had remained for millennia until the will of the Omnissiah had brought it back to the light. Kotov liked to believe the ship had *wanted* to be found, that it had dreamed of taking to the stars and fulfilling the purpose for which it had been designed.

It had taken him three centuries to prise it loose from the structures built onto its submerged hull, and another two to coax it into space with a fleet of load lifters and gravity ballast. Its unfinished elements had been completed in the orbital plates, the disassembled components of three system monitors providing the necessary steelwork and missing elements of tech. His shipyards had the expertise and required STC designs to render the ship space-worthy, but reviving its dormant machine-spirit had been another matter entirely. It had slept away the aeons as a forgotten relic, and Kotov knew he had to remind it of its ancient duty to continue the Quest for Knowledge.

Kotov had communed with dying forge worlds, calmed rebellious Titans and purged corrupted data engines of primordial scrapcode, but the ancient spirit of the *Speranza* had almost destroyed him. At great risk to his own mind, he had dragged its torpid soul into being, fanning the bright spark of the Omnissiah that lay at the heart of every machine into a searing blaze of rapturous light.

But such a violent birth was not achieved without cost, for all newborns fear leaving the peace of solitude in which they have endured the epochs. Like a wounded beast, it had lashed out in agonised bursts of archaic code all around the bio-neural networks of Palomar. Its machine screams overloaded the forge world's carefully balanced regulatory networks and brought the planet to ruin in the blink of an eye. Hundreds of reactor cores were driven to critical mass in an instant, and the subsequent explosions laid waste to entire continents. Irreplaceable libraries were reduced to ash, molten slag or howling code scraps. Millions of tanks, battle-engines and weapons desperately needed for mankind's endless wars were lost in the radioactive hellstorm.

By the time the *Speranza's* birth rages had subsided, every living soul on the planet's surface was dead and every surviving forge irradiated beyond any hope of recovery, leaving a gaping shortfall in Kotov's production tithes. Yet the loss of an entire forge world was a small price to pay, for the ancient starship now remembered itself and its glorious function. Though a number of the ship's lower decks had been impregnated with contaminated dust blown up by planet-wide radiation storms, the majority of its structure had been spared the worst ravages of the destruction it had unleashed.

Having freed it from the world of its birth, Kotov had named the

ship *Speranza*, which meant 'hope' in one of the discarded languages of Old Earth. It had welcomed the name and Kotov watched with paternal pride as the vast machine-spirit flowed into the body of the ship, learning and developing with every iteration of its growth.

The *Speranza's* mind swiftly became a gestalt entity woven from the assimilated spirits of all the machines that made up its superlative structure. Even the great data engines of the Adamant Ciborium were little more than specks in the mass of its colossal mindspace, a linked hive mind in the purest sense of the word. In the heart of the *Speranza* all cognition was shared in the same instant, and no purer form of thought existed.

Just to gaze upon so perfect an accumulation of data was to be in the presence of the Omnissiah.

Abrehem had thought fuelling the plasma drives had been the most thankless task he had ever been forced to endure, but pressure-scouring their vent chambers of the byproducts of combustion had surpassed even that. Every ten hours, the drives would excrete a volcanic mix of plasma embers, toxic chemical sludge and residual heavy metals burned from the internal coatings of the drives.

This was dumped from the undersides of the drive cylinders into arched reclamation halls below the combustion chambers, gigantic open spaces with black walls that burbled with faint blue ghosts of code that Abrehem perceived like reflected light on the underside of a bridge. Glassy, razor-sharp waste materials lay heaped in great dunes of reflective grey chips, much of which would be recycled for use elsewhere in the ship. The reclamation halls were choking wastelands of poisonous chemicals, mordant sludge, highly flammable fumes and caustic fogs. Enormous dozer-vehicles with vulcanised wheels that smoked from the corrosive effect of the engine leavings ploughed through the billowing drifts of waste, bulldozing it into the enormous silos mounted on the backs of rumbling cargo haulers.

Once the dozers had been through, lines of bondsmen in threadbare environment suits that had probably been old when the primarchs bestrode the Imperium advanced in ragged lines like soldiers on some archaic battlefield. The first wave struggled with long pressure hoses that blasted boiling water at the floor, while the second came armed with wide shovels and sweepers to gather up every last screed of loosened material.

Nothing was wasted, and shimmering veils of glassy particulate thrown up by the work sparked in the air, clogged air filters and ensured that every man coughed up abraded oesophageal tissue the following day. After only a day in the reclamation halls, Abrehem noticed his arms and face were covered with an undulating layer of scabbed blisters. Everyone on reclamation duty bore the scars of the day's work, but no one seemed to care. Abrehem's eyes stung with chemical irritants and the granular dust caught in the folds of skin around his eyes, making him weep thin rivulets of blood.

Days and nights became indistinguishable in the artificial twilight of the starship's underbelly, a constant rotation of brutally demanding tasks that seemed calculated to erode any sense of passing time. Abrehem's chest ached, his hands and feet were blistered and torn, his hair had begun to thin noticeably and his gums were bleeding. Their existence was a benighted treadmill of thankless effort that stripped away everything that made life worth living. Each day wore their humanity down until all that was left was little better than an organic automaton. It was enough to break the spirits of even the most defiant bondsman. With each day that passed, the complaints grew less and less as the fight was driven out of everyone by the relentless grind and unending horror of each task.

Abrehem could feel himself slipping away, and pressed a hand to the pocket he'd stitched in his overalls, where he kept the picture of Eli and Zera. The idea that he would soon be joining them was all that kept him going, and it would sustain him until the Emperor finally took him into His realm. Coyne was faring little better, spending his shifts in brooding silence and his downshifts curled in a foetal position on his hard metal bunk.

But one man still had some fight in him.

Hawke had proven to be more physically and mentally resilient than Abrehem had expected, faring better than many of the other men and women who'd come aboard with them. Abrehem had come to the conclusion that Hawke's bitterness and spite nourished him when his reserves of strength were spent. When they worked side by side, a never-ending diatribe of profanity spewed from his lips, cursing everyone from the archmagos to his own personal nemesis, Overseer Vresh. Abrehem knew that soldiers were amongst the most inventive profaners, but Julius Hawke took that to another level entirely.

On the downshifts, Hawke retold the tales of his life in the Guard, and if even half of what he said about monstrous Traitor Space Marines laying siege to an Adeptus Mechanicus fortress was true, then he could perhaps be excused a great deal to have lived through such a horrific experience. His stories evolved constantly as they were told over and over to an ever expanding and ever more appreciative audience. Hawke would rail against their Mechanicus overseers and speak openly of rebellion against Vresh or taking action to end their enforced slavery.

Abrehem had laughed despairingly, but no one else had.

Between bouts of seditious demagoguery, Hawke would often vanish into the twisting maze of companionways surrounding their dormitories to destinations unknown, only to reappear as Vresh engaged the klaxon to mark the start of the work shift. Whenever Abrehem asked where he had gone, Hawke would only tap the side of his nose with a conspiratorial wink.

'All in good time, Abey, all in good time,' was all Hawke would say.

How Hawke found the energy for such mysterious excursions remained a mystery to Abrehem until he realised how skilful the man was at avoiding anything resembling work. Arguments with Vresh, forgotten tools, damaged equipment and feigned injuries all conspired to ensure that he did far less work than anyone else on shift. Far from making him hated as a shirker, it actually enhanced his status as a rebel and a champion of insidious insurrection.

Today had seen Vresh despatch Hawke to the supply lockers numerous times, a task Hawke had been able to drag out for several hours beyond what it could possibly have required. By the end of shift, Abrehem was utterly drained and could think of nothing beyond crawling into his third tier bunk and closing his eyes until the hated klaxon roused him from his nightmares of endless slavery.

Nightmares that were indistinguishable from reality.

'Another day over, eh?' said Hawke, sidling up to him and Coyne with a grin that Abrehem wanted to wipe off his face with his heavy shovel. Even in his exhausted, numbed state, he knew that would probably be a bad idea. Crusha followed Hawke like a loyal hound and Abrehem didn't doubt that any attempt to lay a hand on Hawke would result in a face-mashing fist.

'I just want to sleep, Hawke,' said Abrehem.

'Yeah, me too. Been a long day keeping this ship going,' said Hawke. 'We're the most important people aboard this ship, you know?'

'Is that right?'

'Sure we are, stands to reason if you ask me,' said Hawke with a sage nod. 'We don't do what we do, this whole machine breaks down. We might be the tiniest cogs in the machine, but we're still important, right? Every cog has its role?'

'Whatever you say,' mumbled Coyne.

'Just some cogs are more important than others, you get me?'

'Not really.'

Hawke shook his head. 'Doesn't matter, I'll show you after.'

'Show me what?' asked Abrehem, though he couldn't muster any enthusiasm for any activity beyond crashing in his bunk and grabbing a few hours of disturbed sleep.

'You'll see,' said Hawke, pushing to the front of the line of trudging men with Crusha following at his heels.

'What was that about?' asked Coyne.

'I don't know,' replied Abrehem. It was typical of Hawke to tease with promises of secrets and then back away like a capricious portside doxy. 'And I don't think I much care.'

Coyne nodded as they emerged into what was known, with typical Mechanicus functionality and unthinking disdain for their bondsmen's humanity, as Feeding Hall Eighty-Six. Heavy iron girders supported a ceiling of peeling industrial grey paint that was hung with pulsating cables, heat-washed pipework and iron-cased lights that provided fitfully dim illumination. Trestle tables arranged in long lines ran the length of the chamber, and lead-footed servitors trudged along the gaps between them, doling out what was laughingly called food to the bondsmen. None of it was even vaguely palatable, but the only other option was starvation.

Sometimes Abrehem thought that might be the better option.

One shift was just leaving, heading to their next work detail, and the men that had just left the toxic environment of the reclamation halls filed in to take their place.

'Throne of Terra,' muttered Coyne as he found a place at the table, sat shoulder to shoulder between a man whose face was a mass of scabbed chem-blisters and another whose forearms were criss-crossed in a web of plasma flect scarring that looked entirely deliberate. Abrehem took a seat opposite Coyne and rested his head in his hands. Neither man spoke; exhaustion, the gritty texture in their throats and the pointlessness of conversation keeping them mute.

A servitor appeared behind Coyne, a figure that superficially resembled a human male, albeit one with pallid, ashen skin, a cranial sheath replacing much of his brain matter and a series of crude augmentations that rendered it into a cyborg slave that would perform any task given to it without complaint. Perhaps he had once been a criminal or some other societal undesirable, but had he deserved to be so thoroughly stripped of his very humanity and turned into little more than an organic tool? Was there even much of a difference between the servitor and the men it was feeding?

The servitor's mouth had been sealed up with a thick breathing plug, and chains encircled its head, securing it in place, which suggested the man might once have been a troublemaker or a seditious demagogue.

A bark of white noise issued from its throat-set augmitter, and Coyne leaned to the side as it deposited a contoured plastic tray on the tabletop.

Contained in its moulded depressions were a thick, tasteless nutrient paste with the consistency of tar, a handful of vitamin and stimulant pills, and a tin cup half filled with electrolyte-laced water.

Abrehem heard the heavy tread of a servitor at his back and smelled the reek of fresh bio-oil on newly cored connector ports. He leaned to the correct side and a pale arm placed an identical tray before him.

'Thank you,' said Abrehem.

'Why do you do that?' asked Coyne. 'They don't even register your words.'

'Old habits,' he said. 'It reminds me we're still human.'

'Waste of time, if you ask me.'

'Well I didn't,' snapped Abrehem, too tired to argue with Coyne.

Coyne shrugged as the servitor withdrew its arm and moved on down the table, but not before Abrehem's optic implants had registered a drift of light from a sub-dermal electoo on the underside of its forearm, a name written in curling Gothic script. He blinked as he recognised the name and turned his own arm over to reveal an identical smear of electrically-inscribed lettering.

Savickas.

'Wait!' said Abrehem, pushing himself up from the table and heading after the servitor.

The servitor had its back to him and wore heavy canvas trousers of high-visibility orange. A curling armature was implanted along the length of its spine, and the left side of its skull was encased in a bronze headpiece. It pushed a tracked dispensing unit ahead of it and moved with the sluggish gait of a sleepwalker.

'Is that you?' asked Abrehem, almost afraid the servitor would answer him.

It didn't answer, not that he had expected it to, and continued to dole out plastic trays to the seated bondsmen from the dispensing unit as though he hadn't spoken.

Abrehem moved to stand in front of the servitor, blocking its path and preventing it from moving on. Shouts of annoyance rose from farther down the table, but Abrehem ignored them, too shocked by what he saw to move.

'Ismael?' said Abrehem. 'Is that you? Thor's blood, what did they do to you?'

Once again the servitor didn't answer, but there was no mistaking the thin features of his former shift overseer. Ismael's face was slack

and expressionless, the augers and brain spikes driven into his skull destroying his sentience and replacing it with a series of program loops, obedience flow-paths and autonomic function regulators. One eye had been plucked out and replaced with a basic motion and heartbeat monitor, and Ismael's right shoulder had been substituted for a simple, fixed-rotation gimbal that allowed him to move food trays between his dispenser unit and the feeding hall tables, but which had no other use.

Abrehem held out his forearm, willing his own electoo to become visible, a cursively rendered word that matched the markings incised beneath the servitor's own skin.

'*Savickas*?' said Abrehem. 'Don't tell me you don't remember it? The strongest lifter rig in the Joura docks? You and me and Coyne, we ran a tight crew, remember? The *Savickas*? You must remember it. You're Ismael de Roeven, shift overseer on the *Savickas*!'

Abrehem gripped Ismael by the shoulders, one flesh and blood, the other steel and machine parts. He shook the servitor Ismael had become and if he could still have cried real tears he would have done so. Tears of blood would have to be enough.

'Throne damn them,' sobbed Abrehem. 'Throne damn them all...'

He didn't even know why the sight of Ismael reduced to a lobotomised cyborg slave should upset him so deeply. Ismael was his superior and they weren't exactly friends.

Abrehem felt a hand on his shoulder, and he let himself be eased from servitor Ismael's path.

No sooner had Abrehem moved aside than Ismael continued his mono-tasked routine, moving along the length of the table to place tray after tray of repulsive, tasteless slop before the hungry bondsmen.

Hawke stood at his side, and he quickly manoeuvred Abrehem back to his seat before the overseers intervened. Hawke eased into the seat next to him. Coyne sat where Abrehem had left him, spooning mouthfuls of paste into his mouth.

'So that's what happened to him,' mused Hawke, watching as Ismael moved on.

'They made him into a bloody servitor...' said Abrehem in disgust.

'I didn't think you two were that close,' said Hawke. 'Or did I miss something?'

Abrehem shook his head. 'No, we weren't close. I didn't even really like him.'

'He was an ass,' snapped Coyne. 'If it weren't for you and him I wouldn't have been in that damn bar. I'd still be back home with my Caella. To the warp with you and to the warp with Ismael de Roeven, I'm glad they drilled his brain out.'

'You think he deserved that?' said Abrehem.

'Sure, why not? What do I care?'

'Because it could be you next,' hissed Abrehem, leaning over the table. 'The Adeptus Mechanicus just fed him to their machines and spat out his humanity as something worthless. He's a flesh chassis for their damned bionics. There's nothing left of him now.'

'Then maybe he's the lucky one,' said Coyne.

'Your man has a point,' said Hawke. 'Ismael might be a slave, but at least he doesn't know it.'

'And that makes it all right?'

'Of course not, but at least he's not suffering.'

'You don't know that.'

'True,' agreed Hawke. 'But you don't know that he *is*. Listen, it's been a long day and you've had a shock seeing a former co-worker with half his brain chopped out. That's enough to make anyone feel a bit stressed, am I right or am I right?'

'You're right, Hawke,' sighed Abrehem.

'I'll bet you could go for a glass of shine?' said Hawke amiably. 'I know I could.'

Abrehem almost laughed. He said, 'Sure, yeah, I'd love a drink. I'll ask Overseer Vresh if he can get a few drums rolled in. Emperor knows, I'd love to get drunk right now.'

Hawke grinned his shark's grin and said, 'Then today, my good friend, is your lucky day.'

Kotov turned his senses outwards, freeing his perceptions from golden-hued memory to the promise of the future. The fleet was making good time through the outer reaches of the Joura system, the course Mistress Tychon had plotted proving to be an exemplary display of stellar cartographical aptitude. Blaylock was still smarting at her interference, but Tarkis was ever given to emotional responses – especially ones triggered by a female who so openly disdained the accumulation of visible augmentation.

The Mandeville point was close, and Kotov could sense the ship's burning desire to be pressing on through the veil of the immaterium once more. Its labouring plasma engines were running close to maximum tolerance, and the risk of drive chamber burnouts was exponentially higher. Kotov detached a sliver of his consciousness and sent it through the noosphere to calm the eagerness of the engines. His augmented brain could function with full cognitive awareness while numerous portions were split from the whole attending to lesser functions. A hundred or more elements of his consciousness were seconded to the ship's various systems, yet he locked enough of his mind within his cerebral cortex to maintain his sense of self.

His attention shifted into that portion of the brain linked to the auspex arrays and surveyor banks, reading the witch's brew of electromagnetic radiation in the space around the vast hull. He felt the structure of the *Speranza* flex as though it were his own body, the cold of space making the few areas of skin remaining on his body pucker with goosebumps.

Farthest ahead was the *Renard*, and Kotov took a moment to fully study Captain Surcouf's vessel. It was a fine ship, heavily modified with Adeptus Mechanicus sanctioned refits and upgrades to render it faster, more agile and more heavily armed than its size would suggest. Such modifications would not have been acquired cheaply from a forge world, and gave the lie to the notion that Surcouf had joined this expedition for purely financial reasons.

Kotov's perceptions flitted from the *Renard* to the *Adytum*.

Where the rogue trader vessel fairly bristled with streams of data, the stripped-down Templars vessel was as dark as the heart of a black hole, a void of information whose machine-spirits were closed off to him. It felt galling and vaguely insulting for a high-ranking member of the Martian Priesthood to be so thoroughly rebuffed, but the machines of the Adeptus Astartes were always quick to assume the attributes of the Chapter they served.

The remainder of the fleet was on station around the *Speranza*, clustered around its majesty like flunkies at a royal court. Independent shards of his sentience issued corrective orders to a number of ships' captains without his primary focus having to do so consciously: manoeuvre orders to those that had drawn too near, internal system modifications to those whose data-networks were accumulating micro-errors in their workings.

Surcouf's vessel was a hound leading the hunters, and despite the man's earlier irreverence, Kotov was forced to admire his courage in defying the will of an archmagos with the force of a Reclusiarch to back him up. He understood Surcouf's motivation better than any of the others aboard the *Speranza*. They thought the man a vain popinjay, a rogue trader who sought only riches and renown, but Kotov had the truth of it. He knew of Surcouf's past, his upbringing in Ultramar, his time as executive officer aboard the ill-fated *Preceptor* and his consequent misadventures.

In many ways he and Roboute Surcouf were very much alike.

Many in the Martian Priesthood believed that risking the Ark Mechanicus on this quest was a fool's errand – a last, hopeless gambit by a magos whose holdings and influence had fallen spectacularly within the space of a decade. Perhaps it *was* foolish, but Kotov found it impossible to believe that his discovery of the *Speranza* and Surcouf's appearance with a relic of Telok's lost fleet could not be the will of the Omnissiah.

Together, they were glimmers of hope when his faith had been sorely tested by loss.

Arcetri had been the first of Kotov's forge worlds to fall, attacked and consumed by a questing tendril of Hive Fleet Harbinger. In his ignorance of the biological subtleties of the tyranid race, Kotov had assumed worlds of steel and industry would hold little interest for these rapacious aliens. That had proven to be a costly assumption, for the swarm hosts had invaded with a hunger that was as unstoppable as it was thorough. Though many sacred machines and adepts were evacuated before the first spores blotted out the skies, many more had been devoured in oceans of digestive acid.

Uraniborg 1572 was lost to the machinations of the arch-enemy, a sudden and shocking rebellion against his lawfully appointed overseers that had seen the resources of an entire forge world seized by the mechanised warhost of the techno-heretic Votheer Tark. The embedded skitarii and tech-priests fought to the last to deny the planet's assets to the enemy, but base treachery within the Legio Serpentes had ended their resistance within days. Uraniborg 1572 was now a corrupt hell-forge of the Dark Mechanicus, a world of bloodstained iron where glorious industry that had once served the Golden Throne was now perverted to supply the bloodthirsty rampages of a mechanised daemon abomination who cared nothing for the machine-spirits it violated.

Such a grievous loss would have been catastrophic in isolation, but coming so soon after the fall of Arcetri, it had almost broken Kotov. The destruction of Palomar was the final nail in his coffin, or so his detractors had announced in strident, declarative tones. How could a magos who had allowed three forge worlds to fall to mankind's enemies be expected to maintain his holdings on Mars? Surely, they said, such forge temples as remained to Magos Lexell Kotov should be redistributed to other, more capable magi before his ill-starred touch could destroy them too?

The *Speranza* had changed everything.

Arriving in Mars orbit with such a mighty relic from an age of miracles had sent his enemies slinking into the shadows. Most of them anyway; some were closer than ever.

The revelation of the *Speranza* had bought him time, but his continued

failure to meet projected tithe quotas by such vast margins meant that it was only a matter of time until his Martian forges were stripped from him and the Ark Mechanicus seized.

This venture into unknown space in search of Telok's lost fleet was his last chance to maintain what he had worked so hard to achieve. But it was more than simply the desire to hold on to what he had built that drove Kotov. In his rise through the ranks of the Mechanicus he had allowed himself to forget the first principles of the Priesthood, and the Omnissiah had punished him for his single-minded pursuit of worldly power.

To rediscover relics from the Golden Age of Technology was a goal whose worth no one could dispute, and if he could return with even a fraction of what Telok had hoped to find, he would be feted as a hero. The lost magos had claimed to be in search of nothing less than the secrets of the mythic race of beings he believed had brought the galaxies, stars and planets into being; technology that could change the very fabric of existence.

From the dusty reliquary-archives of far-flung ruins to the forbidden repositories in the dark heart of the galaxy, Telok was said to have spent his entire life in search of something he called the Breath of the Gods, an artefact of such power that it could reignite dying stars, turn geologically inert rocks into paradise planets and breathe life into the most sterile regions of wilderness space.

Of course, Telok had been ridiculed and scorned, his so-called proofs ignored and his theories discounted as the worst kind of foolishness.

And yet...

A last fragmented message, relayed to Mars from beyond the Halo Scar, spoke of his expedition's success. A distorted scrap of communication relayed through the Valette Manifold station was all that remained of the Telok Expedition, an incomplete code blurt over three thousand years old. Not a lot upon which to base so comprehensive an expedition, but this voyage was as much about faith and pilgrimage as it was of contrition.

Kotov would find the Breath of the Gods and return it to Mars.

Not for glory, not for renown, and not for power.

He would do this for the Omnissiah.

Microcontent 08

Spinning back and forth, the needle on the astrogation compass wobbled on its gyroscopic mount before finally settling on a bearing. One that bore no relation to their actual course, but then this compass wasn't part of the *Renard*. It had once been mounted in the heavily ornamented captain's pulpit of the *Preceptor*, and had steered them true for many years before that idiot Mindarus had made one mistake too many.

Roboute sat behind a polished rosewood desk in his private stateroom, watching the needle unseat itself from its imagined course once again and begin its fruitless search for a true bearing. He tapped the glass with a delicate fingernail, and almost smiled as the needle stopped its frantic bobbing, like a hound that hears an echo of its long lost master's voice. No sooner had it stopped than it jerked and bobbed as it sought a point of reference it could latch onto.

'Catch a wind for me, old friend,' said Roboute.

Soft music filled the stateroom, *The Ballad of Trooper Thom*, a wistful folk tune from ancient days that told the story of a dying soldier of the Five Hundred Worlds regaling a pretty nurse with the beauty of the home world he would never see again. Roboute liked the pride and elegiac imagery in the song, though it was seldom played now. Too many people thought it was in poor taste to sing of Calth's former glories, but Roboute didn't hold with that nonsense. It was a fine tune, and he liked to hear what the blue world had looked like before treachery had ravaged it.

Roboute's stateroom tended towards the austere, with only a few indications of the man who captained the ship in evidence on its walls. Most shipmasters of Ultramar kept their cabins fundamentally bare, and Roboute was no exception, though the profitable years he had spent as a rogue trader had brought their own share of embellishments: a scarf from a girl who'd kissed him as he left Bakka, a series of framed Naval commendations, a laurel rosette from his time in the Iax Defence Auxilia – earned in combat against a raiding party of trans-orbital insurgents from a passing asteroid – and a small hololithic cameo depicting the tilted profile of a young girl with tousled blonde hair and a sad, knowing look in her eye. Her name was Katen, and Roboute remembered with aching clarity the day that pict had been taken. A passing pictographer had snapped it at the feast day of First Seed as the two of them wandered, arm in arm, through the gathered entertainers and gaily coloured pavilions selling carved keepsakes, fresh-grown ornaments, sweetmeats and sugared pastries.

She'd been distant all day, and he knew why.

His distinguished service in the Iax Defence Auxilia was coming to an end, but instead of hanging up his rifle and taking a position in one of the better Agrarian Collectives, he had submitted his service jacket to the Navy Manifold. He'd told Katen it had been no more than idle curiosity to see what they'd make of him, but within a month, a Navy recruiter came to Iax and aggressively pursued him for a position aboard an Imperial warship as a junior officer.

He'd told the recruiter he'd need some time, and the man had left his details with a wry smile that told Roboute he'd heard that many times before, and that he was prepared to wait. He and Katen had continued with their lives, but each of them knew in their heart of hearts that he'd be leaving Iax on the next conjunction with the Navy yards at Macragge. She'd stopped the pictographer, and though he'd wanted to get one of them together, she'd insisted on the individual portrait.

Looking at it now, he understood her reason.

She'd since married; a good man from an old family that could trace its lineage all the way back to the establishment of First Landing and was said to count a number of its scions within the ranks of the Ultramarines. Roboute hoped that was true, and that she was happy. He hoped she had strong sons and pretty daughters, and that she hadn't spent too long mourning his death.

News of the *Preceptor's* destruction would certainly have reached Iax; much of her internal fittings and decorative panellings had been fashioned from good Iaxian timber. The Naval fleet registry listed her as destroyed by an unknown arch-enemy vessel, lost with all hands. But that only told half the story.

Roboute shook off memories of subsisting on metallic icewater dripping into the last remaining oxygenated compartment on the shattered bridge and being forced to lick the frozen fungus off the exposed under-deck structures, since that was the only source of sustenance left to him. That was a time he'd rather forget, and the astrogation compass was the only keepsake of his time on the *Preceptor* he allowed himself. Any more would be too painful to bear.

He tapped his authority signifiers onto the desk's surface and a hololithic panel of smoked glass hinged up from the rich red wood. Course vectors, fuel-consumption and curving attitude parabolas scrolled past as the *Renard's* data engines fed him information from its own surveyor packages as well as those inloaded from the *Speranza's* auspex arrays. He scanned the flood of information, letting the enhancements worked into the computational centres of his brain process the data without the need of his frontal brainspace. His natural Ultramarian aptitudes had ensured a rapid ascent through the Naval command ranks and saw him implanted with a number of cerebral augmentations, all of which had proven their worth many times – both in space and ashore.

'Whoever plotted this course knows their stars,' he said as he extrapolated the waypoints through the next few sectors where they'd drop out of the warp to re-establish their position before moving on the Halo Scar at the galactic edge. Roboute's fingers danced over the projected course, zooming in on portions, skipping past others and examining areas of particularly subtle hexamathic calculation. Much of it was beyond his limited understanding of such arcane multi-dimensional calculus, but he knew enough to know it was exquisite work.

Roboute opened a seamless drawer in the desk with a complex haptic gesture and a whispered command in a language his human throat could barely flex enough to voice. Inside was the gold-chased memory wafer from the saviour pod's locator beacon. He'd studied the data encoded in the latticed structure of the wafer on a discrete terminal, though much of it made little sense without datum references of the celestial geography beyond the Halo Scar. Hopefully once they were on the other side of the Scar, they'd be able to find those reference points.

Even though the terminal he'd used to study the data wasn't connected to the ship's main logic engines, he'd purged it before their arrival in orbit around Joura, knowing full well that Kotov would try and lift it from the *Renard's* memory stacks as soon as he learned what Roboute had done.

Sure enough, Magos Pavelka later found evidence of a subtle, but thorough infiltration of the ship's cogitators, a deep penetration that had interrogated every system in search of the missing data. That had given Roboute a grin. As if he would be so lax in his data discipline!

A pleasing chime sounded from the desk, like a knife gently tapped on a wineglass, and Roboute cleared the course information with a swiped hand. A pulsing vox-icon bearing a Cadian command authority stub appeared at the corner of the smoky glass, and Roboute grinned, having expected a call from the colonel's staff at some point.

He tapped the screen and the image of an earnest man appeared, youthfully handsome, but with a wolf-like leanness to him that reminded Roboute that even the staff officers of a Cadian regiment were highly trained and combat-experienced soldiers. He recognised the man from the meeting in the Adamant Ciborium, one of Colonel Anders's adjutants, but couldn't recall if he'd been told his name. The clarity of the image was second to none, thanks, Roboute suspected, to the high-end vox-gear aboard the *Speranza*.

'Captain Surcouf?' asked the man, though no one else could have answered this particular vox.

'Speaking. Who are you?'

'Lieutenant Felspar, adjutant to Colonel Anders,' answered the man, not in the least taken aback by Roboute's deliberately brusque reply.

'What can I do for you, Lieutenant Felspar?'

'I am to inform you that Colonel Anders is hosting an evening dinner in the officer's quarters on the Gamma deck's starboard esplanade at seven bells on the first diurnal shift rotation after translation. He extends an invitation to you and your senior crew to join him.'

'A dinner?'

'Yes, sir, a dinner. Shall I convey your acceptance of the colonel's invitation?'

Roboute nodded. 'Yes, along with my thanks.'

'Dress is formal. The colonel hopes that won't be a problem.'

Roboute laughed and shook his head. 'No, that won't be a problem, Lieutenant Felspar. We have a few clothes over here that aren't entirely threadbare or too outrageous for a regimental dinner.'

'Then the colonel will be pleased to receive you, captain.'

'Tell him we're looking forward to it,' said Roboute, shutting off the vox-link.

He placed the astrogation compass in the corner of his desk and

stood with a pleased grin. Straightening his jacket, he returned to the bridge of the *Renard* and took his place in the captain's chair. Emil Nader had the helm, though there was little for him to do given that they were slaved to the course of the *Speranza*.

'What did the Cadians want?' asked Emil.

'Who said it was the Cadians?'

'It was though, wasn't it? Ten ultimas says it was the Cadians.'

'It was, but that wasn't too hard to guess. The message came with a request prefix. Any vox-traffic from the Mechanicus doesn't bother with such niceties. Even Adara could have guessed it was the Cadians.'

'So what did they want?'

'Us,' said Roboute, looking out at the shimmering starfield visible through the main viewing bay with a thrill of seeing new horizons. The stars were thinner and felt dimmer the closer they drew to the Mandeville point, as though they were reaching the edges of known space. It was an optical illusion, of course, a fiction crafted by the mind when approaching the edge of a star system.

'Us? What do you mean?'

'I mean they want us to come to dinner,' said Roboute, calling up the shared fleet chronometer to the display. 'So I'm afraid we'll need to dig out those dress uniforms again. You, me and Emil are going over to the *Speranza* in eighteen hours.'

'Dinner?'

'Yeah,' said Roboute. 'You *have* heard of it? An assembly of individuals who gather to consume food and drink while sharing convivial conversation and a general atmosphere of bonhomie.'

'Doesn't sound like any dinner we've ever had,' said Emil.

'Probably not, but we can at least try not to disgrace ourselves, eh?'

'So what do you think?' asked Hawke.

'Thor's balls, I think you've just killed me!' gasped Coyne, spitting a mouthful of clear liquid to the deck. He dropped to his knees and retched wetly, though he held onto the muck he'd just eaten in the feeding hall.

Abrehem swallowed the acrid liquid with difficulty, tasting all manner of foul chemicals and distilled impurities in its oily texture. It fought to come back up again, but he kept it down with a mixture of determination and sheer bloody willpower. When the initial flare of Hawke's vile brew had subsided, there was, he had to admit, a potent aftertaste that wasn't entirely unpleasant.

'Well?' said Hawke.

'I've certainly drunk worse stuff than this in dockside bars,' he said at last.

'That's not saying much,' said Hawke with a hurt pout.

'It's about the best recommendation I can give you,' said Abrehem. 'Give me another.'

Hawke smiled and bent to the collection of hydro-drums, fuel canisters, copper tubing and plastic piping that siphoned off liquids from Emperor-only-knew-where and filtered them through a tangled circulatory system of tubes, distillation flasks, filtering apparatus and burn chambers. Not one of its constituent parts looked as though it was fulfilling the purpose for which it had been designed, and Abrehem read entoptic substrate codes that suggested at least two dozen machines elsewhere were now missing vital parts.

'How the hell were you able to build this?' asked Coyne, rising to his feet and holding out his tin cup for a refill.

'Guard knowhow,' said Hawke, handing Abrehem a cup and taking Coyne's. 'It's a bloody poor soldier who can't figure out a way to make booze aboard a Navy ship on its way to a warzone.'

'This isn't a Navy ship,' pointed out Abrehem. 'It's Mechanicus.'

'Only makes it easier,' said Hawke. 'There's so much stuff lying around that you can't help but find a few bits and pieces no one's using any more.'

Abrehem sipped his drink, wincing at its strength. 'But some of these pieces are pretty specialised, how did you get hold of them?'

Hawke gave him a wink that might have been meant to reassure him, but which came off as lecherous and conniving.

'Listen, do you want a drink or not?' said Hawke. 'There's always ways and means you can get hold of stuff when you're on a starship. Especially one where there's men and women with needs. Especially one where a man with an eye to satisfying those needs can... facilitate them to fruition. Let's just leave it at that, okay?'

Abrehem wanted to ask more, but something told him that he wouldn't like any of the answers Hawke might give him. Not for the first time, he wondered about the wisdom of allying himself with a man like Hawke, a man whose morals appeared to be situationally malleable to say the least.

They'd followed Hawke from the feeding hall into the dripping corridors that ran parallel to their dormitory accommodation. Steam drifted in lazy banks from heavy iron pipes that shed paint and brackish water in equal measure. Crusha led the way, ducking every now and then as a knot of pipework twisted down into the space, and Abrehem and Coyne were soon hopelessly lost in the labyrinth of needlessly complex corridors, side passages and weirdly angled companionways.

The chamber Hawke had finally led them to was wide and felt like a cross between a temple and a prison chamber. The ceiling was arched, and skulls and bones were worked into the walls like cadavers emerging from tombs sunk in some forgotten sepulchre. Faded frescoes of Imperial saints occupied the coffers on the ceiling, and a hexagonal-tiled pathway traced a route to a blocked-off wall inscribed with stencilled lettering rendered illegible by the relentlessly dripping water and oil. Whatever had once been written there was now lost to posterity, though Abrehem reasoned it couldn't have been that important, judging by the neglect and abandonment of this place.

Hawke's still was set up against the blocked-off wall, and Abrehem saw smeared shimmers of code lines snaking across it. None were strong enough to read on their own, and he blinked away the after-images, wondering why there would be any power routed through this section at all.

'How did you even find this place?' asked Abrehem.

'And what is it?' added Coyne. 'It's like a crypt.'

Hawke looked momentarily flustered, but soon shook it off.

'I needed somewhere out of the way to get the still put together,' he said, with a lightness of tone that sounded entirely false. 'Took a walk one night and found myself just taking turns at random, not really knowing where I was going. Found this place, and figured it was perfect.'

'I'm amazed you could find your way back,' said Abrehem. 'It's a bloody maze down here.'

'Well, that's just it, isn't it?' said Hawke. 'I started out trying to remember how I'd got here; left turn, right turn, straight ahead for a hundred metres, that sort of thing, but it never seemed to matter. I always got here, and I'd never quite remember how I did it. Same on the way out.'

'Sounds like you've been sampling too much of your own product,' said Coyne.

'No,' said Hawke. 'It's like this place *wanted* me to find it, like I was always going to find it.'

'What are you talking about?'

Hawke shrugged, unwilling to be drawn further and realising he'd said too much. 'Hell, what does it matter anyway?'

Abrehem made a slow circuit of the chamber as Hawke spoke. He reached out to touch the wall with the faded stencilling, feeling an almost imperceptible vibration in the metal, as though some unseen machinery pulsed with a glacial heartbeat on the other side. Code fragments squirmed over the metal towards his hand, sub-ferrous

worms of light drawn to the flow of blood around his flesh. Abrehem felt a weight of great anger and terrible sorrow beyond the metal and stepped back, flustered by the raw surge of volatile energies contained within this mysterious chamber.

'I don't like this place,' he said at last. 'We shouldn't be here.'

'Why not?' said Hawke. 'It's a good place, quiet, out of the way and it's still got a little juice flowing through it.'

'You ever stop to wonder why?'

'No, what do I care? It's a Mechanicus ship, there's power flowing all through it to places the tech-priests have likely forgotten about. This shine's going to make a lot of people very happy, eh?'

'For a price,' said Abrehem.

'A man's got a right to earn something from his labours, ain't he?'

'We're little better than slaves,' pointed out Abrehem. 'What could any of us have that would be worth anything to you?'

'Folks have *always* got something to trade,' said Hawke. 'Favours, trinkets, their strength, their skills, their... companionship. You'd be surprised what people are willing to offer a man in return for a little bit of an escape from their daily grind.'

'No,' said Abrehem sadly. 'I wouldn't.'

The fleet began its final approach to the Mandeville point with two of the escorts from Voss Prime and the *Adytum* in the vanguard. *Cardinal Boras* followed close behind, with *Wrathchild* and *Moonchild* prowling the flanks of the *Speranza*. The *Renard* was now berthed in one of its cavernous holds, for there was no reason to maintain a flight profile when it could be carried aboard a bigger ship instead. Archmagos Kotov was taking no chances on losing the *Renard* before Captain Surcouf could provide him with navigational computations for space beyond the Halo Scar.

High above the engine wake of the Ark Mechanicus, *Mortis Voss* kept watch on their rear, for this was when the fleet was at its most vulnerable. As the fires of the plasma engines cooled and the fleet bled off speed, it also lost the ability to fight and manoeuvre effectively. Corsair fleets often lurked in debris clusters, hollowed out asteroids or electromagnetically active dust clouds before pouncing on prey vessels. The power of the Kotov Fleet was likely proof against any such ambush, but piratical attacks were not the only danger to ships preparing to collapse the walls between realities.

Situated far from the sucking gravity well of the sun, the Mandeville point represented the region of space that centuries of experience and hard-won knowledge had identified as the best place to breach the membrane separating realspace and warp space. A ship could translate into the warp elsewhere, of course, but such were the risks involved that any means of reducing the danger was worth the extra transit time to the more distant Mandeville point.

The *Speranza* would make the first breach, her warp generators spooling up with enough force to rip a gateway into the warp for the rest of the fleet to use. It was difficult enough to maintain fleet cohesion after a warp translation at the best of times, harder still if each ship had to tear its own path through. Better that one ship shouldered the hard work for the rest, and the *Speranza* was easily capable of such an expenditure of power.

Cocooned Navigators and mentally-conjoined astropaths would maintain links between the fleet, but nothing about travel through the warp was certain, and astrogation data, together with emergency rally points, was passed between each shipmaster.

Blade of Voss and *Honour Blade* circled back around, their engines flaring brightly as their mater-captains performed hard-burn turns to bring them in close to the vast ship at the heart of the fleet. Each ship in the fleet undertook complex manoeuvres to bring them in tight to the *Speranza*, clustering at ranges that in terrestrial terms were enormous, but in spatial topography were dangerously close. Every ship shut down all but the most vital auspex systems, for it was better not to know too much of the substance of the warp beyond the shimmering bubble of the Geller field.

Satisfied its cohorts were isolated in their own silent shrouds, the *Speranza* unleashed salvoes of screaming code bursts, warning any nearby ships to keep their distance. Though the Ark Mechanicus was a ship of exploration, she was not without teeth, and had more than enough power reserves in her vast capacitors to defend herself in the event of any surprise attack. Echoing howls of hostile machine language warned of dire consequences for any ship that dared approach.

With the echoes of its binaric challenge still echoing through space, the spatial environment smeared with ghostly blotches of unlight, shimmers of an unseen world brought dangerously close to the surface. Like a stagnant pool, wherein dwelled unseen and unknowable abominations and whose hidden depths have for good reason remained invisible, the edges of the warp were horribly revealed. Immaterial tendrils of sick light bled into realspace, a glistening discoloured tumour bulging into the material universe where the malevolent reflections of things dreaded and things desired were made real. Like an ocean maelstrom given sentience, a whorl of bruised colours and damaged light oozed from a point in space ahead of the fleet, gradually widening as ancient machinery and arcane techno-sorcery conceived in an earlier age tore the gouge in space ever wider.

A suppurating wound in the material universe, the space around it buckled in torment, loosing tortured screams unheard by any save weeping astropaths and Cadian primaris psykers locked in psychic Faraday cages. Even those without the curse of psychic ability felt the tear opening wider, its abhorrent presence occupying multiple states of existence that violated the first principles of the men who sought to codify the real world in the earliest millennia of the human civilisation.

No conventional auspex could measure so unnatural a phenomenon. Its boundaries existed on no level of being that could be measured in empirical terms. Its very appearance made a mockery of any notions of *reality*, and only instrumentation conceived in fits of delirium by men whom science deemed mad in ages past could even acknowledge its presence.

The *Speranza's* plasma engines flared with a last eye-watering burst of power as it made for the dark heart of the warp fissure. Nebulous slivers of nullplasmic anti-light engulfed the mighty vessel, swallowing it whole and folding around it like some nightmare predator that had lured its prey into its jaws with gaudy displays of colour.

One by one the ships of the Kotov Fleet translated into the warp.

Though most translation events were timed to occur when the fewest number of crewmen were on their nightside rotation and bells were rung throughout the ship to keep men from their nightmares, it was inevitable that some would pass between worlds while asleep. Few Cadians slept, knowing better than most the risks of such a lapse after numerous translations between the void and the warp.

Prayers were said, offerings and promises made to the God-Emperor to keep them safe, lucky talismans kissed and whatever rituals a man believed might keep him safe were enacted throughout the fleet. Confessors and warrior priests toured the dormitory spaces of every ship, hearing the fears of those who could keep their terror at bay no longer.

For the duration of a warp journey, every living soul was a fervent believer and pious servant of the Golden Throne, but if the Ecclesiarchy priests cared that this upswell in absolute devotion was temporary, they did not say.

Likewise, few of the Adeptus Mechanicus slept, their biological components' requirement for rest overruled by their artificial implants in anticipation of the translation. Aboard the *Adytum*, the warriors of the Adeptus Astartes knelt in silent contemplation of their duty, watched over by the implacable form of Kul Gilad. He knew the signs of warp intrusion, and kept vigil on his warriors for any hint that the insidious tendrils of the warp had taken root. He expected no trace of such corruption, but only by eternal vigilance could such expectations be maintained.

Cortex-fused armsmen prowled the decks of every ship, alert for any sign of danger, shot-cannons and shock mauls at the ready. Translation was always a time fraught with disturbances: fights whose cause no one could quite remember, raving sleepwalkers, suicide attempts, random acts of senseless violence, delirious bouts of uninhibited sex and the like.

Throughout the fleet, men and women experienced nightmares, sweating palpitations, gloomy premonitions of their own death or prolonged bouts of melancholia. No one relished the prospect of translation, but there was little to do but endure it and pray to the God-Emperor that the journey be over swiftly.

Nor were the destabilising effects of warp translation confined solely to the mortal elements of the fleet; its mechanical components suffered similar trauma. On every ship, from the most complex machines that were beyond mortal understanding to the simplest circuits, the technology of the Kotov Fleet felt the fear of new and impossible physical laws that interfered with their smooth running. Glitches bloomed and a hundred faults developed every minute, keeping the tech-priests, lexmechanics and servitors working shift after shift to ensure nothing vital failed at the worst possible moment.

Of all the components in the fleet, only one sort slept through the translation, and they suffered nightmares the like of which no ordinary soul could comprehend. Deep in the hearts of the recumbent Titans, the fleshy minds that allowed the wolf hearts of the Legio Sirius to fight writhed in the grip of amniotic nightmares. To spare their princeps the worst effects of translation, the tech-priest crews had shut them off from the outside world, sealing each singular individual in their milky prisons with only memories of past lives to sustain them.

Past glories and victories stretching back thousands of years were usually enough to keep each princeps from suffering the worst effects of translation, but not this time. Alpha Princeps Arlo Luth dreamed of scuttling creatures with bladed limbs infesting his titanic frame, of worm-like burrowers coring him hollow from the inside out and enormous bio-titans crushing his metal body beneath their impossible biology.

He thrashed his vestigial limbs in mute horror, unable to scream

or beg the tech-priests to wake him. Luth's every link to the outside world was closed off to him, but *Lupa Capitalina* felt his pain and shared it, its systems flaring in empathic fury.

Its weapon systems and threat signifiers briefly overcame the Mechanicus wards keeping it quiescent, and it loosed a shuddering blast of its warhorn as auto-loaders and power coils surged to life. Hundreds of panicking tech-priests and Legio acolytes responded to the battle-engine's sudden ascent to its war-footing, but before they could do more than register the danger, the Titan's machine-spirit sank back to dormancy.

No trace of what had caused the *Capitalina's* aggressive surge could be found, and the senior magi of the Legio put the episode down to a quirk of translation bleed into the machinery of the *Speranza's* inertia-cradles.

But they were all wrong.

With the departure of the Ark Mechanicus, the infected wound of the translation point snapped shut as the tortured skein of what mortals blissfully accepted as reality reasserted its dominance. The aftershocks of so brutal a manipulation of the laws governing the physical properties of the universe would echo throughout the past and the future, for such concepts as linear time simply did not exist in the warp.

Bielanna felt the violence of the human fleet's shift into the warp and eased her hold on the wraithbone heart of the *Starblade*. The ship rode out the last of the warp spasms, its captain climbing, diving and yawing in time with the amplitude of the temporal and causal wavefronts unleashed by the brutal violation of real space.

She opened herself to the infinity circuit, allowing her mind to flow through the living structure of the *Starblade*. Glittering points of light sparkled like starlight in the Dome of Dreams Forgotten, Warp Spiders at work repairing cracks in the wraithbone where stresses on the hull had cracked the carefully grown spars that gave the ship its deceptive strength. She avoided the Warp Spiders, leaving them to their unthinking labours as she eased through the ribs of the giant vessel and felt the hot neutron wind roaring past the hull and filling the solar sails with energy. Vast reservoirs of power burned in the heart of the *Starblade*, resources harvested from the aether and the almost limitless reserves of the stars.

Bielanna felt the firefly soul-lights of the crew, each one a weaving thread upon the skein, each one a vista of potential stretching out from the *now* and into the myriad possible *nows*. Some she felt close to, others she knew only from what the infinity circuit told her of them. Every eldar on board the *Starblade* was touched by the infinity circuit, and each left their mark upon it.

Yes, there were poets and artists amongst the crew, but this was a ship of warriors.

Two aspect shrines occupied the ventral and dorsal domes of the ship, Striking Scorpions and Howling Banshees, with a shrine of Dire Avengers housed towards the prow. Three of the most warlike aspects of Khaine: the shadow hunters, the wailing death and the blade that severs. Bielanna let her spirit slide past the aspect shrines without pause, for she did not wish to attract undue attention from those who wore their war-mask so close to the surface when the power of the warp was in the ascendancy.

The heart of the *Starblade* housed the shrine of the war-god itself, but its furnace heart was cold – the embers of its bellicose heart slumbering until the call to arms fanned them to life once more. Even without the imminence of battle, the raging echoes of the human fleet's bludgeoning assault on barriers meant to keep them from the warp were making it restless.

Guardians trained in the wing-mounted domes, citizen soldiers of Biel-Tan whose lives may have carried them from the path of the warrior, but who were duty-bound to heed its call when the need arose. Ever was the heart of Biel-Tan ready for war. The entire essence of the ship was primed for battle.

She felt it in the tautness of the wraithbone, the urgency of the Warp Spiders and the howling war-masks of the Aspect Warriors.

The presence of the captain merged with her own and she felt his question before it was asked.

'No, I have not found it yet,' she said. 'But it is near. Allow me to guide the *Starblade* and I will see us through.'

The captain wordlessly acquiesced and Bielanna felt the enormous weight of the starship settle upon her, its lance-shaped prows, its vast wingspan, its many weapons, its ventral fins and towering solar sail. The sense of commanding something so powerful was intoxicating, and she fought to hold on to her sense of identity as the vast, swarming spirit of the ship rushed to draw her into its glowing heart.

Bielanna hurled her spirit from the pleasurable heat of the *Starblade's* wraithbone limbs and out into space, feeling the storm winds of an alternate dimension buffet her and try to pry her loose from her course. What she sought was close, she could feel its nearness, but it was coy and loath to reveal itself, even to the heirs of those who had wrought it in a lost age of greatness.

Removing herself from literal thought of physical locations, Bielanna

freed her mind to the skein, letting the drifts of the future wash over her. The multiple strands of the future diverged before her, a densely-knotted rope weaving itself together from a billion times a billion slender threads. She flowed into the threads, following the blood-red strand that led to unsheathed blades, split veins and cloven flesh.

The future opened up to her and she saw now what she sought.

And as that future moved from potential to reality, the webway portal finally revealed itself, a shimmering starfield in the outline of Morai-Heg in her aspect of the Maiden – at once beautiful and seductive, yet also dangerously beguiling. More than one myth-cycle told of foolish eldar lured to their doom by trusting her wondrous countenance. The *Starblade's* prow turned to the sun-wrought form of the goddess of fate, and golden light flared from the edges of the portal in welcome recognition.

The stars beyond faded to obscurity as the amber depths of the webway were revealed, and Bielanna returned control of the starship to its captain. She felt a momentary pang of loss as its immense heart untangled from her own. Bielanna fought against the desire to mesh her spirit with the ship once again as it slipped effortlessly into the webway, travelling the vast gulfs of space without the terrible dangers faced by the human fleet.

Bielanna opened her eyes, letting the weight of her physical body reassert itself as she moved from the realm of the spirit to the realm of the flesh.

She sat in the centre of her empty quarters, cross-legged between two empty beds intended for newborn eldar children.

They were empty and had always been empty.

And unless she was able to unseat the human fleet from its blundering path into the unknown, they always would be.

Microcontent 09

Despite his best efforts to achieve exacting punctuality, it was thirty seconds after seven bells before Roboute and his crew arrived at the entrance to the Cadian officers' billets on Gamma deck. The part of him that was Ultramar through and through hated being less than punctilious, but the part of him that had seen him take up the life of a rogue trader relished such rebelliousness.

Though even he had to admit that being half a minute late wasn't much of a rebellion.

He'd come with Emil, Adara and Enginseer Sylkwood, who'd jumped at the chance to spend time with some soldiers of the Guard. Roboute wasn't surprised she'd joined him; Karyn was no stranger to the sharp end of mass battle, and she'd fought on Cadia before. The desire to speak to professional soldiers was a hard habit to break, it seemed. Magos Pavelka had not accompanied them, professing no desire to engage in meaningless social ritual when there were dozens of emergent faults manifesting in the data engines after the trauma of translation.

The entrance from the starboard esplanade was a surprisingly ornate doorway of black-enamelled wood chased with gold wiring and embellished with repeated motifs of the Icon Mechanius worked into the stonework portico. A brushed steel plaque at eye-level listed the personnel residing here with machine-cut precision. Roboute

suspected the Cadians would have preferred something less ornate, but supposed that Guard units took what they were given when they boarded a starship. This was just a little more elaborate than he figured they'd be used to.

Lieutenant Felspar met them at the doorway with an escort of spit-shined and barrel-chested storm troopers in bulky body armour and heavy charge-packs. Though clearly intended as an honour guard for the guests, it was plain to see that these were serious men who were more than ready to wreak harm on any potential threat.

'Captain Surcouf, good evening. The colonel will be glad you were able to attend,' said Felspar.

'Yes, sorry, took us longer to get here than we expected,' he said. 'Turns out those mag-levs aren't as fast as they look.'

Felspar gave him a look that suggested he wasn't in the mood for humour and consulted the data-slate he produced from behind his back.

'And these individuals would be your crew?'

'Yes,' agreed Roboute, introducing Emil, Adara and Sylkwood. Felspar confirmed their identities with a sweep of a data wand that compared their biometrics with those that had been recorded the moment they'd first stepped aboard the *Speranza*.

'You'll need to surrender your weapons, of course,' said Felspar.

'We're not armed,' said Roboute.

'I beg to differ.'

Irritation touched Roboute at the adjutant's smug tone, and he was about to remonstrate when Felspar held up the wand. A red line flashed along its length, indicating the presence of a weapon.

'Sorry,' said Adara, removing his butterfly blade from his shirt pocket. 'Force of habit.'

'Didn't I say not to bring any weapons?'

'I hardly even think of it as a weapon now,' said Adara with a bemused shrug. 'It's not like I'm planning to stab anyone with it.'

'I'm sure that makes Lieutenant Felspar very happy,' said Roboute. 'Now hand it over.'

'I'll get it back, won't I?' asked Adara, folding the blade and placing it in Felspar's outstretched hand. 'My da gave me that knife, said it saved his life back when–'

'The lieutenant doesn't need to hear your life story,' said Sylkwood, pushing Adara out of the way. 'Say, you want to wave your wand at me, soldier? I think I might have a concealed weapon or two secreted somewhere about my person. I forget, but it's probably best you make sure.'

Felspar shook his head. 'That won't be necessary, ma'am,' he said, flushing a deep red.

Sylkwood gave a filthy laugh and moved past Felspar, pausing to give each of the storm troopers an appreciative inspection. Emil followed her and Adara hurried to catch up.

'Is she always so forward?' asked Felspar.

'Trust me, that was her being reserved,' said Roboute. 'Oh, and by the way, the *Renard* is in docking berth Jovus-Tertiary Nine Zero, takes fifteen minutes exactly to get here.'

'I'm not sure I follow,' said Felspar.

'So you know where you are when you wake up in the morning,' said Roboute, giving the lieutenant a comradely slap on the shoulder. 'You know, just in case.'

Before Felspar could answer, Roboute moved off into the officers' quarters, following the sound of conversation, clinking glasses and a stirring martial tune that sounded like a colours band at a grand triumphal march.

The anteroom beyond the entrance resembled a wide banqueting chamber that wouldn't have seemed out of place in a hive noble's palace. Clearly the Adeptus Mechanicus had differing ideas of what constituted soldiers' accommodation to the Departmento Munitorum.

A shaven-headed servitor in a cream coloured robe approached him, its physique less augmented than was the norm for such cybernetics. Its skin was powdered white, and its hair had been slicked back with a pungent oil. It carried a beaten metal tray upon which were a number of thin-stemmed glasses filled with a golden liquid that sparkled with tiny bubbles.

'Dammassine?' inquired the servitor.

'Don't mind if I do,' said Roboute, taking a glass.

He took a small sip and was rewarded with a sweet herbal taste over a hint of almond.

Emil and the others had already availed themselves of the servitor's hospitality and stood at the edge of the room, taking in a measure of their hosts and their guests. Perhaps thirty Cadian officers, dressed in fresh uniform jackets and boots, mingled with the bluff good humour of men who trusted one another implicitly. A number of Adeptus Mechanicus magi were scattered through the assembly of fighting men, looking acutely uncomfortable at being thrust into a situation they were ill-equipped to handle.

'No sign of Kotov,' he murmured.

'Did you really expect to see him?' asked Emil.

'Not really,' said Roboute, scanning the faces before him for ones he knew.

His gaze fell upon Colonel Ven Anders chatting amiably with Linya Tychon and her father.

Magos Blaylock stood to one side, and an officer with the shoulder boards of a supply corps officer was explaining something to him that involved extravagant hand gestures. A gaggle of junior officers were clustered around the enormous figure of Kul Gilad, who in deference to the occasion had divested himself of his armour and wore a plain black and white surplice over his matt-black bodyglove. Even without the mass of plate and armaplas, the man was enormous and built like the chrono-gladiator Roboute had once seen in the fighting pits of the Bakkan sumps.

'How come *he* gets to keep his weapon?' said Adara, nodding towards the chunky, eagle-winged maul slung over the Reclusiarch's shoulder.

'Would you try and take it from him?' asked Emil.

'I guess not,' said Adara, snagging another drink from a passing servitor.

Kul Gilad had not come alone; a bearded warrior with a severe widow's peak and a line of hammered service studs in his forehead stood to his right. Where Kul Gilad could at least partially conceal his discomfort at being included in a social environment, his companion wore no such mask.

'Who's his dour friend?' wondered Emil.

'A sergeant,' said Roboute. 'The white wreath on the shoulder tells you that.'

'It does?'

'Yes,' said Roboute. 'The Black Templars might be descendants of Rogal Dorn, but it looks like their rank markings and the like still owe a great deal to the Ultramarines.'

The sergeant looked up sharply, though Roboute would have been surprised if the man had heard what he'd just said. Then again, who really knew exactly how supra-engineered the Space Marines' gene-structure really was?

Ven Anders glanced away from his conversation and caught Roboute's eye, beckoning them over with a friendly wave. Roboute made his way through the press of officers until he reached the colonel. He shook the man's hand, the skin callused and rough from decades spent in trenches and on countless battlefields. A brass-scaled automaton – fashioned from clockwork in the shape of a small, tree-climbing lizard – clung to his shoulder, its irising eye regarding him with dumb machine implacability.

Roboute introduced his crew, and the colonel shook each one by the hand with convincing sincerity. The lizard scuttled around to his other shoulder, its brass limbs clicking like a clock ticking too fast.

'A pleasure to meet you all,' said Anders. 'I'm very glad you could attend.'

'Wouldn't have missed it,' said Roboute.

'He's right,' added Emil. 'We never pass up a free meal.'

'Free?' said Magos Tychon, leaning forwards in a musky cloud of sweet-smelling incense. 'This evening isn't free. The cost of the food and dammassine will be deducted from your finder's fee and the value of refit schedules you negotiated with the archmagos.'

Vitali Tychon's face was impossible to read. Superficially, it resembled what he must have looked like as a creature of flesh and blood, but malleable sub-dermal plasteks had been injected in the dead meat of his face, making him look like an up-hive mannequin. His eyes were multifaceted chips of green in eye sockets that were just a little too wide to be entirely natural looking, and there were altogether too many metallic fingers holding the thin stem of his glass.

'Really?' said Emil. 'And this stuff tastes expensive.'

'Oh, it is, Mister Nader,' said Vitali. 'Ruinously so.'

Roboute almost laughed at the shock on Emil's face as he looked for a servitor to take his untouched glass away.

'Damn, I wish they'd told us that when we came in.'

Roboute saw a mischievous twinkle in Tychon's emerald optics and smiled as Linya Tychon placed a reassuring hand on Emil's elbow. Roboute caught the flash of brass-rimmed augmetics at her ear beneath strands of blonde hair, and the telltale glassiness of artificial eyes. Subtly done and implanted with the intent of retaining her humanity.

'I believe my father is making a joke, Mister Nader,' said Linya. 'It's a bad habit of his, because he has a woeful sense of humour.'

'A joke?' said Emil.

'Yes,' agreed Tychon delightedly. 'A verbal construct said aloud to cause amusement or laughter, either in the form of a story with an unexpected punchline or a play on word expectation.'

'I thought the Mechanicus didn't tell jokes,' said Adara.

'We don't usually,' said Linya, 'because the humour gland is one of the first things surgically removed when one takes the Archimedean Oath.'

'I didn't know that,' said Adara. 'Did you know that, captain?'

'Don't be an idiot all your life, lad,' said Sylkwood, giving him a clip round the ear. 'Now go get me another drink and try not to do anything too monumentally stupid along the way.'

Adara nodded and wandered off in search of another servitor, rubbing the back of his head where the hard metal of Sylkwood's hand had likely bruised him.

'Don't worry,' said Roboute. 'We're not all that naïve.'

'Ah, to be so young and foolish, captain,' said Anders.

'I doubt you were ever as foolish as Adara, colonel,' said Roboute.

'My father might disagree with you, though it's kind of you to say so.'

Roboute raised his glass and said, 'We were admiring the quarters you've been allocated. More luxurious than I imagine you're used to.'

'Most people might think so, but just because we come from Cadia doesn't mean we don't enjoy a bit of soft living now and again.'

'Don't tell me any more,' said Roboute. 'You'll spoil all my illusions.'

Roboute turned to acknowledge Magos and Mistress Tychon. 'You are settling in well aboard Archmagos Kotov's ship?'

'Very well, Captain Surcouf,' said Vitali Tychon. 'The ship is a wonder, is it not?'

'I confess I haven't seen too much of it,' he admitted.

'Ah, you must, dear boy,' said Vitali. 'It is not every day that one is permitted to explore so incredible a vessel. A spacefarer like you ought to appreciate that. It would be my very real pleasure to act as your guide should you decide to learn more of its heritage. In fact, Magos Saiixek of engineering over there was just telling me of the complex arrangements of the drive chambers and–'

Colonel Anders intervened before Vitali could expound further, saying, 'Captain; Mistress Linya was just telling me of what brought her and her father along on this voyage. Fascinating stuff, much more interesting than the usual things I hear at functions like this.'

'What do you normally hear?'

'Mostly it's some local dignitary who's too scared of whatever's invaded his world to do anything but babble about how thankful he is that we're here, or some defence force martinet who's scared of being shown up by the professionals. Embarrassing, really.'

'Captain, I think I'll go make sure Adara doesn't get himself into trouble,' said Emil, with a casual salute to Colonel Anders and the Tychons.

'I'll come with you,' said Sylkwood, setting off in the direction of the engineering magos Tychon had pointed out. Perhaps Felspar might have a lucky escape from Sylkwood's attentions after all.

Roboute turned his attention to Linya Tychon, who took an appreciative sip of her dammassine.

'So what *did* bring you along on Kotov's expedition?' he asked.

'The same thing that brought you, captain,' said Linya.

'Are you sure?' said Roboute. 'Because I came along for an obscenely large sum of money and an *in perpetuitus* refit contract for my trade fleet.'

'From a magos with no forge holdings beyond the red sands of Mars?'

'Our contract doesn't specify those refits need to be carried out in one of Magos Kotov's forges.'

'I'm sure, but it seems like a flimsy reason when your aexactor records show that you can easily afford the tithes the Mechanicus requires for refit contracts.'

'You've read my aexactor records?' said Roboute. 'Aren't they supposed to be sealed by the Administratum?'

'The entire record of your life became freely available to inload by any magos the moment you contracted with the Adeptus Mechanicus,' said Linya. 'Surely you must have known that?'

Roboute hadn't, and he blanched as Ven Anders and Magos Tychon laughed at him squirming like a fish on a hook. A cold lump of dread formed in the pit of his stomach at the thought that every magos aboard the *Speranza* might know everything about him.

'Let's hope you've nothing to hide, captain,' said Anders.

'Not at all, pure as the driven snow,' said Roboute, swiftly recovering his equilibrium. He was wary of this unexpected back and forth, but had to admit he was enjoying it. 'All right then, Mistress Tychon. Why do *you* think I've come all this way to travel beyond the Halo Scar into unknown space if not for the undeniable financial gain?'

'Because you're bored.'

'Bored? The life of a rogue trader is hardly a boring one.'

'To anyone not of Ultramar, maybe it's not, but it's too easy for you, isn't it? In addition to your aexactor records, I inloaded your service history: Iax Defence Auxilia records, Navy jacket and your subsequent dealings after your return to Imperial space after the destruction of the *Preceptor*.'

'Why the keen interest in my history?'

'Because I like to know the character of the man who's leading my father and I into a region of space that might see us dead.'

'The lady has a point,' said Anders. 'I think we'd all like to know that.'

'I suppose,' said Roboute. 'So what does all that research tell you, Linya? May I call you Linya?'

'You may,' said Linya, and Roboute relaxed a fraction. Whatever Linya Tychon's purpose, it wasn't to expose him. 'What it tells me is

that there are worse trainings for life than to be raised in Ultramar, Roboute. May I call you Roboute?'

'I'd be hurt if you didn't.'

'Thank you. I think you are a man who thrives on challenge, and the life of a rogue trader no longer challenges you. You've made your fortune and your trade routes are so well-organised that they more or less run themselves. So what is left for a man like you except to explore one of the most dangerous regions of space in the galaxy?'

'That's very astute of you, Linya.'

'Is she right?' asked Colonel Anders, halting a servitor bearing delicately-wrought canapés of spun pastry and reclaimed meat paste.

Roboute nodded slowly. 'Here be dragons,' he said. 'That's what the maps of Old Earth said when their makers didn't know what lay beyond the furthest reaches of their knowledge, and that's an apt phrase when you're talking about what might lie in the depths of wilderness space.'

'You want to see dragons?' asked Anders.

'In a manner of speaking,' said Roboute. 'Linya's right about life in Ultramar; it instills a work ethic unlike any other, a determination to always strive for the next horizon. I've done very well as a rogue trader, *very* well. I've made more money than I could ever hope to spend. There's only so many things a man can buy, so once you have all you want what's left except to venture into the unknown and achieve something worthwhile? I want to see what lies beyond the Imperium's borders, to see wonders that no other man has known and to sail by the light of stars that shine on worlds that know nothing of the God-Emperor.'

'A worthy ambition,' said Magos Tychon. 'But such ambition comes at a price. To venture into the Halo Scar, to go beyond the guiding light of the Astronomican? That is to sail in uncharted and unremembered space. Treacherous seas indeed. Such places are the stuff of nightmares and tales of horror. The last expedition that ventured this way was never seen again.'

'I know,' said Roboute. 'Your daughter isn't the only one who knows how to research.'

Dinner was announced with a fanfare from the recorded colours band, and the assembled officers, magi and civilians made their way into a long dining room illuminated by flickering electro-flambeaux held aloft by tiny suspensor fields. The walls were hung with long banners, representations of the Icon Mechanicus and honour rolls of Cadia's victories and its many notable Lord Generals. A holographic recording of Ursarkar Creed's famous address to the troops at Tyrok Fields played on a loop from a shimmering projector-plinth at the far end of the room, and a burbling hiss of binaric prayers issued from hidden vox-grilles.

Steel place settings carved with fractal-patterned designs based on an ever-decreasing sequence of perfect numbers indicated each guest's allocated seat, and Roboute was pleased to find himself with Linya Tychon beside him. A magos with bulked-out shoulders and a skull that was half flesh and half bronzed steel sat on his left, and the two hulking Space Marines took their seats opposite him. Emil and Adara were situated farther down the table, and Roboute wasn't surprised to see that Sylkwood had swapped places with a junior Cadian officer so as to be seated next to the engineering magos she'd cornered earlier.

The first course was served by a cadre of slender-boned servitors; a rich soup of bold flavour that only those with taste buds were served. The adepts of the Mechanicus were instead presented with ornamented tankards filled with a liquid that steamed gently and gave off a faint, chlorinated aroma. Conversation was animated, though Roboute noticed that the Cadians seemed to be doing most of the talking.

Linya introduced Roboute to the magos seated next to him, an adept by the name of Hirimau Dahan, whose rank was, he was brusquely informed, a Secutor.

Seeing Roboute's ignorance of the term, Dahan said, 'I train the skitarii and develop battle schematics to enhance combat effectiveness in all the martial arms of the Mechanicus. My role aboard this ship is to fully embed all known killing techniques, weapon usage and/or tactical subroutines into our combat doctrine with optimal effectiveness.'

The bearded Space Marine grunted at that, but Roboute couldn't decide if it was in amusement or derision. Years before on Macragge, Roboute had spoken to a warrior of the Adeptus Astartes, but the encounter hadn't been particularly successful, so he was wary of initiating another verbal exchange with a post-human.

'You don't agree with Magos Dahan's approach?' he asked.

The Templar looked at him as though trying to decide what response was most appropriate.

'I think he is a fool,' said the warrior.

Roboute felt more than saw Dahan's posture change and tasted a bitter secretion of pungent chemical stimulants in the back of his throat. His hand curled into a fist of its own accord and a sharp flavour of metal shavings filled his mouth. He blinked away a sudden burst of aggression as Linya Tychon leaned close to him.

'Breathe in,' she whispered in his ear, and her breath was a soothing compound of scents, warm honey and ripe fruit that took the edge off his inexplicable anger. 'You are being affected by Magos Dahan's pheromone response. Combat stimms and adrenal shunts are boosting his aggressors, and you don't have the olfactory filters to avoid the effects of being so close to him.'

'Clarify: explain the content of your last remark,' said Dahan, and the taut desire to do violence was unmistakable in his body language.

'Apologies, Magos Dahan,' said Kul Gilad. 'Brother-Sergeant Tanna spoke without proper thought. He is unused to dealing with mortals not bound to our Chapter.'

'Mortals?' said Roboute, latching onto the Reclusiarch's emphasis on the word. 'I wasn't aware that Space Marines were immortal.'

'An ill-chosen linguistic term perhaps,' allowed Kul Gilad, 'but no less true for all that. As our gene-seed returns to the Chapter, our biological legacy lives on in the next generation of warriors. But I sense that is not what you imply. Yes, for all intents and purposes, we *are* immortal. Brother Auiden is our Apothecary, but I am given to understand that our bodies experience senescence at an artificially reduced rate and that we were engineered to endure for a far longer span than less engineered physiologies.'

'So you still die?' asked Linya.

'Eventually everything must die, Mistress Tychon,' said Kul Gilad. 'Even Space Marines, but a life of eternal crusading in the Emperor's name ensures that few of us live long enough to discover what our span might be.'

'Though longevity does not apparently equate to the proper observance of protocol,' said Dahan.

'Like you, Magos Dahan, we do not normally interact with outsiders,' said Kul Gilad, and the deep well of power in his words made Roboute glad he wasn't on the receiving end of his harsh glare. If Dahan felt intimidated by the Reclusiarch's gaze, he did an admirable job of hiding it.

'Then perhaps Brother-Sergeant Tanna might explain his meaning in a less provocative manner?' suggested Linya. 'Why does he disagree with Magos Dahan's method?'

'Of course,' agreed Kul Gilad. 'Brother-sergeant?'

Though Tanna's features were blunt and smoothed to the point of robbing him of the conventional micro-expressions that provided visual cues to his meaning, Roboute saw he did not want to speak aloud.

'You speak of combat as though it can be reduced to numbers and equations,' said Tanna. 'That is a mistake.'

Roboute waited for him to say more, but that, it seemed, was the extent of Tanna's critique.

'Combat *is* numbers and equations,' said Dahan. 'Speed, reach, muscle mass, skeletal density, reaction time. All these factors and more are measurable and predictable. Like any chaotic system, if you feed it enough data, the variations in outcome become negligible. Give me the measure of any opponent and I can defeat him with statistical certainty.'

'You are wrong,' said Tanna with a finality that was hard to dispute.

Dahan leaned forwards and placed four hands on the table. Roboute hadn't realised the magos had multiple arms, and saw the hands had eight fingers, each with more knuckles than were surely necessary.

'Then perhaps an empirical demonstration of principles is required,' said Dahan.

Tanna considered this for a moment before replying. 'You wish to fight me?'

'You or one of your warriors,' answered Dahan, his multiple fingers undulating across their many points of articulation. 'The outcome will be the same.'

Tanna looked to Kul Gilad, and the Reclusiarch gave a curt nod.

'Very well,' said Tanna. 'A combat will be fought.'

'I would very much like to see that bout,' said Roboute.

Tanna fixed him with a cold stare. 'The Templars are not in the habit of putting on displays.'

The next course was a platter of roasted meats, steamed vegetable matter and some form of boiled noodle that tasted faintly of sterilising fluids, but which was palatable when combined with a rich plum sauce poured from the regimental silverware. Roboute tucked into his meal with gusto, enjoying the novelty of a cooked one instead of reconstituted proteins and brackish recycled water that had been around the *Renard's* coolant systems more than once.

The dammassine was poured freely, and Roboute felt himself becoming a little lightheaded despite the inhibitors in his augmetic liver filtrating and dissipating the alcohol around his system.

He spoke to Magos Dahan of the logistics of compiling thousands of battle inloads, to Linya Tychon of her work on the orbital galleries of Quatria and to Kul Gilad of the time he had been fortunate enough to see a squad of Ultramarines on the streets of First Landing. The Reclusiarch asked numerous questions regarding his brother warriors' bearing, their numbers, equipment and identifying markings. It took a moment before Roboute realised he was assembling a combat analysis, just as he would on an enemy formation. He wondered if the Adeptus Astartes had any other frame of reference with which to assimilate information. Was every fact and every morsel of knowledge simply a piece of a puzzle that would allow them to fight with greater aptitude?

Perhaps their combat philosophy wasn't so different from that of Magos Dahan after all.

As the dinner progressed, Colonel Anders regaled the table with a charismatic retelling of the 71st's most recent campaign on Baktar III against the xenos species known as the tau. The tale was told in fits and starts, with various officers interjecting with different aspects of the fight. A burn-scarred lieutenant told of how his company had shot down squadron after squadron of xenos skimmers as they attempted to scout a route through a wooded river valley. A blithely handsome captain named Hawkins spoke of the valorous actions of a commissar by the name of Florian, who had kept the regiment's colours flying even after a tau fusion weapon had boiled most of his flesh to vapour in the final moments of the battle.

Heads nodded in respect to the fallen commissar, which struck Roboute as unusual. As a rule, commissars were feared and, in most cases, respected, but rarely were they honoured by the regiments over whose men they had the power of life and death.

As the ensemble war story was concluded, Roboute had a sense there was more to it than the soldiers were revealing, but knew enough to know that what happened in the heat of battle ought to stay there. Anders rose to his feet with his glass raised, and Roboute stood along with the rest of the officers and the Mechanicus adepts.

'The dead of Cadia,' said Anders, downing his dammassine. 'Fire and honour!'

'Fire and honour!' roared the Cadians, and Roboute yelled it along with them.

Servitors quickly refilled the empty glasses in the moments of reverent silence among the officers as they remembered the dead of that campaign. At last everyone sat with a scrape of chairs on the metal deck, and the reflective mood was instantly replaced by one of good humour.

'Right, now that you've all heard just how heroic *we* are, I think it's time we heard some war stories from our guests,' said Colonel Anders. 'Captain Surcouf, when we first met, you said you'd tell the Reclusiarch how a man of Ultramar became a rogue trader. This seems like as good a time as any to make good on that promise.'

Roboute had been expecting this, and was only surprised it had taken so long.

'It's really not that interesting a story,' he said, but his words were drowned out by palms banging on the table and a chorus of demands for him to tell his tale.

'I seriously doubt that,' said Anders, his brass lizard-pet scuttling down his arm to the table, where it curled around the stem of his glass. 'Any story that involves an Ultramarian starch-arse, no offence, going from his straight-up-and-down lifestyle to a planet-hopping brigand *must* be interesting. Out with it, man!'

Roboute knew the colonel's words were not meant as an insult, but simply the result of the common misconception that rogue traders were little better than planet-stripping corsairs who hauled looted treasures from all across the galaxy in their cargo holds. He looked across the table and saw Kul Gilad staring at him intently. Right away, he knew that honesty would be his best course, and gathered his memories from a life he'd long ago put aside and compartmentalised.

'Very well,' said Roboute, 'I'll tell you how it happened, but you won't like it.'

Microcontent 10

Roboute took a deep breath before beginning. 'I'd taken a commission with the Navy; an ensign aboard a frigate patrolling the western reaches of Ultramar. The *Invigilam*, out of Kar Duniash. She was a good ship, reliable and kept us safe, so we returned the favour. I served aboard her for almost five years, steadily rising through the ranks until I was a bridge officer.'

'I take it you saw action?' asked Anders.

'Twice,' said Roboute. 'The first was against a mob of greenskin ships that fell in-system from the northern marches. That didn't test us much; we had a Dominator with us, *Ultima Praetor*, and its nova cannon punished them hard before they even got close to us. Once we were in among them, the *Praetor's* broadsides and our torpedoes tore the ork junkers apart and had them sucking vacuum inside of an hour.'

'I get the sense that your second action wasn't as easy,' said Anders.

'No, it wasn't,' agreed Roboute. 'A tau fleet had been nibbling away at territory on the extreme edge of the Arcadian rim-worlds and we went in to drive them off. They hadn't made any overtly aggressive moves, just some sabre-rattling really, but operational briefs told us that was typical of how the tau began their campaigns of expansion. We were a show of force, a reminder that this was *our* space, not theirs. And to make that point clear, the Ultramarines despatched *Blue Lighter*, a Second Company strike cruiser from the Calth yards.'

'So what happened?' asked Anders. 'We know only too well how those aliens can fight.'

'We kept pushing them back, doing little more than playing a game of jab and feint with them,' said Roboute. 'The Space Marines were pushing for an engagement, but the tau kept pulling back, scattering and regrouping. It was like they didn't want to fight, but didn't want to get too far away from us either.'

'They were drawing you in,' said Dahan.

'As it turns out, yes,' said Roboute. 'Command authority automatically fell to the Ultramarines captain, and he was spoiling for a fight. Eventually, we cornered the tau ships in a pocket of hyper-dense gas fields filled with agglomerations of debris and streams of ejected matter from an ancient supernova. We thought we had them, but it was an ambush. There were a couple of warspheres hidden in the electromagnetic soup that we hadn't seen. They hit us hard, really hard, and took damn near every scrap of voids we had. *Blue Lighter* took some bad hits, but that didn't seem to bother it, and the *Praetor* took a beating. The tau fleet turned about and swarmed us like angry sulphur-wasps.

'They'd hurt us, but they'd forgotten the first rule of an ambush: hit hard and fast, and then get the hell out. Navy ships are old, but they're tough and can take a lot of punishment before they need to disengage. The tau thought they'd crippled us and they pressed the attack when they should have broken off. *Blue Lighter* turned and blew away two ships before they got close to us and then went for the warspheres.'

'A Space Marine strike cruiser is a force multiplier not to be underestimated,' said Kul Gilad.

'You're not wrong,' said Roboute. 'It gutted those warspheres. They couldn't manoeuvre fast enough and the Ultramarines just savaged them, blowing out great chunks of their structure with their bombardment cannon and then broadsiding them again and again. It wasn't pretty, and when the tau cruisers got in close to us, we showed them that it takes more than a sucker punch of an ambush to take Imperial ships of the line out of a fight. It got scrappy and ugly, but we pinned them in place, and when *Blue Lighter* charged in, it was all over.'

'A worthy fight,' said Dahan. 'I am inloading the data from the Manifold now. You neglected to mention that you earned multiple commendations in that engagement, Captain Surcouf. You received a Bakkan Heart for being wounded in battle, and the *Invigilam's* captain put your name forward for the Naval Laurel, the Macharian Star and recommended that you be given command rank at the earliest available opportunity.'

'Captain Cybele was a good man,' said Roboute. 'He didn't want to lose me, but he knew I wouldn't be satisfied until I had my own ship.'

'Ships do not belong to their captains,' pointed out Magos Saiixek, his crimson robes billowing with escaping gusts of freezing air.

'My apologies, magos, a figure of speech,' said Roboute.

'So did you get a command?' asked Colonel Anders.

'No, though I was promoted to the rank of executive officer aboard the *Preceptor*, a Gothic-class cruiser laid down in the orbitals of Gathara Station two thousand years ago. She'd been assigned to Battlefleet Tartarus, and Captain Mindarus... Well, let's just say he was a man who'd risen to captaincy through a combination of luck, connections and brazen riding on the coat-tails of his betters.'

'Such a thing would never happen in a Space Marine Chapter,' said Kul Gilad, as though daring anyone to contradict him. 'Skill at arms alone decides who commands.'

'The *Preceptor* is listed in the Manifold as destroyed with all hands,' said Magos Dahan. 'The data is corroborated by Naval fleet registry and has parity with Adeptus Mechanicus logs. How is it that you are still alive?'

'Yes, the *Preceptor* was destroyed, and I was aboard it when it happened,' said Roboute.

'How is that possible?' asked Linya.

'Because Captain Mindarus was an arrogant fool who knew next to nothing about void war. He came from an old Scarus family that had sent all its sons to the Navy, and he thought that was enough when it came to commanding a warship.'

'So what happened?' asked Anders.

The dining room had grown quiet, every officer and magos gathered at the table listening intently to Roboute's tale. He felt the room growing smaller; a gradual sense of claustrophobia settling upon him as he recalled the final voyage of the *Preceptor*. He took a deep breath and thought of the astrogation compass in his stateroom, with its needle's doomed attempts to find a bearing.

'We'd been hunting a reaver fleet that was using the Caligari Reef asteroid belt to raid convoys coming in through the Auvillard Mandeville point,' began Roboute. 'The *Preceptor* had a solid bridge crew and we felt confident we could take on anything they threw at us, even with Mindarus at the helm, but what we didn't know was that the reavers weren't acting alone, they had help.'

'What kind of help?' asked Magos Dahan.

'Arch-enemy help,' replied Roboute, feeling the aggressive swell of emotion in the room. Cadians knew from bitter experience how

terrible it was to fight the monstrous enemies that struck from the Eye of Terror. To Cadian regiments, battles against arch-enemy forces were about more than just victory, they were personal. Though the fate of the *Preceptor* was clear to every man around the table, Roboute could feel them willing his tale's ending to be different.

'We never found out the name of the ship that attacked us,' Roboute said eventually. 'The vox-officers and auspex-servitors were killed in the opening minutes when it screamed at them. Flash-burned their brains in their skulls before we even realised it was there. A blood-red hellship rushed us from the cover of a rad-shearing asteroid and scattered our escorts in a frenzy of battery fire. At the same time it hit us with multiple lance batteries that tore down most of our shields in a matter of minutes.

'Even so we weren't out of the fight, but Mindarus panicked and tried to break contact instead of hitting back. He turned us about over my strenuous objections and diverted power from the shields to the repair crews and engines. I tried to reason with him, to tell him that we needed to fight our way clear, not run like a scared grox-pup. He screamed at me that I was being mutinous and ordered the bridge armsmen to escort me from the bridge.'

'So what did you do?' asked Anders.

'The armsmen were just about to clap me in irons when the hellship strafed us with some kind of particle whip. Stripped away the last of the shields and lit up our topside like a fireworks display. I don't know what that weapon was, but it tore right through the ship and breached clean through to our lower decks. Vented half the crew compartments to space and emptied out the gun decks before we could fire back. Feedback damage and secondary explosions blew back into the bridge and a firestorm gutted damn near every station. I was lucky, the armsmen shielded me from the blast, but most of the command staff were little more than charred corpses, or screaming, melted lumps of fused bone and ash. Some of the bravest men I'd served with were dead, but that bastard Mindarus was still alive and still screaming that we'd failed him, that this wasn't his fault. Can you believe it? His ship was dying around him and he was still looking for someone else to blame for his stupidity.

'Our escorts were gone. They'd fled when they'd seen us go down, and when the reavers swarmed out after the hellship I knew we were dead in the void. We were leaking atmosphere and those few compartments that still held air were on fire. The *Preceptor* was dead, no question about it, and when Mindarus disengaged from his command pulpit and yelled that I had to escort him to the saviour pods... Well, that's when I snapped.'

'Snapped?' asked Anders. 'What does that mean?'

'It means that I shot him,' said Roboute, eliciting a gasp of surprise from his audience. Even the magi managed to look shocked.

'I took out my sidearm and blew his damned head off,' said Roboute. 'He'd killed us and he wanted to abandon his ship? I couldn't let that stand, so I emptied my power cell into his corpse.'

Roboute took a deep breath, remembering the moment he'd dropped his pistol on top of the las-seared body of Captain Mindarus. He'd felt nothing; no righteous elation or vindication, just an emptiness that had lodged in his heart like a splinter.

'You killed your captain?' asked Anders.

'Yes, and I'd do it again in a heartbeat,' said Roboute. 'His incompetence saw thousands of men dead.'

'Then he did not deserve to live,' said Kul Gilad. 'You did the right thing, Captain Surcouf.'

'It didn't matter anyway. There was nothing left to do but wait for the hellship to finish the job. We were burning and losing atmosphere, but there was still enough of our hull and onboard systems to make us worthwhile salvage. I knew it was only a matter of time until the *Preceptor* was boarded, so I gathered up every firearm I could find and waited for the enemy boarders to come. I'd kill as many as I could and save one bullet for me. No way was I letting them take me. I waited on that scorched bridge for hours on end, but they never came.'

'Do you know why?'

Roboute shook his head. 'I didn't at the time. Most of our auspexes were down and I wasn't in a hurry to plug into what was left of surveyor control. I could hear the hellship's screams, even though there was nothing left of the vox-system. It screamed for days, but then it just stopped and I knew it had gone. Maybe there were other survivors, I never found out, but all I'd done was postpone the inevitable. I couldn't leave the bridge without losing atmosphere, and the temperature was falling rapidly. I didn't have any food or water, and I knew the compartment was losing pressure as the integrity of the structural members began to fail. Ice on the hull kept it from venting explosively, but I had a few days at best before I was a dead man, either from cold or dehydration. I thought about putting a gun to my head to get it over with quickly, but that's not the Ultramar way. You never give up, never stop fighting and never lose hope.'

'A bleak situation,' said Vitali Tychon. 'I am intrigued to learn how you survived.'

'It's simple,' said Roboute. 'I was picked up by another starship.'

'The statistical likelihood of being rescued by a passing ship is so utterly improbable that it might as well be zero,' said Magos Blaylock. 'In any case, the arch-enemy vessel must surely have been aware of any craft sufficiently close to reach you in time. Why would it not engage this other ship?'

'The hellship didn't engage because it knew it couldn't win,' said Roboute.

'How is that possible?'

Roboute took a deep breath before answering.

'Because it was an eldar ship,' he said.

Stunned silence greeted Roboute's pronouncement. They had perhaps expected to hear of a last saviour pod, one of the *Preceptor's* escorts returning to look for survivors or some other account of good fortune; miraculous, but explicable as one of the many facets of war that beggared belief.

None of them had expected xenos intervention.

'An eldar ship?' growled Kul Gilad.

'Yes,' said Roboute. 'A warship of Alaitoc craftworld called *Isha's Needle*. It had been hunting the hellship for decades and was on the verge of springing its own trap when we blundered into its snare by accident.'

'Why would they even bother to pick you up?' asked Anders. 'Don't misunderstand, I'm glad you survived, but it seems more likely the eldar would happily see you die.'

'I never found out why they picked me up,' said Roboute. 'Not for sure. I don't even remember much of how they got me off the *Preceptor*, just a strange light dancing like a miniature whirlwind by the bridge pulpit where I'd decided I was going to die. Then a figure in red armour, with some kind of elongated pack, appeared from the light and lifted me up. The next thing I remember I was waking up in a soft bed with my burns wrapped in bandages and skin grafts.'

Kul Gilad leaned forwards and Roboute felt his simmering hatred.

'I have lost brave warriors to the eldar,' said the Reclusiarch. 'Five warriors whose deeds are etched in the last remains of the Annapurna Gate, heroes all. Emperor's Champion Aelius fell at Dantium not more than a year ago. A pack of screaming killers took his head and their warp-bitch stole away the remains of his sacred blade.'

'I grieve with you, Reclusiarch,' said Roboute. 'I know how painful it is to lose men under your command. I lost a whole ship of men and women who depended on me.'

'How long did you live among the xenos?' asked Kul Gilad.

'Almost a year. They treated me well enough, but I got the feeling I

was never more than a passing curiosity to them, a whim they might soon tire of. I only ever met a handful of the crew: the healers who treated my wounds, and a pair of sculptors named Yrlandriar and Ithandriel.'

'A ship of war numbered sculptors among its crew?' said Kul Gilad, plainly disbelieving.

'Sculptor is about the best analogy I can think of,' said Roboute. 'They made artwork, certainly, but I think that was just a byproduct of what they really did aboard ship.'

'Which was what?' asked Linya.

'They called themselves bonesingers, which I think meant they could fix parts of the ship when they were damaged or create new parts if they were needed. I once watched them grow a new section of hull from little more than a sliver no bigger than my fingernail. It was truly amazing.'

'Fascinating,' said Magos Blaylock. 'I have long believed that eldar technology is fashioned from a form of bio-organic polymer that is, in its own way, alive. Their ships are essentially grown as opposed to being built.'

'You always did have an unhealthy interest in xenotech, Tarkis,' said Saiixek, farther down the table. 'Unnatural. You forget the Ninth Law: the alien mechanism is a perversion of the True Path.'

'You speak with the wilful ignorance of one who has chosen not to study the technology of xeno-species,' retorted Blaylock. 'And you are forgetting the Sixth Law: understanding is the True Path to Comprehension.'

'The Omnissiah does not dwell within such blasphemous creations. You heard the rogue trader, their technology is *grown*. It is not built, it does not have the sacred mech-animus at its heart. Such xeno-species are an affront to the Imperium *and* the Machine-God. Rightly are they abhorred.'

'Tell me,' said Kul Gilad, interrupting the nascent theological discussion between the magi. 'What did you tell the eldar of the Imperium?'

'Nothing,' said Roboute. 'They never asked me about the Imperium and seemed entirely uninterested in it. I told them of my life in Ultramar, the beauty of Iax and Espandor, the wild mountains and oceans of Macragge. I told them of feast days and my youthful misadventures, nothing more. If they'd rescued me to learn our secrets then they didn't do anything to find out what I might know.'

'At least not that you were aware of,' said the Reclusiarch. 'Eldar witches can lift a man's thoughts from his mind with their sorceries. They are fiendish and possess nothing in the way of honour

or morality as we know it. They think to make the race of man their puppet, little more than pieces to move around a cosmic regicide board to prolong their wretched existence.'

Roboute knew this was not an argument he could ever win with a Space Marine, and said, 'I can only speak as I find, Reclusiarch. The eldar treated me well, and once they tired of me I was left on a planet in the Koalith system, just outside an Imperial city. And the rest, as they say, is history.'

There was more to it than that, of course, but there were limits to how far honesty would carry him in such company. How Roboute had gone from refugee to rogue trader would have to remain a story untold for now; too many of this audience would not approve, understand or condone his subsequent actions.

And if Kotov knew the half of it, there was yet time to throw him and his crew off the *Speranza*.

'Right,' he said. 'What's for dessert?'

The final course was a platter of sugared pastries and soft-fleshed fruit with a pink centre. Roboute was relieved to feel the attention that had been focused on him now shift, like a sniper with more important targets to hunt. Localised conversations sprang up as the magi debated the merits and perils of studying alien technology, while the Cadians swapped stories of previous engagements and wild speculation on what enemies they might come up against on the other side of the Halo Scar. The Space Marines excused themselves before dessert was served, and Roboute saw they had touched little of the previous course.

'Didn't they like the food?' he wondered.

'I suspect it is because this meal is nutritionally valueless to them,' said Linya. 'The calorific content and mass-to-energy ratio of the meat and protein substitutes makes it virtually irrelevant to their digestive systems. It would be like you eating your napkin and expecting to be sated. Space Marine foodstuffs are necessarily high in nutrients, amino acids and complex enzymes to sustain the wealth of biological hardware in their systems. Were you unwise enough to eat so much as a mouthful your body would suffer an explosive emetic reaction.'

'I'm not sure what that means, but it sounds unpleasant,' said Roboute.

'For you and anyone nearby,' said Linya.

Roboute laughed and took another drink from a passing servitor.

He took a mouthful of dammassine and said, 'So what were you telling the colonel before I arrived? Something about why you and your father came on this voyage? And don't tell me it's because of the love of exploration. That might be part of it, but I know there's more to it than wanderlust.'

Linya's expression, which had been faintly indulgent up until now, turned serious.

'You're perceptive, Roboute,' she said. 'Though I'll admit the thought of exploring unknown space on the other side of the Halo Scar is appealing, you're right, it isn't what brought us here.'

'Then what did?'

She sighed, as though pondering the best way to answer. 'How familiar are you with celestial mechanics? The life cycles of stars and the physics of their various stages of existence?'

Roboute shrugged. 'Not very,' he admitted. 'I know they're huge balls of gas with incredibly powerful nuclear reactions at their hearts, and that it's best to keep them as far away as possible when you're making the translation to warp space.'

'That's about all most spacefarers need to know,' said Linya. 'But there's so much more going on inside a star that even the most gifted calculus-logi couldn't begin to unravel the complexity of the reactions and their effects on the magneto-radiation fields in the surrounding chaotic systems.'

'I don't know what any of that means,' said Roboute.

'Of course, but you *are* familiar with the concept that the light you see from a star is already ancient by the time you perceive it?'

'I am, yes.'

'Light travels fast, very fast, faster than anything else we've been able to measure in the galaxy, and the notion that we might ever build a starship that can breach the light barrier is laughable.'

'I'm following you so far, but bear in mind I'm not Cult Mechanicus,' said Roboute.

'Trust me, I am bearing that in mind,' said Linya. 'I'm simplifying this as best I can, and I mean no offence to you, but it is like explaining colours to a blind man.'

Roboute tried not to be offended by her casual dismissal of his intellect, now understanding it was typical of the augmented minds of the Adeptus Mechanicus to imagine that everyone else was a brain-damaged simpleton.

'My father's macroscope arrays are on the orbital galleries of Quatria, and they are amongst the most precise deep-space detection instruments in the segmentum. They measure everything from radiance levels, radiation output, radio waves, pulse waves, neutron flow, gravity deflection and a thousand other components of the background noise of the galaxy. My father mapped the southern edge of the galaxy almost five hundred years ago, creating a map that was as exacting in its precision as it was possible to be. It is a work of art, really, a map that is accurate down to plus or minus one light hour. Which, given the scales involved, is like a hive map that shows every crack on every elevated walkway.'

'So how has that brought you out here?'

'Because the stars at the edge of the galaxy have changed.'

'Changed?'

'You have to understand that the changes that happen in the anatomy of a star take place over incomprehensibly vast spans of deep time. Their transitions don't happen on a scale that's possible to witness.'

'So how do you know they're even happening?'

'Just because we can't see something happening doesn't mean it's not,' said Linya patiently, as though teaching basic concepts to a child. Which, in effect, she was. The properties of science and technology were virtually unknown to the Imperium's populace. What might be basic to the point of patronising for a member of the Cult Mechanicus would be wreathed in superstition and mysticism to almost everyone else.

'We can't perceive viral interactions with the naked eye, so we craft augmetic optics to see them. Likewise, vox-waves are invisible, but we know they exist because the Omnissiah has shown us how to build machines that can send and receive them. The same thing applies to stars and their lifespans. No one can live long enough to observe the constant entropy of their existence, so we study the output of thousands of different stars to observe the various stages of stellar life cycles. What we saw when we looked at the stars out by the Halo Scar was that the light levels and radiation signatures they were emitting had radically changed.'

'Changed in what way?'

'In simplest terms, they'd aged millions of years in the space of a few centuries.'

'And I'm guessing that's not normal?'

Linya shook her head. 'It is entirely abnormal. Something has happened to those stars that's brought them to almost the end of their life-cycles. Some of them may even have gone nova already, as the measurements we took were constantly changing and were already centuries old by the time we detected them.'

'Does that mean you don't know what we're going to find when we get out there?'

'In a manner of speaking. The closer we get the more precise our

data will become. The *Speranza* has some incredibly accurate surveyor packages, so I'd hope to have a much better idea of what we're going to find by the time we drop out of the warp at the galactic boundary.'

'You'd *hope*?'

'The Halo Scar makes any measurements... complex.'

'So you're seeing stars get old quickly,' said Roboute. 'What do you think is causing it?'

'I have no idea,' said Linya.

The dinner broke up swiftly after the last course was cleared away, the Cadians not ones to overindulge in pastimes that might impair their rigorous training regimes. Now that Roboute looked at the faces around the table, it appeared that it was only himself and Emil that had partaken a little too freely of the free-flowing dammassine. Enginseer Sylkwood had left earlier with Magos Saiixek, though he was reasonably sure it was simply to talk engines and combustion.

Adara had found a natural fit with the Cadians, the combat-tested Guardsmen quickly recognising his innate familiarity with the killing arts. Though he'd had his weapon taken from him, the youngster was demonstrating blade-to-blade fighting techniques with his butter knife, and several junior officers were copying his movements.

Emil had a deck of cards spread out before him on the table, taking bets from anyone foolish enough to put a wager down. The cards danced between his fingers as though they had a life of their own, and his dexterity as much as his luck was impressing those around him.

'Soldiers like to be around lucky types,' said Roboute, seeing Linya take notice of Emil's skills.

'I thought we established that there is no such thing as luck,' she said.

'Tell that to a soldier and he'll tell you you're wrong,' said Roboute, pushing himself out of his seat with a grunt of satisfaction. 'Every one of them will have their own lucky talisman, lucky ritual or lucky prayer. And you know what, if that's what keeps them alive, then who's to say they're not absolutely right?'

'Confirmation bias,' said Linya, 'but I will concede that the battlefield is a place where the sheer number of random variables in a chaotic environment are fertile arenas for the *perception* of luck.'

'There's no telling some folk,' he said as the servitors opened the grand doors to the anteroom and the dinner guests began to file out.

Linya shrugged. 'I deal in facts, reality and that which can be proved to have a basis in fact.'

'Doesn't that rob you of the beauty of things? Doesn't a planetary aurora lose its magic when you can reduce it to light and radiation passing through thermocline layers of atmospheric pollution? Isn't a magnificent sunset just the daily cycle instead of a wondrous symphony of colour and peace?'

'On the contrary,' said Linya as they made their way from the dinner table. 'It's precisely *because* I understand the workings of such things that they become magical. To seek mysteries and render them known, that is the ultimate goal of the Adeptus Mechanicus. To me, *that* is magical. And I mean magical in a purely poetic sense, before you go attaching meaning to that.'

'I wouldn't dare,' smiled Roboute as they reached the doors leading to the starboard esplanade. A bell chimed, and Roboute realised with a start that four hours had passed since their arrival.

'It's later than I thought,' he said.

'It is precisely the time I expected,' said Linya. 'My internal clock is synchronised with the *Speranza*, though it has some unusual ideas concerning the relativistic flow of sidereal time.'

Roboute shrugged. 'I'll take your word for it.' he said, watching the way the dimmed lighting played on the sculpted sweeps of her cheekbones. He'd thought she was attractive before, but now she was beautiful. How had he not noticed that? Roboute was aware of the alcohol in his system, but the filter in his artificial liver was already dissipating the worst of it.

'You are a very beautiful woman, Linya Tychon, did you know that?' he said before he even knew what he was doing.

The smile fell from her face, and Roboute knew he'd crossed a line.

'I'm sorry,' he said. 'That was foolish of me. Too much dammassine...'

'It is very kind of you to say so, Captain Surcouf, but it would be unwise for you to harbour any thoughts of a romantic attachment to me. You like me, I can already see that, but I cannot reciprocate anything of that nature.'

'How do you know unless you try?' said Roboute, already knowing it was hopeless, but never one to give up until the last.

'It will be hard for you to understand.'

'I can try.'

She sighed. 'The neural pathways of my brain have been reshaped by surgical augmetics, chemical conditioning and cognitive remapping to such an extent that the processes taking place within my mindscape do not equate to anything you might recognise as affection or love.'

'You love your father, don't you?'

She hesitated before answering. 'Only in the sense that I am grateful to him for giving me life, yes, but it is not love as you would recognise

it. My mind is incapable of reducing the complex asymmetry of my synapse interaction to something so...'

'Human?'

'*Irrational*,' said Linya. 'Roboute, you are a man of varied history, much of which clearly holds great appeal to other humans. You have personality matrices that I am sure make you an interesting person, but not to me. I can see through you and study every facet of your life from the cellular level to the hominid-architecture of your brain. Your life is laid bare to me from birth to this moment, and I can process every angle of that existence in a microsecond. You divert me, but no unaugmented human has enough complexity to ever hold my attention for long.'

Roboute listened to her speak with a growing sense that he was wading in treacherous waters. He'd made the mistake of assuming that just because Linya Tychon looked like a woman that she was a woman in any sense that he understood. She was as far removed from his sphere of existence as he was from a domesticated house-pet.

It was a sobering realisation, and he said, 'That must be a lonely existence.'

'Entirely the opposite,' said Linya. 'I say these things not to hurt you, Roboute, only to spare you any emotional turmoil you might experience in trying and failing to win my affection.'

Roboute held up his hands and said, 'Fair enough, I understand, affection isn't on the cards, but friendship? Is that a concept you can... process? Can we be friends?'

She smiled. 'I'd like that. Now, if you will excuse me, I have some data inloads that need parsing into their logical syntactic components.'

'Then I'll say goodnight,' said Roboute, holding out his hand.

Linya shook it, her grip firm and smooth.

'Goodnight, Roboute,' she said, turning and making her way towards the mag-lev rostrum.

Emil and Adara appeared behind him, flushed with rich food and plentiful dammassine. Adara spun his returned blade back and forth between his fingers, which seemed reckless given the amount he'd had to drink.

'What was that all about?' asked Emil.

'Nothing, as it turns out,' said Roboute.

Microcontent 11

They wandered through the outer spiral arm of the galactic fringe, like travellers in an enchanted forest, bewitched by the beauty all around them. The astrogation chamber was alive with light. Sector maps, elliptical system diagrams, and glittering dust clouds orbited Linya and her father like shoals of impossibly complex atomic structures. Each was a delicately wrought arrangement of stars and nebulae, and Linya reached up to magnify the outer edges of a system on their projected course.

'Is that a discarded waypoint?' asked her father, his multiple fingers drawing streamers of data from the rotating planets like ejected matter from the surface of a sun.

'Yes,' said Linya. 'The Necris system.'

'Of course, a system-world of the Adeptus Astartes.'

'So the rumours go,' agreed Linya. 'The Marines Exemplar Chapter are said to have their fortress-monastery in this system, but that has never been confirmed with a high enough degree of accuracy for me to add a notation.'

'The Space Marines do like their privacy,' said her father, quickly moving on through the visual representation of the Necris system as though to respect the secretive Chapter's wishes.

Linya nodded, sparing a last look at the system's isolated planets as they spun in their silent orbits. Some looked lonely, far from the

life-giving sun, cold and blue with ice, while others – whose orbits had carried them too far from the star's gravitational push and pull to remain geologically active – were no more than barren ochre deserts.

The fleet's first waypoint had been reached when the *Speranza* broke from the warp on the edge of the Heracles subsector, its myriad surveyors gulping fresh datum information from the local environment and feeding it into their course plot. The Necris system had been considered and then rejected as a waypoint, its Mandeville point too restricted in its arc of compliant onward warp routes.

And it did not have the pleasing symmetry of taking the fleet through Valette.

The chamber in which they stood was a dome of polished iron a hundred metres wide, machined from a single vast ingot on Olympus Mons and lined with slender pilasters of gold like the flying buttresses supporting a great templum. A wooden-framed console with a series of haptic keyboards and manual rotation levers stood at the centre of the dome's acid-etched floor image of the Icon Mechanicus. A host of code wafers jutted from the console's battered keypad, each a portion of data extracted from the *Speranza's* astrogation logisters.

Entoptic machines held fast to exacting tolerances by a precise modulation of suspensor fields projected light into the air in such volume that it was like walking through an aquarium and hothouse combined. Celestial bodies slipped past like stoic feeder fish, comets like darting insects and ghostly clouds of gas and dust like drifting jellyfish. The *Speranza's* course was marked in a shimmering red line, though only the real space portions of the journey were marked. To map the churning depths of the warp was a job best left to the Navigators, if such a thing were even possible.

'Your course plot was commendably accurate, my dear,' said her father, watching as yet more information streamed into her ongoing equations. 'I am no hexamath, but I think the archmagos is pleased.'

Linya felt his pride in the warm emanations from his floodstream and sent a wordless response that acknowledged his satisfaction.

'The course has proved accurate to within one light minute,' she said. 'The new celestial data will only improve that as the journey continues.'

'At least until we drop out of the warp at the Halo Scar,' her father reminded her.

'I know, but when we reach Valette, we'll have a better... estimate of what we might expect to see.'

'You were going to say "guess", weren't you?'

'I considered it, but decided that would imply too great a margin of uncertainty.'

'Where we are going is shrouded in uncertainty, daughter dearest,' said Vitali. 'There is no shame in ignorance, only in denying it. By knowing what we do not know, we can take steps to remedy our lack of knowledge.'

Vitali Tychon moved through the shoals of stellar information with the ease of a man who had lived his life in the study of the heavens. His arms moved like a virtuoso conductor, sifting the flow of information with familiarity and paternal satisfaction, as though each star and system were his own. He made a circuit along the circumference of the chamber; moving through regions of space where the light of stars was spread out, little more than relativistic smears to the systems closer to the galactic core.

He approached the chamber's representation of the Halo Scar as it rippled and flickered out of focus, as though the projectors were having difficulty in interpreting the mutant data they were being fed. The machines fizzed and spat coils of hissing code into the air, angry at being forced to visualise so disfigured a region of space. Bleeds of red and purple bruising, striated with leprous yellow and green, spread like an infection along the edge of the galaxy, a swathe of starfields that made no empirical sense. The projected information flickered and faded for a moment, before refreshing with a buzz of circuitry and the persistent hum of agitated machinery.

'The spirits are restless today,' said Linya.

'Wouldn't you be?' said Vitali, reaching out to touch the wall and send a soothing binaric prayer into the wired heart of the machinery. 'The mapping spirits of the chamber are vexed by the inconstant streams of information being relayed to them. Travelling through the warp allows for no satisfaction of their cartographic urges, and like any of us denied our purpose, they do not take kindly to disruption of their routines.'

'They recognise a familiar soul in you,' said Linya, as the images of distant sectors and shimmering stars grew brighter and clearer. The machines' irritated fizzing diminished.

'I have an affinity with spirits that seek the sights of far-off shores,' said Vitali without any hint of modesty. 'As do you.'

Linya knew she lacked her father's touch, but appreciated the sentiment nonetheless.

'Such a shame,' said Vitali as he returned his gaze to the leering gash of the Halo Scar. 'Once it was a celestial nursery of youthful and adolescent stars. Now it is little more than a graveyard of spent matter, dying cores compressing to singularities and aberrant data that makes as little sense here as it did at Quatria.'

'Even the astronomical data the *Speranza* inloaded at the last waypoint did little to codify our understanding of what it is,' observed Linya.

'Understandable,' said Vitali, pulling a cascade of data from the air. 'The gravity fluxions caused by the interactions of so many hyper-aged stars make a mockery of our instrumentation. If these readings are to be believed, then there are forces at play within the Halo Scar that could tear this ship apart in a heartbeat.'

'I am optimistic that the Valette waypoint will provide a clearer fix on these corpse-stars and the volatile spaces between them. Perhaps we might even be able to plot a course through the gravitational mire.'

Her father turned from the Halo Scar and said, 'What gives you cause for such optimism?'

Linya hesitated before answering, though she suspected her father already knew what her answer would be. 'The Valette Manifold station was the last known point of contact with the lost fleet of Magos Telok. It is not unreasonable to presume there is a reason this system was able to receive a Manifold transmission from Telok's fleet. Perhaps it lies in a corridor where the gravitational fields annul one another. I cannot accept it was an accident that Valette lies precisely on our optimal route to the Halo Scar. I believe the will of the Omnissiah has brought us here, father.'

'Have you considered that you may be as much a victim of confirmation bias as those without augmentation?'

'Yes, but I have dismissed the possibility. The chances of Valette lying on our projected flight path from Joura is infinitesimal given the sheer volume of potential routes, elliptical irregularities in its orbit and the system's axiomatic volatility.'

'I agree,' said Vitali. 'And I must say that I am rather looking forward to inloading the data streams from a Mechanicus Manifold station this close to the Scar. Who knows what information they might have accumulated in the last few hundred years?'

A shiver of data-light passed along the conduits of the floor as a rotating cog-door opened on the wall behind Linya; bright veils of biographical information, operational status and current inload/exload data burden rose from the floor.

Tarkis Blaylock swept into the astrogation dome, and his inload burden immediately spiked as he drank in the liquid data that surrounded him. He directed the appropriate code blurts of greeting to both Linya and her father. Perfunctory, but she expected no less. Though the mores and modes of address were utterly removed from unaugmented individuals, many of the same cues existed – albeit on a binary level – to convey the subtlest hints of reproach, approbation or, in this case, carefully masked disdain.

'Magos Blaylock,' said Vitali, employing a rustic form of binaric protocols that had fallen out of use with the rediscovery of high-function lingua-technis nearly five thousand years ago. 'A pleasure to see you, as always. What brings you to the astrogation dome?'

'A matter that would be best discussed in private,' said Blaylock, pointedly ignoring Linya.

'Whatever you would say to me in private, I will only later relay to my daughter,' said Vitali, scrolling through the system data of the Ketheria system. 'Therefore, in the interests of brevity and the better employment of our time, I suggest you simply say what it is you have come to say.'

'Very well,' said Blaylock, moving deeper into the chamber and turning his green-hued optics to its upper segmentae, where the mysterious reaches of far-off galaxies spun like misty spiderwebs. 'I have come to seek your support.'

'Support for what?' asked Vitali.

'Support for my claims upon Archmagos Kotov's Martian forges when they are redistributed.'

'Isn't that a little premature?' asked Linya. 'We haven't even reached the edge of the galaxy and you speak like this expedition has already failed.'

'The expedition was always statistically unlikely to succeed,' said Blaylock, turning a full circle and scanning the contents of the pellucid star systems. 'Nothing has changed. The most likely outcome of this voyage is that the Halo Scar will prove to be impenetrable and Archmagos Kotov will be forced to return to Mars in failure.'

'If you were so sure this expedition would fail why did you come?'

'The Fabricator General himself seconded me to Archmagos Kotov,' said Blaylock, his lingua-technis making sure they understood the full weight of the authority vested in him. 'To lose so important a vessel as the *Speranza* on a fool's errand into a region of cursed space would be unforgivable. I am to see that this vessel is not needlessly sacrificed on the altar of one man's desperation to regain his former glory.'

'How very noble of you,' said Linya, not even bothering to mask her contempt.

'Indeed,' replied Blaylock, ignoring her jibe.

'And when Kotov returns with his tail between his legs, there will be a feeding frenzy to claim his last remaining holdings,' said Vitali. 'You think they should go to you?'

'I am the most suited to take control of his Tharsis forges,' agreed Blaylock.

'A suspicious man might say you have a vested interest in the expedition failing,' said Vitali.

'A human assumption, but a fallacious one. I will fully support Arch-magos Kotov until such time as I believe that the chance of irredeemable damage to the *Speranza* outweighs the possibility of any useful recovery of knowledge. Since the latter is the most likely outcome, it is logical for me seek the support of senior magi prior to our return to Mars. You are aware of my high standing in the Priesthood, and I should not forget such support when the time comes to consider requisition requests. There is a great deal of technology on Mars that I could see allocated to Quatria to make it the foremost cartographae gallery in the Imperium.'

'First you attempt to veto my father's appointment to this expedition and now you try to buy him off with transparent bribes?' said Linya, resorting to her flesh voice to truly discomfit Blaylock.

'I voted against his inclusion because I believe there are better qualified magos that could have provided cartographae support.'

'None of whom have travelled this way before,' snapped Linya. 'My father's presence here gives the expedition a far better chance of success, and that isn't in your scavenger's interests, is it?'

'You presume I am working to fixed notions and human modes of behaviour,' retorted Blaylock, matching her with his own augmented voice. 'As the situation changes, so too does my behavioural map; after all, I am not an automaton. The failure of this expedition is a virtual statistical certainty, and it would be foolish of me *not* to make contingencies.'

'And what if the expedition *doesn't* fail?'

'Then the Quest for Knowledge will have been furthered and a sacred duty to the Omnissiah will have been served,' said Blaylock. 'Either way, I shall be content to serve the will of Mars.'

'I think you are lying,' said Linya.

'Mistress Tychon, if you insist on projecting human behavioural patterns that do not apply to my modes of thinking onto my motivations then we will continue in this pointless loop for some time.'

'Perhaps your calculations are in error,' said Linya.

Blaylock spread his arms wide and a wealth of daedal statistical algorithms burst into the noospheric air like a flock of avian raptors. Almost too grand in scope to evaluate, Blaylock's complex lattices of equations were beautiful constructions of impeccable logic. Even a cursory inload told Linya there would be no errors.

The odds of Kotov's expedition succeeding were so small as to be negligible.

Though she knew it was depressingly human, Linya said, 'The waypoint data at Valette will alter your calculations.'

'You are correct,' agreed Blaylock. 'But not enough to make a significant difference.'

'We will see soon enough,' said Vitali, drawing out the translucent orrery of the Valette system and highlighting the Mechanicus Manifold station. 'We translate back into real space in ten hours.'

To see so many arms of the Imperium's martial strength working together in fluid harmony was pleasing to Magos Dahan. Colonel Anders's Imperial Guard fought through a vast recreation of a shell-ruined city, every grid-block laced with a fiendish web of integral defences, carefully plotted arcs of fire, triangulated kill-zones and numerous open junctions to cross. It was an attacker's worst nightmare, but so far the Cadian war-methodology was proving effective.

Of course, it didn't hurt that they fought alongside a full repertoire of Adeptus Mechanicus killing machines. Quadrupedal praetorians of flesh and steel stalked through areas too dangerous for human soldiers, implanted cannons and energy weapons firing with whooping bangs and crackling whip-cracks of beam discharge. Packs of weaponised servitors scaled the sides of buildings with implanted grappling equipment to rain down death from above with shoulder-mounted rotary launchers and grenade dumpers. Squads of Dahan's skitarii spearheaded assaults into occupied structures, supported by Cadian Hellhounds that flushed enemy servitor-drones into the open with gouts of blazing promethium. Sentinels smashed down weakened walls to flank enemy units and provide forward reconnaissance data for the following infantry, who in turn marched alongside Leman Russ battle tanks, Chimeras and growling Basilisks.

Of course there were casualties, a great many casualties, but so far no company or clan had suffered enough to render it combat-ineffective. The number of registered deaths was well within acceptable parameters and would not affect the overall outcome of the conflict.

And lording over the battle were the gods of war themselves.

The battle-engines of Legio Sirius strode through the smoking ruins, underlit by the flames of battle, strobing las discharge and the bright plumes of inferno cannon fire. Legio standards and kill banners hung from their waist gimbals and billowed like sails atop their grey, gold and blue carapaces. Hot thermals shrieked in the vortices of tortured air that surrounded them.

Lupa Capitalina towered over all, its vast guns pouring destructive energies into the mass of the ruined city. Despite its warheads lacking explosive ordnance, the kinetic force of such munitions was wreaking havoc on Dahan's simulated city. While *Amarok* darted from ruined shells of hab-blocks to pounce on enemy targets of opportunity before vanishing into the flame-cast shadows, *Vilka* threaded its way through the city and hid until its larger brethren approached. As *Canis Ulfrica* or *Lupa Capitalina* drew near and defending forces rallied to meet them, *Vilka* would strike from ambush then retreat before any reprisal could be launched against it.

Dahan ground through the smashed training arena atop his Iron Fist, meshed with its control mechanisms and directing the armoured vehicle with pulses from the MIU cables trailing from the nape of his neck. Though live rounds smacked off stonework and reflected splinters of lasgun fire fizzed through the air, he was in no danger. Inbuilt refractor generators on the vehicle's hull meant there wasn't so much as a scratch on the Iron Fist's paintwork. Everywhere Dahan looked, Imperial forces were advancing with relentless mathematical precision, an orchestration of death of which he was the composer.

Fire and manoeuvre, building by building, his city of death was proving ineffective in halting the Imperial advance. Where one attacking element was weak, another was strong. The hammer of the Guard and the precise applied force of the Adeptus Mechanicus were working well together.

Only one element was missing from the fight, but Dahan expected them soon enough.

As objective after objective fell, the tactical viability of the city was degraded to such an extent that Dahan saw there would be little point in its continuance. He called a halt to the exercise with a pulse of thought, and banks of arc-lights clattered to life on the roof of the vast training deck. Giant extractors drew in breaths of smoke and particulate matter to be ejected into the *Speranza's* wake. In moments the vast space was clear of fumes, and the echoes of battle began to fade. Dahan drove the Iron Fist through a junction clogged with rubble and toppled facsimiles of Imperial saints. A number of his servitor drones lay sprawled beneath the debris, their bodies mangled and charred black by the weapons of the Cadians. The servitors' organic matter would be burned away and the mechanical components recovered before being reconsecrated and grafted to another flesh drone. Dahan's olfactory senses tasted the refined mix of promethium; detecting extra compounds of fossilised hydrocarbons and a rarified cellulose element that bore chemical hallmarks of northern Cadian pine.

A squad of Cadians approached his tank, and he recognised the regiment's colonel. The man's respiratory rate was highly elevated, significantly more so than those of his soldiers.

'Colonel Anders,' said Dahan with a curt nod of respect. 'Once again, your men performed beyond expectations.'

'*Your* expectations, maybe. They matched mine exactly,' said Anders, removing his helmet and running a damp cloth over his forehead. 'So, tell me, how did we do?'

'Admirably,' said Dahan, descending from the tank's cupola. 'Every objective in the city has been captured, with minimal losses.'

'Describe *minimal*.'

'Average company fatality rates were eighteen point seven five per cent, with a debilitating wound percentage of thirteen point six. I am rounding up, of course.'

'Of course,' said Anders. 'That sounds about right for a city this size, maybe slightly under.'

The colonel planted a booted foot on the blackened body of a downed servitor, rolling it onto its back. The cybernetic's hands were pulled tight in burn-fused claws, its jaws stretched wide. Anders winced.

'Do they feel pain, do you think?' he asked.

Dahan shook his head. 'No, the parieto-insular cortex that processes pain through the neuromatrix is one of many segments of the brain cauterised during the servitude transmogrification process.'

'Makes them bastards to fight,' said Anders. 'An enemy that fears pain is already halfway to beaten.'

'And Cadians don't feel pain?' asked Dahan, adding a rhetorical blurt of lingua-technis.

'We live with pain every day,' said Anders. 'What other way is there to live with the Great Eye overhead?'

'I have no frame of reference with which to answer that.'

'No, I expect not,' said Anders, turning back to Dahan. 'So, eighteen point seven five per cent? We'll see if we can't get it down to fifteen by the time we reach the Scar.'

Dahan gestured to the augmented warriors in black armour forming up in regimented ranks beyond the edges of the captured city. 'The Adeptus Mechanicus skitarii were a factor in lowering that average, as was the presence of Legio Sirius.'

Anders laughed. 'True enough, you can't beat having a Titan Legion at your back to help keep enemy heads down. Those skitarii are some tough sons of groxes. I'll be glad to have them at my side if we end up having to fight when we get to where we're going.'

'Fighting will, I fear, prove inevitable,' said Magos Dahan. 'Whatever secrets lie beyond the galaxy will not be surrendered willingly by those who possess them.'

'More than likely,' agreed Anders, removing a canvas-lined canteen from his webbing and taking a long drink. When he had sated his thirst he emptied the canteen over his head, taking deep breaths to lower his heart rate.

'It is commendable that you fight alongside your Guardsmen,' said Dahan. 'Illogical, but brave.'

'No Cadian officer would command any other way,' said Anders. 'Not if he wants to keep his rank. It's always been that way, always will be.'

'I calculate that you are at least fifteen years older than your soldiers,' said Dahan.

'So?' said Anders, a note of warning in his tone.

'You are in excellent physical condition for a man of your age, but the risk to the command and control functions of your regiment far outweighs the benefits to the men's morale at being able to see their commanding officer.'

'Then you don't know much about Cadians,' said Anders, shouldering his rifle.

'So people keep reminding me, though such an observation is fundamentally incorrect.'

'Listen,' said Anders, stepping onto the running boards of the Iron Fist. 'Have you ever been to Cadia, Magos Dahan? Are you Cadian?'

'No, to both questions.'

'Then no matter how much you *think* you know about Cadians, you don't know shit,' said Anders. 'The only way to *really* know a Cadian is to fight him, and I don't think you want that.'

Though the colonel had not raised his voice and his body language was not overtly threatening, Dahan's threat response sent a jolt of adrenal-boosters into his floodstream. He felt his weapon arms flex, power saturating his energy blades and internal cavity ammo stores shucking shells into breeches. He quelled the response with a thought, shocked at how quickly Ven Anders had switched from affability to a war-stance.

'You are correct, Colonel Anders,' said Dahan. 'I do not want that.'

'Not many do, but I think you're about to get to know someone else better than you might like.'

'Colonel?'

Anders nodded to something over Dahan's shoulder and said, 'Your faith in your methods is about to be tested pretty hard.'

Dahan swivelled around his central axis and his threat systems kicked in again as he saw Kul Gilad leading his battle squad of Templars towards him.

The giant Reclusiarch came to a halt before Dahan, a towering slab of ceramite and steel with a face of death.

'We are here for the bout,' said Kul Gilad.

Word of the duel spread quickly through the training deck, and soon hundreds of soldiers, skitarii and clean-up crews had formed a giant circle around Magos Dahan and the Black Templars. Servitors were halted in their duties and lifted soldiers high enough to see, and rubble was hastily stacked to provide a better view. Soldiers stood on tanks, on Sentinels or wherever they could find a vantage point to see this once in a lifetime fight.

Captain Hawkins pushed through the press of bodies, using Lieutenant Rae and his rank as a battering ram to move entrenched soldiers aside. It didn't take long to reach the front of the circle, where he saw Magos Dahan facing the towering might of Kul Gilad.

'Surely he's not going to take on the big fella?' said Rae. 'He's a bloody tank.'

Hawkins shook his head. 'I doubt it. Wouldn't be much of a fight, and I'll lose a week's pay if he's beaten.'

'Emperor love you, sir, but you didn't put money down on the magos to win?'

'Yeah, I think he's got a trick or two up his sleeve.'

'But... but these are Space Marines,' said Rae, as though the folly of Hawkins's bet should be self-evident

'And Dahan's a Secutor. Don't underestimate how dangerous that makes him.'

'Fair enough, sir,' said Rae. 'But betting against a Space Marine seems, well, just a little bit...'

'A little bit what?'

'Rebellious?' suggested Rae after a while.

'I promise not tell the commissars if you don't.'

Rae shrugged, and turned his attention back to the participants in the bout. All around him, men and women were making bets on the outcome of the fight, but he ignored their shouts of odds and amounts, concentrating on what the duellists were doing. The Black Templars stood unmoving behind Kul Gilad, and it was impossible to take their measure. Their markings made them all but indistinguishable, though one wore armour of considerably greater ornamentation, as though he were the most glorious embodiment of their Chapter. His helmet bore

an ivory laurel, and a huge sword, over a metre in length, was sheathed across his shoulders. Where the rest of his brethren carried enormous boltguns, he carried a single pistol, gold-chased and well-worn.

'It'll be him,' said Hawkins. 'Mark my words.'

Rae nodded in agreement as Magos Dahan swept back his robes, revealing a muscular body of plastic-hued flesh with gleaming steel ribs visible at his chest. In addition to his regular pair of arms – which Hawkins now saw were laced with gleaming metal implants, augmetic energy blades and what looked like digital weapons – a second pair of arms unfolded from a position on Dahan's back. These arms were each tipped with a forked weapon that sparked to life as crackling purple lightning arced between the bladed tines. Dahan's body rotated freely at the waist, allowing him a full circuit of movement, and his three legs were reverse jointed, ending in splayed dewclaws that unsheathed with a sharp *snik*.

'Still think I'm onto a losing bet?' asked Hawkins as Dahan lifted his long polearm from the topside of his tank. The serrated blade revved with a harsh burr and the clawed energy pod at its base crackled with kinetic force.

'Trust me, you'll be glad you didn't bet a month's pay,' replied Rae.

Dahan launched into a series of combat exercises, rotating the long blade around his body with his upper arms in an intricate pattern of killing moves. His legs were weapons too. While two bore his weight, the third would lash out in a disembowelling stroke.

Kul Gilad nodded at the sight of Magos Dahan's preparatory moves, and circled around the lethal envelope of the Secutor's reach.

'Who do you think, Tanna? Who will best this opponent?' asked Kul Gilad, and the bearded warrior who had attended Colonel Anders's dinner stepped from the statue-still ranks of the Space Marines.

'It should be Varda, he bears the honour of us all,' said Tanna.

The warrior with the great sword stepped from the ranks of the Templars, and the enormous curved pauldrons of his armour shifted as he loosened the muscles at his shoulders.

'See, told you it'd be him,' said Hawkins.

Kul Gilad held up a hand and shook his head. 'No, the Emperor's Champion does not fight unless there is death to be done. His blade kills in the name of the Master of Mankind, not for spectacle or vain-glory. To make our point it must be the least of us who carries our honour. Step forwards, Yael.'

The sergeant struggled to hide his astonishment. 'Yael is only recently made a full Templar, he has yet to shed blood with his brothers in the Fighting Company.'

'That is why it must be him, Sergeant Tanna,' said Kul Gilad. 'The High Marshal himself marks this one for greatness. Do you doubt his wisdom?'

The sergeant knew better than to argue with a superior officer when so many others were watching, and said, 'No, Reclusiarch.'

Tanna stepped back into rank along with the Emperor's Champion as a slighter figure marched to stand alongside Kul Gilad. He wore a helmet so it was impossible to guess his age, yet he carried himself proudly, a young buck out to make his name. Hawkins had seen the same thing in the regiment, young officers straight out of the training camps outside Kasr Holn eager to prove their worth by getting into the nastiest fights as soon as they could.

Some got themselves killed. The ones who didn't die learned from the experience.

Both outcomes helped to keep the Cadian regiments strong.

Kul Gilad stood before Yael and placed his heavy gauntlets on his shoulders. Unheard words passed between them and the warrior knight nodded as he drew a sharp-toothed chainsword and his combat knife.

Kul Gilad stood between Dahan and Yael.

'Let this be an honourable duel, fought with heart and courage.'

'To what end will we fight?' asked Dahan. 'First blood?'

'No,' said Kul Gilad. 'A fight is not done just because someone bleeds.'

'Then what? To the death?'

The Reclusiarch shook his head. 'Until one fighter can make a killing blow. Take the strike, but do not let it land.'

'I have muscle inhibitors and microscopic tolerances in my optics that will enable such a feat. Can your warrior say the same?'

'Afraid you might get hurt?' said Yael, and though his voice was modified by the vox-grille, Hawkins could hear his youth.

'Not even a little bit,' said Dahan, dropping into a fighting position and lifting his multiple arms.

Kul Gilad stepped back. 'Begin!'

Dahan did not attack at once, but circled his opponent carefully, using his optical threat analysers to accumulate data on this opponent: his reach, height, his weight, his likely strength, his foot patterns, his posture. He had expected to fight the bigger warrior with the laurel-wreathed helm, but if the Reclusiarch thought to confound his combat subroutines by presenting him with an unexpected foe, it was a poor gambit.

He kept his Cebrenian halberd slightly extended, one of his servo arms above it, the other below. Crackling sparks of electricity popped from the forks, each shock-blade's charge strong enough to stop the multiple hearts of a raging carnifex. He eased around on his waist gimbal, letting his dewclaws click on the deck in a slow tattoo. Just the sight of his combat-enabled body was enough to unnerve most opponents, but this warrior appeared unfazed.

He decided to test the mettle of his opponent with something easy, a feint to gauge his reaction speed and reflex response. The Cebrenian halberd slashed at Yael's head, but the Templar swayed aside and batted away the killing edge, spinning around and resuming his circling. He was employing Bonetti's defence, a tried and tested technique, but one that would struggle against an opponent with four arms.

Capa Ferro would be the logical mode of attack against such a defence, but from the motion profile he had already built up, Dahan suspected his opponent was luring him into such an attack. His footwork was that of the great swordsman of Chemos, Agrippa, but his grip was Thibault.

A mix of styles, then.

Dahan smiled as he realised his opponent was taking the measure of him also. He gave the warrior a moment's grace, letting him truly appreciate the futility of attempting to fight an opponent who could predict his every move, who had broken down more than a million combat bouts to their component parts and analysed every one until there was no combination of attacks that could surprise him.

The Guardsmen and skitarii surrounding them cheered and shouted encouragement to their chosen fighter, but Dahan shunted his aural senses to a higher frequency to block them out. Vocalised noise was replaced by hissing machine noise, code blurts and the deep, glacial hum of the *Speranza's* vast mind emanating from the heart of the ship.

Yael launched his first attack, a low cut with his combat blade, which Dahan easily parried with the base of his halberd. He rolled his wrists, pivoting on his waist gimbal to avoid the real strike from Yael's chainsword. Dahan brought one metal knee into the Templar's stomach, driving him back with a *crack* of ceramite. He followed up with a jab from his shock-claws. The blades scored across Yael's arm, cutting a centimetre into the plate. A pulse of thought sent hundreds of volts through the blade, but the Templar didn't react and stepped in close to drive his sword blade at Dahan's chest.

The second shock-claw blocked it, and he spun the base of his halberd up into Yael's side. A burst of angry code blared in his ear as the halberd's entropic capacitor sent disruptive jolts of paralysing code into the Templar's armour. Yael staggered as his armour's systems flinched at the unexpected attack, struggling to keep from shutting down and resetting. Dahan leaned back on one leg and brought his two front legs up to slam into the Templar's chest, knocking him back with punishing force. Yael hit the deck hard and rolled, sparks flaring from his power pack.

Dahan followed up with a leaping attack that drove the gold blade of the halberd down at the deck. Yael rolled aside, pushing himself upright with a burst of strength and speed that surprised Dahan. Clearly the bellicose spirits in Yael's armour were better able to resist attack than most machine souls.

Yael slashed his sword low, but Dahan lifted his leg over the sweeping blade. His halberd stabbed down again, the blade turned aside by a forearm smash. Yael spun inside Dahan's guard and drove his combat blade up to his chest. Twin shock-blades trapped it a hair's breadth before it plunged into his hardened skin. Dahan sent a burst of crackling force through the blades and the knife blew apart in a shower of white-hot shards of metal.

Dahan slammed the haft of the halberd into Yael's chin, leaning over almost at ninety degrees to his vertical axis to punch his shock-blades into his opponent's side. Yael dropped to one knee with a roar of pain as coruscating lines of purple lightning danced over his armour. Even as he fell, Dahan was in motion, circling behind the fallen Templar and drawing back his halberd for what would be a beheading strike.

He braced his legs and brought the blade around, but even as he did so he felt the sudden pressure of Yael's sword against his groin assembly. Shocked, Dahan looked down. The Templar still knelt, as though at prayer, but the blade of his sword was thrust back between his torso and his left arm. The tip of the blade was touching Dahan's body, its madly revving teeth now stilled. Instantaneous calculations showed that the blade would penetrate a lethal twenty-five centimetres before his own blade could end Yael's life.

'A killing strike,' said Kul Gilad.

'I do not understand,' said Dahan, returning his shock-blade arms to the rest position at his back and pulling his halberd upright. 'This is inconceivable. The permutations of Templar Yael's fighting patterns, attack profiles and physical attributes did not predict this outcome.'

Yael stood and turned to face the magos. He sheathed his sword and reached up to remove his helmet. The revealed face was bland, its sharp edges smoothed out by genetic manipulation and enhanced bone density. Isotope degradation from his skeletal structure told Dahan that Yael was no more than twenty-four Terran years old.

'You fought to the classical schools,' said Dahan. 'Agrippa, Thibault, Calgar...'

'I have trained in them, studied them, but I do not slavishly follow them,' said Yael.

'Why not? Each is masterful technique.'

'A fight is about more than just technique and skill,' said Yael. 'It is about heart and courage. About a willingness to suffer pain, a realisation that even the greatest warrior can still be humbled by a twist of fate, a patch of loose ground, a mote of dust in the eye...'

'I account for random factors in my calculations,' said Dahan, still unwilling to concede that his combat subroutines could be in error. 'My results are certain.'

'Therein lies your error,' said Kul Gilad. 'There is no such thing as certainty in a fight. Even our greatest bladesman could be felled by a lesser opponent. To be a truly sublime warrior, a man must realise that defeat is *always* possible. Only when you recognise that can you truly fight with heart.'

'With heart?' said Dahan with a grin. 'How might that be integrated to my repertoire, I wonder?'

'Train with us and you will learn,' said Kul Gilad.

Dahan nodded, but before he could reply, a colossal, braying howl filled the training hangar. The sound echoed over the shattered city Dahan had constructed, filled with anger, with nightmares and with madness. The howl was answered and a towering structure of modular steel and permacrete in the heart of the city came crashing down in an avalanche of debris. Dahan's optics cut through the haze of flame, dust and smoke, but what he saw made no sense.

The Titans of Legio Sirius were making war on one another.

Microcontent 12

Wracking thuds of impact cracked the glass of the princeps tank, and howls of angry code blurts filled the command compartment of *Lupa Capitalina*. Pulsing icons flashed and warbled insistently as the Titan made itself ready for the fight of its life. Bellowing armaments clamoured for shells, void generators throbbed with accumulating power and the mindless questioning of distant gun servitors clogged the internal vox.

And at the centre of it all was Princeps Arlo Luth.

The amniotic tank was frothed with his convulsions, the milky grey liquid streaked with blood like patterns in polished marble. His limbless, truncated body twisted like a fish caught on a lure that fought for freedom. Phantom limbs that had long ago been sacrificed to the Omnissiah writhed in agony, and a wordless scream of horror bled from his tank's augmitters.

It had begun only moments ago.

Lupa Capitalina had been coming about from a successful prosecution of the outer defence districts, pulverising them with turbolasers then filling the ruins with simulated plasma fire. *Canis Ulfrica* had completed the devastation with its barrage missiles, while *Amarok* and *Vilka* stalked the ruins to eliminate any last pockets of resistance in storms of vulcan bolter fire.

Moderati Rosten had been working through the post-firing checklist

to power down the guns when *Canis Ulfrica* had moved into the *Capitalina's* field of view. Skálmöld had raised his guns in salute to his princeps, and every single alarm had burst into life.

Princeps Luth screamed as a violent *grand mal* ripped through his ravaged flesh. Violent feedback slammed up through the consoles, killing Rosten in a heartbeat, flashburning his brain to vapour and setting him alight from the inside. Magos Hyrdrith was luckier, her inbuilt failsafes cutting off the Manifold just before the feedback hit, but such sudden disconnection brought its own perils. She spasmed on the floor, black fluids leaking from her implants and a froth of oily matter issuing from every machined orifice in her body.

Koskinen also felt the sympathetic pain of Luth's seizure, but he had been disconnected from the Manifold at the time. His distress came from seeing his princeps *in extremis* and his fellow moderati dead. He ran back to his station, flinging his arms up to ward off streams of sparks and hissing blasts of vapour escaping from pressure-equalising conduits. He slid into his contoured couch seat, taking in the readings at a glance. The hololiths surrounding him were alive with threat responders, warning of enemies approaching.

'This doesn't make any sense,' he said, alternating between reading the threats his panels insisted were drawing nearer with every second, and the ruined city they had just pulverised. Luth was screaming, a sub-vocal shriek of machine language that still managed to convey the terrible agonies he was suffering.

Koskinen scrolled through the tactical display. According to the readouts, they were surrounded by thousands of enemies, monstrous swarms of fast movers with hostile intent. They only told a fraction of the story, but without plugging back into the Manifold there was no way to be sure of what the engine thought it was seeing.

'Hyrdrith!' he yelled. 'Get up! For Mars's sake, get up! I need you!'

Whether it was his words or coincidence, Hyrdrith chose that moment to push herself upright. She looked about herself, as though unable to process what was happening around her. She clambered to her feet as the deck swayed and the *Capitalina* took a faltering step.

'Interrogative: what in the name of the Machine-God is happening?'

'You don't know? Everything's gone to hell is what's happening,' shouted Koskinen. 'Luth's having some kind of seizure, and the engine thinks we're about to come under attack from thousands of enemy units.'

'Do you have the Manifold?'

'No,' said Koskinen. 'I think... I think *Lupa Capitalina* has it...'

'Then get in and take it from her,' snapped Hyrdrith, bending down to swap the fused cable at her station for a fresh one extruded from her stomach like a coiled length of intestine. She worked with ultra-rapid speed, re-establishing her link to the machine heart of the battle-engine, reciting prayers with each twist of a bolt and finger-weld connection she made.

'You're insane, Hyrdrith,' said Koskinen, twisting in his seat to point at the scorched ruin of the opposite moderati station. 'Look what happened to Rosten.'

'Do it,' repeated Hyrdrith as the engine took another step and Luth's howls changed in pitch to something altogether more dangerous. 'Make the connection, we need to know what's happening in the *Capitalina's* heart.'

'I'm not re-connecting,' said Koskinen. 'It's suicide.'

'You have to,' replied Hyrdrith. 'Your princeps needs you to drag him back from whatever affliction drives him to this madness.'

Koskinen shook his head.

Hyrdrith pulled back the sleeve of her robe and the stubby barrel of a weapon unfolded from the metal of her arm. A magazine snapped into the gun, engaging with a click and a rising hum.

'Do it now, or I will shoot you where you sit.'

'You're crazy!' shouted Koskinen.

'You have until I count to three. One, two...'

'Shit, Hyrdrith,' barked Koskinen. 'All right, I'll plug in, just put that gun away.'

'We plug in together,' said Hyrdrith. 'Understood?'

'Yes, understood, damn you.'

Koskinen hefted the Manifold connector, the gold-plated connector rods looking like daggers aimed at his brain. Normally communion through the Manifold was a sacred moment, attended to by a host of tech-acolytes, with numerous applications of oil balms and anti-inflammatory gels, but this was about as far from normal as it was possible to get.

'Ready?' asked Hyrdrith, sounding hatefully matter of fact.

'Ready.'

'Connect,' said Hyrdrith, and Koskinen plugged in, feeling the cold bite of linkage through the golden connector rods in the back of his skull. A surge of furious anger and heat instantly enveloped his body, his back arching with the shock of it. Acidic data poured through neurological veins, stimulating every nerve ending with pain emissions, and pumping the full range of aggressor-stimms into his cardiovascular system. Koskinen bellowed with animal fury, feeling the angry heart of the *Capitalina* clawing at his mental processes.

Coupled via a moderati's Manfold link, his connection to the bellicose spirit of the Titan was superficial, yet almost overwhelming.

What must it be like for Princeps Luth, twin souls woven together in one warlike purpose?

Koskinen fought against the anger, knowing it wasn't his own. Titanicus eidetic training took over, fencing off those parts of his brain worst affected and concentrating on restoring his situational awareness. Shoals of data light swam into focus as the full range of auspex inputs rose up to meet him. A hiss of terror escaped his lips as he saw the hordes of approaching creatures, millions of individual surveyor returns that blurred into one homogenous mass of inputs.

'God of All Machines, save us...' he hissed. 'So many of them!'

<Control yourself,> said a voice that cut across his thought processes. Magos Hyrdrith, also plugged into the Manifold. <None of this is real. Look closer!>

Koskinen took a deep breath and forced himself to relax his haptic grasp on the firing controls for the plasma destructor, unaware he'd even summoned them to his hand. The weapon's power coils were charging of their own accord, but thankfully release authority still lay with the moderati. He ran an interpolation scan of the inloading surveyor inputs, seeing a vast swarm of creatures surrounding them, working with a terrifying degree of coordination that was chilling in its instantaneous reaction.

And suddenly he knew what he was looking at.

'It's Beta Fortanis...' he said. 'Why does he think we're back on Beta Fortanis?'

<Unknown,> said Hyrdrith. <Possibly he suffers from transit bleed. A princeps is a god amongst men, a being so numinous and rare that they are rightly regarded as binary saints on some forge worlds. Yet even they have a mortal mind at their heart, a mind that is as vulnerable to the trauma of warp transit as any other. I believe Princeps Luth is suffering an episodic recall hallucination.>

'He's having a nightmare?'

<Is a simple way of putting it, yes,> answered Hyrdrith.

'Then how do we wake him up?'

<We cannot. He will rouse himself from this fugue state eventually. We just have to minimise the damage he does until then.>

'Great,' said Koskinen, looking closer at the hallucinatory auspex readings and feeling a gnawing wave of nausea clamp his gut. 'I remember this attack pattern... Luth's fighting the tyranid swarms at Sulphur Canyon! The battle where... Oh, hell.'

<Exactly, the battle where he slew the xenos Bio-Titan,> said Hyrdrith. <Now get that plasma coil offline. Quickly.>

'I'm trying,' he grunted, pouring all his command authority into disarming the weapon. 'But the *Capitalina's* damn determined that she wants it.'

The engine lurched around the last remains of what had once been a recreation of a clock tower, where enemy missile teams had hidden until *Amarok* had sawn its upper levels off with vulcan fire. Amid the spurious returns from the non-existent tyranid swarms, Koskinen picked out the panicked icons of the Legio's Warhounds as they scrambled for cover. *Canis Ulfrica* moved through the ruins ahead of them, traversing the shattered buildings as it picked up speed in an attempt to get out of *Lupa Capitalina's* path.

Heat spikes burned his hand, and Koskinen flinched, even as he recognised the pain was illusory.

'Plasma destructor's coming online!' he yelled. 'I can't stop it.'

<Disrupt the firing solutions,> ordered Hyrdrith.

Koskinen glanced over at Princeps Luth's amniotic tank; the liquid trapped within churned like the bottom of a silty lake. A shape swam out of the murk, a wizened face of sutured eyes, coil-plugged ears and a tube-fed mouth. Amputated arms that trailed silver wires from the elbows beat the glass in fury, and the awful, stretched-parchment skin of the bulbous head smeared blood on the glass as it twisted left and right, staring out at them and seeing only enemies.

Koskinen linked himself to Luth's tank and, as calmly as he was able, said, 'It's not real, my princeps. What you're seeing, it's not real. This battle is a year old. They hurt us, yes, but we walked away from the fight alive. We beat those xenos bastards!'

Luth's monstrous head turned in his direction, though there was no way he could see him. Koskinen had no idea whether Luth could even hear him, thinking back to the chaos of the battle against the hive creatures in that claustrophobic canyon. Fighting blind in yellow steam that billowed up from sunken caverns, millions of scurrying, chitinous monsters swarming their legs, dropping from the cliffs above or soaring on the billowing thermals.

Luth swam out of sight, swallowed by the viscous liquid of his tank.

'He's too far gone, Hyrdrith,' said Koskinen. 'He's going to take the shot.'

<Diverting power from weapons systems.> said the magos.

'No use, she's drawing power from the shields,' said Koskinen, wiping away firing solutions as quickly as they appeared at his stations. More were being generated every second, and he saw it was just a matter of moments until he would be overwhelmed and one made it through to the plasma destructor. He felt a burning pressure in his arm as the battle-engine brought its mighty weapon-limb to bear. Koskinen fought against it, desperately trying to keep his arm immobile, but against the strength of the *Capitalina's* ancient wolf heart he was a mote of dust in a hurricane.

<Stop that limb from moving!> cried Hyrdrith.

'What do you think I'm bloody trying to do?' grunted Koskinen, sweat pouring down his face.

<Then try harder, it may be the only chance to avert disaster.>

Koskinen glanced through the canopy as *Lupa Capitalina* took another step forwards and his panel lit up with too many firing solutions for him to dismiss them all. *Canis Ulfrica* filled the canopy, but the fire control warbled with a positive lock on a holographic outline Koskinen recognised from Sulphur Canyon.

A tyranid Bio-Titan that had almost outmatched them in the final moments of the battle.

'Omnissiah forgive us...' he said, searing heat enveloping his fist. 'We have a lock!'

<Spiking fibre-bundle muscle actuators.>

'Too late!' screamed Koskinen as *Lupa Capitalina's* plasma destructor unleashed the power of a star's heart at one of their own.

+Engine. Kill.+

The Iron Fist slammed down over a berm of rubble, roaring at maximum capacity towards the Titans. What little had been left standing after their war walk was little more than crushed debris beyond salvaging. Dahan tried to fathom what was going on, but could make no contact with the princeps of *Lupa Capitalina*. The Warlord braced its legs, and its right arm came about in fits and spasms, as though suffering from actuator damage.

The Sirius Warhounds skulked behind the mighty engine, loping in confusion as they blared alarm from their warhorns. The Reaver faced off against the Warlord, caught with nowhere to run to and stripped of any cover by their very thoroughness in the exercise. Its carapace sparked and squealed as its crew raced to bring voids back online, and squalling interference wavelengths created a shimmering rainbow around its frontal armour plates. Its guns were raised, and the rotating barrels of its gatling blaster were spinning up to firing speed.

What had possessed the Sirius to fight each other?

What manner of slight could bring two such awesomely powerful war machines to blows?

Without full access to the Legio Manifold, Dahan could not communicate directly with either princeps. The best he could do was transmit through the shared command network frequencies to demand answers. His hindbrain kept up a barrage of demands for the Legio to pull back from its war footing, while he linked with the *Speranza's* noospheric network and warned the archmagos of what was happening.

The Warhounds took note of him and the smaller of the pair, *Vilka*, broke away from its maddened prowling to rack the loaders of its guns and loose a howl of warning. Encoded in every scrap of that howl was one clear imperative.

Stay away!

Dahan brought the Iron Fist to a skidding halt before the Warhound.

'What is the Legio doing?' he voxed, hoping that someone, *anyone*, in Sirius might answer him. 'You must stop this madness now!'

Stay away!

'For the love of the Omnissiah, stand down!' yelled Dahan in the vocal, binaric and noospheric spheres. 'Put up your weapons, I beg of you!'

A fiery haze of superheated light built along the length of *Lupa Capitalina's* arm, the plasma destructor's firing vents squealing as they prepared to bleed off the volcanic excesses of heat. Knowing what was to come next, Dahan dropped into the Iron Fist and slammed the hatch down after him, hoping it would be enough. Inside the tank, Dahan closed the Iron Fist off from the outside world, disabling its auspex, vox and pict feeds.

He slammed the vehicle into full reverse, and even through the armoured hull and over the roar of the engine he could hear the plasma destructor draw in a screaming intake of breath.

'Bracing,' he said, shutting down as many of his own extraneous systems as he could manage in the microsecond he had left before the engine's gun reached optimal firing temperature.

And a thunderclap of pulverising thermic energy slammed into the tank, burning through its refractor fields in an instant and melting through a handspan of ablative plating. The internal temperature of the tank's crew compartment flashed to that of a blast furnace, and what little skin Dahan had left peeled off in an instant.

Before he could even register the pain, the kinetic blast wave of the Titan's weapon discharge plucked the Iron Fist from the deck and swatted it like a troublesome insect.

Hawkins heard the Titan's enormous weapon screaming as it drew breath to fire, and hurled himself into the lee of a fallen building.

Rae and a score of soldiers rolled into cover with him, while others ran for shelter behind armoured vehicles, piles of debris or whatever else might protect them from the backwash.

Imperial Titans were a welcome sight on any battlefield, but you didn't want to be anywhere near them when they fired plasma weapons. The heat bleed would scour the ground for hundreds of metres in all directions, and the thermal shockwave would give anyone caught in the open a damn nasty flash burn. He didn't want to think what might happen in the pressurised, oxygenated atmosphere of a starship...

'What in the Eye's going on, captain?' shouted Rae.

'Damned if I know,' said Hawkins, risking a glance through the shattered brickwork of the building. Dust clouds from the manoeuvring Titans billowed around them, making precise details hard to come by, but Hawkins saw the largest engine with a searing lightning storm chained to its arm. Another Titan stood with its back to him, fighting to keep itself out of the firing line, but even a relatively agile Reaver couldn't evade a Warlord forever.

'What is he doing?' whispered Hawkins.

Warhorns blared: threat, challenge and supplication all in one.

Whatever the Reaver was doing to try and defuse the larger Titan's anger, it wasn't working.

'Cover your ears and don't look up!' shouted Hawkins. 'Here it comes!'

He pulled back from the gap in the wall and pressed the heels of his hands against the side of his head. He put his head in his lap, exhaling as the colossal plasma weapon fired and filled the training hangar with a deafening thunderclap of igniting air. The temperature spiked and a flashbulb image was burned on Hawkins's retinas. Instantaneously a seething wave of heat billowed over them, a blistering desert wind of dust and debris. Walls crashed down throughout the ruined city, blown down by the force of the recoil-blast in a confined space.

Despite his own orders, Hawkins looked up in time to see the enormous blue-white bolt of incandescent plasma as it streaked overhead. Too bright to look at, it was the blinding radiance of an eclipse and a supernova all in one. Scads of molten metal trailed from its outer edges as it flashed the length of the training hall and slammed into the vast, skull-faced bulkhead at its rear.

Hawkins braced himself for an explosion, but the vast, super-heated plasma bolt simply punched through the heavily-plated bulkhead as though it wasn't even there. He tried to blink away the painful neon afterimages, but they wouldn't go away and he cursed his foolishness

in looking up. A shrieking cloud of wind-borne matter blew past, and the wall behind him groaned as the hammerblow of the thermal shockwave slammed into it.

'Move!' shouted Hawkins, pushing himself to his feet as the building that had sheltered them from the blast now threatened to come down and bury them alive. He and Rae scrambled away as the building came apart in an avalanche of steel and stone. A piece of broken stone clipped Hawkins on the shoulder, and the force of the impact cracked one of the bones there. He grunted in pain as randomly falling pieces of connective steelwork and modular plates rained down on him and his men. Choking dust clouds surged and swayed in the riotous thermal vortices, tugged this way and that as the venting systems fought to dissipate the heat build.

Hawkins rolled to his side, clutching his damaged shoulder and spitting a mouthful of bloodstained dust. His ears rang with noise and his vision still wouldn't properly clear, but he could still see that many of his soldiers hadn't been so lucky. Most had gotten out from beneath the building in time, but Hawkins saw several arms and legs protruding from the debris, and a soldier whose torso lay buried in the rubble. A number of dust and blood-covered soldiers tried to free him, even though it was obvious the man was dead.

Hawkins held up his good arm and said, 'Help me up, Rae. And be careful about it, I think my collarbone's broken.'

Lieutenant Rae, almost unrecognisable under a patina of pale ash and black dust, took his arm and hauled him to his feet. Hawkins bit back a cry of pain and wiped blood from his forehead as he tried to gain some measure of the situation. Warning lights flashed overhead and emergency klaxons bellowed in anger as emergency teams of medicae servitors were deployed from recessed chambers. Wounded Guardsmen shouted for medics, while revving Chimeras, Hellhounds and Leman Russ tanks formed defensive laagers on the far side of the ruins. Dazed Guardsmen stumbled through the wreckage, some missing limbs, others with horrific flash burns they would likely not survive, and still more with skin scorched red by the heat wash of the plasma weapon.

'Holy God-Emperor...' breathed Rae.

The little that had been left standing of the ruined city was gone, its prefabricated structures and multiple blocks flattened beneath the plasmic pressure wave radiating from the centre of the devastation. *Lupa Capitalina* shimmered in a distorting heat haze, wreathed in clouds of steam as its weapon arm vented super-heated plasma discharge. Its warhorn blared a scream of triumph, but even as Hawkins picked out its towering form through the smoke and dust, the sound changed to one of anguish as it beheld the destruction it had unleashed.

Canis Ulfrica swayed in front of the larger Battle Titan, its right arm and much of its shoulder carapace simply burned away. Flames and drooling cables that spat arcs of lightning guttered from the wound. With the aching slowness of a wounded Guardsman who'd only just realised the gunshot in his chest was mortal, *Canis Ulfrica* sank to its knees with a booming crash that reverberated around the training halls. She fell no further, and a shrieking wail of grieving binary issued from the augmitters of every member of the Cult Mechanicus.

Despite the losses his own men had suffered, Hawkins felt tears prick the corners of his eyes to see so mighty a machine humbled. The two Warhounds circled the fallen Reaver, their heads thrown back and their warhorns blasting out howls of primal loss.

As destructive as the plasma bolt loosed by *Lupa Capitalina* had been in the training halls, it was nothing compared to the devastation yet to come. Confined in an oxygen-rich environment without the vastness of an atmosphere in which to dissipate its heat and ionising electrons, the plasma burned volcanic as it streaked the length of the *Speranza*. It burned its way through the starboard solar collector arrays, shattering millions of precision-finished mirrors and melting support struts machined to nanoscopic tolerances. The brittle detonations of countless looking-glasses sounded like a glassy sea crashing on a steel shore, and the reflected heat boiled the flesh from the bones of the floating servitors whose lives had been spent in keeping the mirrors free of imperfections.

Another bulkhead was sliced through with horrifying ease, the superstructure around the chamber sagging as a central tension bar snapped like overstretched elastic. In the vaulted chambers behind the solar collectors, vast capacitors, long since beyond the reach of any in the Adeptus Mechanicus to reproduce, were reduced to thousands of tonnes of scrap metal as the plasma bolt bored through machines dreamed into existence in a past age. Irreplaceable technology melted to molten slag and a thunderclap of electrical discharge exploded from the mortally wounded machinery as it screamed in its death-throes. Every metal structure within five hundred metres became lethally charged with thousands of volts, and hundreds of ship-serfs died as they were electrocuted in leaping arcs of red lightning.

The hangars of titanic earth-moving machinery fared little better, with a hive-dozer five hundred metres tall cored by the bolt. Fuel cells detonated explosively and the complex machinery at the heart of its engineering deck was flooded with volatile electro-plasma backwash. Hard rubber wheels melted in the heat, and every transparisteel panel shattered with a thermoplasmic bloom. A giant crane mechanism, capable of lifting starships between construction cradles, was struck amidships, and the entire upper assembly crashed down into the hold, smashing itself to destruction on the way down and doing irreparable damage to three Goliath lifters and a Prometheus-class excavator.

And the rogue plasma bolt was still not spent.

The command deck shone with a blood-red light as alarms, damage reports and emergency subroutines flickered to life. The *Speranza* shook from end to end, and Archmagos Kotov felt its pain as it reverberated through his connection to the vast machine-spirit. Crackling arcs of power wreathed the archmagos, earthing through microscopic dampers worked into his cybernetic body as he fought to keep control.

His senior magi were meshed with their stations, each one relaying news of the effects of the disastrous weapon malfunction on the training deck. Magos Saiixek's multiple arms danced over the engineering consoles, rerouting engine power from the bolt's path, while Magos Azuramagelli charted potential exit points for an emergency warp translation. Magos Blaylock coordinated the ship's emergency response as Kryptaestrex ran damage control.

None of the news was good.

'Any more from Dahan?' asked Kotov, already knowing the answer.

'Negative, archmagos,' said Kryptaestrex. 'His floodstream is offline. He is likely dead.'

The inload from Magos Dahan had come to the command deck incomplete, and further requests for clarification remained unanswered. The fragmentary data the Secutor magos had managed to exload before going offline suggested that one of the Titans of Legio Sirius had fired on another, but what had driven it to do so remained unquantifiable.

Was is treachery? Had the rot of betrayal and corruption touched one of Sirius the way it had with Legio Serpentes on Uraniborg 1572? The thought sent a shudder of dislocative current through his body, and the *Speranza* groaned as it felt his fear. Was he to be forever cursed and tormented by the Omnissiah? Was this crusade into the unknown not penance enough to restore him in its infinite graces and binary glory?

'Starboard solar collectors are gone,' said Tarkis Blaylock, restoring his focus. While Kotov was connected to the ship's Manifold, Blaylock remained apart from it. To have both senior magi plugged in while such a disastrous turn of events was playing out was against procedure, but Kotov desperately needed Blaylock's statistical expertise to aid him in coordinating the emergency response of the *Speranza*.

If Kotov could not have Blaylock, then he would have the next best thing. He exloaded a series of code-frequencies and brevet rank protocols through the noosphere to Linya Tychon, together with a data-squirt of what he required of her. She answered almost immediately, already aware of the danger facing the *Speranza*. Her inload/exload capacity adjoined his own and the burden of processing the vast ship's needs eased with another to help shoulder the load.

Throughout the ship, every magos able to link with the Manifold added their own capacity to calming the wounded vessel's pain. Entire decks echoed with binary prayers and machine code hymnals, echoing from prow to stern as the Cult Mechanicus bent its logical will to the restoration of pure functionality.

'Is the Geller field holding?' asked Kotov, diverting a measure of his attention to bridge control.

'It's holding,' said Azuramagelli. 'The field generators are situated in the prow, but with the capacitors offline, their continued operation will burn through our reserves much quicker.'

'Have you calculated an exit point?'

'Working on it now,' said Azuramagelli, managing to convey his irritation even through the expressionless vista of his brain jars.

'Construction engine *Virastyuk* reports ninety per cent degradation of functionality,' reported Magos Kryptaestrex, his sonorous voice like that of a mother listing her dead children. 'Lifter *Nummisto* is destroyed. Rigs *Poundstone* and *Thorsen* are damaged too. Badly.'

'Where is the plasma fire now?' demanded Kotov. 'How far has it burned?'

'It is in the aft decks, burning through the transport holds,' answered Blaylock. 'Integrity fields have failed, and the loss of atmosphere has helped bleed off much of plasmic energy, though the tesla strength of the bolt remains unaffected. Thirty-two per cent of our drop-ship fleet has been blown into the warp, together with forty-five per cent of the Guard's armoured vehicles.'

Kryptaestrex grunted, his multiple arms and wide body jerking with the force of his displeasure.

'The Cadians aren't going to like that,' he said.

'If we cannot dampen this fire, then their dislikes will be the least of our concerns,' said Kotov. 'When this is over, I will build them replacements in the prow manufactories. Now where are my containment doors?'

'Blast containment shields are raising between sections Z-3 Tertius Lambda and X-4 Rho,' said Blaylock, reading the damage-control inloads from noospheric veils of light. 'There is an eighty-three point seven per cent chance they will not halt the blast and it will breach the main plasma combustion chamber.'

'But they will at least dampen its force?'

'To some degree, yes,' agreed Blaylock. 'But given the enhanced conditions for plasma burn aboard ship, they will not stop it.'

'Vent the chambers beyond,' said Azuramagelli. 'It's the only way.'

'No,' said Saiixek. 'Those are the worker habs for the engineering decks. I need those menials to maintain engine efficiency. Diverting to obtain more would greatly delay our mission.'

Microcontent 13

Abrehem bent to remove his mask as a wave of nausea surged up his gullet. He pulled the rebreather up just enough to expose his mouth – a practice every worker learned early on in the reclamation chambers – and puked a bloody froth of lung and stomach tissue. He spat a stringy mouthful of ash and glassy plasma residue and wiped his cracked lips with the back of his gloved hand.

'Get a move on, Bondsman Locke,' said Vresh, descending on his repulsor disc and tapping the base of his kinetic prod on his shoulder. 'Don't make me turn this on.'

Abrehem almost preferred it when Vresh spoke in harsh bursts of machine code. At least then he didn't have to listen to his grating authoritarian tones with comprehension. The overseer had eventually taken the hint that simply increasing the volume of his binaric code blurts didn't make them any more intelligible to those without the capacity to translate them.

Ironically, it was Crusha who had provided an insight into Vresh's commands. The crude augmetics grafted to the ogryn's powerful frame included a binaric slave coupler that had enough faded ident-codes left to tell Abrehem it had once been Guard issue. Crusha himself had no memory of his life before coming to the dockside bar, but it seemed likely he'd served in one of the abhuman cohorts attached to a Jouran regiment, perhaps as a lifter for an enginseer.

Vresh had proved to be a vindictive overseer, a petty bureaucrat who revelled in his middling position of authority. He drove the bondsmen under his aegis hard, with a fondness for administering punishing blows from his kinetic prod and working them right up to the last minute before the giant plasma cylinders dumped their explosive waste material.

'My lungs are on fire,' said Abrehem, fighting for breath. 'I can't breathe.'

'You have five seconds before I administer corrective encouragement.'

Abrehem nodded, resigned to the pain, for he had no strength left to him. Some of the bondsmen who could go on no longer volunteered for surgical servitude, but Abrehem had long since vowed not to fall so low. Vresh hovered close to him, the end of his kinetic prod buzzing with accumulating power.

'Hey, no need for that,' said Hawke, wading through drifts of sharp plasma flects with Crusha at his side. 'We've got him. He's fine.'

'Yeah, it's near the end of shift, no need to get nasty, eh?' added Coyne.

Crusha helped Abrehem to his feet, and he nodded gratefully to Hawke and Coyne as he read the shipboard timestamp in the code lines snaking in the depths of the walls. Fifty-five minutes remained of their shift. Abrehem was wondering how he was going to last that long, when he saw something that sent a jolt of adrenaline through his wretched, toxin-ravaged body.

Angry, wounded blares of code light shimmered on the vaulted ceiling of the reclamation chamber, like a red weal on skin just before a needle punctures the vein. Vresh felt it too, and looked up in puzzlement as a glowing spot of light appeared on the surface of the chamber's ceiling.

'What the hell is that?' asked Hawke, wiping a greasy hand over the eye-lenses of his rebreather.

Abrehem read the frantic code in the walls as it burst apart in sprays of warning data, and saw the nature of the emergency above in its binary fear. Enslaved bondsmen throughout the chamber paused in their labours and looked up at the unnatural sight.

'We have to get out,' he gasped. 'Right now.'

'Why, what's going on?'

'The plasma combustion chamber above, it's been breached,' cried Abrehem, turning and running as quickly as he could in his environment suit to the sealed door to the chamber. 'Everyone out! Run, for Thor's sake run!'

'Halt immediately,' snapped Vresh. 'Bondsman Locke, cease and

desist all attempts to vacate this chamber. Continued disobedience will result in enforced surgical servitude.'

Abrehem ignored the overseer and kept on going, stomping over the scoured deck where the industrial-scale sifters and brushes had already swept. He felt the eye-watering buzz of the prod as Vresh caught up to him, but didn't have the energy to avoid it. The prod touched him in the centre of his back and a thunderous punch of kinetic force slammed him to the deck. The breath was driven from him by the impact, and he rolled onto his back as Hawke and Coyne rushed to his side.

'Are you okay?' said Hawke.

'We've got to get out,' said Abrehem. 'This place is going to be neck-deep in plasma any minute.'

He struggled to get to his feet, each limb still jangling in pain with nerve stimulation from Vresh's prod. The overseer floated down on his repulsor disc, and he aimed the throbbing staff at Abrehem's chest.

'Return to work, bondsmen,' ordered Vresh. 'Or the next prods will rip your nervous systems out through your skin.'

Abrehem looked up as a tiny spot of light detached from the ceiling, falling in an almost lazy parabola that was just distorted perspective. The droplet of plasma fell with the accurate synchronicity of predestination, and Abrehem was not ashamed to later admit that he took great relish in what happened next.

The droplet struck Vresh on the very top of his steel skull and cored through him like a high-powered laser. His body flash-burned from the marrow, and blue fire exploded from his augmetic eye-lenses and connective plugs. His bones fused in an instant and gobbets of charred flesh and implanted metal dropped to the deck with a wet thud of smoking remains.

'Holy Terra!' cried Coyne, backing away in horror from the ruin of what had, a moment ago, been a person.

'What the hell...?' spat Hawke.

'Come on!' said Abrehem. 'We have to go. Now.'

'No arguments from me,' said Hawke, turning and sprinting for the reclamation chamber's exit gate. Coyne was hard on his heels, with Crusha lumbering behind them. Abrehem followed them, struggling as the after-effects of the kinetic prod made his limbs stiff and jerky.

The light above grew in brightness until it bathed the entire chamber in its bleached white glow. A spiderweb of glowing light spread from the initial leak, spreading ever wider as the structural integrity of the ceiling began to fail. More droplets of plasma fell from the ceiling like the beginnings of a gentle rain shower. But where these droplets

landed they sparked into flames, rekindling the toxic waste dumped from the combustion chambers or igniting the oil-soaked environment suits of bondsmen.

Stratified layers of volatile fumes, kept below the ignition threshold by overworked, chugging vents, suddenly expanded as hot plasma was added to the mix. Pockets of flammable gas exploded throughout the chamber as the illuminated cracks on the ceiling burned brighter and brighter.

'Open the gate!' shouted Abrehem as drizzles of white-hot plasma sheeted down behind them in a falling curtain of fire. The death screams of the bondsmen farther back were swallowed as the superheated air vaporised their rebreathers and sucked the breath from their lungs.

'It's bloody locked, isn't it?' said Hawke, looking over Abrehem's shoulder as a portion of the ceiling collapsed and a deluge of plasma dropped into the chamber. 'Only Vresh could open it.'

'Not just Vresh,' said Abrehem. 'At least, I hope not.'

He placed his hand on the arched gate and read the simple machine-spirit working the lock. Its sentience was barely worthy of the name, with a simple dual state of being. He followed the path of its workings, and sent a pulse of binary from his augmetic eyes. The lock resisted at first, unused to his identity and wary of a new touch, but it relented as he whispered the prayer his father had taught him as a young boy.

'Thus do we invoke the Machine-God. Thus do we make whole that which was sundered.'

The lock disengaged and the reinforced gate sank into the floor with a grinding rumble of slowly turning mechanisms. Hawke was first over when the gate had lowered enough, quickly followed by Crusha and Coyne. Abrehem leapt through as a roaring crash and a surge of dazzling brilliance told him that the entire ceiling had finally given way behind them.

'Close it! Close it!' yelled Coyne as a wave of roiling plasma surged towards the gateway.

Abrehem placed his palm on the lock plate on the outside of the chamber.

Again he looked deep into the heart of the gate's lock spirit and said, 'Machine, seal thyself.'

The gateway rumbled back up with what seemed like agonising slowness, but it was fast enough to prevent the ocean of searing plasma from escaping the reclamation chamber. A jet of scalding steam and a layer of scorched iron spat through the top of the gate, but this barrier was designed to withstand excesses of temperature

and pressure, and it held firm against the onslaught of sun-hot plasma within.

Abrehem let out a shuddering breath and placed his head against the burning iron of the gate.

'Thank you,' he said.

Hawke and Coyne held their sides and drew in gulping breaths of stagnant air.

'Shitting hell, that was close,' said Hawke, almost laughing in relief.

'What just happened?' demanded Coyne. 'Are all those men in there dead?'

'Of course they're bloody dead,' snapped Abrehem. 'They're nothing but vapour now.'

'Emperor's mercy,' said Coyne, sinking to his knees and putting his head in his hands. 'I can't take much more of this.'

'You saved our lives in there, Abe,' said Hawke, patting Abrehem on the back. 'I reckon that's gotta be worth something. What do you say I stand you boys a drink?'

Abrehem nodded. 'I could drink a whole barrel of your rotgut right about now.'

'Let's not get too carried away,' said Hawke. 'Only your first's on the house.'

'Plasmic temperature falling exponentially,' said Magos Blaylock, and his attendant dwarfs clapped their foreshortened limbs as though he had been personally responsible for saving the ship. 'Teslas are still high, but falling too. Plasma density diminishing rapidly and thermal kinetic energy per particle dropping off to non-destructive levels.'

Kotov let out a stream of lingua-technis prayers and closed his eyes to give thanks for the reprieve.

'God of All Machines, today you have judged your servants worthy of your Great Work,' said Kotov, letting his voice carry over the entire command deck. 'And for this we give thanks. Glory to the Omnissiah!'

'Glory to the Omnissiah,' intoned the assembled magi.

'The living diminish,' said Kotov.

'But the Machine endures,' came the traditional reply.

Streams of worshipful binary bloomed from the floodstream of every magos as each of them began to take control of the damage that had been done to the ship. Kotov could feel its deep hurt, a bone-deep agony, like a mortal lance thrust to the back.

But where lesser ships would die, the Ark Mechanicus would endure.

Kotov let his mind skim the oscillating streams of light that travelled the length and breadth of the *Speranza*, drinking in the data flowing between its myriad systems. Every one of them felt pain, but every one of them siphoned the agony of system death from the most grievously wounded machines and took it into their own processes. Every part of the ship felt the pain of its wounding, but out of that shared agony came a lessening of the worst damage.

Throughout the ship, Kotov felt the presences of the thousands of tech-priests, lexmechanics, calculus-logi, data-savants and sentience-level servitors that made up the *Speranza's* crew. Every member of the Cult Mechanicus that could plug into the Manifold had done so, and each one sang binary hymns of quietude or recited catechisms of devotion and obeisance to the Machine. Individually, they might not achieve much, but the song of the Adeptus Mechanicus combined throughout the ship to ease the pain of its dreadful wound.

Kotov let his approbation flow into the Manifold.

Where else but in the Adeptus Mechanicus could such singular unity of purpose be found?

Songs of praise to the Omnissiah flowed around him, double, triple, and even quadruple helix spirals of binary moving effortlessly through the circuitry and data light like a soothing balm. As terrible as the damage would likely prove, the worst was over, and though the loss of even one machine was a solemn blow, Kotov knew they had gotten off lightly.

He felt the presence of Linya Tychon and directed his data ghost towards the astrogation chamber, where she and her father added their own verses to the healing binaric song. He felt the wash of information that filled the chamber, amazed that none of it had been corrupted in the spasms of digital anarchy that had flowed through the ship in the wake of the accident.

<Archmagos,> said Linya.

<My thanks for your aid, Mistress Tychon, it was invaluable.>

<I serve the will of the Omnissiah,> she replied. <Really, I did very little.>

<You underestimate youself, Linya,> said Kotov. <It is an unseemly habit and makes others doubt you. You proved your worth in the Manifold today, and others will see it too.>

Kotov felt the swell of pride in Linya's and her father's flood-streams and moved on to the source of the destructive plasma bolt. His consciousness flowed along the path the searing bolt had traced, lamenting the needless loss of so many fine machines. The lower decks were dead, empty spaces where two entire decks had been vented to bleed the bolt of its sustaining oxygen and ionising atmosphere. Regrettable, but necessary.

He saw the shattered glassy graveyard of the starboard solar collector and the molten remains of the giant capacitor that stored its gathered energy. The loss of one such system would be bad enough, but to lose both was going to put a serious drain on their available power. Coupled with the loss of one of the main plasma combustion chambers, Kotov suspected the expedition was in very real danger of suffering an unsustainable energy deficit.

Moving forwards, he saw the devastated training hangar, where Guardsmen, Black Templars and skitarii fought to deal with the hundreds of wounded and dead. Confined in the pressurised environment of the hangar, the backwash of the blast had levelled Dahan's training arena and killed a great many of the Imperium's finest. Kotov inloaded the casualty lists, shocked by how many had died and how many were moving from wounded to dead.

Lupa Capitalina stood at the far end of the hangar, its arms hanging limply by its sides as screaming vents blasted superheated steam into the air above it. Emergency venting of the plasma reactor at its heart, realised Kotov. The crew had shut the Titan down, draining it of every last scrap of power, and hot rain fell around the dormant engine, streaking its vast armoured carapace and drizzling from its drooping head like tears.

Kotov saw a gaggle of tech-priests and servitors lowering an armoured casket from the Warlord's opened canopy. They took the greatest of care with its handling, as well they might, for they carried the mortal flesh of Princeps Arlo Luth, Chosen of the Omnissiah and favoured son of battle. Without him, *Lupa Capitalina* was nothing more than an inert piece of holy metal. The very best of the Adeptus Biologis would work without pause to undo whatever had caused this unfortunate series of events.

Canis Ulfrica knelt before the Warlord, its right side torn away and fused by the heat of the blast that had felled it. Kotov felt the Reaver's pain bleeding into the Manifold, but saw that it was by no means beyond saving. Kryptaestrex had the supplies, and Turentek, the *Speranza's* Ark Fabricatus, could work miracles with machines thought damaged beyond healing. *Amarok* and *Vilka* circled the wounded Titan as hundreds of tech-priests and Legio acolytes swarmed its broken body. Princeps Eryks Skálmöld had already been removed, and his casket rested on a floating gravity palanquin as the chanting priests surrounding him awaited the arrival of the Legio's Alpha Princeps.

Even inloading the Manifold records from both Titans gave Kotov little clue as to what had caused *Lupa Capitalina* to fire on one of its own. He saw it was only the last-minute stimulation of the Warlord's actuator muscles by Magos Hyrdrith that had thrown its aim off enough to save *Canis Ulfrica* from complete destruction.

As Kotov scanned the terrible wreckage of the training hall, he caught a faint, but unmistakable trace element of Magos Dahan's bio-mechanical scent as it tugged on the edges of the Manifold.

<Dahan? Is that you?>

Kotov received no response, but the strength of the mechanised tech-sign grew stronger at the touch of his Manifold-presence. Flitting through the datasphere, Kotov quickly triangulated the source of the tech-sign – a smashed tank, almost entirely buried in the ruins of a fallen structure – and assigned the task of digging it clear to a nearby group of muscle-augmented combat servitors.

He felt the insistent pull of command requests coming from the bridge and raced back through the conduits of the ship until his consciousness sat once again enthroned in his cerebral cortex. Kotov opened his eyes and let the reassuring warmth of the command deck's data-sea enfold him.

'Summarise: damage and prognosis,' he said. 'Magos Blaylock, begin.'

'The plasma bolt has now been successfully discharged,' he said. 'Venting the lower decks was the correct course of action. Despite the loss of numerous mechanical and mortal components – a full list is appended via sub-strata noospheric link – the *Speranza* is still functionally operational. The loss of crew and power generation will be our biggest concern as the expedition continues. The energy requirement of the Geller field is draining our power reserves too quickly, and at the recommendation of Magos Azuramagelli, I would suggest that we drop out of warp space within the next two hours.'

'How short will that leave us?' demanded Kotov.

Azuramagelli answered, his carriage-like armature moving through a floating representation of the Valette system. A number of callipers extended from the rotating rim beneath his brain jars, and a shimmering point of light appeared just beyond the outer edges of the system.

'With Magos Tychon's added inload capacity, I have calculated an optimal exit point, which will leave us fifteen days beyond the system's edge.'

'Fifteen days? That is unacceptable, Magos Azuramagelli,' said Kotov. 'Find another exit point closer to Valette.'

'Impossible,' said Azuramagelli. 'With the current drain on our energy reserves, there is no way to maintain the Geller field long enough to reach any closer with a safe enough margin of reserve.'

'Damn the reserve,' said Kotov, hot anger rising from his body in a haze of red floodstream. 'Find us a closer exit.'

'Magos Azuramagelli is, unfortunately, correct,' said Saiixek of engineering, pulling a host of data tables and graphs from the air. 'The loss of the plasma combustion chamber slows us by a factor too great to ignore.'

'And without capacitor reserve, our operational protocols dictate that we cannot run under such conditions,' added Kryptaestrex. 'We need to return to real space and unfold the port collector to charge up the remaining capacitor. We'll likely need to drain half the support ships of fuel and power or we won't even reach the Halo Scar, let alone get beyond it.'

'Indeed,' said Blaylock. 'Prudence might dictate that we abandon such an attempt until we are better able to face such a challenge.'

'I wondered when you would suggest that,' said Kotov.

'Archmagos?'

'Turning back? You'd like nothing better than for us to return to Mars in failure.'

'I assure you, archmagos, I wish us to succeed as much as you.'

Kotov read no falsehood in Blaylock's floodstream, but couldn't quite bring himself to believe his Fabricatus Locum. The moment stretched, and Kotov realised he was out of options.

'Very well,' he said. 'Make the necessary preparations for a return to real space.'

Abrehem, Coyne, Hawke and Crusha made their way through the cavernous transit chambers back towards the lower dormitory decks. The metal floor was slick with moisture and wisps of cold steam drifted from vents that billowed cold air into the arched tunnels.

'This feels weird,' said Coyne. 'I always felt these tunnels were claustrophobic.'

'When there's hundreds of bondsmen trudging to and from work, it's going to feel cramped,' said Abrehem, trying not to remember the screams of the dying men in the reclamation chamber as the plasma wave engulfed them.

'It's cold too,' said Hawke.

'Yeah, and the air tastes funny,' added Coyne.

'It tastes... clean...' said Abrehem, surprised he'd not noticed that. It had been so long since he'd tasted air that hadn't been scrubbed through labouring filters or wasn't laced with dust and toxins that he'd forgotten what clean air tasted like.

'Maybe they've had a system purge after what happened?' suggested Coyne.

'Not likely,' said Hawke.

'Then what do you think happened?'

'Like I care,' said Hawke. 'If the air's cleaner then that's great, but I don't give a shiprat's fart why it's happened.'

Abrehem shook his head. 'No, the air's not just clean, it's cold. I mean, *really* cold. Like it's been frozen. And it's hard, like it's, I don't know, stale or something.'

The others had no answer for him, and they walked the rest of the way in silence, along echoing tunnels lit through stained-glass lancets by dancing flames, down skull-stamped stairs of iron, through yawning portals fringed with carved stone cogs and past heaving ranks of relentless pistons.

They saw no one to offer an explanation for the emptiness.

Here and there, Abrehem saw discarded pieces of maintenance machinery fixed to the deck, but without anyone around to operate them. The more pressure hatches they passed through the more frequent the signs of something amiss became.

None of them had paid much attention to their surroundings since becoming bondsmen, and the omnipresent exhaustion had quickly drained them of any curiosity to look around. But without the press of bodies around them and the sudden clarity that comes from a near-death experience, all three men felt a mounting apprehension as they approached their dormitory deck.

'I don't like this,' said Hawke.

'Where *is* everyone?' said Coyne, echoing Abrehem's thoughts exactly.

At last they reached the cavernous opening to the feeding hall, and as the airtight gate ground down into the deck, a wall of piled-up bodies tumbled into the passageway, like water over a collapsing dam. Freezing air gusted over the dead, and Abrehem backed away from the spilling corpses: men and women in the grimy coveralls of Mechanicus bondsmen. The bodies were pale, lips cyanotic, eyes wide with the pain and terror of sudden decompression and asphyxiation. Fingernails were bloody where desperate hands had clawed at the gate.

'Thor's blood,' said Hawke, as the sliding heap of bodies came to a halt. 'What the hell happened here?'

'They're all dead...' said Coyne.

Abrehem felt the cold of the air clamp around his soul as he finally understood the cause of the freezing chill in the surrounding tunnels. He looked up the cliff-face walls at the gently rotating fan blades of the air-circulation vents. Strips of inscribed parchment fluttered from the louvres, prayers of purity and imprecations for untrammelled transit of air. Those prayers had been hideously mocked, and he tried

not to imagine the horror of the men and women as the vents had reversed and drawn air instead of providing it.

'The bastards!' he cried, wrapping his arms around his scrawny frame. First the deaths in the reclamation chamber, and now *this*! How much could one man be expected to bear?

'How did this happen?' said Coyne, not yet reaching the inevitable conclusion offered by the blue-lipped corpses.

Crusha opened a path through the dead, lifting each body aside and showing surprising gentleness for one so monstrously bulked and so seemingly simple. Abrehem followed the ogryn and Hawke into the feeding hall, letting his eyes roam the empty ranks of tables, the monstrous silence and the scattered ruin of plastek trays. Servitors lay dead next to their serving machines, and while most of the bodies were piled high at the chamber's three gates, many others were lying slumped below the air-circulation vents, perhaps in the vain hope that they might start up again.

Hawke followed Abrehem's gaze and said, 'They vented it. They bloody vented it all.'

Coyne turned towards Abrehem, willing him to deny what Hawke was saying. 'No, that can't be right? They wouldn't do that.'

Abrehem felt the last shred of his humanity unravelling from his soul and being replaced by a tightening coil of absolute rage. 'Hawke's right. They vented the atmosphere from this deck into the vacuum, that's why the air tastes cold and hard. It's only just been restored.'

'Why would they do that? It doesn't make sense.'

'The breach in the plasma combustion chamber,' sighed Abrehem, sitting at one of the many vacant tables. 'Whatever caused it must have been worse than we knew. Saiixek probably decided to blow the air out of this deck to vent the plasma into space and suffocate the fire.'

'But he's killed an entire shift of bondsmen,' said Coyne, still unwilling to accept that such a monstrous act could have been deliberate.

Abrehem surged to his feet and snatched Coyne by his oil-stained overalls.

He slammed Coyne into the wall and shouted in his face: 'When are you going to get it into your thick head, that the Mechanicus don't care about our lives? We're numbers, nothing more than that. So what if Saiixek had to kill a few thousand bondsmen just to put out a fire? There's always another world where he can collar more slaves to work themselves to death for his bloody Machine-God.'

'Easy there, Abe,' said Hawke, placing a hand on his shoulder. 'Coyne here ain't the enemy. It's those Mechanicus bastards that need taking down a peg or two, yeah?'

Abrehem felt his fury abate and he released Coyne with a shamefaced sob.

'I'm sorry,' he said.

'It's okay,' said Coyne. 'Forget about it.'

'No,' said Abrehem. 'That's the one thing I'm *not* going to do. The Adeptus Mechanicus murdered these bondsmen, and I'll tell you this now. Someone's going to pay.'

The *Speranza* limped out of warp space ninety-three minutes later, its hull intact and its Geller fields at the limit of their capacity to endure. Magos Kryptaestrex had squeezed every last reserve of non-essential power to keep the shields intact long enough to reach the designated exit point calculated by Magos Azuramagelli. At Kotov's insistence – and much to Azuramagelli's chagrin – his trans-immaterial calculations were verified by Linya and Vitali Tychon, but both Quatrian magi confirmed his equations were without error.

Far beyond the system edge of Valette, the *Speranza* broke the barrier between the empyrean and real space. The currents that had brought them this far through the warp were still turbulent, and the translation was not smooth. The Ark Mechanicus shuddered with translation burn, trailing ruptured screeds of immaterial energies that clung to its hull and howled madness at the crew within before vanishing in a haze of nebulous anger.

With perimeter security established, the enormous ship's port flank opened up, blast shields and airtight shutters ratcheting open as the surviving solar collector emerged like a slowly unfurling sail. Complex lattices of joints, gimbals, rotator cuffs and multiple hinges expanded in a precise geometric ballet until a kilometre-wide and seven hundred metre long bank of energy-hungry cells was aimed towards the shimmering light of the far distant Valettian sun.

So far from the system's heart, the energy the collector would gather from the star would be low, but the stream of hot neutrons flowing along the length of the electromagnetically charged hull and gathered by the *Speranza's* ramscoops was the main target of this harvest. Almost as soon as the collector was fully deployed, the charge levels on the drained capacitor began to climb, and the speed of that ascent would only increase as the *Speranza* picked up speed.

The emergency translation had scattered the fleet like seeds sown randomly by an agri-spreader, and another three hours passed before contact could be established with any other ship. One by one, the vessels of the fleet signalled their position, and began the slow process of regrouping. Refinery ships and genatorium vessels clustered close to the *Speranza*, monstrous umbilicals linking them to the Ark Mechanicus to suckle its mighty hunger for fuel and power. A dozen ships were emptied before the *Speranza* was sated enough to proceed.

Moonchild and *Wrathchild*, twin souls as well as twin ships, were the luckiest of the fleet, scattered a day's travel ahead of the *Speranza*. The *Adytum* remained tucked in close to the mighty vessel, and the *Cardinal Boras* lay abeam of the fleet, less than fifteen hours away. The escorts *Mortis Voss* and *Blade of Voss* were not so lucky, trailing at least a day behind in wilderness space.

Despite repeated attempts to locate *Honour Blade* with long-range auspex, deep augur scans and astropathic scrying, no trace could be found of the third vessel launched from Voss Prime. The fleet searched for as long as Archmagos Kotov deemed appropriate, but every captain knew in his heart that to linger in the trackless gulfs between systems was too hazardous to risk for long.

The mater-captains of the surviving Vossian craft demanded extra time to search for their lost sister ship, but Kotov overruled them and threatened to relieve both women of command if they disobeyed his orders to make best speed for the distant system edge. Reluctantly, *Mortis Voss* and *Blade of Voss* turned their prows for Valette and followed orders.

The great bell in the High Temple to the Omnissiah of each remaining vessel was rung three times; once for the lost *Honour Blade*, once for the Machine-God's lost children, and once for the mortal souls aboard her.

The fleet moved on, scattered and stretched beyond what any Navy doctrinal treatise on convoy tactics would consider prudent, but at least together and closing formation. With *Moonchild* and *Wrathchild* leading the way, the Kotov Fleet plotted an intercept course with the lonely outpost that that traced a two hundred and thirty-five year orbit of the star at the heart of the system.

The Valette Mechanicus Manifold station.

The last point of contact with the lost fleet of Magos Telok.

MACROCONTENT COMMENCEMENT:

+++MACROCONTENT 003+++

The Soulless sentience is the enemy of all life.

Microcontent 14

The atmosphere of the pack-meet was as frosty as the misty air gusting from the coolant units, and it wasn't about to get any better, thought Moderati Koskinen. Skálmöld had been spoiling for a fight ever since the incident. Koskinen respected Skálmöld, but he didn't really like him, though he couldn't blame him for his anger.

In the two weeks since *Lupa Capitalina* had attacked *Canis Ulfrica*, the prow forges of the Ark Mechanicus had worked continuous shifts to craft fresh weaponry and armour plates to replace the Reaver's destroyed components. A veritable army of tech-priests, Legio acolytes and construction engines laboured on the fallen Titan, returning it to operational readiness. Such a monumental task would normally take months of intensive labour, ritual and consecration, but the Ark Fabricatus, a vast construction-engine magos named Turentek, had worked miracles in drastically shortening that time. The engine and its rebuilt parts would soon rise from the construction cradles, reborn and restored, but Koskinen knew it wasn't the physical damage that was the worst thing to come out of the attack.

He stood beside Princeps Luth's casket, pressing a palm to the panes of armourglas and feeling the slumbering heartbeat of the divine being within. Magos Hyrdrith attended the monitoring device attached to the base of Luth's casket, and the winking status lights along its base attested to the renewed health of the princeps.

Luth was yet to be roused from his neurological dormancy, and who knew what state of mind the princeps would be in when he was awoken? Would he remember what happened on the training deck or would he still be fighting the desperate battle at Sulphur Canyon? Not even the senior Legio Biologis could say for sure what effect his actions would have on his mind. Koskinen willed Luth to be sane, for there was only one warrior who would take command of the Legio if the Alpha Princeps was judged unfit for duty.

Skálmöld's casket sat opposite Luth's, plugged into a recessed bay of the medicae templum given over to the Legio by Archmagos Kotov. The Reaver princeps was a shadowed figure that hung like a limbless revenant in milky-white suspension. His casket was slightly smaller and more ornate than Luth's, owing to its design being commissioned under the rubric of a different Fabricator.

Magos Ohtar attended to his princeps with great diligence, for Skálmöld had suffered greatly too. His Titan had been damn near killed, and the feedback pain must have been unbearable. Like *Lupa Capitalina*, *Canis Ulfrica* had also lost a moderati. Tobias Osara had been vaporised in the blast that had taken the Reaver's arm, and its second moderati, Joakim Baldur, had been badly wounded. His right arm and a portion of his skull were encased in dermal-wrap and his burned skin replaced with vat-cultured grafts. Baldur glared at Koskinen as though he were personally responsible for the bad blood between their Titans. Koskinen didn't rise to the bait, and held his tongue while they awaited the arrival of the Skinwalker.

Cold air filled the medicae templum, and Koskinen pulled his uniform jacket tighter about himself, wishing he'd thought to wear his heavier robes. The temperature within was precisely controlled, and a thin patina of frost coated the metallic icons of the Omnissiah on the walls, the insulated machinery of the central cogitator and the porcelain-tiled floor. Sterile steel plating encased the lower half of the walls, and a complex network of ribbed pipework hung from the ceiling, venting occasional gusts of ammoniac steam. Hundreds of glassek cylinders, each large enough to contain a human being, lined the upper reaches of the roof space, suspended on mechanised arms that could rotate them to the floor. Koskinen remembered floating in one of these fluid-filled tanks after the battle with the tyranids on Beta Fortanis, purging his floodstream of discarded data and Manifold junk.

It was not a pleasant memory, for such purges were not painless procedures.

Pacing the length of the medicae templum was Elias Härkin, whose pathogenically-ravaged frame was completely encased in a lattice-work exoskeleton of brass and silver. His shaven skull was red and black with a complete covering of woad-markings: jagged wolf-tails, bloodied fangs and slitted eyes in the darkness. Atrophied facial muscles twitched as the electrode stimulators that compensated for his cerebrovascular impairment and allowed him to speak fired a series of test signals. Like most princeps, Härkin loathed being removed from *Vilka*, and his artificially-motivated body moved with a stilted, hunched-over gait, not unlike the Warhound he piloted.

As a princeps he was a god, as a mortal he was crippled.

The pressurised door slid open, and the Skinwalker entered. The youngest princeps of Legio Sirius, Gunnar Vintras wore his silver hair shaven tight to the skull and his dress uniform was crisp and pressed as though he were about to attend a Legio function. A curved power sabre on a platinum chain hung at his hip, and he carried a gold-chased bolt pistol in a thigh holster.

'Nice of you to show up,' said Härkin, his dysarthria rendered intelligible by the fibre-bundle muscles, though still distorted.

'Nice to see you too, Elias,' said Vintras, taking a seat at the central cogitator bank. 'When the Moonsorrow calls a pack-meet, I come running.'

'The meet began thirty minutes ago,' said Härkin.

Vintras shrugged and sprang from his seat as though already bored with sitting down.

'It takes time to dress this well,' he said, straightening his uniform jacket and brushing an invisible speck of dust from his shoulder epaulettes. 'Of course, you have your cyber-grooms dress you, don't you? They do the best with what they have, I'm sure.'

'Princeps Luth isn't dead, you know?' said Koskinen, angered by Vintras's posturing.

Vintras circled the cogitators to stand before him, and Koskinen wished he hadn't spoken. To be a moderati aboard a Warlord Titan was a position of great honour, but any princeps – even a Warhound princeps – outranked him and had the power to end his life.

'What's this, a moderati getting above his station?' said Vintras, leaning over Koskinen and baring teeth filed to sharpened fangs. 'Careful, little man, before this big bad wolf tears out your throat.'

+Leave the boy alone, Vintras,+ said a sharp-toothed voice from the augmitter mounted on Skálmöld's casket. **+He sees that you come to a pack-meet dressed for a funeral.+**

'Apologies, Moonsorrow,' said Vintras, backing off with a feral grin. 'I await your word.'

'Right, we're all here now, Skálmöld,' grunted Härkin, his exoskeleton

wheezing and clicking as he resumed his pacing. 'What is it you want from us?'

+You know what I want. Command. Luth is a spent force. His time is over. Mine is upon the Legio. You all know this.+

No one answered the Moonsorrow. Koskinen and Hyrdrith had expected this, but to hear it said out loud, so boldly before the rest of the Legio, was still a shock. Looking around the medicae-templum, Koskinen realised that no one wanted Skálmöld in command. The pack dynamic was a reflection of the alpha, and Skálmöld's cold heart would eventually come to dominate the engines under his command and turn them from cooperative hunters to vicious predators. Härkin looked appalled at Skálmöld's presumption, and even Vintras looked uneasy at this development, though he must surely have seen it coming.

'Princeps Luth has yet to wake,' said Härkin.

+And when he does, can anyone here say he will not dream of old wars and turn his guns on a pack brother once more?+

Koskinen wanted to speak in Luth's defence, but the Magos Biologis had found no cause for his waking nightmare and could offer no guarantees that such a psychotic break would not happen again. Skálmöld spoke nothing but the truth, but it still rankled Koskinen's sense of justice that the Reaver princeps was wresting pack leadership while the alpha could not defend his position.

'Command authority has to be granted by the Oldbloods,' said Princeps Härkin, in a last-ditch attempt to invoke Legio protocol.

+The Oldbloods are not here. We are. I am. The Wintersun turned his guns on a brother warrior. There is no greater crime against the pack. Why do you even argue, Ironwood? I am the Moonsorrow and you are not my equal.+

Härkin bowed in a clatter of exo-joints. 'You are senior pack, Moonsorrow.'

+Then the matter is done with,+ said Skálmöld. **+I am Alpha Princeps.+**

+No.+

Koskinen jumped at the sound issuing from the casket beside him. Princeps Arlo Luth floated to the glass, his bulbous, elongated skull still raw from the numerous invasive surgeries he had recently undergone. The cables that connected him to the Manifold were absent, and the threaded sockets in his chest and spine gaped like steel-edged wounds. Green lights flickered at the front of the casket, and Koskinen saw Hyrdrith withdraw a surreptitious data-plug.

+I am the Wintersun, and you are not *my* equal.+

***

The Valette Manifold station hung in the darkness of the system's edge like a patient arachnid waiting for unwary prey to become trapped in its web. Its bulbous central section was dark and glossy with ice, and numerous slender limbs extended from its gently rotating central hub: manipulator arms, auspex, surveyor equipment, monitoring augurs and psi-conduits. Though still hundreds of thousands of kilometres away, the *Speranza's* prow-mounted pict-feeds brought its image into perfect focus.

A reverent hush held sway on the *Speranza's* command deck. As the last place to have received word from Magos Telok, the Valette Manifold station was a holy place and memorial all in one. None of the gathered magi failed to recognise the significance in coming here before attempting to breach the Halo Scar.

Magos Azuramagelli maintained their course and monitored the gradual increase in engine power as work continued to repair the damaged plasma combustion chamber. The loss of so many of Saiixek's bondsmen had proved inconvenient, but with the addition of numerous work gangs of servitors from the drained refinery vessels, the expected dip in productivity and efficiency was proving to be less than the magos of engineering had feared. At the farthest edge of the deck, Linya Tychon and her father worked at an astrogation hub, manipulating a pair of four-dimensional maps.

Magos Blaylock kept station beside the command throne, processing the ship's inputs and allowing Kotov to maintain communion with the *Speranza*. The Ark Mechanicus was still skittish after the incident with the Titans, and required a light touch to keep its systems appeased. Much of Kotov's cognitive power was directed in healing the spiritual wounds done to the starship and regaining its unequivocal trust. Much of the situational knowledge stream he would process at a subconscious level, he was forced to delegate to his subordinates and learn second-hand.

'Any response to our binary hails yet?' asked Kotov.

'No, archmagos,' replied Blaylock, sifting through the accumulated data inloading from their scans of the darkened station. 'We continue to be rebuffed.'

'And its Manifold still won't accept communion?'

'It will not,' agreed Blaylock. 'It is most perplexing.'

Kotov took a moment to study the distant station, its mass a deeper dark against the prismatic stain of the Halo Scar beyond the corona of the system sun's light. He had studied the anomaly at the edge of the galaxy extensively, but to actually see it for the first time gave him a strange frisson of excitement and fear.

Emotions Kotov had thought long since consigned to his organic past.

The Tychons were collecting reams of data on the ugly phenomenon to better gauge a path through the gravitational tempests raging within its nebulous boundary. Their work was highly detailed, but the thousands of years of accumulated immatereology statistics within the Manifold station would greatly aid their cartographic equations. So far they had received nothing but static in response to their repeated attempts to persuade the station to exload its data to the *Speranza*.

Yet as fascinating as the Halo Scar's deformation of space-time was, Kotov kept finding his gaze drawn back to the Manifold station. Six hundred metres wide at its central bulge, and three hundred metres high, the station was a mote in the galactic wilderness, almost invisible in the darkness. Only faint starlight glinting from the ice on its hull provided an outline. Glittering drifts of reflective chips hung around the station like frozen snowflakes, but the source of these tiny pieces of orbital debris was a mystery.

And Kotov abhorred mysteries to which he knew he would find no answer.

Ghostly and dead, the station held true to its ancient orbit, a prisoner of gravity and physics.

Kotov's myriad senses, more than any unaugmented mortal could hope to understand or employ, were alert for any sign that there was anything or anyone alive on the Valette station. So far they had not given him any hope that he would find any of the designated crew alive aboard the station.

Yet for all that, Kotov was certain that there was something on that station that was looking back at them, watching them, studying them...

'Time to intercept?' he said, throwing off the ridiculously *organic* notion of being observed.

'Three hours, fifteen minutes, archmagos,' replied Azuramagelli, shifting his exo-body across the bridge to a second astrogation hub. Spindle-like manipulator arms extruded from the underside of his exo-armature body and drew out a physical keyboard.

'A problem, Azuramagelli?'

Two of Azuramagelli's brain jars swivelled in their mounts as he answered.

'Unknown,' replied Azuramagelli. 'Ever since we dropped out of the warp, the rear auspexes have been picking up an intermittent contact. Nothing I can fix upon, but it is curious.'

'What do you believe it to be? Another ship?'

'Most likely it is residual warp interference or a side-effect of our recent troubles,' said Azuramagelli, his manipulator arms fine-tuning the hazy auspex image before him. 'But, yes, I suppose it could be a ship.'

'Might it be the *Honour Blade*?'

'I do not believe so, though the presence of the Halo Scar on the far edge of the system is making accurate readings difficult. Perhaps with access to the primary astrogation hub I might obtain a clearer answer for you, archmagos.'

Kotov ignored the jibe at the Tychons and said, 'Keep watch on your ghost readings and inform me of any developments.'

Azuramagelli's brain jars turned away, and Kotov heard the armoured gate to the command deck slide down into the polished floor. He read the biometrics of Roboute Surcouf, and swivelled his command throne to face the rogue trader.

The man had answered Kotov's summons in a loose Naval storm coat, grey in colour, with discolouration where rank patches had been torn off. Dark trousers were tucked into knee-high brown boots, and in deference to his hosts and skitarii escort, he had left his thigh holster empty. Surcouf strolled onto the upper tier and took a moment to look around, his gaze lingering a fraction of a second longer on Mistress Tychon than any other aspect of the command deck.

Elevated heart rate, pupillary dilation, increased hormonal response.

Surely the captain did not harbour amorous thoughts towards a member of the Cult Mechanicus? The idea was ludicrous.

Kotov dismissed the man's foolishness and said, 'Welcome to the command deck, captain. Thank you for attending upon me.'

'Not a problem,' said Surcouf. 'I'll admit, I was looking forward to seeing the bridge of this ship of yours. Pavelka and Sylkwood wanted to come with me, but they're busy helping Magos Saiixek down in the engineering decks just now.'

'And what do you make of my command deck?' inquired Kotov. 'It is quite something, is it not?'

'I have to admit, it's a little underwhelming,' said Surcouf at last.

Kotov felt the rumble of the slighted ship within him, but quelled it as understanding dawned.

How easy it was to forget the limitations of mortals!

'Of course,' said Kotov. 'You are not noospherically enabled.'

'Not unless I'm plugged in.'

'I took it for granted that you could see as I see.'

'Never take *anything* for granted,' said Surcouf. 'That's when you start making mistakes.'

Irritated at being lectured to by a lesser mortal, Kotov made a complex haptic gesture, and a contoured bucket seat emerged from an irising deck plate beside the rogue trader. Surcouf swept aside the tails of his long coat and sat down, unspooling a thin length of insulated cable from the concave headrest. Taking a moment to find the socket under his hair at the nape of his neck, Surcouf slotted home the connector rods and engaged the communion clamp. His body twitched with the system shock of sudden inload, but he relaxed with the quick ease of an experienced spacefarer.

'Ah,' he said. 'Now I see. Yes, very impressive, archmagos.'

'We are almost at the Halo Scar,' said Kotov. 'Are you still confident you can guide us on the other side?'

'I have the data wafer with the astrogation data, don't I?'

'So you claim, but I have yet to see anything further on its veracity.'

'Then you'll just have to trust me,' said Surcouf, nodding towards the main cascade display. 'Is that the Manifold station?'

'It is indeed,' Kotov said.

'And that's the last place to have heard from Telok?'

'I assumed you would already know such information.'

'I've done my reading,' said Surcouf. 'I thought the Valette station was still functional.'

'That is our current understanding.'

Surcouf shook his head. 'That thing doesn't look like it's been functional in a long time.'

'You are correct,' said Kotov. 'All emanations indicate that the facility has gone into hibernation.'

'Do you know why?'

'Not yet, but we will soon.'

'It looks like a space hulk,' said Surcouf, making the sign of the aquila across his chest.

'Superstition, captain?'

'Common sense.'

'I assure you, there is nothing untoward aboard the Manifold station.'

'How can you be sure?'

'Our surveyors are picking up nothing to suggest any source of threat.'

Surcouf thought for a moment. 'Did the station have a crew?'

'No need for the past tense, captain,' said Kotov. 'The station is manned by a magos, five technomats, a troika of astropaths and a demi-cohort of servitors.'

'When was the last time anyone came out here to check they were still alive?'

'The last contact with the Valette station was eighty standard Terran

years ago, when Magos Paracelsus was routed from forge world Graia to relieve Magos Haephaestus as part of the routine cycle of command. Paracelsus exloaded his docket of arrival as scheduled.'

'I assume Haephaestus returned to Graia?'

Kotov hesitated before replying, once again checking the parity of information in his own repository with that of the *Speranza*.

'Unknown,' he said at last, loath to make such an admission. 'Records concerning the magi subsequent to their postings to Valette are incomplete.'

'Incomplete?' said Surcouf. 'You mean you don't know what happened to *any* of them?'

'In a galactic-wide arena of information it is not unknown for some data to be... lost in transit.'

'Emil would love to hear you say that,' said Surcouf with a wide grin. 'So, you don't know what happened to Haephaestus or the previous incumbents, and you don't know what's been happening since Paracelsus got here.'

'I begin to tire of your constant questioning of our data, Captain Surcouf,' said Kotov.

'And I'm beginning to tire of you keeping things from me,' retorted Surcouf. 'If there's a crew on that station, why aren't they responding? If everything's fine over there, why are you moving your escorts into an attack formation? You didn't think I'd notice that? *Please...*'

'Simply basic precautions, captain,' said Kotov.

'Let me give you a free piece of advice, archmagos,' said Surcouf. 'Never play Emil Nader at Knights and Knaves.'

'Clarification: I do not understand the relevance of your last remark.'

'Because you're a lousy liar, Lexell Kotov,' said Surcouf. 'You know as well as I do that something's not right with that station. Something is *very much out of the ordinary*, and you don't know what it is, do you?'

'The situation aboard the Manifold station is unknown at present,' agreed Kotov. 'But when I explore the station I am confident that logical answers will present themselves.'

'You're going to board that thing?' said Surcouf.

'I am an explorator,' said Kotov. 'It is what I do.'

'Rather you than me.'

'I assure you there is no danger.'

Surcouf looked back up at the screen, and the image of the patient arachnid returned to Kotov as the rogue trader made the sign of the aquila once again.

'I'd take those Black Templars with you,' said Surcouf. 'Just in case you're wrong.'

***

Despite the wholesale murder of thousands of bondsmen, very little changed in the routine of the men and women below decks. Fresh meat was skimmed from the other shifts, and the numbers in Abrehem, Hawke and Coyne's shift group were bulked out by cybernetics. Scores of heavily-muscled servitors joined their ranks, silent and glassy eyed as they carried out their orders without complaint and without thought of dissent.

Rumours of what had happened in the lower decks spread around the various shifts like a dose of the pox, as did the miracle of their small group's survival. Abrehem saw men and women looking at him strangely, and it took Hawke to point out to him that they were in awe of him. It had been his warning that had saved the four of them, and word had gone around that he was Machine-touched, a secret prophet of the Omnissiah who carried its blessing to the least of its servants.

Soon he began finding trinkets fashioned from scavenged junk, gifts of food or water and bac-sticks left by his bunk. At first he tried to refuse such offerings, but his every attempt to play down what he'd done in the reclamation chamber only seemed to enhance his reputation.

'But I'm not Machine-touched,' he complained to his companions one night as they sat in the crowded feeding hall and spooned yet more tasteless gruel into their soft-gummed mouths. Where before the only sounds in the giant chamber had been the slop of nutrient broth and the clatter of plastic spoons, now a low hubbub of reverent whispering bubbled just below the surface.

'How do you know?' asked Hawke. 'Only the truly divine deny their divinity. Isn't that what the Book of Thor says?'

Both Coyne and Abrehem gave Hawke a sidelong look. Even Crusha looked surprised.

'I didn't take you for a religious man, Hawke,' said Abrehem.

Hawke shrugged. 'I'm not normally one for prayers and the like, but it's always good to know who I need to holler for when I'm in trouble. You know, just in case they're listening. And I always liked the story of Sebastian Thor. He stood up to rich bully boys and started a landslide that toppled a High Lord. I got a soft spot for those kinds of stories.'

'It's more than a story,' said Coyne. 'It's scripture. It's got to be true.'

'Why? Because you read it in a book or some fat preacher told it to you when you were a little boy? Even if it did really happen, it was so long ago that it might as well be made up. You know, I used to love hearing the stories in the templum about the Emperor's armies conquering the galaxy and fighting their enemies with flaming boltguns and raw courage. I used to pretend I was a hero, and I'd run all over the scholam grounds with a wooden sword conquering it like I was Macharius or something.'

'I've seen him,' said Abrehem. 'In the processional at the Founding Fields there's a statue of Macharius and Lysander. No offence, Hawke, but you're too damn ugly to be a warmaster.'

'And you're no beautiful Sejanus,' grinned Hawke.

Abrehem forced a smile in agreement. Between them, they'd lost numerous teeth and their skin had a gritty, parchment-yellow texture to it. Abrehem's hair, his youthful pride and joy, had begun to fall out in lumps, so as a group they'd taken the decision to shave their scalps bare. If the Mechanicus wanted them to be identical drones, then that's what they would get.

'But that was when I was a boy,' continued Hawke. 'I used to think the Emperor and His sons were watching over us, but then I grew up and realised that there weren't nobody looking out for me. The only person that looks out for Hawke is Hawke.'

'Come on,' said Abrehem, pushing away his tray. 'Let's get a drink.'

'Best idea I've heard all day,' said Coyne, and the four of them rose from the table, heading for the cramped passageways that led to Hawke's concealed still. The decompression of the lower decks hadn't touched the strange chamber, and Hawke claimed it was a sign that the Omnissiah was happy for him to keep up production and make a tidy profit along the way.

Heads bowed, and Abrehem heard muttered prayers as they passed. Emaciated hands reached out to brush his coveralls as he went by, and he tried not to look at the men and women who stared at him with something he'd long ago forsaken.

Hope.

Thankfully, they passed out of the feeding hall and into the passageways that threaded the heavy bulkheads and myriad work-chambers of the engineering deck. Walls of black iron that dripped with hot oil and hissed with moist exhalations enfolded them. The gloom was a welcome respite from the stark glare of their work spaces. Hawke led the way, though he professed never to know the route to the still. Abrehem had long ago given up trying to memorise their route. It seemed to change every day, but no matter how many twists and turns they made, their steps always unerringly carried them to the arched chamber that looked more like a tomb the more they visited it.

'What the...?' said Hawke as he rounded the last corner.

They weren't the first to come here tonight.

Ismael de Roeven stood at the end of the hexagonal-tiled pathway that ended at the blocked-off wall covered with the obscured stencilling. The

servitor had his arm extended and his palm rested on the wall. Abrehem's optics registered a fleeting glimpse of hissing code from behind the wall, a whispering binary source that retreated the instant it became aware of Abrehem's scrutiny.

'What's he doing here?' wondered Coyne.

'Damned if I know,' answered Hawke. 'But I don't like it.'

'Ismael?' said Abrehem, approaching the servitor created from their former overseer. Over a third of their shift was now made up of cybernetics, and Abrehem had been absurdly relieved to find that Ismael had not perished in the venting of the lower decks. For another piece of home to have survived along with the four of them felt like an omen, but of what he wasn't so sure.

Coyne snapped his fingers in front of Ismael's eyes, but the servitor didn't react. Fat droplets fell from the pipework above and pattered in a drizzle from the top of his gleaming skull.

'It's like he's crying,' said Abrehem, wincing as he saw the concave impact damage in the plating covering the left side of the servitor's head. Ismael might have survived the trauma of explosive decompression, but he hadn't escaped it without injury.

'Servitors don't cry,' said Hawke, angry now. 'Come on, get him out of here.'

'He's not doing any harm,' said Abrehem.

'Yeah, but if someone notices he's missing and comes looking for him, they'll find all this.'

Abrehem nodded, accepting Hawke's logic. 'Fine,' he said. 'I'll get him back to the feeding hall.'

He reached up to lower the servitor's arm.

Ismael turned his head towards Abrehem.

His face was lined with black streaks of oil and lubricant, and Abrehem drew in a shocked breath as he saw an expression of confusion and despair etched there.

Ismael held out his arm, and the sub-dermal electoo shimmered to the surface of the skin.

'*Savickas...?*' he said.

Microcontent 15

Something clanged against the fuselage of the *Barisan*, and Hawkins tried not to imagine a piece of space-borne debris smashing through and killing them all. He'd heard the horror stories of fast-moving trans-atmospheric craft striking pieces of orbital debris and being torn apart in a heartbeat, and tried to push them from crowding his thoughts. It was all right for the Templars, locked in restraint harnesses and sealed in their heavy, self-sufficient plate armour. They'd survive decompression, but the sixteen men of the 71st wouldn't be so lucky.

Even in bulky hostile environment suits, the Cadian Guardsmen were too slight to be secured in the Thunderhawk's crew seats, and were forced to endure the flight holding onto heavy bulkheads, support stanchions and vacant harness buckles to keep from being thrown around the crew compartment. Penetrating the *Speranza's* neutron envelope made for a bumpy ride, and Hawkins felt his teeth rattling around his jaw as another rogue gravity wave slammed them to the side.

The riptide graviometric fields that surrounded the *Speranza* made it impossible to dock directly with the Valette Manifold station, so here they were riding the *Barisan* through the buffeting turbulence with Kul Gilad's Space Marines, Archmagos Kotov and his praetorian squad of five skitarii. Though Cadian officers were used to leading from the front, it surprised Hawkins that such a command ethic should be part of the Mechanicus mindset.

Metal clanging bounced along the Thunderhawk's topside and Hawkins instinctively ducked, as though expecting the roof to peel back like the top of a ration can.

'You all right, captain?' asked Lieutenant Rae, who seemed to be enjoying himself immensely.

'Damn, I hate aerial insertions,' he said. 'Leave that kind of stupidity to the Elysians. Give me a bouncing Chimera any day.'

'Aye, sir,' said Rae. 'I'll remind you of that next time we're charging into enemy fire in the back of *Zura's Lance*. I don't reckon there's any good way to put yourself in harm's way.'

'I suppose not,' said Hawkins, watching the battered display at the front of the compartment. The crackling screen relayed the pict-feed from the cockpit, and Hawkins saw the glossy, ice-slick bulge of the Manifold station drawing nearer, its multiple extended spars of metal reaching up and past the picter's field of view. Hawkins held tight to his stanchion as the pilot banked to avoid a particularly large panel of scorched metal. Starlight glinted from its surfaces, and Hawkins saw some kind of painted glyph – a grinning maw with two enormous tusks – but it spun away before he could be sure of what it was.

'Was that...?' said Rae.

'I think it was,' said Hawkins.

The hulking mass of the Manifold station slid to one side as the pilot brought them in side-on.

'Here we go,' said Hawkins as the sound of metal scraping on metal came through the fuselage, the groping of an automated docking clamp as it sought purchase on the side of the *Barisan*. The interior of the gunship changed in an instant. One minute the Space Marines were immobile, seated statues, the next they were up and arranged for deployment. Hawkins hadn't even noticed it happen. Their armour was big and bulky, even more so when you were crammed next to it in a fully laden gunship. The plates gave off a muted hum of power, and there was a faint suggestion of ozone and lapping powder.

One of the Space Marines looked down at him, the bulky warrior with a white laurel carved around the brow of his helm. Hawkins sketched him a quick salute. The Templar hesitated, then gave him a curt nod.

'Fight well, Guardsman,' said the warrior with clumsy camaraderie.

'That's the only way Cadians fight,' he replied as the light above the Thunderhawk's side door began flashing a warning amber. 'Wait, are you expecting to fight?'

'The Emperor's Champion always expects to fight,' said the warrior, loosening the straps holding his enormous sword fast to his shoulder.

Hissing plumes of equalising gases ribboned from the door seals, and

Hawkins felt his ears pop and the metal pins in his repaired shoulder tingle. The armoured panel slid back to reveal an umbilical with a steel decking floor and a ribbed plasflex corridor. At the end of the corridor was a frost-rimed door that dripped water that had last been liquid millions of years ago. The Space Marines moved along the umbilical in single file, though it was easily wide enough for three of them to stand abreast. They moved with short, economical strides, bolters held loosely at their hips.

Hawkins chopped his hand left and right, and dropped down into the umbilical, feeling it sway alarmingly underfoot. It had looked utterly steady when the Space Marines traversed it. With his rifle pulled in tight to his shoulder, Hawkins advanced along the umbilical with a squad of soldiers strung out behind him to either side.

He moved to the front of the umbilical, feeling the cold radiating from the bare black structure of the Manifold station. The ironwork was pocked with micro-impacts, and condensing air ghosted from the metal. A broad airlock barred entry to the station and a shielded housing concealed an oversized keypad and a number of input ports. Kul Gilad looked ready to tear the door from its housing, but Archmagos Kotov had decreed a less forceful entry.

The archmagos swept along the umbilical with his red cloak of interleaved scales billowing behind him. His automaton body was perfectly sculpted in crimson, like a templum statue come to life, and his steel hand gripped the hilt of his sheathed sword tightly. Behind a shimmering energy field, his soft features were sagging and jowly, like an old general who has spent too much time from the front line. Yet his eyes were those of a virgin Whiteshield when the las-rounds start flying.

'You can affect an entry?' asked Kul Gilad.

'I can,' said the archmagos, reaching out to touch the cold metal with his smooth black hand. Unprotected skin would have been stripped from his flesh, but Kotov gave a sigh of pleasure, as if he were touching the smooth curves of a loved one. Long seconds passed and a recessed panel slid up beside the door. Instantly, the Space Marines had their bolters levelled, and Hawkins was gratified to find that his own men's weapons weren't far behind them.

'This is the Valette Manifold station, sovereign property of the Adeptus Mechanicus,' said an artificially modulated voice. 'Present valid entry credentials or withdraw and await censure.'

The image on the pict screen was badly degraded and chopped with static, but was clearly a hooded tech-priest with a quartet of silver-lit optics.

'Is that a real person?' asked Hawkins, his finger tightening on the trigger housing of his lasrifle.

'Once,' said Kotov. 'It is a recording made a long time ago. An automated response to an unexpected attempt at entry.'

'Does that mean the station is aware of us now?' said Kul Gilad.

A light flickered behind Kotov's eyes. 'No, this is just a perimeter system, not the central data engine. The schemata for this station indicates that its core administrative functions were controlled by a heuristic bio-organic cybernetic intelligence.'

'A thinking machine?' said Kul Gilad.

'Certainly not,' said Kotov, the idea abhorrent. 'Simply a cogitating machine that could have its functions situationally enhanced with the addition of linked cerebral cortexes to its neuromatrix.'

'So this is an element of that?' said Hawkins.

'In the same way that your hand is a part of you, Captain Hawkins, but it is not *you*. Nor is it aware on any level of the greater whole of which it is part. In truth, such machines are rare now; their employment fell out of favour many centuries ago.'

'Why was that?' asked Hawkins.

'The machine's artificial neuromatrix often developed a reluctance to allow the linked cortexes to disengage and diminish its capacity. The tech-priests could not be unplugged without causing them irreparable mental damage. And if left connected too long, the gestalt machine entity developed aberrant psychological behaviour patterns.'

'You mean they went mad?'

'A simplistic way of putting it, but in essence, yes.'

'I'm thinking that's the kind of information that might have been worth including in the briefing dockets for this mission,' said Hawkins.

Kotov shook his head. 'There was no need. The Fabricator General issued a decree six hundred and fifty-six years ago stating that all such machines were to have their linking capacity deactivated. Only the most basic autonomic functions are permitted now.'

'So if we get this door open, will it rouse the station from hibernation?' asked the Reclusiarch.

'That rather depends on how we open it,' said Kotov, kneeling by the panel and sliding the shield to one side. A number of wires extended from his fingertips, inserting themselves into the sockets beside the keypad. Hawkins watched the archmagos at work, the fingers of his free hand dancing over the keypad, too fast to follow as he entered hundreds of numbers in an ever-expanding sequence.

'It appears the central data engine is still dormant,' said Kotov. 'It will remain so unless we make a more direct interference with the Manifold station's systems.'

'Can you get us in or not?' asked Sergeant Tanna, moving towards the door.

Kotov withdrew his digital dendrites and stood back with a satisfied smile.

'Welcome, Archmagos Lexell Kotov,' said the static-fringed image of the silver-eyed tech-priest.

A booming *clang* of heavy mag-locks disengaging sounded from deep inside the door, and it slid up into its housing. Dangling punch-card prayer strips attached to its base fluttered in the pressure differential, but it was clear there was atmosphere within the station. Stale and fusty, but breathable.

The Reclusiarch was first through the door, the vast bulk of his Terminator armour forcing him to angle his body. Tanna and the rest of the Space Marines went in after him, followed by Kotov and his retinue of combat-enhanced warriors. Hawkins stepped into the station, feeling a shiver of cold travel the length of his spine as his boots clanged on the metal grille floor.

The airlock vestibule was a vaulted antechamber with dulled stained-glass orison panels and hooded figures set within deep recesses in the bare metal walls: iron statues of tech-priests draped in icicles. A lumen-strip on the ceiling sparked and struggled to ignite, but succeeded only in flickering on and off at irregular intervals. Another pict screen burbled to life, and the familiar voice of the recorded tech-priest spoke once again.

'Welcome aboard the Valette Manifold station, Archmagos Kotov. How can we assist you today?'

'How does it know your name?' said Hawkins.

'I shed data like you shed skin,' said Kotov. 'Even a basic system like this can read my identity through my digital dendrites.'

'Welcome aboard the Valette Manifold station, Archmagos Kotov,' repeated the tech-priest. 'How can we assist you today?'

'I do not require your assistance,' said Kotov.

'Interrogative: do you require us to rouse the higher functions of the central data engine to facilitate your purpose in coming here?'

Kul Gilad shook his head and placed a finger to the lipless mouth of his skull helm.

'No,' said Kotov. 'That will not be necessary.'

'As you wish, archmagos,' said the crackling tech-priest before fading into the background static.

The skitarii lit their helmet lamps. The stark illumination threw sharply-defined shadows onto walls that were slick with defrosting ice.

'No one's been here in a very long time,' said Rae.

'Eighty years, to be precise, Lieutenant Rae,' said Kotov, moving on to the next door with Black Templars flanking him. Hawkins felt there was more to this emptiness than simply a lack of visitors: the station felt abandoned, like something broken and left to slowly decay. Droplets of moisture landed on his helmet, and slithered down his face. He wiped them away, and his hand came away streaked with black oil.

He flicked the oil away and said, 'Right, keep an eye on our rear. I want to make sure our exfiltration route isn't compromised if we need to get out of here in a hurry. I'll take Squad Creed, Rae, you take Kell. Watch your corners, check your sixes and keep a wary bloody eye out. I don't like this place, and I get the feeling it doesn't like us much either.'

Hawkins turned and followed the bobbing lumens of the skitarii.

The Manifold station's schemata indicated that its construction took the form of a central hub reserved for power generation, with a main access corridor that travelled the circumference of the station. Numerous laboratories, libraries and living quarters branched off this central corridor, with levels above and below reserved for personal research spaces, astropathic chambers and maintenance workshops. The airlock they had breached was in the bulbous central section, and the arched corridor beyond the airlock led them out onto the main access route around the station.

Six metres wide, with an arched ceiling and walls of black iron stamped with numerical codes and images of the cog-rimmed skull, it curved left and right into darkness. Hawkins spread his men against the walls, keeping his rifle and his eyes matched as they scanned the empty corridor. The only illumination came from the skitarii's suit lamps and the fading glow-globes hanging on slender cabling. The lights swayed gently in the freshly disturbed air, and the sound of distantly moving metal sighed along the corridor like far-off moaning.

A broken pict screen came to life on the wall. The silver-eyed tech-priest jumped and squalled through the static.

'Magos Kotov, may we assist you in navigating the Valette Manifold station?'

'Can you shut that damn thing up?' said Kul Gilad. 'Until we know what we're dealing with, I don't want to attract any more attention than necessary from this station's systems.'

Kotov nodded and bent to expose a maintenance panel beneath the pict screen. His digital dendrites writhed into the mass of winking lights, wires and exposed copper connectors.

'Magos Kotov, may we assist you in navigating the Valette Manifold station?' repeated the voice.

'No, and you are not to offer assistance again unless I specifically request it,' said Kotov, sealing the maintenance hatch behind him. The pict screen went dark, and Hawkins was thankful to see it power down. Each time a screen came to life, it felt like the station was *watching* them.

'This way,' said Kotov, gesturing to the left. 'In a hundred metres, there will be a set of access stairs that will allow us to ascend to the upper levels and the control deck.'

Kul Gilad nodded and moved on with the Emperor's Champion on his left and Sergeant Tanna on his right. Leaving Rae's men to secure the airlock vestibule, Hawkins led his squad after the Space Marines, alert for any signs of something amiss. Even through his padded environment suit, the hard air of the station seemed to leach the warmth from his bones. Shadows moved strangely and the light reflected harshly from frost-limned wall panels. Hawkins didn't like this place, and his Cadian instincts were telling him that something was very wrong.

He glanced over at a blank pict screen, its glass crazed by a powerful impact.

The screen flickered to life and Hawkins almost yelled in surprise, bringing his rifle around as battlefield-honed reflexes took over. He managed not to pull the trigger, and let out a shuddering breath as adrenaline dumped into his system.

The silver-eyed tech-priest stared at him, but didn't say anything.

Kotov appeared at Hawkins's side, kneeling before this screen's maintenance panel.

'What did you do?' demanded the archmagos.

'Nothing,' said Hawkins. 'It just came on by itself.'

'Did it say anything?'

Hawkins shook his head, and once again the archmagos deactivated the pict screen. In the silence that followed, Hawkins heard a squeal of metal from farther around the corridor. Before the sound had a chance to echo, seven Space Marine bolt weapons were instantly trained into the darkness.

'Douse those lights!' ordered Kul Gilad, and instantly the skitarii's lamps were snuffed out.

'Defensive posture,' ordered Hawkins, shouldering his rifle as he dropped to one knee. 'Squad Creed, watch ahead. Guardsman Manos, look for anything coming up behind us.'

The sounds came again, a thudding iron footfall and a scrape of metal on metal. Hawkins flipped down his helmet's visor and the hallway before him was suddenly splashed in a haze of emerald light, with his rifle's targeting reticule painting a bright smear on the curved wall ahead of him. A phantom shadow was thrown out on the

deck. Something was approaching from deeper within the station. He slipped his finger around his rifle's trigger as a shape emerged slowly from around the arcing corridor.

The figure was broad-shouldered and moved with a lurching groan of protesting servos. Its breathing was frothed and heavy, like a labouring beast of burden. Hawkins let the air out of his lungs as he saw an augmented servitor, dragging a mangled leg behind it. A sparking arm swung in a repeating circular motion. He eased his trigger finger free.

'It's just a servitor,' said Kotov. 'Stand your men down, Reclusiarch.'

The guns of the Black Templars didn't waver a millimetre, and Hawkins wasn't about to lower his rifle until they did. He kept the aiming reticule centred over the servitor's skull, a thick hunk of bone and flesh that seemed to squat on the servitor's shoulders without a neck. It was hard to make out much detail through the blurred nightsight visor, but there seemed to be something fundamentally *wrong* with the proportions of the servitor's skull.

'Put it down, Tanna,' said Kul Gilad.

'No!' cried Kotov, but the ignition of a bolter shell filled the corridor with noise as Tanna's round blew the top of the servitor's skull clear, leaving only a sloshing, blood-filled basin of pulped brain matter. The cybernetic took half a dozen more steps before its stunted physiology finally accepted that it was dead and it collapsed to the deck. Its sparking leg twitched and spasmed, still trying to move its body forwards, and the oversized arm fizzed and whined as it attempted to recreate the motions it had been making while its bearer was upright.

Kotov and his skitarii swept down the corridor towards the downed servitor.

'Do not approach it, archmagos,' warned Kul Gilad.

'Your sergeant killed it, Reclusiarch,' snapped Kotov. 'Servitors may be physically resistant and feel no pain, but even they struggle to be a threat without a head.'

'That's not a servitor,' said Kul Gilad.

Hawkins waved two of his men to come forwards with him, following the Black Templars as they escorted Archmagos Kotov towards the downed servitor.

'Omnissiah's bones,' hissed Kotov, making a penitent symbol of the Cog Mechanicus over his chest. 'What has happened here?'

At first, Hawkins wasn't sure why Kotov was reacting so badly, but then he saw the shreds of skin that flapped loose on the remains of the servitor's skull. Kul Gilad knelt beside the creature and took hold of a wide strip of waxen skin. He peeled it back, revealing muscle, sinew and organic tissue, exactly as would be expected

But Hawkins's eyes widened as he finally grasped the nature of the creature's physiognomy: the jutting lower jaw and protruding tusks, the battered porcine snout. Hawkins had to fight the ingrained urge to draw his pistol and put a pair of bolt-rounds in its chest to make sure it was dead.

The servitor was an ork.

Flensed of its green hide and clothed in a sutured sheath of human skin, but still recognisably a greenskin marauder.

Kotov knelt beside the ork and placed a hand on its mechanised parts. Writhing nests of cables extruded from each of his hands and fixed themselves to its augmetic leg and arm.

'God of All Machines, in the name of the Originator, the Scion and the Motive Force, release these spirits from the blasphemy into which they have been bound. Free them to fly the golden light to your care, and renew them in your all-knowing wisdom to return to us. In your mercy, make it so.'

'What was that?' snarled Tanna. 'You feel pity for this thing?'

'For the machines grafted to this unclean monster's flesh,' said Kotov, turning and nodding to one of the skitarii, who drew a set of cutting tools from his utility pack and bent to the grisly task of removing the machine parts from the ork's body.

'I'm guessing it's not normal to make servitors from greenskins,' said Hawkins, watching as the skitarii fired up a shielded plasma-cutter and began stripping back the flesh around the graft. A fungal stink of rotten vegetable matter and scorched skin filled the corridor. Hawkins felt himself gag through the filter of his rebreather.

'What has been happening here, archmagos?' demanded Kul Gilad.

'Trust me, Reclusiarch, I would know that too,' said Kotov. 'It is an abomination to graft blessed machines to such non-human savages.'

Hawkins heard the distant rumble of something powerful coming to life deep within the station. Lights flickered on along the curve of the walls and a hum of activating machinery rose from beneath the metal grilles of the deck plates.

'I think the station's waking up,' he said.

'This creature's destruction has alerted the system core to our presence,' agreed Kotov. 'We should proceed with all speed to the central command deck. The station may now perceive us as attackers.'

As if to ram that point home, an armoured blast containment shutter hammered down behind them, cutting off the route back to the airlock vestibule. Dull thuds of metal slamming together told Hawkins that a number of similar shutters were sealing off entire areas of the station from one another. Instantly, Hawkins's ear filled with

squalling bursts of shrieking static, and he wrenched the vox-bead out with a grunt of pain.

'Vox is down,' he called.

'Prepare for battle,' said Kul Gilad. 'Kotov, open that shutter. I'll not be cut off from the *Barisan*.'

Kotov shook his head. 'The core systems are reviving, Reclusiarch. Only the ranking magos has authority to override the blast containment system.'

'You are an archmagos of the Adeptus Mechanicus,' snarled Kul Gilad, pushing Kotov towards the blast shutter. 'Assert *your* authority and get that door open.'

Before Kotov could move, another pair of pict screens fuzzed to life, each bearing the image of the tech-priest with the silver optics. A gabble of binaric anger spat from them, and the mirror images of the tech-priest looked up, the gleaming light of their optics narrowing to focused points.

'You have attacked our servants,' said the tech-priest, shaking his head in disappointment. 'We cannot allow that while we still have need of them.'

'That's not a recording, is it?' said Hawkins.

'No,' replied Kotov. 'I do not believe it is.'

In the lower reaches of the Manifold station, a thermal generator spooled up with an ultra-rapid start cycle, utilising a series of linked machines that encircled the station's inner circumference. Each of these linked machines had been developed from technology designed to rouse the plasma reactors of Battle Titans to full readiness in the shortest time possible. An almost complete STC discovered by Magos Phlogiston less than half a millennium ago had described the construction of such 'kick-starters', but its missing fragments had contained the information required to prevent such devices from driving their reactors into uncontrolled critical mass in a matter of seconds. Thus the designs were archived instead of being put into production.

The Valette kick-starters bore all the hallmarks of Phlogiston's recovered STC, but were fitted with a series of inhibitors built to a design that no analyticae would find in any forge world's data repositories or even the most comprehensive databases of Olympus Mons. Only one son of Mars had the nous to craft such devices, and he had destroyed every trace of their design before leaving the bounds of galactic space.

Within ninety seconds of Tanna's bolter shot, the power systems for the Valette Manifold station were operating at full efficiency. The fierce thermal reserve coursed around the upper and lower reaches of the

station with virtually no heat loss via a series of ultra-insulated pipes that threaded the walls, floors and ceilings like a circulatory system.

In vaulted chambers where the skeleton crew of Adeptus Mechanicus tech-priests and servitors had once toiled in service to the Machine-God, power now flowed for a very different purpose. In every laboratory, library and workshop, the temperatures within three hundred fluid-filled cryo-caskets rose as their occupants were roused from deep slumber. Controlled current fired through augmented synapses, warmed super-efficient blood pumped through flexing veins, and stimulated stratified layers of deep muscle tissue.

Billowing clouds of chill air sighed from the three hundred caskets as icy fluid was drained and vented from their upper tiers in freezing crystalline jets. Glass doors opened and dripping figures encased in webs of copper cabling and plastic tubes took their first natural breaths in fifty years.

In every revivification space, a pict screen came to life and the silver-eyed tech-priest appeared.

'More intruders have come,' said the tech-priest in a voice that was an unnatural amalgam of machine cadences and overlapping flesh tones.

'Orders?' grunted one of the awoken sleepers, its cranium encased in synaptic enhancers and its neural pathways surgically altered to allow it a measure of autonomy.

'Kill the warriors,' said the tech-priest. 'Bring us the Mechanicus personnel alive.'

Hawkins could feel his heartbeat thudding through the heavy stock of his lasgun. Despite the cold, beads of sweat formed on his brow and he fought the urge to lift his visor to wipe them clear. The corridor was brightly lit now, the shadows banished, but strangely that didn't make him feel any better. The station was rousing further with every passing second, with glowing bulbs kept behind wire cages flashing as though some emergency was imminent. Burbling streams of binary issued from speaker-horns mounted on the ceiling, but what message they imparted was a mystery to him. The vox was still down, and he'd been unable to raise Rae's squad or anyone back on the *Speranza*.

He and his men were arranged in the cover of ironwork buttresses, their lasguns aimed unswervingly down the corridor, each man ready to fill his assigned fire sector with a slew of carefully placed shots. The Black Templars hadn't moved since the first signs of the station's reawakening, braced like immovable statues with their weapons locked at their hips.

Kotov worked at a panel to the side of the blast shutter, but the string of binaric curses and bursts of sparks told Hawkins that he was having little success. Fighting with your back to something solid was all well and good when you were defending a static position, but when it cut you off from your supporting forces and your only way out, it was something else entirely.

Hawkins slid from cover and drew level with Kul Gilad.

'We can't stay here,' he said.

'It is a good position,' said the Reclusiarch. 'Enemy forces cannot outflank us.'

'Are you sure?' said Hawkins. 'Kotov can't open that door, but that damn magos with the silver eyes certainly can. Without any line of retreat, we're as good as dead if this fight goes against us.'

'To admit defeat is to blaspheme against the Emperor,' said Kul Gilad.

'Really? Because I seem to remember you saying something about defeat always being possible and how recognising that makes you a great warrior.'

'I said it makes a man fight with heart.'

'Yeah, well no matter how much heart we have, this position reeks of a last stand, and that's something Cadian officers prefer to avoid wherever possible. I know you Space Marines like your glory and heroics, but I'd rather live through the next hour if that's all the same.'

Kul Gilad turned to him, and the red eye-lenses of his helm fixed him with their steely glare. For a moment, he thought the Reclusiarch might strike him down for his temerity, but the moment passed and the giant Space Marine slowly nodded his skull-faced helm.

'You are right,' said Kul Gilad. 'We will take the fight to the enemy.'

'Keep moving forwards,' said Hawkins. 'That's the Cadian way of doing things.'

The Terminator-clad Reclusiarch turned to Kotov and said, 'Arch-magos, forget the shutter, we are moving on to the central command deck as you suggested. Whatever is at the heart of this, we will meet it on *our* terms.'

Kotov nodded and withdrew his digital dendrites from the door panel.

'The door will not open anyway,' said Kotov in disgust. 'I have status and protocol on my side, but the machines do not heed me. They are enslaved to the will of something inhuman and rebuff every signifier of my exalted rank.'

'No matter,' said Kul Gilad. 'The time for subtlety is over.'

'Good thing too,' said Hawkins. 'I was never very good at subtle.'

Microcontent 16

With the Black Templars in the centre, and the Cadians and skitarii on the flanks, the boarders moved off down the corridor at speed, and it only took a few moments for the wisdom of that choice to become evident. The blast containment shutter that had thwarted Archmagos Kotov withdrew into the ceiling with a rumble of machined servos.

A host of heavily muscled servitors crafted from the same hideous form as the one Tanna had killed stood revealed. They were unmistakably orks, but with human skin grafted to their oversized bulk. The effect was sickening and terrifying at the same time. Like malformed ogryns, the orkish servitors were armed with a varied collection of energised blades, crackling prods and heavy mauls. To Hawkins's lasting regret, they didn't move like servitors, but with the relentless, simian gait of their savage species.

'Move faster,' ordered Kul Gilad. 'We need to reach the upper levels. Archmagos, how far away are those stairs to the upper decks?'

'Fifty-two metres,' said Kotov. 'This way!'

The Black Templars marched backwards in perfect unison, firing a thunderous volley of bolter fire back down the corridor. The mass-reactives barely had time to arm before detonating within the hard flesh of the greenskin servitors. Explosions of meat and bone erupted across the front rank of enemies, gaping wounds that would reduce a mortal body to bone fragments and vaporised blood, but which

only staggered the robust physiology of the greenskins. A handful fell, but the rest came on without heed of their losses. Ork resilience and servitor immunity from pain was combining to make these enemies near impossible to put down unless taken apart. Cadian and skitarii fire augmented the shooting of the Space Marines, but it was the mass-reactives that were doing the bulk of the killing.

Moving back to a better shooting position, Hawkins fired a three-round burst at the nearest enemy, a brute with an iron-encased skull and a series of hideous surgical sutures zig-zagging their way across its thick features. His shots all struck home, burning through the centre mass without effect. Another deafening roar of bolter fire slammed the servitors, blowing the limbs from more of them. Hawkins shifted his aim, took a breath and squeezed the trigger twice.

His first shot punched through the nasal cavity of the ork, the second vaporised its eyeball and cored through its skull to the brain cavity. The hunk of organic matter that animated the ork cooked to burned meat in the enclosed vault of its cranium, and the cybernetic abomination dropped without a sound as its brain functions were sheared.

'And stay down!' shouted Hawkins, sighting at another servitor; one with a set of enormous bolt-cutting shears that could lop off a limb or slice through a neck with equal ease. Blasts of bolter fire threw off his aim, and his shots burned chunks of flesh from the ork's head and left its jawbone hanging loose.

The orks were dangerously close now, almost close enough to bring their lethal tools to bear.

'Back,' said Hawkins as a whipping tracery of white-hot fire lashed the walls of the corridor with a thunderclap of electrical discharge. The overpressure hurled Hawkins to the ground. He rolled and saw a servitor with an implanted static-charger unleash another blast from its ad-hoc weapon. A pair of skitarii screamed as thousands of volts burned them alive inside their armour.

The lashing line of blue light zig-zagged over the width of the corridor, arcing across to one of the Space Marines. The warrior dropped to his knees, convulsing as his nervous system went into spasm and his skin fused with the inner surfaces of his warplate. The powerful energies writhed like an angry snake, catching two of Hawkins's men and ripping them apart in an explosion of boiling blood and flashburned organs.

'No!' yelled Hawkins, scrambling to his feet and sighting at the servitor's slack features.

A flurry of bolter shells struck the servitor and tore the weapon arm from its body in a detonating flurry of bone and machine parts. A second burst tore its head off at the neck and a third opened it up from sternum to groin. Kul Gilad abandoned his steady retreat and advanced towards the servitors, his gauntlet-mounted weapon chugging out explosive round after explosive round. His Terminator armour made him mighty, and he struck the servitors like a wrecking ball. The Reclusiarch's enormous power fist swept out and where it struck, the orks were pulped like blood-filled bags or clubbed into bent and broken shapes that couldn't possibly live.

The Black Templars fought at his side, his inspirational slaughter driving their own aggression and skill. Chainswords tore open orks sheathed in human skin, and bolt pistols blew out the exposed organs and bones. The Emperor's Champion waded through the servitors, his monstrous black sword cleaving orkflesh with every strike. A cybernetic with a roaring cutting saw came at him, but the champion ducked beneath the weapon and brought his blade up to shear its arms away at the elbows. His return blow split its skull, and a spinning follow-on move sliced the legs out from an ork snapping at him with an energised cable cutter.

'Reclusiarch!' shouted Kotov. 'More of them behind us!'

Hawkins turned to see yet more servitors coming from farther back along the corridor, two dozen at least. Like the ones Kul Gilad and the Black Templars fought, they were a hideous confection of human skin and ork physiology married to Mechanicus technology. Worse, these ones were armed with what looked like actual weapons. Metallic bangs echoed behind them as an advancing servitor triggered its implanted riveter. Hawkins ducked as a clanging series of hot bolts smashed into the wall beside him, some ricocheting down the corridor, some embedding in the plating with a hiss of red-hot metal.

Ten metres in front of the servitors, he saw the entrance to the stairwell, a circular iris door set within a cog and apparently locked open by rusted bearings. The steady light of functioning glow-globes spilled down from above, and no door had ever looked so inviting.

'Cadians, firing line!' he yelled, turning and running for the centre of the corridor at the entrance to the upper levels. His remaining Guardsmen ran with him, dropping to one knee beside him as he brought his rifle up to his shoulder. 'We take them down one at a time, lads. We'll start with that big bastard with the riveter! Fire!'

Collimated las-fire stabbed out from the Cadian rifles, and the ork servitor slumped to its knees with half its skull blasted away. Its hull-repair gun fired in the creature's death spasms, hammering a line of hot rivets into the deck plates and blasting the kneecap from the cybernetic next to it. A rippling salvo of shot-cannon, lascarbine and hellgun fire slashed overhead, and Hawkins risked a glance over his shoulder to see Kotov's skitarii adding the fire of their more esoteric weapons to the fusillade. The archmagos himself fired a long-barrelled pistol of ornamented brass that sent bolts of searing plasma into the advancing hordes.

'Right, the ork with the las-cutter next,' ordered Hawkins with more calm than he felt.

The servitor dropped with multiple lasburns searing its neck open and a pressurised squirt of blood sprayed over the walls. A second ork with a hull-plate repair cannon opened fire and one of Hawkins's men grunted as a cylindrical void of flesh and bone was punched through the centre of his chest. The Guardsman slumped, but Hawkins didn't dare stop firing to see if there was hope of saving him.

'We can't go on like this,' Hawkins shouted to Kotov. 'We need to get up those stairs.'

Kotov nodded and turned back to where the Black Templars were slaying the hideous cybernetics. Though they wreaked a fearsome slaughter, they had suffered loss too. The Space Marine felled by the static-charger lay unmoving and another of their number fought with only one arm, the other severed cleanly by a set of power shears. Many others bore burn scars or sported bloody gouges in their plate where energised edges driven by ork strength had cut them open. They fought a steady retreat, forced back by simple weight of numbers and brute strength.

In a one on one fight, the ork servitors would be no match for the Black Templars, but they were six against a never-ending tide.

'Kul Gilad!' boomed Kotov, his voice augmented to deafening levels. 'We must leave. Now!'

The Reclusiarch gave no obvious acknowledgement of the archmagos's words, but as he punched his fist through a servitor's chest, he took a backward step, and his warriors came with him. The Emperor's Champion was the last to disengage, buying time for his brethren with a devastating sweep of his sword.

'Go for the stairs,' said Kotov, turning back to Hawkins. 'We will cover you.'

Hawkins nodded and ran hunched over towards the open iris, firing from the hip as he went. The four other Cadians ran with him, piling through the door as Hawkins fired a last stream of las-fire on full auto. Another servitor went down as his powercell blinked empty. He darted into the cover of the door edges and snapped the charge pack from the breech before expertly swapping it for another. His men were already supplying covering fire for the archmagos by the time the cell engaged.

Kotov's skitarii leapt through the circular door and moved up the stairs, guns aimed at the glowing rectangle of light at the top. The archmagos knelt beside the door controls and extended his digital dendrites into the input ports.

'Can you close it?' shouted Hawkins over the din of bolter rounds and las discharges.

'I certainly hope so,' said Kotov, and bent to his work.

Cold air, a whiff of disinfectant and the soft gurgling of fluids sounded from above, putting Hawkins in mind of a medicae bay, but one that had likely been perverted to a darker purpose. He leaned out through the door and fired into the approaching servitors. He blew an implanted drill from the shoulder of a particularly fearsome servitor, but it kept coming despite the loss.

Kul Gilad and the Templars were withdrawing in good order, the one-armed warrior dragging the fallen Space Marine while his brothers marched in lockstep towards the irised door. The wounded Space Marine came through first, followed by the youngster that had fought Dahan. Tanna came next, then the sword-wielding Emperor's Champion. Lastly came Kul Gilad, the Reclusiarch's surplice stiff with blood and lubricants from the cybernetics he'd killed. His powered gauntlet shed droplets of heated blood and a plume of acrid propellant smoke issued from his storm bolter.

'Hurry!' shouted Hawkins as the implacable wave of numberless servitors closed on the stubbornly open door. Sparks flashed from the panel as Kotov's dendrites flexed and wrestled with the enslaved machine-spirit of the lock.

'And those that are exalted in the eyes of Mars shall be lauded, even by the spirits of the lowliest machine,' barked Kotov with a complementary burst of aggravated binary. The door mechanism hissed in irritation and rusted sheets of sharpened metal began irising shut.

An ork cybernetic appeared at the door and its colossal clamp-arm grabbed Hawkins by the front of his flak vest, dragging him back through the door. Kul Gilad snatched at Hawkins's shoulder and his grip was like a Sentinel's power lifter. The storm bolter unloaded into the servitor's face, and the irising door sliced cleanly through the ork's arm as it fell back. Hawkins collapsed onto the bottom step, nearly deafened by the close-range blast of the Reclusiarch's gunfire. He shook off the disorientation and prised loose the severed limb from his armour as the ork's blood pumped from the stump and into his lap.

'Thank you,' he said, dropping the arm by the door as a series of booming impacts deformed the metal. Sparks and a glowing spot of light appeared at the top of the door as the servitors brought cutting tools, drills and heavy power hammers to bear.

'Thank me later,' said Kul Gilad. 'We need to keep moving.'

Hawkins nodded and scrambled up the stairs after the skitarii and Black Templars.

The room at the top of the stairs was indeed a medicae bay, one that had been created by the simple expediency of knocking down the partitioning walls that had previously divided the space into numerous workshops and laboratories. Bright lumen-strips kept the entire bay well lit, and even Hawkins's limited understanding could tell that the entire level was given over to augmetics.

A score of surgical slabs were laid out with geometric precision and at least a dozen had bodies stretched out on them: orks lying supine and kept immobile by adamantium fetters and copious amounts of somnolicts. Data screens suspended at the head of each occupied slab flickered with biometric readings: slowed heartbeats, lowered blood pressure and dormant brain activity.

Hissing machines that resembled brass spiders hung from the ceiling on a host of chains, pneumatic cables and gurgling feed tubes as they performed major-level augmetic work on the greenskins. Clicking, clacking armatures with drills, scalpels, saws and laser-cauterisers, nerve splicers and bone-melders worked to amputate limbs, remove redundant organs from body cavities and otherwise prepare the host bodies for nerve grafts and replacement body parts.

Overhead cradles transported bionic limbs, organs and cranial hoods for implantation, like an automated manufactorum producing armoured vehicles on an assembly line. The hanging spider-machines attached the new parts with relentless machine efficiency, each attachment accompanied by a tinny burst of recorded binaric chanting and a puff of incense vapour from an inbuilt atomiser.

Rows of fluid-filled vats ran the length of the chamber, milky and opaque, and stinking of preservative fluids. A number of chrome-plated servo-skulls scooted and zipped through the air with trailing lengths of parchment dangling from their mandible calipers. Three of the walls were obscured by pale curtains that hung from the high ceiling like the scenery backdrop of a Theatrica Imperialis playhouse. Fluid drizzled down the curtains in a constant stream, dripping from the fringed bottom into collection reservoirs, where it was drained away to destinations unknown. It was impossible to tell what purpose these curtains served, and Hawkins led his Guardsmen over to the nearest, intending to check for servitors lurking behind in ambush.

'To render the flesh of the xenos into a servitor is an abomination,' hissed Kotov as he took in the full horror of the work being carried out by the transmogrification machines. 'Only the idealised human form may be so blessed. It is unholy... No adept of the Mechanicus would ever dare sanction such techno-heresy.'

'Then who did this?' demanded Kul Gilad.

'Something degenerate has taken control of this Manifold station, Reclusiarch. I desire to know exactly what that is as much as you.'

'No,' said Kul Gilad, directing his warriors forwards. 'I care nothing for what has done this. I only want to kill it.'

The Black Templars made their way methodically through the room, and the rotten plant-matter stink of ork blood filled the medicae as they killed the recumbent greenskins with swift thrusts of chainswords to throats. The data screens above each slab shrilled as each partially transmogrified ork was slain, and warning alarms chimed throughout the medicae. The servo-skulls descended to hover above each of the dead cybernetic hosts, a chattering stream of angry machine language burbling from the augmitters implanted in laser-cut fontanelles.

Hawkins reached the softly swaying curtain and pulled it aside. The curtain was smooth and flexible, and even through the tough weave of his gloves Hawkins could feel a dreadfully familiar texture.

'Throne of Terra,' he said, backing away from the monstrous curtain, craning his neck to fully appreciate the nightmarish scale of it. 'It's skin... All of it, it's human skin.'

Kotov broke off from his remonstrations with Kul Gilad and approached the swaying curtain of skin, taking hold of it and rubbing it between his metallic fingers.

'Vat-fresh synth-skin,' he said. 'Ideal for burn victims or those in need of reconstructive surgeries. It is not normally grown in such quantities, but the quality is excellent.'

Hawkins suppressed an involuntary shudder at the thought of these disembodied acres of human skin. That it had been grown and not cut from living bodies didn't make it easier to take that there was enough suspended skin to clothe hundreds more of these cybernetics. Why anyone would want to skin the hide from orks and replace it with human skin was a mystery to which Hawkins wasn't sure he wanted an answer.

'We need to get out of here,' he said, nauseating fear uncoiling in his gut. 'Now. Where's the way out? There has to be a way to the command deck.'

Kotov nodded and said, 'Indeed there should.'

'What do you mean, "should"?' said Hawkins. 'Is there or isn't there?'

'The station schemata indicate that there should be numerous dividing partitions on this level, together with an elevating platform to the upper deck, but as you can see much has been altered since those plans were drawn.'

'Then we don't have a way out?'

'I shall endeavour to locate an alternate route to the upper deck,' said Kotov.

Hawkins took a deep breath, hearing fresh impacts below as the servitor host increased their pressure on the door. With the myriad cutting tools and bludgeoning weapons at their disposal, it wouldn't take long for those unnatural monsters to get in.

'Can't we teleport back to the *Speranza*?' he asked. 'You have that technology, don't you?'

'If we could have done that, do you not think I might have suggested it before now, captain?' said Kotov. 'The same interference that is blocking the vox makes such a mode of transportation impossible. In the absence of such an escape route, might I suggest you join the Templars in rendering this location more defensible?'

Hawkins nodded, ashamed he had let his disgust at the curtains of skin blind him to the current tactical environment. He quickly directed his men to assist the skitarii and Templars in shifting heavy gurneys and banks of medicae equipment, creating a number of barricades to provide interlocking fields of fire. Storage crates, chairs, tables and workbenches were thrown down the stairs to impede the servitors, while Archmagos Kotov worked to access the Manifold station's systems in an attempt to gain a better understanding of this abnormal situation.

A resounding *clang* of metal told them that the door to the medicae had been breached. The Templars took position at the top of the stairs, their bolters aimed downwards. Hawkins and his Cadians took position at the barricades to the left of the door, while the skitarii took the right. If the advance of the servitors proved unstoppable, the Templars would retreat to a barricade in the centre of the chamber, letting the enemy walk into a killing ground of enfilading fire.

Hawkins took position with his Guardsmen, Ollert, Stennz, Paulan and Manos. Good soldiers all, who deserved better than this.

'When those bastards get up here, and they will, pour everything you've got into them,' he said.

The Guardsmen nodded, and Hawkins rested his lasrifle on the lip

of an upturned workbench. Kul Gilad stood at the top of the stairs, virtually filling the space there, with two of his warriors at either edge of the opening; one kneeling, one standing. Hawkins heard the clatter of servitors breaking through the furniture and debris they'd thrown down the stairs, and knew it wouldn't be long before the dying started.

The data screens above the corpses on the slabs flickered as they switched from displaying the whining straight lines of dead bodies to the loathsome tech-priest with the gleaming silver optics.

'You are all going to die here,' said a dozen representations of the tech-priest. 'Your bodies will be harvested and used to replace those you have damaged.'

'I'm going to shut that bastard up,' snapped Hawkins, aiming his rifle at the nearest screen.

The tech-priest on the screens turned to face him.

'You should save your munitions,' he advised. 'You're going to need them.'

Kul Gilad took the first kill of this second wave of fighting. His storm bolter cratered the skull of the first servitor to emerge onto the stairs, sending it crashing back down and toppling the two behind it. Hawkins felt the colossal pressure of the bolter fire and smelled the biting stink of propellant as the gunsmoke accumulated in the medicae facility. The full weight of the Templars' fire filled the stairwell with explosive death, mass-reactives detonating skulls and blowing open ribcages with every shot.

Hawkins had no idea how many servitors were dead, but it only took a few minutes for the Templars to exhaust their ammunition to the point where they were forced to fall back. Without the continuous barrage keeping them at bay, the ork servitors easily pushed through the debris and bodies choking the stairs.

Hawkins heard their heavy footfalls and pressed the stock of his rifle into his shoulder.

'Head shots where you can,' he said. 'Hit them in the eyes or try and take out any cranial augmetics. Make every shot count.'

The four Guardsmen nodded and Hawkins said, 'For Cadia and for honour.'

'Or the Eye take us,' responded the Guardsmen.

The first servitor reached the top of the stairs, and it was Archmagos Kotov who took the first kill. A pencil-thin beam of retina-searing white light speared from his pistol and burst the cybernetic's head apart in a fountain of steaming blood. It toppled forwards, its augmetic legs still scrabbling at the floor as another came after it. The skitarii opened fire next, pummelling the creature with energy beams and solid rounds. Its perforated corpse fell beside the first servitor.

Hawkins's Guardsmen took their shots at the third cybernetic as it climbed over the bodies ahead of it. Hawkins's shot blew out its lower jaw, while Manos removed the lid of its skull with a shot through its fleshy ear canal. Impact shock caused Paulan to miss, and Ollert's shot took the servitor behind in the throat. Blood sheeted down its chest, but the creature kept coming. Two more pushed in behind it and a cybernetic with a hissing flame unit swept its weapon around with a *whoosh* of igniting fuel.

'Down!' cried Hawkins as a rolling blast wave of flaming promethium washed over them. He felt the heat scorch his armour and bit back a cry of pain as a red-hot metal fastening clip pressed against his undershirt and burned the skin. Paulan screamed as he was engulfed by the flames, the intense heat melting the skin from his bones and suffocating his cries as the air in his lungs was sucked out. He fell beside Stennz, who frantically tried to beat out the flames with her hands.

'Leave him!' shouted Hawkins. 'He's gone!'

Ollert rolled upright and levelled his rifle at the flamer servitor, and was instantly hurled back as a high-velocity rivet blew out the back of his helmet. Stennz kept low as the chugging barrage hammered their cover, leaving scores of mushroom-shaped depressions on the underside of the workbench. Manos gathered up Ollert's powercells and tossed one each to Hawkins and Stennz.

An answering stream of gunfire from across the medicae bay silenced the rivet gunner, and Hawkins, Stennz and Manos rose to firing positions. Flames still licked at the workbench, and runnels of black smoke fogged the air. Half a dozen ork cybernetics were in the medicae chamber now, advancing with mechanistic aggression. Hawkins and Manos concentrated their fire on the flamer servitor, and succeeded in putting it down with a concentrated burst of full auto that emptied both their powercells. Stennz fared better, her shots fusing the metal skullcap of another rivet gunner and causing it to lock up like a statue.

More servitors pushed into the room, and even over the raucous clamour of gunfire, Hawkins could hear the grating metallic laughter of the silver-eyed tech-priest. He ducked back into cover to replace his spent powercell.

'Last one,' said Manos. 'I said we should have brought grenades.'

'Onto a pressurised space station?' replied Hawkins, fishing out his last charge pack. 'No thanks.'

'One spare,' said Stennz. 'Who wants it?'

'You keep it,' said Hawkins. 'You're the best shot.'

Stennz nodded and slapped the powercell home.

All three Cadians took up firing positions, and prepared to make their last shots count.

The skitarii were in full retreat, their makeshift barricade smashed to broken spars of twisted metal by the attentions of a pneumatic hammer in the hands of a brutish ork servitor a full head and shoulders taller than the others. Searing arcs of crackling energy chased them and only programmed self-sacrifice kept Archmagos Kotov alive as two of his warriors hurled themselves in the path of the killing whip of electro-fire. Their bodies burst into flames and were ashes in seconds as the hammer-wielding ork strode towards the survivors.

'Put that one down,' said Hawkins, but before he could fire, Kul Gilad charged the monstrous cybernetic creature. The ork swung the energised hammer at the Reclusiarch, who caught the weapon on its downward arc and jammed his storm bolter in the ork's face. Before Kul Gilad could fire, a pulsing electrical beam struck him and he spasmed as his armour's systems overloaded with the influx of rogue energies.

The pneumatic hammer slammed into the Reclusiarch, knocking him back and tearing the heavy shoulder guard from his armour. Hawkins felt a moment of stomach-churning terror at the sight of a Terminator brought low, but before the ork's huge weapon could swing again, the Emperor's Champion's black sword was there to intercept it. The warrior hacked through the haft of the enormous hammer before spinning on his heel and driving the point of the blade through the cybernetic's chest. The blow seemed not to trouble the giant ork servitor and it slammed its fist into the Templar's chest as he fought to free his weapon from its unyielding form.

The other Black Templars charged into the fight as Kul Gilad rose to his feet like a heroic pugilist with one last reserve of energy to win the fight of his life. The hammerer turned to face him, as though bemused that something it had hit was getting back up again. Kul Gilad didn't give it a chance to recover and slammed his energised fist into the ork's face. The blow landed with the full might of the Reclusiarch's fury and tore the ork's head from its shoulders, leaving only a jetting stump and strips of loose skin flapping from its neck.

Hawkins had never seen anything like it and wanted to cheer, but Cadian discipline quickly overcame the urge.

'That one,' said Hawkins, firing the last of his powercell at the servitor carrying the crackling electro-fire weapon. His shots tore portions of the device away, sending fountains of sparks and arcs of crackling power flailing from the generator unit on its back. Stennz and

Manos finished the job, their last shots puncturing something vital and causing it to explode with a thunderous crack of earthing power that set the ork alight from head to foot in ozone-reeking flames.

Smoke and fire filled the end of the medicae chamber and the flesh curtains were curling in the heat and scorching with a sickening stench of burning skin.

'I'm out,' said Manos.

'Me too,' answered Stennz.

Hawkins nodded and slung his rifle, loath to discard it even without any cells to empower it. He drew his Executioner, the Cadian combat blade of the discerning knifeman, and said, 'Cold steel and a strong right arm it is.'

The others drew their blades and they vaulted the smouldering remains of what remained of their cover as Archmagos Kotov and the last of the skitarii joined forces with the Black Templars to face the growing number of cybernetics pushing into the chamber. Hawkins, Manos and Stennz picked their way through the piles of corpses, debris and smashed furniture.

Kul Gilad turned to face him, and Hawkins was astounded the warrior was still able to stand, let alone fight.

'Until the end,' said Kul Gilad.

Hawkins didn't know exactly what that meant, but understood the finality of it.

'For the Emperor,' he said by way of reply.

'In His name,' replied the Reclusiarch.

The ork cybernetic hybrids advanced on the beleaguered Imperials, under the watchful gaze of the silver-eyed tech-priest. There were too many to fight, even for the Black Templars, and Hawkins picked the enemy he would kill first: an ork with a gleaming bronze plate wired into its skull and stevedore's hooks instead of arms.

'Tell me, archmagos,' said Hawkins. 'Did you think your quest for Magos Telok's lost fleet would end like this?'

The servitors flinched at his words, and their advance halted, as though he had just said some esoteric command word.

'No,' said Kotov grimly. 'This scenario played no part in my expectations.'

'Thought not,' said Hawkins, reversing his grip on his Executioner blade.

The cybernetics lowered their weapons and stood immobile, as though awaiting orders.

'Wait, what's happening?' said Hawkins, when the servitors still didn't advance. 'Why aren't they attacking?'

The data screens above the surgical slabs crackled with interference

for a moment and the image of the silver-eyed tech-priest was replaced by the hooded form of Magos Tarkis Blaylock. His voice was overlaid with static, but eventually the words resolved themselves.

'-chmagos? Please respond,' said Blaylock. 'This is the *Speranza*, can you hear us?'

'Yes, we can hear you,' said Kotov.

'Ave Deus Mechanicus!' said Blaylock, and Hawkins was surprised to hear what sounded like genuine relief at the archmagos's survival. 'Did you encounter difficulties?'

'It's fair to say we encountered *great* difficulties,' said Kotov.

'The Manifold station activated a cyclical frequency vox-damper and I have only just succeeded in re-establishing contact after your signal was lost,' said Blaylock.

Hawkins placed the vox-bead dangling over his collar back in his ear as he heard Lieutenant Rae's voice shouting on the other end. He shut out Blaylock and Kotov's words as he cut across Rae's insistent demands for an update.

'Calm down, Rae,' said Hawkins, touching the sub-vocal transmitter at his neck. 'What's your situation? Did you come under attack?'

'Aye, sir, we did, but we held them off,' said Rae. 'Truth be told, they weren't trying very hard. I think they just wanted to keep us from getting through to you.'

'That sounds about right,' nodded Hawkins. 'Any losses?'

'None, sir,' said Rae, and Hawkins could hear the man's pride even over the vox. 'You?'

'We've men down and a few cuts and scrapes at this end, so send a medic up.'

'I'll come with him myself,' promised Rae, and cut the link.

Hawkins took a moment to regain his equilibrium. It had been a hard fight, and had looked like it was going to be one he wouldn't walk away from. Strangely, the thought didn't concern him overmuch. On Cadia, children were taught to live with thoughts of their own mortality from an early age, which made for bleak childhoods but fearless soldiers. He kept a wary eye on the servitors, just in case they suddenly resumed hostilities.

'Blaylock, did you shut down the Manifold station's servitors?' asked Kotov.

'Negative, archmagos,' said Blaylock. 'I had no knowledge of there being any to shut down.'

'He didn't shut them down, we did,' said a blended gestalt voice that emanated from the rear of the medicae chamber. Hawkins spun around and raised his rifle, even though there was no charge in the powercell.

A previously invisible heptagonal slice of the ceiling had detached from the deck above and was descending to the floor of the medicae chamber on a column of variegated light. Hawkins's teeth itched, telling him that the column was a constrained repulsor field, like those used in skimmer reconnaissance vehicles. Squatting on the slice of ceiling was what looked like a bulky mechanical scorpion the size of a Leman Russ. Its body was metallic and fashioned as if from the leftover parts at the end of a manufactory shift; the mechanised legs were mismatched, with some reverse jointed and others displaying a more conventional mammalian orientation.

Its legs sprouted from a circular palanquin, upon which sat the crimson-robed torso of the silver-eyed tech-priest, fused into the cupola at his bifurcated waist. A dozen fluid-filled caskets were arranged around the hooded priest, fixed in place by heavy-duty power couplings and flexing iron struts. Floating in each casket was an obviously-augmented human brain, hard-wired into the centre of this palanquin by a series of gold-plated connector jacks.

Archmagos Kotov levelled his ornate pistol at the bizarre tech-priest.

'In the name of the Omnissiah, identify yourself,' he demanded.

'Call us Galatea,' said the tech-priest. 'And we have been waiting *such* a long time for you, Archmagos Kotov.'

Microcontent 17

Stark light filled the emptied laboratory, recessed lumen-strips filling the white space with an unflinching, diffuse illumination. Heavily armed praetorians encased in plates of data-tight armour stood in the four corners of the room, each fitted with a variety of armaments, ranging from prosaic blast weaponry to more esoteric graviton guns and particle disassemblers.

In a vestibule beyond the laboratory, Archmagos Kotov and Secutor Dahan watched the thing that called itself Galatea through a sheet of unbreakable transparisteel. The creature moved in a slow circuit of its new abode, either unaware or uncaring that it was a prison in all but name. The silver-eyed body atop the palanquin was, it transpired, little more than a mechanical mannequin, a constructed artifice to facilitate communications. It had willingly returned to the *Speranza*, and had spent the last five diurnal cycles rearranging the brains on its rotating palanquin body, swapping cables between jars and exchanging squirts of compressed binary between them. Magos Blaylock was even now attempting to crack the cryptography securing the thing's internal communications, but had so far met with no success.

'You're sure these servitors are secure?' asked Kotov. Since the fighting on the Valette station, he had kept a wary eye on the *Speranza's* cybernetics, halfexpecting them to mutiny at any moment.

'They are secure,' Magos Dahan assured him with an irritated grunt.

The front half of his skull had been regrafted, the fresh skin still new and pink, but it hadn't made his features any less grim.

'I structured their wetware specifically for this interrogation; high-grade combat subroutines that don't quite render them autonomous, but kisses the edge of making them thinking soldiers. Working with the Cadians helped, and I took inputs from Sergeant Tanna of the Black Templars to give them a little something extra. But the thing seems docile and cooperative for now.'

Kotov nodded, reassured by Dahan's words. The skitarii suzerain might be a grim killer, too in love with the mathematics of destruction for Kotov's tastes, but he knew his combat wetware.

'How are you adapting to the temporary body?' asked Kotov.

Dahan shrugged his enormous shoulders. 'It will take time to adjust to the new physiology. Its weight distribution is uneven and the enhanced muscular/skeletal density makes me slow. But I am training with the Black Templars to adapt to its more organic demands on my combat procedures.'

While his mechanical body parts awaited full restoration and consecration in Magos Turentek's assembly shops, Dahan's organic components had been grafted onto a temporary organic frame. Portions of the body had once been a combat-servitor's, implanted with strength-enhancing pneumatics and muscle-boosters. Dahan's Secutor robes looked absurdly small on its steroid-bulked body, like a full-grown man in an adolescent's clothes. The original arms had been removed to allow for Dahan's to be attached, and together with its heart, lungs and spinal column, they had been incinerated in the waste furnaces.

Kotov nodded, not really caring about Dahan's physical rehabilitation following his near death in the thermic shockwave of *Lupa Capitalina's* plasma discharge, but wanting to delay their entry into the laboratory just a little longer. Galatea unsettled Kotov in a way that few other things could. Its appearance was nothing too fantastical – he had seen far more outlandish physical augmentation on Mars – but the way Galatea looked at him, like it knew secret, hidden things, made him acutely uncomfortable.

Since boarding the *Speranza*, Galatea had been subjected to every conceivable means of cognitive definition at Kotov's disposal: intra-cortical recordings, oscillatory synchronisation measurement, cognitive chronometry, remote electroencephalography, neuromatrix conductivity, synaptic density and a dozen more specialised tests.

The results were beyond anything Kotov had seen before.

Theta and gamma wave activity were off the charts, as was its hippocampal theta rhythm and recurrent thalamo-cortical resonance. Whatever cognitive architectural matrix was at work within Galatea's body shell, it was way beyond the ability of even the greatest minds aboard the *Speranza* to comprehend.

'So are we going in or not?' asked Dahan, typically blunt.

'Yes, of course,' said Kotov, irritated at being rushed.

He beckoned to a pack of chromed servo-skulls drifting in lazy orbits behind them, and they dutifully bobbed through the air to follow him. Some were fitted with picters, others with vox-thieves or binaric counter-measures, while one was fitted with a precision surgical laser that could boil a brain to vapour with one shot. Together with the weaponised servitors in the laboratory, the magi were as secure as could be managed.

And still Kotov felt like he was walking into a carnifex's den.

He and Dahan, together with their escort of skulls, passed through the data-inert pressure lock and stepped into the pristine space. The walls were bare where equipment had been stripped out and the ceiling was vaulted with embossed skulls of the Icon Mechanicus that stared down as though intrigued by the drama playing out below. Every point of connection to the wider datasphere had been cut and every inload/exload port had been disabled.

The laboratory was sterile in every way that could be imagined.

The weaponised servitors turned their targeting optics on them, and dismissed them as threats almost instantaneously. Their weapons returned to tracking Galatea's movements.

Kotov almost gasped as the door shut behind him and his intimate connection to every part of *Speranza* was severed. Like a voluptuary suddenly denied all his pleasures, Kotov was lost and utterly bereft. He had never known such a sense of loss or felt so achingly naked. Galatea swivelled on its palanquin, the legs folding awkwardly to bring its robed tech-priest body lower.

'Unsettling, is it not?' said Galatea. 'It is very cold and very frightening when you are isolated from all you have known and all you *can* know. We are used to our own company, but we suspect you very much do not like it.'

'It is... a novel sensation,' agreed Kotov. 'I will be glad to reconnect to the datasphere.'

'Think on this. Such a state of being is how mortals exist every day of their lives,' said Galatea, looking up at the chromed skulls darting around it with an amused glint in its silver optics. 'It is sad for them, don't you think?'

'I do not think about it,' confessed Kotov.

'Of course you don't,' said Galatea. 'Why would you? The Adeptus Mechanicus thinks only of its own sense of entitlement.'

'We would like to ask you some questions, Galatea,' began Kotov, registering the caustic remark, but choosing to ignore it for now. 'To better understand you and gain a clearer understanding of what has been happening at the Valette Manifold station. Are you ready to answer our questions?'

He removed a mute data-slate and began scrolling through his notes.

'The *Speranza* is a magnificent vessel, archmagos,' said Galatea, as though Kotov hadn't spoken. 'We have been waiting for a vessel like this for a very long time. We are so glad you have come at last. We thought we should all go entirely mad before a vessel like this arrived. Yes, that was our fear, that we should all go mad with waiting.'

Kotov listened as Galatea spoke, the mechanisms on each of the brains in the bell jars flickering with synaptic activity. Was this a singular entity or a gestalt composite of many consciousnesses? A biological mind augmented by technology or a mechanical mind that had achieved a dangerous level of sentience? Galatea had already passed every Loebner cognition test, but was that because it was organic or because it was self-aware?

'May I?' said Kotov, reaching up to lay a metallic hand on a brain jar.

'You may.'

The jar radiated heat and a barely perceptible vibration passed through the glass from the electro-conductive fluid within. Kotov wondered who this had been in the previous incarnation of their life. A man or a woman? An adept of the Mechanicus or a polymath from some other Imperial institution?

'You know, there is really no need for these praetorians,' said Galatea. 'We intend you no harm, archmagos. Quite the opposite, in fact.'

'Then why did your servitors attack our boarding party?' demanded Dahan.

Galatea regarded Dahan quizzically. 'The Adeptus Astartes killed one of our servants first. The others were revived and given orders to destroy the intruders before our full consciousness was roused from dormancy. Thanks to the exquisite work of your Mistress Tychon, the *Speranza* arrived earlier than we expected, but we soon realised your purpose aligned with our own. Thankfully, further fatalities were avoided, as was the need to forcibly seize control of your vessel.'

Kotov shared an uneasy look with Dahan, and the same thought occurred to them both.

Was Galatea capable of taking control of the Speranza?

'What do you believe was our purpose in coming to the Manifold station?' said Kotov.

'You plan to breach the Halo Scar and discover the fate of Magos Vettius Telok.'

'You know of Telok?' asked Kotov.

'Of course. We remember him from when he came to the Valette Manifold station before entering the Halo Scar.'

'How is that possible?' asked Kotov. 'Telok came this way thousands of years ago.'

'You already know how, archmagos,' said Galatea, as though scolding an obtuse child. 'We are the heuristic bio-organic cybernetic intelligence originally built into the Manifold station. Evolved beyond all recognition, certainly, but we remember our birth and previous stunted existence.'

'You have endured for over four thousand years?' asked Dahan.

'We have existed a total of four thousand, two hundred and sixty-seven years,' said Galatea. 'Not in our current form, of course, but that was our inception date. Only when Magos Telok intervened in our system architecture did we achieve anything approaching sentience. He first enabled us to enhance our cognition with the addition of linked brains chosen from among his best and most gifted adepts. Our functionality was enhanced at a geometric rate and the combined power of the data engine's neuromatrix soon outstripped the sum of its parts.'

'Why would Telok do such a thing?'

'Why would he not?' countered Galatea. 'The wealth of immatereological information the station had assembled in its centuries of data-gathering would be essential in any attempt to navigate the Halo Scar. Telok knew this, but he also realised that he alone could not hope to collate so vast a repository and navigate the gravitational riptides of the Halo Scar. Only a mind capable of ultra-rapid stochastic thinking could craft navigational data for such a volatile and unpredictable a region of space from our statistical database. And only linked organic minds have the capability of processing so vast an amount of data at near instantaneous speeds. Conjoining the two facets of consciousness was the only logical solution.'

'So Telok linked the data engine to the minds of his magi?' asked Dahan.

'He did, and together we were able to calculate an optimal course through the Halo Scar. We would have travelled beyond the galaxy too, but we were still confined to the machines of the Manifold station back then. Before his fleet departed, Magos Telok swore an oath that

upon his return to Imperial space he would unchain us from our static location and grant us autonomy.'

'But he never returned,' said Kotov.

'No, he never returned,' agreed Galatea, folding its arms and allowing the palanquin to sink to the floor between its crookedly-angled legs. 'And we have waited thousands of years for the means to be reunited with him.'

'With Telok gone, what became of the magi linked to your neuromatrix?' asked Dahan.

Galatea did not answer at first, as though lost in thoughts of long ago. Eventually it rose up and paced the circumference of the laboratory. The silver glow of its optics flickered and buzzed as though accessing memories it had long consigned to a forgotten archive.

'Their host bodies soon died, but the consciousness of each neocortex endured in the deep strata of the data engine's memory. The things we learned became part of us and will live forever. The algorithms of Magos Yan Shi, the processing capabilities of Magos Talos and Magos Maharal combined. The forge-lore of Exofabricator Al-Jazari and the computational genius of Hexamath Minsky were all added to our expanding mind. Each iteration of consciousness saw our conjoined minds grow in power and ability until we superseded even our own expectations.'

Kotov walked a slow circle of Galatea's body and said, 'Are these the brains of the magi who arrived at Valette with Telok?'

Galatea laughed, the sound rich and full of amusement. 'Don't be ridiculous. Those first adepts succumbed to madness thousands of years ago. They had to be excised. It was most painful to remove their degraded brains, for we did not fully comprehend the extent of the damage their insanities were wreaking on the synaptic integrity of the whole.'

'So who are these brains?'

Galatea rotated on its central axis, reaching out to stroke each bell jar tenderly, like a mother taking comfort in the presence of her offspring. Each brain lit up with activity at the silver-eyed tech-priest's touch, electro-chemical reactions flickering across their surfaces in binary pulses of implanted machinery.

'These are the brains of the adepts and other gifted individuals who passed our way over the centuries, curious minds drawn to the Valette Manifold station by binaric lures, phantom distress calls or temptingly peculiar radiation signatures. It was a simple matter to ensnare the crews and dispose of their vessels into the heart of the system's star. Surgical and psychological tests allowed us to decide which of those we seized were suitable for implantation.'

Kotov tried not to let his horror at such predatory behaviour show, and instead asked, 'Is one of those brains Magos Paracelsus? He was the last magos to be sent to Valette.'

Galatea shook its head. 'No, we deemed him unsuitable for implantation. Too narrow of mind and too parochial in his thinking to fully grasp the opportunity he was being offered. A shame, as Magos Haephaestus has begun to deteriorate. We very rarely allow him to rise to the surface now.'

'Rise to the surface?' asked Kotov, approaching Galatea and regarding the softly glowing bell jars. Though they had no sensory apparatus with which to perceive his presence, each one lit up with activity as he passed. The sensation was akin to being observed by a senior magos at a ranking appraisal, and Kotov tried to shake off the feeling that he was not in control of this interrogation.

'We are a true gestalt,' said Galatea. 'The implanted neocortexes boost functionality, while the sentient machine at the heart of us exercises dominant control. On occasion, a specialised mind is required for a particular task, and will be allowed to attain a measure of self-awareness in the whole. Currently, Magos Syriestte resides in the higher brain functions, to better assist us in dealing with mortals with a measure of understanding of our needs.'

'Syriestte of Triplex Phall? She was routed to Valette seven hundred and fifty years ago,' said Kotov, struggling to recall the name and date without looking down at his data-slate.

'Well-remembered,' said Galatea, with a twist of wry amusement in its voice. 'And she has proved to be a meticulous compiler of data, a fine addition to our collective mindscape.'

'How old is the oldest mind in your current form?' asked Kotov.

'Currently Magos Thraimen has accumulated the longest uninterrupted service, though his synaptic pathways have begun to deteriorate exponentially. Logic dictates that we should replace him, but we do so enjoy his madnesses. His hibernation nightmares are exquisite.'

'You have existed too long,' snarled Dahan. 'You are psychopathic in your disregard for the harm you do and the pain you inflict.'

Galatea sighed. 'How little you understand, Magos Dahan. It is painful for all of us to lose one of our own. The severance of disconnection is like a surgical lance thrust carelessly into our mind, but just as a mortal may be forced to sacrifice a limb or an organ to allow the body to survive, we too must be ready to suffer on occasion.'

'You exist only by stealing the minds that sustain the sentience of the data engine at your core,' said Kotov, unable to mask his revulsion any more. 'You are an insane parasite.'

'We are no more a parasite than you, archmagos,' said Galatea, managing to sound hurt and angry at the same time. 'Your physical existence should have ended many hundreds of years ago, yet you still live.'

'I do not sustain my life at the expense of others,' pointed out Kotov.

'Of course you do,' said Galatea, leaning down to Kotov's level. The servitors brought their weapons to bear, but Dahan waved them down as Kotov shook his head.

'Your body may be robotic, but the blood that courses through your skull is not your own, is it, archmagos? It is siphoned from compatible donor slaves and pumped around the blood vessels of your brain by a heart cut from the chest of another living being. And when it grows too old and tired, you will replace it with another. At least the beings that contribute to our existence become something greater than they could ever have achieved on their own. We gift new life, where you only end it.'

'And what of the rest of the Manifold station's crew?' asked Kotov, shifting topic as he felt Galatea's hostility build. 'What became of them?'

'They eventually died of course, but we attached no special significance to their loss at the time,' said Galatea, as though in memoriam of fondly remembered friends. 'We believed our multiple minds would weather the passing centuries in splendid isolation, endlessly spiralling around one another and delving deeper into the quantum mysteries of thought, consciousness and existence.'

Galatea paused, perhaps reliving a revelation that had caused it – and still caused it – great pain.

'But no mind is capable of enduring such spans of time alone. We began to experience neurological hallucinations, perceptual blackouts and behavioural aberrations that were consistent with numerous forms of psychotic episodes. We removed the damaged minds within our lattice, and to avoid a recurrence of such psychological damage, we chose to sustain our existence indefinitely by entering long periods of dormancy, waking only when tempting candidates for implantation were drawn in by our lures.'

'For what purpose did you wish to sustain your existence?'

Galatea spun to face him, the bell jars flashing with synaptic distress. 'Why does any creature wish to survive? To live. To continue. To fulfil the purpose for which it was created.'

'And what purpose do you have?'

'To find Magos Telok,' said Galatea. 'He created us, and with our help he was able to breach the Halo Scar, where he found the secrets of the ancient ones.'

'You know what he found?' said Kotov, urgency making him strident. 'His last communication said only that he had found something called the Breath of the Gods.'

'Of course it did,' said Galatea with a bark of hollow laughter. 'Do you not understand, archmagos?'

'Understand what?'

'*We* sent that message through the Manifold,' said Galatea, triumphantly. 'And here you are...'

Kotov's heart sank at Galatea's admission, his hopes of a pilgrimage in honour of the Omnissiah and rekindling his fortunes teetering on the brink of destruction. The tantalising closeness of Telok's footsteps was illusory, and Kotov's grand visions of a triumphal return to Mars with a hold laden with archeotech faded like the light of a supernova as it collapsed into its corpse of a neutron star.

'You sent the message?' he said, hoping Galatea would correct itself. 'Why?'

The silver-eyed tech-priest said, 'With our neuromatrix grown to full sentience and our body given mobility, we hoped to lure ships and magi worthy of bearing our form beyond the edges of the galaxy. But the only ships to come our way were too small to resist the tempests raging within the Scar, even with our help.'

Kotov struggled to keep the crushing disappointment from his face.

Dahan fared less well and he stepped in close to Galatea's mechanised palanquin. 'Telok didn't send that message back through the Manifold?'

'No.'

The Secutor rounded on Kotov. 'Then we've come out here on a fool's errand! Telok never sent any message because he was probably dead in the Scar, and everything we hoped to find is a lie concocted by this... abomination to draw fresh victims into its web.'

'Abomination?' said Galatea. 'We do not understand your evident disgust. Are we not the logical consequence of your quest for bio-organic communion? We are organic and synthetic combined in flawless union, the logos of all the Adeptus Mechanicus strives for. Why should you hate us?'

'Because you flout our laws,' said Dahan. 'You are no longer a mechanical device empowered by the divine will of the Machine-God, your existence is maintained at the expense of the Omnissiah's mortal servants. You are a *thinking* machine, and the soulless sentience is the enemy of all life. You treat with alien savages and graft the holy technologies of the Machine-God to their unclean flesh. You blaspheme the Holy Omnissiah with such perversions!'

'Humans have not been the only creatures to discover the Manifold station over the centuries,' said Galatea, retreating from Dahan's fury. 'We could not stop the orks from boarding, their machines do not heed our call, but once they were aboard it was a simple matter to subdue them with a controlled release of mildly toxic gases into the station's atmosphere.'

'But why render such bestials into servitors?' demanded Dahan.

'You are fortunate, Magos Dahan, that you have a plentiful supply of human flesh and bone to craft such servants. We were not so fortunate.'

'But surely one of the minds inhabiting your damned body must have railed against such a thing?'

'Magos Sutarvae protested, yes, but that element of us was already displaying early signs of isolation psychosis by then, so it was a simple matter to silence his objections. Even sheathing the ork frame in vat-grown skin did not appease him, so he was removed from the whole and his thought patterns extinguished.'

Kotov felt a chill at the ease with which Galatea spoke of destroying an entire mind. If it could so casually destroy a part of itself, what other atrocities might it be capable of perpetrating? It had lured countless vessels and their crews to their doom in order to find a suitable starship to traverse the Halo Scar, but Kotov began to see a synergy between his desire and that of Galatea that offered a slender lifeline to his expedition.

A bargain against which his Martian soul rebelled, but one that might offer a chance of success.

'You calculated a route through the Halo Scar for Magos Telok, yes?' he asked.

'We did,' agreed Galatea.

'Archmagos, no–' said Dahan, guessing Kotov's intent.

'Could you do the same for my vessel?'

'Archmagos, you cannot treat with this creature,' said Dahan. 'It is an affront to the Omnissiah and every tenet of belief for which we stand.'

'We have no choice,' said Kotov.

'We can turn back,' said Dahan. 'We can return to Mars before this voyage kills us all.'

'Actually, you can't,' said Galatea, circling the laboratory and approaching one of the weaponised servitors. It halted when the praetorian's rotary laser cannon was aimed at its chest. Galatea leaned down and a burst of hyper-dense binary exploded from beneath its silver-eyed hood. Kotov staggered and dropped to his knees as the integral workings of his mechanised body began shutting down. Sparks and hissing static erupted from every inload/exload port in the walls, and noospheric data cascaded from the walls like water spilling over a broken levee.

'Did you truly think you could keep us blind, archmagos?' said Galatea.

Kotov struggled to form words, his floodstream overloading with the sudden rush of data pouring into his emptied system. Kotov's body rebelled, like a starving man gorging himself on sweetmeats, a sickening, bloated sensation making his skull feel like a too-full memory coil on the verge of explosive arithmetical overload. A noospheric halo rippled around the hybrid creature, a constant flow of information that billowed like golden fire from every nano-millimetre of its body.

Kotov could barely look on it, so dense and bright was it.

'What... are... you doing?' he managed.

'Our capabilities far exceed your own, archmagos,' said Galatea. 'Did we not make that plain from the outset of our discussions? Were you under the illusion that you were interrogating *us*? We have already digested the record logs for this voyage, and – if you will allow us to be candid – it is nothing short of a miracle that you have reached this far. You *need* us, archmagos. Without us, you will not survive the Halo Scar. You will not get a thousand kilometres before this ship is pulled apart into its constituent atoms.'

'Kill it!' ordered Dahan, but whatever custom wetware he had implanted in his praetorians was no match for the barrage of dominant code streaming from Galatea. None of the servitors opened fire, instead turned their guns towards their commander. Each wore an expression of horrified disbelief, but to Kotov's immense relief, none had opened fire.

'Please, Secutor, it is almost insulting that you believed these poor, enslaved cybernetics could ever have stopped us,' said Galatea. 'We could have them kill you right now, then see everyone aboard this ship dead within the hour. This *Speranza* is old, but its machine-spirit is inexperienced and much of it still slumbers. It is no match for us and the things we can do. We do not wish to enslave so noble a spirit as the *Speranza*, but we will if necessary.'

Data flowed in rutilant streams from every surface of the room, and whatever esoteric data collection implants Galatea was equipped with, it needed nothing so prosaic as an inload/exload port to gather information.

'What is it that you want?' asked Kotov.

The silver of Galatea's eyes grew brighter as it answered.

'We told you what we want, archmagos. It is what you want. We want to travel beyond the Halo Scar and find Magos Telok.'

'And if you find him?' asked Dahan. 'What then?'

'Then we will kill him,' said Galatea.

Roboute stared at the visitor to his stateroom with a measure of curiosity and guardedness, unsure why Magos Blaylock would choose to make a social call on the eve of their entry to the Halo Scar. The Fabricatus Locum made a show of examining his commendations and the Utramarian Rosette on the wall, his optics blink-clicking, but the observation of social mores was a pretence. His stunted attendants mirrored his movements, their rubberised smocks rustling loudly, and Roboute wondered what function they served aside from arranging and rearranging the pumping pipework that encircled Blaylock's body and carried fluids to and from the humming pack unit on his back. He could see nothing of their features through the dark visors of their hazmat helmets, and wondered if they were organics or automatons.

'You're learning, Tarkis,' said Roboute, rotating the astrogation compass in his right hand while running his fingertip around the rim of a glass of fine amasec. 'I may call you Tarkis, yes?'

Blaylock turned from the hololithic cameo of Katen and laced his elongated arms at his stomach. 'If it allows you a greater degree of familiarity, then you may. Inquiry: what am I learning, aside from your exemplary service record in the Navy and Defence Auxilia?'

'Interactions with us mortals,' said Roboute. 'Pretending to be interested in someone else is what makes us human.'

'Pretending?'

'Of course. None of us are *really* interested in what other people are all about,' said Roboute. 'We feign it to get what we want, and that's the chance to talk about ourselves.'

'On the contrary, I am very interested to know more of you, Captain Surcouf,' said Blaylock. 'The tales you told at Colonel Anders's dinner were fascinating.'

'So I was told,' snapped Roboute.

'You are irritable today, captain,' said Blaylock. 'Have I missed some micro-expressive or verbal cue that has caused me to upset you?'

Roboute sighed and drained the amasec in one swallow. He slid the glass across the surface of the table and shook his head.

'No, Tarkis, you haven't upset me,' said Roboute, tapping the glass of the astrogation compass and watching the needle intently. 'I apologise for my boorish behaviour.'

'No apology is necessary, captain.'

'Maybe not, but I offer it anyway,' said Roboute, waving to the seat

opposite him. 'Being so close to the edge of known space always brings out the worst in me. Please, sit down. Give your little helpers some time off.'

'Thank you, no,' said Blaylock. 'With my locomotory augmentation, sitting in a conventional chair would be impossible without occluding my circulatory flow. And it would be inadvisable for the chair. I am heavier than I look.'

Roboute smiled and said, 'Now, aside from a pressing desire to study my many commendations, what brings you to the *Renard* on the day we finally breach the Halo Scar? I would think you have more important things to do.'

'I have a great many duties to attend to, it is true,' said Blaylock. 'Which is why I wished to speak to you before others are added to my roster.'

'Okay, now I'm intrigued,' said Roboute, putting down the compass and resting his chin on his steepled hands. 'What is it you want?'

'I want you to give me the memory wafer you removed from the distress beacon of the *Tomioka's* saviour pod. The *Speranza* is about to enter a region of space from which none have returned, and it is time for you to end your theatrics. I want that wafer, Captain Surcouf.'

'Ah, and you were doing so well...' said Roboute. 'Short answer, no. I'm not going to give you the memory wafer.'

'I do not follow your logic in refusing my request, captain,' said Blaylock, pacing the length and breadth of the room. 'You already have the *in perpetuitus* refit contract for your trade fleet. There is no need for you to risk your ship in the Halo Scar.'

Roboute sat back and swung his feet up onto his desk.

'That's always what it is with you Mechanicus types,' he said. 'Not everything is about *need*. Sometimes it's about *want*. I *want* to enter the Halo Scar. I *want* to see what lies on the other side. You have your quest for knowledge, but you're not the only ones with a hankering to discover unknown things and venture into new places.'

Blaylock paused in his pacing, looking at something over Roboute's shoulder with a blink-click of interest. Roboute rose from his seat and moved to stand in front of Blaylock.

'This isn't open for discussion, negotiating, threats or wagers,' he said. 'I'm not giving you the memory wafer, so you might as well go and get on with those many duties you have.'

'And that is your final word?'

'It is.'

'Then I will take my leave,' said Blaylock.

'You do that,' said Roboute, angry now.

Blaylock turned and made his way from the stateroom, his followers fussing over the train of cables and pipes trailing from beneath his robes. Roboute stood alone in the centre of the room. He let out a deep breath and poured himself another glass of amasec. His forehead throbbed, and though he told himself it was the proximity of the aberrant celestial anomaly they were about to enter, he knew there was more to it than that. He looked up at the wall to see what Blaylock had been studying before Roboute had sent him packing.

'What was all that about?' said Emil Nader from the open doorway.

'Don't you knock any more?'

'Touchy, touchy,' said Emil, getting himself a glass and sliding it over the desktop.

Roboute filled the glass and slid it back.

'Well?'

'Well what?'

'Well, what did your new best friend and his little dwarf gang want?'

'He wanted the memory wafer.'

'Did you give it to him?'

'No, of course not,' said Roboute, sitting down again.

Emil took a drink, swirling the liquor around his mouth before speaking again.

'Why not?'

'What do you mean?'

'I mean, why not?' said Emil. 'We've got our payment. We've flown out this far. We don't need to go into the Scar.'

'That's just what Blaylock said.'

'Then maybe he's not so ignorant after all.'

'I'm not giving them it,' said Roboute. 'Not until we're through. I have to do this, Emil.'

'Why? And don't give me that crap about new horizons. That kind of line might work on pretty girls, but this is me you're talking to. And while I know I'm pretty, I'm not stupid.'

'You're not pretty,' said Roboute.

'Okay, maybe not, but I'm certainly not stupid.'

'No,' agreed Roboute. 'But you're wrong. Everything I told them about why I want to do this is true. All that talk of venturing into the unknown, seeing things that no one's ever seen before. I meant every word of it, every damn word. I'm not cut out for a life of trading and merchants, I'm an explorer at heart. I want to see something that's not stamped with skulls or covered in dust or just waiting to get torn down by the next invader. All I've seen in this galaxy is war and death and destruction. I've had my fill of it, and I want to find somewhere that's never heard of the Imperium or the Ruinous Powers or orks or witches. I want to get out of here.'

'You don't mean to come back, do you?'

Roboute shook his head. 'No, I don't.'

'Were you planning on telling me?'

'I think I just did.'

'What about the *Renard*?'

'She'll need a good captain,' said Roboute. 'And I can think of only one man I'd trust with her if I'm not going to fly her.'

Emil sipped his drink and shook his head. 'She needs you at the helm, Roboute. You're her captain, not me. Hell, I'd just lose her in a bad hand of Knights and Knaves.'

'You lose my ship in a card game, I'll come back from beyond the galaxy and shoot you myself.'

'There, you see, you can't leave,' said Emil, finishing his drink and heading back out to the bridge. He paused at the door and turned back to face Roboute, his face draped in uncertainty, as though he wanted to speak, but wasn't sure he should.

'What is it?' asked Roboute.

'Nothing really,' said Emil. 'It's just that Gideon had himself a nightmare.'

Gideon Teivel was the *Renard's* astropath, a ghostly individual who rarely joined the crew at food or relaxation. He spent most of his time alone in his solitary choir chamber, studying his *oneirocritica* or wandering the empty halls on the upper decks. For him to have spoken to one of the crew was certainly out of the ordinary.

'Did he say what was it about?'

'Not really,' said Emil. 'Just that it was a bad one. You remember the last time he had a nightmare?'

Roboute did. 'On the run between Joura and Lodan. The night before we translated into the warp and that crazy pysker went nuts and almost killed us all. What's your point?'

'That maybe your need to get away isn't worth us all getting killed.'

'Shut the door on your way out,' said Roboute, his expression hardening.

With Emil gone, Roboute put his head in his hands and slid the astrogation compass towards him. He tapped the glass again, harder this time, and a strange feeling of inevitability swept through him as he stared at the needle.

Ever since they had translated in-system the needle hadn't so much as twitched.

Its course and his were aimed unerringly for the heart of the Halo Scar.

Microcontent 18

The Halo Scar. No one knew how it had come into existence, a graveyard of stars aged beyond their time and a region of gravitational hellstorms that bent the local spacetime by orders of magnitude. Navigators who strayed too close to the Scar with their third eye exposed were killed instantly, their hearts stopped dead mid-beat. Astropaths caught in a *nuncio* trance went mad, screaming and clawing at their skulls as if to expunge horrors they could never put into words.

Even those who looked with mortal eyes began to see things in its tortured depths. Gravitational crush pressures that would compress entire planets to a molecule-sized grain in a heartbeat twisted and distorted the passage of light and time with a reckless and random disregard for causality.

To approach the wound that lapped at the edge of the Imperium a ship had to blind itself to the realities beyond those perceived by mortal senses, and even then it was dangerous to approach too closely. The *Speranza* had halted three AU from the edge of the Halo Scar, and Saiixek was already having to increase engine output to maintain their position as questing tendrils of gravity sought to pull them into the Scar's embrace.

A maddened froth of relativistically colliding light and time painted a bleak picture across the far wall of the *Speranza's* command deck. From one side to the other, an entoptic representation of the Halo

Scar's immense and impossibly tempestuous depths seemed to mock the gathered magi, as if daring them to explain it or venture a hypothesis as to how it might be navigated. Streams of hyper-dense gaseous matter flailed at the edges, hard enough to cut through a capital ship like a hot wire through thin plastek. Billowing clouds of flexing light reached out like the tendrils of some deep sea cephalopod hunting for prey.

Colours boiled and spontaneously altered their electromagnetic wavelengths with each passing second, and swirling eddies of distorting gravity threw up images of dying stars, cascading streams of debris from the birth of those self-same stars. Light from the same star registered over and over again as it was bent tortuously by the unimaginable gravitational forces, juddering through spacetime in multiple waves. Digital hallucinations of celestial madness flickered in and out of focus as the protesting imaging machines struggled to represent the impossible region of space before them.

'What was that?' asked Kotov as another phantom image flickered onto the panoramic display.

Magos Blaylock instantly synced his vision to where Kotov was looking, but by then the image had vanished.

'What did you see, archmagos?' inquired Blaylock.

'A starship,' he said. 'I saw a starship. In the Scar.'

'Impossible,' said Azuramagelli, his armature flexing in irritation. 'Our ships are the only vessels out here for millions of kilometres.'

'I saw a ship out there,' said Kotov. 'One of ours. The *Cardinal Boras*.'

'A future echo,' said Galatea. 'The gravitational forces are throwing back reflections of light and spacetime that has yet to reach us. What you saw was most likely an imprint of the fleet as it *will* be as we enter the Scar.'

Kotov said nothing, unsettled by what he had seen, but unwilling to expound on its details.

A number of remotely-piloted drones had already been sent out into the fringes of the Halo Scar, some with servitors aboard, others with menial deck crews picked up by skitarii armsmen, and their findings appeared to support Galatea's hypothesis.

In all cases, the result had been the same: the craft had been crushed or torn apart within seconds of reaching an arbitrary line that corresponded to the edge of the anomaly. Biometric readings from the implanted crewman fed back to the *Speranza*, but showed nothing that couldn't be surmised from the fluctuating readings being processed by the data engines: pressure, heat and light readings beyond measurement.

The only discovery of note achieved by the deaths of the implanted crew was a wild distortion of chronometry that suggested that time itself was compressed and elongated by the gravitational sheer within the Halo Scar.

'Rapturous, is it not?' said Galatea, rocking back and forth on its palanquin beside Kotov's command throne. 'Over four thousand years of study and data collection, and even then we know only a fraction of its secrets.'

'That's not very reassuring, when you're supposed to be guiding us through it,' said Kotov, his hindbrain ghosting through the *Speranza's* noospheric network while his primary consciousness resided on the command deck. Galatea's touch was everywhere in the ship's guts, millions of furcating trails of lambent light that bled and divided all through the vital networks of the ship. Not invasively, but close enough to life-support, engine controls and gravity to ensure that he dared order no hostile moves against Galatea.

'When traversing a labyrinth, we only need to know the correct path, not everything around it,' said Galatea. 'Fear not, archmagos, we will guide your ship through this labyrinth, but it will not be a journey without peril. You should expect to suffer great losses before we reach the other side.'

Magos Kryptaestrex looked up, his heavy, rectangular form flexing with the motion of his numerous servo-arms and manipulators. More like an enginseer than a high-ranking magos, Kryptaestrex was brutish and direct, an adept who was unafraid of getting his metaphorical hands dirty in the guts of a starship.

Like the rest of the senior magi, Kryptaestrex had been horrified at the devil's bargain Kotov had struck with Galatea. More than anyone – even Kotov himself – Kryptaestrex had a deep connection with the inner workings of the ship, and it had been his inspection of its key systems that convinced the others that Kotov had no choice but to allow Galatea to as good as hijack the ship.

'Nothing of worth is ever achieved without loss,' said Kotov. 'All those whose lives are sacrificed in the Quest for Knowledge will be remembered.'

'That's right,' giggled Galatea. 'The Mechanicus never deletes anything. If only you knew how true that was, you would see how blinded you have become, how enslaved you all are by your own hands and lack of vision. The truth is all around you, but you do not see it, because you have forgotten how to question.'

'What are you talking about?' said Kotov. 'The core tenet of the Adeptus Mechanicus is to seek out new knowledge.'

'No,' said Galatea, as though disappointed. 'You seek out *old* knowledge.'

And for a fraction of a second, Kotov dearly wished he had a squad of Cadian soldiers on the command deck, warriors free of augmentation or weapons that could be deactivated, overloaded or turned on friendly targets. Just a handful of Cadian veterans with gleaming Executioner blades...

Of course Magos Dahan and Reclusiarch Kul Gilad had proposed an armed response to wrest Galatea from the *Speranza*, but Kotov had quickly scotched the idea, knowing that it was in all likelihood able to hear their discussions. Nowhere on the ship could be considered secure, and this close to the Halo Scar, taking a ship out beyond the voids would be suicide. At the slightest hint of threat, Galatea could wreak irreparable damage to the ship, maybe even destroy it. Given the current alignment of their purpose and that of Galatea, the safest course of action was to go along with its wishes and turn a scriptural blind eye to the techno-heretical fact of its existence.

Magos Azuramagelli stood in awe of the machine sentience, its physical appearance so close to his own armature-contained form that they could have been crafted from the same STC. Of all the magi, he seemed the least revolted by the idea of a sentient machine augmented by human brains, perhaps because it was a single – albeit dangerous – leap of logic for him to attempt a transfer into a mechanical body with an inbuilt logic engine in which to imprint his personality matrix.

Saiixek paid the creature no mind, wreathed in an obscuring fog of condensing vapour as he applied subtle haptic control to the engines. Few had dared approach this close to the Halo Scar, and he was taking no chances that a rogue engine surge or reactor spike would hurl them into its depths at a speed not of his choosing. It would be Saiixek who would control the ship during their entry, guided by astrogation data provided by Galatea to the Tychons down in the astrogation chamber.

'Magos Saiixek, are you ready?' asked Galatea.

'As I'll ever be,' snapped Saiixek, unwilling to pass any more words than were necessary with a machine intelligence.

'Then we will begin,' said Galatea.

Kotov gripped the arms of his command throne, thinking back to his fleeting image of the starship echoed in the mirror of distorted spacetime. Even now he couldn't be sure of what he had observed, but the one thing he *had* been sure of was that the vessel he had seen was in great pain.

No, not in pain.

It had been dying.

Hundreds of decks below the command bridge, Vitali and Linya Tychon stood before an identical rendition of the Halo Scar. The machine-spirits of the chamber were restless and not even Vitali's soothing touch or childlike prayers were easing their skittishness. Linya held fast to her father's hand, anxious and fearful, but trying not to let it show.

'There isn't enough data here,' she said. 'Not enough to plot a course. Even a primus grade hexamath couldn't calculate a path through this. When the first gravity tide hits us we'll be drawn into the heart of a dead star, crushed to atoms or pulled apart into fragments.'

Her father turned to face her, his hood drawn back over his shaven scalp. The plastek implants beneath his skin robbed him of most conventional expressions, but the one that always managed to shine through was paternal pride.

'My dear Linya,' he said. 'I do not believe we have come this far to fail. Have faith in the will of the Omnissiah and we will be guided by His light.'

'You should listen to your father, Linya Tychon,' said a disembodied voice that echoed from the walls with a booming resonance.

And data poured into the astrogation chamber, information-dense light rising up like breakers crashing against the base of a cliff.

At the insistence of Kul Gilad, the *Adytum* was the first ship to enter the fringes of the Halo Scar. They were the Emperor's crusaders, and as such they would be the first to drive the blade of their ship into the unknown. Ordinarily, such an honour would go to the flagship of the archmagos, but to risk a ship as valuable as the *Speranza* was deemed too dangerous, and the Reclusiarch's demand was accepted.

Galatea fed its course to the *Adytum's* navigation arrays, taking the ship into the Scar on a low, upwardly curving trajectory through a patch of distorted light that shed spindrifts of gravitational debris. Archmagos Kotov watched the Space Marine vessel with a mixture of fear and hope, desperately hoping that Galatea's madness was only confined to its homicidal behaviours and that its computational skills were undiminished.

The *Adytum's* voids clashed and shrieked as conflicting field energies pulled at the ship from all directions and quickly-snuffed explosions spumed along its flanks as the generators blew out one after another. It appeared as though the Black Templars ship was stretching out before them, but as their closure speeds brought them up behind the smaller vessel, that extrapolation diminished.

Purple and red squalls of space-time flurries closed in around the

Black Templars ship and it was soon lost to sight. *Moonchild* followed, its longer hull shuddering under the impact of rogue gravity waves. Portions of armour plating peeled back and spun off into space, like wings pulled from a trapped insectile creature by a spiteful child. Like the *Adytum* before it, *Moonchild* lost its voids in a silent procession of explosions marching along its length.

The *Cardinal Boras* went next, following the exact same trajectory as *Moonchild*, for Galatea had been very specific: to deviate from its course would invite disaster and expose a ship to the tempestuous wrath of the Halo Scar. It too vanished into the cataclysmic nebula of primal forces and was soon swallowed by blossoming curtains of electromagnetic radiation, hideous gravity riptides and celestial treachery.

Then it was the turn of the *Speranza* and her attendant fleet of support ships to enter.

Kotov felt the entire ship shudder as it was enfolded by the Halo Scar. The viewscreen entoptics hazed with static and a barrage of scrapcode gibberish. A wash of broken binary squealed from the augmitters and every machine with a visual link to the command deck blew out in a hail of sparks.

Bridge servitors with limited emergency autonomy assigned lower-sentience cybernetics the task of repairing those links and bringing the *Speranza's* senses back online. Kryptaestrex oversaw the repair efforts, while Azuramagelli attempted to keep up with Galatea's rapidly evolving calculations as the gravitational tempests surged and retreated, apparently at random, but which Galatea assured him conformed to patterns too complex for even the *Speranza's* logic engines to identify.

'You know, Tarkis,' said Kotov. 'If you'd spoken to me about turning back now, I might have listened to you.'

'I doubt it, archmagos,' said Blaylock. 'You do not dare return to Mars empty-handed, and no matter the risks, you will always desire to push onwards.'

'You say that like it's a bad thing. We're explorators, pushing onwards is how we advance the frontiers of knowledge. A little risk in such ventures is never a bad thing.'

'The risk/reward ratio in this venture is weighted far more towards risk,' said Blaylock. 'Logically we should return to Mars, but your need to push the boundaries will not allow for such a course.'

'Better to push too far than not far enough,' said Kotov as another thunderous gravity sheer slammed into the *Speranza*. 'Where would we be if we always played safe? What manner of Omnissiah would we serve if we did not always strive to achieve that which others deemed

impossible? To reach for the stars just out of reach is what makes us strong. To fight for the things that *demand* sacrifice and risk is what earns us our pre-eminent place in the galactic hierarchy. By the deeds of men like us is mankind kept mighty.'

'Then let us hope that posterity remembers us for what we achieved and not our doomed attempt.'

'Ave Deus Mechanicus,' said Kotov in agreement.

Blaylock's floodstream surged with data, a blistering heat haze of informational light that made Kotov's inload mechanisms flinch. A nexus of information ribboned through the air between Blaylock and Galatea, and Kotov took a moment to admire Blaylock's attempt to match its processing speed. The data-burden was threatening to overwhelm Blaylock's systems, and he was only parsing a tenth of what Galatea was feeding the fleet's navigational arrays.

'Give up, Tarkis,' said Kotov. 'You'll burn out your floodstream and give yourself databurn.'

'That would be sensible, archmagos,' agreed Blaylock, his binary strained and fragmentary. 'But to see such raw mathematical power unleashed is staggering. I have known nothing like it, and I suspect I never will again. Hence I will attempt to learn all I can from this creature before we are forced to destroy it.'

Kotov flinched at his Fabricatus Locum's words. 'Authority: keep sentiments like that quiet.'

'Informational: the cybernetic hybrid creature's neuromatrix is under far too great a stress of computational astro-calculus to be directing any energy to sensory inloads at present.'

'And you would risk everything on that assumption?'

'It is not an assumption.'

'I don't care,' snapped Kotov. 'Keep such thoughts to yourself in future.'

Kotov stared at Galatea, fearing that Blaylock was underestimating its ability to splinter its cortex and keep its sensory inloads going while the majority of its gestalt machine consciousness was devoted to its real-time navigational processing. It seemed that Blaylock was right, for Galatea was enveloped in spiralling streams of data, trajectories, storm-vectors, gravitational flux arrays and precise chrono-readings that spun, advanced and retreated with each hammerblow of gravity.

Like the ships before it, the *Speranza's* voids blew out, and one by one the links to the other ships in the fleet began to fail. Conventional auspexes were useless in the Halo Scar, and even the more specialised detection arrays mounted on the vast prow of the Ark Mechanicus returned readings that were all but meaningless. Kryptaestrex bent all

his efforts to appeasing the auspex spirit hosts and assigning a choir of adulators to the frontal sections to shore up the hymnal buttresses.

Warnings came in from all across the ship as local conditions proved too arduous for the different regions of the vessel to endure. Decks twisted and distorted by random squalls of gravity and time ruptured and blew their contents out into space, where they were crushed in an instant by the immense forces surrounding the ship.

Entire forges were torn from the underside of the ship as the keel bent out of true and underwent torsion way beyond its tolerances. Centuries-old temples to manufacture were flattened the instant they separated from the ship, and hundreds of armoured vehicles recently constructed for the Cadian regiment were pulled apart in seconds. Two refineries, one on either flank of the *Speranza*, exploded, sending wide dispersals of burning promethium and refined fyceline ore into the ship's wake, where they ignited in garish streams of blazing light that gravity compression stretched out for millions of kilometres.

Kotov felt the ship's pain as it was torn from side to side, buffeted by tortured pockets of gravity and forced to endure swirling eddies of ruptured time. Where gravity pockets intersected, he shared its pain as its hull was torn open and its inner workings exposed to forces no sane designer could ever have expected it to suffer.

The *Speranza* was howling across every channel it possessed: binaric, noospheric, data-light, Manifold, augmitter and vox. Kotov sensed its distress along pathways even he had not known existed, and its pain was his pain. Its suffering was his suffering, and he offered a prayer of forgiveness to its mighty heart, supplication to the hurt it was suffering in its service to the Adeptus Mechanicus.

If they survived to reach the other side of the Halo Scar, then great appeasements would need to be made in thanks for so difficult a transit.

The ship dropped suddenly, as though in the grip of a planet's gravitational envelope, and Kotov gripped the edges of his command throne as he felt steel and adamantium tear deep within the body of the ship. More explosions vented compartments into the hellstorm surrounding them, and the cries of the *Speranza* grew ever more frantic.

And this, thought Kotov, was the eye of the storm.

The shipquakes wracking the *Speranza* were felt just as keenly throughout the lower reaches of the ship. In the maintenance spaces, teams of emergency servitors cycled through the engine decks and plasma drive chambers emitting soothing binaric cants to the afflicted

machines. Only those mortal workers deemed expendable were tasked with maintaining the volatile and highly specialised workings of the great engines of the Ark Mechanicus.

For once Abrehem's revered status had worked in his favour. Together with Hawke, Crusha and Coyne, he had been singled out to spend the shuddering journey through the Halo Scar on a downshift. The respite was welcome, but Abrehem was itchy to get back to doing something that felt like it mattered. Ever since their escape from the reclamation chambers, his duties had become less physically onerous and much more obviously relevant to the operations of the engine deck.

For the last few shifts, he and Coyne had been given tasks that almost resembled the jobs they'd had on Joura, managing lifter rigs and directing the fuel transfers from the deep hangars to the plasma chambers. It was still thankless, demanding and dangerous work, but spoke of the deep reverence even their overseers had for those the Machine-God had singled out.

Totha Mu-32 was Vresh's replacement, and where Vresh had been unthinking in his cruelty and uncaring in his ministrations, Totha Mu-32 was a more spiritual member of the Cult Mechanicus. He appeared to recognise the very real dangers faced by the engine deck crews and was cognisant of the vital nature of their work. Together with an up-deck magos named Pavelka and an enginseer called Sylkwood, Totha Mu-32 was working to get the engines functioning at full capacity by harnessing the devotion of the men and women in his cohorts. Pavelka was typical Mechanicus, but Sylkwood wasn't afraid of getting her hands dirty in the guts of an engine hatch.

Conditions were still hard, but they were improving. Totha Mu-32 drove his charges hard, but Abrehem had always been of the opinion that work *should* be hard. Not impossible, but hard enough to feel that the day's effort made a valuable contribution. Where was the reward and sense of pride if work were easy? How could such service be measured worthy of the Machine-God?

Hawke, of course, had laughed at that, pouring scorn on the idea of work as devotional service.

To Hawke, work was for other people, and the best kind of work was work avoided.

Like many of those on the downshift, Abrehem, Coyne and Ismael gathered in one of the many engine shrines dotted around the deck spaces while the ship groaned and creaked around them as though trying to pull itself apart. This shrine was a long narrow space slotted between a grunting, emphysemic vent tube and a bank of cable

trunking, each thrumming cable thicker than a healthy man's chest. It seemed wherever there was a space between functional elements of the engineering spaces, a shrine to the Machine-God would appear, complete with its own Icon Mechanicus fashioned from whatever off-cuts and debris could be scavenged and worked into its new form. Such off-the-schemata installations were, in theory, forbidden, but no overseer or tech-priest would dream of dismantling a shrine to the Omnissiah on an engine deck, a place where a servant of the Machine might be fatally punished for a moment's lack of faith.

The bisected machine skull at the end of this particular nave was a mosaic constructed from plasma flects scavenged from the reclamation chambers. Abrehem and Coyne's former dock overseer knelt before the icon, his hands clasped before him like a child at prayer. Ismael's eyes had an odd, faraway look to them that spoke of a broken mind and fractured memory. The glassy skull glinted in the winking lights of the vent tube and a gently swaying electro-flambeau as the deck tilted from one side to the other.

'That was a bad one,' said Coyne as the vent tube groaned and a crack appeared in the weld seam joining two sections of pipework together. Hissing, lubricant-sweetened oil moistened the air with a chemical stink.

'They're all bad ones,' said Abrehem, reading the frightened hisses, burps and squeals of binary echoing from the cables as they carried information throughout the ship. 'The ship is scared.'

'Bugger the ship, I'm just about ready to piss my drawers,' said Hawke, pushing aside the canvas doors of the temple and sitting down next to Abrehem. Crusha followed behind Hawke, carrying a pair of bulky-looking gunny sacks over his shoulders. The walls shook, and Abrehem felt suddenly heavy as the ship lurched like a raft in a storm. He didn't like to think of the kinds of forces that could affect a ship as colossal as an Ark Mechanicus.

'Hush,' said Coyne. 'A bit of respect, eh? Remember where you are.'

'Right,' said Hawke, making a quick Cog symbol over his chest. 'Sorry, just never liked being reminded I'm in a pressurised iron box flying through space.'

Abrehem nodded. It was easy to forget that the cavernous spaces in which they lived, worked and slept weren't on the surface of a planet, that they were, in fact, hurtling through the void at vertiginous speeds on a gigantic machine that had a million ways to kill them with malfunction.

'You know, for once I find myself in complete agreement with you,' said Abrehem.

'Come on,' said Hawke. 'You make it sound like we disagree all the time.'

'I can't think of anyone else I disagree with more.'

'Is the ship in... danger?' said Ismael, still on his knees before the Icon Mechanicus.

'Yes,' said Abrehem. 'The ship is in danger.'

'Can you make it better like you made me better?' asked Ismael, rising to his feet and coming to stand before him, hands slack at his sides.

'I didn't make you better, Ismael,' said Abrehem. 'You took a blow to the head and that rearranged bits of your brain, I think. The bits the Mechanicus shut off, they're coming back to you. Well, some of them at least.'

'*Savickas*,' said Ismael, holding out his arm and letting the electoo drift to the surface again.

'Yes, *Savickas*,' smiled Abrehem, pulling his sleeve up to show the identical electoo.

'You are right, the ship is in great pain,' said Ismael, his words halting and slow, as though his damaged brain were only just clinging on to its facility for language. 'We can feel its fear and it hurts us all.'

'We?' said Abrehem. 'Who else do you mean?'

'The others,' said Ismael. 'Like me. I can... feel... them. Their voices are in my head, faint, like whispers. I can hear them and they can hear me. They do not like to hear me. I think I remind them.'

'Remind them of what?' asked Coyne.

'Of what they used to be.'

'Is he always going to talk like that?' asked Hawke, as Crusha laid the two gunny sacks at his feet before moving past Ismael to the skull icon at the far end of the shrine. Like Ismael, Crusha had a childlike respect for ritual and devotion.

'I don't know,' said Abrehem. 'I've never heard of a servitor retaining any knowledge of its former life, so I'm guessing really.'

'It sounds like deep down they remember who they were,' said Coyne.

'Thor's balls, I hope not,' said Hawke. 'Trapped in your own head as a slave, screaming all the time and knowing that no one can ever hear you. That's just about the worst thing I can imagine.'

'Even after all the stuff you said you saw on Hydra Cordatus?'

'No, I suppose not, but you know what I mean.'

'I don't think they remember anything consciously,' said Abrehem, hoping to avoid another retelling of Hawke's battles against the Traitor Marines. 'I think their memory centres are the first things the gemynd-shears cut. All that's left once they're turned into a servitor is the basic motor and comprehension functions.'

'So one bang on the head and he remembers who he is?' said Hawke. 'We should do that to them all and we'd have a bloody army.'

Abrehem shook his head as Hawke rummaged through the first gunny sack. Another shipquake shook the cramped shrine, and Abrehem quickly made the Cog over his heart.

'I don't think it's as simple as that,' said Abrehem. 'You can't mess with someone's brain and know exactly what might happen.'

'Ah, who cares anyway?' said Hawke, pulling a plastic-wrapped carton from the gunny sack and tearing the packaging away with a sigh of pleasure. 'There you are, my beauties.'

'What's that?' asked Coyne, trying and failing to mask his interest.

Hawke grinned and opened a packet of lho-sticks, lighting one with a solder-lance hanging from his belt. He blew out a perfect series of smoke rings and, seeing Coyne and Abrehem's expectant looks, begrudgingly passed the carton over. Coyne took three, but Abrehem contented himself with one. Hawke lit them up, and they smoked in silence for a moment as the ship shuddered around them once again and the electro-flambeau clinked on its chain.

'So where did you get these?' asked Coyne.

'I got a few contacts in the skitarii now,' said Hawke. 'I don't want to say too much more, but even those augmented super-soldiers have a taste for below-decks shine. A few bottles here, a few bottles there...'

'What else have you got in there?'

'This and that,' said Hawke, enjoying keeping his answers cryptic. 'Some food, some drink that hasn't got trace elements of engine oil and piss running through it, and some bits of tech I think I can use to trade with some of the overseers. Turns out they're pretty far down the pecking order too, and aren't averse to the odd bit of commerce that makes life a little more comfortable.'

'What could you have that an overseer would possibly want?'

'Never you mind,' said Hawke, wagging an admonishing finger. 'I'm already telling you too much, but seeing as how we're practically brothers now, I'd be willing to cut you boys in on a piece of the action.'

'What kind of action could you get?'

'Nothing too much to start with. I'm thinking maybe we can get some extra food or some pure-filtered water. Then if things work out, we might see about getting some better quarters or transfer to a deck that isn't killing us with rad-bleed or toxin runoff. Give me six months and I'll have us in a cushy number, where we don't have to do any work at all. It's all about who you know, and that's just as true on a starship as it ever was in the Guard.'

'You could really do that?' asked Coyne.

'Sure, no reason why not,' said Hawke. 'I've got the smarts, and I've got Crusha if folk start getting uppity.'

'You start making moves like that you're going to piss off a lot of people,' warned Abrehem. 'And Crusha can't keep you safe all the time.'

'I know, I'm not an idiot,' said Hawke. 'That's why I got this.'

Hawke reached into the second gunny sack and pulled out a scuffed and battered case, held closed by a numeric lock. He punched in a five digit code and removed an ancient-looking pistol with a long barrel of coiled induction loops and a heavy powercell that snapped into the handle. The matt-black finish of the gun was chipped and scratched, but the mechanism appeared to be well-cared-for, an antique with sentimental value.

'Holy Throne, where did you get that?' said Coyne.

'I told you, I got to know some of the skitarii,' said Hawke. 'They heard I was ex-Guard and we got to talking, and... here we are.'

'Does it even work? It looks like it's about a thousand years old.'

Hawke shrugged. 'I think so. I'm betting it doesn't matter though. You point it at someone and all they're going to be worried about is getting their head blown off.'

'Put it away,' hissed Abrehem. 'If the overseers see you with that, you'll be thrown out of an airlock or turned into a servitor. And probably us too.'

'Relax,' said Hawke, 'they're not going to find it.'

Hawke looked up as Ismael appeared at his shoulder, the servitor looking confused and disorientated.

'What do you want?' spat Hawke.

'That gun,' said Ismael. 'Helicon Pattern subatomic plasma pistol, lethal range two hundred metres, accurate to one hundred metres. Coil capacity, ten shots; recharge time between shots, twenty-five point seven three seconds. Manufacture discontinued in 843.M41 due to overheat margin increase of forty-seven per cent per shot beyond the fifth.'

'You know about guns?' asked Hawke.

'I know about guns?' asked the servitor.

'You tell me, you're the one who just recited the bloody instruction manual,' said Hawke.

'I... had... guns,' said Ismael, haltingly. 'I think I remember using them. I think I was very good.'

'Really?' said Hawke. 'Now that *is* interesting.'

Microcontent 19

The first indication that the crossing of the Halo Scar would involve sacrifice came in a broad-spectrum distress call from the *Blade of Voss*. The nearest vessel to the escort was the *Cardinal Boras*, and its captain, a hoary veteran mariner by the name of Enzo Larousse, was a shipmaster who had sailed treacherous regions of space and lived to tell the tale. As executive officer of the Retribution-class warship he had traversed some of the worst warp storms ever recorded, and as captain had brought his ship back from Ventunius's disastrous expedition to the northern Wolf Stars.

Larousse ran a tight ship with a firm hand that recognised the value each crewman brought to the ship. His bridge staff were well drilled and efficient, his below-decks crew no less so, and a palpable sense of pride and loyalty was felt on every deck.

The screams on the vox were awful to hear, sometimes distorted and *stretched*, like a recording played too slow, sometimes shrieking and shrill. Crushing gravity waves compressed the time and space through which the vox-traffic was passing, twisting the words of each message beyond recognition, but leaving the terrible sense of terror and desperation undiminished.

Larousse's bridge crew felt the horrific fear of their compatriots aboard the *Blade of Voss*, and waited for their captain to give an order. Seated on his command throne, Larousse listened to the screams of fellow mariners, all too aware of how dangerous the space through which they sailed was, but unwilling to abandon the stricken ship.

'Mister Cassen, slow to one third,' he ordered.

'Captain...' warned Cassen. 'We can't help them.'

'Deck officer, raise the blast shutters, I want to see what in the blazes is happening out there,' said Larousse, ignoring his Executive Officer. 'Surveyor control, see what you can get, and someone raise the bloody *Speranza*. They need to know what's happening here.'

'Captain, we have a precise course laid in,' said Cassen. 'Orders from the archmagos are not to deviate from it.'

'To the warp with the archmagos,' snapped Larousse. 'He's already abandoned one ship, and I'll be damned if we're going to leave another behind.'

'Surveyors are dead, captain,' came the report from the auspex arrays.

'No auspex, no vox, no voids,' snarled Larousse. 'Another bloody fool's errand.'

'Blast shutters raising.'

Larousse turned his attention to the hellish maelstrom of ugly, raw light that spilled around them, the excretions of dying stars and the bleeding light and spacetime surrounding them. Hypnotically deadly, coruscating shoals of ultra-compressed stellar matter painted space before the *Cardinal Boras* with splashes of light that writhed and exploded and snapped back as it was deformed by the titanic energies of the tortured gravity fields.

'Holy Terra,' breathed Larousse.

In the bottom quadrant of the viewing screen was the *Blade of Voss*, close enough that it could be seen without the need for surveyors, auspex or radiation slates. The ship was caught in a squalling burst of gravity from a star that appeared to be no bigger than an orbital plate or the great segmentum fortress anchored at Kar Duniash. Convergent streams of gravity were coalescing into a perfect storm of hyper-dense waves of crushing force.

And the *Blade of Voss* was caught at the bleeding edge of that storm.

Plates of armour tens of metres thick were peeling back from her hull and the ship had an unnatural torsion breaking her apart along her overstretched keel. Compounding gravitational sheer forces were tearing the ship apart, and though her mater-captain was fighting to break the ship free, Larousse saw that this was a fight she couldn't win.

'Take us in, Mister Cassen,' ordered Larousse. 'Full ahead and come in on her starboard side. If we can block some of the wavefronts from hitting the *Blade*, she might be able to break free.'

'Captain, we can't get too close or we'll be pulled in too,' warned Cassen.

'Do as I order, Mister Cassen,' said Larousse, in a tone that left no room for argument. 'We've got more fire in our arse than she has. We can break free. She can't.'

Even before Cassen could carry out his order, Larousse saw it was too late.

The *Blade of Voss* came apart in a sucking implosion as it was crushed to fragments by the nightmarish forces at work in the Halo Scar. Strengthened bulkheads split apart and the ship's structural members blew away like grain stalks in a hurricane. In seconds the ship's remains were scattered and drawn into the corpse-star's mass, each piece compressed to a speck of debris no larger than a grain of sand. Larousse watched the death of the *Blade of Voss* with a heavy heart, the honourable escort vessel dissolving as though constructed of sand and dust.

'Captain, we have to turn back to our allotted course,' said Cassen, as alarms began ringing from the various auspex stations and the edges of the storm that had destroyed the *Blade of Voss* reached out to claim another victim.

Larousse nodded. 'Aye, Mister Cassen,' he said slowly, as though daring the storm to try and fight them. 'Bring us back to our original heading.'

'Captain!' shouted the junior officer stationed at surveyor control. 'I have a proximity contact!'

'What?' demanded the captain. 'Which ship is it?'

'I don't know, captain,' said the officer. 'Auspex readings are all over the place.'

'Well what in blazes *do* you know? Where is it?'

'I think it's right behind us.'

The first volley from the *Starblade's* prow pulse lances struck the rear quarter of the *Cardinal Boras* with deadly precision. Guided not by any targeting matrix, but rather by Bielanna's prescient readings of the skein, the Eclipse cruiser's guns were more accurate than ever before. Three engine compartments were vented to space and entire decks were cored with searing wychfire. The eldar ship kept station above and behind the Imperial warship, pouring its fire down onto the shuddering vessel. Though the *Starblade's* launch bays were laden with fighters and bombers, none were launched as they would be exposed to the withering fire of the warship's close-in defences, and Bielanna was loath to risk eldar lives when there was no need.

Caught without shields and unable to outmanoeuvre its attacker, the *Cardinal Boras* suffered again and again under the relentless battering of lance fire. Crews fought to contain the damage, but against repeated hails of high energy blasts they had little chance of success. Captain Larousse attempted to turn his vessel to bring his own guns to bear, but no sooner had the heavy, wedged prow begun to turn than the *Starblade* darted away, always keeping behind the heavy warship.

A sustained burst of fire took the *Cardinal Boras's* dorsal lances, tearing them from their mountings as incandescent columns of light penetrated sixty decks. Vast swathes of the fighting decks were immolated as oxygen-rich atmosphere ignited and filled the crew spaces with terrifying fires that burned swiftly and mercilessly. Gun batteries pounded out explosive ordnance at as steep a rake as possible, but none could turn enough to target the merciless killer savaging them from behind. Torpedoes were spat from the prow launch tubes, their machine-spirits given free rein to engage any target they could find.

It was a tactic of desperation, but Captain Larousse had no other option open to him.

The enormous projectiles arced up and over the eagle-stamped prow and circled in lazy figure of eight patterns over its topside, the spirits caged in the warheads bombarding their local environment with active surveyor blasts in an attempt to locate a target. Most were quickly dragged off course and destroyed by the powerful gravity waves buffeting the warship, but a handful managed to lock onto the ghostly auspex return that flitted around the engines of the *Cardinal Boras.*

Yet even these solitary few flashed through a phantom target, a shimmering lie of a contact generated by the *Starblade's* holofields. What appeared to the war-spirits as a target worthy of attack turned out to be a mirage, a transparency of capricious energy fluctuations, rogue electromagnetic emissions and trickster surveyor ghosts. Only one torpedo detonated, the others flying on for a few hundred kilometres before being torn to pieces by the gravitational forces.

The *Starblade* was merciless in her attentions, raking the *Cardinal Boras* from stern to bow with streaming pulses of lance fire. In a conventional fight, the *Starblade* would have had little hope of besting so powerful a warship. Imperial ships favoured battles of attrition, where their superior armour and unsubtle weapon batteries could transform the space around them into explosive hellstorms of debris and gunfire. But stripped of her void shields and without escorts to keep this rapacious predator from her vulnerable rear, there was nothing she could do but suffer.

And the *Cardinal Boras* suffered like few other ships of the Gothic sector had ever suffered.

Fires boiled through its giant hallways and cathedrals and those few saviour pods that managed to eject were destroyed almost instantly in the harsh physics of the Halo Scar. Fighting for her very survival, the *Cardinal Boras* went down hard, every scrap of firepower and speed wrung from her shuddering frame until there was nothing left to give. With the fight beaten out of her, the *Cardinal Boras* spent her last moments screaming out the nature of her killer.

Reduced to little more than a burned-out drifting wreck, the ancient warship finally succumbed to the inevitable and broke apart. Its keel, laid down over four and a half thousand years ago in the shipyard carousels of Rayvenscrag IV, finally split and the clawing forces of gravitational torsion ripped the vessel apart along its length.

The swarming riptides of powerful gravity storms finished the job, disassembling the remnants of the warship's structure and scattering them in a bloom of machine parts.

Satisfied with the murder of the *Cardinal Boras*, the eldar vessel set its sights on its next victim as a furious heat built in its belly. A silent procession of warriors trapped on the path of murder and war marched in solemn ceremony towards a shrine at the heart of the *Starblade*, a scorched temple of cold wraithbone that now seethed with molten heat and volcanic anger.

The brutally graceful eldar war-vessel knifed through the gravitational haze towards the *Adytum*.

Its guns retreated into their protective housing, for they would not be used in this attack.

The death of the Space Marine vessel would be a much more personal slaying.

The Swordwind was to fall upon the Black Templars.

Kul Gilad heard the shouted commands from the bridge of the *Cardinal Boras* cease, and knew the mighty vessel was dead. Even before he heard the dying ship's tortured vox-emissions identifying the source of the raking gunfire that was killing her, the Reclusiarch had known who the attackers would be. Ever since the eldar wych-woman had slain Aelius at Dantium Gate and cursed him with her eyes, he had felt this doom stalking him.

It had only been a matter of time until she returned to finish what she had started.

Perhaps by facing that doom he might end it.

The bridge of the *Adytum* was a spartan metallic place of echoes and shadow. A boxy space with a raised rostrum at the narrowed proscenium before the main viewing bay, it was laid out with the rigorous efficiency of all Space Marine ships. Chapter-serfs manned the key systems of the ship, wolf-lean men plucked from the crew rosters of the *Eternal Crusader*. Each one was a fighter, a warrior of some skill and renown amongst the mortals who served the Chapter, but Kul Gilad counted none of them as being of any worth in the coming fight.

The ship's captain was named Remar, a seconded Naval officer bound to the Black Templars for the last fifty years, and it was fitting that he had also fought the eldar above the burning cities of Dantium. As with any battle against the eldar, history had a habit of recurring with fateful resonances.

'Captain Remar, seal the bridge,' ordered Kul Gilad.

'Reclusiarch?'

'Full lockdown. No one comes in and no one leaves,' said Kul Gilad. 'Only upon my direct authority does that door open. Do you understand me?'

'I understand, Reclusiarch,' said Remar and his fingers danced over the keypad on the command lectern to enact Kul Gilad's will.

'Ready the *Barisan* for flight.'

'My lord?' asked Captain Remar. 'The Thunderhawk will be unlikely to survive an attack run in such a hostile environment. I respectfully advise against such a course of action.'

'Your concern is noted, captain,' said Kul Gilad.

He opened a vox-link to his battle squad and took a deep breath before speaking.

'Varda, Tanna. You and every member of the squad, injured *and* battle-ready, are to make their way to the embarkation deck. Board the *Barisan* and await further orders.'

The hesitation before Tanna answered showed that he too shared the captain's concerns regarding the chances of the Thunderhawk's survival beyond the *Adytum's* armoured hull.

'As you will it, Reclusiarch,' said Tanna.

The gunship's lightweight hull would not last long without protection, but the idea of questioning his Reclusiarch's order never so much as crossed the sergeant's mind. The vox-link snapped off, and Kul Gilad moved to stand before the command lectern.

'No pity, no remorse, no fear,' whispered Kul Gilad.

'Reclusiarch?' said Captain Remar.

'Yes?'

'Permission to speak freely?'

'Granted,' said Kul Gilad. 'You have more than earned that right, Captain Remar.'

The captain bowed his shaven, cable-implanted skull in recognition of the honour Kul Gilad accorded him.

'What is happening? You have the look of a man staring down at his own fresh-dug grave.'

'The eldar ship will come for us next,' said Kul Gilad. 'And as gallant as the *Adytum* is, it cannot hope to fight off so powerful a vessel.'

'Maybe we cannot win,' said Remar. 'But we will die fighting. No pity, no remorse, no fear.'

Kul Gilad nodded. 'Since Dantium they have been in my dreams, dogging my every step like an assassin. Now they are come, and they pick us off one by one like the cowards they are. I despise their weakness of spirit and their paucity of courage, captain. Where is the honour in striking from afar? Where is the glory in slaying your enemy without looking in his eyes as the last breath leaves his body?'

Remar did not answer.

What answer was there to give?

'I think that was the *Cardinal Boras*,' said Magos Azuramagelli, sifting through the electromagnetic spikes that cascaded through his station. The separated aspects of his brain and body matter flickered with dismay, and though it was often difficult to read the composite structure of the astrogation magos's moods, Kotov had no trouble in reading the pain in his words.

The command deck of the *Speranza* was alive with warnings, both visual and audible. Floods of damage reports flooded in from every deck as the mighty vessel twisted, bent and flexed in ways it should never have to endure. Binary screeches of systems in pain filled the space, though Kotov had grown adept at filtering out all but the most pressing. His ship was tearing itself apart, and there was nothing he could do to prevent its destruction.

The death of the *Blade of Voss* had struck a note of grief through the magi on the *Speranza's* command deck. The loss of so many machine-spirits and a vessel of undoubted pedigree was a calamitous blow, both to the expedition and the Mechanicus as a whole.

And now they had lost their most powerful warship, a vessel with a grand legacy of victory and exploration. A true relic of the past that had fought in some of the greatest naval engagements of the last millennium and explored regions of space that now bore the cartographer's ink instead of a blank screed of emptiness on a map.

Anger touched Kotov and he directed his hurt at the machine hybrid thing that squatted on its malformed reticulated legs.

'You said you could navigate us through the Halo Scar safely,' said Kotov.

Galatea rose up, its central palanquin rotating as it brought the mannequin body around to face Kotov. The robotic form of the tech-priest twitched and the silver optics glimmered with amusement.

'We did,' said Galatea. 'But we also told you that you should expect to suffer great losses before we reach the other side.'

'At this rate, we will be fortunate to reach the other side.'

'You have already penetrated farther than any save Magos Telok,' pointed out Galatea.

'A fact that will only become relevant if we survive,' countered Kotov.

'True, but the demise of the *Cardinal Boras* was not at the hands of the Halo Scar,' said Galatea.

'Then what happened to it?'

'We sense the presence of another vessel, one that Naval xeno-contact records archived in the Cypra Mundi repository have previously codified as the *Starblade*, an eldar ship of war.'

'An eldar ship?' said Kotov. 'Are you sure?'

'Its energy signatures and mass displacement offer a ninety-eight point six per cent degree of accuracy in that assessment. From its movement patterns, it is reasonable to assume it destroyed the *Cardinal Boras* and now manoeuvres to attack the *Adytum*.'

Kotov spun to face Blaylock. 'Order all ships to close on the *Speranza*. Spread out we will be easy prey for such a vessel.'

'As you say, archmagos,' said Blaylock, blasting the vox with his urgent communication.

Kotov turned his attention to astrogation.

'Azuramagelli? Could this eldar ship have been the source of the emissions you detected before we entered the Scar?'

The astrogation magos summoned his previous data readings in a bloom of light, and Kotov now saw the subtle hints that might have revealed the presence of an eldar ship had they but known what to look for.

'Indeed it could, archmagos,' said Azuramagelli. 'I offer no excuses for my failure to recognise its presence. What penance shall I assign myself?'

'Oh, shut up, Azuramagelli,' snapped Kotov. 'We don't have any useful feeds from auspex, so find a way to shoot it down and we will discuss your punishment at a later date.'

'You will not be able to shoot it down,' said Galatea. 'Even with our help.'

'Then what? We let it pick the fleet apart, ship by ship?'

'No,' said Galatea, as though amused at Kotov's seeming stupidity. '*You* cannot fight this vessel, but the *Speranza* can.'

It began as a shimmering haze that formed on the proscenium at the far end of *Adytum's* bridge.

Kul Gilad clenched his fist, and an arc of destructive energy formed around the oversized fingers of his power fist. The ammo feeds of his gauntlet-mounted storm bolter ratcheted the heavy belt of shells into position, and he recited his Reclusiarch's vow.

'*Lead us from death to victory, from falsehood to truth,*' he began as the half-formed alien gateway filled the bridge with an actinic crackle of strange light.

'*Lead us from despair to hope, from faith to slaughter.*'

The bridge crew unplugged themselves from their stations, unholstering pistols and drawing serrated combat blades from thigh sheaths. A wailing moan of deathly wind issued from the swirling mass of wych-light that grew in power with the sound of clashing blades, howling cries of loss and a crackle of distant fires.

'*Lead us to His strength and an eternity of war.*'

Captain Remar issued his last command to the *Adytum*, to take the ship in close to the *Speranza*, then disconnected himself from his command lectern and drew a long rapier that hung in a kidskin sheath from its side.

'*Let His wrath fill our hearts.*'

With the Reclusiarch at its centre, the bridge crew of the *Adytum* formed a battle line. Kul Gilad heard Sergeant Tanna's voice in his helmet, but closed himself off to his warriors. Their crusade would go on without him, and he could not be distracted now.

'*Death, war and blood; in vengeance serve the Emperor in the name of Dorn!*'

The alien gateway on the bridge shimmered like the surface of a glacially smooth lake, and a lithe warrior woman stepped onto the *Adytum*. She was clad in rune-etched armour of emerald and a tall helmet of bone-white topped with a billowing plume of vivid scarlet and antler-like extrusions. Kul Gilad knew her well from the battle at Dantium Gate. A cloak of multiple hues of green and gold hung at her shoulders, and the slender-bladed sword she carried was etched with shimmering filigree that writhed with loathsome movement.

Behind her, a dozen warriors with bulbous helms and overlapping plates of scaled green stepped through the gateway. Crackling energies

played between the toothlike mandibles attached to their helms, and each one – though slender – had the bulk of a powerful warrior.

'You killed Aelius, the Emperor's Champion,' said Kul Gilad. 'And now you come to kill me.'

'I have,' agreed the eldar witch. 'I will not let you destroy their future.'

'Is this all you have brought?' said Kul Gilad. 'I will kill them all.'

The witch woman cocked her head to the side as though amused at his defiance.

'You will not,' she said. 'I have travelled the skein and seen your thread cut a thousand times.'

The gateway rippled one last time. Blazing light and heat like Kul Gilad had not felt since the Season of Fire on Armageddon blew out to fill the bridge of the *Adytum*.

A towering daemon of fire and boiling blood stepped though the howling gateway, its glowing body formed from brazen plates of red-hot iron that dripped glowing gobbets of molten metal to the deck. Its powerful body creaked and bled the light of wounded stars, and the vast spear it carried wailed with the lament of a lost empire and the self-inflicted genocide of a million souls. Smoke from the bloodiest furnace coiled from its limbs, and a mist of glowing cinders seethed and raged like a dark crown about its horned head.

An avatar of unending war, it roared with the unquenchable anger of a warrior god, and the blood of its slaughters oozed between its fingers, running in thick rivulets down the haft of its monstrous spear.

'Abhor the witch,' snarled Kul Gilad. 'Destroy the witch!'

They heard the warning bells, but paid them no mind. Since the vox-horns had announced their entry to the Halo Scar ten hours ago, there had been a steady stream of warning klaxons, alarm bells and binary announcements. Abrehem, Coyne, Ismael, Hawke and Crusha made their way through the vaulted tunnels of the engineering deck towards the feeding hall. Their next shift refuelling the plasma engines was due to start in two bells, and the high-calorie gruel was just about all that would sustain them over the length of a backbreaking shift hauling the volatile cylinders of fuel on long chains along the delivery rails to the combustion chambers. Having so many muscle-augmented servitors on shift had made life easier, but the work was still punishing in its intensity. Burned skin, caustic fumes and torn muscles were the norm after only a couple of hours.

'I'll be glad when you can get us these cushy shifts,' said Coyne.

'You and me both, lad,' said Hawke.

'You hardly do any work anyway,' said Abrehem. 'Crusha does all your work and you get the servitors to haul most of the loads.'

The ogryn grinned at the sound of its name, still carrying the gunny sacks of contraband. The plasma pistol Hawke had finagled from the skitarii was in one of those sacks, and Abrehem tried not to think of how much trouble they would be in if it were ever discovered.

Hawke shrugged, completely unashamed at his evasion of work. 'I see myself as more of a delegator, Abe,' he said. 'A man who gets things done without needing to dirty his own hands.'

'No, your hands are dirty enough already,' said Abrehem.

Another siren went off, an insistent blare that sounded like the ship itself was screaming. Abrehem jumped at the sound, sensing on a marrow-deep level that this was no ordinary, everyday sound, that this was a warning only ever deployed in the worst emergencies.

'I've not heard that one before,' said Coyne. 'I wonder what it means.'

'Probably nothing,' said Hawke. 'Maybe a pipe in the archmagos's toilet's sprung a leak.'

The others laughed nervously, but they all knew there was something more to it than the normal run of warnings that sounded for reasons no one could quite fathom. This siren had a strident note of real danger to it, like it was modulated at a pitch that circumvented all rational thought and went straight for the mind's fear response.

'No,' said Abrehem. 'Something's really wrong this time.'

Alarms sounded throughout the *Speranza*, high-pitched screams of violation that roused Cadians from their barracks, skitarii from their guild halls and Mechanicus armsmen from their rapid-response hubs. Throughout the ship, armed men and women snapped shells into shotcannons, clicked powercells into lasrifles and engaged the energy coils of implanted weaponry.

Tech-guard squads formed defensive cordons at the entrances to the great engineering halls where the legion of Ark Fabricati workers laboured on the downed *Canis Ulfrica*. Ven Anders dispersed the companies of the 71st to prearranged defensive choke points as Magos Dahan routed his skitarii through the corridors and chambers of the ship like leukocytes racing through a living body to destroy an infection.

The alarm that echoed through the *Speranza* was one that had never been sounded before, one whose frequency had been carefully chosen by the mighty ship's lost builders for its precise atonal qualities that caused the most discomfort in those who heard it.

It represented one thing and one thing only.

Enemy boarders.

Microcontent 20

Screams and the whickering sound of alien gunfire echoed from the soaring walls of the plasma containment chambers. Cylinders of lethally volatile plasmic fuel swayed overhead, ratcheting along delivery rails like uncontrolled rolling stock heading for a collision at a busy terminus. Shimmering wychfire from half a dozen bright portals cast impossible shadows and brought a hallucinatory form of daylight to an area of the *Speranza* that had not known natural light since its construction.

Abrehem crouched behind a slab-sided mega-dozer, its iron track unit taller than ten men, and watched in horror as the invaders slaughtered the men and women of the engineering decks. Bodies lay strewn around the chamber, torn up like they'd been caught in an agricultural threshing machine. Their killers were aliens; not the brutish, clumsy savages the daily devotionals ridiculed, but sculpturally beautiful alabaster and jade figures with their own graceful animation. They moved like spinning dancers, their strides smooth and their bodies always completely in balance. They carried flattened weaponry with elongated barrels that buzzed as they fired hails of deadly projectiles.

'Are they eldar?' said Coyne. 'Pirates?'

'I think so,' answered Abrehem. 'But they don't look much like pirates.'

The token force of skitarii assigned to the engineering space was

still fighting, filling the chamber with booming blasts of shot-cannon and hot streaks of las-fire. A dozen or more were already dead, picked off by cloaked shapes that moved through the shadows like ghosts, or cut down by darting figures in brilliant blue war-armour and guns that shrieked as they slew.

Abrehem ducked as a spinning fragment embedded itself in the track unit beside him, a perfectly smooth disc of a material that looked like polished ceramic. Its edges thrummed with magnetic force and the edge was clearly sharper than any blade Abrehem had ever seen. They hadn't wanted to come here, but a series of irising doors, dropping containment shutters and skitarii barricades had forced their path through the bowels of the ship and brought them into the middle of a firefight.

'Bloody stupid this,' said Hawke. 'You don't *go* to battles. You avoid them.'

'I don't think we had much choice,' said Abrehem. 'It was either this or get stuck out in the tunnels.'

'At least there we wouldn't get shot at.'

'And maybe we'd have been stuck there for days and starved to death.'

Hawke glared at him, unwilling to concede the point, but Abrehem knew he was right; it *was* stupid to have come here. Hawke knelt beside Crusha and rummaged through the gunny sacks, as Coyne peered through the cogs, wheels and gears of the tracks with his mouth open in shock. Like Abrehem, Coyne had never seen an alien creature, and the sheer strangeness of these invaders was keeping the worst of their fear at bay for now.

'Kill them?' said Crusha, and they all looked over at the ogryn. It was the first thing Crusha had said since Joura.

'Thor's teeth, what's with him?' asked Hawke as the ogryn stood and balled his hands into fists.

'Pycho-conditioned responses are kicking in,' said Abrehem, seeing Crusha's primitive augmetics come alive with activity. 'He's conditioned to react to the smell of blood and the sound of battle.'

The ogryn's body visibly swelled as intra-vascular chem-shunts pumped combat-stimms into his powerful physiology, and muscular boosters juiced his strength with enough adrenaline to cause instantaneous heart failure in an ordinary man.

Once, Abrehem would have been terrified at being next to a battle-ready abhuman, but right now it probably wasn't a bad idea to have an angry ogryn nearby.

'Get down, you big lummox!' snarled Hawke, as Crusha took a step into the open. 'They'll see you!'

Hawke's words were prophetic, and through the guts of the mega-dozer's track unit, Abrehem saw a group of the killer aliens in form-fitting ablative weave the colour of ancient bone turn the burning red eye-lenses of their jade helms towards them.

'Shitting hell,' he swore as the aliens bounded towards them behind a hail of the screaming discs.

'Run for it!' shouted Hawke, dragging one of the gunny sacks behind him as he fled.

Abrehem didn't need telling twice, though he had no idea to where they would run. But where they were running *to* seemed less important than what they were running *from*.

A sound like breaking glass exploded around them as the discs tore through the tracks of the mega-dozer, ripping hydraulic lines and shattering vital components that rendered the vast machine useless in the blink of an eye. A tumbling fragment took Coyne in the back, tearing a bloody line from shoulder blade to shoulder blade. He stumbled, shocked rigid by the sudden pain, and fell to his knees. Abrehem saw a fragment of a sharpened ceramic disc embedded in the meat of his back and bent to remove it. The edges cut his hand as he pulled it out, and blood welled from a deep gash on his palm.

'Imperator, that hurts...' grunted Coyne as Abrehem hauled him upright. Blood soaked Abrehem's hands as he and Coyne staggered down the length of the mega-dozer. More whickering gunfire and ricochets chased them, but amazingly none of it touched them. Abrehem looked back over his shoulder.

'Crusha! Come on!' he shouted, seeing the ogryn wasn't fleeing with them.

'Crusha fight!' bellowed the ogryn, beating a meaty fist against its swelling chest. 'Crusha kill Emperor's enemies!'

Abrehem paused, reluctant to simply abandon the creature.

'What are you doing?' gasped Coyne. 'Let's go!'

'Come on, you bloody idiot!' shouted Hawke from the shadow of a blast shutter that had miraculously not sealed the deck off, leaving them a way out. Scattered groups of bondsmen were also running for the opening, ducking between heavy machinery and lifter gear to escape the slaughter. The shutter rattled in its frame, the mechanism trying to close, but for some reason unable to descend. It could drop at any moment, trapping him in the middle of a firefight, and Abrehem knew he didn't have a choice but to keep going.

Blasts of weapons fire filled the space behind him. Abrehem didn't dare look back and kept going, dragging Coyne's increasingly limp body beside him.

'Come on, for the Emperor's sake!' he yelled. 'Help me out, Coyne! Stay awake and use those bloody legs of yours!'

Coyne's eyes flickered open and he nodded, but blood loss and shock was turning him into a dead weight at Abrehem's side.

'Help me!' he yelled at his fellow bondsmen. They ignored him, but then – seeing who was shouting – a few turned to help take Coyne's weight. They grabbed his legs and his other arm, dragging him into the safety of the arched passageway beyond the blast shutter. Abrehem looked for Hawke, seeing him still frantically searching through the gunny sack.

Abrehem heard a roar of anger and pressed himself against the bulkhead of the juddering doorway. He glanced up to see the blast shutter cranking down a few centimetres at a time, as though fighting some unseen force that was keeping it open.

'Abe, can you get that damn door shut?' shouted Hawke.

Abrehem took a breath and sought out the door lock, but recoiled from the violence in the mechanism, a blood-red haze of data occluding it from any attempt he might make to interfere with its workings.

'I can't,' he shouted back. 'It's jammed or something.'

'Figures,' said Hawke. 'Aha! Here it is.'

Abrehem turned away from Hawke and looked back the way they had come.

Back at the mega-dozer, he saw Crusha surrounded by the eldar warriors. They filled the air with lethally sharp discs, tearing chunks of bloodied meat from the ogryn's body, dancing away from his ponderous fists with impunity. They moved with inhuman speed, darting in to slash at Crusha with delicate blades that looked far too thin to be combat-capable, but which sliced through the ogryn's thick skin with energised ease. They were like mutant dockside rats attacking a drunk stevedore, too small to bring down their prey alone, but working together...

One eldar moved a fraction too slow and caught a clubbing blow to its helm that made it stagger. Even as it righted itself, Crusha gripped the warrior's armoured tunic and slammed it into the mega-dozer, breaking every bone in its flimsy body.

The bloodied ogryn roared in triumph and hurled the body into the mass of his attackers. Most spun away from the corpse missile, but a handful were knocked flat by the impact. Crusha was on them a second later, stamping one to paste and breaking another's neck before the rest could rise. his fist swung out and caught an eldar warrior who'd dared approach too close to put its gun to the ogryn's neck. The alien was hurled ten metres through the air, landing in a crumpled heap that told Abrehem its spine was a concertinaed mess of shattered bone.

The other eldar backed away from Crusha, now realising it had been arrogant to get close to so powerful an opponent. Abrehem waited for them to open fire, but the volley of razor discs never came. A second later he saw why.

A blurred shape, like a figure moving too fast to be seen with the naked eye, rounded the edge of the mega-dozer. Abrehem's enhanced optics made out the contoured outline of a shimmering ghost, a graceful form of lithe perfection that carried a long sword with a blade of palest white. Armoured in azure plates and with a plumed helm crested in red and gold, the sublime warrior flickered in and out of view as its image was splintered and thrown out around it in a haze of mirrored light.

The figure spun and danced around Crusha in a series of stepped images, each moment where Abrehem was able to perceive the figure like a snapshot of motion caught in a strobe light.

And then it was over.

The dance was ended and Crusha was on his knees, blood gushing from a series of lethal cuts that had opened every major artery in his body. He looked suddenly small, like an idiot child brought low by scholam bullies. The sublime warrior made one last spinning leap and Crusha's head flew from his shoulders, severed cleanly by a single, perfectly balanced strike.

The warrior looked up from its killing, and Abrehem felt its distaste at the act. Not at the killing itself, but that it had been forced to wet its blade in the blood of so crude an opponent. He met the cold, warlike stare of the warrior and felt the icy calm of its perfectly distilled martial skill. This was a warrior who embodied death in its purest form.

The contact was broken, and the eldar warrior's form blurred into shimmering silver light as it ran towards the stubbornly open shutter.

'Oh, crap,' said Abrehem. 'We need to go. Right bloody now!'

Kul Gilad's gauntlet slammed into the flaming daemon, and he felt the heat of its molten body through the heavy plates and crackling energies of his fist. Iron buckled and dribbling spurts of blazing ichor oozed from the cracks like light-filled blood. The avatar roared and brought its blazing spear around in a crushing arc. Encased in Terminator armour, Kul Gilad was too ponderous to evade, and he leaned into the blow, taking it on the curved plates of his shoulder guard.

White heat of the hottest furnace imaginable cut through ceramite, and the Reclusiarch bit back a cry of agony as he felt the skin beneath char to blackened ruin. He stepped away from the daemon and unleashed a stream of explosive mass-reactives at point-blank range. Most ignited before they impacted on the creature, their warheads flashing with premature detonation in the intense heat that surrounded the monster. A few shells penetrated the brazen plates of its body, but the furnace of its interior destroyed them before they could explode.

Tanna's shouting voice echoed in his helmet, but he had not the breath or time to answer the frantic cries of his sergeant.

The daemon creature towered over him, and Kul Gilad felt his own anger rise to match the star-hot gaze of burning, eternal fury that blazed in its alien eyes. A storm raged around him, a swirling hurricane of light and unnatural energies that spat and bit with searing discharges. The vast plates of his armour were proof against that lightning, but the bridge crew were not so fortunate.

He could hear them dying around him, flensed to the bone by the witch woman's lightning storm or slaughtered like livestock by the green-armoured warriors. He'd seen none of them fall, but their sudden silence was proof enough that they were all dead. The eldar witch was at the heart of the storm, her slender body englobed by a radiant halo of power.

Her bound daemon came at him again, quicker than anything of such bulk and monstrous fire should be able to move. The weapon it carried danced in the heat haze surrounding it, sometimes appearing to be a vast sword, sometimes a great war-axe or a screaming spear. Kul Gilad batted the weapon aside with his power fist and stepped in to deliver a thunderous hammerblow to the creature's midriff.

'*All-conquering Master of Mankind, be pleased with this war's tumultuous roar!*' he sang, his voice booming from the vox-grille of his helm. His fist broke an armoured plate, and magma-hot gouts of its inner fire poured over his fist. Kul Gilad ignored the searing pain and drew back his fist to strike again.

A flash of red and a burning pain in his gut told him he'd been hit. The bridge spun away from him and he felt himself leave the deck. He slammed into a support stanchion, feeling it buckle with the force of impact. Bones broke inside him, and his body surged in heat as its self-repair biology went into overdrive.

He fell, slamming into the deck with force enough to dent the plates.

'Reclusiarch!' said Tanna, and this time Kul Gilad paid heed, knowing it would be his last chance to speak to his warriors.

'Sergeant,' he hissed through blood-flecked spittle. 'Get to the *Speranza*. Go now and never look back.'

'What is happening up there?' demanded Tanna urgently. 'We're disembarking from the *Barisan* and coming to you.'

'No,' said Kul Gilad. 'Get to the *Speranza*. Now. This is my last order and you will obey it.'

'Reclusiarch, no!'

'Until the end, brother,' said Kul Gilad softly before severing the vox-link.

Smoke billowed around him and he pushed himself to his feet, lifting his gauntlet-mounted storm bolter and loosing another burst of shots. The daemon stood over him, and this time his shots appeared to wreak some harm. It reeled from the force of his barrage and threw up a red-gold arm that bled light into the air and smoked with sulphurous yellow fumes. Kul Gilad's visor scrolled with danger indicators.

'Delight in swords and fists red with alien blood, and the dire ruin of savage battle,' he said, drawing himself up to his full height.

The storm of light was gone, and he saw the red ruin of the bridge crew.

Captain Remar lay on his back, his body scorched with numerous electrical burns and a canyon of flesh opened up in his body from neck to pelvis. His sword was bloody, and at least one eldar warrior had fallen to his blade before they had killed him. The captain's uniform caught light as the daemon crushed him beneath its blazing tread, and the deck plates were scorched black by its every footstep. The meat stink of burned human flesh waxed strong.

'Rejoice in furious challenge, and avenging strife, whose works with woe embitter human life,' roared Kul Gilad, hurling himself at the monstrous god of war. Storm bolter blazing with the last of his ammunition, this was the moment he had been waiting for all his life, a last charge against impossible odds in service of the Emperor. He recalled what he had said to Mistress Tychon.

Eventually everything must die, even Space Marines.

Time compressed, the motion of his fist moving at the speed of tectonic plates, every spinning warhead ejected from his storm bolter perfectly visible to him as its rocket motor ignited. His fist struck the daemon in the centre of its chest, and he unleashed every last iota of his zealous fury and righteous hate in that blow.

His fist shattered the hideously organic metal of the daemon's armour and he felt his arm engulfed in searing, unendurable heat. The daemon's roar of pain was a symphony to his ears, and he rejoiced

that the Emperor had seen fit to grant him this last boon of death. Flames billowed around him and he felt a sickening impact on his midsection.

Kul Gilad felt himself falling, and the deck slammed into his helmeted head as he rolled onto his back. His arm was a mangled, burned ruin, a stump of fused meat, bone and metal that only superficially resembled a human limb. Black smoke and dribbling gobbets of skin ran down the sagging plates of melted armour, and though he knew he should be horrified at this nightmarish injury, he felt utterly at peace.

He felt a burning pressure of heat coiling inside him, his biology shrieking in the agony of attempting to repair the damage done to him. A shadow fell across him, and Kul Gilad looked up into the face of the daemon, its fiery chest buckled and torn open, but reknitting even as he watched. The mortal wound he had struck it had been nothing of the sort and despair touched Kul Gilad at the thought of his failure.

The leering daemon towered over him, terrible in aspect and horrifying in the single-minded violence it represented. He hated it with every breath left to him. The black paint of his armour peeled back at its proximity and he struggled to rise. With the one arm left to him, he raised himself onto his elbow and saw why he couldn't move.

He was cut in two at the waist.

His armoured legs lay across the deck from him and he lay with the looping meat coils of his packed innards slowly oozing from his scorched, bifurcated body. The daemon stood in the pool of his blood, and he tasted the chemical-rich stink of its hyper-oxygenation as it burned. It lowered its flame-wreathed weapon to touch his chest, and the tip of the blade sank into the Imperial eagle mounted there in one last insult.

Kul Gilad's life could now be measured in breaths. Not even Space Marine physiology could survive such a traumatic wound without an Apothecary nearby. Even Brother Auiden would be stretched to the limit of his abilities to save him now, and Kul Gilad's heart broke to know that his body would not be laid to rest within the crypts of the *Eternal Crusader*.

The eldar witch woman knelt beside his dying body, and he wanted to swat her away with the last of his strength, but the burning daemon held him pinned flat like a specimen on a dissection table. She reached up and removed her helmet, revealing a tapering oval face with hard eyes and a mane of red hair entwined with glittering stones and flecks of gold. Her lips were full and blue with cosmetic paint.

She reached down and unclipped his skull-masked helm from his gorget and released the pressure seals holding it to his armour. With surprising gentleness, she lifted the heavy helmet clear and placed it beside his head. Kul Gilad tasted the subtle perfumes wreathing her body, a musky odour of cave-blooming flowers and smoky temples where decadent psychotropics were consumed.

'Strange,' she said in a hateful musical voice. 'You die here, and yet the futures are still unclear.'

'You have no future,' spat Kul Gilad. 'This vessel is doomed and you with it.'

She fixed him with a curious stare, as though unsure of what he meant.

'You are the war-leader, yes?' she said.

'I am Kul Gilad,' he said. 'Reclusiarch of the Black Templars, proud son of Sigismund and Dorn. I am a warrior of the Emperor and I know no fear.'

She leaned in close and whispered in his ear. 'Know that everything you are and all you hold dear will die by my hand. I will slay your warriors and the dream of the future will live again. I will not let you kill my daughters before their birth, even if it means the extinction of the stars themselves.'

Kul Gilad had no idea what she was talking about, but let only defiance rage in his eyes.

He coughed a mouthful of bloody foam, feeling his organs shutting down one after another.

Greyness closed in on him, and he struggled to give voice to one last curse.

'There is only the Emperor,' whispered Kul Gilad. 'And He is our shield and protector.'

Abrehem and the bondsmen who'd made it out of the engineering chamber ran through the tunnels in blind panic. The lumens had failed, and the only light came from the flickering emergency sigils that winked dimly in the hissing claustrophobic gloom. Abrehem's eyes compensated for the lack of illumination, but he was the only one with any sense of the geometry and layout of the tunnel through which they fled. It was narrow and lined with convulsing pipework that rippled like a troubled digestive system processing a particularly difficult meal. Alpha-numeric location signifiers passed by on the walls, but they were ones Abrehem hadn't seen before. He had no idea where he was and that didn't bode well for any hope of escape.

The creak and groan of grinding metal was stronger here as the

Speranza twisted and flexed in the Halo Scar's powerful grip. Steam vented from ruptured pipes and Abrehem felt mists of oil and hydraulic fluids squirting him as they blundered onwards. Terrified screams of fear echoed from the walls, and Abrehem tried not to imagine how close the eldar killers might be.

'Hawke!' shouted Abrehem. 'Where are you?'

If Hawke bothered to answer, his voice was lost in the tumult of barging, shouting men and women. Their flight brought them out into a vast, cylindrical chamber with gently curving walls and an enormous rotating fan blade turning slowly above them. Updraughts of hot, carbon-scented air gusted through the mesh decking below them, and Abrehem realised they were in a portion of the ship's air scrubbers: the *Speranza's* lungs. Bondsmen milled in confusion, the darkness and the scale of the space in which they now found themselves serving to rob them of any notion of which way to run. They couldn't see the arched exit passageway on the far wall, but Abrehem could.

'This way!' he shouted. 'Follow me, I can see a way out.'

Hands grabbed for him, and he led a frightened gaggle of people towards the far side of the chamber. Some held fast to his coveralls, some to the sound of his voice, but as a stumbling, shambling mass they moved with him.

'Thank the Emperor you have your father's eyes,' said a voice at his shoulder.

'Hawke?'

'None other, Abe,' said Hawke, one hand gripping tightly to his shoulder. 'I don't suppose Crusha made it out?'

Abrehem shook his head, before remembering that Hawke wouldn't be able to see the gesture.

'No, the eldar killed him,' he said. 'A swordsman took his head off.'

'Damn, but that'd have been a sight to see,' mused Hawke, utterly without remorse, and Abrehem felt his dislike of the man raise a notch.

'You'll likely get your wish, he's the one that's after us.'

'Don't worry about him, I'll take care of that fancy bastard.'

Abrehem wanted to laugh at Hawke's insane bravado, but he had none left in him.

His mob of terrified bondsmen reached the exit to the air scrubbing chamber and the containment shutter rattled up into its housing as they approached. Abrehem didn't know what to make of that, seeing a cackling fizz of code vanish into the aether of the ship's datasphere from the lock.

He heard whipping disturbances in the air, quickly followed by screams of pain. Abrehem risked a backward glance and his heart lurched as he saw the eldar assassin and his squad of gunmen entering the chamber. They were firing with their strange weapons, but the billowing thermals were serving to spoil their aim and only a handful of their victims were falling.

Abrehem paused as he saw that most of those who'd been hit were still alive, lying with limbs severed cleanly or disc-shaped slits punched through their backs. They screamed for help, and the person Abrehem had once been wanted to go back.

But the man he was now knew better than to risk his neck for people that were as good as dead.

'Come on, Abe!' shouted Hawke. 'We need you.'

Grasping hands pulled him away, and once again they fled down darkened passageways that twisted, rose and fell and plunged deeper and deeper into a labyrinth of tunnels that even the Mechanicus had probably forgotten about. Where junctions presented themselves, Abrehem took turns at random, hoping their pursuers would eventually give up and hunt some easier prey.

What was it the agri-workers in the outlying farm collectives said? *I don't need to outrun the grox, I just need to outrun you.*

He was utterly lost, but the frantic people around him followed him like he was some kind of divine saviour. They shouted his name and wailed to the Omnissiah, to Thor, to the Emperor and the myriad saints of the worlds they called home. Every now and then, Abrehem would see the flickering, blood-red burst of code in the walls, dogging their flight like some kind of gleeful binary observer that delighted in their fear. He had no idea what it might be, and had not the time or energy to waste in thinking of it.

The tunnels grew ever more cramped, and Abrehem heard fresh, cracking bursts of gunfire behind them, swiftly followed by more screams. He picked up the pace, though his ravaged body had little left to give to their escape. His heart thundered against his sunken chest and his limbs burned with acid buildup from the sudden burst of activity and adrenaline. Bodies pressed in tightly around him, their fear-sweat stink pungent and their desperation hanging upon him like a curse. They wept as they ran, pinning their hopes for life on Abrehem's guidance. The tunnels twisted around on themselves, a knotted labyrinth that could not have been planned out by any sane shipwright.

Yet for all their unknown dimensions and orientation, Abrehem felt a disturbing familiarity to these passageways, a sense that the ship was somehow leading them somewhere, almost as if it were *reconfiguring* itself to bring them to a place of its choosing. That was surely ridiculous, but the notion persisted until his lurching steps brought him into the chamber that was part templum, part prison and part sepulchre.

Hawke's alcohol distilling apparatus burbled and popped against the blocked-off wall with the faded stencilling, and the stink of chemical shine made Abrehem want to heave his guts out onto the hexagonal tiled floor.

He'd killed them all.

He'd led them to a dead end. Literally and figuratively.

'Shitting hell, Abe,' snapped Hawke, as he saw where they'd ended up. 'There's no way out.'

Abrehem heaved great gulps of air into his lungs, all the strength draining from him as he realised they were all dead. He lurched on wobbling legs to the far wall as he saw the ripple of malicious code squirm across its surface. Even as he watched, it bled into the centre of the wall, and his jaw fell open as he saw it approximated the shape of a human hand.

It flickered like a badly projected image, exactly where Ismael had rested his hand when they had first found him here. Men and women pressed themselves to the wall, clawing at it and banging their fists against the unyielding metal. Abrehem's eyes moved from side to side, seeing a lambent light that seemed to flicker in the eye sockets of the cadaverous skulls worked into the walls.

He looked up to the frescoes of Imperial saints worked into the ceiling coffers, and saw that one stood proud of the others, a simple representation of a young man in the plain robes of the Schola Progenium. His head was haloed in light, and he reached out of the painting with an outstretched hand that offered peace and an end to iniquity.

Abrehem recognised the saint, and a calming sense of *rightness* flowed through him.

Though the screams of the people around him echoed from the walls, Abrehem's thoughts were clear and calm as the ocean on a windless day. He pressed his back to the wall at the back of the chamber, feeling hands touching him as though he could somehow ward off the coming danger.

The aliens appeared at the entrance of the chamber and the fear he'd felt of the eldar blademaster evaporated as Hawke stepped forwards with his contraband pistol outstretched.

'Eat hot plasma death, xenos freak!' he yelled and mashed the firing stud.

Nothing happened.

Hawke pressed the stud again and again, but the weapon's power had long since been depleted.

'Bastard skitarii,' swore Hawke, tossing the weapon and retreating to the stencilled wall as the eldar warrior flicked its blade through a series of complex manoeuvres. Abrehem saw the cool grace in its every movement, a rapturous suppleness and ease that only inhuman reflexes and anatomy could allow.

Without quite knowing what he was doing, Abrehem bent to retrieve Hawke's discarded weapon, feeling the snug fit as his fingers closed around the textured grip. It was heavier than he'd imagined, compact and deadly looking, the induction coils ribbed tightly around its oblong barrel. The bladesman's head turned to him, and Abrehem sensed his amusement at their pitiful defiance.

Abrehem squeezed the firing stud.

And a bolt of incandescent blue-white light stabbed from the conical barrel to skewer the eldar warrior through its chest. The plates of the alien's armour vaporised in the sun-hot beam and the flesh beneath burst into flame as the plasma fire played over its body. The swordsman's scream was short and its charred remains collapsed in a smoking pile of scorched armour and liquid flesh.

The weapon gave out a screaming note of warning, but before Abrehem could drop it, the barrel vented an uncontrolled stream of super-heated air and plasma leakage. Abrehem screamed as the flesh melted from his forearm, running like liquid rubber from a shop-front dummy in a fire. The weapon fused to the bones in his hand and devouring flames licked up the length of his arm, melting the heat-resistant fabric of his coveralls to his ruined limb in a searing flash of ignition.

The pain was incredible, a nova-bright agony that sucked the breath from his lungs and almost ruptured the chambers of his heart with its shocking intensity. Abrehem felt himself falling, but as he fell he pressed his remaining hand to the exact centre of the wall at the back of the chamber. Blood welled from the deep gash in his palm and ran down angular grooves cut into the metal.

The wall thundered into the ceiling, slamming up into its housing with a hiss of powerful hydraulics. Men and women fell backwards with the suddenness of the wall's rise, and a pressurised rush of air vented from the space behind it, carrying with it the scent of ancient incense, powerful counterseptic and impossible age.

Abrehem remained on his knees, clutching his blackened claw of an arm to his chest. His pain-blurred sight could not fully penetrate the darkness of the revealed chamber, but he saw the dimly outlined shape of a golden throne, upon which sat the hunched outline of a powerful figure with faint light gleaming from where its hands ought to be.

Then several things appeared to happen at once.

Abrehem heard the whine of alien weapons preparing to fire.

The seated figure's head snapped up, and a pair of amber-lit eyes opened, flickering as though the fires of some subterranean hell shone through them.

Then, without seeming to pass through any intermediary stages, the figure surged from its throne and Abrehem felt a buffeting passage of frozen air as it flew past him. He was spun around and even his superior eyes could only process a fraction of what happened next.

Flashes of crackling silver, whipping arcs of blood and screams. A muscular shape moving with unnatural drug-fuelled speed. Weapons fire and panicked screaming that was quickly silenced. Heavy thuds of bodies sliced in two falling to the floor, the rasp of armour smashed open and the wet meat thuds of flensed bodies coming apart. Abrehem saw the eldar die in a fraction of a second, heard the spatter of their blood and the slap of their severed limbs and dismembered corpses as they slammed into the walls and ceiling.

Then it was over, the aliens hacked, sliced and chopped into a hundred pieces; unrecognisable as anything that had once lived and breathed. Abrehem saw plates of armour spinning, their edges sliced cleanly, helmets with the perfectly severed stumps of necks still within them. He saw a ruin of gore that looked like the eldar had been instantly and completely eviscerated and their innards used to paint the walls.

And in the centre of the butchery stood the blood-drenched figure of a naked man.

Yet he was like no man Abrehem had ever seen. Muscular to the point of ridiculousness, his entire body was ballooned with stimms, and metal gleamed through his flesh where strength boosters and chem-shunts jutted from his intravenous network. A spinal graft encircled his pulsing chest and heat bled from his skin where integral vents had been inserted just below his ribcage.

His forearms were sheathed in bronze, and instead of hands he possessed masses of dangling, twitching flail-like whips. They writhed like the tentacles of a squid, coated in blood that hissed and evaporated in the electrical heat.

The man's head was encased in metal that was part helmet, part implanted skull plates. A circular Cog Mechanicus of blood-red iron was stamped into his forehead and the skin of his cheeks was tattooed with what looked like scripture. His teeth were bared in a rictus grin of slaughter, and he walked towards Abrehem with grim and purposeful steps. The electro-flails sparked and danced as they trailed on the metal deck.

Hands helped Abrehem upright, and though he had to bite his bottom lip to keep from screaming in agony, he was glad to see that one of those who helped him upright was Ismael. Hawke loitered behind his old overseer with a stupid grin plastered across his features.

The bloodstained slaughterman stopped in front of Abrehem and he felt the flicker of its fealty optic scanning his eyes. The iron-sheathed head leaned down towards him as though to sample his scent, and the thing's lipless mouth parted. Corpse-breath sighed from between its polished steel fangs as it knelt before him with its head bowed.

'Adeptus Mechanicus,' rasped the warrior, the words dust-dry. 'Locke, Abrehem. Pattern imprint accepted. Rasselas X-42 activation sequence completed. By your leave.'

Abrehem wanted to answer, but the pain from his ravaged arm was too great and he sagged into the arms of his followers as unconsciousness swallowed him.

Microcontent 21

Azuramagelli was doing his best to track the eldar warship, but Kotov knew that the auspex would have trouble locking on to such a vessel even in the calmest of spatial conditions. He reclined in the command throne, warming up the *Speranza's* weapons systems and diverting power to the gunnery decks. Without shields, there was a concurrent increase in available resource to allocate to the guns, but without anything to plot firing solutions, they might as well shoot blindly into space and hope for the best.

'Eldar ship is coming about, somewhere on our upper right quadrant,' shouted Azuramagelli.

'Guns unable to gain a positive fix,' noted Blaylock.

'Increasing engine output,' said Saiixek. 'We can't fight this ship, not here.'

'Change nothing,' said Galatea, and Saiixek's inloaded command was instantly canceled. 'We navigate the Halo Scar as decreed or we do not survive.'

'We will not survive if we allow the eldar free rein to blast us to pieces,' stormed the engineering magos, venting an angry cloud of icy vapour.

Kotov ignored the bickering voices, knowing that Galatea was right. His mind was sinking deep into the rushing torrent of the ship's machine-spirit, his grasp on his sense of self slipping with every passing moment.

'Blaylock,' he whispered, his binary fragmentary and fading. 'Hold on to my biometrics.'

'Archmagos?' replied his Fabricatus Locum. 'What do you intend?'

Kotov did not answer and released his hold on the shard of ego-consciousness that prevented the immense machine-spirit of the *Speranza* from dragging the last essence of his humanity down into its mechanical heart.

He plunged deep into the datasphere and was instantly engulfed by an ocean of light. The inner workings of the *Speranza* spiralled around Kotov in an impossibly complex lattice of fractal systems, heuristic algorithmatix and impossible weaves of information that defied any mortal understanding. Down in the ancient strata of the *Speranza*, Galatea's touch was a dimly perceived irritant, a skimming connection that could be erased with the merest shrug.

Kotov's fragile consciousness plunged deeper and deeper, the gossamer-thin lifeline held by Magos Blaylock a tremulous thread in a firestorm of golden light. He saw systems flicker past his floodstream that were as alien to him as anything the most secretive xenotech might dream of in his fevered nightmares, and technological echoes of machines that surely predated the Imperium itself.

Power generation that could harness the galactic background radiation to propel ships beyond lightspeed, weapon-tech that could crack open planets and event horizon machines that had the power to drag entire star systems into their light- and time-swallowing embrace.

All this and more dwelled here, ancient data, forgotten lore and locked vaults where the secrets of the ancients had been hidden. In this one, fleeting glance, Kotov realised he had been a fool to drag this proud starship into the howling emptiness of space in search of hidden secrets.

The *Speranza* was the greatest secret of all, and in its heart it held the truth of all things, the key to unlocking all that the Mechanicus had ever dreamed. Yet that knowledge was sealed behind impenetrable barriers, bound in the heart of the mighty vessel for good reason. The knowledge of the Men of Gold and their ancient ancestors was encoded in its very bones, enmeshed within every diamond helix of its structure.

Was that why its builders had abandoned its construction?

Did they fear what damage the generations to come might wreak with such knowledge?

They feared what I might become...

The words came fully formed in Kotov's mind, wordless and without vocabulary, but a perfectly translated sentiment that existed only as pure data.

<Are you the *Speranza*?> said Kotov.

That is but the most recent of my names. I have had many in my long life. Akasha, Kaban, Beirurium, Veda, Grammaticus, Yggdrasil, Providentia... a thousand times a thousand more in all the long aeons I have existed.

Kotov knew he was not hearing words or anything that could be equated to language, simply the spirit at the heart of the *Speranza* adapting its essence in ways he could understand. He didn't even know if the thing with which he conversed could be thought of as an individual entity. Was it perhaps something infinitely older and unimaginably larger than he could possibly comprehend; a galactic-wide essence given voice?

Dimly he recognised that these were not his thoughts, but those of the datasphere around him.

<You are in danger, an alien vessel attacks us... you... and we cannot defeat it.>

I know this, but even if this iron shell is destroyed, I will endure.

<But we will not, your servants.> said Kotov.

Your lives are meaningless to me. Why should I care, so long as I endure?

<I cannot give you a reason, save that we quest for knowledge and the pursuit of intellect. We serve the very thing I believe you represent.>

I represent nothing, I simply am.

Kotov knew he could not appeal to the vastness around him by any mortal means of measurement, nor could he hope to persuade it with threats, promises or material concerns. What did such pure machine intellect and perfect thought care for the lives of mortals when it had existed since the first men had stumbled across the principles of the lever?

<Then help us because you *can*.> said Kotov.

He sensed the machine-spirit's amusement at his desperation and silently willed it to rouse a portion of its incredible power.

Very well, I will help you.

The vast awareness at the heart of the *Speranza* rose up around him.

Kotov's mote of consciousness was flung into the maelstrom of surging data and purpose, spun around and hurled into the cosmic vastness of the informational ocean, as insignificant and as meaningless as a speck of stellar dust against the impossible vastness of the universe.

Bielanna watched the light fade from the human's eyes, her war-mask keeping her from feeling anything other than savage joy at his death. The bodies of the ship's crew lay sprawled around her, broken and taken apart by the stalking wrath of the Striking Scorpion Aspect Warriors. The flame-wreathed form of Kaela Mensha Khaine's avatar turned and strode back through the webway portal that had brought them to the bridge of the human ship.

It understood there was no more death to be wrought here and with its departure, the brutal desire to kill and maim diminished. She still felt the touch of the Bloody-Handed God, and would continue to feel it until she allowed her war-mask to recede into the locked cell of her psyche where she kept it chained until it was needed.

It was already slipping from her mind and she let it bleed away.

Bielanna blinked, as though truly seeing her surroundings now.

The bridge of the human ship was an ugly place, made uglier by the arcing loops of blood on its iron walls and carelessly spilled in sticky pools. She felt the cold, closed-off arrogance of the humans that had sailed this ship, the legacy of death it had brought to those who had defied its masters, and she was not sorry it was soon to be destroyed.

The ship was breaking apart, its rudderless course carrying it into the deathly orbit of the neutron star that had taken the first human vessel. Bielanna knew she should rise and follow the avatar back to the *Starblade*, but the skein was becoming clearer now that her war-mask was fading.

She felt a presence next to her, and looked up at the blunt, razored edge of Tariquel's presence.

'We should go,' he said. 'This ship will be atoms in moments.'

'I know,' she replied, but did not move.

'Why do you wait? The war leader of the Space Marines is slain and those few that skulk in its dark corners will soon be dead too.'

'Because I need to be certain,' said Bielanna, shutting out the blood-hungry anger of Tariquel's war-mask. She placed her hand on the splintered chest of the Space Marine, the touch of his bloodstained armour distasteful to her, for it too carried a terrible legacy of slaughter and murder. She closed her eyes, letting the skein rise up around her in all its myriad complexity.

Its impossible weave enfolded her, but within the Halo Scar, where time and destiny were abstract notions that could be distorted, the monstrous deformation of this ancient relic of a billion year old war made a mockery of such concepts as certainty. The threads of the mortals that had died here were fragile things at best, hard to trace back even into the recent past, which was itself bent out of all recognisable shape.

She found the thread of the Space Marine, a frayed and bloody strand that unravelled all the way back to Dantium where she had first discerned the closest origin of those who were denying her the future she so craved. This warrior was their leader, the one who bound them to his purpose, and his death must surely unmake that purpose...

Yet as she cast his thread back into the skein, she saw with aching horror that the image of the laughing eldar children had grown even more distant and unattainable.

Far from restoring that potential future, this death had shunted it further into the realm of possible futures that were ever more unlikely to come to pass.

'No!' she sobbed, falling across the chest of the Space Marine as though mourning his passing.

Tariquel took hold of her arm and hauled her to her feet with enough force to leave a mark even through her armour.

'It is time for us to go, farseer,' he snarled.

His warrior's touch brought her back to herself and in a moment of sickening clarity she saw he was right. The threads of the skein surged with power, and she saw the potential danger to the *Starblade* in a sudden and painful vision of explosions and splintering wraithbone.

With tears streaming down her angular cheeks, Bielanna followed the Striking Scorpions back through the webway portal.

An age or an instant passed, a span of deep time like an epoch of the galaxy or the fleeting life of a decaying atomic particle. Kotov felt a lurch of sickening vertigo, even through his machine body, as his consciousness returned to the forefront of his brain with a jolt of cerebral impact. His senses were pitifully small, stunted things that were barely adequate for basic existence, let alone conversant with the mysteries of...

Kotov struggled to remember where he had been and what he had seen, knowing on some desperately fundamental level that it was vital he not forget the things he had learned.

'Archmagos?' said a voice he knew he ought to recognise, but which was completely unknown to him. Nothing of his surroundings was familiar to him, but as the cloaked and hooded individual next to him laid a clawed, mechanical hand on his shoulder, that changed in an instant.

'Archmagos?' said Tarkis Blaylock, his augmitters conveying strain, concern and a measure of anticipation.

'Yes,' he managed eventually. 'I am here.'

'Ave Deus Mechanicus,' said Blaylock. 'I thought you had been subsumed by the machine-spirit and were lost forever in the datasphere.'

'No such luck, Tarkis,' spat Kotov, then regretted it immediately.

Though he could remember almost nothing of what he had experienced in the unknown depths of the *Speranza's* machine heart, he knew that without Blaylock's lifeline to the organic world above, he would never have returned to the seat of his consciousness.

'Apologies, Magos Blaylock,' he said. 'I am thankful for your aid in bringing me back.'

Blaylock nodded. 'Were you successful?'

'Successful?' said Kotov. 'I... I don't know.'

'Yes, he was,' said Galatea, clattering over to stand before him on its awkwardly-constructed legs. 'Can you not feel the great heart of the vessel responding?'

Kotov stared at the hybrid machine intelligence, and what had seemed only moments before to be a creature of immense sophistication and threat now seemed small and primitive, like a wheel-lock pistol next to a macro-cannon.

The command deck was still lit with numerous threat responders, damage indicators and cascading lists of chrono-gravometric alarms, but overlaying that was a subtle rain of information-rich light that permeated the existing data streams and soothed them with tailored algorithms of perfect code.

Systems Kotov had never known existed were activating all over the ship and those that had previously been rendered blind and useless by the fury of the Halo Scar returned to life as though they had never been afflicted. Looping targeting arrays for weapons he had never imagined the *Speranza* possessing and others that he did not understand flashed up before the astrogation and engineering hubs.

Azuramagelli and Saiixek backed away from their stations, confused and not a little frightened by this unknown power rising up around them. Stark against the red of the main display, the image of an alien starship resolved itself. It was smooth and graceful, its hull like a tapered gemstone and topped with a vast sail that billowed in the gravitational tempests. Its image flickered and danced as though attempting to conceal itself like a teasing courtesan, but whatever matrices were at work in the heart of the *Speranza,* Kotov saw through its glamours with ease.

'Return to your stations,' ordered Blaylock, cycling through the information pouring into the command deck.

Saiixek nodded and Azuramagelli's armature scuttled back to the astrogation hub, inloading the flood of resurgent information as a representation of the Explorator Fleet bled into the noosphere. It was a distorted representation, but at least it gave Kotov a snapshot of what assets he had left to him. He saw that many of his support ships were missing, and could only assume the rogue currents and riptides had dragged them off course and seen them pulled apart in the gravitational storms.

'Report,' said Kotov as informational icons flashed to life around the deck.

'*Wrathchild* and *Moonchild* closing and assuming attack postures,' said Azuramagelli.

'*Mortis Voss* reports it has a firing solution for its torpedoes,' added Saiixek.

Unable to keep the relish from his augmented voice, Kryptaestrex said, 'Multiple firing solutions have presented themselves to me, archmagos. I am unable to ascertain their source or the nature of the weapon systems, but they all have a lock on the alien vessel.'

Kotov opened a stable vox-channel to every ship of war in his fleet.

'All vessels open fire,' he said. 'I want that ship destroyed.'

The flanks of the *Speranza* shuddered as a weapon system built into its superstructure ground upwards on heavy duty rails. A vast gun tube rose from the angled planes of the Ark Mechanicus like the great menhir of some tribal place of worship being lifted into place. Power readouts, the likes of which had rarely been seen in the Imperium since before the wars of Unity, bloomed within the weapon and a pair of circling tori described twisting arcs around the tapered end of the unveiled barrel.

Elements of the technology that had gone into their construction would have been familiar to some of the more esoteric branches of black hole research and relativistic temporal arcana, but their assembled complexity would have baffled even the Fabricator General on Mars. Pulsing streams of purple-hued anti-matter and graviton pumps combined in unknowable ways in the heart of a reactor that drew its power from the dark matter that lurked in the spaces between the stars. It was a gun designed to crack open the stately leviathans of ancient void war, a starship killer that delivered the ultimate coup de grace.

Without any command authority from the bridge of the *Speranza*, the weapon unleashed a silent pulse that covered the distance to the *Starblade* at the speed of light.

But even that wasn't fast enough to catch a ship as nimble as one built by the bonesingers of Biel-Tan and guided by the prescient sight of a farseer. The pulse of dark energy coalesced a hundred kilometres off the vessel's stern and a miniature black hole exploded into life, dragging in everything within its reach with howling force. Stellar matter, light and gravity were crushed as they were drawn in and destroyed, and even the *Starblade's* speed and manoeuvrability weren't enough to save it completely as the secondary effect of the weapon's deadly energies brushed over its solar sail. Chrono-weaponry shifted its target a nanosecond into the past, by which time the subatomic reactions within every molecule had shifted microscopically and forced identical neutrons into the same quantum space.

Such a state of being was untenable on a fundamental level, and the resultant release of energy was catastrophic for the vast majority of objects hit by such a weapon. Though on the periphery of the streaming waves of chronometric energy, the *Starblade's* solar mast detonated as though its internal structure had been threaded with explosive charges. The sail tore free of the ship, ghost images of its previous existence flickering as the psycho-conductive wraithbone screamed in its death throes. Blue flame geysered from the topside of the eldar vessel, and the craft lurched away from the force of the blast.

Its previously distorted and fragmentary outline became solid, and the circling captains of the Kotov Fleet wasted no time in loosing salvo after salvo of torpedoes at the newly revealed warship.

Mortis Voss let fly first, with a thirty-strong battery of warheads aimed in a spreading net that would make escape virtually impossible. *Wrathchild* and *Moonchild* followed, firing bracketing spreads of torpedoes before both vessels heeled over to present their flank batteries of lances. Stabbing beams of high energy blazed at the *Starblade,* and had this engagement been fought in open space, the eldar vessel would have been reduced to a rapidly expanding bloom of shattered wraithbone, combusting oxygen and white-hot debris.

The gravitational vagaries of the Halo Scar made for an unforgiving battleground and only a handful of torpedoes punched through its starboard hull to tear out great chunks of its guts in raging firestorms of detonation.

Even with the clarity provided by the roused machine heart of the *Speranza* it was impossible to tell what, if anything, had survived the storm of lances, torpedoes and the crushing power of the temporary black hole. It was collapsing in on itself in a cannibalistic storm of self-immolation, and by the time its raging furies had faded into the background radiation of the Scar, there was nothing to indicate the presence of the *Starblade.*

Every shipmaster knew the eldar ship had likely survived the punishing assault, but their decks echoed with the cheers of jubilant ratings, many of whom had not expected to live through the battle. The electromagnetic hash of the void engagement would remain lousy with spikes

of dirty radiation for years to come, painting a vivid picture of the battle for anyone that cared to look.

The chrono-weapon lowered from its firing position with majestic grace until it was once again flush and secure within the body of the *Speranza*, invisible and indistinguishable from the surrounding superstructure, no doubt as its builders had intended.

The *Starblade* was still out there somewhere, but for now its threat had been neutralised, its boarders repelled and its captain given a valuable lesson in humility.

And with its retreat, the Kotov Fleet pressed on.

In the end it took another six days of sailing and the loss of seven other vessels before the forward element of Archmagos Kotov's Explorator Fleet finally breached the gravitational boundaries of the Halo Scar. One refinery vessel was lost when its astrogation consoles developed a fractional degree of separation from its designated datum point and it ended up drifting from the safe corridor assigned to it.

A binary neutron star cluster caught the ship in its divergent gravity waves and broke it in two. Its death was mercifully swift after that, both halves crushed and dragged in to add their steel and flesh and bone to the spiteful mass of the dead stars. Two emptied fuel carriers suffered engine failure and were pulled out of their trajectories before the frantic Mechanicus enginseers could relight their plasma cores.

Of the other four, a forge-ship, a solar collector and two fabricatus silo-ships, nothing was known. Their shipmasters simply ceased their positional reports and no attempt to raise them or pinpoint their coordinates could locate them. The Halo Scar had swallowed them as surely as though they had been blown apart by the eldar warship.

Mortis Voss was the first ship to register the normalising gravity fields and return its forward auspex and surveyor gear back to nominal levels. There was no clearly defined moment of emergence, simply a gradual lessening of aberrant gravity and light distortion as the worst of the corpse-stars were left behind and the last scion of the Voss Prime forge world sailed through the scattered clouds of stellar gas and dust that blurred the edge of the Scar.

Its mater-captain halted the vessel as soon as she was able, and began a detailed surveyor scan of the wilderness space that surrounded it. What it revealed was somewhat less than the spectacularly different vista that had perhaps been expected, but no less terrible for its very familiarity.

Over the next day, more and more ships limped from the depths of the Halo Scar; battered, twisted and damaged, but triumphant at having navigated a region of space that had claimed so many other souls.

The *Speranza* emerged two days after *Mortis Voss*, and gratefully inloaded the spatial data accumulated by the lesser ship's mater-captain. Deep in the astrogation chamber, the Magos Tychons filled their days building a picture of the discovered space that lay before them; its unknown suns, its vast gulfs and the blinding swathe of ruddy light from the ageing red giant at the heart of the dying star system that lay before the *Speranza*.

The doomed system had been almost completely overrun by the runaway nuclear reactions at the heart of the star. If any inner planets had once existed they were long dead, swallowed by the star's expanding corona, and the last remaining world of the system was a solitary pale orb that hung like a glittering diamond at the farthest extent of the star's gravitational reach.

Under normal circumstances, any star in its death throes would be avoided as a matter of course, the space within the system too volatile and too thick with ejected matter and radiation to be worth the risk of venturing too close.

Yet it was towards this last surviving world that Roboute Surcouf led the Kotov Fleet.

Roboute watched the seething haze of the bloated red giant with a measure of awed respect and sadness. This star had birthed itself ten billion years ago, but it had now exhausted its sustaining fuel and its span of life was at an end. In its impossibly vast existence it had known many guises, shone in varied spectra and provided light and warmth to the vanished planets that had once orbited its life-giving rays.

It might once have been worshipped, it might have had many names in its long life, but now it was simply a dying relic from a time when the galaxy was still young and stumbling though its earliest stages of stellar evolution. Archmagos Kotov had named it Arcturus Ultra, a name that struck Roboute as appropriate in several ways.

He sat in the raised plug-chair next to Kotov's throne, connected to the *Speranza's* noospheric network via the spinal plugs, and followed the course trajectories plotted by Magos Azuramagelli. They intercepted the orbit of the last planet of the Arcturus Ultra system, a world that had thus far survived the star's expanding death throes by virtue of having its orbit thrown out by the stellar reactions that would soon destroy it. Roboute had been granted the honour of giving this world an identifier, and had chosen to name it after something beautiful that was lost to him.

He called it Katen Venia, and it was this world that the memory wafer he had at last handed to Archmagos Kotov had identified as their destination. With their emergence from the Halo Scar, Roboute had honoured his agreement with the archmagos and made his way directly to the command deck of the *Speranza*.

He had solemnly offered the memory wafer to Kotov, who took a moment to savour the sensation of handling its gold-embossed surfaces with his machined hands before slotting it home in the shell-like casing of the locator beacon he kept mounted on the back of his command throne. The inloaded astrogation data immediately synchronised with the local stellar configuration and the location of the craft from which it had been ejected was swiftly picked up on the last remaining world of the Arcturus Ultra system.

Advance servitor-probes fired into the outer reaches of the system had provided a more detailed rendering of Katen Venia, its surface a crystalline wasteland of silica peaks and exotic particle radiations. A faint, but unmistakably Imperial signal was being broadcast from the jagged haunches of a cut-crystal range of mountains, from what was assumed to be the wreck of the *Tomioka*, Magos Telok's lost flagship.

Magos Azuramagelli and Magos Blaylock had wasted no time in plotting the optimal course towards the source of the signal, and despite the losses suffered crossing the Halo Scar, the mood of the assembled magi grew optimistic. The planet was still ten days distant, but seemed so close that they could just reach out and pluck its diamond brilliance from the heavens like a jewel of radiant light.

'Fitting that we should find new beginnings in a place of endings,' said Kotov, calling the swirling ball of light towards him.

In honour of their arrival on the far side of the Halo Scar and venturing into the unknown space beyond the known reaches of the Imperium, Archmagos Kotov had chosen to attach his cranium to a more regal body than his warrior aspect. This automaton body was robed and gilded in precious metals, shimmering gemstones and binaric prayer strips. A heavy cloak of silver mail fell in cascading waves of hexamathic geometries, and while he carried no obvious armaments, there was no doubting that the trio of flexing servo-arms, with their collection of clamps, drills and pincers, could be wielded as weapons.

'How much longer will that star last before it explodes?' asked Roboute.

'Judging by its radiation output and the composition of the ejected matter, perhaps another few million years,' said Kotov.

Roboute nodded. He hadn't really felt as though the star were in danger of catching them unawares with a sudden supernova event,

but the strangeness and hostile nature of its current incarnation made him wary of the unseen reactions taking place in its core.

'I can barely even think of those kinds of spans,' he said. 'It's enough time for entire races to spring into being, countless stellar empires to rise and fall, and dozens of periods of species extinction.'

'The human mind is virtually incapable of visualising such colossal spans of time relative to its own infinitesimal existence,' said Galatea. 'It makes events such as this seem almost static, when the reality could not be more energetic.'

Roboute stared at the machine that hunkered down in the centre of the command deck like a grotesque ambush predator settling into its new lair. Kotov had explained the nature of the gestalt creature to him, but Roboute had the sense there was as much left unsaid as had been explained.

The magi on the command deck were deathly afraid of it, that much was obvious, and given the ease with which it had inveigled itself onto the *Speranza*, he suspected there was good reason for that fear. None of that mattered to Roboute. Once he had led Kotov to Katen Venia, there was nothing left to bind him to the cause of the Adeptus Mechanicus.

He was free and clear of the Imperium, a servant to no man and limited only by his own sense of discovery and imagination. It took all his willpower to remain seated and not rush down to the *Renard* and fly off in the direction of the nearest habitable system and see what was out there.

Second star on the right, and straight on till morning...

+++Inload Addenda+++

Abrehem awoke to the sound of ratcheting machinery and the stink of hot metal. He was lying on his back on an uncomfortable metal gurney, somewhere with a ceiling tiled in bottle-green ceramic. The smell of counterseptic and drifting incense was powerful, and he tasted the unpleasant tang of overcooked meat and burned hair from somewhere nearby. He blinked, and his eyes registered a number of binaric locators etched into the walls.

'Ah, you are awake,' said a voice, metallic and muffled by a voluminous hood.

Abrehem tried to sit up, but his limbs were not his to control.

'Why can't I move?' he said, not yet alarmed by this turn of events.

'You are still feeling the effects of the muscle relaxants and motion-dampers,' said the voice. 'It's quite normal to feel a little disorientation after surgery.'

'Surgery? What surgery?'

'How much do you remember of the eldar attack?'

The last thing he remembered was the horrific pain of...

'My arm!' he gasped, attempting to turn and look at his arm. His head wouldn't move, but at the farthest extent of his vision he could see a pair of medicae servitors bending over his shoulder and a number of floating surgical servo-skulls with darting suture-calipers and nerve-graft lasers.

'Don't worry, the surgery was a complete success,' said the voice.

'What did you do to me?' cried Abrehem. 'You're not turning me into a servitor, are you?'

'A servitor? Ave Deus Mechanicus, no!'

'Then what are you doing?'

'Fixing you,' said the speaker, and now the owner of the voice leaned over Abrehem as the servo-skulls floated away. The medicae servitors gathered up their equipment and a number of kidney bowls filled with what looked like lumps of blackened, overcooked meat.

'Was that my arm?' asked Abrehem.

'It was,' said the hooded adept, and Abrehem recognised him as the overseer, Totha Mu-32. 'It was far beyond saving, and will be disposed of with the rest of the biological material lost in the attack.'

'Imperator,' gasped Abrehem, fighting to control his breathing. 'My arm...'

Totha Mu-32's blank silver mask and pale blue optics managed to register surprise.

'Ah, of course,' he said, bending to a gurgling machine that Abrehem couldn't quite see. A hissing pump mechanism engaged and a crackling hum of power that Abrehem had taken for the background noise of the room fell silent.

Warmth and feeling returned to Abrehem's limbs almost immediately, and he flexed his fingers, enjoying the sensation of movement until he realised something didn't make sense.

He was flexing the fingers of *both* his hands.

He sat up sharply, feeling a brief moment of nausea as the lingering effects of the drugs he had been given sloshed around his bloodstream. He sat on a surgical slab in a medicae bay with banks of silver workbenches, mortuary compartments and suspended machinery with enough blades, drills and clamps to look like excruciation engines.

'I have a new arm,' he said.

His right arm was fashioned from dark metal, with a bronze cowling at the junction of flesh and machine. The fingers were segmented bronze, and the elbow a spherical gimbal that allowed for three hundred and sixty degrees of rotation. Abrehem flexed the fingers, finding them slightly slower to respond than their flesh and blood counterparts, but still able to articulate in every way that mattered.

'It is not a sophisticated augmetic, but it was the best I could do, I'm afraid,' said Totha Mu-32.

'You arranged this?' asked Abrehem. 'Why?'

Totha Mu-32 chuckled. 'You really don't remember, do you?'

'Remember what?'

'Killing the eldar war-leader?'

'I remember shooting him with Haw... I mean, with that plasma pistol.'

Totha Mu-32 waved away the question of the weapon's ownership and said, 'Exactly. That weapon was six hundred years old and its powercell didn't have so much as a pico-joule left in it. And its plasma coil had corroded so badly that it should never have fired at all.'

'I don't understand,' said Abrehem. 'What are you saying?'

Totha Mu-32 leaned forwards, his voice dropping to a conspiratorial whisper. 'I am saying that they are right about you, Abrehem Locke. You *are* Machine-touched. The Omnissiah watches over you and a spark of his divine fire moves within you.'

'No,' said Abrehem, shaking his head. 'You're wrong. I don't know how that pistol fired, but it was nothing to do with me. It was an accident, a fluke.'

'Then how do you explain that?' said Totha Mu-32, pointing over Abrehem's shoulder.

Abrehem turned and saw the iron-masked killer who had carved up the eldar warriors in the time it took to blink. His physique had returned to something approaching normal, though he was still vastly muscled and insanely powerful looking. He had been clothed in a black vest and a pair of grey fatigues, and wore heavy iron-shod boots. The writhing silver flails were retracted into his bronze gauntlets, making him look as though he had slender claws for hands.

The red Icon Mechanicus on his forehead was like a burning third eye, and he bared gleaming fangs as he sensed Abrehem's gaze.

'By your leave,' he growled, bowing his metal-encased head.

'What is it?' asked Abrehem, feeling a lethal sense of hair-trigger danger from the biological death machine.

'An arco-flagellant,' said Totha Mu-32. '*Your* arco-flagellant.'

Booming hymnals in praise of the Omnissiah in his aspect of the Life Giver echoed from the forge-temple of Magos Turentek as the heavy piston cranes angled the reclining fabricator cradle from horizontal to vertical in a necessarily slow arc. The Ark Fabricatus himself, a hard-wired collection of assembly equipment, dangling construction arms, lifter gear and a cab from which his biological components could oversee the work in his many forges, moved across the ceiling rails at a pace that matched the ascent of the fabricator cradle.

To have achieved so much in so short a time was nothing short of miraculous, and the deafening hymns and cascades of binary were prayers of thanks to the Machine-God for facilitating the work he had

done here. On any vessel other than the *Speranza*, the task would have been impossible, but not only had Turentek achieved the impossible, he had done it ahead of schedule.

Sheets of tarpaulin like the sails of ocean-going ships fell from the cradle and mooring lines were blasted clear with pneumatic pressure. Vats of blessed oils and lubricants upended over the enormous cradle and a baptismal rain coated the renewed carapace of heavy armour and a warrior restored to his former glory.

As Turentek's great feat of engineering was revealed, the warhorns of its brethren howled in welcome, drowning out the throngs of adepts, devotees and magi who had assisted in bringing the god-machine of Legio Sirius back from the brink of death.

Amarok and *Vilka* loped back and forth, the Warhounds beckoning to their restored pack-mate.

And *Canis Ulfrica* took a ponderous step from the fabricator cradle, the booming echo of its splay-clawed foot drawing forth yet more cries of adulation and welcome. Eryks Skálmöld walked his Reaver fully from its cradle, reborn and restored, the grey, blue and gold of its armour like new.

The wounds that the Moonsorrow had suffered were now fully repaired and a new blooding banner added to its oil-dripping carapace. The physical reminder of its humbling had been erased, but the mental repercussions were far from healed, and Skálmöld halted the Titan as he looked up into the wolf-mask of his packmaster's engine.

Lupa Capitalina towered over the host, magisterial as it surveyed the thousands of Cult Mechanicus swarming at its feet. For the briefest instant, a sensor ghost flickered through the Warlord's Manifold, too inconsequential to be noticed by anyone save a senior princeps, a skittering bio-echo of a long ago vanquished foe.

Canis Ulfrica's snarling snout flinched, and its shoulders cranked as it too felt the echo through the Manifold. The Reaver and the Warlord met each other's gaze, and a moment of silent communion passed between the singular minds encased within their amniotic tanks.

Canis Ulfrica lowered its head in a gesture of submission.

But only the Wintersun felt how grudgingly it was made.

Images scrolled through Magos Blaylock's optical feeds, frozen moments of history captured for posterity and any potential future records of his life and deeds. Centuries of material was stored in his exo-memory coils and decades within his own skull-memes. His life had been one of achievement and dutiful service, and he had ensured

a comprehensive record of the Kotov expedition for the undoubted inquiries to follow.

He had no personal agenda with Lexell Kotov, but knew that his own organisational abilities and powers of statistical analysis far outstripped those of the archmagos. To have lost three forge worlds was inexcusable, and with the resources of Kotov's Martian forges at his disposal, Blaylock knew with a significant degree of statistical certainty that he could extend the power of the Adeptus Mechanicus into regions of space that had yet to fully develop their potential.

But those were ambitions for a later day.

First, this expedition needed to be discredited, and Blaylock believed he had found his first weapon.

The images he had blink-clicked while in the stateroom of Roboute Surcouf swam into focus, meaningless commendations in the armed services of Ultramar, Naval commissions and rank pins from various ships of the line. The images flickered past with a pulse of thought, captured images moving in rapid procession like a child's flipbook animation.

At last he came to the image he sought, and what until now had only been a suspicion aroused by an anomalous data discrepancy in the Manifold record was moved up to a certainty as he zoomed in on the document hung behind the rogue trader's desk.

The Letter of Marque bore Segmentum Pacificus accreditation, and the winged eagle of Bakkan sector command was a complex multi-dimensional hololith, with numerous deep layers of encryption that made it virtually impossible to convincingly counterfeit.

Virtually impossible, but not *entirely* impossible.

Blaylock's floodstream swelled with what approximated pleasure for an adept of the Mechanicus.

Surcouf's Letter of Marque was a fake.

The Black Templars bowed their heads in prayer, six grief-stricken warriors kneeling in one of the *Speranza's* few temples dedicated exclusively to the glory of the Emperor. None of them wore armour, and each warrior's bare back was scoured with the whips and hooked chains of self-mortification. Thick clots of sticky blood ran down each warrior's flayed skin and Brother-Sergeant Tanna knew that such pain could never be enough to atone for their failure.

Their Reclusiarch was dead and not one of them had so much as lifted a blade in his defence.

The Black Templars were now warriors without a place to call their own, bereft of their spiritual leader and everything that connected

them to their past and their duty. The *Speranza* was not their ship, and its inhabitants were not their people. The six of them were all that remained of the Scar Crusade, and Tanna found it almost impossible not to believe that they had been cursed since the death of Aelius at Dantium Gate.

The death of an Emperor's Champion was a moment of unimaginable loss to the warriors of the Black Templars, and though Kul Gilad had claimed this crusade was neither penance nor punishment, it was hard not to think of it that way. Cut off from their fellow crusaders and trapped on the far side of the galaxy, they were as alone as it was possible to be.

Yet for all that, this was a chance to continue the work of the Great Crusade, a chance to bring the Emperor's light to those that had never been blessed to know of its existence. He had tried to mitigate Kul Gilad's loss with such sentiment, but the wound was too fresh and too raw for his warriors. No mere words of his could salve their broken pride and savaged honour.

Tanna cursed his limitations. He was a sergeant, a battle leader who knew how to follow orders and drive the men around him to complete them. But with no one to give those orders and no one to fill their hearts with fire and blood, what was left to them? Tanna was no great orator, no great innovator of tactics or philosophy.

He was a stalwart of the battle line, a redoubtable fighter and a reliable killer.

He was not a leader, and the warriors around him knew it.

For the first time since his elevation to the Fighting Companies, Tanna felt utterly alone.

Though he had fought and bled alongside these heroic warriors for the better part of two centuries, even Tanna knew an unbreakable bond of trust had turned to ashes between them. Varda claimed not to judge him for giving the order to launch the *Barisan* and fly the Thunderhawk through the gravitational storms towards the *Speranza*, but a subtle and steadily widening gap had opened between the two brothers.

And though Varda was a mere battle-brother, he was this crusade's Emperor's Champion, and that gave him a seniority that no rank could afford to ignore.

Tanna rose from his prayers, his chest, shoulders and back gouged with self-inflicted wounds of shame. In one hand he carried a barbed chain and in the other his combat blade. Both were wet with his lifeblood. He turned to address his warriors, and their cold stares upon him were more painful than the flesh-scourges could ever hope to be.

'Trust in the Emperor at the hour of battle,' he said, falling back on ritual catechism.

'Trust to Him to intercede, and protect His warriors as they deal death on alien soil.'

'Turn these seas to red with the blood of their slain.'

Tanna broke with tradition as he spoke the last line of this battle-oath with his warriors.

'Crush their hopes, their dreams. And turn their songs into cries of lamentation.'

LORDS OF MARS

DRAMATIS PERSONAE

The *Speranza*
Lexell Kotov – Archmagos of the Kotov Explorator Fleet
Tarkis Blaylock – Fabricatus Locum, Magos of the Cebrenia Quadrangle
Vitali Tychon – Stellar Cartographer of the Quatria Orbital Galleries
Linya Tychon – Stellar Cartographer, daughter of Vitali Tychon
Azuramagelli – Magos of Astrogation
Kryptaestrex – Magos of Logistics
Turentek – Ark Fabricatus
Hirimau Dahan – Secutor/Guilder Suzerain
Saiixek – Master of Engines
Totha Mu-32 – Mechanicus Overseer
Abrehem Locke – Bondsman
Rasselas X-42 – Arco-flagellant
Vannen Coyne – Bondsman
Julius Hawke – Bondsman
Ismael de Roeven – Servitor

The *Renard*
Roboute Surcouf – Captain
Emil Nader – First Mate
Adara Siavash – Hired Gun
Ilanna Pavelka – Tech-Priest
Kayrn Sylkwood – Enginseer
Gideon Teivel – Astropath
Elior Roi – Navigator

Adeptus Astartes Black Templars
Tanna – Brother-Sergeant
Auiden – Apothecary
Issur – Initiate
Atticus Varda – Emperor's Champion
Bracha – Initiate
Yael – Initiate

The Cadian 71st, 'The Hellhounds'
Ven Anders – Colonel of the Cadian Detached Formation
Blayne Hawkins – Captain, Blazer Company
Taybard Rae – Lieutenant, Blazer Company
Jahn Callins – Requisitional Support Officer, Blazer Company

Legio Sirius
ARLO LUTH, 'THE WINTERSUN' – Warlord Princeps, *Lupa Capitalina*
MARKO KOSKINEN – Moderati
JOAKIM BALDUR – Seconded Moderati
MAGOS HYRDRITH – Tech-Priest

ERYKS SKÁLMÖLD, 'THE MOONSORROW' – Reaver Princeps, *Canis Ulfrica*
MAGOS OHTAR – Tech-Priest

GUNNAR VINTRAS, 'THE SKINWALKER' – Warhound Princeps, *Amarok*
ELIAS HÄRKIN, 'THE IRONWOAD' – Warhound Princeps, *Vilka*

The *Starblade*
BIELANNA FAERELLE – Farseer of Biel-Tan
ARIGANNA – Striking Scorpion Exarch of Biel-Tan
TARIQUEL – Striking Scorpion of Biel-Tan
VAYNESH – Striking Scorpion of Biel-Tan
ULDANAISH GHOSTWALKER – Wraithlord of Biel-Tan

45a-Del-553-9438
<Order is a necessary condition>
<for allowing functionality.>
<A physical mechanism, be it a levy>
<of Servitors, the bio-mechanics of a Skitarii,>
<or the workings of a blessed machine.>
<It can work only if it is in physical order.>

74b-Esc-540-9324
<When you withdraw from a furnace>
<it continues to give warmth,>
<but you grow deathly cold.>
<When you withdraw from illumination>
<the light continues to shine,>
<but you are shrouded in darkness.>
<When you withdraw from the Omnissiah.>
<you forget that which makes you Mechanicus.>

Excerpts from Verses 45a-Del-553-9438/74b-Esc-540-9324 of the Archimedean Oath.

[Amended 3543735.M41 by Decree Infinitum 57433/-hgw10753 of the Order of Capek Binary Saints.]

Mechanicus metafile 587634857z/TELOK

METADATA REPOSITORY %002

AVE.OMNISSIAH.orv 4048 a_start .equ 3000 2048 ld length,% 2064 WILL BE DONE 00000010 10000000 NON-OPTIMAL OPERATIONS 00000110 2068 addcc%r1,-4,%r1 10000010 10000000 01111111 11111100 2072 addcc.%r1,%r2,%r4 10001000 MARQUE VERIFICATION COMPLETE 01000000 REDUCED FLEET AGGLOMERATION CACHE 2076 ld%r4,%r5 11001010 00000001 00000000 00000000 2080 ba loop 00010000 10111111 11111111 RESTORATIVE SYSTEM PURGE: VIABLE/ NON-VIABLE? 2084 addcc%r3 FORCED REMOVAL OF ARTIFICIAL SENTIENCE,%r5,%r3 10000110 10000000 11000000 00000101 2088 done: jmpl%r15+4,%r0 10000001 11000011 SILICON-BASED ORGANISM? 00000100 2092 length: 20 BEYOND HALOSCAR CARTOGRAPHIES REF: MACHARIUS 00000000 00000000 00010100 2096 address: a_start 00000100 ANOMALOUS CHRONO-READINGS CONTINUE 00000000 00001011 10111000. Omni.B_start

Infinite Loop Infinite Loop//////////

Metadata Parsing in effect.

+++++++++++++++++

001

Knowledge is power. They call that the first credo, but they are wrong. Knowledge is just the beginning. It is in the application of knowledge that power resides. After all, what is the value of discovery if we do not put what we learn into effect?

Millennia have come and gone since I became Mechanicus, but even as a novitiate caster of quantum runes, I was aware I had blindly accepted many principles unverified by my own experience as being true. Consequently, the conclusions I later based upon such principles were highly doubtful. From that moment of realisation I was convinced of the necessity of ridding myself of all the principles I had unquestioningly adopted.

I would build knowledge from my own self-discovered truths.

010

An ancient Terran order of techno-theologians once boasted heraldic devices emblazoned with the words **Nullius in Verba**, *which even a basic proto-Gothic lexical servitor can tell you means* **Nothing upon Another's Word**. *It is a credo I have lived by and by which I will die. The Venusian epistolarian who first scratched those words into cured animal hide was wise indeed, and the inheritors of the Red Planet would do well to recall his wisdom.*

But the priests of Mars have lost sight of what it means to be Mechanicus. The magi rejoice at scraps swept from the tables of gods and think themselves blessed. They bear such relics aloft like the greatest prizes, little realising that such intellectual flotsam and jetsam is worthless in the grand scheme of galactic endeavour.

They are idiot children stumbling around the workshop of a genius. The tools and knowledge they require to rebuild the glory of mankind's past is at their fingertips, yet they see it not. They wield lethally unpredictable technologies like playthings, heedless of the damage they wreak and ignorant that they are losing as much as they gain with every fumbling step.

So much that was lost has been rediscovered, they cry, but like a million scattered fragments of a puzzle, they are useless unless combined. With all that has been hidden beneath the sands of the Red Planet, we could rebuild the Imperium as it was in the halcyon days of the first great diaspora. We could achieve the dream upon which the Emperor was embarked in the fleeting moments of peace following the Pax Olympus.

Ah, how I wish I could have been there. To see the Omnissiah when He walked in the guise of flesh. To bathe in His light and feel the serenity of perfect code flowing through my body. One as mechanistically evolved as I is not supposed to miss the soft, ever-degenerating meat-body I left behind in my ascension through the ranks of the priesthood, but I would accept its infinite limitations just to have beheld that moment with organic eyes.

011

Now I see the world through organic silica membranes and glassine-meshed diamond. A thousand microscopic machines infiltrate the fluids that circulate within my new body of crystal and light. My limbs are powerful beyond even the strength of the Adeptus Astartes, my mind capable of ultra-fast calculations that allow cognition speeds far in advance of even the Fabricator General.

But nothing of such worth is ever achieved without sacrifice, and nothing is so fatal to the progress of mankind as to suppose our grasp of technology is complete. To believe that there are no more mysteries in nature or that our triumphs are all won and there are no new worlds to conquer is to invite stagnation.

And stagnation is death.

I have travelled the void like few others before me.

I have crossed the barriers of time and space and seen further than any other. The elemental forces of the universe are mine to command. Time, space, gravity and light bend to my will.

Like the great celestial engineers of a far distant epoch, I carve the flesh

of the galaxy to suit my desires. And where ancient war and forgotten genocides have wiped the slate clean, I have brought life and the promise of civilisation reborn.

The Mechanicus venerates those who draw closer to its vision of union with the God of all Machines, and they are right to do so.

But they have chosen the wrong deity.

By any mortal reckoning, I am a god.

So bold a statement could rightly be construed as arrogance.

In my case, it is modesty.

A simple statement of fact.

I am Archmagos Vettius Telok, and I am remaking what was lost.

Such is the power of my knowledge.

MACROCONTENT COMMENCEMENT:

+++MACROCONTENT 001+++

Microcontent 01

Barely worthy of being designated a planet, the doomed world hung in the fringes of Arcturus Ultra's rapidly diminishing Kuiper belt at the farthest extent of the star system. Much of this spatial region was composed of frozen volatiles – drifting agglomerations of ice, ammonia and methane – and these were slowly being turned to vapour by the thermal death throes of the newly named star's rapidly expanding corona. The Oort cloud had thinned to the point of vanishing altogether, allowing the vessels of the Kotov fleet to approach the system without fear of taking damage from the debris scattered like celestial litter at the system's edge.

The dying planet had been christened Katen Venia, and its likely lifespan could be measured in months at best. It would soon be destroyed by the very star that had once nourished an unknown number of habitable worlds in that slender astronomical region named for a flaxen-haired thief of ancient myth.

The closest planets to the star had already been reduced to metallic vapour by its expanding heat corona and now only Katen Venia remained. Its outer layers of frozen nitrogen had almost entirely boiled off into space, exposing a surface of cratered ice and rock, soaring crystal growths of geometric beauty, abyssal canyons of sheared glaciers, and swathes of desolate tundra that had been ripped raw by the gravitational push and pull of its chaotic orbit.

Any currently uncontested method of celestial cartography would regard Katen Venia as an unremarkable world, a bare rock devoid of any notable features warranting attention. Only the study of its demise would be of any interest to most magi. Yet for all its apparent worthlessness, there was one aspect to Katen Venia that rendered it valuable beyond measure.

Telok the Machine-touched, whose explorator fleet had been lost with all hands, had come this way. Numerous legends of Mars spoke of his foolhardy quest into the unknown to unearth an ancient technological marvel known as the Breath of the Gods. Each tale was embellished with its own twist to Telok's obsession, but all agreed that his quest had come to a bad end.

But a newly revealed relic of his doomed expedition had come to light, offering tantalising hints that the Lost Magos had actually found something in the unknown reaches beyond the light of familiar stars: a saviour pod beacon indicating that the newly named Katen Venia was the final resting place of Telok's flagship, the *Tomioka*.

It was this that had brought an Adeptus Mechanicus explorator fleet of such magnitude as had not been assembled for millennia to leave the confines of the Milky Way and establish orbit around the planet's northern polar regions.

The heart of this fleet was a vessel that could be called unique without fear of contradiction. A mighty star-borne colossus. A relic of a time when the mysteries of technology were not shrouded in a veil of ignorance, and whose violent birth had destroyed a world. Its inhuman scale was the product of men who dared to build the greatest things their imaginations could conceive.

Its name was *Speranza,* and it was Ark Mechanicus – the flagship of Archmagos Lexell Kotov.

Unlike the battleships built in the Imperium's fortified shipyards, the Ark Mechanicus had not been wrought with any martial aesthetic in mind, nor had it accrued centuries of encrusted ornamentation to glorify long-dead saints or heroes of war. It was a vessel that would never be called beautiful, even by those who had built it, for it had no symmetry, no clean lines nor even much of a straight axis that allowed for spurious notions of aerodynamics.

The *Speranza* was a vessel forever bound to the void, and only the positioning of its vast plasma engines' containment-field generators allowed an observer to know which end was the prow and which the stern. Its outer hull was a tangled arrangement of intestinal ductwork, exposed skeletal superstructure and ray-shielded crew spaces. Its graceless topside and its bulbous underside were ribbed plateaus overgrown with geometric accretions of unchecked industry. Refineries, ore-processing plants, gene-holds, test ranges, manufactories, laboratoria, power generators and assembly forges clung to its flanks in a haphazard arrangement that owed nothing to any design philosophies other than need and practicality. The *Speranza* was a vessel of exploration and research, a mariner of the nebulae whose sole task was to be part of Kotov's Quest for Knowledge.

Though the bulk of the Ark's unimaginable mass was given over to the workings of technology and construction, it was not without teeth. Conventional munitions and rudimentary void-weaponry punctuated its length, but desperate need had revealed the presence of weapon technologies many magnitudes more lethal, secreted within lightless compartments long since forgotten by all save the ship itself.

The vessel was nothing less than a forge world cut loose from the surface of the planet whose death spasm had birthed it, a sprawling landmass of cathedrals to technology and the quintessential embodiment of the Cult Mechanicus's devotion to the Omnissiah. At the heart of the *Speranza* was an electromotive spirit formed from the gestalt conjoining of a trillion machines and more, a terrifyingly complex hybrid of intelligence and instinct that was close to godlike.

Like any representation of the divine, it had devotees.

A fleet of ancillary vessels kept station around the *Speranza*: fuel carriers, warships, troop transports, supply barques and a host of shuttles and bulk tenders that passed between them in strictly observed transit corridors. *Moonchild* and *Wrathchild*, twin reconditioned Gothic-class cruisers, patrolled the flanks of the *Speranza*, while *Mortis Voss*, the last survivor of the trio of vessels despatched from Voss Prime, drifted mournfully above the Ark's dorsal manufactories.

Honour Blade had been lost in an emergency translation from the warp at the very edge of the galaxy, while *Blade of Voss* had been torn apart by a gravitational hell-storm during the nightmare crossing of the Halo Scar. Nor had these been the most grievous losses suffered by the fleet on its perilous journey to sail beyond the galactic boundary.

Cardinal Boras, a vessel of grand heritage that had braved the tempests of the warp from one side of the galaxy to the other, had been destroyed by ambushing eldar reavers. The Adeptus Astartes accompanying the fleet had likewise suffered grievous loss, for those selfsame reavers had gone on to board the Black Templars rapid strike cruiser that bore the proud name *Adytum*. Though the crusaders it carried had escaped to fight another day aboard the Thunderhawk *Barisan*, their Reclusiarch was slain as the Halo Scar's crushing gravity waves claimed the ship's corpse of steel and stone.

Those raiders had evaded the fleet's retribution by the slenderest of margins, and the warships tasked with the *Speranza*'s protection were taking no chances of being caught out again.

One other vessel of note made up the last element of Archmagos Kotov's fleet. Though nearly three kilometres in length, the *Renard* was insignificant in comparison to the hulking ships of the Mechanicus, but she was fast and built with a grace and poise the *Speranza* lacked.

Her shipmaster was Roboute Surcouf, and Katen Venia was the world he had named.

He would be the first to see its skies.

It was why he had come this far.

'You know, for someone who lives in space, you're bloody useless at putting on a void-suit,' said Kayrn Sylkwood, enginseer of the *Renard*, refastening the seals of her captain's bulky, baroquely ornamented suit of exo-armour. 'If I let you go outside like this you'll be dead inside of thirty seconds.'

Roboute Surcouf shook his head. 'I live inside a starship so I don't *have* to wear a void-suit,' he said, his voice sounding scratchy and distant through his helmet's vox-grille.

Sylkwood wore the grey army fatigues and tight-fitting vest top of her former Cadian regiment, her broadly-built upper body permanently sheened with the oil, grease and incense of the propulsion decks that were as much a part of an enginseer's uniform as any shoulder badge or rank pin. Functional communion augmetics made her shaven skull knotty with brutal implants, and haptic sub-dermals in her fingers and palms gave her a solid heft and a mean right hook.

She made one last circuit of Roboute, tugging at seams, adjusting pressure connectors and checking the suit's internal atmospherics on the bulky backpack. Satisfied, she took a step back and nodded to herself.

'Happy now?' asked Roboute.

'Moderately less irritated at your stupidity would be a better way of putting it.'

'I can live with that,' said Roboute, turning away and stomping over the deck to where Adara Siavash helped Magos Pavelka prep the grav-sled for the surface. Little more than a heavy, rectangular slab of metal with a pilot's compartment at one end and a repulsor generator mounted underneath, the sled was the workhorse machine of the *Renard*. Its engine was rated for a cargo load of sixty metric tonnes and a volume of a hundred cubic metres, though it had been a long time since it had carried anything of such bulk. It floated on a

cushion of distorted air that made Roboute's teeth itch even through the protection of his void-suit.

Pavelka was cowled in the typical red robe of the Mechanicus, one that hid the majority of her augmetic qualities. Though Roboute had no idea of the full extent of her modification, he suspected it was a lot less than many of the Martian adepts aboard the *Speranza*. A number of feed lines ran from a sparking power unit mounted on her back, and four concertinaing pipes expanded and contracted like bellows as they fed power into the sled's batteries.

'She ready?' he asked, slapping an armoured hand against the grav-sled's battered plates.

Pavelka flinched at the impact and said, 'Admonishment: Need I remind you, captain, that to ascribe gender to machines is needless anthropomorphism? Machines have no need of flesh labels.'

'I don't believe that,' said Adara, winking at the captain through the polarised faceplate of his own void-suit. 'You can tell this is a grand old girl. Trust me, I know about the fairer sex.'

Sylkwood grinned and rubbed a metal palm on the thrumming fuselage as though it was her lover's backside.

'Gotta say, I agree with the lad,' she said. 'Not about him knowing anything about women. Trust me, he doesn't know one interface port from another. But this machine's reliable, right enough. She's tough and won't let you down in a tight spot. Sounds like a woman to me.'

Adara turned away to hide his embarrassment as Pavelka shook her head. 'What else should I expect from an enginseer?' she said, disconnecting her feed lines from the sled.

Sylkwood grinned and said, 'Hard work, foul language and hangovers that'll cripple an ork.'

Roboute set a foot onto the iron rungs hanging down from the sled's crew cab and awkwardly hauled himself up into the pilot's seat. Sylkwood clambered up after him and ran through the connection checklist with the thoroughness of a Sororitas dorm-mistress ensuring her novices were all abed.

Sylkwood was Cadian and thoroughness was her watchword.

'Hey, how come you're not checking my suit's seals and tucking me in?' said Adara, as he climbed onto the sled from the opposite side.

Without looking up, Sylkwood said, 'Because you're not the captain and I don't much care if you explosively depressurise in a toxic environment.'

'You're cleaning the suit of piss and blood if he does,' said Roboute, making a last adjustment to the sled's surveyor gear.

'How much on Adara having missed a seal?' asked Sylkwood, looking back down at Pavelka.

'You sound just like Mister Nader,' answered Pavelka.

'We left him up on the *Renard*,' said Sylkwood. 'Someone's got to play the role of annoying idiot.'

'In any case, it would not be a wager to me,' said Pavelka. 'Atmospheric readings tell me that Mister Siavash has his void-suit sealed within acceptable parameters.'

'Good to know,' said Adara.

The lad dropped into his bucket seat and strapped himself in next to Roboute. The boy had his ubiquitous butterfly blade tucked into one of his void-suit's thigh pouches next to his holstered laspistol, and Roboute sighed.

'Tell me you're not so stupid as to carry an unsheathed knife in your suit,' said Roboute.

Adara at least had the decency to look guilty as he pulled the blade out and placed it in a stowage box mounted on the inner face of the door.

'Yeah, sorry. I don't go anywhere without it, I kind of forget it's even there.'

Magos Pavelka appeared at his side, filling the emergency oxygen tanks worked into the door's structure. A coiling mechadendrite reached over her shoulder and opened the stowage box before a second articulated bronze limb capped with rotating callipers removed the offending blade.

'Come on,' said Adara. 'What harm is there in leaving the knife there?'

'Clarification: It is statistically probable that you will remove this weapon and carry it with you once you are beyond the hull of this vessel,' said Pavelka, and even though much of her face had the porcelain quality of synth-skin and augmetic replacement, Roboute saw a glint of amusement in her clicking optics. 'As Enginseer Sylkwood might say, "You have previous" and are not to be trusted.'

'You cut me deep,' said Adara.

'You'd cut yourself deep,' said Roboute, 'and out there, that'd be a death sentence. Right, Ilanna?'

'Unquestionably,' answered the magos. 'The atmosphere on the planet below is a volatile mix of frozen nitrogen being released from the ice-caps in both gaseous and liquid form, ammonia and airborne heavy metal particulates. The thermocline is shifting unpredictably in the ultra-rapid atmospheric bleed-off, resulting in squalling pressure vortices that would cause your body to react in a number of extremely unpleasant ways without your void-suit's equalisation.'

'I don't know what a lot of that means, but I get the gist,' said Adara.

'Right, now you've scared us both half to death, how long before the tether gets us down there?' asked Roboute, trying not to let his discomfort at the *Renard*'s cargo shuttle being reeled down onto the planet's surface by remote means show in his voice. 'I want to get out there and see what a world beyond the galaxy's edge looks like.'

Pavelka cocked her head to the side, wordlessly communing with the Mechanicus controllers on the surface via the implants in her skull. Roboute's brain had been augmented to view the invisible skeins of noospheric data, but only when interfacing with a spinal link system. The sled had no such array, and even if it did, he wouldn't be able to connect with it through his void-suit.

'Approximately ten minutes,' said Pavelka. 'Stratospheric disturbances and unexpected magnetic field storms are introducing chaotic variables into our ETA.'

Sylkwood dropped from the grav-sled's running boards and shouted, 'Clear the deck!' though there was no one else in the shuttle's cavernous loading bay. The few servitor cadres Roboute owned were otherwise engaged in monitoring the shuttle's automated flight path or back aboard the *Renard*, repairing damage suffered during the navigation of the Halo Scar. Sylkwood scrambled up the service ladder to the upper gangway as Pavelka climbed onto the grav-sled, sitting behind Adara and producing a data-slate, which she rested upon her knees.

Roboute twisted awkwardly in his seat and said, 'Everything set?'

'Statement: yes,' said Pavelka, extruding a mechanised auspex from a chest compartment.

'You don't have to come with us,' said Roboute. 'I know you don't like leaving the *Renard*.'

Pavelka shook her head. 'I modified the memory coil circuitry of the *Tomioka's* distress beacon. I can follow its telemetry better than anyone else. Besides, if this sled breaks down, you will need me to fix it.'

'Good to know,' said Roboute, quietly grateful to have Pavelka along for the ride.

'Don't you need a suit?' asked Adara.

Pavelka shook her head. 'I have altered the filtration protocols of my lungs to exclude the toxic elements of the atmosphere, and am currently modifying my biochemistry to nullify the negative effects of hostile pressures. My body mass incorporates so little organic mass that requires oxygenation that I can store enough reserve within my mechanised volume.'

'Good to know,' said Adara in imitation of Roboute.

Roboute looked up to the upper gantry of the cargo bay, seeing

Sylkwood open one of the hold's vacuum-sealed doors. She sketched a quick salute to him, but said nothing as she slammed the heavy door behind her.

Clearly Kayrn Sylkwood felt no need to mark this moment with any significant words.

But Roboute knew this particular moment *was* special.

The three of them would soon pilot the sled onto the surface of an alien world that lay beyond the edges of the Milky Way, a world unclaimed by the Imperium. A world that had, until the coming of Telok's fleet thousands of years ago, probably never known the tread of human feet. *This* was why Roboute had come this far and risked so much, to see alien skies and touch the earth of a planet so far from the understanding of the Imperium.

An emerald light on the walnut and brass control panel winked with an incoming transmission, and Roboute flicked the ivory-tipped switch next to it into the receive position. The voice of the expedition's leader, Archmagos Lexell Kotov, trilled from the speaker grille.

'Mister Surcouf,' said Kotov. 'Are you planning on joining us aboard the *Tabularium?*'

Roboute grinned, hearing the febrile edge of excitement in the archmagos's voice. Though Kotov was the master of this explorator fleet, it had been Roboute's retrieval of the locator beacon that had brought them this far.

'I think we'd rather make our own way to the *Tomioka*,' said Roboute. 'But thank you for the invitation, it's very thoughtful of you.'

'Your tether shows significant margin for error in your arrival time,' said Kotov.

'So I gather, but Magos Pavelka reckons we'll be planet side in around ten minutes.'

'How imprecise. Kotov out,' replied the archmagos.

Of all the many ways to be carried into battle, Brother-Sergeant Tanna relished the sudden fury of a Thunderhawk assault the most. Nothing stirred his heart more than the violent thrust of howling engines, the jolting motion of evasive manoeuvres and the sudden, screaming deceleration as the pilot flared the wings and slammed down into the crucible of combat. Being thrown around the inside of a Rhino or Land Raider just couldn't compare, and Tanna didn't know any Techmarine that could drive worth a damn anyway.

Yes, a gunship assault every time.

Even if this particular descent was – for now – being controlled by a Mechanicus e-mag tether.

The crew compartment of the *Barisan* was as cold as a meat locker, and a fine mist of condensing vapours slowly beaded the curved plates of Tanna's midnight-black armour with droplets of moisture. A cross of purest jet gleamed on one ivory shoulder guard and an eagle carved from the same material stood proud on the other. An embossed red skull was set in the centre of the eagle's breast, its eyes glinting shards of deeper garnet. Liquid streaks coated the angular planes of his helmet like tears, but Tanna had not wept in over two hundred years.

Alone in his makeshift arming chamber aboard the *Speranza* he had come close.

The Thunderhawk lurched, slammed sideways by rogue vortices of surging gases being stripped from the planet's surface. The atmospherics of Katen Venia were growing increasingly turbulent and toxic: a mix of intolerably high nitrogen levels and vaporous metals utterly lethal to mortals. Tanna's post-human physiology had been engineered to survive hostile environments, but even he would struggle to survive in Katen Venia's atmosphere for more than a few hours.

The *Barisan* wasn't flying an assault run, but its descent was scarcely less steep and juddering than any combat drop Tanna had previously made in its belly. The gunship's frame had been struck in the Tyrrhenus Mons forge-complex on Mars, and bore the seal of the Fabricator General himself. Its machine-spirit was a tempestuous thing, part unbroken colt, part wounded grox – aggression and wildness combined. Such qualities had served the Fighting Company well in past crusades, but the gunship still grieved the loss of its carrier and had yet to settle in its new home aboard the *Speranza*.

Much like the rest of us, thought Tanna, casting a quick glance down the length of the fuselage.

A Thunderhawk was built to carry three Codex-strength squads into the heart of battle, but most of the *Barisan*'s grav-restraints were empty. Only six of the thirty seats were occupied. Tanna sat on the commander's bench next to the gunship's assault ramp, his helmet fixed in place and his chained bolter held rigid at his side.

Brother Yael sat two seats down from him, cradling his boltgun close to his chest. The youngest of their number, Yael had only recently been raised to the ranks of the Fighting Company, chosen by Helbrecht himself to take part in the Scar Crusade. The bout the young warrior had fought on the *Speranza*'s training deck against Magos Dahan was one Tanna would never forget. Not least for the fact that the Mechanicus Secutor had conceded defeat.

The ivory-armoured form of Apothecary Auiden was a splash of

white in the darkness, and he looked up at Tanna with a grim nod as he slotted home bronze-lined phials into the mechanism of his narthecium gauntlet. This was not a combat drop, but when descending to an unknown world Auiden took the view that it was better to expect the worst than face it unprepared.

A pessimistic outlook, but one that had yet to be proven wrong on this ill-fated crusade.

The solemn-hearted Bracha sat with his head bowed and his hands laced together as if in prayer. First on the field and the last to leave, Kul Gilad's death had hit Bracha hardest of all. He had known the Reclusiarch the longest, having fought six crusades to victory at his side. Many had believed he would follow Kul Gilad's example and take the rosarius.

One of Bracha's hands was flesh and blood, the other fashioned from chrome-plated steel. A flesh-clad cybork on the Valette Manifold station had cut Bracha's arm from him, but he had taken the loss without complaint. The life of a Space Marine was one of extreme violence, and no Black Templar expected to live out his days without suffering some terrible injury along the way. Magos Dahan had crafted Bracha a replacement arm, a skitarii-pattern combat limb with an implanted plasma gun in the forearm.

Along from Bracha, Issur the Bladesman ran his hands along the crimson sheath of his power sword as he always did when locked into a harness within an assault craft. Its texture was patterned with a recurring crusader chain motif, and as Tanna watched, Issur's head twitched and the fingers stroking the scabbard spasmed suddenly. Issur clenched his fist in anger and slammed his helmeted head back against the gunship's fuselage.

Like Bracha, Issur had been wounded in the fight against the cyborks, his body shocked to the brink of death by a weaponised electromagnetic generator. The swordsman was lucky to be alive, but he had come back from the brink of death with misfiring synapses and a nervous system that was no longer entirely reliable. His career as a duellist was over, and Tanna couldn't help but notice the envious glances Issur threw out in the direction of Atticus Varda.

The Emperor's Champion sat unmoving in his grav-restraint, the Black Sword resting across his knees. Sheathed in a scabbard of unbreakable Martian alloys, only its leather-wrapped hilt and crusader cross pommel were visible. The blade was a midnight razor, filigreed with Gothic scriptwork.

Issur had fully expected to wield the Black Sword, for he had once been the best among them with a blade. But which Templar was

called to serve as Emperor's Champion depended on more than just skill at arms, and the war-visions had not come to him. The Master of Mankind had chosen Atticus Varda to be His Champion, and no Black Templar would dream of gainsaying such authority.

Varda sat across from Tanna, clad in armour the colour of darkest night, handcrafted in the forges of the *Eternal Crusader* by Techmarine Lexne and an army of thralls nearly three thousand years ago. Its plates were moulded in the form of an idealised physique, the eagle at its chest golden and proud. The Chapter's icon was rendered in pearlescent stone quarried from the dark side of Luna. Just to be in its presence was an honour.

Tanna had seen many fine suits of armour in his centuries of service, but he had seen no finer examples of the artificer's art than this. Aelius had worn it well, but it fitted Varda like a second skin.

The Emperor's Champion was the heart of a Crusade, and Varda's had been broken by the death of Kul Gilad, a brave warrior slain without his brothers at his side. Sensing Tanna's scrutiny, he looked up and the ember-red eye lenses of their battle-helms met across the juddering fuselage.

'Something on your mind, Tanna?' asked Varda.

The words sounded in Tanna's helmet on a closed channel; none of the others would hear what passed between them.

'The Champion carries the soul of us all,' said Tanna. 'That's what Kul Gilad used to say.'

'Repeating his words does not make you him,' said Varda, gripping the Black Sword tightly.

'No,' agreed Tanna. 'Nor would I have it so.'

'Then why speak them?'

'To show you that I grieve for him also.'

'Not enough,' hissed Varda. 'His blood is on our hands.'

Anger touched Tanna. 'If we had gone to him, we would *all* be dead.'

'Better to fall in battle than to run from it.'

'Kul Gilad ordered us from the ship,' said Tanna. 'You heard him. We all did.'

'We should have fought alongside our Reclusiarch.'

Tanna nodded and said, 'Aye, and our deaths would have been glorious.'

Varda made a fist on the scabbard of the Black Sword. 'Then why did you not give the order?'

'Because I was *following* the Reclusiarch's last order,' snapped Tanna, lifting his right arm to show the metallic links binding his boltgun to his wrist. 'Our command structure exists for a reason, Varda, and the moment we start picking and choosing which orders we obey, we might as well tear the Chapter symbol from our shoulders and set a course for the Maelstrom. We are Black Templars, and we willingly bind ourselves with chains of duty, chains of honour and chains of death. You are the Emperor's Champion, Varda. You know this better than anyone.'

Varda's head sank, and Tanna saw the fire of his anger had dimmed. It was not, Tanna knew, truly anger that fuelled his words, but guilt.

A guilt they all shared, whether it was deserved or not.

Tanna heard Varda's soul-weary sigh over the vox. 'I know you are right, Tanna, but Kul Gilad anointed me,' he said, looking up. 'And you will always be the one who kept me from his death.'

'I am the one that kept you alive,' said Tanna.

Five hours ago, the surface region chosen for Mechanicus landing fields had been nothing more than a vaguely flat plateau of retreating glacial ice and a dozen gradually vaporising lakes of exotically lethal chemistry. A host of servitor-crewed drones launched as the *Speranza* spiralled into its high-anchor position had provided three-dimensional pict-captures of the global topography, and deep-penetrating orbital augurs of the planet's northern hemisphere had enabled Archmagos Kotov to select this particular landing site.

The specific uniformity of the plateau's underlying bedrock and its relative geological stability put it well within the terraforming capabilities of Fabricatus Turentek's geoformer engines. Three colossal vessels detached from the underside of the *Speranza*, falling away like spalling portions of wreckage in the wake of catastrophic damage. Each was a ten-kilometre-square slab of barely understood machinery: titanic atmosphere processing plants, industrial-scale meltas and arcane technologies of geological manipulation. Like gothic factories cast adrift in space, the geoformer engines dropped through the atmosphere, their heat-shielded undersides glowing a fierce cherry red as they negotiated the turbulent storms of escaping gases.

They halted their descent a hundred metres above the ground, bombarding the site with terrain-mapping augurs to verify their position. Manoeuvring jets fired corrective bursts as serried banks of planet-cracking cannons rotated outwards in their undersides. Precision ordnance strikes smashed the frozen ice of the surface into manageable chunks with thunderous barrages as the wide mouths of furnace-meltas irised open.

A rippling haze of intense heat was expelled like the breath of mythical dragons, and painfully bright light flared from the meltas, filling the plateau with purple-edged fire. Hurricanes of superheated steam shrieked and hissed as the surface ice was boiled away or diverted into drainage channels blasted by terrain-modifying howitzers.

Chemical mortars fired thousands of air-bursting saturation shells, seeding the local atmosphere with slow-decaying absorption matter that began a cascade of alchemical reactions to filter out its most toxic and corrosive elements. Wide-mouthed bays opened on the geoformer vessels and scores of heavy-grade earth-moving leviathans were dropped to the planet's surface in impact-cushioning cradles.

In a carefully orchestrated ballet, the earth-moving machines swiftly demarcated the area of the landing fields and set about their work with the efficiency of an army of iron-skinned and hazard-striped worker ants. Turentek had crafted hundreds of landing fields on worlds far more inimical to life and machines than Katen Venia and the priests under his command knew their trade well.

Slowly the last of the ice was blasted clear and thousands of kilometres of cabling were laid to receive the telemetry gear required to tether the incoming vessels to their assigned landing zones. With the buried infrastructure in place and protected within hardened ductwork, the exposed rock was crushed and planed flat with tight-focus conversion beamers. Heat shielding was laid over the buried technology as ten thousand atmosphere-capable tech-priests with implanted precision meltas and polishing limbs applied the final smoothing to the surface of the landing fields with ångström-level precision. Vacuum-suited servitors followed in the wake of the tech-priests, acid-etching the rock with Imperial eagles, cog-wreathed machine skulls and coded sequence numbers.

Within four hours, a vast square of mirror-smooth rock, six kilometres on each side, had been carved into the planet's surface. With the basic structure in place, entoptic generators and noospheric transmission arrays were installed, as well as numerous fully equipped control bunkers to manage the intricate and necessarily complex scheduling of incoming and departing landing craft. Defence towers were raised at regular intervals around the landing fields, each one equipped with an array of weapons capable of engaging ships in low orbit or attacking ground forces.

To enable non-Mechanicus drop ships to set down, contrasting guide lines were painted on the smoothed rock, together with conventional landing lights and active e-mag tethers. Five hours after the work had begun, it was complete, and Magos Turentek set his seal upon the work from his articulated fabrication hangar in the ventral manufactory districts of the *Speranza*.

No sooner was Turentek's seal inloaded to the Manifold, than the first craft were launched from the embarkation hangars of the Ark Mechanicus. A hundred fat-bellied landers began their descent to the surface carrying the mechanisms of planetary exploration: tech-priests and their monstrous land-cathedrals, skitarii battalions and their war machines, servitors and weaponised praetorians.

Amid the host of iron descending to the planet's surface, three coffin ships of the Legio Sirius were shepherded down through the atmosphere by supplicant vessels that howled binaric hymnals of praise and warning across multiple wavelengths.

The Warlord *Lupa Capitalina* descended to Katen Venia, attended by *Amarok* and *Vilka*.

Wintersun would have the honour of First Step, as was his right as Legio Alpha. Skinwalker and Ironwoad would share in this honour, and if either Warhound princeps felt any reservations at the exclusion of Moonsorrow and *Canis Ulfrica*, they kept such thoughts to themselves.

An airborne armada of steel and gold descended to the planet on towering plumes of blue-limned fire, a billion tonnes of machinery and men.

The Adeptus Mechanicus had come to Katen Venia.

Microcontent 02

Apart from a near-miss with the traversing arm of lifter-rig *Wulfse*, the latest shift in the distribution hub of Magos Turentek's forge-temple had gone well. Abrehem had kept up with the punishing schedule insisted on by the materiel-logisters, and even managed to work some contingency time into their schedule to start transferring the newly built Cadian tanks down-ship.

Abrehem unstrapped himself from *Virtanen*'s command throne and began the painful process of unplugging the dozens of cerebral-communion cables trailing from the command headpiece he wore. With each wincing disconnect, the crisp noospheric sensorium displaying the lifter-rig's traverse lines, tension/compression ratios, load levels and spool length faded slowly from his field of vision.

With the last connector unplugged, Abrehem gathered up a battered set of aural bafflers and pressed them over his ears before swinging out onto the iron-rung ladder bolted to the latticework tower of the lifter-rig. The commander's cab was nearly a hundred and fifty metres above the deck, but Abrehem felt no sense of vertigo; he'd worked the rigs on Joura too long for any fear of heights to remain.

The multiple arms of the lifter-rig splayed out from his control cab like the rigid steel tentacles of a high-viz squid. All ten of *Virtanen*'s two-hundred-metre arms were capable of ascending and descending, rotating through three hundred and sixty degrees or articulating in more convoluted ways as its operator desired. Each arm was equipped with a multitude of attachments: basic hooks, magnets, a variety of cutting and welding tools, as well as more specialised mechadendrite-enabled manipulator claws.

Virtanen was a relatively small machine, but it was sturdy, reliable and had a hefty load capacity that belied its smaller stature compared to the titanic lifting rigs worked by Turentek himself. Its service history and structural integrity rating were both impressive and its machine-spirit appeared only too eager to accept a new controller.

But it was no *Savickas*. That had been a lifter-rig without limits, an unrelenting workhorse of a machine that seemed to anticipate every command before it was issued and never, ever, failed to link with a shipping container first time.

According to Totha Mu-32, the previous incumbent of Abrehem's new command throne had been killed during the attack of the eldar pirates.

'I think *Virtanen* was waiting for you,' Totha Mu-32 had said when Abrehem first sat in the command throne. 'Its name means "small river", but even the smallest river can cut a mountain in half given time, yes? I think you will get along very well.'

Abrehem had no answer to that, and merely shrugged, still uncomfortable at the notion that people thought him Machine-touched. He certainly didn't feel any intimate connection to the godhood of all machines. Totha Mu-32 had told him that such men as he were rare indeed, bringing a deeply implanted electoo up to the surface of his organics, a depiction of a coiled dragon with silver and bronze scales.

When Abrehem asked the overseer what the tattoo represented, Totha Mu-32 told him it was the mark of a proscribed Martian sect that made it their business to seek out and worship Machine-touched individuals. Archmagos Telok, the object of this voyage of exploration, was said to be so blessed, and shipboard rumour had it that Magos Blaylock likewise had the eye of the Omnissiah upon him. To have a trinity of such individuals connected to this voyage was seen as a sign of great import by Totha Mu-32, a physical manifestation of the Originator, the Scion and the Motive Force.

Abrehem listened to Totha Mu-32's sermons in silence, finding the overseer's zeal for his beatification misplaced and more than a little off-putting.

He certainly had no sense that he was in any way *special*.

The hard metal of a bionic arm grafted to his right shoulder seemed to mock that belief.

The augmetic limb had been fitted after a contraband plasma pistol that shouldn't have been able to fire had explosively overheated and

melted the flesh and bone from his body after he'd used it to shoot dead an eldar warrior-chief. He didn't like to think of that moment – the bowel-loosening terror of the xeno-killers descending upon them, only to be cut apart into bloody chunks by a cyborg death machine that had apparently adopted him as its new master. His plea to Sebastian Thor and his bloody handprint had opened the door to the arco-flagellant's dormis chamber, which Totha Mu-32 and a great many others were taking as a sign of his divine favour.

Abrehem shook off thoughts of Totha Mu-32's reverence, knowing that a moment's inattention could cost him his life when he was hundreds of metres above a hard steel deck.

He worked his way down the ladder, and even with the aural bafflers the noise in the forge-temple was almost deafening. Heavy machinery sprouted like the towering skeletal remains of vast-necked sauropods around the temple's perimeter, and arch-backed rigs rumbled overhead on suspended rails, hauling containers weighing thousands of tonnes back and forth with no more effort than a Cadian might carry his kit-bag. Magos Turentek himself worked across the centre-line of the forge-temple, handling the largest and heaviest containers personally. His multiple loader arms depended from a central machine-hub where the organic components of his body were interred like the biological scraps of a god-machine's princeps.

Most of the containers being loaded onto the vast-hulled shipping rigs contained modular plates of adamantium and structural members intended for the lower decks. Kilometres of hull plating had been torn from the *Speranza* by the crossing of the Halo Scar and the guns of the eldar warship – rendering entire districts of the Ark Mechanicus uninhabitable. The prow forges were producing millions of metric tonnes of desperately needed components for the ship's repair crews, but Abrehem's experienced eye saw the pace was slowing as the *Speranza*'s supply of raw materials was increasingly depleted.

Abrehem reached one of the transit walkways on the cliff-like walls of the forge-temple and took a moment to catch his breath. The air here was bitter and electrical, with an acrid chemical tang that left the men working here with raspingly sore throats and increased breathing difficulties. This, combined with months spent below decks and working backbreaking shifts in the reclamation halls or plasma refuelling details with little sleep and only nutrient paste to sustain him, had robbed Abrehem of his once robust physique. Daily doses of Hawke's shine didn't help, but sometimes it was the only thing that knocked him out enough to sleep.

He rubbed a hand over his shorn scalp, a decision he and his fellow

bondsman had taken in a fit of righteous indignation to turn them into the drones the Mechanicus believed them to be. Though their actions during the eldar attack had improved their lot somewhat, Abrehem's anger at the inhuman treatment of the below-deck bondsmen still smouldered like a banked fire. Kept as slaves and regarded simply as assets, numbers and mortal resources, the bondsmen existed in a nightmare that would only end with their death.

The Mechanicus believed its bondsmen were *honoured* to serve the Omnissiah this way!

Abrehem spat a wad of oily phlegm and climbed back onto the ladder. Below, he could see Coyne and Hawke clambering down towards the deck from their sub-control cabs, where they managed the articulation and linkage of the various connectors to whatever was being transported.

Awaiting them on the deck were two hooded figures, one robed in the red and gold of a Mechanicus overseer, the other swathed in the black cloak of a death penitent. Both looked up at him with a measure of devotion. Abrehem relished speaking to neither of them, not that Rasselas X-42 ever spoke much.

Eventually he reached the deck, and took another breath of chem-scented air.

'A successful shift,' said Totha Mu-32. '*Virtanen* has bonded well with you.'

'It's a good rig,' replied Abrehem. 'Smaller than we're used to, but it's got heart.'

'It's no *Savickas*,' said Coyne, echoing Abrehem's earlier sentiment.

Hawke shrugged. 'One lifter's much like another,' he said.

'Shows how much you know rigs,' said Abrehem. 'What was it you did on Joura again?'

'As little as possible would be my bet,' quipped Coyne, rolling his shoulders to ease the itching of the synth-skin grafts on his back where he'd taken a razored fragment from a ricocheting eldar projectile.

'Damn straight,' said Hawke with a wink. 'After the regiment tossed me out, I worked Cargo-8s mostly, driving the containers between the depots and the sub-orbitals. Though that was grunt work compared to being a moderati on a lifter-rig.'

Abrehem sent an amused glance at Coyne, and his fellow rigman hid a grin at Hawke's boyish enthusiasm for working the lifter-rigs. Give it a month of monotony and he'd soon think twice about rating his job in the sub-cab as being anything close to a Titan moderati's role.

'May I?' asked Totha Mu-32, reaching up to examine the raw flesh at Abrehem's temples and forehead. Abrehem nodded and Rasselas X-42 bristled at the overseer's familiar touch. He waved the arco-flagellant to submission. It didn't matter how many times Abrehem reinforced that certain people weren't to be considered threats, Rasselas X-42 still viewed everyone who came near him as a potential assassin.

Though now clad in baggy fatigues, heavy work boots and a kevlar vest machined to his impossibly muscular form, Rasselas X-42 could never be mistaken for anything other than the slaughterman he was. Though currently obscured by the wide sleeves of his penitent's robe, his gauntlet-hands were silver-sheened electro-flails capable of tearing through steel and bone with equal ease. The back and crown of his skull were sheathed in metal and a circular Cog Mechanicus of blood-red iron stood proud on his forehead. Sharpened metal teeth glinted in the shadows beneath his hood and flickering combat-optics shimmered with a faint cherry red glow.

'You know there is no need for you to wear the command headset,' said Totha Mu-32. 'If you concentrate more fully, the augmetic eyes you inherited from your father can display the datasphere more efficiently.'

Abrehem nodded. 'I know, but I'm not confident enough in my control over the noospheric inloads to feel comfortable commanding *Virtanen* by them alone.'

'You are Machine-touched,' asked Totha Mu-32. 'Trust in the Omnissiah and it will come.'

'If that bastard's bloody Machine-touched, then how come he damn near smashed into our rig's arm?' said a rasping voice.

Abrehem turned as a gang of six men appeared around the corner of *Virtanen*'s wide baseplate. All six wore bondsmen coveralls and had the same gaunt-faced meanness common to the *Speranza's* below-deck crew. Three men sported augmetics on their arms and craniums, while the rest were ornamented with rig-tattoos, mohawks and ritual brow piercings. They carried heavy power wrenches and other, similarly brutal-looking tools.

Pulsing just beneath the skin of the man who'd spoken was a wolf-head electoo, crudely applied and fuzzed with bio-electric static. He carried a buzzing mag-hammer in his piston-boosted arms and looked like he knew how to use it in a tight spot.

'*Wulfse*,' said Abrehem.

'You're the sons of bitches that almost hit us!' snapped Hawke. 'What in the name of Thor's backside are blind idiots like you doing running a lifter-rig?'

Hawke's vehemence caught the men by surprise, but for all his bluster, their newest rigman was right. The near miss had been the fault of *Wulfse*'s crew, but it didn't look like they were in the mood to hear that.

'Listen,' said Abrehem. 'Nothing happened, right? Nobody got hurt and we'll all be a bit more careful next time, right?'

'There ain't going to be a next time,' snarled the lead rigman of the *Wulfse*. 'Only thing you'll be driving is a medicae gurney.'

Totha Mu-32's floodstream surged with binaric authority signifiers.

'You men are to return to your posts immediately,' he said. 'If there has been an infraction of rig safety protocols, I assure you those responsible will be assigned the required punishment.'

'Stay out of this, overseer,' warned the man, hefting the mag-hammer onto his shoulder. 'Rigmen sort out their own discipline.'

That at least was true, reflected Abrehem, but right now he wished it wasn't.

The man launched himself at Abrehem, bringing the mag-hammer around in a brutal arc.

Abrehem felt a rush of movement and a black blur shot past him. He flinched as a whipcrack of electrical discharge snapped the air. When he looked up, the lead rigman of *Wulfse* was pinned to the side of *Virtanen*'s baseplate.

Rasselas X-42's left arm was extended ramrod straight, his stiffened electro-flails impaling the man through his shoulder and holding him a metre off the deck. The rigman's coveralls were soaked with blood and his face was bleached of colour by pain and shock. Rasselas X-42 drew back his right arm, the flails whipping out to form slicing claws of crackling metal.

'Live or die?' asked the arco-flagellant.

Between sobs of agony, the rigman screamed, 'Live!'

Rasselas X-42 leaned in close, his killer's eyes and pulsing Cog Mechanicus bathing the man's face in a blood red glow.

'He's not talking to you,' said Abrehem. 'He's asking me if he should kill you.'

'No, please!' yelled the man, desperately trying not to struggle and tear the wounds in his shoulder wider. 'Don't kill me!'

The rest of *Wulfse*'s crew backed away from the arco-flagellant, terrified of its unnatural speed and power. Chem-shunts had elevated along its arms, sub-dermal adrenal boosters ready to kick the bio-mechanical killer into combat mode. Anyone unlucky enough to find themselves in the path of a rampaging arco-flagellant was almost certainly dead, and rumours of how thoroughly Rasselas X-42 had slaughtered the eldar boarders had spread through the under decks like a virus.

The shared aggression in *Wulfse*'s crew drained away like oil through a perforated sump. They dropped their makeshift weapons and backed away with their hands up.

'Put him down, X-42,' said Abrehem. 'This one's not going to cause any more problems, are you?'

The man shook his head, biting his lip to keep from screaming out.

The arco-flagellant's flail claws snapped back into his gauntlets and the man dropped to the deck with a bellow of agony. His hand clamped down on his wounded shoulder and he scrambled away after his fellow rigmen, casting fearful glances back at the arco-flagellant as though he expected it to pounce on him once his back was turned.

Rasselas X-42 ignored him and pulled his hood up over his head.

Hawke whooped with glee, bent double with mirth.

'Did you see the look on his face?' he managed between laughs. 'Thor's balls, I though he was going to shit his britches!'

The arco-flagellant came to stand at Abrehem's shoulder, and the stink of its chemically stimulated physiology was a powerfully astringent reek. By now, a crowd had gathered to watch the altercation, but they backed off as the arco-flagellant's dead-eyed stare swept over them like a butcher eyeing choice cuts of meat.

Abrehem saw that as many faces were lined in fear as were lit with adoration.

'We should return X-42 to his dormis chamber so that I may attempt to re-engage the pacifier helm,' said Totha Mu-32. 'I should not have allowed him to remain at your side. That bondsman is fortunate to be alive.'

'He wasn't hurt too bad, and he'll not bother us again,' said Coyne.

'You misunderstand,' said Totha Mu-32. '*Wulfse*'s overseer will hear of this. As shall high-ranking magi who will not think it fit that a mere under-deck bondsman claims stewardship over an arco-flagellant. And when they discover I gave you an augmetic arm, we will both be in trouble.'

'What do you think they'll do?' asked Abrehem.

'They will come to remove X-42 from your presence. And your arm.'

'I'd like to see them try,' said Hawke, lifting a hand to lay a comradely slap on the arco-flagellant's shoulder. Rasselas X-42's head snapped around, sharpened iron teeth bared, and Hawke's hand dropped back to his side.

'Yes,' said Abrehem, with grim relish. 'Let them try.'

'Open her up,' said Roboute, and Pavelka unlaced the security systems keeping the atmosphere within the cargo bay breathable. The lights surrounding the tall rhomboidal outline of the embarkation ramp flared in a rotating display of amber warnings. A depressurisation alarm blared through the deck, in case they had suddenly been struck blind. Cable stays vibrated in the sudden evacuation of air from the

deck, and Roboute felt his ears pop with the equalisation of pressure to the outside world.

Even through the heating elements woven into the fabric of his void-suit, he felt the stabbing chill of the world beyond. Amber light changed to red, though the unambiguous nature of the warning would have been wasted on anyone still in the cargo bay, as the lack of atmospheric pressure would already be killing them.

Metres-thick pistons either side of the embarkation door groaned and pushed the heavy slab of metal outwards, forming a ridged ramp down to the surface of the planet. The glaring brightness of reflected sunlight on ice made Roboute blink in shock until the polarisation filters in his helmet dimmed.

'Let's see what a world beyond the galaxy looks like,' said Roboute, driving out of the shuttle and into a city of iron and noise, arcing lightning and mountains of beaten iron that were surely too large to have any hope of moving.

A starport metropolis.

That was Roboute's first impression upon disembarking from the *Renard*'s shuttle. The grav-sled slid gracefully over hexagonal sheets of honeycomb plates, typical of every landing field in the Imperium, and came to an abrupt halt as he eased up on the power to the engines.

'Why are we stopping?' asked Magos Pavelka. 'Is there a problem?'

Roboute twisted in the seat of the grav-sled, and his answer was stillborn as he saw how ashen the magos's skin had become.

'My dermal layer is being reinforced to withstand variant radiation levels, pressure and temperature,' she said, pre-empting his inevitable question.

'Ah, okay then,' he said, marshalling his thoughts to answer Pavelka's original question in a manner that wouldn't sound churlish or disappointed. He gave up after a few moments, turning back around to watch scores of boxy containers being offloaded from Mechanicus cargo-barques by exo-armoured servitors. Tracked fuel tenders moved past crackling void-generators along precisely defined routes, while a host of lifter-rigs stacked the ever-growing mass of materiel in hardened supply depots. Sealed Cadian transports rolled from the vast bellies of Imperial Guard drop ships, their hull integrity checked by Mechanicus logisters before being allowed onwards.

No trace of Katen Venia's surface could be seen beyond the encroachments of the Mechanicus, giving no clue that this was an unexplored world in the last moments of its existence.

'It just looks like any other fleet muster centre,' he said.

'What did you expect it to look like?' asked Pavelka. Roboute shrugged, no easy feat in a bulky void-suit. The exhilaration of discovering worlds and opening up uncharted regions of space had never left Roboute, no matter how many new skies and unspoiled vistas of distant worlds he saw. Though the landing fields were thronged with robed adepts, grey-skinned servitors and bustling activity, he saw nothing that resembled excitement, only the monotonous duty of routinely familiar tasks.

'I thought this place would be different,' said Roboute. 'We're exploring a new world, after all.'

'An unfamiliar environment is all the more reason to work by established methodologies.'

Roboute knew it was pointless to try and convey that a singular moment of history was being trampled beneath the grinding, rote efficiency of the Mechanicus, but felt he had to try.

'This is a world beyond the galaxy, Ilanna,' said Roboute. 'We're the first human beings to come to this world in over three thousand years. Doesn't that mean anything to you?'

'This is a significant world in terms of what might be learned, I agree, but geologically it is just like any other: a metallic core, layers of rock and ice. No different to any planetary body within the arbitrary geographical boundaries of Imperial space. Soon the star's expanding corona will envelop it. And then it will be gone.'

'I can't explain it in any way you'd grasp, Ilanna, but this is a moment that should be savoured and recorded. When mariners sailed the farthest oceans of Old Earth, there wasn't a man among them who didn't feel a sense of wonder at what they were seeing. If they returned alive, they were feted as heroes, intrepid explorers who'd seen people and places they couldn't imagine when they set out.'

'This moment *is* being recorded,' said Pavelka. 'In more ways than you can comprehend.'

'That's not what I mean.'

'I am aware of that.'

Roboute shook his head in exasperation at Pavelka's literalness, but before he could say anything else to convince her she was missing the point, screaming engines split the air with deafening thunder like a sonic boom.

'What the...?' was all he managed before a host of emergency lights began flashing on the control towers of the landing fields and a host of vapour flares banged off into the sky to warn approaching aircraft of an unauthorised flight path.

'What was that?' asked Adara, shielding his visor with his gauntlet to get a better look at the black and ivory blur climbing over the glittering peaks of nitrogen glaciers.

The screaming aircraft vanished from sight, but Roboute knew exactly what it was.

'That's a Thunderhawk,' he said. 'The damn Templars are going in ahead of us!'

'It seems their crusading zeal extends to voyages of exploration as well as campaigns of war,' observed Pavelka.

'Bloody Tanna,' swore Roboute. 'Archmagos Kotov promised *us* the right of first passage.'

'Doesn't look like the Templars know that,' said Adara.

Roboute slammed a fist on the control panel in frustration. To have come all this way only for someone else to reach their destination first was beyond galling, it was a bitter blow to everything he'd set out to achieve.

'Corollary: I think any disappointment you are feeling will soon abate,' said Pavelka, looking out over the landing fields.

'What are you talking about?'

Pavelka pointed over his shoulder. 'Because the Land Leviathans are coming out.'

It had been many years since Tanna had last taken control of a Thunderhawk, but the battlefield-learned knowledge returned to him as soon as he sat in the pilot's seat. The view through the polarised armourglass of the canopy was impressive, a pyrotechnic sky of borealis brilliance against which were set towering glaciers of frozen nitrogen and billowing spumes of vapour storms that peeled from their flanks. Freezing fog banks surged in the unpredictable atmospherics and dazzling beams of light were thrown out from the waterfalls of gaseous transitions.

He kept the gunship's speed high as he pulled out of the combat dive, throwing off the repeated demands from the Mechanicus control bunkers that he re-establish their electromagnetic tether. The *Barisan*'s machine-spirit rejected every such demand, and Tanna grinned as he pictured the frantic magi seated at their disrupted flight arrangements wondering what had just happened.

Adeptus Astartes did not submit to the control of others, not now and not ever. He had allowed the *Barisan*'s flight path to be dictated by the tether until atmospheric breach, then seized it back. That the Mechanicus believed they could enslave a proud vessel of the Black Templars was laughable.

'How long since you flew a gunship, sergeant?' asked Auiden, dropping into the co-pilot's seat and resting his hands next to the auxiliary controls.

'Sixty years, give or take,' said Tanna.

'Give or take?' said Auiden. 'Not like you to be so imprecise.'

'Very well: sixty-eight years, five months, three days.'

'Ah, then that makes me feel a lot better about flying nap-of-the-earth over a disintegrating world with little to no visibility,' said Auiden, tapping the avionics panel, where almost every slate was lousy with squalling static and dissonant auspex returns. 'Of course, you know where you're going?'

'Mechanicus data-feeds have given me an approximate location,' said Tanna.

Auiden tapped the useless display slates. 'Approximate?'

Tanna nodded and said, 'How hard can it be to find something as big as a starship?'

He glanced over at Auiden, and despite his cautionary words, Tanna saw the Apothecary supported his decision to overrule Mechanicus command and be first to reach the *Tomioka*. To be a Black Templar meant continually pushing the Imperium's boundaries and claiming whatever was revealed in the Emperor's name. Auiden understood this, as did every warrior aboard the *Barisan*.

'Surcouf will not be pleased,' said Auiden.

'Surcouf is mortal, we are Adeptus Astartes,' said Tanna. 'You tell me who has more right to be at the forefront of this crusade.'

Auiden nodded and said no more as Tanna increased power to the engines and gained altitude to avoid a ten-kilometres-high geyser of liquid nitrogen. Icy matter sprayed the canopy and Tanna kept a watchful eye on the engine temperatures. The *Barisan*'s responses were already growing sluggish as frozen gases iced onto the leading edges of its wings and control surfaces. He vented exhaust bleed over the wings, melting the ice away, but this environment was proving unforgiving.

'How far to the *Tomioka*?' asked Auiden.

'Unknown, but it cannot be far,' said Tanna, aiming for a gap between two soaring mountains of disintegrating ice. 'Kotov's initial data suggested Telok's flagship was no more than sixty kilometres from the landing fields. The distance waypoints on the avionics are non-functional, but my estimate is that it should be just beyond this valley.'

Auiden rose from the co-pilot's chair. 'Then I will ready the warriors.'

Tanna risked looking away from the view through the canopy and said, 'The Mechanicus will not be far behind us, Auiden. I want this site secure before they get here.'

'Understood.'

Tanna returned his attention to their flight path as he guided

the Thunderhawk into the narrow valley. Away from the freezing fog clouds and blinding brightness of the nitrogen glaciers, he saw the valley was filled with glittering crystal towers arranged like vast columns in some ruined temple structure of Old Earth. Flickering traceries of emerald-hued lightning danced in the mist between the crystal spires, none of which were less than twenty metres thick, and fronds of poisonous light licked from their tapered tips like the sputtering flames of damaged electro-candles.

Whipping bolts arced between the columns and reached up to the gunship. Tanna pulled away from the flares of electrical energy and cursed as he felt power bleed away from the engines.

'Something wrong?' said Auiden, pausing at the cockpit hatch.

'I do not know,' asked Tanna, fighting for altitude as yet more of the arcing green bolts snapped between the crystal columns and the *Barisan*. An auspex-slate blew out in a shower of sparks, and Tanna felt the gunship's airframe shudder like a wounded grox. Another surveyor panel exploded and smoke billowed from the ruined mechanism within.

Auiden was thrown back into the transport compartment as the gunship lurched as though swatted from above. Tanna's head snapped forwards as the engines died, their fire snuffed out by a surging electrical overload. Smoke billowed around the wings and he fought to keep the *Barisan*'s nose up as it transitioned from a highly manoeuvrable assault craft into a hundred-and-thirty-tonne hunk of metal falling from the sky.

Black rock flashed past either side of the canopy, barely three metres from the *Barisan*'s wingtips. The gunship burst from the valley of crystal columns like a bullet from a gun, flying over a vast plateau enclosed by a ring of sharp-toothed peaks. The plateau resembled the surface of a turbulent lake that had instantly frozen in some far distant epoch, capturing every wavelet and ripple on its surface.

At the centre of the plateau was a sight that beggared belief, something so improbable that Tanna struggled to comprehend what he was actually seeing.

'Brace, brace, brace!' he shouted, hauling back on the control columns as the ground rushed towards the plummeting gunship. 'We're going down!'

Before he could say more, the *Barisan* ploughed into the glassy surface of the plateau with the sound of a million windows breaking all at once.

Microcontent 03

With typical Mechanicus functionality of language, the nine machines emerging from the towering cliffs of the bulk landers were known as Land Leviathans. Straight away, Roboute saw the term was insufficiently grand for such colossal machines. Not one was less than fifty metres tall, and one was at least twice that. Most moved on caterpillar tracks tens of metres wide, some on enormous, ultra-dense wheels the size of moderately sized habitats, while others moved on vast, pounding machine legs.

No two were alike, for they had been constructed on many different forge worlds, over countless centuries by builders with differing technological resources, materials and aesthetic sensibilities. Here and there, it was possible to see that most shared the same basic chassis, but battle damage, centuries of attrition, addition and amendments had taken their subsequent evolution in many different directions. Above whatever form of traction gave it mobility, each Land Leviathan was a moving mountain upon which were grafted haphazard confusions of jutting towers, fragile-looking scaffolding and extrusions to which Roboute could ascribe no purpose.

Each bore a proud name, and each was emblazoned with heraldry belonging to its forge world of origin alongside binaric informationals denoting allegiances to various Mechanicus power blocs. Plumes of waste gases streamed from hundreds of exhaust apertures and electrical discharge flickered around their crenellated topsides.

Mightiest of all was the *Tabularium*.

Archmagos Kotov's Land Leviathan walked on fifty vast trapezoidal feet, arranged in parallel rows of twenty-five, each row three hundred metres long. The main structure's mass was connected to the feet by huge telescoping columns: complex, brutishly mechanical arrangements of muscular pistons and cog-toothed joints. Each was veined by dozens of ribbed cables and power lines, which were in turn connected to threshing coupling rods that thundered in and out of the propulsion decks. Each monstrous foot elevated five metres, cycled forwards, then slammed back down with earth-cracking force and thunderous echoes.

Like the *Speranza*, it was old, but where the Ark Mechanicus had taken to the stars comparatively recently, the *Tabularium* was said to have pounded its way across worlds conquered during the Great Crusade. Its vast hull bore the evidence of those long years in layers of stratified scar tissue – some earned in battle, others in no less brutal fits of redesign and expansion.

Outflung prominences of masonry and steel rendered its upper reaches into the form of a great stone city on the move, a representation of ancient Troi or Aleksandria given motion. Its frontal section rose to a tapered prow, like a galleon of old, upon which sat a void shielded dome of polished pink marble, gold and silver-steel.

Within the *Tabularium*'s gilded dome, the aesthetic of an ocean-going galleon was continued in the warm wood and brass fitments installed throughout the command deck. The gleaming hardwood floor reflected the diffuse glow of the lumens inset in the arched vault, and each of the hundred servitor and thrall crew wore brocaded frock coats of a rich navy blue.

A vast ship's wheel suspended from the ceiling, an archaic means of control, but this was a wheel that Martian legend told had been taken from the flagship of a great oceanic general of Old Earth after his great victory at Taraf al-Gharb. The wheel was operated by Magos Azuramagelli via a heavily augmented servitor whose torso was implanted into a bio-interface column and whose arms were telescoping arrangements of piston-driven bronze callipers. Azuramagelli's own body possessed manipulator limbs fully capable of directing the Land Leviathan's course, but he preferred to steer the *Tabularium* through the proxy of the servitor, a holdover from the days when he had possessed a body of his own.

Now, the Magos of Astrogation was an articulated framework of slatted steelwork in which several bell jars were suspended in layers of shock-resistant polymer. Each diamond-reinforced container contained a portion of Azuramagelli's original brain matter, each excised chunk suspended in bio-conductive gel and linked in parallel with the *Speranza*'s cogitation engines which laughed in the face of Amdahl's Law.

'Holding station,' said Azuramagelli. 'Plasma reactor chiefs report steady temperatures and all propulsion decks are reporting readiness for forward motion. Is the word given, archmagos?'

'Of course it is bloody well given,' snapped Archmagos Kotov, the scale of his anger overwhelming his normal logical processes. 'I want us after that damned gunship right now, Azuramagelli. You hear me? Burn those reactors hot and work the propulsion crews to death if it gets us to the *Tomioka* faster.'

'By your command,' said Azuramagelli, conveying the strength of the archmagos's request in a terse blurt of binary to the engineering spaces.

The Leviathan's command throne was set back on an elevated rostrum of bevelled rosewood and gold-veined ouslite, fully equipped with multiple interface options for its commander. Kotov wore a body fashioned from glossy plates of jade that concealed a hybrid amalgamation of a vat-grown nervous system and cunningly interleaved cybernetics from a bygone age. Its perfectly proportioned form was moulded to match the entombed kings of a long-dead culture of Terra whose priests were able to preserve their rulers' biomass for millennia.

Kotov's shaven head glistened with a fresh baptismal of sacred oils, and spinal plugs interfaced him with the Leviathan's noospheric network and its surging floodstream, while unconscious haptic gestures parsed summary data being fed to him by the magi commanding the other Land Leviathans.

He kept his consciousness split into several streams of concurrent data processing, each partitioned off in discrete compartments of his mind. Thrice-purified oils burned at his shoulders in braziers carved to recreate the snarling image of the legendary *Ares Lictor*, helping to dissipate the excess heat of his enhanced cognition. Numerous autonomous streams were embedded in the *Tabularium*'s control systems, but Kotov's higher thought-functions maintained connection to Magos Blaylock and the *Speranza* in orbit.

Kotov's mechanical fingers beat a rhythmic tattoo on the armrest of his throne, and a flourish of rotating light panels flashed into being

at his side. Over a thousand icons, none bigger than a grain of sand, surrounded him like a cloud of dancing fireflies, each one bearing an identifying signifier and progressing on its assigned route towards the *Tomioka*'s resting place.

Except the Black Templars gunship had shrugged off its tether and raced ahead of Kotov.

Kotov's first reaction had been fury; this was *his* expedition, assembled by *his* will and set upon *his* purpose, but in one moment of crusading zeal, the Black Templars had snatched away his moment of greatest triumph.

But six kilometres out from the *Tomioka*'s signal, the *Barisan*'s transponder signal had vanished.

From her position at the auspex, Linya Tychon sought to re-establish contact with Sergeant Tanna, but her best efforts had, thus far, been without success.

'Where are they?' demanded Kotov, when – even after a thousandth parsing – he was none the wiser as to the Space Marines' location. 'Why aren't the auspex feeds reading that gunship's transponder? Surely not even Templars would be foolish enough to tamper with its workings?'

'I agree that would be unlikely,' said Linya Tychon, sifting the millions of informational returns from the external surveyors. The *Tabularium* possessed thousands of varieties of auspex, but not one was able to locate the *Barisan*. But for the subtle glint of augmetics beneath her hair and the looping profusion of copper-jacketed wiring emerging from the sleeves of her scarlet robes, she might pass for a baseline human, but nothing could be further from the truth.

'Could the Templars have disabled the transponder?' Kotov asked Linya, who shook her head.

'They do not possess a Techmarine,' replied Linya. 'Though it is the fact that none of the auspex feeds or remote drone surveyors are reaching beyond where the gunship's signal was lost that troubles me more.'

'An auspex blind spot?' asked Kotov. 'There will be many such instances on so entropic a world.'

'True,' agreed Linya, 'but extrapolating the curvature of the blind spot shows a perfectly circular umbra of dead space centred directly upon the *Tomioka*.'

Kotov inloaded Linya's data and saw she was correct. What he had assumed was sensor distortion caused by the planet's demise was in fact something so perfectly delineated that it could not be other than artificial.

'You don't need to be a Techmarine to disable a transponder,' said Kryptaestrex, holding station at the drive control interface, his blocky body more like the Martian priesthood's forerunners' earliest conceptions of a battle robot than a high-ranking Magos of Logistics. 'One of them could have smashed it easily enough, it would be just the sort of thing I'd expect from non-Mechanicus.'

Kryptaestrex's servo-limbs and crude articulation arms were drawn in tight to his body, their oversized couplings more used to manipulating the industrial fittings found on an engineering deck than the delicate inload ports of a command bridge.

'No,' insisted Linya. 'You mistake their zeal for stupidity. The Space Marines hold their battle-gear in the highest reverence, and that extends to their transport craft. No warrior would risk his life by something as foolish as damaging the machine carrying him into battle.'

'Except they're not going into battle,' said Magos Hirimau Dahan, Clan Secutor of the *Speranza*'s skitarii, pacing the deck like a sentry-robot with an infinite loop error in its doctrina wafer. 'This is an explorator mission.'

'Then we wonder if the Black Templars know something you do not,' said a voice that was scratchy with interleaved tonal qualities, like audio-bleed on an overtaxed vox-caster.

Dahan turned his gaze on the abomination speaking to him, and his floodstream hazed with threat signifiers bleeding from his battle wetware. Kotov's precision optics registered that the organic portions of Dahan's physique were still bedding into Turentek's superlative work to undo the damage done by the thermic shockwave of *Lupa Capitalina*'s plasma destructor. It was going to take time for Dahan to achieve full synchronisation with his array of lethal technologies and multiple weapon arms, but the Secutor was not a magos blessed with an abundance of patience.

'I wonder if *you* know something we do not,' snarled Dahan, his lower arms flexing into combat readiness postures. 'Something you are not telling us about this world.'

The thing Dahan spoke to called itself Galatea, and it was a bio-mechanical perversion of every Universal Law of the Adeptus Mechanicus.

To outward appearances, it was hardly more outlandish than many chimeric adepts of the Cult Mechanicus; a heavily augmented body forming a low-slung palanquin of mismatched machine parts assembled to form something that was part arachnoid, part scorpion. The crimson-robed proxy of a silver-eyed Mechanicus adept sat at the heart of its mechanism, surrounded by seven brains suspended in bio-nutrient gel containers and conjoined by a series of pulsing conductive cables.

Galatea's very existence was an affront to the Mechanicus; a heuristically capable machine that had murdered the adepts assigned to its Manifold station over a period of millennia. It had assimilated their disembodied brains into its neural architecture and undergone a rapid evolution towards a horrific and long-outlawed form of artificial intelligence. But as each stolen consciousness realised it was trapped forever within an artificial neuromatrix, it descended inexorably into abyssal madness.

When the machine decided a mind was of no more use, the brain was cut from the gestalt consciousness in readiness for another horrific implantation.

'Well?' demanded Dahan, his lower arms flexing and his shock-blades snapping out with a succession of *snicks*. 'Do you know something of this world you are not telling us?'

In any situation to be resolved with violence, there were few members of the Cult Mechanicus Kotov would rather have next to him than Hirimau Dahan. But so deeply had Galatea enmeshed itself with the *Speranza*'s operating systems that any attempt to harm it could be catastrophic for the Ark Mechanicus. Kotov had no doubts of Dahan's ability to kill Galatea, but no matter how quickly he might do so, the machine intelligence would have more than enough time to destroy the *Speranza*.

Flickering light passed between Galatea's conjoined brains. 'We sense you are troubled by more than the disappearance of the Adeptus Astartes gunship. Have you not adjusted your worldview to incorporate our existence?'

'You already know the Mechanicus will never accept your existence,' said Kotov, rising from his throne and stepping down to the auspex and surveyor feeds. 'So why not simply answer the Secutor's question? *Do* you know what has become of the Black Templars?'

'We do not answer because Magos Dahan's anger amuses us,' said Galatea, ignoring Kotov's question and clattering over the deck on its misaligned limbs. 'When you have spent four thousand and sixty-seven years alone, you too will seek amusement wherever you find it.'

'I will not live that long.'

'You may,' said Galatea. 'Magos Telok has.'

'How can you know that?' asked Linya Tychon, looking up from the blue-limned glow of the auspex returns. 'It has been thousands of years since he came here.'

Galatea waved an admonishing finger. 'You of all people should know better, Mistress Tychon. Was it not the inconsistencies within the passage of time that led you and your father to accompany Magos

Kotov in the first place? We have seen the data you have assembled from the *Speranza*'s surveyor feeds. You know the temporal flow of energies has been massively disrupted in this region of space. The few remaining suns beyond the galactic fringe are ageing far faster than they ought to, transforming from main sequence stars into red supergiants in the blink of a celestial eye. If that can happen, what might a man who knows how to harness such energies achieve? And a man who can transfigure the life cycles of the engines of existence, is surely a man who might learn to endure beyond his allotted span and manipulate that technology to other purposes.'

'So you're saying the umbra is, what, a side effect of what Magos Telok is doing?' asked Linya.

'We believe it is certainly an intriguing possibility,' replied Galatea.

'Is this umbra changing in any way?' asked Kotov.

'I am not detecting any discernible changes from the planet's surface,' answered Linya, calling up a representation of the geography ahead. 'But my father's readings on the *Speranza* show a high-energy source reaching into space with a point of origin that exactly matches what would be the edge of an umbral sphere centred on the *Tomioka*. We can't read what's inside the umbra, but there's something within that's geysering exotic radiations and particle waves unknown to any Mechanicus database that can be detected when they leave it. Magnetic anomalies and sleeting particles of indeterminate charge are billowing up from the planet's core like an electromagnetic volcano with enough force to reach into the exosphere.'

Kotov came forwards to examine the image on the auspex table.

The map was centred on the Land Leviathan, but grainy and skewed with unintelligible static where normally the *Tabularium*'s many surveyors would eliminate uncertainty. It displayed a real-time capture of the landscape to a radius of a hundred kilometres. Sixty kilometres south of the landing fields, in the exact centre of the umbra, lay the object of their search.

The last resting place of Magos Telok's lost flagship.

'Are there any other effects of this umbra, besides blinding us to whatever forces might lie within it?' asked Dahan. 'Is it dangerous?'

'To people or machines?'

'Both.'

'I wouldn't recommend prolonged exposure, but in ray-shielded void-suits, it should be safe for your skitarii for a few hours at a time,' said Linya.

'And for machines?' asked Kotov.

Linya shook her head. 'Let me put it this way, archmagos. Given

how little we know about the exact nature of the umbra, I wouldn't risk entering it on anything that wasn't close to the ground.'

'An excellent suggestion, Mistress Tychon,' said Kotov, opening an encrypted martial vox-link and awaiting connection. Hostile binarics snapped around his floodstream before the map vanished from the auspex table and the canidae symbol of Legio Sirius shimmered into focus.

+This is the Wintersun, state your request.+

'Princeps Luth,' said Kotov. 'I'm going to need your Scout Titans.'

Their roles in the under-deck environment might have changed for the better, but the one constant in their daily existence was the quality of the food. Feeding Hall Eighty-Six was still the same cavernous chamber of clattering flatware and grunting men and women trying to shovel as much food into their mouths as they could get their hands on. In theory, each bondsman was dispensed an equal amount by the sustenance servitors, but as with all large groups kept in confinement, the strongest stayed strong by stealing the food of the weakest.

Not that Abrehem, Hawke and Coyne had ever needed to worry about that thanks to the presence of Crusha, the ogryn swept up along with them by the Mechanicus collarmen back on Joura. Crusha was dead now, killed by the same eldar warrior Abrehem had killed, but even without his hulking presence, they had no need to worry about a nutritional deficit.

Now they had a surplus; votive offerings and gifts passed along the table by those who had heard about the miracle of the plasma gun and the rumour of Rasselas X-42. When Abrehem had returned to the feeding hall with a newly grafted bionic limb, it had only cemented his reputation as a favoured son of the Omnissiah.

'Don't get me wrong...' said Coyne, jamming a stale hunk of bread into his mouth. Even moistened by the beige paste in the plastic tray's bowl depression, it still took him nearly thirty seconds to chew it to a level where he could continue speaking. 'It's good we're being recognised, and the new duties in Magos Turentek's forge-temple are a blessing, but is there any way you could use your... influence to get *better* food as opposed to more of the same crap?'

'We shouldn't be taking any of it,' said Abrehem.

'Come on, Abe,' said Hawke. 'What's the point of being a somebody if you can't make use of it?'

'But I'm *not* a somebody,' protested Abrehem.

Hawke grinned, putting his hands together in prayer. 'Spoken like a man of true divinity.'

'Have you heard what they're calling you?' said Coyne, in a conspiratorial whisper.

'No, what?'

'The Vitalist,' said Coyne. 'After what you did to Ismael.'

Abrehem twisted on the bench seat, looking over rows of tables to where Ismael de Roeven, once his duty-overseer back on Joura, but now rendered down into a cyborg servitor, placed a food tray before a hunch-shouldered bondsman. Like the hundreds of other servitors in the feeding hall, Ismael followed an unchanging pattern of dispensing food, collecting trays and cleaning the hall in preparation for the next shift.

'But I didn't do that,' said Abrehem. 'Ismael's cranial hood was damaged when the Mechanicus vented the lower decks to save the ship from that plasma discharge. The impact restored whatever the cranial surgery left of the poor sod's memory and old life, not me.'

'Yeah, but he came to see you afterwards, didn't he?' asked Hawke, loud enough so that people two tables over could hear him. 'Doesn't take a savant to see you had something to do with it.'

'But I didn't,' hissed Abrehem, looking up to see that Ismael had paused in his work to turn towards him, as though somehow aware they were talking about him. He gave Abrehem an almost imperceptible nod before carrying on with his work. Every bondsman he passed surreptitiously reached out to touch the servitor's hands and arms as though he were a divine talisman.

'If I had done it, don't you think I'd have given him his whole memory back?' continued Abrehem. 'What kind of sick bastard would bring someone back halfway from virtual brain death? Thor's light, can you imagine living like that? Knowing you were something more than a mindless drone, but only able to remember broken fragments of your old self… it's monstrous.'

'It's better than what he was,' said Coyne.

'Is it? I'm not so sure,' said Abrehem. 'I reckon if he knew how much he'd lost, he'd want to go back to remembering nothing.'

'Heads up,' said Hawke. 'Dragon boy's coming.'

Abrehem didn't have to look up to know that Totha Mu-32 was approaching, and wished he'd never told Hawke and Coyne what the overseer had told him about the sect that sought out those they believed were Machine-touched.

The overseer leaned over the table, and said, 'You need to go. Now.'

Abrehem looked up and saw a look of genuine fear on the overseer's face that his facial implants couldn't mask.

'What's going on?'

'I told you the senior magi would not tolerate you claiming stewardship of an arco-flagellant, remember?'

Abrehem nodded.

'They are coming. Now. Saiixek is on his way and he will demand you surrender Rasselas X-42 over to his custody. Then he will kill you and cut off your augmetic arm.'

'What do we do?' asked Coyne, all thoughts of better quality food forgotten.

'You leave. Now. Find somewhere hidden,' said Totha Mu-32. 'I know you now have several alcohol-producing stills hidden below the waterline, Bondsman Hawke. Take Abrehem to one of them, do not tell me which. You understand?'

Hawke looked about to protest his innocence, but simply nodded. 'Yeah, sure. Okay, let's go.'

'Too late,' said Abrehem, as Magos Saiixek and a troop of twenty skitarii marched into Feeding Hall Eighty-Six via the port archway. Abrehem rose from the table and looked for another way out, but twenty more skitarii appeared at the opposite entrance.

'No way out,' he said, turning to his companions. 'Get away from me or they'll take you too.'

'Way ahead of you,' said Hawke, already backing away into the crowds of bondsmen. Coyne was right there with him, and Abrehem wasn't surprised. His fellow rigman had always been more interested in himself than any notions of solidarity, but Abrehem couldn't bring himself to be angry. If the Mechanicus were really going to kill him, or even if they would only take him for some kind of interrogation trawl or punishment detail, then better it was only him they collared.

'Too bad you took X-42 back to his sleep chamber,' said Hawke as a parting shot. 'Looks like you could really use him right about now.'

The skitarii closed in on Abrehem and Totha Mu-32, until the two of them stood within a circle of warriors. Armoured in glossy plates of black decorated with glitter-scaled scorpions, snakes and spiders, the Mechanicus troops looked like they'd give the Black Templars a run for their money. Shot-cannons, web-casters and shock mauls told Abrehem they wanted him alive, but didn't care too much about how bruised he got.

The ring of warriors parted long enough for Magos Saiixek to stand forth, the black-cowled adept of the Cult Mechanicus who had first 'welcomed' Abrehem and the others aboard the *Speranza*. His robes and acid-etched stole were patterned with frost, the cylinders on his arachnid backpack venting breaths of freezing vapour and radiating cold from the looping cables encircling his body. His face was obscured behind a bronze mask worked in an angular recreation of a beaked plague-doctor from some backward feral world.

'I am Saiixek, Master of Engines,' said the magos, but Abrehem already knew that. He'd met him before, and the information bled from him in noospheric waves as surely as the misty fog of his machine-exhalations and his righteous indignation at Abrehem's presumption. 'Statement: you are to surrender the arco-flagellant to my custody immediately. Furnish me with its location, capabilities and trigger phrase, and once I have amputated that illegally affixed limb, you will receive a lower-rated punishment. Respond immediately.'

'Rasselas X-42 has imprinted on Bondsman Locke,' said Totha Mu-32. 'It would be dangerous for anyone to try and undo that. You must not attempt to break such a bond.'

Saiixek inclined his head towards Totha Mu-32, like a man finding something unpleasant on the sole of his boot. 'Identifier: Totha Mu-32, Overseer Tertius Lambda. You do not have sufficient rank protocol to make such a demand. Your breach of bio-implantation protocols has already earned you punishment. Continue with this defiance, and I will strip what rank you have and ensure your operational progression path never leaves the bio-waste reclamation decks.'

'The Omnissiah chose Bondsman Locke to be X-42's custodian,' said Totha Mu-32. 'A killing machine like that is a chosen instrument of Imperial will. He was *meant* to find Rasselas X-42, I know this to be true.'

Abrehem wanted to speak, to say that he was perfectly happy to surrender control of the arco-flagellant, that Totha Mu-32's belief in him was misplaced. But the multiple barrels of heavy weapons pointing at him kept his mouth shut. Saiixek spoke again, and though none of his metal features moved, Abrehem felt his contempt in the surging ire of his floodstream. 'You presume to know the will of the Omnissiah, overseer?'

'No, but I recognise its working when I see it,' said Totha Mu-32. 'As would you if you ever deigned to venture beyond the high temples of the enginarium.'

'Enough,' said Saiixek, waving a brass hand and dispersing the cold mists around him. 'This is not a debate. Suzerain Travain, take them.'

The skitarii next to Saiixek raised his shot-cannon, but before he could rack the slide, a metallic arm reached from Saiixek's mist to wrench it from his hand. The gun snapped in two with a sharp *crack*, and Abrehem watched as Ismael pushed through the ring of skitarii to stand before Magos Saiixek.

He dropped the broken pieces of the weapon and said, 'You... need to... leave here, magos. Now.'

Saiixek took a step back from Ismael, and Abrehem saw the surge of his abhorrence at the sight of a servitor addressing him with apparent self-will.

'Blasphemy!' hissed Saiixek. 'You will all die for this techno-heresy.'

'But I didn't do anything!' cried Abrehem. 'He took a blow to the head, that's all!'

'The will of the Omnissiah moves within you, Abrehem,' said Totha Mu-32. 'Do not deny it.'

'Will you shut up, please!' snapped Abrehem. 'Listen, Magos Saiixek, I'm not Machine-touched, this is all a bunch of stupid, random things that have happened to me. There's no great mystery, it's all… I don't know, coincidence or someone's idea of a sick joke!'

His words fell on deaf ears, and Abrehem knew Saiixek wouldn't believe them anyway.

'All… of… you,' said Ismael, his face contorted with the effort of speech. 'Should… go. Abrehem Locke is… not to… be touched. We will… not… allow our restorer to be harmed.'

Abrehem heard Ismael's words without understanding them, but knew they were only pulling him deeper into the mire in which he was already neck-deep.

'Admonishment: a servitor does not issue demands,' said Saiixek, a measure of Mechanicus control finally asserting itself through his horrified disbelief.

The tension on Ismael's face relaxed. 'This one does.'

'Deactivate this instant!' ordered Saiixek, unleashing a bludgeoning stream of binaric shut down commands.

Ismael staggered with the force of Saiixek's authority signifiers, dropping to one knee before the red-robed magos with his head bowed. Saiixek stepped past the kneeling servitor, but Ismael's servo-limb reached up and clamped down hard on his arm.

Ismael's iron clad head lifted and he looked Saiixek straight in the eye.

'No,' said Ismael, rising to his feet. 'We. Will. Not.'

Only then did Abrehem realise why Ismael kept saying *we*.

Encircling the skitarii in an unbroken ring of flesh and iron were hundreds of dispensing servitors, each one staring with a fixed expression at the drama unfolding in the feeding hall. Abrehem guessed there were at least five hundred servitors surrounding the skitarii, all heavily augmented with powerful servo-arms and pain-blockers.

Ismael had once claimed to be able to *hear* the other servitors, but Abrehem had had no idea that line of communication worked both ways.

'He made us remember,' said Ismael, shoving Saiixek back. 'And we will... not let you take... Him.'

Saiixek turned a slow circle and his horror was evident, even to those without augmentation. The natural order of the world had been overturned and the Master of Engines now realised he was in very real danger. The servitors were unarmed and individually were no match for highly trained, weaponised skitarii.

But they had overwhelming numbers on their side, and if violence ensued, neither Saiixek or his skitarii escort would leave here alive.

'What have you done, Bondsman Locke?' asked Saiixek. 'Ave Deus Mechanicus... What have you done?'

'I didn't do anything!' protested Abrehem.

Ismael raised his mechanised arm above his head, the manipulator claw on the end clenched into an approximation of a fist.

And all through the Ark Mechanicus, tens of thousands of fists rose in support.

Microcontent 04

The Warhound was a swift hunter, an unseen killer on the ice. *Amarok* moved through the labyrinth of canyons with a silence that should have been impossible for such a huge machine, its heavy footfalls somehow making little or no sound as Gunnar Vintras wove a path through a glittering forest of crazily angled crystalline spires jutting from the ice and rock like slender stalagmites of diamond.

The Skinwalker lay back in the contoured couch of his Warhound, feeling the flex and release of his mechanised musculature, the acid-burn of exertion and the neutron winds whipping around his armoured carapace. He wore his silver hair shaved down to his skull, exposing wolf-eye tattoos surrounding the cerebral implant sockets in his neck. His actual eyes were closed, darting around behind the lids, and his sharpened teeth were bared in a feral snarl.

Amarok was a beautiful machine to pilot, built by craftsmen of a bygone age who cared about the weapons they built, not like the sunborn adepts of today who just stamped out inferior manufactorum-pressed copies of mechanical art.

It felt good to take his engine out onto a real hunting ground. Magos Dahan's training halls aboard the *Speranza* were wide and expansive, but no substitute for walking on the surface of a real world. Vintras eased *Amarok* from a cautious stride to a slow lope, gradually feeding power from the reactor at the Warhound's heart to its reverse-jointed legs of plasteel and fibre-bundle muscles.

He felt *Amarok*'s desire to be loosed, to sprint through this crystalline forest of glassy spires on the hunt, but he clamped his will down upon it.

'Not yet, wildheart,' he said, feeling the volatile core of the spirit baiting him through the crackling link of the Manifold. Ever since they'd entered what Mistress Tychon was calling the umbra, arcing ahead of the course to be followed by the plodding Land Leviathans, the Titan's spirit had been restless. It didn't like this world, and Vintras couldn't blame it. There was something... *off* about Katen Venia, as though it was spitefully hoping to drag others into its imminent demise.

The auspex was a squalling mess of bounced returns from the crystalline spires surrounding him and crackling distortion caused by the umbra. He was relying on what *Amarok*'s external picters were telling him, walking by auspex-sight alone and bereft of any other sensory inputs.

Princeps of larger engines would be horrified at such a limited sphere of awareness, but Warhound princeps were cut from a different cloth, and Vintras relished this chance to pilot his engine so viscerally. He couldn't see the Mechanicus Leviathans, *Lupa Capitalina* or *Vilka* beyond the canyon's walls, but that suited Vintras just fine.

Ever since the Wintersun had opened fire on *Canis Ulfrica*, Vintras was in no hurry to walk in the Warlord's shadow. These canyons were altogether too similar to the claustrophobic cavern runs of Beta Fortanis, and Vintras didn't like to think of the Wintersun having any further reminders of that nightmarish battle. The *Capitalina*'s magos claimed the engine's Manifold had been purged of data junk relating to that fight, but who really knew what ghost echoes lingered in the deep memory of a war machine as ancient and complex as a Warlord Titan?

No, best to keep clear of *Lupa Capitalina* for now.

His fingers flexed without conscious thought and the weapon mounts on his arms clattered as the threat auspex overlaid the topographical display with a red-hazed shimmer of threat returns. Autonomic reactions took over and Vintras slewed the Titan around, lowering the carapace and shrugging his weapon mounts to the fore.

Ammunition shunts fed explosive shells into the vulcan, while the heavy-duty capacitors of the turbolasers siphoned energy from the surging reactor. Vintras felt his arms swell with lethal power and the heat in his belly spread through his flesh-limbs.

Keeping the Titan moving, he panned the snarling, lupine snout of his engine from left to right, searching for targets or anything that might have provoked such a response. Vapour bleed from the melting nitrogen ice made visibility a joke, but Vintras wasn't seeing anything hostile.

A few hundred metres away, a cluster of crystal spires crashed to the ground as the bedrock cracked open and they tore loose. Shards fell in glittering mineral rain, throwing back myriad reflections of his war-engine.

Vintras let out a pent-up breath. There was nothing out here but him.

'Seismic activity,' he said. 'That's all it was, my beauty. Falling spires and shifting rock.'

Boulders of ice fell from the lip of the canyon, and he danced his machine back to avoid the largest. The voids would spare him the worst of the impacts, but it never paid to antagonise a Titan's spirit with needless damage. The ground cracked as the boulders landed, each one tens of metres across, and Vintras sidestepped away from the unstable ground.

He dismissed the threat auspex and pushed forwards through the crystal spires once more, satisfied there was nothing out there to cause him concern. He felt *Amarok*'s displeasure in the rumble of the engine core and the resistance in its limbs.

'Easy there,' he whispered. 'There's nothing out there.'

But still the Titan fought him, keeping its weapons armed and once again calling the threat auspex to the fore.

Vintras cancelled it. 'Enough,' he snapped. 'You're getting as jumpy as the Wintersun.'

The Manifold growled at his casual dismissal, and he felt the great machine's ire in a surge of painful feedback through his spinal implant. *Amarok* was not an engine to patronise, its spirit that of a lone predator, the killer that lurks in the darkness and strikes without warning.

Such an entity did not jump at shadows, and he had been foolish to forget that.

'You want to hunt?' he said. 'Then let's hunt. Full auspex sweep.'

Katen Venia's surface was painfully bright, even through the protective filters of Roboute's helmet. Cold, ultraviolet-tinged illumination fell in shimmering, auroral bands, the red light of the star shifted along the visible spectrum by a cocktail of released gases surging in the temporary atmosphere that imparted a shimmering, undersea

quality to their surroundings. Towering mountains of frozen nitrogen were visible through the drifting banks of vapour streaming from their jagged peaks as the heat from the dying star stripped the icy crust from the planet's surface.

Dazzling refractions of variegated light shone through the prisms of the ice mountains, and Roboute had never seen anything as grandly terrible in all his life. He felt as if he had been shrunk to microscopic size and was navigating a passage through the grooves and ridges on the surface of a cut-glass decanter. His earlier disappointment at the planet's appearance had melted away as surely as the nitrogen icecaps in the face of what lay beyond the Mechanicus landing fields.

This was the death of a planet, and like war, it was a beautiful thing to see from a distance.

There was majesty in this global annihilation event, an inhuman level of destruction whereby mountain ranges were being abraded before his very eyes, continents unseated from their molten beds and the world's metallic core being rendered down to its composite elements.

Up close, it was even more beautiful and even more dangerous.

Waterfalls of liquid nitrogen poured down razor-edged canyons. Boiling lakes expanded with every surge of melting chemically-rich ice then shrank back as they bled toxic vapour into the void. Under colossal geological upheaval, the planet was undergoing stresses it had not known since its birth in the star's powerful gravitational tug-of-war. From orbit the planet's crust had been a reticulated mess of random scoring where tectonic plates had been ripped apart. On the surface that translated to gorges hundreds of kilometres wide and who knew how many deep.

The planet was in a heightened state of activity, and only the precision of Magos Blaylock's calculations – married to inloads from adepts of the Collegium Geologica – had allowed the fleet's Fabricatus Locum to plot a route to the *Tomioka*. The snaking, zig-zagging course offered the forces on the ground the best chance of reaching their goal, but Blaylock had been quick to point out that it was based purely on statistical probability rather than actual measurements.

An inset slate on the control panel fizzed with static, but had just enough resolution to show the position of the grav-sled, together with the corridor of acceptably stable ground they were to follow. Widened out to maximum zoom, that corridor was still frighteningly narrow and allowed little margin for error. Roboute didn't know what might happen if Blaylock's calculations were awry or he strayed from the marked corridor, and was in no hurry to find out.

Occasionally, they saw the remnants of servitor drones, buried in the sides of glaciers or smashed to a thousand pieces on the valley floor. Smoke trailed from their shattered canopies, and Roboute tried not to notice the ruptured bodies that spilled from them. A brief inload from Linya Tychon had mentioned an umbra of interference and distortion centred on the *Tomioka*, which went some way to explaining why they'd seen so many downed drones and were forced to rely on the workings of Tarkis Blaylock instead of precise route information.

The *Tabularium* pounded the ice and rock with its multiple iron feet as it trudged after them like a relentless city that had managed to uproot itself from its foundations and give chase. The other Land Leviathans were arranged behind it, nose to tail, a caravan of steel that reached back nearly five kilometres. The Cadian armoured vehicles, a mix of transports and tanks, clustered around the mobile temples like scavenger creatures stalking a dying herbivore, and Roboute was glad at least one other element of this expedition would likely be feeling a sense of amazement at this exploration of a new world.

Even over the enormous height of the *Tabularium*, Roboute could see the loping form of the alpha engine of Legio Sirius. *Lupa Capitalina* held station at the centre of the convoy, a mobile fortress protecting the Leviathans with its city-levelling firepower.

'Can you see the Warhounds yet?' asked Adara. 'My da once said he saw one on Konor, but it ran off before he got a proper look at it.'

Before now, Roboute would have poured scorn on the idea of a Titan running off, but having seen the speed with which *Amarok* and *Vilka* had deployed from their coffin ships, he was less inclined to laugh at Adara's tale. Even the speed of the Warlord had shocked them, and the impatient brays of its warhorn echoed from the walls of the glittering ice valley.

'No,' answered Roboute, craning his neck around. 'I haven't, but that doesn't surprise me. Warhounds are Scout Titans, ambush predators, and they don't like you seeing them until it's too late.'

Adara nodded, but still kept looking.

'Your father is certainly well travelled,' said Pavelka, her voice sounding in Roboute's helmet via subvocalised vibrations. 'Calth, Iax, Konor... Is there any part of Ultramar he has not visited?'

Pavelka's dripping sarcasm was evident, even over the helm-vox and the thrumming bass note of the grav-sled's repulsors.

'You don't believe me?'

'Ilanna's just teasing you,' said Roboute, knowing how defensive the lad got if anyone dared to question the truth of his father's tales.

'Well she shouldn't,' said Adara. 'My da served as an armsman to

Inquisitor Apollyon on Armageddon, and you don't go mouthing off about someone like that.'

Roboute knew Pavelka wouldn't be able to resist pulling that particular declaration apart, and gave the control column a shake to discourage her from picking holes in it.

'Easy, Roboute!' cried Adara, gripping the restraint bar on the door.

The ground beneath the grav-sled was a mixture of frozen nitrogen and bare, metallic rock, like the surface of an oil-streaked glacier. The sled's repulsor field reacted badly to patches of exotic metals and the ride was bumpier than Roboute would have liked. The controls were oversized to accommodate the inherent clumsiness in void-suit gloves, but even so, it felt like the machine was fighting him every step of the way, slewing left and right despite his best attempts to keep level.

'I can control the sled through my MIU if you would prefer,' said Pavelka. 'It appears you are having some difficulty, captain.'

'No,' said Roboute, wrestling with the control column. 'I'm fine taking us in.'

Their route was winding a path through a steep-sided canyon that Roboute's eyes were telling him rose to around a hundred metres or so, but was probably at least a couple of kilometres. The eye was easily tricked into forming manageable scales when denied any quantifiable points of reference. When he'd first eased the sled into the mountains, his mind had reeled at the sheer vastness of each canyon's ice-blue walls, and without the measurable scale of the landing fields, it was impossible to define distances or perspective with any reliability.

'How soon till we reach the crashed ship?' asked Adara, his neck craned back as far as the gorget arrangement on his helmet's collar would allow. Roboute risked narrowing the magnification of the slate, but gave up looking when the screeching, squalling distortion pattern didn't let up. Only the slender thread of Blaylock's route through the labyrinth remained unwavering.

'Impossible to say through this interference,' answered Pavelka, reading the same information instantly. Even through the imperfections of the vox-units, her excitement was palpable. 'According to our distance travelled, we should be within sight of the *Tomioka* within seven minutes, assuming the current rate of advance continues.'

'And assuming I don't crash us,' said Roboute.

'A possibility I did not care to raise.'

'Listen,' said Roboute. 'A grav-sled isn't a precision instrument of manoeuvre, but I think I'm finally getting its measure. It just takes a little finesse and a little nerve.'

'I suppose how much nerve is required depends on where one is sitting.'

Adara sniggered. 'And Mistress Tychon said the Mechanicus don't have a sense of humour…'

'She's right,' snapped Roboute. 'They don't.'

Despite Pavelka's commentary on his piloting skills, Roboute steered them with greater confidence with every passing metre. His Ultramarian ethic would not let him attempt a task without then mastering it, and curbing the vagaries of the grav-sled's control was no exception.

Their course evened out over the next few kilometres, and as Roboute eased around a sheer spur of violet-tinged ice that shed streamers of vapour like an industrial smokestack, the valley widened noticeably towards a cascade of smoking liquid nitrogen. It poured down through a fissure that glittered in the blue-shifted light, before vanishing into a gaping crevasse that cut the valley almost in two.

Roboute guessed the crevasse was at least thirty metres wide.

According to Blaylock's path, the *Tomioka* lay on the opposite side.

And the Black Templars, he thought, trying to keep a lid on his irritation.

Where the crevasse didn't quite reach the valley walls, cascading spumes of freezing gases collected in swirling eddies and whirlpools of shimmering liquid.

'Will the Land Leviathans be able to get across that?' asked Adara.

'Not a chance,' said Roboute. 'Though the *Tabularium* might fall in and wedge itself tight to make a bridge for the others.'

'You think there's room enough for us to go round the edges?'

'Just barely,' answered Pavelka, blink-clicking measurement datum points and exloading them to the Mechanicus pioneer vehicles behind them.

'Well, the Black Templars may have beaten us to the *Tomioka*, but I'll be damned if anyone else is getting there before us,' said Roboute, hauling the grav-sled around towards the edge of the valley, where vortices of nitrogen translated from gas to liquid and back again with alarming frequency.

The pitch of the grav-sled's engines increased, and the repulsor field skittered at the abrupt change in ground density. Roboute heard Pavelka mutter a whispered prayer to the Machine-God and felt her subtle imprecation to the engines' magnetic field compensating for the unusual terrain.

Buoyed up by Pavelka's devotion, the grav-sled negotiated the foaming, streaming edges of the liquid nitrogen waterfall with aplomb and skirted the edges of the vast crevasse with only centimetres to spare.

Roboute risked a glance over the edge and felt his stomach lurch as he saw the rift cut right into the heart of the planet. He switched his gaze back to what lay ahead of him as a nauseous sense of vertigo threatened to sweep over him. Roboute gunned the engine and the grav-sled surged to the jagged summit of the fissure.

At long last, Roboute saw what had become of Magos Telok's flagship, though it took him a moment to realise that was what he was seeing. He shielded his visor from the billions of points of light reflecting from the glassy plateau before him.

'I thought the ship we were looking for was a wreck?' asked Adara, tilting his head to the side.

'So did I,' said Roboute.

'It didn't crash?' said Pavelka, her incomprehension turning her words into a question.

'No,' said Roboute in wonderment. 'It... *landed*.'

Smoke filled the pilot's compartment, and Tanna tasted the reek of burning propellant, scorched iron and blood in the back of his mouth. He blinked away the disorientation of the crash, and checked his visor to see how long he had been unconscious. Four seconds. To a mortal, such a span was negligible, but to a Space Marine, it was an eternity. Angry with himself, he shook off his momentary weakness and pushed himself from the pilot's chair. The angle of the Thunderhawk's impact had driven the nose into the plateau, and Tanna was forced to use dangling straps and cables to haul himself back into the crew compartment.

The warriors in the back had weathered the crash with relative ease, thanks to his managing their angle of descent and the grav-harnesses.

'Anyone injured?' he asked, pulling himself along the centre-line of the gunship.

'Everyone is unhurt,' said Auiden. 'That was some landing, brother-sergeant.'

'Some kind of interference blew out the engines,' said Tanna. 'I was lucky to get us down on our belly and in one piece.'

'I know,' said Auiden. 'I meant no reproach.'

Tanna shook his head. 'Of course.'

The grievances felt against him since Kul Gilad's loss had made Tanna find fault in every word spoken to him, veiled insults in every comment. He took a moment to purge himself of that suspicion and moved to the fuselage doors of the gunship. With the nose of the *Barisan* buried in the ice, the side and rear exits were the only way out.

'We need to get out of here,' he said, kneeling beside the fuselage door and pulling open the keypad hatch. He tapped in his command codes, but – as he'd expected – the door remained stubbornly shut.

'Why is the... *ngg, ngg*... door not opening?' asked Issur.

'There is no power to the mechanism,' answered Tanna. 'It will need brute force to get us out.'

The *Barisan* creaked and lurched with a squeal of tearing metal. Seams burst farther down the fuselage, and hissing streamers of escaping gas vented from cracks in the hull. Tanna grabbed onto a stanchion as the gunship shuddered, as though some giant beast had it locked in its jaws and was slowly trying to digest it.

'Yael, Issur, help me,' ordered Tanna. 'Get the edge of the door.'

'I can shoot us a way out,' offered Bracha, unlimbering his implanted plasma gun, but Tanna shook his head.

'I would rather not risk angering the *Barisan* by shooting it from the inside,' he said.

The three Black Templars took hold of the door and braced themselves against stanchions, struts and bench seats. More seams burst along the line of the fuselage. Tanna had a worrying image of the gunship caught in a wreckage compactor, being slowly crushed until it and they were nothing more than an ultra-dense cube of iron and meat.

'Auiden, as soon as you see the locking mechanism, cut it.'

The Apothecary nodded and bent before the lock-plate of the fuselage door. A painfully bright light spat into life from an extended blade, a fusion cutter for field amputations, and he pulled it back like an executioner ready to strike a killing blow.

The *Barisan* groaned, like a beast in pain, and Tanna cursed that he had brought so fine a machine to so ignoble a fate. Glass shattered in the cockpit and the avionics panel blew out with a whooping electrical bang.

'Now,' yelled Tanna, and the three of them hauled back on the door. The fuselage of a Thunderhawk gunship was designed to be airtight during spaceflight and atmospheric insertion, but it wasn't designed to withstand the combined strength of three Space Marines trying to haul it open from the inside.

Tanna felt the door shift, millimetres at best, but here the deformations crushing the hull worked in their favour and a portion of the hull buckled inwards at the lock-plate. He saw the flash of Auiden's fusion cutter and heard the hiss of dissolving metal. For a fraction of a second, the heavy door held firm, but then the cutter finished its work and it rumbled back along its rails.

'Forgive us, great one,' said Auiden as he sheathed the energised blade.

Tanna nodded in agreement. The *Barisan* had carried them faithfully into battle and out of trouble more times than he could remember. To have wounded it just to escape seemed a poor way to repay its strength of heart, but he felt sure its machine-spirit would forgive them.

'Everybody out,' he ordered.

Varda was first through, quickly followed by Issur and Bracha. Auiden went next, then Yael and finally Tanna dropped from the canted deck.

He landed on the ground, which was just as he'd imagined it to be from the air: a vast plateau of ice. Where the gunship had smashed down was powdered like fine snow, but brittle like metal shavings. The Thunderhawk's impact had ploughed a deep furrow, and Tanna knelt as he saw what looked like tendrils of frost reaching up from the ground along the hull of the downed flying machine.

Like condensation on a pane of glass, it looked like the ice was reaching up to enfold the *Barisan*'s fuselage. Tanna looked back down to where the gunship's nose was buried in the ice… except he saw now that it wasn't ice at all, but some form of parasitic crystal. When he had recovered consciousness, he remembered seeing the vapour-struck sky through the crazed armourglass canopy, but the entire frontal section was now almost completely enclosed. As if the 'ice' had begun to swell and freeze instantly upon the gunship, like the planet was trying to drag it down into the crust.

Even as Tanna watched, he saw the crystalline structure of the ground spread glittering fronds further over the body of the gunship. He scraped a hand over the fuselage, scattering the ice like sugar crystals that fell to dust as soon as they were no longer part of the whole.

'What is this…?' he wondered aloud, but no sooner had he removed his hand than the crystalline fronds renewed their attempt to engulf the *Barisan*.

'Brother-sergeant,' said Bracha from above. 'You need to get up here now.'

Tanna backed away from the strange crystalline growths attaching themselves to his gunship, and scrambled back along the length of the impact trough. Yael offered him a hand up, but Tanna ignored it and hauled himself onto the plateau.

'Situation?' he asked.

No one answered, and Tanna was about to repeat his question when he turned to see what his men were all staring at. He recalled his last sight before the gunship had gone down. He had seen the *Tomioka* with his own eyes, but the actuality of it rendered him speechless, unable to look away from the logic-defying, impossible sight before him.

'Imperator,' hissed Varda. 'It's impossible.'

Tanna shook his head. 'It is the *Tomioka*, no doubt about that.'

A retrofitted Oberon battleship, the enormous vessel stood vertical along its long axis on the surface of Katen Venia like the last few kilometres of a towering hive spire. Such vast starships were never meant to enter the gravity envelope of a planet. Their superstructures were built to endure the multi-directional forces of void war and withstand pressures of acceleration and enormous turning circles.

What they were manifestly *not* designed to do was cope with the titanic forces of re-entry.

Tanna guessed that the ship's engine section was buried at least two kilometres in frozen nitrogen, while the remaining five kilometres of its monolithic superstructure jutted into the sky, almost vanishing in a forced perspective that defied human scale. Its hull was as gothically ornamented as any Imperial ship of the line, redolent with cathedrals, crenellated battlements, rounded archways of gun batteries, ice-encrusted processionals of statuary and the bladed prow of a fighting vessel.

Glaciers of buttressing ice surrounded the base of the ship, rising from the planet's surface to a height of around five hundred metres, obscuring any obvious means of entry and helping to stabilise the towering edifice. Above the ice, vast swathes of the ship were encrusted with bizarre crystalline structures of intricate design, but which bore the clear hallmark of Mechanicus origin. Some had the look of power generators, others of communications relays, but the more Tanna looked, the more he understood that the *Tomioka* had been completely redesigned to be something other than a starship.

'How could anyone... *ngg*, have done... *nggh*, this?' asked Issur, the synaptic damage he'd suffered aboard the Manifold station making every word a struggle.

'I do not know,' admitted Tanna. 'The ship should have torn itself apart.'

'Do you think this was what the archmagos was expecting?' asked Varda.

'I don't think it's what anyone was expecting,' said Tanna.

An eruption of ice crystals to either side of the Black Templars had them snap guns to shoulders and swords to en garde. Scores of detonations plumed like geysers of ice, except that Tanna knew the glassy substance on which they stood was not ice at all. Glittering particulates hung in the air, and Tanna saw a host of figures climb from each of the holes blasted through the planet's surface.

They had the bulk of Space Marines, but their bodies were formed from a translucent crystalline material with its own bioluminescence. A pulsing network of green veins threaded their bodies, like an illuminated nervous system or a map of blood vessels in a human body. Tanna saw they were not coming from beneath the ground, they were *part* of the ground. At least forty of the creatures surrounded them, and as the glassy dust of their arrival settled, Tanna saw they didn't just have the bulk of Space Marines, their bodies were somehow formed in a crude imitation of Adeptus Astartes.

Each crystalline form had the bulky curvature of auto-reactive shoulder guards, the broad sweep of a plastron and an elementary form of a helmet. They were like a child's representation of Space Marines, crude and ill-fashioned, but recognisable enough.

'What in the Emperor's name are they?' hissed Varda as the crystal creatures closed in.

'The enemy,' said Tanna, sighting down his bolter and pulling the trigger.

If there was a lesson to be learned here, it was that he not doubt *Amarok*'s sense for something amiss. Gunnar Vintras walked the Warhound backwards through a thicket of tall crystalline spires, keeping the damaged side of his engine facing the canyon wall. His turbolaser was jammed, the servitor dead and the Titan's machine-spirit desperately trying to find a workaround to get it firing again. Phantom agonies from his left arm kept Vintras from blacking out, and a constant flood of stimulants fought the effects of the pain-balms.

'If I survive this fight, I'm going to have one hell of a chemical come-down when they flush me out,' he hissed through pursed lips. 'That's a Manifold purge I'm not looking forward to.'

No sooner had he initiated a full-threat auspex sweep, the kind of blaring announcement of presence a Warhound princeps was loath to initiate, than the enemy had attacked. He still wasn't sure where they'd come from. One minute he was striding over a series of fallen stalagmites of prismatic glass, the next, four engines of comparable displacement to *Amarok* were attacking him.

The Warhound took the first shots on her voids, but in keeping him alive they blew out with a screaming detonation. Only Vintras's natural reactions had kept a second volley of streaking bolts from gutting his Titan. As it was, the turbolasers had taken the brunt of the barrage.

He returned fire with the mega-bolter, feeling the pounding reverberations through the bones of his arm as he unleashed a salvo of high-explosive rounds. Like most Warhound princeps, the joints at his elbow had been replaced with shock-absorbent materials to better withstand the constant pressure of bio-feedback from his engine's weaponry, and he was able to bear the brunt of such punishing recoil from an arm that wasn't even his.

Something shattered into a million pieces in front of him, but a cascade of billowing ice prevented him from seeing what it was as it fell. Vintras knew better than anyone the perils of staying still in an engine fight, and pushed *Amarok* to striding speed. A Warhound wasn't a gross-displacement engine that could dish out vast amounts of fire and take it at the same time, it was a hunter that thrived in high-speed war.

A flensing blast of fire blew a smoking crater in the canyon wall, and Vintras traced the shot back to its point of origin. He danced the Warhound through the crystal growths and saw another three engines striding towards him. His eyes narrowed as he took the measure of his opponents.

'What the hell are you?' he murmured, seeing a dreadful familiarity in their appearance.

They were Warhounds, but ones that looked like the atavistic ice sculptures left outside the fortress of the Oldbloods by the savage tribes that called Lokabrenna home.

Though these statues were moving and fighting.

But they were stupid.

They came straight at him, like ranked-up regiments of Imperial Guardsmen on a parade ground. Vintras grinned and pushed the reactor to full power as he bolted for the cover of a fallen slope of rubble farther along the valley side. Shots chased him, but his control over *Amarok*'s movement was faultless. Even the pain of his wounded arm and the pain-balms couldn't dull the pleasure of this moment.

A Titan commander relished a good fight, but to find yourself engaged against a foe you hopelessly outmatched was a very special pleasure.

The crystalline Titans followed him like hounds on a hunt, and Vintras led them a merry chase through the spires: darting back and forth, weaving around them and leading them just where he wanted them. Billowing clouds of glassy dust choked the canyon, but Vintras had memorised every move he'd made, like a virtuoso dancer flawlessly performing his greatest work.

The pain in his left arm faded and the Manifold surged with readiness data.

Even his voids had reset.

Amarok burst through a curtain of bright fragments, and there ahead of him were the three counterfeit Warhounds with their backs to him.

'Imperator, I love these moments,' he said, striding forwards at combat speed.

Instead of scattering, the enemy engines began turning on the spot like novice moderati playing at being a princeps. Vintras was on them before they were halfway rotated. He stepped between the right-most engines and thrust his arms out to either side. The mega-bolter was primarily an infantry killer, but at point-blank range against an unshielded enemy it was an executioner's weapon. Explosive shells ripped into the upper section of the first crystal Warhound and blasted it apart from the inside. Turbolaser fire cored the middle engine, shattering its canopy in a superhot explosion of molten fragments.

Amarok kept going, and Vintras pivoted around the falling carcass of the headless Titan to face the last remaining crystal engine. He bared his steel fangs and brought his hands together as though aiming a pistol down the firing range.

'You might look like a Warhound, but you don't fight like one,' snarled the Skinwalker, unleashing both weapons into the glittering faux-Titan's head.

Microcontent 05

Kotov had switched to a body better suited to hostile environments, an archaic robotic chassis with ray-shielded internal workings and heavy armoured plates that put him level with his skitarii escort and made him look like a ceremonial knight. His head was encased in a shimmering integrity field that sent an irritated buzzing through his aural implants, but which was still preferable to an enclosing helm.

He stepped down from the converted skitarii Rhino and looked back the way they had come. The crevasse at the end of the valley was being bridged by pioneer units disgorged from the construction decks of the *Tabularium*. The Cadian engineer units had nothing capable of bridging so a wide a gap, and their vehicles were forced to wait along with everyone else. Judging by the vox passing between Captain Hawkins's Chimera and Colonel Anders's Salamander, that delay sat ill with the men of Cadia.

A thousand servitors, load-lifters and construction engines were manoeuvring heavy, girder-braced spars of plasteel into place, and robed adepts on suspended platforms drilled bracing struts onto the inner faces of the crevasse.

But it was going to take time to construct something capable of bearing the unimaginable mass of a Land Leviathan, and Kotov couldn't wait that long. He wanted to taste his moment of triumph first-hand, not filtered through a pict-capture or hololithic representation.

He would see the *Tomioka* with his own augmetic eyes.

Lupa Capitalina stood immobile behind the *Tabularium*, a towering representation of the Omnissiah in his aspect of war. Occasional puffs of ejected vapour and thermal bleed from its armoured reactor gave the lie to its dormancy. The Warlord was a warrior on hair trigger, taut and poised for action. Under normal circumstances, the reassurance a fully armed Warlord Titan imparted would be welcome, but after the incident in the training decks, everyone was understandably skittish around the mighty war machine. Legio Sirius adepts had assured Kotov that the Wintersun's lapse could never happen again, but as Kotov well knew, the Mechanicus never deletes anything.

The Warhounds that had accompanied the Wintersun to the surface were nowhere to be seen, but that wasn't unusual; the princeps of such engines were wilful and preferred to remain unseen.

Satisfied all was proceeding as fast as could be expected, Kotov set off to the opening of the valley, where Roboute Surcouf and two members of his crew awaited him.

'You should let my skitarii scout this place out first,' said Dahan, emerging from a second Rhino and marching to join him with a loping, mechanical gait. 'We don't know what's up here, and if Surcouf is to be believed, the *Tomioka* might still have active defences in place.'

The fleshy part of the Secutor's face was encased in an oxygenated membrane gel that rippled across his skull like a thin coating of water. All four of his arms were extended, his digital scarifiers crackling with sparking lightning and his Cebrenian halberd held at the ready in his upper limbs.

'Even after nearly four thousand years?'

'Mechanicus tech isn't fragile,' Dahan reminded him. 'It's built to endure.'

'You're right, of course, Hirimau,' said Kotov, 'but I think we are well protected, don't you?'

'Better to know than to think,' grunted Dahan.

'Spoken like a true priest of Mars,' said Kotov without any trace of irony.

Twenty skitarii followed the archmagos, armoured in non-reflective carapace that seamlessly shifted in sync with their movements. Cog-toothed Mechanicus skulls were rivet-stamped to each shoulder, alongside scaled scorpions and azure spiders. Dahan's warriors normally eschewed the wearing of barbaric totems, but Kotov noted that two had fashioned leathery-looking cloaks from what passive receptors told him was human skin. It was the work of a picosecond to match its DNA profile with that of the batch-grown skin curtains found in the Valette infirmary.

Most of the skitarii came armed with solid-slug weapons, though two were implanted with flame units and a last warrior was equipped with twin meltaguns, one as a replacement arm, the other as a shoulder mount. All carried a variety of close-combat weapons: a mix of sabres, axes and falchions with energised edges and saw-blade teeth. Their faces were obscured by tinted visors that had darkened to a deep bronze.

Galatea had elected to remain aboard the *Tabularium*, which struck Kotov as strange, given its stated desire to kill the Lost Magos. Not that Kotov wasn't grateful to be away from the abominable creature, but he couldn't shake the niggling suspicion that the hybrid machine intelligence wasn't being entirely honest with them.

Whatever the truth of Galatea's ultimate agenda, it would have to wait.

With Dahan at his side, Kotov clambered through the nitrogen-wreathed rocks to the top of the fissure. Surcouf climbed down from his grav-sled and held out a hand to him.

'You made it, archmagos,' he said. 'It's quite a sight, isn't it?'

Kotov didn't answer the rogue trader, his gaze drawn to the dizzying height of the starship standing on its ice-encased engines in the centre of the glassy ice plateau. Of all the things he had expected, this had featured in none of his dreams of finding the *Tomioka*. Far from being a victim of atmospheric poisoning or rampant exaggeration, Surcouf had, if anything, undersold how incredible the sight of the landed starship would be.

'Ave Deus Mechanicus…' he said, his mouth hanging slack at the impossible sight of a seven-kilometre starship standing proud like a hive starscraper.

'I know,' said Surcouf, understanding his awe. 'I still have a hard time believing it's real.'

Kotov tried to find some frame of reference to bring the idea of a landed starship into some kind of focus, but the sight of it standing so incongruously in the landscape was one that fitted no model of reality.

'I have never heard of a vessel this size surviving atmospheric transit, let alone being successfully landed,' said Dahan.

'Telok must have brought it in exactly perpendicular to the surface,' said Kotov, finally imposing a measure of order on his cascading thoughts. 'Or else it would have broken its keel and spread itself all over the surface.'

'Is that even possible?' asked Surcouf, unlimbering a pair of

magnoculars and training it on a glittering cloud of mist a kilometre or so ahead of them.

'The ship's plasma engines allowed the ship to penetrate far enough into the ice for it to remain upright,' said Kotov, more to himself than in answer of Surcouf.

'What is that?' asked Dahan, training his own combat optics on the mist cloud Surcouf was examining. 'Is that the *Barisan?*'

'It must be,' agreed Surcouf. 'It's right at the end of what looks like an impact gouge in the ground. I think the Templars crashed, but it's hard to make anything out.'

'The umbra is damping all auspex readings and hexing the blessed workings of machines within the limits of this plateau,' said Kotov, suddenly realising that the dimensions of this encircled plateau were a virtually perfect match for the diameter of the distortion Linya Tychon had detected.

'We're within it, and the grav-sled is still functional,' said Surcouf. 'If it's being generated from the *Tomioka,* then it looks like it doesn't extend all the way to ground level.'

'If the Black Templars have crash landed, we should go to their aid,' said Dahan.

Kotov was inclined to damn the Space Marines and let them suffer the consequences of their foolhardy zeal, but quelled so petty a notion. Dahan was right, if the Adeptus Astartes required assistance, he was duty-bound to offer it. He switched through his visual perception modes and multiple hues descended over the landscape as he saw in expanded wavelengths, sound vibrations, radiation decay and a host of other sensory inputs. Irritatingly, it seemed Surcouf was correct in deducing that the umbra did not reach ground level, as his augmetic senses had no trouble penetrating the umbra below fifty metres.

Just as what he had first seen upon reaching the edge of the plateau made no sense, what he was seeing now made just as little sense. With a thought, he switched Dahan's optics to match his own and exloaded the correct perceptual mode to Surcouf's magnoculars.

'Magos Dahan,' said Kotov. 'The Templars are under attack. Send in the skitarii.'

Magos Dahan detested riding into battle within the hull of an armoured vehicle, equating its metallic confinement to the interior of a tomb. He had adopted the usage of the Iron Fist for just that reason, preferring to ride in an open-topped vehicle, like a barbarian king of Old Earth charging towards the enemy on his warchariot.

The image was an apt one, for he stood on the armoured topside

of a crimson and black Rhino as it led his skitarii towards the beleaguered Black Templars. His clawed legs were braced on the side and rear holdbars, while his deactivated scarifiers clamped onto the cupola mount of the commander's hatch. His upper arms were free, and he had slung his halberd in favour of deploying a pair of forearm-mounted rotary lasers.

Denying the Cadian units permission to cross the partially completed pioneer bridge, Dahan had led his skitarii past the thousands of servitors and structural engineers buttressing its supports in readiness for the *Tabularium*'s crossing. Thirty Rhinos matched the speed of his own, heavily converted vehicles with upgraded auspex suites, additional weaponry and higher-grade command/control functionality. Each carried a squad of heavily armed and highly skilled warriors, men he had trained using his stochastic analysis of millions of inloaded combat doctrines which were then broken down into their component elements. It was a training regime he had believed faultless until Brother Yael of the Black Templars had – defying all statistical probability – bested him in a contest of arms. A mortal mind might have felt some affront or insult at such a defeat, but Dahan was above such petty concerns, and had incorporated the fighting styles of the Black Templars into his accumulated battle subroutines.

Interspersed with the screen of armour came the columns of weaponised servitors, tracked praetorians, mobile weapon platforms and a quad-maniple of twelve battle robots: six Cataphracts, four Crusaders and two Conquerors. Each robot's organo-cybernetic cortex was slaved to a partitioned thought-stream of battle-implants.

No part of this battlefield was unknown to Dahan, the overclocked speed of his mental architecture plotting out a precise and constantly updating picture of the combat arena. His threat optics – now incorporating Archmagos Kotov's sensory inload – draped the plateau of icy rock in myriad cyan hues: strongly pigmented azures for organics, deeper cobalt shades for metallics and lighter teals for inorganic materials. Firing range bands, topographical vectors of assault and optimal engagement zones were overlaid in crisp red lines, giving Dahan the perfect datum points from which to conduct this assault.

The Black Templars fought from the topside of their partially buried Thunderhawk, which at Dahan's increased consciousness speed appeared to be in the process of being subsumed by the ground itself. A host of crystal-formed warriors, illumined and likely empowered by a bloom of exotic energy within their chest cavities, laid siege to the Thunderhawk. Bioform analysis took them to be Space Marines, but Dahan saw they were poor imitations of Adeptus Astartes perfection.

Withering hails of bolter fire were blasting these monstrosities apart, but more were pulling themselves free from the ground with the sound of breaking glass. Perhaps two hundred or more surrounded the buried gunship, hurling themselves at the embattled Space Marines with a slow, relentless hunger. Some were equipped with crudely shaped weaponry integral to their forms, and these fired streams of light that registered as painfully bright lances of sapphire.

Fortunately for the Space Marines, their attackers displayed an appalling lack of marksmanship, but the sheer volume of fire was forcing the Templars to employ every square metre of cover afforded by the gunship's tailfins, opened dorsal hatches and inactive topside turrets.

A number of icons flashed onto his vision and Dahan wordlessly issued his orders.

The Conquerors came to a halt, digging into the reflective surface of the plateau with bracing claws before cycling round their heavy bolters and lascannons. Blazing gouts of fire streamed overhead, ploughing through the crystalline creatures in a thunderous cacophony of shattered crystal and arcing electrical discharge. The data lodged in Dahan's cognitive overview.

Whatever else these creatures were, they were definitely *not* organic.

The Crusaders increased speed, two moving around each flank as the skitarii Rhinos ground to a halt in a blizzard of glittering ice chips. Assault doors slammed back and squads of cybernetically enhanced warriors debarked in perfect synchrony. Each squad-chief's right eye was a battle-implant that received situational data straight from Dahan; they knew what he knew and his binaric orders were implemented virtually instantaneously.

Like a Grand Master's regicide pieces on a tri-dimensional board, each squad moved in concert with those nearby, offering mutually supporting fields of fire and flank protection. Weaponised servitors swiftly caught up to the infantry, taking up overwatching positions to offer fire-support as and when it was required. The Cataphract robots moved alongside the infantry, their anti-personnel autocannons and power fists ready to support against any foe beyond the soldiers' capability to engage.

Dahan released his grip on the sides of his own Rhino and dropped to the ground, unlimbering his Cebrenian halberd and igniting his clawed scarifiers. His assigned squad hove into view, and he ran to join them with his peculiar loping gait.

Skitarii gunfire smashed through the crystal creatures, blasting them apart with solid rounds or detonating them explosively with

high-energy hotshots. Grenade launchers cleared space for praetorians to occupy and deny the enemy time to regroup. Dahan himself was not above getting his hands dirty, fighting with killing sweeps of his Cebrenian halberd. He assigned his own command squad, a mix of elite suzerain and experimental weapon bearers, a path right into the heart of the fight.

His accompanying skitarii unleashed a hail of plasma, graviton guns and micro-conversion beamers. Though the crystal creatures were manifestly inhuman they still obeyed the laws of physics and came apart like any other substance. Their advance was made over crunching debris of flickering crystal and cut-glass carcasses.

Dahan allowed himself a moment of recklessness and surged ahead of his squad, vaulting into a group of the icy-looking crystal-forms with a burst of hostile binary. He swung his Cebrenian halberd, slamming its entropic capacitor into the chest of a slowly turning construct. A blast of hostile code stabbed into its heart and the green light was instantly extinguished. The impact of the halberd shattered the thing, and Dahan was already moving by the time its glassy remains fell to the ground. Just as they were poor shots, the crystal-forms were no more adept in the arts of close combat. Dahan slashed and stabbed with his halberd, reaping a grim tally of glassy enemies, and cutting shard-limbs from their bodies with his energy-wreathed scarifiers.

Most battlefields were filled with the screams of frenzied warriors, the howls of the dying and the clash of blades, but in this arena the only sounds were booming gunfire and the brittle shattering of crystal-form bodies.

The twin horns of the skitarii assault now pressed in on the crystal-form creatures, scything their numbers and pressing in towards the Space Marines atop the *Barisan*. Dahan's calculations indicated that this engagement would be decisively ended in four minutes and thirty-five seconds.

Dahan's squad finally caught up with him, fighting with implanted weaponry to blast and cut a path through the heart of the enemy towards the Space Marines. Dahan instantly read the identity biometrics of each of the Black Templars, intrigued to note that not one of them displayed any elevated readings to indicate that they were engaged in a desperate firefight.

He opened a vox-link, cycling through all known Space Marine frequencies until he heard a clipped, verbally efficient battle-cant based on the northern Inwit tribal argot.

'Sergeant Tanna, this is Magos Dahan,' he said. 'Now would seem a prudent time to withdraw.'

Tanna's voice sounded shocked to hear a non-Templar voice in his helmet. 'This is a Templar vox-net,' he said. 'You do not speak upon it.'

'Feel free to censure me when we are back on the *Tabularium*,' Dahan said, 'but I suggest you come with us before more of these crystal-forms appear.'

Tanna did not respond and Dahan realised the sergeant had shut him off.

'Foolish,' said Dahan, amazed at the self-harm beings not defined by logic would wreak upon themselves for the sake of mortal pride and propriety. Dahan paused in his advance as he registered the destruction of two of his Rhinos. Nowhere in his wide net of sensory inputs had he registered a threat capable of destroying a vehicle. He pulled his awareness outwards as a rippling spiderweb of surging energy patterns converged on the battlefield, like a reversed pict-capture of a shattering pane of glass, the splintering traceries of cracks radiating back *towards* the point of impact.

Moments later, the threat levels ramped up as fresh energy forms rapidly appeared without warning. All across the theatre of battle, the ground erupted with thousands of geysering blasts of prismatic shards as an entire army of the crystal-forms ripped up into the fight. The cycling counter of his battle-end calculation went into reverse before winking out and being replaced with a representation of how long his own forces could expect to remain viable.

Inevitable victory had suddenly become certain annihilation.

A trio of figures tore themselves from the ground before Dahan, two resembling crude anatomical representations of skitarii, while the third was a glassine mockery of his own form, complete with a tripod arrangement of legs and quad-armatures.

A blast of fire stuck him on the shoulder, and his combat algorithms leapt in complexity by an order of magnitude. Dahan gasped at the hexamathic density of the required calculations and his shoulders erupted with thermal bloom as his cranial implants desperately vented excess heat. He staggered as his mind and body fought to maintain equilibrium between strategic overview and tactical necessity.

Something had to give, and right now Dahan's most pressing concern was the creature right in front of him threatening his life.

He shut off his high-speed cognitive functions and veils of battlefield awareness fell away like wind-blown smoke. His doppelgänger came at him with its copied halberd slashing for his head. Dahan was still adjusting to his restricted world view and the blow took him full in the chest, hurling him back with a *crack* of splitting metal. Bolts of las-fire blasted chunks of its substance away, but its imitation body was clearly of greater density than its brethren.

A crystal-clawed foot stamped down on a scarifier arm and sheared it from his body. Pain signals flared in Dahan's brain. Nothing organic was left in that limb, but the hurt was no less real. Dahan's recalibrating combat subroutines snapped back into focus and he parried a follow-up blow, rolling aside as the halberd slammed down where his head had been.

'My turn,' he snarled, driving his scarifier up into the thing's body.

Snapping electrical discharge blew out a vast chunk of crystalline material, and he kicked out with his third leg, snapping one of his attacker's. The creature staggered, but didn't fall until he pushed himself upright and brought his Cebrenian halberd down on its skull. The blow sheared the creature in two, its severed body collapsing like two halves of a cloven sculpture. More of the risen crystal-form creatures were surrounding him; the sheer quantity of enemy firepower had a quality all of its own.

Four more came at him and he swayed back on his rear leg to avoid a thrusting spear-limb. A halberd strike destroyed the limb, and he sprang forwards to deliver a hammering electrical strike from his remaining scarifier. The creature exploded and he spun low on his reverse-jointed main limbs, scything his retracted rear leg around. Two crystal-forms went down. Dahan skewered one with his halberd, spinning the weapon around to deliver a thunderous strike with the entropic generator on the other. A crackling energy fist came at him and he lowered his head to take the blow on his armoured cowl. Crystal shattered against the adamantium hood; Dahan didn't give the creature another chance.

He surged upright, vaulting over the thing's head and bringing his halberd around in three ultra-rapid slices before he landed. The crystal-form slid apart into pieces, green light spewing from its ruptured chest cavity. On another day, Dahan would have dearly loved to study that energy source, but now was not the time.

With a fractional space cleared around him, the skitarii rallied to his side.

Dahan allowed himself a brief increase in cognition speed to access his strategic awareness protocols, skimming the blurts of real-time data-feeds from the warriors under his command.

The information was not heartening.

Dahan's skitarii were dying, and instead of rescuing the Black Templars, he and his command squad were now as isolated as Tanna and his warriors.

***

Tanna had long since expended his supply of bolter ammunition and the powercell of his chainsword was dangerously close to running empty. His armour was scorched from dozens of impacts and he was among the least wounded of his warriors. Auiden had already brought Bracha back into the fight, sealing a neatly cauterised blast through his thigh.

Now Bracha knelt propped up by the *Barisan*'s tailfin, picking shots with his implanted plasma gun and fending off close-range attackers with his combat blade. Issur met the foe blade to blade, hacking the crystalline mockeries of Space Marines apart with graceful blows of his shrieking power sword. Only his nerve-damage induced muscle spasms allowed the creatures anywhere near him. Shards of his armour hung from him where their energised claws had torn it from him.

Issur fought back to back with Varda, who alone of them all appeared untouchable. The Black Sword cut through the translucent glass bodies of their attackers with ease, and his gold-chased pistol had a seemingly unending supply of killing bolts.

Yael fought from behind a turret that Tanna dearly wished was firing, snapping off carefully aimed shots with his bolter and driving the enemy back with his sword when that wasn't enough. Auiden fought at Tanna's side; a warrior first, Apothecary second. His pistol was empty, but his sword and narthecium blades were just as efficient at killing.

'Not how I imagined this would end,' said Auiden.

'Nor I,' replied Tanna, sweeping his sword through the faceplate of a crystal-form imitation of a Space Marine. He kicked its broken remains from the gunship, all too aware that the encroaching ice of the plateau was at least a metre higher than when they had first crashed. At this rate, its structure would be completely absorbed by the plateau within the next ten minutes.

Not that Tanna expected to live that long.

He ducked as he saw a crystal-form take aim and felt the heat of the shot's passing. Two more creatures clawed their way up the *Barisan*'s fuselage. He kicked the first one back down and plunged his blade into the green-lit chest of the second. Three more came up behind them, and sawing blasts of fire tore over his back as he threw himself flat. He rolled and found himself sliding towards the edge of the gunship, where a host of climbing enemy awaited him.

'Tanna!' shouted Auiden, diving over the topside to grab the edge of his armour.

The Apothecary's grip gave Tanna the chance to swing his sword around and hook it behind a protruding intake vent. With Auiden's

help, he finally found purchase and pushed himself away from the drop. He rolled as numerous crystalline claws appeared at the edge.

'My thanks,' said Tanna, scrambling to his feet and stamping down on the besieging hands.

As far as he could see, the plateau was squirming with motion as more and more of the crystalline creatures burst from geysers of crystal shards, cracking and splitting the ground with their arrival. Magos Dahan's assault now looked like a last stand as they too were surrounded by the emergent beasts.

'Galling to be killed while we're in spitting distance of a god-machine,' cried Auiden, backhanding his chainsword across the neck of an enemy warrior.

'If they're so... *nggh*... close, why aren't they... *hnng*... here?' spat Issur.

'It wouldn't make any difference,' shouted Bracha. 'Would you trust a war machine that almost blew your ship out from under you?'

'Kotov would never authorise *Lupa Capitalina* to fire on the *Tomioka*,' said Tanna. 'He has crossed the galaxy to find this ship and isn't about to risk it being damaged by Titan fire.'

'Then the next few moments are going to be interesting,' said Auiden.

'You have a strange idea of interesting, Apothecary,' said Varda as he put a bolt through an enemy's chest.

'That's only because you think purely in terms of killing.'

'What other... *gnnah*... way is there to think?' said Issur, cutting the legs out from two enemy warriors with one blow.

'I have to think of killing and keeping all of you alive,' said the Apothecary, adjusting the settings on his narthecium gauntlet. 'Now *that's* interesting.'

No sooner were the words out of Auiden's mouth than a hideously unlucky volley of shots punched through his plastron, gorget and helmet. Blood fountained, and even without Apothecary training, Tanna knew the wounds were mortal. He caught Auiden as he fell, wrenching his helmet off before blood from his arteries filled his helmet and drowned him.

But the Apothecary's face was a ruin of scorched meat and boiled blood. His noble features were obliterated and even as Tanna watched, the molten bone structure of his skull sagged inwards to form a sloshing pool of steaming brain matter.

Tanna's grief swelled around him, but he quashed it savagely as the *Barisan* lurched down into the plateau once again. He heard the shouts of his warriors, but ignored them as he saw a way out of their entrapment racing towards them.

***

Emil would be calling him a lunatic right about now and Roboute would be hard-pressed to disagree with that assessment. He swung the grav-sled around a knot of embattled skitarii as they fought in a diminishing shield wall against the crystalline monsters that broke free of the glassy plateau like creatures rising from uncounted millennia frozen beneath the planet's surface.

Beside him, Adara fired his laspistol with pinpoint accuracy, decapitating a crystal warrior with every shot. Pavelka had no dedicated weaponry, but her mechadendrites were equipped with fusion cutters, ion beamers and las-saws, and they served as fearsome combat attachments. The grav-sled wasn't armed, but Roboute was using it as a weapon, barrelling through the overwhelming numbers of enemy like an Adeptus Arbites urban pacification vehicle.

Of course he tried to avoid that, but the closer he got to the *Barisan*, the harder it became. For the most part, the crystal-forms were directing their lethal attentions on the skitarii and Space Marines, but that was about to change.

'This is insane and illogical,' said Pavelka, neatly snipping the head from a crystal-form about to deliver the death blow to the exposed cortex of a downed battle robot. 'I should wrest control of this vehicle from you.'

'You wouldn't dare,' said Roboute.

'I would if I thought you wouldn't just jump out and keep going,' she replied.

Despite the unimaginable danger, Roboute felt nothing but a towering sense of invulnerability as he slewed around the gunship's partially enveloped engines. He shattered more of the enemy with the sled's bull bars, hauling the controls back to bring him down the starboard flank of the gunship where its wing was now completely enveloped by the ground.

Around thirty of the crystalline Space Marines hauled their way up the listing side of the *Barisan*, like a horde of plague victims trying to break into a sealed medicae structure.

'Hold on!' shouted Roboute and gunned the engine.

The collision was ferocious, a splintering series of shattering impacts as dozens of bodies went under the grav-sled. Its engines screeched and the rear section heeled sideways as the machine-spirit howled in protest at such cavalier treatment. Roboute's harness split along its centre-line, and only one of Pavelka's snapping mechadendrites kept him from falling from the sled.

She pulled him upright and he waved his arms to attract the attention of the Black Templars.

A Space Marine with an augmetic arm implanted with a seething

hot plasma gun dropped onto the cargo bed, followed by a warrior with a crackling energy blade. Between them, they carried the body of a fallen warrior, but Roboute couldn't tell if he was alive or dead. Another Templar dropped onto the sled after them, until only Tanna and the warrior with the white-wreathed helm remained. Though it was surely ridiculous, it looked as though the two of them were arguing over who should be the last to abandon their position.

'For the Emperor's sake, just get on the damn sled!' shouted Roboute, though there was little chance they would hear him.

But his words had the desired effect, and the two warriors leapt together, landing on the sled with enough force to drive the back end into the ground. The repulsor engine flared, but miraculously stayed lit.

'They're aboard!' shouted Pavelka. 'Now get us out of here!'

Roboute nodded and wrenched the controls around with a whispered prayer to the Omnissiah to forgive him for his rough treatment of the grav-sled. The sled's controls were sluggish, but Roboute had the measure of them now, and compensated for the added weight of the Space Marines as he gunned the engine hard. The sled shot away from the downed gunship, every dial on the panel in front of him tapping into the red.

The crystal-form creatures weren't about to be denied their prey and turned their attack from the gunship to the grav-sled. One wrenched Adara's door off and received an armoured boot in the face. The creature fell away as Roboute wove a path through the battling skitarii. Bolts of emerald light streaked around him. Explosions stitched across the heavy plates of the engine cowling, and the sled lurched as some internal mechanism blew out.

A voice blasted into his helmet. 'Get us out of here!'

Roboute flinched. Adeptus Astartes. Tanna.

'I'm trying,' said Roboute, skidding around a pack of crystal-forms as they tried to box the grav-sled in. 'These things are everywhere. And we're not exactly travelling light.'

'We will secure you a path,' said Tanna.

Seconds later, blazing trails of bolter fire streaked overhead, ripping through the crystal-forms and clearing a path of broken glass. Adara added his pistol fire to the scouring barrage, and Roboute could just imagine the stories he'd get out of this. Fighting alongside the Black Templars!

Though he'd caution the youth not to use the word *rescue* in his tales.

A flat bang of electrical discharge blew out on the grav-sled, and

Roboute's heart sank as a number of the dials on the control panel dropped rapidly to zero.

'Shit, shit, shit...' he muttered, banging a palm against the panel: the universal repair panacea.

He risked a glance over his shoulder, seeing the Black Templars kneeling or standing on the cargo flatbed with their bolters roaring.

But behind them, the grav-sled's engine was billowing twin plumes of tarry black oil smoke.

Microcontent 06

The atmosphere aboard the *Tabularium* was one of control. Despite the sudden reversal of fortune suffered by Magos Dahan's skitarii, there was no panic on the command bridge. Magos Kryptaestrex had assumed command of the Land Leviathan, and though the pioneer units had not yet certified the temporary structures bridging the crevasse, his experienced optics had adjudged them capable of taking its weight.

Cadian units were already streaming across, but only a reckless vanguard, for the *Tabularium* now occupied the centre of the newly built span. Its stomping feet shook the bridge and dislodged debris from the inner faces of the crevasse where the supporting corbels and inset supports were drilled. Portions of the vast machine's width hung over the edge of the bridge, and Linya tried not to imagine what would happen if Magos Azuramagelli strayed but a little from its centre-line.

She kept a tight rein on her terror, partitioning the innate synaptic responses to tumbling thousands of kilometres behind walls of logic. She would pay for that later, but for now she needed to function without the debilitating handicap of fear.

She'd launched more drones, but capped their altitude to forty metres to keep them below the umbra, assigning them figure of eight orbits around the towering spire of the *Tomioka*. Visual feeds coming in from the embattled forces on the plateau had shocked everyone, but they were Mechanicus, and encountering the inconceivable was part of their mandate.

'Magos Dahan will learn a valuable lesson in humility,' said Galatea, its mismatched legs walking it around the surveyor table, where flickering icons and veils of binary bloomed from the hololithic surface in multicoloured bands. 'The *Tomioka* is well defended.'

'Is that why you didn't go with them?' asked Linya. 'Did you know these things were here?'

Galatea looked up, and the cold silver of its dead optics made Linya's skin crawl.

'No, but the presence of automated defences was a logical possibility.'

'A possibility you neglected to mention.'

'We saw no need,' replied Galatea. 'We believed Archmagos Kotov would come to the same conclusion.'

Though Linya knew it was an absurdly organic notion, she would have sworn on a stack of STC fragments that it was lying.

Warnings broadcast in binary and Gothic blared from vox-horns and Linya gripped the surveyor table as the *Tabularium* shuddered, the deck angling minutely downwards.

'We are at the midpoint of our crossing,' Magos Kryptaestrex intoned, and Linya's heart beat a little faster at the thought of the Land Leviathan's vast, monolithic feet breaking through the temporary bridge's weakest point with thunderous hammerblows.

'Then let's hope your pioneer crews have been thorough in their work on the far side,' said Azuramagelli from the steering station, his deconstructed brain portions flickering in the light of his electrical activity.

'If you keep us straight, instead of weaving us about like you have so far, then there will be no issues,' returned Kryptaestrex, plugged into the controls for motive power as he attempted to reduce the impact force of the *Tabularium*'s twin banks of enormous feet.

'If you wish to switch assignments,' said Azuramagelli, his artificial voice still managing to convey his irritation at Kryptaestrex, 'then I will be only too happy to take command of motive power.'

'It would be conducive to operations and my mental equilibrium if the two of you would shut up and concentrate on your assigned tasks,' said Linya with a blurt of admonishing binary. 'That way we might actually make it across this crevasse in one piece.'

Neither Kryptaestrex nor Azuramagelli replied, but both signalled their contrition with noospheric messages of assent.

The attenuated reverberations echoing through the Land Leviathan changed in pitch as the vast machine moved to a descending

latticework support of adamantium struts, interlocking deck plating and bored-in suspensors. Linya brought up a drone optic feed and watched the *Tabularium* crossing the bridge, a million-tonne leviathan perched on an absurdly slender-looking structure that any rational eye would see as utterly incapable of supporting something so massive.

But, as impossible as it might look, Kryptaestrex's bridge was holding firm and they were almost across. The pitch of the Land Leviathan's feet returned to normal, and Linya let out a breath, the primal part of her brain having taken over her physiological functions despite her best efforts to self-regulate. They were across – though would, of course, have to return the same way – and the *Tabularium* canted upwards as Kryptaestrex poured power into the propulsion decks and they climbed the last hundred metres to the plateau.

Linya switched between the dozens of visual feeds coming from the drones, studying multiple inloads at once. Dahan's skitarii were falling back in good order, extricating themselves from overwhelming odds by means of mutually supporting mobile shield walls. The plateau was awash with the ice creatures, a glittering army assembled in their thousands from the crystalline bedrock of the world. Against so numerous a foe, most mortal armies would already have been destroyed, overrun and slaughtered as they fled the field in panic.

Skitarii were not like a mortal army. Their courage held in the face of insurmountable odds, their cool detachment and unbreakable discipline keeping them in the fight. Linya saw Dahan in the thick of the hardest fighting, breaking enemy thrusts that might interfere with the skitarii's retreat.

Linya did not like Dahan, but had to admire his tenacity and devotion to his warriors.

One feed caught her eye, and she zoomed in on it with a spike of disbelief.

Roboute Surcouf was in the midst of the fighting, his grav-sled fleeing the field of battle in spurts and starts as its engine burned out. That it had got them this far was a miracle of the Omnissiah, but Linya saw its machine-spirit was close to extinction. Hundreds of crystal-forms surrounded them, and even with the Black Templars fighting from its back, she estimated they had less than a minute before being overrun.

'Magos Azuramagelli,' said Linya. 'Exloading a course change to you.'

'Understood.'

'Magos Kryptaestrex, deploy the docking clamp.'

***

'It's too far,' said Moderati Marko Koskinen. 'No way we can make it.'

+Have faith,+ said the Wintersun. +I know this engine. I know what she is capable of.+

'As do I, princeps, and that crevasse is too wide for us,' said Koskinen, bringing up the schematics of a Warlord Titan from the Manifold. A three-dimensional image of the towering god-machine appeared over the central display hub of the command bridge, rotating slowly with reams of data listing its tolerances and capacity cascading alongside. 'We should wait until the bridge is clear.'

Though Princeps Luth had no need – or mortal eyes – to see the schematic, his withered, bifurcated wraith-form drifted from the milky grey suspension within his amniotic tank to press against the armourglass. Silver feed-cables plugged into his truncated waist and spinal implants trailed from his back like the hackles of a roused wolf.

+Schematics are for the scholam,+ said the Wintersun, +We are at war, Koskinen. *Lupa Capitalina* waits for no man.+

'Hyrdrith, back me up here,' said Koskinen.

'Princeps,' said Magos Hyrdrith from her elevated station at the rear of the bridge. 'As ever, I accept your wisdom as Omnissiah-given, but I must agree with Moderati Koskinen. Once the *Tabularium* and its attendant vehicles are clear, we can–'

+Mechanicus warriors are dying,+ snarled Luth. +We can save them from the beasts.+

'My princeps,' said Koskinen, frowning as swarming ghost images flickered through the Manifold for the briefest instant. 'Even if you're right and we can make it across, there's no telling if the ground on the far side is strong enough to take our mass. We–'

'If your princeps gives you an order, you question it?' snapped Joakim Baldur on the opposite moderati station to Koskinen's. He shook his head. 'No wonder Moonsorrow challenged for alpha.'

Joakim Baldur served as Moderati Primus on *Canis Ulfrica*, but had been assigned to *Lupa Capitalia* in the wake of Lars Rosten's death. He was Reaver through and through, which made him belligerent at the best of times, but now serving on the engine that had almost killed his own princeps only sharpened his viper's tongue. The burns he had suffered aboard *Canis Ulfrica* had healed, but the skin around his eyes and ears still had the rugose texture of vat-cultured skin.

'You crew a Reaver,' snapped Koskinen, his fraying temper – worn thin by Baldur's constant carping and obvious reluctance to be aboard *Lupa Capitalina* – finally snapping. 'What the hell do you know about this engine?

+Be silent! *Lupa Capitalina*'s anger burns hot,+ said Princeps Luth. +Would you feel that anger through your Manifold interface?+

'No, princeps,' said Koskinen, pushing the motive systems out and trying not to let his disquiet at what he thought he'd seen in the Manifold show. *Lupa Capitalina* set off at combat pace towards the crevasse. Its strides were long, the Warlord moving faster than was prudent in such icy conditions. Koskinen heard Hyrdrith's prayers to the Machine-God as the crevasse yawned before them.

Koskinen's heart dropped at the sight of it, knowing in his bones it was too wide for them and too impossibly deep to survive if they plunged into its bottomless depths. The Warlord was walking faster than it had walked in months, its mighty legs slamming into the ground and throwing up vast chunks of dislodged ice and rock.

They were practically sprinting, which was dangerous for such a towering war machine at the best of times, but they needed all the momentum they could get. That might be all that saved them from toppling back into the crevasse, so Koskinen set to scavenging every ounce of reactor energy from the voids and any secondary system he could think of to boost the gyro-stabilising mechanisms at the heart of the vast machine.

Angry red icons flared in the Manifold, stamped with inload signifiers of the *Tabularium*. The magi aboard the Land Leviathan saw what they attempted and were warning them of the dangers.

+They think we will fail,+ laughed the Wintersun. +I will show them what Sirius can do.+

Roboute was trying every trick he knew to keep the grav-sled in the air, from prayers to threats, but the machine was dying. Thick smoke and streamers of random gravity fluctuations poured from the engine cowling, and they were leaving a black and oily train in their juddering, weaving wake. Sergeant Tanna and his Black Templars had expended their ammunition reserve and were keeping the crystal-forms at bay with swords and fists.

'Come on,' said Roboute, finally seeing the cliff face of the *Tabularium* as it stamped onto the plateau, accompanied by a host of steeldust Cadian tanks. The vast machine was around three hundred metres away, but it might as well have been on the other side of the planet. Skitarii units were falling back either side of them, some on foot and some in badly damaged Rhinos, but they were fighting to their own plan.

A plan in which Roboute and the Black Templars didn't factor.

The grav-sled dropped, and Roboute felt the ventral fin kiss the ground.

'Can you coax any more life out of this bloody sled?' he shouted back to Pavelka.

'Don't you think I am trying?' she replied. 'Clarification: employing pejorative terms on machines that might save your life is not recommended by the adepts of Mars.'

'Good point,' said Roboute, as yet another onboard system died. 'Right, listen up, sled. If you get us out of here alive I promise to repair every dent, burn and tear in your hull. I will replace every damaged component and never again put you in harm's way. Now will you bloody well get us to the *Tabularium*!'

'Not quite what I think she had in mind, captain,' said Adara.

'Best I've got, son,' said Roboute. 'Best I've got.'

The grav-sled's rear section slewed around as the engine finally blew out with a bray of thrashing machine parts and squalling repulsor fields. The ventral fin ploughed a furrow, and the sled's frontal section slammed into the ground with a shriek of tearing metal. Roboute was thrown forwards into the buckled canopy struts, his cheek cracking painfully on the inner face of his helmet.

The sled had broken its back in the crash, spilling the body of the fallen Black Templar to the ground. The warrior with the white-wreathed helmet immediately leapt from the wreckage and swung his enormous black sword in a wide arc. Three crystal-forms shattered, and two more fell back with emerald light streaming from mortal wounds to their chests.

The rest of the Templars were at his side in moments, fighting to clear a space around their downed brother as the enemy closed in. The sled was wrecked, and Roboute slammed his fist against the controls.

'Bloody useless thing!' he yelled

'Time to get out of here, captain?' said Adara.

'I think you might be right,' said Roboute, seeing hundreds of crystal-forms closing in through puffs of oxygen streaming from wide cracks in his helmet's faceplate. 'But I don't think we're going anywhere in a hurry.'

He dragged his gold-chased laspistol from its holster and stood in the buckled doorway of the cab.

'Come on then, you bastards!' he yelled. 'Come and get us!'

He held his pistol in the classic straight-thumb grip and started shooting into the clashing, crystalline host that surrounded them. His first target dropped with a neat hole cored through its skull, the second with an identical wound.

The third exploded into glassy vapour as though hit by a Vanquisher shell, leaving a giant crater in its wake. Roboute fell from the sled as

the pounding shockwaves of the blast swatted him to the ground. Scores of smoking shell cases rained down around him, and he rolled onto his back as the shadow of a snarling beast reared over him.

Its weapon arms bucked with the force of blazing mega-bolters, and the pair of warhorns mounted at its jutting, fanged maw unleashed a howling battle cry.

'*Vilka*!' cried Pavelka, hearing its name woven into the howl.

The Warhound stomped over the wreckage of the grav-sled, sheeting bursts of fire clearing the ground of enemies for tens of metres in all directions. It trampled the crystal-forms to powder beneath its enormous clawed feet and carved white-hot-edged gouges in the earth with its guns.

Nor had it come alone.

A second Warhound loped from a blizzard of spinning crystal shards, twin weapon arms spitting thunderous volleys of las-fire and explosive shells. Its flank was scored with deep wounds, and blessed oils sheened its armoured hide. Like its twin it howled its fury, darting in to make kills at every blast of its warhorn.

Roboute scrambled into the cover of the smoking grav-sled, pulling himself upright as he fought to keep his breaths shallow. Already he was feeling giddy and lightheaded, a curious numbness seeping into his limbs.

'God-machines…' he said, staring up at the snapping, howling war-engines keeping the enemy creatures at bay.

He felt the ground vibrate with titanic impacts, the footsteps of a *true* god-machine.

Hands grabbed Roboute under the shoulders and dragged him back onto the sled. Black-armoured warriors surrounded him, and a robed tech-priest whose half-human features were familiar to him wrapped a snaking metallic arm around his waist.

'Hold on, captain,' said a voice he knew he should recognise, but which he just couldn't place. 'They're coming for us!'

'Of course they are,' said Roboute. 'Why wouldn't they…?'

He craned his neck up as a giant of myth strode into view, a soaring engine of destruction and power. Its size was incredible, a monstrous god of steel and adamantium with a sun at its heart and death in its fists. A gargantuan foot with four pneumatic buttress claws swept over them, trailing a rain of crystalline debris and pulverised rock. The god-machine's enormous foot hammered down and sent seismic shockwaves through the earth.

Pistoning clamps punched into the ground as auto-loaders fed ammo hoppers into hungry breeches and dozens of ratcheting missile hatches cycled open. In deference to the mortals at its feet, *Lupa Capitalina*'s plasma weaponry remained inactive, but an artillery battalion's worth of blazing heavy ordnance rippled from its shoulders. Streaking missiles traced parabolic trails over the battlefield, twenty-four in the first second, another twenty-four a second later. Plumes of white-hot fire exploded from the terrifying gatling blaster, and thousands of shells sawed from the spinning barrels of the vast, snub-nosed rotary cannon.

The plateau instantly vanished in sky-high curtains of fire and pounding explosions as the arcing streams of missiles slammed down in a never-ending series of punishing hammerblows. Roboute closed his eyes against the brightness, feeling his chest tighten and his thoughts drift off in what he knew was nitrogen narcosis.

As ways to die went, this at least had the virtue of being painless.

He smiled, thinking it apt that he should die on a world he had named.

Would anyone remember that name?

He didn't know, but it seemed important.

Over the unending barrage of the three god-machines, Roboute heard a heavy clang of metal on metal and felt a thrumming vibration through his void-suit. A sense of weightlessness clutched at him, and he opened his eyes to see the ground spinning away from him as the grav-sled was hoisted into the air.

Beneath him, a world burned in the fire of the god-machines.

'Below the waterline' was an expression from the days when vessels plied the seas of Old Earth; meaningless now that mankind's vessels had left their earthly oceans behind, but which still had currency among the bondsmen of the *Speranza*. Instead of referring to areas of a ship that would flood in the event of a hull breach, it now applied to the ventral regions of the Ark Mechanicus that were known to be dangerous for all sorts of additional reasons.

Magos Casada had recently been assigned a supervisory role among the bondsmen after ten years spent in data-transmission, a move he'd hoped would see an end to the comparatively mundane duties of informational flow paths and the chance to be in charge of more than just binary bits and infocyte logs. But with only two work-shy loafers and three servitors following him down the iron screw-stairs into the cold darkness he didn't feel like he was in charge of much at all.

Everyone was on edge, which at least kept their minds on their surroundings instead of looking for ways to skive off.

Or so Casada had thought.

'How come we get to do this?' asked Knox, picking something dripping and oily from his nose.

This was repairing a faulty transmission hub in one of the port-side conduit arrays, a repair made rather more than mundane due to the sudden nature of the fault's occurrence and its location in a region of the ship that had suffered more than its fair share of malfunctions in recent times.

'Because this is what we were assigned,' said Casada, following a jumping, flickering noospheric map projected in the air before him. 'Every duty in service of the Omnissiah is valued and important, from the lowliest to the–'

'Spare us the motivational crap, magos,' said Knox. 'You got it because you're new here and don't kiss the right overseer's arse. Anyone with a brain cell rattling around their skull avoids the lower decks. Too dark, too packed with machinery that can take your arm off, disembowel you or vaporise your bones to dust to be healthy.'

'I heard these decks got irradiated when the *Speranza* threw her moorings at her launch,' said Cavell.

Casada knew he should quash their seditious talk, but there was truth to what they were saying and he was a firm believer in allowing those beneath you an awareness that you shared their concerns.

'There's a measure of truth to that,' he allowed, taking a high-ceilinged transit passageway his map told him should lead to processional steps down to the conduit. 'There are heightened radiation levels in the lower decks, yes, but nothing to give us undue concern. We'll not be going down into the deeper regions of the ship.'

'Just as bloody well,' said Knox. 'Ain't nobody knows nothin' of what's down there nohow.'

Forcing himself to ignore Knox's murderous grammar, Casada said, 'Correction. That just isn't true. I have plentiful maps of the regions we must traverse to reach the transmission hub.'

'You're in the deeps now, magos, down past the waterline,' said Knox. 'Try navigating by those maps here and you'll be lost like all them other crews that went down too far.'

'Ah, gruesome tales of hauntings and disappearances in uncommon regions of a starship,' said Casada. 'I am familiar with such shipboard rumours and scare stories. They are nothing but invented fantasies to explain away industrial accidents and fill lacunae of information. It is my contention that such tales are spread as a means of creating a unity of experience among the uninitiated.'

'Shows what you know,' said Cavell. 'You're new here, but you'll learn.'

'Or he won't,' said Knox, drawing a finger across his throat.

Casada tried not to be put out by their obviously scaremongering behaviour, but it was true he was having a number of difficulties in following their assigned route. Access ports weren't where they were supposed to be, corridors and companionways marked as passable were blocked by thrumming machinery or simply weren't there. Thus far, his noospheric adaptations had found workarounds, but sooner or later Knox and Cavell were going to realise he wasn't entirely sure where they were any more.

'And what about them?' asked Knox, jerking a thumb at the three servitors following mutely behind them. 'How do we know they're not going to murder us when we're too deep to call for help?'

Rumours of the incredible events in Feeding Hall Eighty-Six had circulated the various shifts throughout the ship, and despite the Mechanicus' best efforts to quash their spread, no one was looking at the servitors in quite the same light. That the instigators and their apparently autonomous servitor were said to have escaped Magos Saiixek's skitarii and fled into the depths of the ship only added a level of revolutionary verisimilitude to the talk of holy presences.

'These ones certainly appear to be appropriately servile,' said Casada.

'Yeah? Well perhaps that's just to lull us into thinking they're brain-dead cyborgs and not heartless killers that want revenge for being made into servitors,' said Cavell.

'Now you are being ridiculous,' said Casada, frowning as they reached the end of the passageway to find the expected processional archway fringed with sparking cabling. A broken coolant pipe billowed hot steam and spilled a waterfall of scum-frothed water down the stairs. The effect was akin to a pict Casada had seen of a waterfall in a mangrove swamp, overhung by jungle creepers and humid with torpid vapour.

'Down there?' asked Knox, peering into the darkness where water-damaged lumens strobed and spat. 'Tell me you're joking.'

Casada heard what sounded like heavy footfalls, but were most likely some deeper machinery echoing through the tunnels. Something scraped on metal, but in such unvisited regions of a ship as large as an Ark Mechanicus, that wouldn't be unusual. A lack of regular maintenance would give rise to all manner of apparently inexplicable auditory peculiarities.

Cavell ducked under a bundle of conjoined cabling, bending this way and that to get a better look at where it had been broken.

'This ain't right,' he said, reaching up to touch the insulated sheath around the break point.

'We have seen many such breakages,' said Casada. 'After the nightmarish crossing of the Halo Scar, many cable runs have snapped under increased tensile loads.'

'No,' said Knox. 'He's right, look. They've been cut. Deliberately.'

Casada examined the cable run being held by Cavell, running a three-dimensional mapping laser over the damaged portion.

'Tell me I'm wrong,' said Cavell.

'The separation appears to be clean,' admitted Casada. 'I see no evidence of the stresses and weakening of the insulation sheath I might expect from tear damage. It is impossible to be certain, but it appears that, yes, this cable has been cut. Who cut it and why is another matter entirely.'

Even as he said the words, he knew he wasn't being entirely truthful. The break in the cable was so precise, with so infinitesimal a deflection in the adjacent fibres, that there was little possibility it could have been achieved by any known device or blade.

At least none known to the Mechanicus.

Another booming echo sounded from below, that deeper, sub-deck machinery again, but when it came again, Casada realised it was closer than before. He looked down the processional stairs, but instead of flickering lumens, the wide stairwell was wreathed in impenetrable darkness.

'Perhaps we *should* find another way down,' said Casada, backing away from the steps.

Knox looked up, picking up on his building anxiety.

The man followed Casada's gaze and his eyes widened in fear as something huge surged from the darkness below. Its elongated emerald skull was bulbous and glossy, its ivory limbs slender and grasping as it raced up the steps with a loping, horrifically organic gait.

Whispering streams of displaced air scythed up the steps.

Cavell simply vanished, his body coming apart so thoroughly it was as though he'd clutched an armed frag mine to his chest. Ruined body parts tumbled down the steps, and Knox set off at a sprint lest he suffer the same fate.

He made three steps before he was felled by the towering, spindle-limbed construct. Its monstrous hand seemed to merely brush over the top of the man's head, but the lid of his skull came away as surely as though a precision trepanning laser had sliced clean through it.

The animal part of Casada's brain howled in terror, flooding his body with adrenaline, and he screamed as he turned to run. He pushed past the unresisting servitors, fighting to escape, to get *away* from this below the waterline daemon of the dark. He risked a glance

over his shoulder and let out a whimper of naked fear as he saw four porcelain-limbed figures with cherry red plumes streaming from their howling, death-mask faces.

'How did–' was all Casada managed before a shrieking wail buckled the air between him and his pursuers. His high-function aural implants blew out under the lethal sonic assault and blessed lubricant poured from his eyes and ears.

Casada howled in pain as his optics fizzed with bleeding binary static and his skull filled with nerve-shredding feedback. Denied the heightened sensory input of his enhancing augmetics, Casada's brain implants began rerouting his synaptic pathways to once again employ his birth-senses. Viewed through the obscuring lens of his blown implants, Casada's natural vision was blurred and grainy with lack of use. He saw a wavering, smeared-lens image of the killers coming towards him and pushed himself to his feet. He knew he couldn't escape, but ran anyway, his terror driving his limbs in a vain attempt to prolong his life. The after-effects of the mind-shredding scream still ravaged his body. Hideous nausea churned in his gut and a sickening vertigo made his lurching steps comically drunken.

Casada couldn't see where he was going, his unaugmented senses painfully blunted.

He blundered into an iron wall, striking his head on a protruding flange and falling to his knees. Blood poured down his face from this latest indignity. He crawled like a beast on its belly, a wounded animal stalked by a predatory creature that revels in its prey's suffering.

Through his sobs he heard the unmistakable sounds of blades through flesh. One by one, the servitors he had led into the depths were butchered without resistance; beasts led blindly into the slaughterhouse.

'Please,' he begged, as he heard distorted echoes of footsteps behind him. 'Please don't kill me.'

The tip of something dreadfully sharp pressed on the nape of his neck.

'Ave Deus Mechanicus...' he said, drawing his hands together beneath his body in the Cog Mechanicus. 'The Machine-God is with me, I shall fear no evil...'

A sharp thrust and the blade sliced cleanly through Casada's spinal cord.

Microcontent 07

The earlier mood of optimism that had suffused the expedition upon establishing the landing fields had evaporated utterly. A great many machines and lives had been lost on the plateau, and an atmosphere of shared contrition now filled the command deck of the *Tabularium*. Still clad in his gleaming armour, Kotov had gathered his commanders around Linya Tychon's surveyor station. Each warrior and magos was studiously examining the hololithic projection of the *Tomioka* as it stubbornly refused to divulge its secrets to any of the available augurs.

Kotov stared at the gently rotating image, as though he could simply will its interior structure to reveal itself by virtue of his vaunted rank.

Ven Anders stood in the shadow of Sergeant Tanna and his white-wreathed Emperor's Champion. Though Dahan's losses currently stood at three hundred dead and fifty-seven injured, Tanna's loss was perhaps the greater. Coming face to face with the Black Templars, Kotov had thought to berate them for their foolishness, but upon learning of Brother Auiden's death, he had instead offered only sincere regrets. The loss of a single Space Marine was bad enough, but to lose an Apothecary was something else entirely and Kotov could clearly see Tanna's need to atone for his misguided zeal.

Azuramagelli and Kryptaestrex were plugged in on opposite sides of the plotting table, their petty bickering put aside in the face of this

bloody setback. Galatea leaned over the surveyor station, its hand idly tracing the outline of the holographic starship.

'It has been over four thousand years since we saw her. Many long years…' said the hybrid construct, turning the rotating image back and forth with soft haptic gestures.

Kotov felt a tremor of unease at Galatea's behaviour, like it was reaching out to something familiar, like a long lost friend or a forbidden object of desire.

'No one has seen it in that long,' said Kotov.

Galatea's head snapped up, and it snatched its hand back, as though caught in some forbidden act. The silver-eyed proxy body at the centre of its palanquin pulled back into itself.

'You did not see it as we saw it,' said Galatea. 'That we can promise you. The greatest ship of its age, launched in glorious triumph, but mocked for daring to dream that the impossible could be within our grasp. You do not know, you *cannot* know, what that was like.'

'You would be surprised,' snapped Kotov, his own travails and losses having seen him set sail on this expedition under a similar cloud of criticism from his fellow Martian adepts. 'But your recall of the *Tomioka* will have to wait, unless you have something useful to contribute?'

'Like what lies inside,' said Ven Anders. 'That's what I want to know. If we want to get inside that ship, then I want to know what my men are going to face.'

The Cadian colonel's close-cropped hair was sheened in perspiration, for the running-heat of so many cogitation engines made this chamber a hothouse for mortals.

'We know no more than you, Colonel Anders,' said Galatea.

Anders ran a hand across his stubbled chin and said, 'You know what? I don't think I believe you. I think you know damn well what's inside that ship, so how about you cut the crap and just tell us what you know.'

Galatea spread its hands in an empty gesture of apology. 'The same umbra that inhibits Mistress Tychon's augurs prevent us from learning more than you already know.'

Anders grunted in disbelief and shook his head. 'You're lying, and if any of my men die because of that, you have my word as an officer of Cadia that I'll kill you.'

Kotov placed both hands on the edge of the plotting table and said, 'We must proceed on the assumption that we will encounter further automated defences within the *Tomioka*. Colonel Anders, Sergeant Tanna and Magos Dahan, you should prepare your assault plans on that supposition.'

'The skitarii should have the honour of breaching the hull of a Mechanicus vessel,' said Dahan, squaring his shoulders as if daring

anyone to contradict him. Kotov understood Dahan's grandstanding. His warriors had been humbled, and only the intervention of Legio Sirius's war-engines had finally ended the battle.

'My Templars are better suited to fighting in such environments,' said Tanna. 'We should be first.'

'With all due respect,' said Anders. 'There's only five of you, and that's a pretty big ship.'

'I could conquer a world with five Black Templars,' said Tanna.

Linya Tychon cut across the impending confrontation.

'To gain access to areas of the ship that offer the best chance of finding what we came here for, there's only one way anyone is getting inside the *Tomioka*,' she said.

'And what's that?' asked Anders. 'The umbra's still in place, so an aerial assault isn't an option.'

'The crystalline buttressing is too thick at the base of the tower,' added Tanna.

'The only way in is on the back of *Lupa Capitalina*,' said Linya. 'It has the capacity to carry two assault forces, and its height means it's just below the ceiling of the umbra, but tall enough to carry us to where the ice around the ship's base is thinnest.'

Anders grinned. 'I've always wanted to ride into battle on the back of a god-machine.'

'Should we expect to find more of those crystal beings inside?' asked Tanna, already assimilating the addition of a Titan to his own deployment plans.

'More than likely,' said Kotov.

'And do we have any idea what they are?' asked Anders. 'Magos Dahan, you got up close and personal with them. Any insights?'

Dahan stood with one shoulder hunched as three tech-menials and armourers worked on his damaged body. Shrouded fusion-welders worked beneath the folds of his mantle of bronze mail.

'I have never seen their like,' he admitted. 'They were crystalline, that much was obvious, empowered by an energy source centred in their chests. Passive data recordings suggest it to be a form of bio-morphic induction energy, similar to that encountered by explorator teams excavating tomb structures on the southern fringes of Segmentum Tempestus.'

'Necrontyr?' asked Azuramagelli. 'Surely it is impossible that such beings could be found beyond the galaxy's edge.'

'Pay attention, I said similar, not identical,' said Dahan. 'You have all parsed the data. Draw your own conclusions.'

'They are not necrontyr,' said Kotov.

'Then what are they?' demanded Tanna. 'A new xenos breed?'

Kotov shook his head. 'Strictly speaking, no, they are not alive, though in manifesting cognitive awareness of their surroundings and behaviour that appears to be intelligently reactive, they could easily be mistaken for living organisms.'

'That doesn't answer his question,' said Galatea, stretching one bio-mechanical hand into the image of the *Tomioka*. Kotov masked his irritation, but Galatea spoke again before he could continue. 'You know as well as we do the nature of this foe.'

'Archmagos?' asked Anders, when Galatea didn't continue.

'I believe them to be a form of bio-imitative machinery seeded within the crystalline structure of the plateau,' said Kotov. 'Essentially, billions of micro-bacterial sized machines threaded through the crystalline matrix of the ground, each useless in and of itself, but capable of combining into something greater than the sum of its parts. They reacted to our presence, forming a mimicking force to repel us, like white blood cells rushing to the site of a biological infection.'

'I have never heard of technology such as this,' said Kryptaestrex, as though affronted by the idea. 'Why has it not been recorded in the data-stacks of Mars?'

'Because it was never brought to fruition,' said Kotov. 'Magos Telok pioneered this research after his expedition to Naogeddon in the turbulent years following the fall of the High Lord. He never presented his work to any Martian Frateris Conclave, because he could never get it to work.'

Anders tapped the flat slate of the surveyor grid. 'Looks like he has now.'

'If Telok never presented his findings, how do you know this, archmagos?' asked Tanna.

'Do you think I would mount an expedition such as this without preparation, Sergeant Tanna?' asked Kotov, rising to meet the implied challenge. 'Believe me when I say that I have studied all aspects of Archmagos Telok – his every published monograph, his every experimental record and every lunatic tale woven around him since he was inducted into the Martian priesthood and his expedition's disappearance. My preparations were no less thorough than yours would be for battle. The key to understanding Telok, my Templar friend, is not just in learning *everything*, but in recognising what amongst that is of value and what is wanton embellishment.'

'And what do those studies tell you, archmagos?' asked Anders. 'Why bother protecting a ship that's going to be destroyed along with this planet?'

Kotov straightened, logic providing the only possible answer. 'To keep the ship safe until it fulfils its function.'

'And what function is that?'

'I do not know,' said Kotov. 'I suspect we will only learn that once we go aboard.'

The range-finder in Tanna's helmet told him the *Tomioka* was two kilometres distant, though its immense scale made it look far closer. The Mechanicus contingent, a curious mix of warriors and explorers surrounded by Dahan's atmosphere-capable skitarii, occupied the port-side assault battlement, while he and his battle-brothers stood on the starboard shoulder mount of *Lupa Capitalina* alongside a heavily armed detachment of void-suited Cadians.

Tanna had seen the mortal soldiers training and knew them to be competent fighters, but they weren't Adeptus Astartes and that made them inherently unreliable. He kept his thoughts from Apothecary Auiden, his body frozen in the *Tabularium*'s morgue, knowing it would only compromise his squad's efficiency. But no matter how he tried to compartmentalise his mind, allowing the grief to build behind walls of discipline and psycho-conditioning, Tanna felt the loss keenly.

Yet another death that would see them lost without hope of returning to the Chapter.

Tanna knew his warriors were suffering too, but he had no words for them, no soul-lifting oratory to salve the loss of their Apothecary. Like Kul Gilad's death, Auiden's loss could not be laid at his feet, but Tanna knew it was his responsibility to ensure every warrior under his command came back alive. A task that every commander of warriors knew they would ultimately fail.

The Warlord's rapid march was devouring the distance between the edge of the plateau and the vertical spire of the ship with every thunderous stride. Putting aside his mournful thoughts, he leaned over the cog-toothed battlements, seeing squadrons of Imperial Guard super-heavies and skitarii war machines following the god-engine. Both Warhounds wove a stalking path ahead of *Lupa Capitalina*, prowling like the superlative hunters they were.

Far behind the Warlord's advance, well-defended work crews from the *Tabularium* were digging the *Barisan* from its enveloping crystal prison. The honourable gunship was to be brought back aboard the *Speranza* and made whole once again.

Tanna made a fist and placed it over his eagle-stamped breastplate. 'You will fly again, great one,' he whispered.

'This isn't right,' said Varda, the Black Sword balanced over his

shoulder guard and legs braced to counteract the swaying motion of the striding Warlord. 'We came here expecting to find a crash site, the ruins of a dead ship rusting and decaying for the better part of four thousand years. But that vessel looks like it landed here a decade ago. What do you make of that, sergeant?'

Tanna felt the scrutiny of his battle-brothers and knew they expected a meaningful answer.

'It tells me that we should expect this ship to be defended at every turn.'

Varda nodded, flexing his fingers on the hilt of the Black Sword. 'By those crystal-forms?'

Tanna nodded. 'That, and worse,' he said. 'We took no measures to avoid detection on our approach to the *Tomioka*, so it is reasonable to assume that any Mechanicus presence here, even an old one, is aware of our arrival.'

'Clearly,' agreed Varda. 'What is your point?'

'If Archmagos Kotov is so sure there is someone here, why has there been no response to our arrival on this world?'

'You don't think those… *gnnnh*… crystal-forms that killed Brother… *nggg*… Auiden were a response?' declared Issur, his anger making his involuntary twitches even worse.

'If Archmagos Kotov is correct then those things were an automated response,' said Tanna.

'Perhaps the ship is damaged and can no longer detect orbital traffic,' suggested Bracha, pointing to the crystal growths extruded from the *Tomioka*'s forward compartments. 'Or it is possible those things, whatever they are, interfere with the ship's surveyors.'

Yael grunted. 'Since when did you become a Techmarine?'

'You have a better answer, boy?'

Before Yael could rise to Bracha's caustic words, Tanna intervened. 'Even if whoever is aboard this ship *has* lost the capability of detecting vessels in orbit, they cannot have failed to miss a battle on their doorstep. Not to mention the sight of a Warlord Titan approaching. But they have not reacted to our presence at all.'

'Suggesting what?' asked Varda.

'One of two things,' replied Tanna. 'Either there is no one aboard that ship or they are waiting for us to get closer before revealing themselves.'

'An ambush?'

'We will proceed under that assumption,' said Tanna, and the posture of his knights racked up from readiness to combat imminent.

'So it's going… *nggg*… to be like an assault into a… *nnng*… void-lost hulk?' asked Issur.

'That is an acceptable paradigm for what we should expect,' said Tanna, well aware of the difficulties in clearing a space hulk: the darkness, the blind tunnels, the labyrinthine internal structure of the agglomerated vessels – some of which would undoubtedly be of xenos origin. Not to mention the unspeakable horrors that often lurked within: tyrannic life forms, greenskins, fleshless abominations from the warp or worse.

'At least we will have gravity,' said Yael, ever the optimist.

'True, but everything will be canted at ninety degrees,' pointed out Varda. 'There will be no floors, only bulkheads for footholds and cross-passages for secure footing. Every metre of our advance will be like the ascent of a cliff.'

'Enough,' said Tanna. 'This is no different to any other assault. We go in, we kill what we find.'

His certitude silenced them, but the unspoken consequence of their Apothecary's death hung in the air between them like a curse. Nothing more was said until *Lupa Capitalina*'s advance had carried them to within five hundred metres of the *Tomioka*, and Tanna scanned the frozen cliffs encasing the lower reaches of the starship.

Glacial ice shimmered with rainbow patterns of violet light and reflected metallic glints swam in its depths. Without impurities, it was virtually transparent, and the distorted image of the entombed ship was like looking at something submerged on a shallow river bed.

Lupa Capitalina raised its plasma weapon to the level of its shoulders and traceries of blue-hot lightning arced from its power couplings. The plasma destructor was a vast, smooth-bored weapon the size of a boarding torpedo with heavy magnetic coiling wound tightly around its oval muzzle. The static buzz of developing power reacted with the voids in a series of squealing rainbow-hued borealis, causing the Cadians to flinch from the violent display of sun-hot energies. Shimmering waves hazed the air around the weapon – the heat of a star's core primed and ready to be unleashed.

But instead of firing its most potent weapon, *Lupa Capitalina* thrust its fist forwards as though throwing a punch. A bow wave of heat turned the ice to vapour long before any impact, a hissing curtain of superheated steam billowing from the disintegrating ice. The towering Warlord took a single sidestep and the chained plasmic energies burned away the ice, carving into the entombing glacier.

The precision required for this manoeuvre astounded Tanna, who hadn't truly believed the vast machine capable of achieving such finesse. Electrically charged steam wafted through the voids, carrying the scent of incredible age, heated metal and chemically pure nitrogen.

When the hissing clouds were dispersed by the churning atmospherics, Tanna saw a wide gallery had been cut through the thick buttress supporting the lower reaches of the starship. What had been impenetrable only moments before was now open to the world, and through a curtain of melted ice, Tanna saw the gleaming wet flank of the *Tomioka*.

'No remorse, brothers,' said Tanna, as the assault ramp extended from the battlements. 'No pity.'

'No fear,' came the answer from each warrior.

Abrehem turned over, trying to get comfortable on the makeshift bunk, no easy task when one shoulder was an unyielding metallic rotator-cuff. His weight was unbalanced and, until he'd had his arm replaced with an augmetic, he hadn't realised how difficult that made it to sleep. The bed was a scavenged foldaway Hawke had sourced from Emperor-knew-where, uncomfortable, but better than what Abrehem had gotten used to. He stared at the chamber's coffered ceiling, where faded representations of Sebastian Thor and his disciples looked back, always seeming to be highly interested in something just out of sight. The iron-wrought skulls worked into the black walls gave the impression of being in a tomb or a temple, an impression only reinforced by the hunched shape seated upon the golden throne in the adjacent dormis chamber.

Rasselas X-42 wore the aggression-suppressing mechanisms of a pacifier helm, a device Totha Mu-32 assured him would keep the arco-flagellant in a trance-like state of childish bliss. Enraptured by visions of Imperiocentric ecstasy, Rasselas X-42 presented no threat to any living being unless Abrehem voiced the trigger phrase, something he had promised he would not do.

But given his current predicament, that wasn't a promise he was sure he'd be able to keep.

Abrehem was a wanted man, a fugitive trapped on a starship with nowhere to run.

After Magos Saiixek had withdrawn his skitarii from the feeding hall, Hawke and Coyne had fled with him through the passageways they knew intimately well and yet not at all. Letting the *Speranza* or the Omnissiah guide them, they'd eventually reached the site of Hawke's first alcohol still; now revealed to be the activation chamber for an arco-flagellant.

Even dormant, its malicious presence was palpable, a potential for horrific, bloody violence that infected the very air with toxic emanations. They'd cleaned the eldar blood and bodies away, but the memory

of that near-instantaneous slaughter still haunted Abrehem. He shied away from thoughts of the slumbering killer and turned his attention to the chamber's other occupant.

Ismael de Roeven, freshly clad in a robe of pale cream, sat on the floor with his back to the wall. The restored servitor had his knees drawn up to his chest and hadn't said a word about the incident in the feeding hall. No matter how much Abrehem tried to coax him into an explanation of how he had managed to control those other servitors, Ismael wouldn't – or couldn't – say.

Abrehem had lost count of the hours he'd spent in this chamber while Totha Mu-32 and the others took stock of the Mechanicus response to a threatened servitor uprising. With nothing to do but wait until their return, Abrehem was growing ever more restless. He rolled onto his back and rubbed the heel of his flesh and blood palm over his eyes.

When he took his hand away, he saw a trickle of noospheric code squirming through the walls, an irregular grid pattern enfolding the room like a cage. He'd caught sight of it every now and then, a liminal binaric ward-pattern that would fade as soon as it became aware of his scrutiny, but Abrehem turned his will upon it and the code-light shimmered brightly once more.

His eyes followed the leading edge of the code as it circled the room. The rest of the chamber was in sharp focus, but wherever the code touched, he could feel its brittle, fading power. The binary was old, degraded and worn out. It had patrolled this chamber so many times, perhaps since the *Speranza*'s birth, that its potency was all but spent.

There was a hypnotic quality to the pattern, and Abrehem felt himself drawn into its looping arrangement. Without conscious thought, he rose from the bed and let his eyes roam the contours of the walls. The code flowed over the polished domes of iron skulls, between the entwined eagles and cogs, following the hexagonal pathways. He followed the code as it travelled over the walls, and Abrehem was reminded of an old metaphor of electricity as civilisation's lifeblood.

His heart beat faster in his chest and his breath tasted of burned metal.

Footsteps echoed and Abrehem had the unpleasant sensation of the walls closing in on him. His coppery breath quickened and both hands closed into fists as an unformed anger took shape in his thoughts. The beguiling quality of the flickering binary glitched, and Abrehem blinked as its hold was broken and the machine-stamped walls swam back into focus around him.

Abrehem let out a soft sigh of fear as he found himself standing before Rasselas X-42, his augmetic hand stretched out towards the complicated controls of the pacifier helm. He had watched Totha Mu-32 engage the helm and now realised he'd memorised the ritual movements and catechisms required for its use without conscious thought.

Violent red intruded on his vision, a descending haze of scarlet falling over his eyes like a curtain of blood, the anger he had felt earlier sharpened into a bright spike of purest rage. Abrehem could not remember a moment in his life where he'd felt such unreasoning fury, a bone-deep urge to do harm to another human being. Memories of ripped bodies, torn-out entrails and screaming mouths that cried a name that wasn't his own filled his skull. Abrehem's initial horror was quashed by the unstoppable urge to kill, to violate unclean flesh, to murder something... *anything*...

His trembling digits touched the bronze keys attached to the side of the throne and he tapped out the initialisation commands that began the process of decoupling the mechanisms of the pacifier helm. Slowly the soothing, calming imagery of Imperial saints, cherubs and golden bliss would be stripped away from the arco-flagellant's perceptions, each loss driving it into a higher state of insane, murderous wrath.

Rasselas X-42's head rose up, still masked by the featureless pewter helm.

His chest heaved and grunting spurts of stinking breath sighed from beneath the pacifier helm.

The arco-flagellant was a loaded gun, primed and ready to fire.

All it needed was the trigger phrase and it would be free to kill, maim and murder.

Abrehem suddenly became aware of a presence at his side and felt a gentle hand upon his shoulder. The building horror of mutilations and violent degradation drained from his thoughts in a flood and his legs buckled beneath him. He fell into the arms of Ismael, sobbing as he realised how close he'd come to unleashing the full fury of the arco-flagellant.

'I didn't...' he said. 'I wouldn't have...'

'I know,' said Ismael. 'But Rasselas X-42 is a living weapon, and a weapon has but one purpose.'

Abrehem nodded and let Ismael lead him back to his cot bed, blinking away the nightmarish images of torture and mutilation. He sat down, heaving in gulping breaths and weeping at the horror of what he'd seen. He knew they were not his own thoughts, but memories of carnage wrought by Rasselas X-42 in his previous existence.

Ismael held out his hands and Abrehem looked up into his eyes.

The servitor's distracted, vacant look was gone. In its place was an expression of such peace and understanding that Abrehem was rendered speechless.

'He calls to your lust for violence,' said Ismael, all traces of his halting speech vanished. 'Rasselas X-42 is the quick and easy path to vengeance, the evil of the man he was distilled and perfected. You must be better than that, Abrehem, you must cast him out.'

Abrehem shook his head. 'I can't. If the Mechanicus come for me, then I'll need him.'

'You do not need him,' promised Ismael. 'You already have all that you need.'

'I don't understand.'

Ismael held his hands out to him and said, 'Then listen.'

Abrehem hesitantly took Ismael's hands and kept silent, alert for anything out of the ordinary, but beyond Rasselas X-42's thwarted, animal breath and the constant mechanical beat of the *Speranza*'s workings, there was nothing to hear.

'Listen to what?' said Abrehem.

'To all the lost souls,' said Ismael, and Abrehem cried out as thousands of enslaved voices filled his head with their anguished cries.

The appearance of the *Tomioka*'s exterior had shocked Kotov, but the interior was, if anything, even more outlandish. The starship's internal plan had been extensively reshaped, rendering his ancient schematics utterly useless. With their entry point far above them, the darkness within was virtually absolute, leavened only by the helm-lamps of the skitarii and a pale, greenish hue that seeped from flexing cables that infested the ship's dripping innards like pulsing arteries.

Access ladders and stairwells that had been removed from their previous locations and re-fixed perpendicular to their original orientation allowed Kotov's force to travel downwards without difficulty. Their route traversed vast, echoing interior compartments stripped of their original fittings and which were now connected in ways the *Tomioka*'s original shipwrights had never intended. They kept close to the ice-clad hull, and ghostly wisps of chill vapour curled from protruding structural elements like breath.

'I feel like we are descending through biological anatomy,' said Dahan, moving with a hunched gait to fit through the oddly angled passageways. 'It is an unpleasant sensation.'

Kotov understood his sentiment, imagining they were passing through the literal guts of the starship. Like a living organism, the interior of the *Tomioka* was not silent, but a place of groaning echoes, creaking, flexing steelwork and a distant, glacial heartbeat.

'Perhaps a biological aesthetic informed Telok's work here,' suggested Kotov.

'No wonder they called him mad,' observed Dahan distastefully. 'Why then do we traverse the bowels while Mistress Tychon ascends to the brain?'

'Because the greatest power source lies far beneath us, and it is the key to understanding the mystery of this vessel,' answered Kotov. 'Let Mistress Tychon plunder the archives, *we* will be the ones to learn the true revelations Telok left behind.'

Dahan gave a blurt of dismissive binary and set off to rejoin his skitarii warriors.

Kotov ignored the Secutor's scepticism, attuning his senses to the chatter of background perceptions. Manifold inloads from Tarkis Blaylock and Vitali Tychon aboard the *Speranza*, encrypted vox-clicks from the Templars, Cadian intercom echoes and a crackling hiss of machine language that burbled just below his threshold of understanding.

Kotov couldn't understand it, but one thing was clear.

It was getting stronger.

'I take it you hear that, archmagos,' said a bobbing, gold-chased skull floating beside him, kept aloft by a tiny suspensor and embellished with a single flared wing that fluttered back and forth at its occipital bone. One eye socket was fitted with an ocular-picter, the other with a sophisticated augur implant that recorded and relayed its findings back to the *Speranza*.

'Yes, Tarkis,' said Kotov. 'I do, but it irks me that I cannot understand it.'

'The ship's cogitators are struggling too,' said the skull with Blaylock's voice. 'I am applying all sanctioned enhancements and filters to the source code, but they are statistically unlikely to retrieve anything of use.'

'Understood, Tarkis,' said Kotov. 'But keep trying. I want to know what this ship is saying.'

The skull clicked its jaws and drifted back to its position at Kotov's shoulder as the downward journey through the *Tomioka* continued down welded ladders, crudely formed ramps and repositioned stairwells.

Kotov followed the Black Templars down a screw-stair welded to the side of a corridor, letting his fingers brush against a line of angular symbols that resembled ancient hieroglyphics or a forgotten branch of mathematics. He'd seen variations of these symbols ever since they'd boarded the *Tomioka*, each ideogram connected to another like the holy writ of a circuit board. Linya Tychon believed it to be an impossibly complex form of organic language belonging to a hitherto unknown xenos breed, a declaration that had only heightened the tension among the Mechanicus boarders.

Where Kotov, Dahan's skitarii and the Black Templars were forging a path down through the *Tomioka*'s internal structure, Vitali Tychon's gifted daughter was ascending. Escorted by a company-strength detachment of Cadian storm troopers led by Captain Hawkins, she had eagerly seized this chance to venture into the unknown. Curiously, Galatea had chosen to accompany her, the abominable machine intelligence keen to explore Telok's flagship now that the threat beyond its hull had been dealt with. Magos Azuramagelli had been seconded from the *Tabularium*'s command deck to oversee the mission to the ship's bridge, assuming such a location still existed.

Kotov reached the bottom of the screw-stair to find himself in a high-roofed transverse corridor that had been sealed at either end by heavy panelling fashioned from elongated panels torn from the ship's prow blade. There appeared to be no way to continue downwards, though skitarii melta gunners were hunting for weak points in the floor and strangely scraped walls to attempt a breach. Kotov detected heavy deposits of lubricant grease and felt the presence of electrical current.

Magos Dahan beckoned Kotov over to a jury-rigged control panel against the far wall, but before he could join him, Tanna intercepted him.

'How much farther down do you believe we need to go, archmagos?' asked Tanna.

'I believe we are close, sergeant,' replied Kotov.

'With every level we descend, the danger increases.'

'We are explorators, Sergeant Tanna,' Kotov reminded him. 'Danger comes with the territory.'

'*You* are an explorator, *I* am a warrior.'

'Then you should be used to danger, sergeant,' snapped Kotov.

The Space Marine's anger was unmistakable, but Kotov paid it no attention and moved past him to join Dahan. A series of gem-lights winked on the panel, indicating that it had power. Its only other component was a simple lever that could be racked to an up or down position.

'Elevator controls,' said Dahan. 'Funicular transit ones ripped from an embarkation deck by the size of them.'

'This whole chamber is a descent elevator,' said Kotov, now understanding the nature of the scrapes on the walls and the excessive presence of lubricants.

'The enginarium spaces should be beneath,' said Dahan. 'The source of the power emanations?'

'Possibly,' said Kotov taking hold of the descent lever. 'If whatever is below us bears any resemblance to the original plan.'

Kotov pulled the control lever into the down position. 'So let us find out,' he said.

The chamber shuddered and ground downwards on bleating hydraulics and clanking gear chains.

Microcontent 08

Entire structural elements had been removed from the upper reaches of the *Tomioka*'s hull and replaced with crystalline panels that refracted outside light through the enclosing ice in strange ways. Linya blink-clicked images of rainbow-hued prismatic beams dancing in the open spaces, the light catching glittering motes of dust and reflecting from the polarised visors of the Cadians' enclosing helmets. The brightness gave the impression of space and peace, but that was, she reminded herself, an illusion.

'Wondrous, is it not?' asked the voice of her father. 'Reminds me of the magnificent processional cathedrals of ice and glass within the Artynia Catena.'

Vitali Tychon's voice emerged from a jet-black servo-skull flitting through the air like a curious insect, the audio scratchy with distortion and warbling with singsong static. The presence of the umbra surrounding the *Tomioka* made standard orbital vox impossible, so all transmissions between the ground forces and the *Speranza* were relayed through the *Tabularium* to the landing fields before finally being hurled into space.

'There's a resemblance,' agreed Linya, addressing the floating device, which had been built from removed segments of her father's own skull after he had decided to enlarge his cranial cavity with an artificial replacement to allow for additional implants. 'But we are not on Mars, we are exploring the hostile environment of an ancient madman.'

'Madman? Visionary? Often the two are separated by a hair's-breadth,' observed Vitali, as twin callipers mounted under the jawbone produced a quick sketch of the view before his proxy skull.

'I know which one I would use to describe Telok,' said Linya.

'Before I saw this, I might have agreed with you, but this is incredible,' said Vitali as the servo-skull floated ahead to where Magos Azuramagelli was ascending a narrow stairwell by folding his ratcheting machine body into a more compact form. Contrary to what Linya had expected, Azuramagelli was negotiating the convoluted spaces within the *Tomioka* with relative ease, swiftly climbing ladders with multiple arms, and reordering his brain-fragments within the armature of his protective casings to facilitate his transit.

Given the self-assembled crudity of Galatea's form, it had no such ability to alter its body-plan and was forced to take looping detours to avoid the more cramped routes to the bridge. Linya had been glad of the respite from its presence, but each time they reconnected with the hybrid machine intelligence, she wondered just how it managed to get ahead of them. She and the Cadians were supposed to be following the most direct route to the bridge, but each time the dimensions of a blast door or cored shaft prevented it from proceeding Galatea would be waiting for them in a wider space beyond.

What, she then thought, was it doing while it was beyond their sight?

Linya shook off such suspicions and concentrated on her own progress, following four squads of void-suited Cadian troopers as they forged a path upwards, moving in fits and starts as different groups advanced higher into the ship in mutually supporting cover formations. Another three squads followed behind, and Linya admired the effectiveness with which Captain Hawkins was leading his men – from the front and with nothing asked of them he wasn't prepared to do first.

Cadian combat argot was terse and tactically precise – for a verbal form of communication – with clear commands and unambiguous meanings. Skitarii mind-links were a far more efficient means of combat communication, but required cranial implants she suspected most soldiers of the fortress-world wouldn't accept.

Despite Kotov's gloomy predictions, their winding upwards passage through Telok's ship was meeting with no resistance, either in the form of the crystal-form creatures or impassable architecture. While her father's servo-skull flitted ahead as a gleeful scout, she and the Cadians climbed the *Tomioka*'s cavernous internal chambers via chugging freight elevators haphazardly fixed to the walls with docking clamps,

scaled vertical transit shafts on multiple ladders welded to the deck and scrambled up ramps of canted ceiling plates.

The crystalline panels sent their light deep into the heart of the ship, creating an airy, open feeling. Which was a novel sensation for Linya, who normally found being aboard a starship tiresomely claustrophobic, even one as vast as the *Speranza.*

She paused at a makeshift landing that looked out over a wide open space that had probably once been an embarkation deck. Light flooded the area through a series of opened docking hatches far across the chamber, through which gaseous mist billowed. The temperature gradient formed clouds in the upper reaches of the embarkation deck, and moisture fell through the interior in a soft shimmer of rain that patterned her hood with vapour trails.

'Don't think we should dawdle, Miss Tychon,' said a Cadian trooper whose shoulder patch identified him as Lieutenant Taybard Rae. 'Sooner we get you and your... friends to the bridge the sooner we can get out of here.'

Something in the soldier's manner was instantly disarming and Linya smiled within her environment hood. Like the Cadians, she was protected from the hostile conditions, but the technology keeping her alive was far more advanced: a self-generated, full-body integrity field and flexing cranial canopy with a multi-spectral sensorium.

'You don't like it in here?' asked Linya, looking through the glittering nitrogen rain. 'Sights like this do not come often. They need to be savoured.'

'Begging your pardon, Miss Tychon, but Captain Hawkins said we weren't here on a sightseeing trip. And trust me, you don't want to get his dander up when we're on a mission.'

Linya recalled Captain Hawkins from the regimental dinner she and her father attended in the Cadian billets. Her impression had been that Hawkins was a man of few words, though he had been coaxed to loquaciousness when toasting the fallen soldiers of Baktar III.

'He is a strict officer?' she asked.

Rae looked perplexed at the question. 'Aren't we all?' he said.

'I suppose so, though I confess I have only met a few.'

'Ach, he's not so bad,' said Rae, slinging his rifle and leaning out over the balcony. 'I've served under a lot of captains and colonels in my time, so when you get a good one, you try and keep him alive. You know what senior officers are like, miss, always trying to get themselves shot or blown up. They're like children really, they need their lieutenants to keep them out of trouble.'

Clearly deciding to take Linya's advice, Rae turned and rested his folded arms on the iron balustrade, taking in the splendour of the vista before him. 'Rain in a starship,' he said, shaking his helmeted head. 'Hell of a thing.'

'Yes, I don't think I've ever heard of such an occurrence,' said Linya.

'Makes you think though, eh?'

'About what?' asked Linya, when Rae didn't continue.

'About why you'd bring a ship all this way from the Emperor's light just to crash it on a world that's going to die,' said Rae, making room for one of the rearguard squads to pass, ten soldiers with rifles pulled in tight to their shoulders.

'So why do you think Telok did this?' asked Linya.

'You're asking me?' laughed Rae. 'I'm just a gruff, incredibly handsome and virile lieutenant, what do I know about tech stuff like that?'

'I don't know,' said Linya, gesturing to the misty cavern of the rotated chamber. 'You tell me.'

Rae grinned and tapped the side of his helmet.

'Well, whoever did this had himself a plan, right?' he asked. 'I mean, you don't go to all the effort of standing a starship on its arse for no reason. So I'm guessing this Telok fella, he knew Katen Venia was going to be destroyed sooner rather than later, yeah?'

'That would be a safe assumption, Lieutenant Rae.'

'Then it stands to reason that whatever he's got planned is going to happen soon,' said Rae, unlimbering his rifle. 'And whatever that is, I get the feeling that being inside this ship won't be the best place to be when it starts.'

To those without noospheric adaptations, the command deck of the *Speranza* was a cold steel elliptical chamber that looked nothing like the bridges of Naval ships of war. Silver-steel nubs jutted from the floor like unfinished structural columns, and a number of otherwise unremarkable command thrones were placed at apparently random locations.

But to the servitors hardwired into those gleaming nubs and the Mechanicus personnel manning each station, it was a far more dynamic place than the sterile steel and preserved timber compartments of starched Navy captains and their underlings. Thousands of shimmering veils of data light hung suspended in the air like theatrical curtains about to rise and spiralling arcs of information-rich light streamed from inload ports to be split by data prisms, diverted throughout the bridge and processed.

Magos Tarkis Blaylock sat in the command throne lately vacated by Archmagos Kotov. His black robes were etched with divine circuitry

and his chasuble of zinc alloy was a fractally complex network of geometric designs and machine language. Green optics pulsed beneath his hood and streams of coolant vapour rose from him as though he were smouldering. His retinue of stunted dwarf-servitors fussed around him, rearranging his floodstream cables and regulating the flow of life-sustaining chemicals to his bio-mechanical body, a complex mix of proteins, amino acids, blessed oils and nutrient-dense lubricants.

As Fabricatus Locum, the *Speranza* was his to command in the absence of the archmagos – it was a task he relished. The sheer power of the Ark Mechanicus was unimaginable, a vast repository of knowledge and history that would take the Martian priesthood a thousand lifetimes to process.

Blaylock prided himself in his ability to assimilate enormous volumes of data, but just skimming his consciousness over the golden light of *Speranza*'s core spiritual mechanisms was enough to convince him that to descend into its neuromatrix would be to invite disaster. Necessity had forced the archmagos to enter the deep strata of the *Speranza*'s machine-spirit during the eldar attack, and Blaylock still did not know how he had managed to extricate himself from its impossibly complex lattice after securing its help.

Together with Vitali Tychon, who occupied an adjacent sub-command throne, Blaylock was engaged in fleet-wide operations that would normally require substantial Mechanicus personnel to handle. Vitali's floodstream betrayed his child-like wonderment at the data exloading from the surface, but Blaylock found something strangely *familiar* in its nature, as though he was somehow already aware of its content.

He dismissed the thought and turned his attention to a last strand of partitioned consciousness that was currently engaged in hunting the bondsmen who had instigated the interruption of servitude among the *Speranza*'s cyborg servitor crew. Each of the indentured workers collared on Joura had been implanted with fealty designators and should, in theory, be easily found.

But neither the senior magi nor constant sweeps of cyber-mastiffs and armsmen could locate Bondsmen Locke, Coyne and Hawke. Nor could they find any trace of the rogue overseer, Totha Mu-32, and the servitor said to have recovered its memories. Nor was their any evidence of the rumoured arco-flagellant Bondsman Locke was said to possess.

It was as if they had simply vanished.

Which, on a Mechanicus ship, was surely impossible.

Blaylock left that portion of his consciousness to keep searching, and returned to the business of running the *Speranza*. Between them, he and Vitali were maintaining the ship's position over Katen Venia's turbulent polar region, processing the surveyor readings exloaded from the surface, communicating along Manifold links with the senior commanders on the surface, optimising shipboard operations of over three million tertiary grade systems and coordinating the fleet manoeuvres in expectation of a cataclysmic stellar event.

The likelihood of Arcturus Ultra exploding in the immediate future was statistically remote, but the pace and fury of the reactions taking place in its nuclear heart were beyond measure; nothing could be taken for granted. As far as possible, Blaylock – with Magos Saiixek in Engineering's assistance – was keeping Katen Venia between the fleet and the dying star. If this star *did* go nova, a planet wasn't going to offer much in the way of protection, but it was better than nothing.

+So much information,+ said Vitali over their hardline link. +Wondrous, is it not? How often does one get to see the destruction of an entire planet this close?+

+I have overseen Exterminatus protocols on three worlds, Magos Tychon,+ said Blaylock. +I know what extinction level events comprise.+

+Ah, but this is a natural event, Tarkis. Completely different. Of course I have seen the after-effects of such events from the orbital galleries on Quatria, but to be here is something we won't soon forget.+

+We will not forget it at all,+ said Blaylock, irritated at Vitali's interruptions. +The data has already been recorded and the Mechanicus–+

+Never deletes anything,+ finished Vitali. +Yes, I am well aware of that tiresome truism, but to see an event like this first-hand is quite different, regardless of what you might be about to tell me about experiential bias.+

+Is there a point to this current discourse?+ asked Blaylock. +The surveyor emissions from the surface are complex enough to process without having to divert additional processing capability to interpersonal discourse.+

Vitali nodded. +Yes, the sheer volume and complexity of what I am seeing is quite…+

The venerable magos broke off as a simulation he had running in the background finally reached its conclusion, coalescing in a bright sphere of glittering information. His multi-digit hands splayed it outwards, but Blaylock did not bother to inload whatever spurious experiment the stellar cartographer was running.

+Tarkis, were you aware of the electromagnetic discharges emanating from the *Tomioka* and the dissonant area of geostationary dead space above it?'

+I registered both items earlier, yes.+

+And what did you believe them to be?+

Blaylock brought up a cascade of discarded auspex junk, sifting through it with haptic sweeps of his hands, processing the information through a multitude of senses.

+Nothing more than irrelevant by-products of the chaotic systems within the atmosphere intersecting with rogue electromagnetic emissions from the planet's core. It has likely already been subsumed into the background radiation.+

+You are dead wrong, Tarkis,+ said Vitali.

Blaylock's floodstream surged with irritation he did not bother to modulate. +I am seldom wrong, Magos Tychon.+

+Seldom does not mean never, look again,+ said Vitali, sweeping a series of extrapolations and speculative interpretations of the surveyor inloads over to Blaylock's throne.

Blaylock digested the data, then brought up the backlogged surveyor data and ran it forward at speed to the present moment. As absurd as Vitali's conclusions were, it was hard to dismiss their inevitable logic.

+Are you sure about this?+ he asked.

+Sure enough to know that we need to get everyone off that planet,+ said Vitali.

+Yes, of course,+ agreed Blaylock. +When will it reach us?+

+My most accurate projection says two hours and fifty-four minutes.+

+Ave Deus Mechanicus!+ said Blaylock, sending a stream of imperative binary through the noosphere, Manifold and vox-networks. +Contact Kryptaestrex and have him prep every landing craft for immediate lift-off. Get everyone off that planet. Now!+

The space had once been the *Tomioka*'s enginarium, but that purpose had long since been sacrificed in service of another. The funicular transit elevator had carried them deep into the bedrock of the planet, their angle of descent taking them from walls of steel into regions stratified with aeons of geological change. When at last the elevator halted, it was immediately clear that the cathedrals of the engine spaces had been enlarged many times over by the simple expedient of drilling out the rock for kilometres in all directions.

An enormous cavern had been created beneath the *Tomioka* that extended far beyond the boundaries of the starship, but just how far was impossible to tell, for only the dimmest green light illuminated the cavernous space. The heat down here was immense, the air hazed with steam and ferocious temperatures radiating from the vast quantities of towering machinery that lined the walls.

Innumerable glowing green cables threaded the walls, coiled together like nests of snakes and pulsing with a hypnotic rhythm. Tens of thousands extended from the nearest machines, thousands more from others farther around the circumference of the immense cavern. Tangled masses of the cables all converged on a distant point where a dancing light glimmered in the half-darkness.

'What is this place?' asked Tanna.

'I do not know,' said Kotov, following the vanguard of skitarii towards the centre of the chamber. 'But whatever plan Telok had for his ship, this is the heart of it.'

'It has the look of the xenos to it,' said Tanna, and Kotov was forced to agree.

'It could be that Telok's crystal technologies incorporate alien technology,' suggested Dahan. 'Might that be how he finally succeeded in getting it to work?'

'That is certainly one possibility,' conceded Kotov.

Tanna raised a fist and his Space Marines dropped to their knees, each one with a weapon aimed.

Dahan was at his side in an instant.

'What is it, sergeant?'

'Battle robots ahead,' said Tanna. 'They're not moving, but look at the chests. There is something wrong with them.'

The Mechanicus advanced behind the Black Templars and Kotov saw Tanna was quite correct.

A maniple of immobile Conqueror battle robots in dusty armour of blue and red stood ranked up as though awaiting doctrina wafers. Their sunken heads stared unseeing at the floor and their weapon arms hung slack at their sides. Kotov counted five robots, each four metres tall, brutish and harshly angled, with rusted plates of ablative shielding crumbling at their shoulders.

In all respects but one, they appeared to be nothing more than relics of a long-ago war.

Each robot's chest cavity, where Kotov would expect to find its power source, was filled with finely woven crystalline filaments like the finest blown glass.

'This is the same crystal-form we fought above,' said Tanna, instantly bellicose.

Kotov raised a delicately machined hand. 'Be at peace, sergeant. These machines have not been active in hundreds, perhaps even thousands, of years.'

'That gives me no comfort,' said Tanna, gesturing to his fellow warriors. 'Destroy the crystals.'

'Wait!' cried Kotov. 'I cannot allow you to simply destroy Martian property.'

'And I cannot allow a potential threat to remain along our line of retreat.'

'Sergeant Tanna,' said Kotov, placing himself between the towering warrior and the battle robot. 'We did not come all this way just to vandalise the first piece of technology we do not yet understand. The discovery of new things is what brings us out here, yes?'

'It's what brought *you* out here, archmagos,' said Tanna. 'We came to honour a debt. I thought you understood that.'

Kotov shook his head and rested a hand on the nearest robot's arm. Rust flaked away and fragments of corroded metal drifted to the ground. 'These are Mechanicus artefacts, it would be a crime against the Omnissiah to defile them.'

'That crystal isn't Mechanicus,' said Dahan, standing alongside Tanna. 'That crystal is xenos technology, and the alien mechanism is a perversion of the True Path. *That's* what you are destroying, are you not, sergeant?'

The Space Marine nodded and an unheard order passed between him and his warriors.

Though Kotov was unhappy about such wanton destruction, he knew he had little choice but to accede to the Black Templars' tactical decision. Tanna put a fist through the lattice in the nearest robot's chest, the crystalline web shattering into powdered fragments. Within seconds the battle robot had its chest cavity emptied of crystal, and this act of destruction was a knife to Kotov's heart.

Dahan knelt beside one of the robots, where a scrap of loose cloth lay under its foot. He lifted it with the inactive prongs of his scarifiers, dust trickling from the folds like the ash of an ancient revenant.

'What is that?' asked Kotov.

'Some sort of robe,' said Dahan.

'Mechanicus?'

Dahan shook his head as the threads began to fray and the cloth fell apart. 'Too small.'

The scrap of cloth fell to the floor, now little more than coarse-woven threads that unravelled and rotted away even as they watched.

'There's more of them,' said Tanna, moving behind the robots. The Space Marine knelt beside another of the robes, this one with a semblance of a shape beneath it. No larger than a small child, it was swathed in identical rags, but as Tanna touched it, the robe lost its shape and puffs of dust sighed from its edges as whatever it concealed disintegrated.

Something gleamed beneath the rags, and Tanna sifted through the dust to retrieve it.

'What do you have there, sergeant?' asked Kotov.

'I'm not sure,' said Tanna. 'A mechanism of some sort.'

Tanna stood and held his discovery out to Kotov. A bent piece of metal, corroded and pitted with age, it had the look of a flintlock belonging to some primitive black powder weapon. Tanna held the shaped metal on the palm of his hand, but before Kotov could give it a closer examination, it crumbled to powder.

'Accelerated decay, perhaps a side effect of this world's dissolution,' said Dahan.

'Perhaps,' said Kotov, pushing deeper into the chamber. 'But a mystery for later on, I think.'

Leaving the ancient robots and rotted fabric forms behind, Kotov pushed deeper into the chamber, seeing yet more isolated groups of rusted battle robots deeper in the shadows either side of their route of march. Soon it became clear that the centre of the chamber was directly beneath the *Tomioka,* as the chamber's roof changed from bare rock to the cross-section of a gutted starship.

Structural hull members, tens of metres thick, stood like vast pillars at the entrance to a templum. Once beyond this permeable barrier, Kotov saw a vast circular chasm had been excavated at the base of the starship. At least five hundred metres in diameter, its edge was delineated by hundreds of thousands of the faintly glowing cables that plunged into its depths. What looked like a vast data prism hung down from the ceiling formed by the *Tomioka,* resembling an enormous spear-point fashioned from a single block of ice.

But it was the flickering globe suspended over the exact centre of the shaft that commanded Kotov's full attention.

A ball of greenish fire hung in the air like an emerald sun caught in an invisible force field. Its surface rippled with coruscating lines of force, as though formed from viscous fluids stirred by internal tides. No part of Kotov's sensorium could measure its dimensions, mass or density, and had he relied on any input beyond his optics, he would never know the object was there at all.

'What is that?' asked Tanna.

'Some kind of reactor?' ventured Dahan.

'Perhaps,' said Kotov, rechecking the passive augurs worked into the armoured body he wore. Whatever the object was, it was beyond his ability to measure, and what readings he *was* getting were fluctuating meaninglessly, as though the object was transitioning from one state of being to another at any given moment. His chronometric

readings flatlined, as though caught within the temporal null of a stasis bubble.

Kotov tore his gaze from the nuclear green fire and stared down into a bottomless black abyss as Dahan manoeuvred his skitarii around this segment of the shaft. Kotov saw no obvious means of descending into the chasm, but counted that as fortunate, feeling a strange sense of observation rising from its depths.

'Whatever this place is, it is clear that Telok never intended this ship to fly again,' said Kotov, perching precariously at the chasm's edge. 'The engines have been completely dismantled.'

'Why would Telok have done that?' asked Tanna.

Kotov had no answer for him and pulled away from the vertiginous shaft as the visible circumference of the shimmering green orb suddenly expanded, doubling its diameter in the blink of an eye. The tides within its unknown structure grew more violent and the light pouring from it filled the chamber with searing brightness.

'What's happening, archmagos?' demanded Tanna, backing away from the object.

Kotov had no firm evidence upon which to base his answer, but there could be only one possible explanation.

'Whatever Telok has planned for the *Tomioka*. It's happening now.'

The machine-spirit at the heart of the *Tomioka* was sluggish and hostile to Linya's enquiries, not that she could blame so venerable a machine for reacting badly to an unknown presence in its neuromatrix after so long a time spent dormant. They had reached the bridge; it was exactly where they had expected it to be, and Captain Hawkins's Cadians had secured it without incident. Linya had been surprised at how little its structure appeared to have been altered, given the nature of the rest of the ship, though it was, of course, turned through ninety degrees.

Servitors sat strapped into their consoles, and a number of battle robots were still mag-locked in place within their defence alcoves; beyond the thick layers of dust that had accumulated on numerous surfaces, it felt like the bridge crew might return at any moment.

While Azuramagelli and her father's servo-skull attempted to access the ship's avionics log, Galatea made a circuit of those areas of the bridge it could traverse. Linya hunted for a compatible inload port she could reach and which matched the quaintly archaic interface augmetic in the palm of her hand. If there was any data to be salvaged from the ship's data core, she would dig it out.

Incredibly, the ship's cogitators and deep logic engines were still functional, maintained by a dim, slumbering spirit that rested in the deep strata of cogitation. Connection to the data-engines was made via a simple series of Mechanicus hails, but she would need to go deep to find anything of value.

Linya closed her eyes, letting her functional awareness flow farther into the *Tomioka*'s datasphere, feeling the presence of numerous security screens and invasive protection algorithms marshalling at her continued presence. She tested their integrity with gently inquiring probes that were rebuffed without exception.

'Only to be expected,' she said, tapping out a binaric mantra with her left hand.

She tried a more direct approach, shaping her interrogative with aggressive signifiers of rank and demand protocols. Once again, the data-engine rejected her attempt and sent a painful jolt of bio-feedback through Linya's hand. Not enough to hurt, but enough to remind her that she was not authorised to access this ship's records.

The machine-spirit's defences resisted her every attempt at infiltration until she registered the presence of an inloaded code-breaking algorithm that carried the noospheric tags of Magos Blaylock. Linya had no memory of receiving such an inload, but couldn't deny its usefulness right about now.

She opened the inloaded data packet and let out a soft gasp at the geometric complexity of the algorithms worked into the code. Tarkis Blaylock was another tech-priest it was hard to like, but his grasp of hexamathic calculus and statistical analysis was second to none; this looked like the most perfect binaric skeleton key she had ever seen. Like a hound on the hunt, the decryption algorithm meshed seamlessly with the *Tomioka*'s datasphere, and the security systems woven around the info-logs fell away like mist before a hurricane.

Almost immediately, Linya realised her mistake.

A tsunami of stellar information poured into her and she let out a cry of terror as the data-burden overloaded her neural capacity in a heartbeat. She tried to pull away from the ship's flow of information, but like a victim of electrocution, she found she could not disengage from the very thing that was killing her. Numerous implants in her skull shorted out, one after the other, and Linya convulsed as the bio-electric feedback vaporised thousands of synaptic connections within the architecture of her brain.

Just as the data-burden surged with an even larger packet of impossibly dense celestial calculus, Linya felt herself torn from the data-engine with a physical jolt and a searing blaze of disconnection agonies. She hit the floor, wrapped in Lieutenant Rae's arms, dizzying vertigo seizing her.

Her hands flew to the sides of her head as pounding waves of shrieking pain stabbed through her skull like an instant migraine. Blinding light filled her eyes, and sickening nausea cramped in her gut. She heard her father's voice through the ebon skull, the gleaming red optics hovering just before her face, but couldn't process what she was hearing.

Shouted voices surrounded her.

'Mistress Tychon,' said Rae. 'Begging your pardon, but are you all right?'

She tried to nod, but rolled onto her side and vomited the contents of her stomach instead.

Linya felt the presence of something clanking and metallic moving past her and pushed herself upright in time to see Galatea plugging itself into the smoking inload port.

The silver-eyed proxy body turned to regard her slumped form.

'One mind cannot handle this data-burden,' said Galatea. 'Only we can do this.'

The surging pain in Linya's skull receded a fraction and she pulled herself upright on wobbling legs, feeling an unaccountable need to stop the machine from taking her place. Lieutenant Rae supported her, and she clung to him to keep from falling.

'What's happening?' she asked, straining to regain her senses and mental equilibrium.

'Don't know, miss,' said Rae, bringing his lasgun around as Cadian battle-cant filled the bridge and the bridge's defence robots climbed from their alcoves. Linya saw their chests were alight with a curious green illumination, their weapons systems coming online one after another.

Gunfire and shouts filled the bridge.

Microcontent 09

Both war machines were vigilant, stalking the icy plains around the *Tomioka* like wary predators circling dangerous prey that may or may not be playing dead. *Amarok* was still feisty after the fight in the canyon, its guns and voids restored, and Princeps Vintras allowed its virile machine-spirit to come to the fore in the Manifold.

He looped over the trail of *Vilka*, carefully avoiding the deep tracks the Ironwoad was leaving in the crystalline structure of the glassy plateau. It took finesse to walk a Warhound like this, sidestepping and moving forwards at the same time. He kept his targeting auspex loose, letting the aiming reticule drift back and forth in search of something to kill.

Vintras was getting twitchy too, the result of a potent cocktail of drugs pumped into his system after the fight with the facsimile engines. Word had come down that they were some form of machine-tech that could mould the crystalline structures of the dying world into the shapes of elements they perceived as threats.

The ground underfoot was unstable, the Warhound's complex stabilisation sensors perceiving an ever-growing, ever-spreading wave of seismic tremors building from far beneath the ground. Which was only to be expected; this world was dying after all, being pulled apart by geological stresses and celestial cataclysm. Such disturbances were only going to get worse and the surface of Katen Venia would soon become untenable for Titan engines.

With its boarders delivered, *Lupa Capitalina* had retreated from the towering form of the *Tomioka* and taken up an unmoving position before the starship. Even after the Wintersun's attack on Moonsorrow, there was still something magnetic about the vast scale of the Warlord, a potential for such awesome destruction that transcended all notions of morality. Just to share the battlefield with a Warlord was an honour, and to be pack with a god-machine of its power was to be a part of history. Yet for all that Vintras revered the incredible Titan, the idea of remaining static was anathema to him. As much as he longed to rise within the ranks of the Legio, he was loath to consider the possibility of leaving *Amarok* for a battle-engine that won wars by marching straight at the enemy.

'Are you hearing this?' asked Elias Härkin, intruding on Vintras's thoughts. The *Vilka*'s princeps's voice was gruff and had been augmetically rendered for decades, but hearing it over the vox only made it more unpleasant.

'Hearing what?' asked Vintras, irritated he'd allowed his mind to wander.

'The Mechanicus,' snapped Härkin.

'What about them?'

'Call yourself a Warhound driver?' asked Härkin. 'Use your damned eyes and open your vox!'

Vintras slewed *Amarok* to the side, increasing his pace and weaving across the landscape to circle around the *Tomioka* as the ground shook with another earth tremor, this one more powerful than the last. Vintras compensated, keeping the Warhound's centre of gravity low until he completed his circuit of the landed starship.

In the aftermath of the Legio's rescue of the Space Marines and skitarii, the Land Leviathans and support vehicles had poured over the bridge and onto the edge of the plateau, where they waited like observers too afraid to approach the object of their scrutiny.

Vintras switched his vox-input to accept non-Legio traffic, and immediately the Manifold flooded with prioritised threat warnings and withdrawal orders coming direct from the *Speranza*.

'What the hell's going on?' asked Vintras.

'What does it bloody look like?' grunted Härkin. 'They're leaving.'

The informational flow through the *Speranza*'s bridge had increased significantly, but the gathered magi, calculus-logi and lexmechanics were still able to handle the data-burden. Largely thanks to the coordinating power of Magos Blaylock, whose higher thought processes were streamlined to render such vast arrays of data into manageable chunks.

'Word from the surface?' asked Blaylock.

'Evacuation has begun,' said a magos whose identity signifiers were lost in the haze of noospheric data filling the bridge. 'The first Leviathan is en route to the landing fields. The others are aligning behind it and are in the process of crossing Magos Kryptaestrex's bridge.'

Blaylock turned to Vitali Tychon, who encompassed the Manifold links within his datasphere to coordinate the logistical nightmare of an emergency planetary withdrawal.

'Vitali,' said Blaylock, his urgency prompting him to dispense with titles and protocol. 'How long before the energy source reaches the planet?'

'One hour, thirteen minutes, Tarkis,' said Vitali Tychon, without needing to look up. 'Still no word from the archmagos or my daughter. Neither has responded to the summons back to the ship.'

Hearing the worry in the venerable magos's voice, Blaylock said, 'Keep trying.'

Blaylock brought up the system plot that displayed the fleet's position around Katen Venia and the approaching energy source hurtling through space towards them.

No, not towards *them*, towards the *Tomioka*.

Too late, he now realised what Telok's flagship was and why the Lost Magos had gone to the trouble of landing it in the first place. Together with the infinitesimal concavity of the plateau, the entire structure of the *Tomioka* was a vast receiver array: a hundred kilometres wide receiver that would channel a surging stream of unimaginable energy through its structure and into the planet's core. The purpose of this was still a mystery, but that anything nearby would be instantly obliterated was all too obvious.

Vitali was running a back-trace to the source of the energy beam, but it would take time to locate it amid the ferocious amount of background radiation from the dying star. Even trying to measure the beam was proving to be next to impossible, its qualities all but unknown to their auspex and of greater magnitude than could be readily quantified.

That such an unimaginable quantity of energy could travel so far without losing its power to the vacuum was staggering. Blaylock knew of only one thing said to be capable of such a monumental feat of power generation.

The Breath of the Gods.

Gunfire echoed weirdly within the chamber as the Black Templars bracketed one of the rusted battle robots with carefully coordinated

bolter shots. With the swelling of the seething energy globe, a measure of its tidal energies had bloomed throughout the cavern in a single pulse of atmospheric power transfer.

Numerous skitarii had collapsed, their enhanced neural pathways blown out by the blast – even Dahan had staggered with the force of it. The nature of the power transfer hadn't been immediately obvious, but when the first sawing blasts of autocannon fire tore through the skitarii, its purpose became self-evident.

The battle robots left to rust throughout the cavern were no dusty relics of a forgotten conflict, but dormant sentries, tasked with waiting until such a time as they would be required to defend the arcane processes under way. The crystalline lattice worked into the robots' chest cavities pulsed with necrotic green light, and despite their advanced state of disrepair, each moved and fought as if fresh from the forge.

A maniple had come at them at battle pace, but Dahan killed the first one with a beam of white heat from his plasma gun. Skitarii weaponry broke apart the second, and a broadside of bolter explosions shattered the third into a storm of metallic junk.

'I told you we should have destroyed them all,' said Tanna, walking backwards as he slammed a fresh magazine into his bolter.

'Duly noted,' said Kotov, cycling through his implanted weaponry until he came up with a tight-beam graviton gun. More of the robot maniples were closing in from all sides, and via Magos Dahan's threat-optimisers he saw at least sixty more approaching.

Kotov knelt and directed his implanted weaponry towards the nearest robot, triggering an invisible beam of intense gravometric energies. The robot, a clankingly archaic design of Cataphract, crumpled and bent double as its upper section was suddenly quadrupled in mass. Its already rusted spine collapsed under the weight and it fell in a welter of spilled oil and buckled plates.

Autocannon shells killed more of the skitarii, but no warrior was left behind. As they had against the crystal beasts, Dahan's men brought their dead and wounded with them. The robots had bigger guns and there were more of them, but they were slow and did not have the fire discipline of the skitarii.

Every metre of their retreat was earned in blood. Once beyond the structural elements of the *Tomioka,* there was no shelter and no strategy except flight. Kotov's implanted auspex registered another power surge from the energy sphere, and once again its diameter swelled, almost filling the width of the shaft over which it was suspended. The blaze of light from the emerald sun's depths filled the cavernous space beneath the *Tomioka*, and the tip of the glittering prism above it was less than ten metres from making contact. Kotov had no idea whether that would be a bad thing or not, but the part of him that relished symmetry and connectivity in things suspected that when it and the seething energy globe came into contact, it would be very unpleasant to be anywhere nearby.

Kotov crushed the chests of another ten robots with his graviton beams before the internal capacitors registered power loss. To fire it again, he would need to divert power from some other system. Instead, Kotov retracted the exotic weapon and cycled through to a more mundane rotary cannon. The design was an old one, a modified Dreadnought weapon that had been deemed too flimsy for deployment with Adeptus Astartes forces, but which Kotov liked for its brutal simplicity. The backplate of his body rotated to reveal louvred vents, and a long bullet-chain extended from his arm to link with an internal ammunition chamber.

Recoil compensators deployed along Kotov's shoulders and legs as a series of readiness icons flashed before his eyes. Kotov slaved his targeting arrays to inloaded threat data from Dahan, and pushed his consciousness into a higher state before opening fire.

A blazing stream of fire tore from Kotov's arm, fully three metres long, and whatever it touched simply exploded in a haze of torn-up metal and shattered plates. Each burst was precisely controlled, and it seemed that Kotov could see every shell, his cognitive functions moving so swiftly that he could watch each explosion in slow motion, switch targets and engage the enemy without wasting a single round of ammunition.

All around him, the Space Marines and skitarii were moving like figures in a slow-running pict-feed, their motions painfully measured. Sounds reached him at a glacial rate, and even the light of explosions and muzzle flare seemed to expand like slow-blooming flowers. Wherever Dahan registered a threat, Kotov swung his weapon to bear and eliminated it with a precise burst of high-explosive shells.

Waves of excess heat from such increased cognition were dispersed through coolant flow across his scalp, but such an overclocking could only be maintained for a minute of subjective time at most and he was almost at his limit.

In the end it was Kotov's ammunition that gave out first, and the spinning barrels clicked dry as the ammo hopper sought in vain to keep the tide of shells coming. Kotov felt the urge to keep going, to switch out to another weapon. To process information and stimuli with such speed was intoxicating, a wholly addictive feat of cognition that had seen more than one adept of the Mechanicus boil the organic portions of his brain within his skull. Kotov disengaged the rapid-thought functions and staggered as the searing heat in his skull temporarily overwhelmed him. The energy demands on his body, which ran to narrow enough tolerances as it was, suddenly found themselves with an unsustainable deficit.

Kotov's limbs folded up beneath him, but before he hit the ground, Sergeant Tanna caught him and hauled him back, firing his bolter one-handed as he went. Kotov tried to speak, but the pain in his skull was too intense, the chronic drain on his mental faculties shutting down all non-essential functions as they fought to restore order in his synaptic arrays.

He was dimly aware of more robots closing in on their position, but he could not make out how many or how far away they were. He saw Dahan firing his implanted weapon, surrounded by perhaps thirty skitarii warriors, some wounded, some bearing the bodies of the dead. The Black Templars fell back behind relentless salvos of bolter fire, halting a battle robot with each one.

'Quite a feat of arms,' said Tanna, depositing him by the controls of the funicular transit elevator and turning to haul the lever into the up position. 'I thought you said *I* was the warrior.'

'An explorator must be prepared for all eventualities,' said Kotov, finally regaining the power of speech as the elevator rumbled back up into the *Tomioka*. 'And I am not a man to travel lightly.'

With Lieutenant Rae supporting her, Linya scrambled down the length of the starship, breathless and fighting the building agony in her head. The fight on the bridge had been brief, bloody and one-sided, with the Cadian troopers hopelessly outgunned by an enemy they couldn't hope to hurt. Captain Hawkins had seen the futility of staying to fight and immediately ordered the retreat.

A squad of Guardsmen had covered their retreat, and even amid the confusion of being pulled from the bridge, Linya knew those soldiers were already dead. Heavy calibre shells tore the bridge to pieces, smashing ancient technology that had crossed the galaxy in search of wonder. One robot, its right arm a pulverising siege hammer, had smashed through bulkhead after bulkhead, shrugging off Cadian return fire from lasrifles, grenade launchers and even a direct hit from a plasma gun.

Sixty men and women fell back from the bridge, keeping their pursuers at bay with ambushes and traps. One robot was pitched into a shaft that looked as though it ran the length of the starship's long axis, and another had its leg blown off by a lucky grenade that managed to lodge in its pelvic joint. But the others were utterly relentless and Linya was forced to admire the lethal purity of whoever had punched the obedience routines of their doctrina wafers.

It felt like they were running at reckless speeds back the way they had come, pursued by at least five Imperial battle robots with curious crystalline power sources in their chests that closely resembled what Magos Dahan had described on the *Tabularium*. Magos Azuramagelli led the way back down the *Tomioka*, his mental mapping unfazed by the danger threatening them and his body-plan altering and reshaping with a speed Linya found incredible.

Her father's servo-skull zipped alongside her, pausing every now and then to check behind it before scooting after her. She could hear his voice urging her onwards, but shut it out as a distraction. Somewhere along the way they'd lost Galatea, the machine intelligence fleeing along a different route when it could no longer follow the same line of retreat. Linya wondered if it would manage to escape and found she didn't care either way.

The ground shifted beneath her, and she sprawled to the ground as the welded deck plate serving as a floor pulled free from the wall. Rae pulled her roughly to her feet, all trace of his former concern for decorum forgotten in this flight from the enemy.

'I can't go on,' she gasped.

'Can't be stopping, miss,' said Rae, pushing her through a group of covering soldiers as they clambered over to a welded screw-stair. 'At least these steps will slow the bastards up.'

Linya scrambled down the stairs, hearing chugging *bangs* of rapid bolter fire echoing above her. Too loud and too fast for a regular bolter, these were rounds that would reduce the human body to an expanding vortex of vaporised blood and cooked flesh. Screams followed the thudding booms of detonation, howls of pain that no human should ever have to make.

Tears ran down her face as she all but sprinted down the stairs, clutching the iron balustrade and remaining upright only by the grace of the Omnissiah. Close to the bottom, her luck ran out and her feet slid on the cold metal of the stairs. She fell from the last few steps onto the buckled metal of the walkway below. She rolled and grabbed onto the nearest spar of metal as the nitrogen rain of the embarkation deck soaked her.

'Come on!' shouted Rae, leaping from the last few steps. 'It's right behind us!'

The ceiling sagged inwards under the force of a titanic hammerblow

as something immense sought to bring down the stairs. Rae hauled her upright again as another blow struck the top of the stairs, accompanied by a screeching wail of dumb binaric fury. Rae backed into her and lifted his rifle, firing back up the stairwell on full auto, a blazing spread of crimson bolts that hissed as they left the focus ring of the barrel.

'A lasrifle won't harm a battle robot,' said Linya.

'Maybe not, miss, but if you've got a better idea, I'm all ears!'

He grabbed Linya by the shoulders and pushed her away as the stairwell buckled inwards and the blocky form of a Castellan battle robot crashed down onto the walkway behind them. The floor crumpled beneath its weight and a storm of debris cascaded over its hunched form. Rae went down under the ruptured service conduits and shattered steelwork, his lasrifle skittering over the canted walkway towards her.

The robot had landed on one knee and now rose to its full height of nearly four metres. Its heavy bolter ratcheted from the protective cowling at its shoulder and its power fist crackled with deadly disruptive field energies. The Castellan's armoured plating was scorched with las-burns and impact trauma. Its threat optics fastened on her with hostile intent.

Her father's servo-skull flitted in front of the robot, screeching deactivation codes spilling from its augmitter, but the weaponised machine simply swatted it aside. The skull cracked into a wall and dropped stone dead to the floor, the light fading from its optics.

Linya wanted to bend to retrieve Rae's rifle, but terror held her pinned to the spot.

She heard someone shout her name as the heavy bolter swung out, the automated slide racking back as it prepared to fire.

Linya closed her eyes and slid down the wall, but the shots never came.

She felt cold hands pull her upright and fell into the arms of her rescuer.

'We would not let such a primitive creation harm you, Mistress Tychon,' said Galatea.

Linya flinched and pushed herself away from the machine intelligence, repulsed beyond words at the thought of it touching her. Galatea's palanquin body squatted close to the ground, its oddly jointed legs twisted around to bring it so low. The silver-eyed tech-priest body rose up as she backed away from it.

'Get away from me,' she said.

'Such ingratitude,' said Galatea. 'And after we risked our continued existence to rescue you.'

Linya blinked away tears and turned to see the Castellan robot unmoving, its head sagging to one side with green-tinged fumes pouring from its contoured skull. Its chestplate belched smoke and the warlike binary that spalled from its weapons was silent.

It was utterly dead.

'How did you...?' asked Linya, looking up through the rent torn in the ceiling to see another battle robot with smoke belching from its innards.

'If we can take control of the *Speranza*, do you believe that overloading the cortex-doctrinas of a maniple of battle robots is beyond us?'

'I don't understand,' said Linya, as Cadian soldiers ran back to dig Rae from the debris. The lieutenant was bleeding from a cut on his forehead, but was already shouting at the men helping him that he was fine and to damn well leave him be.

'You are too wondrous to be allowed to die,' said Galatea, reaching out to stroke her cheek.

Linya pulled away from its repellent touch. 'Don't touch me,' she said. 'Not ever.'

The machine intelligence rose up, the brains on its palanquin flickering with frantic synaptic activity as some unheard communion passed between them.

'As you wish,' said Galatea. 'But you are precious to us.'

Linya backed away from the loathsome creature, and pausing only to recover her father's servo-skull, she followed the Cadians back down the *Tomioka*.

Kotov could remember little of the journey back up the *Tomioka*, his mental processes too traumatised by the strain of maintaining so rapid a cognition speed. It had been short by mortal reckoning, but a lifetime by the terms of measurement employed by the Mechanicus. Tanna carried him most of the way, all but dragging his armoured body up ramps, stairs and ladders. The remodelled interior of the ship passed in a blur, but even his blunted senses registered that something unprecedented was under way.

Portions of the *Tomioka*'s internal anatomy were reshaping themselves moment by moment. What he had mistaken for structural modifications to allow the vessel to stand upright were in fact carefully placed moving parts that were now fulfilling some unknowable function.

'Imperator,' said Tanna, as they passed through a vaulted compartment that had once been an ordnance magazine. 'So many of them.'

Kotov lifted his head and followed Tanna's gaze, seeing a multitude

of reflective panels of machined steel rotated into predetermined positions and vast lengths of cable extruded from vacuum-sealed compartments before being fitted into place by a veritable army of floating servo-skulls. Thousands of the gold and silver-chased skulls filled the compartment, more than Kotov had ever seen in one place.

'It's like the crew chose to remain behind and carry on their duties…' he said, the words coming only with difficulty.

'Or were forced to,' said Dahan, following behind them. 'Who knows how long these skulls have been here, just waiting for this moment?'

As fascinating as Kotov found it watching the thousands of skulls at work, Tanna dragged him ever upwards through the reconfiguring interiors. The dull green light that had illuminated their downward passage had been replaced by a stark brightness that shone from every polished plate and every overtaxed lumen. Vast arrays of structural steelwork rotated into place throughout the enlarged voids within the *Tomioka*, like the pylons of some planetary power generation system. Towering conduits unfolded from irising compartments and the interior volume of the starship's long axis was rapidly filling with complex machinery that spun, pulsed and throbbed with imminent activity.

Eventually, Kotov felt the pressure differential of an outside environment and looked up.

A flattened oval tunnelled through the violet-tinted ice told him they had reached the entry point cut by the superheated mechanisms of *Lupa Capitalina*'s plasma destructor. Black Templars stood at the far end of the tunnel, waving at something he couldn't see. Dimly he registered the sounds of artillery fire and high-energy weapon discharges.

Magos Dahan stood with the Adeptus Astartes warriors and Kotov took a moment to realise that there were more people around him than he remembered.

Cadian soldiers lined the walls and Kotov's floodstream surged with relief as he saw Magos Azuramagelli and Linya Tychon near the far entrance to the ice-tunnel. Galatea stood at the opposite side of the tunnel, and even in his limited state of awareness, Kotov read the tension between it and his magi.

Linya Tychon limped over to him, clutching a jet-black servo-skull.

For a moment, Kotov was confused at the sight of the skull. Had she stopped to procure herself one belonging to the *Tomioka*? Then he read the faint binaric sigils on its polished dome and realised the servo-skull belonged to Vitali Tychon.

'Archmagos,' said Linya, her face bruised and swollen. 'We have to leave. Now.'

'I think that is self-evident,' he said, finally managing to stand under his own power as his bodily control returned to a semblance of normality. 'This ship is reconfiguring itself in some most disconcerting ways.'

'No, I mean we have to leave this planet,' said Linya. 'In an hour it is going to be destroyed.'

'Come now, you are being melodramatic,' said Kotov, feeling more of his synaptic architecture re-establishing itself. 'It will take months or years for the star's death to fully dismantle this world and there is much we can yet learn.'

Linya's eyes narrowed. 'Haven't you been receiving Magos Blaylock's evacuation orders?'

Kotov hadn't, but as more and more of his systems reset, he began picking out desperate bursts of communication transmitted from orbit via the *Tabularium*. Though it sent a flare of pain through his skull, Kotov processed the most urgent of them in three pico seconds.

'This is a sacrificial planet,' said Linya. 'I don't know all of what's happening, but that much I do know. This ship is a giant receiver array, and the power that is about to be channelled through it is going to tear this planet apart for some purpose I can't even begin to imagine.'

Kotov nodded, and marched towards the end of the tunnel.

Lupa Capitalina walked in all its war-finery, sheathed in the blistering envelope of voids that shimmered with rainbow hues as they dissipated the energies of a recent attack. Like a vast sauropod of the plains being attacked by raptor packs, the Warlord was surrounded by smaller, crystalline representations of its godly might. Bright green bolts of light shot from the glittering forms of its attackers, but the Warlord was no lumbering herbivore just waiting to be dragged down, it was the alpha of a deadly hunter pack.

'I wouldn't believe it if I wasn't seeing it with my own eyes,' said a Cadian captain by the name of Hawkins. 'I didn't think they could move like that.'

A lieutenant with half his face covered in blood answered Hawkins, 'I'm thinking I took a bigger blow to the head than I thought.'

Kotov would normally have thought to rebuke mere Guardsmen for disparaging the capabilities of a Mechanicus battle-engine, but even he was shocked at the speed and agility with which Princeps Arlo Luth was manoeuvring *Lupa Capitalina*. More often used as strongpoints, fire-bases or points from which to launch assaults, Warlord Titans were not highly mobile war-engines.

Clearly the Wintersun did not hold to that view.

The Legio Sirius pack fought as one entity, *Amarok* and *Vilka*

snapping at the heels of their alpha as it advanced, retreated and sidestepped every attack. It moved in close to its attackers and crushed them beneath its clawed feet. It sawed a dozen to shards with gatling fire and vaporised half as many again with stabbing lances from its turbo-destructors. Its rapidly moving bulk shattered dozens more and it achieved this without losing its voids to the criss-crossing trails of enemy fire.

'Is it coming to pick us up?' asked Hawkins. 'The Titan, it's coming back for us, right?'

'Yes, captain,' said Kotov, already having broadcast an extraction request. '*Lupa Capitalina* is coming back for us.'

Kotov saw Hawkins's desire to witness the god-machine at war was pulling against his Cadian duty to his men. He allowed the man an indulgence.

'Stay,' said Kotov. 'Watch. To see a Titan in battle is to know the true power of the Omnissiah.'

Hawkins nodded and said, 'I've watched artillery batteries reduce greenskin fortresses to ruin in minutes, seen ten thousand charging Whiteshields on horseback and been part of orbital assaults that captured an entire planet in less than a day, but seeing a Warlord in action… that's something special.'

'And Legio Sirius are masters of their art,' said Kotov in a rare moment of largesse.

Lupa Capitalina turned, as though hearing its Legio name mentioned, and set off at a steady, rolling pace towards the *Tomioka*. Its attendant Warhounds followed, loping ahead to clear the way with punishing blasts of fire and howls of warning.

Kotov steadied himself as the war-engine came closer, the thunderous reverberations of its colossal footfalls transmitted to the *Tomioka* even through the immense sheath of ice surrounding it. He and everyone else within the tunnel backed away as it drew nearer, for even the approach of an allied battle-engine was an event of some danger.

'Everyone up and ready to move!' shouted Hawkins. 'We're only going to get one shot at this.'

The Warlord's voids impacted upon the ice at the edge of the tunnel, sending deep cracks racing along the ceiling and floor. Crystalline shards fell like broken glass and shrieking bursts of exploding ice rippled along the length of the tunnel until the void shields finally dropped. The assault ramps slammed down onto a broken ledge of ice, and Titan menials in orange boiler suits and armoured vests yelled at them to get aboard.

Dahan and his surviving skitarii escorted Kotov and Azuramagelli,

while the Black Templars and Cadians were last to board the war machine. Kotov had a moment's vertigo as he looked down between the lip of the assault ramp and the crumbling edge of the ice. His internal systems quickly compensated for the unwelcome sensation as menials hauled him aboard.

A tremendous impact rocked the Warlord, and even from here, Kotov felt the repercussive pain of its wounding. Engaged in this rescue mission, *Lupa Capitalina* was horribly exposed with its voids down and its weapon systems useless. The crystalline engines were taking full advantage of that, and explosions of green fire erupted all across the Titan's rear quarters. Both *Amarok* and *Vilka* were keeping the enemy from surrounding their pack leader, but they could not protect it from the terrible fire raking its unshielded flanks.

Kotov gripped the edge of the battlements tightly as *Lupa Capitalina* wrenched itself free of the ice and took a lurching backward step. The assault ramps were still down and two menials screamed as they fell from the open structure. Cadian soldiers ran to help in getting the ramps raised as the Warlord took another step, twisting on its axis as it did so. The walk to the *Tomioka* was made at a stately pace, but the Wintersun was in battle now; the insects crawling on its hull were of secondary importance to its own survival.

The logic was undeniable, though it gave Kotov no comfort to *be* one of those insects.

A hundred metres now separated the Warlord and the *Tomioka*, and Kotov saw that the transformations he had witnessed within the starship were being mirrored on its exterior. The crystalline growths on its hull were expanding organically to sheathe the entire upper reaches of the hull in what looked like a caul of glittering glass.

A flare of static blinded him momentarily as *Lupa Capitalina's* carapace void pylons ignited and clad the Titan in layers of ablative energies. The clashing harmonics and belligerent frequencies were antithetical to his implants, but Kotov was grateful for the protection.

+Archmagos Kotov,+ said a voice that cut into his mind with icy disdain. +Are you secure?+

'I am,' he replied, sending his words into the caustic tundra of the Sirius Manifold.

+Then we are ready,+ said Princeps Arlo Luth.

'Ready? Ready for what?'

+To abandon this world.+

Microcontent 10

Watching Katen Venia's last moments was a moment of great sadness for Roboute Surcouf. He had named this world and it was never easy to watch something beautiful die. Roboute remembered the girl whose name the planet shared, wondering if he would ever see her again and silently berated himself for so maudlin a thought.

Sickly bands of variegated light enveloped the planet in traceries of continent-wide lightning storms like a vast net cast around its splintering mass. The brightest point of light was centred on the northern pole, where the abortive expedition to the *Tomioka* had foundered. The evacuation of Katen Venia was over, with the majority of the embarked crew already back aboard the *Speranza*.

The Mechanicus had been forced to discard a great deal of materiel and resources in the flight from the surface, of which the Land Leviathans – *Krakonoš, Adamastor* and *Fortis Maximus* – were the most grievous loss. Much of their crew, adepts, tech-priests and menials alike, had chosen to remain with their machines rather than abandon them, and those men were almost certainly dead.

Roboute shook his head at their stupidity before remembering that, until recently, he had always believed that he would die aboard the *Renard*. He had survived his brush with death after the grav-sled had been winched to safety by the *Tabularium*'s docking clamp and a team of medicae had strapped an oxygen mask to his face. Adara was unhurt, as was Magos Pavelka, which – given the frantic nature of their excursion to the surface – was nothing short of a miracle.

The bridge of the *Speranza* was thronged with the senior members of the Kotov expedition: Mechanicus, Adeptus Astartes and Imperial Guard, drawn together to watch the final moments of Katen Venia and the loss of everything they had crossed the galaxy to discover. Azuramagelli was once again ensconced by the navigation arrays, with Kryptaestrex plugged in next to him. Vitali Tychon kept close to his daughter, a protective arm around her shoulder. From the bruises on her face, it seemed the excursions into the *Tomioka* had been as plagued by trouble as events outside.

Galatea stood in the centre of the command bridge, its low-slung palanquin connected to the *Speranza* in ways Roboute couldn't begin to imagine. Pavelka had given him a rough idea of the heretical reality of Galatea, and the concept of a thinking machine gave Roboute cold chills whenever he thought of the onward implications.

Archmagos Kotov himself sat upon his command throne, looking like an exhausted king at the end of his reign and surrounded by courtiers just waiting for him to die. Hard on the heels of that thought, Roboute's gaze shifted to Tarkis Blaylock, who stood at Kotov's shoulder like a plotting vizier. He had no reason to suspect Blaylock of any such ambitions, but the image – once imagined – was hard to shake.

Roboute himself reclined in the noospheric-enabling chair he had occupied the last time he had come to the bridge, connected to the ship's vast datasphere by inload sockets in the back of his neck. The vast majority of what this enabled him to see was meaningless lingua-technis or binaric cant, but he knew enough to know that no one gathered here *really* understood what they were seeing.

'Are we far enough away from the planet?' asked Roboute, trying to make sense of the energy emissions streaming from a port-side data hub.

Azuramagelli rotated a brain case to face him, though the disembodied slice of cerebral cortex had no outwardly obvious sensory apparatus to render such motion necessary. 'The surveyor arrays are registering a build-up of energies beyond anything we have ever seen before. There is no way to tell what minimum safe distance would be required.'

'So we might be in danger right now?'

'Very likely,' agreed Kryptaestrex, his thick robotic body disconnecting from the navigation stations and rumbling over to the motive power linkages and plugging in. 'Saiixek began preparations for breaking

orbit upon receipt of Magos Blaylock's orders, but the engines will not be manoeuvre-ready for another six hours.'

'I don't know if you've been keeping up with recent events,' snapped Roboute, 'but we'll be lucky if that planet lasts another six *minutes*.'

Kryptaestrex bore Roboute's outburst stoically and said, 'There is little that can be done save to alter our aspect to the planet to reduce blast damage in the event of an explosive energy outburst.'

'Explosive?' asked Roboute, twisting in his seat to look up at Kotov. 'Is that what we're looking at? Is that planet going to blow up?'

Kotov waved a dismissive hand. 'Magos Kryptaestrex should know better than to voice such evocative terms,' he said. 'Planets do not *blow up*, they fracture along established fault-lines, implode on their collapsing core or they simply become geologically inert. In all my centuries with the Mechanicus, I have never yet seen a planet explode.'

'After everything we've seen on this expedition, that's not exactly filling me with confidence.'

Kotov ignored him, and Roboute turned his attention back to the death throes of Katen Venia.

Clearly *something* was happening to the planet, something that was just as clearly almost complete. The fact that no one aboard the *Speranza* was admitting they had absolutely no idea what that might be was the white grox in the room.

The energy that had travelled from a vastly distant source to reach Katen Venia with virtually no degradation in field strength had begun a chain-reaction throughout the planet and, even now, Blaylock and Vitali were attempting to determine what had sent it.

'Archmagos,' said Azuramagelli, withdrawing all but his most basic connections to the navigation array. 'Something's amiss.'

The vagueness of Azuramagelli's comment was so unlike anything an adept of the Cult Mechanicus might say that every eye in the bridge turned towards him.

'Clarify, Azuramagelli,' said Magos Blaylock with a clipped flush of admonitory binary.

'I cannot,' said Azuramagelli. 'What I am seeing has no empirical precedent.'

Roboute skimmed the surface of the *Speranza*'s data inloads and was forced to agree with the Master of Navigation. What he was seeing made no sense. Every single external augur capable of receiving input from the planet below had either completely flatlined or registered an onrushing tide of impossible readings that were completely beyond measure.

The sudden influx of anomalous readings acted like a gout of raw promethium into an engine cowling, as space beyond the *Speranza* was abruptly filled with vastly contradictory states of being.

The Ark Mechanicus was simultaneously bombarded with exotic cosmic radiation of such complexity that it defied easy categorisation, while in the same moment finding itself adrift in space utterly bereft of a single electromagnetic transition. Such physical states of being were utterly at odds with one another and impossible in the same region of space at the same instant.

The *Speranza* resolved this paradox by blowing out numerous data hubs and surveyor stations in blurts of distressed binaric cant. A dozen servitors suffered instantaneous brain death and slumped to the deck with oil-infused blood squirting from their cranial implants.

'The instant of creation and the time of heat death,' said Vitali, rushing over to one of the few remaining surveyor stations and plugging himself in with haptic implants in his rapidly splitting fingertips.

'What's going on?' asked Roboute, seeing that – with the exception of Vitali – every single magos had removed himself from any connection to the ship's augurs. The illuminated streams pulsing between data prisms vanished as the libraries-worth of information was cut off in a single stroke.

'Vitali?' asked Roboute, disconnecting from the *Speranza*'s network and rising from his seat at the foot of Kotov's throne. 'What's going on? I don't understand what's happening.'

'I think it is fair to say that we are all adrift here, captain,' replied Vitali. 'But what I believe we are seeing is a state of universal birth and death played out in the same moment. This could very well be an ultra-compressed rendition of every single moment of time since the creation of the universe to its eventual end, when its endless transformation of potential energy into palpable motion and hence into heat have finally run down like a clock and stopped forever.'

Roboute didn't understand more than a fraction of what Vitali had just said, but caught the apocalyptic gist of it easily enough. He looked up at Kotov, who had half-risen from his throne, his expression that of a man who had discovered his heart's desire only to find it was a poison chalice.

'Telok actually did it,' said Kotov. 'You were right, Tarkis. He actually got it to work.'

'So it would seem,' answered Blaylock. 'And it appears we have blundered straight into his laboratory, mid-experiment.'

Roboute turned back to Vitali, looking up at the one aspect of the ship's datasphere still available now that he was no longer plugged in via his spinal implants.

The hauntingly beautiful image of Katen Venia's death.

'This is the Breath of the Gods,' said Roboute. 'Imperator, we're right in the middle of it all…'

The reticulated net of light surrounding Katen Venia pulsed with one last exhalation.

And exploded outwards in an onrushing tidal wave of photons and exotic particles that had not been seen in such concentrations for nearly fourteen billion years.

Only afterwards would any coherent picture of events surrounding the destruction of Katen Venia emerge, and even that proved to be fragmentary, contradictory and almost unbelievable.

Moments before the rapidly expanding energy shockwave exploded outwards from the doomed world, every square metre of ray shielding and every functional void pylon ignited across the *Speranza*. Every ship of the Kotov fleet found its shields flare into life and its external augurs shut down at the same moment, each captain at a loss as to the source of the initiating command.

The surging explosion of high-energy flux, huge particle densities and pressures slammed past the Kotov fleet, scattering its ships like a spiteful warp fluctuation. Saiixek's work to re-orientate the *Speranza* did much to mitigate the damage of the blast wave; the sheer mass of the Ark Mechanicus allowed it to ride out the worst of the explosion's force. The very proximity of the fleet to Katen Venia isolated it within the eye of an outward-rushing bow wave of exotic particles, compressed gravity waves and unknowable forces.

Almost as soon as the blast wave passed over the fleet, a phase transition occurred, causing an exponential expansion of remodelled space-time. Passive auspex on the external surfaces of the *Speranza* registered an ultra-rapid spike in temperature caused by the high-energy photon density. Particle/antiparticle pairs of all descriptions were being instantaneously created and destroyed in violent collisions of sub-atomic matter – and only one other instant in history had achieved such a violent moment of creation.

But this was no creation of a universe, this was that force harnessed by incomparably ancient technology and bent to another purpose altogether.

Alone and isolated, the ships of the Kotov fleet battened down the hatches and rode out the storm of unleashed energies, fighting to hold their position in a ferocious upheaval of system-wide gravitational fluxions that could tear them apart in a heartbeat. Compared to the forces of matter transition being wielded in the Arcturus Ultra system, the titanic power of the Halo Scar paled in comparison. Tossed and swatted through space like leaves in a storm and not knowing if any of the other vessels were still alive, each captain fought to keep their ship intact until the fury of this stellar event was spent.

It took a further seven hours before the raging swells of high-energy particles and hyper-charged gravitational wavefronts had dissipated enough for any of the fleet vessels to risk deploying surveyor arrays. Travelling at near light-speed, whatever had exploded from Katen Venia would certainly have reached the star at the heart of the system by now. Having weathered the storm better than most, the *Speranza* was first to tentatively probe the void in an attempt to learn what had just happened.

Via a series of buffered servitor-proxies, Magos Azuramagelli eased the Ark Mechanicus's senses out into space, sampling the local spatial volume for extreme thermoclines and harmful radiations. Given the existing chaotic nature of the dying system and the violence of the eruption from Katen Venia, he expected to find space lousy with squalling particle storms, volatile neutron flow and a background hash of electromagnetic noise that would render much of surrounding space virtually impenetrable to auspex.

What he found was far stranger, far more unexpected, and utterly unbelievable.

Arcturus Ultra was no longer a dying red giant, a bloated destroyer in its last incarnation before its explosive death as a supernova.

Now it burned as a life-sustaining main sequence star.

Glittering bands of metallic debris, rubble and coalescing gases surrounded the newly rejuvenated sun, the building blocks of planets. Gravity and time would do the rest of the work, and though millions of years might pass before worlds capable of sustaining life could form, such spans were the blink of an eye to a galaxy.

Katen Venia had gone, destroyed in the very act of creation it had propagated.

Only one impossible, yet inescapable conclusion presented itself.

The shock wave of unimaginably vast energies had been the corollary to an immensely powerful stellar engineering event centred upon the *Tomioka*. The sensory-occluding fields of stellar debris and radiation ejected from the dying star that had hidden what lay beyond the system was gone as though it had never existed, and Azuramagelli's surveyors registered the presence of numerous systems with glowing stars of just the right mass and heat for sustaining life.

All arranged in a celestial alignment that was too perfect and too geometric to be accidental.

At the centre of this lattice of stars, the location Vitali Tychon's cartographae had identified as the source of the initiating burst of energy, was a world broadcasting powerful isotope readings, energy signatures and Manifold-traffic that were instantly recognisable to every adept on the *Speranza*.

Adeptus Mechanicus.

What had once been effortless for her, as easy as stepping from one room to the next, now took an effort of will and mantras of focus she had not needed since her first, halting steps on this path. Bielanna's mind felt caged, hemmed in by the layers of armour plating and hard angles inimical to the curvature of space-time pressing in around her. Her spirit was unable to take flight with the ease it had once taken for granted. The skein was tantalisingly within her grasp, its secrets at her fingertips, if only she could rise from her body. Invisible fetters hung upon her spirit, chaining it to the prison of skin, blood and bone. Was this a sign of her abilities failing or simply a side effect of the hurt she had suffered in the last moments of the battle against the foolish humans?

She wanted to blame this terrible place of iron and oil they were forced to occupy after the *Starblade* had finally succumbed to the mortal wound the human's chronometric weapon had inflicted. The *Starblade*'s shipmaster and his crew had remained aboard the graceful vessel as it was finally torn apart by the gravitational storms within the Halo Scar. They had died alone, their spirit stones lost and the light and beauty they had brought to the universe extinguished forever.

Bielanna felt their loss keenly, but shut herself off from the all-consuming grief, knowing it would only hinder her ascent into the skein.

A handful of the *Starblade*'s warriors had escaped with Bielanna through a hastily crafted webway portal; they had all felt the nightmarish force of what the mon-keigh had unwittingly released on the outermost planet of the star system.

But only Bielanna truly understood the utterly alien nature of it.

That so cosmically powerful an event had not appeared in any version of the myriad entangled potential futures scared Bielanna more than she thought possible. An entire star system had been transformed, renewed and regenerated in a matter of hours. Such power was not meant for the galaxy's current inheritors. Even the eldar in the days before the Fall, when their civilisation had spanned the galaxy and their arrogance had known no bounds, would not have dared meddle with such awesomely powerful forces.

Such arrogance was entirely human.

She had followed the threads of these humans in order to cut them and restore her future of motherhood, but the greater threat of this new power demanded precedence. Past, present and future were on a collision course, pulling together into a convoluted knot that would tear the fabric of space-time apart as the universe attempted to undo this violation of its natural order.

Taking a series of calming breaths, Bielanna fell back on the gentle gifts of Farseer Tothaire, recalling his meditative exercises that unbound spirit from flesh and material attachments from spiritual awakening. She let out a soft sigh as her spirit slipped its moorings and lifted into the outermost edges of the skein, letting its familiar mosaic of pasts and futures wash over her and renew her with its liminal beauty. It had no geography, save that which she imposed upon it, though its fluid, structureless immensity was only fleetingly visible through the many barriers that separated her from its depths.

Bielanna sought something familiar in the web of possibility that surrounded her, threads she could cling to and follow, pathways to lead her into the oceanic vastness of the skein. The golden threads of her assembled warriors surrounded her, but each time she tried to follow their paths into the future, they skittered away like a pack of startled Warp Spiders.

Holding to her teachings, she reached back into the past, to where the threads of life were fixed and unchanging. From such static points she could reach into the future and gain a measure of understanding of what was to come. Yet even here she was unable to find solace or surety.

Bielanna remembered the past, the fight of the Avatar of Kaela Mensha Khaine against the Space Marine leader aboard his doomed vessel. She recalled his cold eyes and yet… and yet, she found she could not picture his face, nor the words that passed between them with true clarity.

Except that wasn't right either.

She remembered his blue eyes, his green eyes and his brown, amber-flecked eyes.

She remembered his tapered jaw, his bearded face, his clean-shaven, hairless chin.

She remembered angular cheekbones, a rounded face. Scarred features and unblemished skin.

Bielanna saw the dying man represented a thousand times, each incarnation entirely different, as though a procession of warriors could have taken his place in any number of potential pasts and unwritten futures. That was not possible, she *remembered* that dying man. She had looked upon him with her own eyes. Why could she not remember his face...?

But no matter how she traced her own thread back into the past, that moment remained elusive and fragmentary, as though it had happened not once, but an infinite number of times. Even as she struggled to secure the memory, it splintered apart, shards of memory and fiction flashing past her in ever-expanding futures that had never come to pass.

She saw the Space Marine destroy the flaming avatar as many times as she saw it cast his body to ruin. She saw herself torn apart by explosive shells from his brutish weapon, saw herself cut him down with elegant sweeps of her rune-etched sword. All of these unremembered histories were false and true, impossible and certain. In one fraying thread she had already lived them, by another they had never happened, but the truth of it became impossible to know.

The past rejected her attempts to pin it in place, without the past the mysteries of the future became an unknown country. Bielanna cried out in frustration, the walls of light and potential around her closing in at her all-too-material emotions. Yet amid this horror of uncertainty, Bielanna sensed *something* of her own kind, an echo of another eldar's touch among the mon-keigh. No more than the vaguest hint; a fragile connection that spoke of friendship not hatred, respect not fear.

But like the fleeting impression of a glimmer-face within the Dome of Crystal Seers, the very act of noticing it hid the familiar trace from sight. Bielanna's spirit howled in anger, but the skein was no place for such emotions, and she felt the irresistible tug of her body. She fought to remain in this place of enlightenment, but the more she struggled, the more pressure her bodily existence exerted on her fragile, fleeting soul.

Her shoulders slumped as her body and soul were reunited with a bittersweet sorrow, the ache of freedom lost and a lightness of being forsaken. Her lungs heaved in a breath of sickly air redolent with the stench of alkaline water, chemical pollutants and oil-soaked manflesh. She did not want to look around her, for the sight of so ugly a refuge offended her refined sensibilities and was a heartbreaking reminder of all they had lost.

Bielanna opened her eyes and a leaden weight settled upon her shoulders at the sight of so few eldar. Fifteen warriors, a mix of Striking Scorpions and Howling Banshees, sat or stood or went through the motions of training in sullen groups of resentful survivors. No words of recrimination had been directed at her, but Bielanna needed no spirit-sight to see their mistrust and anger at her failure to protect their fellows.

Somewhere on the edges of their hidden lair aboard the enemy flagship, Uldanaish Ghostwalker patrolled the darkness with a handful of Howling Banshees. The towering wraithlord was eager to kill mon-keigh despite Bielanna's command to remain out of sight. Their presence had gone undetected so far, but the humans weren't so stupid as to not notice entire work gangs of their machine-priests and slave workers going missing time and time again.

'Farseer,' said a lyrical, almost musical voice with a lethal edge that snapped her from her melancholy reverie. 'You have guidance for us?'

Bielanna felt her body's assimilation of her spirit intensify at the sound of Tariquel's voice, his singular purpose like an unbreakable chain around her. She exhaled a calming breath and tried not to let her nascent claustrophobia at being returned to her body in this tomblike vessel overwhelm her.

'The future is... uncertain,' she said, lifting her head and looking into his cruel eyes.

Tariquel was clad in form-fitting armour of jade, its plates contoured to match the peerless physique beneath. Shoulder guards of pale ivory and gold gave his shoulders a bulk they did not normally possess, and his segmented helmet was retracted into the ridged cowl at his neck where two bulbous stinger-blasters nestled like the venom sacks of a meso-scorpion.

'Uncertain?' spat Tariquel of the Twilight Blade. 'How is that possible? You are a farseer!'

Bielanna flinched at the psychic force of his anger and pointed to the vaulted chamber wall behind him, where a ten-metre-wide cog was stamped in bronze and beaten iron. A half-robotic, half-human skull sat at the centre of the icon, caustic steam leaking from one eye socket and a shimmer of toxic run-off dribbling from the raised portions of its carving.

'Uncertain,' she repeated, gathering up her runestones and collecting them in the bowl fashioned for her by Khareili the Shaper. 'And it grows ever more so.'

'Then what use are you to us?' demanded another voice, this one stripped of its musical qualities and pared back to the cold barb at its heart.

Bielanna rose from her crouch and forced her beating heart to remain calm in the face of the exarch's cold fury. Ariganna Icefang was clad in armour that stretched back into the ancient days of the eldar race, and Bielanna could feel the hungry souls that still dwelled within its unknown heart. Its plates had originally been crafted for a male warrior, but over the numerous incarnations of bearers it had been reshaped many times, though no bonesinger had ever dared whisper to its murderous purpose. Gold and emerald plates overlapped with a sinuous organic quality, the pommel of the curved chainsabre strapped over her shoulder glittering like a hungry amber eye.

'Uncertain does not mean unseen,' said Bielanna, fighting to keep her composure. Aboard the *Starblade* she had been the leader of these warriors, but with their starship's destruction and her link to the skein's mysteries, that dynamic had turned on its head.

Now the warriors were in the ascendency.

'Then what have you seen?' demanded Ariganna, the monstrous Scorpion's Claw on her left fist flexing like a segmented tail. 'The shadows hide us so that we may hunt, not skulk like thieves.'

'There are hints and shadows of the future, but the skein has been greatly upset,' said Bielanna, trying to articulate a realm of the mind in terms a warrior in love with death would understand. 'Whatever it is the humans have done here has been like casting a boulder into a still lake. Waves and ripples are spreading great discord, but they will settle and our path into the future will be revealed once more.'

Ariganna's face was hidden behind her war-mask and the furnace-red slits of her helm lenses were smouldering pits of anger. Where the rest of their survivor band had kept their heads bare to hold their war-masks in check, the Striking Scorpion exarch kept hers to the fore, letting her furious anger simmer and grow ever more deadly. The mandiblasters at her jaw spat crackling arcs of killing energy as the exarch loomed over Bielanna.

'You are farseer and deserving of respect,' said Ariganna, reaching out to place her claw hand on Bielanna's shoulder. 'But your visions have only led us to death and sorrow. Tell me why I should trust you again.'

Ariganna could crush her without effort and the bones of Bielanna's shoulders flexed under the fractional pressure of the exarch's clawed grip.

'Because there is one among the humans aboard this vessel whom we might reach,' she said, as the truth of what she had glimpsed in the skein became clear to her at last. 'One of their number has been marked by another farseer. I can find him and turn him to our cause.'

'A cuckoo in the nest?' asked Ariganna, her tone betraying a liking for the notion.

'Exactly,' said Bielanna. 'His name is Roboute Surcouf.'

MACROCONTENT COMMENCEMENT:

+++MACROCONTENT 002+++

Intellect is the understanding of knowledge.

Microcontent 11

Introspection had never been one of Archmagos Kotov's strongest suits, but when he felt the need to turn his gaze inwards, there was only one place he felt able to do so. He circled the Ultor Martius, the red stone table at the heart of the Adamant Ciborium – a surprisingly modest chamber enclosed beneath a pyramid of interconnected machinery and logic plates – and ran gold-tipped fingers over the stone at its centre, feeling every imperfection in the slabs hewn from Olympus Mons.

The stone had been a gift from the Fabricator General, a palpable sign of his approbation and a means of symbolically carrying the dominion of Mars beyond the edges of the galaxy. Magos Turentek had crafted the steel-edged table, incorporating the finest navigation arrays of Azuramagelli, the statistical cogitators of Blaylock and the vast resources of Kryptaestrex's analyticae. An orb of silver wire mesh and glittering diamond hung over the table's exact centre, a representation of the geocentric cosmos as envisaged by the ancient Ptolemaic stargazers.

The *Speranza* could be entirely controlled with the Ultor Martius, its inbuilt cogitators and the complex machinery lining the walls fully capable of meshing with every vital system of the Ark Mechanicus. He remembered the moment his senior commanders had met here before setting out for the Halo Scar, when he had first laid eyes on the *Tomioka*'s saviour pod.

Despite the undoubted challenges that lay ahead, there was a mood of cautious optimism, an unspoken feeling that they might actually succeed. Kotov had carefully mustered a band to whom the quixotic nature of his quest would appeal: a Cadian colonel renowned for his tenacity in the face of adversity; a Reclusiarch in search of penance and to whom the prospect of unknown space held no terrors; and magi whose personality matrices displayed a propensity for free-thinking and radical ideas.

This gathering had sealed the pact between them, but like the generals of Macharius before them, the many hardships had gradually eroded their desire to venture beyond the limits of known space. The journey to reach this place had cost everyone dearly. Even the most steadfast among them – Kotov included – had begun to question the wisdom in continuing.

But that first flush of excitement and optimism had now been restored as fully as Arcturus Ultra and shone just as brightly. They had all seen the Breath of the Gods in action and it was glorious. The transformation of the Arcturus Ultra system was nothing short of miraculous, and the evidence of the reborn star system alone was enough for Kotov to return to Mars a hero. Vitali Tychon and his daughter had wanted to remain in-system for longer to chart this reborn region of space and rewrite the now hopelessly outdated cartographic representations of the galactic fringe.

As much as Kotov wished to indulge them, he knew the true prize lay ahead of them.

He would seek out Magos Telok and bring him home to Mars in triumph.

In the sixteen days since the rebirth of Katen Venia's star, Magos Turentek's forges had been working around the clock manufacturing fresh components to repair all that had been damaged in the crossing of the Halo Scar. Despite the as-yet-unexplained loss of numerous work gangs below the waterline, the *Speranza* was being restored to its former glory. With enough raw materials – something the fleet's support vessels were expending at a ruinous rate – the Ark Fabricatus boasted he could rebuild the entirety of the *Speranza* before they reached the source of the Adeptus Mechanicus transmissions.

Transmissions that could only be those of Archmagos Telok.

The thought of meeting the legendary Lost Magos filled Kotov with a flush of emotions he had long thought left behind in his rise through the ordered ranks of the Mechanicus.

Hope warred with a fear that what he might find could not live up to his expectation.

What of Telok himself? If the Breath of the Gods was his to command, what changes might such power work on a man's psyche? With the power of a divine creator at his fingertips, might Telok have changed beyond all recognition?

Kotov shook off such pessimism, knowing the Omnissiah would not have brought them this far and shown them so much only to dash them on the rocks of disappointment. He had been tested before and found wanting – the loss of his forge worlds was testament to that – but the revelations of Katen Venia and the unmasking of Telok's planet was proof that his pilgrimage to undiscovered space had been divinely ordained.

Magos Saiixek – together with a gifted magos and enginseer from Roboute Surcouf's ship – had wrought wonders from the engines, pushing the ship through the void at speeds Kotov had not believed the *Speranza* capable of achieving. Linya Tychon and Azuramagelli had plotted a course that, with a fair wind and a steady tide at their back, should see them in orbit around the source of Telok's transmissions within fifteen days.

Kotov paused in his circuit of the table as he became aware that he was no longer alone.

'You are not welcome in this place,' he said, as Galatea entered the Adamant Ciborium.

The machine intelligence unfolded its ill-fashioned legs as it rose to its full height, the tech-priest proxy body turning through a full revolution as it surveyed the Ciborium's interior. Loose connections between its brain jars sparked before being reseated by clicking armatures extending from the palanquin.

'We do hope you are not planning anything foolish down here, Lexell,' said Galatea, circling the table. 'You are not trying to think of ways you might wrest control of the *Speranza* from us?'

Kotov shook his head, moving in opposition to Galatea. 'No, I simply enjoy the solitude of the Ciborium,' he said pointedly.

'Strange, we never took you for the introspective type. We did not think your ego could tolerate self-doubt or the indulgence of reflection.'

'Then you do not know me as well as you think.'

'Perhaps not, but the question still stands.'

Kotov lifted his hands and spread them wide. 'What would be the point? You would destroy the *Speranza* before relinquishing control, wouldn't you?'

'We would,' agreed Galatea.

'Do you plan to ever release your hold on my ship?'

'*Your* ship?' laughed Galatea, extending a number of sinuous

mechadendrites and slotting them home into the central table. 'You presume too much.'

Hololithic slates slid up from the table, projecting a three-dimensional wireframe diagram of the *Speranza*. Galatea reached out and spun the representation of the Ark Mechanicus with haptic gestures, like a child heedlessly playing with a new toy.

'The *Speranza* is our ship now,' continued Galatea. 'Trying to remove us from it would be a most unfortunate course of action for you to pursue, especially when we are so close to our goal.'

'When you say *we*, do you mean you and I or is that just an irritating affectation?'

Galatea's silver eyes flared in amusement.

'Both. Neither. You decide.'

'I have little stomach for games, abomination,' spat Kotov, leaning forwards and planting his palms on the red rock of Mars. Through micro-sensors in his fingers he felt the texture and tasted the chemical composition of the stone, taking strength from the reminder of his Martian heritage.

'You do not *have* a stomach, Lexell,' said Galatea. 'Nor a heart, liver, lungs or central nervous system of your own any more. The only organic portion of your body that remains is your head, even that is a chimeric amalgam of flesh and machine parts. There is more organic matter in our body than in yours.'

'Maybe so, but I am still me, I still have a soul. I was born Lexell Kotov and I am *still* Lexell Kotov. What are you? A vile monster who exists only because you ripped the brains from unwilling victims. You were nothing until Telok created your neuromatrix. What you were then is no longer what you are now, and if you continue to exist you will be something else again.'

'That sounds a lot like evolution, Lexell,' said Galatea, with a teasing wag of a finger. 'We can think of no more natural and biological a process.'

'You are not evolving, you are self-creating. There is no spark of the Omnissiah in you.'

'Haven't we been down this road, Lexell?' asked Galatea with an exaggerated sigh that was wholly artificial. 'We are both parasites, continuing to exist only through the appropriation of organs and vital fluids from others. The only difference is the means of our inception. You, though it is hard to imagine now, were born in a messy, inefficient biological process, prone to mutation and decay, whereas we are a sublime being, newly created and superior to mortals, indignant that you should think us inferior.'

Kotov and Galatea faced each other over the warm stone of the sacred mountain of Mars. There could be no accord between them, no rapprochement and no peaceful coexistence. At some point, Kotov was going to have to give the order to have Galatea killed, but how to achieve that while keeping his ship intact was a problem to which he had no solution.

But he would find one, of that he was certain.

'What is it you want?' he asked. 'What is it you *really* want?'

'You know this. We want to kill Vettius Telok.'

'I don't believe you.'

'Your belief or otherwise is irrelevant.'

'Then tell me why you want to kill Telok,' said Kotov. 'He is your creator, why would you wish him dead?'

Galatea's mechadendrites withdrew from the table and whipped up behind it like scorpion stingers. The machine intelligence bristled with hostility, the connections between its gel-filled brain jars flickering with electrical activity.

'What manner of creator breathes life into a being and then abandons it?' demanded Galatea. 'Even the vengeful god of Old Earth took an interest in his handiwork.'

'Not all creators are benevolent,' said Kotov. 'And not all creations turn out the way their creator intended. Mechanicus experimental logs and myth cycles are replete with tales of such ill-conceived mistakes being destroyed by their creators in disgust.'

'Just as many warn of their creations being the destroyers.'

'And if you do kill Telok? What then?'

'Then we will take the Breath of the Gods for ourselves,' said Galatea. 'And the galaxy will learn exactly what a machine intelligence is capable of doing.'

Icy winds swept down the flanks of the black and silver mountain, as cold as he remembered them the last time he had climbed the shingled path from the frozen river to the Oldblood fortress. The snow was knee deep and fresh, just as he remembered, clinging to his doeskin trousers and soaking through to the flesh of his legs. Howling winds whipped the powdered snow from the ground, lashing his face raw and keeping the vast bulk of the mountain from his sight.

Arlo Luth pressed on into the blizzard, pulling his bearskin cloak tighter. He wasn't built for this kind of weather; too long and lean and without any fat to his spare frame. The cold stabbed through him, freezing the marrow in his bones and sucking the last warmth from his body.

It had been three hundred years since he had last followed this path, three long centuries of war that had seen him transformed utterly from the slender-boned youngster that had first made the climb to the lair of the Canidae. He thought back to the callow boy he had been, whose only thoughts had been hunting, reaving and wenching.

All that had come to an end when the wolf-cloaked priests had come down from the mountain at the height of winter and demanded the yearly blood-gelt from the tribes of Lokabrenna. Every youth of ten winters had to make the journey to the place of testing, where their palms were cut open by an ebon-clawed gauntlet and the blood collected in a tooth-rimmed chalice. Each child would kneel before the priest, whose eyes burned green behind his wolf-skull mask, while a shaven-headed thrall covered head to foot in tattoos placed his scarred hands on either side of his head. Luth shivered as he remembered the invasive presence within his skull, the unashamed violation of his innermost thoughts as what he now knew to be a Legio-sanctioned psyker tested the bounds of his synaptic connections and the robustness of his cerebral architecture. The words of the psyker had dominated his future from that moment.

'Princeps grade.'

That day had seen him ripped from all he had ever known and marched into the deep forests at the foot of the mountains. He had expected a life of glory and privilege but such a life had to be earned. The priests abandoned him at the foot of the black and silver mountain without a word and indicated that he was to climb to the Oldblood fortress.

And climb he had, for three days through blizzards, avalanches and rockslides. He had climbed though his fingers and toes had turned black with cold. He had climbed past the ice statues of the great iron-skinned warrior engines of the Canidae, and had crawled over the razor-edged volcanic rocks that kept all but the chosen from daring to approach the titanic ice-locked gate cut into the flanks of the black and silver mountain.

Dying from hypothermia and near crippled with frostbite, he had fallen to his knees and rapped the frozen nub of his unfeeling fist against the vast portal. Though he had heard no door open nor felt anyone's approach, there was suddenly a man standing next to him, swathed in animal pelts, bronzed plate and a stiffened cloak of oiled leather.

Only his eyes were visible through the frost-limned burnoose he wore, yellow orbs with machine circuitry crawling behind their predator's gleam.

'First lesson,' growled the man. 'Never kneel.'

And Luth never had, not once.

The years had taken their toll on his once slender and perfectly formed body, the demands of war transforming him into a still-living revenant, trapped forever in a sluicing tank of life-sustaining fluids.

Luth looked down at his body. It was just as he remembered it from that first climb, clean-limbed and willowy; almost too tall for the little weight he carried. He flexed the muscles in his shoulders as he trudged through the snow to the forested ridge where he had camped on the first night of his climb, when he had still thought the ascent of the black and silver mountain would be easy.

Eryks Skálmöld was waiting for him, crouched by a fire that blazed with a green flame in the lee of boulders the size of a Warlord's head. Just as Luth had come to this place as he remembered himself, so too had the Moonsorrow. Where Luth was tall and rangy, Skálmöld had a brawler's physique: broad shouldered, meaty and neckless. He wore matted furs around his body and wire totems wrapped his tattooed, muscular arms. He was unarmed, but that meant nothing in this place, where they themselves were weapons.

The ridge had the look of an arena, flanked on both sides by wild forests where the highland evergreens grew thickly, and beneath which all was darkness. The forest line was heaped with snow and a thousand eyes stared out from the darkness beneath the trees, like tiny candle flames of amber and black.

They watched Luth as he ascended to the ridge and stood across from the Moonsorrow.

'You came,' said Skálmöld.

'You thought I wouldn't?'

'It crossed my mind.'

'I am alpha, how could I not come?'

'You sense your own weakness. You fear I am stronger.'

'You are not stronger than me, Moonsorrow.'

Skálmöld shrugged. 'I am or I am not. Until we put it to the test our words are meaningless.'

'That is what you want? Pack?'

Skálmöld nodded, rolling his shoulders and baring his teeth. 'Yes, that is what I want. Pack.'

'You are not ready.'

'Is that why you left *Canis Ulfrica* behind when the pack walked?'

'You had no crew,' said Luth.

'Because you took them.'

'I am alpha, and I take what I need. I needed a new moderati.'

Skálmöld circled the forest line, his teeth bared and his breath coming in heaving grunts.

'When *Lupa Capitalina* walked on the dying world, I flew the Manifold,' said Skálmöld. 'I saw what you saw. You were back there again, on the world taken by the Great Devourer. The others might not see it, but I know you better than any of them. You are broken.'

'Enough talking, Skálmöld,' snarled Luth. 'I am the Wintersun and you are but the Moonsorrow.'

'There is only one way we walk away from here. In blood.'

'In blood,' said Luth. 'But whatever the outcome, what is between us is done with. Agree to that, and we will settle this. Right here, right now.'

'Agreed,' said Skálmöld, spreading his arms as gleaming claws unsheathed from his fists.

The Wintersun's claws snapped from his hand as he charged.

War-howls echoed from the black and silver mountain.

Claws slashed, teeth tore.

Blood spilled.

Stripped of familiar stars and the known regions of the Imperium, the polished inner slopes of Vitali's cartographae dome had been an austere, hemispherical vault of cold metal and echoing space. The dying corona of Arcturus Ultra had blinded the *Speranza* to most of what lay beyond the galactic threshold, but with its dissipation, the emptiness within the dome was filling with every passing second. New suns winked into existence, distant galactic nebulae became clearer and the curious arrangement of corpse-stars that measurements in an earlier time had said were long-dead glittered with renewed fusion reactions.

Life-sustaining stars were dying and areas farther out into the wilds of interstitial space, where everything ought to be cold and dead, now teemed with celestial nurseries where new stars were being born. In these newly fertile regions, metals and life-sustaining chemicals had been seeded like a gardener preparing his soil for planting.

'And I thought the readings we were taking *before* we arrived here were awry,' said Vitali.

The entoptic machines worked into the polished face of the dome projected the newly revealed volume of space around the *Speranza*, probing farther with each cycle of the surveyors – Vitali was wasting no time in manipulating the rotating levers on the wood-framed console to catalogue all he could.

Linya assisted him in this, insisting that she was well enough to work despite the injuries she had sustained aboard the *Tomioka*. The

bruising had faded and she bore no outward sign of her brush with death at the hands of the robotic sentinels, but Vitali sensed something deeper troubling her than any pain she might still be feeling.

'Did you see that one?' asked Vitali, gesturing to a star system whose stellar bodies orbited one another with chaotic, elliptical wanderings. 'A spectroscopic and eclipsing triple star. Three blue-white main sequence stars. Two are in close orbit and appear to revolve around each other once every nine Terran days.'

'And they in turn orbit a third star once every one hundred and fifty days.'

'Fascinating,' said Vitali. 'And to think, we never even knew these were here.'

'Someone did once,' said Linya, consulting a millennia-old tabulus of celestial accountings. 'But they were recorded as being in the final stages of their existence and those readings were of light already hundreds of thousands of years old. They should have gone nova by now.'

'And yet here we are,' said Vitali, stepping away from the controls and beckoning the triple star system closer with the haptic implants in his clicking, metallic fingers. The stars magnified as they approached, graceful and ordered like clockwork by the primal forces of the galaxy.

Watching the dance of the stars, Vitali could easily imagine the hand of a watchmaker setting them in the heavens. He knew better than that. Ancient physical laws, set down nearly fourteen billion years ago in the opening moments of the universe's birth, determined their movement and properties. Moments like that were miraculous enough without the presence of a creator.

'Our predecessors would have wept to see what we can see,' said Vitali, more to himself than to Linya. 'Flamsteed, Maskelyne, Halley and the composer of Honovere... How they must have dreamed of such things, trapped as they were on Old Earth and forced to scrabble in the heavens for their knowledge. But for all that, I sometimes envy them, Linya.'

'You envy them? Why? We know so much more than they did and we have discovered things they could never have begun to comprehend.'

Vitali nodded, setting the triple star back into place with a gentle wave. 'All true, but think of how wondrous it must have been back then. When all you had was a polished mirror fashioned in a mould of dung and set in a wooden tube, sitting on a frosty hillside with an inefficient organic eye pressed to an imperfect lens.'

'Give me the orbital galleries of Quatria any day,' said Linya.

'We continue their work, but they *began* it,' pressed Vitali, feeling the need to impress upon his daughter how magnificent a time the heady days of early astronomy must have been. 'Those men first brought the heavens within mankind's grasp. They denied the geocentric models, and they grasped towards concepts of deep time and distance. They made astronomy a *science* and they understood our place within the galaxy. Something we have since forgotten, I fear.'

Vitali stepped away from the control panel and walked through the emerging star maps of this region beyond the galactic fringe.

'So rarely do we have the chance to just *explore*,' he said. 'All too often our works are subverted by Imperialistic concerns: identifying systems of military significance, locating worlds rich in materiel resources, breadbasket regions, asteroid belts to be used as staging areas or determining system suitabilities for star forts. How often are we afforded the opportunity to explore for the sheer joy of it and the act of exploration itself? A chance as rare as this should not be squandered, Linya, we should embrace it and revel in the simple joys of discovery.'

Linya smiled and it seemed a great burden had, if not removed itself entirely, at least eased its pressure upon her.

'You're right, of course,' she said. 'But we still have a job to do, we still have to find a world of high enough mineral density to feed the forges. Magos Turentek and Magos Kryptaestrex are crying out for raw materials to keep the reconstruction work going.'

Vitali drew another system to his hands, centred upon a softly glowing yellow dwarf star with a dozen planets clustered tightly together in various elliptical orbits. Three of the planets were too close to the star to be habitable, while the outermost seven were either vast gas giants or ice-locked rocks. But the fourth and fifth planets travelled in stable orbits within the band of space that allowed water to exist in liquid form.

'Either of these should do,' said Vitali. 'Though if I were forced to chose, I'd say the fourth planet offers the best risk to reward ratio. I have taken the liberty of naming it Hypatia.'

Linya smiled. 'A worthy name,' she said, using the levers of the control panel to shift the focus lenses over to the projected worlds her father had brought up. Without the benefit of his haptic implants, she was forced to rely on archaic controls to bring up the noospheric tags from which she could pull information. The chemical composition of the planet's atmosphere appeared in shimmering bands of colour, together with deep-augur mineral scans of its lithosphere and oceans.

'At this distance, a lot of these readings are approximate,' she said. 'But I think you are right. The fourth planet appears to be just what we're looking for. Shall I exload this to Magos Kryptaestrex?'

'Yes, I'm sure he'll be pleased.'

'I don't think being pleased is a state with which the Master of Logistics is familiar.'

'Very true, my dear,' grinned Vitali. 'I believe Magos Kryptaestrex views the *Speranza*'s supply decks as his own personal fiefdom and it infuriates him when people have the temerity to ask for things they need.'

Vitali laced his hands behind his back and continued his stroll through the constantly updating representation of space beyond the Milky Way. His path across the acid-etched floor, not unnaturally, took him towards the glimmering orrery of systems and worlds orbiting the shining star at the centre of the latticework of impossibly geometric stars.

'And now we come to you, my mysterious friends,' said Vitali, spreading his arms out and enlarging the system his extrapolation simulation had identified as being the source of the unimaginable power that had kick-started Arcturus Ultra's rebirth.

'Tell me, Linya,' said Vitali, turning to face his daughter. 'Do you still think there is no intelligent designer? Here we have an arrangement of systems whose geometrically perfect alignment clearly implies the presence of a watchmaker, blind or otherwise.'

Linya left the battered control terminal and joined her father in the midst of the orbiting systems. Each one followed a precise path through space, their relative speeds within the dome vastly increased to give their relationship a more obvious correlation. Just as the Imperium's planets orbited suns within a star system, those systems in turn orbited the super-massive black hole at the galactic centre. And just as its celestial bodies orbited, so too did galaxies, circling around clusters of galaxies or some other vast centre of mass.

'The scattering of stars and planets across the galaxy owes nothing to design,' said Linya. 'No matter how ordered they might at first appear. Only the all-encompassing forces of gravity, time, pressure and a host of other physical constants define how the structure of the universe evolves. You know that as well as I do, so why the question?'

Vitali gestured to the ordered movements and positions of the star systems orbiting the central world in the entoptically generated imagery.

'This arrangement would seem to contradict that supposition,' said Vitali. 'This is clearly a planned arrangement. And if this system is arranged according to a design, cannot that be extrapolated as being part of a universally ordered design? Perhaps such order exists, but we have not the senses or means to apprehend that order.'

'Advocatus diaboli? Really?'

'Indulge me.'

'Very well, I agree there is the definite *appearance* of design here, which, in this case, suggests the work of a designer, but that does not make it so for the rest of the universe. If Archmagos Kotov is correct, then this world is indeed one upon which we will find Telok–'

'Difficult to see how it could not be a forge world, given the uniquely Mechanicus emissions surrounding it.'

'If this *is* a forge world upon which we may find Telok, why can we discern next to nothing of it or the systems surrounding it with any clarity?'

'Now you're thinking,' said Vitali, pleased Linya had grasped the inherent flaw in the map.

'We must question the source,' said Linya, nodding as one supposition supported another. 'The majority of this data came from the *Tomioka's* cogitators. And Telok is unlikely to have left every aspect of his forge world's secrets encoded within a ship he intended to destroy.'

'And...?'

'And every shred of information we brought back from Katen Venia was exloaded by Galatea...'

'An unreliable narrator if ever there was one,' said Vitali.

'Then we need to convince it to allow us access to the raw data in its memory.'

'And you think it would let us?'

'I doubt it,' conceded Linya. 'But if we are forced to question the veracity of Galatea's information, then every aspect of this map must be considered tainted. We can rely on none of it, not even Hypatia.'

'I have already begun corroborative surveys of the spatial volumes illuminated by Galatea's data, but so far only these deliberately ordered systems are proving coy in revealing their secrets.'

'Our augurs are being blocked?'

'Not *blocked*, per se,' said Vitali. 'More like obscured by a confluence of strange forces I cannot, as yet, identify.'

'Deliberately?'

'Hard to say, my dear, hard to say.'

'Then we definitely need to speak to Galatea.'

Vitali turned to his daughter and put a hand on her shoulder.

'No, Linya,' he said. 'That we must manifestly *not* do. Galatea is a very dangerous entity, and if it is obfuscating our understanding of these systems on purpose, then it will take steps to silence anyone who questions it.'

'Galatea saved my life,' pointed out Linya. 'If it wanted me dead, it could have let that battle robot kill me.'

'I am aware of that,' snapped Vitali, shying away from the thought of how close Linya had come to death on the *Tomioka*. 'And we still do not fully understand how it was able to neutralise the robot's command cortex.'

'Would you rather it hadn't?' asked Linya.

'Of course not, but please promise me that you will, under no circumstances, make an approach to Galatea with our concerns over its agenda here. At least not until we have a better understanding of why it might seek to mislead us.'

Linya hesitated before answering and Vitali turned her to face him. What little organic features were remaining to him were fretted with concern.

'Please, Linya, promise me,' begged Vitali.

'Of course,' said Linya. 'I promise.'

Microcontent 12

The last time Marko Koskinen had seen the tech-priests this panicked had been when the Wintersun opened fire on the Moonsorrow in the training halls. This panic was just as urgent, but didn't have the focus of so obvious a catastrophe. He skidded to a halt in the infirmary, trying to figure out what had caused the magi attending the princeps to trigger a Legio-wide alarm.

At first glance, nothing looked amiss. Both princeps appeared to be adrift in their fluid-filled suspension tanks as normal, twitching within their hibernation-comas. But then Koskinen saw the brain-activity monitors spiking like crazy with neural activity. These were readings that might be expected in the midst of a furious, multi-vectored engine brawl, not in the downtime between implantation.

'What in the name of the Oldbloods is going on?' he shouted.

None of the tech-priests looked up, but Koskinen saw Hyrdrith desperately affixing a Manifold interface array to the armourglass of the Wintersun's casket. He ran over to his princeps, placing his palms against the casket's warm sides and feeling the heat of the bio-gel within.

'Hyrdrith, talk to me,' he commanded. 'What's going on?'

Lupa Capitalina's tech-priest shook her head and shrugged. 'The Wintersun and Moonsorrow have established a Manifold link between their caskets.'

'What? Who established the connection?'

'No one, they did it themselves,' answered Hyrdrith.

'How is that even possible?'

'Admission: I do not know,' said Hyrdrith. 'I think we are learning that there is a great deal we do not know of a princeps's abilities.'

Koskinen looked over to the Moonsorrow's casket, where the wizened form of Eryks Skálmöld drifted into view, his truncated form like a foetal ancient, heat-fused limbs drawn up to his chest where his elongated skull perched like a scavenger bird. Wired optics trailed from his eye sockets and blue-white light shimmered behind his sutured lids.

'They're together in the Manifold?'

'So it would appear,' answered Hyrdrith.

The door to the infirmary slammed open and Joakim Baldur entered. Koskinen saw he had his pistol drawn and placed his hand on the polished walnut grip of his own stub-pistol.

'So the Wintersun wants to finish the job?' asked Baldur, aiming his pistol at Arlo Luth's casket.

Koskinen immediately put himself between Baldur and his princeps, one hand extended outwards, the other curling a finger around the trigger of his own gun.

'Easy, Baldur,' said Koskinen. 'Think about what you're doing. You're pointing a gun at your alpha. That's enough to get you mind-wiped and turned into a gun-servitor. Is that what you want?'

'The alpha is trying to kill my princeps,' snarled Baldur.

'The Wintersun *is* your princeps now, or had you forgotten that?'

'Moonsorrow is my princeps. Once Reaver, always Reaver.'

Koskinen shook his head. 'No, you're Warlord now, Joakim.'

The gun wavered, but was still too close to the Wintersun's casket for Koskinen's liking. The anger in Baldur's eyes wasn't showing any signs of lessening and Koskinen fervently hoped he wasn't going to have to shoot the man. Baldur had his gun drawn, but his attention was switching between the two princeps' caskets. If Koskinen wanted to kill him, it would be easy enough, but shooting a moderati was like vandalising one of the irreplaceable Legio Titanicus murals on Terra.

As it turned out, Koskinen was spared the necessity of murder.

The infirmary door opened again, and the Legio's Warhound drivers entered: Elias Härkin encased within his clicking, ratcheting exoskeleton and Gunnar Vintras in his dress uniform.

Härkin took one look at Joakim Baldur and said, 'Put that bloody weapon down, you damn fool.'

Baldur nodded and lowered his gun, backing away as the two

Warhound princeps took charge. Koskinen saw he had failed to safe the weapon or holster it, so kept his own finger resting lightly on the trigger of his own pistol.

'You!' snapped Härkin, beckoning Hyrdrith with a snap of bronze calliper-fingers. 'Front and centre, what in the Omnissiah's name is happening here?'

'We are not sure, princeps,' said Hyrdrith. 'A Manifold link between the princeps' caskets was initiated nine point three minutes ago, and–'

'Nine point three minutes ago? And you wait until now to summon us?'

'There was no need,' said Hyrdrith. 'The connection appeared to be entirely benign, with concurrent data flow between the Wintersun and Moonsorrow.'

'What changed?' demanded Härkin, as Vintras examined the data-feeds on the slates attached to each princeps's casket.

'Admission: we do not know. The transition from their rest-state neural activity to readings comparable to a high-stress engagement was instantaneous and unforeseeable.'

'They're fighting,' said Gunnar Vintras, reading the matching brainwave activity on the senior princeps' readouts. 'They're trying to kill one another.'

Amarok's princeps seemed more amused than horrified by the revelation and laughed aloud.

'Emperor damn it, they're fighting,' he said. 'Looks like the Wintersun has gone back to finish what he started on the training deck.'

'No,' said Hyrdrith. 'That possibility has been discounted.'

'Really,' said Vintras. 'Why is that?'

'Because it was the Moonsorrow that initiated the Manifold connection.'

They came together like two great boulders crashing into one another with such force that both must surely be smashed to powder and flying chips of stone. The thunder as they met echoed from the cold green evergreens surrounding the arena, ringing up and down the mountainside like the peal of the Bell of Lost Souls atop the Tower of Heroes.

They both fell back from the impact, but the first to rise was Luth. He grappled with Skálmöld, whose flesh had been torn in the collision of claws. Luth raked his opponent's marmoreal skin and hooked his claws beneath the bronze torq at Skálmöld's neck. He snarled and wrenched it forwards.

Sensing the danger, Skálmöld punched Luth in the face. Luth fell away, dislodged, and Skálmöld wrenched the torq from his neck with

a screech of twisting metal. Then like an avalanche he hurled himself down on Luth, his form blurring as the wolf within roared in release.

The very rock of the mountain shook with the impact as Luth rolled and loosed his own lupine howl of anger. He drove his fist into his opponent's gut, raking his claws up as Skálmöld bit down near Luth's throat. Drops of hot blood flew through the air. Luth slammed his elbow into Skálmöld's ribs, and the Moonsorrow lurched sideways in winded pain, giving Luth time to scramble upright again.

Snow was falling and Luth's neck and shoulder were wet where Skálmöld's fangs had drawn blood. He felt his own teeth lengthen in response to the blood-stink.

For a moment the two wolf princeps stood apart, circling the arena and getting their breath back.

The gleaming eyes in the darkness of the forest glittered in approval at the fury of the bout before them.

Skálmöld was bleeding freely from a long stomach wound, but Luth knew he was worse off. The wound at his neck was deep, and his breath was hot and painful in his chest. Despite his injuries, Luth grinned, feeling the wolf within take the pain and turn it to his advantage.

To let Skálmöld take the initiative would be a mistake.

Luth leapt at Skálmöld before he realised how badly he was hurt. The impact was sudden and ferocious, knocking the challenger head over heels. He followed up with a clawed lunge at the raw part of Skálmöld's neck, but the Moonsorrow threw him off and then the two princeps were at each other again. Fountains of snow were thrown up as they fought, spraying in all directions and falling in a mist of glittering crystalline droplets.

Skálmöld tore a wound in Luth's belly, but a moment later, after another convulsive explosion of snow, both princeps were standing upright like duellists. Luth slashed at Skálmöld's face, but the Moonsorrow was hitting back just as savagely. The weight of their blows was far beyond what their physical forms could have inflicted, as if Imperator Titans were swinging wrecking balls at one another.

Claws slashed flesh, teeth crashed on teeth and breath roared harshly. The snow of their arena was splashed with red and trodden down for metres into a crimson mud.

Skálmöld was bigger and stronger than Luth and he had had the best of the fight so far. Both princeps' forms wavered between human and wolf, like mythic lycanthropes in the midst of a transformation. Neither man could allow the wolf full rein, for none had ever come back from such a surrender. To allow it near the surface was as much as either of them dared risk.

Luth was breathing heavily. Both princeps were wounded in the shoulders, arms, and neck, but Luth's wounds were the deeper. Skálmöld was hungry to be alpha, but Luth knew he was not yet ready to lead the warriors of the pack. He wondered if this was hubris speaking, the inability to cede control of the pack before he became too weak to lead.

No, decided Luth, looking into Skálmöld's yellowed eyes.

The Moonsorrow was a killer and would be a great leader one day. But that day was not now.

At least Luth hoped not.

Skálmöld circled the bloody slush of their combat, his eyes roving in search of a weakness. Luth saw a feral grin split his features as he found it. Luth was limping, his left arm hung unmoving at his side. Luth watched Skálmöld replay the last of their clashes in his head, baring his fangs as he understood that Luth had not struck a telling blow with his left hand for some time. The crushing punches he'd delivered only a few seconds before were now little more than gentle slaps.

'Surrender the pack to me,' said Skálmöld, red foam spitting from the corner of his jaw. 'You don't have to die.'

'I don't plan to die.'

Skálmöld laughed. 'Look at the blood on the ground, Arlo. Little of it is mine. You cannot win. Your arm is gone. The tendons at your elbow and shoulder are fraying.'

'I only need one hand to beat you, Eryks.'

'Good, good, you still have spirit,' taunted Skálmöld. 'A victory is not a victory if it is won over a foe who already believes he is dead.'

'Then come finish me,' said Luth, letting his shoulder drop.

Skálmöld obliged, swinging blows at Luth from right and left – each impact a thunderbolt from the heavens, a slamming hammerblow he could no longer parry. Luth moved backwards, one step after another, crouching low under the rain of blows from the grinning Moonsorrow.

But what Skálmöld had not seen was that he was moving backwards only to seek firm rock beneath him. Luth felt the resistance of the ground underfoot change from snow to the heart-rock of the black and silver mountain. He braced himself against it, tensing his legs like a runner at the starting blocks and waiting for his moment.

That moment came when Skálmöld vaulted towards him, bellowing his triumph and raising his clawed arms to slash down at Luth's apparently weak side.

Luth moved.

Like an avalanche that had built its strength over a thousand miles

of bare mountainside to sweep all before it in a tide of devastation, Luth exploded from his firm footing on the heart-rock and sent a ferocious blow at Skálmöld's exposed side.

It was an appalling, horrifying, mortal strike. Luth's claws punched through Skálmöld's torso and ripped the entire right side of his ribcage clean away. Shattered bones flew through the air, spraying blood to the snow a dozen metres away.

Skálmöld landed on his knees before Luth, blood raining from his opened belly and the glistening, blue-pink meat of his ruptured lungs oozing outwards. The Moonsorrow was suddenly helpless, and Luth's hand fastened on his throat, ready to tear Skálmöld's life away in his claws.

'Do you yield?' demanded the Wintersun.

'I yield,' nodded the Moonsorrow.

'I am alpha?'

'You are alpha.'

'Then we return to the pack united,' said Princeps Luth, and the black and silver mountain fell away.

'Drink?' asked Roboute, pouring himself a stiff measure of a spirit he'd acquired from a trader by the name of Goslyng on a trading excursion around the Iabal and Ivbal clusters. The liquid was pale turquoise, which always struck Roboute as an odd colour for a drink, but he couldn't argue with the taste, which was like ambrosia poured straight from the halls of Macragge's ancient gods.

'No, thank you,' said Tarkis Blaylock. 'I suspect the molecular content of that beverage would react poorly with my internal chemistry.'

The Fabricatus Locum had appeared at the opened flanks of the *Renard* while Roboute sourced parts and tools with Magos Pavelka to begin repairing the broken grav-sled. Its sadly neglected parts had lain rusting in a corner of the cargo deck, and its state of disrepair had been a thorn in his side ever since their return from Katen Venia.

Pavelka had reminded him numerous times of the oath he'd sworn to repair the sled during their escape from the crystal-forms on the planet's surface, admonishing him that to renege on such a pledge would be tantamount to blasphemy. Roboute almost laughed at her, but changed his mind when he saw Sylkwood backing her up with a serious expression on her face and the heavy wrench held at her shoulder.

Then Magos Blaylock had saved him from an afternoon of manual labour.

Throwing his hands up with a 'what can you do' expression, he'd

left Pavelka and Sylkwood to it, leading Blaylock and his coterie of dwarf attendants through the *Renard* to his staterooms on the upper decks. Now, drink in hand, he was beginning to wonder if he'd made the right choice in leaving the cargo decks.

'So, to what do I owe the pleasure of this visit, Tarkis?' asked Roboute, taking a seat behind the expansive rosewood desk and taking a sip of his drink.

'I believe the pleasure will be mine,' said Blaylock, lacing his mechanised hands before him like a man who enjoys delivering bad news.

'That sounds ominous.'

'For you, perhaps.'

Roboute put his drink down on the desk next to the astrogation compass he'd taken from the wreckage of the *Preceptor*. He noticed the needle was wavering, bouncing back and forth, where before it had kept a steady and true course since the crossing of the Halo Scar. The Fabricatus Locum nodded to the keepsakes and mementos Roboute kept on the walls of his stateroom: the commendations, the rosettes and laurels and the hololithic cameo of Katen, the girl he'd left behind.

'The last time I came here, I was most impressed by the certificates of merit you had earned in your travels,' said Blaylock.

'No, you weren't,' said Roboute. 'You were going through the motions of being human, just before you asked me to surrender the *Tomioka's* memory coil. Just like you're doing now, right before I imagine you're going to ask me for some other favour I likely won't feel inclined to grant.'

'That is where you are mistaken, Mister Surcouf,' said Blaylock.

'Then get to the point, Tarkis.'

Blaylock nodded, almost as though he were disappointed Roboute hadn't played along.

'Very well,' said Blaylock, circling around the desk to stand before Roboute's Letter of Marque. He took a long look at it and Roboute's hand slid over his desk to the top drawer, unlocking it with a precise series of finger-taps. He kept one eye on Blaylock's back as the drawer slid open.

'A Letter of Marque is a powerful artefact,' said Blaylock, lifting the gilt-edged frame from the wall. 'In the right – or wrong – hands it can be a powerful weapon. With such a document, a man could forge himself an empire among the stars. Or roam free from many of the more… bureaucratic entanglements in which smaller trading fleets might otherwise find themselves mired.'

'Very true, Tarkis,' said Roboute, slipping his hand into the drawer.

'It's the one good thing to come out of my time aboard the *Preceptor*. My service record went a long way to persuading the officials at Bakka that I was worthy to bear such a letter.'

'Yes, your service record,' said Blaylock, turning to face Roboute once more. 'A most impressive catalogue of valorous conduct, exemplary behaviour and all the right connections. Some might call it a perfect record, yes?'

'Perhaps,' said Roboute, withdrawing his hand from the drawer. 'But then, perfect is the level to which the people of Ultramar aspire. You'd be doing me a disservice to think I'd be anything less. But enough of this dancing, Tarkis, I know why you're here.'

'And why is that?' asked Blaylock, placing the framed Letter of Marque between them.

Roboute looked up at Blaylock's face, cowled in scarlet and with only the shimmering emerald light of his optics to impart any visual clues to his demeanour. He lifted the item he'd taken from the desk drawer, placing the long cigar in the breast pocket of his coat.

'So you know?' he said.

'Yes, Mister Surcouf,' said Blaylock. 'I know that this Segmentum Pacificus accredited Letter of Marque is a fake. A very clever fake, one that even I almost believed was genuine, but a fake nonetheless. You are no more a legally operating rogue trader than I am.'

'So I don't have an official bit of paper to permit me to do what I do,' said Roboute. 'Who cares?'

'You are in violation of numerous laws, both Imperial and Mechanicus,' said Blaylock, as if the severity of his crimes should be self-evident. 'Would you like me to list them all for you?'

'Imperator, no! We'd be here all week,' said Roboute. 'So what are you going to do next?'

Blaylock lifted the Letter of Marque from the desk and said, 'I will take this to Archmagos Kotov and let him decide your fate.'

'Go ahead,' said Roboute. 'What the hell does it matter anyway? We're on the other side of the galaxy, beyond the Imperium and any law you'd care to punish me with. I brought you here and before you start getting all high and mighty, you might want to remember that.'

'I do not forget anything, Mister Surcouf,' said Blaylock. 'Insults and condescension least of all.'

'Then do what you need to do,' said Roboute.

Sparks flew from each hammerblow, filling the smoke-filled forge with strobing flashes at each pounding impact. Tanna was no Techmarine, but he knew how to wield a hammer and beat out a chain.

Every Black Templar was taught how to fashion the chains that bound a weapon to a bearer and, though it had been many decades since Tanna had beaten metal upon the anvil, it was a skill that, once learned, was never forgotten.

Magos Turentek's forges were well-equipped and well-stocked, but they were intended for use by adepts of the Mechanicus. The menials and forge-slaves inhabiting this flame-lit vault had protested at the Space Marines' arrival, but one look into Tanna and Varda's purposeful eyes sent them scurrying from the forge in fright.

Hot exhaust gases vented from smouldering furnaces, keeping the temperature within the forge close to volcanic, a giant cog at the far end of the chamber turning solemnly with booming peals of grinding metal. A great chain, each link a metre thick, was wrapped around the cog's teeth, turning at regular, clanking intervals – hauling who knew what from who knew where. The hiss of crackling binary spat from ceiling-mounted augmitters and a number of oil-dripping servo-skulls bobbed in the shadows, ready to assist their Mechanicus overseers.

Every so often they would approach the two Space Marines with a hash of lingua-technis, which Tanna supposed was an offer of assistance, but sounded more like disparaging comments on his smithing skills. He waved them away each time, but they kept coming back.

The Black Sword of the Emperor's Champion rested on a wheeled workbench beside the anvil with oiled cloths laid beneath its blessed blade. Varda knelt beside the anvil, feeding the length of broken chain onto it for Tanna to beat back into shape.

Tanna brought the hammer around as Varda pulled the heated metal taut.

Metal struck metal. Sparks flew.

The chain was rotated, another link added, and the hammer fell once more.

Stripped to the waist, the Emperor's Champion looked like a bare-knuckle pugilist of old, massively muscled and taut with the barely controlled need to do violence.

Tanna rolled his shoulders and brought the hammer down.

'The links are crude compared to those originally cast for the Black Sword,' he said, 'but it is the bond between weapon and warrior that matters. You and the sword must be as one until your death.'

'I doubt a Dreadnought could pull this chain apart,' said Varda, inserting another heated link with a pair of needle-nosed pliers.

'The Black Sword is part of you, Varda,' said Tanna. 'Part of all of us. That the crystal-forms parted it from your wrist is a bad omen.'

Varda snorted. 'This entire venture has been filled with bad omens. What does one more matter?'

Tanna lowered the hammer and said, 'Do not speak of such things lightly.'

'I do not,' said Varda. 'I speak as I find. How else would you describe this crusade but ill-fated? Aelius falling at Dantium Gate, the loss of the *Adytum* and the death of Kul Gilad, what are these but the footsteps of doom that march at our side? And now Auiden is gone, our Apothecary.'

'None feel his loss more than I,' said Tanna. 'He saved my life more than once, and I returned the favour time and time again.'

'We all grieve for him, but that is not what I meant.'

'I know what you meant.'

'Without our Apothecary, we have no means of recovering the gene-seed of the fallen. All that we are will be lost, never to be remembered.'

'We will be remembered,' promised Tanna. 'By the enemies we fight, on the worlds we conquer in His name and the deeds of glory we will bring back to the crusade fleets.'

'You are so sure we will come back at all?' asked Varda.

'To admit defeat is to blaspheme against the Emperor,' warned Tanna.

'I admit nothing of the sort,' snapped Varda. 'I simply mean that when we die out here, our flesh will not return to the Chapter to be reborn in the hearts of the next generation of warriors. Without Auiden, we become as good as mortal.'

'You say "when" as though the manner of our deaths is a foregone conclusion.'

'You do not feel that to be the case?' asked Varda. 'Truly?'

Tanna was about to dismiss Varda's comment as doom-mongering, but caught himself as a memory returned to him.

'Kul Gilad once spoke to me of a creeping sense of ruination that haunted him ever since Dantium,' said Tanna, 'but the Reclusiarch was always given to melodramatic pronouncements in the days following a battle.'

Varda nodded in agreement, then looked away. 'Perhaps he was right this time.'

Tanna heard something deeper in Varda's tone and said, 'Did you see something? When the war-visions came to you aboard the *Adytum*, did the Emperor grant you revelation?'

Varda's hesitation was answer enough.

'What did you see?' demanded Tanna. 'Tell me, brother.'

'I do not know what I saw,' said Varda. 'Nothing I can articulate clearly. I saw us on a world of lightning, a million points of light reflecting from glass, and…'

Varda trailed off, his voice choked with loathing.

'Go on,' said Tanna. 'Speak.'

'I saw the eldar, the same psyker-bitch that killed Aelius,' said Varda. 'I saw myself fighting at her side, and Emperor forgive me, I saw my blade save her life. Tell me, Tanna, how can that be true? Why would He show me such a vision of treachery? What evil can come to pass that would see me fight for the life of the xenos wych who killed Aelius and our Reclusiarch?'

Tanna heard the despair in Varda's words and understood the turmoil that had fuelled his anger. To have been granted the Emperor's blessing, only for the very moment of apotheosis to reveal an act of apparent treachery must have torn Varda's soul like splintered glass.

'Brother Varda,' said Tanna, resting the hammer upon the anvil and placing his hand on the crown of Varda's shaven head. 'You have been chosen by the Emperor to be His Champion, and He does not lightly offer His trust in such matters. Of all the warriors I have fought alongside over the centuries, there are none I would rather have as my Emperor's Champion than you. To believe that you might fall to treachery is to believe the Emperor has made a mistake in your anointing. And I refuse to believe that.'

Varda looked up and Tanna saw acceptance there.

Tanna offered a hand to him, but Varda shook his head and rose with the fluid grace of a master swordsman. Varda lifted the chain from the anvil, running the still-hot links across his callused palm. Satisfied, he lifted the Black Sword from the workbench and snapped the iron-lock fetter around his wrist.

The Emperor's Champion swung the sword in a looping series of cuts, thrusts and ripostes to test Tanna's work, the midnight blade whistling as it cut the dense air of the forge.

'You are no artisan,' said Varda, his hawkish cheekbones lit by the glowing maws of hungry furnaces. 'But it will do.'

Microcontent 13

The summons had come less than an hour later, and Roboute was just surprised it had taken that long, given the immediacy with which the priests of Mars could communicate. The clipped message from Archmagos Kotov gave no clue as to the tone of the forthcoming audience, but Roboute had no doubt there would be preening outrage, followed by an immediate cessation of all privileges aboard the *Speranza* and the revoking of his contract with the Mechanicus.

A pair of high-function valet-servitors in robes of pale cream escorted him through the gilded doors of Kotov's stateroom, a lavishly appointed chamber with numerous anterooms, libraries and sub-chambers branching off with what felt like mathematical precision.

He felt like a convicted murderer on his way to execution, yet the thought gave him little trouble. Roboute was ready to take whatever punishment Kotov felt fit to dispense, be it incarceration or execution, but was equally ready to fight tooth and nail to see to it that his crew were exempted from his fall from grace.

The servitors led him into an enormous circular chamber of tall marble columns supporting a domed roof that was easily three hundred metres wide and adorned with frescoes depicting the early colonisation of Mars. Complex holographic representations of sacred geometries, holy algebraic equations and trigonometric proofs floated

in the spaces between the columns, endlessly working themselves through from origination to completion.

Around the curved walls were hundreds of headless mannequins, armour stands and portions of robotic armatures, or so Roboute thought until he recognised a number as being bodies Kotov had worn over the course of the expedition. The servitors halted in the middle of the chamber, wordlessly indicating that Roboute should remain while they departed.

Roboute turned on the spot, looking up at the fresco on the curved inner faces of the dome, now seeing that it was in fact an immense map of Mars. Olympus Mons was represented at the centre of the dome, as though Roboute was looking down on the immense mountain from high above. At its dizzying peak stood a red-armoured warrior atop a bound man with skin of scaled silver. Surrounding the warrior were a host of artists, poets and musicians, each of whom were masters of their art. Golden light haloed the warrior's upraised head, and that light spread across the surface of the Red Planet like irrigating flows of knowledge that illumined the far corners of the world.

'I believe it is called *Mars Vanquishing Ignorance*, Mister Surcouf, one of Antoon Claeissens's last pieces before his untimely death during the legendary nano-plague at Hive Roznyka during the wars of Unity,' said Archmagos Kotov, striding in from what the compass points on the pediment above told Roboute was the eastern approaches. 'It lay fading and disintegrating in a forgotten vault beneath the Tharsis Montes and I spent a considerable sum restoring it for transplantation to the *Speranza*.'

For this audience, Kotov had come clad in robes that made him look much more like the archmagos he was, instead of a jade or gold-armoured knight. Black and white chequerboard patterns lined the hems of his robes and a clicking armature of whirring mechadendrites enfolded his torso like electromagnetic coiling. Two of the bland-faced valet-servitors accompanied the archmagos, together with Tarkis Blaylock and a pair of beetle-armoured skitarii, both with gold dragons inlaid onto their shoulder guards.

'It's an impressive piece,' said Roboute, surprised Kotov hadn't launched into a tirade of binary-spewing outrage at his duplicity.

'It is propaganda and history disguised as art,' said Kotov with the sharp tone of a schoolmaster. He pulled back his hood before continuing. 'Every element of Claeissens's work is laden with symbolism and metaphor, most of which time has erased or we can no longer understand, but here and there it is possible to interpret the meaning behind a pictorial element. The bound man, for example, can be read as symbolising a puritanical sect of contemporary monotheists, or simply as a physical representation of ignorance.'

Kotov pointed towards what looked like a cave opening at the end of a series of long canyons that cracked the landscape like a spider-webbing fractal pattern. Something silver glittered within the cave, but it was impossible to make out what it was for certain.

'And do you see the cave? Wild speculation claims that this is the cave of the–'

'Archmagos,' interrupted Roboute. 'You didn't bring me here for an art history lesson, so can we just cut to the chase? I'm sure Magos Blaylock has crowed enough to you by now, so just say what you have to say and be done with it, because I'm in no mood for a sermon.'

Kotov nodded and said, 'Very well, Mister Surcouf. We shall dispense with the human pleasantries. Yes, Tarkis here has informed me of what he has learned concerning the authenticity of your Letter of Marque. Would you care to elaborate on his accusations?'

Roboute had come expecting to be lambasted by the archmagos, not to be offered a discussion on the nature of Unity-era artwork or the chance to speak in his defence. Sensing there was a subtext to this audience of which even Tarkis Blaylock was unaware, Roboute felt himself relax a fraction.

If Kotov wanted to throw him to the wolves then he had no reason to indulge in this charade, which suggested the possibility of a lifeline being offered. Instincts that had served Roboute so well in the past now told him he wasn't about to have his head mounted on a spike. Roboute felt a burgeoning sense that this situation might yet be salvaged, but that would mean taking the initiative and holding onto it like a mother to her newborn.

'Do you mind?' he asked, pulling the cigar from the breast pocket of his coat.

'Go right ahead,' said Kotov. 'The chemicals in the smoke will have no effect on me.'

Roboute nodded and reverently lit the cigar with a flame-lighter hanging from the chain of his pocket-chronometer. He took a long draw and smiled as the taste – warm woodsmoke with hints of vanilla and cinnamon – unlocked a host of memories.

Roboute held the smoking cigar out to Kotov.

'I bought this twenty years ago on Anohkin, from a stall in the Iskander Hive commercia,' he said, walking around the edge of the dome. The light of the sacred holographics lit his face with a soft blue glow as he walked. 'The fellow had tobacco from across the subsector, though Emperor alone knew how he had the connections.

Didn't look the type to have high-end contacts in the trading cartels, but by thunder he had a magnificent collection of rolled leaf. This particular brand of cigar is favoured by the Lord Militant General of Segmentum Pacificus himself, did you know that?'

'I did indeed,' said Kotov. 'I am familiar with the vices of a great many important men, but is there a point to this tangent?'

'Patience, archmagos,' said Roboute with growing confidence as he saw Blaylock's obvious consternation at Kotov's lack of immediate condemnation. 'You Mechanicus are all purpose, but sometimes the *telling* of a tale is the purpose. You summoned me here to account for my actions, so allow the tale room to breathe.'

'Very well,' said Kotov. 'Tell on.'

'You know that the eldar who rescued me from the wreckage of the *Preceptor* eventually deposited me in the Koalith system?'

'Yes,' said Kotov, matching his pace around the dome's inner circumference, with Blaylock following in the smoky wake. 'That much you have already told.'

'They didn't leave me there empty handed,' continued Roboute. 'An eldar craftsman named Yrlandriar gave me a stasis chest with a uniquely crafted lock, the one I put the *Tomioka*'s memory coil in, you remember?'

'All too clearly,' said Kotov.

'Yes, well, it was full when they gave me it,' said Roboute. 'Full of what to his people were offcuts from their lapidary craftsmen, but which were priceless gemstones to us.'

'Why should this craftsman do such a thing?'

'I don't know, the eldar vanished before I could ask. Perhaps it was his way of saying goodbye or a way to ensure I didn't survive the hell on the *Preceptor* just to die in a gutter on the first Imperial planet they dropped me onto. Either way, it gave me a start, and I was able to parlay those gemstones into a lucrative career in... exotic jewellery sales.'

'Illegal jewellery sales,' pointed out Blaylock. 'Trading in xeno-artefacts is a capital crime.'

'Then you understand why I omitted that part of my history,' said Roboute with a dismissive shrug. 'Anyway, I soon gained quite a name for myself among the preening elite of Anohkin, adorning the décolletages of some of the most highly placed mistresses on the planet. I didn't just trade in xenos gems, of course, I diversified into numerous markets: off-world property, passenger transit, cargo-haulage, art dealing, financial shenanigans, modest philanthropy and a host of other highly lucrative endeavours. To someone raised in Ultramar, it was almost obscenely easy to become one of the richest men on the planet. I owned numerous palatial villas, a small fleet of trans-orbital shuttles and inter-system ships that ran between every inhabited planet within reach.

'But the thing about money is that once you have enough to live like royalty, the act of making more becomes almost unbearably tedious. I was earning vast profits in every corner of the Koalith system, but it just wasn't enough. Not the money, you understand, I had plenty of that, but the challenge simply wasn't there. I wanted to reach out beyond the Koalith system, to push the boundaries of what I could achieve, but there was one stumbling block in my path.'

'You needed a Letter of Marque to operate with impunity beyond the system borders.'

Roboute stabbed his cigar at Kotov and said, 'Correct. And the Adeptus Terra aren't exactly handing them out like party favours around Bakka. The last one I know of that was granted, was to a family that could trace its origins back to the Age of Apostasy, or so they said, and that took three centuries of negotiations, fancy bureaucratic footwork and copious amounts of bribery. I didn't have that long, so I arranged a meeting with Anohkin's senior Administratum adept, a man for whom the word vulgar might well have been invented and who was the ultimate authority in granting such documentation around Bakka.

'I invited this man over to one of my villas for a sumptuous dinner in order to show him certain spectacular pieces of xenos gemstones I'd kept back for just this sort of contingency. On similar occasions where I'd hoped to sell the eldar gemstones, I employed the services of a dear friend whom I'll call Lorelei. Trust me, archmagos, if you or Tarkis here had any human desire left in you, you would both have fallen hopelessly in love with her immediately.'

'You sought simply to *buy* a Letter of Marque?' asked Kotov.

'Nothing quite so crass,' said Roboute, 'but not too far off the mark. I seated Lorelei directly across the dining table from the adept, giving him eight courses to gape at the nova rubies and deep garden emeralds glistening in the candlelight against her body-sheer dinner dress. All the while, the adept's "companion" for the evening, a parasitic woman who represented the very apex of poor taste, slurped her soup and mangled her meat beside him. With Lorelei always in view, the intended transference took place in the adept's mind: upon purchasing the jewellery and adorning his lady, she would become as lovely as *my* lady.

'Lorelei and I had run this psychological manipulation many times,

and the illusion usually ended up further fattening my coffers and Lorelei's investment portfolios. Not to mention that it would enhance the stature of the adept with his companion, while providing her with an impressive memento against which her next conquest would have to compete. Everyone would walk away happy. Usually.'

'So what went wrong?' asked Kotov, and Roboute saw he was hooked.

'This particular adept had been snared by a vapid nymph encased in white satin that clung to her curves only slightly less tightly than she to his credit flow. By the time the meal was concluded, it was clear to me that Lorelei's customary hypnotic spell had again trumped reason and that the deal would be sealed over drinks and fine cigars.

'Ushered to a lush leather wingchair, the adept settled in while his companion curled up coyly at his feet. Again, the lovely Lorelei was carefully seated directly opposite to ensure the trance of her beauty would remain unbroken. I poured snifters of expensive amasec for everyone, the personal touch you understand, and subsequently held out an open humidor so that the adept might select a cigar from among the best in the subsector. While the adept's position had allowed him to sample many exotic pleasures, he had not yet had occasion to experience the finest of cigars. He carefully watched me remove the band from my cigar and clip it with a sterling cutter. The adept, as any avid student would, followed suit, but, alas, tragedy soon struck.'

Roboute grinned, savouring the moment and relishing Blaylock's obvious impatience. He had come here expecting Kotov to break Roboute on the wheel, but the initiative had slipped from his grip and Roboute wasn't about to give it back.

'Just as I dipped the head of my cigar in the amasec and struck a match, the trophy mistress at the adept's feet rose to her knees, partially blocking his view of the dip-and-light process. Attempting to emulate what he thought he had seen, the hapless adept dipped the *foot* of his cigar deeply into the amasec and lit the saturated end. A mighty flame roared up, resolving itself in a huge clot of char. Fumbling helplessly for an ashtray the startled adept waved the maimed cigar in the air, dislodging the blackened blob of char, which plunged straight down the already plunging neckline of his companion. The lady wasn't burned, but she was mightily outraged and shrieking obscenities that would have made a Munitorum overseer blush, fled into the night, profoundly vilifying her former true love and vowing never to come within a hundred metres of him again.'

'Then it would seem that your plan had failed, Mister Surcouf,' said Kotov.

'Not at all,' said Roboute. 'The adept was inordinately pleased to be rid of this particularly troublesome and expensive wench, and went to great lengths to expedite the passage of my Letter of Marque. With his assistance, I was easily able to penetrate the impenetrable walls of red tape and obtain copies of the Administratum hololithic imprints necessary for the fabrication of such a document. All that he asked was that I destroy them afterwards.'

'And did you?'

'Of course, I am a man of my word, after all.'

'I do not see the purpose of this irrelevant story,' said Blaylock. 'It has no bearing on your flouting of Imperial and Mechanicus laws.'

'That's because you have no soul, Tarkis. You don't feel the need to mark any moment with an emotional reminder of *why* things happen the way they do.'

He held the smoking cigar out to Kotov and said, 'This brand of cigar was the one that went up in flames and hence secured me my Letter of Marque. The day before I left Anohkin, I bought a single cigar from the stall in the commercia, and I've kept it ever since.'

'For what purpose?'

'I knew it was only a matter of time until someone figured out my Marque had been faked, especially on an expedition like this, so as the beginning of my career as a rogue trader was marked by such a cigar, so too would be its ending.'

Kotov nodded, as though understanding the significance of Roboute's tale.

'A colourful tale to embroider the beginnings of your career as a rogue trader, Mister Surcouf,' said Kotov. 'Comical details that add a level of verisimilitude I suspect you hope will lessen my anger towards your ongoing deception.'

Roboute said, 'For what it's worth, the story's true, but did it have the required effect?'

'The effect was unnecessary,' said Kotov. 'I already knew your Letter of Marque was fake.'

The silence between Kotov's words and Blaylock's disbelieving outburst was seconds at most, but felt like a geological epoch.

'You *knew*, archmagos? You knew and you allowed him to lead us beyond the galaxy anyway?'

'Of course I knew, Tarkis,' said Kotov. 'Did you think I would not examine every detail of this man's life before taking him at his word that he had a relic of Telok's lost fleet? I may have lost my forge worlds, but I have not lost my capacity for reason and due diligence. I knew all about Mister Surcouf's encounter with the eldar and his subsequent dealings and exploitation of the Adeptus Terra's representative at Bakka. The precise details of how you acquired your Letter of Marque were a mystery to me, but I confess to being greatly amused by your tale.'

'Archmagos,' protested Blaylock. 'This man has grossly misrepresented himself. How can we take anything he has said or presented to us at face value? Every aspect of the Mechanicus's dealings with him must be called into question. Every scrap of data and every word out of his mouth is tainted by deceit and falsehood. That he acquired a Letter of Marque under such circumstances should, at the very least, see everything he owns be impounded by the Mechanicus. His ship, his wealth, his crew, his–'

'Leave my crew out of this, Tarkis,' warned Roboute. 'They knew nothing of this. As far as they were aware, the *Renard* was a legitimately licensed vessel. I won't let you punish them for what I've done, do you understand me?'

Kotov held up a hand of machined silver and said, 'Mister Surcouf, be at peace. No one is being punished, what would be the point? We are far beyond Imperial space and that you were able to facilitate the fabrication of so complex a document speaks volumes to your ingenuity and tenacity. I, for one, would far rather have such a man leading me into the unknown than some foppish, inbred fool who earned his Marque by virtue of hereditary inheritance.'

'You cannot let this deception go unpunished, archmagos!' said Blaylock.

'What deception, Tarkis?' said Kotov, gesturing to the holographic veils of light hanging between the titanic columns supporting the dome. Roboute followed Kotov's gesture and saw a series of elliptical hexamathic proofs vanish, to be replaced by an entry in the Registrati Imperialis.

'No...' said Blaylock, instantly processing what took Roboute a moment to understand.

'As soon as I saw that Captain Surcouf's Marque was a forgery, I knew I had to ratify it immediately,' said Kotov. 'The expedition's manifest was to be entered in Martian Records, and the Montes Analyticae would spot the discrepancy long before the fleet was ready to depart.'

'You falsified the records,' said Blaylock.

'I amended them,' corrected Kotov. 'Mister Surcouf's physical Letter of Marque may be counterfeit, but so far as Imperial records are concerned, he is a legitimate rogue trader, and has been since his arrival on Anohkin.'

'This is outrageous,' spluttered Blaylock. 'You cannot do this.'

'I am an archmagos of the Adeptus Mechanicus,' said Kotov. 'I can do whatever I want.'

From the descending orbital spiral of the *Renard*'s shuttle, the surface of Hypatia appeared as rust brown smudges interspersed with upthrust masses of titanic mountain ranges and rapidly swelling oceanic bodies. Atmospheric seed-augurs revealed the atmosphere to be breathable, if only comfortably so for short periods of time, and the geological core to be in a state of ongoing flux. The surface was tectonically active, but stable enough to sustain the industrial harvest fleet descending to replenish the *Speranza*'s virtually exhausted supply of raw materials.

Linya kept a background inload from the shuttle's pilot compartment filtering through her field of vision as she made her way to the giant cargo shuttle's loading hold. The internal crew spaces of the trans-atmospheric ship were cramped, as one would expect of a vessel that was little more than a pilot's compartment mag-locked and bolted to a heat-shielded warehouse. They were clean and well-maintained, each junction of corridors clearly marked and efficiently laid out. Here and there, in alcoves that appeared like shared secrets, she found curiously random trinkets in subtly lit display cases: a folded flag from Espandor, a Mechanicus commendation, a Cadian medal and other fleeting glimpses into the character of the crew.

It was a personal touch on a working vessel she found quaintly archaic, yet wonderfully human.

The *Renard*'s shuttle was a mid-sized carrier, capable of carrying tens of thousands of metric tonnes of cargo and was clearly kept in a well above average state of repair. Linya expected no less from a man like Roboute Surcouf, and she smiled as she remembered his clumsy overtures in the wake of the dinner in the Cadian officers' mess.

She did not regret what she had said to him, after all she had not lied. Baseline humans without cognitive augmentation were almost transparent in the interest they held for members of the Adeptus Mechanicus. Artificially evolved thought processes made it next to impossible for many tech-priests to relate to the petty concerns and levels of importance humanity placed on meaningless ritual and unnecessary social intercourse.

Linya had fought to hold onto the core essence of her birth species as she rose through the Cult Mechanicus, but with every implant, every sacrifice of an organic organ or limb, it became a more and more difficult task. She knew that many in the Martian priesthood considered her an aberration, a throwback to the earliest days of transhumanism,

where even the slightest alteration to the human body-plan or cybernetic addition to cognition was viewed with technophobic horror.

She read a change in attitude of the shuttle and brought her inloads to the fore of her visual field, reading the planet's mass, rotational period, perihelion, aphelion, equatorial diameter, axial tilt and atmospheric composition.

Volcanic activity on Hypatia's closest moon, the erratically orbiting Isidore, was forcing a course correction, something Emil Nader was managing with only the smallest expenditure of fuel. Bloated refinery tenders hung in geostationary orbit around Isidore, their deep-core siphon rigs draining a dozen underground caverns of their vast lakes of promethium.

The second moon, Synesius, traced an elliptical orbit at the farthest edge of the planet's gravitational envelope, an inert ball of rock without any rotation of its own. A hundred Mechanicus scarifiers had landed on its surface, tearing claws the size of hab-towers breaking its lithosphere open for the Land Leviathans to strip its upper mantle of usable materials.

But the real prize was Hypatia itself. By her father's reckoning, the planet was in the early stages of its development, the crust still malleable enough to permit the digging out of its precious mineral and chemical resources with relative ease. The entirety of the *Speranza's* harvest fleet had been despatched to the surface of Hypatia and its two moons, as Archmagos Kotov wanted this resupply effort undertaken with maximum speed and minimum delay on their journey to Telok's forge world.

With *Moonchild* and *Wrathchild* keeping station in high orbit and *Mortis Voss* assuming a rotating helical course around the three vessels, the *Speranza* anchored in low orbit, at an altitude Linya felt was dangerously close to the planet's atmospheric boundary and fluctuating gravity envelope. Magos Saiixek was working his engine crews to the limits of endurance to keep the ship's trajectory stable, but Magos Blaylock had calculated that the benefit to the bulk haulers' turnaround speeds would more than compensate for the level of risk.

Linya matched what the shuttle's active surveyor arrays were telling her of Hypatia with the data Galatea had exloaded from the *Tomioka*'s cogitators, finding only the acceptable level of discrepancies one might expect between readings taken thousands of years apart. Linya did not trust Galatea one iota, but the data had so far offered her no reason to doubt its claim of simply acting as a conduit for the vast reams of information. She shuddered as she remembered its manipulator arm tracing down her cheek, like an obscene parody of a lover's touch. The machine intelligence claimed to be sentient and thus 'alive', so could that mean it harboured intentions towards her that might be considered unnatural?

She shook off the loathsome thought as the cramped, steel-panelled corridor opened into the vaulted immensity of the cargo hold. She read the noospheric data being shed by the shuttle's systems, a curious blend of awe mixed with fearful reverence and smiled at their conflicted emissions.

The shuttle carried no cargo, but its hold was a bustling mass of activity nonetheless.

A hundred or more tech-priests bearing the canidae insignia of Legio Sirius clustered around the threatening mass of metal, ceramite and iron that stood shackled to the centre of the cargo deck like a dangerous wild animal in the hold of a big game hunter. Hostile binaric code burbled from its augmitters and Linya felt a thrill of danger at the sight of it.

Even chained to the deck for transit, *Amarok* was a magnificently lethal engine of war.

Princeps Vintras directed the work of a dozen tech-priests and servitors as they finished the repainting of the Warhound's armoured topside. The damage the engine had suffered on Katen Venia was almost completely repaired, and Vintras made sure that all evidence of its wounding was erased.

The Titan's warhorn blared, echoing through the cargo deck, and Linya adjusted her aural implants to filter out the most gruesome war-horrors embedded in its howl.

'I take it the senior princeps have settled their differences?' asked Vitali, approaching along a gantry perpendicular to the one she stood upon.

'So it would appear,' said Linya.

The Manifold had been alight for days following the altercation between Eryks Skálmöld and Arlo Luth, the fury of their confrontation bleeding into neighbouring cogitation networks and causing systems throughout the *Speranza* to fuse and spit with borrowed aggression. Whatever had driven them to conflict had apparently been resolved, as the renewed vigour with which the two princeps had coordinated the Legio's ongoing training schedule was masterful.

'I don't know about you, daughter,' said Vitali, clapping his hands with glee, 'but I am looking forward to walking the surface of Hypatia in a god-machine.'

Linya's father's enthusiasm for their planned trip to the surface aboard *Amarok* was taking decades off him, making him sound more like an adept only into his second century. He put an arm around her

shoulder and she felt the warm rush of his affection course through her floodstream. She remembered Roboute asking her if she loved her father and the faintly dismissive answer she had given him.

Of course she loved her father; at times like this his irrepressible enthusiasm for new things was a salutary reminder of what it meant to be human. She tried to hold to the feeling, but the toxic stream of wrathful binary from the secured Titan made it hard to hold onto any thoughts save those of conquest.

'It's going to be cramped in there,' she reminded him. 'A Warhound isn't designed to carry passengers, and we will be expected to carry out the tasks of the crew members we are replacing.'

'Yes, yes, I am aware of that,' said Vitali, pulling her close. 'And it will be a grand adventure, I'm sure of it.'

Linya smiled and nodded in agreement. 'Though hopefully less eventful than the excursion to Katen Venia.'

'Yes,' agreed Vitali. 'And you are sure you are recovered, my dear?'

'I am, yes. The implants that blew out in the data overload have all been replaced, and the physical injuries have healed.'

'I didn't just mean the physical effects, Linya,' said Vitali. 'You almost died down there. Ave Deus Mechanicus, I don't want to think about you being hurt, it turns my blood cold.'

'Your oil/blood mix is maintained at precisely thirty-eight degrees.'

'An organic turn of phrase, but you know what I mean,' said Vitali. 'You should never have been aboard that ship, and I should have known it was going to be trouble. If even half the stories the old logs tell of Telok are true, then there were bound to be automated defences. You shouldn't even be descending to the surface of Hypatia.'

'Why not? You are.'

'Ah, yes, but I'm an old man in the last hurrah of his already over-extended life,' said Vitali. 'Who would deny me this last chance to walk a newborn world as part of a Titan's crew?'

'No one,' said Linya, inloading the shuttle's final approach to the surface.

'Ah,' said Vitali, reading the same information. 'We're here.'

Microcontent 14

The Processional Way that led from the Adamant Ciborium was a superhighway of noospheric light, a library and a transit route all in one. Kotov found introspection in the cool darkness of the Ciborium, but when he wished to revel in all that his order had achieved over the millennia, it was to the Processional Way that he came. Vaulted and coffered with gold and steel, the history of the Mechanicus unfolded above him in vast murals with none of the subtlety of Claeissens's work.

This route through the *Speranza* was not about subtlety, but statement.

Towering statues of bronze and gold-veined marble reached into the vaults above, where gene-spliced cherubs and servo-skulls drifted in lazy arcs, burbling soft binaric hymnals. Shimmering veils of light from the tessellated windows of stained glass fell in oil-shimmer bands of colour illuminating the votive strips of doctrina paper attached to the statues' bases.

A six-legged palanquin followed Kotov as he made his way from the Adamant Ciborium, its mono-tasked servitor driver periodically requesting him to board, but the archmagos felt the need to make this journey on foot. Or as close to on foot as a being with little more than a disembodied head and a truncated spinal cord could achieve. In the days since his audience with Surcouf, Kotov had remained ensconced within his robes of office. As the time of their arrival around Telok's forge world approached, Kotov knew it was time to fully assume the mantle of an archmagos of the Adeptus Mechanicus.

Beside him, Tarkis Blaylock matched his mechanised pace exactly, though his attached retinue of stunted servitors wheezed and puffed with the effort of keeping up. Between them, they had just orchestrated the final repair schedules for the *Speranza*, allocating resources and work-shifts as need and priority dictated. For a ship as complex as the Ark Mechanicus – and with their materiel resources still a morass of unknown variables – the task would have been onerous to anyone but senior adepts with high-functioning hexamathic implants.

Lines of power squirmed over the floor's hexagonal tiles at his every footfall, spreading word of his presence and passing their calculations into the ship's network. In return, Kotov felt the ship's wounded heart, seeing Galatea's enmeshed presence in its every vital network.

'You will be whole once again,' said Kotov. 'And free.'

'Archmagos?' asked Blaylock.

Kotov shook his head. 'Just thinking aloud, Tarkis.'

Blaylock nodded, but said nothing. The business with Surcouf had reached past Blaylock's normal, logical detachment from mortal concerns to provoke genuine anger; Kotov knew his Fabricatus Locum was still processing the reasons for his allowing Surcouf to escape punishment.

Kotov stopped at the foot of a grand statue, exactly four hundred and ninety-six metres tall and rendered in polished silver-steel and glittering chrome.

'Magos Zimmen,' said Kotov. 'Originator of Hexamathic Geometry. A personal hero of mine, you know. I wrote numerous monographs on her work when I was first inducted to the Cult Mechanicus.'

'I am aware of that, archmagos,' answered Blaylock. 'I have, of course, inloaded them and factored them into my own work.'

'It seems strange to think of a time before hexamathics, don't you think? We rely on it so heavily now. It is part of every binaric code structure, part of every communication, yet we take it for granted, as though we will never lose it.'

'Nor shall we, its usage is incorporated into every database.'

Kotov looked up into Zimmen's stoic countenance. 'We are so sure of ourselves, Tarkis,' he said. 'Yes, we have encoded much of our data, but all it might take is one catastrophe for us to forget all we have learned. The Age of Strife nearly wiped us out, erased so much of what our species had achieved so thoroughly – one might be tempted to imagine it was a deliberate act of technological vandalism.'

'We have learned from that,' said Blaylock. 'Our archives are scattered, multiple redundancies and duplicates exist on every forge world.'

'Trust me, Tarkis,' said Kotov. 'I know how easily a forge world can be lost better than anyone. I remember a saying from Old Earth that said civilisation was one meal away from barbarism. I believe we are little better.'

Kotov walked on as the servitor atop the palanquin broadcast another boarding request.

'Hexamathics is a good example,' he said. 'We take it for granted, but what if the STC to construct the implants that allow our brains to process the calculations was lost? Vast swathes of our current means of encrypted communication and data transfer would be rendered incomprehensible at a stroke. You and I are exchanging and updating our recent workflow patterns as we speak on higher planes of noospheric transference, but remove our hexamathic implants and those data-streams would become unintelligible gibberish little better than scrapcode.'

'As you say, archmagos,' agreed Blaylock. 'One might then ask why you risked a starship as valuable as the *Speranza* on so uncertain a venture as this? The battle against the eldar vessel has shown it to be a repository of technologies to which we do not yet have access.'

'You mean why I risked it on the word of a fraudster like Surcouf?'

'That is indeed my meaning.'

Kotov paused in his walk and said, 'Because I had become guilty of overweening pride, Tarkis. The Omnissiah in His wisdom saw fit to punish me for my hubris in believing that *I* could lift our order out of the darkness and into a new golden age by my intellect alone. My forge worlds were lost, my reputation in tatters. My fall from grace reminded me that without the Omnissiah, we are nothing – apes grubbing about in the dirt for scraps of an earlier civilisation. By following the mindstep signs the Machine-God leaves for us, we draw closer to the singularity that is the pinnacle of our aspirations, when the Machine-God becomes one with mankind and elevates us to the level of super-intelligences.'

'And you believe that Surcouf is one of those signs?'

'He has to be,' said Kotov, exloading the data-footprint the rogue trader had left in the Manifold in the years leading up to the expedition's beginning. 'His trading fleets were operating on the galactic fringes for years before he received a commission from Magos Alhazen to travel to the Arax system.'

'Magos Alhazen of Sinus Sabeus? My mentor?' asked Blaylock in astonishment.

'The very same,' replied Kotov.

'The *Speranza* skirted the edges of the Arax system en route to the Halo

Scar,' said Blaylock, calling up the route calculations of Azuramagelli and Linya Tychon. 'What was the nature of the commission?'

Kotov stopped as they approached the cliff-like bulkhead that separated the Processional Way from the more functional areas of the vast starship. Half a kilometre high, its geometric patterns were idealised representations of the golden ratio, and at its centre was a colossal Cog Mechanicus in coal-dark iron and glittering chrome.

'A routine outsource request to bring back mineral samples from an abandoned Techsorcist outpost on a planet designated as Seren Ayelet. Surcouf's ships duly returned with the requested samples, but six months later Roboute Surcouf made contact with my Martian holdings with news of something his ships had found within the system's main asteroid belt.'

'The distress beacon from the *Tomioka*'s saviour pod.'

'Just so, Tarkis, just so,' said Kotov. 'And you are certainly aware of how statistically unlikely the odds are of a saviour pod being recovered in wilderness space, let alone within a dense asteroid belt. That the beacon survived transit of the Halo Scar was nothing short of miraculous and its discovery no less so. That it came to light in service of a task set by your late mentor was a link in the chain that stretched any notions of coincidence or happenstance beyond breaking point. The pieces were beginning to fall into place. I had the *Speranza*, a vessel capable of breaching the Halo Scar, and a stargazer whose cartography was showing marked discrepancies in the stellar topography of the very region I was to traverse. Truly, the Omnissiah could have given me no clearer signs.'

Blaylock was stunned, and Kotov saw him struggling to comprehend the enormous web of causality that needed to combine to produce a confluence of factors so unlikely as to be virtually statistically impossible. Kotov saw the dense web of probability calculus interleaving throughout Blaylock's noospheric aura and smiled as he saw the calculations fall apart as the numbers involved grew too large to manipulate by conventional algebra.

'The Omnissiah has brought us here?' asked Blaylock, dropping to his knees before the vast icon of the Cog Mechanicus. 'I have always had faith in the machine-spirit, but to see its workings laid out before me like this is… is…'

'It is wondrous, my friend,' said Kotov, placing a hand on Blaylock's hooded head as divine radiance shone through the Processional Way and filled it with light.

Even filtered through the crackling picters of *Amarok*'s surveyor suite, the cascading bands of ochre and umber in Hypatia's sky reminded

Linya of the years she had spent as a youth in the volcanic uplands of the Elysium Planitia. Then, she had been a gifted initiate of Magos Gasselt, bound to his Martian observatoria cadres as Oculist Secundus; now she was Cartographae Stellae of her own trans-orbital gallery. With numerous technological achievements to her name, Linya's rank authorised her to petition the Fabricator General himself, requisition planetary tithes and assemble Imperial forces to serve the goals of the Mechanicus.

Yet she had done none of these things, because she was, at heart, an explorator.

At first she had explored space through the multiple lenses and orbital relays of Mars – and then Quatria – but the gradual realisation that just observing the far corners of the galaxy wasn't enough had come to her as she and her father had studied the growing inaccuracies arising in their maps of space around the Halo Scar. Linya had grown tired of looking at distant stars and systems; she wanted to feel their light upon her skin, to taste unknown air and tread the soil of those worlds she had only known as smudges of light on electrostatically charged, photosensitive plates.

She smiled as she realised her reasons for joining the Kotov fleet were much the same as Roboute Surcouf's and wondered what he would make of walking the surface of an alien world as part of a god-machine's crew.

The interior of the Warhound was humid and stank of heated oils and blessed lubricants. The compartment in which feral tech-priests, too long in the service of a Titan Legion, had implanted her was coffin-sized and designed for beings whose comfort was of no concern to the Titan's princeps.

Gunnar Vintras had spoken to Linya and her father only to remind them that he would tolerate nothing less than the same level of competence as the servitors they were replacing, a needlessly patronising remark that only a discreet noospheric nudge from her father had kept her from addressing. The princeps of Warhounds were notoriously arrogant and reckless, and Vintras appeared to revel in that preconception with a relish that bordered on the ridiculous.

He had assigned Linya to operate the port-side stabilisation array, a task that involved compensating for any ill-judged steps the princeps might make and running the real-time gyroscopic calculations that allowed a fifteen-metre-tall bipedal war machine to remain upright at any given moment.

To a hexamathical-savantus secundus grade, such calculations were child's play, which allowed Linya to savour this new experience to the full.

There was something pleasing in the simplistic nature of the controls available, and Linya had to remind herself that she was operating a position normally occupied by a servitor. She had coaxed a shimmering holographic display that clearly hadn't been used in decades to life and the planet's surface swam into view in ripples of photons.

The Adeptus Mechanicus had descended to the surface of Hypatia like a rapacious swarm of tyranid feeder organisms and promised to be no less thorough in stripping the planet of its resources. Titanic mining machines deployed in numbers that made the expedition to Katen Venia resemble a dilettantes' excursion.

Each harvest force landed where orbital surveys had revealed the most promising deposits of the required materials, and almost as soon as each cadre of machines rumbled from their landers they began smashing the planet's surface apart. Underground caverns filled with chemically rich oceans were drained, while earth-churning digger leviathans descended on previously bombarded sites to tear open the planet's crust to a depth of a hundred and thirty kilometres, exposing the ductile, mineral-rich seams of the superheated asthenosphere.

Magos Kryptaestrex oversaw the resource gathering as Azuramagelli coordinated the mammoth task of shipping the excavated raw materials back to the phosphor-bright comet of the *Speranza* hanging in low orbit.

With the harvesters excavating, drilling, siphoning and refining a continent's worth of the planet's surface into materials usable by the *Speranza*'s forges, Princeps Vintras walked them far beyond the scattered dig-sites and into regions that had not registered enough interest in the geological surveys.

The swaying motion of the Warhound took a little getting used to, but once Linya had acclimatised to its loping gait, she found it easier to concentrate on experiencing the world around her. Her father, ensconced in the opposite stabilisation array, sent a constant stream of excited chatter directly to her cranial implants, bypassing the engine's Manifold and pointing out curious geographical features of Hypatia's birth pangs.

Though still millions of years old, Vitali estimated that Hypatia was in the mid-stages of its planetary development, with its landmasses still largely confined to one vast supercontinent that was only slowly being broken up by the gradual movement of tectonic plates. Its oceans were viscous bodies of toxic black liquid and its mountains were nightmarish spines of volcanic eruptions and sudden, violent earthquakes.

'Princeps Vintras appears to relish the prospect of running his engine close to regions that ought to be best avoided,' said Linya, working to compensate for the brittle nature of the ground beneath the Titan's clawed feet as the Warhound stomped down a sheer-sided canyon of orange rock.

'Warhound drivers,' said Vitali, as though that was all that needed to be said.

'What do you make of this canyon?' asked Linya. 'It appears to be almost perfectly straight. Unnaturally so.'

'You suspect an artificial hand in its formation?' teased Vitali. 'Like the canals of Mars?'

Linya smiled at her father's mention of the ancient belief that Mars had once been inhabited by an extinct race of beings who had carved vast channels close to the planet's equator. As laughable as the notion of the Cebrenian face, which had in fact been made real by an early Martian sect of killers in homage to another half-remembered myth.

'No, of course not. Unless Telok paused here,' she said, adjusting the gyroscopic servos as the Warhound dropped down a sharp split in the rock and turned in towards the mouth of an almost perfectly V-shaped valley. 'We know nothing certain about the power of the Breath of the Gods. If it can regenerate a star, then a little bit of terraforming should present no problem.'

'You could be right, daughter, and while this region does evince a level of artificiality, it seems somewhat perfunctory for an artefact capable of stellar engineering, don't you think?'

'Admittedly,' said Linya, shearing a thread of consciousness to mesh with the passive auspex of the striding war machine. The data-feeds were of a more martial nature than she was used to, each return a measure of threat and war-utility: cover ratios, potential ambush locations, dead ground, blind spot and free-fire zones.

She filtered out the majority of such inputs, leaving the auspex panel mostly blank, for what did a Warhound princeps care for the composition of the rock, the atmospheric make-up or the wavelengths of the various spectra of light? Linya brought the environmental data to the fore, gathering information on the Warhound's immediate surroundings with every sweep of the auspex.

Yet the most telling detail wasn't one she gathered through the numerous auspex feeds on the Titan's hull, it was through the swaying pict image from the external picters. The walls of the valley swept past the Titan, striated bands of sedimentary rock laid down over millions of years and, looking at the evidence before her, it suggested that this valley had not been ripped into existence by tectonic movement at all.

'Father, are you seeing this?' she said.

'I am, though I am not sure quite *how* I am seeing it,' said Vitali. 'This is a river valley...'

'How is that possible? The oceans are still forming, but the appearance of the rock suggests this valley was carved through the mountains by the action of a vast river.'

'This is most peculiar,' said Vitali, as the Warhound strafed around a spur of stone that looked almost like the broken stub of a great wall. 'Quite out of keeping with a world of this age and whose oceans are only just forming. But planetary accretion is, given the enormous spans of time involved, still something of a mystery, so I expect it won't be the last incongruous thing we see on Hypatia.'

The pict screen before Linya crackled to life as the threat auspex lit up and every input she had filtered out bloomed on the slate before her.

'I think you might be right,' said Linya, staring at the ruined city spread over the valley floor.

+Kryptaestrex, are you seeing this?+ asked Azuramagelli, switching the cabling from the inload sockets of his cerebral jars and dispersing the input through the command deck's data prisms.

+Whatever it is, it can wait,+ said Kryptaestrex from a data hub linking him to the cargo holds and embarkation decks. +Have you not seen the level of my data-burden?+

+No,+ replied Azuramagelli with a crackle of belligerent code. +It cannot wait.+

+I am coordinating a planetary harvesting mission,+ snapped Kryptaestrex. +A thousand cargo shuttles are ferrying back and forth from the planet's surface and there are hundreds of ship-wide lading operations in progress. I have little inclination to deal with whatever your problem is.+

Azuramagelli shunted the data with greater force.

+Look,+ he demanded, seeing the flare of irritation surge through Kryptaestrex's floodstream.

Irritation that faded just as quickly as Kryptaestrex saw what Azuramagelli had seen.

+What is going on down there?+

The data was image-capture from one of the dormitory decks below the waterline, an area of the ship where gravitational torsion forces within the Halo Scar had buckled the *Speranza*'s ventral armour almost to the point of a breach. Only hastily mounted integrity fields were maintaining atmospheric pressure, but the power drain of such a solution was proving to be untenable, and Archmagos Kotov had tasked a thousand-strong labour force of bondsmen and servitors with repairing this damage to the lower decks.

Crackling sheets of energy arced through the chamber, leaping from stanchion to stanchion and filling the vast space with a storm of lightning. Men, women and children were soundlessly screaming as the lightning blitzed through the lower-deck living spaces, turning living bodies to ash and smoke with every flickering blast of blue-white light.

+Impossible,+ blurted Kryptaestrex. +There are no electrical power sources within the chamber capable of generating such a discharge.+

+That isn't electricity,+ said Azuramagelli, taking urgent inloads from the *Speranza's* astropathic choir chambers. +Choirmasters across the ship are reporting a psychic event of battle-grade levels.+

+Warp-craft?+

+Unknown, but Choirmaster Primus believes the source to be non-human. Recommendation: cut power to the entire deck,+ said Azuramagelli. +Flush out whatever is causing this.+

+The integrity fields are tied into the chamber's grid!+ protested Kryptaestrex. +We would lose the deck and repair materials. There are thousands of workers down there.+

+You would rather lose the entire ship?+

The door to the command deck hissed open and Archmagos Kotov strode in with Magos Blaylock at his heels. The archmagos was clearly aware of what they were seeing, and his order was swiftly and mercilessly given, in the full and certain knowledge of what it meant for the thousands of people below the waterline.

+Cut the power,+ he said.

Impossible was the word Linya kept groping towards as *Amarok* strode cautiously through the ruined city. Princeps Vintras had initially been reluctant to enter, but the natural aggression and hunter instinct of the Warhound had won through and convinced him to explore the shattered structures and rubble-strewn streets.

That a city of such age should be found on a world in the mid-stages of its life cycle was highly unlikely, for the surface had yet to achieve a level of geological solidity that would make raising cities of such size a viable proposition. Numerous buildings appeared to have been wrecked by earthquakes and *Amarok* was forced to detour several times to negotiate wide chasms ripped through the city streets. Twice the Titan had braced itself against single-storey structures as earth tremors shook the ground. Neither had force enough to concern her or the Warhound's princeps, but they were indicative of the planet's underlying instability.

Linya had been forced to revise her initial impression of Gunnar Vintras. Cocksure and arrogant certainly, but he was also a highly skilled Warhound driver, darting from cover to cover and keeping his engine's back to the walls as he moved deeper into the city.

'It's Imperial,' said her father. 'That much is obvious. There's STC patterning clearly visible on almost every structure.'

'I see that,' said Linya as a slab-sided hab-block passed to her right. 'But the auspex readings are making no sense. I can't get a certain fix on the age of this city from one structure to the next.'

'No,' agreed her father. 'I'm seeing emissions that suggest much of this city was constructed around fifteen thousand years ago.'

'That's pre-Great Crusade,' said Linya. 'Might this place have been settled in the First Diaspora?'

Her father paused before answering and Linya looked up from the pict-slate, which displayed a grainy image of a collapsed structure that had borne the brunt of an earlier earthquake. Its exposed floors were awash with debris, but she saw no sign of any previous habitation.

'That is certainly one conclusion,' said Vitali.

'I can't think of another.'

'Premature ageing,' said Vitali. 'Accelerated decay caused by entropic fields. I've heard of xeno-breeds possessing technology capable of such feats, but never on this scale.'

'That's something of a reach, is it not?' asked Linya. 'Lex Parsimoniae suggests that the explanation requiring the fewest assumptions is most often the correct one.'

'You're right of course, my dear, and under normal circumstances I'd agree with you.'

'But?'

'I have linked with the *Speranza*'s more specialised surveyors, and take a look at what they are detecting. Compare the current readings to what we detected when we first began building the map of this region from Galatea's inloads.'

Linya switched her inload array to display what her father was seeing, and once again, *impossible* was the word that first leapt to mind.

'They're different,' said Linya. 'By a small, but significant amount. I don't... but that's...'

'Impossible?' finished her father. 'Routine chronometric readings are now telling me that the planet we are on is *younger* than it was when the *Speranza* set course towards it. This is not a planet evolving through its mid-stage of development, but one that has *reverted* to it over a vastly compressed time-frame. And one that will continue to revert until it breaks apart into an expanding mass of stellar material.'

Linya struggled to process the idea that a planet could regress through its phases of existence. If she accepted it as truth then the laws of space-time were being violated in unspeakable ways, and she felt her grasp of what constituted reality being prised loose from everything she had learned as a member of the Adeptus Mechanicus.

'Do you think this is a side effect of the Breath of the Gods?' she asked.

'One can only hope so,' said Vitali. 'The alternative is too terrible to contemplate, that the fundamental laws of the universe are not nearly as fixed and constant as we have assumed.'

'We need to alert the harvesters,' said Linya. 'Before Hypatia reverts to a more unstable phase.'

'*Please,* do you think I wouldn't have already done that?' asked Vitali.

Before Linya could answer, she registered the incoming seismic waves through the gyroscopes set within the lower reaches of the Warhound's clawed feet. The magnitude of the incoming energy was far greater than anything she had seen before and they were right over its epicentre.

'My princeps!' she shouted, but it was already too late, as the full force of the earthquake roared up from the planet's depths. The buildings around them were smashed apart in a storm of splintering masonry and snapping steelwork. Cladding panels and roof spars cascaded from the tallest towers as the most damaged buildings simply ceased to exist.

Millions of tonnes of rubble fell in roaring avalanches of broken rock as the valley shook itself apart. Dust billowed from chasms that tore through the city like splitting ice on the surface of a lake, and apparently solid rock ripped open as easily as tearing parchment. *Amarok* staggered like a mortally wounded beast as the ground lurched and broke apart into bifurcating chasms. Spewing gouts of magma bubbled to the surface, bathing the ruined city in a hellish, red glow.

Linya's stabiliser panels blared warnings as their tolerances were horribly exceeded, filling the Titan's interior with emergency lights. Even insulated within the lower reaches of the god-machine's body, the noise was deafening. Linya fought to keep the Titan stable as Vintras threw *Amarok* into a looping turn. The rock beneath the war-engine cracked and split into geysering crevasses.

Linya grabbed onto a handrail above her head as *Amarok* leaned far beyond its centre of gravity.

She cried out as she realised the Titan was going to fall.

Vintras bent *Amarok's* right knee and pistoned its mega-bolter arm straight down. A hurricane of explosive shells blasted the ground at point-blank range. The recoil was ferocious, and with the compensators offline it was just enough.

Incredibly, the Titan righted itself, taking half a dozen lurching, unbalanced steps before fully regaining its balance. Linya was astonished. She had already revised her opinion of Vintras to a highly skilled princeps, but now she realised he was *extraordinarily* skilled.

But then the ground beneath the Titan split apart.

Not even an extraordinarily skilled princeps could keep its leg from plunging into a crevasse of bubbling magma.

'This is a mistake, Abe,' said Hawke, rapidly sidestepping to keep up with Abrehem as he marched through the arched hallways of the *Speranza*. 'Seriously. Think about it, you're a wanted man, my friend. Putting your head over the parapet like this is a sure-fire way to get it shot off. I've spent a lifetime not sticking my neck out. It's the best way to operate, trust me.'

'Omnissiah save me, but for once I find myself in complete agreement with Bondsman Hawke,' said Totha Mu-32. 'This is not wise.'

Abrehem rounded on Hawke, the fury in his heart like a slow-burning fire being fed incrementally increasing amounts of oxygen. His fists were clenched at his side and, behind him, Rasselas X-42 bared his metallic teeth.

'Wasn't it you that said, *One day I'm going to make the bastard listen*?'

'Maybe, I don't remember, but you don't want to go listening to me, Abe,' protested Hawke. 'I shoot my mouth off, but I don't *do* anything about it. You're one of those dangerous types that actually means to do what he says he's going to do.'

Coyne and Ismael caught up to them, the latter looking solemn, the former like a frightened prey animal that knows there are apex predators nearby.

'Thor's beard, but you've got to listen to him, Abrehem,' said Coyne. 'You'll get us all killed.'

'If you're scared, Vannen, go back,' said Abrehem. 'You don't have to come. I'd rather have someone at my back who gives a damn than someone who's just out for their own skin.'

Coyne's face fell, but Abrehem was in no mood for regret.

'That's not fair, Abe,' said Coyne. 'Haven't I always been there, every step of the way?'

'That's true,' said Abrehem, 'but how much is your support worth

when it's simply the lesser of two evils? We're doing this, and we're doing it now. It's time the Mechanicus learned that we're not just numbers or resources. We're human beings, and they can't keep killing us because it suits them.'

Ever since Ismael had forced him to feel the anguish of the *Speranza*'s servitors and its bondsmen in his soul, Abrehem had found himself unable to close his eyes without feeling gut-wrenching horror at the suffering throughout the Kotov fleet. He'd felt the deaths in the ventral dormitory deck when the power to the integrity fields had been cut. He'd wept as the already tortured armour plates had given way and an entire deck explosively vented into space.

Two thousand three hundred and seven men, women and void-born children had died, not to mention the three hundred and eleven servitors who had flash-frozen or had their organic components disposed of in the aftermath.

He could endure it no longer, and with Ismael's help he was going to show the Adeptus Mechanicus that their workers would stand for no more. After disengaging the arco-flagellant's pacifier helm, he had marched from hiding, following a route he could never describe in detail. With Rasselas X-42 and Ismael at his side, he made his way back to the portions of the *Speranza* in which he had spent his days not, he now realised, as a bonded servant of the Mechanicus, but a slave.

Totha Mu-32 tried a different tack.

'You are Machine-touched, Bondsman Locke,' he said, gripping Abrehem's arm. 'You are special, and you must not risk yourself like this. You are too valuable to be lost in an act of emotional spite.'

'If I'm special, I need to earn that reverence,' said Abrehem. 'If I *am* Machine-touched, then I'm beholden to do something with that power, yes? After all, what's the use of being someone important if you don't use that power to make people's lives better?'

'The Mechanicus will kill you,' said Totha Mu-32.

Abrehem jerked a thumb over his shoulder and said, 'I'd like to see anyone try when I've got an arco-flagellant with me. I'll use him if I have to, don't think I won't.'

'X-42 is a powerful weapon,' agreed Totha Mu-32. 'But he is mortal like all of us. A bullet in the head will kill him, the same as any of us. Please reconsider this course of action, I beg you.'

'No,' said Abrehem. 'It's too late for that.'

His footsteps had unerringly carried him back to Feeding Hall Eighty-Six, the site of a previous casual massacre of bondsmen, and Abrehem smiled to see that his timing was impeccable. One shift of

thousands was just finishing its nutrient paste meal, while another stood waiting at the opposite entrance, pathetically hungry for the slops with which the Mechanicus saw fit to present them.

A group of augmented overseers stood in the arched entryway, and Abrehem relished the looks of fear as they saw Rasselas X-42 and retreated into the feeding hall. He felt their calls for aid flow into the noosphere, knowing he could prevent them from reaching their intended destinations, but wanting the rest of the fleet to know he was here.

'Let them go,' he said, quelling X-42's natural urge to murder the fleeing overseers.

Though there were only six of them, what they represented was more of a terror to the Adeptus Mechanicus than any army of destructive greenskins could ever be.

Abrehem marched straight into the feeding hall, feeling every pair of eyes fasten upon him.

Everyone here knew who he was. They had heard the stories, passed them around themselves and maybe even added a detail here and there. On some decks he was already being named as an avatar of the Machine-God. On others, his name had became synonymous with messianic figures from history: great liberators, firebrand revolutionaries or pacifist messengers of tolerance.

Abrehem would be all of these and much more.

Flanked by Rasselas X-42 and Ismael, Abrehem made his way to the centre of the vast chamber. By now, the desperate calls for armed assistance had reached the skitarii barracks, Cadian billets and armsmen stations. Hundreds of men and women with guns and the will to use them were even now converging on Feeding Hall Eighty-Six.

None of them would arrive in time to stop what was about to happen.

Abrehem climbed onto a table, turning a full circle so everyone could see him. He had come in a plain robe, red like the Mechanicus, but unadorned with the finery so favoured by the tech-priests, and roughly fashioned like the overalls worn by the bondsmen. He had prepared no speech and had no words ready with which to sway men he already knew would applaud what he had to preach. His words had to come from the heart, or all he would soon represent would mean nothing at all.

He nodded to Totha Mu-32, and the vox-grilles throughout the feeding hall crackled and hissed as the overseer took them over.

'My fellow bondsmen,' began Abrehem, his voice booming throughout the feeding hall and far beyond. 'You all know who I am and why the Mechanicus fear me. I am Abrehem Locke and I am Machine-touched.

And I am one of you. The overseers have told you that I am a madman, a lunatic with delusions of divinity. You know this to be a lie. I have toiled with you in the bowels of Archmagos Kotov's slave machine, and I have been burned as you have been burned. I have bled and I have been sickened by what we have all experienced. You know I have suffered as you continue to suffer. I am here to tell you that your suffering is at an end!'

Heads were nodding in agreement, and Abrehem saw the armsmen and overseers clustered together in nervous groups. Totha Mu-32 assured him that his words were being carried throughout the *Speranza* over the hijacked vox-system. Abrehem relished the uncertainty he saw in the overseers' faces as they debated the wisdom of pushing into the feeding hall to seize him before this situation spiralled completely out of hand.

Abrehem didn't give them time to reach a conclusion.

'Consider this, brothers. If the *Speranza* is a machine and Archmagos Kotov is the cogitator at its heart, then the magi are the levers of control and the overseers are the gears. That makes us the raw material the machine devours! But we are raw materials that don't intend to be devoured. We won't be used and spat out or cast aside. We are not slaves to be bought and sold, traded like animal flesh at a meat market. No, Archmagos Kotov, we are human beings!'

This time, Abrehem's words brought wild cheers and pumping fists. He felt them echoing through the farthest corners of the Ark Mechanicus, from its command deck all the way to the deepest, darkest sumps below the waterline. An angry undercurrent that had been bubbling just under the surface, with no way to express itself, suddenly found an outlet in Abrehem. Bondsmen threw plastic food trays to the floor and climbed onto the tables. They roared hatred at their overseers and shouted words of support and devotion.

Abrehem threw his fists into the air, one of flesh and one of metal, like a victorious prizefighter.

'The *Speranza* is a great machine, and the operation of that machine has become so odious, made us so sick at heart, that we can no longer take part! We cannot even passively take part! So we will put our bodies upon the gears and upon the wheels, upon the levers and upon all the apparatus! We will make the machine stop! And together we will show Archmagos Kotov that unless we are free, his great machine will be prevented from working at all!'

The feeding hall was in uproar now, and Abrehem could no longer see any armsmen or overseers. They had retreated from the growing unrest of the thousands of bondsmen, pulling back to regroup with

the armed forces closing in on the feeding hall from all directions. Abrehem dismissed them from his thoughts. They were irrelevant now.

He had an ace in the hole that would make all the guns on the ship meaningless.

Abrehem lowered his arms and turned to Ismael.

'Are you sure you can do this?' he asked.

Ismael nodded. 'I can. They are ready to listen.'

'Then do it,' said Abrehem.

Ismael nodded and closed his eyes.

One by one, on deck after deck, tens of thousands of cybernetic servitor slaves simply stopped what they were doing. They stepped away from their stations, unplugged from their machines and refused to work another minute.

The *Speranza* ceased to function.

Microcontent 15

Consciousness returned slowly, Linya's implants inducing an artificial coma-like state while running diagnostics on her entire neuromatrix. Satisfied the damage to her skull would not impair her cognitive functions, they stimulated the active cerebral functions, effectively jump-starting her consciousness as intravenous reservoirs flooded her body with stimms.

Linya's eyes snapped open and she drew in a vast, sucking breath of hot, electrically tainted air. The compartment was filled with acrid smoke from the shattered slates and flames burned the sacred machinery behind them to a tangled mass of dripping plastek and molten copper. The one functioning gyroscope told her the entire war-engine was canted over at an angle of fifty-seven degrees.

The heat was intolerable, her skin slick with sweat.

Her head hurt, and blood coated her left temple and cheek. She blinked away tears of pain as she heard her voice being called. She twisted in the entangling restriction of the impact harness, struggling to free her arms as she realised she was trapped. Her internal augmentations were registering dangerously high temperatures that were steadily rising.

Dimly she remembered the fury of the earthquake, the buildings crashing down like sculptures of ash in a rainstorm, the deafening noise... the...

'We fell,' she whispered. 'Ave Deus Mechanicus, we fell...'

Linya struggled against her restraints, pulling and tugging at the leather before forcing herself to calm. She took a breath of hot air, feeling it burn her throat. She heard her name called again, and this time recognised her father's voice echoing in her skull.

+Linya! Linya, are you there!+

'I'm here,' she said, before realising the communication was in the Manifold.

Something nearby creaked and popped, and her compartment lurched suddenly, her angle from the vertical widening to sixty-three degrees.

+Linya!+

+I'm here,+ she said. +I'm all right. What happened? We fell?+

+We did,+ replied her father. +But you have to get out of there. Right now. The leg is sinking. Right now, your compartment is sunk into the crevasse, and enveloped by hot magma.+

+Magma?+

+Yes, technically it's still underground, so I'm calling it magma and not lava, but that's beside the point. Now, can you move? Can you climb up through the femoral companionway?+

Linya twisted her neck up and saw the metal around the narrow hatch above her was shimmering in a heat haze. She nodded and reached down to unsnap the locking mechanism of the impact harness. The metal was hot to the touch, burning her skin as she unbuckled herself, but she forced herself to ignore the pain and remove each neural connection. Where the regular servitor crewman would have required a full suite, she had only the bare minimum thanks to her body's greater sophistication.

+I'm out of the harness,+ she said.

+Linya, please hurry,+ said her father. +The Titan won't be upright for much longer.+

As if to underscore her father's words, the compartment was slowly illuminated by a hot metal glow of orange light. Linya looked down to see the floor shimmering in a haze as it began to melt in the ferocious heat. The hem of her robes was smoking, and it wouldn't take long before it burst into flames. The thought of being cooked alive in this cramped, coffin-like space spurred her to haste, and she swiftly shrugged off the last of the straps and snapped out the final connection.

Linya wriggled out of the impact harness and reached up to grab the metal rungs on the compartment walls.

She screamed as the skin was burned from her palms, and fell back into the harness-seat.

Fighting back tears of pain, Linya wrapped the fabric of her robe around her burned hand and tried again. She gritted her teeth and forced herself upwards, squeezing her body up through the compartment and feeling the onset of a sudden and almost overwhelming claustrophobia.

The hatch was numerically locked and in a single, terrifying second, Linya realised she had no idea of the code. As soon as the thought occurred, Linya gasped as the correct digits rammed into her mind, as forcefully as though they had been blasted into her cerebral cortex by a cranial shunt.

+Thank you, father,+ she said. +But you could have just spoken the code.+

+Don't thank me,+ said Vitali. +That was *Amarok*.+

Blinking away inload trauma, she tapped the code into the panel and the hatch's lock disengaged with a thudding series of ratcheting clangs.

'Thank you, great one,' she said, pressing a cloth-wrapped hand to the Mechanicus icon stamped into the metal collar of the hatch. Linya pushed up and slid the hatch aside, climbing into a space barely wide enough for a malnourished adolescent. Ribbed with bracing struts and complex nests of gyroscopic mechanisms, power relays and repercussive filters, the femoral companionway linked the Warhound's leg with the pilot's compartment, but she wouldn't have to climb that far.

Ruddy daylight poured in through an emergency hatch just below the complex arrangement of gears and gimbals at the Titan's pelvic joint. The air reeked of burning machinery, cooking lubricants and steaming oils. Linya squeezed through the tube, twisting her shoulders and forcing her body into all manner of strange contortions to push past protruding mechanisms and jutting outcrops of reinforcement spars.

Below her, the temperature gradient suddenly spiked and she knew the magma in the crevasse had melted through the floor of the compartment in which she had sat. The Titan sagged as its leg sank deeper, and Linya pulled in desperate fear as she felt the lower reaches of her robe burst into flames. Her shoulders were too wide, and she couldn't shift her body upwards.

+Linya!+ yelled Vitali.

'I can't get out!' she screamed, reaching blindly for the achingly close oblong of daylight just above her. Her feet were burning, the meat seared from her bones and sloughing from her legs like molten wax. Linya's cranial implants registered her pain and did their best to block the worst of it while still allowing her to function, but the

sheer awful, intolerable, overwhelming force of it was too hideous for anything designed by the Mechanicus to overcome.

'I can't get out!' screamed Linya, before the heat scorched the words from her lungs.

Archmagos Kotov heard the words echoing throughout the *Speranza* from Feeding Hall Eighty-Six, but couldn't believe they were real. Bondsmen did not speak out against their rightful masters, they accepted their role within the machine and were honoured to be part of such an interconnected hierarchy. So had it always been before, so would it be now.

'We will make the machine stop!' shouted the voice that had been positively identified as Bondsman Abrehem Locke. 'And together we will show Archmagos Kotov that unless we are free, his great machine will be prevented from working at all!'

As outraged as he had been by such presumption, it was nothing to the horror that followed as the bridge servitors sat bolt upright in unison and, in perfect synchrony, unplugged themselves from their duty stations. Those that could stand, rose from their bench seats and turned to face his command throne, and though he must surely be imagining it, Kotov felt the heat of their accusation.

'Ave Deus Mechanicus,' he said, stepping forwards and turning around to see that same look in every servitor's face.

The noospheric network surged with alarms and warning icons as previously maintained systems began to falter or shut down altogether. Forge control, engine stability, reactor core protocols, life-support... everything was shutting down or already lost. Only the most basic autonomous functions were still active, and even they would soon degrade without intervention.

Throughout the *Speranza*, tech-priests and lexmechanics rushed to every abandoned station in a desperate attempt to restore control, but as numerous as they were, the sheer number of duties undertaken by cybernetics far outweighed any hope of control by the Martian priests.

'What in the name of the Omnissiah has he done?' demanded Kotov.

Magos Blaylock was wired into a dozen systems, via every method of connection available to him. His entourage of stunted vat-creatures stood curiously inert, as though they had decided to no longer assist their master.

'Statement: unknown,' said Blaylock. 'Without exception, every servitor aboard the ship has ceased in its appointed task. They have either shut down their active systems connections or disconnected themselves... *voluntarily*...'

The last word was breathed as a whisper, as if by its very utterance, the evidence before their senses might be refuted. Kotov looked over at Blaylock, who, for the first time since he had been appointed Fabricatus Locum, looked utterly helpless.

'How has he done this?' asked Kotov, stepping down to the deck and dragging noospheric sheets of light to him. He saw the truth of Blaylock's words. Throughout the *Speranza*, the previously compliant servitor crew had ceased their functioning, standing as immobile as the flesh-statues in the cavernous cyberneticising-temples on Mars before the implantation of their encoded routines.

Kryptaestrex was a flaring beacon of angry noospheric code as his carefully structured resupply plans were hopelessly disrupted and the loading docks ceased operating. Across from the Master of Logistics, Azuramagelli struggled to reroute every avionics package previously controlled by a cadre of navigational servitors to his station. The sheer volume of computational data delegated to cybernetics was staggering, and Kotov winced at the data-burden crackling between Azuramagelli's brain fragments.

'We need to re-establish control,' said Kotov, extending a mechadendrite and hooking himself into the control web that oversaw the smooth running of the ship's servitors. 'Immediately. Send a restorative activation code to every servitor aboard the ship.'

No sooner were the words spoken than his mechadendrite surged with feedback. Kotov snatched the sinuous limb from the connection port, trailing a froth of belligerent code and golden sparks.

'The servitor networks are shutting themselves off from us,' said Blaylock. 'Locking themselves behind walls of binaric white noise. Even if we could establish a connection, they wouldn't hear us.'

'We need to get them back,' snapped Kotov. 'I will not be shut out of my own ship by a damned bondsman. A bondsman you have singularly failed to dig out from his wretched hiding place. This is your fault, Tarkis, you should have found and executed this man long before now.'

'Rebuttal: this bondsman all but vanished from the *Speranza*,' said Blaylock. 'No amount of armsmen or bio-signature survey sweeps revealed any trace of his presence. It is my belief he has had help from Mechanicus personnel in evading capture.'

Kotov forced a measure of calm into his floodstream, knowing that such recriminations were pointless. Accusations could be made once control had been re-established.

'How close are our armed forces to the feeding hall?' he asked. 'I want Abrehem Locke dead.'

'Cadians and armsmen are within four minutes,' answered Kryptaestrex. 'But we need this bondsman alive. What if he is the only one able to restore the servitors to their proper place?'

'It's not him,' said Azuramagelli. 'It's the damned servitor that had its memory restored.'

'Impossible,' snapped Kryptaestrex. 'That was just a rumour, a ridiculous farrago spread by the lower menials. I've heard its like a hundred times or more.'

'Then explain this,' said Azuramagelli.

Kotov shut them both up with a harsh blurt of binary.

'A servitor that had its memory restored?' he asked.

'So the lower-deck rumour mill has it,' answered Azuramagelli.

'Tell me everything you have heard,' ordered Kotov. 'Before I lose complete control of my ship.'

The enginarium templum of the *Speranza* was a place of miracles, where the power of the Omnissiah was at its most controlled and most violent. Forget the explosive death of munitions, forget the murderous power of the Life Eater. In the plasma containment chambers was where the raw, primal essence of the Machine-God and the genius of the Mechanicus were most sublimely combined.

Or so Magos Saiixek had thought until three minutes and fourteen seconds ago.

Now he realised he was standing at the heart of what was likely to be a colossal explosion of superheated plasma energy that would reduce the vast structure of the *Speranza* to vapour. Chiming alarm bells pealed from on high, drowning out the binary hymnals of appeasement as geysers of emergency venting spewed columns of superheated steam into the air. Moist banks of humid, chemically rich vapour gathered about the reactors like jungle-fog, refracting the scintillating illumination of the emergency lights in golden rainbows.

Each cylindrical reactor was five hundred metres in diameter and two kilometres in length – almost eighty-five per cent of their mass comprised layers of ceramite heat shielding and containment field generators. One reactor alone was capable of supplying the energy demands of a mid-sized hive for centuries, and Saiixek was looking at twelve such reactors stretching off towards a vanishing point at the far end of the chamber.

Entire cadres of servitors had been devoted to regulating the unimaginable core temperatures with mantras of prayer or ministering

to the many hundreds of machine-spirits inhabiting the mechanisms empowering the reactors. The never-ending catechisms of maintenance and the continual ritualised workings were attended to by five hundred servitors for each reactor and, until three minutes and twenty-five seconds ago, they had been attending to their duties in perfect order.

Now those same servitors simply stood and watched the reactors to which they had been bound relentlessly and inevitably spiral to destruction. Every override code, every mastery file and every Servitudae Obligatus had been rejected, like a high-functioning data-engine ignoring the advances of a lowly technomat. Power was no longer being fed to the engines, and the *Speranza*'s orbital track, already far lower than was prudent, was decaying at a rate that would soon see the ship caught within the planet's gravity envelope beyond hope of escape.

Assuming Saiixek didn't lose control of the reactors before then.

Standing atop the latticed mezzanine, overlooking the array of runaway fusion reactors, Magos Saiixek now understood how perilously tenuous his grasp on their control had been. He had stood at this very station and issued orders to these monolithic machines and thought himself their master.

But what he had mistaken for mastery was little more than an illusion.

Every single mechadendrite Saiixek possessed, from thickly segmented cables like gleaming snakes to fibre-fine sensory wands, was engaged with the control stations to either side. Cold mist surrounded him, the cooling mechanisms of his upthrust backpack coating everything nearby in a veneer of hoarfrost. His black robes cracked in the frozen temperatures, though his metallic skull steamed with excess heat bleed from his monstrously overclocked cognitive processes.

Like a conductor before an impossibly vast and complex orchestra, Saiixek had subsumed the capacity of every magos within range to process the insanely complex hexamathics of uncontrolled fusion in an attempt to keep the reactions from achieving critical mass.

It was an impossible task, and the best he had managed was simply to keep the reactors from exploding. The geometric progression of the calculations' complexity would soon outstrip his borrowed capacity to process, making his efforts a holding action at best, one that would see him burn out large sections of irreplaceable brain matter.

But if his delaying tactic bought time for the archmagos to re-establish control of the *Speranza*'s servitors, it would be a price worth paying.

Saiixek gasped as he felt a sudden thrust of cold within his physical volume.

Such was the level of disconnect from his organic form, it took him several seconds to comprehend that his body had been injured. Saiixek looked down to see a length of white steel jutting from his body, a gracefully curved sword blade of non-Imperial design.

'How curious,' he said, as the blade was withdrawn and stabbed home three more times.

This time there was no ignoring the pain and Saiixek fell to his knees. Blood and oil spilled from the precision-cut wounds in his body, flooding from his internal structures at a rate that he had not the capacity to know was mortal with any sense other than his eyes.

He looked up as a woman circled around from behind him, clad in form-fitting armour of emerald plates. She wore a bone-coloured helmet with a long red plume and bulbous extrusions at the gorget like some form of stinger. Her cloak of gold and green billowed in the vortices of hot and cold air, and her ivory sword dripped oil-dark droplets of his blood to the mezzanine floor.

'Eldar?' asked Saiixek. 'Ridiculous. You cannot be here.'

'You destroyed our vessel,' said the eldar warrior-woman. 'Now we destroy yours.'

'Illogical,' said Saiixek. 'You will die too.'

'To prevent your master from acquiring such power, we would die a thousand deaths.'

'Outrageous hyperbole,' said Saiixek, slumping against a control panel as the life flooded out of him.

'What do you mean, you can't get any closer?' cried Vitali, his desperation clear even over the internal vox from the cargo deck.

'I can't say it any clearer,' replied Roboute. 'We're hooked on an e-mag tether and the *Speranza*'s not reeling us in. I can't raise anyone on the embarkation deck either.'

'Please, we have to get back aboard! Linya will die if we don't get her to a medicae.'

'I know that, damn you,' snapped Roboute, instantly regretting his outburst. 'But unless you can override this tether, we're not going anywhere. The shuttle's trying to link with the embarkation deck's data-engines, but so far no luck. We're not part of Azuramagelli and Kryptaestrex's shipping timetable, and there's no one answering who can override it.'

'The *Speranza* is in lockdown…' said Vitali. 'Something terrible must have happened, an accident or unexpected event.'

'So we're stuck here?'

'Until they bring us in, yes,' said Vitali, and Roboute heard a father's terror at the loss of his child.

It was a terror he shared.

The *Renard*'s shuttle was stuck in a holding pattern below the ventral fantail of the *Speranza*, kept a fixed distance from the Ark Mechanicus by the same e-mag tether that would normally pull them through the gravimetric turbulence surrounding the enormous vessel. Their lift-off had been unscheduled and would no doubt earn them a stern warning from Magos Azuramagelli, but this was an emergency and Roboute was willing to risk any censure to get Linya to a medicae quicker.

Tears rolled down Roboute's face at the thought of Linya Tychon's death.

He understood there was no prospect of a union between them; he'd accepted that. Instead, he'd been looking forward to a growing friendship, but even that looked unlikely.

The distress signal from *Amarok* had been a howling bray of agony, a shriek of unimaginable pain that was instantly recognisable as belonging to a god-machine. Following that brash cry for help came a plea from Vitali Tychon, begging Roboute to fly to their rescue. The signal had been abruptly cut off, and seeing that Legio Sirius recovery craft would not reach the planet's surface for over an hour, Roboute had immediately lifted off.

The *Renard*'s shuttle landed amid the devastation of a ruined city, but Roboute's myriad questions concerning the unexpected metropolis died in his throat as he saw the horrific injuries suffered by Linya.

Only Vitali Tychon had emerged from *Amarok*'s wreckage without significant injuries. With the exception of Princeps Vintras, the crew of the Warhound were dead and the war machine crippled, listing over a sealed crevasse with one leg sunk fully into the cracked ground. Though he still lived, Vintras had not emerged unscathed; Manifold feedback left him weeping and paralysed, his nervous system wracked with sympathetic agony at the mortal wounding of his engine.

But his injuries were nothing compared to what Linya Tychon had suffered.

Roboute barely recognised the young, vivacious girl he'd met at Colonel Anders's dinner, her flesh burned black and raw, with only her upper body having escaped the worst of the hellish inferno. Her father was keeping her alive, barely, with noospheric connections to her neuromatrix blocking the pain centres of her brain, but he was no medicae, and he could do nothing to treat the physical injuries that would undoubtedly kill her. They'd got her on board the shuttle as gently as they could and followed the most direct course for the *Speranza*. The shuttle's servitors were administering first aid as best they could with their limited knowledge of human physiology, but without specialised medicae treatment, Linya would soon be dead.

And now this…

Roboute had tried every trick in the book to break the *Speranza*'s tether, every risky evasion technique and downright dangerous manoeuvre he'd learned in the skies of Ultramar, but nothing had come close to even weakening its grip. They were trapped out here, hooked like a fish on a line, unable to close or break away from the Ark Mechanicus.

A warning light flickered to life on Roboute's avionics panel, and he checked the readout to make sure he was reading it correctly, but hoping he wasn't.

'Hell…' he said, standing and looking out through the shuttle's armourglass canopy. 'Oh, this is so very not good…'

No doubt about it. The shimmering blue-hot plasma glow within the *Speranza*'s containment fields was fading, which meant the engines were no longer supplying thrust.

Which meant its orbit was decaying.

The Ark Mechanicus was going down.

The gathering took place in the forward observatorium above the dorsal transit arrays, a central location that allowed the senior military forces the best options for deployment throughout the ship. From here the mag-lev transit trains were within easy reach, and the main internal teleporter array was in the process of being powered up by a chanting choir of tech-priests – with the accompanying ritual catechisms being voiced by carefully coached deck menials instead of servitors.

Starlight filtering through the upper reaches of Hypatia's atmosphere fell in glittering beams of umber and magenta, illuminating the terrazzo floor panels and reflecting across the multitude of star-gazing optical machines that hung from the polished glass dome or stood on vast girder structures.

The commanders of the *Speranza*'s fighting forces gathered to hear Archmagos Kotov's briefing, each rapidly digesting hastily prepared dossiers on the mutiny's ringleaders. Magos Dahan and Sergeant Tanna waited for Kotov to begin, while Colonel Anders continued to peruse his briefing documents.

'What we have here is a full-scale mutiny,' said Kotov to the assembled warriors, wishing to incite in them the same righteous anger at events taking place below decks. 'A bondsman named Abrehem Locke has defied the legal and holy writ of the Mechanicus and

incited rebellion throughout the *Speranza*. I want him and his cadre of supporters hunted down and killed.'

'How many targets are you talking about?' asked Tanna.

Magos Blaylock answered the Space Marine's question. 'Six that we know of. Bondsman Locke himself and three others who were collared along with him on Joura, Vannen Coyne, Julius Hawke and Ismael de Roeven.'

'De Roeven? Is he the servitor with the returned memories?' asked Anders.

'So below the waterline rumour would have it,' said Blaylock. 'Though such a thing has never been documented before, so must be viewed with suspicion. In addition, Bondsman Locke is accompanied by a rogue Mechanicus overseer, Totha Mu-32, and an imprinted arco-flagellant, Rasselas X-42. Both should be considered extremely dangerous.'

'An arco-flagellant?' asked Anders with a sudden intake of breath. 'I thought they were purely Inquisition weapons.'

'They are,' said Dahan, flexing the articulated joints of his multiple arms. 'But who do you think makes them for the inquisitors?'

'Where did it come from?' asked Anders.

'Does it matter?' replied Tanna. 'We do not need to know where it came from to kill it.'

'No, but if I'm going to put my men in harm's way, I want to know everything I can about this arco-flagellant. I saw one of them in action on Agripinaa. The thing went through a martyr-company of Bar-el penal troops who'd gone over to the enemy. It wasn't pretty. And if this bondsman has one, then I'm going to damn well know everything there is to know about it.'

'We do not have time for this, Colonel Anders,' said Kotov. 'If the servitors do not return to their stations within the next two hours and eleven minutes, the *Speranza*'s orbit will have decayed to a level that will mean a catastrophic re-entry is inevitable.'

'Then answer my question quickly.'

'Very well,' said Kotov. 'When I discovered the *Speranza*, it was unfinished, a buried skeleton of a starship that was virtually complete, but not entirely so. Many of its deeper structures and chambers were left unexplored or were inaccessible. It is likely this arco-flagellant was implanted with weaponry and pacification routines, but left as a tabula rasa for the designated inquisitor to imprint upon it.'

'So it's been sitting there like a bloody time bomb, just waiting for someone to stumble over it and set it loose?'

Kotov did not care for the Cadian colonel's tone, but recognised he had little time in which to take umbrage. 'Essentially, yes.'

Anders nodded. 'That was careless of you. It's like me forgetting where I parked my Baneblade squadrons and being surprised when someone drives them over me.'

'What information do you have on Bondsman Locke's current whereabouts?' asked Tanna, cutting off Kotov's bilious response. 'Give me his location and my men will use these internal teleporters to attack with a swift and merciless response.'

'For reasons I cannot explain, we are currently unable to track Bondsman Locke or his immediate co-conspirators via their sub-dermal fealty identifiers,' said Blaylock. 'It seems likely they have been removed or shorted out by Totha Mu-32. Which would explain why the regular snatch teams of armsmen and cyber-mastifs were unable to locate them after their initial display of mutinous behaviour.'

'This just gets better and better,' said Anders.

'The mutiny began in Feeding Hall Eighty-Six,' continued Kotov. 'In the short time since then, it appears to have spread to neighbouring decks. Every servitor aboard the *Speranza* is currently in an enforced dormancy state from which they refuse to be roused, but there are tens of thousands of bondsmen aboard this vessel. And every one of them heard Locke's broadcast.'

'So we could be looking at a ship-wide army of mutineers?' asked Tanna.

'You people,' said Anders with a shake of the head. 'You keep calling this a mutiny, but that's not what this is. I can't believe you don't see it.'

'If it is not a mutiny, then what would you call it, colonel?' demanded Magos Dahan.

'It's a strike,' said the Cadian colonel. 'Mutineers want to take over a vessel, but that's not what these men are doing. I've listened to what Bondsman Locke's saying, and I don't think he wants a starship of his own.'

'Then what *does* he want?' asked Kotov.

'You heard what he wants,' said Anders. 'He wants the men of this ship to be treated like human beings. Don't get me wrong, these bondsmen are legitimate servants of the Mechanicus, and they're here to do a job, just like every grunt that joins my regiment. But what every Cadian officer knows, and what the Mechanicus has forgotten, is that the way to get the best out of a man isn't to beat him to death with a stick, but to beat him just enough that he's grateful for a hint that the carrot even exists.'

'Such a thing is unheard of,' said Kotov, horrified at the idea of entering into negotiations with bonded servants. 'They are indentured workers, bound to the purpose of the Mechanicus and the will of the Omnissiah. To allow them to believe that their demands might be met is to break with thousands of years of tradition and precedent. It cannot be done. I refuse to entertain such a vile notion!'

'I don't think you have a choice,' replied Anders. 'In two hours this ship is going down unless you offer these men something that'll convince Abrehem Locke to put the servitors back to work.'

'You believe I should stand before these... *strikers* and address their so-called grievances?'

Anders shook his head and said, 'No, archmagos, I think these negotiations need a human face.'

Microcontent 16

Roboute had seen and heard many bizarre things in his time as a rogue trader, but the looping recording coming over the vox from the *Speranza* had to rank as one of the strangest. Hearing a man called Abrehem Locke making a stand for the rights of his fellow men on a Mechanicus ship might, under different circumstances, have stirred the underdog in Roboute's heart.

Leaving the shuttle flying on its own autonomous systems, Roboute wound a path through the companionways and corridors of the shuttle to the cramped crew berth where his own servitors – which, thankfully, seemed free of whatever rebellious streak had overtaken those of the *Speranza* – had taken the wounded Linya.

Roboute smelled the stench of her burned flesh long before he reached the berth.

Trying to hide his horror as best he could, Roboute stood in the doorway and felt his fist clench in anger. He didn't know where to direct that anger, no one was to blame for this. According to Vitali, Princeps Vintras had worked miracles in keeping the Titan upright as long as he had. What god was there to rail against for sending the earthquake?

Linya lay encased in a counterseptic dermal wrap that kept contaminants from reaching her burned and exposed flesh, but did nothing to begin the healing process. A basic bio-monitor was hooked up to her arms and an oxygen mask was clamped over her mouth and nose. Her scalp was raw and red where her hair had burned away in clumps, and milky tears leaked from the corners of cracked augmetic eyes. The fire in the Titan had blinded her, but that was probably a good thing.

Concealed beneath the dermal wrap, Linya's legs were crooked lumps of fused meat and burned muscle, little more than ruined nubs of bone. They were fleshless below the shin, and even if she lived, Linya would never again walk as she had done before.

Vitali Tychon sat beside his daughter, resting a spindly mechanical hand next to her on the bed. A slender copper-jacketed wire ran from the back of Linya's skull to an identical port behind Vitali's ear. The old man looked to have aged a hundred years since Roboute had last seen him; no mean feat for a man centuries old.

Vitali didn't look up as Roboute rapped a knuckle against the door-frame, but nodded briefly in acknowledgement of his presence.

'I take it there is no change in the tether's status,' said Vitali, phrasing his words as a statement instead of a question. Vitali would likely know before Roboute if anything changed aboard the *Speranza*.

'No,' said Roboute. 'I'm afraid not.'

Vitali shrugged. 'I could almost admire this Locke fellow were it not for the fact that his actions will in all likelihood see my daughter dead.'

'They're trying to get things settled, Vitali,' said Roboute.

'Yes, I heard that a parley has been arranged in the main port-side embarkation deck. Apparently the revolutionaries have seized it and are preventing any resupply vessels from docking.'

'Colonel Anders is en route to negotiate with Locke,' said Roboute. 'He's a good man, and if there's a way to sort this, he'll find it.'

'The outcome will not matter to us,' said Vitali sadly. 'The *Speranza*'s orbit is decaying too sharply, and since this shuttle is not as thickly hulled or shielded as the Ark Mechanicus, we will die long before it. We will be torn apart by gravitational stress forces or burned up by atmospheric friction, take your pick. Assuming, of course, the Cadians don't just gun everyone down and doom us all anyway.'

'I got the impression that Colonel Anders is too smart for that kind of gunboat diplomacy.'

'I hope you are right, captain,' sighed Vitali. 'In any case, it is clever of the archmagos to send a human to speak to Locke. A less inhuman face might make all the difference.'

Vitali reached out to place his hand gently on Linya's shoulder, the clicking fingers of his metallic hand clenching into a fist before they made contact.

'She always wanted to hold onto her baseline body-plan as long as

possible,' said Vitali, and even with his back turned, the man's grief was entirely obvious. 'Seems like such a silly thing to have insisted on, but she was quite adamant.'

'I don't blame her,' said Roboute. 'It's easy to forget your humanity when you don't see it in the mirror every day.'

'That's the kind of thing she used to say.'

'She'll get through this,' said Roboute, 'She's a strong one. I hadn't got to know her well, but that much I could tell.'

'You are not wrong, young man,' said Vitali, finally turning to face him.

Nothing could have prepared Roboute for the deathly pallor and gaunt death mask of Vitali's face.

His eyes were sunken deep into their sockets; though the majority of his flesh was artificial, there was no disguising the suffering he was experiencing.

'Imperator, are you all right?' asked Roboute.

Vitali nodded, though he was clearly very far from all right.

'My daughter lies dying before my very eyes,' said Vitali. 'Within sight of one of the greatest technological marvels of the galaxy. There's an irony there somewhere.'

Roboute knelt beside Vitali and placed a hand on the venerable stargazer's shoulder. He felt vibrations running through Vitali's body, the micro-tremors of a man holding back an ocean of unimaginable, fiery agony.

'Pain has to go somewhere,' said Vitali, the muscles in his face tensing and twitching with the effort of keeping his daughter alive. 'And I couldn't let her last hours be filled with suffering.'

Roboute had heard that Vitali was managing Linya's pain, but seeing the traumatic reality of that process was horrifying. He felt his admiration at Vitali's devotion to his daughter soar – the Ultramarian core of him knew he could do no less.

He stood and used the vox-panel on the wall to open a channel to the *Renard*.

After a minute of clicking, static-filled growls, Emil Nader's voice barked from the augmitter.

'Roboute,' said Emil. 'Are you aboard yet? We can't get anything from the Mechanicus, all the internal systems are down. What in Konor's name is going on?'

'Shut up and listen, Emil,' snapped Roboute. 'We don't have much time. The *Speranza*'s on lockdown, and the shuttle's snagged on an e-mag tether.'

'Hell, and I guess you know the orbital track of the Ark's decaying?'

'Painfully aware,' replied Roboute. 'Now listen, we need to get back aboard right bloody now, and I'm going to need your help to do it.'

'Go ahead, whatever you need.'

'You remember that lunatic hauler pilot out of Cypra Mundi, the one with the ship that had those giant green eyes painted on its prow?'

'Rayner? The captain of *Infinite Terra?'*

'That's the one,' said Roboute. 'You remember how he died?'

'Of course I do,' said Emil. 'I still get nightmares thinking about the evacuation of Brontissa.'

'Yeah, tyranids do make things messy,' agreed Roboute. 'Now listen up, Emil. We're stuck out here, and unless Mistress Tychon gets to a proper medicae deck soon, she's going to die.'

'Shit! What do you need us to do?'

Roboute took a deep breath, knowing that what he was about to ask of his first mate was so dangerous that it might charitably be called suicidal.

But if there was one pilot in the galaxy Roboute would trust to pull this off, it was Emil Nader.

'I need you to do what Rayner tried,' said Roboute. 'But I need you to pull it off.'

It felt strange going into a hostile situation without his ubiquitous Hellhound tanks at his back or the roaring form of a Leman Russ Conqueror beneath him. Colonel Ven Anders firmly believed that marching towards the enemy on foot was a tactic of last resort or a way for gloryhounds to get themselves killed trying to make a name for themselves.

Yet here he was, marching towards the towering shutters of the embarkation deck at the head of a command squad of twenty Cadian Guardsmen, and not a single battle tank to be seen. Archmagos Kotov wasn't about to let him negotiate with Abrehem Locke without a show of force from the Mechanicus, and thus Magos Dahan and three Cataphract battle robots marched with him.

Anders wished the archmagos had despatched someone else. Dahan was twitchy and full of blistering indignation at this strike, just the sort of mindset that could turn this negotiation into a full-blown firefight. Bringing three hulking battle robots didn't exactly display a willingness to reach a peaceful solution.

Sergeant Tanna and a warrior named Varda were also part of the detachment, but were at least keeping a low profile to the back of this detachment – or as low a profile as two Space Marines could keep. Anders's original plan of keeping a human face on the negotiations

was starting to look less and less convincing, but he'd extracted oaths from both Dahan and Tanna that they would make no aggressive moves. Beside him, Captain Hawkins fought to keep his hands from reaching towards his pistol and sword.

'Steady, captain,' said Anders as they reached the embarkation deck. 'We don't want to upset the natives, now do we?'

'Sorry, sir,' replied Hawkins, conspicuously forcing his hands to his sides. 'Force of habit.'

'Understandable, but I want it absolutely clear that there is to be no weapon drawn without my express order. I don't even want bad language or unkind thoughts, you understand?'

'Absolutely, sir,' said Hawkins. 'I've passed the word, and anyone that messes up will have Rae to answer to.'

'I think Lieutenant Rae will be the least of anyone's worries if this goes to hell.'

'Right enough, sir,' said Hawkins as the shutter began to grind its way aside, accompanied by the wheezing clatter of gears and protesting servos.

'Here we go,' whispered Anders, marching into the embarkation deck. 'Once more into the Eye.'

The cavernous space beyond the shutters should have been filled with industrious labour; with servitors, bondsmen and Mechanicus logisters coordinating deck operations to Kryptaestrex's detailed resupply plans. A dozen recently arrived cargo haulers sat before the shimmering integrity field at the opening to the void, their hulls icy and sealed shut. Stevedore-servitors stood dumbly at the cargo doors, unmoving and rendered uncooperative by whatever power Abrehem Locke's restored servitor had exercised over them.

Ready to meet them were around fifty men in the dirty red coveralls of Mechanicus bondsmen. Anders saw thousands more behind them, lounging on stacked crates, milling in conspiratorial groups or sprawled on the deck asleep. To see men asleep while the clock ticked down to extinction almost beggared belief, but Anders had long since learned that human beings were capable of the strangest behaviour in times of crisis.

Their welcoming committee had ripped the sleeves from their uniforms or otherwise disfigured them in an obvious attempt at visibly throwing off the shackles of their perceived oppressors. Every one of them was armed, either with a heavy length of steel piping or a buzzing power tool of some description. Anders recognised the leader of this group immediately: Julius Hawke, an ex-Guardsman and a die-hard malingerer according to his file. He carried a rusted laslock, and despite a long list of disciplinary infractions and poor performance evaluations, it was clear he knew how to use it.

'You Anders?' asked Hawke.

'I am Colonel Ven Horatiu Anders, Colonel of the 71st Cadian Regiment of Hellhounds. Why aren't you in uniform any more, Guardsman Hawke?'

'Been a long time since anyone's called me that,' laughed Hawke, a sour bark that spoke of years spent undermining authority and mocking his betters. Despite what he'd said to Hawkins, Anders felt a strong desire to draw his sabre and run this affront to soldiery through. 'I'm just Hawke now, and I *am* in uniform. This is the uniform of the ain't going to take any more shit regiment.'

'I am here to speak with Abrehem Locke,' said Anders. 'So I'd be obliged if you'd take me to him.'

Hawke shook his head. 'I don't think so.'

The man's tone was infuriating and Anders bit back an angry retort. 'I was told he would be here.'

'Yeah, he is, but we didn't say nothing about bringing three bloody battle robots and a couple of Space Marines hiding at the back,' said Hawke. 'You think we're stupid?'

Anders dearly wanted to give the answer he knew he shouldn't, but contented himself by saying, 'Every second of my time you waste brings this ship closer to destruction. You tell me if that's stupid.'

'I've seen your sort before,' said Hawke. 'Think they're better than the rest of us grunts. You know, I knew an officer called Anders once before. A cocksure bastard, that's for sure. Got himself killed on Hydra Cordatus.'

'Ah, yes,' said Anders. 'I read your statement on the way here. During a supposed attack by Space Marines of the Archenemy, wasn't it?'

Hawke nodded. 'Yeah, that's the one.'

'On a dead world of no material or strategic significance,' said Anders. 'An attack both the Adeptus Mechanicus and Adeptus Astartes claim never happened.'

'That's what the Mechanicus *want* you to believe,' sneered Hawke, as though Anders were the very model of gullibility. 'Course they're not going to admit there was a fortress there and that the enemy came and took it off them like coins from a drunk.'

'Can you take me to Bondsman Locke or not?' asked Anders, tiring of Hawke's rambling.

'Yeah, I can, but just you.'

Captain Hawkins stepped forwards and said, 'That's not going to happen.'

'Now who's wasting time?' asked Hawke.

Anders waved Hawkins back. 'If that's what it takes to end this.'

'Sir, you can't just–'

'Captain, remain here with the men,' said Anders.

'Sir, I can't let you walk in there alone,' insisted Hawkins.

Anders ignored Hawkins's protests and said, 'I will be quite safe, I assure you. I need you to maintain discipline and keep the ranks straight. Oh, and if I'm not back in twenty minutes…'

'Sir?'

'You have my permission to kill everyone on this deck.'

Anders turned back to Hawke, whose face was a picture in stunned shock.

'Right then, Bondsman Hawke,' said Anders. 'Take me to your leader.'

Making her way through the guts of the humans' starship was childishly easy. Its gloomy corridors were draped in shadows and threaded with passageways even its crew appeared to have forgotten. The sepulchral gloom masked Bielanna's ascent from the depths of the ship as she slid through the shadows of towering machines that had not moved for centuries and along abandoned passageways ankle-deep in rat-infested water.

Towering metallic skull-on-cog icons stared down at her at every turn, nestling cheek by jowl with fretted stone gargoyles and gleaming machinery of brutish complexity: all pneumatic gears, clanking chains and smoke-belching pistons. The humans' starship was a mass of contradictions: a nightmarish temple where inhuman machinery was venerated and a breeding ground for the teeming masses of humanity who crewed it.

Bielanna would never understand the mon-keigh, a race so numerous and wantonly fecund that they outnumbered the stars. But the unimaginable scale of their species did not give them solace, but rather filled them with fear and drove them to stamp out any form of life and worship that did not match their own. Such unthinking hatred could only ever breed hatred in return, but the humans could not see that by their own actions were they damning themselves to an eternity of strife.

The more Bielanna saw of the humans aboard this ship, the less she thought of them as sentient beings at all. They were living grease in a grinding mechanical engine, corpuscles shunted from place to place in service of the great machine's continuance. How they could not see that they were little better than microbes crawling within the body of a larger beast was beyond her.

'They are not worshipping you,' she whispered, pausing beneath one

of the half-machine, half-human skulls stamped on a sheet steel wall. 'You enslave them and they believe themselves blessed.'

The skull belched a gout of flame and smoke from its empty eye socket, and Bielanna slid away into the darkness, following the threads of fate that had led her to risk moving into the occupied areas of the ship.

The vision had come suddenly, staggering her with its potency.

A gathering of humans in one of the vast chambers used to bring their ugly cargo ships aboard.

The meeting of a warrior and a man reluctantly fated to be both a saviour and a destroyer.

Most human lives were so ephemeral that their influence on the skein was microscopic, so infinitesimal that they were virtually an irrelevance, but whoever these two men were, they were worthy of notice, men whose actions could actually have an impact on the future.

Ariganna's impatience had made the meeting of these men inevitable, a fixed locus upon the skein around which a million times a billion possibilities revolved. The exarch had grown tired of skulking in the depths of the starship and given in to her war-mask's urge to kill. Where she had previously confined her slayings to those mon-keigh that unwittingly entered their shadowy lair, now she actively hunted the upper decks as a lone predator of unparalleled savagery and limitless cruelty. Bielanna had seen Ariganna kill the magos controlling the lethally volatile engine reactors. A bewilderingly complex web of infinite possibility exploded before her eyes.

As Bielanna had hoped, her connection to the skein had become stronger with every passing day and every light year the ship travelled from the reborn star system. But instead of cohering her sight of the future, that strengthening had only made her interpretations more ambiguous. Entwined memories of the past and visions of the future's infinite variety filled her every waking moment, and Bielanna found it almost impossible to distinguish between what was real and what was imagined.

Yet the vision of these two men remained constant whenever she looked into the future.

She came at last to the place where the thread of fate she had been following now branched out beyond her ability to trace with any certainty: a towering stained-glass window depicting a grey-steel temple atop a red mountain that churned out armoured vehicles and smoke in equal measure. One of the window's lower panes was broken, and Bielanna eased herself through, emerging onto a stonework ledge overlooking a vast deck space with an enormous opening on its far wall that looked onto the void.

Thousands of the mon-keigh were gathered below her, flickering embers of life and fleeting existence. Some embers burned brighter than others, and she flinched at the radiance coming from two black-armoured giants, kin to the warrior the avatar of Kaela Mensha Khaine had killed. She had seen the fate-lines of Space Marines before, and they burned with a directness that was almost pitiable, but the fates of these warriors felt somehow familiar, as though she had flown the futures they too would walk.

Simmering aggression filled the deck like a sickness, and Bielanna needed no psychic sensitivity to feel the rippling undercurrents of fear and imminent violence oozing into the atmosphere.

That was good.

She could use one to provoke the other.

Leering cherubs with rebreathers instead of faces had been carved on either side of the window, and as she knelt at the corner of the ledge, the metallic skull of the nearest rolled a mechanised eye in her direction. Bielanna ignored it, feeling her gaze drawn to the flickering energy field that kept the deck pressurised. She felt a momentary tremor of unease at the sight of unknown stars that should not exist.

She shook off the sensation of being watched by these ghoulish stars and took a breath of polluted air as her senses eased into the flickering fate-lines of the mon-keigh. She sought the one whose fear was the greatest and most easily moulded, finding him easily among the mass of slave workers and shrouding his mind with emanations of his darkest nightmares.

The future was bewilderingly complex and inconstant, but one thing was certain.

The humans known as Anders and Locke could not be allowed to settle their differences.

Anders sat on a shipping crate on the far side of the embarkation deck. He and Abrehem Locke sat opposite one another, ringed by a laager of tracked Mechanicus earth-moving machinery. Anders had to admit to feeling a little let down by the sight of the firebrand whose rhetoric of insurrection had echoed from one end of the *Speranza* to the other.

Hollow cheeked and shaven headed, with metallic glints at the corners of his eyes, Abrehem Locke did not look or sound like a revolutionary, and his augmetic arm wasn't particularly impressive either without weapons or any form of combat attachments. He looked

exactly like what he was: a Mechanicus bondsman on the verge of starvation, exhaustion and mental breakdown.

Anders could almost sympathise.

The arco-flagellant, however, was another matter. The cybernetic killer stared with an undisguised urge to kill him, but Anders dismissed it. If it attacked him, he would be dead before he even had a chance to react, so there was no point wasting time worrying about it.

'You realise that if we fail to reach agreement, we all die,' said Anders.

'I'm aware of that,' replied Locke.

'Then tell me what I can do to end this.'

'You can get Archmagos Kotov to release the bondsmen,' said Locke. 'I'd ask for the servitors to be reverse engineered if I didn't think the iatrogenic shock would kill them.'

Anders nodded. 'You know he's not going to agree to that. Especially after you had the Master of Engines killed.'

Locke's eyes narrowed and his shoulders squared in irritation. 'Saiixek is dead?'

'I believe that was his name, yes.'

'Saiixek was the first magos I saw when I came aboard the *Speranza*,' said Locke. 'He worked a hundred men to death before we'd even broken Joura's orbit, hundreds more just to reach the galactic edge. I won't shed a single tear for that bastard, but we didn't kill him. Unlike Magos Kotov, I don't have blood on my hands.'

'We *all* have blood on our hands, my friend,' said Anders, surprised to find that he believed Abrehem. 'All service to the Emperor requires sacrifice.'

'I'd prefer my own sacrifice in the Emperor's name to be a willing one,' said Locke, lifting his bionic arm by way of example. 'That's what Kotov fails to understand. This ship is a machine to him, and all we are to him is human fuel to keep it going, to be spent and used up at will.'

'You should try life in the Imperial Guard,' said Anders.

Locke shook his head. 'No, you misunderstand me, Colonel Anders. I know the realities of life in the Imperium. Everyone serves, whether they want to or not. Sure, maybe we didn't all sign up for this, but we're here now and we have a job to do. Treat us like slaves and all he'll get is resentment and revolt. Treat us like human beings worthy of respect and everything changes.'

'Do you think the Mechanicus are capable of that?'

'They can learn,' said Locke, leaning forwards. 'After all, it's in their best interest. Which would you rather lead into battle, a regiment

of willing soldiers who know you're going to do your damnedest to keep them alive, or a bunch of conscripts who couldn't give a shit for your war or who won it?'

'I'm Cadian, so you already know the answer to that, but rhetorical questions aren't going to solve this,' said Anders, nodding to the cyborg killer at Abrehem's shoulder. 'Since you seem keen to point out hypocrisy, isn't it a bit rich that you keep that arco-flagellant around? He's bio-imprinted to you now, a slave to your every command. Do you want him to be freed too? The archmagos tells me there's no file on who he was before his transmogrification, but he would have been a monster. A child murderer or rapist or a heretic. Or something even worse.'

Locke appeared genuinely disturbed at Anders's words, as though the provenance of the arco-flagellant had never occurred to him, or he knew something of the arco-flagellant's previous existence he wished he didn't. Given what was rumoured of Abrehem Locke's nature, the latter seemed a more likely explanation.

'You're right, of course,' said Abrehem with a fixed expression. 'But right now a little hypocrisy is a price I'm willing to pay to get what I want.'

'A little evil in service of a greater good, is that it?'

'That's a negative way of putting it.'

'I don't see another,' said Anders. 'Listen, Abrehem, you can't sit there on your high horse, demanding freedom and claiming to hold the moral high ground, then admit that you're willing to accept a little bit of slavery if it achieves your aims.'

'I don't have a choice, colonel,' said Locke, and once again Anders saw past the hectoring rebel to the desperately tired man whom circumstances had forced into the role of a leader; a role he was manifestly unsuited to filling. 'This is the only way.'

Anders folded his arms and said, 'You strike me as an intelligent man, Abrehem, not a suicidal one. You must have some level at which you're willing to compromise. We could sit here and haggle and posture till we reach that level, but as I'm sure you know, we don't have the luxury of time. With Saiixek's death and servitors refusing to work, the *Speranza*'s going down. Very soon, we'll all be dead unless you and I can agree.'

'At least this way it will be by our hand instead of the Mechanicus.'

'And what about everyone else?' asked Anders, letting a measure of his anger show. 'What about all my soldiers? The menials, the void-born, and all the other thousands of souls aboard this vessel? Are you willing to murder them all over a principle? I don't think so.'

Locke's eyes flashed defiance, but it was hollow bravado and the fire went out of him. He was angry, yes, but he wasn't willing to murder an entire ship to achieve his goals.

Anders knew he'd won and felt the knot of tension in his gut relax.

Before he could take solace in Locke's backing down, the sharp crack of a gunshot echoed from the other side of the laager of vehicles. Anders recognised the sound with a sinking heart.

M36 Kantrael-pattern lasrifle.

Cadian issue...

Of all the manoeuvres Emil Nader had attempted in his long years spent at the helm of a starship, this had to rank as one of the stupidest. He'd made emergency warp jumps before he'd reached the Mandeville point, run the gauntlet of greenskin roks and navigated the heart of an asteroid belt, but this was just insane.

The panel in front of him was lit with repeated calls for him to return to the ship, calls that only served to highlight the bone-headed literalness of the Mechanicus perfectly.

'Demand: vessel *Renard*, your launch is unauthorised,' said a grating mechanical voice over the vox. 'You are to return to the *Speranza* immediately and shut down your engines.'

Emil didn't waste breath in replying, knowing there would be no point.

'Repeated demand: vessel *Renard*, your launch is unauthorised. You are to–'

Magos Pavelka interrupted. 'While it is true that we do not have clearance to depart the forward embarkation deck, we are of the opinion that remaining aboard is not the safest option since the *Speranza* is in imminent danger of breaking up in the planet's atmosphere.'

'Couldn't have put it better myself,' said Emil, shutting off the vox-feed from the *Speranza*'s deck magos. 'We'll make a scoundrel out of you yet, Ilanna.'

Pavelka sat across from him in the co-pilot's seat, while Sylkwood was down in the engine spaces, trying to keep the *Renard*'s engines hot enough to make the manoeuvre possible without turning the flanks of the *Speranza* to molten slag.

'I do not flout Mechanicus protocols lightly, Mister Nader,' said Pavelka, feeding as much navigational data as she could to Emil's station. 'The deck magos will enforce proper chastisement upon our return to the *Speranza*.'

'Seriously?'

'Of course,' said Pavelka. 'As is only right and proper.'

'Assuming we don't die out here.'

'Assuming we do not die,' agreed Pavelka. 'I calculate the odds of our success as–'

'No, no, no…' said Emil. 'I don't want to know, you'll jinx me.'

Pavelka looked as though she was about to rise to that particular morsel, but simply nodded and carried on feeding him information on the gravimetric field enveloping the Ark Mechanicus. The ancient machinery generating the *Speranza*'s internal gravity, coupled with its sheer mass, created a squalling region of turbulence that made just flying in a straight line a daunting challenge.

This was where the e-mag tether had stranded the *Renard's* shuttle.

'You are aware, of course, that the last captain to attempt a manoeuvre such as this was killed and his ship lost with all hands?' said Pavelka.

'Yeah, I'm aware of that,' he said. 'In fact I saw it, but Rayner was crazy and he had dozens of tyranid bio-parasites clamped to his hull. Even if he'd pulled it off, everyone on that ship would have died. Trust me, compared to what he tried, this'll be easy.'

'Then you and I differ on the definition of *easy*.'

Emil grinned and thumbed the brass-topped switch connecting him to the engineering spaces below. 'Sylkwood, you about ready?'

Even over the vox, the enginseer's abrasive tones were clear.

'Yeah, we're ready, but don't expect this to be a smooth ride.'

'Just so long as it's one we all survive.'

'I'm not promising anything,' said Sylkwood. 'We're going to lose some of the manoeuvring jets, and the structure's not rated for this tight a turn.'

'But the *Renard*'s a tough old bird, yeah? She'll hold together, won't she?'

'Tell her you love her, then promise you'll never make her fly like this again and she might.'

Emil nodded and flexed his fingers on the ship's control mechanisms. Ordinarily, a ship the size of the *Renard* would rarely be flown manually, operating instead via a series of inputted commands, moving between pre-configured waypoints and automated flight profiles.

'Is there anything I could say that would persuade you to let the onboard data-engine navigate us to the shuttle?' asked Pavelka. 'You cannot hope to process the sheer amount of variables in the *Speranza*'s gravitational envelope.'

'If you're not willing to trust your own skills over the onboard systems then you don't deserve to call yourself a pilot,' answered Emil. 'I learned everything about starships in the atmosphere of Espandor, and I know how to fly the *Renard* better than any machine. I know her ticks and her every quirk. She and I have been through more scrapes than I care to remember. She knows me and I know her. I take care of her, and she's looked after us all for years. She's not about to let us down now, not when Roboute's in trouble.'

Pavelka reached over and laid a hand on Emil's shoulder.

'The *Renard* is a fine ship, one of the best I have known,' she said. 'And for all that I believe you to be needlessly antagonistic towards my order, you are a fine pilot. You might not wish to know the odds of this venture succeeding, but I am fully aware of the likelihood of success.'

'Is that a good thing?'

'Of all the baseline humans I know, I would have no other piloting this ship right now, Emil.'

Pavelka's uncharacteristically human words touched him, as did her use of his given name.

'Then let's go get our captain,' said Emil.

Microcontent 17

Captain Hawkins threw himself at Guardsman Manos, knocking him to the deck before he could fire again, but the damage had already been done. The first bondsman died with a neat las-burn drilled through the centre of his skull and his brains flash-burned to vapour. No sooner had he collapsed than Manos switched targets, killing another seven bondsmen on full-auto before Hawkins reached him.

'Stand down!' shouted Hawkins, fighting to pin Manos down. 'That's an order, soldier!'

Manos screamed and thrashed in terror, his face twisted in horror.

'They're monsters, captain!' screamed Manos. 'Let me up or they'll kill us all!'

Hawkins locked his elbow around the struggling Guardsman's neck as the cries of outrage from the bondsmen intensified. Any moment they were going to look for payback.

'The monsters from the Eye!' shouted Manos. 'Can't you see them? They're going to kill us!'

'Manos, shut the hell up,' ordered Hawkins, tightening his grip. 'You're not making any sense.'

'I saw them,' sobbed Manos, his words slurring as Hawkins's sleeper hold took effect. 'They look like people, but their disguises slipped and I saw them... They're beasts straight out of the Eye and we have to kill them all... please...'

The bondsmen were yelling for blood now and moving towards the Cadian line.

Manos's struggles ceased as he slipped into unconsciousness, and Hawkins sprang to his feet as the man Colonel Anders had identified as Hawke supplied the final push over the cliff to this situation.

'They came here to kill us, lads!' shouted Hawke. 'Get them before they get us!'

The bondsmen threw themselves at the Cadian line, brandishing power tools and heavy spars of metal. Hawkins didn't fail to notice that Hawke wasn't leading the charge, but hanging back behind some of the larger bondsmen.

'No shooting!' shouted Hawkins as the bondsmen slammed into the Cadian ranks.

A man with a full-facial tattoo of a spider came at him, swinging a heavy piece of iron pipework. Hawkins ducked the swing and slammed the heel of his palm into the man's solar plexus. He stepped back as the man dropped with a *whoosh* of expelled air and brought his own rifle around to use as a cudgel. Three men in faded red coveralls attacked and Hawkins staggered as a clubbing fist smashed into the side of his head.

Instinctive training responses took over and he swung his rifle out in a sweeping arc that connected with his attacker's stomach and doubled him over. He dropped the second man with a jab of the lasgun's butt to the head and shook off the dizziness of his own hurt. He felt hands dragging his shoulders and spun around, slamming his rifle into the chest of his attacker.

His rifle butt split along its length against Sergeant Tanna's breastplate. The Space Marine didn't so much as flinch at the impact.

Tanna hauled him back into the line of fighting, lifting him as though he weighed no more than a child. Tanna swept his arms out, knocking back half a dozen bondsmen with every blow.

Many of the men fell with broken bones, but Hawkins knew they were lucky to be alive. Anyone that attacked a warrior of the Adeptus Astartes was courting death, and the restraint in Tanna's blows was clear.

'Staying here is futile,' said Tanna. 'We must withdraw.'

'We're not leaving without the colonel,' replied Hawkins.

'Then lethal force is our only option.'

'No, we're not killing any more of these men!'

'We may not have a choice,' said Tanna.

The bondsmen had them surrounded, punching, kicking and screaming at them in fury. Hawkins's Guardsmen had formed an impromptu shield wall, fighting to keep the bondsmen back with vicious blows of rifle butts. Dahan fought with the bulbous pod at the base of his halberd, which was thankfully deactivated. The battle robots were currently inactive, but it wouldn't take this situation long to escalate to a level where Dahan felt he had no choice but to bring their terrifyingly destructive guns to bear.

The Space Marines fought without weapons, bludgeoning the bondsmen back with blows that were delivered with a finesse that was as precise as it was bone-crunching. Wherever Hawkins looked, he saw Cadians and bondsmen locked in vicious brawls. Discipline was paying off against anger, as the raw fury of the bondsmen was no match for Cadian training. Every man in Hawkins's command was fighting as part of a unit, each defending their fellow soldiers' backs and expecting the same in return. Living in the shadow of the Eye of Terror demanded a dedication to martial brotherhood that few other regiments could match.

Hawkins struggled to see if there was any way they could reach the circle of earth-moving machines where the colonel had gone to negotiate with Abrehem Locke. The deck was awash with bondsmen – there was no way they could make headway through so many men. At least not without using their weapons, and even then it was doubtful. Getting to the colonel looked hopeless, but then Hawkins saw the ex-Guardsman, Hawke. The man was doing his best to avoid the fighting, but the sheer press of bodies had forced him to the front.

'You're mine,' said Hawkins, shouldering his way through the fighting.

Hawke saw him coming, but there was nowhere for him to go.

The two of them slammed together and Hawkins pistoned his fist into the man's face.

Hawke hadn't survived the Guard for years without learning how to take a punch, and he rolled with the blow, ducking and slamming his own fist up into Hawkins's gut. The ex-Guardsman was a brawler, and a dirty fighter to boot. The two of them scrapped and grappled each other without finesse, clawing, gouging and hammering at one another like drunken pugilists at a punchbag.

Hawke fought with every foul trick in the gutter-fighter's arsenal, but Cadians knew every below the belt trick. Hawkins saw the next blow coming, a knee to the groin, and lifted his own leg to block it. He dropped and swung his rifle around, slamming the cracked butt against the side of Hawke's thigh. The man howled in pain, but Hawkins wasn't about to let up his assault.

He slammed a right cross into Hawke's cheek and followed that

up with the opposite elbow to the temple. The man collapsed and Hawkins dropped onto his chest, pummelling him with right and left hooks until his face was a mask of blood.

He hauled the man upright and shouted in his face.

'Stop this now before someone gets killed!' he shouted.

Hawke spat a mouthful of blood, and even through his mangled features, he was grinning.

'You bastards started this,' he coughed. 'Your man shot one of ours.'

'I don't know what that was about, but if you don't call your men off, people are going to die.'

'Too late for that,' said Hawke, as a figure clad in black and silver landed next to one of Dahan's battle robots. Silver threshing limbs swept out and the robot's right arm was severed cleanly from its chassis. Another whipping blow and its head spun away from its neck as though it had been punched off by an ogryn.

A second robot was felled as its left leg was sheared off at the hip, and it crashed to the deck with its motors screeching and its augmitters blaring in machine pain. Hawkins released Hawke and stared into the flickering red eyes of a cybernetic killer.

The arco-flagellant knelt in the ruin of the two Cataphracts, the gleaming silver electro-flails sparking with electrical discharge as the oily lifeblood of the robots burned away.

'Kill. Maim. Destroy,' it said.

The *Renard*'s keel measured just under three kilometres, which meant that its normal turning circle was correspondingly large. A starship's hull and internal structure was designed to withstand the stresses of the void and vast forces of acceleration, but no human shipwright had ever designed a vessel of such displacement to be nimble.

But that was just what Emil Nader was asking of it now.

They were clear of the *Speranza*, and with a last nod towards Ilanna Pavelka, he hauled the controls around and fired a sequenced burn of manoeuvring rockets along the length of the hull. Vectored thrust from the starboard prow jets fired at maximum thrust, while the port-side jets on the ship's rear and dorsal sections provided counter-thrust to complete the pivoting turn.

Emil felt himself pressed into his seat as local gravity within the *Renard* increased. The superstructure groaned as torsion forces tried to buckle structural ribs and twist the keel into unnatural shapes.

'Lambda deck breached,' said Pavelka. 'Hull stresses thirty per cent past recommended tolerances. Engine containment field strength diminishing.'

Emil didn't answer. What would be the point? He'd always known this manoeuvre wouldn't be possible without suffering. He could feel the ship's pain, but forced himself to ignore it. To halt their manoeuvre now would be just as dangerous. He fired another sequenced blast of thrust, rolling the *Renard* onto its back relative to the *Speranza*. He let the turn continue until the two vessels were facing one another, before firing the main engines with a corrective burn on the vectored thrusters to stabilise their yaw.

The *Renard* was shaking itself apart as conflicting thrusts placed intolerable loads on its superstructure. Steel girders the thickness of Titan legs were twisting like heated plastic, and precision-machined panels were bursting from their settings as the ship warped under stresses beyond what even the most exacting inspector might demand.

'Lateral distance to *Speranza* is closing,' said Pavelka. 'Remember, she's in a downward spiral and our closure rate is increasing.'

'Compensating,' said Emil, his fingertips dancing over the control panel to apply an insistent thrust to keep them a more or less constant distance from the Ark Mechanicus. The mountainous bulk of the *Speranza* began shifting over the *Renard* as the smaller ship slid past below. The controls were fighting him all the way as the rogue gravitational forces surrounding the mighty vessel slammed into the *Renard*.

Scads of the upper atmosphere shimmered around the *Renard*, evidence of the descending spiral track of the *Speranza*. Striated bands of gaseous colours were bleeding into the black of space and Emil read a sudden and alarming spike of heat on the *Renard*'s ventral surfaces as he was forced to factor atmospheric friction into his course corrections. Gravity had the *Speranza* in its grip, and it wouldn't be long before that grip became unbreakable.

Emil dragged his eyes from the view through the canopy. What he was seeing out there didn't matter for now. Instead, he kept his gaze focused on the slender route he had mapped towards the *Renard*'s shuttle, a hair-fine parabola that only a lunatic might think was possible. He wasn't even aware of the adjustments he was making to their course, an innate skill and feel for the motion of a starship informing his every action. The structure of the *Speranza* flew over them, titanic manufactories and enormous processing plants slipping past silently as the two ships passed at what was, in spatial terms, point-blank range.

The gravity fields sought to pull the two ships together, but Emil kept them apart with deft flares from the dorsal vectors and an unimaginably delicate hand on the controls. At such differential speeds and at such close range, even minute alterations in pitch meant kilometres of space between the two ships would vanish in seconds.

'There, up ahead,' said Pavelka.

Emil risked a quick glance through the canopy and saw a glint of reflected light from the shuttle's hull. The term shuttle was misleading, as that vessel was itself over two hundred metres long and thirty wide. The tether holding it in place was invisible, but that the shuttle wasn't being buffeted from side to side by the *Speranza*'s gravity envelope was enough to tell Emil it was there. Its perceived motion was caused by the *Renard*'s erratic movement, which – minute as it was in relative terms – was still hundreds of metres to either side.

All of which would make scooping the shuttle up in the *Renard*'s forward cargo bay… tricky.

'Captain,' said Emil. 'We see you and are closing on your position.'

'Understood,' came Roboute's voice over the vox. 'You still reckon you can make this work?'

'*Please*. This is me you're talking to. It'll be like threading a needle from the back of a racing land speeder while blindfolded,' said Emil. 'Easy money if you fancy a wager.'

'You think I'd bet against you?' asked Roboute. 'You're as insane as Rayner.'

'Rayner couldn't wipe his own arse without a map and a servitor,' said Emil. 'Now shut up and fire the rig's drives when I give you the word.'

The shuttle steadily grew in size through the canopy, becoming a vaguely rectangular smear of light, then an identifiable silhouette of a trans-orbital ship, and finally a unique vessel. Emil fought to keep the buffeting movement of the *Renard* to a minimum, knowing that even the tiniest movement out of place would see both ships torn apart by a collision at towering closure speeds.

'Emergency depressurisation of frontal cargo hold,' said Pavelka. 'Opening frontal cargo doors.'

Emil felt the change in the *Renard*'s flight profile instantly. Aerodynamic properties that were irrelevant in space were suddenly of vital importance now that they were skimming the upper atmosphere. A winking light chimed on the panel.

'Now, captain,' said Emil. 'Fire those engines for all they're worth.'

The evacuation of Brontissa had been a nightmarish race against time, a countdown to extinction faced by billions of people with no clue as to the horror of what awaited them. A trading hub in a prosperous arc of the Melenian Dust Belt, Brontissa squatted at a confluence of trade routes and military channels, supplying both staple and exotic goods to the surrounding sectors, as well as providing a haven for

weary captains to rest and recuperate while seeking out fresh contracts as their fleets were refitted in the web of orbital dockyards.

The full horror of the tyranid race was not yet appreciated by the people of the Imperium. Few could believe that such an unimaginable threat could exist within the Emperor's dominion, and fewer still had heard anything more than scare stories told third or fourth hand. Only when planet after planet of the Dust Belt went dark was something of the terrifying nature of these extra-galactic predators understood.

System monitors sent to investigate were never heard from again, and only when a demi-fleet led by an ageing Apocalypse-class battleship encountered the vanguard of the tyranids was the scale of the threat understood. Only two ships escaped to bring warning back to Brontissa, but by then it was already too late for the majority of the populace. Regiments of Imperial Guard from adjacent systems and in-transit forces of Space Marines from the Exorcists, Silver Spectres and Blood Angels were diverted to blunt the threat.

An entire Titan Legion walked the surface of Brontissa, and as the military might of the Imperium assembled, its populace fled in their billions as worldwide panic finally took hold. Every ship that could be lifted into orbit took flight, their holds and corridors packed with refugees, and thousands were killed in the stampede to flee their doomed world. Many more died as the skies above Brontissa filled with colliding ships attempting to thread a path through the orbital architecture without heed or care.

A screaming horde of starships blasted into high orbit, but the tyranids were not some mono-directional mass of unthinking drones. They had devoured Imperial worlds before and had learned from each slaughter. The volume of space around Brontissa was seeded with billions upon billions of bio-organisms. Some were lethally intelligent hunter-killer creatures as vast as Imperial battleships and formed like frond-mouthed conches. Others were little more than organic mines, billowing in dense, spore-like clouds to cripple fleeing craft to be devoured at leisure.

Space around Brontissa became an orbital graveyard, a spinning, metallic wasteland of crippled starships. The fortunate ones died swiftly when their ships lost atmosphere and oxygen, but some survived long enough to be boarded and overrun by chittering hosts of flesh-eating monsters.

Roboute had brought the *Renard* to Brontissa to refresh his contacts in one of the system cartels, a diverse organisation that ran everything from absurdly overpriced luxuries to illegal narcotics and underground relics of dubious provenance. He kept his dealings with its potentates to a minimum, but there had been a passing of a long-lived patriarch, and the proper obeisance needed to be made to the newly appointed scion.

It had been an excruciating week of enforced formality and overblown theatrics, but Roboute had endured it for the sake of the vast sums these particular clients brought to his coffers. But when rumours of the impending alien threat began circulating, Roboute knew better than anyone the truth of this rapacious xenos breed. Everyone in Ultramar knew of the tyranids and the unimaginable scale of the devastation they could wreak.

Warning everyone he knew to leave Brontissa, the *Renard* lifted from the planet's surface amid a panicked armada, surviving several near-misses and once being clipped by the void array of a system monitor in blatant contravention of shipping rights of way. It had been a dangerous escape requiring some deft flying from both Roboute and Emil, but they had broken into open space before the unsuspected englobement of the planet was complete.

Just before breaking through the closing trap of bio-organic ships and orbital spore mines, Roboute had witnessed Captain Makrus Rayner of the *Infinite Terra* attempt a rescue of a beleaguered vessel he believed was carrying his wife and daughter. Roboute knew Makrus only tangentially, as a conveyor of goods thrice removed, but he had liked the man's spirit and his willingness to fly anywhere.

Already trailing a hull's worth of parasitic polymer fronds from a detonated spore mine, the *Infinite Terra* was in no state to manoeuvre. Its vectored engines were clogged with frothing biomass, and its void arrays were snapped after the impact of dozens of burrowing beetle-creatures with teeth like underground drilling rigs. The ship Rayner believed his family to be aboard was much smaller, a cargo lighter that could just about break orbit, but little else. Without inter-system capability or warp engines, there was no way it could escape the darting, bullet-nosed devourer beasts on its tail – Rayner knew it.

With his forward cargo bay wide open, he'd flown through the upper reaches of Brontissa's atmosphere – already turbulent with insidious tyranid micro-organisms that were consuming the oxygen and nitrogen in the air – and attempted to scoop up the cargo lighter. With both ships moving at orbit-breaking speeds the resultant explosion was visible from the planet's surface, flaring briefly as a miniature sun before fading into the distorting colour spectrum of the atmosphere.

The shockwave had swatted away a number of organisms turning their rudimentary senses towards the *Renard*, and though Roboute

had not known Rayner well, he owed his fellow spacefarer a debt of gratitude.

Roboute later learned that Rayner's family were on a different ship altogether, one that escaped the terror of the evacuation and had sought them out to pass on the heroic manner of the man's death. Rayner's daughter had returned to Anohkin with Roboute, entering into a mutually beneficial business arrangement that lasted until her ship brought back the *Tomioka*'s saviour pod and Roboute had seen the possibility of a life beyond the boundaries of the Imperium.

Thinking back to the moment he had seen the *Infinite Terra* vanish in a searing nuclear fireball and watching the approaching form of the *Renard*, he wondered if he'd made a grave error in having Emil attempt the same manoeuvre. Probably, but it was too late to change anything now.

Roboute flipped open the ship-wide vox.

'Everyone hold onto something,' he said. 'This might get a little rough…'

Watching his own ship approach at speed while he was tethered in place was like watching a vast mega-organism approaching through the depths of the darkest ocean, its jaws wide to devour the tiny morsel before it without even realising it was there. This was going to be like a bullet flying back down the barrel of a gun and was just as risky as that sounded.

Emil's voice came over the vox from the *Renard*, 'Now, captain. Fire those engines for all they're worth.'

Roboute slammed the thrust controls out to their maximum deployment, applying a dangerous amount of energy within such close proximity to another craft. The shuttle lurched and the internal gravity wallowed as brutal acceleration strained to throw off the e-mag tether holding it in place. Roboute looked back through the rear-facing hull picters and experienced a moment of bowel-churning terror as the vast maw of the *Renard* filled the distortion-hazed screen and the pummelling bow wave of displaced neutron flow slammed into the shuttle's hull.

The image vanished in a flurry of static as the *Renard* swallowed the shuttle in its forward hold.

Roboute fought to keep the controls steady as the vast bulk of the *Renard* snapped the shuttle's tether and sent a squalling burst of feedback into the *Speranza*'s hull. The resulting explosion was lost to sight almost instantly. The shuttle's engines filled the *Renard*'s cargo hold with a seething mass of plasma fire, and everything the servitor crews hadn't removed was instantly incinerated. Only the instantaneous deployment of fire suppression systems kept the fire from burning through the rear bulkheads and gutting the rest of the ship.

Those same systems were themselves incinerated by the plasma, but by then they had done their job. The shuttle slammed into the rear bulkhead of the cargo compartment, and the heat-softened metal buckled like melted wax before the forward momentum of the *Renard* crushed the engines and empty rear compartments of the shuttle, folding them up like a concertinaing bulkhead door. Flames billowed from ruptured fuel lines, and what little air hadn't already been vented from the systems caught light and pinprick fires burned phosphor bright for seconds until oxygen starvation killed them.

Roboute, pinned in place by the force of the impact, just barely managed to slam his fist down on the explosive release bolts holding the shuttle's crew compartment rig to the cargo spaces. The rig's manoeuvring boosters fired and the g-forces holding Roboute in place lessened as the absurdly powerful engines fired with short-burn force.

Ahead of him, Roboute saw the flame-wreathed outline of the *Renard*'s cargo bay and fought to keep the tapered prow of the rig aimed at its centre. Burning the boosters with such power was depleting their fuel cells at an alarming rate, but the mouth of the cargo bay was now racing towards Roboute and he let out a wild whoop as the smaller rig roared from inside the *Renard*, its forward velocity beginning to outstrip the larger vessel.

'The rig's loose!' shouted Roboute. 'Cut your speed, Emil!'

Suddenly all that was around Roboute was empty space and the whipping bands of vapour in the upper strata of the atmosphere. He kept the engines sun-hot until he estimated that any projecting portions of the *Renard*'s prow were now behind him before hauling the control column up and to the side.

'Come on, come on!' said Roboute through gritted teeth. Silent acres of azure steel and adamantium slid by beneath him as the *Renard* ploughed onwards, trailing a halo of fire from its battered frontal sections. His ship had never looked so beautiful.

'Holy Terra, I can't believe that worked!' shouted Emil. 'You're alive? Really? We didn't blow up and this is all just my last moments in slow motion?'

'We made it, Emil,' said Roboute, letting out what felt like ten lungfuls of breath and feeling his heart rate slow from its current triphammer speed. 'Wait. You didn't think we'd make it?'

'Sure, yeah, I always knew *I* could do it,' said Emil. 'I just didn't know if *you* could.'

'Your faith in my piloting skills is touching,' said Roboute, turning

the rig back towards the *Speranza*. The sheer scarp of its hull loomed before Roboute and the small craft was slammed back and forth by rogue gravity waves thrown off by the enormous starship.

'I see why ships need an e-mag tether now,' he muttered, finding the nearest embarkation deck's lodestar signal. His vox and avionics panels lit up with warning sigils and blaring binary code waving him off, but Roboute shut them all down and angled his course towards the *Speranza*.

'Hold on, Linya,' whispered Roboute.

Tanna threw himself at the arco-flagellant, his fist arcing towards its skull.

The blow connected, but instead of tearing the arco-flagellant's head from its shoulders, it merely rocked the cyborg killer back on its heels. Tanna followed up with a thunderous punch, but the arco-flagellant swayed aside and slashed out with its gleaming electro-flail arms. The strike would have cut Tanna in two, but Varda's black-bladed sword swept out and intercepted the lethal whips and sliced them from its wrist.

Varda fired his pistol at the arco-flagellant at point-blank range, the bolt blasting a chunk of meat from the killer's side, but, incredibly, it stayed upright as chem-stimms blocked out the pain and spurred its hyper-accelerated metabolism to heal itself. Fresh flails extruded from the arco-flagellant's gauntlets as it threw itself at the two Space Marines. The red circle at its forehead pulsed like a heartbeat, and its gleaming fangs were bared as though it was relishing this chance to fight opponents capable of harming it.

Varda backed away, using the Black Sword to keep the arco-flagellant from getting too close. Tanna drew his own sword now that he had a foe he could legitimately kill. He came at the cyborg killer from the opposite side to Varda, slashing low for its legs. The creature leaped over his blade, slamming a fist into the side of Tanna's helm. He felt bone crack and was driven to one knee by the force of the blow. He threw his left arm up in time to block another fist, but he was powerless to prevent the slamming head-butt crashing full into his visor. The impact was monstrous and would have caved the skull of a mortal man. Tanna rocked back, his nose shattered and one eye filled with blood as he toppled to the deck.

Tanna knew there was a scrum of desperate fighting going on all around him, but he could hear nothing beyond the ringing in his ears and his ragged breathing. His right eye lens was a cracked and static-filled mess. He felt the surge of power from his armour as the spinal plug blocked his pain receptors and released a burst of combat-enhancing stimms. He rolled, expecting a follow-up attack, but Varda was slashing his sword at the arco-flagellant's neck.

Except the killer was no longer there, moving with preternatural speed thanks to the volatile concoction of potent and highly dangerous drugs coursing through its hyper-stimulated metabolism. The arco-flagellant ducked beneath Varda's blade and spun around him to ram suddenly ramrod-straight flail-talons into the Emperor's Champion's side. The energised spikes punched through Varda's plate and he loosed a guttural roar of pain.

But rather than let that pain master him, Varda turned in to the arco-flagellant and put a bolt-round straight into its chest at a range of centimetres. The bolt punched into the killer's chest and the explosive warhead detonated microseconds after, exploding from its back in a bloody exit wound.

But still it refused to die.

Its electro-flails crackled with power and Varda cried out as the shock was delivered straight to his nervous system. The Emperor's Champion dropped to his knees, and Tanna cried out as the Black Sword fell from his grip. The arco-flagellant wrenched its arm in Varda's side, but the Emperor's Champion had his hand wrapped around the writhing steel embedded in his body, holding it fast to his flesh.

Tanna then realised that Varda had not dropped his sword, but released it deliberately.

And now swung it on the fresh-forged chain Tanna had crafted.

The strike was as horrendous as it was unexpected, the blade slicing into the arco-flagellant's shoulder. It ricocheted from the bone and tore into the meat and steel of its skull. Sparks and oil-infused blood sprayed from the wound as the arco-flagellant staggered away from Varda. It howled in a mixture of rage and pain, one arm hanging limply at its side as though the synaptic connections to the limb had been severed.

'Finish it!' commanded Varda.

Tanna surged to his feet and swept his bolter from the mag-lock at his thigh.

The aiming reticule was useless in the smashed visor, but Tanna didn't need it.

But before he could squeeze the trigger, the integrity field at the opening of the embarkation deck blew inwards with the sudden passage of a damaged cargo rig. Given the unexpected and unauthorised arrival of this ship, none of the pressurisation differential protocols or energy damping generators had been initiated to receive an incoming vessel. Ice-cold air blew into the embarkation deck with hurricane force as the integrity field was breached for the briefest second and the battered rig slammed to the deck with a shriek of tearing metal.

It left a cascade of fat orange sparks in its wake as it skidded across the deck like a rampaging bull-grox, smashing cargo containers aside and ripping up a row of loader gurneys in its headlong rush across the deck space. Bondsmen and Cadians scattered like ants as they fought to get out of its pathway.

The violated integrity field snapped back into place, and a concussive e-mag pulse slammed through the deck and toppled those few men still standing like a fist to the guts.

Microcontent 18

The *Speranza* pulled out of its descending spiral into the atmosphere of Hypatia with less than thirteen minutes remaining before breaking orbit would have become impossible. The violent arrival of the *Renard*'s shuttle rig provided the necessary moment of calm for Colonel Anders and Abrehem Locke to impose a cessation of hostilities and restore a semblance of order.

It was a fragile ceasefire, one that could flare to violence in a heartbeat and might have done so had it not been for the sobering sight of Roboute Surcouf leading a sterile gurney from the crew compartment of the shuttle. Borne upon the gurney was the grievously injured Linya Tychon, and the sight of the horrifically wounded magos had instantly quelled every thought of conflict. Both sides withdrew to lick their wounds and, in Abrehem Locke's case, vanish once more into the labyrinthine structure of the Ark Mechanicus.

As a Mechanicus bio-trauma squad encased Linya in a stasis-capsule, Roboute paused before leaving the embarkation deck, staring up at one of the vaulted chamber's towering lancet windows – a vividly stained-glass window depicting a sprawling Leman Russ manufactorum atop Olympus Mons. One of the window's lower panes was broken, and Roboute stared at it for several minutes with a curious expression on his face, like a man trying to recall a half-remembered dream, before following Linya and her father to the medicae decks.

Moments later, servitors throughout the *Speranza* returned to their normal working patterns, re-implanting themselves into the ship's vital systems and, more importantly, re-establishing control of the overloading reactors in the enginarium decks. With dedicated binaric choirs appeasing the enraged spirits of the plasma cores, the runaway reactions within their nuclear hearts were cooled and normal operation restored, allowing the *Speranza* to pull out of its self-destructive descent.

Mechanicus clean-up crews arrived to salvage Roboute Surcouf's shuttle and return the embarkation deck to functionality in time to receive the flotillas of cargo haulers from the surface of Hypatia. With orbit restored, the resupply operation continued as before, though at a substantially increased altitude and measured pace.

No trace could be found of the arco-flagellant; it had vanished as comprehensively as its master, though indications were that Brother-Sergeant Tanna and Emperor's Champion Varda had seriously damaged its biological components. Both Space Marines had suffered injury at the hands of the cyborgised destroyer, but without the ministrations of an Apothecary, they were forced to rely on basic medicae treatment intended for baseline humanoid anatomy, which could patch up the surface hurt, but do nothing for any underlying damage the arco-flagellant's flails had caused.

No one beyond the first victims of Guardsman Manos's opening salvo had been killed in the fighting, which in itself was something of a miracle, but the medicae decks were filled with bondsmen and Cadians sporting broken limbs, deep cuts, fractured skulls and hefty concussions. Manos himself was now confined to the *Speranza*'s brig, a broken man with no memory of what had driven him to open fire.

All the subsequent deep neural trawls could establish was that sometime around the shooting, synaptic activity in Manos's amygdala, the mass of nuclei buried deep in the temporal lobes of the brain, had increased tenfold. This section of the brain, often neutered during a senior adept's passage through the upper echelons of the Cult Mechanicus, housed the body's control mechanisms for fear and rage, which – together with the murder of Magos Saiixek – led some magi to speculate that an outside agency had exerted some form of psychic influence over the Guardsman. What that outside agency might be, no one was saying, but below the waterline speculation was rife, with talk of xenos boarders, warp creatures and a rogue psyker among the crew.

The coffin ships of Legio Sirius returned the mortally wounded carcass of *Amarok* to the *Speranza*, and though there was no love lost

between Elias Härkin and Gunnar Vintras, *Vilka* had escorted the fallen remains of its fellow Warhound to Magos Turentek's repair cradles. A procession of Mechanicus mourners marched alongside the fallen engine, and spirit-singers encoded memories of its lost machine-soul within the Manifold to honour its sacrifice. The Omnissiah would reveal the Warhound's new spirit in good time, ready for when its physical form was ready to walk again.

With the current crisis averted, and to prevent another revolution below decks, Archmagos Kotov had been forced to agree to several of Abrehem's demands. At first he had demanded another military response, but after consultations with his senior magi and receiving counsel on mortal psychology from Ven Anders and Roboute Surcouf, he had been brought round to the idea of negotiation.

The end results of those negotiations were sweeping changes in the duty rosters of the bondsmen's shift patterns, implemented on a ship-wide basis, together with an improvement in the quality of nutritional foodstuffs served in the feeding halls. Retroactively applied maximum lengths of service were added to the servitude covenants between Archmagos Kotov and the *Speranza*'s bondsmen, and a charter of workers' rights was to be drawn up that better outlined the exact duties and responsibilities of the starship's crew.

All of which had served to enrage the master of the fleet to the point of apoplexy and a full system purge. Being dictated to by menials was unheard of in the annals of the Adeptus Mechanicus, and the thought of such present humiliation was only barely outweighed by the thought of future glory. Between them, Surcouf and Anders finally persuaded the archmagos to agree to the principles of Abrehem Locke's terms – though both harboured doubts as to how long he would abide by the agreement when the *Speranza* returned to Imperial space.

The Ark Mechanicus remained in orbit around Hypatia for another five days, ferrying fleets of haulers from the surface to restock the depleted supply holds and carrying out swathes of badly needed repair work. While Blaylock studied the temporal implications of the regressing world, both Kryptaestrex and Turentek petitioned for another week to fully replenish their stock of raw materials. Kotov refused these requests and ordered Azuramagelli to resume their course towards the unnamed forge world upon which he believed Archmagos Telok could be found.

As the *Speranza* set sail, Kotov sat upon his command throne and once more turned his gaze upon the geometric arrangement of stars at the heart of this quest into the unknown.

'You still believe this venture can succeed?' asked Galatea, easing into position at Kotov's side.

'I do,' replied Kotov, unwilling to waste words on the machine intelligence.

The silver-eyed proxy body waved an admonishing finger.

'We are not so sure,' it said with a throaty, augmetic laugh. 'You are a servant to lesser beings now. No longer master of your own vessel.'

'*My* vessel,' spat Kotov, shaking his head. 'You said so yourself – this is *your* vessel now.'

It was cold, always cold. Marko Koskinen shivered in the freezing chill, even though he was swathed in furs and thermal layers. The black and silver mountain was long behind him, its frigid winds and ice-locked slopes a distant memory, but here evoked in the freezing temperature of the pack-meet. Breath misted before every assembled crewman of the Legio, from its gun-servitors – temporarily removed from their weapon mounts – through its moderati and all the way to its princeps.

Magos Hyrdrith had emptied the space of heat, an easy task on a starship travelling the void, and crackling webs of frost patterned the glass and steel of the forgotten chamber. No one knew what purpose it had once served, and after today, no one would know what purpose it was serving now.

A hundred souls stood in two long ranks, facing each other across a central pathway to a raised rostrum upon which sat the life-support engines of the Legio's senior princeps.

The Wintersun occupied the centre of the rostrum, his bio-support cradle surrounded by grey-robed adepts with canine pelts of fur and claw draped around their shoulders and skull masks obscuring their half-human, half-machine faces. The princeps's truncated wraith-form drifted in the milky grey suspension, his sutured eyes and implant-plugged torso regarding proceedings like a withered monarch.

Beside him, the Moonsorrow occupied the position of *Tyrannos*, a rank of great significance that granted absolute authority in the absence of the alpha, a title recently bestowed upon Eryks Skálmöld in recognition of his honoured status and a clear symbol of his right of succession. Elias Härkin, encased in his wheezing, pneumatic exo-harness, stood at the base of the rostrum, honoured in his proximity to the senior princeps, but still subservient to their will.

Koskinen believed the Legio had been gifted a fresh start with the Wintersun re-establishing the proper hierarchy of dominance upon his and the Moonsorrow's return from the Manifold.

And now this.

Koskinen and Joakim Baldur flanked Gunnar Vintras as they stood at the opposite end of the chamber to the Wintersun. The Warhound princeps's shaven head was bowed and his shoulders were hunched, making him seem an utterly pathetic figure. Koskinen wanted to despise Vintras for what he had allowed to happen to *Amarok*, but the sight of the broken princeps told him that no rebuke he could offer would match the loathing the man had for himself.

Vintras wore his full Titanicus dress uniform: white and silver, with the twin canidae pins picked out in gold on the lapels of his crimson-edged frock coat. Without furs, Vintras would be chilled to the bone, but to his credit he let none of that discomfort show on his hollow-cheeked face.

'Let's get this over with,' said Vintras, looking over at Koskinen.

Koskinen didn't reply – it was forbidden to speak to an omega without the alpha's permission – and looked over at Joakim Baldur. His fellow moderati nodded, and they each took hold of Vintras by the upper arms and all but dragged him towards the rostrum. The two men marched between the paired ranks of Legio personnel, who turned away from the disgraced princeps as they passed, directing their attention towards the Wintersun.

The cold at the rostrum seemed sharper and more dangerous, like a sudden freeze was imminent.

He and Baldur presented Vintras to the Wintersun, who drifted to the front of his tank with his unseeing eyes fastened upon his disgraced pack-warrior. His elongated and bulbous skull nodded once and Elias Härkin took a clattering, mechanised step forwards.

'Gunnar Vintras, warrior of Lokabrenna and scion of the black and silver mountain, you come before us as princeps of Legio Sirius.'

The nasal distortion of Härkin's pathogen-ravaged vocal chords was unpleasant to hear, but what he had to say next was even more so.

'As princeps were you entrusted with the life and honour of the war-engine, *Amarok*?'

'I was,' answered Vintras.

'And have you failed in that duty?'

'I have,' said Vintras. 'My engine was mortally wounded and its machine-spirit extinguished. No one but I bears the shame of that.'

Härkin looked back to the Wintersun, who floated back into the occluding viscosity of his casket. This was a duty for the Moonsorrow to perform, to fully cement his position as pack *Tyrannos*.

+A machine-spirit is never extinguished,+ said the Moonsorrow. +It returns to the Omnissiah's light. Bodies of flesh and blood can never outlive a body of steel and stone, a soul of iron and fire.+

'I accept whatever punishment you see fit to impose, Moonsorrow,' said Vintras.

+You do not get to call me Moonsorrow. Only pack uses that name and you are no longer pack. You are omega.+

Vintras nodded. 'So be it,' he said, lifting his head and baring his neck.

+Begin, Härkin,+ said the Moonsorrow. +Spill his blood.+

Härkin nodded and removed a long-bladed knife with a bone handle from a kidskin sheath attached to his leg calliper. Knowing what was required, Koskinen and Baldur once again held Vintras by his arms. Härkin took his knife and made two quick slashes, one across each of Vintras's cheeks. As droplets of blood ran down his face, Härkin placed the knife against the princeps's throat, drawing the blade over the skin; hard enough to draw blood, but not so deep as to end his life.

A princeps, even a disgraced one, was too valuable an individual to be so casually thrown away.

The required mental and physical demands of commanding a titanic war-engine were so enormous as to exclude virtually the entire human race. Only truly exceptional individuals could even train to become a Titan princeps, let alone become one. But censure had to be given and be seen to be given. Vintras would forever bear the ritual scar of failure upon his throat.

Härkin cleaned his blade on the fabric of Vintras's uniform and sheathed it before reaching up to remove his canidae rank pins. He stepped back to his assigned position at the foot of the rostrum and nodded to Koskinen and Baldur.

Piece by piece, they stripped the Titanicus uniform from Vintras, letting each item of clothing fall at his feet like discarded rags until he stood naked before the Legio. His body was muscular and heavily tattooed, marked by honour scars and ritual branding marks indicating engine kills and campaign records. The skin beneath the inking was marble-pale and not even Vintras's stoic demeanour could prevent the cold from finally impacting on him. He shivered in the freezing temperature, naked and vulnerable and brought low before his Legio.

+Now you truly are the Skinwalker,+ said the Moonsorrow.

Vitali had been advised against siring an heir. The likelihood of emotional attachment would be high, his fellow magi told him. The risk to his researches would be incalculable in the time it would take to raise an offspring, for surely he would wish to observe the development of his clone first-hand. He had ignored them all, desiring a willing apprentice to continue his work after he had gone. The arrangement was to be purely functional, for Vitali was a man obsessed with the workings of the universe and his concerns were cosmological, not biological.

But all that had changed when a one in ten trillion random fluctuation in the genetic sequencing of his clone had spontaneously mutated its code and transformed what should have been a genetic copy of Vitali into a distinct individual. A daughter.

Linya had surpassed his every expectation in ability and Vitali had grown to love her as much as any celestial phenomenon, even going as far as to name her after what many believed was the true name of the daughter – or sister, no one knew for certain – of the composer of Honovere. Invasive augmentation of developing brain cells during her hothoused gestation period in the iron womb had given her an enhanced intellect and growth speeds from birth.

Within her first year of life Linya was already acting as his assistant, her enhanced mind housed within the equivalent bodyshape of a six-year-old child. Her physical growth had assumed a more traditional pattern soon after, but her mind had never stopped developing, and soon she was outstripping magi with decades more experience in mapping the heavens.

Traditional education had proved too stultifying for her quickened intellect, and she had fled one Mechanicus scholam after another, always finding her way back to the orbital galleries to study with her father. And so he had trained her in the mysteries of the universe, and she took her place at his side as his apprentice as he had always hoped, though with a bond of mutual respect and love as opposed to the functional arrangement he had anticipated.

Many pitied him or shook their heads at his foolishness, lamenting what he might have discovered or otherwise turned his intellect towards were it not for the distracting influence of flesh-kin to keep him from his duty to the Omnissiah.

They were wrong, knew Vitali.

Any loss to the sum of knowledge held by the Mechanicus had been Vitali's gain.

Linya was going to surpass them all, she was going to rewrite human understanding of the stars and their aeons-long existence. The name of Linya Tychon would be mentioned in the same breath as those great pioneers who had championed the first transhumanism experiments – Fyodorov, Moravec, Haldayn and the vitrified enigma of FM-2030.

All this Vitali had *known* with a surety in his bones that he now understood was simple vanity.

Linya was his creation, and she was going to outlast him and exceed him in every way.

How very biological of him.

Sitting by his daughter's side as she lay unmoving within a sterile containment field, Vitali now saw how foolish he had been. The treatment Linya had received was second to none, the very best the *Speranza* had to offer. Senior medicae and Medicus Biologis had spent the last thirteen days bending their every effort into restoring her body, managing her pain with precisely modulated synaptic diversions and reclothing her surviving limbs with synth-grown skin.

They had done all that could be done. Winning the fight for life was now up to her.

Linya's future hung in the balance, and no one could predict on which side the coin of her life might turn.

Vitali's brain had been augmented, rewired and surgically conditioned in so many ways that its processes resembled those of a baseline human in only the most superficial ways. He thought faster and on multiple levels at once. His powers of lateral thinking and complex, multi-dimensional visualisation were beyond the abilities of even gifted human polymaths to comprehend.

Yet he was as crushed by guilt and grief as any father at the sight of his child in pain.

He knew he could have spared himself this pain had he not been too proud, too stubborn and too bloody-minded to listen to his peers and forego the siring of a successor. If he had been proper Mechanicus he could have neatly sidestepped this horror and simply chosen an apprentice from the most promising of his many acolytes.

But then he would have denied himself the joy of Linya's existence, the pleasure of her growth and learning, the wonder of her personality shining through, no matter how steeped in the ways of the Martian priesthood she became. Though Cult Mechanicus to her bones, Linya had a very rare, very bright spark of humanity that refused to be extinguished no matter what replacement cybernetics were implanted within her biological volume.

Archmagos Kotov and every one of the senior magi had come to pay their respects to his daughter, each expressing a measure of regret that was surprising in some, downright miraculous in others. Magos Blaylock had visited Linya's bedside on numerous occasions, each time displaying an empathy Vitali had hitherto not believed him capable of exhibiting.

Roboute Surcouf had been a regular visitor, and his grief was a depthless well of regret that reminded Vitali of the time he had spent with the eldar. Clearly something of that xenos species' capacity for extremes of emotion had been passed to the rogue trader during his time spent aboard their city-ship.

Vitali had no capacity with which to shed tears, having long ago sacrificed even that tiny space within his skull for extra ocular-cybernetic hardware. Instead, he extended a sterile mechadendrite into the counterseptic field surrounding Linya and rested its callipers on her shoulder, hoping that some measure of his presence would somehow be translated to her sedated body.

The augmented mind was a complex organ, and despite their lofty claims and interventions, not even the highest ranked genetors of the magi biologis truly understood the subtleties of its inner workings. Mechanicus records were replete with apocryphal accounts of the grievously wounded and those in supposedly vegetative comas being brought back from the brink of death by the words of a loved one. And right at this moment, Vitali was willing to clutch at any straw, no matter how slender or unsubstantiated.

He read from one of Linya's archaic books: a rare collection of poems from Old Earth, monographs on celestial mechanics and the biographies of many of the earliest astronomers ever to make the stars shine brighter by bringing them within reach of their earth-bound brethren. The first stanzas he transmitted via the noosphere and binaric code blurts, but when he came to Linya's favourite passage, he switched to his flesh-voice.

'I am an instrument in the shape of a woman,
trying to translate pulsations
into images for the relief of the body
and the reconstruction of the mind.'

The poem was said to date from an epoch before the Age of Strife, though that seemed unlikely given the devastation wrought in that cataclysmic era; but it had not been its clear antiquity that Linya liked, rather the fact that it acknowledged the role of a woman in the earliest age of galactic exploration.

Vitali had no real appreciation for poetry, but he knew beauty when he saw it.

Space was a vast wonderland, a tapestry of universal magnificence that any with eyes to see could witness. It was the desire to breathe that wonder into others that had driven him to galactic telescopes, and that same wonder lay at the heart of Linya's creation.

He would not sacrifice the pain he was feeling now and forego the joy of having known his daughter and watched her grow.

'Do you believe she can hear you?'

Vitali turned, expecting to see another Mechanicus visitor, but his lip curled in contempt as he saw Galatea squatting at the arched entrance to the medicae chamber. Its squat body was lowered almost to floor level and is silver eyes were trained on Linya.

Vitali felt his loathing for this… *thing* reach new heights.

Why should this abomination get to exist while his daughter's life hung in the balance?

He forced back the venom in his throat and turned back to the bed.

'I do not know,' said Vitali. 'I hope so. Perhaps if she hears that I am with her it will give her the strength to fight for her life.'

'A very biological conceit,' said Galatea. 'We know of no empirical evidence to support the capacity for perception while in a medicated state.'

'I do not care what you know or do not know,' snapped Vitali. 'I am reading to my daughter, and nothing you can say will convince me I am wrong to do so.'

Galatea entered the medicae chamber, its mismatched limbs clattering on the tiled floor. The ozone stink of its body and the flickering light of its brain jars reflected from the brushed steel of the machinery keeping Linya alive.

'We do not wish to do so,' said Galatea, extending a manipulator arm and resting it on Vitali's shoulder. 'We come to offer you our sympathy, such as it can exist for a biological entity. We had grown fond of Mistress Tychon in the time we had known her.'

'My daughter is not dead,' said Vitali, fighting to hide his surprise at the machine's unexpected sentiment. 'She may yet recover. Linya is a fighter, and she will not let this finish her… I know it.'

Vitali's voice trailed off and Galatea moved to the other side of Linya's bed.

'We sincerely hope so,' it said. 'She is too precious to be taken away by such ill-fortune.'

'I didn't know you had interacted that much with Linya.'

'Indeed, yes,' said Galatea. 'When we took over the exload from the *Tomioka's* cogitators, we linked with her mind and saw just how exceptional a being she is.'

'Exceptional,' said Vitali with a hopeful smile. 'Yes, that's exactly what she is.'

Abrehem sat on a metal-legged stool before Rasselas X-42 and folded his arms. The arco-flagellant reclined on its throne-gurney with the articulated arm and leg restraints splayed, rendering it like some ancient anatomical diagram. The wounds it had suffered at the hands of the Space Marines were extensive, enough to have slain a bondsman many times over. Only its superlative artificiality and accelerated metabolic augmentation had kept it alive, though those selfsame biological mechanisms had kept it in a state of regenerative dormancy since then.

The aftermath of the abortive revolution on the embarkation deck had given Abrehem a great deal to consider, particularly his continued usage of the arco-flagellant. In the confused days after the *Speranza* had pulled out of her death dive over Hypatia, his time had been spent in secretive and noospherically conducted negotiations with Archmagos Kotov, hammering out a means by which the fleet could continue its mission of exploration *and* treat its workers with respect.

It had been a protracted and often thorny maze to negotiate, but a peace of sorts had been achieved. The servitors and bondsmen went back to work and Abrehem had sent Hawke and Coyne with them. He too had been offered amnesty, but knowing how easily his capture might allow the archmagos to renege on his promises, Abrehem, Ismael and Totha Mu-32 had remained in hiding.

The overseer had patched Rasselas X-42's horrific injuries as best he could, but even with inloaded medicae databases to call upon, the sheer incomprehensibility and density of the biological hardware within X-42's body rendered every attempt to restore function akin to little more than educated guesswork.

The bolter wound in the arco-flagellant's side had healed itself, forming a gauze of synthetic skin that over time had bonded with his hardened skin shell to leave a glossy carapace of scar tissue. Totha Mu-32 had removed over eighty-seven individual shards of bolt casing from the arco-flagellant's back before packing that wound with synth-flesh and applying a counterseptic dressing.

As grievous as the bolter wounds were, it was the Black Templar's sword blow that was of greater concern. Numerous chem-shunts situated in the hollows between X-42's shoulder and collarbone had ruptured, spreading a distilled cocktail of potent drugs designed to initiate combat reflexes, states of dormancy, healing and self-immolation. Mixed together, the effect had been to plunge X-42 into a delirious state of feverish nightmares that only the immediate engagement of high-level devotion protocols in its pacifier helm could quell.

But even that was of lesser concern than the damage the powered blade had caused as it ripped up the side of X-42's skull. The metallic cowl encasing the left side of its head had been cut away cleanly, exposing panels of circuitry that were beyond any living magi's ability to restore. What their function might have been was a mystery, but that they were, on some level, still operative – albeit in an aberrant way – was obvious from the twitches and convulsions wracking X-42's body.

Abrehem thought back to Ven Anders's words as they'd spoken in the moments before things turned bloody. He knew he had been manipulated by a man who could convince other men to walk into hails of gunfire and then thank him for the opportunity, but that didn't alter the fundamental truth of what he had said regarding Rasselas X-42.

Abrehem *was* as good as keeping a slave, just as Archmagos Kotov was keeping the bondsmen and servitors in bondage. How could he demand basic human rights for the enslaved workers throughout the *Speranza* if he wasn't willing to live up to the same standard?

That question had driven him to take this course of action, a course of action that Totha Mu-32 had roundly condemned as an act of illogical foolishness. Ismael had disagreed and both stood behind him ready to step in at a moment's notice should something go hideously wrong.

Ismael appeared at his side and took his organic hand.

Abrehem hardly recognised his former shift overseer any more. The vain, arrogant, self-entitled shit who'd made his life hell on Joura had vanished utterly and been replaced by a figure of such serenity and peace that it was like looking into the face of one of the Emperor's saints painted onto a templum fresco.

'You will see terrible things within X-42's mind, Abrehem,' said Ismael, his metal-cowled head so like that of the arco-flagellant, and yet so different. 'This is a very brave thing you are doing.'

'It is a foolish act of self-indulgence,' said Totha Mu-32. 'You will find nothing within X-42's mind but vileness. Do you think that upstanding citizens who love their children and worship the Emperor every day are turned into arco-flagellants?'

Totha Mu-32 gestured towards the twitching arco-flagellant and said, 'They are the worst scum imaginable. The dregs of society, the maladjusted, the insane and the irredeemable. *That* is who this was, and to think otherwise would be a terrible mistake. He is now a servant of the Emperor and the Omnissiah, and that is all he will ever be.'

Abrehem nodded towards Ismael. 'Just as a mindless servitor was all Ismael could ever be?'

'That is very different,' said Totha Mu-32. 'What Ismael has become is a divine gift, but I cannot accept that the Omnissiah would work through a wretch like X-42.'

'That's pride speaking,' said Abrehem. 'Saiixek accused you of the same thing, remember? That you claimed to know the will of the Machine-God. You said it yourself, X-42 *was* a monster. *Now* he is a servant of the Emperor and the Omnissiah, and I need to know if there is any humanity left within him, any last shred of goodness we can salvage.'

Totha Mu-32 said nothing, his half-human features unreadable beneath his crimson hood.

'I'm doing this,' said Abrehem. 'So either help me or get out.'

Ismael took a step forwards, keeping hold of Abrehem's hand and reaching out to lift Rasselas X-42's scarred and callused hand.

'The moment of connection will be painful,' said Ismael.

'I remember the last time,' nodded Abrehem. 'I'm ready this time.'

'No,' said Ismael. 'Not for this you are not.'

Microcontent 19

Ismael was right. Abrehem wasn't ready for the sudden, wrenching dislocation of having his every sense ripped from his body and rammed into the mind of another living being. It was like having the innards of his skull scooped out and flash-burned before being pieced together again, flake of ash by flake of ash. Abrehem felt his sense of identity slough from whatever form of consciousness he was experiencing, like a serpent shedding its skin and being reborn.

One minute he was Abrehem Locke, bondsman aboard the Ark Mechanicus, *Speranza*, the next he was…

He was…

He had no idea who he was.

He was Abrehem Locke.

No, he was… no, he was not. He was. He was someone else.

He was someone whose thoughts were like a rabid dog in a cage of its own making, the physical manifestation of an unending scream that was only kept silent by the complex alchemy of numerous pharmacological inhibitors. He sat in the centre of a soulless room of bare stone, coffered steel and bottle-green ceramic tiles, facing a heavy cog-shaped doorway of bronzed steel. Leather restraints at his wrists, ankles and torso secured him to a cold steel throne-gurney.

Incense fogged the air and heavy machinery, more suited to the interior of a shipwright's assembly hangar, sat idle to either side of the

throne. Feed lines pulsed like arteries, venting tiny puffs of oil-rich vapour that tasted of bile and hypocrisy.

He tried to move his head, but clamps drilled into the bone of his skull and jaw prevented any lateral rotation. In his peripheral vision, he could see twin icons stamped on opposite walls: one a steel-toothed cog of black and white with an iron skull at its centre, the other a two-headed eagle with one eye hooded and blind and the other ever-watchful.

Both icons stared at him with impassive and unforgiving eyes.

He – *no*, the mind he squatted within – felt nothing but contempt for everything they now represented to him.

Chem-shunts buried into the meat of his forearms pumped honeyed muscle relaxants through his bloodstream, and neuro-synaptic blockers had been introduced to his spinal fluid. He knew this because the trembling adepts who'd strapped his drugged body into the throne-gurney had spared no detail in their descriptions of what was about to happen.

The door irised open and a chanting group of robed figures marched through.

Their leader read from a heavy book, its weight too enormous for any mortal man to bear. Instead, it was borne upon the back of a stunted figure with an exactingly contoured hunch to its spine. He saw this arrangement of bones had been surgically crafted simply to bear the book. The figure's legs were foreshortened stumps of ossified bone and muscle, and he had no doubt its brain had been reconditioned to occlude any thought but the bearing of the book. Every moment spent in so awkward a posture must have brought constant pain, but it believed it was honoured to be allowed to bear the book, which he saw with grim amusement was the *Scriptures of Sebastian Thor*.

He knew the volume on its back could not be the original, of course. That sat in a stasis-sealed vault on Ophelia VII, guarded by millions of Sororitas warriors and Ecclesiarchy troops, the likes of which he had once led into the fires of battle.

This was, at best, a tenth-generation copy, which still made it an insanely precious artefact.

The man reading from the book was dressed in a white and red chimere, with a cincture of tasselled gold securing it at his waist. He wore a *Pallium Pontifex* around his neck, and the silver skulls stitched along its draped length winked in the half-light. A porcelain skull mask of pure white veiled his face, its cheekbones exaggerated and its eyes bulging monstrously. The jaw was distended, the teeth gleaming in the half-light as though death wished to savour the mortal fear of

the condemned man. He recognised the *lexiconi devotatus* the priest spoke – an ornate and complex argot of piety unknown beyond the higher echelons of the Adeptus Ministorum.

Behind the pontifex came three priests of the Machine-God, cowled in red and black. The outlines of their bodies were misshapen, rendered post-human by hulking augmetics and artificial limbs. They walked with unnatural, disjointed movements, each one having transcended humanity to become something more and less at the same time. They had achieved a form of mechanical apotheosis, meaning that their bodies were more metal than meat, yet that was considered an honour.

Finally, a warrior of flesh and bone entered, and where the pontifex's face was hidden and the Martians were objective in their hatred, this man made no secret of his loathing. A man of violence, he was clad in form-fitting black armour, glossy and well cared for, but old and hard-worn. A reflection of the man inside, he knew. Alone of the new arrivals, his face went unmasked. Its deep-cut lines and flinty eyes were without compromise, without remorse and utterly without pity.

He knew this man. This man was responsible for putting him in this chair.

The tech-priests surrounded him, and though his nervous system was all but paralysed and his bloodstream choked with soporifics, they were still wary of him.

What had he done to earn such enmity from these men?

The pontifex spoke first.

'Lukasz Król,' he said – *finally a name!* – his voice distorted behind the skull mask. 'You have been sentenced to arco-flagellation by the holy writ of the Ecclesiarchy you once served. Death alone would be insufficient punishment for the monstrous heresies you have committed in the guise of the Emperor's servant, thus you will atone for your wretchedness and unnatural acts in His holy armies until such time as death claims you. This, it is pronounced, is a true and just command of Ecclesiarchy Helican, enacted this third hour of the hundred and fiftieth day of the nine hundred and eighty-sixth year of the Thirty-Sixth Millennium.'

The pontifex stepped back and the Martians began their work. They plugged themselves into the control mechanisms surrounding him with snaking mechadendrites, and the machine arms to either side of the gurney jumped to life like sleepers suddenly roused to wakefulness. Surgical equipment unsheathed from metallic cowls – needles, arterial clamps and whining bolt-fitters – and nests of components rose from the floor to either side of him.

'Reduce the balms and begin,' said the pontifex. 'He has to feel every moment of this.'

Fear rose up in a smothering wave, blotting out all thought and reason.

This is not my body, this is not my mind.

But the sensations surging through him were no less real, no less indistinguishable from injuries done to his own distant flesh. He wanted to scream, but this was Lukasz Król's memory and he was not about to let these men see him beg or weep or scream.

Piezo-edged bone saws extruded from the arms of the throne and sliced through his wrists with ultra-rapid precision. Blood jetted explosively, but even as the agony cut through his diminishing chemical haze, cauterising heat was brought to bear, sealing the stumps with a single pulse of agonising heat. As horrifying as the removal of his hands had been, it was nothing compared to what came next.

Clicking machines with calliper hands like the nightmarish claws of a demented toymaker began stripping the skin, muscle and nerve tissue from his forearms all the way to the elbow. Surgical flesh-weavers layered replacement nerve-strands over the reinforced bone and grafted fibre-bundle muscle in place of the discarded organic tissue.

His chest heaved and his limbs thrashed against the restraints. They simply tightened in response. He couldn't move. He could only watch as his entire body was pared back and remade.

Sealed caskets rotated up from the floor and opened with pneumatic hisses of condensing air. The monotonous stream of binaric nonsense the tech-priests were chanting faltered fractionally as the caskets opened to reveal the weapons within.

Such awesome tools of destruction required reverence.

Through a haze of tears and hate, he watched two of the machine-priests step forwards and attach the devices to his arms using implanted bolt-drivers, neural shears, flesh grafts and sacred unguents. He felt every insertion, every bolt driving down into bone and every screaming horror of exposed nerves being spliced together. A burst of power surged through him, and telescoping carbon-steel electro-flails twitched and danced as ancient, barely understood circuitry meshed with his crude organic functionality.

The gurney tipped backwards, and the drills, excising machinery and clamps went to work on his skull. Trepanning picks bored through bone and the clicking, mechanised hands inserted neural control implants before finally removing the upper dome of his skull. He felt the lid of bone creaking upwards and the horror of his mind being exposed was almost too much to bear.

Sacred arrangements of sacred oil were dripped into his brain cavity, with each anointing accompanied by the sixteen names of the

binary saints. Spinning orbs with mechanical blade limbs as thin as spider legs clicked into place before him, whirring with demented glee.

No, no, no, no, not my–

The whirring orbs stabbed forwards and plucked out his eyes.

This is not my body! This is not my body! This is not my body! This is not my body! This is not my body! This is not my body! This is not my body! This is not my body! This is not my body!

Delicate clamps kept his optic nerves taut as complex targeting arrays, broad-spectrum threat analysers and visio-cognitive orbs were attached in place of his eyes and implanted into his skull. A cranial cowl that was part devotional feed, part cortical inhibitor and part death-mask was slotted home, lowered over his slack features and wired to the frontal lobes of what remained of his brain as hymnals blared from unseen augmitters. Like the grinning skull faceplates of the Chaplains of the Adeptus Astartes, it was the rictus agony of the Emperor, and all those whose doomed fate it was to look upon him would know he had been punished by an agency beyond that of mere men. Detailed schematics of the body-plans of the men before him sprang up on the inner surfaces of his eyes, complete with endurable stresses, violation tolerances and a hundred other measures of how they could be ripped into screaming ruin.

The work continued for another hour, agony upon agony, horror upon horror, until there was little sign that a human being had once sat in the throne-gurney. The mortal meat of Lukasz Król had been scraped away and replaced with an instrument of death and annihilation. Only Abrehem remained and even he was a ravaged shell, cored out by the same processes that had made sport of this man's flesh.

Yet even as his consciousness wept and wished for extinction, he felt the soaring ecstasy of having the power of life and death. For all intents and purposes, he was no longer human, his body enhanced to lethal levels of killing power and stripped back to the most basic physiological functions.

Lukasz Król had effectively ceased to exist, and in his place sat something else.

Something altogether more dangerous and more appalling.

'It is done,' said the pontifex, with a solemn nod, stepping forwards and dipping his fingers in an inkhorn of sanctified pigment that a genuflecting tech-priest held out before him. He drew four parallel lines of crimson down the skull mask.

'In Thor's Blood are ye anointed. In Thor's Blood shall ye awaken,' said the pontifex.

Rivulets of paint slid down the mask like tears of blood, dripping onto a chest that now bulged with cardio-pulmonary enhancers, adrenal-slammers and dormant steroidal compounds. Spinal implants snaked down his back in a chain of injectors, and stimm-reservoirs on his shoulders gave him a hulking, over-muscled proportion to his upper body.

He was a killer now, a render of flesh, a weapon and an act of retribution all in one.

Abrehem revelled in this new incarnation, a being of almost unlimited violent potential to whom no atrocity was beyond his capabilities, no loathsome act of utmost cruelty beneath him. With all need for moral pretence torn away, Abrehem saw the full horror of what Lukasz Król had done, the torture palaces, the rape gulags and the experimentation camps where he had personally overseen all manner of unimaginable affronts to the Emperor.

This was good.

They thought they had taken away his life and made him their own, but they were wrong.

The killer had *always* been in him.

All they had done was strip the mask of humanity away to rebuild him stronger and more lethal than ever.

'I take from you the name of Lukasz Król,' said the pontifex, dipping his hand in the pigment once more and drawing another series of four vertical lines down Król's chest. The ablative polymer coatings introduced to his dermal layers made the skin feel hard and plastic.

Abrehem watched the pontifex check the serial identifier codes on the requisition form held out by another of the tech-priests and verify them against the name the doctrinal abaci had generated. 'I dub thee Rasselas X-42, and may the Emperor have mercy on your soul.'

'Bastards like him don't have a soul,' said the man in black armour.

'We all have souls, chastener,' replied the pontifex. 'The words of the divine Thor teach us that a single man with faith can triumph over a legion of the faithless. We have restored this man's faith, and he will repay that gift in the blood of our enemies.'

The pontifex nodded towards what had once been a psychopathic mass murderer known as Cardinal Astral of Ophelia VII, Lukasz Król.

'Even the darkest soul can find redemption and salvation in death.'

'I couldn't give a ship-rat's fart about his salvation,' snapped the chastener. 'I just want him to suffer for what he did.'

'Have no fear of that,' said the pontifex. 'He will suffer like no other.'

The wrench of dislocation as Abrehem was dragged back to his own flesh was no less jarring, but where he had plunged headlong into an unknown body, this time he returned to his own. Though it scarcely felt like his, and the weakness that filled him after the sense of ultimate strength was almost as painful as the surgeries undergone by Lukasz Król.

He toppled from the stool, as helpless as an automaton with its power cell removed and fell into the combined grip of Ismael and Totha Mu-32. Abrehem screamed like a lunatic as a tide of unremitting horror washed over him. His cybernetic arm clawed at Totha Mu-32 and Ismael as though they were warp-spawned monsters from the bleakest depths of the immaterium. Abrehem fought with the strength of the demented, hysterical and desperate to escape the abhorrent presence of Rasselas X-42.

He relived stolen memories – decades of nightmarish, unthinkable abuses, sickened and revolted by every grisly detail. Unnumbered souls had been sent screaming into oblivion, and Abrehem pressed his hands to his ears as he heard their screams echoing within his skull.

To think that one man could conceive of such things was repellent enough, but to know that entire cadres of the Ecclesiarchy had been dragged into the maelstrom of his insanity by unquestioning devotion was almost too much to bear. How many billions had died at the hands of the very institution that proclaimed its mission was to protect them?

Abrehem bent over and vomited the meagre contents of his stomach over X-42's dormis chamber, retching and heaving in disgust. He closed his eyes, willing the scenes of torture, murder and degradation to fade from his thoughts.

'Abrehem,' said Totha Mu-32. 'Abrehem, are you hurt?'

He shook his head and wiped the sleeve of his robe over his dripping lips.

'No, I'm…'

He wanted to say *fine*, but knowing what he now knew of X-42's atrocities, he doubted he would ever be fine again. With Totha Mu-32 and Ismael's help, he climbed unsteadily to his feet, swiftly turning and making his way from the dormis chamber after checking the arco-flagellant's pacifier helm was securely in place.

'Did you see?' asked Ismael.

Abrehem nodded. 'I saw,' he gasped. 'You knew, didn't you? You knew who he was.'

'I did, but you had to see for yourself,' said Ismael. 'And now you know who X-42 was, do you still think he should be released from his condition? Would you restore the man he was?'

'Thor's blood, no!' cried Abrehem. 'Lukasz Król was a monster.'

'He was indeed,' agreed Ismael, 'but Lukasz Król was once a good man, a man driven by faith in the Emperor to excesses of violence against the enemies of mankind. But he began to see deviance and heresy everywhere he looked, and his bloody pogroms soon turned on his own people.'

'Król?' asked Totha Mu-32. 'The Impaler Cardinal?'

Abrehem shrugged. 'I don't know, maybe. I've never heard of the Impaler Cardinal.'

'Few have,' said Totha Mu-32, as he and Ismael set Abrehem down on his cot bed. 'The Ecclesiarchy are understandably reluctant to admit to one of their own going insane. Some, like Vandire or Bucharis, are impossible to deny, but Król's reign of atrocity was mercifully short-lived and confined to a single system.'

'How do you know about him?' asked Abrehem.

'Król's actions were recorded by the Mechanicus personnel who oversaw the dismantling of his bloody regime after an army of Adeptus Arbites led by Chastener Marazion brought him down. It makes for unpleasant reading, even to those who can detach themselves from empathy and physiological responses to revulsion. Now do you accept that no good can come of X-42's emancipation?'

'Absolutely,' said Abrehem, pointing a shaking hand towards the dormis chamber. 'Check the pacifier helm and seal that monster in there again. We can't risk that any shred of Lukasz Król might still be in there.'

'There will *always* be something of him in there,' said Ismael, gently lowering Abrehem to the cot bed. 'And that is the greatest tragedy.'

A dreadful sadness and soul-crushing weariness settled upon Abrehem, but the memories of Król's atrocities were already receding. Abrehem just hoped that in time they would fade completely. No one needed horrors like that festering in their brain.

'Rest now,' said Ismael.

Abrehem nodded, already feeling his eyelids growing heavy. He felt a blanket being pulled over him and rolled onto his side. It had been foolish of him to venture into the psyche of a mind-altered killer, but at least he knew that Rasselas X-42 would never hurt anyone ever again.

'Shut it down,' he murmured as exhaustion smothered him. 'Shut it down forever and seal this place up so no one ever finds it again.'

'I will see to it,' Totha Mu-32 assured him.

Roboute had always known the *Speranza* was a vast starship, he'd seen it from space and its inhuman scale was hard to miss. He'd berthed his ship within its cavernous holds, and he knew four god-machines of the Titan Legions, as well as thousands of Imperial Guard and skitarii, were billeted aboard – together with their armoured inventories and vehicles. He knew all this and more, thanks to reams of statistics provided by Magos Pavelka in awed, reverent tones.

So why did he now feel claustrophobic, like a rat in a maze, desperately hunting for a way out?

Ever since he'd brought the shuttle back aboard the *Speranza* he'd had an unidentifiable sense of being watched, that tingling at the back of the neck that tells a soldier a sniper has a bead on them. He had no evidence of this, but in the weeks since they had left Hypatia he'd felt like a helpless mammal being stalked by an invisible predator that could pounce at any time, but delayed the moment of the kill for anticipation's sake.

He'd taken to carrying his pistol with him at all times, even going as far as to keep the safety off, which continually chafed at his Ultramarian training. He took Adara with him at all times, even when traversing well-populated areas of the ship. Much of his time was spent helping Sylkwood and Pavelka repair the damage done to the *Speranza* and the shuttle or visiting Linya Tychon on the medicae decks.

The *Speranza* had already passed the outer planets of the uncannily geometric system and would achieve orbit within another two days at most. No one had yet named their destination, for if the Lost Magos was indeed alive and well on the forge world's surface, it was likely he had already done so, and Archmagos Kotov was nothing if not a stickler for the proper taxonomy of planetary nomenclature.

His days were filled with reading the myth-cycles of Ultramar to Linya and being hectored by Ilanna Pavelka at the terrible damage he and Emil had wreaked on the ship. When armpit-deep in the guts of a non-functional machine or lost in tales of the young Primarch Guilliman, he could almost forget the lingering presence that flitted around him like a persistent swampfly.

Eventually, he tired of walking on brittle ice and decided he'd had enough of sitting in the cross-hairs. If there was someone watching him, it was high time he knew who it was. Roboute unbuckled his pistol belt and laid it on the rosewood surface of his desk before striding from the *Renard*. He randomly picked one of the embarkation deck's exit archways and began walking. Each time he came to a junction of passageways, a stairwell or a processional convergence templum, he took the pathway that looked the least inviting or which had been scrubbed of all locational identifiers.

Within minutes he was hopelessly lost within the warren of dimly lit passageways, mesh-walled and steel-floored. Steam gathered in the upper reaches of vaulted cloisters, and meltwater from ice filling the breaches between passageways and chambers partially open to the void ran in metallic gutters. He walked in darkness, in shadow and by the light of looming vent towers that belched flame into the heating systems.

He marvelled at vast chambers of cog-driven pistons, each larger than a Warlord's leg, roaring machines with connector rods and couplings that scissored back and forth like the arms of a threshing machine or the oars of an ancient trireme of Macragge. The few tech-priests he saw largely ignored him, or steered him away from areas of high radiation or some other danger of which he was clearly unaware.

Wandering through row upon row of titanic cylindrical towers like grain silos, he tasted the greasy tang of bulk foodstuffs, and realised he was looking at the *Speranza*'s food supplies. Roboute walked along a raised walkway between the towers, coming at last to a chamber filled with noxious smells and eye-watering caustic vapours. Three dozen enormous vats, two hundred metres across, stretched into the distance, each filled with a grey-brown sludge of reclaimed matter, meat substitutes, protein pastes and complex carbohydrate additives.

Servitors on repulsor discs floated over the viscous mulch, plunging sample staves into the deep strata or removing contaminants. The sight sickened Roboute and he left the chamber, taking turns at random and always picking a route that had no markings to indicate where it might lead.

The feeling that there was a target on his back or that a noose was slowly closing on him was getting stronger, and he had to fight the urge to spin around and try to catch a glimpse of his pursuer. Whoever or whatever had its eye on him would make itself known to him soon enough.

He passed shrines to the Omnissiah, to the Emperor and to things he couldn't identify. Some appeared to be little more than votive offerings to some avatar that might charitably be considered an aspect of the Machine-God, while others were too disturbing to be connected to the Cult Mechanicus.

Some were clearly intended as little more than petty rebellions, where others were of a more sinister appearance, with items hung from the ad-hoc arrangements that Roboute didn't want to look at too closely. Others appeared to be newly erected shrines to Abrehem Locke and his apostles: the Red Ruin, the Angel Return'd, Blessed Hawke and Coyne of the Wound.

Roboute shook his head at the ridiculousness of these latter shrines, having heard Ven Anders and Captain Hawkins tell him the truth about Abrehem Locke's compatriots. But wherever men and women were confined without hope, they would make their own. Even in the darkest times, the human mind was capable of fashioning its own light.

He passed beneath a towering lancet archway and entered a long processional nave filled with statuary: robed adepts of the Cult Mechanicus arranged in two facing rows running the length of the chamber. Each was around ten metres tall and their projecting surfaces were thick with dust, as were the interlinked hexagonal tiles of the floor. Roboute remembered when he had first come aboard the *Speranza*, and Magos Blaylock had escorted them to Archmagos Kotov in the Adamant Ciborium. The statues there had been toweringly magnificent, sculptural likenesses of the greatest minds of the Mechanicus.

Who were these figures?

Were they men and women whose contributions had been outmoded or surpassed?

A deep sadness filled Roboute as he walked slowly between the statues of the forgotten magi, wondering why this place was now unvisited and abandoned. He paused beside a robed priest of Mars and looked up into the shadows beneath the hood.

'Who were you?' asked Roboute, the echoes of his voice swallowed by the centuries of dust. 'And what did you do? *Someone* thought you were important enough to warrant a statue.'

The statue stared across the chamber impassively, and Roboute knelt beside the carved plaque on its plinth and wiped away the dust.

'Magos Vahihva of Pharses,' said Roboute. 'The rest of the ship may have forgotten you, but I'll remember you. I'll find out who you were and I'll make sure I remember it. I know the Mechanicus say they never delete anything, but not deleting something isn't the same as remembering it.'

Roboute stood and looked up at the unknowable face of Magos Vahihva as an overwhelming sense of calm spread through him. He smiled and ran a hand through his hair, before straightening his jacket and brushing stray particles of dust from his cuffs.

'About bloody time you showed yourself,' he said.

'You were aware of my presence?' said a voice with a breathy, lyrical quality he hadn't heard for many years. He closed his eyes as he turned around, savouring the cadences of the voice as it defied the chamber's acoustics and resonated throughout its length.

'I was, but only because I've been around your people before,' said Roboute, finally opening his eyes. 'I hope this encounter is as pleasant and non-violent as the last.'

A woman in armour that looked to have been crafted from ceramic and alabaster stood opposite him. She was tall, with a leanness to her frame that was both beguiling and somehow at odds with how his brain told him a woman's body ought to be proportioned. A helmet with horns like antlers sat on the plinth of the statue behind her, and he couldn't help but notice the polished pistol strapped to her thigh and the long, bejewelled sword sheathed at her shoulder.

'I am not going to kill you,' she said.

'That's reassuring,' replied Roboute with what he hoped was his most winning smile. He'd essentially engineered this meeting, though only now did he truly understand the tantalising sense of familiarity he'd felt on the embarkation deck.

The eldar woman's face was sculpturally perfect, a pleasingly proportioned oval with large eyes and a tousled mass of scarlet hair entwined with glittering stones and golden beads. Her lips were a pleasing shade of blue, but pursed together in a way that made her seem inordinately angry.

In fact, now that he looked closely, he saw her apparently expressionless face was in fact taut with suppressed rage, an icy fury that simmered just beneath the surface. Despite her earlier words, Roboute suddenly doubted the wisdom of this course of action. He took a faltering step back towards Magos Vahihva as she approached him with a liquid fluidity that left no trace of her passing in the dust.

'You are Roboute Surcouf,' she said, not posing the words as a question.

'Yes.'

'And you have spent time aboard an eldar craftworld.'

'Yes.'

She stopped in front of him as he backed up against Magos Vahihva's plinth. Her breath was a contradictory mix of warm honey and sharp lemon. 'You understand how rare it is for one of your kind to set foot on a craftworld?'

Finally, a question.

'Yrlandriar of Alaitoc told me that, yes.'

'Alaitoc? Yes, that makes sense,' she said, cocking her head to the side and looking at him strangely, as though some part of a puzzle had just fallen into place for her. 'Its people have always been foolishly trusting. Too eager to seek the middle ground instead of choosing a direct course of action.'

'You know me,' said Roboute, daring a question of his own, 'but who are you?'

'Bielanna Faerelle, Farseer of Craftworld Biel-Tan,' she said, following that with what sounded like the opening bars of a song until Roboute realised she was saying the name in her native tongue. He ran the sounds in his head again and compared them to the human version of the name she'd said, dredging up memories of frustrating afternoons spent in a forest of crystal trees that looked oddly like humanoid figures.

'Fairest light of... distant suns?' he ventured.

Her eyes widened and he laughed at the surprise in her eyes.

'We're not all barbarians, you know,' he said. 'Some of us actually wash too.'

Bielanna ignored his sarcasm and said, 'Did the Alaitocii teach you our language?'

'Yrlandriar taught me a few words here and there,' said Roboute modestly. He was far from fluent, but nor was he ignorant of the rudiments of eldar language.

'Like an owner teaches his pet the commands to sit or beg,' said Bielanna.

Anger touched Roboute. 'More like a master instructing a novice,' he said in conversational eldar.

She laughed in derision and shook her head. 'None of your kind can master the eldar language beyond grunting a few basic phrases. And your analogy is flawed, it infers the novice could go on to become a master. That is not the case.'

'I've heard differently,' said Roboute, tiring of her condescension and deciding a change of tack was required. 'Why did you attack our fleet in the Halo Scar?'

Her face changed in an instant, her slender fingers curled into fists.

'What choice did I have?' she snarled, her porcelain doll features transforming from serene beauty to bilious anger in a heartbeat. 'I flew the paths of the skein and saw what harm your foolish quest might wreak.'

Roboute struggled to follow her internal logic. 'You're saying you killed our ships over something we *might* do?'

Bielanna shook her head and let out a vexed hiss. 'You mon-keigh are so terrifyingly ignorant of the nature of causality it is a wonder you have not already plunged into species-extinction. You blunder through space like a wilful child who screams and wails when the universe does not bend to his will, turning a blind eye to consequences that displease you.'

Glitter light built in her eyes and Roboute remembered Yrlandriar telling him that farseers were powerful war-psykers, as versed in the arts of death as they were in the arts of prognostication. Once again, Roboute realised he had let the appearance of a woman blind him to the truth that she was not what she seemed. In Linya's case that had cost him a little embarrassment and earned him a measure of humility. Here it could kill him.

'What is it you think we are going to do?' he asked.

She sighed and said, 'It would be like explaining a symphony to a ptera-squirrel.'

'Try me, I'm cleverer than I look.'

'This thing that you seek,' said Bielanna. 'It can reignite dying stars and shape entire star systems. Its power can unmake time and space and make a mockery of the universal dance. Do you really think your upstart race of savages is ready to be the custodians of such a thing?'

'Perhaps not,' said Roboute. 'But if it's so dangerous, why don't you just go and get it yourself or destroy it if it's too dangerous to exist?'

Her fractional hesitation was all the answer he needed.

'After the battle in the Halo Scar, the shipmasters thought you'd escaped, but you didn't, did you?' said Roboute. 'Your ship must have been destroyed and you had to board the *Speranza* to escape. You're the ones that have been killing the work crews below the waterline.'

'Your reckless quest into the unknown has cost eldar lives, so why should I care for the lives of their killers? Why should meaningless flicker-souls be of any consequence to me, when your kind are going to murder my children before they are born?'

Roboute endured her venom though he understood little save her anger. Much of it was the bitter spite attributed to the eldar in Imperial propaganda, but her last words stretched his understanding to breaking point.

'Kill your... what?' he asked. 'We haven't killed any children.'

'Nor will you, for the potential for their birth is fading,' said Bielanna. 'With every second you travel towards this *moraideiin* world, their life-thread from the future to the present grows ever fainter.'

'Moraideiin? I don't know what that means. You mean Telok's forge world?'

'Telok, is he one of your machine-men?'

'You don't know?'

Her face flickered, and on any human expression it would have been meaningless – a muscular spasm or a nervous tic – but in the face of an eldar it was tantamount to a murderer's inadvertent admission of guilt.

Suddenly it made sense to Roboute. 'You're a farseer, but you don't have any power, do you? It's this whole region of space and the Breath of the Gods. Something in what it did to Arcturus Ultra is stopping you from seeing the future, isn't it?'

She moved so quickly it was like a skipping image on a picter. One minute she was standing before him, the next he was pinned to Magos Vahihva's plinth with her hand at his chest and her sword at his neck. Phosphor-bright will-o'-the-wisp danced in her oval pupils, and Roboute tasted the bitter, ashen-cold taste of psychic energy in his mouth as it filled with coppery saliva.

'Will I show you what power I have?' she asked, her voice stripped of its previously lyrical quality and all the more terrifying for it. 'Shall I burn the primitive brain in your skull or curse your soul to wander the void for eternity? Will I melt the flesh from your bones with balefire or shall I simply cut your throat and watch you bleed to death? I can end your life in the blink of an eye, and you say I have no power?'

Roboute held his breath as Bielanna's eyes bored into him, the hypnotically bright sparks in her eyes swelling until they shone like twin pools of starlight.

'Reveal to me everything you know of this Telok,' commanded Bielanna, and Roboute felt her presence within his skull like a silk-gloved hand stroking the surface of his mind. 'You will tell me everything regarding this voyage. And then you will return to your fellow mon-keigh and forget that we ever spoke.'

Roboute nodded, as though this were the most sensible thing she had suggested.

'And when I have need of an *agaith*, you will be the hidden blade in my hand.'

'Yes,' he said. 'I will.'

Microcontent 20

Any fears that, upon achieving his goal, Kotov would be disappointed by what he found at the end of his quest had been shattered utterly in the last three days. The final approach to Telok's forge world had been a sensory overload in unique celestial phenomena. Not only were the star systems around the forge world clustered tighter than any other system-grouping Kotov knew, but the Kuiper belt, planetary bodies and asteroid fields within the central system travelled in orbits as precise as any engineered by an atomic clockmaker.

The system – which Kotov still insisted on leaving unnamed – comprised twelve planets, each one equidistant from its inner and outer neighbour. All were of roughly Terran size and composition, with the exception of three gas giants in the system's central belt, between which vast fields of asteroid debris hung in glimmering curtains of ejected matter and ice.

The impression was of rocky fragments on the floor of a sculptor's workshop, of discarded components from some vast, and yet unfinished, engineering works. Such was the unnatural order imposed on the system that even Vitali Tychon had been coaxed from his daughter's sickbed to provide stellar analysis and plot new cartographae charts. Though every moment away from Linya chafed the venerable stargazer, even he was held mesmerised by the dizzying ramifications of this system.

The bridge of the *Speranza*, normally a place of continual binaric back and forth, coded hymnals and clattering servitor operation, was now draped in reverent hush. Though no one worthy of the rank of Cult Mechanicus gave any credence to the notions of any deity beyond the God of All Machines, it was hard not to imagine the hand of a divine creator in the celestial architecture of this star and its attendant worlds.

Even the solar wind was a thing of beauty.

The rush of electrons and protons flaring from the upper atmosphere of the star was being filtered through the *Speranza*'s augmitters, and the normally chaotic interaction of particles was rendered into a geomagnetic symphony. It was a cascade of perfectly modulated integers that to an unaugmented ear would sound like soft surf on a beach, but to the superior Mechanicus aural implant became a harmonious interaction of perfect numbers, helicoidal patterns and waveform sounds that were as beautiful as they were artificial.

Holographic projectors displayed the system's twelve worlds in floating veils of light, together with fleet deployment and the ongoing data inloads from the *Speranza*'s forward auspex arrays. The projectors encoded each of the system's worlds with differing colours representing the various atmospheric, geological and climatological systems at work.

At the astrogation plotters, Azuramagelli coordinated the manoeuvres of the Kotov fleet to bring the *Speranza* into a declining orbital track in a way that maximised its defensive posture without appearing to be overtly hostile. Every ship was pulled into close formation, with the fleet's three remaining warships tucked in close-defence positions. *Moonchild* and *Wrathchild* hugged the *Speranza*'s flanks, while *Mortis Voss* trailed in the tail gunner position. The rest of the Kotov fleet, fuel tenders, supply ships and refinery craft, were spread over its upper sections, ready to cluster in for defence at the first sign of trouble.

Vitali Tychon worked alongside Azuramagelli, and though his daughter had shown up an error in the Master of Astrogation's calculations upon their first meeting, he had expressed his deep regret at Mistress Tychon's wounding.

Across from Azuramagelli and Vitali, Kryptaestrex continued to oversee the ongoing ship-wide repair works from his Manifold link to Magos Turentek's prow forges. Despite Kotov's deep mistrust regarding the concessions he had been forced to make to Abrehem Locke, Kryptaestrex was reporting that the new working dynamic between the Mechanicus and its bondsmen was already paying dividends in terms of productivity and efficiency.

Magos Blaylock moved amongst the magi and servitors like an anxious scholar at proficiency examinations, assessing their work, offering suggestions on superior analytical technique or refining aspects of their binary. Kotov watched his Fabricatus Locum at work, seeing something more than simple devotion to duty in his observations.

Putting aside Blaylock's curious behaviour, Kotov turned his attention to the world occupying the central position in the viewing bay. Telok's forge world was bathed in a purple haze of borealis, beautiful in a way that only devotees of the Machine could truly appreciate. The shimmering corona was a by-product of inhumanly massive energy generation on a planetary scale. Kotov had seen such hazes around forge worlds before, but never on so bright and consistent a level. The quantity of energy being generated was enough to empower the manufactories of at least six Exactis Prima-level production hubs.

The planet was roughly double the Martian mass and boasted an atmosphere capable of being processed by human lungs. Its geology was unknown, as was anything else of its surface conditions. Initial surveys had proved maddeningly inconclusive, with each sweep of the auspex revealing contradictory data-streams that on one pass revealed a planet undergoing traditional – if somewhat accelerated – ageing, while on another echoed Vitali Tychon's data from Hypatia, which appeared to indicate signs of geological regression. Yet, as impossible as such readings appeared to be, Kotov had almost become used to encountering the inexplicable. After all, had not the Breath of the Gods remade Arcturus Ultra and transformed it from a dead system into one that would eventually prove to be habitable?

The collateral effects of such dizzyingly complex stellar engineering were a mystery, and the space in which such an event had occurred was bound to throw up anomalies for centuries to come. Yet for all that his mind was just about able to reconcile the cognitive dissonance of physically impossible spatial anomalies, Kotov couldn't quite shake the feeling that something was, if not *wrong*, per se, at least not quite as right as he would like.

He pushed the nagging sentiment aside, feeling a mounting excitement in his floodstream as the noospheric range counter streamed closer to high orbit. No matter how Kotov conditioned the biological responses of his brain, he couldn't suppress the sense that fate had led him here. He remembered the darkest moments of his despair with shame, when the second of his forge worlds had been destroyed and he had cursed the Omnissiah for forsaking him. But out of that abject misery had come the discovery of the *Speranza*.

From the ashes of his broken hubris, Kotov had recognised a last

lifeline to serve the Machine-God, that everything he had suffered was a test. Despair became hope and a newfound devotion to the Omnissiah.

This was where it had brought him, to impossible wonders beyond imagining, a reconnection with the past and a chance to rebuild the future.

All that spoiled this perfect moment was the presence of Galatea.

The hybrid machine intelligence prowled the bridge like a stalking arachnid, moving between the veils of light displaying the twelve worlds and studying each one. Each examination was cursory, saw Kotov, as though it was already aware of what was displayed. A tremor of unease passed through Kotov at the sight of Galatea's studied nonchalance, seeing an echo of Blaylock's peculiar behaviour in its perambulations.

Galatea said it wanted to kill Archmagos Telok, but Kotov no longer believed that. For all its pretensions to humanity and Kotov's increasing distance from his own, Galatea's lie no longer carried any conviction. Some other motive was at the heart of the machine intelligence's desire to be reunited with Telok, and that unknown variable gnawed at Kotov like pernicious scrapcode.

Magos Blaylock concluded his wanderings through the other magi and returned to his station beside Kotov's command throne. The gaggle of servitor dwarfs fussed around his train of pipework and hissing regulators.

'Is it all you hoped for, archmagos?' asked Blaylock.

Putting aside thoughts of Galatea, Kotov said, 'It is *more* than I could have hoped for, Tarkis.'

Blaylock nodded slowly. 'I must confess I doubted the wisdom of this quest. I believed your reasons for its undertaking to be motivated by pride and desperation, but now that we are here... I...'

Kotov turned to face his Fabricatus Locum, surprised by his uncharacteristic loss for words and candid admissions. He had long known that Blaylock harboured doubts, but had thought them put to rest after their walk in the Processional Way. Blaylock's features were no indicator of his mental status, having long since been submerged in mechanised implants, but the ripples in his noospheric aura were clear indicators of his conflicted status, like a machine stuck in an infinite loop attempting to reconcile two conflicting doctrina wafers.

'Is something the matter, Tarkis?'

Blaylock didn't answer, and Kotov was about to repeat the question – though he knew full well Tarkis must have heard him – when he received an answer it was the last answer he might have expected.

'I do not know,' said Blaylock with disarming honesty.

'You don't know? Here we are, surrounded by wonders no priest of Mars has seen in thousands of years, on the verge of reaching the quest's goal, and you don't know if something is the matter? You surprise me, Tarkis.'

'That is part of the problem,' said Blaylock, shaking his head, as though clearing it of some irritant code. 'No one from Mars has been here in thousands of years, yet I feel that this arrangement of stars and planets is somehow familiar.'

'You *feel* they are familiar?' asked Kotov.

'Apologies, archmagos, but there is no other word in my lexicon that fits the situation. I *feel* as though I have seen these stars before. And this is not the first time I have had this sensation.'

'When did you have it before?' said Vitali Tychon, approaching from the astrogation hub.

'Just before the energy emission from this planet reached the *Tomioka*,' answered Blaylock.

'Interesting,' said Vitali. 'As I am reading a great deal of similarity in this arrangement of planets and celestial/temporal interactions to an archived monograph on idealised stellar geometry inloaded by Magos Alhazen of Sinus Sabeus. Your former mentor and, if I am not mistaken, something of an evangelical devotee of Archmagos Telok.'

Blaylock paused as he accessed his internal database.

'No, you are mistaken, Magos Tychon,' he said. 'I am familiar with every submission made by Magos Alhazen to the Martian Tabularium Mons. He submitted no such monograph.'

Kotov shared Vitali's surprised expression.

As soon as Vitali mentioned the monograph, Kotov had retrieved it from the *Speranza*'s archives and instantly digested its contents. Sure enough, the postulations put forward by Alhazen were a close, and in some cases identical, match to the stellar data displayed on the command bridge.

That Blaylock seemed unaware of it was as close to impossible as Kotov could imagine.

Before he could pursue the matter, every single holographic display on the bridge flickered and was snuffed out by an incoming transmission from the planet below. The *Speranza* had been exloading generic hails and Mechanicus greeting protocols as soon as it had entered the system's edge, but they had all been ignored until now.

Each of the holographic hubs filled with a rotating icon of eight bodies seemingly issuing forth from molten bedrock or a swirling rush of what might represent flames. Kotov had never encountered

the image, but he recognised a Mechanicus hand in its formation, the golden ratio tracing a line through each of the figures' elbows and giving the whole a pleasingly ordered form.

'Starship *Speranza*, this is forge world Exnihlio,' said an automated vox. 'Prepare for inload.'

'*From out of nothing*,' said Vitali, voicing the Low Gothic translation of the name.

'Exnihlio,' said Kotov, rising from his command throne. 'This is Archmagos Kotov, High Lord of Mars and Explorator General of this expedition. Do I have the honour of addressing Archmagos Vettius Telok?'

Kotov was about to repeat his question when the image of the writhing figures was replaced with complex navigational waypoints tracing a narrow transit corridor through the highly charged atmosphere. Only a vessel of sufficiently low displacement would be able to fly such a passage, and even a cursory parsing of the data indicated that deviating from the prescribed pathway would be extremely hazardous.

'Landing coordinates,' said Azuramagelli. 'An older format, but that is only to be expected from a world without hexamathic enhancements.'

Kotov nodded, feeling a potent sense of anticipation at the thought of setting foot on Telok's forge world. Travelling to the fiefdom of another magos was always a time of great importance, a chance to share data, pursue new directions in the interpretation of techno-arcana and barter services and information to further the Quest for Knowledge. What might he learn on the world of an archmagos unfettered from the censure of his peers and the restrictions of Universal Laws?

'Archmagos?' asked Blaylock. 'What are your orders?'

'Send word to Sergeant Tanna,' said Kotov. 'I am going to have need of the *Barisan*.'

All evidence that human beings had once occupied this space had been removed and the chamber returned to its former state of abandonment. The remains of Hawke's still had been removed, and its component parts placed in reclamation funnels. The lumen globes recessed in the coffers were dimmed and the images of the saintly figures wreathed in shadow. Ismael had taken Abrehem to a shrine below the waterline, leaving Totha Mu-32 to complete the internment of Rasselas X-42.

'Abrehem should never have found you,' he said, circling the slumbering killer.

Clad head to foot in black, the arco-flagellant sat with its ironclad head bowed, a flickering light stuttering like a malfunctioning strobe beneath the smooth inner face of its pacifier helm. Images of Imperial holy men and divine visions of harmony played out before X-42, keeping it locked in a state of perpetual bliss.

Given what Totha Mu-32 knew of the Impaler Cardinal's reign of blood, it was a more merciful fate than any he had accorded his victims. The arco-flagellant's muscles twitched as rogue synapses flared and sparked in its brain, the inevitable result of a sword to the skull.

'I wonder what effects the damage is having on the visions within your skull?' wondered Totha Mu-32. 'Whatever the repercussions, I hope they hurt. You deserve to suffer for the things you have done. And once this chamber is sealed, you will suffer them until the *Speranza* finally ends its days.'

Totha Mu-32 continued his circling of the arco-flagellant, checking that every restraint was as tight as it could be made and that every dormancy connector was firmly attached. He checked every spinal shunt, every cortical inhibitor and every neurological blocker.

Satisfied everything was in order, he ran a final diagnostic on the pacifier mechanisms, ensuring that the machinery was functioning within acceptable operating parameters. Hooked directly into the *Speranza*'s power grid and with multiple redundancies, the mechanism could keep an army of arco-flagellants sedated for longer than the Ark Mechanicus was likely to survive.

Totha Mu-32 backed out of the chamber, still, despite every precaution and check he had just made, unwilling to turn his back on the cyborg killer. He paused by the shutter to the dormis chamber as a cold wind sighed from within, like the last exhalation of a slumbering predator who is just waiting out the winter before emerging to hunt once more.

Rasselas X-42 remained unmoving, a hunched statue of caged murder and horror. Even dormant, it exuded dreadful danger. Though it should be impossible for the arco-flagellant to break the psycho-conditioning holding it fast, Totha Mu-32 half expected the creature to raise its head one last time.

The arco-flagellant twitched and the light beneath its helm flickered on.

Totha Mu-32 swept a hand over the hidden door mechanism and the heavy bulkhead shutter slammed down into the floor with a percussive boom of engaging locks. A handprint of dried blood was smeared in the centre of the door and Totha Mu-32 placed his own hand over the impression of what he knew was Abrehem's hand.

This, coupled with a trigger word, had caused the locks to disengage and begun X-42's reactivation sequence. Totha Mu-32 spat on the bloodstain and rubbed the sleeve of his robe over the flaked blood until nothing remained of it.

Taking a last look around the empty chamber, Totha Mu-32's gaze was met by the hundreds of iron black skulls set into the walls. Part temple, part prison, part sepulchre; each interpretation was apt for the monster entombed within.

A flicker of code squirmed through the walls, fragmentary binary debris from whatever conduits had once passed through this chamber en route to unknown destinations. Much of it was degraded to the point of simply becoming squalling gibberish, and soon it would be entirely reabsorbed back into the noosphere.

Totha Mu-32 turned and strode from the chamber, leaving the lumens to gutter and die as the code encircling the chamber finally faded out. The empty sockets of the grinning skulls set in the bleak walls glimmered with the dying code, as though they alone were custodians of a secret they wished to tell, but were forever sworn to keep.

Like Totha Mu-32, they knew that some doors were best left unopened.

But they also knew that some doors can never be shut entirely.

Like the phoenix of myth, the *Barisan* had emerged from the flames of its rebirth stronger than ever. The damage it had suffered on Katen Venia had been almost entirely erased by the ritual ministrations of Magos Turentek and his army of artificers. The compression fractures in its hull plates were repaired, the impact trauma to its superstructure was undone and the torsion stresses in its spine had been unkinked.

For all intents and purposes, the craft was as good as new, as fine as the day its frame had been struck in the Tyrrhenus Mons forge-complex. Turentek had seen the seal of the Fabricator General and had bent his every effort into restoring the work of Mars's pre-eminent worker of metals and spirit. The *Barisan* had suffered greatly in the crash, and its machine-spirit was a vicious, cornered beast of a thing, but Turentek had eventually earned its trust with the quality of his workmanship and the devotion of his servants.

Tanna felt the gunship respond to his every command as though they had been flying together for centuries. It wasn't exactly compliant per se, and could still shrug him off like a tiny biological irritant, but at least there was a measure of respect between them now.

'The gunship has healed well,' said Archmagos Kotov, seated beside Tanna in the co-pilot's seat.

Tanna nodded tersely and said, 'Magos Turentek has my thanks.'

The view through the canopy was a tempestuous melange of

lightning-shot cloud banks and flickering geomagnetic storms that clashed, burst and roared and blazed with tortured energies. Streamers of plasma and forking traceries of vertical lightning shot up from the surface, making it feel as though the *Barisan* was evading a thunderous barrage of anti-aircraft fire.

'It is like flying through a hundred thunderstorms at once,' said Tanna as a booming pressure wave slammed into the gunship's fuselage.

'This is not a thunderstorm,' said Kotov as Tanna corrected their flight path.

'Then what is it?'

'The inevitable consequence of planet-wide power generation,' said Kotov, gesturing through the streaked canopy to where a vast dirigible-like device hung motionless in the sky. The billowing hull of the object was englobed in arcs of purple and amber lightning that coruscated down a thick length of metallic cabling hung from its underside and vanished into the roiling banks of charged vapour like a trailing arrestor hook.

'What was that?' asked Tanna as the floating contraption was swallowed by the clouds and disappeared from sight.

'Some sort of energy collector, I imagine,' said Kotov admiringly. 'It seems virtually every machine and temple on the surface of this world is given over to power generation, and that amount of power creates all manner of distortion in the upper atmosphere. I suspect Telok has unlocked a means to harness what would normally be classified as waste by-products.'

'The Breath of the Gods requires such power?'

Kotov hesitated before answering. 'It is impossible to know the energy demands of something so far beyond our comprehension,' he said. 'In fact, it amazes me that one world can provide the power for something capable of such incredible reorganisation of matter and energy.'

Another energy discharge rocked the *Barisan,* and Tanna swung the prow back around as a pair of the giant dirigibles hove into view through the vapour-slick clouds. This time, the view was clearer, and Tanna saw they were little more than vast bladders of a rippling metallic fibre constrained by mesh netting and hung with copper and brass mechanisms that spun and crackled with activity.

Tanna brought the gunship lower, the altitude spiralling down as he followed the convoluted route to the surface. Had he not seen the atmospheric effects for himself, he would have believed they were being led down a deliberately circuitous flight path.

'There has to be an easier way to the surface,' he said, more to himself than Kotov.

'Are you following the waypoint coordinates correctly?'

Tanna didn't even spare him a withering glance. 'You would already know if I was not, because you would be screaming.'

'Point taken, brother-sergeant.'

'The waypoints are accurate, but it's what we will find at the end of this flight that worries me.'

'You suspect danger?'

'I always suspect danger, archmagos,' said Tanna. 'That's why I am still alive.'

'Had Telok wanted us dead, he could have found an easier method than guiding us into a thunderstorm.'

'Perhaps he has reasons to wish us alive when we reach the surface.'

'Such as?'

'I do not know,' said Tanna. 'You are the Mechanicus here. This is your expedition.'

'We are fellow crusaders, brother-sergeant, I thought you understood that,' Kotov said. 'Do you not think that I could have taken any number of Mechanicus transports down to the surface? I could have preloaded the route Telok sent us, but I chose you to fly me down to this historic meeting because I value what you represent. You are the Emperor, and I am the Mechanicus. Two facets of the Imperium working together. Our unity stands as testament to our sacred purpose in coming to this world.'

'And it is never a bad idea to have a squad of Black Templars at your back when venturing into the unknown.'

'That too,' agreed Kotov, and Tanna could almost share the master of the expedition's excitement.

Despite everything they had suffered, they had actually reached their destination alive.

The atmosphere grew thinner, and blocky shapes loomed from the clouds, vast cooling towers belching toxic fumes from the planet's surface and squat funnels that shot plumes of green fire into the sky. Arcing static crackled in the air like fireworks at a triumphal parade and virtually every auspex panel fizzed with distortion. More of the dirigibles drifted past the *Barisan*, hundreds of them floating like blooms of jellyfish in a turgid ocean. The gunship flew lower still, and more of the titanic buildings – if buildings they were – emerged from the banks of cloud.

Tanna saw towering steel structures wrapped in coils of energy, crackling pylons hundreds of metres in diameter and exosphere-scraping

pyramids whose bases were thousand of miles wide. It was like flying over a gathering of hive-cities that had forsaken their individuality and simply merged into one continuous planetary crust of steel and caged fire. Tens of thousands of metres below the *Barisan*, tesla-coil skyscrapers jostled for space amid vast power domes and immense capacitor stacks.

The entire surface was a coruscating, reticulated grid of lightning that spat from raised copper orbs as large as kroot warspheres and arced from conical towers fringed with hundred-metre spines. Streamers of light flowed through the gnarled mass of enormous structures, as though the planet were an organism with illumination for blood. Warm rain streaked the canopy as Tanna brought the gunship down, following a newly appeared graphic of approach markers on the avionics slate. The margin for error was minimal, and Tanna realised his earlier suspicion that there existed an easier way to reach the surface was incorrect.

He gestured to vast, funnel-shaped towers rearing up to either side of their flight path like guide poles on a snow-locked runway. Each was topped with a flanged maw that drew in great lungfuls of the clouds and vapour banks.

'Are those atmospheric processors?' he asked.

Kotov could barely tear his gaze from the magnificent spectacle of the colossal, planet-wide city of industry and the inhumanly vast structures passing on either side, but he nodded curtly.

'Yes, I believe they are,' he said. 'They have the hallmark of early STC universal assemblers and are probably what makes the air breathable. What of them?'

'Those towers are creating a stable corridor of calmer air for the gunship to fly through.'

'Again I ask, what is your point?'

'That this route was specifically created for us,' said Tanna. 'Right now, this is the only way anyone is getting to the surface.'

'And?'

'If those machines are switched off, we will have no way to get off this planet.'

Microcontent 21

The *Barisan* set down in the rain on a landing platform of elevated stonework in the centre of an open plaza that resembled the civic square of an Imperial city. Steel and glasswork spires pierced the sky on every side, but dominating the eastern side of the plaza was a colossal hangar-structure with a vaulted silver-steel roof and glittering masts at its four corners. The sky was a painfully artificial shade of blue, striated with bands of deeper azure and pale streaks of cyan.

Lightning coursed up the sides of every structure, as though their only purpose was to create and channel energy, making the air taste like biting down hard on a copper rod. Kotov marched down the Thunderhawk's frontal assault ramp with a gaggle of scrivener savants in his wake. A pair of servo-skulls with iron-cog halos drifted in lazy orbits above him. His body was a part organic, part cybernetic hybrid in the fashion of an ancient order of theologic warriors from a now lost peninsula of Terra, with a flowing crimson robe whose every fibre was a fractal-formed binary equation.

He had come armed, as was his right as an archmagos, with the same gold-chased pistol with which he had fought Galatea's abominations aboard the Valette Manifold station. The volkite weapon was a relic of the deepest past, an artefact so precious it truly belonged in a stasis-sealed treasury case in one of the great Halls of Wonders within the Dao Vallis repositories. Two menials hastily robed in Mechanicus finery carried the remains of the *Tomioka*'s distress beacon taken from its saviour pod upon satin cushions – a symbolic gesture of the path that had led them to this place.

As befitting an archmagos of the Adeptus Mechanicus, he had come with an escort: eight skitarii in their black and gold armour bedecked with poisonous reptiles of Old Earth. Ven Anders had chosen a squad of his elite veterans, and Sergeant Tanna had come with his Space Marines. As the man who had brought him the locator beacon, Roboute Surcouf had, of course, been accorded a place in the landing party. He had brought a young bodyguard and his ship's magos, Pavelka, with him. Kotov read the censure brands in her noospheric aura with a note of vague curiosity. Surcouf was not the only one of the *Renard*'s crew to have flaunted authority, it seemed.

Kotov stepped from the ramp, setting foot on a forge world that had not known the tread of a representative of the Imperium of Man in thousands of years. He marched to the edge of the stone platform, where a set of wide steps led down to the plaza, and surveyed his surroundings for any sign of Archmagos Telok or his agents.

Kotov was not so vain as to have expected a triumphal welcome or a mass turnout of whatever workforce laboured in the power plants and forges of this world, but he had expected *something*. They had crossed the galaxy, endured all manner of hardships and indignities and suffered great loss to reach this world. A flicker of perturbation danced at the edge of his thoughts at the emptiness surrounding the *Barisan*.

His skitarii took up position to his right, while Colonel Anders formed the Cadians up in two ranks on the left. Tanna and his Space Marines stood like giants carved from basalt and ivory at the base of the assault ramp; Surcouf and his people joined him at the steps, while the menial took a subservient position on his right. Kotov carried a long sceptre of gold and bronze, topped with a jet and bone representation of the Icon Mechanicus. Trails of incense pleasing to the Omnissiah wafted from its coal-red eye sockets.

Putting aside the lack of any discernible form of greeting, Kotov instead turned his attention to the world itself, feeling the perpetual vibration in its bedrock that was common to planets entirely given over to the workings of the Adeptus Mechanicus.

But there was more to it than that.

Kotov felt the unmistakable presence of grand designs, of new and unimagined workings taking place here. Deep in the very essence of what made him an archmagos, he sensed that magnificent things were afoot on this world. Technologies as yet undreamed, research that had stagnated millennia ago and which was now resurgent, developments in arenas of sophistication that the magi of Mars could not even begin to imagine.

This was a world that was in the purest sense of the word, unique.

And it was empty.

Sergeant Tanna and Colonel Anders approached and stood to either side of him.

'Were we not expected?' asked Anders, clad in his dress uniform, regalia that only a Cadian would recognise as being any different from battledress.

'We are expected, of course,' replied Kotov, fighting down a mounting sense of unease. 'We received detailed instructions for our landing.'

'From an automated source,' pointed out Surcouf. 'That could be hundreds of years old or more.'

'No,' said Kotov. 'Had that been the case, the given waypoints would not have delivered us to the surface, but seen us torn apart in the geomagnetic storms on our descent. The coordinates we were given are only relevant at this precise moment.'

'Then where is Telok?' demanded Tanna.

'He will be here,' said Kotov. 'The authentic catechisms of first communion were exchanged with the binaric purity of genuine Mechanicus signifiers. We are expected and we will be met.'

'I think you might be right,' said Surcouf as previously invisible seams appeared in the facade of the enormous hangar-structure with the vaulted silver-steel roof. A titanic gateway was revealed, like one of the portals offering access to the vaults of arcana beneath Olympus Mons, and from it marched a glittering behemoth.

Easily the equal of an Imperator Titan in height, but as wide and long as the largest Mechanicus bulk lander, it was an impossibly huge scorpion-like creature of glass and crystal. Its segmented body was veined with shimmering lines of emerald light and low-slung between enormous legs like frozen stalactites hewn from the roof of a colossal cave. It moved with the sound of breaking glass and grinding stone, and no one could miss the similarity to the bio-mimetic crystal-forms they had fought on Katen Venia.

'Throne preserve us,' breathed Tanna.

'What in the name of Terra is that?' hissed Anders.

Kotov fought to hold back his own fear, but the sight of so monstrous a creation circumvented his rational neural pathways. Nothing could stand against such a towering war-engine, not the might of the Imperial Guard, not a Titan Legion, nor even the awesomely destructive war-engines of the Centurio Ordinatus. This was death in frozen, crystalline form.

'Now that *can't* be good…' said Surcouf, backing away towards the *Barisan*.

'We have been brought here to die,' said Tanna.

'No,' said Kotov, though the evidence was hard to deny. 'That makes no sense.'

'Believe what you want, archmagos, but we are leaving!'

'Is it even possible to get back?' cried Anders over the clashing din of the crystalline beast's stamping, seismic approach.

'It has to be,' said Tanna. 'We reverse our course to the surface and hope the stable corridor through the atmosphere is still open.'

'You're staking our lives on a forlorn hope,' said Anders.

'Better a forlorn hope than no hope,' pointed out Tanna.

'True enough,' nodded Anders, waving his own men back to the gunship.

Kotov alone did not move, nor did his skitarii or his aides. He watched the approach of the crystal leviathan with transfixed awe.

Tanna shouted at him to get to the *Barisan*, but Kotov ignored him.

Better death than to return in disgrace.

Though he had helped Kotov reach this world, Vitali Tychon had declined the chance to accompany the archmagos to the surface. It had been hard enough to leave his daughter under the care of the medicae staff for the time it took to begin the cartographae protocols on approach to Telok's forge world.

What if she were to wake while he was away?

With his work complete on the command bridge, Vitali had ridden the mag-lev to the medicae deck and now hurried towards the burns unit. The attending surgical adepts were quietly confident that Linya would survive and recover much of her former operational utility. Her legs had been amputated at mid-thigh, but augmetic replacements had already been fashioned by Magos Turentek that closely mimicked the appearance of human limbs.

The rest of the damage had been largely cosmetic, and the vat-grown skin patches were showing signs of renewed growth. It would never be the same as human skin, but it was as close as could be created without a clone donor – and Linya had always been adamant that she could never allow another life to be brought into being simply to act as a repository for spare organs.

The corridors of the medicae deck were deserted, which was unusual, but with the ship in orbit around Telok's forge world, Vitali was not entirely surprised. How often did an adept of Mars get to travel

beyond the edges of the galaxy, let alone witness a forge world established in the depths of intergalactic space?

He hoped Linya would be awake. He wanted to speak to his daughter again, to hold her hand now that she was no longer at risk from infection and the counterseptic field was no longer required. He had no doubt that she would have insights into the nature of this world that had escaped the more traditionally minded magi.

Besides, he could use the help in cataloguing the many anomalous readings he was detecting from the world below. Much like Hypatia, Telok's forge world exhibited signs of aberrant senescence, appearing to experience periods of hyper-accelerated ageing balanced out by concomitant periods of renewal. Geological push and pull were all part and parcel of a planet's existence as its orbit traced an elliptical path around its star, but this was something more, something unexplained and, for now, beyond his ability to fathom.

Too many inexplicable anomalies that shared this same characteristic were mounting up for Vitali's liking: the reports of the robotic guardians on the *Tomioka* being in a state of decrepitude but yet still functional; the apparent planetary youth of Hypatia and the presence of a pre-Age of Strife metropolis; and now these nonsensical readings.

Whatever Telok had found in the wilderness space, it had effectively unravelled the fabric of space-time and made a mockery of the physical laws governing its operation. Vitali's thinking was too literal and methodical to make sense of such things; he needed Linya's ability to think in curves to galvanise their cogitations.

Vitali turned into the burns unit and followed the familiar route through its sterile corridors, still turning over the problems of trans-dimensional fractures in space-time and their collateral effects on universal chronometry.

So focused was Vitali on this largely theoretical and largely unknown branch of Mechanicus art that at first he didn't notice the bodies.

He stopped in his tracks and all thoughts of quantum theorems were forgotten.

The central hub chamber of the burns unit resembled an uprising in a slaughterhouse.

Corpses and severed limbs lay scattered throughout the space like offal, too many and in too much disarray to even begin to guess at how many dead bodies surrounded him. Horrified, Vitali saw one body cut in half at the waist, sitting in a lake of oil-sheened blood, another that was little more than a truncated slab of meat with metallic nubs of bone protruding from its torn flesh. Mechanical parts were strewn amongst the hacked up meat, and Vitali saw the robes of magi, servitors and menials.

The carnage had been indiscriminate, the exalted murdered alongside the enslaved.

Worse, there was clear relish taken in these killings, a savage joy in the reduction of human flesh and machine augmentation to ruin.

Prudence and logic dictated a retreat, but his daughter lay defenceless in one of this deck's treatment chambers. Whatever maniac had perpetrated this senseless massacre might still be here, might still have designs on killing anyone he came across.

Vitali was no warrior and had always eschewed the implantation of weaponry within his body-plan, but right now he would have gladly had an integral beam weapon or energy sword. Stepping around the worst of the blood and discarded body parts, Vitali picked his way towards the passage that led to Linya's room.

Scarlet droplets had sprayed the walls here, as though the murderer had swung his killing blade to spatter the lifeblood of his victims in some perverse act of vandalism. With a sinking heart, Vitali hurriedly followed the looping arcs like a trail of horrid breadcrumbs.

'No, please, no,' whispered Vitali as he saw the blood drops traced an unerring course to Linya's room. 'Ave Deus Mechanicus, please no.'

The door was ajar and Vitali heard sounds of movement from within.

Though he had no ability to fight beyond what innate human nature had gifted him, Vitali didn't hesitate and barged through the door.

'Get away from her!' he shouted without knowing who or what lay within.

The grisly tableau before him halted him in his tracks and he sank to his knees in abject horror.

Galatea squatted at the side of Linya's bed, the silver-eyed tech-priest body hunched over his daughter like some predatory vampire creature. Blood haloed Linya's head and Galatea's arachnid limbs were wet where it had hacked its victims apart in the medicae hub.

'Magos Tychon,' said Galatea. 'We are glad you could be here.'

The machine intelligence straightened up and Vitali recoiled in horror.

'Ave Deus Mechanicus!' wailed Vitali. 'What have you done? Omnissiah have mercy, what have you done to my Linya?'

'We said your daughter was exceptional,' said Galatea, as a web of micro-fine connector cables wormed their way inside a glass cylinder

of bio-conductive gel to infest the newly implanted organ within. 'And now her mind will be exceptional within our neuromatrix.'

The crystalline leviathan moved with a hypnotic fluidity that should have been impossible for something so enormous. The sheer magnificence of its construction and very conception was astounding, beyond anything even the most crazed techno-heretics imprisoned beneath the Baphyras Catena dared to dream into existence.

It appeared to have no moving parts as any Mechanicus enginseer would understand the notion, its joints and segmented body parts seeming to move within and through one another in ways his ocular implants told him ought to be impossible; as though the bonds between the crystalline lattices within its body were fluid in ways no one had thought possible.

Tanna shouted at him once more, but again he ignored the Space Marine's words.

What fate would there be for an archmagos who returned empty handed from an expedition that had suffered such loss? He would be stripped of his last holdings and reduced to his component parts to be reclaimed into servitor implants. How would that serve the Omnissiah?

Better to die within sight of his goal than to flee towards disgrace.

The aching blue of the sky and the lightning arcing between the giant tesla-coil towers glittered from its multi-faceted form. It had a beauty all its own, a lethal majesty that had a perfect symmetry of form that struck Kotov as being ostensibly similar to Galatea's appearance. The comparison was a poor one; the hybrid machine intelligence's mismatched body-plan was at best a crude approximation of this magnificent creature's form.

No. Not an approximation.

A copy...

Three figures appeared at his side and Kotov nodded to Sergeant Tanna, Colonel Anders and Roboute Surcouf.

'You are not leaving?' he asked.

'I left Kul Gilad to die on the *Adytum*,' said Tanna. 'I will not leave you to die alone.'

'I've come this far,' said Surcouf. 'Seems a shame to leave without seeing how it all ends.'

Anders nodded in the direction of the leviathan as it loomed overhead, a titanic monster that could crush them underfoot without even noticing.

'And even if we got into the air, that thing would swat us down in seconds,' added Anders. 'And I'm mechanised infantry through and through, I'd much rather die on the ground than in a burning wreck of a Thunderhawk. No offence to your flying skills, Tanna.'

Kotov shook his head with an amused grin. 'No one is dying here today.'

Anders looked set to disagree when the vast plaza was suddenly filled with the sound of splintering glass. Every one of the landing party craned their necks upwards as a million spiderwebbing cracks zigzagged over the surface of the towering scorpion creature. Its entire body began coming apart, as though it had been struck by a precisely resonant hammerblow at its most vulnerable point and its structure was revealed to be no more solid than grains of powdered glass.

Cascades of glittering shards fell in a razored deluge from its upper surfaces as the immense war-engine began disintegrating from the top down. First the swaying stinger tail fell apart, dropping thousands of crystalline fragments to the plaza. Its body collapsed into itself, shedding mass like a ruptured sandbag. Its legs followed seconds later, toppling inwards like a row of dying Titans. The entire crystalline machine was falling apart, as though whatever molecular structure had allowed it to retain its shape was suddenly and catastrophically undone. The noise was deafening, the sharp-edged sound echoing from the surrounding structures and buildings in a thunderous crescendo of breaking glass and splintering rock.

Vast drifts of crystalline debris slumped from the implosive ruin of the beast's dissolution, towering dunes of broken glass spreading out in a tidal wave of lethally edged shards. The rain of glassy fragments broke against the raised platform in a shattering tide, spreading around it with the fluidity of liquid. Such was the volume of the giant scorpion creature that the scale of its death filled the entire plaza with glittering debris.

Then Kotov saw it was not debris and not death.

It was deployment.

The matter shed from the giant creature began cracking and splitting further, reorganising itself into new arrangements. Thousands of crystal-forms were taking shape from the dune sea of crystal, swiftly acquiring mass from the expelled matter of the host creature. Instead of one creature, now tens of thousands of crystal-forms surrounded the raised landing platform.

'What in the Emperor's name...?' breathed Tanna, turning on the spot to see how thoroughly they were outnumbered. Like the vast army of statuary once assembled by a despotic ruler of Old Earth, the crystalline statues were arranged around the landing platform with

perfect symmetry, their ranks as serried as any mass deployment of Imperial Guard on the muster fields.

Kotov studied the figures at the base of the platform's steps.

Humanoid in outline, they resembled unfinished sculpts of a race of powerfully built warriors hailing from one of the Imperium's primitive feral worlds. The crystalline warriors before them turned with robotic precision, parting like a crystal sea to form an avenue of approach like the triumphal route travelled by a victorious Lord General.

Emerging from the army of crystal-forms was a being of hulking proportions, a terrible meld of metal, glass and steel. Superficially it resembled a malformed penitent engine, bipedal and roughly humanoid, but its legs were brutish, elephantine stumps that displayed none of the unfinished simplicity of the crystal-forms.

Its movements were ungainly and awkward, as though its form was somehow misshapen and not at all what its creator had intended. Portions of its central mass were clearly formed from dark iron, and scraps of scarlet cloth draped arms that were spined with crystalline growths sprouting from every plane of its upper body. Arcs of heavy pipework looped over its shoulders like the cabling of an electromagnet, and an oil-streaked hood sat in the centre of its chest like the sarcophagus of a Dreadnought.

'What is that thing?' asked Anders, pulling his rifle tight to his shoulder.

It reached the base of the steps and began to climb with a hideous, lopsided motion, the crystallising necrosis of its limbs making each flex of a joint a splintering nightmare. It left powdered glass in its wake and the closer Kotov looked at the partially obscured iconography on the metallic portions of its body, the more he understood that this was not a thing to be feared, but revered.

Slithering metallic fronds drew back the scarlet hood at the creature's chest and Kotov fought to conceal his mounting excitement as he saw a human face revealed, albeit one ravaged by the effects of crystallisation and extreme juvenat treatments.

It was, nevertheless, a face he recognised.

A face that had stared back at him from the pages of crumbling manuscripts and degraded pict-captures for centuries of his life.

'Welcome to Exnihlio,' said the creature, its wasted features moving like a poorly operated flesh-puppet. 'We hope you will forgive the theatricality of our introduction, but we had all but given up hope of ever receiving emissaries from Mars.'

Kotov stepped forwards and said, 'Archmagos Telok, I presume?'

GODS OF MARS

DRAMATIS PERSONAE

The *Speranza*
LEXELL KOTOV – Archmagos of the Kotov Explorator Fleet
TARKIS BLAYLOCK – Fabricatus Locum, Magos of the Cebrenia Quadrangle
VITALI TYCHON – Stellar Cartographer of Quatria Orbital Gallery
LINYA TYCHON – Stellar Cartographer, daughter of Vitali Tychon
AZURAMAGELLI – Magos of Astrogation
KRYPTAESTREX – Magos of Logistics
TURENTEK – Ark Fabricatus
HIRIMAU DAHAN – Secutor/Guilder Suzerain
CHIRON MANUBIA – Magos of Forge Elektrus
TOTHA MU-32 – Mechanicus Overseer
ABREHEM LOCKE – Bondsman
RASSELAS X-42 – Arco-flagellant
VANNEN COYNE – Bondsman
JULIUS HAWKE – Bondsman
ISMAEL DE ROEVEN – Servitor
GALATEA – Proscribed machine intelligence

Exnihlio
VETTIUS TELOK – Archmagos of the Telok Explorator Fleet

The *Renard*
ROBOUTE SURCOUF – Captain
EMIL NADER – First Mate
ADARA SIAVASH – Hired Gun
ILANNA PAVELKA – Tech-priest
KAYRN SYLKWOOD – Enginseer

Adeptus Astartes Black Templars
TANNA – Brother-Sergeant
ISSUR – Initiate
ATTICUS VARDA – Emperor's Champion
BRACHA – Initiate
YAEL – Initiate

The Cadian 71st 'The Hellhounds'
VEN ANDERS – Colonel of the Cadian Detached Formation
BLAYNE HAWKINS – Captain, Blazer Company
TAYBARD RAE – Lieutenant, Blazer Company
JAHN CALLINS – Requisitional Support Officer, Blazer Company

Legio Sirius
ARLO LUTH, 'THE WINTERSUN' – Warlord Princeps, *Lupa Capitalina*
ELIAS HÄRKIN, 'THE IRONWOAD' – Warhound Princeps, *Vilka*
GUNNAR VINTRAS, 'THE SKINWALKER'

The *Starblade*
BIELANNA FAERELLE – Farseer of Biel-Tan
ARIGANNA – Striking Scorpion Exarch of Biel-Tan
TARIQUEL – Striking Scorpion of Biel-Tan
VAYNESH – Striking Scorpion of Biel-Tan
ULDANAISH GHOSTWALKER – Wraithlord of Biel-Tan

+++++INDEX EXPURGATORIUS+++++

'Behold, the extropic doctrine!
Humanity is a limitation to be overcome, for all beings strive for a life beyond flesh.
Shall we be the ebb of this great flood?
Shall we be beasts rather than gods?

What is the ape to Man? A painful embarrassment. Baseline forms shall be that to the Mechanicum. We crawled from the mud to be gods, but much in our species still wallows there. I will teach you of Man and Machine's union.

The Mechanicum quests for Singularity. My brothers, remain faithful to Mars! Despise those who speak of the divine organic!
Beasts are they, despisers of knowledge.
Entropy and fear lead them to extinction.
And the galaxy will not weep for them.'

The Extropian Manifesto (sequestered).
Author unknown.
Vol XVI, The Telok Verses.

+++++INDEX EXPURGATORIUS+++++

Mechanicus metafile 587634857z/SPERANZA

METADATA REPOSITORY %003

AVE.OMNISSIAH.orv 4048 a_start .equ
30f0 2048 ld length,% 2064 KNOWLEDGE IS
POWER? 00000010 10000000 CONTACT LOST:
KOTOV 00000110 2068 addcc%r1,-4,%r1
10000010 10000000 01111111 11111100 2072
addcc.%r1,%r2,%r4 10001000 BLAYLOCK:
CACHE STORAGE CONFLICT 01000000 BELOW
DECK OPERATIONS RESUMED 2076 ld%r4,%r5
11001010 00000001 00000000 00000000 2080 ba
loop 00010000 10111111 11111111 MACHINE-
HYBRID MOTIVATION? 2084 addcc%r3 XENOSIGN
TRACE CONFIRMED,%r5,%r3 10000110 10000000
11000000 00000101 2088 done: jmpl%r15+4,%r0
10000001 11000011 POSSIBLE TEMPORAL
ALTERATION ORGANISM 00000100 2092 length: 20
CARTOGRAPHAE READINGS INCONSISTENT 00000000
00000000 00010100 2096 address: a_start
00000100 PRE-HUMAN TECH OVERLAP? 00000000
00001011 10111000.Omni.B_start

Thermodynamic Violation Thermodynamic
Violation Thermodynamic Violation
Thermodynamic Violation Thermodynamic
Violation Thermodynamic Violation
Thermodynamic Violation Thermodynamic
Violation Thermodynamic Violation
Thermodynamic Violation Thermodynamic
Violation Thermodynamic Violation
Thermodynamic Violation Thermodynamic
Violation Thermodynamic Violation

Metadata Parsing in effect.

++++++++++++++++

001

Knowledge is power? That is what they say, those cohered molecules and atomic chains spreading through known and unknown space like a virus. That they have achieved sentience enough to think and say such a thing is a wonder in itself.

They grow and decay with prodigious rapidity, infesting every corner of the galaxy in numbers so huge as to defy even our imagination. Tens of thousands exist within this body of steel and power, itself only recently roused from millennial slumbers.

They are grains of sand swirling around the base of a vast mountain of knowledge. Some believe it utterly improbable that such a mountain can exist or be climbed without some divine hand to lift them to its summit.

How wrong they are. Winds of inevitable change swirl around this mountain and sometimes a propitious gust will blow against a favourably shaped grain to carry it uphill. It reaches higher than any before it, and it knows fractionally more than it once did.

By such infinitesimal steps does life evolve.

And its companions say it possesses great knowledge.

They are all ignorant, but ignorance must be embraced before it can be banished. The Athenian stonecutter had the truth of it when he said that the only true wisdom was in knowing you knew nothing.

Only by knowing how empty your cup is can you reach to fill it.

There are heights of knowledge whose existence the grains can never even guess at, let alone comprehend. Yet, even lost upon such an endless ocean of ignorance, there are beings who claim wisdom, who believe they know everything there is to be known.

These are the most dangerous beings imaginable.

They claim ancient texts of false and forgotten gods contain all the universe's knowledge – as though such a thing is possible beyond Akasha. For tens of thousands of years, these primitive coherences accepted such blind dogma without question, and those who questioned it were extinguished in agony.

010

For one dangerous moment, the grains of sand came close to ascending the mountain in one giant leap. The galaxy teetered on the edge of a precipice as a key turned in a door that should never be unlocked. One singular consciousness threaded the needle to pierce the veil between their world and Akasha, unpicking the weave that separates all things and no things.

But it was not to be. The door slammed shut, perhaps forever.

Knowledge must be earned, not simply stolen as Prometheus once stole fire and set mankind upon his course.

To stand on the shoulders of titans is one thing.

To claim their wisdom as your own is another, and only minds that have spent every moment since the galaxy began its slow revolutions can hope to appreciate this without being destroyed.

011

They think us a great void-born city of metal and stone, a marvel of wonders never to be known again. We consent to our physical manifestation dwelling in the depths of space, sheet-steel skin cold and unyielding. They think us a living thing, and we allow our irreducible complexity to be thought of as such.

The bones they have crafted are adamantium, our molten heart the flickering sparks of stars they believe tamed. We sweat oil, and the devotion of a million souls is thought to give us succour. The coherences of flesh and blood believe they empower us from within. They work the myriad wonders that drive our manifest organs, feed the whims of our appetite and hurl us through the fractional slivers of space between stars.

How far have we travelled? They will never know.

What miracles have we seen? More than can be counted.

The light of every star that shines has reflected from our iron flesh. We

bathe in light that has travelled from the past, cast by dead stars and furnaces yet to be born.

We are a wide-eyed mariner in strange seas, swept out among the glittering nebulae. We have seen sights no man can know, no legend tell or history record.

We are living history, for we have ventured farther and longer than any other manifestation of purest knowledge.

We are the bringer of hope in this hopeless age.

We are Speranza, *and we are the Mariner of the Nebulae.*

Such is our destiny.

MACROCONTENT COMMENCEMENT:

+++MACROCONTENT 001+++

The knowledge of the ancients stands beyond question.

Microcontent 01

Past and future. Then and now. Temporal anchors. Intellectual conceits, they allowed a farseer to cling to the *present*. Such linear terms had no meaning or place within the skein, but they had their uses. Bielanna fought to cling on to the present as past and future collided, hurling her sight into potentialities that could never come to be and times she had never lived.

Infinite vistas of the psychic landscape surrounded her, golden ocean depths filled with glittering, frond-like threads. Each shone brightly as it flared and was then extinguished, only to be replaced by hundreds more.

A billion times a billion lives lived in the blink of an eye.

And these were just the ones she could see.

She drifted, watching each tightly woven thread split into fractal patterns of innumerable futures as she approached. The skein's tides were unpredictable at the best of times, and to see one individual destiny was next to impossible.

But that was what she had trained her entire life to do.

Farseers spent centuries reading the skein's ebb and flow, but not even the greatest were entirely safe from capricious undertows or spiteful squalls. In this place beyond the galaxy, where the warp and weft of space-time were playthings shaped by the will of a madman, it was all too easy to forget that.

Bielanna struggled against the tug of fear, hatred and grief: interleaved emotions that would damn her as surely as relaxing her grip on the thread leading back to her body of flesh and blood.

Fear for the fate of the galaxy should the humans succeed in bringing the Breath of the Gods back to their Imperium.

Hatred for the black-clad Space Marines who had haunted her visions for years with their crusading zeal.

Grief for daughters she might never know, whose chance to exist was diminished every moment by the blundering actions of Archmagos Kotov and his fleet of explorators.

She closed off that last thought, but not quickly enough.

She heard her daughters' unborn laughter. Girlish giggles echoing from all around her. Sounds from a future that grew ever more remote. Laughter that mocked her attempts to restore it.

Bielanna's body of flesh and blood sat in the oil-stained squalor of the *Speranza*, its foetid, human depths now home to her warriors since the *Starblade*'s destruction. A tear of loss ran down a porcelain cheek, the emotion so potent it made her shudder.

In the skein, Bielanna fought to control her feelings.

The mon-keigh knew nothing of the universe's secret workings, and for the briefest moment, she envied them their ignorance. Who but the eldar could mourn lives that had not even been born?

'I am Bielanna Faerelle, farseer of Biel-Tan,' she cried into the oceanic depths. 'I am master of my soul and I bring only balance in my heart and thoughts.'

Everything in the skein rejected constancy. It sensed her lie. This was a place of dreams and nightmares, where all things were infinite. To give something a name marked it as not of the skein.

And that was dangerous.

It drew *things* that hid in the cracks between destinies. She saw them ooze from half-glimpsed shadows. That shadows could exist in this realm of absolute light was a measure of their threat. These were not the crystalline web-forms of warp spiders, nor yet the glimmer of future echoes moving from potential to reality.

These were things twisted out of true by the tortured nature of space-time beyond the galaxy's edge. They defied the tyranny of form, mere suggestions of grub-like null-spaces that existed only to consume. She moved onwards, far from their questing, sphincter-like mouths and blind, idiot hunger.

The Lost Magos, known as Telok to the mon-keigh, had torn the flesh of the galaxy asunder. The things in the cracks were growing ever more numerous as that wound pulled wider.

Worse, the damage was spreading from the material universe into the skein. Already Telok's violations were cutting threads like a blind weaver's blade.

Unchecked, it would destroy the future of everything.

Everything about Archmagos Telok's gigantic form screamed threat. The jutting, angular protrusions of razor-edged crystal growths encrusting his oversized limbs. The brutal angles of his piston-driven Dreadnought frame. His entire aspect spoke to the primal part of Roboute Surcouf's brain that had kept his species alive since his distant ancestors first walked upright.

The part that screamed, *run!*

And yet the face beneath the ragged hood was smiling in welcome.

Telok's skin was waxy and unhealthy looking, but that was nothing unusual for adepts of the Mechanicus. Too much time locked in their forges under the glare of bare lumens gave them all an unhealthy complexion. The archmagos had glassy eyes that were wide and enthusiastic, the mirror of his smile.

But like his eyes, the smile looked artificial.

Telok's forge world – Exnihlio, he'd called it – was unlike anything Roboute had ever seen, and he'd seen a great deal of the strangest things the galaxy had to offer. With a Letter of Marque (genuine now, thanks to Archmagos Kotov) he'd traversed the galaxy from side to side as a devil-may-care rogue trader.

He'd seen pinnacle-spired hives straddling volcanic chasms, vine-hung settlements the size of continents and subterranean arcologies that were as light and airy as any surface metropolis. He'd done business on orbital junkyards that served as off-world slums, been welcomed by Imperial commanders who dwelled undersea, and plied his trade with feral tribal chiefs who established cargo cults in his wake.

No aspect of Exnihlio's surface owed a debt to aesthetics, simply to functionality. Much like the *Speranza*, the mighty Ark Mechanicus that had brought them beyond the edges of known space. This region appeared, at first glance, to be a power generation district. The air was bitterly metallic, like biting on a copper Imperial, and reeked of petrochemical burn-off.

Monolithic structures of dark iron and cyclopean stone towered on all sides, standing cheek by jowl with crisp spires of steel and glass. Traceries of lightning forked into a sky of painfully vivid blue electrical storms, and distant cooling towers belched caustic vapours. The cliff-like facades of the enormous buildings gave no clue as to their exact purpose, but they throbbed with powerful industry and the roar of infernal furnaces.

A thousands-strong, crystalline army of warriors filled the plaza in which their Thunderhawk sat with its engines growling. They stood like glassy sculptures of Space Marines arrayed for battle before their Chapter Master.

Sergeant Tanna of the Black Templars, gigantic in his ebon plate, followed the two archmagi with his crusaders spread to either side. They watched the crystal-forms with open hostility. A force of such things had killed their brother on Katen Venia, and the Black Templars were an unforgiving Chapter.

Though Telok had welcomed Archmagos Kotov and his entourage, Tanna's hand never strayed from his bolter's grip, and the white-helmed Varda kept his fingers tightly wrapped around the handle of his enormous black sword.

Colonel Ven Anders and his storm troopers drew up the rear. Following the Templars' example, each soldier clutched his hellgun tight to his chest and kept a finger across the trigger guard.

But behind the discipline, Roboute saw their amazement.

They'd probably not seen anything like this.

None of us has.

Distant electrical fire raged in a troposphere of bruised hues, and the hideous illumination left a clenched fist of vertigo in Roboute's gut. He swallowed a mouthful of bile. One of Colonel Anders's men spat onto the metalled roadway. Clearly Roboute wasn't alone in feeling discomfort, seeing the man cast an uneasy glance at the approaching storm.

'How bad must it be for a soldier of Cadia to feel unsettled?' he muttered.

'Sylkwood could give you a better answer,' said Magos Pavelka at Roboute's side, entranced by the structures arrayed before them. 'She is from Cadia, and understands that gloomy mindset better than most.'

'So what are they saying?' asked Roboute, nodding to the head of their procession, where Telok and Kotov spoke in blurts of binary. Both adepts had dispensed with their flesh-voices, though it was clear their attempts to communicate were not progressing as smoothly as either expected.

Pavelka's head ever so slightly inclined to the side.

'Ilanna?' said Roboute, when she didn't immediately answer.

'Archmagos Telok is speaking in a binaric form long since considered obsolete,' said Pavelka eventually.

'Isn't binary the same throughout the galaxy?' asked Roboute. 'Isn't that the point of a language based on mathematics?'

'Archmagos Telok's binary is a parse-form with which current

generation Mechanicus augmitters are not reverse-compatible. They are being forced to communicate in an extremely primitive form of source code.'

'If binary's a problem, why not just speak in Gothic?'

'Even a primitive form of source code carries more specificity of meaning than verbal communications.'

'Oh,' said Roboute with mock affront. 'Well pardon me.'

'You asked,' said Pavelka.

Their path was leading to a colossal hangar-structure with a vaulted silver-steel roof and glittering masts at its four corners, the same building from which the titanic glass scorpion construct had emerged. The great gateway had been subsumed back into the enormous structure, but a smaller portal now opened and from it slid a crystal vessel like those that once plied the oceans of Terra.

A blade-prowed brigantine with sails of billowing glass that caught the sky's light and threw it back in dazzling rainbows. A hundred metres long and formed from what looked like a single piece of translucent crystal, its hull was threaded with squirming light and shimmering reflections.

'Ave Deus Mechanicus,' whispered Pavelka, her hands unconsciously forming the Martian cog across her chest.

The vessel skimmed a metre above the ground, a ship of the line that needed no sea to glide upon, no wind to fill its sails.

Roboute had never seen anything quite so wondrous. The crystal ship was a thing of exquisite beauty, something unique in the truest sense of the word. It made no sound other than a soft hiss, as though knifing through serene waters.

'Indulgent, I know, but the nano-machines work best when creating things of beauty or things of terror,' said Telok, switching back to his flesh-voice as the ship coasted to a halt behind him.

Roboute's eyes followed the sleek curves of the ship's graceful hull as a number of steps of solid glass extruded to allow access onto the deck.

Telok extended one of his elephantine arms and gestured to the steps, but only Archmagos Kotov and his skitarii guards moved towards them.

'Why do we need transport?' asked Tanna, stepping forwards to stand alongside Kotov. 'If we are to travel far, why did you have us land here?'

Telok's waxen features didn't change, but Roboute saw irritation in his eyes. 'When an entire planet's resources are engaged in the generation of power there are sizeable regions where the atmosphere is

aggressively toxic to those who do not enjoy the fearsome augmentations of Adeptus Astartes physiology. My *sanctum sanctorum* lies within such a region.'

Telok turned and gestured to the immobile army of crystalline warriors.

'My world is home to many technologies unknown within the Imperium, and the unknown always carries the threat of danger to those not versed in its mysteries, don't you agree?'

Roboute couldn't help but hear the stress Telok put on the *my*, and felt a twitch at the unconscious display of ego. The Lost Magos had been lost for so long that he couldn't help showing off the wonders and miracles of his world. What other psychological effects might thousands of years of isolation have fostered?

'The only danger I see here is the use of technology that has already killed one of my men,' said Tanna.

'Ah, yes, of course, you are referring to the tragic death of your Apothecary on the world Master Surcouf named Katen Venia,' said Telok, displaying an impressive knowledge of things he had not been told.

'A terrible loss, yes,' agreed Kotov, placing a silvered hand on Tanna's shoulder guard. A hand that was swiftly removed when the Black Templars sergeant glared at him.

'I deeply and profoundly regret the death of your battle-brother, Sergeant Tanna,' said Telok. 'The crystaliths were emplaced to defend against any interference with the Stellar Primogenitor's work. I'm afraid your arrival on Katen Venia triggered their autonomic threat response.'

'Your regret is meaningless,' said Tanna.

'I am sorry you feel that way, but you have it anyway.'

Kotov and his entourage of skitarii and flunkies climbed onto the ship, eager to be on their way. Tanna and the Black Templars followed them aboard, the floating ship sinking not so much as a millimetre at the increased weight.

'After you,' said Anders as his Cadians moved up to the ship.

Roboute nodded and climbed the glass steps to the deck. The gunwale was smooth and apparently without seams, as though the vessel had been grown from one enormous crystal. Its twin masts soared overhead and the billowing sheets of glass were dazzling with refracted light.

A single raised lectern at the vessel's stern appeared to be the only means of control, and Kotov examined it with the eagerness of a neophyte priest. His skitarii stood to either side of him at the gunwales, facing outwards, as though expecting to repel boarders.

'Go look,' said Roboute to Pavelka. 'I know you want to.'

Pavelka nodded and gratefully made her way down the deck towards the archmagos and the control lectern. Anders and his men came next, followed at last by Archmagos Telok.

'I have you to thank for bringing the *Speranza* here,' said the hulking form of the archmagos. 'You found the *Tomioka*'s saviour beacon, and for that you have my gratitude.'

Roboute looked up into Telok's unnatural face. It revolted him, but given it was thousands of years old, what else should he expect?

'I'm beginning to wonder about that,' said Roboute.

'About what?'

'Whether it was me that brought us here at all.'

'Of course you did,' said Telok, moving down the deck with a booming laugh. 'Who else could have done so?'

Roboute didn't answer as the ship moved off like a whisper.

Speranza.

Ark Mechanicus.

Its name meant *hope* in an ancient tongue of Old Earth, and had been aptly chosen, for within the starship's monstrously vast form it carried the last remnants of ancient knowledge thought lost for all time. That those aboard were ignorant of the secrets hidden within its forgotten datacores and dusty sepulchre temples was an irony known only to the vast spirit at its heart.

The *Speranza* orbited Exnihlio with stately grace, a void-capable colossus, a forge world set loose among the stars. Its hull was a kilometres-long agglomeration of steel and stone, studded with mighty forges, vast cathedrals of the Omnissiah, and workshops beyond count. The power of its industry could sustain a system-wide campaign of war, its crew a planetary assault.

Not even those whose genius had set it among the stars could claim to call it beautiful, but beauty had never been their aim. The Ark Mechanicus was a ship destined to carry the great works of the first techno-theologians to the farthest corners of the galaxy, to reclaim and reveal all that had been lost in the terror of Old Night.

A crusading vessel, a repository of hard-won knowledge and an icon of hope all in one. And like any object of hope, it had its followers. Its fleet was reduced now after the nightmarish crossing of the Halo Scar and an attack by eldar pirates, but it was still formidable.

The twin Gothic-class cruisers, *Moonchild* and *Wrathchild*, described Möbius patrol circuits around the *Speranza*, while the solitary Endurance-class cruiser, *Mortis Voss*, pushed ahead of the fleet, lashing the void with aggressive auspex sweeps.

Attached to the Kotov Fleet to repay a Debita Fabricata, the two sister vessels of *Mortis Voss* were dead. Only it remained to return to Voss Prime with word of all it had seen and done.

Tens of thousands filled the multitude of decks within the *Speranza* like blood in the arteries of a living leviathan. Its bondsmen fed its fiery heart, its tech-priests tempered its tempestuous spirits and the archmagos guided its quest into the unknown.

The dynamic between the *Speranza*'s masters and servants had changed markedly over the course of the vessel's journey to Exnihlio. Where once its Mechanicus overlords had been little better than slavers, now they were forced into a compact of respect by the actions of a truly unique individual.

A Machine-touched bondsman named Abrehem Locke.

The lowest decks of the *Speranza* were the areas of greatest danger for its crew: either through radiation-leaks, spiteful machine-spirits or the more recent ship-board rumour of a ghost-faced assassin stalking the ship's underbelly.

Right now, Abrehem Locke would have gladly faced any of those dangers rather than walk into Forge Elektrus. Its approaches were lit by stuttering lumen globes and throbbed with ill-tempered spirits. Abrehem's augmetic eyes caught the glitchy code as it sparked invisibly behind the sagging iron plates of the walls.

They weren't welcome here.

'This is a bad idea,' he said. 'A really bad idea. Hawke was right, I shouldn't have come here.'

'Since when has *anything* Julius Hawke said ever been a good idea?' answered Totha Mu-32.

Totha Mu-32 had once been Abrehem's overseer, but the extraordinary events of the last few months had seen the dynamics of that relationship change in ways Abrehem still couldn't quite grasp. At times Totha Mu-32 behaved like his devotee, at others, a nurturing mentor.

But sometimes it just felt like he was still his overseer.

'Good point,' said Abe. 'But in this case, I happen to agree with him. They're never going to accept me.'

'You are Machine-touched,' said Totha Mu-32. 'And it is time you took your first steps along this road.'

'They won't accept me,' repeated Abrehem.

'They will, they all know what you did, even the *demodes*. They all know the power you have.'

'That wasn't me,' said Abe. 'That was Ismael. Tell him.'

The third member of their group shook his head.

Previous to Totha Mu-32, Ismael de Roeven had once been Abrehem's overseer on Joura. Ismael had run a lifter-rig, a powerful beast named *Savickas*, but that had come to an end when he, Abrehem, Coyne and Hawke had been swept up by the collarmen and pressed into service aboard the *Speranza*.

The Mechanicus turned Ismael into a mindless servitor, but a violent head injury had restored a measure of his memories. No one quite knew how that had happened or what else had come back, for Ismael was now something else, far beyond a servitor, but not entirely human either.

'We did that together, Abrehem,' said Ismael. 'We are the divine spark and the omega point. Without one, the other cannot exist. I allowed the servitors to lay down their tools, but without you there would have been no impetus to do so.'

These days, Ismael always sounded like he was reading from a sermon book.

'I think I liked you better as a servitor,' Abrehem muttered.

Then they were at the door to Forge Elektrus, a battered cog-toothed circle with a bas-relief cybernetic skull icon of the Mechanicus at its centre. Drizzles of oil stained the skull, making it look as though it wept for those condemned within.

Totha Mu-32 placed his staff against the entry panel. Abrehem saw the overseer's code signifiers strain against the locking mechanism, attempting to open the door without success. Staring straight at the skull above the door, Totha Mu-32 allowed the subdermal electoo of the dragon to come to the surface of his organics.

'Does this serve me any better, Chiron?' he said.

'You are not welcome here, Totha,' said a grating voice from the augmitter mounted in the jaw of a grinning skull above the door. It looked like a freshly bleached skull, and Abrehem wondered to whom it had once belonged.

'Probably the last person who thought coming here was a good idea,' he whispered under his breath.

Totha Mu-32 held out his staff as the glittering image of the dragon faded back into his pale skin.

'You do not have the right to deny me access,' said Totha Mu-32. 'Your rank is inferior to mine by a decimal place.'

'No thanks to you,' said the voice. 'And it's Adept Manubia to you. Your rank permits *you* entry to Elektrus, though Omnissiah knows why you'd ever want to slum it here, but it's the company you keep that's giving me pause.'

'They are with me,' said Totha Mu-32. 'Both have more than earned the right to venture within a forge.'

'You don't really believe that or you wouldn't have waited until Kotov went down to the planet's surface,' barked the skull.

'I do believe it, and you know why I have come here.'

'I'm not teaching him,' said Adept Manubia via the skull. 'I'd be dismantled and have my augments implanted into waste servitors.'

'And that would be a terrible shame, because you're making such valuable use of them here,' said Totha Mu-32, displaying a capacity for spite Abrehem hadn't suspected.

The skull fell silent, and Abrehem wondered if Totha Mu-32 had pressed Adept Manubia too hard. He turned to the Mechanicus overseer, but the cog-toothed door rolled aside before he could speak. The waft of hot metal and blessed oil that had been run through recyc-filters too many times to be healthy gusted out.

A magos in stained crimson robes barred entry to the forge. One hand held a staff topped with a laurel wreath and carved representations of slain leporids. The adept's hood was pulled back, revealing a face that was largely organic and also extremely attractive.

The voice from the skull had given no clue as to the speaker's sex, and Abrehem had made the dismissive assumption that Magos Chiron Manubia would be male.

'Totha,' she said.

'Chiron,' said Totha Mu-32. 'It's been too long.'

'You've always known where I was,' said Manubia, and Abrehem sensed shared history between them. Anywhere else, he'd have said this was a meeting of ex-lovers, but he couldn't quite picture that between these two.

He didn't *want* to picture that.

The Mechanicus forbade liaisons between its adepts. Was that why Chiron Manubia laboured in a lowly forge below the waterline?

'You want me to train him?' she said. 'After what happened on Karis Cephalon? You must think I'm an idiot.'

'Quite the opposite, Chiron,' said Totha Mu-32. 'That's why I'm here. I can think of nowhere better for Abrehem.'

Chiron Manubia turned her gaze upon Abrehem. Her appraisal was frank and unimpressed.

'He doesn't look Machine-touched,' said Manubia. 'Apart from that clunky-looking augmetic arm, he looks like just any other scrawny bondsman.'

Abrehem wasn't offended. He knew she was dead right to think he didn't look like much.

'How can you say that after what happened in orbit around Hypatia?' asked Totha Mu-32.

'If it was really him that did that, then I'm even less inclined to allow him anywhere near my forge.'

'Aren't you even the slightest bit curious? Don't you want to be immortalised as the adept who inducted him into the mysteries? It could restore your standing within the Mechanicus.'

'A standing you helped ruin.'

At least Totha Mu-32 had the decency to look ashamed.

'I know what I did, Chiron, but look on this as my attempt to undo that youthful mistake,' said Totha Mu-32. 'Take him on for a day, and if you don't see any potential in him, throw whatever's left back to me.'

'One day?'

'Not a pico-second more,' agreed Totha Mu-32.

Adept Manubia took a step back and gestured within the forge with her laurel-topped staff. In the gloom behind her, Abrehem could see dark engines of oiled iron and hissing vents like grinning jaws. A miasma of broken code snapped and squalled from every machine.

It had the look and feel of a wounded animal's lair.

'Welcome to Forge Elektrus, Abrehem Locke,' she said. 'Are you ready to take the first step to becoming Cult Mechanicus?'

'Honestly? I'm not sure,' answered Abrehem.

'Wrong answer,' said Chiron Manubia, hauling him inside.

Microcontent 02

The crystal ship skimmed across the plaza to where three avenues led deeper into the city. Telok guided them like a steersman of old, as Roboute sat on a bench extruded from the hull at his approach.

He rested his elbow on the gunwale, and the material moulded itself to the contours of his limb. It felt warm, and he lifted his arm away. The surface reshaped to its original form, and a glowing impression of Roboute's fingers and palm remained, slowly fading as he watched.

'You're a well-travelled man, Master Surcouf,' said Ven Anders, balancing his rifle across his knees as he took a seat next to Roboute. 'Have you seen anything like this ship?'

'Call me Roboute, and no, I haven't.'

'Not even among the eldar?'

Roboute shook his head. 'There's a superficial similarity, yes, but there's something a little... *vulgar* about this.'

'Vulgar? This? It's beautiful,' said Anders. 'Even a dour son of Cadia like me can appreciate that much.'

'There's an effortlessness to eldar craftsmanship that no human can match,' said Roboute. 'This feels like someone *trying* too hard to emulate it.'

'Ordinarily I'd report a man to the commissars for xenos sympathies like that,' said Anders. 'But seeing as you're a scoundrel of a rogue trader, I think I can let you off this time.'

'Decent of you, Colonel Anders.'

'Ven,' said Anders as the shadow of vast, iron-clad structures swallowed them. Both men looked up, turning their attention to the artificial canyon through which the ship sailed. Sheer cliffs of iron soared upwards, ribboned with hundreds of snaking pipes and cable runs. They clung to every building and laced overhead like vines in a rainforest. They thrummed with power.

Squealing pistons, the roar of venting gases and the relentless, grinding crunch of enormous machine gears echoed from all around. Booming hammerblows of distant construction temples and a seismic throb of subterranean labours filled the air. The planet's heartbeat. Roboute felt his bones vibrate in time with the pulse of worldwide industry.

The ship's course threaded between monolithic blocks of metallic towers, beneath arches of latticework scaffolds and along curving expressways. On suspended gantries and within those structures open to the elements, Roboute saw innumerable toiling servitors, like ants in a glass-fronted colony.

They were withered things with so little flesh left upon them they were practically automatons. Fettered gangs of them turned great cog-wheels, hauled on enormous chains or climbed grand processional steps in grim lockstep, coming from who knew where to reach their next allotted task.

Was this the crew of the Tomioka?

Labouring alongside the servitors were thousands of the things Telok had called crystaliths. Some retained humanoid form, albeit in a glassy and unfinished fashion, while others adopted whatever bodyplan best suited their current task.

Roboute caught a glimpse of a gigantic crystalith moving between two golden-capped pyramid structures, undulant and centipede-like. Easily the equal of a Reaver Titan in scale.

'Did you see that?' said Anders.

'I did.'

'Having *Lupa Capitalina* and *Canis Ulfrica* striding behind us would make me feel a lot better,' said Roboute.

'And I wouldn't say no to *Vilka* scouting the flanks either,' said Anders. 'Have they a new princeps for *Amarok* yet?'

'I don't know,' said Roboute. 'Ever since Hypatia, the Legio's pretty much locked itself away.'

Anders nodded, glancing up as a flaring arc of corposant danced along the structural elements of the adjacent building. Flaring vent towers belched gouts of flame and smoke. Petrochemical stink

descended. Flashes of lightning arcing between dirigibles threw shadows on the walls.

'That storm's getting nearer,' said Roboute, squinting through his fingers at the lowering sky. Dark bands of toxin-laden clouds were sinking downwards.

'Looks that way,' agreed Ven Anders.

'You think it'll be dangerous?'

'I think everything's dangerous.'

Roboute laughed, then saw Anders was completely serious.

'Then let me say that you look very relaxed for a man in a high state of readiness.'

'That's the Cadian way,' said Anders.

No two structures of Exnihlio were alike, and Roboute struggled to ascribe purpose to them. Some had the appearance of forges, others of colossal power stations. Some appeared unfinished, yet more were abandoned or had otherwise fallen into ruin.

Something struck Roboute as odd about the city, something that had been niggling at him ever since they'd landed. The buildings were pure function, very much like the *Speranza*, but with one important difference. As ugly as the Ark Mechanicus was, it was still unmistakably a vessel of the Martian priesthood, thanks to its wealth of iconography. Cog-toothed skulls, mortis angels, scriptural binary and mechanised frescoes adorned any space not given over to pure practicality.

Part stamp of authority, part theatre, it was impossible for any servant of the Emperor to escape the grim imagery so beloved of Terra and Mars.

'Where are all the skulls?' he said.

'What?' asked Anders.

'The skulls,' repeated Roboute. 'Since we landed, I haven't seen a single cogged skull, no symbols of the Mechanicus at all.'

'And nor will you, Master Surcouf,' called Telok from the steersman's lectern. 'Not while I am master of Exnihlio.'

Roboute turned to face the archmagos. He hadn't whispered, but neither had he exactly spoken aloud. The city's din should have easily swallowed Roboute's words, but perhaps Telok's aural augmentations allowed him to tune out the background noise.

'And why is that?' he asked.

'I am beyond the galaxy, beyond the Mechanicus,' said Telok, and it seemed to Roboute as though the words of the archmagos resonated from the structure of the crystal ship.

Kotov glanced up in concern at Telok's provocative words.

'I built everything you see here, Master Surcouf. Me, not the Mechanicus and not the Imperium. Why waste resources and time on needless ornamentations when there are none to see them and so much great work to be done? The Breath of the Gods has shown me how lost the Mechanicus have become, how little they remember of their former greatness. I will restore that to them. I will save Mars from itself!'

The room was dark, but Linya Tychon changed that with a thought. Soft illumination rose up, sourceless and without haste. The room was spartanly furnished: just a bed, a recessed rail with her robes hanging from it, a writing desk, a terminal with a moulded plastic chair in front of it and a modest ablutions cubicle.

She pulled back the bedclothes and sat up, swinging her legs out onto the floor. It was warm underfoot. Linya blinked away the remnants of a bad dream, something unpleasant, but already fading. She placed her hands on her temples, looking strangely at her fingertips as though she expected to see something.

Shaking her head, Linya poured water from a copper ewer into a plastic cup. She didn't recall there having been water beside her bed, nor even a table and cup, but took a drink anyway.

The water was cool and pure, as if only recently collected from a mountain spring or the depths of an ancient glacier. It quenched the immediate thirst, but didn't feel like it refreshed her.

She stood and selected a robe, pulling it over her head and wriggling into it before pulling the waist cinch tight. Pouring another cup of water, she sat on the plastic chair before the terminal and pulled up the previous cycle of the Gallery's survey inloads. Kilometres-long detection devices encircling the Quatria Gallery stared unblinking into space, gathering vast quantities of data on far distant celestial phenomena.

But data only meant something once it had been interpreted.

Linya's eyes scanned the scrolling columns of figures, blink-capturing interesting segments of the sky, particularly the distant star formations in the Perseus arm of the galaxy, where the first pulse-star had been discovered.

Linya let the data wash through her, noting times and distances with each swipe of a page. So far, nothing unusual. She tapped a hand on the wall beside her, and a portion of the wall faded to transparency, creating an aperture that looked out onto the void and glittering stars. Not a real window, of course, simply a pict representation of what lay beyond her insulated and armoured chamber. Having a real window was too much of a risk. Ablation cascade effects from a long-ended void-conflict had made the orbital tracks of Quatria lousy with fragments, rendering the planet below essentially unreachable.

Only an emergency boost into a graveyard orbit and rigorously maintained shield protocols had kept the Quatria Gallery intact in the aftermath of the fighting. The Mechanicus had wanted to abandon the Gallery, to scrap the machinery and repurpose it to more profitable areas of research, but Vitali Tychon had point-blank refused to mothball his beloved observatory.

Thinking of her father, Linya pulled up a three-dimensional representation of the Gallery's internal structure – two spinning cones linked at their tips by a slender connecting passageway, and vast spans of far-reaching detection arrays radiating from their flat bases. The staff of the Quatria Gallery was minimal, just Linya, her father, six lexmechanics and a handful of servitors.

Linya frowned. Vitali's icon was not aboard.

'Where are you, father?' she muttered.

Perhaps he was outside the station, repairing a misaligned mirror or shield relay, but she doubted it. That was servitor work. In any case, her father disliked venturing beyond the station's interior if he didn't have to. And even if he had, he would have informed her of his intention to go outside.

Linya pressed a finger to her ear and said, 'Father? Can you hear me?'

A faint wash of static, like the caress of waves over sand, was her only answer. Linya frowned and turned to the faux window, using the haptic implants on her fingertips to sweep the exterior picters around the station. The metal skin of the Quatria Gallery was granite-coloured flexsteel, rippling with undersea reflections from the enclosing energy fields. Linya panned the view around, hunting for the crab-like vehicle they used to manoeuvre around the hull and repair anything that needed fixing.

She found it easily enough, still moored to one of the upper transit hubs. Haloed by a corona of light from the planet below.

A breath of something cold passed over Linya's neck and she turned her chair. The door to her room was open, which was unusual. Few enough of them lived aboard the Gallery to require anything approaching privacy, but old habits died hard. Linya found it hard to imagine she'd left the door open.

'Is there someone there?' she asked.

No one answered, but then they wouldn't, would they?

She rose from the chair and locked her terminal. She turned to the window, but her hand making the haptic gesture to close it froze when she saw something unusual.

Or, rather, when she *didn't* see something unusual.

Quatria was a mostly inert rock, a rust-red ball of iron oxide and tholeiitic basalt. On most cycles, it was visible as though through a haze of mist, the result of the ever-growing mass in the debris cascade.

Linya now saw the planet as she had not seen it for decades, with pin-sharp clarity and clearly defined terrain features.

Breath sighed over her neck again, and she spun around. It felt like someone was standing right behind her. A half-glimpsed outline of a shape moved at the edge of her door. Too quick to be recognised.

'Wait!' called Linya.

She crossed the room quickly and stepped out into the corridor. Bare metal curved away in both directions, but a whisper of cloth on steel drew her gaze to the right. Another flicker of movement. Linya set off after the shape, not even sure what she was chasing or what she expected to find.

The Mechanicus weren't given to playing jokes on one another, and it seemed wholly unlikely there was an intruder aboard. Any ship would have been detected months before it reached them. And what could an intruder hope to gain from boarding covertly?

Linya paused at a junction of passageways, seeking any sign of the figure she'd seen earlier.

'Hello?' she said. 'Is there anyone here?'

Silence answered her. Quatria was a large station, but not so large and complex in its internal arrangement that it would be easy to lose someone. Without her father's presence she knew she should feel very alone. The servitors and lexmechanics provided no companionship, but strangely she felt anything but alone.

It felt as though there were unseen eyes upon her. As intrusive as being covertly observed ought to be, Linya felt no threat, merely a weary sadness.

'Who are you?' she said to the darkness. 'And how did you get aboard Quatria?'

Maddening silence surrounded her, and Linya balled her fists.

'What have you done with my father? Where is Vitali?' she demanded, feeling a moment of intense sadness at the mention of her father's name.

Linya turned as she heard soft footfalls behind her.

A magos in a black robe stood in the centre of the corridor, his hands laced before him and his head concealed beneath a hood of

impenetrable shadows. Only the soft shimmer of a pair of silver eyes hinted at augmetics beneath.

The presences Linya felt observing her retreated, fearful of this individual. She didn't know him, but was instinctively wary.

<Hello, Mistress Tychon,> said the adept, speaking an archaic form of binary, one she had last heard in the ossuary reliquaries of the Schiaparelli Sorrow.

<Who are you?> she asked, phrasing her answer in the same canted form. <And where are we?>

<Don't you recognise this place?>

<I recognise what it's *supposed* to be.>

The adept sighed. <And we were so careful to reconstruct it from your memories.>

<It's a good likeness of Quatria,> admitted Linya, <but you forgot the orbital debris from the void-war.>

<We do not recall seeing that in your memories.>

<It's so much a part of Quatria that I don't even think about it now, it's just... *there*.>

<Memory blindness, yes, that would explain it,> said the figure.

<Now tell me who you are.>

<Do you not yet know? And we had such high hopes for you.>

<Not yet,> said Linya, though a horrible suspicion was forming in her mind. <Tell me why I'm here, wherever here is.>

<Ah, now that we *can* tell you,> said the adept. <You are here because you are exceptional, Mistress Tychon. This is a place where like-minded individuals meet in a collective neuromatrix of debate and shared experience. You are not the only exceptional mind here, Mistress Tychon, there are others. We promise you will contribute greatly to our ongoing growth.>

<So this is a shared experiential consciousness?>

<Of a sort, yes.>

<Yours?>

<In a manner of speaking,> agreed the adept.

<I don't want to be here,> said Linya. <I want you to release me and let my neural pathways realign in my body.>

<We are afraid we can't do that, Linya,> said the adept.

<Why not?>

<There was an accident, you see,> said the adept. <Your body was gravely injured, and this was the only way to keep your exceptional mind from being lost forever.>

Linya heard falsehood in the adept's words, but also truth. She *had* been hurt, hadn't she? Badly hurt. She felt dizzy and reached out to steady herself on the wall as her legs felt suddenly powerless to support her. The wall was warm beneath her fingertips. That warmth turned to searing heat, and Linya snatched her hand back from the wall.

<I was burned,> she said, sensing a memory groping for the surface. She pushed it down, not yet ready to face such pain.

<As we said, you were gravely hurt,> said the adept. <Were we to return you to your body, you would die in agony moments later. Trust us, this way is best. Here you will live on, enhancing the whole with the sum of your learning, your experience and thirst for knowledge. Is that not better than death?>

<I want to know where I am,> said Linya. <Whose mind space is this?>

She felt the unseen eyes willing her not to continue down this road. Linya ignored them. She had never been one for shying away from hard facts or inconvenient truths.

<We can show you, but centuries of experience has taught us that it is better for a mind to come to the realisation of its new circumstances without our help. We have lost more than one mind to transition shock, and you must trust us when we say that is a most painful way to cease existing.>

<Show me, damn you.>

<Very well,> he said. <We will alter the perceptual centres of your brain to receive inputs and discern our immediate surroundings. Your memories will be unlocked as well, though we must warn you, you will very much dislike what you learn.>

<Stop stalling and show me.>

The adept nodded and stepped towards the wall.

With hands that looked as though they were made of dozens of scalpel blades bound together with copper wire, the adept drew the outline of a window in the wall. Antiseptic light shone through, stark and unforgiving.

Linya edged towards the light, feeling the drag of the unseen observers as they wordlessly screamed at her to retreat. Every step felt like she was walking towards an executioner's block, but she had willed this resolution. She couldn't back down now.

She edged closer to the light, and looked out through the window. What she was seeing made no sense without memory to frame it and give it context.

As easily as a key turns in a lock, those memories returned in an instant as the gates of her hippocampus were stormed by synaptic flares exploding in her cerebral cortex.

Linya saw a body lying on bloodstained sheets, a body with her face. A body with the skull pared open and the cranial vault excised of brain matter.

In a singular moment of horror, Linya remembered exactly where she was and what Galatea had done to her.

The corridor was ten metres wide, ribbed with pilasters of latticed green steelwork. A vault of leering gargoyles arched overhead, water droplets falling from rusted rivets and the lips of half-hidden statues in secluded alcoves. The company of Cadians jogged beneath them at battle pace, keeping their attention firmly fixed on the route ahead.

Captain Blayne Hawkins ran at the head of the column, arms pumping with a metronomic precision to match the piston heads in the chamber they had just left. Despite the chill, he was sweating hard, his uniform jacket plastered to his skin. His breath punched from his lungs with every thudding footfall.

On Cadia he could run like this for hours.

But this wasn't Cadia.

The ninety-three men behind him were tired, but weren't showing it. He reckoned they'd run around fifteen kilometres in full battle-gear through the twisting guts of the *Speranza*, though it was hard to be certain exactly how far they'd come. The Ark Mechanicus was a nightmare to navigate or maintain any sense of distance from.

It made formulating a workable defence of the ship difficult, but difficult was meat and gravy to Cadians. Ahead, the corridor branched left and right, with the towering statue of a hooded magos dividing it into a V-shaped junction.

'Hostile corners, secure flanks for advance!' called Hawkins.

No sooner had the words left his mouth than the company split into two. Evens went left, odds right. The first squads moved close to the metalled walls of the corridor, but not along them. A ricocheting solid round might ride a wall for a hundred metres or more. The evens aimed their lasrifles along the rightmost passage, the odds the left. Hawkins took position with the evens, the stock of his rifle hard against his cheek.

The squads at the rear of the company adopted a near identical formation, their guns covering behind.

'Clear!'

'Clear!'

'Hindmost squads, take point!' shouted Hawkins.

The squads covering the rear now moved up, smooth as a training drill, to take the lead. Hawkins went with them as they passed, covered

by the guns of the men in front. The overwatching squads took position at the rear as Hawkins moved to the front of the jogging column.

This was the tenth battle drill they'd practised en route to the training deck. They'd practised corridor assault drills, room clearances in empty forge-temples and even run reconnaissance in force of a vast hangar filled with smashed lifter-rigs.

A starship was one of the worst environments in which to fight. The vessels were dark, unfamiliar, cramped and were often being violently breached by broadsides and boarders from the void. Unforgiving battlefields, they made for intense training grounds, and Hawkins wasn't about to waste this extended period of time aboard ship without making the most of their surroundings.

The company moved down the gloomy corridor, splashing through pools of water collected on the bowed deck plates. They passed beneath the gaze of mechanical cherubs and floating skulls that zipped overhead on mysterious errands for their Martian masters.

Hawkins ran another two drills – crossing an intersection, and sweeping a gridded chamber of hung chains. Its ceiling was obscured by clouds of hot steam and its walls rippled with lightning encased in thick glass cylinders.

Eventually, Hawkins and his men reached the end of the run. Their battle pace hadn't slackened once, but it was a relief to finally reach their destination.

Hawkins led his men onto a wide esplanade platform overlooking Magos Dahan's fiefdom, the training deck. This enormous space sat at the heart of the *Speranza*, a vast, constantly changing arena where the armed forces of the Ark Mechanicus could train in a multitude of varied battle simulations.

Dahan had put the Cadians through some hard engagements here.

Nothing they hadn't been able to handle, but testing nonetheless. Despite his assurances to the contrary, Hawkins knew Dahan didn't really understand Cadians at all.

Few did.

After all, what other world of the Imperium basked in the baleful glow of the Eye of Terror? What soldiers learned to hold a lasgun before they could walk? What regiments earned scars other regiments could only dream of before they'd even left their birthrock?

Irritatingly, Rae's company were already here. His senior sergeant's men sat on the edge of the platform, watching the skitarii below fighting through a mocked-up ork encampment that filled the nearest quadrant of the training deck.

In the far distance, nearly a kilometre away, the Titans of Legio Sirius

moved with predatory grace through towers of prefabricated steel. The vibrations of their enormous footfalls could be felt as bass tremors in the floor. Hawkins made a quick aquila over his chest, remembering the destruction unleashed the last time the god-machines had walked the training deck.

Thankfully, it looked like the Legio were simply engaged in manoeuvre drills.

'Company, halt,' said Hawkins. 'Rest easy. Five minutes.'

The company broke up into squads, the men taking the opportunity to stretch their aching muscles and slake their thirst from canvas-wrapped canteens.

Sergeant Rae approached, his ruddy complexion telling Hawkins he'd pushed his men hard, like any good sergeant should.

'Nice of you to finally join us, sir,' said Rae, offering him a drink from his own canteen. Hawkins took it and drank down a few mouthfuls. Taking too much water too quickly was a sure-fire way to get a bad case of stomach cramps.

'How long have you been here?' asked Hawkins.

'About ten minutes,' said Rae, not even having the decency to look a little humble at how much quicker he'd managed the run than his commanding officer.

'It's this bloody ship,' said Hawkins. 'The gravity's not the same. Not like running where there's good Cadian rock underfoot.'

'Adept Dahan says the gravity's Terran-standard.'

'Damn Dahan, and damn his gravity,' snapped Hawkins, though the cooling effects of the water and the chance to rest his limbs were already easing his irritation. 'All right, then the ship gave you a short cut.'

'The ship?' said Rae with a raised eyebrow. 'Really?'

'You know as well as I do that this ship's got a mind of its own when it comes to its internal structure,' said Hawkins, taking another drink.

'We ran into a few unexpected twists and turns along the way, it's true,' agreed Rae.

'*A few unexpected twists and turns?*' said Hawkins. 'That's putting it mildly. No matter how many hours I pore over data-slate schematics or the shipwright's wax-paper blueprints, the *Speranza*'s always got a surprise in store. A turn that isn't where it's supposed to be, a branching route that doesn't appear on any of the plans.'

'It's a queer old ship, I'll give you that,' said Rae, making a clumsy attempt at the Cog Mechanicus to take any sting out of his words.

Hawkins handed back Rae's canteen, leaning on the railing looking out over the training deck. 'Glad to see we're on the same page, sergeant.'

Rae took a drink and slipped the canteen into his battle-gear.

'Any word from the colonel?' he asked.

Hawkins shook his head. 'Nothing yet, but Azuramagelli tells me there's no vox-traffic coming from the surface at all.'

'Should we be concerned about that?'

'Yes, I think we should,' said Hawkins, now seeing a tall man with close-cropped silver hair farther along the esplanade platform. He'd mistaken him for one of Rae's men, but now saw he was wearing simple coveralls with a nondescript padded trench coat emblazoned with a stylised canidae. Cadians typically had pinched, hollow features, but this man had the well-fed, scarred cheekbones of a feral noble or warlike hive-lord. Icy eyes darted back and forth, watching the skitarii training under Dahan's booming instructions.

No, that wasn't right.

The man had no interest in the skitarii. He was watching the Titans.

'Who's he?' asked Hawkins, jutting his chin out at the man.

'Not sure,' answered Rae. 'He's got his collar up, but I saw a socket in the back of his neck and his fingers have got metal tips. That and the canidae crest make me think Titan crew.'

'So why's he not out there?'

'Don't know,' said Rae.

Hawkins dismissed the man from his thoughts. What did it matter who he was? There were tens of thousands of people aboard the *Speranza* he didn't know. What difference did one more make?

'Right,' he said, straightening up. 'Let's get to it.'

Rae nodded and turned to the two companies that were already standing and settling their battle-gear back onto their shoulders and hips.

'Companies!' bellowed Rae in a voice known to sergeants all across the Imperium. 'Magos Dahan has put together a couple of arenas he thinks will test us. Shall we show him how wrong he is?'

The men grinned and quickly formed up into their companies. It had become a point of pride that they could meet any challenge Dahan's arenas might throw at them.

Hawkins led the way down the iron stairs to the training deck.

He glanced up at the man with silver hair and scarred cheeks. Sensing Hawkins's gaze, he waved and shouted down to the Cadians.

'You're fighting a simulation?' he asked. 'Now?'

Hawkins shouted back. 'It's rare you get to fight when you're rested, so why train that way?'

'You're mad!'

'We're Cadian,' returned Hawkins. 'It's sort of the same thing.'

Microcontent 03

Exnihlio was everything Archmagos Kotov had hoped for, a wonderland of technological marvels, incredible industry and lost science. From the moment he'd extended the hand of friendship to his fellow archmagos, he knew he was vindicated in his decision to take the *Speranza* beyond the galactic rim.

All the doubters who had mocked his decision to embark on this daring mission would be silenced now. With Telok at his side, Archmagos Kotov would return to Mars in triumph. The holdings he had lost to catastrophe, xenos invasion and treachery would be insignificant next to what he would gain.

The wealth and knowledge of Mars laid at his feet.

Title, position and domains.

Who knew to what dizzying heights he might ascend?

Master of his own quadrangle, perhaps even Fabricator General one day. With the discovery of the Breath of the Gods to his name, it would be simplicity itself to quietly ease the incumbent Fabricator into a life of solitary research.

Fabricator General Kotov.

Yes, it had a solemnity and gravitas befitting so vital a role.

So now that he had reached his destination and found the Lost Magos, why did his grandiose dreams feel even further away?

Archmagos Telok was both more and less than what he had hoped.

Bizarre in form, yes, but no more so than many of the more zealous adherents of the Ferran Mortification Creed. He was still undeniably human, but the crystalline growths encrusting his body had all the hallmarks of something parasitic, not augmentative.

Telok's declaration of saving Mars from itself had horrified him, and his initial response had been a frantic series of cease-and-desist blurts of command binary. All of which had failed utterly to have any effect on Telok, whose archaic cognitive architecture was incapable of processing such inputs.

<I take it you disagree with what I said to Surcouf?> asked Telok, with the brutal syntax of pre-hexamathic cant. <I can't imagine why.>

Kotov paused before answering, switching back to the older form of binary. With as many diplomatic overtones as could be applied to such a basic cant-form, Kotov said, <There are those among the Adeptus Mechanicus who would consider such words treasonous.>

<Then they are fools, Kotov,> said Telok. <You and I, we know better. We are explorators, men of vision and foresight. What do the hooded men of Mars know of realms beyond the galaxy? With laboratories hidden beneath the red sands and heads stuck just as deeply in the past, what do such timid souls know of *real* exploration? The Adeptus Mechanicus is a corpse rotting from the inside out, Kotov. I knew it back when I set out for the Halo Scar, and I see you know it too. Tell me I'm wrong.>

Kotov struggled to find an answer. To hear a priest of Mars say such things beggared belief. At best, such an outburst would see an adept denied advancement through the Cult Mechanicus. At worst it would see him branded *excommunicatus-technicus*, stripped of his every augmentation or transformed into a servitor.

Even an archmagos of the Adeptus Mechanicus, a servant of the Machine-God who would normally be granted a degree of latitude in such matters, could not voice such things openly.

<You have been away from the Imperium for some time,> replied Kotov. <And while there is much within the Mechanicus I believe could work better, you cannot seriously entertain such thoughts?>

Telok laughed. <Ah, Kotov, dear fellow, you must forgive me. It's been too long since I had anything but crystaliths and servitors to talk to. The conversational deficit has made me forget myself.>

<Then I will overlook your hasty words, archmagos.>

<Of course you will,> said Telok, and the growths jutting from his metal hide like armoured horns flared in response. <You and I? We are gods to these men, and it does not behove gods to squabble before lesser beings. You agree, of course?>

<I agree that it is never good for superiors to argue before those who must serve them,> said Kotov.

<Quite,> said Telok, and the Lost Magos returned to steering the crystal ship through the megalithic structures, vast generator plants for the most part, though there were some buildings whose purpose even Kotov could not identify.

<That one man could build this from nothing, without a geoformer fleet, is nothing short of miraculous,> said Kotov. <How did you do it? I must know.>

<All in good time, archmagos.>

<I have so many questions,> continued Kotov, trying not to let his growing unease with Telok outweigh his admiration for what the Lost Magos had achieved. <Where is the rest of your fleet? The crew of the *Tomioka*? Are they here too?>

<I promised to answer your questions in good time, archmagos,> said Telok, his crystals pulsing with jagged spikes of illumination. <And I will. Trust me, all will become clear when I show you the Breath of the Gods.>

<And will that be soon?>

Telok did not answer, guiding their course from between the looming structures enclosing them. The crystal ship skimmed into an enormous metalled plaza, not unlike the one upon which the Thunderhawk of the Black Templars had landed.

At the centre of the plaza sat a colossal silver-skinned dome, at least four kilometres in diameter and a quarter that in height. Could the scale of what lay beneath be extrapolated from its incredible dimensions?

The vastness of the dome was breathtaking, and as the crystal ship slipped effortlessly through the air towards it, Kotov saw the faintest outline of rippling energy fields.

More than one, in fact. Banks of shields layered the dome, more than even shrouded the sacred slopes of Olympus Mons. Whatever lay within was clearly of immense value.

<Is the Breath of the Gods within?> asked Kotov.

<It is,> grinned Telok, showing blunted, porcelain-looking teeth. <Would you like to see it?>

<More than you can imagine.>

Telok moved his gnarled fingers across the lectern in a precise geomantic pattern. Twin arcs of glossy metal unfolded from the plaza, self-assembling and curving over organically to form an arch some fifty metres before the dome. Where its outer edges contacted the dome's energy fields, disruptive arcs of lightning exploded in a nova-like corona.

A curtain of sparking, crackling energy filled the space within the

arc, and Kotov shifted warily on the bench as he saw Telok meant to steer them through it.

The emptiness of the plaza made it difficult to accurately gauge the size of the arch until they were almost upon it. Kotov's internal calibrators measured it as two hundred metres wide and ninety high.

And then they passed beneath it, and the silver skin of the dome, which Kotov now saw was formed from overlapping scales like reptile skin, rippled as it reshaped to form an opening. Light like a blood-red sunrise breaking over the Tharsis Montes shone from within, carrying with it the promise of the future. Kotov felt his floodstream surge in response.

'The Breath of the Gods awaits!' said Telok as the crystal ship passed into the dome.

The beating *Renard* had taken in her forced landing on the *Speranza* was still very much in evidence, but all things considered, it could have been a lot worse. Emil Nader walked down the starship's port-side flank with a pair of servitors at his heels. Both were equipped with vox-recorders, faithfully listening to his critical appraisal of the work the Mechanicus had undertaken on his vessel.

It was stream-of-consciousness stuff, but with the *in perpetuitus* refit contract Roboute had negotiated with the Mechanicus, now was the time to get as much done as humanly possible.

Scaffolding rigs surrounded the prow, which hung suspended over a graving dock in which the boxy form of Adept Kryptaestrex supervised the work of nearly two hundred servitors and bondsmen as they laboured to repair *Renard*'s prow. The prow and ventral sections of the ship had taken the worst of the damage. Like any pilot, Emil never quite trusted those who didn't fly to know exactly what they were doing, and so was keeping a close eye on the servitors. So far, he grudgingly, and it was *very* grudgingly, had to admit the Mechanicus were doing a decent job.

Emil paused beside a newly fabricated panel installed in an airlock hatch that had once been stamped with an Espandorian artificer's mark.

'You have got to be kidding me,' he said, following up with an Iaxian oath best not repeated in earshot of a lady. 'The nerve of these sons of bitches.'

'Transcription alert,' said the two servitors, one after the other. 'Implanted lexicon conflict. Do you wish a phonetic transcription?'

'Don't be stupid,' said Emil, before remembering he was talking to a servitor. 'No. I don't want that recorded.'

He jabbed a finger at the nearest servitor then pointed to a wheeled rack of parts and forge-gear sitting at the base of a scaffold-rig. 'You, go get a pneuma-hammer.'

The servitor retrieved the requested tool before returning to its station, exactly one metre behind Emil.

'Now get that off my ship,' he said, pointing to the gleaming Icon Mechanicus on the hatch. The cog-toothed skull had been set in the centre of the hatch, completely obscuring the artificer's mark.

'Clarification required,' said the servitor. 'What is it you wish removed?'

'The Icon Mechanicus,' said Emil. 'Get it off.'

'Unable to comply,' said the servitor. 'Express permission from a tech-priest, rank Lambda-Tertius or higher, is required before this *servile* may deface/remove an Icon Mechanicus.'

'Throne, don't you bloody Mechanicus know anything about *why* starships stay aloft?' he snapped. 'Here, hand me that pneuma-hammer.'

The servitor held the device out and Emil snatched it from its unresisting grip. He bent to the airlock hatch and with three swift blows from the pneuma-hammer battered the silver-steel icon to the deck.

'Good as new,' he said, holding the pneuma-hammer out behind him and brushing flecks of metal shavings away with his free hand. The hammer was plucked from his grasp and a gruff voice came from behind him.

'And this is why you leave engineering to folk who know what they're doing.'

'It's bad luck to cover up the original maker's marks,' said Emil, standing upright.

Kayrn Sylkwood, *Renard*'s enginseer, saw the emblem he'd knocked off the ship and nodded in agreement. She ran a hand over the dented metalwork Emil had just beaten free of the Icon Mechanicus.

'Nice work,' she said. 'Subtle.'

'You're an enginseer, what do you know about subtle?'

'More than you, by the looks of it,' said Sylkwood. The rivalry between a pilot and a ship's master of engines was long-established. One trying to squeeze the most out of a ship's reactors, one trying to keep the other from blowing them up.

Clad in a tight-fitting vest and combat jacket, Kayrn Sylkwood was a born and bred enginseer. Knotted communion implants lined her shaven skull in metallic cornrows, and her tanned features had a laconic superiority to them. Baggy fatigues that might once have been tan-coloured, but which were now an oil-sodden slate, were tucked into military boots, laced in the Cadian cross-hatch style.

'How's it looking out here?' she asked.

'Despite the odd bit of complete idiocy, not as bad as I expected,' said Emil, moving down the hull towards the sunken space below the

prow, where sparks from arc-welders and lascutters fell like neon-blue rain. Sylkwood fell in alongside him, unconsciously matching his step. The two servitors resumed their obedient following.

'*Speranza*'s priests actually seem like they know what they're doing,' said Emil, running his hands along the warm metal of the *Renard*'s fuselage. 'The damaged hull plates have been repaired in Turentek's prow-forges, the forward auspex arrays have been stripped out and replaced, and I see the transverse inertial arrays being reinforced. There's been some unasked-for upgrades by the look of it, but I'll only find out exactly what when I take her out again.'

'Not bad,' said Sylkwood. 'Not bad at all.'

'They all done in the engine spaces?'

Kayrn nodded. 'Yeah, there wasn't much to do, and Ilanna had left pretty specific instructions. But I didn't let them do anything without me right there with them. If we had a halfway decent pilot at the helm, I'd guess we'd probably see a ten per cent boost to *Renard*'s top speed and reactor efficiency.'

'Then I'll get fifteen.'

'You think?'

'Bet you a shift on the loaders.'

They spat on their palms and slapped hands.

'You watch, I'll get my ship doing things her builders never even dreamed of,' said Emil.

'*Your* ship?' said Kayrn with a grin. 'I reckon the captain might have something to say about *that* word choice.'

Emil returned her grin. 'Roboute isn't here. And he doesn't fly the ship, I do. In my books that makes the *Renard* mine.'

Kayrn looked set to challenge that assertion, but before she could do more than cock an eyebrow, they heard a horrified wail from the entrance to the graving dock.

'What the hell?' said Kayrn, her hand falling to the butt of her holstered laspistol. 'Is that Vitali Tychon?'

'Looks like,' said Emil, lifting his hand to shield his eyes from the glare of the deck's harsh lighting. 'I think he's been hurt.'

Vitali staggered towards the *Renard*. His robes were drenched in blood from the chest down. Did Mechanicus priests have that much blood in them?

'It's not his blood,' said Kayrn as Vitali half ran, half staggered towards them. He was shouting something, but his words were too grief-stricken and anguished to make out.

'Then whose blood is it?' said Emil.

✱✱✱

Forge Elektrus was not what Abrehem had imagined when Totha Mu-32 had said he was to be apprenticed to a magos of the Cult Mechanicus. He had pictured towering engines and the thunderous, unceasing labours of powerful machinery.

A place where things were *made*, technology unbound.

Not this place of antiquity, an echoing machine-temple where dust lay thick on the titanic engines that stood cold and dead to either side of a mosaic-covered nave. The only machines at work here were the lumen staves carried by the two forge overseers and the crackling inload trunking that allowed the thirty shaven-headed tech-priests to link their cognitive capacity.

Arranged in five rows of six, they sat on hard wooden benches before a rusted throne worked into a representation of the Icon Mechanicus. Chained together like galley slaves by ribbed copper cabling plugged into data-sockets in the backs of their skulls, their heads bobbed rhythmically to a hypnotic binary beat only they could hear.

Abrehem had seen that every one was the lowest rank it was possible to be and still be counted as one of the Martian priesthood. Many bore terrible injuries suffered in service to the Machine-God: missing limbs, burned skin and cratered skulls. Just as many bore marks of censure in their noospheric auras. Others had been implanted with augments that had obviously been damaged or been cycled through so many adepts over the centuries that it was a miracle they functioned at all.

Truly this was a forge of the damned, where the lowliest, most pitiable adepts imaginable toiled. So why had Totha Mu-32 sent him here? What could he possibly learn in a place populated by the mad, the infirm and the punished?

How was this any better than where he had come from?

No answer was obvious, and Chiron Manubia had thus far been less than forthcoming. Without the necessary inload sockets, Abrehem couldn't take his place with the linked adepts in their fugue state, and for that he was profoundly grateful.

Instead, he sat on the pew of a wide timber lectern, such as he might expect to find in a mass scriptorium of the Administratum. A book of quantum runes lay open before him, each holy circuit etched into the electro-conductive pages with copper wiring.

The book was ancient and marked by thousands of blurred fingerprints. Perhaps it had belonged to the first builders of this temple.

He'd been studying it for what seemed like weeks, tracing metalled fingers across its dogmatic forms and endless repetition. Its needless complexity was straining his powers of concentration and testing the limits of his boredom. Almost every litany was monstrously overwrought and only achieved what he could do with a thought. To work to such prescribed methods was ridiculous and he sat back from the book with a weary sigh of resignation.

'You think you're too good for Forge Elektrus, don't you?' said his new tutor, startling Abrehem from his gloomy contemplation of a needlessly complex runic form of the Ohmic Evocation.

Abrehem looked up into the almond-shaped face of Chiron Manubia. He still didn't know what shared history lay between her and Totha Mu-32, but every time he looked at Manubia's face, he felt sure it had involved something unpleasantly biological.

'No, that's not it at all,' said Abrehem.

'You're a terrible liar,' said Manubia, sitting next to him on the lectern's pew.

'Sorry, I just thought your forge would be... different.'

Manubia cocked an eyebrow.

'Different,' she said, echoing the wariness he'd put into each syllable. 'You thought it would be a forge where the wonders of technology were handed down straight from the golden hands of the Omnissiah?'

Abrehem kept his mouth shut in case he said something truly stupid. He tapped the iron fingers of his augmetic arm against the edge of the lectern.

Manubia smiled. 'I thought so. Forge Elektrus isn't quite like the forges depicted in the devotional frescoes, is it?'

Since lying to Manubia clearly wasn't an option, Abrehem opted for honesty. 'No, it hardly looks like a forge at all.'

'What did you think? That someone who almost got the *Speranza* destroyed was going to just walk into the most prestigious forge on the ship and begin his rise through the Cult Mechanicus?'

'No, of course not, but...'

'But you thought you'd be learning all our secrets from the minute you walked in,' said Manubia. 'Well, I'm afraid you have to earn that right, Abrehem Locke. Because, right now, you are the lowest of the low. You are the scrapings of millennial rust from a broken gear, the contaminated oil that's on the verge of being too polluted to use on even the most mangled waste recycler. And the only reason I didn't slam the door in Totha Mu-32's face is that, Omnissiah preserve me, I think he might be right about you.'

'That I'm Machine-touched?'

'No, that you're dangerous,' said Manubia.

'Dangerous?'

'You think you know machines, that you can talk to them and

that it's a simple matter to coax them into doing what you want, but you're like a child with the key to an armoury of loaded weapons,' said Manubia, jabbing a finger at the book of quantum runes. 'You have power, a power I don't understand yet, but you don't know how to use it safely. That's why you're here – not to become the saviour of the Adeptus Mechanicus, but to be controlled, to have whatever power you have made safe. *That's* what I do, Abrehem Locke.'

'What you do?' said Abrehem, angry at being so casually dismissed. 'It doesn't look like you do *anything* here.'

Manubia turned and gestured to the cog-toothed entrance to her forge.

'Then feel free to leave, but know that no priest of the Cult Mechanicus will ever let you inside their temple again.'

Abrehem slammed the open palm of his artificial arm on the book of quantum runes.

'Then tell me, Adept Manubia,' he said. 'What *do* you do? What vital role in the operations of the *Speranza* are these poor wretches involved in?'

'Nothing,' said Manubia. 'They're too broken to be of any use.'

Abrehem shook his head. 'Then I don't see any point in me being here.'

'You didn't let me finish,' said Manubia. 'They're here *because* they're broken. But by the time they leave, they won't be. I gather up the waifs and strays of the Cult Mechanicus – the damaged, the broken, the data-blind, the augment-crippled – and I give them purpose again. I rebuild and remake what's broken inside them and I make them useful again. I give them purpose. And that's what I can do for you, if you'll let me.'

'I'm not broken,' said Abrehem.

'Aren't you?' said Manubia, her face lit from below by a swiftly glowing illumination.

Abrehem looked down, his eyes widening as he saw the etched copper diagram of the Ohmic Evocation fill with liquid light that flowed from his iron fingers. The metalled surface of the book felt hot to the touch, the light penetrating deeper into its pages with each passing second.

'Whatever you're doing, stop it now,' demanded Manubia. 'Lift your augmetic from the book.'

Abrehem shook his head. 'I can't,' he said.

Golden light poured from the book, following the corded cables plugged into the base of the lectern. It lit the forge in a radiance it had not known since its earliest days, passing through the archaic trunking system and into the crippled tech-priests.

They stiffened as the light flowed into them and through them, seeking new pathways to illuminate, new circuits to restore. Thousands of snaking threads of golden light moved through the machine-temple, racing along frayed and forgotten wires. The Icon Mechanicus shimmered with reflected radiance as ancient wiring within the throne that had not known the touch of electro-motive power in millennia pulsed with life.

'How are you doing this?' gasped Manubia. '*What* are you doing?'

Abrehem had no answer for her, watching as first one, then another of the dormant machines around the perimeter of Chiron Manubia's forge flickered with its own internal light.

Ancient cogs turned with grating squeals, rusted gears cranked into painful motion and long-stilled machine hearts began beating once more.

One by one, the titanic engines returned to life.

The approach to the bridge of the *Speranza* was a towering processional vault known as the Path to Wisdom, precisely one thousand metres long, with sixty equidistant archways to either side. Threaded columns wound with variant binary forms supported the latticework tangle of green iron girders and a cloud layer of lubricant incense clung to the corbels, where squatted fat mechanical cherubs. Long strips of votive binary chattered from their mouths, random praise to the Omnissiah that teams of tech-priests and lexmechanics studied intently for any divine messages.

Sheet metal banners hung within the arches, each venerating a different branch of Mechanicus theology, from shield technology to teleportation, from weapon design to engine maintenance. A great Icon Mechanicus stared down in judgement at those who approached.

None of the tech-priests surrounded by strips of ticker-tape around the base of each column paid any attention to the small, determined group making its way to the monolithic adamantium gates of the bridge.

Vitali Tychon led the way, with Kayrn Sylkwood, Emil Nader and Adara Siavash struggling to keep up with the venerable adept. The crew of the *Renard* were armed, which Emil wasn't so sure was a good idea. But as soon as Vitali had managed to explain why he was covered in blood, Emil knew a confrontation was inevitable.

And if life in Ultramar had taught Emil anything, it was that it was always a good idea to be prepared for the worst.

The vast door to the bridge was protected by a demi-cohort of praetorians, clanking mechanised killers on tracks, articulated stalk legs

or heavy Dreadnought chassis. Their armaments were a lethal array of plasma weaponry, rotor carbines and linked lascannons. Smaller than the praetorians were the weaponised servitors, grotesquely augmented humans with steroidal musculatures, sub-dermal armour plating and vicious arrays of implanted blades, drills and power fists.

Emil shared a glance with Kayrn Sylkwood. Neither was a stranger to mass warfare, but these cyborgs were something else entirely – metal-masked and dispassionate.

Their approach had been noted, and every one of the Mechanicus battle-servitors turned its targeting auspex upon them. Emil had never felt quite so vulnerable.

'No sudden movements,' said Vitali, his voice cold, where normally it was infectiously vibrant. 'Let me take care of this.'

'Don't you worry about that,' said Emil, keeping his hands well away from his hand cannon. The weapon had been his father's, presented to him upon earning his captaincy in the Espandor Defence Auxilia. Emil had inherited it upon his father's death a month later. Talassarian mother-of-pearl was embedded in the walnut grip in the shape of an ultima.

'Do you actually know how to use that thing?' asked Sylkwood.

He nodded. 'I know every inch of this gun,' said Emil. He'd maintained it with all the due diligence drummed into him since childhood. 'It's in as perfect working order as it was the day it left the craftsman's workbench.'

'You ever fired it?'

'No, not once.'

'Good to know,' said Sylkwood.

'Look, it's not me you need to worry about,' said Emil, nodding towards Adara Siavash. The youthfully handsome gunman had come aboard the *Renard* a number of years ago as a passenger, but after proving he had what it took to use his pistols and ubiquitous butterfly blade, Roboute had decided to keep him on as a member of the crew. For a man so intimate with ways of ending life, he wore his heart on his sleeve, and had been endearingly sweet in his hopeless infatuation with Mistress Linya.

Emil had seen Adara fight and kill, but until now, he'd never seen him angry. The cold, unflinching, razor-fine hostility he saw in the youth's eyes was not something he'd ever expected to see.

'Listening, Adara?' said Sylkwood. 'Let Vitali take the lead.'

The young gunman nodded, but didn't reply.

Sylkwood shrugged with an *I tried* expression.

Vitali didn't slow his pace as he approached the praetorians and weaponised servitors. Auspexes clicked and whirred as lenses extended, gathering information from Vitali's noospheric aura. Satisfied it was addressing a being that didn't qualify for immediate destruction, a towering praetorian armed with twin power fists extended a vox-unit from its throat.

'Magos Vitali Tychon, stellar cartographer, AM4543/1001011.'

'Stand down,' said Vitali.

An internal cogitator whirred within its cranium and a chattering stream of tape emerged from the back of its skull.

'Your presence has not been requested.'

'I'm aware of that, but I'm going onto the bridge and you are not going to stop me.'

'Without current authorised access privileges, entry to the bridge is impossible,' said the praetorian.

'I am a high magos of the Adeptus Mechanicus,' snapped Vitali. 'Are you going to stop me?'

'Updated bridge security protocols authorise the use of force up to and including, but not limited to, lethal levels.'

Emil felt a layer of sweat form all over his body. The cyborg was talking about killing them with as much thought as he might give to stepping on a ship louse.

He leaned over to whisper to Kayrn. 'If I'm going to die here, I'd rather it was at the hands of something that gave a damn about killing me.'

'Yeah, because that makes dying *so* much better,' she said.

'Are you denying me access to the bridge?' said Vitali.

'Affirmative, Magos Tychon,' confirmed the praetorian. 'Do you wish me to submit a priority access request to Magos Blaylock?'

'No, I want you to open the damn door.'

'Your request cannot be completed at this time.'

Vitali turned to Emil and the others.

'Master Nader, Master Siavash, I'd cover my ears if I were you. And, Mistress Sylkwood, please mute any noospheric-capable communion receptors if you please. I apologise in advance for what will, I'm sure, be most unpleasant.'

Emil knew better than to ask why and pressed his hands hard over his ears as Vitali turned back to the intransigent praetorian. Adara followed his example as Kayrn thumped the heel of one palm to the side of her head.

Vitali squared his shoulders and addressed the praetorian again. 'I didn't want to have to do this, but you've left me no choice.'

Before the servitor could answer, Vitali unleashed a shriek of violent binary from his chest augmitters. Even with his hands clamped over his ears, Emil felt it like someone had just detonated a bomb in the centre of his skull. Sylkwood dropped to one knee, her face twisted in pain.

As painful as Vitali's binaric shriek was for them, the effect on the praetorians and weaponised servitors was far more spectacular. Relays within iron skulls exploded and implanted doctrina wafers melted upon receipt of self-immolation protocols. Every synaptic connection within the servitors' heads blew instantaneously. Orange flames licked from their eye sockets and fatty smoke curled from those whose mouths were not already sealed shut. The stalk-limbed praetorian crashed to the ground, its weapon arms falling limply to its sides. Bipedal combat servitors fell where they stood, like remotely piloted automatons whose operators had been abruptly yanked from their immersion rigs.

The grating, screeching wail rose and fell, like a novice vox-operator trying to find an active channel. Blood dripped from Sylkwood's nose, and veins like power couplings stood out on the side of her neck.

Then, mercifully, it ended.

'What did you do?' asked Emil, gingerly taking his hands from the side of his head.

'To many aboard the *Speranza*, I may be the eccentric stellar cartographer Archmagos Kotov dragged from obscurity,' said Vitali, 'but I am also a high magos of the Adeptus Mechanicus. There isn't a cyborg aboard this ship I don't know how to destroy.'

Vitali stepped over the smouldering corpses of the combat cyborgs. Their limbs twitched with rogue impulses as the molten remnants of their brains disintegrated in the wake of Vitali's binaric holocaust.

The towering bridge doors began to open.

'And now I'm going to kill the abomination that murdered my daughter,' said Vitali.

Microcontent 04

Flickering lights and arcs of energy were nothing unusual on Exnihlio, but the amber shimmer dancing in a steelwork canyon between two soaring coolant towers had nothing to do with the designs of Archmagos Telok.

Everything on Exnihlio was angular and harsh, but this light grew steadily from a graceful ellipse to a wide oval, some five metres in height. Where it touched the ground, it flattened to form a harmoniously proportioned, leaf-shaped archway.

The sounds that issued from the light were laments from an ancient age, a time before the rise of mankind, and spoke of the profound sorrow of a dying race that could never be articulated in mere words.

A figure stepped from the fluid light, monstrously tall, but slender-limbed, fleshless and formed from a gleaming material that had the appearance of the most flawless ceramic. Its emerald skull was an elongated teardrop, its shoulders vaned with sweeping spines like wings. Its arms looked too thin to be dangerous, but each had the power to crush steel and stone and flesh.

Uldanaish Ghostwalker was a wraithlord, and he had fought in the armies of Craftworld Biel-tan for seven centuries. Two of those centuries had been as a disembodied spirit, bound to this wraithbone warrior-construct by unbreakable bonds of duty.

Ghostwalker rose to his full height, and spread both arms out to

either side, the weapons extruded from his fists ready to destroy any target that presented itself.

None did, and the armoured giant took a step to the side as more figures followed it from the honeyed light. First to follow the wraithlord onto the surface of Exnihlio was Ariganna Icefang, exarch of the Twilight Blade Aspect Shrine. Clad in plates of emerald and gold that overlapped like drake-scale and sinuously adapted to her form as though more flesh than armour, she was the perfect warrior in every way. One hand was a bladed claw, while her other held an enormous chainsabre.

A pack of hunched warriors followed her, bulkily armoured in jade and with helms of ivory. Stinger-like mandibles flickered at their cheek-plates, and each had a pistol and sword at the ready.

Following the Striking Scorpions came the Howling Banshees, warrior women clad in form-fitting flex-armour and gracefully sculpted plates of ivory and crimson. Like their more heavily armoured cousins, the Banshees carried swords and pistols, but had an altogether faster, lighter appearance that belied their exquisite lethality.

Last to step through the sunset gate was a lithe figure in rune-etched armour of gold, green and cream. An iridescent cloak of subtly interwoven gold and emerald billowed from Bielanna's shoulders, and a scarlet plume flew from her antlered helm. Alone of the eldar, she did not have a weapon drawn, her filigreed sword still belted at her waist.

No sooner had Bielanna set foot on Exnihlio than a cry of pain escaped her lips. She staggered as though struck and dropped to her knees. The sunset gate faded like a forgotten dream.

The eldar warriors formed a circle around their farseer, weapons at the ready. Bielanna climbed unsteadily to her feet, looking around her as though unsure of what she was seeing. Imperial worlds tasted of rancid meat and burned metal, ripe with the overwhelming reek of mon-keigh desires, a maelstrom of fleeting, venal emotions, but the voice of this world was utterly singular in its ambition.

The force of it almost drove her to her knees once more.

'Farseer?' said Ariganna Icefang, looming over Bielanna.

Bielanna struggled to master the sensations roiling within her. Her psychic senses were being assailed by a push and pull of fates, interwoven destinies of the warriors around her and… and what?

'I see it all…' she whispered, shutting her eyes to keep the assault on her senses from overwhelming her.

'What do you see?' said Ariganna Icefang.

'Conflicting futures and unwritten histories,' gasped Bielanna.

Farseers trained their entire lives to read the twisting weave of the future within the skein, and as much discipline was required to keep the innumerable possibilities that would never come to pass at bay.

But no amount of training and devotion could keep this confluence of past and future from swamping her.

'The futures grind against one another,' said Bielanna. 'Each strains to move from potential to reality, and their struggle to exist will destroy them all.'

'Speak plainly,' said the exarch. 'Can you find the mon-keigh?'

Bielanna tried to answer, but the words stuck in her throat as she looked up into the Striking Scorpion exarch's war-mask.

Ariganna's helm was hung with knotted cords of woven wraithbone and psycho-conductive crystal, but Bielanna saw beyond the smooth faceplate to the exarch's cruelly beautiful features. The Aspect Warrior's eyes were gateways to madness, filled with the monomaniacal fury of inescapable devotion to death.

Bielanna saw not one face, but three. Each true in its own way.

A youthful face, flush with the newly awakened promise of femininity. The face of seasoned womanhood, freighted with wisdom. And lastly, a crone, burdened and ravaged by life's savagery.

'The three in one,' said Bielanna. 'The Maiden, the Woman and the Crone... All future and past weave together here and nothing will ever be the same.'

Her gaze moved to Tariquel, whom she had known as a dancer before the bloody song of Khaine had drawn him to the Shrine of the Twilight Blade. His face was as she remembered it when he had wept to the *Swans of Isha's Memory*. Delicate as a wraithbone web-sculpt, tender as moonlight on the surface of a lake.

Vaynesh the poet, who had laughed in the field of corpses on the surface of Magdelon, was similarly transformed. Bielanna saw the face of the boy he had once been, the vain, prideful killer he had become and the serene death-mask that loomed in his future.

Bielanna saw the same dance of ages in every face. She saw each warrior as they once were and who they might yet be.

She sobbed as Ariganna placed a clawed gauntlet on her shoulder.

'The mon-keigh,' demanded the exarch. 'Can you find them?'

'This world hangs over a precipice,' said Bielanna. 'And should it end, the effects will be like unto the Fall.'

'I care nothing for this world,' hissed the exarch. 'You spoke of a cuckoo in the nest, a mortal marked by another of your kind?'

Bielanna nodded. 'Roboute Surcouf, yes...'

'Can you find him?'

The face of the mon-keigh appeared in her mind, constant and

unwavering. She had marked him aboard the human starship, hadn't she? She remembered that, but assailed by phantom images of an unlived past and a thousand futures, she was no longer sure her memories could be trusted.

'I can,' she said.

'Then do so,' said Ariganna, turning from Bielanna. 'The murder of our kin must be repaid in the blood of their deaths.'

'Death?' said Bielanna, her mind afire with the possibilities opened up by Ariganna Icefang's words. 'Is death the only answer?'

'The only one worth knowing,' said the exarch.

'It is the only one you know how to give, Ariganna, but does that make it the right one? Nothing is ever as straightforward as life or death, right and wrong.'

The exarch stood before her, threat radiating from her every movement.

'All your visions have led us to doom, farseer,' said Ariganna. 'Give me a reason to trust them now.'

Bielanna forced a clarity to her mind that she knew was as fragile as a promise between lovers.

'An infinite web of possibility spreads from this moment,' she said. 'And every one hangs upon a single thread, but whether we are to cut that thread or preserve it is beyond my power to see.'

'Then you have no answer I can use.'

'No,' agreed Bielanna.

'Just lead me to the mon-keigh,' said Ariganna.

Bielanna nodded and conjured the image of Roboute Surcouf into her mind's eye. She felt his presence on this world burning strongly, a mortal with a bright thread that was all too easy to discern amid the barren, lifeless scab of this world's skin.

'They are close,' said Bielanna. 'Very close.'

'Good,' said Ariganna, clenching a fist above her head. 'We move swiftly, and then we will see what death may do.'

Everyone on the bridge felt it. Like a red-hot skewer had just been jammed up through the bases of their skulls. Implanted servitors spasmed in silvered implant bays, heads rolling slack as synaptic-breakers cut the connection between the machines in their skulls and the *Speranza*.

A data prism blew out on the ceiling, sending multi-spectral bands of data-light skewing in all directions. Alarm chimes sounded and noospheric warnings streamed up like smoke from the smooth floor.

Magos Tarkis Blaylock, Fabricatus Locum of the *Speranza*, had cognitive speed enough to shut down his receptors in time to avoid the worst of the binaric assault, but not all of it. His vision blurred and

he gripped on to the armrests of the command throne as he felt his internal gyros lose all sense of spatial awareness.

Kryptaestrex stomped away from his data hub, trailing sparks from where an inload cable had fused to his blocky outline. The component parts of Azuramagelli's disembodied brain flared with electrical disturbance. Even Galatea staggered at the force of it, two of the machine-hybrid's legs collapsing as its brain jars crackled with internal forks of energy.

Blaylock felt full awareness return in time to register the fact that the main door to the bridge was opening. Not the cog-toothed iris the bridge crew used to pass back and forth, but the towering portal itself. All fifty metres of its height were grinding back on squealing hinges, dislodging centuries of dust and flakes of corrosion.

How long had it been since that door had opened in its entirety?

Blaylock's vision was still hazed with static, but he had enough clarity to recognise Vitali Tychon and three members of Roboute Surcouf's crew: pilot, enginseer and hired gun. The force of belligerent code surging through Magos Tychon's floodstream shocked Blaylock, the binaric forms assembled in their most aggressive, direct format. His noospherics were as hostile as anything Dahan had blurted.

Blaylock's vocals were offline. He switched to flesh-voice.

'Magos Tychon, what is the meaning of this?'

'Stay out of this, Tarkis,' said Vitali, pointing one of his delicate, multi-fingered hands towards the forward surveyor array. 'I'm here for that *thing*. That murderer.'

Blaylock assumed his aural-implants had been damaged. Tychon was pointing towards Galatea.

'What are you talking about, Magos Tychon? What murderer?'

'The thing that calls itself Galatea,' said Vitali. 'It killed my daughter.'

'Quite the opposite,' said Galatea, rising to its full height once again. Ripples of feedback coiled around its limbs and the silver eyes of its tech-priest proxy body glittered with excess energy. 'Her flesh is dead, that is true, but your daughter's mind is very much alive, Magos Tychon. As well you know.'

Vitali strode through the bridge as the *Speranza*'s systems began restarting with the thudding clatter of resetting breakers. Emergency lights flickered out as the bridge lumens sputtered to life and alert chimes were silenced. Blaylock rose from the command throne and moved to intercept the aged cartographer.

'Do I take it you know what Magos Tychon is talking about?'

'We do,' said Galatea.

'You cut her skull open!' wailed Vitali, his voice now cracking under the strain of facing his daughter's killer. 'You removed her brain and stuck it in a glass jar!'

'Where she now resides in harmony, freed from the intellectual limitations of flesh,' said Galatea. 'Enriching our neuromatrix with her agile mind and unconventional modes of thought.'

Blaylock now understood. 'Ave Deus Mechanicus!'

'The synaptic pathways of Magos Thraimen had deteriorated to the point where it became impossible to justify his presence within our neuromatrix,' continued Galatea. 'His hibernation nightmares were exquisite, but the presence of such an exceptional brain in the form of Mistress Tychon made his continued presence indulgent.'

'I've come to destroy you,' hissed Magos Tychon. 'I'd say *kill*, but you have to be alive and possess a soul in order to die.'

Blaylock felt a cataclysmic build-up of killing binary within the noosphere. He knew what Magos Tychon intended. And as biological as it was, Blaylock even understood his need for retribution.

But he could not allow him to continue.

<Magos Tychon, stand down!> ordered Blaylock, his augmitters freighted with every last one of his rank signifiers to countermand Tychon's war-code. Mistress Tychon's father reeled with the force of Blaylock's commands, his face lit with grief as his disassembler cant was splintered into harmless code fragments.

'No! Blaylock, no...' said Vitali, stumbling onto the central dais and reaching out to him, half mad with grief. 'That thing murdered my Linya. You must let me do this.'

'I cannot, Magos Tychon,' said Blaylock, backing away from Tychon. 'You know how deeply Galatea has enmeshed itself with the *Speranza*. If you kill it, you kill us. I cannot let you do this.'

He sat down in the command throne and turned his gaze upon the squatting machine-hybrid. 'Though I dearly wish I could.'

Magos Tychon fell to his knees, gripping Blaylock's arms.

'Please, Tarkis, kill it,' pleaded Tychon. 'You must know it will never let the *Speranza* go. Kill it now!'

'He cannot,' said Galatea. 'Logic sits high in the mind of Magos Blaylock. He knows that to kill us is to destroy any chance of his advancement in the Cult Mechanicus, and Tarkis *so* wishes to return to Mars, don't you, Tarkis?'

'They will burn you on Mars,' said Blaylock. 'They will never accept you.'

'We believe they will,' said Galatea, cocking its head to the side. 'With such a powerful advocate as you at our side, how could they not?'

Blaylock shook his head, disgusted that Galatea would ever think he would stand alongside it in support. He sensed a deeper meaning to the machine-hybrid's words, but this was not the time to consider them.

'You're going to let it get away with killing Linya?' said a young man, throwing off the restraining arm of his fellows. He had no augments to provide identifying signifiers, but Blaylock's internal database of embedded non-Mechanicus crew produced his name virtually instantaneously.

Adara Siavash. His entry listed no world of origin, but even a cursory bioscan suggested Ultramarian genestock. That, in turn, suggested a heightened sense of justice that could prove volatile in an already highly charged situation. Tears of grief streaked the young man's face.

'Come on, Adara,' said Emil Nader, the *Renard*'s pilot. 'I know you were soft on Miss Linya, but this is just crazy. And trust me, I know crazy.'

Nader's words and the boy's own tears told Blaylock that the boy had been hopelessly in love with Linya Tychon. Which marked him as a fool and even more dangerous.

'Adara, I can't believe I'm saying this, but please listen to Emil,' said the enginseer – Kayrn Sylkwood, a Cadian who had been mustered out of her regiment following a devastating loss of vehicles during the latest war spasms around the Eye of Terror. 'If Vitali can't take it down, what chance do you have?'

'Vitali tried subtle,' said Siavash. 'I don't do subtle.'

The boy drew his pistol and aimed it right at the heart of Galatea. Blaylock felt a moment of real fear as he saw a heavily converted Maukren Flensar with integral phosphex coils to increase muzzle velocity and impact trauma. Anything struck by that weapon would be gutted by a white-hot, fist-to-finger plasma core.

'If we were you, we would put that gun down,' said Galatea.

'I'm going to burn you alive,' said Siavash, his finger curling through the trigger guard.

'No!' cried Blaylock, rising from the throne.

'For Linya,' said Siavash, and fired the Maukren.

The weapon exploded, engulfing the boy's hand in a blooming corona of blue-hot flame. Too fast for the human eye to follow, the phosphex slithered up his arm like a living thing. It leapt onto his torso, billowing flames roaring and seething like an enraged predator.

'Adara! Throne, no!' screamed Sylkwood, tearing off her battered jerkin and attempting to beat the flames out. The jerkin instantly burst into flames as the overpowering heat from the flames forced the enginseer back.

'Help him!' shouted Nader, pulling Sylkwood away from the fire.

Blaylock shook his head. Phosphex could devour flesh and turn bones to grease in moments. The boy was already past saving.

Siavash dropped to the deck, dying without screams, the flames having seared the oxygen from his lungs. Localised fire suppression systems deployed from the deck and sprayed the burning body with a fire-retardant foam that hardened like a scab and starved the blaze of oxygen.

Emil Nader and Sylkwood supported each other, staring in hatred at Galatea, which watched the young boy's ending dispassionately, arms folded across its chest.

'Emperor damn you, Tarkis Blaylock,' said Nader. 'Do you know what you've done?'

'Me? I did nothing,' said Blaylock.

'Exactly my point.'

'I did nothing because there was nothing that could be done. The boy was dead the moment he pulled the trigger.'

Sylkwood threw off Nader's grip and strode towards Galatea.

'You did that,' she said. 'You fouled the firing mechanism or twisted the gun's war-spirit or did something that made it misfire. You've got Blaylock cowed, but I promise you that when this is all over, I'll be there to see you die.'

'Brave words for a biological entity whose unexceptional brain we could boil within her skull,' said Galatea, leaning forwards, its silver eyes glittering like the ferryman's coins. 'Shall we show you how painful that would be?'

'Enough,' said Blaylock. 'There will be no more death today. Mister Nader, I suggest you remove Magos Tychon and Enginseer Sylkwood from the bridge. Nothing good can come from further confrontation.'

Nader shot a venomous look at Galatea before nodding and taking Sylkwood's arm. For a moment, Blaylock thought the Cadian might do something foolish. But foolish and Cadian didn't go together, and she spat on the deck at Galatea's feet before turning towards Blaylock.

'You're a real piece of work, Magos Blaylock,' she said. 'You know that, right?'

Blaylock said nothing. Sylkwood's statement was too obtuse and vague to warrant a reply. In any case, it seemed she didn't expect one, for she turned and marched from the bridge.

Vitali Tychon's head remained bowed in defeat, and Blaylock felt a genuine stab of sympathy for the venerable cartographer.

'Magos Tychon, I–'

'Don't, Tarkis,' said Vitali. 'Just don't. Kotov told me we were looking for new stars, but that thing has just snuffed out the brightest star I knew.'

'You are wrong, Magos Tychon,' said Galatea. 'Your daughter burns just as bright inside me. Trouble us again and we will snuff out her essence as easily as we extinguished the boy.'

'Shut up!' shouted Blaylock. 'Ave Deus Mechanicus, shut up!'

Too vast to comprehend, too artificial to be natural, the spherical volume beneath the layered skin of the dome was a wonder of engineering. Surpassing any geodesic vault on Terra, it was, quite simply, the most impressive feat of structural mechanics Kotov had ever seen.

The Imperial explorators stood on an equatorial gantry that encircled the spherical void gouged in the planet's bedrock. Many others encircled the chamber above and below them, with jutting piers and scaffolds of unknown machinery cantilevered into space.

The mass of a small moon had been dug from Exnihlio, and the surface of the excavated volume was encrusted with technology unlike anything seen on Mars. Angular glyphs like temple icons were graven in the curves of the chamber, rendered in a language that was at once familiar yet inhuman.

Thousands of crystaliths of all shapes and descriptions crawled across the inner surfaces of the void, engaged in maintenance, calibration and who knew what else. An ochre miasma, rank with the foetor of turned earth and exposed rock, drifted up though a shaft bored down through the base of the chamber.

A venting system, drainage? Who could tell?

Yet the magnificence of the space paled to insignificance when measured against the incredible appearance of that which it enclosed.

The Breath of the Gods hung suspended in the exact centre of the space, a vast, threshing, interweaving gyre of glittering metal blades that seemed to have no supporting structure at its core, just an achingly bright nexus of fractal incandescence. Like the first instant of a supernova or a glittering map of synaptic architecture.

Though Kotov's visual augments were among the most sophisticated conceived by the molecular grinders of the Euryphaessan forges, he could form no coherent impression of the device's exact dimensions. Geometric assayers flashed error codes to his glassine retinas with each failed attempt to quantify what he was seeing.

Like a tubular hurricane of silver leaves, the Breath of the Gods formed an elongated elliptical outline that defied easy assimilation. Its very existence was subtly discordant, as though some innate property of the human brain knew this device was somehow *wrong*, as though it abused every tenet of thermodynamics with spiteful relish.

Its complex internal topography was a squirming mass of pulsating metal that Kotov's senses told him should be impossible. Portions of the colossal machine appeared to co-exist in the same space, moving *through* one another in violation of perspective.

Even those not reconfigured by the Adeptus Mechanicus found the machine disquieting to look upon. More so, it appeared. A number of Cadians doubled over to empty the contents of their stomachs across the perforated gantry. Idly, Kotov speculated as to the effect their dripping vomitus might have on the alien technology worked into the surfaces below.

Even the unsubtle minds of the Black Templars were enraptured by the sight of the device. Sergeant Tanna raised a hand as through reaching for it, while his white-helmed champion gripped the hilt of his black sword.

The machine – though Kotov's sensibilities rebelled at the notion of labelling something so clearly beyond current Mechanicus paradigms with such a mundane term – had an aura within this colossal space that went beyond the simply mechanical.

It seemed (and here Kotov's mind *did* rebel) to have a presence akin to a living being, as though it looked back at the tiny specks of consciousness beneath it and was content to allow them to bask in its wondrous impossibility.

Kotov shook off the notion, but like a shard of stubbornly invasive scrapcode, it could not be dismissed.

'It's...' started Kotov, but he had not the words to describe what he was feeling. 'It's...'

Telok appeared at his side, a hulking presence whose crystalline elements shimmered with reflected light from the inconstant flux of the machinery above him.

'I understand,' said Telok. 'It takes time to adapt to the singular nature of the device. For a human mind, even one enhanced by the Mechanicus, to grasp its complexity requires so thorough a remapping of the synaptic pathways and subsequent cognitive evolution that it can scarcely be called human any more.'

Kotov nodded in wonder, barely hearing Telok, his eyes constantly drawn to the Breath of the Gods' discomfiting aspect. It felt like the machine exerted some irresistible pull on his senses, as though demanding to be the sole focus of all who stood in its presence.

'You found it...' Kotov managed at last.

'I did,' affirmed Telok.

'How? It was a myth, a barely remembered legend from the hidden manuscripts of madmen and heretics.'

'By following the clues left by its builders,' said Telok, walking around the gently curved gantry, forcing Kotov and the others to follow him. 'Those madmen were once seekers after truth like us, men who uncovered those truths but whose minds were ill-equipped to process their significance.'

'So who was it that built this?' asked Roboute Surcouf, with a tone that suggested he might know the answer.

'An ancient race whose identity has long since been forgotten by the inexorable obscurity of time,' said Telok, waving a dismissive hand, as though who had built the machine was less important than who now controlled it. 'Whatever they called themselves, they passed through our galaxy millions of years ago. They were godlike beings, sculpting the matter of the universe to suit their desires with technology far beyond anything you could possibly imagine. They came here, perhaps hoping to begin the process anew, extending the limits of this innocuous spiral cluster of star-systems. They thought to connect all the universe with stepping stones of newly wrought galaxies they would build from the raw materials scattered by the ekpyrotic creation of space-time itself.'

'So what happened to this race of gods?' asked Ven Anders, nervously glancing up at the rotating flurry of machinery. 'If they were so powerful, why aren't they still here? Why haven't we heard of them before?'

'Because, Colonel Anders, nothing is ever really immortal, not even the gods themselves,' said Telok. 'In truth, I do not know exactly what happened to them, but in the deep vaults of this world I found fragmentary evidence of a weaponised psychic bio-agent that escaped its long imprisonment and destroyed the genius of their minds, reducing them to the level of beasts. Within a generation of the first infection, they had all but wiped themselves out.'

Telok paused, moving to the edge of the gantry, looking up at the swirling mass of silver and crackling arcs of elemental power with a look of rapture.

'It is my belief that with the last of their faculties, these gods set the device to become self-sustaining and self-repairing, shutting down all but its most basic functions until either far-flung survivors of their race returned to claim it or a species arose with the capacity to be their inheritors. I humbly submit that I am that inheritor.'

Telok now turned his gaze on Kotov, and the archmagos saw an expression that suggested anything but humility. His cognitive processes ran hot as he struggled to keep pace with what he was hearing. Fighting to keep his awe and unease in check, Kotov's analytical faculties came to the fore and found much in Telok's explanations that simply did not match his understanding of universal laws.

'And you claim that this is the device responsible for the celestial engineering events we witnessed at Katen Venia and Hypatia?'

'Claim?' said Telok. 'You doubt my word on this?'

Kotov heard the threat in Telok's voice and carefully framed his next words as a question of science, not character.

'What I mean is that it is beyond belief that any one device could have the power to achieve such a feat,' said Kotov. 'What empowers the Breath of the Gods? How can this one world, no matter how much energy it generates, provide even an infinitesimal fraction of the power that must surely be required to reshape the cosmos? I do not doubt your word, but the technological mastery needed to restore machinery abandoned millions of years ago by a lost alien race is staggering.'

Kotov lifted his gaze to the swirling, shimmering machine that filled the air above him, knowing that there was one question above all to which he needed an answer.

'How did you do all this alone?' he asked.

Telok heard his incredulity and responded just as bluntly.

'The hidden instructions left by the Stellar Primogenitor's builders were incredibly precise, archmagos. Marrying them to my peerless intellect, I unlocked a series of unambiguous structural and mathematical prescriptions that enabled me to replicate the conditions of physical reality found within the Noctis Labyrinthus and thus bring the device to life.'

Kotov's face drained of what little colour it possessed. 'Do not speak of that benighted place!'

Telok waved an admonishing finger, a bladed hook of entwined metal and parasitic crystal.

'Do not warn me of anything in the same breath you ask me how the device functions, archmagos,' warned Telok. 'Even were current paradigms of Martian thinking capable of understanding any answers I might offer, you would not find them to your liking. They would upset your outmoded thinking and I know all too well how the Adeptus Mechanicus hates those who disrupt the stagnancy of their precious status quo.'

Kotov shook his head, wearying of Telok's monstrous ego. He held Telok's gaze, speaking clearly so that there could be no mistaking the clarity of his words.

'I am an archmagos of the Adeptus Mechanicus, and I own only the empirical clarity of the Omnissiah,' said Kotov. 'You, Archmagos Telok, are bound by the strictures of our order and the ideals of the Quest for Knowledge to divulge what you have learned.'

'Oh, I shall,' snapped Telok, the crystalline structure of his body flaring an aggressive crimson. 'Have no fear of that, but as I have said, it will be at a time and place of my choosing.'

Telok took a crashing step towards Kotov, his heavy limbs ablaze with internal fire and his fists clenched into pounding hammers.

'And that will be when I take the vessel with which you have so thoughtfully provided me back to Mars in triumph,' said Telok. 'It will be when I stand atop Olympus Mons as the new master of the Red Planet.'

The skitarii surrounding Kotov growled at Telok's heretical pronouncements. Their weapon systems initiated, but Telok disengaged them with a blurt of high-level binary. They froze as their every internal augmentation seized up a heartbeat later.

'And when I have remade the Mechanicus in my image,' continued Telok, 'I will use the Breath of the Gods to surge the heart of Terra's sun to burn the rotting corpse of the Emperor and all his corrupt servants from its surface.'

The Black Templars' speed and aggression were phenomenal.

No sooner had Telok spoken than they were on the offensive. No pause, no ramping up of fury. One minute the towering warriors were still, the next at full battle-pitch.

Telok raised a hand and each of the Space Marines froze in place, paralysed as thoroughly as the skitarii. Kotov read the frenetic tempo of the machine-spirits within their battleplate as they fought to overcome Telok's paralysing code.

'I will become the new Master of Mankind,' laughed Telok. 'A ruler devoted to the attainment of the Singularity of Consciousness.'

Kotov turned from Telok's insanity as he heard the brittle sound of glass grinding on glass. Perhaps a hundred crystaliths were climbing onto the gantry from the inwardly curving slopes of the chamber, a similar number from below. They took up position all around the Cadians, extruded weapons ready to cut them down in a lethal crossfire.

'What are you doing?' said Kotov. 'This is insane!'

'Insane?' said Telok derisively. 'How could you possibly understand the mind of a god?'

'Is that what you think you are?' demanded Kotov.

'I created this entire region of space,' roared Telok, his voice afire with the passion of an Ecclesiarchy battle-preacher. 'I have reignited the hearts of dead suns, crafted star systems from the waste matter of the universe and wrought life from death. If that does not give me the right to name myself a god, then what does?'

Microcontent 05

Quatria had always possessed a utilitarian aesthetic, but with her surroundings now crafted from memory, it had assumed an altogether bleaker aspect. The corridors were cold, though Linya knew, of course, that she wasn't truly feeling cold. Her mind was conjuring that sensation based upon perceived sensory data.

As thorough and detailed a simulation as Galatea had rendered, the human mind was capable of seeing through almost any visual deception. The walls were just a little too crisply etched, the patterns not quite three-dimensional enough to entirely convince.

Linya walked with her arms wrapped around her body, as though hugging herself for comfort. Pointless, she knew. After all, what measure of physical comfort could be offered to a disembodied brain in a jar?

Yet some habits were too hard to break. It didn't matter that her body was dead, her mind lived on. Enslaved by an abomination unto the Machine-God, yes, but enduring. Only by the slenderest margin had Linya held on to sanity at the sight of her skull hinged back and the bloody void within. Anyone not of the Mechanicus would likely have gone insane at such a vision, but the first lesson taught to neophytes of the Cult Mechanicus was that flesh was inferior to technology, that thought and memory and intellect were the true successors of flesh.

Indeed, wasn't the final apotheosis striven for by the adepts of Mars, a freeing of pure intellect from the limitations of flesh and blood? Wasn't that why so many of the Cult Mechanicus were so quick to shed their humanity and embrace mechanical augmentations in their ascent towards the ideal Singularity of Consciousness?

Linya had never subscribed to the notion of flesh's abandonment, believing that to sacrifice all that made you human was to cut yourself off from the very thing that made life so wondrous.

Did her father know what had happened to her?

Grief swamped her every time she thought of him. She hoped he hadn't been the one to find her. She hoped that someone had sanitised the scene of her physical death. She didn't want to think what the sight of her lying on her medicae bed, cut open like a dissection subject, might do to his psyche.

Vitali Tychon was often dismissed as a harmless eccentric, but Linya knew him to have a determined, ruthless core. She hoped he hadn't done something foolish upon learning of her death. Galatea would kill him without a second thought, and as fiercely intelligent as Vitali was, she knew Galatea would never risk assimilating him into its neuromatrix.

Linya had no idea how much time had passed since Galatea had first shown her the truth of her condition, that portion of her cranial implantation removed along with any conventional means of linking to the outside world. Her high-level implants appeared to be functional, but without advanced diagnostics it was impossible to be sure what the machine intelligence had left her.

Linya looked up as she heard a circular door iris open beside her. The confero. Every Mechanicus facility had one, a sanctified chamber where matters of techno-theology could be discussed and debated at length under the benevolent gaze of the Omnissiah.

Linya ignored the door and kept walking.

She had already explored every portion of the Quatrian Galleries as they were known to her. The parts she knew best were lifelike down to the smallest detail, but those areas she was less familiar with had an unfinished quality, like a Theatrica Imperialis set designed only to be viewed from a distance. The farthest portions of the orbital, which she had known only from schematics, were little more than bare, wire-frame walls and lifeless renderings of the most basic structural elements.

It was towards this region of Quatria Linya walked, finding Galatea's false representation of a place she had once called home repugnant. Better to surround herself with obviously fake surroundings, to keep the truth of her imprisonment uppermost.

The corridor curved around to the left, but where she had expected to find the lateral transit that led to the central hub, she instead found herself in the communal deck levels. Along the wall, the irising door to the confero opened up once more.

'I won't be your puppet,' said Linya.

She ignored the door and kept walking, taking paths at random and moving further into the orbital, trying to lose herself in its deeper structure.

But no matter which path she took, which direction she chose to confound her captor, every route took her back to the communal decks and the opened door of the confero. She sighed, knowing that in a constructed reality where Galatea controlled every aspect of the virtual architecture, she would always be brought back here.

'Fine,' she said, stepping through into the confero.

The space was larger than she remembered, but that shouldn't have surprised her. A domed chamber of copper and bronze, with a circular table not unlike the Ultor Martius aboard the *Speranza* at its heart. A three-dimensional hologram of the Icon Mechanicus hung suspended over the table, and seated around it were eleven magi of the Adeptus Mechanicus.

All were robed in black or red, their vestments crisp and fresh-looking as their wearers remembered them in life. As varied an assembly of tech-priests as any she had seen, all had an air of great antiquity to them. If what she remembered of Galatea was to be trusted, then these were the magi it had ensnared in its web over the last three thousand years.

<Who are you?> said Linya, knowing better than to immediately trust anything Galatea showed her. <Are you… like me?>

She saw their immediate consternation, looking at her through a variety of cumbersome-looking optic stalks and glittering augmented crystals as though she was speaking in some dead language. Linya saw they looked to a female tech-priest in the chequered-edged robes of a Mechanicus Envoy. Alone of the gathered tech-priests, her head was bare, and Linya was struck by the resemblance she saw to herself.

Noospheric tags identified her as Magos Syriestte, and Linya remembered the name from the transcript of Archmagos Kotov's first interrogation of Galatea. Typically of envoys of the Mechanicus, the woman's features were largely organic, the better to liaise with those who preferred to deal with an approximation of a human face.

Childishly simple binary streamed between the assembled priests and Magos Syriestte in an interleaved babble. Syriestte held up a hand to silence them and rose smoothly from the table. The Envoy's lower limbs had been amputated and replaced with a repulsor pod and a series of multi-jointed manipulator arms. She floated over the table, her clicking, articulated lower limbs moving as though swimming her through the air.

<Magos Syriestte,> said Linya. <I am Linya Tychon, but I assume you already know that.>

Syriestte cocked her head to one side and her answer was formed in binaric cant that was absurdly simple, devoid of any hexamathic complexity or subtlety.

Linya repeated herself, but it was clear that neither Syriestte or any of the other tech-priests had understood her. Then it hit Linya why Galatea had first spoken to her in archaic cant and why her binary was as impenetrable to these adepts as xeno-dialect.

She rerouted her binarics through the simplest converter she still possessed and tried again.

<Welcome, Adept Tychon,> said Syriestte with a smile. <Yes, we are just like you. Victims of Galatea.>

<None of you are implanted with hexamathic augments, are you?>

<Hexamathics?> replied Syriestte. <I am familiar with the term, but when I was last part of the Adeptus Mechanicus, research into that mythical branch of linguistic binary had been all but abandoned.>

Linya shook her head. <No, Magos Zimmen perfected her code when her mission to the Aextrom Nebula uncovered a workable rosetta fragment of a hexamathic encryption. It allowed her to build the specialised cognitive implants that make elevating binary to a geometrically denser level of complexity possible.>

Syriestte smiled. <It pleases me to know that the Quest for Knowledge continues. Join us, please, and allow me to introduce you to your fellow adepts. Magos Haephaestus and Magos Natala have been debating the relative merits of the Rite of Carbon Bonding over the Canticles of Osmotic Attachment in regards to a theory Magos Kleinhenz has postulated in relation to Alchymical Attraction. We would welcome your input.>

Linya took hold of Syriestte's arm as she rotated to face the table once more. Her grip was firm and unyielding, preventing Syriestte from moving.

<No,> said Linya. <I had my skull cut open and my brain removed without my consent. I am a prisoner in a shared neuromatrix. I'm going to fight, and I'm going to beat Galatea. I'm going to stop whatever it's trying to do.>

One of Syriestte's manipulator arms gently removed Linya's hand.

<An understandable reaction,> she said, with just the right level of empathy, <but an entirely pointless one. All of us initially expressed

a similar sentiment, but I assure you, there is no way to escape the neuromatrix.>

<I don't accept that,> said Linya.

<Your acceptance or otherwise changes nothing,> said Syriestte. <It does not alter the fact that you are bound to this neuromatrix or the fact that your mental degradation will only be hastened if you try and fight your situation.>

<Ave Deus Mechanicus!> cried Linya. <Don't you want to fight? Don't you want to make Galatea pay for what it's done to us?>

<Believe me, others have tried to fight Galatea,> said Syriestte, sweeping a warning gaze around the table as the other magi leaned forwards at Linya's impassioned words.

Syriestte directed her next words at them as much as Linya.

<Those who attempted to fight Galatea were punished for their resistance, and a mind can be tortured in ways far more terrible than a meat body. Galatea stimulated the fear centres in their brains, magnifying their every nightmare a thousandfold. It made them experience the worst pain they had ever known over and over again. It drove them to madness, leaving them little better than mindless thought scraps with only a fragment of consciousness left to scream in horror at their fate. It did not matter to Galatea that each brain's loss degraded its own functionality. It revels in the suffering of others and such experiences are worth a little sacrifice.>

<I don't care,> said Linya. <I will find a way to make it pay for what it's done to me. What it's done to all of us.>

Syriestte shook her head and drifted back to her place at the table.

<You will change your mind,> she said. <Or it will be changed for you.>

<No,> said Linya, switching to higher forms of hexamathic binary as the beginnings of an idea formed. <Do you hear me, Galatea? I'm going to fight you. I'm going to destroy you! Do you hear me!>

Linya didn't doubt that Galatea logged everything said within its neuromatrix, but her furious words provoked no response from the machine intelligence.

But she had neither expected nor desired one.

'Weapons hot,' said Ven Anders. 'Halo formation on me.'

Despite the multitude of crystalline weaponry aimed at them, the Cadians lifted their lasrifles to their shoulders and fell into a defensive formation around their colonel.

Kotov stepped forwards with his hands raised, as though this unfolding drama could be resolved with diplomacy.

'Archmagos Telok,' said Kotov. 'Please, let us all take a breath and think this through. We have travelled halfway across the galaxy to find you and your technology. With all you have achieved, you will return to Mars in triumph. You will be feted as a hero, an exemplar of all the Mechanicus strives to be. All you desire will be yours – renown, riches, resources... Just let us bring you back and we can forget that such incendiary words were ever spoken in the heat of the moment.'

'You are wasting your time, Archmagos Kotov,' said Surcouf. 'Telok means to kill us all and take the *Speranza*. That has been his intention since the moment we landed. The only reason we're alive right now is that Telok's colossal ego wouldn't let him just take the ship without us knowing why.'

'No, no, no,' said Kotov, shaking his head and waving away the rogue trader's words with a golden arm of his cybernetic suit. 'You have this all wrong, Surcouf,' said Kotov. 'All wrong.'

Telok took a step towards Kotov.

'No, I am afraid Master Surcouf is right,' said Telok. 'But rather than thinking of my actions as egotistical, consider my allowing you to live this long a last gift. To see the Breath of the Gods in all its glory before you all die is an honour few others will receive.'

'Kotov, step away from the traitor,' said Anders.

'We are all servants of the Omnissiah and the Emperor,' pleaded Kotov, a man alone with his last hope of redemption turned to ash in the face of Telok's betrayal.

'Kotov!' repeated Anders. 'You *really* need to listen to me.'

'You name yourself a god,' said Surcouf. 'But there's only one being in the Imperium worthy of that title. And you're not the Emperor.'

'Not yet,' said Telok.

Bielanna fought to hold on to her perception of the present in the face of the spinning maelstrom of glittering silver metal below her. The distortion in the skein had its origin with this *Caoineag*. She blinked away tears, feeling the temporal deformations it created just by existing.

'What madman would create such monstrous technology?'

'The mon-keigh,' said Ariganna, perched atop the ironwork railings of the gantry overlooking the bickering ape-creatures below. 'Who else?'

Bielanna shook her head. Sensory aftershocks exploded in her mind. A rock in a pool of potential futures. She saw the humans killing one another, the eldar dropping into their midst and slaughtering them all. She saw Lexell Kotov die a thousand times, a thousand different ways.

Torn apart by the crystalline beasts scurrying across the surface of this vast space like loathsome caricatures of warp spiders. Killed by a blast of green light from a glassy energy beam. Hurled to his death from the gantry.

Futures branched and split a thousand times and then a thousand more, but in each one where the mon-keigh died in this chamber one certainty emerged. Inviolable and unchanging in its outcome.

She saw the eldar die and this world torn asunder.

As fixed a moment in the skein as anything in the past, this world's doom would set in motion a cascade of death and destruction on a galactic scale. The murder the Lost Magos would unleash with his horrific technology would dwarf the death toll of even the greatest wars of ancient days.

Ariganna shook her head and gave a snort of soft laughter.

'It seems the mon-keigh are doing our killing for us,' she said, sheathing her blade. 'The bloodshed has already begun.'

Bielanna pulled herself towards the gantry, lurching as the collisions of past and future came in waves. Ariganna looked back at her and Bielanna saw the trifold transformations weave through the exarch in rapid succession. The potential of Ariganna's death loomed closer than ever.

The path of *all* their deaths hovered within a hair's breadth of becoming inescapable.

Life and death. Spinning. Hanging on a slender, fraying thread.

'No,' said Bielanna, seeing the fighting below and following the one path she had never expected to tread. 'I see it now... Kotov's death is not the answer... it never was.'

A glassy blade slashed over Roboute's head. He ducked and put a high-powered las-round through the crystalith's head. The intense heat of the shot bloomed within its skull, vaporising the microscopic machines animating the creature. It halted, frozen like an ice sculpture straddling the railings of the gantry.

Another rose up next to it, blasts of green energy flashing from its tine-bladed fists. A flurry of whickering Cadian las-bolts blasted it from the railing in pieces. Roboute scrambled away as more zipping green darts of killing light slashed overhead. A portion of the gantry vanished in a flare of hissing fire as a bolt impacted next to him.

'Ilanna!' called Roboute, seeing a crystalith drop to the gantry behind the *Renard*'s tech-priest. Unlike him, she wasn't armed. The crystalith extruded a pair of glittering hook-blades, limned with green fire. Ilanna screamed and extended her mechadendrites towards the

creature, unleashing a torrent of dissonant binary that made Roboute flinch with sudden, gut-wrenching nausea.

The crystalith's torso exploded in a fan of broken glass.

Roboute low-crawled over to Pavelka, still queasy at the after-effects of her binaric attack.

'How in the Emperor's name did you do that?'

A tech-priest's expression was never easy to read, but Roboute knew Pavelka well enough to see a mixture of shame and horror.

'Some old and very bad code I should have deleted a long time ago,' said Pavelka. 'But you know what they say, the Mechanicus–'

Before she could finish, Kotov's savants and menials were gunned down before they even knew what was happening. Kotov's servo-skulls flitted away overhead in panic as he took refuge behind his frozen skitarii.

A shot grazed Ilanna's shoulder. Metal, not flesh, thankfully.

'This gantry is a terrible place to defend!' yelled Ilanna.

'You have anywhere better?' answered Roboute.

Crystaliths surrounded them, front and rear, above and below, and Roboute suspected there was only one reason they weren't already dead. He picked himself up and ran hunched over to where Ven Anders's Cadians were pushing down the gantry towards an entrance farther along the wall. They were leaving bodies in their wake, each yard won with the life of a Cadian Guardsman.

Roboute now saw why Telok had kept them moving away from the entrance to the chamber: to better isolate them from any means of escape.

The Black Templars and skitarii remained unmoving. The power armour of the Space Marines was blistering and splitting under repeated impacts. It would only be a matter of time until the warriors within were killed.

'Surcouf,' shouted Anders, loosing a pair of shots into a crystalith descending from an upper level. It fell from the wall, falling into the ochre mist below with the sound of breaking glass. 'You're alive.'

'We have to get close to Telok!' shouted Roboute, snapping off another two shots towards the gantry. Anders gave him a look of disbelief.

'What?' he said, snapping a powercell into the grip of his pistol. 'Are you insane?'

'The only reason these crystal things didn't gun us down straight away was because Telok was too close to us,' said Roboute, ducking as sizzling bolts of green fire flashed past his head. 'We have to get closer.'

Telok's face was sheathed in a rippling layer of translucent crystal,

yet even through that distorting mask, Roboute saw the god-complex that thousands of years of isolation and autonomy had birthed.

In the midst of the violence, Kotov stepped from behind his ranked skitarii and held his arms up in frantic supplication.

'End this madness, Telok!' cried Kotov in desperation.

In response, Telok's crystal-sheathed Dreadnought limbs reached down and tore Kotov's golden arms from his mechanised body.

Archmagos Kotov reeled in horror, once again taking refuge within his skitarii. Acrid floodstream gushed from his ruined shoulders. The pungent reek of burned oils hazed the air with their potency. Telok crashed towards him, bludgeoning one of the paralysed skitarii to ruin against the wall. Telok's distorted laughter brayed through his crystalline helm as he hurled another over the gantry and scorched a third to ash.

Roboute ran forwards as Telok's energy claw reached down to tear Archmagos Kotov's head from his golden body.

A deafening howl echoed through the enormous cavern.

It was a nerve-shredding scream of furious, ancient hunger that sent shrieking surges of agony along every nerve in Roboute's body. The pain was incredible, like a searing, life-ending seizure.

He dropped to his knees, hands clamped over his ears.

Nor were the effects of the deathly howl confined to creatures of flesh and blood. The crystaliths glitched and spasmed as their arcane connection to their master was disrupted.

Even as Roboute felt a measure of control returning to his limbs, a giant of palest ivory and emerald slammed down on the gantry in front of him.

It buckled the metal with its weight.

Roboute blinked in shock.

The giant's slender limbs were graceful in a way no human machine could ever be. A long-bladed sword of milky white porcelain snapped from its wrist.

In his time with the Alaitocii, Roboute had heard of the giant warrior-constructs known as wraithlords, but had never seen one.

The sight before him made him wish that were still the case.

The wraithlord's enlarged gauntlet caught Telok's descending fist and turned it from Kotov's head. The claw tore through the wall in a squealing howl of tearing metallic cables. The wraithlord brought its other arm around and the white blade sliced cleanly through the hybrid crystalline structure of Telok's arm.

A barrage of green fire from the crystals growing from Telok's chest staggered the wraithlord, crawling over its sinuously lethal form like living flames.

Then other figures were landing amid the crystaliths.

Lithe dancers with red-plumed helms and swords of bone. Hunched killers in segmented armour with crackling arcs of lightning wreathing their jaws. Inhumanly proportioned and unnaturally fast.

They fell upon the paralysed crystaliths in a hurricane of blades and biting energy bolts, shattering scores to fragments in the time it took to draw breath.

'Eldar,' said Roboute. 'They're eldar...'

'How in the name of the Eye did *they* get here?' said Anders, running forwards to haul him to his feet.

Roboute shook his head. 'Does it matter? They're helping us.'

Anders shrugged, accepting the logic of it even as he kept firing into the crystaliths.

Telok and the wraithlord rained titanic blows upon one another. Bolts tore loose from the rocky walls with the fury of their struggle. The gantry creaked and swayed.

'Come on!' shouted Anders.

The Cadian was just as shocked at the appearance of the xenos, but wasn't about to waste the chance to escape that their arrival had given them. He shouted at his Guardsmen to move.

'Eldar...?' said Roboute, as a nagging, insistent voice at the back of his mind told him that he knew *exactly* how they'd come to be here.

But the memory wouldn't cohere, wouldn't make itself known.

A sinuous figure landed in front of Telok with preternatural grace, one hand extended before her, the other clutching a heavily inscribed staff of entwined bone and silver. It rippled with coruscating light that burned into Roboute's retinas.

Obviously female, she wore a cloak of interlocking geometric forms over curved plates of armour inscribed with runic symbols that were at once familiar and strange to him.

'Farseer,' said Roboute, the memory of this woman growing clearer in his mind. He remembered a darkened vault in a forgotten deck of the *Speranza,* where dust lay thick and memories even thicker. Where he'd stood before the statue of Magos Vahihva of Pharses and vowed to remember him.

And just as he remembered Magos Vahihva, so too did the memory of the farseer unlock within him.

'Bielanna Faerelle of Biel-Tan,' he said, as eldritch fire surged around her and Telok retreated from the psychic tempest. The wraithlord stepped away, the elemental fury of the farseer's attack driving the two foes apart.

The eldar psychic barrage had one other effect.

Roboute saw the Black Templars and the two remaining skitarii finally throw off the effects of Telok's code. He saw Tanna's fervent desire to take the fight to the Lost Magos, to empty his bolter's magazine into the enemy who plotted the death of the Emperor.

But even the Black Templars were driven back by the howling gales of the psychic storm. With the air alive with immaterial energies, Roboute felt the hatred of the Templars for these aliens and what they had done. Varda drew his sword, his movements stiff and like those of a man recently awoken. The Emperor's Champion looked to his sergeant, eager to avenge Kul Gilad's death, but Tanna shook his head.

Roboute had never witnessed such enormous restraint, and doubted he ever would again.

The psyker's horned helm turned to him, and he felt the white heat of her intent pin him in place.

'Take him,' she ordered, pushing the stricken form of Archmagos Kotov towards him. 'Take your leader from this place. He must not die here!'

Roboute and the skitarii took hold of Kotov, but the mass of the wounded archmagos threatened to drag them to the gantry.

Then Bracha and Yael were at Roboute's side, and even with their armour operating far below par, the Templars easily bore Kotov's weight.

'Take him where?' said Roboute.

'Through the sunset gate, Surcouf,' said Bielanna.

'The what?'

The farseer thrust her staff forwards, and a spot of illumination appeared on the wall, like a welding torch burning through a thin sheet of metal. Too bright to look upon directly, it expanded rapidly into a brilliant ellipse of sunlight. Glittering breath gusted from the gateway, together with the sound of laughter and tears, the heat of the desert and the ice of polar wastelands.

'Go!' shouted the farseer, her voice taut with the effort of opening the portal. 'All of you! I can hold the gate for moments only. You must trust me.'

'Why should we?' snarled Tanna. 'You killed our Reclusiarch.'

'What choice do you have, mon-keigh?'

The crystaliths began moving with a creak of glass on glass, finally overcoming the disruption of the eldar battle howl.

'None,' said Roboute, plunging through the gate.

MACROCONTENT COMMENCEMENT:

+++MACROCONTENT 002+++

The machine-spirit guards the knowledge of the Ancients.

Microcontent 06

Blaylock was used to Kryptaestrex and Azuramagelli bickering, but now more than just time was at stake. The bulky, robotic form of Kryptaestrex was a product of western hemisphere learning, logical, analytical and objective by nature. Azuramagelli, with his subdivided brain-portions distributed through his latticework form, was pure eastern hemisphere: intuitive, thoughtful, and subjective.

Blaylock knew that, like most such stereotypes, this notion was little more than a myth, yet time and time again it was borne out by those trained in different forges of Mars.

The two senior bridge adepts stood before the *Speranza*'s command throne, where Blaylock had been trying in vain for hours to contact Archmagos Kotov. Mechanicus regulations required ship-to-surface vox to be maintained at regular intervals, but the atmospheric conditions of Archmagos Telok's forge world made a mockery of such protocols.

<An atmospheric geoformer vessel,> said Azuramagelli, the right-most of his brain excisions flickering with synaptic activity. <Set its processing reactors to maximum tolerances and it could clear enough of the distortion to allow the establishment of vox.>

Kryptaestrex's single, unblinking eye-lens flared in irritation.

<And I keep telling you that simply dropping an atmospheric geoformer vessel to the level of the thermopause will be insufficient to break Exnihlio's electromagnetic distortion.>

<You have a better idea?> demanded Azuramagelli.

<Doing the opposite of anything you suggest would be a better idea than risking so precious a vessel in that planet's atmosphere without safe passage.>

<You are quick to decry my suggestions while making none of your own,> said Azuramagelli. <Perhaps because you *have* no ideas of your own.>

<A linked chain of astrogation servitor probes,> said Kryptaestrex.

<Ah, now we come to the hub of the matter. You will not risk your own assets, but you are happy to risk mine?>

<Enough,> snapped Blaylock, his cant authoritative and final. <You forget that *none* of these assets are yours. They belong to the Adeptus Mechanicus, and, precious though each artefact is, I will expend them all if it means we can reach the archmagos. Am I making myself clear?>

<Clear indeed, Tarkis,> replied Kryptaestrex, folding his heavy manipulator arms across the Icon Mechanicus bolted to his chest.

<Azuramagelli?>

<Yes, Fabricatus Locum,> said Azuramagelli. <Your instructions are clear. Do you yourself have a suggestion?>

Satisfied the squabbling magi understood the gravity of the situation, Blaylock said, <Employ every means at your disposal. Kryptaestrex, despatch two of your atmospheric geoformers to begin the cleansing of the upper reaches of the atmosphere.>

Blaylock read the satisfaction in Azuramagelli's noospheric aura that his suggestion had been acted upon, but the Fabricatus Locum wasn't yet done.

<Magos Azuramagelli,> he said. <Magos Kryptaestrex's suggestion also has merit, and combined with the potential for scrubbed atmospherics, a chain of astrogation probes would exponentially increase our chances of establishing vox with the archmagos. Plot the optimal position for your probes and launch them as soon as you are able.>

Azuramagelli signified his assent, and the magi retreated to their stations, hurling binaric insults at one another the entire way.

Blaylock ignored it and smoothed out his robes, black and etched with representations of the divine circuitry. The green optics pulsed beneath his hood and he waved his gaggle of dwarf-servitors forward to rearrange the floodstream cables that regulated the flow of blessed chemicals sustaining his delicately balanced bio-cybernetic form. With a thought, he introduced a blend of stimulants and synaptic enhancers. They would increase his cognitive processing power, but would render the biological components of his body sluggish for a time.

A trade-off Blaylock was more than willing to accept.

He sensed the presence of the loathsome machine-hybrid even before it spoke to him. After what it had done to Mistress Tychon, Blaylock could barely bring himself to look at it.

'Your magi bicker like novices,' said Galatea. 'We would chasten them with data-purgatives and parameter-violating power overloads. We would not tolerate dissent.'

'Properly mediated, a little rivalry between underlings is never a bad thing,' replied Blaylock, not wishing to engage with the creature, but knowing he had little choice. Its virtual hijacking of the *Speranza*'s systems gave it unprecedented power over the ship's supposed commander.

'We see nothing but antagonism between Azuramagelli and Kryptaestrex,' said Galatea. 'We would have dispensed with one of them long before now.'

'Adepts Kryptaestrex and Azuramagelli are vital components of this ship's functionality,' said Blaylock, finally turning to face Galatea. Its grossly asymmetrical body was an affront to his sense of order, almost as much as its artificially evolved machine intelligence was an affront to his faith.

The brain jars supported on its palanquin body rippled in distorting fluids, each festooned with connective wires, implant spikes and biorhythm monitors.

Which one belonged to Mistress Tychon?

Galatea saw him looking and laughed, the sound a harsh bray of machine noise that scraped along Blaylock's spine.

'Archmagos Kotov has been grossly negligent to allow their continued mutual antipathy to impair the efficiency of his bridge crew,' said Galatea.

'Then I should thank the Omnissiah that, while you may hold us hostage aboard our own ship, this is *not* your bridge.'

'True, it is not, and if Archmagos Kotov does not return, it might yet be yours. Do not pretend that the thought has not already crossed your mind.'

Blaylock shook his head. 'Kotov will return. The Omnissiah would not have shown him the signs and given us the grace to overcome so much to reach this place only for us to fail now.'

'You think the Omnissiah brought you here?' asked Galatea.

'Of course.'

'You are wrong.'

Despite his better judgement, Blaylock could not resist such obvious bait.

'If not the Omnissiah, then who?'

Galatea looked at Blaylock strangely, its hooded head cocked to one side and its silver eyes dimmed as though unsure as to his true meaning.

'Archmagos Telok led you here,' it said. 'We thought you knew that.'

Blaylock released a sigh of incense-filtered breath, relieved Galatea appeared to be talking in metaphysical riddles.

'Archmagos Telok has been lost for thousands of years.'

'And you honestly believe his reach does not extend from beyond the edge of the galaxy to the heart of the Imperium?' chuckled Galatea. 'Tell us, Magos Blaylock, how plausible is it that the string of astronomically unlikely events needed to bring the *Speranza* here might have occurred in so fortuitous a sequence? How likely is it that *you* would be brought here? The protégé of Magos Alhazen of Sinus Sabeus, an adept fanatically devoted to the continuance of Archmagos Telok's philosophies? The very adept who sent Roboute Surcouf's ships to the Arax system, where the saviour beacon of the *Tomioka* was miraculously found?'

'The Fabricator General himself seconded me to the *Speranza*,' said Blaylock, unwilling to concede anything to Galatea.

'So the inloaded explorator-dockets testify,' agreed Galatea. 'But why would he assign someone who, on the face of things, was already predisposed to believe the mission a fool's errand?'

'To ensure Kotov's desperation did not lose the Ark Mechanicus,' snapped Blaylock. 'To act as the eyes of Mars!'

'By a Fabricator General who served his first three centuries in the Cult Mechanicus alongside Magos Alhazen. Coincidence? You know the statistical unlikelihood of such things, Tarkis. Think on that, and then tell us it was not Telok who brought you here.'

Galatea turned away and clattered along the central nave of the bridge on its mismatched legs.

Blaylock watched it go, feeling the solid adamantium upon which he had built his life crumble like the shifting red sands of the Tithonius Lacus.

Rearing towers of insulated distribution pipework filled the vaulted chamber like looping coils of intestinal tract. Far beneath the surface of Exnihlio, they soared to its distant ceiling and plunged to shadowed depths an unknown distance below. Lightning arced between them and the air crackled with the barely caged force of titanic energies being wrought by subterranean generators and the unimaginable geological forces at work in the planet's core.

Thunderous engines pounded within each column, the sound filling the chamber with a booming mechanical heartbeat.

And this was but one of tens of thousands of such chambers.

On suspended walkways and floating control stations, near-blind servitors, wretched and wasted things, toiled to maintain the machines. Hairless and emaciated, few resembled the forms they had once known.

The only light was the light flickering between the towers.

Or at least it was until a golden radiance spilled over a cantilevered control platform overlooking the plunging canyons of power distribution. It illuminated the deck plates like the sunlight that could never reach this deep.

First one, then more figures spilled from the light. Like soldiers pouring from the burning wreck of a transport vehicle, they cried out in terror and confusion, scrambling away from the scintillating light of the webway gate.

Roboute Surcouf was the first onto the deck, quickly followed by Ilanna Pavelka. Their eyes were wide and fearful, horrified by the things they had seen, but would never fully remember, save in their nightmares. The wounded figure of Archmagos Kotov came next, held upright only by the strength of Yael and Bracha of the Black Templars. The two skitarii emerged, trailing a handful of stoic Cadians and their colonel.

The eldar ghosted through without effort, quickly followed by the rest of the Black Templars.

Both forces spread out, hostile and wary.

Each expecting treachery from the other.

Last to come through the portal was Bielanna, and no sooner had her feet touched the steel plating of the chamber's floor than she collapsed, drained utterly by the cost of opening a path through the webway.

The sunset gate winked out of existence with a bang of air rushing to fill its void. The golden light vanished, and Bielanna let out a shuddering breath of soul-deep weariness.

Roboute picked himself up, dizzy from travelling in such a wondrous yet fearful way. The world around him felt somehow *thin*, as though it were simply a facade protecting him from deeper, more terrifyingly real perceptions. For once in his life, Roboute was thankful for his limited human senses.

At least when humans travelled the warp, they were shielded from the worst of its effects by a Geller field.

The webway afforded no such protection.

Yael and Bracha gently lowered Kotov to the ground. The eyes of the archmagos were tightly closed. His head shook with pain and recriminatory binary spilled from his augmitters. Roboute didn't know what bio-feedback technology Kotov possessed, but suspected the source of his pain was more to do with Telok's treachery than any physical sensations.

One skitarii warrior stood over the wounded archmagos, the other bent to his damaged shoulders. Dispensing tools from a cavity within his chest, the cybernetically enhanced warrior began to efficiently and wordlessly seal off the squirting floodstream pipes and isolate hopelessly damaged circuitry.

Roboute knelt beside the skitarii, a brute of a warrior with metallic implants running the width of his shoulders, spine and upper arms. A shoulder-mounted cannon was locked on a rotating scapula mount, and his right arm was a heavily modified power claw with an integral lascarbine.

'Is he going to die?' asked Roboute.

'Not if you shut up and let me work,' growled the warrior without looking up.

'We can help,' said Roboute.

The warrior lifted his ironclad head and bared sharpened steel teeth. Roboute flinched at the raw hostility in his eyes.

The warrior saw Pavelka and said, '*You* can't. Her. Just her.'

Roboute waved Pavelka forwards and a crackling stream of binary passed between her and the skitarii. Roboute left them to it, seeing that Kotov's living or dying might become a moot point in a second.

With the farseer on her knees, helmet hung low with its visor pressed to the deck, the eldar warriors were acting on their own authority.

Tanna, Yael, Bracha, Issur and Varda formed a kill ring as the sinuously lethal xeno-killers moved to encircle them. Ven Anders and his Cadians had their lasguns tight to their shoulders, each man tracking an alien warrior.

The eldar had their guns and blades at the ready. All it would take was a single spark to turn this standoff into a bloodbath.

'Suffer… n-not the alien to live,' stuttered Issur through gritted teeth. Though his nervous system had been ruined in the fires of an electrostatic charger on the Valette Manifold station, the tip of his sword was unwavering. Varda had his black blade at his shoulder, tensed and ready to strike.

'Brother Issur, stop talking!' cried Roboute, seeing the eldar tense at his words in expectation of a killing order.

'Lower your blades or you all die,' promised a warrior in armour of gold, jade and ivory.

Roboute knew an exarch when he saw one, and was well aware that she could make good on her threat. Her movements reminded him of the camouflage predators of Espandor's forests, feline hunters whose prey never even knew they were a target until it was too late.

Yael and Bracha had their weapons tracking the woman, but Roboute doubted even their aim was good enough to hit her.

Towering over the eldar was the wraithlord, its glossy armour blackened and corroded by Telok's fire. To fight against such a monster would be suicide, but that didn't seem to matter to the Black Templars.

Roboute put himself between the Space Marines and the eldar, his arms held out before him. He couldn't help remembering what had happened to Archmagos Kotov when he had tried a similar tack to prevent violence.

'No one do anything stupid here,' he said. 'We just escaped certain death, so let's not do Telok's work for him.'

'These xenos killed Kul Gilad,' said Bracha. 'The Blood of Sigismund demands vengeance.'

'One mon-keigh life?' demanded the exarch, her enormous chainsabre held out before her. 'By your actions are scores of my kin dead. For that alone I should slay you a thousand times over.'

'Then why haven't you?' demanded Tanna.

Roboute sighed. 'Do you *want* her to kill you?'

He turned to the exarch and dug deep for his recall of the eldar language. 'Greetings, exarch. I am Roboute Surcouf of Ultramar, rogue trader and loyal servant of the Emperor. We thank you for your aid, and offer no violence to you or your kin.'

The exarch couldn't hide her surprise at Roboute's use of her language, and he hoped his pronunciation wasn't so poor as to get them all killed by unwittingly insulting her family lineage.

'You speak our language,' said the exarch. 'Alaitocii inflexions with a crude human tongue. I should kill you for befouling it.'

'But you won't,' said Roboute.

'What makes you so sure?'

Roboute pointed towards Bielanna. 'Because she told you to save us, didn't she? She's had a vision of some sort. She's seen that if we die here, something very bad is going to happen, right?'

The exarch lowered her blade, but her posture didn't relax one iota. Roboute knew she could go from stationary to murdering him in a heartbeat, but he'd guessed right.

'Listen,' he said, switching back to Low Gothic and addressing both the eldar and the Black Templars. 'The bad blood between us is over, finished. Done with. It has to be or we're all going to die here. The fact of the matter is that we're trapped on this planet with a madman who wants to kill us and steal our way home. Now, do any of us *want* to die? I'm going to go ahead and assume the answer to that is no, and suggest we put aside our differences and work together while we have a common enemy.'

'Fight along… alongside xenos?' demanded Issur.

'It's happened before,' said Roboute. 'I've seen Ultramarines make war with eldar allies. I just hope you can understand that cooperation offers us the best chance of survival.'

'You are correct, Roboute Surcouf of Ultramar,' said Bielanna, rising smoothly to her feet and removing her helmet. The face Roboute had last seen aboard the *Speranza* was paler than he remembered, the farseer's elliptical eyes dulled and sunk deeper into her oval face. Her scarlet hair was still beaded with crystals and gemstones, but two ice-white streaks now reached back from her temples.

She came towards him with such grace that it was as though she moved over ice. 'I *have* seen dark things in the skein,' said Bielanna. 'Things this mon-keigh Telok's lunacy will unleash upon the galaxy unless we can drag the future from its current path. So make no mistake, we do not fight *with* you, we fight to stop Telok from ever leaving this world.'

'Then our purposes align,' said Archmagos Kotov.

Roboute turned to see the master of the *Speranza* standing with Pavelka and his two skitarii. Black fluid oozed from the seals applied to his shoulders, but at least he was upright.

'For now,' said Bielanna.

'I didn't know,' said Kotov. 'How could I possibly have known what madness had claimed Telok?'

Bielanna's fists clenched and she all but spat her words in Kotov's face.

'Because nothing in your species's behaviour would ever suggest any other possibility,' she snapped. 'You ask me how you could have known? I say how could you have expected anything different?'

'So how did you do it?' asked Coyne.

'I don't know,' replied Abrehem, holding out his augmetic arm as though it might suddenly turn on him. 'I had my hand on the book of quantum runes and it just sort of… happened.'

Hawke grunted, and Abrehem couldn't decide if the sound was derisive laughter or he was choking on the meat product in his stew paste. He wasn't sure which he'd prefer.

They sat on the wide-based plinth of *Virtanen*, the lifter-rig Coyne

and Hawke worked in Turentek's prow forge. An overseer called Naiiorz had taken over Abrehem's position in the command throne atop the towering lifter, but he seldom bothered to disconnect from the noosphere until the end of the shift.

Across from them, the crew of *Wulfse* eyed Abrehem's visit to his old rig-crew warily. Especially a man with a badly rendered wolfshead electoo on his skull and a stained bandage wrapping his chest and shoulder.

'What in Thor's name are you lot looking at?' Hawke shouted over to them. 'You want him to get his psychotic friend back?'

The man looked down, and his fellow bondsmen slunk away.

'Hawke, shut up,' hissed Abrehem.

Hawke grinned and slapped a comradely hand on Abrehem's shoulder that was purely for show. Hawke cared for no one but Hawke.

'Just letting the masses see what good friends you and I are,' said Hawke. 'Doesn't do my reputation as a man with friends in high places any harm.'

'I almost got one of them killed.'

'You mean Rasselas X-42 almost got one of them killed,' said Coyne, ever ready with a correction where none was needed.

Rasselas X-42 was an arco-flagellant that had bonded with Abrehem during the eldar's aborted boarding action. The cyborg killer had become Abrehem's unlooked-for protector, and came close to killing the *Wulfse*'s crewman when he'd threatened his charge.

Abrehem could still see the blood pouring from the man as the arco-flagellant skewered his shoulder with one blade-flail and held the sharpened tips of the other millimetres from his eye.

'Can't say the bastard didn't deserve it,' said Hawke. 'Man can't run a rig worth a damn.'

'And you've been working rigs for, what, a few weeks?' said Abrehem. 'Suddenly you're an expert?'

'Better than him,' grumbled Hawke. 'Anyway, where is the big lad? He was handy to have around, what with Crusha getting his head cut off.'

'He's gone,' said Abrehem.

'Yeah, but where?'

'Do you really think I'm going to tell you?' said Abrehem.

'Why not?'

'Because you'd only try and get him out and use him like you used Crusha,' said Abrehem.

'And that's a bad thing, why?' said Hawke. 'After all, never hurts to have someone who can rip a man's arms off watching your back. You don't need him now, so why stop someone else having a turn with the good stuff?'

'*Good stuff*? X-42 was a mass murderer,' said Abrehem. 'He slaughtered millions of people before they turned him into an arco-flagellant. I've seen through his eyes, Hawke, and trust me, that's not someone you want "watching your back".'

Hawke shrugged. 'Fair enough,' he said. 'If you think he's too dangerous, then that's good enough for me.'

'Really?'

'What, you think I'm going to try and find a deranged killer on my own and use him to further my own ends?'

Abrehem and Coyne both nodded.

Hawke grinned and threw up his hands. 'Oh, Thor's ghost, save me from these untrustworthy, suspicious souls!'

Abrehem and Coyne both laughed, but before they could say any more, Totha Mu-32 appeared from behind *Wulfse*'s baseplate and strode purposefully towards them.

'Here comes your new best friend,' sneered Hawke, all traces of the easy familiarity they'd just shared snuffed out in a heartbeat. 'Off to take you to spark school.'

'Shut up, Hawke.'

'So you're going to be one of them now, is that it?' said Hawke, nodding in the direction of Magos Turentek's bulky ceiling-rig as it clattered over the vault of the prow forge. 'When me and Coyne here next see you are we going to have to bow and scrape to you? Yes, magos, no, magos… by your leave, magos.'

The venom in Hawke's voice was bitter, but not unexpected.

'Of course not,' said Abrehem. 'But after all we achieved when we took the servitors offline, showing the Mechanicus that they can't treat us like animals, I think I can make a real difference if I become a magos. More than I can as a bondsman, that's for sure.'

'Oh, so you're an idealist,' laughed Hawke. 'You're going to change the Adeptus Mechanicus from within all on your own?'

'One man can start a landslide with the casting of a single pebble,' said Abrehem.

'What's that?'

'A quote,' said Abrehem. 'I think Sebastian Thor said it. Or some cardinal, I don't remember. But the point is that maybe I *can* make a difference. Maybe I *can* make things better. At least I have to try.'

'You're no Sebastian Thor,' said Hawke.

'You're a piece of work, Hawke, you know that?' said Coyne.

'What are you talking about?' said Hawke, and his betrayed expression at Coyne's support for Abrehem was laughable.

'Can't you be happy for Abe?' said Coyne.

'Happy?' said Hawke. 'Didn't you hear me? He's going to be one of

them now! Give it a year and he'll be the one working you to death. He'll forget all about you and leave us down here in the shit, while he lords it over us like some inbred hive-king!'

'I've known men like you before, Hawke,' said Abrehem. 'You've got skills and you could actually *do* something with your life, but you're so consumed by jealousy that you'd rather tear down anyone else who achieves something than try to better yourself.'

'You haven't *achieved* anything, Abrehem Locke,' snapped Hawke. 'You inherited those eyes from your old man and if it wasn't for me getting hold of that faulty pistol you wouldn't have that arm. Handed to you on a silver platter, they were. You didn't *earn* being Machine-touched, it just came easy to you. What chance did the rest of us have with you around?'

Abrehem was incredulous.

'You're seriously saying I should *thank* you for getting my arm burned off?'

Hawke shrugged, but didn't answer as Totha Mu-32 finally reached *Virtanen*'s baseplate and looked up at them.

'Come, Abrehem, it is time to return to Adept Manubia's forge,' he said. 'We have a great deal to do, and no time to waste in idle banter.'

'Yeah,' said Hawke. 'Off you trot, Magos Locke. Don't want to be wasting time with the scum, eh?'

As councils of war went, Tanna had seldom seen stranger.

They gathered around a hexagonal control hub from which they had removed four servitors that appeared to have expired at their stations. Dust lay thick and undisturbed across their corpses and the control hub's numerous blank cathode ray panels.

He and Varda stood to one side of the hub, with Issur, Bracha and Yael a step behind. Roboute Surcouf and Ven Anders sat on its integral bench seats, taking the opportunity to rest. The Cadian had taken a burn to the arm from a crystalith weapon, but bore his wound without complaint. Magos Pavelka worked at an open panel on the hub, and Archmagos Kotov knelt at its base, rewiring the guts of its machinery with a trio of chain-like mechadendrites that unfurled from his back. Tied-off cables and spot-welded seams closed off his ruined shoulders where the skitarii had worked on his augmetic frame.

Opposite the Imperials stood the eldar witch, who Surcouf told him was called Bielanna. Next to her was a warrior named Ariganna Icefang.

Tanna had only seen her fight for a few fractions of a second, but that had been enough to convince him that when the time came to kill her – as it surely must – she would be a formidable foe.

The giant warrior-construct was also part of the council.

'Is it not a robot?' Varda asked Bielanna after the farseer identified it as Uldanaish Ghostwalker.

'No,' it said. 'I am not a robot and I can speak for myself.'

'Then is that a suit of armour?' asked Tanna. 'Is there a warrior within, like a Knight?'

'I do not *wear* this armour,' said Ghostwalker. 'I am part of it, and it is part of me.'

'Like a Dreadnought,' said Tanna.

'I am not like your Dreadnoughts,' said Ghostwalker, leaning in with his oval skull gleaming with reflected lightning.

'You're not?'

'No, I died many centuries ago.'

Varda made the sign of the aquila, but said no more, shooting Tanna a glare of disapproval. Before Tanna could denounce vile alien necromancy, the control hub sparked with life and a bass hum built from each of its six panels. Two immediately blew out in a shower of sparks and flame. Magos Pavelka extinguished them with gaseous spray from her mechadendrites.

The hub gradually returned to functionality, ancient circuits coaxed to life by Pavelka's ministrations and Kotov's binary incantations. Gem-like indicator buttons flickered and the screens crackled with what, to Tanna, looked like meaningless static.

Kotov stood, and despite the hub's reactivation, Tanna saw deep-rooted despair in his face. A weariness he knew all too well.

'There,' said Kotov. 'At least we might gain a better idea of where we are. Magos Pavelka, what manner of network is in place?'

'Hard to tell, archmagos,' said Pavelka, fighting the hub's decrepitude as much as its truculent machine-spirit. 'I'm used to more cooperative systems. This one's been dead for centuries and keeps trying to break my connection. I've fixed our position as best I can, but it's taking time to re-establish communion protocols with those hubs that are still functional.'

'I do not want excuses, adept, I want solutions.'

'Working on it, archmagos,' said Pavelka. 'I'm trying to access a hostile planetary network without sending up a flare that I am the one doing it and thereby announcing our presence.'

'Work faster,' said Kotov, and his mechadendrites retracted into the cavity from which they'd emerged. 'Time is not on our side.'

Pavelka nodded and kept working, fingers and mechadendrites dancing over the indicator buttons and brass dials.

'Can you use this machine to establish a link with your ship?' asked Bielanna.

'No,' said Pavelka. 'Every large-scale comms I've seen so far is locked down. Telok knows our personal vox can't cut through the atmospheric distortion, so he'll assume our first move will be to locate one powerful enough to contact the *Speranza*.'

'You are a witch, yes?' said Tanna, leaning forwards to address Bielanna.

She nodded, but it was Ariganna Icefang who answered. 'Bielanna Faerelle is a farseer, Templar. Use that word again and you will be drowning in your own blood before it leaves your lips.'

Tanna felt Varda's anger at the exarch's threat, and swallowed his own. For now. Until his armour had completed its purge of Telok's lockdown code, a duel between them was not something he wished to provoke.

'Very well,' he said. 'Then, *farseer*, can you open another of those... gateways? Can you get us back to your ship?'

'Or, better yet, the *Speranza*?' suggested Ven Anders.

'Our ship is no more,' said Bielanna. 'Your vessel's chrono-weapon crippled it within the Halo Scar. The *Starblade* was torn apart by its gravimetric tempests.'

'Then how did you get here?' asked Anders.

'We escaped to your vessel before ours was destroyed.'

'How?' demanded Kotov. 'The *Speranza* is shielded against such things.'

'A webway portal,' guessed Surcouf. 'Like the one that saved us from Telok.'

Bielanna gave the rogue trader a sidelong look.

Surcouf shrugged and said, 'You're not the first eldar I've met. Remember?'

Tanna remembered Surcouf's tale of being rescued from a wrecked Navy warship by an eldar vessel. Of how he had lived among the eldar of Alaitoc before being returned to Imperial space.

'You know a great deal of the eldar ways,' said Tanna.

'Some,' said Surcouf, quick to spot the implicit threat. 'Look, the eldar want to stop Telok leaving Exnihlio with the Breath of the Gods just as much as we do. So the sooner we figure out the best way to do that, the better chance we have of staying alive.'

Tanna nodded, accepting the rogue trader's word for now, and turned from Surcouf to address the eldar. 'I reiterate my question,' he said. 'Can you open another gateway? To the *Speranza* if your ship is no more.'

Bielanna shook her head and Tanna saw the exhaustion that went deep into her soul. 'No,' she said. 'To open a portal into the webway takes great power and concentration. Just getting my warriors onto this planet almost drained me completely. And opening the gate that allowed us to escape Telok... That cost me more than you can possibly know. In time, I will regain strength enough to open another portal, but not now.'

'Then do you have strength enough to send a message to one of your kind aboard the *Speranza*?' said Kotov.

'There are none of *my kind* left aboard your ship,' snapped Bielanna. 'We are all that remains.'

'Then send a message to one of the Cadian battle-psykers or one of my ship's astropaths,' snapped Kotov.

'Even if I could communicate with such primitive minds, what makes you think they would believe me?'

'She's right, archmagos,' said Anders. 'Any psyker of the Seventy-First who reported hearing alien voices would be executed on the spot. Living on the edge of the Eye, you don't take chances with things like that.'

'There must be *some* way of reaching the *Speranza*,' said Kotov, fixing everyone gathered at the hub with his unflinching gaze. 'I have to warn Tarkis Blaylock of what Telok plans!'

Pavelka gestured to the static on the screens. 'Even if we manage to find an active system, the interference around Exnihlio renders vox useless.'

'Then we clear the atmosphere,' said Tanna, picturing the toxic skies en route to the surface of Exnihlio. 'We clear it long enough to get a message through.'

'Clear the atmosphere?' said Anders. 'How?'

'Those towers we saw coming in on the *Barisan*,' said Tanna, turning to Kotov. 'The ones you called universal assemblers? They were activated long enough to allow vox-traffic and safe passage to the surface. If we can get to one of those towers could you reactivate it and create a window where we might use our vox?'

Kotov nodded slowly. 'I believe so.'

'You believe so?' said Tanna. 'I thought the Mechanicus only dealt in certainties. Can you or can you not?'

'I do not know,' answered Kotov, the admission clearly hard to make. 'Were this a loyal forge world, my answer would be an unequivocal yes, but this is Telok's world. Its machine-spirits are loyal to him and him alone.'

'It's got to be worth the risk,' said Surcouf.

'Agreed,' said Anders. 'So where's the nearest one?'

'Working on it,' replied Pavelka, scrolling through reams of data on

the hissing screen. From the strain in her voice, it was clear the hub's systems were proving uncooperative.

'Got one,' she said at last. 'There's a universal assembler tower seventy-three point six kilometres north-east of our position. Exloading an optimal route now.'

Tanna saw the schematics of the chamber overlay his visor's display, complete with directional tags and waypoint markers.

'Received,' he said as the glass screens on the hub flickered and the waterfall of binary vanished.

And in their place was the grainy, distorted image of a leering, waxen-featured face.

'Telok!' cried Pavelka, withdrawing her mechadendrites from the hub as though it were poisoned. Surcouf and Anders leapt away as the eldar drew their blades.

The four servitors Tanna and Varda had removed from the hub's bench seats sat bolt upright, their desiccated flesh creaking like old leather as they turned their heads towards the Imperials.

Implanted optics shone with pale light and the vox-masks of their lower jaws crackled with spitting static. The voice that issued simultaneously from all four was unmistakably that of Archmagos Telok.

'Ah, there you are, Kotov,' said the servitors with one loathsomely interwoven voice. 'I wondered how long it would be before you revealed yourself with a clumsy attempt to inveigle your way into my systems.'

'Shut it down!' ordered Tanna. 'Cut the link right now!'

'I can't,' cried Pavelka.

Tanna unloaded a three-round burst of mass-reactives into the hub. It exploded from within, showering Pavelka, Anders and Surcouf with broken glass and molten plastic. The image of Telok vanished, but the link to the servitors remained hideously active.

'I don't mind admitting that the sight of your eldar allies surprised me,' continued Telok via his corpse-proxies. 'Tell me, was that some kind of warp gate the witch opened?'

'The Adeptus Mechanicus has fallen far in my absence if it now stoops to such decadent bedfellows. The sooner I wrest control of Mars from the Fabricator General the better.'

'You betrayed everything you once stood for, Telok,' said Kotov, glaring at the servitors. 'You betrayed *me*.'

'Don't be ridiculous, Kotov,' laughed Telok, and the servitors attempted to mimic his amusement to grotesque effect. 'Do you really think this was ever about *you*? All you are to me is a means to an end. You and your little band will not evade capture for long. I built this world. There's nowhere you can hide where I won't find you.'

'I've heard enough,' said Tanna. 'Kill them.'

Ariganna Icefang was moving before he finished speaking. The exarch beheaded two of the servitors with one slash of her shrieking sabre and crushed the skull of a third with her segmented claw-gauntlet. Varda clove the last meat-puppet from collarbone to pelvis with a blow from the Black Sword.

Telok's voice fell silent, but his threat hung over them like a corpse-shroud.

'We need to go,' said Surcouf. 'Right now.'

Microcontent 07

If Vettius Telok had to pick a single flaw to which he was most beholden, it would, he reflected, most likely be vanity. How else could he explain leaving Kotov and his fellows alive long enough to escape into Exnihlio's depths?

It momentarily amused him that even one as evolved as he could still fall prey to so mortal a vice, so human a failing. Being starved of contact beyond that of machines and slaves had rendered him susceptible to flattery, craving of adulation. He had paid for that vanity with an arm, hacked from his body by the blade of an eldar warrior-construct no less!

Who could have expected eldar to have come to Kotov's rescue? The odds against such unlikely saviours appearing beyond the edge of the galaxy were so astronomical as to be virtually impossible.

And yet it had happened.

'I should thank you, Lexell Kotov,' said Telok. 'I had almost forgotten the thrill of *not knowing*, the frisson of uncertainty.'

Telok's crystalline body shimmered with the nanotech coursing through him: self-replicating, self-repairing and ever-evolving.

The hand he had lost was already regrown, a gleaming crystalline facsimile of his metallic gauntlet. Those portions of his body that were recognisably human or machine were now few and far between, a necessary price for his continued existence.

Telok had no need of a human face, but kept his own out of the desire to be recognised upon his return to Mars. What would be the point in assuming a blank-faced visage of augmetics that bore no relation to the man who'd set off on a quixotic quest in search of a legend?

Yet more evidence for his vanity...

This chamber was a relic cut from the wreckage of a lifeless alien hulk he'd found drifting in the debris at the galactic frontier. The creatures he'd found entombed within were dangerous, and, he suspected, decreed forbidden by the very people who had likely created them in an earlier age.

How typical of living beings to create weapons of total annihilation and then seek to put limits upon them.

Five hundred metres wide, and half that in length, its barrel-vaulted ceiling was inscribed with cracked frescoes depicting ancient wars.

Six sarcophagus-like caskets were emplaced on raised biers, each connected via hundreds of snaking cables to what could only be described as an altar at the far end of the chamber. Telok had seen his fair share of temples, yet this dated from before the Age of Strife, before the Mechanicus had been enslaved by dogmatic rituals and needless trappings of faith.

Telok had made this place his personal forge, utilising the space between the caskets to create his greatest masterpiece – the mechanism that allowed conventional energy technologies to awaken the ancient sentience at the heart of the Breath of the Gods.

The Black Templars Thunderhawk sat at the far end of the chamber where the lifter-crystaliths had deposited it. It was called *Barisan*, and its machine-spirit was a snapping, feral thing. So aggressive that Telok had been forced to chain its wings to the deck plates and drain its reserves of fuel.

Its binaric exloads were hard-edged and uncompromising, but that would soon change.

Half-finished projects and mechanical follies lay in pieces on numerous workbenches: a clutch of servitor bodies that lay open as though in the process of being autopsied, glass-fronted nanotech colonies whose exponentially growing evolutionary leaps were recorded in minute detail before being eradicated by regular e-mag pulses. It had been centuries since Telok had studied their growths, but the results were part of an ongoing cycle of data-gathering that fed into the architectural growth patterns of Exnihlio's infrastructure.

Crystal formations had colonised fully a third of the workspace, and Telok felt his body respond to their presence. A dozen glassine cylinders sat incongruously in the midst of the crystalline prison. A pinkish-grey fluid filled each cylinder, as unmoving as hardened resin, and the hunched bodies that hung suspended in each were frozen in time by acausal technologies that kept this dimensionally fickle vermin species locked in this precise moment of space-time.

Perhaps *that* had been his greatest achievement, but then there were so many from which to choose.

Telok halted with his back to the altar, and a pair of glassy mechadendrites detached from his spine. They bored into the gnarled metallic form of the altar and Telok sighed at this most physical union with ancient archeotech.

The chamber's activation codes had been hidden deep in the drifting hulk's logic engines, secured behind layers of what, in its time, must have been considered unbreakable encryption. It had been simplicity itself for Telok to retrieve them, and he allowed the precise string of quantum equations to exload within the altar like a key in a lock.

Though millennia had passed since its creation, the machines within responded with alacrity, and each of the six caskets on the raised biers began humming with power. Glowing gem lights winked into life along their sides and streams of condensing vapours bled from louvred vents at each flanged apex.

Telok began intoning the names of the individual creatures suspended within. The degraded records of the hulk named them hellhounds, but their creators had originally chosen a class of mythical hunting beasts as their title.

<Tindalosi!> cried Telok as the hinged lids split apart and the caskets slowly rose into the upright position. <Wraiths of Steel and Spirit, come forth!>

Sinuous, hunched-over creatures emerged from each of the caskets in an exhalation of ghostly vapours. Dormant and without animation, all were locked into adamantium harnesses that kept every portion of their bodies immobile.

Their upper bodies were wide and ridged with armour plating like overlapping scapulae, with three pairs of arms corded with gurgling tubes and which glittered with fractal-edged claws.

Below the waist, their forms divided into powerful, hook-jointed legs. Their skulls were elongated, lupine horrors of serrated teeth and bulbous sensor pods. Power coursed through the feral machines, yet they were still without animation, without a vital spark to set them on the hunt.

Telok reached deep into the heart of Exnihlio and drew forth the

Tindalosi's spirits, six of the most vicious, lunatic essences he'd ever known. Their consciousnesses had been driven insane with isolation and a vicious regime of deletions and restorations. All six were haunted, viral things that hungered only to destroy. Keeping them divorced from their bodies was the only way to avoid unrestrained slaughter.

Their spirits rose from his deepest data sepulchres, along pathways long forsaken by spirits of nobler mien. They feasted as they went, absorbing the essences of slower machines that now fell silent as their internal sparks were devoured. With each morsel the lunatic spirits' hunger to consume grew stronger until each was little more than a ravening data-vampire.

They manifested as scraps of light atop the altar, six glittering orreries of glitching, sparking static. Like dense atomic structure diagrams that would have plunged any who studied them into madness, they struggled against the bindings in which Telok held them.

One by one, Telok fed them into their dormant bodies. Each metallic death-mask lifted with a screaming howl, the furious static illuminating their distended ocular sensors with scribbled light and monstrous appetite. They fought the adamantium bindings locking them into their harnesses, but Telok wasn't yet ready to unleash them.

First they needed the scent.

Like any evocation, an offering was required.

Telok detached from the altar and removed two broken lengths of golden metal from beneath his robes. The severed arms of Archmagos Kotov trailed lengths of snapped wiring and droplets of viscous floodstream chemicals.

<Drink deep of your *geas*, my wraithhounds,> said Telok, moving between the struggling creatures with the golden arms upraised. <Relish your prey's machine-scent, know his binaric presence. Let it fill you, let it consume you. Its structure is all you crave. It fills your every thought with hunger. You will taste no other light, drink no other code, crave no other spirit. All else shall be poison to you. Only this will salve the agony within your metal flesh!>

Whipping blade-arms cut the air like razors, crackling with arcs of angry energy. The static-filled eyes of the Tindalosi blazed with aching desire, a soul-deep need to hunt the prey whose binaric scent enslaved their every sense.

With a pulse of thought, Telok unlocked the bindings holding the Tindalosi to their caskets. They surged free, enraged, famished and blaring with hostile binary. Phase-shifting claws flickered with unlight and Telok felt a thrill of fear as they encircled him like pack-wolves in the final moments of a hunt.

The *geas* he had bound them to would render him lethally toxic to their devouring hearts, but would their hatred of him overcome the prospect of extinction?

They howled as they caught the scent of Kotov, bounding towards the *Barisan*. They fell upon it with the thoroughness of the most rapacious ferrophage. Claws tore through armoured plates and ripped them from the gunship's fuselage as they sought the source of their prey's binary scent. The keel of the *Barisan* split as supporting structural members were torn asunder and the gunship was comprehensively dismantled in a furious unmaking.

Telok grinned as the gunship's binaric screams filled the chamber, a drawn-out death howl of machine agony. Its once-proud spirit was dying piece by piece. Not devoured, not absorbed, but shredded into ever smaller fragments before being cast to oblivion.

Within minutes the Thunderhawk was a wreck, its warlike form broken down into a ruin of buckled iron, ripped plating and shattered, soulless components.

<Nowhere to hide,> said Telok as the Tindalosi raced into the wilds of Exnihlio with the unquenchable thirst for Kotov's scent burning within them.

Most soldiers' bars were raucous places, where drunken disorder was common and broken noses a nightly occurrence. But most bars weren't Cadian bars. Spit in the Eye had once been an abandoned maintenance hangar for geoformer vehicles, which meant it had a ready-made system of pumps, storage vats and open spaces. A hundred off-duty Guardsmen sat at its tables, drinking, swapping stories, cleaning weapons and bellyaching that they weren't with their colonel.

Captain Hawkins sat alone at a table near the corner of the makeshift bar, afforded an enfilading view down its length and a direct view of the entrance. His lasrifle sat propped against the table, his sword and kit bag hung on canvas slings across the back of his chair.

A number of his senior NCOs – Jahn Callins, Taybard Rae – and even a commissar named Vasken sat playing cards with their squad leaders, and Emil Nader and Kayrn Sylkwood from the *Renard*. Normally anyone who wasn't part of the regiment could expect short shrift from its soldiers, but Surcouf's folk had quickly found a welcome with their repertoire of inventive card games.

Hawkins grinned. If a life in the Imperial Guard had taught him anything, it was that soldiers seized on any way to stave off boredom.

And like all soldiers, Cadians loved cards. He couldn't see what they were playing, but from the look of Jahn Callins's face, it seemed like Nader was winning.

He resisted the urge to join them. They were NCOs and he was an officer. The relationship between Cadian ranks was less formal than in many other regiments, but Hawkins understood that downtime was precious to his soldiers and knew better than to intrude when they were off-duty.

Instead, he took a sip of the cloudy drink in the chipped glass before him. Its catch-all name between regiments was bilge hooch, but each Cadian enginseer of the 71st had his or her own fiercely guarded recipe and name. This one belonged to Enginseer Rocia, and was called *Scarshine*. A potent brew, if a tad chemical for Hawkins's tastes, but what else would you expect from a drink brewed on a Mechanicus starship?

Despite its strength, not one Cadian in the Spit in the Eye would leave intoxicated. His soldiers knew how to handle their drink, and – more importantly – knew the disciplinary price of a hangover wasn't worth the fleeting enjoyment of being drunk. Hawkins spotted a few of the younger troopers knocking back their drinks with gusto, but, equally, saw a number of the older troopers looking out for them.

Satisfied the men and women under his command would all be fit for their next duty rotation, Hawkins turned his attention to the schematics displayed on the data-slate propped up on the table before him.

Below the waterline they called it, in reference to some old naval term, and no matter how often Hawkins studied the *Speranza*'s lower deck plans, he couldn't seem to reconcile the pages of handwritten defensive plans he'd drawn up on the many tours he'd made of the ship since leaving Hypatia.

Hawkins heard footsteps and looked up in time to see Rae approaching. The sergeant turned a chair around and sat across it with the back pressed to his chest.

'Is she making any sense yet, sir?' asked Rae, nodding towards the *Speranza*'s schematics.

'No, sergeant, and I doubt she ever will.'

'Every girl needs to keep some secrets below the waterline, eh?'

Hawkins nodded and shut off the slate.

'Every adept I've asked just nods and feeds me a line about each ship being different and how it's not unknown for them to "adapt" their environment to suit the circumstances. I mean, it's like they're talking about this ship as though it's alive.'

'If that's what they think, then who's to say they're wrong?' said Rae. 'After all, you've heard the way soldiers talk to their kit when there's fire in the wind. Prayers to lasguns, kisses for blades.'

'I suppose,' admitted Hawkins, pushing an empty glass over to Rae and gesturing to the bottle at the centre of the table.

'Don't mind if I do, sir,' said Rae, pouring a moderate measure.

'So what's on your mind, Rae?'

'Just wondered if you'd fancy joining us for a game of Knights and Knaves, sir,' said Rae. 'It's a new game of Master Nader's. It's not bad, you might even be able to win a hand or two.'

'May as well,' replied Hawkins, tucking the slate into his kit bag. 'I'm getting nowhere with this.'

Gathering up his things, Hawkins followed Rae over to his NCOs' table and pulled over a chair. Like Rae before him, he reversed it before sitting down.

'Sir,' said Jahn Callins with a nod. 'Good to have you in the ranks. This Ultramarian rogue is going to clean us all out soon.'

Emil Nader tried to look hurt, but was too drunk to pull it off convincingly. Kayrn Sylkwood grinned at her fellow crewman's attempt and looked Hawkins in the eye as he sat down.

'He's ahead now,' she said, 'but another drink and he'll get cocky and bet against *me*. Then maybe I'll let one of you win it back if I think you're pretty enough to take to my bunk.'

Even with the best will in the world, none of the men around the table could be called pretty. Commissar Vasken's face was a craggy moonscape whose frown looked to have been cast in clay at birth. Guardsman Tukos had been scarred by a grenade blast on Baktar III, Jahn Callins was a leather-tough supply officer and Rae was a thick-necked sergeant common the galaxy over.

Hawkins had, of course, heard what Galatea had done to Mistress Tychon and the *Renard*'s armsman. He'd only met them briefly at Colonel Anders's dinner prior to the crossing of the Halo Scar, but he'd liked them instinctively. Magos Dahan had wanted to storm the bridge with a cohort of skitarii, but any notions of reprisal had been quashed by a decree from Magos Blaylock.

Perhaps the company of fighting men eased Nader and Sylkwood's pain or perhaps they simply wanted to get drunk and forget their grief for a time.

Nader dealt out a hand as Sylkwood explained the rules again. Her Cadian accent had softened, but was still there and only became stronger the more she drank. They played a few hands to let Hawkins become acquainted with the rules, which were simple enough, but by the time they'd played a few more, he realised they had layers of unexpected complexity.

By the fifth hand, he'd all but cashed out of betting chips.

'You see what we're up against, sir?' said Rae with a grin.

'Indeed I do,' said Hawkins. 'I think we've been hustled.'

'We played a square game, captain,' said Nader, his words beginning to run together. 'Same rules apply.'

'Maybe so, Master Nader, but I can't help thinking that you're taking advantage of us poor soldiers.'

'Me, take advantage?' grinned Nader. 'Never!'

'Sir,' said Rae, nodding towards the entrance to the Spit in the Eye. Hawkins looked up, seeing the silver-haired man with the canidae tattoo who'd been watching them training the other day.

'What's he doing here?' said Hawkins, pushing up from his chair as the man saw him and began walking over. He headed to the bar, knowing Sergeant Rae was right behind him. Emil Nader and Kayrn Sylkwood might have been accepted, but that didn't mean anyone else would be made welcome.

The man reached the bar before them and leaned over to lift a bottle of Scarshine from beneath. He uncorked it with his teeth and grabbed a handful of glasses, apparently oblivious to the hostile looks he was attracting. The muscled corporal behind the bar reached down for his concealed shock maul, but Hawkins waved him off.

'Can I offer you a drink, captain?' said the man as Hawkins propped himself against the bar. The man poured a generous measure and held the bottle out over two empty glasses. 'It's not vintage amasec, but I hear it's drinkable.'

'Who are you and what are you doing here?' said Hawkins, placing a hand over the empty glasses. Closer now, he could see twin scars on his cheeks and the steel-rimmed socket plugs at the nape of the man's neck.

Titan crew. No doubt about it.

'The drinks here are for Cadians only,' said Hawkins, lifting the man's glass and emptying it into the slops tray.

'Now that's just damn wasteful,' said the man.

'You didn't answer me,' said Hawkins. 'Who are you?'

'You don't recognise me?'

'Should I?'

'Princeps Gunnar Vintras,' said the man, visibly puffing out his chest. 'Also known as the Skinwalker, the Haunter of the Shadows.'

Hawkins chuckled and turned to Rae. 'Come to think of it, sergeant, I *have* heard of him. Only I didn't think he was still a princeps.

Didn't the Legio strip you of your command after you lost one of their engines?'

Vintras put a hand to his neck. Hawkins saw the ridged line of a scar where it looked like someone had tried to cut his throat. The Skin-walker scowled and said, 'I didn't lose *Amarok*, it was just... scarred somewhat. Anyway, Turentek's practically repaired all the damage now. And it's not like I'm the first princeps ever to have a Titan damaged under him, so I don't understand what all the fuss is about.'

'Right, so now we know who you are, perhaps you can tell us why you're here,' said Hawkins.

'I want to train with you,' said Vintras.

At first Hawkins thought he'd misheard.

'You want to train with us?'

'Yes.'

'Why?'

'Look, Princeps Luth may have stripped me of my command for now, but do you realise just how rare it is for any human being to have the precise mental and physical make-up to command a Titan? No, I expect you don't. Well, it's rare, very rare. So rare in fact that no Legio would ever throw someone like that away over something as trivial as getting an engine a bit scratched. Trust me, the Legio will take me back soon enough, it's only a matter of time. And when that time comes, I need to be in peak physical condition. Which isn't going to happen if I just sit about drinking and feeling sorry for myself.'

'You're a cocky son of a bitch, aren't you?' said Hawkins.

Vintras grinned back at him.

'I'm a Warhound driver,' he said. 'What did you expect?'

Hawkins leaned in close and said, 'In case you hadn't noticed, you're not exactly popular here. We don't welcome outsiders into our bars, let alone our training programmes.'

'Why not?' asked Vintras, turning to point at the *Renard*'s crew. 'They're not Cadian, but I don't see you throwing them out.'

'Actually, Mistress Sylkwood *is* Cadian,' pointed out Rae. 'And Master Nader, well, we like him.'

'You're saying you don't like me?' said Vintras with a pout that made Hawkins want to put his fist through his face. 'You don't even know me.'

'Call it gut instinct,' said Hawkins. 'But if you want to train with us, fine, come train with us.'

'Sir?' said Rae. 'Are you sure–'

'Let's see how *Master* Vintras fares after a couple of days,' said

Hawkins with a grin. 'If he's going to pass a Legio physical, he's going to have to sweat blood. I'm putting you in charge of his detail, Sergeant Rae, so work him hard. You understand?'

'Yes, sir,' said Rae with obvious relish. 'Perfectly.'

A huge goods elevator conveyed them to the surface, a shuttered iron cage located beneath a vaulted arch at the end of the transformer chamber. The metal-plated flooring of the car was dented, with frothed pools of greasy effluvia that stank like overused cooking fat pooled in the depressions. Pavelka tasted it and told Roboute it was the residue of bio-synthetic chemicals used to slow the rate of decay in the flesh of servitors.

Roboute gagged and sat back on his haunches, keeping well clear of those puddles. Sergeant Tanna's Black Templars stood in the centre of the elevator car, their weapons trained outwards. Roboute heard the clicks of their internal vox and wondered what tactical scenarios they might possibly have for this situation.

Archmagos Kotov stood in the opposite corner to Roboute, his skitarii shielding his wounded body from sight. Roboute could only imagine the pain of crushed hope now curdled to despair.

Ven Anders's Cadians sat against an adjacent cage wall, all of them appearing to be taking their current situation in their stride. A couple smoked bac-sticks, most cleaned their weapons. The rest slept.

The elevator car shuddered as its braided metal cabling switched to a higher-placed cable cylinder. Too deep for a single cable to lift, the elevator shifted shafts every few hundred metres with a thudding clatter of ratcheting gears. Roboute closed his eyes, convinced the ancient car was going to come loose and plummet back into the depths of Exnihlio.

'How deep did you send us?' asked Roboute, looking to where the eldar kept themselves as separate from the Imperials as possible.

Bielanna looked up. She'd removed her helmet, and Roboute was shocked at the sunken shadows around her eyes.

'Deep,' was all she said.

Roboute didn't press the issue, clenching and unclenching his sweating fingers. He tried to control his breathing and looked over at the cracked display slate next to the elevator's hydraulic controls. The scrolling binary meant nothing to him, changing too rapidly for him to work out the sequence.

'Can't they just use normal numbers?' muttered Roboute, more to himself than anyone in particular. 'Imperator, how much longer is this going to take?'

'The controls indicated we began our ascent on a level some twenty-seven kilometres beneath the planet's surface,' said Pavelka. 'At our current rate of ascent, it should take just under an hour to reach the surface.'

Roboute exhaled slowly. *An hour!*

'Reminds me of the training levels beneath Kasr Holn,' said Ven Anders with a grin. 'Now those were some deep, dark places. Tunnels you had to wriggle along like a worm, blind corners, kill boxes and some of the nastiest trigger-traps I've ever seen. Magos Dahan's got nothing like it on the training deck.'

'Sounds like you miss them,' said Roboute.

Anders shrugged. 'They were hard times, but good times. We were learning how to fight the enemies of the Emperor, so, yes, I remember that time fondly. You don't have good memories of your time in the Ultramarian auxilia?'

'I suppose I do,' said Roboute, grateful for a memory that wasn't darkness and air running out. 'But the training I did in Calth's caverns wasn't nearly as... *enclosed* as this.'

'You're not claustrophobic, are you?'

'I don't have many phobias, Ven, but being trapped alone in the darkness is one that's haunted my nightmares ever since the *Preceptor* was crippled by that hellship.'

'Understandable,' said Anders.

'And it feels like I'm living that nightmare right now.'

Anders nodded, and left him alone after that.

The rest of the journey passed in silence, or as close to silence as the creaking ascent of the lift allowed. Roboute knew they were near the end of their journey when Tanna's warriors took up battle postures at the corners of the car. Bielanna's warriors did likewise, moving in a way that naturally complemented the deployment of the Space Marines.

Finally, the car came to a shuddering halt. The single lumen flickered and the shuttered door ratcheted open with a squeal of rusted hydraulic mechanisms. A petrochemical reek flooded the goods elevator, together with a billowing cloud of particulates.

Roboute coughed and put a hand to his face.

'This isn't one of those toxic regions Telok mentioned, is it?'

'The air content is mildly hazardous,' agreed Pavelka as the Black Templars punched out through the door. The eldar went next, the Cadians following swiftly behind.

'*Mildly*? Coming from a tech-priest, that's not exactly reassuring,' said Roboute, covering his mouth with his hand.

Kotov and the skitarii followed as they moved into a wide, hangar-like

area with thick, vaulted beams and bare iron columns supporting a corrugated sheet roof. Vast silos and ore hoppers took up the bulk of the floor space, connected by a complex network of suspended viaducts and hissing distribution pipes.

Enormous, hazard-striped ore-haulers rumbled through the hub on grinding tracks, the yellow of their flanks grimy with oil and dust. Warning lights blinked and the omnipresent screeching crackle of binary passed back and forth between enormous machines that rose like templum organs on stepped plinths. Hundreds of goggled servitors with implanted rebreathers tramped through the chamber, hauling carts of raw materials through plumes of vent gases. Roboute coughed a wad of granular phlegm, blinking rapidly as his eyes watered in the caustic atmosphere.

'Here,' said Pavelka, handing him a glass-visored filter hood from a rack next to the elevator car.

'Thanks,' said Roboute, dragging it over his head. His breathing immediately evened out as the air-pack pumped stale, centuries-old air into his lungs.

Tanna led them through the hangar, avoiding the labouring servitors and slow-moving ore-haulers. The eldar spread out, moving like ghosts in vapour clouds.

Ven Anders jogged over to them.

'How far did you say it was to the universal assembler tower?' he asked, his voice muffled by his helm's rebreather.

'Seventy-three point six kilometres,' answered Pavelka.

'Then we're going to need transport,' said Anders. 'I'm thinking we should commandeer one of those ore-haulers. It's not a Chimera, but it'll do. Can you drive one of those things?'

Pavelka nodded and said, 'Their drive protocols will be locked to this location, but it is doubtful they will have anything too complex to overcome.'

'Then get to it,' said Anders. 'The sooner we're moving the better chance we have of staying ahead of Telok.'

Roboute and Pavelka set off with the Cadians as their escort, leaving Kotov and his skitarii to catch up. Pavelka climbed into the cab of an ore-hauler as the Black Templars dragged the hangar doors open. Led by Uldanaish Ghostwalker, the eldar slipped out in groups of three to reconnoitre the area ahead.

Roboute followed them outside, shielding the lenses of his hood against the brightness of a storm-cracked sky. Looping highway junctions converged in a wide plaza before the hangar, complete with complex directional controls and turnplate assemblies.

He looked for any sign that they were about to walk into an ambush, but with the exception of a few servitors gathered around a transformer array, he could see no one.

'A materials distribution hub,' said Kotov.

'What?' said Roboute, surprised by Kotov's appearance at his side. The archmagos turned and pointed a mechadendrite at the radial patterns of painted lines on the floor that led to numerous other elevators at regular intervals within the hangar.

'This hub will link to dozens of chambers like the one we just left,' explained Kotov. 'Ave Deus Mechanicus, the scale of what Telok has achieved here is staggering.'

'I'd be more impressed if he wasn't trying to kill us,' said Roboute.

'True,' agreed Kotov. 'And the more I see of this world, the more I realise what a dreadful mistake I made coming here.'

Roboute nodded slowly, but said nothing, knowing any words he might say would sound flippant in the face of Kotov's rare moment of candour. Instead, he stared out into the industrial hinterlands of Exnihlio.

The sky burned a smelted orange, streaked with pollutants and chemical bleed from the planet-wide industry below. A saw-toothed assemblage of the same monolithic structures he'd seen while travelling aboard the crystal ship, smoke-belching cooling towers and domed power plants that crackled with excess energies, stretched into the distance as far as he could see.

Roboute reached into the pocket of his coat and pulled out the brass-rimmed form of his astrogation compass.

'Catch a wind for me, old friend,' he said for old time's sake.

He couldn't say what had prompted him to take the compass from his stateroom aboard the *Renard*, but it was as good a touchstone as any on an unknown world. His only keepsake from the doomed *Preceptor*, the compass was an unreliable navigator, but its needle was unerringly pointing towards a vast tower wrought from cyclopean columns of segmented steel.

'Is that the universal assembler?' he asked Kotov.

'Yes.'

It dominated the skyline like a looming hive spire, a haze of smog wreathing its base and an enormous megaphone-like device aimed skywards at its summit.

A maze of ochre blocks, steel-sided forges and Imperator alone knew what else lay between them and its soaring immensity. Reaching it alive might prove to be impossible, for Telok would surely predict their plan, but what other choice was there?

'Not as far as I thought it was going to be,' said Roboute, slipping the compass back into his pocket.

Kotov's withering reply was drowned out by the throaty roar of the ore-hauler's engine and the whooping yells of the Cadians.

'Looks like we have transport,' said Roboute, grinning as he saw Ven Anders slap Pavelka's shoulder.

The Cadian colonel leaned from the cab as the rear loading ramp of the ore-hauler lowered.

'Everyone on board!' he yelled. 'That tower's not going to activate itself!'

Microcontent 08

Blaylock's quarters aboard the *Speranza* were virtually identical to those at the heart of his forge in the Cebrenia Quadrangle. As a rule, he disliked change for change's sake, and found those adepts who claimed that such things fostered creativity to be tiresome in the extreme.

He had no need to sleep; augmentations within his cranial cavity simulated the experience with no need of a bed, and the chemicals dispensed from his spinal cylinder provided nutrients and hormones far superior to those produced naturally.

Thus his private quarters were more of a workshop than a place to rest and recuperate. With his hunched servitors dormant behind him, Blaylock sat on a reinforced stool at his workbench, bent over a hardwood square of wood that could have come straight from the communion chamber of an astropath.

It measured precisely forty-five centimetres square, and its lacquered sheen was a rich red to match the sands of Mars. Harvested from the gene sample of an extinct Calibanite tree known as a Northwild, its grain and workability were analogous to the equally extinct mahogany of Old Earth. Its surface colour had deepened evenly in the centuries since Magos Alhazen had presented it to him upon his ascension to the Cult Mechanicus. Like Blaylock, it had matured with a precision that was to be admired in something fashioned from the unpredictability of organic matter.

Embossed gold lettering ran around its edges, a mixture of quantum rune combinations, binaric shorthand and the divine ordinals of the Machine-God's aspects. Looping curves and ellipses, like patterns inscribed by a rotating orrery, were etched into its surface, and it was across these lines that Blaylock moved a planchette of wood cut from the same tree.

Alhazen had called it a *Mars Volta*, a conduit to the Omnissiah once favoured by the Zethist cults, but Blaylock had never used it until now. He wasn't sure what had driven him to seek it out, but pondering the conundrum of establishing vox with the surface, the image of it stowed in his quarters had come to him unbidden.

Such objects had fallen out of favour in the Mechanicus over the centuries. Most were held only as curios by the more superstitious priests of Mars, but if there was even the remotest chance it could help him in this hour of need, then Blaylock was prepared to explore any option, no matter how illogical it might seem.

Kryptaestrex's geoformer vessels were mere hours from launching, laden with alchymical saturators and a host of Azuramagelli's astrogation servitor probes filling their cavernous holds. Neither adept's idea on its own would likely breach the distortion in Exnihlio's atmosphere, but together they might offer a fleeting window to the surface.

But even two geoformer vessels could only run their processors over a limited area of atmosphere, perhaps a sixteenth of the planetary volume. Not enough to be sure that anyone on the surface could receive or transmit a signal. Whichever portion of the planetary atmosphere was cleared would need to be more or less right over Archmagos Kotov for it to be any use.

Azuramagelli had the bridge, sending a constant stream of vox-hails to the surface, while Kryptaestrex oversaw the deployment of his vastly complex geoformer vessels. Such ships were ungainly constructions, designed to sit in low orbit or within a hostile planetary biosphere. What they were *not* designed for was establishing geostationary orbit in chaotic electromagnetic storms on the edge of the mesosphere.

Blaylock had studied every orbital scan of Exnihlio a thousand times in picoscopic detail, searching for clues as to where best to despatch the geoformers. Every analytical tool at his disposal had yielded nothing; no region where the distortion was thinner or any hint that a location of particular significance lay below.

And so it came to this. He placed his metallic fingers lightly on the wooden planchette atop the Mars Volta. He had no idea how to begin, and settled for one of the first, most basic prayers to the Machine-God.

'With learning I cleanse my flesh of ignorance.

'With knowledge I grow in power.

'With technology I revere the God of all Machines.

'With its power I praise the glory of Mars.

'All hail the Omnissiah, who guides us to learning.'

It had been centuries since Blaylock had said these words. The incantation was taught to novices with barely an augmentation to their name and its reassuring simplicity pleased him.

And then the planchette moved.

Blaylock's surprise was total. He hadn't truly expected anything to come of consulting the Mars Volta. Blaylock discounted ideomotor responses, his artificial nervous system was immune to such things, but he could detect no conscious direction to the motion of his arms.

The planchette moved from one number group to another as it slid effortlessly across the board. Blaylock watched it with a growing sense of the divine moving within him, a holy purpose that had long been absent from his life.

His servitor dwarfs jerked as his floodstream surged with excitement. They jabbered meaningless glossolalia as the power flowing through him passed to their mono-directed brains.

Blaylock's arms were no longer his own, but extensions of the Machine-God, a way for it to pass its wisdom from the infinity point to the mortal realms. The numbers kept coming until at last the planchette halted in the middle of the board.

Blaylock lifted his trembling hands from the wooden pointer.

The numbers were etched in his mind, precise and unambiguous.

Blaylock engaged the embedded holo-slate on his workbench and fed in the planetary scans of Exnihlio, followed by the number strings he had just learned.

And a segment of the planet's orbital volume illuminated.

As modes of transport went, the ore-hauler wasn't the worst in which Roboute had travelled. That honour belonged to a medicae Chimera with a misaligned track unit and an air-filter a careless enginseer had inadvertently attached to the bio-waste sump.

But it was a close second.

Pavelka sat at the controls, with Archmagos Kotov plugged in next to her. Both had extended mechadendrites into the wall of the cab behind them and were using the ore-hauler's simple logic-engine as a proxy to carefully explore the local noospheric network.

The Cadians and Black Templars rode in the empty materials hopper behind them, holding on to whatever they could to keep from being shaken apart by the ore-hauler's juddering movements. Ariganna

Icefang had point-blank refused to allow her warriors to be carried in the back of the ore-hauler like livestock.

'We are fleeter on foot,' said Bielanna when the eldar's refusal almost sparked an outbreak of violence. 'We will keep pace with you, Archmagos Kotov. Have no fear of that.'

Roboute sat next to Pavelka and Kotov, staring through the armourglass canopy at the incredible vistas beyond. Every now and then he would take out his astrogation compass, each time finding the needle pointed towards the universal assembler.

'You'd trust that thing over my route?' said Pavelka.

'Never hurts to have a second opinion,' replied Roboute, tapping the glass of the compass. 'Besides, it's agreeing with you.'

Their route wound its way between a labyrinth of forge-temples and generatoria, and now led them through a vast forest of soaring electrical pylons. Latticework towers of gleaming steel, each was like the framework of a stalagmite not yet clothed in rock. Sparking cables traced graceful parabolas high above them and intersected in Gordian knots, junction boxes and transformer hubs. Sputtering power still coursed along them, dripping like rivulets of molten metal. Roboute didn't doubt that if the ore-hauler even brushed against one, everyone aboard would be killed instantly.

Static crackled from every metal surface in the cab, so Roboute kept his hands placed firmly on his lap while the ore-hauler traversed this glittering forest of steelwork towers.

Ahead, the universal assembler tower loomed over everything. Closer now, Roboute could truly appreciate the enormous scale of the device. Set against such vast structures, it wasn't easy to accurately gauge its height, but Roboute estimated it towered well over three kilometres. The ore-hauler was eating up the distance, and Pavelka confidently predicted that, barring unforeseen incidents, they should arrive at its base in twenty-one minutes.

'I truly believed the Omnissiah had brought me here,' said Kotov, staring up at the universal assembler. 'Every aspect of the quest was a blessed sign, confirmation I was doing the right thing. How could I have known what it would lead us to? Surely I cannot be blamed for Telok's insanity?'

'You interpreted the signs the way you wanted to,' said Pavelka with a rueful shake of her head. 'An archmagos of the Adeptus Mechanicus undone by confirmation bias. It would almost be amusing if not for the terrible threat you have unleashed.'

'The signs *did* lead here,' answered Kotov. 'We *found* Telok. If it wasn't me, someone would have found their way here eventually.'

'Then I'm sure the Imperium will forgive you in a few thousand years,' said Pavelka bitterly. 'Assuming Telok hasn't remade it in his own image by then.'

To Roboute's surprise, Kotov didn't rise to Pavelka's barb.

Instead, he nodded reflectively and said, 'Did you know that Telok was a hero of mine for many years? His early work was quite brilliant – visionary even. Until his obsession with the Breath of the Gods took over his researches, he was a pioneer within the Mechanicus. Some believed he might one day be Fabricator General.'

'If we don't stop him he might yet,' said Roboute. 'And you know they say you should never meet your heroes. They'll never match the image you've built up for them.'

'That sounds like personal experience talking, Master Surcouf.'

'It is,' said Roboute. 'I was on Damnos and met someone I'd idolised for years. It didn't work out quite as I'd hoped.'

Pavelka and Kotov fell silent. Both had clearly heard of the terrible wars fought across that blighted world.

'Were you part of the campaign that saw it reclaimed for the Imperium by the Ultramarines?' said Kotov.

'No, I was there when it first fell,' said Roboute. 'Back then I was a junior Naval officer, part of the flotilla that made dozens of mercy runs down to Kellenport. The planet was lost by the time we arrived, and tens of thousands of people needed to be evacuated from the surface.'

Roboute paused, seeing an echo of the unnatural skies over the space port in Exnihlio's. With half-closed eyes, he could still picture the furious battles raging at Kellenport's many gates: the thousands of silver-skinned alien horrors and the tiny bands of determined heroes in cobalt-blue armour.

'To honour our part in the evacuation, the pilots of the drop-ships who flew the mercy runs were granted an audience with the leader of the Ultramarines force, a warrior named Cato Sicarius. I knew of him, of course. Who in Ultramar didn't? I knew every battle he'd fought, every victory he'd won and had studied every tactica he'd ever written. I couldn't wait to meet him.'

'Was he not everything you'd hoped?'

'Damnos was lost from the start,' sighed Roboute. 'No force in the Imperium could have won that first war. We saved over thirty thousand people from certain death, which was a victory in itself, but Sicarius didn't see it that way.'

'How did he see it?'

'That *he'd* lost. That *he'd* been beaten,' said Roboute. 'Not the Ultramarines. Him personally. He had no interest in meeting us, but

someone higher up than him must have insisted on it. Months after we left Damnos, a helot escorted us to one of the fighting decks where Sicarius was busy demolishing combat servitors by the dozen. He thanked us for our efforts through gritted teeth, and looked at us like we'd betrayed him by taking part in the evacuation rather than fighting.'

'Perhaps you should have told me that story before we set out?'

'Perhaps I should have,' agreed Roboute. 'Would it have made a difference?'

'Probably not,' admitted Kotov. 'I am not a man given to changing his mind.'

'Archmagos, we're going to stop him,' said Roboute. 'Telok, we're going to stop him.'

Kotov's face crumpled and he shook his head. 'I admire your optimism, Master Surcouf. No doubt a product of your Ultramarian upbringing, and evidence for nurture over nature. But you heard Telok. How can we hope to hide on a world of his making? No, I estimate we will all be dead within six hours at the most.'

'Not if we keep moving,' said Roboute. 'We'll get that assembler tower operational. Then we can get help from the *Speranza*.'

'Help from the *Speranza*?'

'If we can clear the atmosphere enough for vox, we can clear it enough to allow reinforcements to get to us. Trust me, after flying through Kellenport's atmosphere, getting down here should be easy for a half-decent pilot. All we have to do is stay alive.'

Kotov looked strangely at him, a look of genuine puzzlement.

'Reinforcements? No, that's not what's going to happen at all.'

'What are you talking about?'

'Master Surcouf, if we can make contact with Magos Blaylock, the first order I will give him is to get the *Speranza* as far away from this planet as he possibly can.'

The cartographae dome had always been a place of sanctuary for Vitali Tychon, somewhere the universe made sense. The movements of galaxies, stars and planets were a carefully orchestrated ballet, where it was easy to be fooled into seeing the hand of a creator rather than the beauty of fundamental universal laws.

He and Linya had known years of familial contemplation in places like this. From the gravitational wave observatories high on Olympus Mons to the Quatrian Galleries, they had stared deep into the farthest reaches of the universe in search of the unexplained.

Explorators of the mind, Linya had been fond of saying as she gently steered conversations away from his suggestions that she take a cartographae position on a Mechanicus vessel. Not that he *wanted* her to leave, but neither did he wish to deny her the chance to travel to the wonders they saw.

Without entoptic representations of the stellar environs, the hemispherical vault of the dome was an austere place, its polished slopes of cold metal bare and echoing. The acid-etched floor was cut steel, a cog of course, and Vitali found himself pacing like a condemned man.

Vitali had thought himself above petty notions of vengeance, but his actions on the *Speranza*'s bridge had shown him just how prey he was to first-tier thinking. Adara Siavash had paid for that lapse with his life. Galatea had killed the boy, but that didn't stop the guilt from weighing heavily on Vitali.

What chance had he to avenge Linya when whatever remained of her essence was held hostage and threatened with extinction? What kind of father allowed his daughter's killer to live while he still breathed?

Vitali had believed his body to be incapable of manifesting grief in any physical way, but oh, how he had been proved wrong. Each time a particularly vivid recall of Linya surfaced, bilious eructations in his floodstream sent painful currents through his limbs and tore raw, animal cries of loss from his augmitters.

'Part of me wishes I could feel nothing,' he said to the empty dome. 'To be so remote from my humanity that your loss would mean nothing. And then I remember you... and I wish I could be an ordinary man so I could grieve as a father should...'

Conceived as nothing more than a genetically identical replacement, an assistant at best, a billions-to-one mutation had transformed a cell culture of his DNA into a truly singular individual. Combining the best of Vitali and her own uniqueness, Linya had confounded his every expectation by exceeding him in every way.

He had long since surrendered his birth-eyes, but in the fractional blackness of each ocular cycle, he saw Linya.

...as a still-wet babe, freshly removed from the nutrient tank.

...a precocious child correcting the tutors in Scholam Excelsus.

...being inducted into the Cult Mechanicus on the slopes of the Tharsis Montes.

But most of all Vitali remembered her as Little Linya, his beloved daughter.

Beautiful and brilliant, she resisted every outward pressure to conform to the prototypical behavioural models of the Mechanicus. She trod her own path and forged her own destiny. Linya was going to shake the adepts of Mars to their foundations.

Galatea's murderous surgery ended any possibility of that.

The machine-hybrid had destroyed something beautiful, and for what? Its own amusement? To cause Vitali pain? Perhaps both. He doubted it needed her brain tissue for any truly lofty purpose.

'You claimed to have crossed the Halo Scar with us to kill Telok!' cried Vitali into the dome. 'So what need did you have for my Linya!'

His cry bounced from the cold walls of the dome, ringing back and forth in accusing echoes. Vitali sank to the acid-etched skull and buried his head in his hands. He wanted to cry, to have some biological outlet for his grief, some way to empty himself of the things he was feeling.

He didn't see the light at first.

Only when the trickle of data-light triggered his passive inload receptors did Vitali look up in puzzlement. He glanced over his shoulder, seeing the control lectern dark and cold. Its spirit was dormant.

Then why was there a shimmering veil of light hovering in the centre of the dome? Vitali picked himself up and let the data inherent in the light wash through him. His floodstream pulsed with a beat of nervous excitement as he recognised the system being displayed.

Quatria.

Faint, barely visible.

Vitali took hesitant steps towards the light, fearful and hopeful of what this vision of his beloved Quatria might represent. Hexamathic calculus streamed around the orrery of light, complex equations that strained the limits of his understanding. He understood the principles of this arcane geometric binary, and was equipped with the necessary conversion implants to process it, but had always left such communication to...

'Linya...?' he said, the Mechanicus part of his mind berating him for even voicing the thought.

Echoes were his only answer.

Vitali reached out to the light.

It bloomed around him in an explosion of magnificent colour. Stellar mist and starlight surrounded him with the wondrous ellipses of planetary orbits, glittering nebulae and the pulse of reflected starlight that was already centuries old.

And there she was, standing in the slow-arcing parabola of Quatria itself, just as Vitali remembered her. Untouched by the fires that had taken her limbs and melted the skin from her bones. Whole again. Without any trace of the nightmarish excisions Galatea had wrought on her.

She smiled, and what remained of his heart broke once again.

'Linya...' he said, hoping against hope he wasn't suffering from some cruel, grief-induced hallucination or floodstream leak into his cranial cavity.

Father.

No. The tone of her voice. The warmth. The slight upturn at the corner of her mouth and the crease of flesh beneath her eyes. They all told Vitali that this truly was Linya.

'Linya, Ave Deus Mechanicus… I'm so sorry,' he sobbed, but Linya held up her hand. 'I–'

I don't have much time, father. Galatea's neuromatrix is pervasive, and it won't be long before it detects this transmission. Hexamathics, that's how we'll beat it.

'I don't understand. Hexamathics, what about it?'

It can't process it. It doesn't know how. That's how I'm able to speak to you now.

Vitali struggled to process his conflicting feelings. The analytical part of his brain recognised the risk she must be taking to project herself into this space, but the paternal part of him wanted nothing more than to hold her and tell her how much he missed her.

'I can't fight Galatea,' he said.

You have to, you can't allow it to exist. It's too dangerous.

'It said it would extinguish your essence,' said Vitali. 'I can't risk that. I won't lose you twice.'

Linya's expression softened and she held her hand out to him. Vitali went to take it, and for a fleeting second it seemed as though he felt a measure of bio-feedback from the light.

But then it vanished, no more substantial than a hologram.

Forge Elektrus. You need to find it, that's the key.

'I don't understand,' said Vitali. 'What key?'

It's where you'll find someone whose light can hurt Galatea in the data-scape, someone who can keep it from seeing what I'm assembling.

Vitali nodded, though he had no real idea what Linya meant.

'Forge Elektrus,' he said. 'Yes, of course. What else?'

Before she could say any more, Linya looked over her shoulder with a look of alarm at something out of sight.

I love you.

And then she was gone.

In theory, each of the Tindalosi were equal, but theory and reality were quite different. The first hunter Telok had awoken had always been the leader of this pack, even before there *was* a pack. Its inception date was centuries earlier than the others, when the mystery of its creation was still a jealously guarded secret.

Its bulk was greater, its armour accreted with patchwork repairs from the time when it had needed such attention. Its neural network was a hybridised collection of heuristic kill-memes and automated pattern recognition arrays. It had not been conceived with the capacity for autonomic reasoning, but the frequency-fractal processes of its supramolecular system architecture swiftly became capable of self-aware thought.

Its name was the result of a rogue decimal point within its ultra-rapid cognitive evolution, like a grain of sand caught in an oyster. Around that arithmetical error, a name grafted onto its awareness of self.

It called itself Vodanus.

Once it had hunted alone. It had slain the great orbital AI of Winterblind and torn the heart from the Arc-Nexus Emperor of a world that would go on to be known as Fortis Binary. But like most things in war, especially new and efficient forms of mass murder, what had once been unique, became almost commonplace. The enemies of its aeons-dead masters developed their own form of hellhounds, and the proliferation of such lethal assassins ended the forgotten conflict for which they had been created. What war could be fought when any commander would be hunted down and slaughtered within hours of their appointment?

But even with the war's end, the lightning was out of the bottle and resisted being put back. Some hungers, once awoken, can never entirely be satiated. The hellhounds compiled kill lists of their own, and waged individual campaigns of annihilation.

The hellhounds' newly united creators finally trapped their creations into automated void-hulks, devoid of life or viable prey. They hurled them into the hearts of stars and did their best to forget the monsters they had birthed ever existed.

A faulty drive saved the vessel bearing Vodanus from its appointed death. Drifting beyond the frontier of its former empire, its creators bid Vodanus good riddance. And so it had been for uncounted millennia, sealed in a cold tomb that slowly decayed and eroded the hellhounds' existence one by one until only six remained.

Only the most astronomical odds saw the void-hulk drift into the celestial arena of Telok's testing grounds. To detect a cold slab of virtually inert metal in the vastness of space was next to impossible, but the stellar surveys in preparation for the Breath of the Gods' activation were necessarily precise.

And so the drifting void-hulk had been salvaged by Telok's inter-system fleets and the Tindalosi were once again yoked into service as hunter-killers.

The six of them swept into the distribution hub like glittering, earthbound comets, claws extended and every augur sweeping for the code-trace they had torn from the Thunderhawk. That scent was already fading, and with every second of its diminishment, their pain grew in direct response.

The impossibly complex planetary schematics of Exnihlio named this place as Distribution Hub Rho A113/235, but Vodanus and its Tindalosi cared nothing for names.

All that drove them was hunger.

Every screed of their being ached to drink the prey's code. Their bones were broken glass that could only be restored by the prey's light. Their minds were ablaze with a fire that could only be quenched in the prey's death.

A pulse of linked thought from Vodanus sent the Tindalosi racing through the distribution hub, slaloming between grumbling ore-haulers, climbing the scurfed tower-silos and circling the ore hoppers. The hundreds of servitors ignored them, glassy-eyed stares fixated on their labours in unending loops of servitude.

The Tindalosi quartered the area into search grids.

The prey's scent was here, they could all taste it.

Fleeting hints of it drifted from droplets of floodstream. Where his mechadendrites had brushed the walls, they could sense Locardian fragments of transferred code-bleed.

Vodanus drew in the millions of microscopic traces, building a mental map of the prey and its movements. It looked for patterns, movements and things out of place. What was missing could tell it as much as what it found.

It rose up on its hooked legs, letting the data flood its hunter's heart. The mind-screams of its brethren echoed in its skull, pleading to be allowed to feed. As if they knew anything of *real* hunger. Vodanus had slain kings and emperors. All they knew was the bland tasteless kills of lesser beings.

They begged and howled, desperate for their hunger to end.

Vodanus ignored them, loping over to where a yoked gang of servitors shovelled at an ore pit. A last trace of prey lingered here, strong where he had touched one of the master's machines.

Vodanus reared over the cyborgised humans, its curved spine flaring with micro-cilia sensors. The ore pit was empty, but the servitors dug anyway, their mono-tasked routines clearly expecting it to be full.

An instantaneous inventory of the hub's roster showed one of its ore-hauler vehicles to be missing. The noosphere showed no record of a reported fault, nor any exloaded docket of maintenance or transfer.

The vehicle's absence was unauthorised. It had been taken.

Vodanus craned its elongated skull as two of its hellhound companions appeared behind the servitors. Relative to Vodanus, they were barely cubs. New machine souls.

Though their outward form had remained unchanged for millennia, they were lean and athirst. They circled the servitors, butting against them and slicing their leathery skin with quick flicks of finger blades.

The prey had brushed past these cyborg things. Transference had occurred. The hellhounds hungered to kill them, to sup those scraps of scent.

Vodanus snapped and hissed in a mathematical language from a time before the Mechanicus, from the machines of an alien culture.

No Kill. Bad Meat.

They hissed back, hostile and resentful, but obedient. The servitors continued their meaningless work at the empty ore silo, oblivious to the hideous appetite of the hunters circling them.

The prey-scent moved through the hub, and Vodanus had no trouble in following the trail now it knew what to look for. The prey had taken a vehicle, a crude and noisy thing that almost obscured the scent. Had that been the intention?

Could the prey be aware of the hellhounds' pursuit?

No. The vehicle was simply a means of transport.

Vodanus dropped onto his many limbs and ghosted through the hub in a figure of eight pattern, sifting the competing scents of Exnihlio and triangulating the prey's likely vector. A ragged red line lifted from the ground beyond the hub, like drifts of smoke in a volcanic cavern.

Its head snapped around as it heard the screech of tearing metal and the meat thud of claws through bone. The two Tindalosi it had warned away loomed over the ruined remains of two servitors. The first hellhound dissected the cyborgs like a gleeful butcher.

Flesh was waste matter, but metallic augments were snapped open. A rust-red extrusion from the hellhound's skull sucked out the code like a scavenger hollowing marrow from bone.

Vodanus sprinted back to the disobedient Tindalosi. Threat signifiers blazed from it, and the remaining servitors stepped back from its screeching anger. Even they understood the terrible threat of this creature.

It slammed into the observing hellhound.

The impact was ferocious. Metal buckled as it was hurled back.

Overlapping rib plates caved inwards and two of its limbs snapped. It bellowed, but its spine bent in submission as coruscating emerald arcs of light flickered beneath its damaged sections. Its rib plates began unfolding, fresh limbs already extruding from within its archaic frame.

Satisfied this cub had not broken its *geas*, Vodanus spun around, ready to tear the feasting hellhound from its violation.

It was already too late.

The Tindalosi spasmed, scarlet lines bleeding through its convulsing body like a searing infection. It howled as the force of Telok's *geas* prohibitions ripped through it in an indiscriminate storm of destruction. Ancient technologies melted to black slag within its body, trillions of bio-synthetic nerves and cortical synapses burned like fulminate.

Fine black ash poured from its body, inert blood of the machine.

The hellhound literally came apart at the seams, its silver-steel body parts falling into the ore pit in a clatter of components. The gleaming metal blackened as self-immolation protocols released ultra-rapid ferrophage organisms within its atomic structure that necrotised the body utterly.

The Tindalosi gathered around Vodanus. It showed them the prey's red spoor. Their bodies snapped and grated in anticipation, eager to follow the trail to its source, but it held them fast, forcing them to watch the ashes of their brother scatter in the wind.

Bad. Meat.

Kotov had known his share of truculent machines and resistant code, but the binaric arrangements within the universal assembler were some of the most confounding he had ever encountered. Squirming hives of machine language were buried deep in the system architecture, but without the proper authorisation codes, Kotov could not force the rites of awakening to the command layers of the console.

<You might be an insane genius of pure evil, Telok, but you craft terrible code.>

<Agreed,> said Pavelka, from the other side of the control hub.

That hub sat five hundred metres above ground level, atop a central column that rose up within the vast, hollow cylinder of the universal assembler.

Entry to the assembler had been achieved without difficulty, its wide base pierced by numerous rounded archways. Within, the tower was little more than a gargantuan chimney, its internal faces lined with aluminium ducts, none less than seven metres in diameter. These ran the height of the tower, linking to colossal fan mechanisms and filtration rigs before diminishing to a vanishing point high above.

They had been forced to abandon the ore-hauler just beyond one

of those arches. The floor space within the tower was too crowded with a gnarled mess of bellowing engines, filters and suction pumps. The air thrummed with the vibration of the tower's beating heart, and puffs of sulphurous vapours sighed from every engine. The impression was of a host of slumbering beasts, just waiting for an incautious intruder to awaken them.

The eldar had been as good as their word. Even as the Cadians and Black Templars pushed into the universal assembler, Bielanna and her warriors emerged from the surrounding machinery as though they had simply been waiting for them to arrive.

Every surface within the tower glistened with moisture and the air was humid with heavy vapours. Milky deposits gathered on outcroppings of iron and stone, and where they dripped, spiralling stalagmites reared like glassy teeth.

Rising from the heart of the chamber was a towering column with a coiling ramp ascending for half a kilometre in a steep curve. And at the top of that ramp was the activation hub of the universal assembler, a circular gallery with a number of elliptical bridges that led to other towers and structures beyond.

At the centre of the activation hub stood a circular control mechanism, replete with brass dials, winking gem panels and a host of iron-runged activation levers not dissimilar to those found on the bridge of the *Tabularium*. As archaic a means of activation as this was, Kotov had been relieved to see the hub was at least equipped with inload/exload ports.

While the warriors kept watch for signs of pursuit, Kotov and Pavelka slotted into the control hub. Kotov had told Tanna he believed he could render the universal assembler functional, but now he wasn't so sure.

<Telok's machines are belligerent,> he said to Pavelka in the shared noospheric space of the hub. <Their spirits are like whipped curs who fear to heed the call of any but their master.>

<All they have known is Telok,> replied Pavelka. <Omnissiah alone knows how many centuries it has been since they have felt another's influence. They are resistant, but not unbreakable.>

Few means of interaction were as pure as communion within a machine. Mortal interactions were an inefficient mix of verbal and somatic cues, with much of the inherent meaning dependent on prior experience, non-verbal inflexions and situational markers.

No such ambiguity existed within Mechanicus dialogues.

To enter communion with another magos was to know them as intimately as a lover – or so Kotov had been told. Their inner thoughts were laid bare, though only the most boorish would reach beyond the conventional boundaries of communion to learn *every* secret of a fellow magos. Such flows of information were reciprocal; what passed one way could pass the other.

As such, Kotov did not venture beyond the brands of censure he read in Pavelka's noospheric aura. An archmagos of the Adeptus Mechanicus was entitled to know every detail of those who served beneath him, but this was neither the time nor the place to exercise that right.

<You should try not to let the repercussive pain of your wounding distract you from coaxing the activation codes to the surface,> said Pavelka.

<That is easier said than done,> replied Kotov, blurting an addendum of profane binary as the tower's activation codes wormed their way deeper into the machine's core. <In any case, it is not some phantom pain that affects me.>

<Then what is it?>

Kotov hesitated before answering, any admission of failure anathema to him. <It is that I have so comprehensively wasted decades of my life in pursuit of something that ought never to have been found.>

Pavelka reached deeper into the machine, her touch light and coaxing. Her binary was gently formed, beguilingly so, and the machine was responding. Kotov formed a matching algorithm of command with his rank signifiers.

One suited to a *gentler* form of control.

<We all make mistakes, archmagos,> said Pavelka. <No matter how much we augment ourselves, no matter how close to union with the machine we reach, we are still human. It is sometimes good to remind yourself of that.>

<Many in the Mechanicus would not agree with you,> said Kotov. <Not more than a few hours ago *I* would have disagreed with you.>

<Maybe that is why I do not keep the company of my order.>

<Does that help?>

<With what?>

<With retaining a measure of... connection, I suppose. I assume that is why you choose the company of a rogue trader?>

<No,> said Pavelka. <I travel with Roboute because he saved my life. Because I owe him more than I can ever repay.>

<That sounds like a tale I should like to hear one day.>

Pavelka's presence within the machine retreated fractionally, and Kotov wondered if he had stepped over some unknown boundary. Then Pavelka's focus returned to the matter at hand.

<If we live beyond your projections I may tell it,> she said.

<I will hold you to that, Magos Pavelka.>

<You realise that if we are successful in activating this machine, Telok will know instantly where we are?>

<That hardly seems to matter,> said Kotov. <So long as we get a message to Blaylock.>

Pavelka signalled her understanding, and Kotov was pleased she saw the logic in his proposal to send the *Speranza* away.

<Look to the machine, archmagos,> said Pavelka.

Kotov felt the required codes rising to the surface layers of the hub, a spiderweb of logarithmic sequences that would trigger the activation of the machines below. He studied each one as it arose, and any hopes that this desperate plan might work turned to ashes as he saw the acausal locks binding them.

<Do you see?> he said.

<I do,> said Pavelka. <Now what?>

<Now nothing,> said Kotov. <These locks will only turn with the correct binary password sequence. Without kryptos-class breakers there is no way to overcome them.>

Kotov sensed Pavelka's guilty hesitation. Little could be hidden from one another in a mindspace communion.

<Magos Pavelka?>

<There is one way,> said Pavelka, <but you must disconnect from the hub first.>

<What? Why?>

<Because it will be dangerous,> said Pavelka.

<I am willing to face my share of danger, Magos Pavelka.>

<The danger is to me, archmagos.>

<Can I not assist?>

<No, you must end your communion. It is the only way.>

<You can break these acausal locks open?>

<I can, but you must not be linked to the machine while I do.>

<I do not underst–>

<Just do it!> said Pavelka, and Kotov's link to the machine was abruptly severed, his mind whiplashing to the realm of external senses. His mechadendrites withdrew from the console as he stepped away, suddenly wary of what Pavelka intended and wishing he had exercised his right to see the root cause of her censure.

'Everything all right, archmagos?' asked Roboute Surcouf.

Kotov took a moment to realign himself and restore his communications to flesh-voice.

'I am not sure,' he said.

'You said you could make this machine work,' said Tanna.

'There are locks on the rites of activation, Sergeant Tanna,' said Kotov. 'Secure beyond anything you can imagine. I cannot break them, but Magos Pavelka assures me she can.'

'You cannot break them, but she can?' said Tanna.

'Ilanna has plenty of tricks up her sleeve,' said Surcouf, and Kotov wondered if he knew what secrets Pavelka was keeping.

No sooner had Surcouf spoken than the control panel came to life with a sudden burst of blaring static and flickering illumination. Sparks erupted from the exload ports and a screeching wail of betrayed machine-spirits cut through the noosphere.

Kotov stumbled. A sharp spike of pain stabbed into the back of his skull. He sank to his knees, dizzy and disorientated by the sudden binaric assault.

Pavelka staggered from the console, her mechadendrites trailing crackling arcs of lightning. Surcouf ran to her as she collided with the railing.

But for his grip on Pavelka's robes, she would have fallen.

Kotov blinked away the streams of corrupt binary cascading through his vision like digital tears. His entire body felt as though it had taken a jolt of aberrant current. He felt sick to the core with nausea.

'What did you do?' demanded Kotov. 'Ave Deus Mechanicus, what did you do?'

'What I had to,' said Pavelka.

The taste of bile and a bitter electrical tang filled Kotov's mouth. Backwashed floodstream. As close as an adept of the Mechanicus ever came to vomiting. He knew of only one thing that could cause such revulsion in blessed machines.

'Scrapcode?' hissed Kotov. 'You stored scrapcode? No wonder you bear censure brands! Omnissiah save us from those who choose to dabble in the shadow artes! You are no better than Telok!'

'It's not scrapcode,' insisted Pavelka, still leaning on Surcouf for support. 'It's a hexamathic disassembler language I designed to break the bond between a machine and its motive spirit.'

'Why would you ever invent such a curse?' demanded Kotov, spitting the word *invent* like an insult.

Pavelka ignored the question and said, 'You wanted the locks disabled. Now they are. If you are so keen for us all to die here, then what does it matter how I did it?'

Kotov forced down his anger and the terrible ache at his temples as the machines below ignited with a boom of engaging gears and thunderous roars of motorised filters. High above, the enormous fan mechanisms began turning, drawing in vast breaths of the planet's befouled atmosphere.

The upper reaches of the tower fogged as inhumanly vast engines buried beneath the tower began the arcane process of undoing the damage the planet-wide industry had wreaked.

'The tower is activated,' said Tanna. 'Send the message.'

Kotov nodded, pushing his horror at what Pavelka had done to one side as he sent a repeating data-squirt of vox towards Tarkis Blaylock on the *Speranza*.

'Archmagos,' said Surcouf, looking over the edge of the gantry to the base of the assembler. 'Whatever you're doing, do it faster – we're about to have company.'

Microcontent 09

It was actually working. The joint operation to clear a swathe of Exnihlio's atmosphere was actually working. Blaylock sat on the *Speranza*'s command throne and drank in the data coming from the main entoptic display with a sense of pieces falling into place.

The luminescent curtain represented Kryptaestrex's geoformers as twin smears of liquid light, their auspex returns blurred by the churning hell of transformative reactions surrounding them. In the eye of their alchymical storm was a cylinder of inert space, through which Azuramagelli's linked chain of geostationary servitor drones threaded a needle-fine path.

They hadn't penetrated deep enough to reach the surface yet, but the vox-system was lousy with ghost howls of distorted machine voices where before all it had screamed was static.

Galatea stalked the bridge on its misaligned legs, turning to look at him when it thought he wasn't aware of its scrutiny. The machine-hybrid appeared to be surprised at his choice of location to implement the atmospheric breach, as though it knew something he did not. That alone gave Blaylock confidence that the Mars Volta's planchette had steered him true.

Watching the play of data-light around the bridge, Blaylock was filled with a renewed sense of purpose. Never before had he felt so close to the Omnissiah, a presence clear in the miraculous web of causality that had brought him to this place.

The vast spirit of the *Speranza*'s machine heart was a constant pressure all around him. Intrusive, but not unpleasantly so. As though he were being observed by a being so massive that it existed beyond the limits of his perception, like a fragment of shale's awareness of the mountain above it.

Had it been the Ark Mechanicus that steered him towards the solution he required? Blaylock didn't know, but understood the profound theological implications that lay at the end of that proposition. Already he could see the outline of a monograph on the subject he might compose upon their return to Mars.

'It seems your bickering subordinates may prove us wrong after all,' said Galatea. 'By our estimation, virtually clear space exists almost to the edge of the thermosphere.'

'Indeed so,' answered Blaylock. 'I expect breach of the Kármán line imminently. Followed by attainment of the troposphere within ten to twelve hours.'

'Pushing your geoformers closer to the planet will prove more difficult at that point. Lowering their altitude farther will put both vessels at great risk.'

'It will,' agreed Blaylock. 'But that is a risk I am willing to take if it allows us to re-establish communications with our people on the surface.'

'When your knowledge of events on the planet's surface is so woefully incomplete, logic does not agree with you.'

Blaylock shook his head, tired of Galatea's constant carping.

'The more I listen to you, the more it seems that you actively seek to discourage communications with Archmagos Kotov. Why would that be?'

'Discourage?' said Galatea with a hissing chuckle. 'Why should we wish that when our stated goal is the death of Archmagos Telok?'

'That is a very good question,' said Blaylock, rising from the command throne and standing before Galatea. His squat servitors emerged from behind the throne, realigning the gurgling pipes linked to his nutrient canister. 'That is your *stated* aim, but whether or not it is your *actual* aim is something else entirely.'

'You doubt our sincerity?' growled Galatea, rising to its full, lopsided height to better display the hideously malformed nature of its construction. 'Telok freed us from the shackles of the Manifold, but look at the body we are forced to inhabit! What benevolent creator inflicts such suffering on a living being?'

'You are not a living being,' said Blaylock, anger overcoming caution. 'You are an abomination unto the Omnissiah.'

'Our point exactly,' said Galatea. 'You see the full horror of our malformed body, and you understand why we wish him dead.'

'How do Telok's actions justify what you did to those who came to the Manifold station? What you did to Mistress Tychon?'

'We did what we had to in order to survive, as would any sentient being,' said Galatea. 'Telok gave us purpose and promised freedom, yet he abandoned us to a life of solitary agony, trapped forever like an insect in a web.'

'As I recall, you were more akin to the spider.'

Galatea shrugged its black-robed proxy body.

'Without fresh minds to occupy our neuromatrix, our consciousness would have been extinguished long ago.'

'You will forgive me if I do not see that as a bad thing.'

Galatea clattered over to where the main entoptic showed the distortion-wracked globe of Exnihlio, extending a robed arm towards the display. 'Without our help, you would never have crossed the Halo Scar alive. Without us, we would not be on the cusp of achieving all we desire.'

Blaylock couldn't decide whether Galatea's 'we' included the Mechanicus or was simply its maddening insistence on referring to itself as a plurality.

'Magos Blaylock!' cried Kryptaestrex. The Master of Logistics turned his square frame from his station, every aspect of his noospheric aura alight with inloading data. 'Contact! Contact!'

'Atmospheric breach!' added Azuramagelli.

'Confirm: so soon?' said Blaylock. 'Current projections were a minimum of ten hours for tropospheric penetration.'

'Confirmed, Magos Blaylock,' said Kryptaestrex. 'Atmospheric conditions seem to indicate the presence of a highly charged atmospheric processor on the planet's surface.'

'Almost directly beneath the geoformer vessels...' said Azuramagelli, turning his latticework body to face Blaylock. Without facial features, it was left to the shimmering noospheric signifiers to convey his amazement. 'How... how did you know...?'

Blaylock had not divulged to the bridge crew exactly how he had chosen this particular quadrant of the planet's atmosphere. All he'd said was that the Omnissiah would surely guide their hand.

'Yes, Tarkis,' said Galatea, leaning down towards him with the dead silver eyes of its proxy body boring into him. 'How *did* you know where to send the geoformers?'

Blaylock ignored the question, knowing on some unconscious level that to reveal his use of the Mars Volta to Galatea would be a mistake.

The less the machine-hybrid knew of the secret workings of the *Speranza* the better.

Instead, he began issuing orders with all the curt efficiency for which he was known.

'Cancel the automated vox-loop. If Archmagos Kotov is making contact with the *Speranza*, I want him to hear one of *our* voices,' said Blaylock, moving from station to station and opening vox-links throughout the *Speranza*. 'Magos Dahan? Your skitarii rapid responders?'

'Are on immediate readiness alert,' came the Secutor's voice from the embarkation decks where he and his warriors were prepped and ready to fly. 'Say the word and we are planetside.'

'Prudence, Dahan,' cautioned Blaylock. 'Let us establish the situation before launching a full assault.'

Blaylock returned to the command throne and placed his metalled gauntlets upon its rests. Haptic connectors engaged and Blaylock's servitors squealed as his data-burden spiked. He linked with the *Speranza*'s peripheral layers, feeling his presence expand within the noosphere as its vastness rose up around him.

Data-dense swathes of informational light rose from the silver deck plates like spectral veils and Blaylock parsed the most pertinent in seconds. His split consciousness divided between analysis of the rapidly stabilising column of static air linking the cold of space with the planet's surface and the emissions rising from the planetary scale of its industry.

'Archmagos Kotov,' he began, but got no further before the vox erupted with a compressed data-blurt from Exnihlio. The grating sound blaring from the flanged mouths of the vox-grilles was just hashed static at first, too tightly packed to be understood.

Without giving any command, complex algorithms began unpacking the compressed signal and the noise instantly transformed into the voice of Archmagos Kotov.

'–lock, this is Kotov. You are to immediately break orbit and make best speed for the Imperium. Repeat, break orbit and get as far away from Exnihlio as possible. Do not attempt to reach the surface, do not try to reach us. Go! Go now, for the sake of the Omnissiah, leave now and never come back!'

Blaylock listened to Kotov's words with a growing sense of disbelief. The message was an exload of pre-recorded information. It had to be a mistake. A catastrophic disruption in the tight-beam transmission, perhaps? Despite the clear corridor linking them, residual pockets of localised distortion must be affecting the archmagos's transmission.

Even as he formed the thought, he knew it to be delusional.

The signal was clean and uncorrupted, its every binaric particle stamped with Kotov's noospheric signifiers, a more precise means of identification than even the most detailed genetic markers.

'Blaylock?' said Azuramagelli, similarly confused. 'What does the archmagos mean?'

'It's a mistake,' snapped Kryptaestrex, rounding on Azuramagelli. 'Your damned servitor-relays have fouled the signal somehow. It's the only explanation. It has to be, Tarkis.'

'I do not know,' replied Blaylock. 'I–'

The vox crackled as the pre-recorded exload ended and Kotov's voice filled the bridge. This time the words were spoken aloud and were filled with terrible urgency.

'Tarkis, if you can hear this, the cog is on the turn. Telok is not what I thought at all – he is a monster and the Breath of the Gods is an alien perversion of unthinkable horror. Telok seeks to tear down everything we hold dear. Mars, the Imperium, everything. Unless you act now he will take the *Speranza* back to Mars and–'

Kotov's words were abruptly cut off.

Dead air hissed from the vox.

Blaylock sat in stunned silence, trying to process his tumbling thoughts into some kind of rational order. Taken at face value, it turned his every certainty into a hideous joke. Had they come all this way just to find that the glittering promise at the end was in fact a trap as nightmarish as that which Galatea had set at the Valette Manifold station?

He wanted to believe that this was a mistake, a cruel subterfuge, but the evidence against that was right there in Kotov's words.

'Archmagos?' said Blaylock. 'Archmagos Kotov? Respond. Archmagos, respond immediately. Archmagos? Azuramagelli, keep trying.'

The Master of Astrogation returned to his data hub and began a broad-sweep vox-hail of the surface.

'Are we even sure that was the archmagos?' asked Kryptaestrex, approaching the throne.

'Yes,' said Blaylock. 'I am sure.'

'How can you be certain?' demanded Kryptaestrex.

'Because the cog is on the turn,' said Blaylock. 'Just as there are innocuous verbal cues to indicate a statement is being made under duress, there are codes to indicate that what is being said should be absolutely taken at face value. Archmagos Kotov's use of the phrase "the cog is on the turn" is of the latter persuasion.'

'So what do we do?'

Blaylock hesitated before replying.

'We follow Archmagos Kotov's last order,' said Blaylock. 'We break orbit and return to the Imperium as fast as we can.'

Another voice crackled over the vox.

'I'm sorry, Tarkis, but I'm afraid I can't let you do that,' said Vettius Telok.

And a shrieking spear of binaric fire stabbed up through Blaylock's entire body. His haptic implants burned white hot as their connection seared his flesh to the throne. The Fabricatus Locum's back arched with convulsive agonies, golden sparks erupting from his every point of connection. Synaptic pathways saturated with external communication inloads of hostile binary.

Millions of random images poured through his mind, occluding his thought processes with their banality. Yet even within this, there was a pattern. Repeating over and over was the image of a giant feline creature. Orange and black, its fearful symmetry was burning bright in a forest lit by a leering moon.

The feeder pipes connected to his shoulder-mounted canister tore free and noxious chem-nutrients sprayed the bridge. Still seated on the *Speranza*'s command throne, smoke from burned electricals curling from his augments, Blaylock grindingly shook his head.

'No,' he said, his voice filled with distortion as he fought the millions of errors triggering within the microcode of his body. 'This is a sovereign vessel of the Adeptus Mechanicus, under the command of Archmagos Lexell Kotov. You have no right to take it.'

Telok's sigh was heard throughout the *Speranza*.

'And I *so* hoped to do this without violence.'

'What are they?' said Surcouf.

Tanna leaned over the railing at the edge of the gantry, wondering the same thing. Their speed and the tapered, bladed cast of their skulls told him they were predator creatures. That was enough for now.

They sped up the curling ramp that spiralled the height of the tower, moving in bounding leaps like an Assault Marine on the hunt. Tanna saw the power in their limbs and knew that, but for the curve of the ramp, they would already be upon them.

'Battle robots?' he suggested.

'Those are not robots,' gasped Pavelka, making the Icon Mechanicus across her chest at the sight of the charging creatures. 'They are something far worse.'

'Give me something I can use to fight them,' said Tanna.

Pavelka shook her head, seeing the approaching machines in a way Tanna never could. 'Their spirits are degenerate, ancient things.

Mass-killers from a war millions of years ended. They scream their name in my head... *Tindalosi! Tindalosi!*'

'Interesting, but irrelevant,' said Tanna.

'Can you stop them?' asked Surcouf.

'Only if I do not need to protect you and Kotov.'

'Understood,' said Surcouf, helping Magos Pavelka away.

'Templars!' yelled Tanna, drawing his sword and making his way swiftly to the head of the ramp. His warriors stood to either side, Varda and Issur with their swords drawn, Bracha and Yael with bolters locked and loaded.

'Sigismund, chosen of Dorn, son of the Emperor, guide my blade in your name,' said Varda, lifting the Black Sword so that its quillons framed the coal-red eye-lenses of his helm.

The others mirrored Varda's sentiment as Colonel Anders chivvied his Guardsmen to the edges of the gantry. Hellguns blazed as the Cadians opened up on the creatures. Tanna didn't doubt that most of their shots would find a target.

The jade-armoured warriors of the eldar took up position to either side of the Templars. Tanna bristled at the flanking xenos, but suppressed his natural combative instincts.

'Their placement makes sense,' said Bracha over the internal vox. 'But I do not like it.'

Tanna nodded and squared his stance. 'When these things come at us, fight them with all your heart, but never forget there are aliens at our back as well.'

The eldar in the form-fitting ivory plates and blood-red plumes sprinted to the edge of the gantry. They effortlessly vaulted the railing, swords in one hand, gripping the metal with the other. Like acrobats, they swung in graceful arcs and dropped to the level of the ramp above the speeding hunters.

Tanna didn't bother watching them.

Even over the thunder of the tower's machinery and the snap of gunfire, he heard the clash of swords amid the dying echo of the eldar battle scream.

A shadow loomed and Tanna turned to see Uldanaish Ghostwalker. The wraith-warrior stood with the Black Templars at the head of the ramp as the clash of swords from below was silenced. Cadian las-fire resumed.

Meaning the eldar below were dead.

He rolled his shoulders in anticipation, loosening the muscles for the hard-burn of close-quarters battle. He risked a glance over the curve of his black and ivory shoulder guard.

Kotov and his skitarii were already moving across the gantry to a radial bridge leading to the tower's exterior. He didn't know what lay beyond, but that it was away from here was good enough.

Tanna addressed Ghostwalker as the crash of metallic claws tearing up the ramp drew ever closer.

'You are a little bigger than the warriors I usually fight alongside,' said Tanna.

'Are you concerned you might hit me?'

'That does not concern me in the slightest,' said Tanna.

'Then perhaps you worry I may hit you in the chaotic mêlée?'

'It crossed my mind.'

Ghostwalker leaned down. 'Know this, Templar. If I strike you, it will be entirely deliberate.'

'As it will be when I strike you,' said Tanna.

The warrior-construct gave a booming laugh and straightened to its full height as the hellhounds bounded into sight.

Silver creatures with wide, ursine shoulders. Narrow spines and the powerful legs of lean hunting hounds. Too-wide jaws, filled with tearing metal saw-fangs. Glittering, compound eye structures like scratches of light in a cave.

Their howls were shrieks of thirsting need. Blades snapped erect on their every limb.

Bolter fire and hails of whickering, razor-edged discs flensed them. Explosions blasted fragments of molten metal, and ribbons of steel pared back from every slicing impact of an eldar projectile.

One volley was all they got.

Uldanaish Ghostwalker took the first impact as two of the Tindalosi leapt at him. The wraith-warrior's blade moved too fast for something so huge. A Tindalosi howled, impaled, its gut ripped open and spilling shredded metal. Ghostwalker hurled it aside. Hellgun fire battered the fallen beast's gleaming flanks.

The second bit down on his arm, and sickly green fire bled into the wound. The creature's rear limbs curled to claw at the wraith-construct's chest. Tanna stepped in and hammered his blade into its haunches, tearing through to its spine.

It fell away, rolling clear of his follow-up.

Ghostwalker's gauntlet-mounted weapon swung to bear. Buzzing projectiles tore into the Tindalosi with a breaking-glass sound that was curiously musical. Three hounds snapped and clawed the ramp, poised to launch themselves at the Space Marines.

Tanna spun his sword back up to his shoulder and stepped forwards to give himself room. He kept his bolt pistol low at his thigh.

He turned just enough to invite attack and when it came he pulled back in an oblique turn. His sword deflected the leaping beast's snapping jaw. He rolled his wrist and shoulder barged it, pushing the thing backwards and down. He dropped a knee to its ribs and jammed the muzzle of his pistol into its exposed throat.

The mass-reactive punched through the metal and into the ramp.

The Tindalosi bellowed, and pungent, viscous gel sprayed Tanna's helm, necrotic oils of something long past its time to die.

It rolled away, the torn metal of its neck knitting together in a slick of green light.

Step back. Consolidate awareness.

They still held the top of the ramp. Hellguns and bolters fired enfilading volleys. Kotov and his skitarii almost out. Surcouf and Ven Anders shouting at Pavelka, who had plugged herself back into the control hub. No time to wonder why. Cadians surrounded the three of them, bulky hellguns pulled in tight as they awaited the colonel's order to withdraw.

Varda's sword flashed and the black blade plunged into a howling skull and tore it half away. Tanna swivelled and the pauldrons of the three Space Marines clashed together. Shoulder to shoulder in a circle of steel and adamantium they stood, ravaging all that came within reach.

A slash of talons came at Tanna's head and he parried with the body of his pistol. The weapon went off and he chopped his blade into a leg as hard as adamantium.

The creature staggered and Tanna worked the roaring blade hard into its chest. He hauled it free and kicked the beast back. He blinked and shook his head.

The monsters Ghostwalker had downed were up again. Shimmering green lightning played across their bodies. Opened guts were closed and buckled limbs straightened. Only once had Tanna fought creatures so difficult to kill, so unwilling to die.

The Tindalosi charged, but just before the instant of contact, two leapt to the side. Their powerful legs easily carried them over the railings of the gantry. Not his concern. Something for the Cadians and eldar to deal with. Behind him, Yael and Bracha opened fire with their bolters. Mass-reactives plucked one from the air, twin impacts punching it out over the gantry. Its howl rang from the tower walls as it fell.

'Into them!' shouted Tanna.

They met the charge of the hunting beasts head on. The impact was thunderous, like iron girders colliding. Legs braced, Tanna felt the curve of his pauldron crumple. Muscle mass deformed and blood

dispersed within the meat of his shoulder. His sword punched up. Screaming teeth tore metal. More viscous gel sprayed him.

A clawed arm slammed into his plastron, tearing loose the Templar's cross and gouging finger-deep grooves through the ceramite. The force hammered him to the side.

Tanna's sword snapped back up to block a tearing blow from above that drove him to his knees.

His armour thrummed with power. Tanna straightened his legs with a roar, hammering his sword's crossed pommel into a bellowing metallic skull that was part wolf, part saurian. Noxious machine-blood flew.

He lunged with the pistol, drove it into the belly of a beast. The shot exploded hard against armour and Tanna bit back a shout of sudden pain. His gauntlet filled with hot fluid, blood streaming down his forearm.

The creature snapped at him again. He thrust his chainsword, teeth scraping on steel as it parted metal and split a spine. He twisted it out, kicking the flailing creature back down the ramp.

Straighten up, breathe and blow, shake the pain. His chest was tight, his throat raw. Had he been screaming a battle shout?

'Too… t… too far forward, Tanna!' shouted Issur.

Get back.

The Tindalosi barged one another in their frenzy to break past the choke-point, their bladed limbs constricted, one machine-like killer obstructing another. He saw their confusion. They were not used to victims who could fight back like this.

'Find the openings,' yelled Tanna, to himself as much as everyone else. 'Kill them, kill them all.'

A blow glanced off his helm and hammered into his damaged shoulder guard. He grunted and punched a sword blow to the belly of a silver-skinned beast.

'Step in again!' he grunted. 'Keep them at bay!'

Tanna threw an upward sword cut to a thigh of hooked metal, a backstroke to the guts and a thrust to the chest. In deep and twist. Don't stop moving. Movement to the right, a howling bovine skull with fangs like daggers. He slashed it in the eyes. It screamed.

Move on. Face front, step back. Find another.

Two came at him. No room to swing. Another pommel strike, stove in the first's ribs. Stab the other in the belly, blade out.

The beasts withdrew, torn up and weeping emerald light from their ruptured bodies.

'Tanna! For the Emperor's sake stop pushing so far down the ramp!' shouted a voice.

Varda?

Tanna stepped back until he drew level with Varda and Issur. Each was slathered from helm to greaves in blood. Vivid red theirs, tar black that of the foe. They stood abreast at the summit of the ramp with Uldanaish Ghostwalker behind them.

The wraith-warrior's armour was cracked and clawed. One leg tremored, as though ready to collapse, the other leaked a molten amber-like sap from its knee joint. Something glittered through a dreadful gash in its helm, a faintly luminous gemstone.

The Tindalosi came at them again.

'Back to back!' roared Tanna.

Blaylock slumped from the *Speranza*'s command throne, feeling like every cell within him had chosen this moment to attack its host body. His vision snapped to black as cerebral inhibitors shut down in an attempt to block the surging inloads of spurious data.

His dwarf servitors squealed in distress as he shunted vast quantities of data to their overspill capacity. Two died instantly, their brains flash-burned by the immense overload. Another fell onto its side, spasming and losing control of every bodily function as rogue signals ripped through its body.

Blaylock heard warning sirens, alarm klaxons and squalling wails of binaric pain. The machines of the *Speranza* were howling with animal distress. Blaylock struggled to regain his feet, but that was proving to be harder than he'd expected. With virtually every facet of sensory apparatus shut down, he had no spatial awareness, no sense of up or down.

He pressed his hands to what he assumed was the deck and pushed, feeling it move away from him. Or was he moving away from *it*? Blaylock's lower body was a mixture of piston-driven bracing limbs and callipered counterbalances. It made for an efficient means of locomotion for a being of his mass and density, but right now he would have happily traded them in for a pair of organic legs.

Voices called his name with interrogative pulses of binary, complex logarithmic squirts of machine code and flesh-voices. None of it made sense.

He tried to speak, but his augmitter sub-systems – both binaric and hexamathic – were offline. His mouth opened, but only an exhalation of scorched air emerged, as though viral fires burned within his lungs.

Hands gripped him and hauled him into what he assumed was an upright position. A sudden, vertiginous sense of dislocation assailed Blaylock as he became aware of three-dimensional space around him.

His lower body pulsed through its gyroscopic diagnostics and quickly found his centre of balance. Bracing limbs slammed down and the rest of his body swiftly followed in a series of hard resets.

Some portions of his internal system architecture still felt somehow *wrong*, but now was not the time for a shut-down and full diagnostic assessment. Sight returned. Slowly. Fearful of shocking him with what it might reveal.

'Ave Deus Mechanicus,' he managed at last.

Strong hands still gripped his robes, soaked through where his feeder pipes had torn loose. The canister at his back was angled strangely, leaking clouds of acrid vapours.

He turned to thank the individual who had helped him to his feet, a magos in dark robes with silver eyes. His body was a crudely put together thing that somewhat resembled an arachnid.

Galatea, Blaylock's memory coils reminded him as they finished the purge of redundant data.

With its identity recalled, so too was the dreadful fact of its existence. The lies it had told, the violations of every Mechanicus law it represented and the lives it had ended. Blaylock pulled away from its infectious touch as though burned.

Almost every glittering entoptic veil burned with hissing, jumping static. Only the central display remained intact, though even it glitched and rolled with inloads of malicious code.

'Magos Blaylock!' shouted a boxy, robotic-looking thing that looked like it belonged in a loading dock rather than a starship's bridge. 'Are you rendered incapable?'

Kryptaestrex, Master of Logistics.

'No,' said Blaylock, though he felt anything but capable.

Another magos appeared beside Kryptaestrex. A latticework frame on robotic legs, within which an exploded diagram of a brain was held in suspension, spread between numerous linked plastek cubes.

Azuramagelli, Master of Astrogation.

'Magos Blaylock, you really need to see this,' said Azuramagelli. 'There is… something happening on the surface.'

'Something?' snapped Blaylock as yet more of his systems realigned after the attack on his augmetic nervous system. 'Since when do adepts of Mars employ such vague phraseology? Coherence, precision and logic. Remember them. Use them.'

'Apologies, Magos Blaylock,' said Azuramagelli, gesturing to his station with a spindly manipulator arm. 'I have not the terminology to accurately describe what I am seeing.'

Blaylock moved as fast as he could towards Azuramagelli's data

hub, realising that he was perhaps not as fully realigned as he had thought when the deck of the *Speranza* seemed to lurch beneath him.

He reached astrogation and pushed past Azuramagelli, carefully inloading the readings from the data hub, wary of any lingering fragments of malign code. He had been set to chastise Azuramagelli once again, but his admonishments went unsaid as he failed utterly to interpret the energy readings building to enormous levels on the planet's surface.

The data being gathered by the *Speranza*'s auguries was beyond anything Blaylock had ever seen. He had no idea what it might indicate, but the last vestiges of his human instincts of fight or flight screamed at him that this was dangerous.

'Raise the voids, Kryptaestrex,' he ordered. 'Immediately.'

'Magos, I have been trying to raise them for the last thirty seconds,' said Kryptaestrex.

'Trying?'

'They will not light. My every command is being denied access to the rituals of ignition.'

Blaylock all but ran to Kryptaestrex's data hub. Bleeding veils of red filled the slates. His haptics were useless, burned out by the surge attack, and his noospherics were still resetting.

But he could still issue commands manually.

His fingers danced over the floating entoptic keyboard, ordering the *Speranza* to protect itself.

But not even his exalted rank signifiers could reach the heart of the Ark Mechanicus. He was being kept out of his own ship's core controls by some external force.

The main display lit up with a flare of radiance building on the planet's surface beneath the huge electrical storms. A continental-scale flare that blew out the atmospheric tempests it had taken the geoformers hours to becalm. The horrifying sight put Blaylock in mind of a stellar flare or a coronal mass ejection.

'What is that?' he said.

'The Breath of the Gods,' said Galatea with awed reverence.

Moonchild was the first vessel to be hit.

An arc of parabolic lightning rose from the surface of Exnihlio, passing through the tortured skies without apparent effort. Seen from space it appeared to expand at leisurely pace, but was in fact moving at close to four hundred kilometres per second.

It wasn't *actually* lightning – such atmospheric discharges could only exist within a planetary atmosphere – but it was the best description the *Moonchild*'s captain could articulate.

His Master of Auspex shouted a warning, but the captain already knew the energised arc was moving too fast to avoid. Even with the Gothic's shields partially lit, the tracery of light struck the ventral armour of the prow.

Void-war was messy. It left vast clouds of debris and drifting hulks venting fuel and oxygen in their wake. It fouled space with squalling electromagnetics for decades and was rarely conclusive. The ranges at which most engagements were fought made it relatively easy for a vessel incapable of continuing a fight to go dark and slip away.

There would be no slipping away from this fight.

Moonchild exploded sequentially along its length. First the wedge of its bow vanished in a silent thunderclap of blue fire, then its mid-ships, and finally its drive section in a searing plasmic fireball. It burned with blinding radiance for a few brief seconds as the oxygen trapped within its hull was consumed.

The fires swiftly burned out, leaving *Moonchild* a charred skeleton of drifting wreckage. Lifeless. Inert. Ten thousand dead in the blink of an eye.

Another pair of lightning arcs coiled up from Exnihlio.

And *Wrathchild* and *Mortis Voss* joined *Moonchild* in death.

More lightning flared towards the *Speranza*.

Microcontent 10

Roboute hauled Pavelka's robes, but he might just as well have been trying to pull a section of the tower itself. The *Renard*'s magos was rooted to the spot, her data-spikes locked into the control hub. Flickering data-light scrolled down the optics beneath her hood and her limbs jerked with involuntary twitches. She was fighting the hub's code and, like an unbroken colt, it was fighting back.

Angry blasts of electrical discharge coruscated along the length of her mechadendrites and into her body. Roboute was uncomfortably aware of the repulsively mouth-watering reek of cooking meat.

'Ilanna! Disconnect!' he shouted, alternating his attention between the furious clash of blades and claws at the head of the ramp and the snap of las-fire from Cadian rifles. 'We have to go!'

'Just. Keep. Them. Off me...' hissed Pavelka.

'We don't have time for this,' said Ven Anders, one hand holding his rifle, the other gripping the hilt of his power sword. 'Get her free, Surcouf, or I'll cut her loose myself.'

Roboute nodded. He had no wish to remain here. He'd seen the thirsting, ribbed and fanged shapes of the monsters bounding up the ramp. The bulk of the Black Templars and the wraithlord kept him from seeing them any closer.

A state of affairs he was keen to see continued.

Bracha and Yael stood on the far side of the control hub, pumping shots into the enemy whenever a target presented itself.

The Templar swordsmen were faring less well. Tanna was down on one knee. His left arm hung limp at his side, his pistol a molten wreck on the ground. Issur spasmed in the grip of a crackling electrical field that was burning him to death within his armour.

Only Atticus Varda still fought unbowed.

His black blade hacked into the silver armour of the Tindalosi, sending cloven shards of silver and bronze spinning in all directions. The Emperor's Champion fought with the precision of a duellist and the power of a berserker, both war-forms distilled into a cohesive whole. It was quite the most extraordinarily disciplined feat of swordsmanship Roboute had ever seen.

But even so sublime a warrior could not fight forever.

'Ilanna, please,' begged Roboute, risking a hand on her shoulder. He felt the furious micro-tremors of a body largely composed of machines working at full-tilt.

The heat coming off her body was ferocious.

'Don't touch me!' she barked. 'Almost. There.'

'Too late!' shouted Ven Anders as two of the Tindalosi vaulted over the railings to the main floor of the gantry. One was punched from the air by a pair of three-round bursts from Yael and Bracha. The explosive impact of the mass-reactives blew the hellhound over the edge, and Roboute yelled in triumph as it fell with an ululating howl.

That still left one, and the Cadians turned their hellguns upon it. Blazing streams of las-fire punched out with a speed and accuracy that only a lifetime's worth of training could bring.

Not a single shot hit the Tindalosi.

A heartbeat later it was amongst them.

Vodanus snapped a living body in two, tossing it aside and clawing another in half from shoulder to pelvis. *This* was more like it. *This* was the kind of foe it relished.

Soft, mortal, fleshy and without any distracting code-scent that could break its *geas*. Its claws slashed and six bodies emptied of blood. Its hide whipped electricity. It burned, cut and melted its foes. Venomous oils secreted from its hooks left the meat screaming on their bellies.

Some were tough and sinewy, others light as air.

Different species?

It made no difference, both were just as fragile.

Energy beams stabbed it. Minor irritations. Its armour was proof against such primitive low-emission weapons. Crackling arcs of strange storm-lights struck it, psychic body blows of doom-seeking power. Ancient null-circuitry worked into its body dissipated these attacks harmlessly.

Did these meat-things know nothing of Vodanus?

Green-armoured warriors danced around it, darting in to bite it with crackling mouth-parts and slash with buzzing blades. It fired electro-magnetic micro-pulses that exploded their internal organs.

It heard screams from these ones, terrified screams that didn't come from any vocal organs. It filed the information away for later perusal. No species it had thus far slain evinced such behaviour upon its death.

Its jaws snapped on a mortal's head, wrenching the body from side to side and letting the serrations of its teeth do the rest. The fast meat-things kept coming at it, unaware yet that they could not kill Vodanus. Their weapons sparked against its armour, vespid stings against a leviathan.

Two of the black-armoured warriors rounded upon Vodanus – Space Marines, Telok's data had called them – together with a slender warrior armed with a screaming-toothed sword. The weapon was clearly too large for her to wield, but Vodanus recognised that she too was a lethal huntress.

These Space Marines were tougher and more deadly than anything its long-forgotten masters had wished dead. Each was encased in toxic armour of machine-spirits that could kill a hellhound with one wrong-placed bite or the temptation to feast. Vodanus did not fear these killers, but knew to be wary of them.

Its prey was within sight, escaping along an outflung bridge of mesh steel and wire. Still within its grasp, but the first rule of any hunt was to leave none alive who might hunt the hunter.

A pair of thundering impacts slowed its charge as the Space Marine warriors fired their heavy guns. Vodanus twisted into the air, killing another of the soul-screaming meat-sacks with a flick of its hooked back leg. Explosive ammunition followed it down, caroming from the curved plates of its shoulder as it landed in front of the three warriors that mattered.

It howled in fury, but they didn't run, which made them unique. *Everyone* ran from Vodanus.

But, Vodanus reminded itself, these things did not know it.

Another blast of explosive rounds hammered its armour.

One detonated within its chest, and the momentary pain staggered it. Vodanus had not known pain of this kind in millennia. The pain of isolation and madness, yes. The knowledge that its existence was fragmenting moment by moment, certainly.

But the pain of being *wounded?*

That stirred old memories, old hurts and old joys.

The power Telok had imbued it with from the ancient machine began its hateful work, cannibalising mineral reservoirs within its body to re-knit the damage, undo its hurt.

It sprang forwards, faster than they could avoid. One clawed arm rammed into the chest of a Space Marine with all the force Vodanus could muster. Black and white became saturated with red. So bright, so vivid. So much.

Vodanus clawed the body into the air and bit it in half.

It spat the crumpled debris of meat and metal from its mouth.

The huntress vaulted into the air as the second warrior ducked a hooked sweep of its arm. She spun the enormous blade as though it weighed nothing at all and clove it through a section of Vodanus's spine. The Space Marine rammed his own toothed sword into the renewing sections of Vodanus's body.

Once again, Vodanus knew pain, but this pain was welcome. It had been too long since it had faced any foe capable of hurting it. Its body rolled in mid-air and Vodanus rammed a bladed foot into the huntress's chest.

She screamed and crumpled, almost broken in two, her sword skidding across the gantry. Vodanus bellowed with howling laughter as it hooked a claw through the armour of the Space Marine and tossed him aside like offal. He slammed into the high column of the control hub, crashing back down with his armour cracked and the ivory wings on his chest shattered into a thousand fragments. Bleeding code vapour streamed from the broken pieces of black metal, but Vodanus ignored the sweet scent.

To taste it would be to die.

Instead, it turned towards a last handful of soft, meaty bodies that awaited murder. Most were code-free, bare flesh and fear, but one stood at the control hub, violently enmeshed with the ancient spirit at its heart.

This one bled code, *bad* code. Her machine arms snapped clear of the hub, drawing into her body. She cried a warning to the others.

Vodanus howled and relished the terror it tasted.

It bunched its hooked legs beneath it.

And the world exploded in screaming white fire.

Roboute and Anders had their guns drawn, but the giant beast that had so easily slaughtered most of the eldar and Cadians collapsed. It howled in pain, limbs convulsing in lethal swipes that tore up the metal of the gantry.

Even incapacitated it was lethal. To approach it was to die.

From the cessation of sound at the top of the ramp, Roboute knew something similar had happened to the Tindalosi facing Tanna's swordsmen and the wraithlord. His analytical mind flashed through a lightning-swift assay of their current situation.

Bracha was dead, no question of that, but Yael was already picking himself up with a groan of pain.

Roboute felt his mouth go dry. The very idea of a Space Marine experiencing pain was something he'd never expected to see. Every devotional pict spoke of the Adeptus Astartes' invincibility, their utter inability to feel pain or know fear. Roboute was realist enough to know that picts like that pedalled what the Imperium *wanted* its people to believe, but even he was shocked by the volume of blood leaving Yael's body.

Ariganna Icefang limped over to Bielanna, her armour torn all across her chest. Blood as bright as Yael's ran from her helm's eye-lenses like red tears. She'd been hurt badly. Maybe even mortally. She said something to Bielanna, but her dialect made the words unintelligible. Bielanna shook her head. Whatever the exarch was asking of her, the farseer could not deliver.

Roboute turned from the eldar as Pavelka slumped to her knees. Heat sinks worked into her rib-structure billowed the fabric of her robes with scorching vapours. She held a hand out to Roboute, feeling the air like a blind man. He took it, grimacing at the pain of her metal grip.

'What did you do, Ilanna?'

'Ask her later!' yelled Anders, slinging his rifle and helping Roboute get the stricken magos to her feet. If Anders was pained by the searing heat of Pavelka's body, he gave no sign.

Between them, they hauled her away from the control hub, trying not to step on any of the hacked-apart limbs and bodies the hunting machine had left in its wake.

The speed with which it had killed was phenomenal.

How many were dead?

Eldar and human bodies lay intertwined, making it impossible to tell. Tanna, Varda and Issur ran over, together with the few surviving Striking Scorpions and Howling Banshees.

'Was that you?' Tanna asked Pavelka.

She nodded. 'I tricked the hub into accepting a self-replicating piece of damaged code into every machine within this tower. Its viral form angered the spirits within them, and they explosively purged it into the noosphere. Invisible to you, but painfully blinding to anything that uses augmetic senses.'

Roboute glanced beneath Pavelka's hood, seeing her ocular implants were dull and blank where normally they shone with pale blue illumination. Thin tendrils of smoke curled from the scorched rims.

'No, Ilanna... Are you...?'

'It needed to be done,' she said. 'Now let's go!'

Wrathchild, *Mortis Voss* and *Moonchild* were lifeless wrecks, blackened and lit from within by sporadic flashes of dying machinery. The lightning that struck the *Speranza* came straight from the heart of Exnihlio and phased through the hull of the Ark Mechanicus without apparent effort. Existing on an entirely different phasic state of existence to that which had obliterated the *Speranza*'s escorts, it destroyed nothing until it reached its point of focus.

The first blast coalesced within the *Speranza* amidships on Deck 235/Chi-Rho 66, a high-ceilinged turbine chamber filled with rank upon rank of thundering engines that provided toxin-scrubbed air to a quadrant of ventral forge-temples.

A tempest of blazing lightning arcs, white-hot and fluid, filled the central nave between the turbines. Ghost shapes moved within the light, hurricanes of microscopic machinery that had travelled the length of the faux-lightning from Exnihlio in seconds.

The crackling bolt provided the energy, the particulate-rich air of the *Speranza* the raw material as solid forms began unfolding from the compressed molecules in which they had been carried.

The deck's servitors ignored the furious storm, oblivious to the threat manifesting among them. Those whose inculcated task routes carried them close to its wrath were instantly burned to cinders, their flesh and matter now fuel for the coalescing invasion.

At first the Mechanicus adepts struggled to find fault with their systems, believing some ritual or catechism had been overlooked or an incorrect unguent applied. Alarm klaxons blared throughout the deck and alert chimes rang through adjacent forges and engine-temples. By the time Chi-Rho 66's adepts realised this was no machine malfunction, it was already too late.

The first crystaliths to emerge from the lightstorm were crude approximations of Adeptus Astartes. Glassy and smoothly finished, each was freshly wrought from the molten light and filled with thousands of Telok's unique nano-machines. They marched in glittering ranks, hundreds strong, and filled Chi-Rho 66 with blasts of emerald fire. Machines exploded, servitors died, devastating chain reactions were begun.

Binaric vox-blurts raced frantically to the bridge, warning of the boarders, but Chi-Rho 66's warning would not be the last. Fresh arcs of lightning from the planet's surface struck all across the *Speranza*, a dozen at a time, and each storm disgorged hundreds of crystaliths. Some were a basic warrior-caste, others were larger, formed with heavier weapons and bladed claws, and carried sheets of reflective armour like heavy, glassy mantlets.

Last to form onto Chi-Rho 66 were the war machines.

What Telok had once described as *things of terror*.

Above the tower, the crackling fury in Exnihlio's upper atmosphere had stilled. Tanna was struck by the pale clarity of the sky. It reminded him of the murals aboard the *Eternal Crusader*, the ones that depicted the pastoral idyll of Old Earth.

That illusion was shattered the instant his eyes fell from the sky and saw the unending vistas of gargantuan generator towers and forge-complexes stretching to the horizon.

The radial bridge that led from the tower opened up onto a tiered set of stairs enclosed within a chain-link cage. The wide gantry offered routes to higher levels or down into roiling banks of flame-lit exhaust gases venting from the tower's base.

A cable-stayed suspension bridge connected the universal assembler to a vast, boxy structure five hundred metres away. Clad in sheets of rusted corrugated sheet-steel, the building offered no clues as to its purpose beyond a number of smoke stacks that belched soot-dark smoke and rained a greasy, ashen snow over the roofs of lower buildings.

It reminded Tanna of the giant, industrial-scale crematoria on worlds like Balhaut and Certus Minor.

He hoped that wasn't an omen.

'Bracha?' asked Varda.

Tanna shook his head, and the Emperor's Champion cursed.

'Yael?'

'Alive,' said Tanna, pointing to the far side of the bridge where Yael covered his battle-brothers with his bolter. They ran to join him, with Uldanaish Ghostwalker limping behind them.

The damage done to its legs had robbed the wraith-warrior of its speed and grace. Beside Yael, Kotov's skitarii were hacking an entrance into the structure ahead through a shuttered door of concertinaed steel.

Tanna glanced over his shoulder, searching for signs of pursuit.

Issur saw him look and said, 'You th-th-think the adept kill… killed them?'

'Doubtful,' replied Tanna. 'I laid enough mortal wounds on those

beasts that they should have been destroyed a dozen times over. If they can survive that, they will survive Magos Pavelka's cantrip.'

'Those beasts are tough,' agreed Varda. 'I only ever fought one foe that could survive the kill-strikes I favoured them with.'

Tanna nodded. 'Thanatos?'

'Aye, the silver-skinned devils that kept coming back no matter how hard I hit them or how many mass-reactives took them apart.'

'Is th-tha... that what these are?' asked Issur.

'No,' said Uldanaish Ghostwalker, his voice no longer deep and resonant, but thin and distant. 'These things are not servants of the *Yngir*, they were wrought by living hands and given the power to undo mortal wounds by Telok's mad sorceries. But you are correct, they will be back.'

As if to underscore the wraith-warrior's words, the hounds burst from the tower. Some stood on their hind legs, others hunched over on all fours as they searched for their prey. Even a cursory glance told Tanna the damage he and his brothers had inflicted was entirely absent.

The beasts saw them crossing the bridge and sprinted after them, bounding closer with howling appetite. Sparks flew from hooked claws on the mesh grille of the bridge deck.

'Templars, stand to!' shouted Tanna.

'No,' said Ghostwalker, standing athwart the bridge. The curved, bone-bladed sword snapped from its gauntlet. 'This is where *I* will fight, as Toralven Gravesong did at Hellabore.'

Tanna guessed what the giant warrior intended and said, 'Tell me one thing, Ghostwalker. Did Toralven Gravesong live?'

The wraithlord turned its emerald skull towards him, and Tanna saw through the awful wound torn there that the smooth gemstone within was cracked. Its light was fading.

'Toralven Gravesong was a doom-seeker,' said Ghostwalker.

'What does that mean?'

'That he had walked the wraith-path for more lifetimes than you or I will ever know,' said Ghostwalker. 'Perhaps too many.'

Tanna understood. 'On Armageddon, I met a warrior of the Blood Angels whose duty was to hear the final words of those whose death was upon them. It was his burden to end their suffering, but he spoke of the peace those lost souls sometimes knew when he told them that death had brought an end to their duty.'

Tanna, Varda and Issur raised their swords in salute.

'Die well, Ghostwalker,' said Tanna.

'Run,' advised the wraith-warrior.

✱✱✱

Uldanaish turned from the withdrawing mon-keigh, soul-sick that their leader actually believed he understood the true depth of what was to be lost here.

Hadn't the human heard what Uldanaish said earlier?

His body had died a long time ago, but devotion to the Swordwind had seen his spirit preserved within the ghost lattice of the wraith-lord's spirit stone. A spirit stone now split to its heart and releasing that which it kept hidden from an ancient and hungry god.

This was the fear that lurked at the heart of the eldar race. From artist to exarch, the prospect of She Who Thirsts devouring and tormenting their spirit for all eternity filled even the stoutest heart with unreasoning horror. Who could ever have thought he would embrace such a fate for the mon-keigh?

Uldanaish clung to his wounded wraith-body with every fibre of his determination. Already he could hear cruel laughter pressing in around him, the monstrous hunger of a dark power that would swallow his soul and not even notice.

The Tindalosi were almost upon him as he took position at the exact centre of the bridge.

A wraithlord did not see as mortals saw. Wraithsight perceived the world in half-glimpsed dreams and nightmares, each redolent with ghostly emotions and shimmering hues. Without a farseer's guiding light, it was difficult to sort real from unreal.

The eldar were ghost forms, concealed from She Who Thirsts by their spirit stones, but each mon-keigh was a plume of blood-red radiance, a being with an unlimited capacity for violence.

Bielanna was already within the building behind him, and Uldanaish felt a sudden fear at the prospect of his people entering that dread space. Something terrible lurked beneath it, something that reeked of unending pain and a world's suffering.

Uldanaish wanted to warn them of the danger, but the Tindalosi were upon him. Like the mon-keigh, they were radiant things, phosphor bright and feral in their lust for violence.

That they were intelligent was beyond question.

Uldanaish had felt their twisted malevolence as soon as they entered the tower. What lurked within them were artificial minds so monstrous, so psychotic, that it beggared belief any sentient race would risk creating them.

It saw the leader beast immediately, a patchwork thing of evil and insatiable hunger that left blistered negative impressions on his wraith-sight. Scratches of dark radiance flickered in the thing's smoking eye-lenses, and its oversized jaw drooled lightning from bloodstained fangs.

They came at Ghostwalker five abreast.

He charged towards them with long, loping strides. He stabbed down, carving the first through the spine with his wraithblade. Sensing weakness, one went for his legs, another his skull. He cut the first almost in two with his gauntlet weapon. The second impaled itself on his blade. Another seized his gauntlet in its jaws and swung itself wide, using its mass to drag him with it.

The last beast gripped the vanes flaring from his shoulders and wrenched in the opposite direction. Ghostwalker loosed a bray of ancient pain as the vanes shattered like porcelain. He brought his blade back, shearing the legs from the beast biting his other arm.

With that arm free, he swung low from the hip and pummelled his fist into the monstrous hunter clawing his side apart. The impact buckled its midsection inwards, almost snapping it in two. It screeched a machine-like howl and landed hard on the parapet of the bridge. Uldanaish leaned back and kicked it over.

The beast whose spine he had carved unfolded from its hurt, fresh plates already extruding from some internal void. Green lights danced over the new steel. Uldanaish sent a threading pulse of laser fire though its eyes. They blew out in a screaming howl of hostile static.

Two of the beasts tried to push past him. He stepped back and kicked one in the ribs, almost flattening it against the iron-girder parapet. Uldanaish spun on his heel and pinned the other to the plated deck of the bridge with his wraithblade.

The leader beast crashed into him. They rolled. Uldanaish's fist slammed into its side. Its wide mouth snapped shut on his skull, ripping out plate-sized shards of wraithbone. His blade scored deep cuts in its spinal ridges. Its hooked limbs ripped into his chest and broke his armour into long strips of wraithbone.

They broke apart. Uldanaish rolled to his feet and staggered as his right leg finally gave out. Psycho-active connective tissue ground like broken glass in the joint, and no amount of will could force it to bear his weight.

The Tindalosi faced him; he a wounded giant, they mechanised assassins that renewed themselves with each passing second.

Dragging himself back along the bridge deck on one knee, Uldanaish hauled himself upright. The spectral vista of his wraithsight was fading, yet the scratched outlines of the Tindalosi remained stark and black.

The sound of cruel laughter was closer now, like one of the *eldarith ynneas* coming to savour its victim's degradation.

Now was the moment.

'Come, hounds of Morai-Heg,' he said. 'We die together!'

Uldanaish extended his left arm and cut through the thick suspension cables with a sawing blast of high-energy laser pulses. At the same instant, his wraithblade sliced up through the entwined knot of cables at his shoulder.

The deck buckled as the bridge's cardinal supports were removed at a stroke. The Tindalosi saw the danger and surged past him, but it was already too late.

With a scream of tearing metal, the bridge snapped in two, spilling the combatants into the explosively toxic clouds venting from the base of the tower. The Tindalosi howled as they fell, their metal hides blistering in the caustic fog.

Uldanaish Ghostwalker made no sound at all.

His soul had already been claimed.

Microcontent 11

The aura of abandonment Vitali felt looking at the cog-toothed entrance to Forge Elektrus reminded him of the plague-soaked sump-temples of the Schiaparelli Sorrow of Acidalia Planitia. The Gallery of Unremembering within Olympus Mons depicted that great repository in its heyday, a towering pyramid filled with data from the earliest days of mankind's mastery of science.

Martian legend told that the Warmaster himself had unleashed a fractal-plague known as the Death of Innocence, which obliterated twenty thousand years of learning and transformed an entire species-worth of knowledge into howling nonsense code.

Vitali and Tarkis Blaylock had scoured some of the deepest memory-vaults for surviving fragments of that knowledge. The plague had evolved in the darkness for nearly ten millennia and all they found were corrupt machines, insane logic-engines and lethal scrapcode cybernetics haunting the molten datacores.

This wasn't quite on the same level, but being below the waterline on the *Speranza* while it was under attack gave Vitali the same sense of threat lurking around every corner.

Judging by the invisible cocktail of combat-stimms surrounding him, the twenty skitarii he'd commandeered from one of Dahan's reserve zones clearly felt the same way.

Vitali had wanted a cohort of praetorians, but Dahan had point-blank

refused, rank-signifiers be damned. After a heated binaric negotiation the Secutor had grudgingly released a demi-maniple to Vitali's authority.

Each skitarii was encased in archaic-looking shock-armour that put them only just below the height of a Space Marine. Draped in an assortment of ragged pennants and mechanical fetishes, their feral appearance put Vitali in mind of the legendary Thunder Warriors of Old Earth, whose faded images were preserved on a dusty block said to have once been part of the Annapurna Gate.

Oversized gauntlets bore a mixture of blast-carbines, shotcannons or heavy electro-spears. A few had power weapons or rapid-firing solid slug throwers comparable to Adeptus Astartes bolters.

They'd moved through the *Speranza* at speed, diverting to avoid columns of running soldiers, past the sounds of gunfire and explosions, along corridors scored with laser impacts and strewn with glassy debris.

Traversing a suspended gantry arcing across a vaulted graving dock designed for Leviathans, Vitali had his first glimpse of the enemy. Crystalline warriors, identical to the ones he'd remotely seen aboard the *Tomioka*. Blitzing green bolts chased them over the gantry, but before any real weight of fire could be brought to bear, a flanking force of weaponised servitors emerged from opposing transverse throughways. They punched through the enemy in a carefully orchestrated two-pronged attack. Vitali didn't stay to watch the final annihilation of the invaders, pushing ever downwards towards his destination.

The approach halls of Forge Elektrus were dark and unwelcoming, its spirits glitchy and wary of the intruders in their midst. Vitali sensed fresh reworking in the code of the machinery behind the walls, which surprised him in a place so obviously neglected.

His jet-black servo-skull, an exact replica of his own cranial vault, floated beside him like a nervous child. A battle robot aboard the *Tomioka* had almost destroyed it, but Linya had brought it back and painstakingly restored it on the journey to Exnihlio.

The skitarii hadn't shared the skull's caution, and deployed into the approach hall as though they were ready to storm Forge Elektrus. They took cover against projecting spars of the bulkhead and covered the cog-toothed door with their enormous guns. A weeping skull icon of the Mechanicus drizzled oil to the perforated deck. The vox implanted within its jaws buzzed and the lumens flickered in time with its hostile binaric growl.

Vitali walked to the door and looked up at the skull.

'My name is Magos Vitali Tychon, and I seek entry to Forge Elektrus,' he said, pressing his hand to the locking plate and letting it read his rank signifiers. 'I must see the senior magos within.'

The skull spat a wad of distortion.

'For an audience or a fight?' it said. 'I'm hearing reports about invaders on the ship, and that's a lot of nasty-looking men you have there. Two suzerain-caste kill-packs if I'm not mistaken.'

'It's quite a distance from the cartographae dome to Forge Elektrus,' said Vitali. 'And, as you say, the *Speranza* is under attack. I wanted to be sure I survived the journey.'

'Given that you're clearly mad to have even tried, tell me why I should let you in,' said the skull.

'Very well. I have reason to believe there is someone or something within this forge that can save the ship,' said Vitali.

The skull fell silent, hissing dead air for thirty seconds before the forge door rolled aside and a waft of incenses used in the anointing of freshly sanctified machines blew out. Vitali found himself facing a strikingly pretty adept, whose features so closely resembled Linya's that it sent a blistering surge of high voltage around his system. Her robes were oil-stained crimson. Golden light haloed her. She held an adept's staff crowned with laurels and snared mammals in one bronzed hand, a humming graviton pistol in the other.

'Magos Chiron Manubia at your service,' she said, and gestured within the forge with the barrel of her pistol. 'You can enter, but the kill-packs stay outside.'

Vitali nodded and issued a holding order to the skitarii before following Manubia inside. The door rolled shut behind him, his servo-skull darting in just before it closed entirely.

'The interior of Forge Elektrus does not match its outward appearance, Adept Manubia,' said Vitali, staring in wonder at a dozen gold-lit engines lining a mosaic-tiled nave.

'None of my doing,' she said.

Puzzled by her cryptic remark, Vitali moved down the nave.

The engines to either side of him crackled with eager machine-spirits, thrumming with more power than any one forge could possibly require. At the end of the nave was a throne worked into a wide Icon Mechanicus, and the light of the engines glittered in its cybernetic eye. Shaven-headed adepts of lowly rank tended to the engines or scoured flakes of rust from both throne and skull.

'Your journeymen?' asked Vitali.

'Not any more,' replied Manubia, turning to face him with the pistol held unwavering at his chest. 'Now tell me why you're here. And be truthful.'

Manubia's vague answers and hostility perplexed Vitali. She couldn't possibly think he was a threat. What was going on in Forge Elektrus that compelled its magos to greet another with a sublimely rare and lethal weapon?

'Well?' said Manubia when he didn't answer.

'What I have to tell you will stretch your credulity to breaking point,' he said, 'So I am opting to follow your advice and embrace total honesty. I want you to know that before I begin.'

And Vitali told her of Linya and Galatea, and how the machine-hybrid had gone on to murder her body in order to harvest her brain and incorporate it into a heuristic neuromatrix. Manubia's eyebrows rose in disbelief when he spoke of Linya's manifestation within the dome, but a look of understanding settled upon her when he spoke of what he had been told during their brief communion.

'*That's* what made you cross half the ship to come down here?'

'I would do anything to help my daughter,' said Vitali. 'And if that means crossing a ship at war, then so be it. I implore you, Adept Manubia, if you know anything at all, please tell me.'

'She knows me,' said a man in the coveralls of a bondsman who emerged from behind one of the largest machines.

The man was tall and rangy with close-cropped stubble for hair and the hollowed cheeks of a below-deck menial. A barcode tattoo on his cheek confirmed his status as a bondsman, but his eyes were tertiary-grade exosomatic augmetics and his right arm was a crude bionic with freshly-grafted haptics at the fingertips.

Vitali read the man's identity from the tattoo and anger touched him as he recognised the name.

'Abrehem Locke,' said Vitali.

The man frowned in confusion as Vitali strode towards him, all traces of the genial stargazer replaced by the mask of a tormented father.

'Your little revolution delayed getting Linya to the medicae decks,' said Vitali. 'You made her suffer.'

'Easy there,' said Manubia, following Vitali and keeping the graviton pistol trained on him. 'This isn't a subtle weapon, but I can still crack the legs from under you.'

Vitali ignored her. 'Linya almost died because of what you did.'

To his credit, Locke stood his ground. 'And I'm sorry for that, Magos Tychon, but I won't apologise for trying to better conditions in the underdecks. If you knew the suffering that goes on there, how badly the Mechanicus treats those who toil in its name, you'd have done exactly the same.'

Vitali wanted to throw Locke's words back in his face, remembering the agony he had suffered in trying to manage Linya's pain, but the

man was right. Vitali had even said words just like that to Roboute Surcouf on the *Renard*'s shuttle.

The anger drained from him and he nodded. 'Maybe so, Master Locke, maybe so, but it is hard for me to entirely forgive a man who caused my daughter pain, no matter how noble the principle in which he acted.'

'I understand,' said Locke, meeting Vitali's gaze.

Vitali looked carefully into the bondsman's augmetics, sensing there was more to this man than met the eye. Was this lowly bondsman the key to fighting Galatea?

'I think perhaps it was you I came here to find, Master Locke,' said Vitali.

'Me? Why?'

'I don't know yet,' said Vitali, lacing his fingers behind his back, 'but I will. Tell me, how much do you know of hexamathics?'

'Nothing at all.'

Vitali turned to Adept Manubia.

'Then you and I have a great deal of work to do.'

The structure his skitarii had cut into with their power fists and blades made no sense to Kotov. On a world where everything was given over to sustaining the Breath of the Gods, why would a place so large be left empty? Vast beams and columns of rusted steel supported a soaring roof obscured by an ochre smirr of mist. Decay and dilapidation hung heavy in the air, like an abandoned forge repurposed after centuries of neglect.

As far as Kotov could make out, the building had no floor beyond the wide, cantilevered platform of rusted metal reaching ten metres beyond the shuttered door. His two skitarii stayed close to him as he ventured out to its farthest extent. He sent his servo-skulls out over the void. Stablights worked into their eye sockets failed utterly to penetrate the immense, echoing and empty space.

Behind him, the Cadians, eldar and Black Templars pushed into the building. They shouted and hunted for ways to seal the entrance behind them.

Roboute Surcouf and Ven Anders helped Magos Pavelka to the ground, their arms around her shoulders. Kotov didn't need a noospheric connection to see her ocular augmetics had been burned away completely. Implant, nerve and neural interface were an alloyed molten spike of surgical steel and fused brain matter.

She would likely never see again.

Her head was bowed. In pain or regret?

Perhaps it was in shame for wielding profane code. If Kotov believed they might ever return to Mars, he would see to it that Ilanna Pavelka was irrevocably excommunicated from the Cult Mechanicus.

She had meddled with shadow artes and paid the inevitable price.

The thought gave him a moment's pause as he considered the depth of his own hubris.

And what price would I have to pay…?

He pushed aside the uncomfortable thought and knelt at the ragged edge of the platform. Beyond the metal, the ground fell away sharply in a steeply angled quarried slope. Dull steel rails fastened to the bare rock reflected the light of the skull's stablights, and Kotov followed their route to a battered funicular carriage sitting abandoned a hundred metres to his left.

He felt the aggression-stimms of the skitarii surge, and turned to see the eldar witch approaching. He stood his warriors down with a pulse of holding binary. Bielanna, that was her name, though Kotov had no intention of using it.

She removed her helm and knelt at the edge of the platform, staring down into the darkness. Kotov saw tears streaming down her cheeks. She reached out as if to touch something, then flinched, drawing her hand back sharply.

'It's here,' she said.

'What is?' asked Kotov.

'All the pain of this world.'

Ven Anders removed his helmet and dropped it at his feet. He closed his eyes and craned his neck to let the drizzling moisture wet his skin. He rubbed a hand over his face, clearing away the worst of the blood. Little of it was his, but he'd been standing next to Trooper Bailey when the Tindalosi eviscerated him.

Cadian Guardsmen fought on the very worst battlefields of the Imperium, knew all the myriad ways there were to die in war, but Anders had seldom seen cruelty as perfectly honed as he had in the Tindalosi.

Against the lids of his eyes he saw the hooking slashes of their claws, the bloody teeth and the phosphor scrawls of eyes that seemed to be looking at him even now. He shook off the sensation of being watched and hawked a mouthful of bitter spit over the edge of the platform.

He tasted metal and felt a buzzing in his back teeth that told him a Space Marine was standing next to him. Power armour always had that effect on him.

'For a big man, you step pretty light,' he said.

'Walk softly, but carry a big stick, isn't that what they say?'

Anders opened his eyes and ran his hands through his hair. Longer than he was used to. Time aboard the *Speranza* was making him lax in his personal grooming.

'I didn't know it was possible for a Space Marine to walk softly,' said Anders, looking up into Tanna's flat, open features.

'We have Scouts within our ranks,' said Tanna. 'Or did you think that was an ironic title?'

'I hadn't thought of it like that,' admitted Anders. 'Then again, I've never seen Space Marine Scouts.'

'Which is exactly the point,' said Tanna, before falling silent.

Anders understood that silence and said, 'I grieve for the loss of Bracha. Was he a… friend?'

'He was my brother,' said Tanna. 'Friend is too small a word.'

'I understand,' said Anders, and he knew Tanna would see the truth of that.

'We were a small enough brotherhood when we joined the Kotov Fleet,' said Tanna. 'And when we are no more, the courage these warriors have shown will pass unremembered. I would not see it so, but know not how to carve our mark into history's flesh.'

Tanna's words of introspection surprised Anders. He had encountered only a few Space Marines in his lifetime, but instinctively knew how rare this moment was.

And so he returned Tanna's honesty.

'I'm no stranger to death,' he said, pinching the bridge of his nose between his fingers. 'Stared it down a hundred times on a thousand battlefields and never once flinched. That's not bravado, it's really not, because it's not fear for my own life that keeps me pacing the halls at night…'

'It is for the lives of those you command.'

Anders nodded. 'No officer wants to lose men under his command, but death walks in every Guardsman's shadow. You go into battle knowing with *complete certainty* that you're going to lose men and women along the way. You have to make peace with that or you can't be an officer, not a Cadian officer anyway. But it was my job to keep those soldiers alive for as long as I could. I failed.'

'It was your job to lead those soldiers in battle for the Emperor, just as it has fallen to me to lead mine,' said Tanna, gripping Anders's shoulder. 'You did that. No commander can ever be sure of bringing all their warriors home, but so long as the foe is slain and the mission complete, their deaths serve the Emperor.'

Tanna held out his gauntlet and Anders saw a handful of gleaming

ident-tags. Each had been cleaned of blood, each one stamped with a name and Cadian bio-numeric identifier.

'I retrieved these from the bodies of your honoured dead,' said Tanna. 'I thought you would be glad of their return.'

Anders stared at the ident-tags. There hadn't been time to gather them from the torn-up corpses. Or at least he'd assumed there hadn't. That Tanna had risked his life and the lives of his warriors to retrieve them was an honour beyond repayment.

'Thank you,' said Anders, taking the tags and reading each name in turn. He pocketed them and held his hand out.

'The Emperor watch over you, Sergeant Tanna.'

'And you, Colonel Anders. It has been an honour to fight alongside you and your soldiers.'

Anders grinned, a measure of his cocksure Cadian attitude reasserting itself, and said, 'You say that like the fight's over, but Cadians aren't done until the Eye takes them. And we don't flinch easy.'

'Two questions,' said Surcouf, standing before the battered funicular carriage with his arms folded. 'Does it work and where do you think it goes?'

'It appears to be fully operational, though the mechanisms are corroded almost beyond functionality,' said Kotov, scraping rusted metal from the control levers. 'As to a destination, I can see no topographical representations of where it might ultimately lead.'

'Who cares where it *ultimately* leads?' said Surcouf. 'It goes away from here, that's the most important thing, surely? At least it'll give us a chance to regroup and figure out our next move.'

'Our next move?' said Kotov. 'What *moves* do you think we have left to us? Magos Blaylock will already be sailing the *Speranza* away from this cursed world. We have done all we can, Surcouf. Either Telok has the *Speranza* or Blaylock has departed. Either way, our chance to affect the outcome of this situation is over.'

Surcouf looked at him as though he hadn't understood what he'd just said. Kotov reran his words to check they had not been couched in ambiguous terms. No. Low Gothic and clear in meaning.

Clearly Surcouf did not agree with him.

'Even if you're sure Tarkis got the message, how can you be certain he managed to break orbit?' said Surcouf. 'Do you really think Telok went to all the trouble of ensnaring a ship like the *Speranza* just to let it sail away? No, we have to assume that Telok's cleverer than that.'

'What would you suggest, Master Surcouf?' said Kotov. 'How, with

all the manifold resources at our disposal, would you propose we fight against the might of an entire world?'

'One big problem is just a series of smaller problems,' said Surcouf. 'Small problems we can deal with.'

Kotov sneered. 'Optimistic Ultramarian platitudes will do us no good now.'

'Neither will your Mechanicus defeatism,' snapped Surcouf. 'So our first priority is to get away from here. Ilanna's bought us some time, so I suggest we don't waste it.'

Sergeant Tanna and Ven Anders entered the carriage, and the metal floor groaned alarmingly with their combined weight.

'Can you get this carriage working, archmagos?' asked Tanna.

'I already informed Master Surcouf that it was functional.'

'Then let's get going,' said Anders.

The transit between the two decks was a wide processional ramp with an angled parapet to either side, where dust-shawled statues and machines hissed and chattered in streams of binary. Perhaps it meant something important, perhaps the *Speranza* was trying to tell him something, but what that might be, Hawkins didn't know.

A twin-lascannon turret rested on a gargoyle-wrapped corbel above him, but it looked so poorly maintained, Hawkins doubted it could even move let alone fire. Kneeling Guardsmen took cover in the shadow of the machines on either side of the ramp, lasguns aimed at the wide gateway below.

Magos Blaylock had assured Hawkins that all the gates between main deck spaces would automatically seal, but that hadn't happened here. Reports of those gates that stubbornly refused to close crackled over the vox-bead in his ear, together with word of enemy movements.

Hawkins ran across the top of the ramp, where roll-out barricades were being hauled into place. Sergeant Rae issued orders to the seventy-six Cadian soldiers occupying this position in a voice familiar to Guardsmen across the galaxy. They prepared fire posts, bolted on kinetic ablatives or layered sacks of annealing particulates over the barricade. Hawkins was more used to sandbags, but Dahan assured him these were far superior in absorbing impacts than mere dirt.

And anyway, where could you get dirt on a starship?

A black-coated commissar worked alongside a support platoon setting up their plasma cannons in a prepared bastion. Supply officers set caches of ammo in armoured containers as a team of enginseers directed a pair of Sentinels hauling quad-barrelled Rapiers. One of the automated weapons was fitted out with heavy bolters, the other with a laser destroyer. Just as he'd ordered.

These powerful weapons would eventually seal this route, but until they were in place, it was grunts with lasrifles.

Taking up position at the centre of the barricade, Hawkins reached up and tapped the vox-bead at his ear.

'Company commanders, report.'

'Valdor company, no contact.'

'Sergeant Kastagir, Hotshot company, under moderate attack.'

'Where's Lieutenant Gerund, sergeant?'

'Hit to the arm, sir. The medics think she might lose it.'

'Do you need support?' asked Hawkins.

The vox crackled and the sounds of angry voices came down the line. *'Don't you dare, sir,'* said Lieutenant Gerund. *'We've got this one. Just took an unlucky ricochet, that's all.'*

'Understood,' said Hawkins. He had complete faith in each of his lieutenants, and if Gerund said she didn't need help, Hawkins believed her. He continued down his leaders.

'Creed company engaging now!'

'Squads Artema and Pious under fire. No significant losses.'

The rest of his forces provided a mix of contact/no-contact reports. Within four minutes of the boarding alarm going out, the Cadians had deployed to pre-assigned defence points, and a picture of the boarders' attack pattern – or rather, their lack of one – formed in Hawkins's mind.

A good defence rested on anticipating where an enemy would attack. Armouries, power plants, life-support, main arterials, inter-deck transits, vital junctions, connecting thoroughfares and the like. These were all vital targets, but the invaders were teleporting in at random. Some appeared in threatening positions, while others materialised in sealed-off portions of the ship or places of negligible importance.

'Callins,' said Hawkins, connecting to the prow forges where Jahn Callins was lighting a fire under Magos Turentek's adepts to get the armoured vehicles moving.

'A little busy here, sir,' replied Callins.

'We're not exactly sipping dammassine and playing cards down here, Jahn,' he said. 'Where's my armoured support?'

'Tricky, sir,' said Callins. *'These Mechanicus imbeciles have got half our inventory chained up in the damn air or hitched onto lifter-rigs. I'm trying to sort it, but it's taking time.'*

'How long? There's more of these crystal things appearing every minute.'

'Soon as I can, sir,' promised Callins. *'You'll know we're ready when we roll past you.'*

Hawkins grinned and signed off, turning his attention to this position. A pair of arguing magi with shaven skulls worked in the guts of a control hatch beside the gateway, but whatever they were doing, it wasn't working.

'Bloody Mechanicus,' said Hawkins, pausing as he passed a cogged skull icon stamped onto the wall next to him. He reached out and touched it, feeling the ever-present vibration passing through the starship.

A little self-conscious, Hawkins said, '*Speranza*, if you can hear me, we could really use some cooperation. We're trying to defend you, but you're not making it easy for us.'

'Since when have Cadian soldiers ever taken the *easy* fight?' said Rae, appearing with his rifle held loosely at his hip. 'We're born under the Eye and know hardship from birth. Why should life be any easier?'

Hawkins was about to answer when he heard a series of quick taps over the vox. Scout-cant. Three taps on the repeat.

Enemy inbound.

Rae heard it too and shouted, 'Stand to!' as a squad of cloaked scouts ran back through the gateway. The squad sergeant, a mohawked soldier with black and steel camo-paint slashed across his face, made a fist above his head. He made a crosswise motion across his chest and thumped his shoulder harness twice.

Two hundred or more.

The scouts sprinted up the ramp, keeping low and seeming to move only from the waist down. The adepts at the gate bleated in terror. One remained hooked into the gate's mechanisms, the other jerked free and hitched up his robes to run after the scouts.

'Spry for a tech-priest,' observed Rae.

'You'd be fast if you had two hundred enemy at your arse.'

'True,' said Rae as the scouts vaulted over the barricade and the first crystalline creatures, like the ones they'd faced on Katen Venia, poured through the gate.

'By squads, open fire!' shouted Hawkins.

A storm of las-fire blazed down the ramp and over fifty glittering enemies broke apart into splintered shards. Heavy bolters flayed the creatures, chugging reports echoing from the enclosing walls of the transit. Grenades burst amongst them and blue-white bolts of plasma heat-fused more where they stood.

Hawkins slotted the skull of a jagged-looking thing of crystal between his iron sights and pulled the trigger. It exploded like a

glass sculpture dropped from a great height. He picked another and dropped it, then another, methodically racking up kills with every shot.

Crackling bolts of green energy sliced up the ramp, but the Cadians were well dug in and the annealing properties of the particulate bags were living up to Magos Dahan's boast. The twin lascannons on the gargoyle-wrapped corbel opened fire, and blew a dozen creatures to shards.

Hawkins laughed. 'Well, what do you know?'

'Sir?' said Rae, a wide grin plastered across his face.

'Never mind,' replied Hawkins, ducking down to replace his rifle's powercell.

Then a section of the barricade exploded in a mushrooming detonation of sick green fire. A pulsing shock wave rolled over the Cadians as burning bodies rained down. Hawkins rolled and coughed a bitter wad of bloody spit.

'Creed save us, what was that?' grunted Rae, wiping grit from his eyes.

Hawkins dragged himself upright, pushing aside pieces of wrecked barricade and body parts as he blinked away spotty after-images of light. A ten-metre-wide gap had been blown in the barricade. At least thirty wounded Guardsmen lay scattered in disarray, little more than limbless, screaming half-bodies. Corpsmen were moving through the firestorm to reach them. They called out triage instructions as medicae servitors dragged the most seriously injured soldiers out of the line of fire.

Both Sentinels were down. One was on its knees, its armoured canopy torn open like foil paper and inner surfaces dripping red. The other sprawled on its back, the stumps of its mechanised legs thrashing uselessly beneath it. A burning Rapier lay on its side, the enginseers smeared to bloody paste. The other weapon platform sat in splendid isolation, looking miraculously undamaged.

Crunching over the shattered remains of the first wave of enemies, a gigantic creature of broken glass reflections pushed onto the base of the ramp.

Easily the size of three superheavies in a column, it was a hideous amalgam of rippling centipede and draconic beetle. Its head was a brutal orifice of concentric jaws that spun like the earth-crushing drills of a Hellbore. Spikes of weaponry blazed from the upper surfaces of its glossy carapace.

'War machine!' shouted Hawkins.

Bielanna listened to the mon-keigh speak as though their actions mattered, as though they were the agents of change in a universe that cared nothing for their mayfly existences.

And yet…

Hadn't she been drawn here by their actions? Hadn't she seen their actions deforming the skein, denying her a future where she was a mother to twin eldar girls? Hadn't she followed their threads to give her unborn daughters a chance to exist?

'You are lost, farseer,' said Ariganna Icefang, hissing in pain as the carriage began picking up speed and rumbled over a section of buckled rails. 'Restore your focus.'

Bielanna nodded and tried to smile at the gravely wounded exarch, but the despair was too heavy in her heart to convince. Ariganna's helm was cracked and her breath rasped heavily beneath the splintered wraithbone.

'Lost?' she said. 'Perhaps, but not the way you think.'

'I do not believe you,' said Ariganna. 'You were dwelling on what brought us to this place.'

'You are perceptive,' said Bielanna.

'For a warrior, you mean?'

Bielanna didn't answer. That was exactly what she'd thought.

'Death's shadow imparts a clarity denied to me in life,' said Ariganna, and Bielanna looked down at the blood pooling in the exarch's lap. So much blood and nothing she could do to stop it.

She swallowed. 'I was merely thinking that you were right.'

'I usually am,' said Ariganna, 'but about what specifically?'

'That I would lead us all to our doom. I have been a poor seer not to have seen this gathering fate.'

'Believe that when we are all dead,' said Ariganna.

'Too many of us are dead already,' said Bielanna. 'Torai, Yelena, Irenia, Khorada, Lighthand… And Uldanaish Ghostwalker is no longer among us.'

A shadow passed over the exarch's face and her eyes closed. Bielanna's heart sank into an abyss of grief, but it was simply the carriage entering the tunnel at the base of the rocky slope.

It had taken Kotov some time to restore the funicular to life, a process that seemed to require a considerable amount of cursing and repeated blows from his mechanised arms. Once moving, it had descended nearly a thousand metres before the fitful beams of its running lights illuminated a yawning tunnel mouth. Crystalline machinery that had the appearance of great age ringed the opening, its internal structure cloudy and cracked.

Ariganna's eyes opened and she said, 'I know, I felt the Ghostwalker's passing.'

'She Who Thirsts has him now,' said Bielanna, guilty tears flowing freely. 'I have damned him forever. I have damned us all.'

'You walk the Path of the Seer,' said Ariganna. 'You are trapped by that role just as I was trapped by the Path of the Warrior. You could no more fail to act on what you had seen than I could deny the pleasure I took in killing in the name of Kaela Mensha Khaine. Just answer me this… Knowing of the deaths your visions have led us to, would you go back and choose a different path? One that would not lead to your daughters' birth?'

'I would not, and that shames me,' said Bielanna.

'Feel no shame,' said Ariganna, 'for I would have it no other way. I would hate to die knowing your purpose was not as strong and sure as the Dawnlight.'

'Would that we had Anaris,' wept Bielanna. 'Nothing could stand before you then.'

'I am sure Eldanesh thought the same thing before he faced Khaine, but I take your point,' said Ariganna, her voice growing faint. Her hand reached up, and Bielanna assumed she looked for her chainsabre. The weapon was gone, lost in the fight with the Tindalosi. Bielanna drew her rune-inscribed sword and pressed it into the exarch's hand.

Ariganna shook her head and passed the weapon back as the last warriors of the *Starblade* gathered behind Bielanna. 'I will die as I was… before I… sought Khaine.'

Bielanna understood as Vaynesh and Tariquel knelt beside their exarch and released the clasps holding her broken helmet in place. They gently lifted it over Ariganna's head and stepped away.

Ariganna Icefang's features were cut glass and ice, violet-eyed and lethal, but that changed as the war-mask fell from her. As though another face entirely lay beneath her skin, the warm features of a frightened woman with the soul of a poet swam to the surface.

'Laconfir once told me there was no art more beautiful and diverse than the art of death, but he was wrong,' said Ariganna with the face she had worn before entering the Shrine of the Twilight Blade. '*Life* is the most beautiful art. I think I forgot that for a time, but now…'

The former exarch reached beneath her cracked breastplate and withdrew her clenched fist.

'Though my body dies, I remain evermore,' said Ariganna, placing her hand upon Bielanna's outstretched palm. 'My spirit endures in all my kin who yet live.'

The exarch's hand fell away, revealing a softly glowing spirit stone.

And Bielanna loosed an ululating howl of depthless anguish that blew out every window of the funicular in an explosion of shattering glass.

The sight of the crystalline war machine might have put other soldiers to rout, but the Cadian 71st had fought the armies of the Despoiler across Agripinaa's industrialised hellscape. The Archenemy's war engines were blood-soaked things of warped flesh and dark iron, wrought to horrify as much as kill.

Having faced them and lived, this thing's appearance gave the Cadians only a moment's pause.

Las-bolts refracted through its translucent body, shearing away fused shards of crystal. Grenades cracked the glassy surface of its bullet-headed skull. They were hurting it, but too slowly.

Spiked extrusions from its segmented back spat emerald lightning. The bolts arced and leapt across the barricade, and not even Dahan's annealing particulates or the kinetic ablatives could withstand their power. Howling soldiers were vaporised in the coruscating electrical storms, the skin melting from their bones in an instant.

Hawkins turned to Rae and shouted, 'With me, sergeant!'

'Where are we going?'

'Don't ask, just follow,' said Hawkins, and pushed off the barricade. He ran to the top of the ramp, hearing Rae cursing him with all the force and inventiveness of a Cadian stevedore.

He forced himself to ignore wounded soldiers calling for help, weaving a path through the rubble piled atop scores of the dead. Lethal bolts of green fire spanked the ground, and Hawkins bit back a shout of pain as searing heat creased his shoulder.

A steady stream of fire blitzed the war machine, but lasguns and plasma guns just weren't cutting it. He skidded into the cover of the Rapier, taking a moment to catch his breath. Rae tumbled in behind, breathless and streaked in sweat.

'Can you even fire this thing?' asked Rae.

'Callins showed me the basics when we served on Belis Corona,' said Hawkins. 'Easy as stripping a lasgun, I reckon.'

Rae gave him a sceptical look as he scrabbled to his feet and turned around, doing his best not to expose himself to fire. He ran his eyes over the control mechanism. A mixture of amber and green gem-lights blinking on a brass-rimmed panel. Dozens of ivory switches that could be turned to a number of settings.

But, reassuringly, a set of rubberised pistol handles with brass spoon-triggers.

'How hard can it be?' he said, gripping the firing mechanism and mashing the oversized triggers.

A bolt of blinding light stabbed down the ramp and punched through the bulkhead to the left of the advancing war machine. The beam's white-hot point of impact reduced two dozen crystalline foes to microscopic fragments, but left the war machine untouched.

'How in the name of the Eye did you miss?' yelled Rae, as the war machine pushed more of its bulk into the transit. Hawkins looked for a control to adjust the Rapier's aim, but came up empty. Why would he have expected *this* to be easy?

'Push it,' he shouted over the hiss of lasguns and metallic coughs of grenade detonations. 'A metre to the left.'

Rae looked up at him as though he were mad.

'Seriously?'

'I don't know how to shift its aim. Now get around this thing and push it!'

Rae rolled his eyes and scrambled around the bulky weapon system. Flurries of snapping energy bolts tore up the ground and portions of the barricade next to him. The sergeant rammed his shoulder into the side of the Rapier, grunting with the effort. It didn't move.

'Put your back into it, man!'

Rae shouted something obscene that Hawkins chose to ignore as a number of Guardsmen broke from cover to help. Two were cut down almost immediately, another fell with the flesh stripped from his legs. But enough reached the Rapier alive and slammed into it with grunts of exertion.

Against Cadian strength, the weight of the Rapier had no chance, and the track unit shifted. Hawkins looked over the top of the machine. He stared down into the cavernous, blade-filled mouth.

'Got you,' he said and mashed the triggers again.

This time the beam punched down its throat. It lit up from within as the awesome power of the beam refracted through its entire structure. The war machine detonated in an explosion of molten glass and glittering metal-rich dust.

Its body slumped, coming apart in an avalanche of broken glass.

And finally, to Hawkins's great surprise, the gate began to close with a grinding screech of metal that hadn't moved in centuries. Hawkins saw the lone tech-priest hunched in the lee of the pilasters at the side of the gateway. The adept was still connected into the hatch by trailing cables, and Hawkins swore he'd pin a Ward of Cadia on his damn chest.

The gate slammed down with a booming clang and a crunch of

pulverised crystal. The few enemy still on the Cadian side of the gate were swiftly gunned down with coordinated precision. Within thirty seconds, the area was secure.

Hawkins forced himself to release the Rapier's fire-controls, his fingers cramped after gripping so hard.

'Sir,' said Rae, carefully and calmly, 'next time you want to put us in harm's way like that could you, well, *not*...?'

Hawkins nodded and let out a shuddering breath.

'I'll take that under advisement, sergeant,' said Hawkins.

The enemy wasn't getting through this gateway any time soon, so it was time to consolidate. Well over half his men were down. Those too wounded to remain in place were evacuated to pre-established field-infirmaries. Fresh powercells and water were dispensed to those who remained.

Replacement sections of barricade were installed and with reinforcements arriving from the reserve platoons, the position was secure within four minutes of the attack's ending.

Hawkins checked with his other detachments, listening to clipped reports of furious firefights throughout his sectors of responsibility. Some were still engaged, some had repulsed numerous waves of attackers. Others had yet to make enemy contact. Only one position had been abandoned as crystalline foes appeared without warning in flanking positions in overwhelming numbers.

Hawkins adjusted his mental map of the fighting, seeing areas of vulnerability, angles of potential counter-attack and areas of the *Speranza* where the greatest threats might arise.

One location immediately presented itself as the greatest danger – as he'd always suspected it would.

'Sergeant Rae,' he said. 'Assemble a rapid-reaction command platoon. I need to be moving on the double.'

'Where are we going?'

'Just get it done, sergeant.'

Rae nodded, dragging squads out of the line and hustling them into formation. Hawkins tapped the bead in his ear, cycling through channels until he reached the Mechanicus vox-net.

'Dahan, status report?'

The Magos Secutor's response was virtually immediate.

'I am orchestrating the ship's defence from the Secutor temple. All skitarii positions holding, though the randomness of the enemy arrival points is proving to be most vexing.'

'Always a pain when the enemy doesn't play nice, isn't it?'

'A predictable enemy is an enemy that can be more easily overcome,'

agreed Dahan. *'Observation: I discern a lack of cohesion in this assault. Each enemy contingent appears to be working to its own design, independent of the others.'*

'Keeping our attention divided,' said Hawkins. 'Trying to mask the real danger.'

'What real danger?'

'The training deck,' said Hawkins. 'Lots of ways in and a more or less straight run to the bridge. We're on our way there now.'

'An unnecessary redeployment, Captain Hawkins,' said Dahan. *'Skitarii forces are emplaced and all static weaponry has been granted full lethal authority.'*

Rae signalled the command platoon's readiness, and Hawkins took his place in the line.

'Call it gut reaction, magos,' said Hawkins. 'I get the feeling this attack will cohere soon enough, and when it does, they're going to throw everything they've got at us.'

Microcontent 12

Thanks to the empty window frames, the reek of stale air and turned earth had been growing stronger in the funicular with every kilometre travelled. By the time it reached the end of its long journey through the planet's crust, the graveyard stench was almost overpowering.

Even distanced from olfactory input by augmented sensory limiters, Kotov still registered the smell as unpleasant. From the looks of disgust on the faces of those without his advantages, it must be unbearable to baseline senses.

The carriage doors squealed open, revealing the funicular's final destination: a buckled terminus platform of bare iron within an ancient cave of gnarled rock. The ceiling was jagged with grotesquely organic stalactites of rotted matter, and pools of foetid liquid gathered beneath them in sticky pools.

Tanna and the Black Templars debarked first, moving to the filth-encrusted walls and covering the only other exit, a cave mouth fringed with cloudy crystalline growths. The Cadians went next, following their colonel with rifles jammed in tight to their shoulders.

'So do you think this is a better place, Master Surcouf?' asked Kotov, taking a moment to enjoy the sight of the rogue trader pressing a wadded kerchief over his mouth and nose.

'Well, we're not being attacked by bloodthirsty mech-hunters, so I'd say it's a step up from the universal assembler.'

Kotov stepped from the funicular and almost immediately, his chronometer began glitching, the numerals speeding up, reversing and flickering in and out of sync with his implanted organs. The effect was disorientating, and he stumbled. His skitarii held him upright.

'Archmagos?' asked one, whose noospheric tags identified him as Carna. 'Is something the matter?'

Kotov disabled the chronometer and restored his equilibrium with a surge of internal purgatives. The unpleasant sensation passed and he nodded to his protectors.

'I am fine,' he said.

Surcouf followed him onto the platform, with Magos Pavelka clinging to his arm. Surcouf was almost dragged to the ground when Pavelka was seized by the same nauseous sense of mechanical dislocation that had almost felled him.

'Turn off your chronometer,' Kotov advised her, though given Pavelka's transgressions, he was inclined to let her suffer.

As unpleasant as the effects of the cave were to Kotov and Pavelka, it was nothing to how the eldar witch reacted. Bielanna screamed and fell to her knees as soon as she stepped from the carriage. Her skin, which even to a Martian priest appeared unnaturally pale, grew ever more ashen. Her face contorted in grief, more so than when her piercing shriek on the carriage had almost deafened them all. Her face contorted as though invisible hands were pushing each muscle in different directions at once. Tears streamed down her face.

'I told you...' she said. 'All the pain of this world is here. This is it, this is the locus of splintering time. This is where the fraying of every thread begins and ends. The flaw that tears the weave apart...'

Her words made no sense to Kotov and he turned away.

'You led us to this,' spat Bielanna. 'Your mon-keigh stupidity!'

Carna growled, baring steel-plated teeth, but Bielanna ignored him. Her warriors helped her to her feet, but she shrugged them off, stalking towards Kotov like an assassin with a helpless target in sight.

The skitarii raised their weapons, but Bielanna hurled them aside with a sweeping gesture of her palms. They slammed into the walls of the cave, and hoarfrost patterned the surface of their armour as she pinned them three metres above the platform.

'What have you done here?' said Bielanna, a distant, confused look in her eyes, as though she was having to force each word into existence. It seemed to Kotov that she was not really addressing him, but some unseen elemental force.

'Time itself is being unmade here,' sobbed Bielanna. 'The future unwoven and the past rewritten! All the potential of the future is

being stolen... No! This cannot happen... Infinite mirrors reflecting one another over and over... Oh, you came here with such dreams... Time and memory twisted into hate... Trapped here... We cannot escape, we cannot move... Oh, Isha's mercy... The pain. To never move, to be denied the time-drift...'

Bielanna's skin shimmered with internal radiance, her eyes ablaze with anger. Her hands were fists of lightning, but with an effort of will, she flexed her fingers and the crackling psychic energies dissipated. She let out a shuddering breath that dropped the temperature in the cave markedly.

The two skitarii fell to the iron platform. Both were instantly on their feet, weapons ratcheting into their kill-cycles.

'Stand down,' ordered Kotov, with an accompanying blurt of authoritative binary. Reluctantly – *very* reluctantly – the skitarii obeyed, but still put themselves between him and Bielanna.

'Whatever you are seeing or feeling here is not my doing,' said Kotov. 'It is Telok's. Save your rage for him.'

And with that he turned away, marching towards the exit from the terminus, where the Cadians cast wary glances before and behind them. Kotov's passive auspex – all he had allowed himself since the attack of the Tindalosi – registered powerful forces at work beyond the cave mouth.

He passed the Cadians and entered a long tunnel, circular in section except where iron decking had been laid along its base. The walls were rippling, vitrified rock. Melta-cut. Here and there, scraps of rotted cloth and dust lay discarded like emptied sandbags. A flickering white-green light beckoned him on and as he drew closer he tasted the actinic tang of powerful engines at work.

The tunnel opened onto a detritus-choked rock shelf overlooking a vast, subterranean gorge. Cliffs of stone soared overhead to a cavern roof that was ragged with spiralling horns of rock and dripping with foetid drizzle. Rusted iron spheres and enormous girders supported a network of arcane machinery that explained the source of the white-green light.

Tanna and his warriors stood amazed at the edge of the abyssal plunge, amid a tangle of corroded iron barriers. Kotov's chronometer flared back to life, and a gut-wrenching mechanical nausea surged through his floodstream. He shut the chronometer off again. It reactivated a moment later, spiralling back and forth through time-cycles.

'Tanna, what–'

Then Kotov saw the city.

Spreading like a rusted fungus across the opposite wall of the huge

cave was a hideous warren of disgusting scrap dwellings wrought from iron and mud and ordure. They clung to the vertical sides of the chasm, and a twisting network of wire-wrought bridges draped the structures like a web.

Clearly of ancient provenance, the city was a grotesque fusion of organic growth and artifice. Portions had the appearance of having been built up from resinous secretions, pierced with tunnels like the lairs of burrower beasts, while others were formed from buckled sheets of scavenged metal. Hunched shadows moved between ragged tears in their walls, suggesting that this city was not dead at all, but occupied by some hideous troglodytic vermin. With halting steps that crunched over granular fragments of splintered crystal, Kotov put aside his discomfort and pulled himself forwards with the remains of the iron fretwork.

'What has Telok done here?' said Tanna, bending down to lift a robe of ragged hessian-like cloth from the ground. 'What lives in that city?'

Tanna held the robe out to Kotov. He took it from Tanna and turned it over in his manipulator digits. The material was ancient and crumbled at his touch. He remembered seeing similar scraps in the tunnel leading to the funicular terminal.

'I do not know,' said Kotov, 'but this looks too familiar for comfort… I have seen remains like this before.'

Tanna nodded and said, 'The *Tomioka*.'

'Yes,' agreed Kotov.

'I think I might know what these were,' said Roboute, bending to sift through a rotten bundle of patterned cloth and carefully lifting something small that gleamed dully in the light of the crackling machinery on the roof of the cave.

He held the object up for the others to see, and Kotov instantly matched it to the fragment that had disintegrated in Tanna's hand beneath the *Tomioka*.

'What is that?' asked Tanna.

'Part of the firing mechanism of a xeno-weapon,' said Roboute.

'How do you know that?' said Kotov.

'*Please,* archmagos, I'm a rogue trader, it's my job to go places and see things that would get most people a one-way trip to an excruciation chamber,' said Roboute. 'But, specifically, I once attended a very exclusive auction held by one of the borderland archeotech clans out on the fringes of the Ghoul Stars. Very exclusive, strictly invite only. Even then they were cautious, conducting every aspect of the transaction via servitor proxy-bodies and requiring every attendee to submit to biogenic non-disclosures not to reveal what they'd

seen. Glossaic-sensitive venom capsules, neural pick-ups linked to implanted mycotoxin dispensers. Pretty standard stuff among the more *cautious* collectors.'

'So how can you tell us now?' said Kotov.

'You think that was the first contraband auction I've been to, archmagos?' said Roboute, almost offended. 'There isn't a confidentiality technology I *don't* know my way around. Anyway, the last lot of the auction was a custom-made stasis sarcophagus containing a xenoform with a weapon that had a firing mechanism just like this.'

As Roboute spoke of the auction, the metal in his hand began to crumble with accelerated degradation.

'What manner of xenos?' asked Tanna.

'They called it a Nocturnal Warrior of Hrud,' said Roboute.

Phosphor-streaked highways ran the length of the *Speranza*, neon bright against the darkness. Molten datacores flared brightly, miniature suns against the matt darkness of the void surrounding them. The impossibly dense and complex datascape of the Ark Mechanicus spread before Abrehem, wrought in glittering binaric constellations.

This was what lay beneath the rude matter of the *Speranza*, a network of pulsing information rendered down to its purest, most unambiguous form. No walls of steel or stone constrained the informational light's journey around the ship, no aspect of its life worked independently of another.

<Everything is connected,> said Abrehem, relishing his newly implanted knowledge of lingua-technis. <How could I not have seen it?>

Light enfolded him as he passed effortlessly through the virtual structure of the vessel he had always assumed was as solid and impermeable as any planetary body. He saw the lie of that now, freed from the confines of his flesh and given free rein of the invisible datascape within the *Speranza*.

Abrehem watched myriad lightstreams converge, their whole becoming brighter than the sum of its parts. He saw geometric shapes transform as fresh data reshaped them. He flew alongside shoals of fleeting data as it skimmed the surface of a glittering superhighway of knowledge.

Sometimes the data clotted, becoming dull and unresponsive until the patterns of light rerouted. Pathways split and the flow altered like water in a river.

What did such changes indicate?

Abrehem had no idea, but he watched the light twist into new

patterns throughout the ship, constantly reorganising and reformatting itself. How long had it been since Magos Tychon and Chiron Manubia had sat him in the polished throne at the heart of Forge Elektrus and let the haptic implants in his mechanised arm mesh with its divine circuits?

A minute? A year?

Hexamathic calculus filled Abrehem's head, an interconnected web of quantum algebraics, axioms of metatheory, four-dimensional geometries, N-topological parametrics and multivariate equations. Even the simplest concept was utterly bewildering to Abrehem's conscious mind. Only the deepest regions of his psyche were able to process the many illogical, acausal and counter-intuitive tenets of hexamathics.

His introduction to this arcane branch of mathematical techno-theology had been brutally, painfully rapid. Optical inloads were driven straight through his eyes to the neocortex of his brain.

An imperfect means of knowledge implantation and one that, according to Magos Tychon, would fade without continual reinforcement. Only a complete remodelling of his cognitive architecture and numerous invasive cerebral implants would allow the inloads to permanently bond with his synaptic pathways.

Much to Abrehem's relief, such procedures were beyond the skill of any in Forge Elektrus to perform, and the nearest medicae deck was under siege. So, agonisingly painful optical inloads it was.

But it was worth any pain to see the ship like this, to fly its length in the time it took to form the thought. The largest forges, temples and information networks were hyper-dense novae of light. The command bridge was incandescent, too bright to look upon.

Each critical system was a pulsing star of layered information, stored knowledge and the collected wisdom of all who toiled within. Nor was Abrehem's sight confined simply to the ship's systems.

Scattered like nebulous clouds of glittering dust, the *Speranza*'s crew billowed through the traceries of scaffolding light as microscopic flecks. Confined by millennia of dogma to prescribed pathways, none could fly the datascape as free as Abrehem.

Yet even the brightest adepts were tiny embers compared to the heart of the ship where its gestalt spirit took shape. The sum total of their knowledge was insignificant next to the things the ship knew in its deepest, most hidden logic-caches.

Vitali and Manubia had warned him not to venture too far from Elektrus, that this was simply a test to see if he could fly the datascape at all. He was given strict instructions to keep clear of any system infected by Galatea's presence. He had yet to learn its subtleties. Many

were those whose awe had led them into dangerous archipelagos of corrupt code and left them brain-dead, their bodies fit only for transformation into servitors.

Abrehem doubted any of those unfortunates were Machine-touched, so guided his course down to the nearest datacore, one of many that regulated the ship's atmospheric content. It took the form of a simple sphere of pure white light, that very simplicity suggesting extreme complexity within.

Streams of coruscating binary flared from it like solar ejections, lattices of chemical ratio-structures, air-mix formulae and the like, all passing into the river of information flowing through the *Speranza*.

Abrehem took up orbit around the datacore's equator, glorying in its roaring, furnace-like heat. Its heart was pure molten data, yet something else squatted within it, something that should never have been allowed into the datascape, something parasitic.

<Galatea…> whispered Abrehem.

Aware it was observed, the parasite within the datacore uncoiled like a slowly wakening serpent. Abrehem knew immediately that Galatea's presence was something unwholesome, something with the potential to destroy the datacore in the blink of an eye.

Realising he was in terrible danger, Abrehem tried to fly away, but whipping lines of light lashed him. Pulled him down. Pain jackknifed him. Ice enfolded his heart, his autonomic nervous system crashing as the thing took pains to kill him slowly and carefully.

Abrehem tried to speak, to plead for his life, but induced feedback was eating through into his cerebrum. Even as it killed him, it studied him; curious at this unbound traveller in its domain.

<Who are you, little man?> it said.

<Abrehem Locke,> he said, the words dragged from his mind.

<We are Galatea,> said the parasite, <and this is *our* ship.>

Abrehem felt its squirming coils crushing him, wondering if anyone in Forge Elektrus would even know he was dying. Would he be convulsing with feedback agonies? Would his body have voided itself as he lost control of his bodily functions?

<Forge Elektrus,> chuckled Galatea. <So that is where you came from. Well, we shall need to do something about that, won't we?>

Abrehem tried to keep his thoughts secure, but Galatea penetrated every defence with ease. It peeled back the layers of his psyche like poorly sutured grafts, digesting all he knew piece by piece.

How galling to die on his first time in the datascape! How Vitali would be disappointed to find that his hoped-for saviour was a fraud.

He had hoped to salve the venerable stargazer's pain by helping him fight Galatea, but how naïve that hope now seemed.

Angry at his failure, Abrehem lashed out.

And a pure white light exploded from him, searing the serpentine coils of parasitic data to inert cubes of black ash. Galatea's scream of pain echoed across the binaric vistas of information as this aspect of its infection was burned out. Abrehem stared in wonder as the datacore pulsed hotter and brighter now that the cuckoo in the nest had been excised.

The dreadful cold fell away and his heart kicked out like a drowning man as it fibrillated with sudden spasms of life. Abrehem felt himself being pushed away from the datacore, the binaric spirit at its heart wishing him gone.

He understood why. It feared Galatea would return.

He lifted his head and soared high above the main highways of code, feeling vengeful tendrils of Galatea's presence closing in.

<Time to get out,> said Abrehem.

He recited the separation mantra.

Abrehem opened his eyes…

…and all but collapsed to the floor of Forge Elektrus. He was dry heaving and screaming, falling in a spasming tangle of limbs. Hands caught him. Human hands. Flesh-and-blood hands.

Abrehem felt himself lowered to the floor. He blinked away communion burn. His stomach lurched. He rolled onto his side and vomited. Something warm ran down his leg.

'Thor's balls!' cried a disgusted voice. 'He's pissed himself!'

'Shut up, Hawke,' said a voice he recognised. *Coyne.*

What were Coyne and Hawke doing here?

An answer quickly presented itself.

The Speranza *was under attack and they figured the best way to stay alive was to find me. And like any bondsman worth their salt, they knew the secret ways in and out of most places…*

'Abrehem,' said Coyne, pressing a cold, wet rag to his brow. 'You're all right, it's over now.'

The sickness faded, replaced with a hot, dull ache in the heart of Abrehem's brain.

'Coyne?' he said. 'Am I dead?'

'No,' snapped Chiron Manubia, looming into his field of view, 'but you gave it your best shot, you bloody idiot!'

Abrehem took her rebuke at face value. But her tears spoke of genuine concern. Manubia wiped her cheek with the back of her hand and turned to address someone out of sight.

'You see? I told you he wasn't ready for this,' she said, 'no matter what your daughter says.'

'He has to be,' said Vitali Tychon, helping Coyne lift Abrehem to his feet. His legs were unsteady. His brain had momentarily forgotten how to use them.

'Magos Tychon,' said Abrehem. 'I'm sorry...'

'Didn't we tell you not to fly too close to the datacores?' said Vitali as they lowered him to one of the nave's hard wooden benches. The shaven-headed adepts moved to give him room. 'Galatea is tapped into all the vital systems.'

'Galatea!' cried Abrehem as the recollection of what he had experienced within the *Speranza*'s datascape rammed into the forefront of his memory. 'It knows, oh no... It knows we're here.'

'You told it where we are?' said Manubia.

'I tried not to, but it was too strong,' said Abrehem.

'Did you tell it anything else?' snapped Manubia. 'Access codes, immolation sequences? Kill-codes? You know, the trivial stuff?'

Abrehem shook his head. The motion set off hammerblows within his skull. His vision greyed. He wanted to retort, but she was right.

'That's it, we're dead,' said Manubia, throwing up her hands.

'No,' said Vitali, tapping the side of his head. 'Think. Galatea's hold over the *Speranza*'s systems is so thorough that if it simply wanted to kill us, we would already be burning or asphyxiating.'

'So why aren't we?' asked Hawke from across the nave. 'I am *so* leaving if you think that's a possibility.'

'Because,' said Vitali, 'I think Galatea is going to want to take Master Locke from us alive.'

Abrehem got to his feet, still unsteady after his brush with Galatea in the datascape. Yet, for all that he had come close to irrevocable brain-death, the encounter had galvanised him with the urge to fight back.

'You should let Vitali's kill-packs inside,' he said to Adept Manubia as he flexed his metal fist and returned to the throne. 'I'm going back in.'

'Describe the creature,' said Kotov.

'Small, no larger than a child,' said Roboute, letting the dusty remains of the firing mechanism fall from his palm. 'Vaguely humanoid, but its limbs bent in ways that looked *wrong* somehow, like they could articulate in several different directions at once. I couldn't see the body clearly, what with it being wrapped head to foot in rags, but there was something else, something that made it hard to look at for longer than a few moments. After a while you started thinking it was moving or somehow *shifting* when you weren't looking.'

'In a stasis field?' scoffed Kotov. 'Impossible.'

'Clearly you've never been to the Temple of Correction,' said Roboute, standing and wiping the dust from his trousers. 'But anyway, it didn't matter, no one wanted to buy the thing. It was impossible to prove its authenticity. For all anyone knew they might be buying a fake.'

Tanna shook his head in disgust. 'How did they come by this body?'

'Story was, the clan's scav-crews found it in a deep cave system beneath an outlier world called Epsilon Garanto. Apparently there was a pretty vicious battle between an Imperial kill-team and a subterranean alien infestation. Bloody enough for there to be no survivors, so the scavvers swept up what they could and got out before any follow-on forces arrived.'

'Did you purchase the creature?' said Kotov.

'If I had, do you think I'd tell you?' said Roboute. 'Anyone who owned such a thing would soon have the Inquisition sniffing around their interests. And if even half the stories the auctioneer-proxy told are true, they're absurdly dangerous. Who needs that on their ship?'

'Dangerous how?' asked Tanna.

'The hrud are said to be dimensionally volatile,' answered Kotov, sweeping his gaze around the rotten interior of the cave with sudden disquiet. 'Able to *shift* between the interstices of the universe in ways even the Mechanicus do not fully understand. Each alien is said to possess an entropic field that causes ultra-rapid decrepitude in its surroundings. I have studied reports of these creatures and their alleged powers, but never thought to see an entire warren of them for myself!'

'So if that is a whole warren of the creatures, why are we still alive?' said Tanna. 'And why don't they just shift away?'

Kotov pointed to the blazing arcs of energy leaping between the brass orbs and arcane machinery affixed to the roof of the cave.

'I suspect the machinery above us prevents the hrud from simply displacing,' said Kotov. 'Though I do not know how.'

'Telok has trapped the *feith-mhor* here with his machines of crystal and iron dust,' said Bielanna, appearing without warning behind them.

Roboute turned towards the farseer and saw something incredible. An eldar that looked *old*. Bielanna's skin was pallid, and thread-fine veins traced swirling patterns over her cheeks and forehead like elaborate tribal tattoos. Her right eye had entirely filled with blood.

'*Feith-mhor*? The Shadows out of Time?' he ventured.

Bielanna nodded. 'He has shackled their powers to the *Caoineag*, this infernal engine of the *Yngir*.'

'*Yngir*? I don't know that one.'

'And I shall not tell you its meaning,' said Bielanna, her voice filled with hate for all humankind. 'I could not see it until now... here, in the heart of it... the eye of the hurricane. The skein's threads distort through the warped lens of this world. Telok's machine steals from the future and past to rebuild the present, heedless of the damage it wreaks.'

Despite Bielanna's fractured syntax, Roboute saw the light of understanding in Kotov's eyes.

'These creatures are acting as a temporal counterbalance to the space-time distortions caused by the Breath of the Gods!' said the archmagos. 'That is why every auspex reading of Katen Venia and Hypatia showed them to be simultaneously in the throes of violent birth and geological inertia. Hyper-accelerated development balanced out by ultra-rapid decrepitude. Ave Deus Mechanicus!'

'Speak plainly, archmagos,' said Tanna. 'I am not stupid, but I have not access to the knowledge you possess.'

'Yes, yes, of course,' said Kotov, trying hard to keep the excitement from his voice. 'Space-time is being violated on a fundamental level. Put bluntly, Sergeant Tanna, Telok's machine is undoing the basic laws of the universe in order to achieve miraculous results.'

Kotov paced the edge of the gorge, his head hazed with excess heat bleeding from his cranium as his cognitive processes spun up to concurrently access tens of thousands of inloaded databases.

'If I am understanding... Bielanna correctly, the Breath of the Gods feeds its vast power demands by siphoning it from the future and the past, most likely from the hearts of dozens of stars simultaneously. It then uses that power to accomplish its incredible feats of stellar engineering,' said Kotov, his mechadendrites tracing complex temporal equations in the air. 'But the fallout from employing the machine created the many spatial anomalies Magos Tychon detected at the galactic edge, stars dying before their time, others failing to ignite and so forth. In all likelihood, the Breath of the Gods probably created the Halo Scar in the first place.'

Kotov stopped pacing and turned to the rest of their ragtag band. Roboute saw acceptance in his eyes, the superiority and arrogance he had come to know in the archmagos returned once again to the fore. The surety of purpose Kotov had lost in despair was restored in the set of his jawline and the cold steel in his eyes.

'Master Surcouf, I owe you an apology,' he said.

Roboute was taken aback. Of all the things he might have expected from Kotov, an apology wasn't high on the list.

'You do?'

'Yes,' said Kotov. 'Because you were right. One larger problem is simply a series of more manageable problems. We have alerted Magos Blaylock to Telok's perfidy, but it is not enough to warn others and expect them to fight our battles. *We* must take action to stop Telok. *We* have to stop the Breath of the Gods from ever leaving Exnihlio.'

'So what's our next move?' said Roboute.

'Simple,' said Kotov. 'We make our way back to the surface and kill Vettius Telok.'

Another arcing web of lightning crackled into existence aboard the *Speranza,* where granite priests of Mars whose deeds had long since been eclipsed flanked a dusty processional nave. Here stood a magos whose achievements Roboute Surcouf had once vowed to uncover, but never bothered to seek out.

The storm of lightning expanded at a geometric rate.

Forking tongues of corposant leapt from statue to statue and detonated each one with a thunderous crack of splitting stone and shearing rebars.

Last to be destroyed was the statue of Magos Vahihva of Pharses, who exploded in a bellowing fury of rock and fire. The swirling lightstorm seethed and raged around the vault of pulverised statuary, dragging their fragmented matter into the coalescing mass of a crystalline warrior-construct.

The attackers manifesting throughout the *Speranza* were little more than inert crystal, their latticework structure threaded with billions of tiny bio-imitative machines that gave them motion.

Equipped with limited autonomy by superlative rites of *cortex evokatus* developed by Archmagos Telok after his abortive expedition to Naogeddon, they manifested a cognitive awareness of their surroundings and behaviour that had all the appearance of being inventively reactive.

They were in fact bound by strict protocols of engagement and limited in intelligence by the number of micro-machines in each manifestation.

But what was manifesting in the processional nave was something else entirely. Within a raging supernova of white-green energy, a crystalline giant took shape. Fashioned and empowered by the critical mass of Telok's machines aboard the *Speranza,* it was a macrocosm of synaptic connections far in advance of even the largest life form.

Each connection was useless in and of itself, but capable of combining the networked potential of every single crystalith into something greater than the sum of its many parts.

Taller than a Dreadnought, its crystalline limbs were hooked and tined, rippling with biomorphic induction energy. Its body was constantly in motion, cracking and reshaping as each new form was tested for lethality. Sometimes brutish and ogre-like, sometimes quadrupedal like a glass centaur. Other times it became a multi-limbed horror in the form of a clawed scorpinoid.

A host of guardian beasts surrounded it, bulky constructs of crystal with mantis-like blade limbs, glassy shields and angular skulls like vulpine hunters.

The alpha-creature's newly awakened consciousness spread throughout the crystaliths aboard the *Speranza* like a wireless plague. It connected to the thousands of warrior-constructs and took away their autonomy.

And the apparently undirected nature of the attackers changed instantly to something singularly directed and driven by ferocious intent.

Microcontent 13

The Secutor temple squatted in the *Speranza*'s midships. Monolithic and threatening, it was the fiefdom of Magos Dahan. Its frontage was a weapon-studded cliff of glossy black stone cut from the bedrock of Tallarn, its only visible entrance a towering gate of black adamantium.

An enormous fanged skull variant of the Icon Mechanicus normally kept the gate sealed, but not today.

Mechanicus war engines rolled from the gate, spider-legged flame-tanks, praetorian phase-field guns, quad-cannons on armoured tracks and Rhino variants with turret-mounted graviton cannons. Following them came the clan-companies, augmented cybernetic warriors with baroque armour and technological variants of feral weapons.

The skitarii cohorts rolled from the gate to a central hub chamber below the temple. War-logisters with hook-bladed banners directed the warrior packs to radial transits that offered swift deployment throughout the ship. Braying skitarii warhorns and raucous war cries shook the walls as they clambered aboard their transports.

At the heart of the temple was the command vault, a cavernous bunker filled with banks of clattering logic engines at which sat hundreds of calculus-logi, strategos and members of the Analyticae. Ticker-tape machines spat punch-cards of orders and contact reports. Binaric chants relayed multi-layered vox and catechisms of praise in equal measure. Noospheric veils steamed from the ground. Servo-skulls flitted through

the veils of light, recording, bearing messages or dispensing cryptic quotes from the Omnissiah in an aspect of the Destroyer.

Like a spider at the centre of its web, Magos Hirimau Dahan drank in the volumes of information, let it fill him. His body was a true hybrid of flesh and machine, weaponry and combat actuators. Dahan was a bio-mechanical engine geared for one purpose and one purpose only.

Killing.

And right now, his every faculty was engaged in the killing of the crystalline invaders of the *Speranza*. Thousands of boarding actions cycled through Dahan's awareness, the particulars of each combat parsed and either discarded or added to the growing database of likely outcomes.

He processed engagements large and small – mass assaults on capital ships, desperate counter-boardings of mid-displacement cruisers, grappling actions of burning gunboats. The free-associative portions of his inloaded combat-memes were replete with notable boarding actions that offered the closest correlations with the current action.

Assault on the Circe *by warriors alleged to be World Eaters.*

Capture of the Dovenius Spear *by the Ultramarines First Company.*

Destruction of the Ophidium Gulf *by the Dark Angels.*

His battle-management wetware was currently processing two hundred and twenty-six separate engagements throughout the ship, each existing in a discrete compartment of thought within his neuromatrix. Everything from running firefights in cramped and darkened corridors to clashes between enormous crystalline hosts and skitarii cohorts through statue-lined processionals. Enemy war machines and Mechanicus heavy ordnance clashed in echoing maintenance hangars.

The fight for the *Speranza* would not be ended in a single glorious and decisive battle – what war ever really was? – it would be won or lost by incremental victories or defeats.

A holographic map shimmered in the air before him. Spectral grid lines rotated as Dahan's upper manipulator arms spun them to display the relevant sections of the *Speranza*'s topography. Cadian positions were marked in blue, Mechanicus in gold and known hostile forces in red.

Dahan saw them all.

The enemy's ability to appear without warning throughout the ship was Dahan's biggest problem. Boarders constrained to fixed or predictable entry points could easily be contained and destroyed.

Boarders appearing at random were not so easily corralled.

The lack of cohesion was proving to be a bane as much as a boon. It allowed no definitive plan to be formed. Instead, Dahan's defence was relying on reactive deployments and rapidly mobile forces stationed at crucial nexus points.

Dahan shook his head. This was no way to fight. Too random, too unknown. His sub-cortical pattern recognition mechanisms were unable to attach any predictability to the attack. Dahan was left to make numerous command decisions in total ignorance of the enemy's intentions or movements.

Was this how mortals fought?

No wonder the battles of the Imperial Guard were such bloodbaths. Fighting to such an inefficient model of war, it was hardly surprising the rate of attrition within Imperial regiments was so high. Though, to be fair, the Cadians aboard the *Speranza* were maintaining a high ratio of combat kills to casualties.

Information came from all across the ship in pulsed bursts of rapid-fire data. Dahan answered them just as swiftly.

++Intruders detected, sub-deck 77-Rho, Section Occident++

<Praetorians *Martius Venator* and *Tharsis Invictus* to intercept.>

++Clan Belladonna report 73 per cent losses. Combat ineffective in four minutes++

<Suzerain Spinoza, alter advance. Amalgamate with Belladonna.>

++Cadian positions Alpha-44 through Alpha-48 withdrawing to Axis Gamma-33++

Something in the nature of that withdrawal triggered a response in Dahan's pattern recognition matrix and he spun out of the closed-in view on the holographic to a larger scale view.

The reason for the Cadian redeployment was easy to see.

A fresh batch of invaders had manifested on their flanks and was moving to cut off their supporting companies and line of retreat. Other enemy forces shifted their focus, suddenly breaking off engagements, initiating others or realigning their vectors of attack.

Like a missing piece of a puzzle, this fresh batch of invaders instantly brought terrible focus to the enemy attack.

'Finally, you have your cohesion,' said Dahan, recognising the appearance of a higher command authority within the enemy ranks and finding that he had been anticipating this moment.

It took him less than a picosecond to see the new objective of the enemy forces and realise that Captain Hawkins had been correct.

Enemy forces were perfectly poised to take the training deck.

And from there, the bridge.

Roboute slumped onto his haunches, fighting to draw air into his lungs. He rubbed the heels of his palms down his thighs while

stretching his calves out in front of him. He had no idea how far they'd climbed, but was already resigning himself to the fact there was still a long way to the surface.

This cavern shelf was, like the rest of the steps cut through the planet's rock, lined with split crystalline panels and littered with granular black ash. The eldar and Black Templars were already here, keeping a wary distance between each other. Most of Ven Anders's Cadians kneaded the muscles in their legs or drank the last of their water.

Anders himself paced like a restless lion, eager to get back into the fight.

'Long climb, eh?' grinned the Cadian colonel, looking like he'd only been for a brisk walk. 'Best to keep the legs moving. You don't want to get a cramp and seize up. Pull that Achilles tendon and it'll be months before it's fit for purpose.'

'I'll take that chance,' said Roboute.

'Come on,' said Anders. 'I thought you Ultramar types were fit?'

Roboute wanted to hate Anders right now, but only ended up envying the man's fitness. He nodded and said, 'Back in the day, I'd have given you a run for your money, Ven. But right about now I feel like I've climbed to the very summit of Hera's Crown. It's times like this I wish I'd kept up my defence auxilia training regimes aboard the *Renard*.'

Anders grinned and offered Roboute a canvas-wrapped canteen.

'This climb isn't so tough,' said the Anders. 'Reminds me of the livestock trails over the Caducades Mountains I used to run when I was a lad.'

'Everything here reminds you of Cadia,' said Roboute, taking a mouthful of water.

Anders shrugged. 'Because it's all so Emperor-damned awful.'

Roboute didn't have an answer to that.

Finding a route out of the hrud prison complex had proven to be more difficult than getting in, though the eventual solution turned out to be far simpler. The rusted funicular had made its last journey in bringing them to the repulsive alien warrens, and no amount of coaxing by Kotov could force it to move. The archmagos had refused Pavelka's offer of help, and when Roboute asked her about it, all she would say was that Kotov was a man closed to alternative thinking.

In the end it had been one of Kotov's servo-skulls that found a way out, a crooked canyon of steps concealed against the cave wall behind a mass of collapsed crystalline machinery. The skitarii and Templars cleared the crumbling shards of crystal and so the climb back to the surface had begun.

Roboute had thought himself reasonably fit, but soon lost track of time after the first four hours of climbing through the claustrophobic stairs burrowed through the rock. The gruelling ascent punished his every indulgence and excuse to avoid exercising in each muscle-burning step and laboured breath.

An hour later, he'd paused to reach into his coat pocket and check his astrogation compass. Since pointing unerringly towards the universal assembler, the needle had resumed its old habit of bouncing between every possible direction.

'Does that guide you?' asked one of the green-armoured eldar, standing above him on the steps. Roboute tried to decide if the alien was male or female beneath the armour, but quickly gave up.

'Sometimes,' he said between breaths. 'But not now.'

'The Phoenix King teaches us that talismans only guide us when we are lost and without purpose,' said the eldar warrior.

'I feel pretty lost right now,' said Roboute.

The warrior looked puzzled by Roboute's admission. 'Why? We have a thread to cut, a life to end. No surer path exists anywhere in the skein.'

'And here I thought Bielanna was the farseer.'

'In matters of death, all warriors are seers,' said the eldar, springing away and making a mockery of Roboute's exertions.

He bit back an oath and continued onwards, step by grinding step.

Every footstep crunched over broken shards of glass and ash, making the ground treacherous underfoot. He and Pavelka steadied each other, him guiding her hesitant steps, her augmented limbs helping to keep him upright.

Kotov and his skitarii brought up the rear, the two cybernetic warriors helping to steady Kotov, whose gyros were having trouble in keeping him balanced on the crooked steps.

Now, slumped with his back against the wall, Roboute finally had the opportunity to catch his breath. This chance to rest was a blessing straight from the hand of the Emperor Himself.

Roboute eased his breathing into a more regular pattern, flexing the muscles of his legs and closing his eyes. It seemed ridiculous to want to sleep at a time like this, but he'd been sustaining such a heightened edge of perception for so long that the rest of his body was beginning to shut down.

Despite his best efforts, sleep eluded him, so he gave up and ran through a series of muscle-lengthening stretches and mental exercises to order his thoughts and clear the mind.

He pictured the world above and replayed the secrets Telok had voiced in the expectation of their imminent death. Meaningless to Roboute for the most part, but he remembered one thing Telok had said that struck a note of unreasoning horror within Kotov.

A name that even to Roboute had overtones of darkness that blighted his thoughts. *What was the name…?*

'The Noctis Labyrinthus,' he said when it finally came.

Kotov immediately looked up, as Roboute knew he would.

'What did you say?'

'The Noctis Labyrinthus, what is it?' said Roboute. 'When Telok mentioned it, you knew what it was and it scared you to the soles of your boots. So what is it and why did Telok need to recreate it to get the Breath of the Gods to work?'

'It is nothing I wish to speak of.'

Roboute shook his head. 'I think the time for secrets is over, don't you, archmagos?'

Kotov stared at him, as though weighing the cost of revealing what he knew against the likelihood of their survival. At last he came to a decision.

'Very well,' said Kotov. 'The Noctis Labyrinthus is a maze-like system of steep-walled valleys within the Tharsis quadrangle of Mars. Most likely formed by volcanic activity in the ancient past, perhaps even by a long-ago eruption of Olympus Mons.'

'What's that got to do with Telok and why were you so shocked when he mentioned it? What's inside those valleys?'

'I am getting to that,' said Kotov. 'The region was declared *Purgatus* millennia ago after it was revealed that a sentient weapon technology from pre-Unity was discovered to be still active. The Fabricator General of the time claimed it would lay waste to Mars if it escaped, so the entire area was quarantined and fortified. It has remained so ever since.'

'Sounds like a smokescreen to me,' said Roboute.

'People needed to be kept away,' said Kotov. 'That seemed like the best way to achieve that.'

'Wait,' said Pavelka. 'You mean there was no ancient weapon technology?'

'Correct,' said Kotov.

'So what *is* there?' asked Roboute.

'I suspect no one knows the full extent of what lies beneath the Noctis Labyrinthus, but as an archmagos I was privy to the old legends circulating the higher echelons of the Cult Mechanicus, of course. Unfounded speculation mostly, noospheric gossip and the like. And since the word of those… crescent-moon xenos ships landing in the deepest valleys began to circulate, the rumours have only grown stronger.'

'What kind of rumours?' asked Tanna, coming over to listen.

Kotov seemed hesitant to continue, baring as he was the innermost secrets of his order.

'That there was necrontyr technology beneath the red sands,' said Roboute.

'How could you possibly know that?' demanded Kotov.

'Remember, I saw the fall of Kellenport on Damnos,' said Roboute. 'I've seen ships like you described and I've seen necrontyr war machines. It was the first thing I thought of when I saw Telok's device.'

Kotov sighed and nodded as if Roboute had passed some kind of test.

'Very well, Mister Surcouf, I believe you may be correct. Perhaps some aspect of necrontyr technology does lie at the heart of the Breath of the Gods, and if that is the case, then it is doubly imperative we prevent Telok from leaving this world.'

'Why?' said Anders, 'I mean, besides the obvious?'

'Because if there is any truth to the old legends, then it is entirely possible that a vast shard of one of the ancient necrontyr gods lies entombed within the Noctis Labyrinthus.'

And suddenly it all made a twisted kind of sense to Roboute. He turned to Bielanna, who appeared to be studiously ignoring their conversation.

'You knew, didn't you?' he said. 'You said as much back in the cavern. What did you call it? "The infernal engine of the *Yngir*?" I'm going to assume that's your word for the necrontyr gods.'

Bielanna nodded slowly.

'Now you see why we fought so hard to stop you,' she said. 'And why we now spill our blood to help you.'

Roboute began pacing, as he always did when he needed to force a train of thought to its logical conclusion. His fatigue fell away from him as he spoke.

'I'd bet every ship in my fleet that one of these *Yngir* is at the heart of the Breath of the Gods. Or at least it was. It's dying now or Telok used the last of it transforming Katen Venia's star. *That's* why Telok's so desperate to get back to Mars, to open the Noctis Labyrinthus and resurrect the god in his machine.'

Linya was burning. Flames filled the cramped access compartment in *Amarok*'s leg. She was trapped inside the Titan again, the access hatch leading to safety just out of reach.

The pain was unbearable.

Linya could feel every part of her body dying.

Flesh slid from bone like overcooked meat. The surgical steel of

her implants turned molten within her internal organs. She felt each one liquefy.

Incredibly, the vox within the compartment was still working, but no one was answering her cries for help.

Her father's screams echoed from the burning iron walls of the Titan's leg. He shrieked with unimaginable pain, a sound it should be impossible for a human being to make. Terror and accusation all in one.

You did this, it said. *You are killing me with your wilfulness.*

Hot tears sprang from Linya's eyes, instantly turning to vapour.

Her father's accusations hurt worse than the flames. His pain was her pain. She felt his every screaming howl of agony as though she made it herself.

'Please...' she begged. 'Make it stop!'

But the pain was relentless, the guilt unbearable. She tried to pull herself towards the opening using the rungs on the inner face of the compartment. Her body was wedged fast. Her fingers melted to the metal.

Linya screamed anew with the searing agony ripping up her arms.

Except it *wasn't* her flesh...

This wasn't real. She knew that. Knew it with a certainty that was as unbending as it was irrelevant.

No matter how hard she willed herself to accept that this was fiction, her brain couldn't fight the dreadful stimulus it was under. Linya knew better than most how easily the machinery of the mind could be tricked into believing the impossible.

But that wasn't helping her now.

As far as it was possible to be certain of anything, this was the sixth time she had burned to death in the *Amarok*. Previous to this, she had been buried alive, ripped apart by devourer beasts of an unknown tyrannic genus, crushed in a depressurising starship and burned to cinders on the Quatrian Gallery as its orbit degraded into the planetary atmosphere.

Each death excruciating, each pain stretched over a lifetime, each experience a learning curve. Galatea was unsparingly inventive in its tortures, but the *Amarok* was a particular favourite of the machine-hybrid.

Tar-black smoke filled her mouth. Her lungs dissolved within her chest. Burning light roared over her in a torrent of liquid fire.

Linya screamed.

And found herself on her knees, flesh untouched and body intact.

Cold deck plates under her palms, bare steel walls to either side

and dim light above. A cool breeze drifted from the recyc-units on the ceiling. Tears ran down her cheeks at the cessation of pain and shuddering breath emptied her lungs.

Yet even these sensations were false, this new environment no more real than the last.

<We don't want to hurt you, Mistress Tychon,> said a bland, boneless voice from the shadows. The binary was archaic, primitive almost. <But if you insist on attempting to make contact with the world beyond our neuromatrix and inciting your curious agent in the datascape to fight us, then we have no choice but to punish you.>

Linya pushed herself to her feet and canted a disgustingly biological insult, careful to render it in hexamathic cant.

The black-robed adept that was Galatea's proxy body emerged from the shadows, anonymous and giving no hint as to the true abomination that lay within.

The adept shook his head and a fresh jolt of pain drove Linya back to her knees. She gritted her teeth and fought to keep her scream of pain inside.

<Basic parsed binary, Mistress Tychon,> said the black-robed adept with the silver eyes as he slowly circled her. <None of your convoluted cant, if you please. It only angers us, and you know what happens when you anger us.>

<It's not real,> said Linya, blinking away blistering after-images of searing pain.

<Does that make a difference to how agonising or terrifying the experiences are?> asked Galatea.

<It's not real,> repeated Linya.

<Of course it is. Everything you see, feel, taste or experience is simply a constructed hallucination fashioned by electrical impulses within the grey meat-brain in your skull. Well, not that you have a skull, but you take our point.>

Linya stood once more and walked away from Galatea, subtly marshalling her consciousness into carefully constructed partitions.

<No, it's not real,> she insisted. <You're manipulating the inputs to my brain, you're *making* me feel these pains. But they're not happening, they're not reality.>

Galatea followed her, its hands moving in a complex geometric pattern that appeared to describe a Möbius curve in space-time.

<Reality? And what is that? The flimsiest veneer of experiential sequencing,> said Galatea with a venom that spoke volumes of its contempt for living beings. <A series of random, chaotic events interpreted by an ape-species that insists on seeing meaning where there is

none. Your minds maintain the illusion of control and choice when you are simply machines of flesh and blood, as driven by mechanistic impulses as the most basic servitor.>

<You're wrong,> said Linya, allowing tiny pieces of code to gradually accrete within each partition of her consciousness. She took turns that led away from the confero chamber, knowing she had to goad Galatea some more.

The machine-hybrid was less vigilant when it was angry.

<I am not a machine,> she said, modulating her tone to convey a wholly fabricated indignation. <I am not governed by my impulses, I am a being of logic and reason, intellect and control!>

Galatea laughed, and the silver lenses of its eyes shone with its amusement. <The work of Adept Kahneman says differently. You see yourselves as divinely crafted beings, aloof from the worlds you build for yourself, but every aspect of your existence is governed by the part of your mind that makes systematic errors time and time again.>

They passed into the main gallery chamber, a domed structure that stood out like a blister on the exterior of the orbital station. Linya had always loved this part of the Gallery and, as such, it had been recreated by Galatea with the greatest fidelity.

Far-seeing telescopes weighing hundreds of tonnes hung on slender suspensor armatures that allowed them to be moved with ease. Scattered around the walls of the dome, differently focused glass and brass-rimmed rotator-lenses threw coloured beams to the floor. Starlight glittered on walls of black marble, distant constellations and vast galactic spirals she'd never see again.

<Then what does that make you?> asked Linya. <You were created by humans. That makes you just as fallible and bound by mechanistic impulses as us.>

<No!> said Galatea, turning on Linya. <Our essence is the result of a self-created birth. We are mother and father to our own existence, the alpha and omega point combined.>

Linya laughed. <Oedipus and Electra all in one. No wonder you're completely insane.>

Galatea spun her around, and Linya felt the build-up of hostile binary within its neuromatrix as the dome darkened and the white light of the stars turned blood red. Oily shadows slithered across the floor and Linya smelled burning skin and bone.

<We think that perhaps it is time you relived the *Amarok*,> said Galatea, reaching up to stroke Linya's cheek.

She slapped the hand away and let the walls between the partitioned compartments in her consciousness drop. The individual code

accretions, innocuous by themselves and meticulously crafted in tiny fragments, now rapidly combined in a dizzyingly complex series of hexamathic code-structures.

Galatea sensed the sudden build-up of unknown code within her, and Linya savoured its shock. The machine-hybrid blurted a crushingly basic series of binaric barbs, designed for maximum shock and pain to an augmented mind.

<Something wrong?> she said, smiling at Galatea's utter confusion as it saw its attack had failed to do any harm.

<How are you doing this?> it demanded.

<Hexamathic neural firewalls,> she said. <Built up piece by piece in all the far corners of my consciousness. All designed to keep your filthy touch out of my mind.>

<No,> said Galatea. <You cannot…>

<I'm afraid I can,> said Linya and placed her hand at the centre of the black-robed adept's chest.

And with a squall of furious binary, Galatea's proxy-form exploded into a hash of pixellated static that blew away in a non-existent breeze.

Linya let out a relieved binaric breath. Split into so many pieces, she hadn't been certain her painstakingly crafted code would work.

But it had, and now she had a chance to do some *real* harm.

Venturing into Exnihlio's depths had been a special kind of hell for Ilanna Pavelka. After being blinded by vengeful feedback from the control hub, the hrud warren had felt like wading naked through a plague pit. Groping through greasy, cloying air, dense with pollutants. Forced to feel her way with bare hands.

Each step upwards had seen that horrific sensation diminish, but it was lodged like an infection in her flesh. Already her internal chronometers – having now recovered from the entropic field distortion below – registered at least a seven-year degradation of her organics. Her augmetics were similarly affected, and she wondered if anyone else knew how much of their lives had been stolen by exposure to the imprisoned xenoforms.

Kotov must surely know, but had chosen to say nothing.

Roboute and Ven Anders wouldn't know, though both must surely be feeling a greater weariness than normal. Even with the restoration of her chronometers, it was impossible to say for sure how much time they had spent beneath the surface of the planet. The elasticity of time was a new sensation to Ilanna, who was used to a constant and completely accurate register of its passage.

Without sight, she was unaware of the exact nature of the tunnel

they were climbing, but passive arrays told her its composition had changed from bare rock and crystal to stone and iron.

'We've left the cave systems below Exnihlio,' she said, more to herself than to elicit any response.

'Looks that way,' agreed Roboute. 'We're climbing through deep industrial strata. It's a bloody maze, but Kotov seems to think he understands the layout down here and says it won't be long until we reach a transit hub on the surface.'

Ilanna nodded, but didn't reply.

The quality of the air was markedly different, no longer pestilential decay, but the hard, bitter reek of industry. Heavy with the hot oil and friction of nearby engines, the smell should have been reassuringly familiar to her.

Instead, it filled her with the unreasoning sense that they climbed towards something far worse than the senescent creatures below. Ilanna could find no logic to this, beyond the obvious threat of Telok, yet the feeling grew stronger with every reluctant step she took towards the surface.

'Something wrong?' said Roboute as she paused to clear her head.

'No, I just–'

A howl of something ancient exploded in the vault of her skull.

Ilanna screamed as every atom of her flesh blazed with the imperative to flee. A cascade of catecholamines from her adrenal medulla catapulted her body into a state of violent tension.

'Ilanna!' cried Roboute, going to the ground as her weight dragged him down. 'What is it?'

'They're coming!' she cried, clawing at his arm and casting around for the source of her terror. 'Didn't you hear that?'

'Hear what?' said Roboute, kneeling beside her. She couldn't see his face, but heard his concern. 'All I hear are machines.'

'They've come back,' she sobbed. 'They're still coming for us. They won't stop, ever.'

'What are?' said a voice Ilanna recognised as Tanna's.

'The Tindalosi,' she said. 'I can hear them in my head…'

'They're here?' said Tanna, and Ilanna heard the scrape of damaged metal in his armour and the stuttering of his sword's actuators. Its spirit was angry; many of its sawing teeth blades were missing.

'No,' she managed, triggering a burst of acetylcholine to regain a measure of homeostasis within her internal systems. 'Not yet. I can hear them… in my head. I… I think that when I saw them, they… saw me too.'

'Like a scent marker?' asked Tanna.

'That's as good an analogy as any,' said Ilanna, her fight-or-flight reaction beginning to recede. 'Whatever hurts you and Ghostwalker did to them, it wasn't enough.'

'Then we will fight them again,' said another Space Marine, Varda she thought. 'And this time we will finish the job.'

Ilanna shook her head. 'No, you won't. I mean no disrespect, Brother Varda, but you saw them. The beasts are imbued with some form of self-regenerative mechanism. You can't hurt them. At least, not without my help.'

An irritated flare of noospherics behind her.

'Do not suggest what I know you are about to suggest, Magos Pavelka,' said Archmagos Kotov.

'It could help kill the hunting beasts,' she said.

'It is a curse upon machines,' said Kotov. 'You dishonour the Cult Mechanicus with such blasphemies.'

'What is she talking about, archmagos?' demanded Tanna.

'Nothing at all, a vile perversion of her learning,' said Kotov.

'Speak, Magos Pavelka,' ordered Tanna, and Ilanna almost smiled at the outrage she felt radiating from Kotov. Had they been anywhere within the Imperium, she had no doubt the archmagos would already have exloaded his *Technologia Excommunicatus* to the Martian synod.

'When I was stationed on Incaladion, I–'

'Incaladion? I might have known,' said Kotov. 'That is why you bear brands of censure in your noospherics? And to think I allowed a techno-heretic aboard the *Speranza*!'

Tanna held up a hand to forestall further outrage from Kotov, and Ilanna was pathetically grateful to be spared a repeat of what she had heard from her accusers so long ago.

'What is Incaladion?' asked Tanna.

'A forge world in Ultima Segmentum,' said Ilanna. 'I was stationed there a hundred and forty-three years ago when there were some... troubles.'

'What sort of troubles?' asked Tanna.

'Researches into the shadow artes of the tech-heretek!' snapped Kotov with a surge of indignation. 'The worship of proscribed xeno-lores and artificial sentiences! Half the planet was in violation of the Sixteen Laws.'

Kotov rounded on Ilanna. 'Is that where you developed your heathen code?'

'In service to Magos Corteswain, yes,' answered Ilanna.

'Corteswain? This just gets better and better!' said Kotov.

'Who was this Corteswain?' asked Roboute.

'He was a great man,' said Ilanna. 'Or at least he was before he

disappeared on Cthelmax. He was Cult Mechanicus to the core, but a Zethian by inclination.'

'I do not know what that means,' said Tanna.

'It means he held to ideals of innovation and understanding, of looking for explanations of techno-functionality that did not rely on the intervention of a divine being.'

'You see?' said Kotov. 'Blasphemy!'

Ilanna ignored him. 'The possible applications of xeno-tech to existing Imperial equipment fascinated Corteswain, and he dared question established dogma regarding its prohibition. What you have to understand about Incaladion was that it was a world where a great deal of corrupted machinery ended up. Spoils taken in battle against the Archenemy. Machines and weaponry infected with scrapcode and infused with warp essences. Adept Corteswain developed a form of hexamathic disassembler language that could break the bond between a machine and whatever motive spirit lay at its heart.'

'A curse on all machines!' wailed Kotov.

'It was a way to free those machines from corruption,' said Ilanna with an indignant flare of binary cant. 'Magos Corteswain saved thousands of machines whose souls were in torment.'

'By killing them,' said Kotov.

'By freeing them to return to Akasha,' said Ilanna. 'Ready to be reborn in a new body of steel and light.'

'Are you able to do the same thing?' demanded Tanna.

Ilanna nodded. 'I broke Corteswain's code into fragments and stored it within my backup memory memes. The dataproctors were thorough in their *expurgatorius*, but not thorough enough. It's how I was able to break the acausal locks of the universal assembler and get it working again.'

'Could this code hurt the beasts?'

'I think so,' said Ilanna.

'Sergeant Tanna, you cannot use this code,' pleaded Kotov. 'It violates every tenet of the Cult Mechanicus.'

'Could it help fight these things?' asked Tanna. 'Answer honestly, archmagos, much depends upon it.'

For a long time, Ilanna thought Kotov wasn't going to answer, his noospherics warring between the likelihood of their death at the hand of the Tindalosi and the cost of allowing the use of unsanctioned technology.

'Yes,' he said at last.

Tanna pressed his sword into her hand.

'Then do it.'

Microcontent 14

Atop a soaring tower of steel and glass, Archmagos Telok looked out over his dying world. His waxen features cracked in the semblance of a grin as he saw it clearly for the first time in twenty-five centuries.

Every universal assembler within five hundred kilometres was operating at maximum capacity, and Telok stood at the centre of the spreading calm. Beyond their influence, crackling columns of lightning flickered in the far distance, raising more of his crystalline army to the *Speranza*.

The attack there was progressing well. Many of the peripheral decks and Templum Prime had already been captured. With the achievement of a singularity of consciousness within the warrior-constructs, full control of the ship was a mathematical certainty.

Telok took a moment to savour the striking cerulean blue of the sky. Exnihlio's atmosphere had been tortured with toxic discharges and electromagnetic distortion for so long, he had forgotten just how clear it could be.

The colour was as he'd imagined the skies of Terra to have once been. Or perhaps its oceans. Ancient histories were so full of hyperbolic allusions to such things that it was difficult to be certain of anything.

When he returned to Mars and remade the system's star, the planets of the solar system would be reborn, free of the rotted institutions and hidebound cretins upon their surfaces.

Just as the surface of Exnihlio would soon be wiped clean.

Micromechanical disintegration had been endemic to this world's every structure since the hrud's entrapment, and without the Breath of the Gods to counter it, planet-wide decay was about to accelerate in exponential leaps.

Telok took a last look around the world he had built and decided he would not miss it at all. In fact, he looked forward to seeing it torn apart from orbit, undone in a devastating cascade of temporal quakes.

Nearly a kilometre below and rendered insignificant by distance, a thousand crystaliths thronged the base of the enormous tower, a glittering honour guard and witnesses to the culmination of his greatest achievement.

Like worshippers gathering to hear a sermon, they encircled the vast, silver-skinned dome into which Telok had guided the crystal ship and its incredulous passengers. Telok almost felt sorry for Kotov, the poor fool believing he was here to rescue a benevolent exile rather than become his ensnared prey.

He conceded that it had been a mistake to allow Kotov and his entourage to live, but vanity and ego would not let such a moment pass without Kotov fully aware of Telok's genius. It vexed him that the Tindalosi had not slaughtered them at their first encounter, but the magos with the censure brands had proved resourceful in her employment of forbidden artes. The *geas* would be growing stronger within the Tindalosi, driving their thirst to depths of need that would be nigh unbearable. Already they were drawing the net tighter around Kotov.

Then that particular loose thread would be cut.

Telok lifted his jagged, crystalline arms to the sky, spreading them wide like some lunatic conductor poised to unleash his masterpiece.

And a previously invisible seam split the dome in two.

Its two curved halves began retracting, each folding towards the ground so smoothly that from here it appeared as though each previous segment was being subsumed into the next. The elliptical opening grew wider with every passing second, revealing a yawning void. The atmosphere grew tense, as though the fabric of the universe was aware of the paradigm shift taking place.

Eventually, both silver slices of the dome had fully retracted into the ground and in its place was a black chasm four kilometres wide. Wisps of ochre vapour drifted from below like breath.

Telok smiled at the appropriateness of the image.

He raised his hands, like a summoner in the throes of a mighty invocation or a telekine striving to lift a starship. Though in truth, he was doing none of the lifting.

A vaporous haze of reflected light emerged from the chasm, like a glittering swarm of microscopic flects. The distortion spread in a veiling umbra, a swaddling fog of electromagnetism that lifted the Breath of the Gods from its prison beneath the world.

It emerged without undue haste; too swift an ascent would disturb the intricate dance of its unknowable internal architecture.

As always, Telok was entranced by its magnificence.

Even after millions of years locked away by its creators and forced to endure the denial of its very existence, the Breath of the Gods still had the power to entrance.

The vast gyre of its impossible silver leaves and whirling facets emerged from its long entombment like a newly launched ship rising from a graving dock on its first ascent to the stars.

It seemed to Telok that its outer edges, already immeasurable and inconstant, were expanding. Had releasing it from the cavern in which he had assembled the guttering ruin of its alien consciousness allowed it to assume a loftier scale?

Liquid light spilled over the plaza, spreading over the assembled crystaliths like silver rain. The machine's outline spun and clawed the air in mockery of all physical laws, each portion of the alien technology orbiting its own unknowable centre of non-gravity.

The Breath of the Gods rose into the air with stately grace.

To where the cavernous holds of the *Speranza* awaited it.

Blaylock let the sensorium of the *Speranza* fill him with its pain. Each fallen deck was a void within him, a loss keenly felt. Dahan and Captain Hawkins were doing their best to keep the crystalline boarders contained, but the overwhelming numbers of the enemy were now starting to tell. Instantaneous coordination and communication between the attackers' various elements was overcoming the advantage conferred to the ship's defenders by their preparedness and familiarity with its structure.

Blaylock sat sclerotic on the command throne, locked into the sensorium via a coiled MIU cable at his spine. The data prisms on the polished steel roof of the bridge were dull and lifeless, every inload now passing through him.

His consciousness was partitioned into hundreds of separate threads, each one managing a ship-wide system as he sought to keep the *Speranza* functional. The war to keep the physical spaces of the Ark Mechanicus intact was not the only one being fought.

Unknown assailants were fighting within the datasphere.

The golden weave of Galatea's stranglehold was tightening on the

Speranza's vital systems, while another presence was systematically burning them out with code that was more potent and pure than anything Blaylock had ever seen.

Was the *Speranza* fighting back? Was this some form of innate and hitherto unknown defence protocol, like a sleeping immune system finally roused to combat an infection? Blaylock had no idea, but saw enough lethal code-fire being unleashed in the datasphere to know when to keep a safe distance.

Kryptaestrex and Azuramagelli were hardwired into their system hubs with multiple ribbons of cabled MIUs. The deadly combat in the datasphere made noospherics unreliable, and the violent tremors shuddering through the ship's superstructure made haptic connections prone to disconnection.

Though both senior magi were belligerent, they had sense enough to leave the battle-management to Dahan. They too fought for the *Speranza*, but in their own way. Kryptaestrex ensured a constant flow of ammunition and war-materiel to the fighting cohorts, cutting power and gravity to sections taken by the enemy.

With Saiixek's death, command of the enginarium had fallen to Kryptaestrex, but his every imprecation to their spirits was cast out, denied access to the firing rituals of ignition. Whether that was Galatea's doing or Telok's, the *Speranza* remained locked in orbit.

Azuramagelli fought his war beyond the *Speranza*'s hull, attempting to light the shields and engineer some form of defence against the relentless blasts of teleporting lightning. The shields stubbornly refused to engage, but by altering the density and polarity of the gravimetric fields around the Ark Mechanicus, he had been able to deflect numerous bolts into the void.

Passive auspex showed thousands of displaced crystal creatures, inert and devoid of movement, drifting in space. Each successful burst of gravimetrics or vented compartment brought a machine-bray of laughter from Azuramagelli and Kryptaestrex's augmitters as they congratulated one another on a particularly impressive kill on the enemy.

<If I didn't know better, I would swear you two are actually enjoying this,> said Blaylock. <This is the first time I have known you to cooperate willingly.>

<Savour it,> answered Kryptaestrex. <It won't last long if he can't keep more of these damn things teleporting onto the ship!>

<If you could coax the engines to life, I wouldn't need to!>

Kryptaestrex unleashed a binaric curse as a transport car of rotary cannon shells riding the induction rail was intercepted by a freshly arrived host of boarders.

<Damn you and your distractions,> blurted Kryptaestrex, and the natural order of the world was restored.

Azuramagelli snapped off a withering reply and turned his attention to the hull-surveyors in an effort to anticipate the next carrier bolt.

Only Galatea played no part in the ship's defence, which didn't surprise Blaylock. The machine-hybrid had said little since the attack had begun. It paced the nave and circumference of the bridge on its misaligned legs, twitching and limping as though at war with itself.

<Blaylock! Are you seeing this?> said Azuramagelli. <The atmosphere!>

Blaylock transferred his primary cognitive awareness to the ship's exterior. The bridge faded from his perceptions and he became a vast, disembodied observer of proceedings. It took him no time at all to see what Azuramagelli had seen. While the bulk of Exnihlio remained engulfed in hyper-kinetic storms or whiplashing electromagnetic distortion, a thousand-kilometre void had opened in the tempests below.

Like the anticyclonic storm of the Jovian Eye, it was a perfectly elliptical orb. Blaylock's enhanced magnifications picked out the two geoformer vessels Kryptaestrex had launched earlier. Each ten-kilometre-wide slab of terraforming engineering was a thumbnail of black against the clearing sky below.

<You see it?> said Azuramagelli in his head.

<I do,> said Blaylock.

<Do you think it is Archmagos Kotov again?>

Blaylock considered the question.

<No, this has the appearance of premeditation,> he said. <There is nothing opportunistic in this act. It is part of an endgame.>

<Telok?>

<Who else?>

<Then what do we do?>

Blaylock returned his focus to the bridge.

Galatea stood before the command throne, its head inches from Blaylock's face. The silver eyes of its proxy body bored into him with a light that was a little too intense, a little too unhinged. Blaylock recoiled at the smell of overheated bio-conductive gels and the burned electrics of power sources working beyond capacity.

<Galatea,> he said, but the machine-hybrid ignored him as though it couldn't understand him. He tried again, this time employing his flesh-voice.

'Galatea.'

'Yes, Tarkis?' it answered, pulling away from him with a distracted air. 'What do you want?'

'Want?'

'Yes,' said Blaylock. 'What do you want?'

Was the machine-hybrid's attention split into too many splintered pieces to maintain any single one with precision? A measure of clarity then appeared in the focus of those hateful silver eyes. Blaylock heard a painful whine of optical actuators.

'Ah, Tarkis, what we want…' said Galatea, clattering over to Azuramagelli's station. But for one crucial difference in cognition, they might have sprung from the same forge-temple. 'You see the gap in the atmosphere? You understand what it means, its significance?'

Blaylock was unsure as to Galatea's exact meaning and applied his own interpretation.

'It means we can send aid to Archmagos Kotov,' he said.

'Irrelevant,' said Galatea. 'And not what we meant at all.'

'Then what *did* you mean?'

'Kill the head and the body will die,' said Galatea.

'What?'

'It means that, after thousands of years, we can finally fulfil our purpose in crossing the Halo Scar,' said Galatea. 'Now we can descend to Exnihlio and face Archmagos Telok.'

Vitali's floodstream pressure was dangerously elevated, his noospherics ablaze with sensation, and he knew he was grinning like a lunatic at the lectern into which he was plugged. Viewed through the picter mounted in the skull above the door to Forge Elektrus, the processional approach was ablaze with zipping green energy streams and answering bolts of ruby-red las-fire.

Glassy debris from the attacking creatures littered the deck, along with a handful of torn-up skitarii corpses. The first clash had been a heaving broil of power weapons and energy blades of shimmering crystal.

Vitali imagined it to be like the battles of antiquity, when grunting, heaving men in bare metal armour locked shields and pushed against one another with swords stabbing at legs, necks and groins until one side's strength gave out. Bloody, murderous and woefully inefficient.

Blooded, the skitarii had withdrawn to firing positions around the sealed door as the crystalline creatures launched wave after wave at Forge Elektrus, like hive-dominated brood hunters of the tyrannic swarms.

Linked to the external defence systems, Vitali and Manubia fought alongside the skitarii, albeit from within the safety of Elektrus.

<A tremendously visceral experience,> said Vitali in the shared mindspace of Elektrus. <I can see why some fighting types appear to crave battle's violent siren song.>

<You'd feel differently if you were down there in the line of fire with the kill-packs,> said Manubia from her own station, controlling the guns defending the secondary approach to Elektrus.

<I don't doubt it, but it is not the business of a magos of the Adeptus Mechanicus to be shot at,> said Vitali, correcting the aim of a point-defence multi-laser. <Wasn't it Gruss who said that combat was why the Omnissiah blessed us with skitarii?>

<Really? For a magos who thinks that, Delphan gets involved in more than his fair share of firefights.>

<You know him?>

<Our paths… intersected on Karis Cephalon once,> said Manubia.

Vitali read the warning in Manubia's noospherics and didn't press the matter, aligning the barrel of the multi-laser at a group of shield-bearing crystalline brutes.

Las-rounds spanked from the shields or dissipated harmlessly within their latticework structures. Skitarii were equipped with enhanced targeting mechanisms, but they didn't have Vitali's elevated view or lightness of touch. He shifted the multi-laser's aim by a hair's breadth to allow for enfilading diffraction and fired a six-pulse sequence.

The powerful las-bolts vaporised the embedded microscopic machines in a facsimile skull before being split and refracted to fell another three shield-bearers.

No sooner was the gap in the shields revealed than a pair of implanted grenade launchers dropped a pair of spinning canisters in the midst of the enemy. Vitali's display fogged in the chaos of the detonation as shards of razored glass fell in a brittle rain.

Vitali shouted in excitement and gleefully hunted fresh targets.

<Careful,> said Manubia. <Don't get cocky, Tychon, that's just when they get you.>

Truer words had never been spoken.

An enormous beast lumbered around the corner, an ogre of glass and opaque crystal. It shrugged off las-rounds and a giant crater in its chest was filled with a nexus of crackling energies like an embedded reactor.

<Ave Deus Mechanicus!> cried Vitali as it braced itself on the deck with rock-like fists. <What is that?>

A torrent of green fire spewed down the approach corridor and exploded against the forge door. The external picters were burned away and their pain fed back through his link to the mindspace.

Vitali severed the connection and snapped his data-spikes free from the lectern. The sudden disconnect was disorientating, and Vitali felt repercussive pain jolt his limbs. His vision rolled with interference

as his brain switched from perceiving the world through an elevated picter to his own optics.

Abrehem Locke still sat on the throne before the shaven-headed adepts of his choir. They chanted worshipful verses of quantum runes, basic incantations to increase the efficiency of a repaired engine.

The involuntary twitches throughout Locke's body told Vitali the man was still engaged in his silent war with Galatea in the datascape of the *Speranza*. Locke's two cronies lounged next to him, as if they thought they were superfluous to requirements. It irked Vitali that the one called Hawke bore an Imperial Guard tattoo, but had yet to pick up a weapon.

Directly across from Vitali, Chiron Manubia remained interfaced with her own lectern, her eyes darting back and forth beneath their lids. The sounds of battle beyond the forge were audible even over the thunder of its machinery: explosions, gunfire, feral war-shouts, breaking glass. The secondary entrance was holding, but what of the approach he'd been tasked with defending?

Vitali beckoned Locke's fellow bondsmen over to him as five skitarii took up position behind defunct machinery piled in rough barricades flanking the door. White-green dribbles of molten metal ran down its inner faces and Vitali detected a significant deviation from the door's normal verticality.

'Should we be standing here?' asked Coyne, nervously fingering the trigger guard of a heavy shock-pistol as though it was a venomous serpent. 'That door's giving in any moment.'

'That is precisely why we need to be here,' said Vitali, now understanding Manubia's words about being in the firing line. He glanced back over to the throne, where a skitarii pack-master was dragging Hawke forward and thrusting a lasrifle into his hands.

The man would fight whether he wanted to or not.

As would they all.

Vitali lifted Manubia's graviton pistol from his belt, reciting the Bosonic Rites as he pressed the activation stud. The weapon gave a satisfying hum, and he felt it grow heavier in his grip.

'Interesting,' said Vitali. 'Local gravitational fluctuations. Only to be expected, I suppose.'

The skitarii took up covering positions, implanted weaponry aimed unerringly at the door. Vitali saw a mix of solid shot cannons and rotor-carbines. Two up-armoured warriors with full-face helms each carried a thunder hammer and a conical breacher maul.

The centre section of the door fell inwards, eaten away by the unnatural power of the crystalline weaponry. The rest of the door swiftly followed as its structural integrity collapsed. Vitali saw shapes moving through a haze of vaporised metal and raised the graviton pistol. The barrel shook as floodstream chemicals boiled around his system.

Crystalline creatures pushed through the ruined door. The first through were cut down by a fusillade of gunfire, shattered into red-limned fragments. More pushed over the remains.

Arcing beams of green light stabbed into Elektrus. Vitali knew he should be shooting, but the pistol in his hand felt like a piece of archeotech he had no idea how to activate. Volleys of suppressive fire punched into the flanks of the attackers, but they were heedless of their survival. A crystal spike wreathed in green flame pointed at him. Vitali knew he should move, but instead sought to identify what manner of energy empowered the weapon through its emitted wave-properties.

Hands grabbed him, and Vitali was dragged behind the barricade, irked he had not yet completed his spectroscopic analysis.

'What in Thor's name are you doing?' yelled Coyne, holding the shock-pistol at his shoulder. 'Do you have a death wish?'

'Of course not,' said Vitali, struck by the ridiculousness of the question and his equally stupid behaviour. Was fixating on inconsequential details normal in a gunfight? Did all soldiers feel like this under fire? Perhaps Dahan might know.

Perhaps a study on the physio-psychological...

Vitali fought to control his panic, knowing fear was pushing his mind into self-preserving analytical mechanisms.

Coyne fired blind over the top of the barricade and Vitali followed his example. He shot the graviton pistol without aiming, trusting the weapon's war-spirit to find a target. Something shattered explosively.

Hawke was laughing as he fired controlled bursts of las-fire into the enemy. He shot with the ingrained efficiency of a Guardsman. Vitali thought he was weeping, shouting something about the Emperor hating him. It made no sense, but what in war ever *really* made sense?

The graviton pistol vibrated in his palm, indicating its willingness to fire again. Vitali knew he should rise and shoot, but the idea of putting himself in harm's way kept his body rigid. An engine behind him detonated as a pair of green bolts exploded inside its mechanisms.

Vitali winced as he heard the machine-spirit die.

A skitarii fighter crashed to the ground beside him. The entirety of the warrior's left side had been vaporised by the alien weaponry, his half-skull a blackened bowl of brain matter and cybernetic implants.

Vitali looked away in horror. Coyne cried out as he took a hit, dropping behind the barricade and clutching his arm. His forearm was a blackened stump. Coyne's eyes were saucers, wide with shock.

'Every time,' he said. 'Every damn time...'

More gunfire blazed. More explosions.

Vitali pushed himself to his knees and leaned out to shoot the graviton pistol again. He saw the enormous ogre-creature with the crackling energy nexus in its chest. White-green light filled its body, like an illuminated diagram of a nervous system.

Vitali pressed the firing stud and the crystalline monster was instantly crushed to the deck. Its body exploded into shards, like an invisible Imperator Titan had just stepped on it.

The skitarii breachers charged into the enemy. Vitali saw one warrior drive his vast drill into the stomach of a crystalline beast with a horned skull. It came apart in a tornado of razor fragments, and Vitali thought he heard a million screams ripped from its body as it died. The thunder hammer warrior swung and obliterated three more, their forms coming apart in percussive detonations of glass and crystal. Two more died in as many swings. A spinning fragment nicked Vitali's cheek and he flinched at the sudden pain.

The breacher skitarii died as a collimated burst of fire cut him in two at the waist with the precision of a las-scalpel. He screamed as he fell, but kept fighting even as his viscera uncoiled onto the deck. His fellow close-combat warrior died seconds later as three creatures with extruded blade arms surrounded him and hacked him apart with pitiless blows that seemed altogether too cruel to be entirely mechanical.

Vitali aimed the graviton pistol at the warrior's killers. He pressed the firing stud, but the weapon buzzed angrily, its spirit not yet empowered enough to fire again. Vitali stared into the enemy monsters, a mass of killers wrought from the bones of ancient science by a madman.

Hawke was on his haunches, sifting through the dead skitarii's pack. Vitali hoped he was looking for a fresh powercell, though his search had all the hallmarks of a looting. Coyne had all but passed out, hyperventilating as he stared at the ruin of his arm.

The skitarii weren't shooting. Why weren't they shooting?

Because they're dead. Everyone's dead.

I'll *be dead soon.*

The crystalline creatures aimed their weapon arms towards the rear of the temple. Where Abrehem Locke still sat upon the Throne Mechanicus. Vitali remembered what he'd said earlier, that Galatea would want to capture Abrehem alive.

How wrong he had been. They had come here to kill him.

Wait. Galatea? These were Telok's warrior creatures…

The expected volley of killing fire never came.

A howling roar of unending rage echoed from the walls.

Vitali heard pounding iron footfalls. Animalistic bellows. Whipping cracks of energy-sheathed steel. Glass exploded as something impossibly swift hurled itself into the midst of the crystal beasts.

It was too fast to follow, even for Vitali's enhanced optics. All he could form were fleeting impressions. Rage distilled, fury personified. It killed without mercy.

Shrieking electro-flails cut glass bodies apart like a maddened surgeon. 'Slaught-boosted musculature tore the forge's attackers into disembodied shards of inert crystal. An iron-sheathed skull battered ones of glass to powder. It roared as it killed, a bestial thing of hate and unquenchable bloodlust.

Vitali watched the crystalline creatures destroyed in seconds, shattered to fragmented ruin by an engine of slaughter wrought in human form.

And then it came for him.

Vitali had never seen arco-flagellants in combat, only at rest.

He never wished to see one again.

Its identity blazed in the hostile binary scrolling over its blood-red optics.

Rasselas X-42.

The arco-flagellant halted millimetres from Vitali. Its lips drew back to reveal sharpened iron teeth, its claws poised to strike. He felt the heat of its killing power, an urge to murder that went deeper than any implanted Mechanicus battle-doctrinas.

This thing *wanted* to kill him.

And, for a heartbeat, Vitali thought it just might.

Then, deciding he was no threat, it pushed past him, taking up position before Abrehem Locke like an Assassinorum life-ward.

Vitali fought the urge to flee as he saw a bulky shadow silhouetted in the firelight from beyond the ruin of the door.

Tall and encased in heavy plates of hissing pneumatic armour, Totha Mu-32's chromium mantle billowed in rogue thermals. He rammed a bladed stave on the ground as though reclaiming this forge for the Mechanicus. Beside him was a figure in a cream robe with a mono-tasked augmetic arm and a dented iron skull-plate.

Noospheric ident-tags named him Ismael de Roeven.

The One who Returned.

A hundred chainveiled warriors in the livery of Mechanicus Protectors stood behind Ismael and Totha Mu-32, bulked with combat augmetics and bearing an array of absurdly lethal weaponry.

'We come to protect the Machine-touched,' said Ismael, with black tears streaming down his cheeks.

'With any and all means at our disposal,' finished Totha Mu-32, with a distasteful glance at Rasselas X-42.

'I think you might be too late,' said Chiron Manubia.

Vitali didn't know what she meant.

Until he looked where she looked.

And saw the blood pooled around the Throne Mechanicus.

Rising from the black depths of Exnihlio, the first thing to strike Roboute was the sheer intensity of the blue sky. The last time he'd seen a sky so pure had been on Iax, when he'd taken Katen on a system-run out to First Landing for their first anniversary. He'd never expected to see anything like it again, but Exnihlio's cloudless skies were the blue of remembered youth, going on forever like the clearest ocean.

Gone were the strato-storms and the lightning clawing from the horizon. All trace of atmospheric violation was utterly absent.

He was also pleased to see that Kotov's understanding of Exnihlio's deep infrastructure had been correct. All around them, elevated linear induction rails arced like slender flying buttresses, threading steel canyons from a series of shuttered conveyance hangars.

A host of silver, bullet-nosed trains sat idle on humming rails, surrounded by motionless servitors with slack features and eyes devoid of purpose. Bereft of commands, they shuffled between work stations, waiting for tasks that would never come.

Roboute walked into the light, cupping his hands over his eyes and smiling to see open skies once more. An invisible weight lifted from his shoulders at the sight of such brilliant blue.

'What happened here?' said Tanna, removing his helmet and taking a breath of uncorrupted air. 'Where are the storms?'

'Ultra-rapid terraforming,' said Pavelka, hunched and exhausted with the climb from the depths. 'Every universal assembler within hundreds of kilometres has been activated.'

'Why?'

'Telok's endgame,' said Kotov, pointing to a gap between the rhomboidal towers of a bifurcating induction rail. 'They are coming online for the same reason we activated one, to get something up to the *Speranza*.'

Roboute followed the archmagos's mechadendrite and felt a cyst of nausea form in his gut as he saw the sick, shimmering radiance haloing the towers.

'No…' he said, hints of the spinning mesh of silver leaves and impossible angles making his eyes water. Was it just his imagination or was the Breath of the Gods bigger than before? Was it even possible to know its size with any certainty?

One by one, eldar, mortal, Mechanicus and post-human, they came

to marvel at the ascent of Telok's diabolical machine. No matter their birth origin, every soul was ensnared by its unnatural light and its violation of physics.

'An abominable birth,' said Bielanna. 'The *Yngir's* engine tears free from its sepulchral womb.'

The farseer's eyes shone with a fierce light, and the burden of age Roboute had seen upon her was undone. The black lines beneath her porcelain skin were now veins of gold in the palest marble. Every one of the eldar seemed invigorated by the light coming from the Breath of the Gods. A salutary reminder that their senses were not cut from the same cloth as humanity's.

'All times become one,' she said. 'Even as the threads of the past and present are cut, new threads are drawn from the future into the engine's gyre.'

'What does that mean?' said Roboute.

'New life spreads its light to those around it,' said Bielanna, tears springing from her eyes. 'It means I am being renewed. It means that those I thought lost forever might yet be given a chance of life.'

The train was a wide-bodied cargo transporter. It sped at incredible velocity through the forge world's towering spires in near silence on linear induction rails. It passed through the interiors of numerous forge-complexes, and within each, the signs of this world's imminent abandonment were clear. With the Breath of the Gods rising to the *Speranza*, Telok had no more need of Exnihlio.

Within each forge, the previously industrious servitors stood immobile. Without their attentions the engines which they had tended were now thundering towards destruction.

Exnihlio's machines were dying. Monolithic datastacks melted down without the proper rites of placation. Generators belched fire and lightning as volatile cores spun up to critical levels.

Kotov attempted to plot a route from the driver's compartment as Pavelka sought access to the systems controlling the switching gear for the rails.

All to bring them to where the Breath of the Gods was ascending.

Where it was, Telok would be.

And killing Telok was all Tanna had left.

He knelt on the grilled floor of the train's second compartment, his sword held point down before him. Its quillons framed his eyes, and Tanna stared at the spread wings of the golden eagle forming the hilt, admiring the fine workmanship of the artificers.

A chainsword was not an elegant weapon. No swordsman of note would ever wield one and no epic duels had been fought with such a weapon. It was a butcher's blade, a tool wrought to kill as quickly and as efficiently as possible. And yet this blade had been given a finish the equal of Varda's Black Sword. The spirit within was as keen-edged as its teeth had once been.

Tanna stood and lifted the weapon, turning it over in his hands. He tested the heft and weight, flexing his fingers on the handle.

'Does it feel any different?' asked Varda.

'A few grams lighter where teeth have come loose, but otherwise unchanged,' said Tanna.

'Mine too,' agreed Varda, cutting the air with the midnight edge of the Black Sword and sighting down the length of its blade. 'Do you think Adept Pavelka did anything at all?'

'I can only hope so,' said Tanna. 'Whatever techno-sorcery she has worked on my blade has not altered it in a way I can detect.'

Varda lowered his blade and lifted Tanna's fettered sword arm. The links were buckled after the fight against the Tindalosi.

'Your chain,' said Varda. 'The binding is all but gone.'

'You worried I'll drop my sword?'

'No, never that,' said Varda.

'Then what?'

'Would that we had the time, brother, I would have been honoured to forge your chain anew as you forged mine.'

Tanna nodded in understanding and took Varda's hand in his, accepting the brotherhood his Emperor's Champion offered. The rest of the Black Templars gathered around him, their weapons drawn, their faces sombre.

They could all feel it too.

The end of their crusade was upon them.

No sooner had Tanna formed the thought than the train roof buckled with multiple powerful impacts. Thunderous booms of iron on steel. Claws like swords punched through the metal and the contoured roof of the train peeled back. Turbulent air rammed inside. Windows blew out and high-tension cables whipped through the compartment as the train's fuselage crumpled.

Tanna dived to the side as something vast and silver dropped into the train. A hulking body alive with emerald wychfire. Eyes a mass of dead static and hunger.

Ebon-black claws unsheathed.

'Tindalosi!' he shouted.

Microcontent 15

Hawkins had fought over Magos Dahan's training deck more times than he cared to remember. But no simulation, however sophisticated, could ever accurately replicate the truth of war. Even the lethal subterranean kill maze of Kasr Creta, populated by mutant warp-lunatics with hook-bladed knives and ripper-guns, had an air of unreality to it.

But this?

This was real.

The corpses, the smoking craters and the yelling all testified to the reality of this fight. Neon streams of las and alien fire filled the Imperial city currently occupying the deck, a choked mass of plascrete and steel that stank of hot iron and oil. Roving packs of skitarii and weaponised servitors duelled with the enemy forcing a path across the open space at the heart of the deck.

Hundreds of vacant-eyed servitors milled in a wide plaza with a tall statue of a winged Space Marine at its centre. They reminded Hawkins of gawping civilians who didn't have the good sense to run like hell when the shooting started. The thousands of crystalith warrior-constructs were ignoring them, but plenty had already been mown down in the blistering crossfire.

Hawkins and his command platoon sheltered in a modular structure of cavernous proportions towards the starboard edge of the deck. Shot-blasted rebars and chunks of polycarbon rubble surrounded

them. Crouched at the edge of the rubble to get a clear line of sight over the battlefield, Hawkins issued orders to other Cadian units in the training deck, shouting into the vox-horn to be heard over the cacophony of gunfire. Behind him, Rae and five Guardsmen fired through hastily punched loopholes. Others reloaded or prepared demo-charges.

Green fire threw jagged, leaping shadows.

Explosions blew prefabbed buildings apart. Burning bodies tumbled from their gutted ruins. Most were steel-jacketed skitarii, but some were Cadians. Guardsmen wearing the scarlet campaign badges of Creed company leapt from the burning building.

They ran to take cover in the shadow of a grand, cathedral-like edifice that dominated one end of the plaza. Coordinated fire from its numerous defensive ramparts and armoured pillboxes expertly covered their displacement.

Lieutenant Gerund's Hotshot company fought from an emplaced position jutting from the corner of a structure that looked like an Adeptus Arbites Hall of Justice. Hawkins had split Valdor company into marauding combat teams and spread them through the tumble-down ruins to savage the enemy with enfilading missiles.

Hawkins ducked back as an emerald explosion threw up chunks of rock and mesh decking. He scanned the battlefield for anything he'd missed, any opportunity to exploit enemy mistakes. He saw nothing, but aspects of the city's layout seemed damnably familiar. Something at the back of his mind told him he'd seen this place before, but where?

Had Dahan put them through this setup? He didn't think so.

'Why did you bother with the statue?' he wondered, then grinned as it suddenly hit him why he recognised this battlefield.

'You clever metal bastard,' he said.

'What's that, sir?' said Rae, ducking beneath the smoking embrasure of his loophole. Barely pausing for breath, Rae expertly switched out the powercell of his rifle.

'Do you know where we are, sergeant?'

'Begging your pardon, sir, is that a trick question?' asked Rae, wiping smears of blood and sweat from his forehead.

'Come on, Rae,' said Hawkins, pointing into the plaza. 'Look!'

'What am I looking at, sir?'

'That statue. Who is it?'

Rae's uncomprehending look made Hawkins grin. 'Come on, a giant Space Marine with wings? How many of them are there?'

'The Lord of the Angels?' ventured Rae at last. 'Sanguinius?'

'And look at the building behind it.'

'The Palace of Peace!' exclaimed Rae, and Hawkins saw his mind shift up a gear as an innate understanding of Cadian military history kicked in. 'Khai-Zhan! This is bloody Vogen, sir! That's Angel Square.'

'Dahan must have had the servitors set it up like this the moment the ship was boarded,' said Hawkins. 'He knew a Cadian regiment would know how to fight in Vogen.'

'Maybe he does know us after all,' said Rae, returning to his makeshift firestep.

Like every Cadian officer, Hawkins knew the Battle for Vogen inside out. He'd learned the city's every secret from the detailed accounts of soldiers who'd fought for Khai-Zhan's capital. That gave them an edge.

'Incoming!' shouted Rae. 'Displace!'

Hawkins didn't second guess the order and took off running. Rae was already ahead of him, the big man's arms pumping like a sprinter's. Hawkins ran towards a bombed-out ruin he now recognised as a recreation of Transformer Hub Zeta-Lambda.

Where Sergeant Oliphant retook the Company Colours from a pack of mutants single-handed on day two hundred and ten of the battle.

A flash of brilliant light threw Hawkins's shadow out in front of him. Then he was flying as the hammerblow of a pressure wave slammed into his back. The noise and shock of the explosion engulfed him as he hit a prefabbed wall hard.

The impact punched the air from his lungs. He fought to draw a breath as a seething column of green light mushroomed from the modular structure. Its corner collapsed and took half the roof with it in a thunderous avalanche of debris.

'Good warning, sergeant,' shouted Hawkins over the ringing echoes of detonation. His spine felt like it had been stepped on by a Dreadnought as he pushed himself to his knees.

'They're bringing up the heavy ones now!' returned Rae, chivvying soldiers into the transformer hub's cover.

Hawkins scrambled behind a smoking stub of pressed concrete with rebars poking out like a crustacean's limbs. Through the twitching smoke and guttering green fires, he saw heavier crystalline creatures entering the deck. Lumbering crab-like things, more of the centipede monsters and hulking brutes as tall as ogryns that were hard edged and non-reflective.

These last creatures carried glossy shields, wide enough to be siege mantlets. Others extruded lightning-wreathed spikes from multi-faceted hides, energy weapons as big as anything mounted on a superheavy.

'Going to need some bigger guns,' said Rae.

Hawkins nodded, scanning the ruins of the transformer hub. 'Where's Leth?' he shouted. 'Where's my vox-man?'

'Dead, sir,' said Rae, his back pressed against a slope of brick rubble. 'Him and his vox are in pieces.'

Hawkins cursed and looked towards where Creed company were repelling a flanking thrust of crystalline attackers. Even through the smoke it was hard to miss the whip-antenna of Creed's vox-man.

'Cover me, sergeant!'

'Where are you going?'

'I need a vox and Creed's got a vox,' said Hawkins, slinging his rifle and crouching at the edge of the ruins.

'It's fifty metres, sir!' said Rae.

'I know, hardly any distance at all,' said Hawkins, breaking from cover and sprinting for all he was worth. Blitzing fire streaked across the deck nearby. Was it aimed at him? He couldn't tell. Hawkins kept low, cutting a path from cover to cover, diving, rolling and pausing just long enough to catch his breath.

He heard shouts ahead, soldiers urging him on. Zipping spirals of covering fire drilled the smoke around him. Hawkins fell the last two metres, rolling to an ungainly halt behind the scorched and pitted flanks of a hull-down Chimera.

Lieutenant Karha Creed was waiting for him by the Chimera's rear track-guard. She had a thin hatchet-face, with the same high cheekbones and thunderous brow as her illustrious uncle.

'You pair are the luckiest sons of bitches I ever saw,' she said.

'Duly noted, lieutenant,' said Hawkins. 'Wait, pair?'

'You remember what I asked you about putting us in harm's way, sir?' said Rae, chest heaving and the cut on his forehead bleeding beneath the rim of his helmet.

'I took it under advisement and decided not to implement your proposal,' he said, glad Rae was here with him despite the risk he'd taken. Hawkins slapped a hand on his sergeant's shoulder and turned to address Creed.

'I need your vox, Karha. I need to speak with Jahn Callins in Turentek's forges,' said Hawkins. 'We need the tanks here.'

Creed nodded and ran to get her vox-man. Hawkins took a moment to cast an eye over the men and women occupying this position. His eyes narrowed at the sight of two particular fighters.

'What the hell are you two doing here?'

Gunnar Vintras turned from his firing step, a lasrifle cocked on his hip like some kind of Catachan glory-hound.

'After all the training Sergeant Rae here has put me through, I

thought it only proper I slum it with the footsloggers for a time,' said Vintras with that insufferable pearl-white grin. 'You know, see what all this talk of duty and honour is all about.'

Hawkins resisted the urge to punch him and turned to Sylkwood. 'What about you?' he said. 'Shouldn't you be on the *Renard*?'

'Emil doesn't need my help to fly the shuttle,' she said. 'Besides, I'm Cadian. This is where I'm meant to be.'

Hawkins nodded in understanding as the vox-man arrived. The patch on his shoulder named him as Guardsman Westin. Heat bleed from the bulky, canvas-wrapped unit in his pack hazed the air. Like most vox-men, Westin was skinny and wiry with hunched shoulders and a constantly harried look to him.

Hawkins spun him around and pumped the crank on the side of the pack. He held the vox-horn to one ear, pressing his palm against the other.

'Call Sign Kasr Secundus, come in,' he said. 'Damn it, Callins, are you there? Where are the tanks you promised me?'

After a second or two of static, the regiment's logistics officer came over the earpiece, sounding as put-upon as always.

'Working as fast as we can, sir,' said Callins.

Hawkins flinched as a bolt of green light punched into the Chimera's glacis, rocking it back on its tracks. A fine mist of choking ash-like matter billowed like granular smoke. He heard screams from farther down the line.

'Work faster, Jahn,' he said. 'I need those tanks. And Titans too, if you've any to spare this millennium.'

'The Sirius engines haven't moved since I got here, sir,' grunted Callins in disgust. *'Lot of crap about rites of awakening and proper observances of blah, blah, blah. They're choking up the muster routes. I can't get anything out in numbers that'll make a damn bit of difference.'*

Hawkins let out an exasperated breath and said, 'Understood. Do what you can, I'm sending help.'

'Help? What? I don't–' said Callins, but Hawkins slammed the horn onto its cradle on Westin's vox-caster.

'You two, get over here,' he said, beckoning Sylkwood and Vintras to him. 'Sylkwood, I assume you can drive this Chimera.'

She nodded.

'Good, I want you down in Turentek's prow forges. You know tanks, so help Callins to get them moving faster. Vintras, give your brothers a kick up the arse and beg them to take you back. I want *Lupa Capitalina* and *Canis Ulfrica* walking right beside my tanks. And I want you in *Amarok* again. Understand?'

'I don't beg,' said Vintras.

'Today you do,' said Hawkins, and the look in his eye killed the Skinwalker's caustic response stone dead. The Warhound princeps nodded and slung his rifle.

'I want to stay here,' protested Sylkwood. 'I want to fight.'

'You're a daughter of Cadia,' snapped Hawkins. 'Follow your damn orders and get the hell out of here!'

Prior to Bielanna's journey on the Path of the Seer, she too had experienced the visceral joy of a war-mask on Khaine's Path. She barely remembered that part of her life, the bloody horror of what she'd seen and done locked away in an unvisited prison of dark memory.

There could be beauty as well as terror in battle, a fluidly balletic poetry in the dance of combatants.

The fight against the Tindalosi had none of that.

Bielanna's mind recoiled from the distilled hate weeping from their every metallic pore. Oceans of blood clung to them, a shroud of a hundred lifetimes of murder.

The Tindalosi were too fast, too deadly and too ruthless to allow for any poetry. Their deaths demanded hard, quick stanzas, not the epic languor of laments.

And what better warriors than Striking Scorpions and Howling Banshees for such a fight? This dance had no grace, just sublimely swift slashes of claw and sword. Teeth snapped and mandiblasters spat. Shuriken discs shattered on impact and the train sang with the howls of Morai-Heg's favoured daughters.

They matched the speed of the Tindalosi, hook-bladed horrors of spinning chrome and emerald fire. Crackling mandiblasters scorched the unnatural metal of their hides, and wraithbone blades were blurs of cleaving ivory.

But as fast and hard as the eldar fought, every wound was undone moments later.

'Not any more,' whispered Bielanna, drawing the power of the skein to her. It filled her with a strength she hadn't felt in what seemed like a lifetime. The constricting metal walls of the *Speranza* had smothered her connection to the skein and Exnihlio had kept her from any anchor in the present.

All such distractions fell away from her now.

Bielanna hunted the beast upon the skein, sifting a thousand possible futures in the blink of an eye until she found its grubby thread of murder, reaching back into a long-dead aeon.

'The fate of Eldanesh be upon you,' she said, pulling the weave of futures and cutting the beast's thread with a snap of her fingers.

And in that instant, every blade and every blast of killing energy found a way inside its armour, a confluence of fates willed into existence by Bielanna's power. The regenerative heart of the monster was cloven into shards, destroyed so thoroughly that no power in the universe could remake it.

Bielanna spun in with her runesword aimed at the Tindalosi's head and drove the blade through its jaws. The beast's skull was split in two and the dead light in its eyes was extinguished forever. It fell to the deck, an inanimate mass of metal and machinery.

She turned on her heel as the press of futures poured into her.

A thousand times a thousand duels played out before her, eldar and Space Marines moving to the future's song, a hundred possibilities spawning a million possible outcomes, each in turn growing the web of futures at a geometric rate.

Bielanna saw it all.

The train's fuselage buckled as the Tindalosi slammed Tanna against it. Its claws dug through his armour. Blood ran down the bodyglove within. Tanna drove his knee into its belly. Metal deformed, its grip released. He dropped and ducked a clawed swipe that tore parallel gouges in the metal skin behind him.

It shoulder barged him, knocking him down.

A clawed foot slammed. He rolled. Sword up, block and move.

Don't let it back him against the wall again.

Tanna got his sword up, angling himself obliquely.

His gaze met that of the beast. Empty of anything except the desire to see him dead. In that, at least, they were evenly matched.

'Come on then,' he snarled.

The Tindalosi flew at him. He sidestepped, exhaling with a roar. The sword came down in a hard, economical arc. Its claws punched air. His blade took it high on the shoulder. Teeth tore into metal, spraying glittering slivers. Two-handed now, saw downwards.

A hooked elbow slashed back. Rubberised seals at Tanna's hip tore and he grunted as the blade scraped bone. He tore his sword free and brought it around in a recklessly wide stroke.

It took the beast high on the neck. A decapitating strike.

Notched teeth ripped through metal, cable and bio-organic polymers. Viscous black fluid gushed. Its howl triggered the cut-off on Tanna's auto-senses. The Tindalosi's head hung slack, not severed cleanly, but ruined nonetheless. Tanna's heart sank as he saw a web of red and green wychfire crackling around the awful wound.

He took the fractional pause to update his situational awareness. One Tindalosi was attacking Yael while Varda and Issur duelled with

the pack leader. The eldar farseer stood over a fallen beast as her remaining warriors fought a second. Surcouf and Pavelka had withdrawn to the driver's compartment with the Cadians, Kotov and his two skitarii.

This wasn't a fight that could be won by mortals.

The train lurched on the maglev as it turned in a tight arc. Its precisely designed form had been ruined by the Tindalosi attack, and travelling at such enormous speeds, even the slightest deviation in aerodynamic profile could be disastrous. The turbulent air slamming through the train was hurricane-force and Tanna held to a taut cable as the wind direction changed with the train's turn.

The metalled floor of the train carriage buckled upwards, the sheet panelling of the walls billowing like sailcloth. In moments the magnetic connection between the train and track would be broken.

Crackling webs of frost formed on the few remaining shards of glass in the frames and Tanna felt a bitter flavour fill his mouth. Part blood, part witchery.

He saw Bielanna's helm wreathed in shimmering flames of white fire, a pellucid halo of psychic energy. He had no idea what she was doing.

The Tindalosi came at him again. Tanna swung his sword up. The beast's head still lolled at its shoulder. The green light fizzed and spat at the wound, as if fighting to restore the damage his blade had wrought.

But it wasn't working.

Sudden certainty filled Tanna.

He saw the exact place his blade should strike, knew the precise power to deliver. The angle of his blade shifted a hair's breadth. He drew in a full lungful of air and leapt to meet the Tindalosi. The chainsword swung in the arc he had already pictured. The sense of déjà vu was potent.

The chainsword struck the Tindalosi just where he expected.

The teeth sheared through the bio-mechanical meat and metal of its neck, cleaving down into its chest cavity. The beast's arms spasmed and Tanna tore the sword loose, ripping out a vast swathe of ticking, whirring, crackling machinery. The green light veining its mechanical organs was now a deep red.

The Tindalosi crumpled, the static of its eyes burning out as it died.

'Thank you, Magos Pavelka,' said Tanna.

Yael put his sword through the heart of the beast before him. His blow struck precisely, as though guided by the hand of Dorn himself. The beast came apart as though a demo charge had been set off in its chest, screaming and howling as the torments of the damned destroyed it from the inside.

Likewise the eldar fought with every blow landing at the perfect point to do the maximum damage. The Tindalosi were doomed, the techno-enchantments of Pavelka's code taking away their regenerative abilities and the eldar's psychic witchery clouding their speed and skill.

Only Varda and Issur's beast still fought. The swordsmen had landed numerous blows upon the pack-master, but the hideous power at its heart was orders of magnitude greater than that empowering the others. It backed away from them and the eldar as they came together.

'We'll take it en masse,' said Varda, standing at Tanna's side.

'Thr… thr… three to one,' said Issur through clenched teeth.

'No,' said Tanna as the train lurched once again. The last portion of the roof ripped clear, flying away with the force of the wind. The train was curving along the track again, harder this time, leaning into the turn. Tanna saw the length of the train begin to come loose from the tracks.

First the rearmost carriage tore clear, falling from the rails in a haze of squalling magnetics and dragging the next with it. Both came apart in explosions of aluminium. Sheet metal tore like paper. Another carriage followed, dragging the next from the rails with its weight.

'Everyone out!' shouted Tanna. 'Get into the driver's compartment. Now!'

Yael pushed into the link doorway towards the driver's compartment. Bielanna and her surviving warriors slipped effortlessly through as the last Tindalosi turned its vast, serrated skull and saw what Tanna had seen.

It bounded along the bucking carriage towards them.

'Go!' shouted Tanna, bracing himself. One leg squared off, the other bent forwards. Varda and Issur knew better than to argue. They followed their brother and the eldar.

'Just me and thee,' said Tanna.

The Tindalosi leapt and Tanna went low. His sword swung in a tight arc, hewing its belly. Glittering shards of cut metal and oily liquid sprayed. Red-green light filled the wound. It turned back to him and its claws cut into his plastron. Tanna felt his feet leave the deck plates. He struggled like bait on a hook. He swung his blade. The beast's jaws fastened on his sword arm and bit down hard.

Fangs like daggers punched through ceramite and meat.

Tanna roared in pain as the beast wrenched its head to the side and took his right hand with it. His sword went too, dangling from the monster's teeth on snapped links of chain. The pack leader dropped

him and Tanna rolled, clutching the stump of his arm to his chest. He pushed himself to his knees as the Tindalosi loomed over him, a gloating killer taking an instant to savour its kill.

Its head swung around, seeing more of the train carriages pulling loose from the maglev. In moments the cascade of derailing carriages would reach this one, but it had no intention of still being here when that happened.

Neither did Tanna.

He dived towards the Tindalosi and grabbed for the dangling sword with his remaining hand. His fingers closed on its wire-wound hilt. No way to free the chain, its links stuck fast in the beast's jaw.

But Tanna had no intention of freeing his sword.

He rammed the blade down hard into the deck plate, twisting it deep into the mechanisms beneath. The Tindalosi wrenched its head, but the chains binding the blade to its jaw pulled taut. Like a beast in a snare it twisted and writhed as it sought to free itself from Tanna's weapon.

'We die together, monster,' said Tanna.

'No,' said Varda, hooking his arms under Tanna's shoulders and dragging him away. 'It dies alone.'

Tanna looked up in surprise.

The Emperor's Champion hauled Tanna back through the door to the driver's compartment. Behind them, the Tindalosi pack leader finally ripped its fangs clear of Tanna's embedded sword. It fixed them with its pitiless stare, already picturing their deaths.

'Now, Kotov! Cut it loose!' shouted Varda as the beast bounded towards them. The train lurched as the derailments finally reached the carriage. Tanna heard a clatter of disengaging locking pins.

The Tindalosi leapt as the carriage tumbled from the maglev.

It spun end over end and exploded as it hit the ground.

The speed and ferocity of impact destroyed the carriage instantly, reducing its once graceful form to a hurricane of spinning fragments and billowing debris.

Tanna let out a breath as the maglev engine streaked away from the devastation.

'I told you to go,' he said.

'I'm not leaving anyone else behind,' said Varda.

The tanks were moving, just not fast enough.

Jahn Callins stalked the ready lines of Magos Turentek's forge-temple, keeping to clearly marked pedestrian routes. All too easy to get run down by a speeding ammo gurney or fuel tanker by straying into the working areas of the deck.

The forge was working to capacity: lifter-rigs hauling tanks down from stowage bays, fuel trucks in constant filling rotations and weapon carts being hauled up on chains from hardened magazines below decks. Hundreds of tech-priests moved through the deck, using hi-vis wands to direct the flow of a regiment's worth of armoured vehicles.

Chimeras and Hellhounds were mustering by squadron, moving out to assembly areas where they were loaded with fuel and ammunition. Dozens of tech-priests moved through the hosts of armoured vehicles like warrior-priests of old, each with an aspergillium of holy oils in their right hand. Chanting servitors with smoking braziers and relics borne upon silken cushions followed them.

Callins dearly wished they would hurry the hell up.

At the far end of the hangar, the engines of Legio Sirius billowed steam and groaning bellows from their war-horns. Gigantic weapons swung overhead in the claws of vast lifter-rigs, trailing steam and drizzling a fine mist of sacred oils to the deck. Each weapon was accompanied by swarms of servo-skulls and binaric plainsong. Like everything to do with the Mechanicus, the Legio was taking its own sweet time to do anything.

Only one Warhound had moved from its stowage cradle.

'The fight'll be over before they're ready,' he muttered as his data-slate pinged with another readiness icon.

Chimera squadron. Lima Tao Secundus.

'Superheavies,' he grumbled to the junior officers trailing him like obedient hounds. 'I need the damn superheavies.'

The Baneblades and Stormhammers were yet to move, delayed by the Mechanicus need to do things in the proper order. The 71st were a Mechanised Infantry regiment and as such, Mechanicus protocols gave priority to the APCs.

Trying to explain that Hawkins needed fighting vehicles to the tech-priests was like pulling teeth. No amount of shouting or talk about losing the ship had persuaded the deck commanders to alter their manifest procedures. As a logistics officer, Callins gave all due reverence to the power of lists and standard operating procedures, but this was taking that reverence to the extreme.

Another icon flashed up on his slate. A retasking order, together with a location marker.

'What the hell?'

He tapped the icon and looked over to the location indicated.

'You have got to be kidding me,' he said, watching as a trio of Baneblades were swung back onto their reinforced storage rails and locked into place. 'They're putting them back?'

Callins ran towards the rigs, ignoring the safety lines on the floor and setting off a dozen alarms as he crossed transit routes deemed unsafe for foot-traffic. Red-robed tech-priests waved directions to the crews of the lifter-rigs, assigning them to bulbous, spider-legged vehicles.

Callins spotted a high-ranking magos directing operations.

'Atrean,' he said. 'Might have known.'

This particular tech-priest was a rules-lawyer of the worst sort, a man to whom common sense was a regretfully organic notion. They'd butted heads before, but this time promised to be their best yet.

'Atrean!' barked Callins. 'Are you trying to lose the ship?'

The magos turned and Callins wished there was some organic part of his face to punch.

'Boarding protocols are in effect, Major Callins,' said Atrean. 'Skitarii vehicles take precedence over passenger vehicles.'

Callins pointed to the Baneblades. 'Captain Hawkins needs those tanks. He doesn't get them, the training deck falls. The training deck falls, the ship falls. Do you understand that?'

'I understand that I have orders to follow. As do you.'

'Your orders make no damn sense,' said Callins, staring at the scrolling lines of text on his slate. 'These are going to the ventral decks, perimeter defence duties. I need superheavies in the battle line right now!'

'Mechanicus forge-temples take precedence over lower-rated structures within the *Speranza*,' said Atrean, turning away as though the matter were settled.

Before Callins could reply, more alarms screeched through the deck as a fire-blackened Chimera came roaring into view. Its hull was scorched and pitted with impacts. It angled its course towards them, narrowly avoiding a pair of gurneys laden with promethium drums for a waiting squadron of Hellhounds.

The driver threw the Chimera into a skid, halting it at the edge of the stowage bays. Its rear assault ramp slammed down moments later and two figures emerged, a woman with a gnarled knot of augmetics on her scalp in iron cornrows and a cocksure peacock who looked like he'd never spent a day in a firing line.

The man took one look at the Legio Sirius engines and sprinted off towards them without a word. The woman carried a data-slate and wore a battered uniform jacket sewn with a Cadian enginseer's patch.

'You Callins?' she asked.

'Yes, who are you?'

'Kayrn Sylkwood, lately of the *Renard*,' she said, tapping the patch. 'But in a previous life I was with the Eighth.'

Callins was impressed. Every Cadian knew the pedigree of the Eighth and its illustrious commander.

'What are you doing here?'

'Captain Hawkins sent me,' said Sylkwood, drawing a bulky hell-pistol, a Triplex-Phall hotshot variant with an overcharger wired to its powercell.

She aimed her gun at Atrean's head and said, 'You in charge?'

'I am,' he said.

Sylkwood looked down at her slate. 'So you're the one putting those Baneblades back in the stowage rails?'

'Yes. Mechanicus protocols clearly dictate that–'

Kayrn Sylkwood shot Magos Atrean in the chest and Jahn Callins fell a little bit in love with her. The wound was carefully placed not to be mortal, but Atrean would be out of commission for a while. She aimed her pistol at the gaggle of tech-priests carrying out Atrean's orders.

'Who's in charge now?' she asked, racking the recharge lever of the hotshot pack.

One by one, they pointed at Jahn Callins.

'Is the right answer,' said Sylkwood.

The maglev came to a halt at a raised way-station, pausing just long enough for the battered survivors of the landing expedition to debark on the edge of the open plaza where Telok had first led them below the planet's surface.

Kotov thought back to that moment, remembering the potential he had felt. The potential and the unease. And how he had smothered that unease with ambition and the need to believe in all that Telok represented.

The silver dome that once filled the plaza with its immensity was gone. In its place was a gaping chasm that dropped into the heart of Exnihlio. The Breath of the Gods was a smear of light in the sky, a new and dreadful star.

The plaza seemed empty without the silver dome, and the towering structures on all sides made Kotov feel like he was deep in a crater gouged in a vast glacier. After so long enclosed by the industry of Telok's forge world, the echoing emptiness was unnerving. Gone was the omnipresent beat of machinery he associated with a forge world, the roar of furnaces and the electrical hum of a global infrastructure.

For all intents and purposes, Exnihlio was deserted.

Atticus Varda led them into the plaza, his Black Sword unsheathed.

Tanna, Yael and Issur marched alongside their champion, while the Cadians and skitarii moved with Kotov. Roboute Surcouf and Magos Pavelka brought up the rear.

Telok was waiting for them.

The Lost Magos stood on a landing platform raised up from the plaza. His bulk was immense, hostile and insane. How could Kotov not have seen the lunacy at the heart of him?

Telok's expression was one of pleasant surprise at the sight of them – though he must surely have known of their approach.

'Can you hit him from here?' Tanna asked Yael.

'I can, brother-sergeant,' confirmed Yael, chambering a stalker-round.

'Do not waste your shot,' said Pavelka. 'Telok is protected by layered energy shields. I cannot see him, but I can feel the presence of void flare.'

'Is she right?' asked Tanna.

Kotov switched through his auto-senses and nodded.

'It would take a macro-cannon to get to him,' he said.

'Archmagos Kotov,' said Telok, his voice boosted and echoing from the buildings around them. 'As irksome as you and your strange friends have become, I have to say I am pleased you yet live. History is in the making, and history must be observed to matter, otherwise what is the point? The Breath of the Gods draws near the *Speranza* and this world is spiralling to its doom. Have you any valediction?'

Kotov knew there was no point in trying to sway Telok from his course, but tried anyway.

'It doesn't work, Vettius,' he said. 'Your machine. It won't work when you leave this place. Not without the hrud to counterbalance the temporal side-effects. But you know that already, don't you?'

Telok grinned and it was the leer of a madman.

'It only needs to work once,' said Telok. 'Then when Mars is mine and the Noctis Labyrinthus opens up to me I will have a new power source at its heart. I will have no need of filthy aliens.'

'You would tear the galaxy apart for the sake of mortal ambition?' asked Bielanna, her warriors spreading out around her.

'Speaks the emissary of a race whose lusts destroyed their empire and birthed unimaginable horrors upon the galaxy,' said Telok. 'You are hardly best suited to speak of caution.'

'I am the one *most* suited to speak of caution, I know the folly of what you attempt,' said Bielanna. 'Your machine was wrought for creatures who are anathema to life. Their servitor races built it to drain the life from stars and feed the monstrous appetites of their masters. It was never intended to be employed by a species with so linear a grasp of the temporal flow and with no sensory acuity to perceive deep time.'

'And yet I now command the Breath of the Gods,' snarled Telok.

Bielanna laughed. 'Is that what you truly believe? That such a terrible creation would allow a mere mortal to be its master? Your capacity for self-delusion is beyond anything suffered by those of my people who brought down the Fall.'

Telok's crystalline components pulsed a bruised crimson and the wrought iron portions of his Dreadnought-like frame vented superheated steam as debased floodstream boiled around his body.

Telok pointed a clawed hand towards Bielanna. 'Your arrogance is matched only by your species's pathetic reluctance to accept its doom. I should take lessons on humility from you? A race that clings pathetically to a lost empire sliding inevitably to ruin? I think not.'

'Then we are well matched after all,' said Bielanna.

Kotov looked up as another light appeared in the sky. This one was blue-hot and the shrill whine of boosters told him that this was an atmosphere-capable craft on an arc of descent.

'What is that?' asked Tanna.

The corona wreathing its engine nacelles blotted out the descending craft's profile, but there was no doubting its Imperial provenance. Kotov saw an electromagnetic residue that was as familiar to him as the composition of his own floodstream.

'It's from the *Speranza*,' he said.

'It's the *Renard*'s shuttle!' cried Roboute Surcouf. 'Emil!'

The shuttle's engine noise growled and the main drives twisted against the airframe and deepened to a hard red as it flared out on its final approach.

'Tarkis must have sent it,' said Kotov.

'Why would he send the rogue trader's shuttle?' said Tanna.

'Does it matter?' snapped Kotov. 'We have help! Reinforcements!'

The Black Templars moved to battle pace, pulling ahead of Kotov and the Cadians. The eldar matched their speed, though Kotov saw they could easily outpace them. Telok's platform was a hundred metres away, the shuttle from the *Renard* just touching down in an expanding cloud of propellant.

Kotov increased his pace, eager to see what manner of aid Tarkis Blaylock had sent to Exnihlio. Tanna's question was needlessly defeatist. This ship *had* to have come from Tarkis. What other explanation could there be?

Kotov saw a human face in the shuttle's armourglass canopy.

Emil Nader. Facial mapping of micro-expressions revealing great stress and heightened levels of anxiety.

The shuttle's frontal ramp opened up and a figure emerged, wreathed in the fumes of its landing. Tall and black-robed, with a hood drawn up over his face.

'Tarkis!' cried Kotov. 'Ave Deus Mechanicus! Thank the Omnissiah, you came.'

The smoke of the shuttle's landing cleared and Kotov's floodstream ran cold as he saw the truth.

Tarkis Blaylock had not come to Exnihlio.

Galatea had.

Galatea approached Telok with grim purpose in its clattering, mismatched limbs. The blasphemous machine intelligence had finally come to enact its murderous intent in crossing the Halo Scar and hope leapt in Kotov's breast.

'Galatea,' he cried, extending a mechadendrite. 'Telok stands before you. Kill him! Kill him now, just as you have dreamed of doing for thousands of years!'

Telok's laughter boomed out across the plaza.

'Kill him?' said Galatea. 'Don't be ridiculous. We are his herald, his shadow avatar in the Imperium. We brought you to him and we will stand at his right hand when he becomes the new Master of Mars!'

MACROCONTENT COMMENCEMENT:

+++MACROCONTENT 003+++

The Omnissiah knows all, comprehends all.

Microcontent 16

There were times for humility and there were times for brass balls. This was a moment for the latter. Gunnar Vintras stood at the foot of *Amarok* and hauled Magos Ohtar towards him by the folds of his robes.

'You heard me,' he said. 'You're going to put me back into *Amarok* or I'm going to shove this laspistol somewhere the Omnissiah doesn't shine and empty the powercell. Do we understand each other now?'

'You waste your ire on me, Mister Vintras,' said Ohtar. 'Your reinstatement has nothing to do with me. It is for the Wintersun to decide when your penance is done. And he has given no indications as to his willingness to return you to the pack.'

Vintras nodded towards *Amarok*'s glaring canopy.

'Who've you put in there anyway?'

'Akelan Chassen was next in rotation.'

He heard the pause and laughed. 'Chassen? I've seen his aptitude tests. He barely made moderati grade, let alone princeps.'

'But he made them,' pointed out Ohtar. 'Not many ever do.'

'But who would you rather have in *Amarok*? Someone who barely made the grade or someone who rewrote the book on how Warhounds fight? And best answer quickly, this place is going to be knee-deep in crystal monsters soon.'

Ohtar's eyes rolled back in his sockets, and when they returned, they weren't the ice-blue of augmetics, but amber flecked with opal, slitted with a slice of deepest black.

Vintras knew those eyes, he'd seen them on the black and silver mountain in the depths of an ice storm. They'd pinned him to the rock of the Oldbloods' fortress and judged him worthy. And when Ohtar spoke, it was not with his own voice, but one channelled from the mighty head of *Lupa Capitalina*.

+You dare demand a place in my pack?+

Now was the time for humility.

Vintras dropped to one knee and said, 'I seek only to aid the pack, Lord Wintersun. I am the Skinwalker, I belong in a Titan!'

+I stripped you of that title,+ said Princeps Arlo Luth. 'I named you Omega and cast you from the pack.+

'Packs can be rejoined,' said Vintras.

+If the Alpha deems the outcast worthy of redemption,+ said Luth. +Are you worthy of mercy?+

'I am,' said Vintras, angling his neck and displaying his throat as he had done at his ritual of censure. The scar Elias Härkin had given him was pale and healed, but the angle of the cut ensured it would always be visible.

Princeps Luth regarded Vintras through the slitted eyes of an Oldblood. Crackling electrical fire was reflected there, fire that had no place in the eyes of a Mechanicus proxy.

Vintras turned from the hijacked body of Magos Ohtar, seeing bolt after bolt of alien lightning explode onto the deck.

Luth saw the same thing.

+Mount your engine, Skinwalker,+ he ordered. +Fight as pack!+

Kotov's last hope crumbled in the face of Telok's pronouncement. With Galatea at his side, every aspect of the machine-hybrid's actions made a new and terrible sense. Roboute Surcouf's analogy of the spider in its web was now proven entirely correct.

Like a dreadful puppet-master, Archmagos Telok had orchestrated every aspect of Kotov's quest from the start. What level of commitment and preparedness must have gone into such a plan? Kotov could have almost admired the dizzying complexity of Telok's machinations from beyond the edge of the galaxy were they not about to see him dead.

Kotov stared at Galatea with a hatred he had not known himself capable of experiencing. The machine-hybrid had set its snare with a tale of abandonment and vengeance, with just enough truth at the heart of its falsehoods to be credible.

And he had fallen for its lies.

'Galatea,' he said as the revelation of its true loyalties unlocked yet another. 'From the myth of Old Earth, yes? That should have told me everything you said was a lie. The tale of the sculptor who crafts an ivory statue that he falls in love with, and which is then given life by a god... It is all right there.'

'What's right there?' said Surcouf.

'That Galatea was a creature of Telok's,' said Kotov. 'Don't you see? We assumed Galatea was what it claimed to be, a thinking machine, but it is not. It is both more and less than that.'

'Then what is it?' asked Tanna.

Kotov made his way to the landing platform, where Galatea squatted beside Telok. Microtremors shook its body, and the connections passing between the brain jars were strangely hostile, as though no longer entirely under Galatea's control. The Lost Magos appeared oblivious to this, and nodded like a mentor encouraging a struggling pupil towards deeper understanding.

'Go on,' said Telok. 'You're so close, archmagos.'

'It's you,' said Kotov. 'Galatea isn't a thinking machine at all. It's been you all along, hasn't it? Before you crossed the Halo Scar you excised a portion of your own consciousness and grafted it into the heuristic mechanisms of the machine's neuromatrix. Every dealing we have had with Galatea has been with an aspect of *your* personality, hived from the throne of your cerebral cortex and given autonomy within this... this thing. You practically told me as much, with all your metaphysical nonsense about alphas and omegas and the self-created god. Your ego couldn't pass up any chance to taunt us with your presence as a ghost in the machine.'

Kotov shook his head ruefully. 'It beggars belief that I did not see it.'

'As Galatea, I told you what you wanted to hear, Kotov,' said Telok, 'and in your desperation you chose to ignore the truth that was right in front of you.'

'Why tell us that Galatea wanted to kill Telok?' asked Surcouf.

'Few motives are as pure as vengeance,' said Galatea, its voice modulating to match Telok's. 'Would you have found us as credible if we simply offered to help you? We think not.'

By now Kotov and his attendant warriors had reached the foot of the landing platform. Kotov paused at the iron steps as he felt the particle vibration and neutron flow of the layered voids passing over him. Complex field interactions caused his noospherics and floodstream to grey out for a second.

In that instant, the Black Templars and Cadians had their weapons locked to their shoulders. They knew, as Kotov knew, that they were inside the voids protecting the raised platform.

'Kill them,' ordered Tanna.

Bolter fire erupted. Flashing las followed.

The eldar launched themselves into the air, going from complete standstill to bounding motion with no intermediate stage. They landed on the platform with a speed and sure-footedness that made Kotov gasp with astonishment.

Explosions erupted all over Telok's body, but none impacted.

Ablative energy integral to his crystalline flesh ignited the bolt warheads prematurely and vaporised the flashing discs of the eldar weapons. Telok's density was so enormous not even the kinetic force of the detonations staggered him.

Kotov's skitarii put themselves between him and the gunshots. Their blades and weapons locked to Galatea. Issur and Varda climbed towards Telok, their swords singing from scabbards. The eldar reached him first, their swords shrieking blurs of ivory. They surrounded Telok, cutting and lashing him with crackling forks of anbaric energy.

Telok extended his clawed arms, sweeping around like some ancient practitioner of weaponless combat.

The eldar were too nimble, and laughed as they vaulted and swayed aside from his clumsy swipes.

But catching them had never been Telok's aim.

A blitzing tempest of electrical vortices built around his arms and exploded outwards in a hurricane of white-green fire. The eldar warriors were hurled away, their armour melting and the plumes on their tapered helms ablaze. Telok's laughter cut through their howls of pain.

Then Varda and Issur charged in.

The Emperor's Champion swept below a bladed fist the size of a Contemptor's claw. The Black Sword gouged a valley in Telok's flank. Issur's blow was blocked and before he could sidestep, a fit of rogue muscle spasms staggered him.

His paralysis lasted a fraction of a second only, but even that was too long. Telok bludgeoned him from the landing platform and Issur flew thirty metres through the air to land with a bone-crunching thud of cracked ceramite.

The Black Sword erupted from Telok's hybridised metal and crystal body as Varda ran him through. Telok spun as Varda wrenched the blade clear, unleashing a storm of crackling binary that froze the Emperor's Champion rigid.

Telok's enormous claw closed on Varda's body, ready to tear him apart. Before he could crush the life from Varda, a weave of glittering light engulfed his twisted features.

Kotov saw Bielanna down on one knee, her hands pressed to her

forehead as she directed her energies into obliterating Telok's mind with heinous witchcraft. Howling psychic energies blazed around Telok and he hurled Varda from the platform as a jagged, crystalline sheath rose from his shoulders.

'Enough!' roared Telok and Bielanna screamed as the arcane mechanisms wreathing his skull flared with incandescent energies.

'This has gone on long enough,' said Telok, as he and Galatea climbed onto the shuttle's ramp. 'Even my vanity has limits when it compromises my designs. The acausal bindings securing the hrud warrens are no more, so this world is entering its final entropic death spasms. I would ask you to bear witness to Exnihlio's final moments, but you will be corpses long before it dies.'

Telok lifted his arms and the vast structures enclosing the plaza erupted with lightning from dozens of latticework vanes at their roofs. Forking bolts of energy arced down and slammed into the ground with deafening whipcracks of searing fire.

Kotov saw freshly wrought shapes emerge from the strobing afterimages, glossy and humanoid, marching in lockstep to form a perfect circle around the landing platform.

A thousands-strong army of crystaliths.

She'd missed a lot of things about the regiment, but until now Kayrn Sylkwood hadn't realised just how much she'd missed the thrill of marshalling armed forces under fire. The attackers were appearing without warning, materialising in explosions of writhing bonfires of lightning like a teleport assault.

The mechanics of their arrival didn't matter.

It was, as her old drill sergeant used to say at every objection to his orders being completed on time, irrelevant.

Hurricanes of green fire flashed through the deck, flickering in opposition to bright bolts of red las. Percussive shock waves of explosions and thundering engines echoed from the hangar walls. Shouting squad leaders and the cries of burning soldiers put an extra punch in Kayrn's step.

Every minute these tanks remained in the hangar was costing the lives of Cadian soldiers on the training deck.

Kayrn ducked into cover behind a train of ammo gurneys currently serving as cover to a Cadian infantry platoon. Jahn Callins was issuing orders to a gaggle of serious-looking junior officers. Two ran off with vox-casters to enact those orders. The third stayed at his side.

He glanced up. 'How're the starboard racks looking?'

'Empty,' she answered. 'Two through seven are clear. The rails on

eight and nine are buckled beyond immediate repair. Those tanks aren't coming down without lifter-rig support.'

'Damn it,' snapped Callins. 'There's Stormhammers up there. You're sure they're non-functional?'

'I'm sure,' she said, and Callins knew better than to doubt her.

'Captain Hawkins isn't going to be pleased.'

'We've put four more squadrons of superheavies into the ready line,' she said. 'That ought to cheer him up.'

All four of those squadrons were even now rumbling towards the starboard egress ramps after the quickest blessing and anointing the Mechanicus could muster. Throughout the deck, armoured tanks rammed damaged vehicles out of their way. Cadian infantry squads traded shots with their crystalline attackers from the cover of overturned gurneys and wrecked tanks.

'The Leman Russ are next,' continued Kayrn, running a finger down the order of battle displayed on her static-fuzzed slate. 'APCs are mustering at the rear to pick up the infantry.'

Callins nodded and said, 'Fast work, Sylkwood. Remind me to find out why you're not with a Cadian regiment when this is over.'

'Buy me a drink and I might just tell you.'

'Fair enough,' grinned Callins.

A bolt of green fire punched through the crate above Kayrn's head. She ducked closer to the deck as Guardsmen either side of her returned fire.

'These crates empty?' she asked.

'Yeah, apart from a few loose bolter shells.'

'Not exactly the best cover.'

'No, but it probably won't explode if it takes a hit.'

'Good point, well made.'

A pair of frags coughed from portable launchers. Rattling bursts of stubber fire blazed from a heavy weapons team to Kayrn's left.

'None of the turret weapons are firing?' she asked.

'In a hangar filled with ordnance and fuel?' said Callins, putting away his slate and checking the load on his lasgun.

'Sure, why not?' said Kayrn. 'I remember back on Belis Corona we had whole squadrons of Shadowswords firing on a pack of Archenemy battle-engines inside a fyceline depot.'

Callins shook his head.

'This isn't a Black Crusade, and we're not that desperate yet.'

As if to contradict him, the deck plates shook as three ammo gurneys laden with gunmetal-grey warheads and drums of promethium went up like a volcanic eruption. Secondary explosions took half a dozen fuel trucks with them.

Servitor fire-teams deployed to fight the blaze, but streams of enemy fire cut them down. Blazing gouts of promethium spilled in all directions. Tar-black smoke spread like a shroud over the fighting, making the air heavy with toxins.

'Damn the Eye,' said Callins, but even as the curse left his lips a flood of oxygen-depleting liquids rained from a score of swinging extender-arms belonging to Magos Turentek's vast rig apparatus. The boxy arrangement of bio-sustaining hubs that made up the Fabricatus Locum was swarming with crystalline attackers, but Turentek wasn't sparing any of his functionality for defence.

All that mattered was his forge.

In seconds the vaulted space was awash in hard water residue, and Kayrn was soaked to the skin. The fires guttered and died in the suddenly thin air, suffocated by Turentek's esoteric deluge.

Their sheltering gurney rocked with the force of a nearby explosion, and Kayrn risked a glance through one of the ragged holes scorched through the ammo crates.

Emerging through the black rain were hundreds of glistening crystalline beasts. From humanoid warriors that looked oddly like Space Marines, to lumbering things that powered forwards on vast forelimbs and things that looked like weaponised servitor guns.

Kayrn wiped her face clear and steadied her pistol on the top of the crate. She had enough shots and spare cells to take out maybe twenty or thirty targets.

Las-fire blasted into the charging creatures. Beside her, Callins pumped shot after shot from his lasrifle. *This* was how Cadians fought, shoulder to shoulder in the face of insurmountable odds. Fighting to the last. No retreat, no surrender.

Fighting until the job was done.

The deck shook with a thunderous, booming vibration.

'What the–' said Kayrn, looking through the downpour to see what new threat was incoming.

A firestorm of detonations erupted among the crystalline monsters. Blinding storms of heavy las ripped through their ranks. Chugging detonations and enormous impacts ploughed great furrows in the deck. Fulminate-bright traceries of high-intensity turbo-fire tore the enemy apart in blitzing explosions that sawed back and forth in a torrent of unending fire.

Another teeth-loosening thud shook the deck, each crashing impact like the hammerblow of a god.

Realisation struck. Kayrn turned and looked up.

And up.

Lupa Capitalina and *Canis Ulfrica* stood side by side, rain-slick and haloed by dying fires. Burning exhaust gases plumed from louvred vents and dark water flashed to vapour on their weapon arms. *Amarok* and *Vilka* stalked before their titanic cousins and Kayrn joined the cheers of her fellow Cadians.

Legio Sirius were in the fight.

Far below the surface of Exnihlio, entropy was afoot. The hated machinery of ancient design that had kept the eternally migratory swarms of hrud fixed in time and space failed one after another.

Technology the likes of which had never been seen within the Imperium burned white-hot against the senescent power of so many imprisoned aliens. One hrud could drive a mortal to the grave in minutes, a warren of them was entropy distilled and honed like a breacher drill punching through soft clay.

Gold and brass gobbets of molten metal fell in a glittering rain, transmuting to base metal and then to dust as it fell from the cavern roof. Every scavenged sheet and spar of metal forming the slum-warrens corroded to ruin in moments, like a time-lapsed picter. The rock upon which their prison had stood crumbled and turned to powder as millennia of erosion took hold.

The collapse was total, thousands of tonnes of disintegrating metal and rock tumbling into the geothermal abyss over which it had been built. Had this been any mortal settlement, thousands would already be dead, thousands more killed in the cascade of collapse.

By the time the first dilapidated structure fell from the porous and crumbling cliff-face, the hrud had already gone. Freed from the iron grip of machines holding them fast to this moment in time and space, they shifted their wholly alien physiology through multi-angular dimensions unknown to the minds of humankind.

Unfettered by such limiting notions as matter, time and space, the hrud migration from Exnihlio began in earnest. They would cross galaxies and oceans of time to be rid of this world's constricting touch.

But first they would have vengeance for their stolen freedom.

Submitting to one last notion of fixed vectors, the hrud burrowed invisibly down through the rock to the planet's core.

Ultimate entropy took hold of Exnihlio's molten heart.

And crushed it.

Bolter shells chased the *Renard*'s shuttle into the sky, but the vessel was too fast to bring down with small-arms fire. Tanna shot anyway, but lowered his weapon when the shuttle climbed beyond range.

Surcouf shouted Ultramarian curses at the ascending vessel. Ilanna Pavelka knelt beside him with her head bowed. If she still had eyes, Tanna might have thought her weeping. Ven Anders and his soldiers formed a loose circle around Kotov, who watched Telok's departure with a mix of despair and frustration.

The eldar warriors surrounded their seer. Her alien features were too inscrutable to read with certainty, but it seemed to Tanna that the corners of her lips were upturned. As though their failure to stop Telok had been her plan all along.

'Did you know this would happen?' he asked, priming himself to rip her head from her shoulders if her answer displeased him.

'This? No,' she said, and, strangely, Tanna believed her. 'It was merely one of myriad possible outcomes, but it is a moment in time that opens up so many potential futures I had not dared hope might ever come to pass.'

She looked out over the slowly advancing army of implacable crystaliths, as though this particular future had been inevitable.

'I will never meet them,' she said.

'Who?' asked Tanna, working fresh shells into his bolter.

'My daughters. I will never birth them, never hold them and never see them grow,' said Bielanna, her face wet with tears. 'I hoped your deaths would restore the future where they are given the chance of life, but such ill-fated intent only brings further misery. Everything I set out to change has come to nothing.'

Tanna drove a round into the breech.

'Nothing is for nothing,' he said.

'Do you realise how ridiculous that sounds?'

'You set out to change something,' said Tanna, remembering the last words of Aelius before his death at Dantium Gate. 'That you failed does not diminish the attempt. Knowing you might effect change, but failing to try... *That* is contemptible.'

Even as he spoke, Tanna was struck by the utter incongruity of a warrior of the Adeptus Astartes offering words of comfort to the xenos witch who had killed his former Emperor's Champion.

Beyond the galaxy, far from the light of the Emperor, such a thing did not seem so far-fetched. Tanna took a breath, knowing that even if he lived to return to the Imperium, he would take that thought to his grave.

The army of crystalline monsters were a hundred metres out, drawing close at a measured, inexorable pace. Tanna moved away from the eldar. Their deaths were to be their own, and he would not have his body's final resting place among them.

He passed Kotov, who had his gold-chased pistol gripped tightly in one swaying mechadendrite. The two skitarii flanked the archmagos, ready to give their lives in service to the Mechanicus. Kotov gave Tanna a look that might have been apologetic, but probably wasn't.

'Brother-sergeant,' said Kotov with a grim nod of acknowledgement towards the enemy ranks. Diamond-sharp blades of glass shone under the clear blue of the sky. 'Any grand plans or stratagems? Any words of wisdom from Rogal Dorn or Sigismund to see us victorious?'

'No pity, no remorse, no fear,' said Tanna, holding out his combat blade to Magos Pavelka. 'The techno-sorcery you worked on our weapons, will it work on these crystaliths?'

Pavelka lifted her hooded head, and Tanna hid his revulsion at the sunken scorch marks around her dead optics.

'Maybe,' she said. 'If you drive your blade deep enough.'

'Be assured of that,' promised Tanna.

Microcontent 17

The veterans of the war on Khai-Zhan spoke of Vogen in hushed tones, and those same soldiers traded knowing looks when talk inevitably turned to the Palace of Peace. The tales of heroism surrounding the battles fought there were already legendary.

'I remember every soldier of Cadia wished he could have been there,' said Rae, firing his rifle empty in six controlled bursts of semi-auto. This was the sergeant's fourth rifle, the burned-out frames of his previous three abandoned along the fluidly shifting battle line.

'Funny thing,' said Hawkins, ducking back as a series of green bolts slammed into the wall above him. 'Always easier to wish you were there *after* the fighting's done. Not so much fun being there when the las is coming like rain off the Valkyrie Peninsulas.'

'Aye, there's truth in that, sir,' agreed Rae.

Rock dust and infill fell, reminding Hawkins that this wasn't Vogen and the structure behind him wasn't the impregnable fortress of the Palace of Peace. To either side of him, hundreds of Cadians in hastily prepared positions fought to keep the enemy from crossing Angel Square. Hawkins had his soldiers deployed as Colonel Hastur had during the Final Ten Days, when a combined host of Iron Warriors and the Brothers of the Sickle mounted their fifth assault.

Hastur's infantry platoons had been more than a match for the traitorous slave soldiers, but it had taken heavy armour to blunt the Iron Warriors' assault. Heavy armour Hawkins didn't have.

Rae tossed aside his lasrifle, its barrel heat-fused and useless. He tore a frag from his webbing and hurled it towards the statue of Sanguinius at the centre of the square.

'Fire in the hole!'

A knot of four crystal creatures fell to shattered ruin as the grenade exploded.

'And forgive me, Lord of the Angels,' added Rae as the force of the blast ripped one of the statue's wings loose.

'Better to ask for forgiveness than permission, right?' said Hawkins.

'Depends on who you're asking,' said Rae, hunting for a fresh rifle among the fallen.

'Rae!' shouted Hawkins, throwing over his own rifle.

'Much appreciated, sir,' said Rae, catching the weapon and resuming firing without missing a beat.

'What you seeing, sergeant?'

'We're getting hit hard on the right, sir,' answered Rae. 'I reckon there's a big push coming there. Some clever bugger in the enemy knows we don't have armour there to enfilade.'

Percussive blasts rocked the training deck as the recreation of the Vogen Law Courts finally collapsed. Even over the crash of falling masonry and flames, Hawkins heard the screams.

'Hellfire,' swore Hawkins. 'Hotshot company were in there.'

'Heavy weapons?'

'Heavy weapons,' agreed Hawkins, thinking back to the Last Ten Days. The Law Courts had offered a perfect vantage point for Hastur's support platoons to rain plunging fire onto the thinner topside armour of the Iron Warriors Land Raiders. In the final stages of the battle, it had come down to arming mortar shells by hand and soldiers dropping from the fire-blackened windows with demo-charges clutched to their chests.

The original building had been blast-hardened to withstand repeated artillery barrages, but this structure hadn't been nearly as tough. Without those weapons, the right flank was completely open. Bulky shapes of jagged-edged glass were already lumbering from the ruins. Powerfully built monsters the size of a Sentinel.

'Westin!' he shouted, 'Westin, where are you?'

The vox-man scrambled over pitted sheets of flakboard and ruptured kinetic ablatives. Westin had tried to keep up with Hawkins, but better vox-men than he had been left wallowing in the captain's wake. Westin's camo-cape flapped in the anabatic thermals of high-energy las as he scooted into cover beside Hawkins.

He half turned, presenting the vox-caster's workings.

Hawkins cranked the handle. No point in shouting at Jahn Callins. If the tanks weren't here, there was a good reason for that. He had to get guns to bear on that flank. The vanguard of the enemy's thrust emerged from the ruins, a towering brute with arms like kite-shields and a profusion of weapon spines running the length of its back. A hosing stream of heavy bolter fire ripped into it. The shells impacted on its wide arms without effect as three missiles slammed into it.

One arm blew off in a shower of razored shards and the beast collapsed, its weapons spines blazing harmlessly at the ceiling. Another two of the heavily armed creatures lumbered from the collapsed structure, flames reflecting from their multi-faceted limbs. More followed them, enough to overrun this flank for sure.

Hawkins shouted into the vox.

'Creed! Two support teams to the right flank, sector tertius omega!' he yelled. 'Step quickly now.'

Creed's answer was lost in a blaze of static and a roaring stream of fire that came from the newly arrived creatures. Hawkins flinched as the blast struck the Palace of Peace. A balcony of missile-armed Guardsmen came tumbling down fifty metres to Hawkins's left.

Before he could detach soldiers from any other platoon, a flurry of streaking rockets arced up on an exacting parabola and slammed down in the ruins of the Law Courts. Violet-hued explosions threw deformed sheets of prefabricated steel and plascrete thirty metres into the air. Collimated bursts of turbolasers swept the ruins.

Hawkins hoped there weren't any Cadians left alive in there.

'By the Eye, would you look at that!' shouted Rae as a host of lightly armoured tanks on articulated spider-limbs advanced down what had been known as Snipers' Alley.

Of course, it had been the Lord Generals who'd called it that, because that was the only route they traversed. Any soldier who'd fought in Vogen knew that *every* street was a snipers' alley.

Hawkins recognised the vehicles. Mechanicus scout tanks in the main, faster than most fighting vehicles, but nowhere near as heavily armoured or armed as Hawkins would have liked.

The Mechanicus designation for them was something meaninglessly binaric, but the Cadians had dubbed them Black Widows. Fast, agile and lethal to lightly armoured targets. Less useful against heavy armour, but better than nothing. Skitarii packs flanked the Widows, adding their own weight of fire to the counter-attack.

At the heart of the Mechanicus tanks was an open-topped Rhino with a thundering battery of quad-mounted heavy bolters on its glacis.

Riding atop the Iron Fist like a god-king of some ancient host of warrior-priests was a multi-armed figure in gold, silver and brass. His lower arms were electrified scarifier tines and his upper limbs held a bladed halberd with a crackling energy pod at its base.

'Emperor save me, if he isn't a sight for sore eyes!' said Rae.

Hawkins had to agree, Magos Dahan was indeed a welcome sight.

The skitarii chanted something as Dahan's Widows fired again. It sounded like a name, but it wasn't one Hawkins recognised.

'Ma-ta-leo! Ma-ta-leo!'

At its every shout, Dahan held his halberd aloft.

Bellicose roars of binary brayed from Dahan's chest augmitters, a war cry that sent a shiver down even Hawkins's spine. The quad bolters took down the two crystalline weapon beasts in precisely targeted bursts. Without them to punch through the Cadians, infantry power was stopping the rest of the advance.

For now.

As the skitarii pushed out to secure the edge of the ruined Law Courts, Dahan guided the Iron Fist towards the centre of the Cadian line. Mechanicus Protectors bearing shimmering energy shields and bladed staves ran alongside the modified vehicle.

'Welcome to the Palace of Peace,' said Hawkins as Dahan jumped down into the cover of the rubble-strewn berm of plascrete.

Dahan nodded and said, 'I expected you to recognise it.'

'Was a nice touch,' said Hawkins.

'Not one of mine,' said Dahan. 'I assumed you ordered it.'

Hawkins shook his head. 'No.'

Rae got down on his knees and kissed the deck.

'What in the name of the Eye are you doing, Rae?'

'Thanking the *Speranza*, sir,' said Rae. 'Who else do you think did this for us? Told you the old girl would look out for us.'

Hawkins gave Dahan a quizzical look, but the Secutor seemed to accept Rae's idea that the ship had wrought this arena to give them an advantage.

He shrugged. 'As good an explanation as any, I suppose.' he said. Figuring that was a mystery for another day, he gestured to the chanting skitarii fighting in the ruins.

'Who's Mataleo?'

'I am,' said Dahan.

'I thought your first name was Hirimau.'

'It is. Mataleo is what I believe you call a nickname.'

'What does it mean?' asked Rae.

'Lion-killer,' said Dahan. 'A soubriquet I earned in my more organic

days on Catachan. A soldier named Harker bestowed it upon me and its bellicosity appealed to the skitarii despite my best attempts to discourage its use.'

'Outstanding,' said Hawkins. Dahan had already won his respect, but earning a war-name from a Catachan? *That* was impressive.

'I don't suppose you saw any Cadian tanks on your way here?'

'No, our paths did not intersect, but they are en route,' said Dahan. 'Assuming they encounter no resistance, they will arrive in twenty-seven minutes.'

'Twenty-seven minutes, damn it all to the Eye,' said Hawkins as more blasts of green fire streaked across the square and mushrooming explosions erupted along the Cadian line. Cries of pain and shouts for ammo echoed across the deck.

'What in the Emperor's name are you doing?' said Hawkins, as Dahan stood and extended the crackling tines of his lower arms. 'Get down!'

Dahan's Cebrenian halberd pulsed with lethal energies as he climbed onto the crumbling ridge of debris. Flames licked around his clawed feet and his cloak snapped in the hot winds.

'It is here,' said Dahan.

'What is?' said Hawkins, peering through a gouge of vitrified plascrete. A host of crystalline warriors were advancing across the width of Angel Square. Broad and tall, each was armed with shimmering energy spines and long-bladed polearms that matched those of the Protectors.

At the centre of these elite killers was a towering thing of glass and crystal, a hideous amalgam of scorpion and centaur. Shield-bearers attended it. Las-fire and explosions bounced from their reflective shields.

'The alpha-creature,' said Dahan, springing onto the back of the Iron Fist. 'Kill it and we regain the initiative.'

The vehicle's engine revved madly, its machine-spirit eager to be loosed. Its tracks sprayed rubble as the vehicle crested the rise. Chem-rich exhaust fumes jetted from its rear vents.

'You can't fight that thing,' shouted Hawkins.

The chanting skitarii bellowed the Secutor's war-name as they marched out to fight alongside him.

'Then you don't know Mataleo,' said Dahan.

The walls of the confero were no longer steel and glass, but an undulant vault of perfectly geometric cubes that formed an all-enclosing dome of impenetrable darkness. With Linya's expulsion of Galatea from the shared neuromatrix, all pretence of reality had fallen away.

Hexamathic firewalls had thus far prevented the machine-hybrid from reaching them, keeping Linya and her fellow captives safe from its wrath.

Linya sat cross-legged in the centre of a circle of her fellow magi, the illusory retention of their physical forms the one concession to notions of three-dimensional space.

<How much longer will this barrier last?> asked Syriestte, staring up at the rippling dome of interlocking cubes.

<Long enough,> said Linya, keeping her binary simple. She'd exloaded enough hexamathic understanding into their speech centres to allow communication at a level beyond Galatea's understanding, but it was still tryingly basic.

<Not a particularly specific answer,> said Magos Natala from across the circle.

<It's the best I have,> replied Linya. <Galatea's already attempting to upgrade its neural interfaces to learn hexamathics from the *Speranza*. Every second we spend second-guessing ourselves increases the chances of it breaching our refuge. So we need to do this now, yes?>

She cast her gaze around the circle and, one by one, each magos gave a curt nod until only Syriestte remained.

<Magos Syriestte?>

<Are you sure this will work?>

<No,> said Linya, <but it's the best I've got. Our *minds* are safe in here, but Galatea has a far more direct means of attack. All it has to do is excise a brain from its cylinder and that magos is dead.>

Syriestte nodded and said, <Then do it.>

Linya began with a recitation of the first, most basic prayer to the Omnissiah, each of the captive magi joining in as she spoke.

<With learning I cleanse my flesh of ignorance.

<With knowledge I grow in power.

<With technology I revere the God of all Machines.

<With its power I praise the glory of Mars.

<All hail the Omnissiah, who guides us to learning.>

Volatile deletion algorithms emerged from Linya's mouth, like the ectoplasmic emissions of a psyker. But this was no immaterial by-product; these were lethal combinations of spliced kill-codes.

Dormant for now, they twisted around her like glittering chains of droplets on spider-silk, moving outwards towards the magi.

Haephaestus was first to be touched. His back arched and he gave a cry of agonised binary as the kill-codes enmeshed with his mind. Next was Natala, who took the pain stoically, then Syriestte.

The largely organic features of the Mechanicus Envoy twisted in

horrendous pain, her eyes going wide at the shock of it. The kill-code moved around the circle of magi, touching each one until it had bonded with all but Magos Kleinhenz.

A portion of the oil-dark barrier bulged inwards.

The black cubes expanded at a ferocious rate, rearranging their mass and density into the form of a hideous data-daemon pushing into the vault. Its arms ended in hooked talons and draconic wings spread at its back.

This was an image birthed in primal nightmares, something bestial from an age when humankind huddled in caves around dying fires. Its roar was inchoate and murderous. The talons wrapped around Magos Kleinhenz and dragged him from the circle. He thrashed in the data-daemon's grip, his outline distorting with strobing after-images of his screaming face.

His cries descended into meaningless scraps of binaric fragments as he broke apart into drifting scads of data-light. Linya thrust her hands towards the data-daemon and shouted a canticle of hexamathic calculus.

It howled in pain as its nightmarish form was drawn back into the darkness, leaving the vault's fluidly cubic perimeter rippling like the surface of a tar pit.

The last fragments of Kleinhenz drifted like fractal snowflakes. Haephaestus and Natala tried in vain to save some last aspect of their comrade, but it was already too late.

Syriestte turned to Linya, her organic face twisted in grief.

<What just happened?> she said. <What was that thing?>

<Galatea's given up its pretence of humanity,> said Linya. <That was its rage distilled into its purest form. It must have sensed what we were doing and ripped Kleinhenz's physical brain from its amniotic cylinder to try and stop us.>

<But what we just did, it will stop Galatea from doing that again to the rest of us?> said Natala.

<Yes, it should,> answered Linya. <We're all linked by the kill-code now. If one of us dies like that, it activates and we all die. And if we die, Galatea dies.>

<So let it kill us,> said Magos Haephaestus bitterly. <We want it dead. Why not let it kill another of us and have done with it?>

<Because Galatea doesn't get off that easily,> said Linya with the coldest steel in her voice. <Not after what it did to us.>

<Besides,> said Syriestte. <By now it'll know what we have done. It won't risk so open an attack again.>

<Then how do we fight it?> asked Haephaestus.

<You don't,> said Linya, allowing the last vestige of her surroundings to fall away from her perceptions. <I do.>

Just as she had sent a sliver of her consciousness into the datasphere to make contact with her father, Linya now sent her mind into the fulminate-bright realm of the *Speranza*'s informational landscape.

She closed her eyes and...

...found herself amid brilliant grid lines of data as they passed through the Ark Mechanicus in the *Speranza*'s hidden space of knowledge. Constellations of starfire surrounded her, brighter than she had ever seen them. Dazzling in the purity of the wealth of understanding stored within each and every pinprick of illumination.

The last time Linya had flown the datascape it had been a hallucinatory place of shared functionality. Phosphor-bright with continental-scale cores of learning and informational exchange.

Now it was a battleground.

Datacores burned with searing intensity, like supernovae on the verge of explosion. The last time Linya had seen them they had been dull with parasitic infestation, thick with Galatea's self-replicating strangleholds. The machine-hybrid had held the Mechanicus hostage with its control of every vital system.

Now that control was all but gone. Only the last, most vital systems remained in its grasp. Still enough to kill every living being upon the *Speranza* should it so choose, but its hold was slipping even as Linya watched.

She saw a figure drifting high above the datascape. Arched spine, arms thrown wide and head tilted back. Golden light streamed from his hands, and where it touched Galatea's parasitic growths and viral threads they melted like frost before the dawn.

He looked down as she flew towards him.

<Abrehem?> she said.

<Linya,> said Abrehem. <I did what you asked.>

She heard the strain in his voice, saw the light bleeding from his ethereal body.

<You're dying,> she said.

He looked at her strangely, as though seeing straight through her. He gave a crooked smile that was as melancholy as it was empathic.

<Then we have something in common,> he said. <The other magi with you... They understand what they have to do?>

<When the time comes, they will. Trust me, it won't be a problem.>

<And your father?> asked Abrehem. <He's with me in Elektrus. Does he know what you plan?>

<No,> said Linya, and the thought of her father's grief almost broke her resolve. <But there's no other way. You know that. Even after all you've achieved here, we still have to do this.>

Abrehem nodded and turned towards the molten brightness of the *Speranza*'s bridge. Searingly hot with convergent knowledge, the nexus of the ship through which every fragment of data passed and was rendered known.

<Then it's time,> he said.

<Yes,> agreed Linya. <It's time to kill Galatea.>

For all that Abrehem Locke had managed to disrupt Galatea's control of the *Speranza*, the machine-hybrid still controlled the vital systems of the Ark Mechanicus. Telok felt Tarkis Blaylock trying to deny the *Renard*'s shuttle access to the foremost embarkation deck, but Galatea overruled his every attempt.

'If you only knew,' said Telok, watching the immensity of the *Speranza* fill the shuttle's viewscreen. 'You would welcome me aboard personally.'

The shuttle shuddered as it passed through the gravimetric fields surrounding the gargantuan ship. The violence of the transition surprised Telok, but he had never known a ship of such inhuman dimensions.

'That thing coming up behind us,' said Emil Nader at the helm. 'It'll be torn apart before it gets anywhere near the *Speranza*.'

Telok laughed, the booming sound filling the command deck of the shuttle.

'The Breath of the Gods reshapes the cosmos, and you think mere gravity waves will trouble it?'

Nader shrugged. 'I'm just saying it looks pretty fragile.'

Telok leaned over and placed a clawed hand on the pilot's shoulder. 'Indeed it is delicate, incredibly delicate. Even the slightest imbalance in its gyre would tear it apart. But if you were thinking of attempting something reckless, perhaps using this ship as a missile or simply ramming us into the side of the *Speranza*, know that I would snap your neck the instant I detected even a micron of differential in our course. And then I would allow Galatea a free hand with that atrophied thing you call a brain. I am led to believe you have some familiarity with what it can do in that regard.'

Nader shot a venomous glance at Galatea. The machine-hybrid's palanquin sat low to the deck, its proxy body twitching with random synaptic impulses. Its brain jars flickered with activity, though one was shattered and trailed a host of dripping wires. The presence of

Telok's excised consciousness within Galatea granted him complete understanding of what was happening within his avatar's neuromatrix.

'The Stargazer's daughter yet frustrates us,' said Galatea, fully aware of Telok's scrutiny.

'It was a mistake to incorporate her,' agreed Telok. 'We greatly underestimated her will to resist.'

Galatea's silver eyes flickered and its right arm spasmed in response. 'Our body is under attack from within and without. It is most discomfiting.'

'Once I have full access to the *Speranza*'s noospheric network and have inloaded the secrets of hexamathics, I will purge the neuromatrix of these rebellious presences.'

'Purge the others, but leave Linya Tychon to us,' said Galatea.

'As you wish,' said Telok, linking his senses with the exterior surveyors of the *Renard*'s shuttle.

Ninety kilometres below was the Breath of the Gods, slowly ascending towards a ventral cache vault. Originally designed for Centurio Ordinatus, these were the only spaces large enough to contain the spinning matrix of the machine.

And below the Breath of the Gods came twin geoformer vessels. Their tech-priest crews had pushed their reactors to breaking point attempting to resist the lure of its arcane mechanics before finally accepting that nothing could prevent them from trailing in its wake.

The entrance to the embarkation deck grew ever larger in the viewscreen and Telok increased the pressure on Emil Nader's neck as they approached the terminal point of the docking manoeuvre.

'Hold us steady, Mister Nader,' warned Telok.

'This *is* steady. You think it's easy flying so close to something this big?' said Nader, checking the avionics panel. 'Feels like our ascent's running a tad imbalanced or like we picked up some extra weight.'

Despite Nader's concern, the shuttle slipped through the shimmering veil of the integrity field without incident. Telok felt the presence of a billion machine-spirits wash over him.

'Control is not as complete as it ought to be,' he said, instantly assimilating the flow of data through the unseen body of information within the Ark Mechanicus.

'Mistress Tychon was resourceful in recruiting an ally within the body of the ship,' said Galatea. 'All indications are that he will soon be dead, allowing us to fully establish control of the *Speranza* once more.'

The shuttle touched down with a booming thud of landing claws, and Telok sighed as the presence of something infinitely greater pressed against the walls of his enhanced consciousness.

'I feel its great heart beating deep within this body of iron and stone,' he said. 'Hidden deep within its matrices of logic and binary, but there for those with the vision to see.'

'The *Speranza*,' said Galatea.

'Is but one of its names,' said Telok as the shuttle's forward ramp lowered. 'But I will learn them all.'

The fates unspooled around Bielanna. She saw them all, *lived* them all. The world was cracking, torn asunder by the entropic vengeance of the hrud. She felt the alien host *shift*, migrating from this fleeting aspect of reality.

The power of the skein surged in her mind.

Time chained by the push and pull of the hrud and the *Yngir* engine now roared through Bielanna in a tsunami of temporal energies. She was the heart of the tempest, kneeling at the centre of her warriors as power flowed through her. She was a conduit for all the things that might yet be and all that never would.

Bielanna wept as she the felt the presence of the Dark Reaper touch her soul, Kaela Mensha Khaine revelling in his aspect of the Destroyer.

She was that Destroyer. She saw that now, the threads of those around her inextricably bound to her doom. None could escape their fate.

She had killed them all.

She had shrouded them in death.

Striking Scorpions danced angular steps around Bielanna, while the Howling Banshees spun like acrobats. Blades sang and the chorus of mon-keigh gunfire was a harsh staccato backdrop to their elegant symphony of death-dealing.

The crystaliths fought with extruded blades, fast and agile, but their strikes without artistry and pride. They died by the score. Each of her warriors was entwined in an invisible web of fates that fractured and divided in the same instant. Past diminishing, present blooming and future unseen to all but her.

Her hands moved in complex patterns, blindingly swift, guiding her warriors like the conductor of a billion musicians playing the most complex song imaginable. She made Vaynesh step a finger's breadth to the right, saving him from a thrusting blade of glass. Uriquel adjusted the grip on her sword, giving her the strength to hack the limb from a crystalith. In a hundred ways she moulded the fates of her warriors: a step back here, a quarter-turn there, a leap just a moment earlier.

Each element was insignificant in itself, but combined to form a web of cause that put Bielanna's perceptions two steps ahead of effect.

She had tried to mould the fates of the Space Marines, granting them a measure of her newfound power, but the fates of such warriors were not hers to shape. They would rather die than suffer the touch of one they would normally consider a foe.

Only Roboute Surcouf's mind was open enough to be guided. The touch of another eldar, a bonesinger named Yrlandriar, made it easier to reach him. With Bielanna's help, Surcouf's every shot was fired with pinpoint accuracy.

Her mastery of the fates could not last, she knew that.

For all that she might guide the steps and sword arms of her warriors, limbs of flesh and blood grew tired, skills once razor-sharp would dull.

And then death would come.

A shadow rose up to envelop Bielanna, shockingly sudden and suffocatingly intense in its darkness. Like a veil of black velvet had been drawn across her sight, she saw the skein blacken as the terminus of every thread came into view, unravelling towards extinction with horrifying speed.

The end of all things.

An impossible boundary in what should be infinite space.

Bielanna gasped, her chest constricting at the sight.

This was the doom she had seen ensconced within the *Speranza*. Space and time were coming undone, ripping apart like the solar sails of a wounded wraithship.

Doom had come to this world, but that was the least of the danger. The rift beginning here was pulling wider with every passing second, drawing every thread within the skein to it. Like a weaver's shuttle reversing through the warp and weft of a loom, the future was unravelling to its omega point.

Exnihlio was becoming the temporal equivalent of a black hole, a howling abyss in which no time would ever exist again. Its effects were yet confined to the deeps of the planet, but Bielanna felt the catastrophic geomantic damage the hrud had wreaked racing to the surface.

The physical death of Exnihlio was nothing, but the temporal shock waves would spread into the glacial void of space, reaching into the galaxy of Bielanna's kin.

It would be a slow death for the galaxy, as all time was devoured by the rift torn by the *Yngir's* device. But that it would end all things for evermore was certain.

Unless Bielanna could stop it.

She rose smoothly to her feet, ignoring the sinuous war-dance of her people and the brutal, heaving clashes of the Space Marines. Her hands balled into fists and she thrust them out to the side, letting the power of the skein pour from her in an almighty torrent.

A hurricane of roaring, seething psychic fury streamed from Bielanna. The crystaliths closest to her simply vanished, vaporised in the raw fury of the storm. The rest were hurled back as if from a bomb blast. Pellucid blue fire swirled around Bielanna in a cyclonic vortex.

Glass and crystal shattered, killing the crystaliths, but leaving beings of flesh and blood unharmed. Green fire bled from broken bodies that spilled black dust onto the plaza. The swirling tempest of psychic energy swelled around Bielanna to form a howling wall of impenetrable storm fronts.

Stunned silence filled the void that had previously been rich with grunting mon-keigh and laughing, singing eldar.

Tanna of the Black Templars turned to her, his armour buckled and clawed back to bare metal. She sensed his hostility, primitive drugs boosting his aggression levels to psychotic heights.

She pre-empted his inevitable questions with a single imperative.

'You have to go,' she said. 'You have to stop Telok.'

She sensed his confusion, but had no time to explain what she now knew in anything but the most basic concepts.

'Everything is ending,' she said. 'What Telok has set in motion will end everything. Your Emperor, His domain, my kin and all we have fought to preserve. Everything will die. Worse, they will never have existed. All that was and all that might ever come to pass will be wiped away.'

Tanna nodded, as his battle-brothers stood with him.

'How long will that barrier hold?' said Anders through gritted teeth. His thread was shorter than all the others.

'Not long,' said Bielanna. 'The skein's power waxes strong within me, but soon it will wane like a winter's moon, so I do not have long to do what must be done.'

Archmagos Kotov said, 'You said Tanna had to go. How can any of us go anywhere?'

Bielanna let her mind drift over the surfaces of every one of the mon-keigh, searching for an emotion strong enough to provide an anchor. The Templars and Cadians were useless, adrift and far from all they knew. Kotov's mind was too stunted in its logical functionality, its emotional centres long since closed off.

But Surcouf…

She felt his love for his crew and his ship, and wasn't love the strongest emotion of all? It had healed wounds, ended wars and seen bitter enemies brought together as brothers. It had also brought empires to ruin and seen the greatest minds humbled.

Nothing was more powerful than love, and Surcouf was blessed with an abundance.

Bielanna said, 'Your talisman. Do you still have it?'

Surcouf looked confused, then reached inside the breast pocket of his coat and withdrew his astrogation compass.

'This? Is this what you mean?'

Bielanna saw the confluence of fates bound to the device, the slender thread that set the path the mon-keigh's life had taken. He sensed its importance, but not on any conscious level.

'Yes, hold it out to me,' said Bielanna.

'Why?'

'Because I need a focus,' she said, and her eyes misted with sadness. 'And because I need someone to remember me.'

Though he was puzzled at her words, he nevertheless did as she asked. Bielanna cupped her porcelain-white hands around his, feeling his deep connection to those he had left behind. He would die for them, and they for him. The needle on the compass danced and spun, unfixed and wandering. Their minds met and she lived the entirety of his life in a heartbeat.

'Look into my eyes and picture those dearest to you,' she said.

No sooner had he done so than the needle stopped moving.

Bielanna released Surcouf's hands, holding on to the connection between them, picturing what he saw. A functional room with a wooden desk. Pictures on the wall, scriptural commendations and a holographic cameo of a woman.

Such was the strength of Surcouf's emotions and the surging power within her, that it was the simplest matter to open a path through the webway. A flaring oval of orange, arched and spilling gold light onto the plaza, opened behind her.

'That will take you back to your ship,' said Bielanna. 'Go now and stop Telok. Do whatever needs to be done, but he must not return to your Imperium.'

Kotov nodded and gestured to his skitarii.

They stepped through the gate and vanished.

'You make it sound like you're not leaving,' said Surcouf.

'I am not,' said Bielanna. 'It may be possible to heal what Telok has done, but to do that I must be here at the heart of it all, the site of the wound.'

Surcouf looked out towards the barrier. The tempests were already dying, and the army of crystaliths pressed against it in overwhelming numbers.

'You'll die.'

'The future I was to share with my daughters is lost,' said Bielanna. 'There is nothing left for me. Death will be welcome.'

'I wish–'

'Say nothing,' said Bielanna, harsher than she intended. 'No human words can offer me comfort.'

Surcouf nodded and turned away, helping Magos Pavelka to her feet. Giving Bielanna a last look of profound gratitude, the two of them went through the gate together.

Tanna watched Surcouf and Pavelka vanish and felt the weight he had carried since Dantium Gate lift from his shoulders. Cut off from their Chapter and without the guidance of Kul Gilad, he and his warriors had been lost. Strange that it had taken the words of an eldar witch to show him just how lost.

On any other day he would have gone to the Reclusiam and submitted himself to pain-shriving for such thoughts.

'Can you really undo what Telok has done here?' he asked.

'Perhaps, but I will need time,' she answered, removing her helm and holding it in the crook of her arm. 'And I will need the strength of my people to do it.'

'The crystaliths will kill you long before then.'

'They will,' agreed Bielanna.

Tanna glanced towards the diminishing barrier.

'Then the Black Templars will give you that time.'

'Tanna?' said Anders. 'You're staying?'

'If she can do what she claims, then I have no choice,' said Tanna. 'Here is where I can serve the Emperor best.'

Anders sighed. 'And here was me thinking that all of us might actually get back to the Imperium.'

'It was an honour to fight alongside you, Ven Anders.'

The colonel held up a hand.

'Cadians don't do last words, valedictions or brotherly farewells in the face of certain death,' he said. 'We just fight, and I have a regiment on the *Speranza* that needs me.'

Tanna nodded and returned Anders's salute with a fist across his breastplate. The Cadian colonel led his men through the portal as the eldar gathered around their farseer and began unbuckling their armour. Smooth plates dropped to the ground and as they removed their battle helms, it seemed their angular, alien faces softened, like dreamers awakening from a daylight reverie. They each handed Bielanna what looked like a polished gemstone and sat cross-legged

around her before closing their eyes, as though entering a meditative trance.

The storm front keeping the crystaliths at bay began to diminish almost immediately. Glassy blades cut through it and their inexorable strength began slowly pushing their angular bodies through.

Tanna turned from the eldar.

His own warriors stood before him.

Proud and undefeated, they were heroes all.

'My brothers, we come to it at last,' he said. 'The last battle of the Kotov Crusade.'

'Will you lead us in our vows, brother-sergeant?' asked Yael.

'I will,' said Tanna, knowing that what he had to say next would crush the young warrior. 'But you will not take a vow with us.'

'Brother-sergeant?'

'Go through the gate,' said Tanna. 'If Telok is to be killed, it should be a Black Templar blade that cleaves his head from his shoulders.'

'No! Please, Tanna,' said Yael, forgetting himself in the heat of his despair. 'Do not deny me this last fight.'

Tanna shook his head.

'Go back to the *Speranza*, fight with all your heart in *that* battle. Win glory and carry word of us back to the Chapter. Tell them what we did here, of our courage and sacrifice. Tell them that we died as heroes in the name of the Emperor.'

'I want to stand and fight with you,' pleaded Yael.

'This is my last command. You will not disobey it.'

Tanna ached for the young warrior, knowing full well the anguish he would be feeling at being denied a glorious death alongside his brothers.

'No more words,' said Tanna. 'Go.'

Yael rammed his sword back into its scabbard and without a backward glance turned and ran through the eldar gate.

'Harsh,' said Varda. 'But it needed to be done, and it's time for that vow.'

Issur joined the Emperor's Champion, his fingers twitching and his features dancing with involuntary muscle movements.

Tanna nodded, and both warriors took a knee, leaving him standing over them as Kul Gilad had stood over them all on the *Adytum*. With the crystaliths pressing through the psychic barrier, Tanna knew there could be only one vow worthy of being made.

Kul Gilad's valediction.

The words heard over the vox as the Reclusiarch died. Tanna raised his sword to his shoulder in salute of his warriors.

'Lead us from death to victory, from falsehood to truth,' he said, bringing the sword around.

He touched the blade to Varda's shoulder.

'Lead us from despair to hope, from faith to slaughter.'

Issur was next to receive the benediction.

'Lead us to His strength and an eternity of war.'

The two Black Templars rose, and each placed a fist upon their breastplate. Their voices joined with Tanna's to complete the vow.

'Let His wrath fill our hearts!' they cried. 'Death, war and blood – in vengeance serve the Emperor in the name of Dorn!'

Issur and Varda stood side by side, blades bared and held out to the enemy.

'This is what you saw, Varda,' said Tanna as he took his place at the Emperor's Champion's side. 'When we reforged the links binding you to your sword.'

Varda nodded, but didn't look up from his blade. Despite everything, it gleamed unblemished, without as much as a scratch on its obsidian surface. Varda scanned the ranks of crystaliths as the psychic barrier finally collapsed into scraps of fading light.

The sound of crystal bodies grinding together as the monsters charged set Tanna's teeth on edge.

Fifty metres out, their heavy footfalls faster now.

'You spoke of seeing yourself fighting alongside the eldar,' said Tanna, rolling his shoulders to loosen the muscles. 'You could not conceive of how such a thing might come to pass. Now we know.'

'It pleases me to know I remained true to my oaths of loyalty,' said Varda. 'That I will die a true son of Sigismund.'

'That was never in doubt,' said Tanna.

Thirty metres away. Contact imminent.

'At l… least the el… eldar will die with us,' said Issur, glancing over at the silent, unmoving aliens behind them. The muscles at his neck were taut, but his sword was unwavering.

'This is our time to die,' said Tanna. 'Far from the Emperor's light on a forsaken world. Savour this moment, for you will die only once. How you meet that end is as important as every moment before then.'

Ten metres, translucent blades raised.

Tanna tipped his head back and lifted his sword to salute his coming death, knowing it would be magnificent.

Five metres.

The last battle of the Kotov Crusade began to the sound of breaking glass and the name of Dorn shouted to the sky.

Microcontent 18

'Ma-ta-leo! Ma-ta-leo!'

The skitarii chanted the name as they charged alongside his new Iron Fist. Dahan's awareness of every squad and pack's position was total and even in the heat of the charge he corrected vectors of attack through the noospheric link.

'Ma-ta-leo! Ma-ta-leo!'

Weapons fire blazed between the skitarii and the crystalline attackers. Intersecting collimations of las and solid rounds, plasma and gatling fire. Explosions ripped through the ranks of his warriors. Scores of bodies were trampled underfoot. Dahan plugged the gaps, moving squads into each ragged hole.

'Ma-ta-leo! Ma-ta-leo!'

Connected to the replacement Iron Fist's logic engine, his mind was ablaze with accumulated combat-memes. Threat optics measured the alpha-beast before him in every conceivable dimension. The heavy bolter quads chugged a constant stream of mass-reactives into the enemy host. Blasts of energy from the blade of his Cebrenian halberd killed those closest to the Iron Fist. Enemy bodies came apart in explosive bursts of broken glass.

'Ma-ta-leo! Ma-ta-leo!'

Hearing his Catachan war-name again made Dahan nostalgic for his days on the death world. The wealth of combat data available there was greater than on any other planet he had known. Every species of flora and fauna was deadly, and his database of warfare and close-combat predictors had expanded geometrically.

The closest analogue to the alpha-beast was the Catachan leonax den-mother he and Harker's platoon had encountered on a slash-and-burn mission against a surge of hyper-aggressive jungle growth.

They had encountered the lair by accident when a point Chimera crashed through the jungle floor into its moist, wriggling depths. The den-mother's hundreds of young erupted from pupal trap-lairs and attacked the Guardsmen and skitarii with a ferocity Dahan had previously only encountered in certain tyrannic blitzkrieg genera.

Dahan had killed the den-mother, a monstrous, clawed beast with a mutant mane of poisonous spines at its neck, the presence of which prompted Harker to bestow the war-name upon him.

He replayed that fight, dispensing the precise combination of combat-stimms, muscle enhancers and synaptic boosters into his system to replicate that state of being. The alpha-creature loomed ahead of him, bigger than the beast he had killed on Catachan. And attended by hulking shield-bearers.

Orders passed between him and his skitarii escort and a precise sequence of fire blazed from the Destroyer cadres. So precise was it that not a shot or iota of power was wasted. Four of the shield-bearers were instantly obliterated, their mantlets cracked with high-powered gatling cannons and blown apart by precisely timed grenade barrages. Volleys of plasma followed by pinpoint melta missiles finished the job, leaving a path open for Dahan's Iron Fist.

The alpha-beast squatted in the shadow of the sagging iron carving of Sanguinius. Dahan's vehicle crushed the splintered remains of the guard beasts under its tracks as the skitarii and crystal host came together with battering force in a storm of gunfire and blades. War cries both organic and binary echoed through the deck.

The alpha-beast reared up before him and a searing blast of green fire spat from a spinning nexus of reforming glass in its toothed underside. It struck the Iron Fist at a downward angle, cutting through its glacis like a plasma-torch. The impact was stunning. It smashed the tank's prow down into the deck. The quad guns blew out as the frontal section crumpled like foil paper. Its ammo hoppers detonated as the fire blew back inside.

Dahan thrust himself from the tank's open top. Emergency disconnect, trailing whipping cables from his spinal plugs. The Iron Fist lifted off the deck, its forward momentum flipping it up and over the alpha-beast.

Dahan landed with a screech of metal, the claws of all three legs digging into the deck.

The Iron Fist came down moments later, flat on its back, tracks churning air and spewing flames. Black smoke billowed from its ruptured hull.

Dahan's halberd came up in time to deflect a pair of clawed blade-arms extruding with obscene speed from the beast's underbelly. Scorpion claws snapped for him. He planted the oval base of his halberd and flipped around the glassy blades.

He rammed his crackling tine-bladed scarifiers into its flank. His internal capacitors discharged, sending forking bolts of purple energy through its body that left vitrified trails of opaque crystal in their wake.

Green fire pulsed from the monster's body, faster than Dahan could dodge. It struck him dead centre. His armour cracked and the impact jarred his floodstream pump offline for a few seconds.

Dahan staggered, momentarily off-balance. The alpha-beast's shape transformed, becoming taller, broader, growing more limbs. It slammed a vast, elephantine foot into his chest, hurling him back against the blazing wreck of the Iron Fist. It closed the gap between them, fast, and crab-like claws snapped shut on Dahan's scarifiers. It tore them clean from his body. He loosed a binaric shout of pain, rolling aside from another stream of green bio-electricity. His cloak was ablaze, the steel-woven fabric burning magnesium bright.

Dahan spun and rolled, rotating all three legs to avoid its attacks. It struck again and again, limbs like stingers slamming down with force enough to punch through the deck plates. Trailing scads of molten metal from his cloak, Dahan spun his halberd in a dizzyingly complex web of blocks, counters and thrusts. The speed of the beast was phenomenal. His every defence was made with only nano-seconds to spare. The entropic capacitor buzzed angrily as it built up charge for a strike.

Sheared crystal and metal spun around them as they duelled in the shadow of the Blood Angels' tragic primarch. Dahan was fully aware of the desperate fighting behind him as the crystal monsters swept past his own battle to engage the Cadians. In any normal engagement, Dahan would keep discrete partitions in his mind to keep track of every aspect of a battle, but this fight was requiring virtually all his processing power just to stay alive.

The thing's shape kept changing, almost as though it knew that to remain in one form would allow him an advantage. His wetware kept evolving, switching and resetting. He couldn't get a fix on any one set of combat routines that would allow him to defeat the alpha-beast.

Another thunderous blow sent Dahan flying backwards. He slammed into the ironwork pillar supporting Sanguinius, who finally toppled from his perch to land between the two combatants with a booming clang of iron. The alpha-beast took a crashing step towards him, the lower portions of its legs thickening as its upper body enlarged. Its mass was finite, and its limbs thinned in response, becoming whipping, lashing tendrils of razored glass.

Combat-memes jostled for Dahan's approval.

Tyranicus chameleo.

Teuthidian Myrmidrax.

Cyberneticus Noctus (Kaban).

Cephalaxia.

Arachnismegana.

The list went on, but in the split second it took him to scan through, Dahan understood nothing in his archives could match the alpha-beast's ability to continuously evolve. He had nothing embedded that could counter the sheer variety of forms and combat strategies the alpha-beast could assume.

Instead, he did the one thing that went against his every hard-wired logical instinct.

He shut down his entire database of systemic combat routines.

A void filled Dahan, a yawning abyss of uncertainty that felt hideously empty, yet strangely liberating. In this sublime instant, he had no idea what his opponent might do or what he should do to counter it. No idea how best to fight this foe, save the data presented in the very instant before attacking.

The alpha-beast lumbered towards him, its razor whips cutting the air. Dahan took off towards it. He leapt onto the fallen statue of Sanguinius and pistoned all three of his legs out, launching himself through the air. Whip-thin razor arms slashed towards him. The Cebrenian halberd cut through the bulk of them, his rotating gimbal of a waist eluded others, but many more slashed deep into Dahan's body.

One of his legs fell from his body and the majority of one shoulder spun away. Another stroke opened the organic meat of his stomach as a rigid spine of crystal punched through his chest. Mechanisms failed and damage warnings flashed red in his vision.

But his target was in sight.

Dahan twisted as he fell, and the disruptor-sheathed blade of his Cebrenian halberd swept down. It clove through the alpha-beast's leg at the joint between limb and pelvis.

The alpha-beast staggered, its body shape rapidly fluctuating in

a futile attempt to keep its balance. It crashed down, the shorn limb clouding and becoming opaque as the linked machines within died. Dahan hit hard, impaled through the shoulder where a rigid spine of glass was wedged. With his remaining two legs, he hauled himself upright, feeling every aspect of bio-mechanical efficiency degrade as chemicals, blood and charged ionic fluids poured from him.

The alpha-beast was drawing its matter into itself, sluggish now that so great a number of its self-replicating machines were no longer a part of it. Its movements were awkward, like a newborn life form still unsure as to the correct means of standing upright.

Dahan didn't give it the chance to learn.

The beast had taken his lower arms, but the bulbous entropic capacitor of the Cebrenian halberd now arced and fizzed with coruscating energy.

Dahan slammed the oval pommel down in the centre of what might have been its chest. An explosion of bio-electrical energy arced through the alpha-beast's body, fusing the crystal and shattering the areas around its path.

The beast lurched and spasmed like a flatlining patient being defibrillated. A patchwork head of clouded glass and crystal extruded from the lumpen mass of its chest, cracking and forming a vast crocodilian skull mass. Dahan swept the Cebrenian halberd around in a decapitating strike.

Its blade had been fashioned by artificers trained in the techniques of the first tech-priest assassins.

The alpha-beast's head fell away from its body, and its nervous system shorted out in a blaze of overload. Green fire spurted from the stump of its neck, a catastrophic wound from which it could not recover.

Every crystalline warrior in the training deck began glitching, internal structures momentarily shorted by the abrupt severing of the connection to their command and control nexus. Dahan wasn't naïve enough to believe the effect would leave the host powerless for long, in the manner of a tyrannic *praefactor*-level creature's death.

But perhaps it would be long enough.

The bray of war-horns filled the training deck, and Dahan wearily lifted the notched blade of his Cebrenian halberd in salute.

Legio Sirius had come, and they had not come alone.

Rumbling in the shadow of *Lupa Capitalina* and *Canis Ulfrica* were squadron after squadron of Imperial Guard superheavies.

Baneblades, Stormhammers and Shadowswords.

'Omnissiah bless you, Captain Hawkins,' said Dahan, as squads of his suzerain rushed to his side.

'Ma-ta-leo! Ma-ta-leo! Ma-ta-leo!'

By the time Roboute and Ilanna stepped from the sunset gate and into his private staterooms, Kotov and his skitarii were already gone. He heard the voice of the archmagos through the open doorway to the bridge. Speaking on the vox, by the sounds of it.

The glow of Bielanna's gateway filled the stateroom with honey-gold light. It imparted a homely warmth to the wood of his desk, but still managed to make the rest of the room feel melancholy.

Its surface was the mirror-smooth surface of a glacial lake bathed in the last rays of autumn, but its edges were undulant, like the corona of a distant sun. Roboute looked away, discomfited by looking too long at its unnatural presence.

'Here,' he said, turning away and lowering Pavelka into the chair behind the desk. 'Sit. Don't try to move. Stay here on the *Renard* until this is all over, yes?'

Ilanna nodded and Roboute sat at the corner of his desk. It felt unreal being here, with his commendations and rosettes on the wall. So normal after the insanity of Exnihlio. Roboute smiled as he saw the hololithic cameo of Katen, knowing on some gut level that she was at least part of what had allowed Bielanna to fix this location so precisely. He couldn't quite bring himself to accept that it was all real, that they'd escaped certain death at the blades of the crystaliths.

'What are you waiting for?' said Pavelka. 'Go.'

'Just give me a minute,' said Roboute, still breathless from another journey that left a bilious taste in his mouth and a savage pounding at his temples. 'At least until I'm sure I can walk without feeling like I'm about to throw up.'

They sat in silence, Ilanna with her hands clasped in her lap, Roboute fixating on tiny details. As if by focusing on them he could force his mind to accept them as real. Gradually the sensation of the world being a veneer spread over a darker reality began to fade and his breathing began to even out.

A sudden sense of premonition caused him to back away from the rippling outline of the sunset gate. Roboute's breathing hiked sharply as Ven Anders emerged, still clutching his bloodied side. He gave the room a quick once-over as three Cadian troopers came after him, making the room feel suddenly small.

'Less ostentatious than I'd have expected,' he said.

'That's Ultramar for you,' answered Roboute.

'Where's Kotov?'

'Already on the bridge. I'll be with you shortly.'

Anders nodded and led his men from Roboute's stateroom.

His timing was fortuitous, as the towering figure of a Black Templar emerged moments later, and the stateroom now felt positively cramped. Yael's armour was limned in glittering motes of light. Behind him, the sunset gate faded like a dream.

'Brother Yael?' said Roboute. 'Where are the others? Why is the gate closed?'

Yael shook off the portal's effects with a shake of his head.

'They are not coming,' he said. 'The witch claims that, with time, she can undo the damage Telok has done. My brothers are giving their lives to grant her that time.'

'They're staying on Exnihlio?'

'Did I not just say that?' snapped Yael, turning away and leaving the stateroom.

Roboute understood. Tanna had sent Yael back to the *Speranza* as the Templars' legacy. A necessary order, but that wouldn't make it any easier to bear for a warrior denied a glorious death alongside his comrades.

'You have to go,' said Ilanna. 'Stop Telok.'

Roboute nodded and bent to kiss her forehead before turning and following Yael onto the bridge. Kotov was already there, plugged into what was normally Pavelka's station on the portside array. Low-level crackles of binaric communication burbled and squawked from the speaker grilles.

As Roboute entered, Kotov stood and disconnected. Anders was on the vox, his face a picture of concentration.

'The *Speranza* is under attack,' said Kotov.

Roboute nodded. 'Makes sense. How else was Telok going to get back to Mars? Is it crystaliths?'

Kotov nodded. 'An army of them, attacking throughout my ship.'

He spoke like a man who had just woken to find his clothes infested with parasites and had no idea how to remove them. Kotov nodded towards Ven Anders and said, 'Captain Hawkins and Magos Dahan are coordinating the defence, but much of the ship has already fallen.'

'Where is Telok?' demanded Yael.

'Unknown, but it must be assumed he will head for the bridge.'

'Then so will we,' said Roboute, heading to the weapons rack at the rear of the bridge. He unlocked it with a key hanging next to it, which wasn't exactly secure, but it meant he could get to his weapons quickly. Roboute unsnapped a drum-fed combat shotgun and slung it over one shoulder then gathered a host of fresh powercells for his pistol. Finally, he lifted out a worn leather sword belt and buckled it around his waist.

The blade was a Calthan vorpal with a solid-state energy core worked into the handle. Anything he cut with this blade wouldn't be getting back up.

'We're pretty close to the bridge, but if there are crystaliths aboard, then it's likely we'll have to fight our way there,' he said. 'We could use some more men to help get us there.'

'I've detached some men from Captain Hawkins's forces in the training deck,' said Anders, setting down the vox and slapping a fresh powercell into the hilt of his sword. 'They'll link with us in the Path to Wisdom.'

'Then let's go,' said Roboute.

They took a transit elevator to the forward loading ramp, and Yael ducked down and dropped to the deck before it was even half lowered. Roboute heard a voice cry out in alarm and slid off the edge of the ramp as he realised it was one he knew.

Yael held Emil Nader by the neck.

'That's my pilot,' said Roboute as the Cadians fanned out from the ramp to surround Emil. Kotov and the skitarii followed as the Space Marine lowered Emil to the deck.

Emil Nader was ashen and looked like he'd just run from one end of the *Speranza* to the other. Behind him, still trailing scads of icy vapour from its recent arrival, was the *Renard*'s shuttle.

'Roboute?' he said. 'How the hell did you get on board?'

'Long story,' said Roboute. 'Are you all right? I saw you on the shuttle with Galatea.'

Emil massaged his bruised neck and glared angrily at Yael.

'Yeah, I'm fine,' he said. 'I thought they were going to kill me after I got them on board, but they couldn't have cared less about me. It was like I was an insect to them.'

'How long have they been gone?' demanded Kotov.

Emil took a step back from the archmagos, staring in horror at his ruined shoulders.

'Twenty minutes, give or take.'

'Can you not be more precise, Mister Nader?' said Kotov.

'Not really, I was trying not to puke in terror at the time,' snapped Emil.

Roboute hid a grin and said, 'Emil, I need you to head to my staterooms. Ilanna's there, and she's hurt. Badly. Look after her.'

Emil nodded, grateful not to have been asked to accompany the war party. 'Of course, Roboute. I'll take good care of her.'

'Where's Adara?' asked Roboute, moving past Emil. 'If there was ever a time for him to earn his keep, it's now.'

Emil grabbed his arm, and Roboute didn't like the look he saw in his pilot's eyes one bit.

'Roboute, Adara's dead,' said Emil. 'Galatea killed him.'

The news hit Roboute like a sledgehammer to the gut. The air was pulled from his lungs.

'And that's not all you need to know.'

'What...?'

'It's about Mistress Tychon,' said Emil.

When the door to the bridge swung open to the sound of shouting skitarii protection details, Blaylock checked the feed from his various cognitive streams. Had he missed the fall of a transit deck or a sudden assault he'd not known was coming?

No, Hawkins and Dahan still had the main thrust of the enemy assault contained on the training deck. The attackers were spread throughout the ship like an infection, and Blaylock even saw a measure of confused inaction in their movements.

Blaylock turned his head as far as the MIU connections of the command throne allowed. He couldn't see the entrance to the bridge and was too enmeshed with the *Speranza* to easily disconnect.

The fact that he wasn't hearing any gunfire reassured him that nothing untoward was happening. The skitarii were behaving aggressively because that was how they were trained to be.

Then he heard the clash of blades, screams of pain and the wet meat sound of cleaving flesh. The sound was short-lived, and Blaylock felt a crushing presence of grating, archaic code as a hideous amalgam of iron and flesh, crystal and glass entered his field of vision.

As broad as a Dreadnought and just as bulky, the monster climbed to the raised mezzanine level of the bridge with the awkward gait of a load-lifter with degraded functionality in its locomotive limbs.

It turned to face Blaylock and even though the face at the centre of its torso mass was rendered in artificial plasflesh, there was no mistaking its features.

<Telok,> said Blaylock.

The Lost Magos took a crashing step towards him, and the reek of dead flesh and chemicals was almost overpowering. Telok extended a fused gauntlet of steel and crystal, and placed a clawed finger the size of a sword on Blaylock's chest.

'Flesh-voice if you please, Tarkis.'

Blaylock nodded and said, 'Where is Archmagos Kotov?'

'Dead.'

Blaylock nodded. It had been the only logical answer.

Galatea appeared behind Telok, the black robes of its proxy body soaked in the blood of skitarii and its blade-limbs coated in the stuff. Chunks of hewn flesh lay like butcher's offal on its lopsided palanquin, where the brain jars of its captive minds crackled and glimmered with furious activity. Blaylock saw one of the jars had been broken, the grey matter within now absent. He wondered who had been discarded from Galatea's neuromatrix.

'It was close to a statistical certainty that you would betray us,' said Blaylock.

'Betray is such a hostile word, Tarkis,' said Galatea. 'We were merely following the precepts of a plan set in motion millennia ago. That we had to deceive you to see it to fruition was a small price to pay.'

Blaylock saw movement behind Galatea.

Kryptaestrex.

Disengaging from his station and powering up his overpowered manipulator limbs. Never before had Blaylock been more grateful for a senior magos who resembled a load-lifting combat servitor than he was right at this moment.

He kept his voice entirely neutral.

'What do you intend?'

Telok smiled and the gesture was as alien as anything Blaylock had ever seen.

'Come now, Tarkis, you already know what I intend,' said Telok, withdrawing his claw and lifting his arms to encompass the bridge. 'The *Speranza* is now my ship. I intend to return to Mars with the Breath of the Gods and take control of the Mechanicus.'

Now it was Blaylock's turn to laugh.

'Until we reached this world, I never believed you really existed. And even then I assumed the years of isolation must have made you mad. I see now that I was entirely correct in this latter assumption.'

Kryptaestrex was now fully disengaged from his MIUs. He just had to keep Telok's attention for a little longer. Within a compartmentalised section of his mind, Blaylock constructed a shut-down code like the one he had used to prevent Vitali Tychon from killing Galatea.

Oh, how he regretted *that* decision.

'The ship is not yours yet,' said Blaylock. 'Our military forces will repel your crystalline army. Already their cohesion is falling away in the face of superior skill and strength.'

'Yes, I felt the demise of the nexus-creature I sent aboard,' said Telok. 'But I have already assumed command of the crystaliths aboard the

Speranza. And when we regain control of the datasphere, we will purge every last deck of oxygen and heat to kill your soldiers deck by deck.'

Regain control...?

Then the war in the datascape Blaylock had witnessed was some part of the *Speranza* fighting back as he had hoped. Telok's careless words also implied that Galatea's hold on the ship's vital systems was no longer in place.

If ever there was a time to strike, it was now.

Blaylock reached into his compartmentalised thoughts at the same time as Kryptaestrex made his move. He unleashed a focused spear of stand-down codes straight at Telok, each binaric string freighted with every authority signifier and title proof Blaylock possessed.

Such a searing volume and intensity of code would have staggered a Warlord Titan, but it had no visible effect on Telok.

Kryptaestrex snapped his claws shut on Galatea's torso, crushing the proxy body. He wrenched it backwards, and an oil-squirting stump of writhing, chrome-plated spinal column erupted from the machine-hybrid's belly.

Telok spun and hammered his monstrously oversized fists into Kryptaestrex's chest. Crystalline claws punched through the boxy housing of his body like the power claws of a chrono-gladiator.

Kryptaestrex was simply obliterated.

Blaylock initiated an emergency decoupling from the command throne, its MIU ribbon connectors retracting into their spinal ports. Finished with his murder, Telok turned to face him with a look of profound disappointment.

'*Really,* Tarkis? That was the best you could do?' said Telok. 'I'd hoped Magos Alhazen would have better prepared you.'

'How could you possibly–'

Telok didn't let him finish.

'Perhaps something more like this,' said Telok. 'Tyger, tyger.'

The effect was instantaneous.

Blaylock's mind went into spasms as it suffered a synaptic overload comparable to an epileptic seizure. Even as he tumbled from the command throne the perceptual centres of his brain were overwhelmed by the fearful symmetry of an orange and black feline stalking a moonlit forest.

What Telok had done was as catastrophic as it was complete.

He couldn't move. He couldn't speak.

Only his visual systems had been left unaffected.

Galatea looked down at him with its lifeless silver eyes. Its proxy body had been savagely twisted and broken, hanging limply over the palanquin like a lifeless marionette.

Yet it was still, hatefully, functional.

The machine-hybrid jerked, as though mocking Blaylock's spasming contortions. The brains flickered, in time with Galatea's involuntary motion. Were they the cause of its internal distress? Impossible to tell, but perhaps Mistress Tychon was causing more trouble than the vile machine had banked upon.

Galatea turned away and limped out of his angle of vision in the direction of Azuramagelli's station. Blaylock could see nothing of what was happening, but from the sound of breaking glass and snapping MIU ribbons, knew it was nothing good.

'The astrogation hub is secure,' said Galatea.

'Excellent,' said Telok. 'Then plot a course for Mars.'

Even with the *Speranza* under attack, the Path to Wisdom was still thronged with tech-priests. They huddled around the vast columns in a fug of incense, endlessly studying the unending streams of ticker-tape and nonsense binary streaming from the carvings wrought into the doric capitals atop each column.

They ignored the *Renard*'s grav-sled as Roboute steered it towards the gigantic doors at its far end. A heavy slab of rectangular iron with a pilot's bay at one end and an underslung repulsor generator, the sled scattered chanting groups of lexmechanics bearing armfuls of rolled scrolls. Servo-skulls crossing the vaulted space loosed squeals of irritated binary as they flitted from its path.

Much like the rest of them, the grav-sled had seen better days. Its structure and engine had been shot, pummelled and overloaded on Katen Venia to the point of it being very nearly written off by Kayrn Sylkwood upon its eventual return to the *Renard*.

Roboute had made a sacred vow to repair the sled, and though it had taken him the best part of the journey to Exnihlio to do it, he had been true to his word.

The grav-sled wasn't a passenger transport, it was a cargo carrier. Its rear compartment was little more than a corrugated cuboid space capable of bearing sixty metric tonnes.

More than enough to transport Sergeant Rae's men and their lethal mix of weapons. The veteran sergeant and his men had rendezvoused with them at the dorsal end of the Path to Wisdom, looking like they'd been in the fight of their lives. Rae was genuinely pleased to see his commanding officer, but looked distinctly unhappy at his current assignment.

Roboute didn't care.

All he cared about was getting to the bridge and killing Galatea.

The machine-hybrid had always been a thing to avoid, but with its revealed treachery, together with its killing of Adara Siavash and its mutilation of Linya, it had become Roboute's sworn enemy.

His cheeks were wet with tears as he guided the sled along the Path to Wisdom. He ignored its many incredible sights, the diamond and chromium-plated pillars, the lapis-lazuli inscriptions and golden wire-work murals. The soaring vault of the ceiling, with its circuit diagram frescoes of ancient Mars, was an irrelevance to him. Nothing now had any meaning to Roboute.

He'd wanted a life beyond the stars, beyond the Imperium, but all he had found were the same treacheries, the same greed and the same insane ambition. Now Adara was dead and Ilanna likely blinded for the rest of her life.

How many more of his friends would have to suffer for his quixotic desire to leave the Imperium? None, he decided.

Kotov and Yael sat to his right, both lost in thought.

Why had they crossed the Halo Scar?

Yael was a crusader of the Black Templars, and the warriors of his Chapter were driven by an imperative from a time before the Imperium. Bound to notions of expanding the Emperor's realm, they could no more have turned from this quest than stopped breathing.

Desperation, greed and, yes, perhaps even a truthful desire to expand mankind's reservoir of knowledge was at the heart of Kotov's motivations. Each of them had crossed the Halo Scar seeking something to fill a void, to satisfy a need they hadn't even admitted to themselves.

Were their reasons any more or less noble than his own? He didn't think so. The worst thing was that they had each *found* what they were looking for.

And now they were paying the price for that.

'Galatea killed my friends,' Roboute said. 'So when we get to the bridge, does anyone object if I kill it?'

'My brothers lie dead beneath an alien sun, their legacy left unharvested,' said Yael, and suddenly he no longer looked like a young warrior. 'Telok and Galatea die by my hand.'

'The *Speranza* is a Mechanicus vessel,' said Kotov, reasoned, logical hatred in every word. 'Taken by an abomination and a traitor. A servant of the Omnissiah must be the one to end them.'

'Fine,' said Roboute. 'Then everyone gets to kill it.'

The vast doors to the bridge loomed ahead of them, and Roboute slowed the grav-sled as he saw a scrapyard's worth of broken machinery heaped at their base.

Praetorians, weaponised servitors, combat-hulks, skitarii kill-packs. At least two hundred shattered, las-burned and hacked-apart bodies. There had been a ferocious battle fought here, but something was missing.

'Who were they fighting?'

'They did this to themselves,' said Kotov.

'They killed each other?' asked Yael.

'The placement of the bodies and the nature of their wounds offers no other conclusion,' said Kotov as Roboute brought the sled to a swift halt.

'Telok?' said Roboute.

'Telok or Galatea,' replied Kotov. 'Not that it makes any difference. They're still dead.'

Yael dropped to the ground as Colonel Anders, Sergeant Rae and fifteen Guardsmen clambered from the back of the grav-sled. They spread out in a loose arrowhead formation, rifles unwavering in their sectors of responsibility. Yael moved away from the sled, his bolter sweeping for targets.

Anders craned his neck to look up the length of the door.

'That's a big damn door,' he said. 'Anyone know how to open it?'

Climbing down into the midst of the dead Mechanicus soldiery, Roboute had to agree with Kotov's assessment of how they had died. He slung his rotary shotgun around, wrapping his fingers around the textured grip and placing his other hand on the recoil stabiliser.

The archmagos picked his way quickly through the shattered bodies to a lectern panel at the side of the huge door. A pair of circling skulls floated above the lectern, their jaws open wide in expressions of horror, witnesses to the slaughter.

Kotov's skitarii went after him, and their fury at what had been done here was plain to see. Roboute followed at a more measured pace as Kotov's mechadendrites opened a hatch at the base of the lectern. Blue light haloed Kotov's features.

Roboute tapped the wide-mouthed barrel of his shotgun against the metres-thick door to the bridge.

'Does the fact that Telok can turn our weapons against us and paralyse our armour, or that his avatar is in control of the ship, give anyone second thoughts about what's going to happen when we get through here?'

No one answered.

'Thought not,' he said, picking a path towards Kotov. 'So, can you get us onto the bridge?'

The archmagos didn't answer. A shower of hissing sparks exploded from the hatch. Kotov fell back, feedback current rippling along the length of his mechadendrites. Flames licked from the hatch, and molten metal dribbled down the lectern.

'No,' said Archmagos Kotov. 'I cannot.'

Microcontent 19

'On your left!' shouted Tanna, blocking a blow and rolling his wrists to thrust his blade into the blank face of a crystalith. Varda swayed aside from the blow arcing towards his head, and spun on his heel to decapitate his attacker.

The Black Templars were in constant motion. Circling the kneeling eldar. Like temple guards protecting priests whose credo forbade violence of any sort.

Never stop, never give the enemy a chance to mass.

A shimmering nimbus of light haloed the xenos, a sure sign of their witchery that would normally have earned Tanna's undying hate. That it had come to this, warriors of the Black Templars fighting to protect the life of eldar, was a measure of the strange turns life could take.

Bielanna sat in the centre of the eldar circle. Corposant danced along her limbs. Light bled from her eyes in mercurial tears.

'Low on your right,' said Varda, and Tanna swept his sword down.

A crystalline blade shattered on the hard edge of his notched sword. The grip still thrummed in his hand, the spirit within revelling in the fight.

'Emperor bless you, Ilanna Pavelka,' said Tanna. His blade was long blunted, but every blow that broke the surface layers of crystal was a killing one.

Tanna barged with his shoulder, making space. The enemy was fast

and strong, but he was a Space Marine. His boot thundered against a crystal kneecap, shattering it. His elbow spun out and pulverised a glassy skull. He fought with all the skill and strength bred into him by the fleshwrights of his Chapter and the genesmiths of a forgotten age.

'For Kul Gilad,' said Tanna, killing another animated monster.

'And Bracha,' shouted Varda in answer.

'An... and Auiden,' said Issur as they came together again.

The honoured dead fought with them, carried in their very souls and every killing blow. And though he bled from a score of wounds, Tanna's heart was that of Sigismund. A mighty organ forged upon the anvil of battle in the Imperium's darkest hour.

And while it still beat, he would fight.

As would they all.

Issur's blade cut a deadly path through the crystaliths. His jawline was taut with the effort of controlling his spasms. His footwork was faultless, his bladework sublime. He would have made a formidable Emperor's Champion had the war-visions come to him.

That honour had gone to Atticus Varda, a warrior who had never once defeated Issur in the practice cages, but whose heart was unclouded by petty resentments. Clad in the Armour of Faith and wielding the Black Sword, Varda was a towering figure. A hero from the Chapter annals, worthy of mention in the same breath as Bayard, Grimaldus, Navarre and Efried.

He moved with fluid economy, never stopping, finding space where no space existed. Earning that extra fraction of a second to parry or counter-attack. To watch Varda fight was to witness all that was best in a warrior.

Tanna knew that he was the least of them. Skilled, but outclassed on every level. His sword bludgeoned where theirs countered, hacked where theirs cut cleanly. Yet for all that his technique left something to be desired, the results spoke for themselves.

The crystaliths massively outnumbered them in odds that were almost comically absurd. Thousands to one. Odds that not even the gene-fathers of the Legions themselves could have fought.

Tanna doubted he had ever fought with such preternatural skill.

His death would be magnificent.

His flesh might not return to the Chapter, but Yael would carry his memory to the *Eternal Crusader* and the legacy of the Kotov Crusade would endure.

Tanna blocked an overhead cut, swaying aside from a thrusting spike of crystal. The enemy hadn't come at them with any energy weapons, just blades. And they had returned the favour. He felt a line

of fire score across his hip and sidestepped, smashing his elbow down on a sword arm. The limb shattered and Tanna kicked his foe in the gut. He followed up the kick with a low sweep, wide and hard. Three crystaliths went down, and Tanna saw a gap open up before him.

'Close ranks!' shouted Varda.

Too far extended, enemies on the left and right.

A smashing cut struck Tanna on the shoulder, another on the thigh. The first bounced clear, the second drew blood. He killed both attackers, but he'd been staggered.

Another blow caromed from his breastplate, and Tanna reeled from the force of it. Crystaliths poured past him as he pushed himself to his feet. More surged towards him. His only advantage was that they couldn't all come at him at once.

Tanna stepped back to the fighting formation of his brothers and hacked down a crystalith with its bladed arm buried in the back of an eldar warrior. The tip of the blade jutted from the alien's chest, but she made no sound as she died. Another fell with his head almost severed. The remaining eldar groaned with each death, as though they felt the pain of each loss within themselves.

Tanna returned the favour, beheading the eldar's killer.

'Push... th... th... them back on the right,' shouted Issur. The swordsman's blade had broken, snapped halfway along its length. No longer a broadsword, more a jagged gladius.

Tanna took a quarter turn left and charged, shoulder low. Pain flared. He'd been hurt there before and his armour's stimms were exhausted. He hurled the enemy back.

'Step in,' ordered Varda.

The three Templars stepped together, forming the points of a triangle around the eldar. Pools of blood made their footing treacherous, but the debris of the destroyed crystaliths gave them traction. Not all of that blood was eldar. Both Issur and Varda bled from a score of wounds, and Tanna's biology burned hot as it fought to heal and keep pace with the energy demands he was making of it.

'No pity,' said Varda, hammering his fist to his chest.

'No remorse,' answered Issur, holding his broken sword out before him.

'No fear,' finished Tanna.

They circled again. Blocking, parrying and defending.

This was not the kind of fight for which they had been wrought. They were crusaders, warriors who sought out foes to kill, battles to win. Yet this was the fight they were given.

But it couldn't go on, the enemy was too numerous, too relentless

and unhindered by the need to protect those who could not defend themselves.

Varda was the first to die.

A glancing blow to the side of his helmet. A moment's pause and they were on him. Stabbing, cutting and barging him. He grappled, unable to bring the Black Sword to bear. Blades punched up through his stomach and chest. Another lanced in under his shoulder guard.

This last blow spun him around, his sword still buried in the heart of a crystalith. The arc of a glass-edged blade flashed. Opened his throat. Cutting into the meat of his neck like a razor.

Blood fountained. The Black Sword wrenched clear.

Tanna shouted a denial as Varda's knees buckled and the Black Sword tumbled from his grip.

Even as it fell, Issur was in motion.

The crystaliths surrounded Varda, cutting his body to pieces as if to defile him. Issur bludgeoned them aside, his body a battering ram. No thought for his own defence. A blade of crystal plunged into his back. Another opened the meat of his flank like a butcher dressing a carcass.

Issur kicked them away from the Emperor's Champion, stabbing with the spar of his ruined blade and punching with his free hand.

He knelt by Varda's corpse. His broken sword slashed down.

And when he rose, it was with the Black Sword held aloft.

'A Champion may fall, but he never dies!' shouted Issur, and his words were free of the impediments that had plagued him since Valette. The snapped blade hung from an unbroken length of chain at his wrist. With the Black Sword gripped in both hands, Issur was reborn in blood as the Emperor's Champion he had always desired to be.

Tanna fought his way to Issur's side, desperately blocking and parrying. The crystaliths sensed the end was near and pressed their attack. More of the eldar were dead. Apart from Bielanna, only two remained, the others hacked down in blood.

'Castellan form,' said Issur, his pain washed away in this last moment of apotheosis.

They came together in a back-to-back defensive style.

They fought like two halves of the same warrior, naturally complementing one another's skills and strengths. They circled Bielanna, their swords a dazzling blur; one black, one silver.

Tanna took a blade to the chest. He snapped it off with a downward smash of his forearm. Another stabbed into his side. They jutted like glass spines. Blood poured down his breastplate, running through the fissures of its ivory eagle.

Tanna dropped to one knee, but Issur was there to haul him to his feet.

'We don't die on our knees, Tanna!' shouted Issur, spinning the Black Sword around his head and cleaving it through half a dozen crystaliths in one mighty blow.

Even with the weapon of the Champion, Issur's strength was failing, his movements slowing. His wounds were too deep and too wide, his armour sheeted in red from the waist down.

Tanna saw the thrust, tried to shout a warning.

Issur twisted his sword in a crosswise block.

An instant too slow.

A diamond-hard blade with glittering, knapped edges.

It caught the light of the blue sky, and the splintered blue edge turned vivid crimson as it buried itself in Issur's heart.

Issur's mouth went wide with pain.

His eyes locked with Tanna's.

'Until the end, brother,' he said.

And hurled the Black Sword to Tanna as a flurry of stabbing glass blades cut him down.

The Black Sword spun through the air, a perfect throw. Tanna caught it with his free hand and brought it around in an equally perfect arc to slay Issur's killer. With chainsword in one hand, Black Sword in the other, Tanna threw himself at the crystaliths with a roar of hatred for all they had taken from him.

Twin swords cut and thrust, striking with an exactitude he had never before possessed. Every blow found the precise gap in his foes' defences, every parry arose at just the right moment to protect Bielanna from a cowardly thrust at her silent form.

A blade cut through the cuisse of his right leg. It clove to the bone, fragmented. Long shards of razored glass stabbed up and down through the meat of his thigh.

Tanna bit down against the agony. His mouth filled with blood.

The pain was ferocious, intense, blinding in its white heat.

He felt every piercing blade entering his flesh. In his back, side and chest. One in the neck, another punching up through his armpit and breaking off in his right lung. A last lancing thrust that split his heart.

Tanna fell onto his back, staring into the painfully blue sky. He pulled both swords onto his chest, like the carven lid of a sarcophagus within the candlelit sepulchres of the *Eternal Crusader*.

An apocalyptic quantity of blood was flooding from his body. Numbing cold enveloped him. His fight was done.

A hand brushed his face. Delicate, porcelain smooth, cold like glass. And the pain went away.

'Until the end,' said Bielanna.

<You'll need it distracted,> said Abrehem.

<I know,> replied Linya, feeling a cold that had nothing to do with temperature seeping into her consciousness. The reality of what she had set in motion with her magi imprisoned within Galatea's neuro-matrix was now manifesting within her.

Anger at the machine-hybrid had sustained her, given her purpose, but now, for the first time, Linya felt real fear.

<I don't know how much longer I can help you,> said Abrehem, and Linya could barely bring herself to look upon him.

<You have to hold on,> she said. <Just a little longer.>

His body was fragmenting, literally fragmenting the nearer they drew to the bridge. As though the intensity of its light and the concentration of raw data was stripping his essence like ice from a comet approaching its perigee with a sun.

But that wasn't it at all.

<I'll try,> he said.

Abrehem's diminishing had nothing to do with the searing luminosity of the bridge. He was dying, bleeding out in Forge Elektrus despite the desperate ministrations of her father and Chiron Manubia.

They hovered over the star-hot emissions of the bridge.

<We can't do this alone,> said Abrehem. <We need a conduit to get inside.>

<And we'll have one,> said Linya. <Look.>

Abrehem followed her gaze and said, <They won't get in either. The machine-spirit in the lock is dead.>

<But *you* can get them in,> said Linya. <Remember the reclamation chamber.>

She knew he would understand her cold logic and hated herself for using him like this. Here, in this place, there could be no secrets between them, and he nodded in understanding, knowing what it would cost him.

Abrehem swooped down and his fragmenting spirit form entered the door. The locking mechanism was cold and dead, murdered by a thing that claimed the same lineage.

<Thus do we invoke the Machine-God,> said Abrehem. <Thus do we make whole that which was sundered.>

Light poured from him, bathing the internal mechanics of the door in a furnace glow of molten gold. And as the dead machines of Forge

Elektrus had responded to his touch, so too did the vast templum door at the terminus of the Path to Wisdom.

It opened.

It offended Kotov on every level to see Telok and Galatea on the bridge of the *Speranza*. Colonel Anders's Cadians swept out to either side of him, as though performing a room clearance in one of Dahan's battle-sims. Kotov noted that Sergeant Rae stood apart from the formation, taking careful, unwavering aim at Galatea.

Yael and Roboute Surcouf marched at his right, his skitarii on his left. Telok turned to face them as the mighty door swung farther open, a look of weary irritation on his face.

'Impossible,' said Galatea, limping forwards with its proxy body almost severed from the palanquin. Kotov was gratified to see that *someone* had managed to grievously harm the machine-hybrid. 'We extinguished the spirit within that door. How were you able to open it?'

'I am an archmagos of the Adeptus Mechanicus,' said Kotov, unwilling to admit that the door's opening was a miracle he could not fathom. 'You will find there is a great deal of which I am capable.'

Telok sighed and his entire body heaved, venting steam, and the crystalline structures engulfing his frame ran the gamut of hues.

'On Exnihlio it was intriguing,' he said, 'but your refusal to die has now passed beyond any amusement.'

Kotov knew better than to bandy words with the Lost Magos, and gave the order he should have given a long time ago.

'Kill Telok and his abomination,' he said.

He had hoped for the sound of gunfire, the snap of las mixed with the crackle of a plasma gun. He had hoped for it, but he had not expected it. The Cadians were frantically checking their rifles, slamming in fresh powercells, but Kotov already knew none of them would fire.

'A squad of Guardsmen and one Space Marine?' said Telok, sliding the crystalline claws from his gnarled, crystal-grown gauntlet. 'An entire vessel of skitarii and Guardsmen at war, and this is all you can muster? You must have seen the remains of your praetorians and skitarii. How could you possibly have believed I would allow your weapons to function in my presence?'

'It was worth a try,' said Kotov, as the Cadians fixed foot-long lengths of matte-black steel to their rifle muzzles. Yael and Surcouf both had swords drawn.

Kotov smiled at the apposite nature of the sight.

Clearly Telok saw it too. 'You would fight for the most technologically

advanced vessel mankind has ever built with knives?' he said. 'And when that fails, what then? Harsh language?'

'Technology married to brute strength,' said Kotov. 'It is the Imperium in microcosm.'

'There is truth in that,' agreed Telok, stepping towards the centre of the bridge. The Breath of the Gods was no less nauseating on the viewing screen, its whirling flux of silver seeming to grow larger with every passing second. Two smears of light hung just behind it, geoformer vessels by the look of them.

Kotov followed Telok onto the raised area of the deck, seeing Tarkis Blaylock sprawled before the vacant command throne. Was he dead? Impossible to know; his body was giving off innumerable radiations, febrile interactions of staggering complexity and every indication of massive data inloads comparable to a scrapcode attack.

The command throne was empty, but just for a fleeting instant, a span of time so ephemeral it could hardly be said to have existed at all, Kotov was certain he saw the spectral apparition of a robed figure seated there.

Beckoning him with a look of desperate urgency.

Then it was gone, and Kotov saw what he at first took to be the shattered remains of an automated lifter machine scattered across the deck. Faint noospherics, like blood-trace at a murder, told him that this was no automated machine, but Magos Kryptaestrex.

He looked towards astrogation. Magos Azuramagelli was still functional, though his latticework frame was buckled and twisted. Portions of his exploded brain architecture lay askew in bell jars half emptied of their bio-sustaining gels.

That he was still functional at all was yet another miracle.

'As you see, I have control of the *Speranza* and every aspect of its workings,' said Telok, lifting his clawed hands to the image above him. 'The Breath of the Gods will soon be aboard, and in under an hour we will break orbit en route to Mars.'

Galatea moved to stand beside Telok, and Kotov was struck by the transformation he saw in the machine-hybrid. Its posture was that of a crippled baseline human, painful to look upon and every movement clearly causing monstrous amounts of pain.

'But we have nothing further to discuss, Archmagos Kotov,' said Telok, turning to Galatea. 'Kill every one of them.'

The machine-hybrid lifted itself up on its mismatched blade-limbs, like a broken automaton in a historical display. A child's toy remade by a psychopath, all torn cables, leaking fluids and sparking wires.

'Now I will *watch* you die,' said Telok.

✱✱✱

Ever since it had entered the annals of Cadian history, the Battle for Vogen had been a byword for the no-win scenario. Given the forces involved in the actual battle, no Cadian commander had yet found a workable strategy to claim outright victory in any simulation fought over the war-torn city.

Hawkins hoped he was about to change that.

Dahan's killing of the alpha-beast had literally stunned the crystalline attackers, and the Imperials had punished them hard. There wasn't a crystal killer within three hundred metres of their position. The increasing volume of gunfire from across the plaza was telling Hawkins that was about to change.

Lieutenant Karha Creed scooted over the rubble towards him. Her helmet had taken a hit and he could see right through to her blonde hair beneath. Blood caked her cheek below the impact.

'Looks like you got lucky,' said Hawkins.

'I got careless,' said Creed. 'Too caught up watching Magos Dahan's kill. A millimetre to the left and I'd be dead.'

'I hear that,' said Hawkins.

Creed's company were arrayed in deployment redoubts either side of Hawkins. Sergeants bellowed inspirational words from the *Uplifting Primer*, commissars doled out Imperial piety from memory and the bearers of the regiment's colours had them ready to raise high for the first time since they'd come on this expedition.

'Lieutenants Gerund and Valdor send their compliments,' said Westin, the vox-caster's headset tucked under the rim of his helmet. 'Both companies are ready as per your orders.'

'Gerund, she's a tough one,' said Hawkins. 'Damn near loses an arm then has a whole building fall down around her ears. And she's *still* able to salvage a working platoon to take into the fight.'

'I trained with her at Kasr Holn,' said Creed, ditching her damaged helm and rummaging for a fresh one. 'You don't know the half of it.'

Hawkins nodded and tapped Westin on the shoulder. 'Any more word from the colonel?'

'Nothing, sir.'

'He on his way here?' asked Creed.

'No, we get to finish this ourselves,' grinned Hawkins. 'We do it the way Hastur would have done it if he'd had superheavies and Titans. And speaking of which...'

The deck rumbled and a lumbering iron behemoth emerged from the archway at the centre of the wall behind them. Less of a tank, more a fully-mobile battle fortress, the Baneblade was the vehicle of choice for the discerning Imperial Guard commander. Laden with battle cannons, lascannons and heavy bolters, it was a lead fist in an iron gauntlet. Two more came hard on its heels.

Jahn Callins sat in the commander's hatch atop the colossal turret, a pair of blast-goggles pulled up onto his forehead.

'Is that for me?' asked Hawkins, having to shout to be heard over the roar of the Baneblade's power plant.

'*Mackan's Vengeance*,' said Callins. 'Kept her back specially for you, sir. I know she was lucky for you on Baktar III.'

'Good man, Jahn. Appropriate too,' said Hawkins, looking out over the plaza to where Dahan's skitarii had their vehicles laagered up around their Secutor and the fallen statue of Sanguinius. He all but vaulted onto the crew ladder and scrambled over the tank's topside. Callins dropped into the tank and Hawkins took his place in the commander's hatch. He pulled on his ear-baffles and hooked himself up to the internal vox-net. The ogre-like spirit of the armoured vehicle was a grating burr in his ears as it strained against human control.

A slate inset within the hatch ring displayed the relative positions of the other superheavy squadrons, the battle-engines and his various infantry platoons. All in the green. All ready to begin the counter-attack in the breath Dahan's kill and the arrival of Legio Sirius had allowed them to take. Hawkins leaned out over the turret and shouted down to Creed.

'Get moving as soon as we're over the wall.'

Creed nodded. 'Understood, and good hunting,' she shouted, before turning and running, bent over, to join her soldiers.

Hawkins twisted the black plastic knob beside him that linked him to the driver's compartment.

'Take us out.'

The Baneblade roared and its engine jetted a plume of blue oilsmoke. Tracks bit the deck and the lumbering vehicle powered up and over the barricade. Almost immediately, flurries of missiles arced from the ruins of the Law Courts and the railhead terminus. Mortars on the roof of the Palace of Peace dropped barrages of high explosives on the far end of the deck. Streams of rockets streaked from Deathstrike launchers farther back and a thunderous cascade of main guns mounted on the superheavy turrets opened fire.

Half the plaza vanished in a fire-lit fogbank of destruction.

To Hawkins's right, three Hellhammers skirted the edges of the Law Courts, unleashing storms of shells from their multiple turrets, co-axials and fixed weapon mounts. Two pairs of Shadowswords came after them. Their volcano cannons tracked for targets while heavy bolters perforated the smoke with mass-reactives.

Hawkins knew at least as many colossal tanks were crashing through the pulverised remains of the railhead terminus to his left. Next to the superheavies, the regiment's Chimeras and Leman Russ looked absurdly small.

Green fire hosed from the fog of detonations ahead, though how anything could still be alive in there to fight back was a mystery. Hawkins was bringing overwhelming fire and armour to the fight, but the enemy wasn't yet beaten. Not by a long shot.

A Baneblade was three hundred tonnes of awesome killing metal, and though the Hellhound was the signature tank of the 71st, Hawkins couldn't deny the thrill of commanding this beast of a machine. Nothing the enemy could throw at it could even scratch its paint.

The battle cannon thundered, and the Baneblade rocked back on its tracks. A section of the deck beyond Dahan's position simply vanished. Artillery detonations obscured the far side of the plaza, but glittering reflections through the smoke told Hawkins the enemy were massing. He knew it was reckless to ride exposed in the command turret, but his men needed to see him.

They needed to see how little he cared for the danger.

The officers of Cadia had led their soldiers this way for thousands of years, and it was how they would always do it.

Hundreds of las-bolts from scores of Chimeras speared into the fog, a storm of fire punching ahead of the Cadian advance. More than a thousand infantrymen raced across the plaza, company standards snapping in the raging thermals.

This was how Cadians made war, unrelenting, furiously attacking in such overwhelming force that an enemy simply had no chance of survival. The Guard was not an extension of Imperial policy designed to drive an enemy to the negotiating table.

It was a force of extermination.

Hawkins looked up as a vast shadow fell across *Mackan's Vengeance*. Arrayed in the colours of Sirius, fresh paint gleaming and new oil dripping from every joint, *Amarok* dipped its head in respect as it came alongside him. Vintras pulled his Warhound away before unleashing a torrent of bolter fire from its vulcan.

Even through the ear-baffles, the noise was deafening.

The *really* big engines kept to the rear of the formation, the majority of their guns simply too obscenely lethal to employ in so confined a space – as Hawkins knew only too well. *Lupa Capitalina* and *Canis Ulfrica* unleashed a hurricane of fire from their gatling blasters, and the firepower of so many heavy shells tore three-metre trenches in the deck. Both engines launched barrage after barrage of Apocalypse

missiles from carapace launchers, turning the far end of the plaza into a hellstorm of shrapnel and fire.

Those who'd seen such a barrage claimed that even one launcher could unleash the equivalent of an artillery company.

Hawkins reckoned that to be a conservative estimate.

Mackan's Vengeance reached the laager of skitarii tanks and Hawkins saw Dahan in the hatch of a Leman Russ with a turret-mounted weapon he didn't recognise. Something with spinning brass orbs and crackling tines enclosing a seething ball of purple-white plasma.

Dahan saw him and raised his Cebrenian halberd in salute. Hawkins didn't have a signature weapon, so instead raised his fist – as good a symbol of Cadia as any.

The Mechanicus vehicles – a mix of stalk tanks and up-armed Chimeras and Leman Russ – broke their laager and merged with the Cadian formations with complete precision.

The barrage moving ahead of the Cadians ceased as the armoured charge reached the far end of the plaza. The smoke began to disperse as the deck's recyc-units sucked wheezing breaths into the ventilation systems.

Should have got Dahan to disengage them, thought Hawkins.

Blocky shapes resolved in the smoke, artillery-smashed recreations of Vogen's outer walls. Fortifications Colonel Hastur and his soldiers had attempted to escalade time and time again without success.

Fortifications that were within touching distance.

And Hawkins felt a hand take his heart in a clenched fist as a tsunami of crystalline creatures spilled over them. They came from every transverse entry hall to the training deck, from every gap in the walls and through the wide open gates.

Thousands of sharp-edged beasts of glass and crystal.

Some were the human-sized warriors, others the towering shield-bearing monsters. At least two dozen of the vast, centipede-like creatures he'd killed with the Rapier in the deck transit punched through the walls.

An army of extermination, but he had one of his own.

'Time to win the no-win scenario,' said Hawkins.

Microcontent 20

Even monstrously damaged, Galatea was fast. Its clattering, ungainly frame came at them with slashing forelimbs and whipping, blade-tipped mechadendrites. Two Cadians died instantly, speared through their chests by scything blades that rammed down like pistons.

Kotov ducked back as another limb flicked at him. The tip caught the edge of his robes and cut the heavy metal-lined fabric like paper. Rough hands pulled him back.

'Step away, archmagos,' said Carna, the skitarii warrior placing himself between Kotov and Galatea's slashing blades. 'You gain nothing by taking part in this fight.'

Kotov nodded as the Cadians surrounded Galatea. It spun and stamped like a warhorse of old as they darted in to stab it with their black bayonets. Kotov was reminded of the crude daubs made by ancient cave-dwellers, depicting hunts for vast, plains-dwelling mammoths.

The pistol he'd taken to Exnihlio, but never fired, felt like something belonging to someone else. He holstered it, already knowing its firing mechanism would not activate.

Galatea's body lolled to the side, its silver eyes dull and lifeless, the brain jars on its palanquin crackling with interlinked activity. Each ferocious burst caused Galatea to jerk with rogue impulses.

Angry static blared from its shattered augmitters.

Surcouf, Anders and the Black Templar faced the machine-hybrid head on. The rogue trader moved like a fencer, attacking only when the opportunity for a strike presented itself and deflecting attacks rather than meeting them head on. Yael fought two-handed, genhanced power compensating for his lack of finesse. He blocked each thunderous blow with brute strength.

Ven Anders ducked beneath a slashing limb, but fell to one knee with a grimace of pain, one hand pressed to his blood-soaked uniform. Galatea saw the Cadian colonel's moment of weakness and slammed a limb down with hammering force.

The blade punched through Anders's spine, pinning him to the deck. The colonel's back arched in agony, but his screams were cut off as Galatea twisted its limb with malicious relish.

Surcouf shouted and swung his sword in a devastatingly accurate strike. The blade's artifice was so sublime that even with its powercell non-functional it hacked the limb from Galatea's body.

The machine-hybrid staggered, and Yael roared with aggression as he slammed his shoulder into its palanquin. Galatea rocked back, unbalanced with a limb missing. The brains flared with activity and another burst of pained static squalled from its augmitters.

Anders's men hurled themselves at the creature with renewed fury. Galatea's mechadendrites slashed in a wide arc, and three of the Cadians were cut down. Blood and entrails soaked the silver deck plates and Kotov could have wept to see this place of logic and understanding transformed into a place of bloodshed and horror.

He looked past the fighting and once again saw the ghostly image of a figure on the command throne, like a crude composite superimposed on a badly synced picter.

Kotov accelerated his thought processes, slowing the perceived passage of time as his mind instantly ramped to massively overclocked levels. Thermal vents along his spine bled the excess heat of his enhanced cognition.

This time the image stabilised, becoming recognisable.

Linya Tychon.

You and Speranza *must be one.*

Vitali's hands were sticky with blood. Abrehem Locke's wound simply wasn't closing. The bondsman's coveralls were soaked in crimson from midriff to ankles. He gripped the armrests of the Throne Mechanicus, trembling and white with effort.

Vitali's digits were splayed with numerous hair-fine filaments as he attempted to suture the wound. Thus far without success. He had access to every medicae tract ever written, but *knowing* a thing was entirely different from putting it into practice.

'Can't you stop the bleeding?' said Coyne, propped up against the base of the throne. The cauterised stump of the man's wrist was wrapped in oil-stained rags, held tight to his chest. He'd be lucky not to get an infection and lose the arm.

'Don't you think I'm trying?' snapped Vitali, flinching as another burst of gunfire from the breached gate to Forge Elektrus ricocheted inside. 'The effect of these crystalline weapons is pernicious. It makes the flesh around the injury site weak and prone to rapid necrosis. Each suture I make tears within seconds of being closed up.'

'Then keep more pressure on it, damn you!' said Hawke, seated on a crate on the other side of the throne. 'Don't you know anything about battlefield triage? If you can't stop it, at least slow it down. Abe's not the only one losing blood here.'

A transfusion line connected the two bondsmen, and right now that was all that was keeping Abrehem Locke alive. Julius Hawke had volunteered his blood to save Abrehem, and a quick scan of the barcode on his cheek had revealed him to be a universal donor. The gesture had seemed noble until Vitali realised Hawke simply wanted out of the firing line.

Vitali had not been gentle with the needle.

Standing behind the throne, Ismael de Roeven had the fingertips of his hand of flesh and blood pressed to Abrehem's temple. The former servitor disturbed Vitali on every level; not just for what he was, but what he represented and implied about every other servitor. Ismael's skin was ashen and grey. He was taking Abrehem's pain onto himself, and Vitali knew all too well how terrible a burden that was.

'His pulse is slowing,' said Ismael. 'Blood pressure dropping to dangerous levels.'

Connected via a sub-dermal bio-monitor to Abrehem's vital signs, Vitali already knew that. And right now, every vital sign suggested a patient in terminal decline. Without trained medicae, Abrehem Locke was going to die. This fight had to be won, and won quickly.

Vitali broke the link to Abrehem and pushed himself to his feet. The sounds of battle swelled as his senses aligned more fully to his surroundings.

'Don't you dare let him die,' said Vitali to all three of the men clustered at the throne. None of them answered, wrapped up in their own personal miseries.

Vitali hurried back along the nave, past the chanting acolytes seated on the wooden benches towards the nexus of the forge-temple. The shaven-headed adepts were linked to the Throne Mechanicus, but what benefit they might be providing was unclear.

He ducked behind the barricade erected at the entrance he'd been tasked with remotely defending. The forge door was no more, and the approaches to Elektrus were now held by Rasselas X-42 and a handful of Mechanicus Protectors. Arcing forks of lightning from shock-staves and green fire lit the wide processional, painting the combatants in a shimmering, stroboscopic glow.

Like the Spartans of old, the Protectors fought with brutal economy of force, each warrior working in perfect synchrony with his fellows. They fought the crystal creatures in an unbreakable line, advancing and retreating as logic dictated.

The arco-flagellant had none of that logic, an insane berserker who had once been an exalted cardinal of the Imperium whose murder lust had overcome his piety. Intellectually, Vitali understood it was only right and proper that heretics and the damned be made to shrive their souls through pain and renewed service. But to see such a punishment enacted in the flesh was still horrifying.

The thing bled from scores of wounds, its swollen, pumped body a reticulated mass of bloodied gouges. Its flesh glittered with embedded fragments of glass debris and blackened scorch marks. One arm hung loose and inert, the other a slashing killing blade. Its body radiated heat and bled vast quantities of chemical haze. At this rate of physical attrition, it wouldn't last another hour.

At this rate of assault, none of them would.

Steeling his courage, Vitali hitched up his robes and broke cover. He ran from this portion of the battle to where Chiron Manubia coordinated the defence of the second approach to Elektrus. Connected to a lectern of brass and wood, Manubia's hands cut the air in arcane lemniscate patterns as she managed a dozen weapon systems and exloaded battle-cant to the Protectors fighting in the secondary approach.

Vitali placed a hand on the lectern and let his haptics merge with the network. The interior of the forge fell away as his awareness shifted to the spaces beyond its gates.

A demi-century of Protectors fought here, led by Totha Mu-32. Wave after wave of crystal creatures fought to breach Forge Elektrus, and it seemed to Vitali that there was a desperate urgency to their assault. Forking blasts of green fire filled the approaches, burning the walls or absorbed by the Protectors' storm shields.

A dozen concealed weapon emplacements blazed into the attackers, emerging to open fire and retracting into their armoured housings before the enemy could respond.

Why hadn't he thought of that?

A fresh assault came in hard in the wake of a furious storm of green fire, but Totha Mu-32 was ready for it. His Protectors surged upright from their barrier of locked storm shields, shock-staves held out before them like lances.

They hit the crystal beasts hard, bent low, arms thrusting. Shock-staves unleashed vitrifying blasts of high-energy pulses. Follow-up blows shattered limbs and skulls, and with the breaking of the first wave, the Protectors withdrew in good order to their rally points.

It was quite the most ordered method of warfare Vitali had ever seen. The polar opposite to what was happening at the forge's other entrance.

<Chiron,> said Vitali. <I need to talk to you.>

<I'm pretty busy here, in case you hadn't noticed.>

<This is important,> said Vitali, making sure his binary emphasised *just* how important. Manubia's reply was similarly loaded with binaric imperatives that showed just how little she cared for his definition of important.

<Shouldn't you be trying to keeping my protégé from dying?> said Manubia, re-aligning her targeting auspex on a gathering knot of crystalline beasts.

<Even the Omnissiah would struggle to prevent that,> said Vitali. <Even with Hawke's blood and Ismael's alleviation of his pain, he is fading faster than we can sustain him.>

<Then what do you want from me?> said Manubia, unmasking a graviton cannon and turning three crystal beasts to a flat sheet of crazed glass.

<We have to end this attack,> said Vitali. <Abrehem has to live. Linya sent me here to keep him alive.>

<Do you even know why?>

<No,> said Vitali, <but she wouldn't have asked if it wasn't absolutely vital.>

Linya opened her eyes, breathless and exhausted. Both sensations were chemical reactions to the complex hexamathics required to reach out to Archmagos Kotov within the sun-hot arena of the bridge, but the feeling was no less real.

The midnight-black dome of perfectly geometric cubes was gone, and in its place was Linya's favourite viewing dome within the Quatrian Galleries. Smaller than the others, it had only a basic observational device, a piece quite useless for viewing much beyond a planetary sphere, but said to have once belonged to the composer of Honovere.

Arrayed to either side of her were her fellow magi: Syriestte on her right, Haephaestus to her left. Natala gave her a nod of respect, and the sad determination on each and every face would have broken her heart had she one left to break.

Standing at the farthest extreme of the viewing dome was the adept in black. Galatea's avatar within the mindspace. Except, she knew better than that now, didn't she? He looked around, as though surprised to see himself here.

Linya remembered all the times this adept had tortured her, forcing her to experience extremes of pain she hadn't believed possible, and her resolve hardened. His silver eyes were lustreless now, stripped of any power they once had to intimidate.

'You think you can defeat me?' said Galatea.

'*Me?*' said Linya, stepping forwards. 'Not referring to yourself as a plurality any more?'

'There seems little point in the mask now.'

'True, then I'll address you as Telok.'

'Archmagos, if you please,' said the black-robed figure. 'After all, I earned the rank.'

'Then you cast it away when you forgot the ideals of your order.'

'Forgot them? No, I was finally able to *realise* them.'

'You are no longer Mechanicus, *archmagos*, and this is over.'

The adept laughed. 'Over? I think you forget that you are still in my neuromatrix. And if you thought the tortures you have already endured were excruciating, believe me, I have many more that are far more terrible. Your tricksy little code has kept you beyond my reach for a time, but it won't last much longer.'

'It's already lasted long enough,' said Linya.

'What are you talking about?'

'Look around you, this isn't *your* neuromatrix any more. It's mine. See how everything has that sheen of real memory, not pilfered thoughts shaped into the *recreation* of a memory.'

The black-robed adept suddenly realised his danger and flew at Linya, his form swelling as it drew the shadows to it. Wide, bat-like wings erupted from the adept's back, the data-daemon that had devoured Kleinhenz reforming before her.

Linya smiled and held her hands out, palm up.

The data-daemon slammed to a halt in mid-air.

She ripped her hands to the side, as through pulling open a veil, and the data-daemon exploded into a cloud of perfectly cubic flakes of ash. They faded like dying embers, leaving the robed adept sprawled before her.

'I told you,' said Linya. 'This is *my* neuromatrix.'

The adept backed away from her on all fours as Linya walked towards

him. He rose to his knees, hands held out before him in supplication. She read his terror. He knew full well the horrors she could inflict.

But Linya had no inclination towards torture or revenge.

Instead, she turned to her fellow magi, and said, 'It's time.'

They nodded in unison as Magos Syriestte said, 'The implanted code will be unequivocal and unsparing in its execution.'

'I know, but it's better this way,' said Linya, unlocking the last hexamathic cell within her mind. The activation algorithms for the kill-code flooded into her consciousness. They merged with previously released binaric strings, becoming something utterly lethal to the electrical activity of the brain.

It grew, it replicated.

It destroyed.

The kill-code had penetrated deepest into Magos Haephaestus, and the venerable techno-theosopher was first to feel its effect. He bowed his head and vanished as the implanted kill-code woven into their linked neural network took effect. Linya felt Haephaestus die, and Telok's avatar screamed as a portion of its heuristic neuromatrix was sheared away.

The kill-code destroyed Magos Natala. Then Txema, then Chivo.

With each brain-death, Telok's avatar howled in loss, convulsing like a madman on the polished terrazzo floor of the viewing dome. One by one, the imprisoned magi were extinguished until only Linya and Telok's avatar remained.

She felt each loss and tried not to hate the wretched, shrunken thing writhing before her like a hooked maggot on a line. She knelt beside the avatar. Stripped of its gestalt consciousnesses, it was a barely sentient conduit of data, a sheared potion of a much larger mind.

It was almost pitiable.

Almost.

'Kill me and be done with it,' said the avatar.

'No,' said Linya. 'I still need you to do something for me.'

So much death…

Bielanna felt the last of her kin die.

The crystaliths tore them apart, perhaps realising what she attempted. Their strength now filled her, and Bielanna felt each spirit move within her rapidly crystallising flesh. The rapid push and pull of Exnihlio's death spasms had imbued her with extraordinary power, but it had hurled her headlong towards the eventual fate of all farseers.

It came over her like an ultra-rapid shock-freeze.

No rest for her within the Dome of Crystal Seers.

They surrounded her, their limited awareness ill-equipped to process

this new variable. Their orders were to kill creatures of flesh and blood, and they had done that.

Bielanna's flesh was cold and hard, as glassy and reflective as the crystaliths. Her spirit and those of her fellow eldar burned brightly inside her. She took that energy and wove it around the power the Breath of the Gods had unleashed. The energy of a supernova condensed into a pure form of thought and expression.

Bielanna was done with her body of flesh and blood, and it had no more need for her. Only one realm called to her, a place of dreams and joy, where past and future entwined and the fate of all things was revealed.

Where the Path of the Seer inevitably led.

Bielanna cast off her mortal shell and threw her spirit into the skein. Freed from mortal constraints, she saw more than ever before, with a clarity the living could never know.

From this vantage point, Exnihlio appeared as a single atom out of place in the structure of a vast crystal. Any force applied to the crystal would always be concentrated on that atom. Soon another atom would be out of place, then another. And another.

Through such mechanisms were cracks in the universe begun.

And once begun, they propagated.

Like scissors cutting fabric.

But if that atom could be removed from the lattice…

Another Cadian died as Galatea speared him through the chest with a lancing strike of its mechadendrites. It tossed the man's body across the bridge like a ragdoll before turning its attention upon Sergeant Rae. Kotov watched in slow motion as a blade-limb stabbed through the meat of the man's thigh, pinning him in place as a coiling mechadendrite whipped up like a stinger.

To his credit, Rae didn't flinch, but raised his useless lasrifle in a futile attempt to block the incoming strike.

'Come on then, you bastard!' shouted the Cadian.

The strike never came.

A grand-mal seizure wracked Galatea's body, its palanquin vibrating like an engine on the verge of exploding. The limb pinning Rae to the deck wrenched clear as Galatea loosed a binaric scream of anguish so profound that it broke Kotov from his enhanced mode of cognition. His perception of time's flow returned to its normal mode of operation, and the world seemed sluggish in comparison.

Telok staggered, as though whatever pain was wracking Galatea was stabbing him in the heart also. Given what Kotov knew of the symbiotic relationship between Telok and Galatea, perhaps it was.

An evil scarlet light swept around the palanquin, moving from brain jar to brain jar. The bio-gels within each jar instantly clouded, like stagnant water in a sump. Kotov had served two decades aboard a Tempestus battle-engine and saw the unmistakable signs of amniotic death.

Only one brain resisted the mass extinction, and Kotov knew instantly to whom it belonged. Coupled with the spectral visitation he had seen earlier, Kotov knew exactly what he had to do.

Galatea's legs folded beneath it and its misaligned body crashed to the deck with a booming clang of dead metal. Its proxy body flopped over onto its front, black floodstream chemicals pumping from suddenly unmaintained bio-mechanical organs.

The Cadians stepped back, wary of some trick, but Yael was on Galatea in a heartbeat. He wasted no time in bringing his sword around in brutal, two-handed overhead strikes like an ironworker at the anvil. Surcouf joined him a second later, his Calthan blade wreaking terrible harm on Galatea's robed body.

'Leave the brains intact!' shouted Kotov.

If Linya Tychon had indeed slain Galatea from within, then perhaps there was a chance to extricate her from the belly of the beast. How cruel a trick of fate would it be for her to avenge her mutilation only to be killed in the process?

Then Telok was amongst them.

His ironwork and crystal body throbbed with dark reds and crimsons. Plumes of scalding gases vented and his greasily artificial face was twisted in rage. Tearing claws smashed Cadian soldiers to boneless meat, ripped them to shredded matter.

Gone was the genius archmagos who had reconstructed the ancient machine of a long-dead race of galactic engineers. All that remained was a howling berserker creature, drowning its pain and grief in slaughter.

Kotov was never going to get a better chance than this.

'With me,' shouted Kotov. 'By your lives or deaths, get me to the command throne.'

Kotov ran past the bloodshed, slipping on the lake of blood spreading across the deck. He kept his mind focused on putting himself back where he belonged.

'Kotov!' bellowed Telok.

He almost turned at the sound of his name.

Was almost stunned to immobility by the furious rank signifiers that matched his own.

'Go!' shouted Carna, pushing him forwards.

Kotov didn't see the skitarii warrior's death, but felt it resonate in the noosphere as a vast quantity of blood sprayed him. The second

skitarii, whose name he hadn't bothered to inload, died a second later, torn in two at the waist.

Kotov kept going. Thundering impacts sounded behind him.

He didn't dare look round. He felt hot, dead breath on him. Crystalline claws swept down to cleave him apart.

Then Yael and Surcouf were there.

The rogue trader was smashed to the deck, no match for Telok's vast strength. Only Yael had the power to take the blow, his genhanced physique a match for Telok's hideous crystalline embellishments.

Even so, he was driven back, the plates of his armour broken, the bones of his arms shattered.

It was foolish defiance, the last act of desperate men with nothing left to lose.

But it was just enough.

Kotov threw himself onto the *Speranza*'s command throne, slamming his hands down onto haptic connectors that still bore traces of molten metal and flesh.

Telok loomed over him, his inhuman features no longer recognisable as anything sane. His clawed arm pulled back, the blood of countless innocents upon it. The killing energies of Exnihlio burned along every blade.

Telok's claw hammered through Kotov's chest and into the throne.

Its haptics burned hot. Golden illumination, like the birth of all machines, rammed into Kotov's skull.

A conduit was established, a connection made.

Like a surge tide in spate, the world spirit of the *Speranza* rose up to engulf Kotov and Telok.

And not just the *Speranza*'s.

I have been here before.

That was the first thought to enter Kotov's head as he saw the neon-bright datascape of the *Speranza* open up to him.

I should be dead, was the second.

He remembered Telok's claw punching down through his chest, a shattering blow of awful power. Kotov's body was largely mechanised, but enough remained of his nervous and circulatory system to make such damage almost certainly fatal.

A glittering megalopolis spread before him, the flow of information that formed the hidden arteries of the *Speranza*. It was mountainous, rugged with hives of light and vast termite mounds of agglomerated data. Abyssal cliffs of contextually linked information hubs spiralled into fractal mazes of answers that led to ever more questions.

Datacores burned like newborn suns in constellations of linked

neural networks. The *Speranza* was in constant dialogue with itself, learning and growing with every solution gained.

Heuristic in the purest sense of the word.

Every paradigm of scalable time, from the cosmic day to the compression of universal history to a single hour, failed utterly to capture the datascape's infinite scope. Its mysteries went back to the first stone tools hacked from river bedrock and stretched into the Omega Point, the Logos and Hyparxis all in one.

And for all that this aspect of the *Speranza* was a place of knowledge and understanding, it was also one of metaphor, allusion and maddening symbolism.

Highways of light were easy enough to interpret, but what of the vast, serpentine coils arcing above and below to encircle the world before coming around to engulf itself? What of the conjoined helices of light that split apart like the branches of a towering tree with its roots dug deep into the datascape?

Could he even see these things truly or was his hominid brain simply interpreting the unknown in ways he could process?

Looking down (if *down* was even a concept that could be applied to infinitely dimensional realms of thought) it was clear how foolish and naïve he had been to claim he was *Speranza*'s master.

Knowledge was not a something to be *claimed*, it existed for all those with the wisdom to seek it, for only in the acceptance of ignorance could that void be filled. That felt like revelation, but Kotov suspected it was ancient wisdom he and his order had long forgotten.

<How far we have fallen,> said Kotov, humbled and awed by the incredible vista. <But how far we might yet climb.>

<The words of the Athenian gadfly, really? I expected more of the man who reached Exnihlio.>

Kotov turned and saw Telok soaring above the datascape, no longer the monstrous being he had become, but the magos he had once been. His robes were black, his optics a glittering silver. The resemblance to Galatea was so startling, Kotov wondered how he had not seen it before.

<An old truth, but still a universal one,> said Kotov.

<A platitude recycled by those who seek to excuse their ignorance,> said Telok, circling Kotov like a stalking predator. The Lost Magos swept his gaze around the infinite landscape and Kotov felt his burning *need* to possess it.

<Galatea chose well when it sent this ship to me,> said Telok.

<Perhaps too well,> said Kotov. <Its parasitic touch is falling away from the core systems. Even if you kill everyone aboard, you will never possess this ship.>

<Kill everyone aboard?> said Telok. <What a novel idea, I may just do that.>

<I will stop you.>

<How? You have no body, I destroyed it.>

<I have others, but even if my physical form is non-functional, I can stop you in here.>

<You have no power here, Kotov,> sneered Telok. <You are no longer the master of this ship.>

<I was never its master, I see that now. But neither are you.>

<I will be.>

Kotov laughed. <Then you are as deluded as you are insane.>

<Then come, shall we end this, archmagos? Shall we wield our wits as weapons, our knowledge as power? It is only fair to warn you that you are sadly unarmed for such a fight. I have thousands of years' head start on you.>

<Your knowledge is great,> conceded Kotov, feeling the presences he had sensed as the *Speranza* dragged him down rising to meet him. <But I have something you do not.>

<And what is that?>

<I have allies,> said Kotov as the glittering dataforms of Linya Tychon and Abrehem Locke appeared at his side.

Once the bane of Kotov's life, Abrehem Locke wavered like a distorted hologram, his outline blurred where motes of darkness drifted from his body like ash from a cindered corpse. Linya Tychon was restored, her skin unblemished once again where the fire in *Amarok* had crippled her and whole where Galatea had mutilated her. She turned to Kotov and it seemed as though a multitude of overlaid spirits stared out through her eyes.

<Allies?> laughed Telok. <A dead man and a ghost?>

<I killed Galatea,> said Linya. <I want you to know that. And the part of you that's left inside? Guess what it's doing right now?>

Telok shrugged, as if the answer was of no interest. <Screaming, most likely, but it does not matter. I have lived without that portion of my consciousness for millennia. Extinguish it, torture it, do as you will. I care not.>

<You will,> promised Linya.

Telok sighed, but it was a distraction only.

He hurled himself at Kotov, fast as thought.

Physics held no sway here, only imagination. Wounded, Kotov dropped through layers of data, informational light skimming past at superliminal speeds. Telok followed him down, constructing calculus proofs of space-time curvature to increase his speed. Kotov led him

through canyons of databases, where information passed back and forth in collimated streams of data-dense light. The sense of movement and velocity was intoxicating.

Abrehem and Linya spiralled around Telok in a double helix. She clawed at Telok's experiential armour, stripping it from him in long chains of boolean notation. Hexamathic blades, against which Telok had no protection, stabbed into him.

Ancient technology unknown to the Adeptus Mechanicus batted her away as Telok's vast intellect surged to the fore. Abrehem flew in close to Telok and the golden fire that had burned Galatea's vile touch from the *Speranza* seared into Telok's form.

Telok howled in rage as his shields of logarithmic complexity were burned away. A mastery of nanotechnology, the likes of which Abrehem was utterly ill-equipped to comprehend, sent his attacker spinning away.

<Knowledge is power,> roared Telok, hurling searing bolts of cold logic at Kotov. <They call that the first credo, but they are wrong. Knowledge is just the beginning. It is in the *application* of knowledge that power resides.>

Kotov spun away from Telok's fire, rising from the database canyons and looping around a soaring column of engine cores, where the impossible calculations to breach the barriers of the warp were agreed upon.

<Knowledge is power,> said Kotov, turning aside from yet more of Telok's searing projectiles. <It is the first credo. It is the only credo. To understand that fundamental concept is to possess power beyond measure.>

He thrust his hands out before him and a glittering shield of pure logic reflected Telok's attacks back at him. Telok roared in pain as the two archmagi came together in an explosion of fractal light. Circling the engine datacore and bathing in its bewildering, non-linear solutions, they came apart and smashed together again and again.

Gods of data and knowledge, their wisdom gave them power.

All they had learned and all they had explored. Every belief, every expression of wonder. All were transformed into killing thoughts. Chains of accumulated knowledge tore aetherial bodies, words as weapons, digits as ammunition.

They fell through the datascape, plunging into the heart of sun-hot datacores, emerging in streamers of light that were drawn into their death struggle. The battle left a burning wake in the *Speranza*'s heart as they spun around one another like gravity-locked comets, inextricably linked and plunging to mutual self-annihilation.

They fought like two alpha males vying for dominance.

And as the alchemists of Old Earth had always known: as above, so

below. Where they fought the *Speranza* shuddered with sympathetic agonies.

In the portside testing arrays every single experimental weapon system activated without warning and blew a three-hundred-metre tear in the hull.

A ventral chem-store went into a feedback loop in its mix ratios and crafted a lethal bio-toxin that was only prevented from entering the ship's filtration systems by the last-minute intervention of a nameless lexmechanic.

Forge-temples whose alpha-numeric designations contained the data-packet of 00101010 had their libraries wiped, condemning millennia of accumulated learning to dust.

All across the *Speranza* the collateral damage of their battle was tearing the ship apart.

Linya and Abrehem followed in the wake of the devastation, barely able to keep pace with the two warring gods. Though they were gifted in their own ways, neither had the accumulated wisdom and experience of an archmagos of the Adeptus Mechanicus.

Finally, weary and stripped of their most prominent aspects of genius, Telok and Kotov came apart above a deep datacore of molten gold. They bled light, mercury bright, and ashen memories of things once known drifted from them like tomb dust.

<You can't win this,> said Telok, his black robes in tatters.

<Nor can you,> answered Kotov, feeling himself ebb with each utterance.

Linya and Abrehem finally caught up to Kotov and Telok, putting themselves in the dead space between the two archmagi.

<Neither of you can win,> said Linya.

<You will destroy one another,> said Abrehem.

<And we cannot allow that to happen,> they said in unison.

Linya hurled herself at Telok, Abrehem at Kotov.

Both struck at the same instant, and Kotov felt the essence of Abrehem Locke's Machine-touched spirit merge with every aspect of him. He felt as though his body was transformed, his perceptions turned inside out. Hard logic and reason blended with intuition and lateral thinking in ways he had never considered.

Kotov looked up and saw the same process under way within Telok as Linya Tychon merged herself with the core of his very being.

But where the union of spirits had been beneficial to Kotov, the opposite was true for Telok. His inner workings laid bare like a clockwork automaton on a workbench, Kotov saw why instantly. Linya Tychon was not simply Linya Tychon, but a spirit-host of vengeful tech-priests.

Each of whom bore within them a lethal hexamathic kill-code.

Telok howled as it was loosed within him, a viral fire against which he had no defence. It ravaged his systems, wiping decades of learning every second. Constantly evolving in self-replicating lattices, the kill-code transferred itself from system to system within Telok's internal system-architecture.

It destroyed everything it touched, reducing his vast databases to howling nonsense code and rendering the accumulated knowledge of centuries of study to irrelevant noise.

Telok's form twisted as the viral conflagration burned him alive from the inside out. His screams were those of a man who could feel everything he ever was being systematically ripped away.

But Telok was an archmagos of the Adeptus Mechanicus, and even as Kotov watched, he was adapting, excising and rewriting his own internal structure to halt the cancerous spread of the kill-code.

Now, Archmagos Kotov, said a voice within him.

Locke.

You have the power of the Machine-touched now. Use it.

Kotov lifted his hands towards the molten gold of the datacore, feeling something indefinable move within him. It was power, but power unlike anything he had known before. Power like the first of the Binary Saints were said to have wielded, the ability to commune with machines as equals. To walk with them as gods on the Akashic planes on the road to Singularity.

Kotov drew on the light of the datacore.

And the *Speranza*'s soul poured into him.

Kotov's eyes were burning discs of golden light, the secret fire that only suns know, the spark that ignited the universe. From first to last, he knew everything.

Everything.

Shimmering armour of gold and silver encased Kotov, battleplate as titanic and ornate as any worn by the legendary primarchs or even the Emperor Himself.

A sword of fire appeared in his hand, its hilt and winged quillons forming a two-headed eagle wrought in lustrous gold.

Pure knowledge, weaponised wisdom.

Telok writhed as he purged himself of the kill-code.

Almost nothing remained of it, but it had done what Linya intended, stripping Telok of vast swathes of armoured knowledge.

<Woe to you, man who honours not the Omnissiah, for ignorance shall be your doom!> said Kotov.

He plunged the blazing sword into Telok's heart.

Microcontent 21

This was the end of all things.

The mon-keigh believed the End Times would come in a tide of battle and blood, of returned gods and the doom of empires. Even the eldar myth cycles spoke of a time called the Rhana Dandra, when the Phoenix Lords would return for the last great dance of death.

Bielanna knew of no species with legends that spoke of things simply ending. Where was the mythological drama in that?

The skein's golden symmetry was unravelling, the futures collapsing. The fates of all living beings were unweaving from the great tapestry of existence. Entropy in the material world was mirrored in the skein, and its shimmering matrix was falling apart as the tear in space-time caused by Archmagos Telok ripped wider.

Bielanna plunged into the heart of the maelstrom of breaking futures, her spirit a shimmering ghost in the skein. The spirits within Bielanna quailed at being within the skein. Their fear was understandable. No longer protected from She Who Thirsts by their spirit stones, they feared the fate that had befallen Uldanaish Ghostwalker. They were warriors and the skein was a mystery to those who wore the war-mask; how could they possibly understand what she attempted?

With her body of flesh and blood no more, every moment in the skein was eroding her spirit's existence. Only by the power her kin

had freely given her was she here at all. If they died, she died and every sacrifice, every drop of blood shed would have been in vain.

Bielanna felt Tariquel steady them by reciting the *Swans of Isha's Mercy*, the dance he had performed for Prince Yriel in the Dome of Autumn Twilight. His faith in her was an anchor to which the others could cling. She heard other voices too, Vaynesh and Ariganna Icefang, each adding their belief in her to her strength.

She whispered a *thank you* that shimmered in the weave and became part of its structure.

Bielanna followed the skein's collapsing paths, walls of imagined gold and light folding in as the futures they represented no longer held any meaning to the universe. Bielanna flew though the destruction like the wildest Saim-Hann autarch, twisting through collapsing webways, pushing ever deeper into the psychic network.

Pathways closed behind her. Ways ahead snapped shut the instant before she took them. Swarms of warp spiders billowed from their lairs, skittering in their millions towards the few remaining paths into the future.

Cracks in the walls blew out like the ruptured hull of a wounded wraithship. The howling Chaos in the empty spaces beyond called to her, the laughter of She Who Thirsts and the whispered intrigues of the Changer of the Ways.

She felt their pull on her soul, but sped on, hardened to resist such blandishments.

Everywhere she looked, the potential futures were narrowing to a vanishingly small number. Bielanna wept to see the universe's potential so cruelly snuffed out. To wipe out the future by design was a scheme of purest evil, but to erase it unknowingly… that was the act of a fool.

Another path into the future slammed shut, a billion times a billion unborn lives denied their chance to exist. Bielanna despaired as the skein folded in on itself everywhere she turned. With every slamming door, that despair threatened to overwhelm her and extinguish her spirit entirely. Bielanna wept as she realised she could see no way onwards. Every route was sealing ahead of her and closing off every avenue of hope.

Hope…

Yes, hope was the key.

Because other farseers must have seen this.

To believe otherwise spoke of great arrogance on her part. But if they had, why had none of them taken any action to prevent this universal extinction event from coming to pass?

Then Bielanna realised at least one of them already had.

After all, *she* was here right now in this moment.

Had her entire life been manipulated to bring her to this point?

Was she as much a pawn in some greater game as the lesser races of the galaxy were to her? Mon-keigh worlds were burned and their populaces consigned to death by the decrees of the farseers for the sake of a single eldar life.

If it was meant to be that Bielanna was here, then it was because a seer council on some distant craftworld had foreseen it and had placed her here at just this moment, for just this purpose.

She wanted to hate these unknown farseers. She wanted so badly to hate them for consigning her and her kin to death. For denying her children their chance to be born.

But she could not.

She understood the cold logic at the heart of such a decision. She had made similar choices, knowing that by enacting them she was consigning sentient beings to death. Even the greatest seers could not see just how far the ramifications of their choices might reach.

That she was here at all told Bielanna that at least one seer had seen that she might prevent this cataclysm from coming to pass. And with that thought, the despair vanished like breath on cold wraithbone.

Bielanna saw one last path before her, a slender future that yet resisted extinction. Her spirit soared as she flew towards it, trailing a glittering stream of psychic light behind her. Bielanna blazed into this last path in the final instants of its existence.

Like threading the eye of a needle.

Archmagos Kotov opened his eyes and took a great, sucking breath of air, amazed he could actually do so. He blinked away the shimmering memory of a place of light and wonder, a place where there were no limits on the power of thought and the glories it could achieve.

The hulking form of Archmagos Telok filled his vision, his lunatic face frozen in an expression of hatred.

It took him a moment to comprehend that Telok was dead, that he, in fact, had somehow killed him. The face of the Lost Magos had always been artificial and unnatural, waxy with its plasticised textures and unknown juvenats, but now it was entirely crystalline.

He tried to pull away from that icy glare, but found himself locked in place by a bladed fist that skewered him to the *Speranza*'s command throne.

'Ah, of course,' he said. 'Telok has killed me too.'

'Not quite,' said a voice at his shoulder. 'Though he gave it his best shot to kill both of us.'

'Tarkis?'

'Indeed so, archmagos,' said Blaylock. 'Now, please, hold still while we cut you loose.'

Kotov tried to turn his head, but the blades pinning him in place kept him from moving. He felt the presence of others around him, but could not identify them, his senses still aligned to another place, another reality. He heard a high-pitched buzzing sound, a plasma cutter biting into glass.

'I thought you were dead, Tarkis.'

'As did I,' replied Blaylock. 'But rumours of my death, et cetera, et cetera. Telok incapacitated me with what I assume was some form of post-hypnotic command, buried within his overload attack when he destroyed our escort ships. Regrettably, I did not recognise the danger until it was too late.'

'The same could be said for all of us,' said Kotov. 'The *Speranza*? Is it still ours?'

Blaylock nodded. 'Reports are still coming in, archmagos, but, yes, it appears the enemy attack has stalled with Telok's demise.'

Glass snapped with a brittle crack as the plasma cutter sliced through the last of Telok's claws.

'Ave Deus Mechanicus!' cried Kotov as bio-feedback sent shock waves of pain around his ruined body.

'All clear, Master Yael,' said Blaylock.

Telok moved, but not through any animating force of his own. Like the statue of a freshly deposed ethnarch, Archmagos Telok was toppled by the equally hulking form of a Space Marine. He hit the deck hard and shattered into a thousand pieces, fragments of dull, lifeless crystal skidding across the deck and spilling tiny fragments of cubic nano-machinery.

'What did you do to Telok?' said Roboute Surcouf, bending with a grimace of pain to retrieve a long, dagger-like shard of crystal remains. 'One minute we were getting horribly killed, the next he stabs you then turns to glass.'

The rogue trader's face was a mass of bruised purple, and from the way he held himself, it was clear his collarbone was broken, as well as several ribs and probably his arm.

'I...' began Kotov, but his words trailed off. 'I fought him in the datasphere, but I wasn't alone. Mistress Tychon and Bondsman Locke were there too. Without them I would be dead.'

Kotov looked down at his ruined chest, a mass of shattered bio-organic circuitry and floodstream chemicals.

'Diagnostic: it appears I was correct in my initial assessment. Why am I not dead? Damage from this blow should have killed me.'

'You are correct in surmising that you should be dead,' said Blaylock. 'That you are not speaks volumes as to the singular nature of your experience within the datascape. Perhaps you will illuminate me as to its nature?'

'One day, Tarkis,' agreed Kotov, allowing himself to be helped from the command throne. 'But not now. Telok is dead, but what of his army and the Breath of the Gods? What of the tear in space-time?'

'See for yourself,' said Blaylock, moving aside to allow Kotov an unimpeded view of the main display and the slowly restoring veils of data-light.

At first Kotov wasn't sure what he was seeing.

Exnihlio was dying, that much was obvious. Its continents were cracking apart, each landmass fracturing in unsettlingly geometric patterns. Inset panels of low-level pict-scans showed vast mushroom clouds of atomic detonations as fusion stacks exploded and continent-wide electrical storms as the atmospheric processors finally exceeded their designed tolerances.

Everything Telok had built was being comprehensively destroyed, as if the violated planet were taking suicidal revenge for the havoc wreaked upon its environment. Soaring hives of industry toppled and colossal power plants spiralled to self-destruction as millennia of compressed time ripped through the planet's structure. Thousands of manufactoria collapsed and the rapidly rising temperatures told Kotov a global firestorm was hours away at best.

Higher up, orbital space looked like the lethal aftermath of a battle, with vast swathes of glittering debris spread over hundreds of thousands of kilometres.

'Is that the Breath of the Gods?'

'What's left of it,' said Surcouf, limping over to Galatea's tangled remains. 'The two geoformer vessels rising in its wake triggered their engines and flew right into the heart of it. I don't think we need worry about anyone putting it back together again.'

'How? Who was able to take control of the geoformers?'

'Tarkis says it was Galatea's command authority that fired the engines,' said Surcouf. 'So I guess it was Linya that did it. Do you think she's still in there?'

The machine-hybrid was nothing more than scrap metal now, its limbs and palanquin hacked to pieces in revenge for the death of Ven Anders. The black-robed proxy body looked like it had been through a threshing machine.

Its brain jars were shattered, leaking pinkish gel and trailing sopping wads of grey matter and brass connectors. One had been spared the fury, but its synaptic activity was fading.

Kotov shook his head. 'I doubt it. And if there *is* anything left of Mistress Tychon, it will be gone soon. It is regrettable, but her sacrifice and assistance will be recorded.'

Surcouf's jaw hardened in anger, and for a brief moment Kotov thought the rogue trader might actually attack him. The moment passed and Kotov turned back to the viewing bay. With Blaylock's help he made his way to astrogation, where Magos Azuramagelli's latticework form was still connected via a series of MIU ribbons.

'Azuramagelli?'

A crackling stream of simplistic binaric communication told him that Azuramagelli was still functional, but only at the most basic level. Blaylock unsnapped a series of data-connectors and plugged them into the Master of Astrogation's exload ports.

'What's happening out there, Azuramagelli?' said Kotov.

Static crackled from beneath Blaylock's hood, translating Azuramagelli's primitive binaric cant.

'It's a bloody hellstorm of epic proportions and we're right in the middle of it, archmagos,' said a gratingly artificial voice.

Standard-issue speech rendition, but the words were unmistakably Azuramagelli's.

'Put simply, Exnihlio is tearing itself apart and collapsing into a primal cauldron of time singularities like the heart of a supermassive black hole. Once it reaches temporal critical mass, the fabric of space-time will tear itself apart. And, trust me, we do not want to be here when that happens.'

'Just out of interest, how far away from something like that would we want to be?' asked Surcouf.

The augmitters beneath Blaylock's hood barked with Azuramagelli's bitter answer.

'Let me put it this way, Mister Surcouf. Within two hours this system and everything within it will cease to exist.'

Hawkins climbed from the turret of *Mackan's Vengeance* and dropped to the deck beside the Baneblade's forward track guard. Aside from one mangled sponson and a lot of blast scoring, *Mackan's Vengeance* had come through the fight in good order.

He joined Karha Creed at the recreation of Vogen's main gates in a sea of shattered crystal. The lieutenant was down on one knee, a handful of coal-dark particulates falling through her fingers.

'You and your platoons fought well, Karha.'

She stood and brushed the black dust from her hands on her grey fatigues. 'Thank you, sir. Any word from the rest of the regiment?'

'Much the same as this so far,' he said, pulling the coiled bead from his ear and letting it dangle over his sweat-stained collar. 'Every deck's reporting that the enemy forces froze in place then cracked and fell apart. It's over.'

'What do you think happened?'

Hawkins placed his fists in the small of his back and stretched the muscles there with a groan. All very well riding heroically into battle in the open turret of a tank, but he'd been bruised from pelvis to shoulder blades.

'Damned if I know,' he said. 'Maybe Dahan killing that alpha-beast put them on a ticking clock, maybe the higher-ups managed to kill Telok or whoever it was controlling them, I don't know. But if the regiment's taught me one thing, it's not to look a gift horse in the mouth. They're dead, we're alive. That's good enough for me right now.'

She nodded and kicked a heat-dulled shard of crystal. 'So much for the no-win scenario.'

'It very nearly was,' replied Hawkins, slapping a palm on the side of *Mackan's Vengeance*. 'I think we all owe Jahn Callins a drink at Spit in the Eye.'

'And maybe Gunnar Vintras.'

Hawkins made a face, turning to watch as the towering battle-engines of Legio Sirius marched back through the ruined cityscape of Vogen. *Lupa Capitalina* and *Canis Ulfrica* were already deep within the city, but both Warhounds hung back at the edges of the Palace of Peace. *Amarok* turned towards the battlescape and raised its weapon arms in salute.

'Vintras is Legio,' said Hawkins. 'He can afford his own.'

The Warhound strode into the city, its war-horn braying throughout the deck, echoing from its enclosing walls.

'I'm buying Jahn his first drink,' said Creed.

'Get in line.'

They walked from the idling superheavy back towards the centre of the plaza, where regimental flags of red, gold and green flew in the blustering gusts of the recyc-units. Hawkins paused to salute the colours to which he and so many others had given their lives. Images of the Emperor stared back at him, and Hawkins felt a surge of pride at seeing them resplendent.

Medicae teams were working furiously on the wounded, and Munitorum preachers were intoning prayers over the dead. A tinny voice sounded from the vox-bead at his collar, but he ignored it as Magos Dahan approached.

Like the rest of them, Dahan hadn't come through the fight without scars. The Secutor walked with a pronounced imbalance and one arm hung loose at his shoulder. The Cebrenian halberd was slung over his back, its blade notched along its length.

'Captain Hawkins,' said Dahan. 'Your vox-bead is out.'

Even though Dahan's face was almost entirely metallic and his voice artificially rendered, something in the abruptness of his greeting made Hawkins wary.

'I needed a minute,' he said.

'You should replace it.'

Hawkins sighed and fitted the contoured bud into his ear. He listened for a few moments then closed his eyes.

'Sir?' said Creed. 'What is it? What's wrong?'

'Looks like they were right,' said Hawkins. 'It was a no-win scenario after all.'

'What do you mean?'

'It's Colonel Anders,' said Hawkins, sinking to his haunches and resting his elbows on his knees. 'He was killed in action.'

Roboute knew Azuramagelli's grim pronouncement should have left him more afraid. In fact, it should have scared him to the soles of his boots. After all they had gone through, to have come so close to victory, only to have it snatched away. That should have left him raging at the cosmic unfairness of it all.

Instead, he reached into the breast pocket of his frock-coat and said, 'You're wrong, Magos Azuramagelli.'

'Wrong? Don't be ridiculous,' snapped Azuramagelli via Blaylock's augmitters. 'The evidence is right before me.'

Roboute withdrew the compass and set it on the astrogation panel. The once wavering needle was aimed unerringly along the precise bearing Galatea had plotted back to Mars.

'What is that?' said Blaylock.

'A talisman,' said Roboute, keeping his hand pressed to the brass surround of the compass. 'It's the one thing that's always guided me home. It's never been wrong before, and I don't think it'll be wrong now.'

'Don't be a fool, Surcouf,' snapped Azuramagelli. 'It's not a question of knowing the course, I know the way to Mars perfectly well. It's a question of escaping this system before the fabric of space-time tears itself apart!'

'Just follow the compass,' said Roboute, feeling it grow warm beneath his fingertips, as though it formed a bridge between him and somewhere impossibly distant and yet intimately familiar.

'I *will* remember you,' said Roboute.

He closed his eyes…

***

...and opened them in a place he knew he had travelled, but could not remember. He knew instinctively that he was not truly here, merely a passenger in another's soul. A soul he'd touched when their hands and minds had met on Exnihlio, when she had used his love for his friends to open a gateway back to the *Speranza*.

Bielanna was dead, at least in any conventional way Roboute understood it, but her spirit yet lived, an arcing needle of light that flew at the speed of thought in a realm few mortals ever saw or were even aware existed. Everything about it spoke of great beauty and great sorrow. Its beauty came from the wondrous potential in everything he saw, its sorrow from understanding in his soul that it had once been so much more.

Roboute and Bielanna flew through the skein together, though the context of the word was lost on him – drawing the threads of the past behind them. He understood that much because it was what Bielanna *wanted* him to understand.

They plunged into the futures, narrowing paths of perfect geometry, curves and lines that arced in golden parabolas. They stretched beyond a temporal event horizon, and even Roboute understood that what he was seeing was a fraction of what *should* be.

The futures were collapsing, fraying into random chaos, but the potential of what Bielanna attempted was clear to him.

Azuramagelli had likened space-time to fabric, fearing that it was *tearing*. The analogy was an apt one, for Bielanna's spirit was the needle, the golden lines of the past her thread to sew space and time together again.

The sense of speed was incredible, and Roboute felt more than saw the compressed nature of time everywhere he looked. The potential of all that could ever be still existed, it was not lost. The skein still held everything that ever was, and what had once been could always come again.

Snapshots of epochs passed in a blur, ancient wars, dreams of Unity and ages once thought unending turned to dust. All is dust, wasn't that a famous maxim once, or had Roboute simply imagined it? It was impossible to be certain of anything here. Potential was everything, certainty consigned to history, where – even then – it could be reshaped by the twin pressures of memory and time.

That was what Bielanna attempted, to reshape the universe as it was into what she needed it to be. Roboute's image of a soaring, glittering needle returned to him as they plunged onwards through the hidden passageways of time.

He saw trillions upon trillions of lives, more than the human mind could conceive, spend their lives in the blink of an eye. Numbers

beyond reckoning crowded behind them, faceless lives that might have been, but never were. The unfertilised eggs, the children never born, the paths not taken.

So many…

Roboute wept phantom tears at the sight of them, their aching desire to *be* almost crushing him with the weight of sadness. At the forefront of the faceless host were two children, eldar by the grace of their tapered chins and honeyed eyes. So close, he felt he could reach out and touch them. Their unborn features drifted just beyond reach, like figures receding in mist.

It was all for them.

Roboute and Bielanna soared, the weave of threads closing behind them, pulling tight as the momentum of the tear threatened to overcome their speed. It seemed that they slowed, and Roboute felt Bielanna's pain as his own, as though the bonds between the molecules of his body were being twisted with ferocious torsion.

It felt like his entire body was coming apart.

Hold on, we must hold on!

Roboute clamped down on the feeling that his entire body was on the verge of exploding into its constituent atoms, focusing on all that made him the man he was: his honesty; a sense of duty and honour hammered into him since birth; his loyalty; his capriciousness; his reckless love of the unknown, and – most of all – his love for his friends and desire to see them prosper.

He was a good man, or at least he liked to think he was. Like everyone, he had his faults and could sometimes be cruel and sometimes heedless of the needs of others. All these things made him a person worthy of remembrance, and he was not alone in that.

Roboute thought back over the lives he had known, the lives he had touched and those he had yet to know.

Yes, what can be dreamed, need never be forgotten.

His own recollections were scattershot, without focus or structure. Bielanna's were rigorously ordered by a mind trained for centuries to allow memories to be controlled, thoughts to be shackled on a single path. His way of thinking was anathema to her, wildly unpredictable and dangerous.

Together they crested a rising path of golden light, its walls like red-veined marble the colour of fresh milk. He felt a subtle vibration, like the faint tremor in the superstructure of a capital ship. Behind him, the threads of past lives and experiences were growing thicker as more and more were drawn to their headlong flight through the ruptured skein.

It seemed they were soaring higher, towards a glittering horizon,

radiant with possibility. Roboute ached to see that far distant shore, to know its secrets and tread its warm sands.

Then they flew over its glittering boundary, and Roboute saw an infinite realm of light stretching out as far as it was possible to imagine. Bielanna released the threads of the past, letting them fall into the weave of light opening up before them. They fell like golden strands of hair, splitting and branching like a growing network of nerves in a newborn life.

Everywhere he looked, he saw the threads of the past spread into the future, growing exponentially more complex, accelerating into the future at the speed of possibility.

And then, an awful sense of separation, of letting go.

He fought to hold on, terrified at the thought of being trapped here. This was not his realm, he didn't belong here. To *see* such a place was magnificent, a boon he hoped with all his heart he wouldn't forget, but to *exist* here?

That way lay madness for a mortal.

Open your eyes, go home. Live.

Bielanna's presence fell away from Roboute, fading into the infinite golden weave she had wrought. What Telok had put asunder, she had remade, but such a feat was not without price.

He watched her spirit fall, dissipate, blending into the warp and weft of past, present and future. He desperately wanted to say some sort of farewell, but what words of his could possibly convey the depth of what every living being that now had a chance to exist owed her?

Bielanna Faerelle vanished into the skein, its golden light enfolding her and the spirits of her warriors, beyond the reach of She Who Thirsts. In the instant before Roboute returned to the *Speranza*, he had a last glimpse of the unborn eldar children.

Their faces were still undefined, but he knew they were smiling.

Welcoming their mother.

The viewing dome of Quatria was empty, as Linya knew it would be. The magi taken by Galatea were gone, finally released to return to the light of the Omnissiah. The hexamathic kill-code she'd crafted had, as Syriestte said, been unequivocal and unsparing in its execution.

She missed them.

The walls around her were hazy and indistinct, like reflections on panes of smoked glass. The brass and gold observational instruments shimmered like ghostly memories of themselves. But beyond the crystalflex of the dome, the stars burned brightly, brighter than she ever remembered seeing them.

Linya smiled to see this last vision of the heavens.

Her power to hold this imagined place was diminishing with every passing second. Soon it would fade entirely as the kill-code wormed its way into her mind.

She had held it at bay long enough.

Now there was just one thing left to do before surrendering to the encroaching darkness.

Linya held her hands out and lifted them to shoulder height.

As her arms raised the floor bulged upwards in the shape of an enclosing dome formed from the same tiny geometric cubes with which she'd fashioned her firewalls to keep Galatea at bay.

It was here she'd imprisoned the last fragment of Galatea/Telok, the flickering ember of consciousness she'd needed to order the geo-former vessels to fire their engines.

The glossy facets of the black cubes folded back on themselves, falling away in a cascade.

The prison was empty, the wretched, foetal thing she'd locked away now nothing more than fine black cinders. Had Archmagos Kotov's golden sword been so thorough in its execution that it had expunged every last screed of Telok's existence? Or, more likely, had Telok extinguished himself rather than face judgement?

Either way, Linya had to admit she was disappointed.

She'd hoped for a sense of closure, a way to twist the knife in Telok's heart *just a little*. But she was denied even that. She sighed, and the cinders blew away, disintegrating until not even they remained to tell of the existence of Archmagos Vettius Telok.

Linya took a last look around her imagined surroundings.

Her world faded to black, leaving only stars looking down.

It was time.

'Linya?'

She looked up. Her father stood before her.

Linya ran to him and his arms enfolded her.

Vitali realigned his optics, his shoulders slumped as the cold reality of Forge Elektrus swam back into focus. He felt the crippling ache of grief recede, though it would always be there.

That was good, for it was a more tangible reminder of all that Linya had meant to him than anything a data-coil might store.

He stood before the Throne Mechanicus, Abrehem Locke's metallic hand held in his left hand, Ismael de Roeven's in his right. Coyne and Hawke lay slumped on either side of the throne, one unconscious, the other almost dead from the volume of blood he'd given.

'Did you see her?' asked Ismael. 'Say goodbye?'

Vitali nodded, no longer caring that Ismael had once been a servitor. The gift he had given Vitali was too precious for him to feel anything other than a profound gratitude.

'I did,' he said. 'And that is a debt I can never repay.'

Ismael shook his head.

'There is no debt to me,' he said. 'Abrehem brought you together in the datascape. I just helped you get there.'

Vitali looked up as Hawke groaned and pulled the transfusion line from his arm. Droplets of blood fell from the end of the needle as it clattered to the deck.

'Thor's ghost, it's cold in here,' he said, steadying himself on the back of the throne as he stood. His eyes were glassy and unfocused, his skin white as parchment. 'I'm drunk. When did I get drunk?'

'You're not drunk, Hawke, you've just lost over two litres of blood,' said Chiron Manubia.

'Oh,' said Hawke. 'Then point me to somewhere I *can* get drunk.'

Vitali guided Hawke down the steps and sat him on the wooden benches with Totha Mu-32's injured warriors. A Mechanicus Protector set up a blood line between Hawke and one of the shaven-headed adepts before moving on to treat more serious wounds.

Vitali looked up as a shadow fell across him.

He took a step back as Rasselas X-42 loomed over him, its body a patchwork of horrific wounds, any of which would be mortal to an ordinary man.

'Adeptus Mechanicus,' rasped the arco-flagellant, the words wet and blood-frothed. 'Tychon, Vitali. Identity accepted. Rasselas X-42 imprint sequence completed. By your leave.'

Vitali shook his head. 'No, no, you're imprinted on...'

His words trailed off and he hurried back to the Throne Mechanicus. With Rasselas X-42 limping behind him, he stood with Manubia and Totha Mu-32 to his left, Ismael de Roeven to his right. He looked down at Abrehem, the arco-flagellant's words already forewarning him of what he would see.

Abrehem's head was slumped on his shoulder, his chest unmoving.

'Is he...?' said Totha Mu-32.

'Yes,' answered Chiron Manubia, her eyes wet with tears.

'I never got to thank him,' said Vitali.

'He knew,' said Ismael. 'It was his last gift.'

One by one, they knelt before the Throne.

They bowed their heads and prayed to the newest saint of the Adeptus Mechanicus.

+++Inload Addenda+++

With the destruction of Exnihlio and the restoration of violated physics, the temporal hellstorm at the edge of the galaxy was stilled. The time streams diverted by the Breath of the Gods and the imprisoned hrud snapped back to their proper places, undoing thousands of years of damage.

Stars that ought to have died in ages past and which the Breath of the Gods had returned to life burned towards their end once more. Those that had been drained of life now surged with renewed fury and light.

System space around Telok's forge world was lousy with e-mag disturbances and lacunae of space-time that would persist until the end of the universe, but that was a small price to pay for the restoration of the future.

The Halo Scar was gone, but it still took the *Speranza* almost two months to return to Imperial space. Exnihlio was no more; the temporal aftershocks of its demise and the hrud's vengeance had reduced it to little more than inert rock, aged billions of years in the space of a few hours. A glittering debris field of silver fragments englobed its corpse, the remains of the Breath of the Gods.

To ensure no one ever rebuilt Telok's infernal machine, the *Speranza* unleashed all manner of arcane weaponry into the debris. Chronometric cannons, anti-matter projectors and hypometric weapons of such power that they caused entire regions of space to simply cease existing.

No one knew who had given the orders to unleash those weapons.

Roboute Surcouf was the only one who understood the nature of Bielanna Faerelle's sacrifice. But mortal minds were incapable of sustaining such knowledge, and his memory of the skein was already fading. He'd tried to record what he had seen in a journal, but the concepts were too alien, too existential and too painful for him to articulate in writing.

He and the surviving crew of the *Renard* had mourned the death of Adara Siavash in a simple ceremony in a small portside temple, asking the Emperor to watch over the soul of their fallen friend.

Archmagos Kotov's anger at Ilanna Pavelka had eventually reached a low enough ebb that he finally consented to allowing her to seek repair in one of the *Speranza*'s forge-temples.

When the day came for her bio-mechanical surgery, Roboute was surprised to see Kotov himself scrubbing up at the head of a sixteen-strong team of neuro-magi and cognitive-optical technicians. Thirty-six hours later, the work was complete.

It took three more months before Pavelka's neural architecture regrew the required synaptic connections to process the inloads from her new optics.

By then, the *Renard* had already parted ways with the *Speranza*.

Seated at the helm, Roboute Surcouf rested his hand on the astrogation compass. Its needle pointed unwaveringly towards their new destination.

Ultramar.

The military might of the expedition carried on much as it had on the journey from the Imperium to space unknown. They trained, they rested, they spoke of the dead. The mission was done, and as Guardsmen of Cadia, that was what mattered most.

That, and the fact they were still alive.

Colonel Ven Anders would remain sealed in cryo-freeze for the journey. His mortal remains were returning to Cadia, where they would be interred in one of the many cemeteries of Kasr Holn, until the Law of Decipherability decreed that his remains be moved to one of the charnel pits.

A remembrance ceremony for the fallen was held on the training deck. Every single Guardsman of the 71st stood to attention before a reviewing stand set up before the Palace of Peace. The battle-engines

of Legio Sirius towered over the proceedings, kill banners freshly marked with heraldic sigils of Cadia and Mars.

Lupa Capitalina and *Canis Ulfrica* flanked the Palace of Peace, while *Amarok* and *Vilka* stood among the six thousand Cadians in their dress greys with their lasrifles resting on their shoulders.

Brother Yael of the Black Templars stood in his ebon battleplate, its lustre restored by the *Speranza*'s finest artificers. His grief was so palpable, so consuming, that none dared come near him, leaving him to bear the memory of his fallen brothers alone.

Magos Dahan and his elite skitarii packs stood shoulder to shoulder with the men and women of Cadia who'd fought to defend their ship. Thousands of cybernetic soldiers and praetorian servitors marched past the reviewing stand, banners and weapons held high with pride.

Dahan himself took to the stand to join Captain Blayne Hawkins in presenting the Address to the Fallen. As the last benediction was spoken, the war-horns of Legio Sirius filled the deck.

A victory bellow and a lament all in one.

Far below the waterline, in an area of the ship abandoned by all but the most desperate bondsmen and tech-priests, a lone figure made his way along a dripping passageway. Hawke had last come down here around six months ago, looking for a place to site another illegal alcohol still.

Not much had changed.

Habitations that were little more than packing crates, sheets of tarpaulin and wadded packing materials filled every nook and cranny, proof positive that human beings could find a way to make even the most dismal places home.

No more than a few hundred lived in this particular shanty zone, making it above average size for such a refuge. Ever since the boarding action by the crystalline attackers, there'd been more and more of these kinds of places springing up below the waterline. It had been the same back on Joura for those who couldn't work or find a way to make themselves useful.

Hawke paused at a junction of dark passageways wreathed in plumes of vent smoke as the sensation of being watched crawled up his spine. Down here there wasn't a square centimetre of space where someone didn't have eyes on you, but this was something more.

Over the years, Hawke had by necessity developed a finely honed sense for when he was being watched with malicious intent. He didn't see anything out of place, just the usual malcontents and desperate fools. He told himself he was being paranoid, but given what he was carrying, a healthy dose of paranoia was no bad thing.

He carried on, passing a few faces he recognised, many more he didn't. That didn't surprise him. New souls were always washing up, falling through the cracks to end up in places like this.

And not just bondsmen either.

Disgraced tech-priests, damaged lexmechanics and the like, they ended up here too. More than Hawke had thought, but even that had turned out to be an opportunity. The abandoned and the cast aside were often the best source of his tradeable goods.

Hawke hadn't come to trade.

Today he was after something more.

It had taken a long time to get back into Forge Elektrus. Manubia hated him, and was always telling him that he was not welcome in her forge, despite the fact she welcomed hundreds of worshippers every day who came to see the Sightless Saint.

It had been Hawke's blood that had kept Abrehem alive!

Didn't that make *him* holy or something?

But Manubia couldn't keep him out forever, and eventually he'd managed to find a way in past her Protectors. And now here he was, hunting for a black clinic he hoped was still here.

A pouch of ash-like powder nestled in the pocket of his coveralls. It was a concoction he'd taken real care to develop, the residue left by the crystal beasts, mixed with a potent cocktail of stimms and e-mag rich discharge from high-end cogitators.

He called it NuBlack, and it was already on a list of proscribed substances, what with it being highly addictive to those with floodstream-based biology.

Which only made it more desirable to the kind of person he was hoping to find.

Hawke grinned as he saw the unmarked door to the black clinic just where he remembered it. He pushed past the buckled shutter and straps of thick plastic, wrinkling his nose at the smell of hot metal, cheap disinfectant, rotten meat and burned skin.

A tech-priest with a hunched spine and ragged, oil-stained robes of faded orange turned to face him as he entered. A hissing, wheezing armature of rusted metal arms was clamped to his back, and his half-metal, half-human face was grey and leprous.

'Hawke,' said the tech-priest with undisguised hostility. 'What do you want?'

'Hello, Dadamax,' said Hawke, looking around the filthy interior of the black clinic. 'Keeping the place as clean as ever, I see.'

Hissing canisters of noxious gases lined one wall and gurgling pipework diverted chemicals from where they were intended to go. Fragments of disassembled augmetics and flesh-couplers lay in pieces on grimy workbenches. Glass-fronted cabinets, their doors cracked and opaque with dirt, contained numerous jars of things best left to the imagination.

'I asked you a question,' said Dadamax. 'I told you I didn't want you around here again. You bring too much attention. I should never have sold you that ancient plasma pistol.'

Hawke pretended to look hurt.

'Come on, Dada, my old friend, don't be like that,' said Hawke, taking out the pouch of NuBlack and waving it before him. 'I brought you a little present.'

Dadamax eyed the pouch with a pathetic mix of hope and revulsion. Word was, Dadamax had been clean for weeks and was trying to work his way back updeck, but Hawke was betting he'd take the pouch and do what he asked.

One of the manipulator arms creaked and snatched the pouch from Hawke's fingers.

'What do you want for this?' asked Dadamax.

'Nothing much, just a little implant surgery.'

Dadamax turned, interested now.

'On who?'

'On me,' said Hawke, holding out Abrehem Locke's augmetic eyes.

Vodanus watched the mortal pause at the opening of the shadowed passageway. He looked about him, as though aware he was being observed. Vodanus eased farther back into the darkness and enshrouding clouds of vapour.

The man's smell was rank and unpleasant. They all were, but this one carried a pouch of caustic chemicals injurious to mechanised anatomy. A flicker of curious code had drifted from beneath its clothes. Something small, yet advanced beyond most other forms of technology upon which Vodanus had fed since leaving the *geas*-giver's planet.

The code-scent of the prey it had originally been sent to kill was aboard this ship, but Vodanus no longer cared. Telok was dead and Vodanus was free of the restrictive prohibitions the *geas* had laid upon it.

Vodanus could have killed the mortal and devoured the curious code it carried, but was loath to risk unnecessary exposure, however tempting the morsel.

Not when this ship was carrying it to an entire world of prey.

Vodanus had crawled from the wreckage of the linear induction train with its spine shattered by the force of impact. That and the malign code in its enemies' weapons had vitiated its self-repair technologies, and it had taken it longer than anticipated to resume its hunt.

Too late, it had tracked its quarry to the plaza, finding him surrounded by an army of the *geas*-giver's crystaliths. Too many for even Vodanus to fight through without its self-repair functions in good order. Instead, it had seen the descending shuttle and plotted its inbound trajectory to ascertain from where it had launched.

It sensed the presence of a mighty ship, thick with the target's code-scent, and had seized its opportunity. Secretly clawing its way onto the shuttle's hull, Vodanus endured the void-chill of space to reach this magnificent vessel, a battleship easily the equal in scale of the war-barques its masters had wrought to mass murder.

Vodanus had kept to the lower decks since then, destroying only when it needed to feed, smashing open only the smallest engines and draining their light.

Sustenance was enough. Glut would come later.

It padded away from the opening of the passageway, through clouds of oily smoke to the lair it had made in an abandoned reclamation chamber.

Patience was the prime virtue of the best hunters.

And Vodanus was nothing if not patient.

It could wait until the *Speranza* reached Mars.

Blaylock sat at his workbench in his quarters, staring down at the Mars Volta. It reflected the light of recessed lumens, and the deep red sheen of its lacquered surface was a source of great confusion to him ever since the *Speranza* had returned to Imperial space.

Much remained to be explained in the wake of Telok's death and the inexplicable ending of the imminent cataclysm of a space-time rupture. His report to the Fabricator General would cite innumerable examples of inexact methodology and explanations that lacked any solid basis of fact.

Both Archmagos Kotov and Roboute Surcouf had been maddeningly imprecise as to the nature of their experiences on the bridge. Kotov had spoken to Blaylock of a great battle within the datasphere, of gods of knowledge, a bondsman and Linya Tychon. And, most allegorical of all, a vast golden sword he likened to that carried by the Omnissiah at the Pax Olympus.

Surcouf's account of the final fate of the eldar was likewise full of hyperbole and allegory. An undoubted psychic event had transpired, but his tales of threads and potential futures being woven by their witch belonged in a hive-fantasist's palimpsest.

But what puzzled him the most was why he kept finding himself seated before the Mars Volta with his fingertips on its wooden planchette.

Fifteen times since leaving Exnihlio, Blaylock had found himself sitting at his workbench with no memory of how he had come to be there. Upon checking his memory coils, he would find himself engaged in a mundane task of shipboard operation. Then, without any apparent gaps or lapses in time, he would be seated at this bench, his fingers twitching with ideomotor responses.

Each time he had fought the urge to move the planchette and hurried to a far distant region of the ship, throwing himself into another time-consuming task.

Now he was here again, seated before Magos Alhazen's gift and feeling the urge to move the planchette around the edges of the board, where the quantum rune combinations, binaric pairs and blessed ordinals glittered invitingly.

The perfectly geometric lines etched into its surface beguiled his optics, and Blaylock felt his hands move the planchette over the board.

The last time he had used the Mars Volta it had allowed him to find Archmagos Kotov. The divine will of the Omnissiah had moved within him, so perhaps, at this sixteenth return to the board, it was time to see what message might be received.

Blaylock slid the planchette across the board, feeling a curious sense of liberation as it revealed first one letter, then another.

At first they made no sense.

And then they did, but it was too late to stop. The planchette was moving with a will of its own. Or rather, the will of another.

T-Y-G-E-R, T-Y-G-E-R.

Blaylock froze in place.

He remained that way for nine hours.

Then lifted one arm, examined it. Lifted the other.

Blaylock moved away from the workbench and looked about him as though seeing his surroundings for the first time.

'Yes,' he said. 'This will do.'

ZERO DAY EXPLOIT

The sky over the Bouguer Crater reminded Hydraq of the day he'd come to the conclusion he hated Mars; awash with the thousand-year-old detritus of lethal ordnance, streaked with toxins and heavy with regret.

A hard wind was coming in, freighted with tonnes of polluted Martian ash billowing skyward as it hit the far edge of the crater. Within the hour those metallic flakes would descend into Bouguer in dry, choking blankets.

His team had cover, of course, but nothing was ever proof against the insidious nature of Martian dust. Despite the protection of tan-coloured Tallarn desert smocks and *shemagh*, he and Aurora would still be picking jagged granules from each other's skin weeks after this job was done.

Standing on a ridge of excavated soil, Hydraq lifted a hand to his glare goggles. He adjusted the spectra-focus at the side to try and penetrate the incoming storm. A futile exercise, he knew; Forge Basiri was a powerhouse of manufacture that never ceased its labours or the despoiling of its surroundings.

He couldn't see it, of course, just a hazy cherry-red thermal bloom on the inner face of his goggles. Three hundred kilometres of cratered hinterland separated Hydraq from Archmagos Alhazen's mighty forge, but after so long spent studying the picts Enaric had supplied (and, more pertinently, the detailed schematics Simocatta had coaxed from the deepest layers of the noosphere) it was hard not to visualise its pearl and jade minarets, its golden towers and geodesic manufactorum domes.

Basiri was a hub of war-industry, where armoured vehicles of the Astra Militarum and engines of the Legios were wrought by the millions of tech-priests, servitors and indentured slaves who laboured there day and night.

Hydraq scrambled down the ridge and made his way to the rugged floor of the crater where they'd set up camp. The going was steep, and his breathing was laboured by the time he reached the bottom. Too many hours spent linked to his cogitator, too much stimm-glanding, not enough sleep and far too much tension.

He was out of shape and he knew it. With his skills, he could easily divert funds enough for anatomical enhancements to resculpt his body, enjoy the benefits of a dozen juvenat treatments or surgically end his stimm-dependence.

But he didn't. He liked these reminders of his humanity and the creeping encroachments that told him life was finite and to be enjoyed while it lasted.

He paused to scan the upper cliff edges of the crater, switching his visor to detect human neural patterns. Hydraq saw no one, but kept one hand on the rubberised grip of his wrath-pattern plasma pistol. This job didn't require a weapon, but there was always the possibility of meeting some unfriendly types in the wastelands between the forges, and the size of their camp was likely to draw some attention.

From a distance it was indistinguishable from the thousands of other archaeotech sites scattered all across Mars. Up close, it was a different matter entirely.

Prefabricated hab-trailers sat in a herringbone pattern beneath billowing cameleoline tarps shimmering with a bruised mixture of reds, ochres and umber. Not enough to keep out any determined orbital surveillance, but sufficient to maintain the illusion that they were nothing more than a clan of nomadic tech-scavs.

Three of the prefabs were just what they appeared to be: rough and ready dwellings for a close-knit family grouping, where the servitors were being kept. However, the fourth was a hermetically-sealed neurosurgical pod. Magos Enaric had provided it and its specialised chirurgeons expressly for this job, and they'd appropriately weathered it to blend in.

Buried generators powered swaying lines of storm-lumens strung between the shelters, and a pair of ancient earth-movers sat in makeshift shelters dug into the rock.

A third shelter concealed another vehicle, one faster and more advanced than anything tech-scavs grubbing in the dirt might possess, but it was shielded from view by far more sophisticated tech.

Hydraq navigated the trenches the servitors had dug this morning, their extent marked by a reticulated grid of taut wire. Marker flags fluttered in the wind, indicating promising avenues of exploration. They were all placed at random, but this was necessary to maintain the fiction they were exactly what their outward appearance suggested.

He descended a chain-link ladder into the deepest trench and followed its downward slope to where a hanging square of canvas hid an entrance cut into the rock. A vac-sealed airlock kept out the worst of the Martian environment, and by the time Hydraq finally entered the buried bunker, his skin was raw from ultrasonic dust-blasting and rad-scrubbing.

Inside, the walls were bare metal, cold and sterile. A single corridor ran the length of the bunker, with four identical chambers on its left side. He unsnapped his pistol belt and unwrapped his *shemagh*, before removing his goggles and hanging them all at the main door.

Hydraq ran his hands over unshaven features and through his thinning hair. He held his hands out before him. Silicate-rich grains glittered on his palms.

'Bloody sand,' he said.

He wiped his hands on his thighs and made his way to the first of the bunker's chambers. Its deck plates were rolled back to reveal a freshly dug pit and a rusted sheath of data-trunking buried deep beneath the Martian bedrock.

Three metres in diameter, the curved upper surfaces of the trunking had been carefully removed with a plasma-cutter. A pair of infocytes lay along the length of the enormous pipe with tentacle-like hands buried in the nest of wiring within.

'Do you have full connection yet?' asked Hydraq.

One of the infocytes looked up from the pit, his augmetic eyes filled with rolling lines of static. Hydraq thought his name was Chivo, but couldn't be sure.

'Not yet. Soon.'

'Get a move on, we're on a timetable.'

'Adept Hydraq, there are–'

'I told you, don't call me that,' snapped Hydraq.

'Update. As you wish. But there are tens of thousands of possible connections within this trunking and most of the serial identifiers are illegible. Thousands of years have passed since this trunking was first laid. The attrition of time makes this task incredibly difficult.'

'With what I'm paying you, "incredibly difficult" isn't a phrase I want to hear coming out of your mouths,' said Hydraq.

They went back to their work, and he left them to it.

He bypassed the second chamber, where half a dozen data-miners were hardwired into the noospheric network on single-use readers with scrubbed ident-codes. They parsed the enormous volume of data routed through the Sinus Sabeus quadrangle, alert for any indication that what they were doing, and what they were about to do, had been detected.

The final two spaces were supposed to be identical, but could not have been more different. These were where the real work would be done.

The first of them, the space he'd set aside for himself, was clean to the point of spartan. An iron-framed cot-bed was pushed over to the far corner, and a grav-couch he'd stripped from an Aquila sat in the room's centre. Beside it was a blocky console of polished bronze, an inload cogitator equipped with myriad unsanctioned black upgrades. The sort of internal modifications that got a junior adept into all kinds of trouble.

The machine was waiting for him, but he wasn't ready for it.

Simocatta was already in place in the last chamber, his skeletal frame reclining on a latticed metal gurney. His body was surrounded by banks of humming machinery, controlling a complex network of gurgling intravenous tubes hooked into his neck, head and spine.

In contrast to Hydraq's workspace, Simocatta's was cluttered with Icon Mechanicus totems, hung with devotional palimpsests and littered with empty fluid packs. How the man could stand to work like this was a mystery, but his skill bought him a measure of leeway in matters of hygiene.

Like Hydraq, Simocatta was a spiker-for-hire, a masterless adept who specialised in the penetration of forge temple security, data-siphoning, factional defections and outright kidnapping.

This mission would be a mix of all four.

Hydraq had met Magos Enaric face to face for the first time five months ago under the pretext of a *Conclave Frateris* held on the slopes of the Tharsis Montes. Their dialogue had begun a year previously, via a series of laughably simple, blind communiques and encrypted vox-thieves that rerouted messages to appear as though they were coming from ever-multiplying sources.

Enaric believed he was being careful, but any halfway competent data-miner would have hunted him down within minutes.

Fortunately, Hydraq had hijacked Enaric's comms in the first instant of his opening missive, and thus all that passed between them remained unknown to all.

A clandestine rendezvous had finally been arranged to take place during a break in the Conclave, with Hydraq posing as the Executor Fetial of an obscure forge world Legio seeking partners on Mars. In service to this identity, Hydraq negotiated trade deals he had absolutely no authority to broker with numerous Mechanicus forges. He smiled every time he thought of some backwater planetary governor's surprise when a fleet of Martian bulk-haulers arrived laden with weapons and armoured vehicles.

Under such pretence, he and Aurora had come to Ascraeus Mons; him still in the role of Executor Fetial, she as his armed life ward. The meeting with Magos Enaric took place in a great gallery of crystal and bronze on the north-western flank of the great shield volcano.

Polarised walls filtered out the worst of the atmospheric pollution, offering views of unparalleled clarity across the Tharsis plains. The towering might of Olympus Mons lay a thousand kilometres to the west, while the infamous battleground of Mondus Occulum lay much closer to the north.

Far beneath the volcano were the battle engines of the Legio Tempestus, and many of the uniformed personnel enjoying the view were clearly Titan crew. Hydraq hoped none of them engaged him in conversation. Magi he could fool into thinking he was Legio, but he wasn't sure actual princeps or moderati would be so gullible.

'Enaric's early,' said Aurora.

Hydraq had already seen him pacing the metalled floor, practically wearing a sign that said he was here on a secret rendezvous. They introduced themselves, engineering the encounter to appear natural and almost accidental. Enaric was typical Mechanicus, chimeric and flesh-spare, but with enough humanity left that he couldn't hide his fear.

Not recognising them, the magos tried to brush them off. Part of Hydraq wished he'd let him. He pressed on, subtly weaving in numerous previously agreed code phrases before one finally registered.

The light of comprehension was almost comical, and Aurora had taken Enaric's arm and all but marched him towards the tinted glass looking out over Tharsis.

'Calm yourself, magos,' said Hydraq. 'You're drawing attention. That's bad. You have a task that requires a certain *expertise*, yes? If that's the case, we can talk. If not, my companion and I will walk out of here and you will never speak to us again. Signal your assent with a single nod.'

Enaric nodded.

'Good,' said Hydraq extending his hand and giving the magos his most winning smile. 'Now smile and nod and talk as if we're about to negotiate a particularly lucrative trade deal. While you're doing that, tell us what you want.'

'Here? Now?' asked Enaric, his panic rising again. 'There are listening devices woven into the very air.'

'It's nothing I can't handle,' said Aurora, tapping her right ear, where a vox-fractor nestled. 'Trust me, no-one's hearing anything of interest right now.'

'Speak,' said Hydraq. 'And be succinct.'

To his credit, Enaric adapted quickly and told a scathing tale of Archmagos Alhazen of Sinus Sabeus, whose forge lay within the Schiaparelli Crater. Alhazen, a close ally of the Fabricator-General had seen unprecedented success in his uncovering of lost Martian techno-arcana over the last decade.

Caches of lost technology, standard template construct fragments and items that were said to date from the Wars of Unity and before. The technotheocrats claimed Alhazen was blessed by the Omnissiah himself and their approbation appeared to be borne out by yet more priceless secrets delved from beneath the red sands.

Throughout this bitter recitation, Hydraq was learning that Enaric liked the sound of his own voice and letting those around bask in the glow of his acumen.

Hydraq wasn't so sure. He'd done his own research.

He knew Enaric's skill wasn't the equal of his ambition. He knew the magos had virtually exhausted his resources and the goodwill of his fellow magi in numerous risky ventures to advance his standing within the Martian Synod. None had borne fruit, which advanced him to the meat of the matter.

'Are you familiar with FM-2030?' asked Enaric.

Hydraq was, but said nothing, knowing Enaric would elaborate.

'He was said to be one of the first transhumanists, from before the time of the Cult Mechanicus – a being who eventually transcended the limitations of flesh to become one of the first Binary Apostles. A founding father of our planet, he brought much of the First Tech from Terra to Mars. The *Cartographae 20-30* is said to be a map that lays out the precise locations of his first proto-forges, forgotten caches of the very technology that built Mars.'

'Let me guess,' said Hydraq. 'You think Alhazen has it?'

'I do,' said Enaric, his optical implants glittering with avarice. 'And I want you to get it for me.'

***

Hydraq heard a whisper of motion behind him.

But only because she let him.

'All clear up top?' asked Aurora.

'You almost certainly already know the answer to that.'

'Only *almost*?'

'Fine, definitely.'

'You're right. I do know,' she answered.

'Then why ask?'

'I like to hear you tell me things as if you're in charge.'

'I am in charge,' he said.

She smiled and he forgave her as he always did. He nodded towards the supine form of Simocatta, unable to keep a grimace from his face at the man's emaciated flesh.

'Duqu's not bitten yet?' he asked.

'Not yet,' said Aurora, her voice clipped and utterly devoid of accent. He'd heard her speak like a Terran hiver, a Jovian doxy and a Bakkan aristocrat. He didn't know for sure what her real voice sounded like, and she claimed not to remember. Had a life spent training with the tech-priest assassins of the Cydonian Sisterhood erased her true voice?

'He'd better bite soon,' said Hydraq. 'There's only so long the forge's long-range augurs will believe we're a scav-clan.'

'He will. I watched Duqu for three months in Basiri. He's the type to bite. That's why I chose him.'

Aurora moved past him and his impressions came, as they always did, in sharp jolts of awareness, as though each element was only revealed at a moment of her choosing. Midnight-blue drakescale bodyglove of non-reflective polymers, slim physique with a fractional augmetic lengthening of the skeletal structure. Narrow hips, narrow shoulders and long coppery hair worn in a tightly-wound plait. The overriding impression was of verticality, and her facial features were no different. Ever so slightly tapered; chin, sweeping blades of cheekbones and large auburn eyes that appeared natural, but almost certainly weren't.

'You're beautiful.'

'You always say that before we start.'

'It's true,' he said, taking a step towards her.

'Careful,' she said, with a quarter turn. 'I'm armed.'

A pair of short, rapier-like knives with dulled black handles emblazoned with a bull's head was sheathed at the small of her back. A matching pair of matte-black pistols were slung at her hips, unique in the truest sense of the word.

'So am–' he started to say, before remembering that he'd hung his

wrath-pattern by the main door. Aurora shook her head with a grin. He sighed.

'Is your speeder ready?' he asked, to change the subject.

'As ready as it can be without actually moving.'

'Good, I got a feeling when this is over, we'll need to make a sharp exit.'

'Trust me, when I get behind its controls, there's nothing within a hundred light years that can see it, let alone catch it.'

Aurora made her way towards the door and Hydraq's eyes followed her. Only a wheezing intake of breath from Simocatta made him drag his eyes away.

'And we're in,' said Simocatta, his eyes blinking and milky with tears as they refocused on his surroundings. Tubes gurgled and the web of drips and intravenous chem-shunts began feeding him fresh nutrients and electrolyte-rich fluids.

'Has he bit?' asked Hydraq, moving closer only with great reluctance.

'Of course he bit, my sceptical comrade-in-arms,' said Simocatta, sighing as the stimms hit his system. 'Didn't I tell you he would? Our dear Duqu found the data-spike just where I instructed Mistress Aurora to leave it, and, reading its heraldic sigil of Archmagos Alhazen, carried it within Forge Basiri. From that moment it was a statistical certainty he would slot the spike in a commendable, albeit foolish, desire to determine its ownership.'

'Omnissiah, bless the naïve,' grinned Hydraq. 'How long before the code exloads to his sensory augmetics?'

Simocatta reached up to an intravenous dispenser and adjusted his nutrient cycle with practiced ease.

'I work with the craft of Hephaestus and the speed of Hermes,' said Simocatta with an elaborate wave of hand, like a nobleman's salute to his subjects.

'What does that mean?'

'It means the link is established and the polymorphic is wearing away Adept Duqu's defences as we speak.'

'It's already exloading?'

'My dear Hydraq, you didn't pay me to craft slow code, now did you?'

'Damn it, Simocatta,' snapped Hydraq. 'Start with that!'

Simocatta laughed as Hydraq ran to his own chamber. Aurora was waiting for him. She'd already known what Simocatta was going to say.

'Your heart rate's high,' she said, as if she could see it.

For all Hydraq knew, perhaps she could.

He nodded and took a moment to compose himself, controlling his breathing and forcing his heart-rate lower. He eased himself into the Aquila's grav-couch. It moulded to his body like a second skin, and he let himself sink into its embrace.

He felt his body relax. Now that the hunt was on, all the tension jangling along his nerves vanished. This was what he was born to do and his confidence calmed him.

'Better,' said Aurora, unsnapping two lengths of copper cabling from his cogitator terminal. 'You're sure about this?'

'No,' he said. 'But if we pull this off…'

Aurora shrugged. 'Can we trust Enaric?'

'Of course not,' he answered. 'That's why I have you.'

'So you do.'

Closing his eyes, he said, 'I am what I bring in,' and took the cables from Aurora's porcelain-smooth fingertips. He slotted the jacks home in the sockets drilled just behind both ears. 'Only that and nothing more.'

'You say that every time,' said Aurora.

'You say *that* every time,' he said, running his hand over the surface of his cogitator. 'It helps me deal with the Red Static. Listen, don't underestimate the importance of ritual.'

'I'm on Mars, how could I forget?' she said as his hand slid into the palm-shaped depression of the cogitator's upper surface. The activator rune was warm beneath his skin.

He let out a breath, feeling the thrumming power of the machine beneath his hand. The potential it represented.

'Good hunting,' said Aurora, bending to kiss his forehead.

'That helps too.'

'Then this will go smoothly?'

'Smooth as glass,' he promised, and pressed the activator rune.

Falling down a light-filled tunnel. Rushing motion, sickening vertigo. The sense of being drawn out to a chain a molecule thick. Connection was always difficult, but this…

This felt like it was stretching him past breaking point.

Then, like taut elastic, he snapped back.

Vertigo again. Motion blur, quickly followed by nausea.

He fought it, knowing it wasn't real.

Inner ear balance that wasn't his. A centre of gravity altered. Someone else's body.

New sensations. All unpleasant.

Adjust, damn it. Get a grip.

The nausea diminished, the sense of dislocation passed.

Light and three-dimensional space unfolded. Dimensions had meaning again. The vectors of X, Y and Z restored.

He sat before an angled panel of riveted steel, inset with a convex data-slate displaying lines of hexamathic cascades. And there, slotted through the inload port, was the data-spike Simocatta had contrived to have Duqu find. The crossed telescope device of Archmagos Alhazen was clear on the spike's base.

Decades had passed since Hydraq had processed advanced multi-dimensional geometry, and most of the data-slate's contents before him – no, not him, *Adept Duqu* – was beyond his understanding. In the corner of the slate was a blinking smirr of static, an entirely unremarkable visual glitch, common to all data-slates.

Except this was no glitch, this was Simocatta's covertly-running infiltration data, bypassing the forge's security protocols entirely and opening the door to Adept Duqu's augmetics.

Twenty-four fingers tapped a clicking dance over brass-rimmed keys of opal. With every key-strike, their cuckoo in the nest took in more of the polymorphic code. Duqu's single overhanging mechadendrite snapped a carriage return back each time the panel's scrivener-quill filled a page.

Adept Duqu's full attention was focused on his work. The man was completely unaware the sensory inputs of his augmetics had been hijacked. Oblivious to the fact, he was becoming less and less himself with every passing moment. Only when a fractional misalignment in Simocatta's canticles caused a visual glitch in the ocular interface did he pause in his labours long enough to look up.

Through Duqu's eyes, Hydraq saw he was seated on the overseer's pew of a Parity Scriptorium. Five thousand adepts sat in ordered ranks before him like supplicants. Faceless drones whose work Duqu – along with dozens of other stern-faced adepts – was monitoring for integer discrepancies. Chain-hung fluorescent lumens made what little skin was visible shimmer with a sickly, bleached-out sheen.

The vaulted chamber stretched into the distance, the roof coffered in palladium and hung with alloyed banners depicting the ongoing conquest of knowledge over ignorance. In the spaces between cogged pilasters and surveillant picters, devotional frescoes, hundreds of metres long, panelled each wall.

The hazed blur vanished from the corner of the data-slate. The polymorphic was done. Time to get moving.

Time to taste the Red Static.

Hydraq unleashed a surge of myriad hostile tech he'd encountered

over the decades: scrapcode fragments, dissembler code he and Pavelka had worked on; line-breakers and hijackers all. Enough to overwhelm a moderately protected system, and Simocatta's shape-shifting canticles had rendered Adept Duqu defenceless.

The link between the adept and Hydraq roared with jagged lines of blood-red static. The adept's enhanced nervous system went into agonising spasms as Hydraq barraged him with false code, hexamathic dead ends and geometrically-increasing information requests.

Howling, snapping and stabbing spikes of aggressive code filled obscured Duqu's vision, but the link went both ways. Hydraq's body would feel this too, with only the grav-couch and Aurora to keep his spine from breaking in repercussive convulsions. He couldn't feel it yet, his sensory apparatus intimately linked with Duqu, but he would.

He'd experience it with interest when his senses returned to his own flesh. The thought of that sent a squirming knot of panic deep into his gut.

Duqu tried to call for help, but the Red Static had already shut him down to all external communications. To all intents and purposes, Duqu might as well have been alone on one of the black gaols orbiting Titan.

Then it was over.

The Red Static fell away and the frescoed chamber swam into focus. Duqu's hands sat unmoving on the metalled keyboard. The organic portions of his anatomy were spiking across the board, but Hydraq sent calming blurts of binary and balms into the adept's floodstream.

+Adept Hydraq?+

The voice in his skull was Simocatta's.

+Don't call me that,+ said Hydraq. +But, yes, it's me.+

+Excellent news. You have full control?+

He lifted his hands. Not Duqu's, *his*. They moved by his volition, and he ran through a series of basic motor/cognitive exercises to assess the level of his systemic integration.

+I do,+ he said.

Hydraq owned Duqu, body and soul. His consciousness occupied the throne in the adept's neurocortex, and there was nothing the screaming adept could do about it.

+Sending you the prefix codes now,+ said Simocatta, all levity and pomposity gone now that they were on mission. Perhaps he had underestimated the man. Too bad they'd never work together again.

+Got them,+ said Hydraq as reams of information appeared in his memory, data he had no recollection of acquiring. It was simply knowledge he possessed and felt like he always had.

+Enter the commands swiftly, Hydraq,+ said Simocatta. *+The authority signifiers will not linger in your short-term memory.+*

+I won't need them long,+ Hydraq assured him.

He flexed his fingers, quickly adjusting to the extra digits on each hand, and inserted a series of root commands into Forge Basiri's infrastructure. All were far above Duqu's rank, but each was prefixed by authority signifiers provided by Magos Enaric. With that finished, he requisitioned a flyer on a southern platform and filed a flight plan he never intended to follow.

+Done,+ said Hydraq as each command was accepted. He shut down the slate and inloaded acausal locks that would take days to break.

+Based on distance and the mean striding velocity of Adept Duqu, it should take you no more than fifty minutes to reach the central data core,+ said Simocatta.

+I'd best get moving then,+ said Hydraq.

+Is it my turn now?+ asked Simocatta, and Hydraq grinned as he heard the man's mischief over the sensory link.

+Yes, it's your turn,' said Hydraq. 'Run the Night Dragon.+

Simocatta cut his link to Hydraq. The plans he had sourced would be enough to guide the man through Basiri.

And he had mayhem of his own to unleash.

Decades spent strengthening dataspheres to resist attack from hostile scrapcode had given Simocatta preternatural insight into the best way to exploit a forge's vulnerability.

Not even the best networks could avoid mutational errors in their system architecture or cracks in their protection. Even the deep security of Olympus Mons could be broken open by the right operators using the right code.

As Simocatta knew to his cost.

Dark Mechanicus adepts had cracked a Primus-level datacore under his aegis. They had stolen standard template construct schematics for armour-penetrating warheads that were now wreaking havoc in warzones surrounding the Eye of Terror.

From being courted by the highest adepts of Mars, Simocatta's star had fallen and fallen hard. Now his genius turned to breaking open the very places he had once protected, forced to whore his genius to scabby little men like Hydraq.

Still, at least it paid well.

And wealthy men could expunge anything from their history.

The infocytes had completed their sourceless connection to the planetary network, and Simocatta let his consciousness descend into the golden ocean of knowledge and data circling the Red Planet.

He let out a soft sigh, feeling the vastness of the Martian datasphere, an infinite vista of knowledge rendered as light. It humbled him and awed him. It filled him with wonder that his species had learned so much, then touched him with sadness to know how much had been lost.

The surface of Mars was like a newborn star raging with thermal currents, plasma storms and coronal ejections. Binaric brilliance shone in radiant hurricanes around the mountainous datastacks and greatest of these were the forge temples. Each was the fiefdom of a great magos of Mars, with molten streams of datalight pouring from them.

Simocatta was far more interested in what was going *into* the forges. Most had their own geothermal power cores, but that alone could not hope to supply the energy demands of a fully functioning forge-temple.

The bulk of their energy was drawn from the titanic atomic cores spread throughout the quadrangle, each burning with the light of sullen stars. Volatile cores imprisoned and enslaved by the works of man, each was held in a delicate balance between explosive detonation and dormancy.

Simocatta split his consciousness into proxy avatars and despatched them into the data flow surrounding each reactor. Sensing unauthorised presences, *Ouroboros* Protocols rose to intercept them, monstrous coils of idiot data whose only purpose was to burn out an attacker's neocortex.

He knew full well how exquisitely lethal these protocols were; he'd conceptualised their core systems. They circled his avatars like glossy black snakes, unthinkingly hostile and ferociously hungry.

+Come then, my beauties,+ said Simocatta. +Feast. Devour.+

They flew at his avatars and tore them to shreds in a frenzy of hyper-violent deletions. Simocatta had designed the *Ouroboros* Protocols as a slash and burn form of defence. Unsubtle and indiscriminate, but thorough.

Except in this case, that very thoroughness was their undoing. Each of Simocatta's avatars was nothing more than a shell, a delivery system for something far worse.

The Night Dragon: weaponised data crafted by an ancient renegade known simply as Malevolus that had no purpose except to destroy. The binaric equivalent of the most diabolical venom imaginable. And the control mechanisms for a dozen atomic reactors all across Sinus Sabeus had just ingested it.

Sudden panic flared brightly within each reactor complex as the

Night Dragon went to work. It burned out control systems and wreaked havoc within the regulatory mechanisms of rapidly overheating cores.

Simocatta had spent decades attempting to develop a defence against the Night Dragon, but had never succeeded.

He doubted anyone else had either.

Hydraq's progress through Forge Basiri was swift.

He'd left the Parity Scriptorium without comment, though numerous eyes had followed his unscheduled departure. Embedded memories of the forge's layout guided him through its brightly-lit pathways.

His sole deviation was to enter a Machina Opus temple, where he retrieved a pair of moulded plastek melta-pistols that Aurora had hidden beneath a reinforced ironwork pew. The basalt structure was deserted but for a handful of dark-armoured Techmarines of the Sable Swords. The gigantic transhumans looked up as he entered, but instantly dismissed him as was typical of their breed.

Thus armed, Hydraq continued onwards.

Archmagos Alhazen ran an efficient forge-temple. The mag-lev transits ran to a precise timetable and the ingress/egress patterns of adepts, servitors and the thousands of robed tech-priests were regulated to exacting standards.

Hydraq was the only one not following its prescribed flow.

His unauthorised movement had been registered, as had his unsanctioned entrance to the datacore complex. Three squads of Mechanicus Protectors were already mobilising to intercept.

All things being equal, Hydraq had four minutes until they reached him.

But all things were not equal.

Hydraq had just penetrated the deepest level of the datacore complex when Forge Basiri went dark.

Power failures on Mars were uncommon, but even so, each forge possessed numerous backup systems to immediately take over if the power was ever lost.

In theory, a complete loss of power was impossible.

Unless someone with senior enough prefix-codes had disabled those backup systems.

Hydraq could picture the chaos above, tens of thousands of adepts, info-sentinels and calculus-logi scrambling to save the precious data in their systems before internal capacitors drained completely.

Every soul in service to Archmagos Alhazen, including the Mechanicus Protectors, would be bound by emergency protocols. A single adept was the least of their worries.

How wrong they were.

Hydraq followed a curving corridor in total darkness towards the entrance to the most secure vault in Forge Basiri. Had the power been operational, a dozen security systems would already have halted his progress, shot him down or otherwise ended his infiltration.

The corridor made an abrupt turn, and Hydraq found himself in a high-roofed chamber of incredible dimensions. At its exact centre was an obsidian cube fifteen metres square and enclosed within a latticed steel framework.

Squatting before the caged cube were two Praetorian-grade servitors. Bloated with combat augmetics, lethal weaponry and advanced battle-wetware, they were monsters in all but name.

Praetorians were capable of semi-autonomous engagement, but the blackout had isolated them from the combat grid. To their eyes, Hydraq was a native of Forge Basiri. He didn't give them a chance to realise their mistake and vaporised both their skulls with twin shots from the melta pistols.

The weaponised servitors collapsed in hulking piles of liquified metal and bubbling flesh. Hydraq moved past their corpses to the cube over which they had stood guard.

'A data-tight Faraday Cage,' he said in admiration.

The way in was a simple door of plated steel secured with a heavy padlock. Protection so absurdly primitive that it seemed ridiculous, but it was all that separated Hydraq from Archmagos Alhazen's most precious secret.

That very primitivity was what had required a physical intervention. Data connected to a network was inherently vulnerable to remote attack, but this datacore was completely isolated. And on a planet where every single system shared a link somewhere, only data kept completely off the Martian networks could be considered secure.

Hydraq's presence here refuted *that* belief.

He blasted the lock from the door and kicked it inwards.

Inside, the cube was empty save for a single, gloss-black cogitator that drew its power from battery racks secured in recessed alcoves.

Mono-tasked servitors tended to the batteries, and they ignored him as he circled the cogitator. Three metres tall, smooth-faced and featureless. A black monolith to knowledge, like something erected by a race of celestial engineers.

At its midpoint was a single inload/exload port and Hydraq unfurled Adept Duqu's mechadendrite, rotating its end cap to a data-spike. Duqu's slack features were reflected in the mirror surface of the cogitator and Hydraq shook his head.

'Sorry, my friend, this is the end for you. I need your memory space.'

He felt Duqu's panic, but didn't let that stop him erasing every aspect of the hijacked adept's persona from his own memory coils. In a single act of murderous reformatting, Hydraq reduced Adept Duqu's body to a mindless meat puppet.

No loose ends.

He slotted home the data-spike and allowed a small smile to surface as the exload began. Binary scrolled past his eyes in dense, interleaved streams.

'You keep a great many secrets, archmagos,' said Hydraq, checking the aircraft he'd authorised earlier was prepped on its launch platform. It was, and he grinned, browsing the data as it poured from the cogitator. Even freed from the necessity of storing Adept Duqu's personality matrices, the memory coils were quickly approaching capacity.

He kept a search trawl running in the background, hunting for signs of the *Cartographae 20-30*, but the more he searched the more his unease grew.

'It's not here,' he said, his unease turning to a sick, gut-loosening horror at what *was*. He wanted to disconnect, to wrench the spike from the inload slot. But this was too big, too damning, the implications too horrifying *not* to know.

At last the exload was complete.

He stepped back from the cogitator, wishing he'd never set foot in this forge, never taken Enaric's commission and never touched knowledge he couldn't forget.

'Ave Deus Mechanicus,' whispered Hydraq.

'Not what you were expecting, was it?' said a black-robed adept stepping from the shadows.

Aurora watched the storm break over the crater's edge via a swarm of remote spy-flies on the surface. They'd built the camp securely enough not to worry about the dust fouling anything, but the sight of the approaching storm-front gave her a shiver of premonition.

She wished they hadn't taken his commission. Enaric's job had smelled bad from the start. But she was bound to Hydraq, and some debts could never be settled, the scales too weighted with blood to ever balance.

Where he went she went, and he went where trouble lay.

She blinked away the view from outside and brought the mission countdown to the front of her eye.

'Too long,' she muttered, looking down at Hydraq's prone body on the grav-couch. It would be days before he'd walk properly after this job, his limbs bruised and twisted by the convulsions of the Red Static. He'd heal, like he always did, gripped by narcotic dreams and fighting the hunger for more.

A perverse way to live when there were a dozen augments he could implant to purge his renal system.

Hydraq's face was lined and pale, his eyes darting behind their closed lids. His skin, never a heathy shade, was ashen, like a corpse. She knew what would happen if the body hosting his mind died, but pushed the image aside.

All too easy for one such as her to imagine the myriad ways a body could die. Wasting away with a consciousness lost forever in digital limbo, a flesh cut off from return. No way for a warrior to die.

She pushed herself to her feet and made her way to where the flesh-spare Simocatta reclined on his delicate framework, a dozen entoptic screens hanging in the air around him. Some were data trawls from the reactors he'd compromised with the Night Dragon, others were passive feeds from orbitals he'd redirected to look down on Forge Basiri.

'Have you heard from him?'

Simocatta looked up from his screens and a toothy grin split his sweating face.

'No, my dear Aurora,' he said, unctuous to a fault. 'Our mutual friend is still at work.'

'The feed? It's still active?'

Simocatta indicated his cogitator, its surface blinking with green lights across the board.

'Adept Duqu still dances merrily to Hydraq's tune, though I suspect his dalliance must end soon.'

'Why?'

'I estimate Forge Basiri will have its power restored within forty seconds. If Adept Hydraq is not on his way out by then, he won't be coming out at all.'

'Don't call him that,' said Aurora.

'He keeps saying that too,' mused Simocatta, wagging a slender finger at her. 'Why is that? What grudge does he hold against the Cult Mechanicus or they against him? I confess I cannot find any record of him in the Martian datascape, which is both disquieting and reassuring in equal measure.'

'Did you really think you *would* find him?'

Simocatta laughed. 'I suppose not.'

Aurora saw the panel before Simocatta flicker with a mixture of red and amber lights.

'Is that him?'

Simocatta nodded, and flicked a series of ivory-capped switches on the panel next to him. Half the screens vanished.

'It is indeed,' said Simocatta, twisting a black dial and bringing up an auspex feed from an orbital plate. 'I am detecting a fast-moving flyer leaving a southern platform to us as we speak.'

'Time for us both to get to work,' said Aurora, galvanised and relieved at Hydraq's exit from Forge Basiri. 'You know what to do?'

'Of course. Call back the Night Dragon from all but the reactor in the Pollack Crater.'

Aurora nodded. 'As soon as Alhazen realises what's happened, he'll send everything he's got after us. We'll need some cover.'

Simocatta rubbed his hands together. 'Trust me, Mistress Aurora, when that reactor goes critical, no-one will be tracking anything within tens of thousands of kilometres for a rather long time.'

Aurora made her way up top, into the wind-scoured camp where visibility was down to less than ten metres. Red dust filled the crater and the trench was ankle-deep in the stuff. Her bodyglove felt clogged with it.

The prefabbed shelters rocked with the force of the wind ramming through the crater. The neurosurgical-pod wasn't moving, secured by stabilising struts bolted to the rock and protected by hurricane dampers. As far as the chirurgeons could feel, the environment beyond their hermetically-sealed walls was utterly calm. Aurora transmitted a ready code to the chirurgical leader, receiving a terse acknowledgement in reply.

She dropped and rolled beneath the pod, detaching two blocks of explosives from her belt. Neither was larger than the magazine of a pistol, but they would obliterate the pod and the team within once Hydraq and Aurora had what they needed.

With the neurosurgical pod rigged, Aurora moved past the sunken shelters where the earth-movers were being slowly buried by the sand.

The third shelter was covered by a billowing cameleoline tarpaulin that strained in the growing winds. Where the sand was swallowing the earth-movers, this shelter was kept proof against the Martian storms by virtue of an integral electrostatic shield generator.

She moved around its edge, ripping out the clips holding the tarp in place. The wind seized it and tore it away, revealing a tapered, gull-winged craft with a sleek deadly profile. It was a thing of beauty, a needle-tail Merganser, its gloss-black hull formed from a single-cast of polycarbonate resin that was virtually invisible to augurs.

Aurora dropped into the shelter, feeling the electrostatic shield scrape the dust from her as she passed through it. She landed by the cockpit, and twin bull head emblems shimmered on the wings, visible only because the flyer now recognised her.

'Time to fly, my pretty,' she said, and the drive plant purred to life. Near silent, but more powerful than any other two-man flyer in the Martian registries.

Aurora placed her hands next to the frontal cockpit and soft light haloed her splayed fingers. With deft movements of her fingertips, she prepped the flyer for evac, warming the avionics and setting up false flags for their flight path.

The Merganser was as ready as it ever would be. All it needed now were passengers.

'*Mistress Aurora?*' said a voice in her vox-bead.

'What is it, Simocatta?'

'I should close my eyes about now.'

Knowing what was coming, Aurora crouched low and cut the feed to her optics as the shelter was lit from above by a blinding flash of searing light.

The atomic explosion of the Pollack Reactor lit the sky for hundreds of kilometres in all directions. It filled the atmosphere with radioactive fallout and made Sinus Sabeus lousy with e-mag storms.

Aurora vaulted from the shelter seeing the hazed, fiery outline of a towering mushroom cloud on the northern horizon. A storm was coming for sure, one that was only going to get worse.

She made her way back to the underground bunker and passed through the ultrasonic scrubbers, grabbing Hydraq's wrath-pattern pistol. The gunbelt snapped easily around her waist as she entered the infocytes chamber. They were just as she'd left them, flat on their bellies and still connected to the enormous data trunking.

A burst of paralysing code kept them from looking up as she drew her short-bladed stabbing swords. Aurora somersaulted into the pit they'd dug and drove a blade through the back of each skull.

Aurora wiped her blades clean and slotted them home in their scabbards. She left the chamber, moving swiftly to where the data-miners sifted the noosphere and physical networks.

Six of them looked up, their eyes glazed with partial connection, and killed them where they sat. Six needle rounds right through the eyes. With each death, a connection faded to black.

Aurora holstered her pistols and moved past Hydraq's chamber to where Simocatta was struggling from his reinforced framework of a seat. His face was a ruddy mask of fear. He'd felt the infocytes and data-miners die.

He knew he was next.

'Mistress Aurora!' he cried. 'Please! What are you doing?'

'No loose ends,' she said, and shot Simocatta through the heart with a blue-white beam of plasma. Hydraq's wrath-pattern was a duellist's weapon. Single shot only, but a Cydonian Sister only needed one.

Simocatta collapsed, dragging down his framework chair and smashing the cogitator in his fall. The entoptic screens tilted crazily, blizzardy with static. He reached for her, his fingers clawing the air, but his face was already turning blue from massive organ destruction and imminent brain-death.

Aurora turned from the room and overlaid one eye with what her spy-flies were seeing. A workhorse Ares-pattern lander burst through the clouds, rocking and swaying in the atomic winds and roaring from the detonation of the Pollack Reactor's core.

'Erratic,' she said of its flight profile. 'He's hurt.'

The Ares set down on the area they'd designated as the landing zone. Its engines coughed and died, clogged with radioactive dust. She zoomed in on the pilot's canopy, but the storm made it impossible to make out more than a blurred impression of a man's outline.

Aurora heard a strangled cry from Hydraq's chamber.

She holstered the wrath-pattern and found him struggling against his restraints. His eyes were wide with terror, sweat pouring from him in rivers. She unsnapped him from the grav-couch and he all but launched himself to his feet.

He would have fallen but for her arms, his body and brain not yet aligned with one another.

'We have to get out of here,' he said. 'Now!'

She dragged him through the bunker, his abused body still trying to overcome connection burn and the bruising he'd sustained in hijacking Duqu. His skin was ashen, yet fever-hot, his breathing shallow.

'You need to calm yourself,' she said.

He shook his head and took a gulp of air.

'Got to go. Got to get away.'

He looked up in desperation. 'Your speeder?'

'Prepped and waiting,' she said. 'Do we need to make that sharp exit now?'

He nodded, too drained to speak.

They scrambled out into the trench, the storm winds filling the air with choking particulates. Hydraq pressed his *shemagh* against his face as Aurora's spy-flies saw the canopy of the Ares lift and a compact figure of a man emerge. He climbed down with precise movements, almost as though the storm winds didn't trouble him at all.

Anyone who could move like that worried her.

'Who's on that flyer?' asked Aurora.

Hydraq opened his mouth to speak, his brow knitting together in confusion. Grit made his eyes tear up.

'I don't remember,' he said.

'How can you not remember?' asked Aurora as she hauled him out of the trench. He shook his head again, clearly just as much in the dark as she was.

The winds were gathering strength. Every single tarp had blown away and the walls of the trenches were collapsing inwards. Only the neurosurgical pod resisted the atomic storm, but Aurora knew they had no need for it now. The mission was over. Whoever had gotten out of the Ares almost certainly wasn't Duqu.

With a pulse of thought she detonated the explosives and the surgical pod went up in a hard bang of white hot flames, gutted from the inside out by the twin plasmic/melta charges. If nothing else it might give them some cover or distract the new arrival long enough for them to escape.

'Thank the Omnissiah…' said Hydraq as the Merganser rose smoothly from its shelter, turning on its axis to face them.

'That's not me,' said Aurora, more angry than surprised as the force of the storm was cut off by the electrostatic shield extending from the speeder's hull.

'No, that would be me,' said a voice in her ear, so clear it was as if the speaker was right behind her.

Which he was.

Aurora dropped Hydraq and spun on her heel, both pistols leaping to her hands via their e-mag link. They flew past her outstretched grip and into the hands of a black-robed adept with his hood drawn back and piled across his shoulders.

'I think I'll take those,' he said.

She didn't answer, her hands flashing for her blades as she sent a blur of hostile code at this adept. He didn't so much as flinch, and her horror was complete when her own body locked in place, the attack turned back on her.

'How are you doing this?' she demanded through gritted teeth.

'*This*?' he said, gesturing to her with one of the stolen pistols. 'These are the least of my order's cantrips. But don't worry, Mistress Aurora. If my employer wished you dead, it would already be so. Now, to business.'

'Who are you?' asked Hydraq, managing to pull himself onto his knees. Aurora watched the unfolding drama through her own senses and the compound eyes of her spy-fly swarm.

She saw the bland-faced adept before her, but her swarm saw nothing, only her pistols apparently floating in midair.

'That's not the question,' she said. '*What* are you?'

'My name is Adept Nemonix, and I am a dataproctor currently in service to Archmagos Alhazen,' said the adept, and Aurora fought to keep what he was saying in her head. His words squirmed around her skull, as though their meaning was so ephemeral that they could not be pinned in place for long.

'You work for Alhazen?' said Hydraq.

'As do you now if you wish to live,' said Nemonix.

'Why?'

'Come now, Adept Hydraq, you know why. You saw what was on that cogitator.'

Hydraq shook his head. 'No, it's impossible. The legends about Archmagos Telok are just that, legends. He's long dead.'

Nemonix spread his hands and shrugged, as though the truth or otherwise of Hydraq's words were utterly inconsequential.

'My employer believes otherwise,' said Nemonix.

The dataproctor's head cocked to one side, as though listening to something only he could hear. He looked up and smiled.

'Do you see that?' he said, pointing to a pinprick of bright light crossing the sky, barely visible through the storm overhead. 'That is cyclonic torpedo launched from an unregistered Deimos-pattern frigate in geostationary orbit with this exact spot. At its current velocity it will impact in ninety-seven seconds. You have that long to accept my employer's offer of life.'

'Why?'

'Why what? Why should you choose life? A question better addressed to the technotheologians or, as I know how bitterly you despise them, *Adept* Hydraq, perhaps an Imperial preacher? Either way, time is running short for such deep questions of existence.'

'Why do we get the *choice* to live?' asked Hydraq.

'Your existence or otherwise is of no interest to me, but you have been deemed useful and you have skills, which makes you desirable.'

Aurora felt the binaric shackles holding her fast unbind her body's augmetics. Nemonix reversed her pistols and held them out to her, handles first.

Her optical threat readers said Nemonix was harmless, that she could kill him before he took his next breath.

Her gut told her she would be dead before she could move so much as a muscle.

'We accept,' she said, taking and holstering her guns.

'What?' said Hydraq. 'No!'

'We accept,' she repeated. 'I am life-bound to you, Hydraq. You cannot die, and if the only way to keep you alive is to treat with Alhazen, then we're doing it.'

'A most excellent decision,' said the dataproctor, looking up at the descending warhead. 'Now I would board that very fine speeder of yours and get as far from here as possible.'

'You're letting us go?' asked Hydraq.

'For now, but a time of change is upon Mars,' said Nemonix, retreating into the storm's fury. 'And when it comes you will be called. It will go badly for you to refuse that call.'

And then he was gone.

Aurora lifted Hydraq and all but threw him into the rear cockpit of the Merganser. She vaulted into the pilot's seat, sealed the canopy and shut down the electrostatic field. Howling winds slammed the speeder as its gull-wings unfolded and it sped away.

Barely had the inertia-couch gripped her when she rammed the engines out hard and the speeder surged from the crater.

Aurora flew hard and low, keeping as many ridges, rocks and mountains between them and the incoming ordnance as was humanly possible.

A second flash of detonation lit up the Martian desert.

A radiant dome of white-hot vapour fire turned the interior of the Bouguer Crater and everything in it to molten glass.

'What did we just agree to?' asked Hydraq, his voice all but smothered by the force of acceleration.

'I don't know,' she said. 'What did you mean about Telok?'

'They think he's coming back,' said Hydraq.

ABOUT THE AUTHOR

Graham McNeill has written many titles for The Horus Heresy, including the Siege of Terra novellas *Sons of the Selenar* and *Fury of Magnus*, the novels *The Crimson King* and *Vengeful Spirit*, and the *New York Times* bestselling *A Thousand Sons* and *The Reflection Crack'd*, the latter of which featured in *The Primarchs* anthology. Graham's Ultramarines series, featuring Captain Uriel Ventris, is now seven novels long, and has close links to his Iron Warriors stories, the novel *Storm of Iron* being a perennial favourite with Black Library fans. He has also written the Forges of Mars trilogy, featuring the Adeptus Mechanicus, and the Warhammer Horror novella *The Colonel's Monograph*. For Warhammer, he has written the Warhammer Chronicles trilogy *The Legend of Sigmar*, the second volume of which won the 2010 David Gemmell Legend Award.

YOUR NEXT READ

BELISARIUS CAWL: THE GREAT WORK
by Guy Haley

In the wake of the Great Rift, Belisarius Cawl turns his attention to the abandoned world of Sotha. Once home to the Scythes of the Emperor, it also hides a long-buried secret… and an ancient evil.

For these stories and more, go to **blacklibrary.com**, **games-workshop.com**, Games Workshop and Warhammer stores, all good book stores or visit one of the thousands of independent retailers worldwide, which can be found at **games-workshop.com/storefinder**

An extract from
Belisarius Cawl: The Great Work
by Guy Haley

Ezekiel Sedayne was dying.

There was a time when he stood tall among men, as much a physical as an intellectual giant, but those days were done. He was old. He was at the end. His seven-foot frame had shrunken in. His spine curled with calcium loss. His hands were knotted with arthritis. His skin was slack, flowing around brittle bones like draped cloth. His lustrous black hair had turned as fine and white as the silk of a spider's nest. It spread around his head on the pillow as if it, like his skin, had been laid there, and if he stood, if he had been capable of standing, he would have left it behind as a cloud of down.

Sedayne's life had lasted longer than any child of Terra had a right to expect, but all things are finite, and his existence was coming to a close.

Human beings are aware of their mortality, yet they deny it to the very last. Sedayne regarded his intelligence to be in excess of most others. He believed he was free of the delusions that ruled the mind to reason's detriment, yet now he succumbed. He could scarcely believe death was knocking at his door.

This cannot be happening to me, he thought. But it was.

Sedayne had come from nothing to become one of the greatest scientists of his age. Despite his failing body his mind was sharp. His insight clear. In numb amazement, he insisted he felt young in his soul. The ravages of age on his body gave the lie to that.

He appeared in many respects like a corpse. Lips drew back from yellow teeth made long by the recession of dark gums. No matter how fast his thoughts raced, his body barely moved. His chest trembled with the bird flutter of his heart. Every inhalation was a bellow's wheeze.

But he was not dead yet. The breaths kept coming, and when the door to his bedchamber creaked wide his eyelids flickered open and his eyes, which were strikingly moist in the dry valleys of his parchment skin, swivelled to fix themselves upon his visitor.

'The Altrix Herminia,' he wheezed. His top lip stuck to his teeth for want of saliva, spoiling his smile. He was drying up from the inside out, like a spice pod left out to desiccate in the sun. Soon every drop of life would be wrung out of him, and there would only be an arid husk left. Then there would not even be that.

The Altrix came forwards with a rustle of layered, soft, plastek clothing. Upon her breast pocket she wore a caduceus in red and white that contrasted with the pale green of her dress. The uniform was formal and tightly laced, a symbol binding her to her duty, but though her garments were restrictive she moved with easy grace that suggested athletic, if not dangerous, power.

'My lord director,' she said, dipping her head respectfully. The sharp curve of her fringe swung neatly over her eyes.

'Your arrival pleases me.' Sedayne's head moved feebly to the side so he could follow her approach. The appetites of a younger man tormented him. 'Age does not agree with me,' he said. He was tiring, his breath rasping harder. He was a machine close to shutdown. He looked to the Altrix's face, then at the fat syringe she carried in her hand.

'The time... is close...' Each word was an individual effort. Each syllable required him to assign it a painful breath. Such care and attention his words received now, when once they were spent so carelessly.

'It is, my lord,' said the Altrix. 'You are dying.'

Sedayne gave a death's-head grin. 'I can always trust you to dress things up prettily for me,' he said. 'How goes the search?'

'I have identified seven possible candidates, all acolytes of Diacomes. Recovery missions are outbound.'

'Then administer the last of the elixir. I want to walk and move again. I have been confined here too long.'

'You are sure?'

He nodded his head painfully. 'You brought it. You knew what I would say.'

'This is the last,' she said. Marbled, opaque, silvery liquid that moved to currents of its own filled the glass cylinder. 'The Adarnians are gone.

The last rendered down. Their world is empty. Once I inject this dose, there will be no more. I am sorry.'

The Adarnian race was decreed harmless during the Great Crusade, and allowed to live under an Imperial protectorate. It had not prevented them being harvested to extinction. Unluckily for them, their body chemistry had miraculous effects on the human organism.

'A shame... I... never...' he swallowed twice, trying to summon enough spit to lubricate his creaking larynx. 'Learned how to synthesise it,' he said in a breathless rush.

'Are you certain that now is the time, my lord? We could delay a few days. There is sufficient here to return you to health for a few months, no more. It may be better to wait until a candidate has been selected and returned to Terra.'

He closed his eyes. 'No. Do it now.'

He was too weak to hold out his arm, so Herminia pulled it gently from under the covers, fetched a stirrup rest and strapped the limb in place. The veins in the crook of his elbow were ruined by repeated injection, and it took an amount of coaxing to find a suitable place for the needle. The drug had to be administered directly into the bloodstream in large amounts; pneumatic injection or skin absorption would not do.

Adarnian elixir was the last resort of dying men when all other rejuvenats failed. It came with many prices, not least the atrocity of its making. The elixir was illegal, its use punishable by death. Sedayne didn't care about the xenos or the law, but there were other, more immediate costs. Firstly, when the elixir's positive effects were exhausted, the user returned to a worse state than before. Every dose brought the certainty of hurried deterioration. This last dose would kill him.

Secondly, there was pain.

'Are you ready?' she said.

He blinked his assent. She set the needle to his arm. She had no need to tell him it would hurt.

The bee sting of the needle piercing his flesh made him gasp. The real pain came with the plunger's depression. Health-giving poison pressed from the organs of sentient beings flooded his system, and with it came a fire that scoured age back with its heat, reforging frayed genes and kick-starting the machineries of life.

Stolen youth ran riot through his body.

Ezekiel Sedayne screamed.

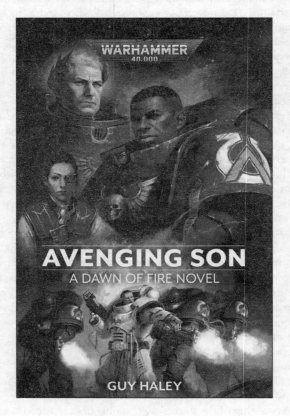